Trapped on Kzinhome

❖

The Swiftwing rocked as another tank round hit it, and a second tank penetrator slammed into the already wrecked storage building behind Ayla, spraying razor shards of fibercrete, knocking her to the ground. She looked up, momentarily dazed. Pouncer and T'suuz had vanished; Brasseur lay sprawled on his side where the concussion of the first impact had thrown him. No time to worry about that now; the kzinti couldn't be far, and they wouldn't leave without her.

She reached up to key her comlink but the concussion had torn her lapel mike away. She cursed, willing the pilot to do as she had told him, and she sighed in relief as the Swiftwing pitched up and then boosted skyward, shrinking to a silver dot in seconds, leaving behind the double *bang* of a sonic boom. Incandescent lines stabbed after it and she held her breath, fearing the sudden fireball that would signal the death of her lover. It didn't come, but she watched the empty patch of sky where the ship had vanished for long seconds after she knew it had to be safely out of range.

There was a momentary silence and a strange feeling came over her. Her ticket off-world was gone. She looked down and met Brasseur's gaze, glassy and unfocused. They were in serious trouble, trapped on this alien world and surrounded by heavily armed and now thoroughly enraged enemy carnivores.

She shook herself. Time to succumb to that later; first she had to get the hell out of the spaceport.

THE MAN-KZIN WARS SERIES
CREATED BY
LARRY NIVEN

The Man-Kzin Wars
The Houses of the Kzinti
Man-Kzin Wars V
Man-Kzin Wars VI
Man-Kzin Wars VII
Choosing Names: Man-Kzin Wars VIII
Man-Kzin Wars IX
Man-Kzin Wars X: The Wunder War
Man-Kzin Wars XI

The Best of All Possible Wars

Destiny's Forge (by Paul Chafe)

Also by Paul Chafe from Baen Books
Genesis (forthcoming)

THE MAN-KZIN WARS

DESTINY'S FORGE

PAUL CHAFE

DESTINY'S FORGE

Copyright © 2006 by Paul Chafe. "Man-Kzin Wars" universe is
used by permission of Larry Niven.

A Baen Book

Baen Publishing Enterprises
P.O. Box 1403
Riverdale, NY 10471
www.baen.com

ISBN 10: 1-4165-5507-2
ISBN 13: 978-1-4165-5507-0

Cover art by Stephen Hickman

First Baen paperback printing, October 2007

Distributed by Simon & Schuster
1230 Avenue of the Americas
New York, NY 10020

Library of Congress Cataloging-in-Publication Data: 2006007462

Printed in the United States of America

10 9 8 7 6 5 4 3 2

For Maggie, my mom.

The Tyger

Tyger! Tyger! burning bright,
In the forests of the night,
What immortal hand or eye
Could frame thy fearful symmetry?

In what distant deeps or skies
Burnt the fire of thine eyes?
On what wings dare he aspire?
What the hand dare seize the fire?

And what shoulder, & what art,
Could twist the sinews of thy heart?
When thy heart began to beat,
What dread hand? & what dread feet?

What the hammer? What the chain?
In what furnace was thy brain?
What the anvil? What dread grasp
Dare its deadly terrors clasp?

When the stars threw down their spears
And water'd heaven with their tears,
Did He smile his work to see?
Did He who made the lamb make thee?

Tyger! Tyger! burning bright,
In the forests of the night,
What immortal hand or eye
Dare frame thy fearful symmetry?

—William Blake

The Roots Of Kzinti Culture, Language And History.

The kzinti culture is both more homogenous and richer than human culture. In a very real sense there are not one but many human cultures, since civilization arose not once but several times on Earth, each time in complete isolation and independence, separated by insurmountable geographic barriers. By contrast, both linguistic, historical and (where available) genetic evidence indicate that civilization arose on Kzinhome only once. In geocultural terms, this can be explained by Kzinhome's relatively small (~50%) percentage of water cover and proportionally larger contiguous continental area, combined with the smaller range of climatic conditions over the non-polar regions of the planet. This is caused by the denser atmosphere and the tropical wind belt phenomenon, which acts to pump heat from the equator to the mid-latitudes. This arrangement can be expected to have facilitated the movement of trade and technology over isoclimatic lines with relative rapidity. At some point relatively early in the civilization cycle the primary kzinti culture was established

and thriving planetwide. On genetic evidence it is certain
that the kzinti species passed through a population bottleneck approximately ten thousand generations ago for
unknown reasons.

Given the evidence of a single start point for kzinti civilization, we can argue that an evolutionary stress caused
the bottleneck and triggered runaway sexual selection of
intelligence with resultant rapid and concurrent development of bi-quadrupedal posture, language, and tool use as
species traits. It seems likely this stress was a massive
climatic shift brought about by the slight eccentricity in
Kzinhome's orbit caused by gravitational interactions with
the gas giant Hgrall. This posited orbital shift, occurring
approximately 200,000 years ago, would have increased
average solar flux, in turn increasing the average surface
temperature as much as 3 degrees Celsius, extending
growing seasons and accelerating the rate of water circulation through the atmosphere and hydrosphere. The
combination of these effects formed extensive rainforests
throughout the tropical and temperate zones.
Simultaneously large sections of the continental interiors
were reduced to desert. The higher rate of photosynthesis
has led directly to the high (~30%) oxygen levels seen in
Kzinhome's atmosphere today. A general rule of planetary
evolution states that the average mass of animal species
increases with increased solar energy flux. This is due to
both the greater availability of food through increased
plant growth, which supports a heavier food chain, and
the greater availability of oxygen due to increased photosynthesis, which allows the high metabolic rates necessary
for large, active animals to exist.

Although humans are accustomed to seeing the two-meter kzinti as large predators, in their native ecosystems they are small in relation to most high order fauna in their ecological range, small with respect to their primary prey species and small with respect to other predators with which they compete. Typically, large land predators take prey no more than twice their weight, and usually less than their weight. By contrast, lone kzinti will stalk and kill *zerkitz* up to ten times their weight, and hunting parties will take *a'kdzrow* of up to twenty-five metric tons. In most cases where evolutionary forces lead to an increase in prey species size we expect to see the predator species increase along with them. However, in the case of the kzinti the large predator niches remained occupied by competitors such as the *v'speel* stalker and the pack hunting *grlor*.

This suggests that the kzinti were forced into the intelligence niche because their customary prey animals increased in size with the climate change but they themselves could not because the large predator niches were already occupied. As their prey grew larger the large predators flourished at the expense of the smaller early pre-kzin, driving them to the edge of extinction. This would have pushed the pre-kzin toward the cooperative hunter niche, which requires the development of complex signaling and a basic social structure. These developments set the stage for the evolution of intelligence. This picture is plausible but incomplete, and it is important to understand that while the individual links in this chain of reasoning have all been verified, to the extent possible through kzinti documentation, the actual proof of the

cause and effect relationships asserted will have to await
detailed research on Kzinhome itself.

Regardless of the root causes of the genetic bottleneck
event, the effects on kzinti development are clear. The
kzinti speak a single language, although there are many
dialects, and extremely separated dialects have difficulty
communicating. Given the limits imposed by speed-of-
light communications in an interstellar empire, identical
linguistic groups have had ample time to diverge but have
not. It could be argued that this lack of linguistic flexibility
is evidence of a more instinctive, less flexible language
facility, hinting that kzinti are less intelligent than humans.
However the Hero's Tongue is a fully combinatorial
language in the sense of Gödel, i.e., a formal system capable
of making statements of arbitrary complexity. There is
therefore no thought that cannot be expressed in the
Hero's Tongue. Further, kzinti are gifted mathematicians,
which again requires thought processes capable of handling
problems of arbitrary complexity. In addition, both the
language areas and visual cortex in the kzin brain are highly
developed and both larger and more finely structured
than in humans.

This last fact may provide an answer to the puzzle of
the Hero's Tongue's strange cohesion. It is known that the
kzin population is richer in telepathic adepts than the
human population, and it is known that the brain processes used in telepathy make extensive use of both language
and visual circuits in humans. In the visual system this is
known to correspond to the high demands of the active
predator ecological niche. The low genetic diversity of the
kzin race may have facilitated the emergence of a telem-

pathic sense due to the high degree of correlation of thought and emotional processes between individuals. There is then a natural evolutionary pathway toward making use of the processing power of both visual and language brain circuits in order to extract increasingly detailed information from the telempathic sense. This development can in turn have *locked in* those brain circuits to the demands of telempathic processing. In the visual cortex these effects may not be noticeable, since the visual cortex is also locked into processing patterns that correspond to a verifiable external reality; however, there is no single "correct" combinatorial language system, which leaves the language centers of the brain free to select any of an infinite number of equally valid symbol systems.

This is the case in humans, and human languages drift and evolve rapidly. However, in kzinti we may conjecture that the telempathic sense has effectively locked in the language centers to its (still poorly understood) demands, which would go far toward explaining both kzin linguistic homogeneity and telepathic prowess. As a side note, hallucinatory experiences are common in human telepathic adepts, which may be due to the telempathic and other senses competing for the same brain processor resources. Kzinti telepaths also suffer from numerous cognitive difficulties, and this may explain why telepathy evolves rarely and is seldom a highly developed sense in any species despite its obvious evolutionary advantages: Its cognitive costs simply outweigh its survival benefits. The largest exceptions to this rule, the now extinct Slavers and the sessile Grogs, both show clearly the cognitive drawbacks of a highly developed telempathic sense.

Kzinti share with humans the ability to form hierarchical mass societies, but they are orders of magnitude less social. Any society can be seen as a series of opportunities to cooperate or compete, and in kzinti the balance falls more heavily on competition than in human society. This fact imposes strict limits on the forms of society that the kzinti can successfully use, and in fact we can see that kzinti culture shows much less variation than human culture does in terms of structure. The reasons for this are complex, but ultimately, for any evolved organism, the final measure of success is the number of offspring injected into future generations *in relation to the number of offspring injected by competitors*. There are two basic strategies available to achieve this, and we may categorize species as K (named because the population total is characterized by K, the carrying capacity of the environment) and r (named because the population total is characterized by r, the reproductive rate). K species are characterized by a small number of large offspring, long lifetimes with late maturity, and high levels of parental care. Type r species have a large number of small offspring, short lifetimes with early maturity, and low or no parental care.

In species with sexual reproduction we see two strategies, individuals who produce a small number of large gametes (females) and those who produce a large number of small gametes (males). This tendency usually generalizes so that we see females invest a large amount to ensure the success of a small number of offspring, and males invest a small amount in any given offspring in order to maximize the total number of offspring. Since the child-bearing capacity of females is the ultimate limit on the reproductive potential of any given generation, we usually see a situation in which males compete for females. In a species like the Wunderland gagrumpher, males invest no parental care in their offspring, and as a result we see a large sexual dimorphism, with males averaging five times the weight of a female and possessing specialized neck dewlaps, which serve both as an intimidation mechanism in male/male conflicts and as a sexually selected attractant to females. There are exceptions to this rule. In some bird species the male and female form long-term pair bonds and there is very little (although not zero) mate competition. As a result males and females are nearly identical in body plan and require an expert (or a con specific) to differentiate them. In a few fish species the technical details of reproduction dictate that males provide all or the bulk of parental care, and in these cases females compete aggressively for access to males, reversing the normal pattern.

In almost all mammalian species, males compete for females, but humans are an extreme case of the K strategy and this changes the equation. Due to the limitations of the female pelvis and the human specialization of large brain size, human infants are born almost completely helpless and require two decades to reach full maturity. This tremendous reproductive burden requires the dedicated assistance of the male to ensure the survival of the offspring in a primitive environment, and the males best able to provide this assistance then become objects of competition for females. Because of this almost unheard-of female competition, the degree of male competition is reduced. As a result male humans mass only about 50 percent more than females and females possess secondary sexual attractant displays that are almost universally confined to males in other mammals. Under these conditions cooperative, coalitional behaviors in both sexes are cost effective, and it is these behaviors that make human society possible. Through this process intelligence itself has become a sexually selected characteristic as well as a naturally selected characteristic. At this point in human evolutionary history it seems likely that sexual selection has become the dominant driving force behind the development of human intelligence, as witnessed by the tremendous costs involved in bearing large-brained infants (including a significant death-in-labor and infant mortality rate under primitive conditions) and rearing them to adulthood. Such high-cost evolutionary features, like peacock tails and moose antlers, are generally only seen in cases of runaway sexual selection, where a trait evolves until the evolutionary cost of displaying it counterbalances the tremendous reproductive advantage it confers.

The kzinti are even more extreme *K* strategists than humans. Kzinti kits are normally born as brother/sister twins from a single egg, although there are rare cases of quadruplets or single births, and are typically nursed for eight to twelve (standard) years, during which time the female remains infertile. A fertile female kzin may have only three or four estrus cycles in her lifetime. As a result kzin population growth is extremely slow and kzin males compete strenuously both for females and for the resources to support them. A high proportion of kzin male deaths are due to challenge duels resulting from this competition, and in the adult population females outnumber males in a ratio of between two to one and three to one. In other words, between 50 and 75 percent of male kzin kits can expect to die in combat. Of these, most can expect to die at the hands of older and more established kzin, although among those Great Prides involved directly in the Man/Kzin wars almost 50 percent are killed in combat with humans or other species. Combat death among males begins in late adolescence and rises to a peak in young adulthood, declining steadily thereafter. This single fact dominates the entire kzinti social structure, and in fact the entire Patriarchy is built around the requirement to redirect the aggression of young males outward to prevent them from completely destabilizing the hierarchy. It is this high death rate that allows the extended polygamous mating structure that is the core of kzinti social life. Paradoxically this system has given the kzinti 50,000 years of cultural stability and an interstellar empire unmatched in Known Space. Unfortunately these achievements are little comfort to any particular adolescent kzin who, regardless of station of birth, can only look forward to a lifetime of status-driven combat with a better than even chance of violent death.

Kefan Brasseur
Senior Fellow for Nonhuman
Studies
Kardish University
Alpha Plateau
Plateau

THE ANVIL

We are Kzin-ti because we are wild, born of Savannah and Jungle. We are Kzin-ti because we are hunters swift and silent, cunning and strong. We are Kzin-ti because we are warriors, with honor won in battle and proved in blood. We are Kzin-ti, we are the hunters, we are Kzin-ti.
—Saga of the Fanged God

The *zitragor* paused, head coming up to scan the area, delicate nose sniffing inquisitively. The beast seemed nervous, as though it sensed something wrong, but after a long moment it lowered its head to the rivulet to drink.

Watching from his concealment on a rock behind a spreading burstflower bush, Pouncer twitched his tail unconsciously, eyes locked on his prey. It was a good four leaps away, drinking where the little stream narrowed and speeded up before disappearing around a bend in the canyon. It wasn't the easiest place for the *zitragor* to drink, but it was safer by far than the larger pool where Pouncer was waiting.

Had it scented him? No, the light breeze was still in his face, and it would not have stayed if it knew a predator was in the area. Its nervousness was just well applied caution. Would it come closer? The air smelled of ozone, alive with the promise of a gathering storm, but overhead the sun burned hot in clear blue sky flecked with a few white clouds. Somewhere nearby a charge suppressor

13

was neutralizing high-altitude ions to prevent the clouds from building up to thunderheads. That allowed the wind to carry the uncondensed moisture over the high Long Range mountains to moisten the Plain of Stgrat beyond them, but the ground here in the foothills was parched as a result. The *zitragor* was feeling the effects of the drought, and it was thirsty, very thirsty. Pouncer settled lower on his rock, his hunt-cloak blending with the vegetation around him. He waited. It needed to come closer. A *v'pren* blurred past, its wings a high keening note. Pouncer looked up sharply, ready to run, but it was alone. A single *v'pren* bite was a trivial annoyance, but when they swarmed they were lethal.

The *zitragor* looked up again and seemed to hesitate. Had it heard the *v'pren*? Had it seen his motion? Four leaps was a long way to go if he wanted to ensure his kill. A *zitragor* could outrun a kzin with a four-leap head start, seven times in eight. It looked around, flicking its ears, then bent to drink again. Pouncer gathered himself for the leap and willed the beast to come closer. It swallowed in quick gulps, looked up, twisting its long neck around to scan behind it. A swiftwing rustled in the bushes behind it, and it started, half turning. This was it! But the *zitragor* didn't run and Pouncer didn't leap. It scanned the area again, scenting the air, then returned to drink again. It was agitated, but its thirst was stronger than its fear. Perhaps it had scented the rest of the hunting party on the plateau above the canyon. His father and brother and the others were hunting as a group, but Pouncer preferred his own company. He might not gain as many kills by himself, but they were his own, and that was important. Politics claimed more attention than prey when the Patriarch led a hunt, and Pouncer had little liver for the toadying of courtiers trying to gain his father's favor. In two days the Great Pride Circle of all the Patriarchy met, and Great-Pride-Patriarchs and double-named Emissaries had been arriving from beyond the singularity for the last Hunter's Moon. Many of them had never been to Kzinhome before, and they came with strange foods and stranger customs, retinues of retainers, trains of slaves, and any number of demands, pronouncements, propositions, and intrigues. And all of them wanted nothing more than to share a hunt with the Patriarch, or failing that, his oldest heir. When Younger-Brother mentioned this water-hole, Pouncer had leapt at the chance to lead himself on his own private hunt.

The *zitragor* looked up nervously, then went back to drinking. If only it would come closer! Unconsciously Pouncer's lips curled back from his fangs. Not that Younger-Brother's suggestion was free of intrigue itself. He knew Pouncer's preference for solitude, and with First-Son-of-Meerz-Rrit away by himself, the attention would fall to Second-Son. Pouncer licked his chops, concentrating on the *zitragor*. Let him play his palace games of *strakh* and precedence. Today was a day for the chase.

The *zitragor* turned and jumped into the bushes. Pouncer screamed and leapt. The kill scream was meant to paralyze prey, but this victim was simply galvanized into full flight. Four leaps later it had a five-leap lead, clearing a fallen tangletree and dodging sideways. Pouncer kept his eyes focused on its hindquarters, running on all fours, putting every sinew into every stride. He managed to close the distance to three leaps, gulping air in deep pants, and then his quarry dodged sideways and the distance widened as his claws dug into the dirt to make the turn. No! It would not get away! His muscles were already screaming with fatigue, but Pouncer drove his legs forward, gained back a leap when it half-stumbled over a boulder, gained another when he anticipated a dodge and cut the corner as it tried to shake him. *It is tiring too*, he told himself. He could almost taste it, fresh meat in his fangs, blood squirting warm and rich down his throat. His kill! A single leap in front of him. It would not get away. Half a leap!

The *zitragor* burst through a line of shrubs and Pouncer followed, fangs extended for the kill. A gray wall loomed in front of him, ivory tusks gleaming, huge bodies milling aimlessly as they grazed.

Tuskvor!

Pouncer skidded to a stop, nearly falling. The exhausted *zitragor* dodged between two of the hulking beasts. Agitated by its passage, one of the herd-mothers bellowed. Pouncer dropped to the ground, still as death, letting his hunt cloak settle over him. *Tuskvor* rarely came so high out of the jungle below, but it was late summer, fodder was scarce, and they would be migrating soon. Farther back in the herd another bellow answered the first, and the herd began to stir. Pouncer's heart pounded. If they charged he would die, it was that simple. A *tuskvor*'s lumbering walk was not much slower than a kzin could run, and they could walk all day. A herd charge mowed down all before it. He slowly adjusted his hunt cloak around his body to conceal himself better.

In front of him a vast herd-grandmother turned ponderously, tossing the air with her tusks. She must have outweighed him eight-cubed to one, big as a scout craft from her long neck to her armored tail. The great beast turned slowly to face him, her huge eyes staring. The gentle breeze carried her heavy musk to his nostrils. She snorted, thrusting her tusks in threat display. *Tuskvor* had good vision, but hunt cloaks were nearly perfect camouflage. Had she seen him? Pouncer began to back slowly away, seeking the cover of the bushes behind him. A smaller herd-mother bellowed, and her young crowded close behind her for safety. The beasts stirred restlessly, and the grandmother angrily uprooted a bramblebush. She knew something was wrong, but she hadn't seen him. Not yet.

Slowly he raised himself to all fours and carefully, paw by paw, crawled backward, keeping low, using what cover he could. The grandmother flapped her ears and seemed to settle down. One of the young began to drink from its mother's teats, and Pouncer allowed himself to relax slightly. Behind him a swiftwing called as it launched itself into the air. It banked overhead, riding the rising air currents out of the mouth of the canyon. The clouds were piling up in the sky overhead, converging into pillars that climbed for the top of the atmosphere, and the scent of ozone was stronger now. Despite the charge suppressors there would be a storm in the afternoon, a big one. The swiftwing banked again as the wind changed, rippling through Pouncer's fur.

The wind! It would carry his scent . . . Even as he thought it, the herd grandmother snorted, head coming back around to peer at him. She snorted again at the rank scent of carnivore and bellowed, the booming cry echoing from the canyon walls. The others in the herd answered. Ponderously the beast started toward him, her momentum building. Others moved with it; the herd was charging. Pouncer turned and sprang into a run. Fire burned in his legs, already spent from the *zitragor* chase, but the growing rumble behind him was reason enough to ignore it. Bellow after bellow shook the air. He leapt over the same trunk the *zitragor* had in its flight, breath coming now in gasps. Behind him the rumble grew to thunder. He risked a glance backward and saw the herd bearing down on him like a living avalanche, half obscured in its own dust. He had enough of a lead to escape, perhaps, if he could run until the charge ran out of momentum. Ahead of him the canyon narrowed and the vegetation thickened. That would slow him down but not the herd. Exhaustion weighed on his legs, but he drove himself forward, angling toward a clearer corridor. Behind him the pounding feet drew nearer, the herd grandmother bellowing in rage. They had his scent, and they weren't going to stop until they overran him. At the head of the canyon large rocks had fallen from the cliffface, too big for a *tuskvor* to tumble, too high for them to gore him. If he could get on top of one of those he would be safe, if he reached them with enough strength to leap to the top.

He risked another look back, saw the herd-grandmother's narrowed eyes fixed on him. If he reached them at all . . . The herd had noticeably narrowed the gap. Saplings snapped like twigs as they came to the heavier vegetation, and thick bramblebushes were pounded into the dirt.

Nothing survived a herd charge, it was common

knowledge. Nothing a kzin could carry could take down a *tuskvor*, save for a lucky head shot, and a herd held eight-cubed of the beasts.

The body follows where the mind leads. Guardmaster's training ran through his brain. Pouncer's legs were spent but he ran on, inexorably slowing. He came on the stream where he'd waited so patiently for the *zitragor* and leapt it without hesitation, putting everything he had into it. On the far side a rock rolled under his foot and he tumbled, slamming hard against the rocks as he fell, just as the herd-grandmother bellowed in rage. Pain flared in his hip as he came to his feet. They were almost on him and he could run no farther.

"Sire!"

His head snapped around at the shout. A gravcar! Guardmaster! It swooped down ten leaps ahead of him and he put every sinew into one last burst of speed, ignoring the pain, feeling the ground trembling under the herd behind him as they splashed into the stream. He leapt for the car's open back, Guardmaster's paws pulling him inboard even as the pilot lifted out. The car jolted sideways as the herd-grandmother's tusks slammed into it in a vain attempt to wrench her quarry from the sky. One paw slipped free and for a moment he dangled, not enough strength left to keep himself from falling into the churning mass of flesh below, then he was grabbed again, hauled bodily into the vehicle to lie panting on the floor. Concerned eyes looked down into his.

"Myowr-Guardmaster!" He could barely get the words out. "Thank the Fanged God!"

"Sire! Are you injured?" His mentor's worry was clear.

"Only my pride." Pouncer panted, recovering himself. He ran a paw down his side to his hip. Pain flared again but nothing seemed broken.

"Only a fool stalks *tuskvor*."

"It was a *zitragor*, but it knew where to run for safety." Pouncer breathed in heavy gasps. "I owe you my life."

"Meerz-Rrit would end my line if I let his eldest son be trampled."

"Where is my father?"

"He made his kill. He's returning to the Citadel. I was coming to let you know that."

"Fortune is with me in your presence."

"You shouldn't hunt alone. Not even here, much less the jungle."

"You know about that?" Pouncer had thought his private expeditions to the dangerous jungle verge were his own secret.

Guardmaster rippled his ears in amusement. "I know everything. I was once my father's eldest."

"Hrrr." Pouncer grimaced. "Then you know my thoughts on Patriarchal hunts."

Guardmaster rippled his ears again. "Second-Son does not share your reticence."

"Black-Stripe yearns for the *strakh* of the Patriarchy. If he felt the burden of its responsibility he would be less eager."

"It would not hurt you to practice your diplomacy. Balancing the factions is vital."

"When I am Patriarch I will outlaw factions. I want no one currying favor with me."

Guardmaster's whiskers twitched, and he turned a paw

over to contemplate his claws. "Some things even the Patriarch cannot command."

The older kzin turned to give direction to the pilot, and Pouncer looked out over the side as the gravcar slid over the hills, south toward the Hrungn valley. The *tuskvor* herd had eaten a huge swath through the savannah and into the foothills where they had started their charge. From that point forward the ground was churned, vegetation and everything else crushed into the dirt. Pouncer looked away. It could have been him down there. It *would* have been him, save for blind luck. Some things not even the Patriarch could command.

The Great Prides require a great master.
—Si-Rrit

Stkaa-Emissary paced restlessly, impatient and nervous at once, waiting in the Patriarch's quarters for the Patriarch to get back from his hunt. Occasionally he stopped to take in the vista. He had never been to Kzinhome before, but everything about it, the smells, the colors, the very air, told him he was *home*, home in a way that even his native W'kkai had never been, much as he missed it. Still, the panorama gave him no pleasure. The Patriarch's Tower was the tallest structure in the Citadel by design and the tallest on the planet by decree. Its windows gave him a panoramic view of the vast fortress and the rolling countryside beyond it. Surrounding the Citadel were small groups of low buildings built of stone and stonewood, the homes and shops of smallholders and crafters who served those who served the Patriarch. Farther out he could see great expanses of ripening fields, *hsahk* and *meeflri* for the grazing meat beasts. The vista was broken up by the huge tracts of forestland that marked the hunt parks of the Lesser Prides of Kzin, whose smaller strongholds were scattered across the plain like children's toys. Everywhere the riding lights of gravcars sparkled like flashflits in the early dusk, shuttling between the splashes of light that marked communities and enterprises big and small. On the eastern horizon the last rays of the setting sun glinted from the steady stream of freighters shuttling to the spaceport called Sea-of-Stars from the orbital dockyards invisible overhead. At regular intervals sat the domes of space-defense weapons, firepower enough to rip a fleet from orbit. Eight-to-the-sixth kzinti and eight-to-the-seventh slaves occupied half a continent here, churning out products from wine to warships. The Plain of Stgrat was the single greatest concentration of military and economic power in the Patriarchy.

To Stkaa-Emissary it seemed insignificant. He had been to Earth.

The doors opened and he spun around, expecting the Patriarch's advance guard. There was only a single kzin, followed by a buzzing Whrloo slave and a floating servitorb.

"Where is . . ." He began, then caught sight of the crimson sash and the sigil on it. "Patriarch! I abase myself."

Meerz-Rrit waved away his crouching obeisance. "Stkaa-Emissary, welcome to my home."

Stkaa-Emissary studied Meerz-Rrit carefully. *The Patriarch comes without guards, without retainers. Does this mean I have his trust, or is he simply that confident?* The Patriarch was tall and very fit. The handle of his variable sword was well worn, its scabbard made for ease of use and not ostentation. His belt held no more than a pawful of ears. *He does not need to duel often*, Emissary decided, *but when he does he wins*.

"Clean kill I trust, Patriarch?"

There were half a dozen ornate *prrstet* in the room, set around a low obsidian table polished to a mirror gloss. Meerz-Rrit hopped on to one and reclined, inviting his guest into another with an open paw.

"Clean kill, Emissary. It was a satisfying one, a prime *zitragor*." Four Kdatlyno filed into the room, carrying the still warm kill on a large platter, now cut into thick slices and seasoned. A pair of pointed *skeceri* blades skewered the meat so it could be handled and cut without bloodying the paws.

Stkaa-Emissary jumped up and settled himself carefully. "It is an honor to share it with you, Patriarch." He began carefully, pausing to spear a section of haunch with his *skeceri* and tear at it, savoring the juices and spice. It was prime indeed, like nothing he had ever tasted on W'kkai.

"I trust you find your chambers comfortable." Meerz-Rrit was solicitous, polite to a fault.

"The House of Victory is both spacious and lavish."

"And your colleagues are congenial, I trust."

"It is an honor to meet the leaders of the Great Prides, and fascinating to see how our species has adapted to life among the stars. There are more ways to be kzinti than I ever imagined." He paused before getting down to business. "My goal here is simple, Patriarch. As you know, Stkaa Pride has borne the brunt of the campaign against the monkeys."

"With honor, if not success." The Patriarch beckoned to the Whrloo, which picked up a decanter and two flagons from the servitorb and buzzed to the table with them. "This is *shasca*."

"Thank you Patriarch." Emissary lifted his flagon and sipped; the rich blending of fresh blood and fermented berry was exquisite on his palate. "It is excellent." *I am evolved for this world*, he thought, and drank more deeply before continuing. "The *kz'zeerkti* present us a unique problem. Not only have we been unable to conquer them, but we have lost entire worlds to their counterattacks. Now our base on Ch'Aakin has fallen, and W'kkai itself is suffering grievously under human embargo. Even this we retain only because they have not chosen to take it."

"Hrrrr. In the time of my thrice-grandsire they besieged Kzinhome itself. Their forbearance is surprising."

"It is not mercy that stops them." Emissary paused for emphasis, drank again from the flagon. "The situation is not acceptable, not for Stkaa Pride, not for the Patriarchy, not for our species. We must finally subjugate them."

"A worthy goal, and one I am surprised Stkaa Pride has not already accomplished." Stkaa-Emissary flattened his ears at the implied criticism. "What will you ask of Rrit Pride in this regard?" Meerz-Rrit speared a hunk of *zitragor* haunch and wolfed it down.

"The humans represent a threat such as our species has never experienced before. I believe they now pose a threat not only to Stkaa Pride but to the entire Patriarchy. When the Great Pride Circle meets I intend to ask for the participation of all the Great Prides in an extended

campaign to eliminate the monkey menace permanently."
Stkaa-Emissary made the open-pawed gesture of deference.
"With your support, Patriarch, I am sure we will get it."

"And your dispute with the Cvail Pride?"

"Cvail Pride presents a problem. Chmee-Cvail hopes
to strangle us in order to gain for himself what we have
lost."

"With some considerable success, I understand."

"Unfortunately true, Patriarch. A key factor in the loss
of Ch'Aakin was our difficulty in moving supplies due to
the intransigence of Cvail Pride."

Meerz-Rrit turned a paw over in contemplation. "So
perhaps Rrit Pride should throw itself behind Cvail Pride.
Their success is a measure of a prowess that perhaps you
lack."

"No!" Emissary's ears snapped up and forward.
"Patriarch, this is no longer a matter of gaining *strakh*
enough for a world or a fleet. Great Pride rivalry weakens
us, and we are in grave danger. This is a matter of species
survival."

"The monkeys possess only a pawful of worlds. Your
pride's inability to defeat them speaks poorly of you, and
now you inflate their prowess to excuse your incompetence." Meerz-Rrit fixed his gaze on Emissary. *We shall
see how he defends himself.*

"It is not the number of worlds that counts, Patriarch,
but the number of sentients. Their homeworld numbers
thrice-eight-to-the-eight-and-three individuals. Thrice-
eight-to-the-eight-and-three! Their military potential is
tremendous and their savagery unimaginable."

"Savagery." Meerz-Rrit flipped his tail dismissively.

"How much ferocity does an herbivore need to catch a root?"

"As herbivores they do not understand the dangers of unrestrained aggression. These creatures do not fight wars like any other species. They fight without regard for spoils, they do not try to capture slaves, possess no concept of honor. They give no thought to the use of the land they acquire and thus use conversion weapons without restraint. Their single focus is the annihilation of their enemy, of *us*. They destroy utterly what they cannot possess, even what they simply do not care to possess."

"Surely you exaggerate."

"I wish I did, Patriarch. On Hssin they ruptured the domes from space; slaves and warriors alike drowned in their own blood. It was not a battle, not a conquest, just honorless slaughter; they did not even bother to scour the ruins for booty. It was the same on Ch'Aakin. I was there, and few enough of us escaped with our lives."

"So you say. And yet time and again they have failed to follow up on their initial success. If they were as fearsome as you claim we would long ago be their slave race."

"As herbivores they do not understand the folly of leaving wounded quarry alive. Believe me when I speak of their ferocity. They have no interest in slaves or booty. What does the *tuskvor* want with meat? But when the hunter draws close the herd will charge and trample all before it, not for gain but for safety."

"Yet surely leading the entire Patriarchy in hunt-conquest cannot fail to enhance the *strakh* of Stkaa Pride at the expense of Cvail Pride." Meerz-Rrit narrowed his eyes. "Perhaps even at my own expense."

"*Strakh* is no use to slaves, or to the dead. When we met the *kz'zeerkti* we enjoyed tremendous advantages in technology and space warfare experience. We failed to conquer them. Each new attempt has been better organized and better equipped, and yet now we lose ground. Their technology has become fully the equal of our own."

"It is not technology that wins wars, it is the courage of the warriors."

"Only where the combatants meet with honor, Patriarch. The way the monkeys wage war, only raw industrial strength counts. Already on their few worlds they match the entire Patriarchy. They never duel among themselves, so nothing slows their growth rate but lack of space, and they are content, even eager, to crowd closer than a basketful of kits."

"Hrrr. I have seen the images." *Not that I have quite believed them.* Emissary had too much status to lie, but Meerz-Rrit had no doubt he was presenting the truth to his pride's best advantage.

"I have been there! I went to negotiate with their rulers on Earth, in a city called Nyewrrk. In a structure the size of this tower eight-cubed, even eight-to-the-fourth might live." He gestured out the tower windows. "And from here to the horizon was nothing but more buildings larger still, immensely larger, dwellings stacked like *pirtitz* on a platter."

Meerz-Rrit wrinkled his nostrils. "My nose is offended already."

"You cannot understand, Patriarch!" Stkaa-Emissary fought down the urge to gag at the memory. "They wallow in their own filth. The sky is literally brown with pollutants, and their drinking water reeks of the chemicals they must use to strip their own sewage from it. I could not eat for days. But this is how they live. And from space you can see the lights at night, every continent is a solid mass of light! The entire planet is populated like this."

"I am convinced of their decadence, Emissary. What is your point?" *And what is his aim here? What is the deeper game?*

"We are no longer the predators here, we can no longer scream and leap. They breed like *vatach*, so fast that on Earth they must have reproductive laws to prevent them drowning in the flesh of their offspring. On a colony the population doubles and redoubles as you watch! Unchecked they will inevitably expand into our sphere and overrun us as casually as the *zitragor* moves to fresh stands of grass. They have no liver for conquest, but their social system makes it inevitable."

"As does ours."

"Exactly, Patriarch. One species must be conquered by the other, there is no other way. I am naturally convinced that it should be ours that prevails."

Meerz-Rrit extended his claws and contemplated them. "Your arguments are compelling, Emissary."

"The facts speak for themselves, Patriarch."

"They do. My question is, what facts aren't speaking now?"

"I don't understand."

"Let me give you the scent. Stkaa Pride has fought this conquest war for generations now and has failed miserably. Cvail Pride seeks your ears."

"Cvail Pride's ears will swing with ours on the monkey's belt."

"I understand they have declared *skalazaal.*"

IIe knows! Stkaa-Emissary managed to control his reaction. Did the Patriarch know, or merely suspect? "The Honor-War is a pride matter. I cannot speak for my patriarch."

"Of course not." Meerz-Rrit quaffed his flagon, inhaling the rich taste of the *shasca.* The smell masked the subtle hint of fear that had crept into Stkaa-Emissary's scent, but that had already been enough to confirm his theory. Patriarch's Telepath had been correct, and Cvail Pride was at Stkaa Pride's throat. *Skalazaal* had returned to the Patriarchy. That had serious implications for Rrit Pride. He looked out the windows at the flitting lights in the darkening sky. And if half of what Emissary was saying about the monkeys was true, the Patriarchy faced a dangerous adversary even as its internal frictions rose. *I must have Rrit-Conserver's counsel on this, and I must see the monkeys for myself.* Soon enough he would meet a monkey, when his brother Yiao-Rrit returned from his own mission to the *kz'zeerkti* patriarch in Nyewrrk, but there was no need for Stkaa-Emissary to know that. He raised his flagon to Emissary. "The *shasca* is excellent, is it not?"

All warfare is based on deception.

—Si-Rrit

Through the panoramic windows of *Distant Trader'*s bridge the spidery gantries of the Patriarch's Dock loomed vast, scout ships and streamlined lighters gliding past transfer stations like swiftwings in a forest. Raarrgh-Captain and Lead-Pilot muttered back and forth to Docking Control as they slid into position. Behind them, Kchula-Tzaatz watched the scene spin slowly as the freighter gave way to a pair of Hunt class battle-ships, bulking huge as they cleared the docks, one behind the other. Their armored hulls slid past so close that Kchula could see the gunners in their turret blisters. He repressed the urge to duck; he could not allow him-self to show fear in front of inferiors. Kzinhome itself backdropped the scene, a beautiful blue-white sphere looming overhead, new continents coming into view with the ponderous grace of its rotation. Kchula-Tzaatz raked his claws across the vista. *Soon, very soon now, it will be mine.*

The battleships floated clear of the docking area, hung there for a long, pregnant moment as their navigators confirmed their courses, then vanished to pinpricks, eight-squared gravities of acceleration taking them out of sight in an eyeblink. An instant later they had faded to invisibility, heading for the edge of the system, for hyper-space, for death or glory on some unknown mission at the Patriarch's behest.

Kchula-Tzaatz purred to himself in ill-concealed pleasure. Two less to deal with when the time came, not that it mattered. Ship-to-ship battle against the might of the Rrit fleet was not the way to victory. It was cunning, not strength, that would bring him to power.

And before that could happen, he had to face his enemy. His purr faded and his ears flattened unconsciously. Before he could secure power he would have to face the

Patriarch in his own stronghold. Already parts of the scheme were in motion. If any of them failed he would be vulnerable.

"Our arrival is late, Raarrgh-Captain." Not that it mattered, but upbraiding his subordinate served to relieve his worry.

"My apologies, sire. Traffic is heavy." Raarrgh-Captain showed a disappointing lack of submission in his reply, concentrated as he was on the docking procedures.

Kchula twitched his tail in ill-suppressed agitation, unable to think of a reason to castigate Lead-Pilot as well. Finally he turned on his heel and strode from the navigation bridge to the command deck.

"Telepath!"

Kchula's Telepath lolled on a low *prrstet* in a corner, eyes partially unfocused and carrying the yellowish staining characteristic of his addiction to the *sthondat* lymph extract that brought his powers to life and chained him to a life of statusless servitude.

"Sire!" The bleary eyes struggled to focus.

"What is in the Patriarch's mind?"

The eyes unfocused, and Telepath drifted away long enough for Kchula to become impatient. Eventually he came back to awareness. "Apologies, sire. The range is far too great and my talents are not that strong."

Kchula snarled. "Don't dishonor yourself with deception. I can tell when your mind is connected."

"I sense only Patriarch's Telepath, sire. His presence is great even here."

"Well, what is that *sthondat* thinking then?"

"I sense only his presence. His mind is too strong to

penetrate. He blocks his thoughts from me, and the thoughts of those around him."

Kchula kicked at the hapless addict. "What use are you?"

"I serve to the best of my abilities, sire."

"Useless cur!" He aimed another kick at Telepath, who cringed backward.

Ftzaal-Tzaatz moved forward, black fur sleek over lean muscles. He raised a paw to intercede.

"Telepath may yet prove a valuable resource, brother." His voice was a silky purr. "Perhaps patience is a valid approach here."

Kchula-Tzaatz slashed the air in annoyance. "You would counsel patience to a stone." Nevertheless he desisted in his assault on Telepath, who took the opportunity to infuse more *sthondat* extract. "I lack power. Why do I lack power? Because I am surrounded by incompetents. The Patriarch does not contend with such inadequacies."

"It is inevitable that Meerz-Rrit's resources exceed yours. Were it not so you would not desire his station."

"You give me empty philosophy, brother. You've spent too long with the Black Priest cult. I need information. I will be on that planet in his stronghold. I will be vulnerable, do you understand? What if we have been compromised?"

"We would know by now. The Patriarch would have acted and our informants would have passed on the information"

"Your faith in your informants is touching."

"I have no faith in any single source. But put together,

yes, I am confident we would learn of anything important."

"Perhaps the Patriarch has laid a trap." Kchula's hind claws extended on their own, digging into the resilient flooring.

"Are you nervous, brother?" Ftzaal kept his voice carefully neutral.

"Nervous." Kchula looked up sharply, searching the black kzin's face for any sign of impertinence. "Don't be ridiculous."

"I and my *Ftz'yeer* will be your shield." Ftzaal lifted the ornately carved pommel of his variable sword from his belt and hefted it.

"As skilled as you are, two-eights of *Ftz'yeer* will not stand against a fortress full of Rrit."

"They will when the Rrit are busy defending the walls from our warriors. Great rewards demand great risks."

"Great risks are managed through control of information." Kchula snapped the words. "We lack any."

"We have what we need."

"Ktronaz-Commander's Heroes?" Kchula-Tzaatz changed the subject before it came any closer to his own fears

"They will leap on your command."

"The *rapsari* are prepared?"

"Rapsarmaster has been industrious. The beasts are thawed and ready, and the assassin is already in position."

"You are certain of that?"

"As certain as possible. It was launched; I have had no word of its interception."

"It is set then." Kchula paused, realizing that he was

now merely hesitating. "Curse the Fanged God, I wish I knew what was in the Patriarch's mind." He spat at the now comatose Telepath.

"We have the traitor. If everything else fails the traitor will not."

"Yes, we have the traitor." Kchula breathed deep to calm himself. Ftzaal-Tzaatz's words were meant to soothe, and so he responded as if they had worked. There was no point letting his brother see concern turn to fear, but inwardly he remained unconvinced. There was always a balance to be struck between risk and reward. In this case the reward was tremendous, the risks . . . acceptable. In games of stealth you could never be sure who was the stalker and who was the prey. The hidden blade was the deciding factor, but was the traitor really theirs?

There was no way to know, and no point in delaying. Kchula turned and strode back onto the navigation bridge. "Raarrgh-Captain, have my shuttle prepared!" His voice was harsher than it needed to be. *Better they fear my wrath than sense my fear.* Great rewards demand great risks, Kchula-Tzaatz well understood the dynamics of power. Usually he managed to arrange it so the reward fell to him while the risk fell to someone else. Not this time.

The warrior is known by the clarity of his thoughts and the purity of his purpose. To clear your mind you must rise above your emotions. Fear is death, for fear brings paralysis, leaving you helpless before your foe. Rage is death, for anger brings the kill fury, which slays first your own judgment. The warrior stands his ground

with clarity of purpose, attacks without rage,
defends without fear. The warrior can never be
less than honorable, for the warrior chooses
with clear mind a purpose higher than himself.
                                    —Conserver's teaching

The arena floor was deep in sand—difficult footing. The smell of hot dust filled Pouncer's nose as he shifted his rear leg, the pommel of his variable sword in rest position. He thumbed its extend button and the almost invisible magnetically stiffened wire slid from the coil inside to its full length. He centered the weapon between his breastbone and groin and tilted his grip until the blue marker ball at its tip was aligned precisely on his opponent's nose: *v'scree*, the resting guard position of the single combat form.

A leap and a half away Myowr-Guardmaster's eyes narrowed to slits, ears flat on his skull as he changed stance to receive the attack.

"You're a coward." he spat. "You don't deserve the name of Rrit."

The insult stung, and Pouncer dropped to attack crouch and leapt to avenge it in a single, fluid motion. His weapon came back, kill scream echoing from the bare stone walls. He landed and let his momentum carry him forward, sweeping the sword at his adversary's throat where there was a gap in his mag armor, but Guardmaster was already dropping to a knee and his own sword was coming around to amputate Pouncer's legs. Pouncer leapt vertically, and the blow went under his feet. He swung again on his way down but the blade glanced off

Guardmaster's mag armor. Guardmaster kicked up from his position on the ground and connected with Pouncer's wrist, sending his variable sword flying. Pouncer fell back, empty-handed as his opponent rolled to his feet and advanced on him, variable sword raised for the kill. *Fear is death,* he told himself, picturing the ground behind him as he moved backward, watching not his opponent's weapon but the shoulder of the arm that held it. Before the weapon could move the arm must move. Before the arm could move the shoulder must move.

"You don't deserve the name of *sthondat!*" Guardmaster spat the words in disgust.

And before the shoulder can move, the mind must move. Myowr-Guardmaster was confident, his stance solid. Pouncer could sense his developing attack . . .

There! He screamed and leapt before his opponent could, claws extended as though they could rip mag armor. Guardmaster pivoted out of the way and Pouncer went past, to roll and recover and attack again, but Guardmaster fell back and countered. As he did, Pouncer dropped sideways to the ground, kicked out, and connected with his opponent's ankle. Guardmaster tumbled forward, overbalanced with his forward momentum, and Pouncer rolled to one side to avoid the molecular blade coming down at his head. He flipped to his feet, only to be knocked backward as his opponent back-kicked from below and swung around. He found himself flat on his back with the tip of Guardmaster's variable sword a paw-span from his nose. *Fear is death,* he told himself again, but fear was not the only emotion that led to death, and he could see his own face snarled in kill rage in the perfect mirror of Guardmaster's breastplate.

"Your line ends here, *sthondat*." Guardmaster's words were laced with contempt, and Pouncer knew he had lost.

"Hold!" By the wall First Trainer had his arms upraised, stopping the duel. "First positions."

Panting hard, Pouncer retrieved his variable sword and made the chest-to-nose-to-chest gesture that acknowledged his opponent's victory. Guardmaster responded in kind. "Well fought, Pouncer. Well fought, but you leapt with anger again."

"You taught me yourself, when in doubt, attack."

"And were you unsure of what I was going to do?"

"I knew you were about to attack."

"I know you knew, I saw it in your eyes. So you had no doubt, but you attacked anyway. When you are sure of your opponent's intent, anticipate it in order to defeat him. When you are unsure, attack to make him unsure also, but do not overcommit yourself."

Pouncer moved back to his starting point. "You insulted me, Guardmaster."

The battle scarred warrior rippled his ears. "Of course. I fight to win, and if I can cloud your mind with anger I *will* win. Insults will not kill you, but losing self-control is fatal. Rage is death. Anger makes you fight hard, but you cannot win if your mind is not clear."

"It is easier to say than to exercise."

"One day you will be Patriarch, Pouncer, and then you will have no one but yourself to keep your rage in check."

"I will do better, Guardmaster." Pouncer took a deep breath to ready himself for the next bout. "Again, First

Trainer?" He moved to resting guard position in anticipation of the command.

"Again! *V'scree!*"

"Wait!" All three of them looked up to the gallery that ran around the top of the arena. Second-Son-of-Meerz-Rrit was there watching them. Pouncer's younger brother had the same Rrit-characteristic orange/black coat as he did, but he was short and broad compared to Pouncer's lean form, with a distinctive series of black bands along his shoulders and back.

"Your training time is long over, Elder-Brother. This is my time for the Arena."

A momentary annoyance washed over Pouncer. Second-Son was right, but as always his manner was unnecessarily hostile. He raised his ears and kept the irritation from his voice. "Of course, Black-Stripe, I am tired of looking up at Guardmaster's blade anyway."

Second-Son's lips curled in a suppressed snarl at the sound of his hated familiar-name but he too kept his voice level. "Rrit-Conserver is expecting you."

"My test is tomorrow, brother."

Guardmaster watched the exchange in distaste, offended by Second-Son's antagonism. He trained First-Son because he enjoyed it and Second-Son because it was his duty. He hefted his variable sword and cocked an ear in not-quite-sincere invitation. "Would you care for a bout, Second-Son?"

"I will confine myself to the training drone." Second-Son's voice held an arrogance he was entitled to by birth if not by ability. "Guardmaster, First Trainer, you are dismissed."

Guardmaster swirled his tail in indifference. "As you wish." Trainer gathered his training aids, turned to Guardmaster and Pouncer, and gave a claw-rake salute.

"Sires, until tomorrow." He left through the training gate.

Guardmaster turned to Pouncer. "A quick hunt in the Darkmoon Park might make a meal."

Pouncer depowered his mag armor, the perfect mirror surface reverting to lustrous copper, and tossed it aside for the pierin training slaves to collect. "The Hero's Square Market has easier prey for a tired student." He rippled his ears in amusement.

Guardmaster twitched his tail as he depowered his own armor. "Hrrr. You know I disapprove of the risk."

"What risk, with you as my sword and shield?"

"I'm too old to duel on some *kzintzag's* whim." Guardmaster twitched his whiskers grumpily. "But I'd better come so you don't get yourself lost."

On the gallery above them Second-Son watched them leave, his lips curling up over his fangs in distaste. He had been watching them for some time from the shadows of the gallery, his impatience growing steadily. First-Son used the arena as though it belonged to him, as he acted about all things in the Citadel of the Patriarch. The knowledge that one day it *would* belong to him, along with the Patriarchy and all that went with it galled Second-Son. The jotok beside him sensed his displeasure and tried to slip away, but a curt gesture stopped it. He ignored her, his thoughts occupied with his brother. It pleased him to see Guardmaster administer humiliation to his father's favored son, but there was no denying Pouncer's skill at single combat. Second-Son disdained the rigors of the formal combat form and its emphasis on self-restraint. Instead he preferred live meat. There was little danger in a duel between a hapless slave and a noble equipped with mag armor and a variable sword, but much excitement. Dueling slaves was forbidden, and First-Son lacked the liver to defy their father's edict, but simple obedience was not what it took to wield the power of the Patriarchy. For now there was little that Second-Son could do but bear his brother's unfounded arrogance and keep his trophies well hidden, but one day his moment would come. When Second-Son was Patriarch he would wear his ears with pride, and everyone who saw them would know he backed his rule with his own claws.

With a gesture he ordered the cowering slave onto the arena floor and then screamed and leapt from the balcony, his variable sword a blur of slash attacks as he channeled the rage he felt at his brother into his weapon.

> *Generosity gives a generous life.*
> —Wisdom of the Conservers

The sun was up and on its way down again, filtering soft light through the high canopy of sheetleaf trees in the Eastern Park, warm on Pouncer's fur as he and Guardmaster went over the burbling Quickwater at the River Gate bridge in the outer fortress wall. Once the Citadel had sat on an island in the river, but the fortress had long since outgrown its boundaries. Only at River Gate was the Citadel's outer wall still protected by water. Upstream the other fork flowed through an ornate portcullis in the Middle Rampart to form the centerpiece of several of the parks and gardens within. Around River Gate smallholdings were scattered, visible here and there between the huge, gray sheetleaf trunks, largely the homes of those who served at the Citadel. Pouncer threaded his way down the wide paths, enjoying the stretch of his muscles after the hard training session.

"One day you will be challenged here." Guardmaster reemphasized his disapproval. The safety of the Patriarch's heir was his responsibility.

Pouncer rippled his ears. "I imagine myself equal to it with you by my side." Guardmaster's deadly precision with a variable sword was legendary across all of Kzinhome.

"A wise warrior chooses his opponents, sire. He doesn't let his opponents choose him. You are the Patriarchy."

Pouncer waved a dismissive paw. "My father is the Patriarchy. I am only his son, and he has many sons."

"You are the oldest, and by far the most worthy to succeed him."

Pouncer rippled his ears, understanding the implied comparison with his next-oldest brother. "Black-Stripe is young yet. I remember when you took another unruly and disobedient kitten into training."

Guardmaster's irritation faded at Pouncer's humor. "That one has improved with the seasons."

"And has some improving yet to do."

"You are too hard on yourself, sire. You have mastered a great deal for your age."

"My father cannot walk in the market." Pouncer changed the subject, uncomfortable with praise for a performance he felt was substandard. "His leadership is too important to risk. But the *kzintzag* will see his son and know the Patriarchy doesn't hide behind the Citadel walls. It is important."

Guardmaster was silent. *He is right*, he thought to himself. *Which does not mean I have to like it.*

It was some distance to the market, but the breeze was heavy with its scent, the urine marks of the stall holders, hot metal from a coppersmith's booth, leather from a cloak vendor's, frightened prey animals in display cages, ozone and oil from gravcars, fresh plasteel from component shops. Pouncer inhaled the scent, sampling each of its notes with pleasure. There were times, more and more frequently of late, when he thought it would be easier to live as a crafter did, his days bound by nothing more than the cycle of trade and tradition. It was a thought without honor, he knew, but he could not deny its attraction.

The Quickwater bent around into their path once more and the trail took them over an ancient bridge of mossy stone. Over the rise beyond it was a vast clearing in the canopy, Hero's Square, the ancient intersection of four great trackways. Once it had been a walled fortress itself, though unlike the Citadel's continually updated defenses the walls were now more tradition than protection, breached with walkways over and tunnels through. Workshops crowded tight along the concentric rings of stone, suntiles gleaming on the rooftops to power the machines inside. There was an audible buzz, machines and slaves and kzinti, working and bartering and gossiping among the bustling stalls. Gravcars hummed overhead, bringing goods from all over the plain, from all over the planet, from the edges of the Patriarchy and beyond. If you couldn't find what you wanted in Hero's Square you could always find someone who could get it for you.

Pouncer sniffed the air, licked his chops, delighted at the sight. "Come, I'm hungry. Let's go here." He pointed to a *grashi* vendor's stall on the less fashionable side of the square.

Guardmaster rippled his lips in distaste. "We can find better than that farther along."

"Hunger has no time or place." Pouncer headed for his chosen booth.

"I serve the Rrit, sire." Guardmaster's tone was smooth, but his annoyed tail flip made his feelings clear.

It was not the poorest stall in the market, but far from the most lavish. Heavy jars of thick, pungent sauces lined a polished stonewood countertop attended by an old kzin, his ears tattered and scarred and his fur faded. Behind the counter were stacked cages of *grashi*, sniffing and scrabbling behind the bars. Below them larger cages held eights of close-huddled *vatach* and a handful of some exotic off-world prey that Pouncer didn't recognize, dappled gray fur and long ears, whiffling noses. Pouncer leaned on the counter, inhaling the rich scents of the booth. It might not have been the most refined venue, but if his nose was any measure it served fine food.

The vendor moved to serve them, then made a startled claw-rake salute when he recognized the Sigil of the Patriarchy tattooed on Pouncer's ears.

Pouncer acknowledged the salute, waved a paw as the old kzin started to abase himself. "What have you today, Provider?"

"Sire, my humble offerings are surely not worthy of your palate." The vendor continued to abase himself.

"Hunger exalts the simplest food." Pouncer ran his eye over the sauces on display on the counter and the ranks of caged burrowers behind the vendor. "Are your *grashi* wild?"

"They are, sire. My son hunts beyond the Mooncatchers for them." The vendor stood, somewhat hesitantly, and came to the counter.

"What sauce do you think best?"

Provider ladled a dish full of dark red sauce from one of the containers and slid it across the counter. "This is made with *tunuska*, very tangy but smooth. Please try it." Expertly he fished a wriggling burrower from one of the cages, beheaded it, and drained its blood into the bowl. Pouncer took the offered bowl and dipped the still warm body into the sauce, then popped the burrower into this mouth, enjoying the fresh crunch.

"Your sauce is excellent!"

"I have new *vatach* as well, Patriarch, also wild-caught, if you care to sample them." He was already pulling another jar of sauce forward. "This one is made with *nyalzeri* eggs." Serving First-Son-of-Meerz-Rrit would bring him more *strakh* than a whole season of his usual custom. Now that his surprise was gone he was anxious to impress.

"They could not be better than your *grashi*. Two bowls of this *tunuska*, and twice-eight of *grashi* each."

"Of course. You'll have my finest." The aged kzin ran a practiced eye over his stock, choosing carefully. Finally satisfied, he expertly fished his quarry from their cages into two wriggling bags and slid them across the counter.

He ladled another bowlful for Guardmaster. "I am honored by your patronage, sire."

"I am honored by your hospitality, Provider." Pouncer took the *grashi* bags and handed one to Guardmaster. They walked in silence for awhile. Toward the center of the square the market plaza opened into a park with low stone tables under widespread tangletrees. Pouncer disdained them, choosing instead to relax on a shaded hillock. He set his bowl down carefully, opened his bag and let a *grashi* run, pouncing on it like a kitten before dipping it in the bowl. The *grashi* had the deep, musky flavor that farmed *grashi* lacked, and the sauce accented it perfectly. His companion ate slowly, his eyes far away.

"Something is troubling you, Guardmaster."

Guardmaster looked at Pouncer and concealed his surprise. He had not meant to express his concerns, even nonverbally. *The heir is perceptive, more perceptive than I give him credit for.* He weighed his answer carefully before speaking. "It is not fitting, sire, for the Patriarch's son to share honor with a streetvendor."

Pouncer made a dismissive gesture. "Are the *grashi* not fresh enough for you?"

"The *grashi* are excellent, as are the sauces, but for the First-Son-of-Meerz-Rrit to eat from a market stall . . ." Guardmaster swept a paw to take in the vast expanse of the square. "There are many fine places here eager for the patronage of the Patriarch's line, vendors who have spent years building their reputations, even vendors with halfnames. To squander the *strakh* of Rrit Pride on a stall merchant, this is not done."

Pouncer rippled his ears. "You would rather spend the

day reclining on a padded *prrstet* being hand fed by trained kzinretti, is that it?"

He knows better than this, thought Guardmaster. *He is testing. Why?* "The order of things is not lightly defied, sire. The Lesser Prides are very traditional and they compete keenly for the honor of the Patriarch. If Rrit *strakh* is casually dispensed to street rabble there will be talk, and Rrit *strakh* will be worth less. Your father needs their solid support now more than ever."

"And the support of the *kzintzag* is not equally important? Provider's *grashi* are excellent, his sauces rich and finely spiced. Does he not also deserve a measure of the *strakh* so greedily hoarded by those fortunate enough to be born to a half-name? Today First-Son-of-Meerz-Rrit was his customer. By this evening the whole market will know. By tomorrow he will have not a stall but a house, and if his quality remains this high, his *strakh* will be no more than he deserves."

"In three days your father sits with the Great Pride Circle, and he will be asked why his son gives honor to a stall vendor when he would be a welcome guest at any pride on the Plain of Stgrat. Degrade the honor of Rrit Pride and you degrade the honor of every pride that swears fealty to us."

"And no doubt my father will say that the Patriarchy gives honor to any who deserve it, regardless of station. Perhaps the Lesser Prides will put more effort into earning their positions and less into parading what they already have."

Guardmaster was silent, but he looked at Pouncer with new respect. *He is impetuous perhaps but he is growing out of that, and his political sense is already keen. He did not do this casually. He calculated the effect this would have quite finely, and on every level. He is sending a message to his father and the Lesser Prides and the kzintzag as to the sort of leader he will be. And to me. Tomorrow he faces Rrit-Conserver's test. I wonder if he is ready?*

Steel is no stronger than the sinew that wields it.
— Si-Rrit

It was twilight, and Third-Guard stood at his post by the River Gate, mag armor gleaming in the fading light, variable sword held at the ready. His post was mostly ceremonial; the Citadel's weapons systems reached into high orbit and its sensors extended across half-eight-squared octaves of the electromagnetic spectrum. He was the last line of defense before the walls of the Citadel itself, and the chance that he would stop an enemy who had somehow evaded the sophisticated layers of protection above him was vanishingly slight. Nevertheless he took his post seriously. He served the Rrit, one of the elite *zitalyi* of the Patriarch's personal guard. It was an honor, and he would prove himself worthy of it. His equipment was well maintained, his stance alert and ready.

"Sire! Myowr-Guardmaster!" Third-Guard leapt to attention and claw-raked. The Patriarch's Son and the leader of the *zitalyi*! It was well that he presented himself as a warrior should. The Rrit rewarded fealty and competence above all.

"Good watch, Third-Guard?" Guardmaster's critical

eye took in his warrior's equipment and deportment at a glance, and finding nothing lacking, carried on without comment. Approving silence was high praise from the taciturn commander. Third-Guard was pleased with himself. He practiced his combat drills daily. He was lethal with anything from heavy beam weapons to his bare teeth and claws. It was his place to be that way, now more than ever that the Great Pride Circle was meeting. The leaders of the Great Prides could not see the gamma ray lasers and mag launchers that protected the Citadel. They could see Third-Guard, and it was important that what they saw impressed them. More than one had commented on the discipline and bearing of the Patriarch's Guard, wishing their own Heroes were at such a standard. That was heady talk, coming from the double-named rulers of worlds and star sectors.

And they impressed him! Kzinti whose ancestors had left Kzinhome eight-cubed generations ago! The white-pelted ice-warriors of Churrt Pride, their fur thicker than a *tuskvor*'s, the tall and lean Vdar of Meerowsk, Dcrz Pride of ancient Kdat with their rarefied rituals. Some of the newcomers' dialects were barely understandable, their customs uniformly bizarre. The other day Chmee-Cvail himself had swept through, with a retinue of odd-faced Pierin slaves of a noticeably different breed than those who belonged to the Rrit, and just before watch he had traded stories with a retainer of Kchula-Tzaatz, heard tales of jungle hunts on steamy Jotok and the Puppeteer first contact. It was stuff to fire the imagination, and he had decided then and there to get on the next available ship headed anywhere. There was a universe out there to conquer, if he only had the liver for it. In the service of the Rrit he could not fail to win honor.

There was a splash from the Quickwater beneath the bridge. Was it just the play of the waves against the pilings? It was not repeated, and any other night he would have ignored it. Tonight . . . tonight it was worth investigating. He leapt easily to the riverbank, tapped his keypad, and brought up a spybot. A moment later one floated down from perimeter patrol, grav polarizer whining quietly. He beckoned it forward and gestured under the bridge. Its AI chirped its acknowledgment and the seeker tilted, slid sideways, and dropped over the rail, searching. A moment later it popped back up again.

All clear.

Good enough. The seeker hummed back up to its patrol circuit and Third-Guard relaxed, went back to his alert post, and allowed himself a little fantasy of a vast estate on some distant, yet unconquered world. He would have a name and his kits, yes, his many kits would have names too. End of watch soon, then back to the barracks and food, and tomorrow he'd see about getting signed on to an assault ship. He was *zitalyi*, and any seasoned commander would be glad to take his pledge.

Another splash—there *was* something down there. Third-Guard went to the rail and strained his eyes in the gathering gloom. The water burbled against the bridge supports. He saw tumbled rocks, the gray stone wall of the citadel rising vertically from the river shore, nothing else.

Something moved in his peripheral vision. He jerked his head up but there was nothing, just more rocks. He looked closer. *Was that rock there before?* Something was wrong. He didn't bother with the spybot, though its sensors were better than his eyes could hope to be; he just leapt the railing and dropped to attack crouch, beamer ready.

There was a flash of movement, something large and dark coming fast. He swung his weapon up and around, but too slow. Razor fangs dug into his neck and he felt burning pain and numbness. He tried to cry out but couldn't. Something dark and scaly filled his vision, its skin rough and rock textured, blending perfectly with the stone of the citadel wall, and then it faded into invisibility in the twilight as the world dimmed to blackness.

It is said that Telepath knew the minds of his enemies, and so became a great warrior. Because he also knew the minds of his Pride he became a great leader. None could stand against him, and so his strakh grew until he was Pride Patriarch, then Great Patriarch, and then finally Patriarch. And because he knew the minds of ally and foe alike he was a wise Patriarch, but Telepath's ambition outweighed even his great wisdom, and his yearning for power would not be stilled. He envied the Fanged God, who had dominion over the entire world and the moons and the stars, and so he tried to know the mind of the Fanged God that he could then challenge him and take his place. But no mortal Hero can know the mind of the Fanged God and retain his reason, and so when Telepath Saw what the Fanged God can See he was driven insane. The Fanged God could have killed him then, but he gives honor to those brave enough to challenge him, and so spared Telepath's life in the duel. His reason gone, Telepath was transformed from Patriarch to outcast czrav in a single day, with no strakh, with no Pride. Cjor became Patriarch, and Telepath was forgotten. He wandered eight times around the seasons, reduced to hunting sthondats just to survive. One day he wandered to the Temple of the Black Priests, who took him in and cared for him. Because he had been eating sthondats this is what they fed him, and when his reason returned they found a place for him at Cjor's side as his Telepath. And to this day it is the duty of the Black Priests to care for the telepaths, and to this day they take the lymph of the sthondat and sit by the Patriarch's side.

—Kitten's Tale: The Legend of Telepath

Pouncer woke early and splashed himself in his bathing pool before allowing his Kdatlyno groomer to dry and comb his pelt. He was uneasy about his upcoming meeting with Rrit-Conserver. Tests were not unusual in his life but this one was different, and not only because he had no idea of its nature. The Great Pride Circle was meeting in two days, Pride-Patriarchs and Emissaries from all the worlds of the Patriarchy gathered in his father's Great Hall. It was the first such meeting in his lifetime, only the second in his father's. The Patriarchy was changing; power structures as fixed as the constellations were now in flux. Even he could see that. What that meant wasn't clear, but he knew it would require him to be a strong and competent Patriarch, stronger and more competent perhaps than he was capable of being. His mood did not improve as he left his chambers and walked through the arching stone pillars in the Hall of Ancestors. The Hall was lined with portraits and statues of long-dead Patriarchs, and their eyes seemed to follow him as he walked. He felt history bearing on his shoulders like some vast weightstone. It was an increasingly common reaction in him, an acute instance of the inescapable effect of the imposing bulk of the Citadel of the Patriarch. The fortress was ancient beyond memory and huge beyond easy comprehension, a vast warren of towers, walls, courtyards, and passages. The Rrit Dynasty was thrice-eight-cubed generations old at least, and the Citadel had been their stronghold all that time. Its origins were long lost in the dim past but it certainly predated space travel. It had been extended and rebuilt and re-rebuilt so many times that it was doubtful any of the original construction remained. Even so, the stone floors of the Inner Fortress were worn deeply concave by the paw pads of countless Patriarchs. How many First-Sons had walked the Hall of Ancestors? They didn't bear counting.

Pouncer had grown up in the Citadel, explored its myriad corridors as a kitten, played in its secret spaces, dutifully learned its history from the stern Rrit-Conserver. At first the structure had been as pervasive and unnoticed as the air he breathed, but as he matured he had slowly come to understand what the vast fortress represented, and was increasingly unable to escape its implications.

It was about *power*, nothing more and nothing less.

The Citadel was built to protect what belonged to its keepers and aid them in taking what belonged to others. Every detail of its construction, from the ancient stone battlements of the Inner Fortress to the mag field generators and laser cannon of the Outer Fortress, was aimed at that goal. Every tapestry, every holo, every sculpture in it told a part of that story of conquest. It was a nexus of control, its influence radiating from the Command Lair protected deep within its heart to the very borders of the Patriarchy, no less than fifty light-years in any direction you cared to point. That control stretched to vast fleets of warships, uncountable legions of Heroes, orbital dockyards, bases, colonies, entire star systems, eight sentient slave species, eight-squared Great Prides. All of them swore fealty to the Patriarch.

And it was certain that Meerz-Rrit deserved that fealty. He was a fearless warrior, cunning tactician, consummate diplomat. His honor was beyond question and his wisdom beyond measure. He was everything a Patriarch should, no, *must* be to exercise control over that vast empire. When he died there would be no lack of heroic deeds to immortalize in stone and steel, no shortage of tales of valor and victory to add to the eight-to-the-fourth stanzas of the Rrit Pride saga.

But when Meerz-Rrit died, Pouncer would become Patriarch. From his earliest realization of that fact he had applied himself diligently to master the skills he would need to rule his father's empire, but the more he learned the more he found he had yet to learn. He had long since despaired of achieving his father's greatness. Recently he had come to despair of reaching even minimal competence. He would have given a lot to have been born to a less demanding role. He rippled his ears at the irony, his mood lifting slightly. There were few in the Patriarchy, he knew, who would not have eagerly traded places with him, even, no *especially* Black-Stripe. His half-brother's ambition was clear, but Second-Son was young yet. A few more years trying to gain the skills required of a Patriarch would leave him happy to accept the role of trusted *zar'ameer*, the Patriarch's right hand, as his uncle Yiao-Rrit did for his father.

His steps brought him through the armory hall to the Puzzle Garden, a great courtyard within the walls of the Middle Fortress. An intricate hedge maze of manicured scentvine filled most of it, its configuration changed every High Hunter's Moon by means of clever gates that were themselves puzzles to open. You could lose a day, or several, trying to find your way through its convolutions to the amusing surprises the Jotoki tenders hid throughout it, but the maze itself was the least challenging puzzle in the garden. The best work of the Conundrum Priests came to the Puzzle Garden. Some of the sculptures were generations old, and some of them had never been solved.

Rrit-Conserver was waiting on a bench near the maze entrance. "You are late, First-Son-of-Meerz-Rrit."

"I abase myself, Rrit-Conserver. I must confess no eagerness for today."

"So I surmised. And how was yesterday's discipline with Guardmaster?"

"I have much to learn yet. Sometimes I fear I will never master the formal combat forms."

Conserver nodded. "This is good. You are improving."

"I don't understand, Conserver."

"Single combat, like many disciplines, can never be fully mastered. You may only strive for continuous improvement. Knowledge of your limitations is the first step to maturity. From maturity comes self-discipline, which will allow you to excel at the warrior's art."

Pouncer twitched his whiskers. "Your words don't fit my ears."

"In time they will."

"I am here for my test, Conserver. How may I prepare myself?"

"There is no preparation. You are going to visit Patriarch's Telepath." Rrit-Conserver rose, the blue robe and sash of his station swirling as he led the way to the maze entrance.

A tremor of not-quite-fear ran through Pouncer as he followed. Like all of his kind, Patriarch's Telepath could hold no rank or status, crippled as he was by his addiction to the *sthondat* blood extract that enhanced his inborn talent. Unlike other telepaths he was treated respectfully, even deferentially. In the Patriarch's court it was whispered that his Gift could reach to other stars, that he could read the thoughts of the recently dead, that he could *become* the minds he probed. If the rumors were true it spoke volumes for his strength of will that his Gift hadn't claimed his sanity. Pouncer for one believed them. You had only to stand once in the presence of Patriarch's Telepath to know the truth of his power. It was a presence he systematically avoided.

Not today. A Whrloo slave was waiting at the maze entrance for them, no taller than Pouncer's knee, carapace iridescent in the afternoon sun. Conserver pointed. "This slave knows today's route to the center of the maze. Telepath is waiting for you there."

"I will do my best."

"I know you will." For a moment Pouncer thought he detected a note of concern, even compassion, in his gruff mentor's manner. Rrit-Conserver's disquiet did nothing for his sense of equanimity. The Whrloo buzzed into the air. Wings blurring, it twirled on its axis and headed down the arching scentvine corridor. Pouncer hurried after it.

The route the Whrloo took led quickly into the heart of the maze, past intricate gardens whose flower arrangements hid route clues and carved game stones whose solutions coded hints to other mysteries. The puzzle gates had been set, Pouncer realized, to allow fast access to the maze center, if you happened to know the turnings. Another Whrloo buzzed heavily past and as Pouncer turned to watch its iridescent flight he saw a five-armed Jotok resetting one of the gates behind them. Anyone who happened to wander into the maze later would find his route impossible to follow and, he had no doubt, the center impossible to find. His test would be held not just in the inherent security of the Citadel, not in a closer privacy ensured by guards, but in subtle secrecy. Who might command *zitalyi* set by Rrit-Conserver to stand aside? Only his father, and his father was occupied preparing for the Great Pride Circle. So it was not just the test itself but the very fact that the test was occurring that was secret. *It is serious, very serious*, he thought to himself, and the knowledge was unsettling.

The slave led him quite quickly to the center of the

maze. There was a larger garden there, shaded by tangle-trees, and a water-clock. A fountain at its top splashed streams through a bewildering array of troughs and basins, driving wheels and levers to move the gears that turned its bronze dials. The motion was ever changing and chaotic but the clock itself kept perfect time. Ordinarily Pouncer could have spent half the afternoon enjoying its motion. Today it didn't merit a glance.

Patriarch's Telepath lay curled in the sun beside the clock, lying on a polarizer-lofted *prrstet* and tended by two silent Kdatlyno. His body was wasted, muscles melted away and fur thinned by the toxic side effects of the *sthondat* drug. His eyes were huge in his shrunken face, seeming to stare at nothing as he lay there. Other telepaths entered the mind-trance only when the drug was on them, but Patriarch's Telepath seemed to never leave it. A thin strand of drool stretched from his lips to the *prrstet* and his breath came with obvious difficulty. To Pouncer he seemed to be dying, but he always seemed to be dying and perhaps death would have been a release from the strange and painful reality he inhabited.

"Approach me, First-Son-of-Meerz-Rrit."

An involuntary shudder ran through Pouncer as the crippled kzin turned his vacant gaze on him. He stepped forward, not wanting his inward hesitancy to show. *Not that I can hide it from him.* Patriarch's Telepath was blind, Pouncer knew, but he didn't need eyes to see more than most could ever dream of.

"You will be Patriarch." Telepath said it flatly, as if it were already fact. His voice was low and rasping.

"Yes, Telepath."

"We are here to learn if you are worthy to assume that role. You will be tested."

"Of course, Telepath."

"Are you ready?"

"Yes." *No!*

"You are far from ready." Patriarch's Telepath examined him through blind eyes. "You may recall the Black Priest's test. This test is more difficult."

"I was just a kitten then." Pouncer remembered the huge black-furred figure, his mother's anxiety as he was taken away.

"You are a kitten now. Nevertheless events overtake us. There are tremendous forces at play. The future holds chaos."

"What forces?" It could only have to do with the Great Pride Circle. There would be ample intrigue there, as the Prides jockeyed for position and status, but Telepath's words hinted at something weightier than the order of precedence. "Does my father know?"

"I am sworn to serve your father. Sometimes the best service is silence. I am doing all I can for him. Right now I will test you."

"I am . . ." He stopped. It was said Patriarch's Telepath could not help knowing a mind in his presence if he tried. Why say anything at all? "Let us begin then." Even as he wondered what form the test would take, the world disappeared and he was alone in a void that had not even the solidity of darkness. He was vaguely aware of his knees buckling beneath him, and then even that touchstone was gone. He flailed wildly, managed to knock his head, and pain flared momentarily, a beacon of reality in the endless nothing.

Panic gripped him and he struck himself again, deliberately and harder this time, but the pain was less and he felt himself drifting away, losing himself. He fought down the urge to slam his head against the ground. There was a limit to how much pain he could inflict on himself, and he knew it wouldn't be enough to save his sanity.

Fear is death.

He couldn't feel himself breathing, and the drowning terror gripped him.

Fear is death. He felt as if he were already dead. *I must be calm,* he told himself, but he had nothing on which to anchor his awareness and the raging animal at the back of his brain screamed in inarticulate terror.

Fear is death. He repeated the phrase like a prayer while panic savaged reason in his mind. He fought it like a physical thing. *Rage is death.* But it was all he had to fight the panic with. Rage and terror fought in his mind like wild beasts while his awareness cowered and struggled feebly to make itself felt.

His brain spun and there was no sight, no sound, no smell, no touch. His body was gone and he was dead. More than dead, he was—*erased*—his very being utterly obliterated; he had never been and never would be, and the universe was vast and empty and uncaring and the nameless horror that dwelled at its center reached out for him and plucked the fragile thread of his ego from his shriveled mind and cast it into that vastness to drift forever screaming, and he yearned for oblivion to end the infinite nothingingness. The warmth and intimacy of simple death would be welcome beside it.

And in that moment he realized he was free. The

emotions at war within him were not him. He could not suppress them, but they did not control him. Death could not bring fear, could not bring rage. Death could only bring release, and it welcomed him into its close embrace, and consciousness faded to nothing.

All human beings are born free and equal in dignity and rights. They are endowed with reason and conscience and should act towards one another in a spirit of fellowship.
—Article 1 of the United Nations
Universal Declaration of Human Rights

The UNSN battleship *Crusader* dropped out of hyperspace and drifted. Captain Ayla Cherenkova looked out into the star-dusted night, watching as the scene slowly rotated in the transpax. She was hoping to pick up 61 Ursae Majoris, Kzinhome's star. From this distance it would be a brilliant flare, powerful enough to cast shadows, easy to find. If she was on the command bridge she would have known whether *Crusader*'s rotation would bring it into view, because she would have known *Crusader*'s orientation.

But she was not on the command bridge, she was in the targeting control blister, observing over the shoulder of the gunnery officer as a passenger. *Crusader*'s weapons systems were powered up, but if she was seriously expecting a fight Cherenkova would have been required to be in the crash position in her stateroom. It wasn't an arrangement she was comfortable with and it rankled, not for the first time on the voyage. Trying to find their destination star was just a distraction to quell her desire to be on the bridge. *Crusader* already had a captain. She didn't need two.

After half an hour of searching she gave up. If Kzinhome's star was in her field of view, she couldn't pick it out. She was just about to turn away from the window when a kzinti battleship appeared out of nowhere and halted, decelerating from who knew what velocity to zero relative in an eyeblink. The gunnery officer was strapped into his combat couch, but Cherenkova jumped backward reflexively, although if the maneuver had turned into a collision the reaction wouldn't have saved her from two million metric tons of warship coming through the transpax windows at some hundreds of meters per second. She picked herself up off the floor and looked at the alien warcraft. She was not five hundred meters away, bristling with weapons and absolutely stationary, velocity vector completely killed with respect to *Crusader*. The kzinti captain had tremendous faith in his navigation computer.

Cherenkova allowed herself a wry smile. *It may be the ratcat has tremendous faith in his pilot*. It wasn't beyond the kzinti to do a precision approach on manual. They might even see it as a point of honor.

"It's huge." Major Quacy Tskombe had come up behind her, tall, broad shouldered, dark complexioned in an age where social mobility had blenderized most racial markers. He was intelligent and articulate as well; his refined surface made him well suited for a diplomatic mission, though his eyes hinted at dangerous depths to his character. She was used to military men, but war in space was not ground combat, and the difference showed in the way he moved, as lithe and powerful as a kzin, a lethal force restrained by will. He was undeniably attractive—more than that, he was *intriguing*—but Cherenkova carefully avoided showing even the slightest hint of interest. A liaison would be a pleasant diversion for the duration of their mission, but the mission itself was too important to muddy the interpersonal waters with sex.

She nodded, pointing. "See the paired launch tubes? That's a Hunt class battlewagon." She paused to figure out the dots-and-commas script on the warship's prow. "*Fanged Victory.* She's got terawatt gamma ray laser turrets and a spinal mount meson cannon as primary weapons. She carries four wings of dual-role fighters, eight heavy assault landers, and a brigade of shock troops."

"All kzin are shock troops." Tskombe wore the Valor Cross for the defense of the Kirlinkon base on Vega IV. He would know. "Could we stand up to it in a fight?"

"*Crusader* could. You and I might not survive it."

He paused to examine the other ship more closely. The kzin warcraft had the beauty of raw power. She was watching his eyes, saw them widen. He pointed. "Could we stand up to two of them?"

She followed his finger. A second battleship had appeared, this one not quite so close. She shook her head. "We'd make them know they'd been in a fight, though."

He nodded silently, his finger unconsciously tracing the long scar that ran across his cheek from ear to chin where a kzin he'd thought was dead had come within inches of decapitating him. *Crusader* was here in kzinti space by invitation, safe passage guaranteed. Nevertheless the display of firepower could not help but be intimidating, a physical reminder of the magnitude of the task they were undertaking.

Tskombe turned. "We should go. The ambassador is ready in the docking bay."

"If we must." Cherenkova was a line officer, command experienced, combat blooded, with more than enough success on her record to warrant command of a ship like *Crusader*. Her mistake had been learning to speak the Hero's Tongue, or rather in allowing that fact to be put on her personnel file. Now instead of a line command she was here as the naval attaché to the Special Mission to Kzinhome. It was, she had been told, a great honor to be among the first group ever formally invited to be in the Patriarch's presence under flag of truce. She would rather have been offered the battleship; her form of diplomacy worked better with seeker missiles. So far as she was concerned, it was the only kind that worked with kzinti at all.

The shuttle was waiting for them, and Lars Detringer was there to see them off.

"Good luck, Captain." He offered his hand.

"Thank you, Captain." Ayla shook it. *Might as well be professional.*

He didn't let her hand go, met her eyes. "I mean it, Ayla. Be careful down there."

"I will." She gave him a warmer smile than she'd intended to, squeezed his hand with feeling. She and Lars had walked the thin edge between friendship and rivalry since the Academy. His assignment to *Crusader* had stung, and the way he'd landed it hadn't made her happy. *But that's the way the game is played, and he just recognized that earlier than I did.*

She moved on as he gave more formal best wishes to Tskombe. They were the last ones into the passenger compartment. Kefan Brasseur was studiously reading last-minute reports on the diplomatic situation on W'kkai. He was the ambassador, an academic from Plateau of aristocratic Crew descent and the nominal leader of their group. His bearing bordered on arrogant but there was no disputing the tremendous knowledge he had accumulated in a lifetime of studying kzin culture. Across from him, large enough to make Tskombe look small, was Yiao-Rrit, the Patriarch's Voice, his fur the characteristic tiger-striped dark orange of the Patriarch's line. He was clearly cramped in the confines of the shuttle but seemed relaxed enough. He was wound far less tightly than she had expected him to be, being almost offhand with his offering and receipt of honorifics. She was not entirely comfortable dealing with kzinti on friendly terms, and she had consistently avoided being drawn into the poetry games he and Brasseur played to pass the time in hyperspace.

They waited in silence while the ramp was sealed and the pilots did their cross check. Then the bay doors slid open and the shuttle lifted and slid out into space. Cherenkova's stomach tightened. They had crossed the point of no return. She was walking straight into the stronghold of her enemies.

"I smell your anger, Cherenkova-Captain." Yiao-Rrit's voice was a purring rumble.

She looked up sharply. "A great many lives have been lost . . ." She stopped before she said what she wanted to say. Her anger was more personal than that. "A great many more hang in the balance here." *I have learned to speak like a diplomat.*

"I have no doubt you will perform as a warrior should."

She nodded. "Perhaps too many of us have been performing too well as warriors." *Where did that come from?* She wondered a little at her own thought processes. She had trained half her life for starship command, dreamed of it since she was a little girl. She had worked hard, very hard, to get where she was, and she took tremendous pride in herself as a combat commander.

But the job of a warrior was to destroy the enemy. *In the end all I am is a hired killer for the state.* She was by now worldly wise enough to know that the UN government was not as pure as it made itself out to be. The higher she rose, the more duplicity and corruption came into play. At the rank of senior captain, politics played as much role in assignment and promotion as ability, which was why Lars Detringer was standing on *Crusader*'s command bridge instead of her. At the rank of admiral considerations of status and power began to take priority. At the level of the General Assembly . . . She didn't want to think about that. The holocasters uncovered scandal after scandal, nepotism, patronage, influence peddling, bribery, blackmail, theft in the millions, fraud in the trillions, and not infrequently murder to cover it all up, but nothing ever changed. Before the kzinti came the UN had used liberal applications of psychodrugs and extensive and intrusive surveillance to keep its citizens in line. After the kzinti a continuous alternation between war and the threat of war had been sufficient excuse to keep the rights of the populace from interfering with the prerogatives of power. The armed forces served to protect humanity from the kzinti, but they also served to protect the government from humanity, and Cherenkova was all too aware that frequently the second role was more important than the first.

Perhaps that's why I'm so uncomfortable around Yiao-Rrit. He was the Patriarch's brother, a major force in the rule of the Patriarchy, and he had pledged his honor to her safety as her escort. Yiao-Rrit lived by his honor code, and she was quite sure he would die by it if that became necessary, which was more than she could say of any politician and most of her command structure. She owed her loyalty to her race and her anger at kzinti aggression ran deep, but where did it leave the honor of her service when her enemy was more worthy of her respect than her own chain of command?

It took under a minute for the shuttle to cover the short distance between the two craft, another couple for the kzinti hangar to be sealed and pressurized. Yiao-Rrit took the opportunity to rummage in his travelbag. He handed them ornate crimson sashes with a heavy metal badge on front and back.

"You must wear these at all times."

"What are they?"

"This symbol is the sigil of the Patriarch, demonstrating that you are under his protection. Without these you may be killed as game."

Tskombe didn't look pleased, but said nothing. He too was accustoming himself to speak as a diplomat. Brasseur had been chosen because of his knowledge of kzinti culture, and Cherenkova was sure he was an intelligent choice for the role. She and Tskombe had been picked because it was felt the kzin would respect their considerable combat experience. The wisdom of that decision remained to be seen.

The ramp hissed and slid open, and Cherenkova looked out into a sea of predatory faces. *I have nothing to be afraid of.* Her hands were slick with sweat as she put the sigil over her head.

Yiao-Rrit sniffed the air and looked at her. "You are in no danger, Cherenkova-Captain. You are under the protection of the Patriarch."

He was right, of course. That didn't stop the danger signals leaping from her hindbrain to her adrenal glands. The lead kzin came aboard and performed a ritual cringe before Yiao-Rrit.

"I abase myself, sire. I am Chmee-Captain. I trust your journey was successful."

Yiao-Rrit returned the salute with a relaxed paw wave. "It was, Chmee-Captain."

"We have quarters prepared for your guests, and entertainments for the in-fall."

"Excellent." Supple-armed Jotok slaves took the humans' baggage and led them into the depths of the ship.

Cherenkova found their quarters spacious. In fact everything aboard the alien warcraft was spacious by human standards, but the gravity was set too high and the lighting made everything orange. The kzinti had expected her to share accommodations with Tskombe. Brasseur had been given his own stateroom as leader of the mission. She felt a little thrill at that news, and the conflict in her heart between desire and duty rose a notch, but Brasseur chivalrously volunteered to trade his own. She hadn't expected that of him, but he was Plateau Crew. It was probably noblesse oblige. She couldn't protest, and though the move spared her from temptation she couldn't help but feel a twinge of disappointment.

Sleeping arrangements were a couch as big as a king-sized bed, covered in pillows and blankets. The washroom was a high-technology sandbox in an alcove paneled in scented wood; she'd figure that out when she had to. Food was waiting for her, thick slices of alien meat piled high on a platter, elaborately prepared and seasoned and absolutely raw, with a thin-bladed knife as the sole eating utensil. They'd given her a hydrogen torch to cook it with.

She considered it at some length. *It can't be more alien than squid*. She wasn't that hungry yet.

The door slid open and a kzin stood there, all fangs and claws, pupils contracted to narrow slits. What were kzin protocols about knocking and privacy? Brasseur had lectured them endlessly on kzin history and society, but it was the small details that mattered. She realized she had much to learn if she was going to do her job properly, and she was going to have to learn it in a hurry.

"You are the *kz'zeerkti* Cherenkova-Captain?" Its words were slurred but intelligible. *Kz'zeerkti* was the common semi-slang term for humans in the Hero's Tongue, the name of a tree-dwelling, vaguely monkeylike species on Kzinhome. It could be used as an insult, or simply descriptively.

"Yes." She nodded, reflexively, not sure if the kzin would understand the gesture. Would Brasseur be as lost as she was? Academic knowledge was not practical experience, but he had lived twelve years on W'kkai.

"I am Second Officer. At the invitation of Chmee-Captain, there is a dance display in honor of Yiao-Rrit's return."

A dance display? She tried to imagine the huge carnivore before her dancing and nearly laughed at the image. That would be bad. Laughing showed teeth, and showing teeth meant challenge; she knew that much at least. She considered, looked again at the bloody slabs of meat on the platter, looked at her beltcomp. It was more than twenty hours until planetfall on Kzinhome. Watching the display would give her something to do, and might give her some new understanding of kzin culture.

And it certainly would be an experience she'd never have again in her life. That decided her.

"Yes, I'll go."

Second Officer gave her a claw-rake salute and left, and Cherenkova decided that he had meant *kz'zeerkti* in its purely descriptive sense. He was probably as uncomfortable with interspecies protocols as she was. *We call them ratcats anyway, because they look like naked-tailed tigers, and that's both descriptive and derogatory.*

The display was held in a large room with wide tiers going down to a circular stage area in the center. The tiers were padded for reclining, too large to be easy steps for a human. She clambered down to where Brasseur and Tskombe were already waiting and exchanged greetings. A tier below them Chmee-Captain and Yiao-Rrit snarled amicably back and forth, their voices quasi-musical in the room's excellent acoustics. She had the déjà vu experience of a night out at the opera, waiting for the show to begin while the orchestra tuned up. She made herself comfortable, sitting back against the next tier. The padding material was resilient and warm and as she settled, the lights suddenly went down and a rhythmic beat began.

For several minutes that was all there was. The music built in tempo and volume, and then a spotlight came on and a kzin leapt onto the stage, pelt a uniform tawny gold and small, at least by kzin standards, with a distinctive dark tail-tuft. The dancer looked left, then right, pounced forward and then crawled, head low to the ground, tail twitching from side to side. Perhaps the dance simulated hunting.

Brasseur pointed excitedly. "I've heard of this; I've never seen it. This is a stylized version of the offering display where a female is gifted from pride to pride."

Female? Cherenkova looked, saw for the first time the prominent teats. All of a sudden she saw the dancer's movements in a whole new light.

"Aren't the females non-sentient?"

Brasseur nodded. "In relative terms they are, but they're smarter than chimpanzees, just to put them in human perspective. They have language and tool use. These dances take months of training, and skilled trainers command considerable *strakh.*"

"What's *strakh?*"

"Reputation or status, more or less. Kzinti have no currency; they trade based on *strakh.* If you have high *strakh* you will be offered fine goods by the best craftsman, invitations to high-profile hunts, even fealty by other kzinti. By accepting you enhance the *strakh* of the giver as well as your own. Only the finest crafters have their work accepted by the nobility. If you have lower *strakh* you wouldn't be made the offer in the first place."

"How do they keep track of it?"

"How do you keep track of who owes you a favor? It's their culture, they just do." He pointed at the stage. "Shh, it's the next sequence."

Another kzinrette had joined the first and the dance became an intricate pairing of symbolisms, mother and kitten, hunter and prey, male and female in mating. Some of the meanings were unclear, but there was a sensuous, powerful beauty to the way the lithe females swayed and stretched in syncopy with the rhythm. A third leapt in and the movements became more complex, the three circling nose to tail, reversing, leaping outward. Again the movements clearly symbolized roles, maybe entire stories, but they were now too abstracted for Cherenkova to tell what they meant.

One of the dancers leapt upward and yowled, a long, earsplitting wail. Cherenkova clapped her hands over her ears. Brasseur's fascinated absorption with the display didn't waver, but beside him Tskombe grimaced. The intricately unfolding dance was beautiful, the steady percussion rhythm compelling. The wail cut across the experience like a rusty band saw. The kzinrette sounded like nothing more than a wildcat in desperate heat. The next dancer in the circle leapt upward and yowled, if anything louder and longer than her sister.

Cherenkova looked at Yiao-Rrit and Chmee-Captain in front of her, leaning forward, tails twitching with ill-concealed eagerness, and realization dawned. The kzinretti *were* wildcats in desperate heat. She was watching an alien strip show. The third dancer leapt and wailed. She looked at her beltcomp. They were still more than twenty hours from Kzinhome.

> "Where does honor come from?" asked Conserver.
> "It comes from skill," said the first kit.
> "Very good," said Conserver. "You shall be Artisan," and then again he asked, "Where does honor come from?"
> "It comes from courage," said the second kit.
> "Very good," said Conserver. "You shall be Warrior," and then again he asked, "Where does honor come from?"
> "It comes from integrity," said the third kit.
> "Very good," said Conserver. "You shall be Patriarch." And as he said it, so it was.
> —Kitten's Tale: The Lesson of Honor

All at once the void was gone and Pouncer found himself lying on the ground in the Puzzle Garden maze. His throat hurt and he realized the scream echoing from the distant fortress walls was his own.

His throat was ragged, raw. How long had he been screaming? How long had been lying there? The shadows were long. Evening then, but as his vision swam into focus he realized that was wrong. The air was rich with dew scent. He found Forgotten Tower, high on the edge of the Middle Rampart, followed its shadow. It pointed west. It was morning.

He'd been there almost a full day? Was that possible?

In his mind it had seemed an eternity. He became aware of a presence. Patriarch's Telepath was staring down at him.

"I was dead. My mind was gone . . ."

"You have passed your test." Telepath's voice was flat and tired, exhaustion heavy on his wasted features.

"I felt as though I couldn't breathe."

"Many times you did not breathe."

Not breathing? That thought gave him pause. "Patriarch's Telepath."

"Yes?"

"That place I was in . . . Could I . . . would I, have died there, had I not passed the test?"

"To survive is to pass the test, to die is to fail it."

Anger came over Pouncer, but washed out, faded anger with no strength behind it. "That is too dangerous. You must not do that again. Not to me, not to anyone." He tried to stand and failed.

"Not all necessary things are safe."

"I nearly died. I wasn't ready."

"I knew you would not fail."

"Then why the test?" Pouncer would have screamed, if he had had the strength. "Why put me through that?"

"You also had to know you would not fail." Telepath's head dipped to his couch and his eyes slid closed. "The maze path has been changed." *I already know this*, thought Pouncer. *I am more observant than he thinks*. Patriarch's Telepath waved a paw wearily. "You are exactly as observant as I think. Your mind is oppressive. Leave me now. Events are beyond immediate control. I have much to do, and I need to rest."

Pouncer started to say something, thought better of it, and stayed silent. With an effort he found his feet. The waiting Whrloo buzzed into the air and Pouncer followed it again. Unlike the route in, the route out past the changed gates was long and convoluted, and the sun was almost down before he made it back to the outer Puzzle Garden. Pouncer was not entirely surprised to find Rrit-Conserver still waiting for him at the maze entrance, for all he could see, in the exact same position he had been in when Pouncer left.

"You knew what was going to happen." The anger Pouncer had been unable to muster at Telepath spilled over onto his mentor.

"I knew as much as Patriarch's Telepath would tell me."

"What did he tell you? That he would gut my brain like a prey animal? That I might die in battle with my own mind?"

"He told me you would pass."

"He told me that himself, afterward." Pouncer shivered involuntarily. *The blackness.* "I am not convinced."

"Rage is death."

"Rage is . . ." Pouncer's lips twitched over his fangs and he felt the kill rage coming over him at the platitude, but regained self-control with an effort. *He is right. I am acting from anger. I have passed, whether they knew in advance or not, whether I might have died or not, I have passed, I have survived.* He breathed deeply and repeated the mantra. *Rage is death Fear is death.* Telepath's test had been more trying than simple annoyance with Conserver.

After a long moment he spoke, his voice level. "Have you been tested like that yourself, Conserver?"

"Telepaths will not share minds with Conservers."

"Why is that?"

"It is against the traditions."

"You taught me that no tradition exists without reason."

"Hrrr." Rrit-Conserver looked at First-Son with care. *He is gaining wisdom. He will make a good Patriarch.* He composed his answer carefully. "They have their reasons, I am sure. They are not well treated by our culture, and we Conservers hold the keys to that culture, we and the Priesthood. They work for the long term, as do we. It is not necessarily the same long term."

"He said events were overtaking us. What events?" *Why was I tested so early?*

"The Great Pride Circle is meeting. The Patriarchy is at a turning point. Our growth has been checked by the monkey-humans. Worse, we have gained the hyperdrive . . ."

"Hyperdrive is not new."

"Its use throughout the Patriarchy has reached a saturation point. Its reliability approaches absolute, and it is now the dominant means of transport. We cannot continue as we have before."

"The humans have shown nothing but advantage in possessing it. We now communicate faster than light, mass forces in an instant. How can this fail to aid us?"

Conserver waved a paw hand down, *this-does-not-follow*. "This technology does not serve us as it serves them."

"Technology is neutral. It is up to us to find its best application."

"You must understand the difference between ourselves and humans. We feed at the top of the food chain, and it is very difficult for us to move lower. At the bottom of the chain are photosynthetic plants. They provide the totality of energy available to the system. Every layer above them represents a drop in available energy of nearly eight-squared times. When you eat a *grashi* burrower you are using energy only one-over-eight-to-the-sixth as efficiently as the plants eaten by the insects that the *grashi* eat."

"I fail to see the connection."

"Each kzin require a tremendous amount of resources. We are large, warm-blooded carnivores. We require a tremendous amount of energy, all of it filtered through several layers of food chain. The sheer physical space required to support that many plants is a major constraint on our population density. We are evolved to live in these low population densities, and so we respond poorly to crowded conditions. The amount of a planet's surface we can use is small compared to the amount humans can use."

"This is irrelevant to the application of the hyperdrive."

"It is key!" Conserver held up a paw. "As our population expands we must have more space, or fight each other for what we already have. We were fortunate to gain gravity polarization before population pressure forced us to repeated internal wars. Ever since, the Patriarchy has been stabilized by its ability to expand."

"So hyperdrive can only aid us in that."

"No, hyperdrive is tremendously destabilizing."

"How so?"

"Before hyperdrive, speed-of-light placed serious constraints on communications. The head of a Great

Pride bent on conquest had strictly limited information on potential adversaries. Imagine yourself in his position. Ahead of you is the unknown, unexplored worlds, unconquered species. Behind you is the might of the Patriarch, immense fleets patrolling worlds we have already fully populated. Where should you direct your Heroes?"

"Outward, of course."

"Yes, outward. Our history shows us that we have always conquered as we expand. What fool would take the risk of turning against the Patriarch when external conquest is both easier and more profitable."

"This is still true."

"No. The *kz'zeerkti* have shown us that our victory is not inevitable. And with hyperdrive communications the Patriarchy is no longer a vague but immense monolith of power at the backs of the Great Prides. Now the Pride-Patriarchs can gauge our strength with fine accuracy. Now they have the means to communicate among themselves. The Rrit remain more powerful than any single Great Pride, but if four or eight band together the equation changes radically."

"Would any Pride-Patriarch worthy of his name contemplate such treason?"

"In matters of power honor becomes increasingly flexible. And the rules of *skalazaal* apply to the Rrit as much as to any Great Pride."

"*Skalazaal!* There hasn't been a War-of-Honor since Kzan-Rrit!"

"The tradition exists, the rules are defined. Cvail Pride is making ready to leap on Stkaa Pride."

Pouncer's ears swung up and forward in surprise. "I haven't heard of this!"

"Stkaa doesn't care to advertise their weakness, nor does Cvail want their ambition made clear."

"Conserver, this is too much to absorb."

"Absorb it quickly. You have been tested far too early. Patriarch's Telepath was insistent it be done at once."

Pouncer cocked an ear. So it was not Rrit-Conserver who had pushed him into the test. That was interesting news. "Why?"

"Hrrr . . ." Conserver waved a paw. "Many minds come together in Telepath's. With so much information he can judge how events will unfold far better than you or I. He felt it important. That was sufficient for me."

"He didn't share his reasons?"

"Patriarch's Telepath seldom does."

"I will sleep with this tonight."

"Your father wants you at the Great Pride Circle tomorrow."

"I am his son." Pouncer made the gesture-of-abasement-to-the-Patriarch-in-his-absence and took his leave, intending to put the day out of his mind. Far too much had happened to deal with at once, but he found he could not push his disquiet away. *The Patriarchy is reaching a turning point. Events are overtaking us.* If Conserver and Telepath were this concerned he should be too, but he lacked information. That had to be fixed immediately. Tomorrow he would begin research.

The farmer labors long in the field and is bitten by gnats. Each day he bends his weary back to

the mud to tend the crop. The builder strains to lift stones and breathes the dust of his hammer; his hands are dirty and cut. The soldier carries great loads slung around his neck, like that of an ass. He thirsts and hungers and is beset by enemies. Be therefore a scribe, and lift nothing heavier than a stylus. The Pharaoh shall seek your advice, and reward you with wealth and slaves.
—Egyptian inscription from the rule of Amenemhet IV of the Twelfth Dynasty of the Middle Kingdom

Kefan Brasseur smiled to himself. The House of Victory was huge and ancient, framed in black, dense-grained timbers a meter on a side with walls of cut and dressed boulders taller than he was. The furniture in the human delegation's apartment was exquisitely carved, the walls of their rooms covered in pelts and heads and weapons. Kdatlyno touch sculpture, vases from the dynasty of the mighty Si-Rrit, exquisite ply-murals crafted by the legendary Pkrr-Pkrr while humans were still scrawling on cave walls—the opulence was endless. At least ten thousand years of Patriarchal history was laid out on display. Their rooms were high up in the structure, the view through the huge windows showing all the varied architectures of the Middle and Outer Fortresses, and beyond them the sweeping vista of the Plain of Stgrat. He could spend the rest of his career in the House of Victory and never stop learning.

Even the normally impassive Tskombe was impressed, examining ancient weapons and suits of armor with fascination. Only Cherenkova seemed indifferent, her attention focused on her beltcomp. She had grown progressively more withdrawn on the voyage to Kzin, and now that their audience with the Patriarch was about to begin she had lapsed into brooding silence.

"You don't like being here, do you?"

She looked up. "Since you ask, no, this wasn't my choice of assignment."

Brasseur raised an eyebrow. "Why not?"

"I don't believe there's any point to negotiating with the kzinti."

"I have to ask again, why not?"

"You might as well negotiate with a polar bear. It isn't that they aren't intelligent, it isn't that they don't have a role to play in the arctic ecosystem. It's just in their nature. Polar bears are the top predator in the food chain. If one gets hungry, it'll eat you. That's what polar bears do."

"You think that's what kzinti do?"

"I know it is. I've seen it." Unbidden, the images burned into her brain at Midling research station came into her mind's eye and her jaw clenched as she looked away, not wanting him to see her expression.

"You hate them."

"They think we're animals. I think they're animals." Cherenkova spoke with more intensity than she'd meant to.

"Both views are correct. It's a human conceit that we're somehow better than anything else in the galaxy. The kzinti have had a spacefaring civilization for fifteen thousand years at least, maybe fifty thousand. We have a tremendous amount to learn from them. Just consider—"

Cherenkova cut him off. "Have you ever studied ruins, professor? Buried cities, anything like that?"

"Of course. I was an anthropologist before I switched to studying the kzinti."

"Did you learn a lot from them?"

"Yes . . ." Brasseur's answer was hesitant; he was unsure where she was leading.

"Well, maybe their civilization needs ruining." There was venom in her voice. "Just think what you could learn."

The academic just looked at her and Ayla looked away. *I've said too much, let my emotions interfere with my judgment.* The silence dragged out to an awkward length. It was relieved by the heavy door swinging ponderously open. Yiao-Rrit came through, halted and gave a claw-rake salute. "I present my brother, Meerz-Rrit, Patriarch of Kzin."

Behind him another kzin entered, this one wearing a deep blue cloak with a scarlet sash bearing the sigil of the Patriarchy. Yiao-Rrit stepped aside to allow his brother forward. Behind him was a third kzin, this one dressed in Conserver's robes. Brasseur came to attention and returned the salute. "I am Kefan Brasseur of Plateau, representative of humanity."

Yiao-Rrit made a gesture and half a dozen slaves bustled into the room, carrying trays laden with delicacies. Brasseur recognized three Jotoki and two Kdatlyno, but the sixth was completely alien to him. It was a six-limbed cross between a turtle and a rhinoceros beetle, perhaps a meter high with long eyestalks, flying clumsily on buzzing, translucent wings. It seemed to be in charge, directing the other slaves in their tasks. *It must be a Whrloo.* He had heard them described in passing, but had never seen so much as a holo of one. He knew they were both rare and prized as slaves and nothing else about them. He watched its heavy, bumbling flight with fascination. It wore a grav-belt to help it fly; its homeworld had to have low gravity in order to allow a creature so heavy to hover, as it was clearly designed to do. Its delicate structure implied the same thing. The gravity was a third more than he was used to on Plateau, not an unbearable strain but enough to make his feet tired at the end of the day. *It can't be happy here on Kzinhome.* His distraction was short-lived. Meerz-Rrit padded to an immense skin rug by the room's enormous fireplace and reclined, completely relaxed. No human could be in the company of any kzin without being awed by their lethal grace and power, but the Patriarch stood out even among his peers. He had *presence.*

"Sire, I present the Emissaries of Earth." Yiao-Rrit spoke in the formal tense, indicating each of the humans in turn. "Kefan-Brasseur-Leader-of-Negotiations, Cherenkova-Captain of the UNSN, and Tskombe-Major, representing the UNF."

Brasseur went to a *prrstet* and tried to emulate the Patriarch's quiet, powerful confidence. He was less than successful; the room was too large and the interpersonal distances too great for human social comfort. He glanced at Tskombe and Cherenkova and saw they weren't completely at home either. They had all grown used to kzin-scale furnishings aboard *Fanged Victory* on the flight from the edge of the singularity, but those were cramped and utilitarian by kzinti standards. The House of Victory was built to be grandiose. *I had forgotten this from my time on W'kkai.* He would do well to remember quickly.

Meerz-Rrit spoke, his voice a calm rumble. "The situation our races face is dire, Kefan-Brasseur. Worlds may die if war occurs again."

Brasseur collected himself, very aware he was representing all of humanity in these vital negotiations. "The decision to fight is not ours, Patriarch."

The Patriarch made a dismissive gesture. "We do not besiege your planet as you besiege W'kkai."

"Your incursions into our space continue. Ships destroyed. People kidnapped and enslaved."

"The MacDonald-Rishshi treaty allows this."

Across the room Cherenkova flushed. "It does not! It specifically states humans may not be enslaved by kzinti!" There was anger in her voice.

Brasseur looked up at her sharply. Clearly something had touched a nerve in her, but top-level diplomatic negotiations were not the place for personal emotions. "My colleague is correct. Kzin violations of the treaty have been constant. War is inevitable if these are not stopped immediately."

"You question my honor . . ." The Patriarch's tone was halfway between question and statement. He was giving Brasseur the chance to back away from a breach in protocol.

Brasseur chose his words carefully. To insult the Patriarch would be diplomatically disastrous, if not personally lethal. At the same time, he had to convey the seriousness of the human position, or the negotiations would fail. "Your honor is beyond question, Patriarch. Unfortunately the incidents we have documented are also beyond question. We must find a way to prevent them from recurring."

"The Passenger liner *Freedom* . . ." Cherenkova was reading from her beltcomp, ignoring the ongoing conversation. ". . . captured by the kzinti cruiser *Long Leap*. The Hercules deep space research base, raided by an unknown kzinti warship with its personnel enslaved on W'kkai. Belt Resources mining station on the asteroid Persephone at Farstar, raided and pillaged by forces from the attack carrier *Chosen of the Fanged God* . . ."

The Patriarch held up a paw and interrupted. "Rrit-Conserver, please clarify the relevant provisions of the MacDonald-Rishshi treaty."

The robed kzin stood and spoke. "Provision twice-eight-and-five of the MacDonald-Rishshi treaty forbids the use of armed force between the forces of the Patriarch and those of the United Nations. Provision thrice-eight-and-one forbids the enslavement of any legal entity by the forces of the Patriarchy, legal entities defined as follows . . ."

The Patriarch made a gesture and Rrit-Conserver fell into silence. "As you can see there is no relationship between the provisions of the treaty and the incidents referred to here."

Cherenkova stood up, anger in her voice. "All of these incidents are documented, Patriarch. We have statements from survivors, investigators' reports, damage assessments . . ."

"I am sure your research is thorough, Cherenkova-Captain." Meerz-Rrit leaned forward, muscles unconsciously tensing to pounce. The time to back away from protocol breaches was rapidly passing.

"If you do not dispute the facts then you must admit your responsibility, Patriarch."

"Hrrrr. You suggest I dishonor myself. That has no merit." Meerz-Rrit's lips twitched over his fangs, and Brasseur felt his stomach muscles tightened. The Patriarch was angry, and these negotiations were too important to risk that outcome. He shot a warning glance at Cherenkova, but her own face was flushed, her expression grimly triumphant, and she wasn't looking at him. He held up a hand to speak.

"Perhaps if you could explain your understanding of the treaty, Patriarch."

The big kzin's eyes bored into Brasseur's. "The intent of the treaty and its wording are both clear. My implementation of it, and that of my warriors, have been comprehensive. There is no meat in leveling these accusations at me."

"And yet these incursions continue." Tskombe broke in, his voice flat.

"These are Heroes on conquest, the name-seekers of Stkaa Pride, perhaps even Cvail Pride. They are not the forces of the Patriarchy."

The tall soldier shrugged elaborately, a gesture almost certainly lost on the kzinti. "They scream and leap in your name."

"Of course they do. I am Patriarch. This does not imply they act on my commands."

"The distinction is lost on the UN, Patriarch."

Meerz-Rrit waved a paw, palm down. "The treaty was forged at the insistence of the UN, and its provisions were written by humans to meet the requirements of humans. Now humans have come to quibble over the words that they wrote." The Patriarch's tail twitched in annoyance. "Of what use are words written on paper? If you have faith in my honor you do not require written words. If you have no faith in my honor then no words will change that."

"The issue is not your honor, Patriarch." Again Brasseur chose his words carefully. "The issue is the prevention of another war. The words are simply a tool. Written or spoken, their purpose is to convey meaning and build understanding. If the words fail at their task they must be exchanged for words that succeed. That is the purpose of this conference."

"Hrrr. I will overlook the insults implied by your presentation here today. I will not hear any further accusations." The Patriarch's lips twitched over his fangs, and his claws extended of their own accord. He was deeply angered, Brasseur could tell. Best not to push him further.

"I abase myself, Patriarch." Brasseur made the gesture. "No insult was intended."

"We may now turn to the issue of human honor." Meerz-Rrit's fanged smile relaxed, but his eyes remained fixed on Brasseur, making him feel like a prey animal. "The UN has taken the colony world Ch'Aakin, in flagrant violation of the treaty. There is no room for misinterpretation here. Military action against W'kkai and its subject worlds must cease immediately."

Cherenkova answered before Brasseur could. "This action was taken because the Patriarchy has not acted to prevent Heroes from screaming and leaping in its name." Her repressed anger came out as sarcasm. "Ch'Aakin was identified as the base for many of these attacks."

"The treaty does not require the Patriarchy to do any such thing." The Patriarch's tail lashed as he spoke. "However it does require the UN to respect kzinti worlds.

The actions of the UN, Cherenkova-Captain, are contrary to both the letter and the spirit of the treaty. If humans value words so highly then humans should let their actions follow their voices." The Patriarch's lips twitched over his fangs again. Brasseur felt a thrill of real fear go through him as he saw the negotiations foundering on the Patriarch's hair-trigger honor and Cherenkova's ill-repressed hostility.

"If I may interject." Rrit-Conserver had raised a paw. "The issue is simple. War is imminent, it has in fact already begun in the destruction of Ch'Aakin and the siege of W'kkai, though we characterize these as skirmishes to avoid the larger implications. If we in this room cannot find a solution, the toll in death and destruction to both our species will be immeasurable. We cannot alter the past; we might yet alter the future."

For a long moment there was silence. Cherenkova looked down again, studying her beltcomp intently. Meerz-Rrit's eyes narrowed, and he leaned back in his *prrstet*. He looked over the humans dispassionately. Finally he spoke. "My adviser speaks wisely. This is a negotiation. What is it precisely the UN wishes to negotiate for?"

Brasseur took a deep breath. "Our position is simple, Patriarch. Kzinti raids against humanity must stop. It does not matter who is responsible, it only matters that they cease."

Meerz-Rrit nodded slowly. "And what does the UN offer in return for this forbearance?"

Brasseur carefully kept himself from smiling. When a kzin asked for an offer there was room for bargaining.

"What does the Patriarchy demand?" Let the Patriarch put something on the table.

"Hrrr. The return of all of our colony worlds from Ch'Aakin all the way back to Hssin, the cessation of the siege of W'kkai, an agreement limiting the sphere of expansion of human space, an agreement limiting the number of warships deployed by the UN, a program of reparations to redress the atrocities committed by human forces; these are the primary requirements. Yiao-Rrit will provide you with a detailed list."

Tskombe's eyes widened. "I can tell you now, Patriarch, the UN will not the able to meet that list."

Meerz-Rrit switched his gaze to Tskombe from Brasseur. "Why is that?"

Tskombe shrugged. "It will not be politically possible."

The Patriarch growled, a deep rumbling sound. "It is necessary. What you are asking requires that I restrict the freedom of the Great Pride of Stkaa, and by extension of all the Great Prides. This they will not accept easily. Tomorrow the Great Pride Circle meets, and there are pressures building within the Patriarchy. If I cannot show them quarry wrested from the enemy they may not follow where I lead."

Brasseur's eyebrows went up. The Patriarch was as good as admitting he did not have complete control over his Great Prides. The pressures must be great indeed. That meant danger. "If they do not follow you to peace, they will lead us all to destruction."

"Then you must give me the tools to ensure they follow."

"The UN will not do that. The populace will see it as

paying ransom. If the General Assembly agrees, even against their own feelings, they will be voted out of office. The Secretary General will not countenance it, regardless of his personal views on the matter."

"You must understand. My great-grandsire negotiated the MacDonald-Rishshi treaty with care to ensure he could keep the promises he made." Meerz-Rrit leaned forward. "You are now asking me to overstep the traditional limits of Patriarchal power. I can in principle decree what I like. In practice"—the Patriarch twitched his tail—"space is vast. My Great Prides control worlds of their own, and they have their own imperatives to follow. To deny them hunt-conquest against your species I must offer them rich game elsewhere."

"You say the Great Pride Circle convenes tomorrow?"

"It does. You were invited here so we could resolve these issues prior to its meeting."

"Patriarch! It will take hours to get a message to our ship at the edge of the singularity. The meeting will be over before it can be relayed to Earth, let alone answered. And that answer will not come so quickly. It will take weeks, months of discussion before the General Assembly comes to any conclusion, let alone an agreement."

"You're not empowered to speak on behalf of your race?" Meerz-Rrit's ears swiveled up and forward, his voice mingling anger and incredulity in equal measure. He turned to face Yiao-Rrit. "Brother, why is my time so wasted? If the monkey lords wish to insult me to war they are succeeding."

"Sire!" Yiao-Rrit raked his own claws across his nose. "I abase myself, the fault is mine. Simply arranging with the

UN for these representatives to accompany me took far longer than I anticipated. I specifically stated that those chosen be empowered to speak on behalf of their government. I should have verified this was true. It did not occur to me that the monkeys would not deign to comply."

The Patriarch turned his gaze on Brasseur, tail lashing angrily. "Why then have my emissary's stated requirements not been met? Does Earth not consider the Patriarchy worthy of this respect?"

"There has been a miscommunication, Patriarch." Brasseur felt himself sweating. The situation was spinning rapidly out of control. "We are empowered to speak, and to negotiate. We are not empowered to make binding decisions on behalf of our government. Not even the Secretary General can make that decision; he can only put forward his recommendation. The General Assembly reserves the prerogative of decision for itself."

"Your masters expect me to negotiate with emasculated lackeys." Meerz-Rrit slashed the air with his claws, and Brasseur prayed he would not choose to scream and leap.

"Patriarch, I assure there is no insult intended here. The General Assembly does not possess the power to delegate its decision-making in the kzinti style. I might add that Secretary General Desjardins is undertaking considerable political risk in undertaking negotiations at all. There are those in the General Assembly who see war as the only solution, and call negotiation appeasement. We *must* give them a better option."

"A negotiator who cannot bind his government has no goods to trade." Rrit-Conserver's tones were even, but even he showed annoyance.

Meerz-Rrit laid his ears flat and returned his attention to Brasseur. "Advise me then, human. What will you have me present to my Pride-Patriarchs tomorrow morning?"

"We must negotiate the terms under which our species can live in peace. Give them those terms and tell them the UN intends to ratify them. They need only accept them provisionally. The agreement can be formally accepted at the next Great Pride Circle."

Brasseur was not prepared for what happened next. All three kzin rippled their ears, the kzinti equivalent of laughter. "And when do you think that will be, human?" Meerz-Rrit's anger seemed to have evaporated. "My son will be Patriarch before the Great Pride Circle convenes again."

Brasseur felt himself flushing red. The kzinti were laughing at him, and both Cherenkova and Tskombe were looking at him intently. He was supposed to be the expert on kzin affairs, and this critical negotiation was about to fail because of his lack of understanding. At least the tension had dissolved.

"Does the Patriarchy want peace with humanity?"

There was a long pause. Meerz-Rrit had not expected the question, and the answer circumstances required him to give was not the answer he felt in his liver. He lashed his tail unconsciously. "Of course."

"Our species are on the way to war precisely because of the misunderstandings we are experiencing today. If you want peace you must do whatever is necessary to prevent your Pride-Patriarchs from acting against humanity in any way. There may be nothing we can do here to support you in that, save assure you that our species also wants only peace." Meerz-Rrit's ears moved to relaxed attention, and Brasseur spoke quickly, needing to get his point across before communication broke down again. "There are those on my world who do not believe the kzinti capable of peace and who therefore advocate preemptive conquest." Brasseur took a deep breath. "I know you also have to contend with forces that drive your species to conflict. Any fool can run at the front of a mob following the road to war and justify every step as simple prudence. It takes a leader to take the risks required to obtain peace."

Meerz-Rrit snarled. "Do you imply I am a fool, Kefan-Brasseur, or simply that I am not a leader?"

"I imply nothing. I merely state facts. I find no fault in principle with the Patriarchy's requirements. I will pledge my honor to do my utmost to see them adopted by the General Assembly. I cannot promise any result, but the most powerful tool you can give me is a cessation of kzin-initiated hostility. Peace requires the will for peace. If we do not have that here in this room then our races are doomed to war."

The Patriarch growled deep in his throat. "What you ask is difficult. It will require drastic measures. It may in fact be impossible." He paused, his eyes far away for a moment as he thought. "I will consider what can be done."

Brasseur breathed out, only then realizing how tense he had been. "It is our only way back from the brink of oblivion."

As skatosh tests the strength and skill of warriors, skalazaal tests the strength and skill of Prides. In skalazaal as in skatosh, no slave may carry weapons for its master, though it may otherwise serve the Pride in any way. As in skatosh, no warrior may use a weapon that does not strike with his own strength. As in skatosh, no Patriarch shall leap his pride without the challenge scream. As in skatosh, skalazaal must be declared and open for all to bear witness to the honorable combat of the contending prides. As in skatosh, skalazaal sees no victory without honor. As in skatosh, skalazaal is judged by the Conservers and their edict is final.

— The Dueling Traditions

Back in his chamber Pouncer splashed again through his bathing pool, then lay on his side on his *prrstet* while a Pierin combed out his fur. Was it the same one who had served him in the morning? He looked closely but couldn't tell. Slave Keeper would know of course, but to Pouncer the individuality of a slave was barely relevant, and yet this creature was a being as intelligent as himself. What did it think? Was it content to serve well, or did it live in fear of the hunting park?

He dismissed the slave with a paw wave, leaving his coat half brushed. The unchanging ritual of morning and evening was somehow wrong after the experience of his test. Everything was in flux, he could sense that now, though the ancient stones of the Citadel were indifferent. He closed his eyes but his mind would not quiet. Perhaps he should summon the slave again.

He rolled over and examined his pelt. It didn't need more grooming. The style among the young nobility was symbols dyed into the coat and emphasized with intricate braidings. The symbols signified prowess, accomplishment, or fealty. Pouncer preferred to keep his fur simply brushed out. It was more practical, and he disliked the naked boasting the symbols amounted to. Rrit-Conserver and Guardmaster administered too many lessons in humility for him to feel otherwise. And it was also true that he had done nothing heroic enough to be worthy of a future Patriarch, and thus preferred to keep his lesser accomplishments to himself.

Research! He must understand the Honor-War, kzin against kzin with nothing more than sinew and steel. Certainly it had happened in the histories, but so long ago. Yet Conserver felt there was a risk of it surfacing again. He needed understanding, more details! It couldn't be a threat to the Patriarchy now, could it? And the *kz'zeerkti* with their Outsider-gifted stardrive, what role would they play? The Great Pride Circle would determine the shape of the power structure he would soon rule, and the details of the intrigue and conflict that would challenge that rule. He had to know more. He called up information on his wall and began to study, the Pride-Patriarchs and their advisors, their capabilities, their strengths and weaknesses, their goals, their traditional alliances and enmities. His eyelids grew heavy but he kept at it. He would be at the Circle in the morning, and much might depend on his awareness of a subtle detail and its import. There would be no second chance to get it right.

Something tugged at the edges of his awareness. Something was wrong; he was not alone in the room. He froze, ears up and swiveling slowly, nose twitching for a hint of the other. There was no sound, no scent, but there was a *presence*, cold, reptilian, and hostile. A nameless dread rose in him and he fought down the urge to turn and flee. *Fear is death,* he reminded himself. *It's waiting,* he thought, *waiting for me to turn my back, waiting for me to drop my guard.* At the same time another part of his brain wondered how he knew that *it* was there at all. Slowly he rolled from the *prrstet* and dropped to *v'scree* stance, moving only his eyes to search the room, his ears tracking his gaze automatically. His chamber had few places to hide and he shifted his attention to each in turn, his well padded *prrstet* and its cushions, the wall tapestries, the cabinet that held his ceremonial armor, his compsole and books, the few simple furnishings, the grooming stand. Nothing moved but the ripples in his bathing pool. He sniffed the air again, found nothing but the familiar odors of ancient stonewood and fabric.

There was nothing, and it made no sense that there would be anything here in the heart of the Citadel. He willed himself to relax, to push the awareness of the other out of his mind. *I am tired,* he thought. *I am tired and unsettled and that has me jumping at shadows.* He breathed deeply. Fear was death, not only in the paralysis it brought to crisis but in its unrelenting erosion of normal life. If he allowed every potential threat to so disturb his equanimity he was not fit to be Patriarch. Fears alone in the night were for kittens, not warriors.

With an effort he straightened himself. There was a flash in the corner of his eye and he pivoted to catch something exploding out of the bathing pool, had time only to register pasty gray flesh and razor fangs before it was on him, talons extended to rake his belly open. Off balance, he dropped to the floor and the thing flew over him, one long hind talon slicing into his arm to leave burning pain behind. He rolled awkwardly away as it landed a body length behind him and turned. He flipped to his feet and back into *v'dak* stance. His upper arm was numb where the thing had clawed him. He expected a second's respite while the thing recovered from its leap and reassessed its attack but it gave him none, launching itself from the wall, talons again reaching for him. He pivoted and spun sideways, allowing it to pass and using the energy of his pivot to drive a disemboweling kick. He connected with its side and was rewarded with a satisfying crunch as bones shattered under the impact. His claws dug in and flesh ripped. The thing landed and rolled, half its side torn away. It showed no hesitation as it turned to attack again but its injury slowed it and gave Pouncer an instant to assess his enemy.

It was a horror, built for killing and nothing else. It was half his size but powerfully muscled, moving on its hind legs alone, counterbalanced by a short, heavy tail. Its mouth gaped wide to expose its fangs but it seemed to have no tongue. The eyes were large, black and pupilless, staring from beneath heavy protective brow ridges in a bony domed skull over a short, wrinkled snout that drew long, hissing breaths. Its forelimbs were powerful with dagger-curved claws, and now that it was wounded Pouncer could smell the tangy metallic pungency of its blood.

The searing pain spread up his arm to his shoulder, leaving numbness behind it. He found he could barely move it. Paralytic poison on its talons, he realized. *I must finish this now, while I still can.* The thing's fangs were narrow and pointed, designed to penetrate rather than tear flesh. *Every battle is to the death.* Would they inject poison if it bit him? He couldn't allow that to happen.

It leapt for him again and again he pivoted aside, but the thing had anticipated the move this time and its fore-claws caught in his sash, yanking him over sideways, and then it was on top of him, fangs questing for his throat. Its breath in his nostrils stank of enzymatic poisons and he could see the oily droplets of venom dripping from the ends of its teeth. Pouncer grabbed at its throat to hold it away, but it sank both its foreclaws into his shoulders and held on. He roared in pain, willing his talons to close, but the strength was fading from his arms as the paralysis seeped through them. In desperation he kicked his legs up to its belly, claws seeking flesh but unable to strike home. His grip began to slip and the thing's jaws gaped wide, reaching for his throat.

He half rolled, feeling its claws rip from his shoulders, and kicked upward, his own claws finding its belly this time and sinking in. He pushed, digging them in, and it went flying backward. He finished his roll and dropped to attack crouch, streaming blood from both shoulders, both arms numbed and nearly useless. There was an ornamental spear on the wall, part of a display and more decorative than functional. He grabbed it down, tried to level it, but it was all he could do to keep it from simply falling from his unresponsive fingers. Across the room the thing had been disemboweled by his kick, and the landing had frac-tured a hind leg. It was breathing in bubbling gasps, entrails dragging, obviously dying, but its dark, staring eyes were locked on Pouncer, and incredibly it was staggering forward, lurching on its one good leg to come at him again. Training evaporated and the kill rage swept over him, stronger than fear, stronger than discipline. The rage brought enough strength back to his arms to use them and he screamed and leapt, raising the improvised weapon in midleap. The thing reared back on its good leg as Pouncer's feet smashed into its muzzle. It fell backward and raked at him but missed, and then Pouncer was on it, slamming its head to the ground and the spearhead down through the top of its brain case.

The blow was ill coordinated and weak, but it had the momentum of his leap behind it and he felt the blade strike the stonewood floor beneath and dig in, pinning the creature there. Even then it scrabbled and fought to free itself, rear limbs kicking in a fruitless attempt to rake him. Exhausted, he fell back as the room started spinning around him. An armspan away the thing tore its own skull apart in its struggle to get at him, but he couldn't summon the strength to either get away or finish it. The paralysis his rage had held at bay swept over him again, and he collapsed to the floor, losing the struggle to fight it off. How much poison had he received from the thing's talons? How much was lethal? He needed immediate medical attention. Gathering his will he crawled toward the door and collapsed, breathing heavily. *Discipline is mind over body*, Rrit-Conserver taught. He remembered when he was a kitten and his mother, M'ress, would groom him with her tongue. *Move the mind and the body will follow.* But his body would not follow his mind, and his mind would not stay focused. The stonewood was cold beneath him, but he remembered the softness of M'ress's fur and the comforting scent of her nipples as he suckled with T'suuz, his litter-sister. *"K'vin veer ce aros zheer, marli?"* he had asked. *Will it always be this nice, Mother?* "Always," she had told him. "Always," and the kittens had cuddled close to her, hoarding her body heat as the darkness fell, as it was falling now, and he felt her warmth engulfing him again as his breathing slowed and his awareness faded. Behind him the creature had finally died, and already its body was beginning to dissolve into foul-smelling slime.

Secretary General, my fellow assemblyists, I ask you, what are the kzinti? They are animals, nothing more. Their technology is produced by their slave races. Without them they would have no more culture than a chimpanzee. I will not hear arguments that they are sentient beings under the Declaration of Rights. I will not hear arguments that they are entitled to Charter protection. They are not only animals but dangerous animals. They are vermin, plague rats, and yet we question what we should do with them. I for one am tired of debating a question with only one answer. The time for words is over. Hear me now! The kzinti must be exterminated!

—Assemblyist Muro Ravalla
before the UN General Assembly

"This system was adopted four generations ago. It no

longer reflects the realities of today!" Graff-Kdar's voice
echoed down the Great Hall of the Patriarch as Meerz-
Rrit listened with half an ear. The Great Hall of the
Patriarch was immense and ornate, the ceiling held up by
carved marble pillars and the walls paneled with oiled
stonewood, and it had heard far too many speeches just
like Graff-Kdar's impassioned declamation against the
ruinous and unfair allocation of hyperdrive engines his
pride was receiving. The Patriarch scanned the hall again,
seeking a familiar face. *Where is First-Son?* Second-Son
was there, showing an uncharacteristic interest in the art
of rulership, though the way he was toying idly with his
wtsai showed his obvious disinterest in its realities. *And
why is Second-Son carrying a* wtsai? The ceremonial
blade was an honor that came with a name, and Second-
Son had yet to earn his. *I must speak to Rrit-Conserver.* It
was not the first time Second-Son had shown casual disre-
gard for proper form.

     ". . . there is no honor in this! It weakens us all . . ."
     Today the hall was packed with Pride-Patriarchs from
every star system in his empire, each with his own agenda,
each with his own speech. The speeches were mere
formality of course, the statement for the record of each
Pride's position, what they wanted, what they offered. The
real negotiations would take place in small groups behind
closed doors far from the hall. Nevertheless, they had to
be listened to and considered, or at least appear to be considered. The honor of the final word fell to Meerz-Rrit,
and there was nothing Graff-Kdar could say about hyperdrive that could change what he was going to present to
the assembly. Where was First-Son? He felt nervous

despite himself. The human Kefan-Brasseur was correct of course. If another monkey war was to be avoided he needed to seize the Great Prides by the scruffs of their necks. That needed to be done anyway, before some upstart Pride-Patriarch decided to test his strength against that of the Rrit. Stkaa-Emissary's proposal was more appetizing. A monkey war would cost high in blood and treasure but, if he led the entire Patriarchy against them, the humans would be enslaved once and for all, and that leadership would secure the Rrit's position for generations to come. He, Rrit-Conserver, and Yiao-Rrit had spent the entire night in the Command Lair arguing strategy, and even now the best course was not clear. Balancing the present and future was not easy, and the greatest threat to his empire was not obvious. He was growing old for this kind of game, and Graff-Kdar's lengthy droning did nothing to keep him awake. He stretched to keep the circulation going to his limbs. The seasons would not go around many more times before First-Son would be ready to take his place as Patriarch.

"Patriarch! I appeal to you, as I do to all of my brothers assembled here, correct this injustice before it does irrevocable harm to the very fabric of our Patriarchy."

Graff-Kdar sat down, obviously pleased with himself, although the roars of approval from the assembly were no more than polite.

It was time. Meerz-Rrit waited for the noise to die down, waited longer, until the silence stretched out to painful length. Whatever came of this Great Pride Circle, it was ultimately about power. Making the Pride-Patriarchs wait for his words was a palpable demonstration of the power of the Rrit, and it would remind them of their places. That was important. He scanned the assembly slowly, meeting each and every gaze with his own. *Where is First-Son? He should be here to witness this, to see how power is exercised.* All the fleets in the Patriarchy were insufficient to rule with if you lacked the liver to meet the gaze of your adversaries.

Too late to wait for Pouncer now. He stood, let the silence stretch further, looking down the vast hall. Heavy banners of fine woven *hsahk* dyed Patriarchal crimson hung down the cut stone walls from the point where the huge and ancient stonewood crossbeams held up the grandly arched ceiling. Gem-set chandeliers hung down over the audience, unnecessary now with the sunlight spilling through the immense windows, arrogantly wide with hand-cut ripple glass. The Hall itself demanded words strong enough to be worthy of its magnificence. He would not fail it.

It was time. "Honored Cousins!" He paused while the word echoed down the length of the hall. "All of you have spoken today. And all of you have listened. And while all of you have raised issues of tremendous importance to the Patriarchy"—he nodded to Graff-Kdar—"I am sure that nothing has seized your livers as strongly as noble Stkaa-Emissary's call to arms against the *kz'zeerkti*."

There were muted whispers from the floor, and he paused to make sure he had their attention. "Before this gathering I spoke at length with honored Stkaa-Emissary. The Great Pride of Stkaa has been on hunt-conquest against the monkeys since before my great-grandsire's time, and they have suffered serious reverses in that campaign, most recently the loss of Ch'Aakin. W'kkai itself may yet fall."

He paused again to let that sink in, took in the faces looking at him, studied them. There was no doubt he had their attention now. There was no event in all the Patriarchy larger than the monkey wars.

"Honored Cousins! We are a race of warriors, of predators! Throughout our long history we have had setbacks and losses. Never before have we suffered so serious a defeat." There was general snarling from the floor and the atmosphere thickened with fight-scent. "There are those who doubt the competence of Stkaa Pride. There are those who doubt their courage and honor, in their failure to subdue a race of herbivores." He let his gaze fall on Chirr-Cvail, let it rest there a long moment. "I am not one of those. Let us not forget that it is Stkaa Pride who gave us the hyperdrive and opened the entire galaxy to us. Stkaa-Emissary has spoken of the unique danger the monkeys present, and I am convinced he is correct. He has asked me to lead the Great Prides as one against them. He is certain they cannot stand against the combined might of the Patriarchy. I am certain that he is correct." Again he paused while snarls of agreement rose throughout the chamber. "With the combined might of the Patriarchy devoted to their conquest, the spoils of the monkey worlds are ours for the taking. Who here doubts this?"

There was silence from the assembly, but everywhere ears were up and swiveled forward, the Pride-Patriarchs hanging on Meerz-Rrit's words. He looked to the high, hidden gallery where the *kz'zeerkti* delegation watched the assembly in secret. They would be afraid now, as they watched him speak of unrestricted war and saw the eagerness of the Pride-Patriarchs to follow him down that road. Their fear was a necessary thing, for they would carry it back their homeworld, and their overcomplex government would be convinced of kzinti resolve through it. He looked again to the assembled Pride-Patriarchs. *I must deal with two audiences here.* This would have to be played with both caution and boldness if he was to achieve the result he wanted.

"Who here would stand with me for such a hunt?"

Stkaa-Emissary leapt to his feet. "Stkaa Pride stands with the Patriarch!"

There was a long pause, and Meerz-Rrit held himself calm. *Now is the time . . .*

"Cvail Pride stands with the Patriarch!" Chirr-Cvail's need to demonstrate his loyalty showed in his eagerness.

"Tzaatz Pride stands with the Patriarch!" Kchula-Tzaatz, there was one to watch. The dam broke and tumult of voices filled as the assembly stood almost as one.

"Kreetsa Pride . . ."

"Prrrtz Pride . . ."

"Mroaw Pride . . ."

Meerz-Rrit raised his arms, pleased at the reaction but not allowing himself to relax. His first goal was accomplished; they were committed. The harder task came now. He waited for the commotion to settle, and when he spoke his voice was lower. "I am honored by your loyalty, brothers. I am pleased to see the warrior spirit is alive in the Great Prides." He paused to meet all their gazes. *This is the critical moment; my leadership turns on this instant.*

He raised his voice. "It is my decision to turn away from this path. It is my command to Stkaa Pride that they seek and maintain peace with the *kz'zeerkti*."

There was a stunned silence, then an undertone of snarls as the Pride-Patriarchs confirmed with each other what they had just heard. Stkaa-Emissary leapt onto his desk, challenge in his voice. "The warriors of Stkaa Pride will not stand for such cowardice, Patriarch! We have the obligation of vengeance to our dead. We have suffered grievously in the service of the Patriarchy. The Patriarchy cannot abandon us!"

"Do you doubt my honor, Emissary? Do you call me a coward in my own hall, before this assembly here?" Meerz-Rrit held Emissary's gaze, daring him to challenge leap.

"Your honor speaks for itself, Patriarch." Well played, neither a challenge nor an insult that could invite challenge, but nevertheless making his position clear.

"As does your wisdom, Emissary." And a worthy reply.

Kchula-Tzaatz stood up. "Stkaa Pride has enslaved this species, Patriarch, and to my knowledge they have paid their fealty in full measure. The humans are theirs to conquer as they will." His voice was smooth in Meerz-Rrit's ears. What was his game?

"They are a spacefaring race with all the power that implies." The Patriarch kept his voice even.

"With primitive technology and a pawful of worlds." Kchula-Tzaatz twitched his tail dismissively.

Meerz-Rrit slammed his clenched paw on the podium, abandoning restraint. "They swarm those worlds at a density of thrice-eight-to-the-eight-and-three! Would you

provoke the *tuskvor* where they can herd-charge the den?
Stkaa-Emissary, tell him of the attack on K'Shai."

Emissary was shaken, being called on to attack his own
position. He had been swept up with Meerz-Rrit's initial
proposal, thinking he had won his point. He stood to
address the assembly "Patriarch, I stand with . . ."

"Tell him!"

"Patriarch, this is common knowledge . . ."

"Tell him!"

Reluctantly, Stkaa-Emissary spoke. "They used kinetic
energy missiles from their home world."

"Arriving at nearly light speed! Continents laid bare,
oceans half vaporized. Only strenuous efforts prevented
ecological collapse. Am I not correct?"

"The damage was contained . . ." Emissary's voice was
plaintive.

"And K'Shai was lost! A fraction of their weapons
struck home. Had they been more accurate they would
have sterilized the planet. And remember, K'Shai was
their colony world. Tell him of the attack on Hssin."

"They ruptured the domes from space." The defeat was
clear in Emissary's voice.

"And Ch'Aakin?"

"Saturated with conversion weapons, Patriarch."

Meerz-Rrit raised his paws to the assembly.
"Conversion weapons! Used not on ships but on a world!
Hear him, Honored Cousins! Hear him and hear the
tuskvor thundering toward your kits."

"W'kkai has not yet fallen." The desperation was clear
in Emissary's voice "We too possess the power to destroy
planets, Meerz-Rrit."

"Shall we become monkeys and trade conquest for extermination? Shall we abandon our warrior's honor and slaughter what we fear?"

Emissary raked the air with his claws. "Honor demands vengeance!"

"And when your honor is satisfied shall I grant you lands on the newly barren Earth? Or would you rather the greater honor of an estate here on Kzinhome? I will have many to give you when the humans have finished stripping the crust in their barbarity."

"These are herbivores, Patriarch! Where is the honor of a warrior who accepts less than victory over a prey species? Stkaa Pride is loyal. We have suffered grievously. We ask only . . ."

Meerz-Rrit cut him off with a snarl. "I am not blind to your sacrifice, Stkaa-Emissary, nor to the obligations of fealty. I am stalking bigger game here."

"Patriarch, I . . ." Emissary was tense, poised to leap. Perhaps he would challenge after all, but that would not aid the Patriarchy.

"Enough!" Meerz-Rrit's gaze was hard, his eyes narrowed. If it came to a fight, he had no doubt he would win. For a long moment the tableau held, then, trembling with barely restrained rage, Stkaa-Emissary slowly sank back to his seat. Meerz-Rrit turned back to the assembly, breathing deeply to keep his own anger under control. "Honored Cousins! There are those who will call me a coward behind my back." And so branded themselves cowards, now that he had made the declaration. "The monkeys we can conquer, though the blood-price will be high. But the monkeys are not the greatest danger facing us. We have made contact now with the Puppeteers, whose technology is so far beyond ours that we have not even theories to explain it. We have met the Outsiders who gave that knowledge to the Puppeteers in the first place. We have learned of the Thrint, whose empire once encompassed the galaxy, and of the Tnuctipun war, which ended the line of every sentient race in all of that vastness."

Kchula-Tzaatz stood again. "Patriarch, we have nothing to fear from races long extinct. The Outsiders want nothing that we do. As for the Puppeteers"—he snorted in disgust—"I have met a Puppeteer. Its cowardice knew no bounds."

"Open your eyes! Courage is not power! The cowering Puppeteers could end our line to improve their sleep."

"Kittens' fears! When the time comes we will take their technology and hunt them for sport. When have the children of the Fanged God failed to conquer?"

"The Q'ryamoi must have thought the same before the herbivores destroyed their world."

"We have only the Puppeteers' word that the Q'ryamoi existed at all."

"I bow to your wisdom, Kchula-Tzaatz." The Patriarch's voice dripped sarcasm. "Tell me where the Puppeteer homeworld is, and I will launch a conquest fleet tomorrow."

"Just because we haven't found it doesn't mean we never will."

"And in the meantime? Even the monkeys can raze a world. Do you doubt those herd animals could do the same?"

Zraa-Churrt stood. "If I may speak for my honored cousins, Patriarch . . ."

"You may speak for yourself."

"I have seven sons. My elder will inherit my name and my Pride. My second will advise him. The other five must command warships in hunt-conquest to justify their names. If that road is closed they will fight each other for my inheritance."

Graff-Kdar stood up. "I stand with Zraa-Churrt. Eight-to-the-seventh Heroes pledge fealty to Kdar Pride. I could not deny them conquest if I wanted to."

Meerz-Rrit flipped his ears. "This is a matter of leadership. You must lead your Prides as I lead you. You have heard my decree. Will any here challenge me?" He scanned the assembly again, meeting their gazes. None of them were happy, but none of them were willing to challenge his rule. Meerz-Rrit allowed himself to relax. The critical moment was past, and he had won. "So you must lead your Prides. We now possess the hyperdrive. You can send your fleets farther than ever before, find planets where no sapient will contest your claims. We have slave species enough as it is. If you want more slaves, breed them. Replace war prizes with construction. We shall not repeat the error of the Thrint. We shall not become so feared in the galaxy that we motivate other species to our extinction." He paused to let his words sink in. "I want to make something very clear, Honored Cousins. There are those of you who will see opportunity here, opportunity to make gains at the expense of others in this circle, even at the expense of Rrit Pride." He held up a paw as some of the assembly started to rise. "No, do not protest your loyalty. There are traditions that govern duels and those same traditions govern the Honor-War. The traditions will be followed in detail, and I stand behind them with fang and claw. *Skalazaal* will be declared and open for all to see and judge, and the traditions adhered to explicitly. The Patriarchy is made strong by conflict, but I will not see it destroyed by dishonor." He paused for emphasis. "Mark my words, my Honored Cousins. I will command the full might of the Rrit against any who overstep those boundaries." He had their attention now, and he met their gazes with his own narrowed eyes. "We are not monkeys, we are Heroes. We duel with sinew and steel, claim victory with honor. If any of you here today violate the traditions, I will end your line."

Meerz-Rrit took in the assembly, looking at him now with stunned silence. It was the effect he needed to end on, and he turned and strode from his dais without another word. Behind him the Great Hall exploded into snarls as voices rose in argument. Let them debate it between themselves. He was Patriarch, and none would dispute his rule. Second-Son followed him out, looking sour for who knew what reason. He glanced again to the hidden gallery where Yiao-Rrit sat with the humans. Most important, the monkeys would know that he could have launched a war, and that he had chosen not to. They would know they need not strike at the kzinti out of fear, and they would also fear to strike themselves. It had been a good assembly. The results could not have been better. He should have felt pleased, but he didn't. *Where was Pouncer?*

Without honor there is no victory.

—Si-Rrit

Kchula-Tzaatz left the assembly immediately after the

Patriarch, leaving the swelling storm of protest behind him. He went as rapidly as dignity allowed back to his retinue's quarters in the House of Victory. As soon as he arrived he ordered his guards into discreet defensive positions. Nothing must be obvious. They were all Ftzaal-Tzaatz's elite *Ftz'yeer*, disguised as retainers and diplomats though each wore *Ftz'yeer* red and gold somewhere, here a sash, there a brassard, to meet the demands of honor. Nevertheless they were far too few to stand long should Meerz-Rrit decide that he wanted Kchula's head.

That done, he retired to his private chambers. They were lavishly appointed; Meerz-Rrit treated his guests well. No sooner had he entered than a silent Kdatlyno brought in a spiced platter of fresh killed *pirtitz*, their blood rich in a decanter of *shasca* beside it. A pair of well trained *prret* curled on cushions by the window, swishing their tails suggestively and *chrowl*ing for his attentions— pleasant distractions to offset the stresses of the Great Pride Circle. He ignored them. Rage and fear alternated in his brain, and once he stopped moving, their scents mingled thick in the air around him. It was supposed to happen during the meeting of the Circle. He had been ready, and then nothing. Nothing! He had been reduced to some weak platitude about courage.

So close! He had delayed speaking as long as possible. The drop capsules should have been landing around the Citadel even as he made his declaration of *skalazaal*.

They had not, but the assassin would have struck by now, and the Rrit be alerted to danger. Now they would be looking for the guilty, and first suspicion would fall to

him. He had to take immediate action, and for that he
needed an ally. He pointed to one of his own Jotok
attendants, waiting silently for orders. "You. Come."
Obedient and silent, the slave moved up beside him, its
five multijointed limbs waving like tentacles to make it
walk. He scribbled a note on his beltcomp and dumped
the hardcopy, handed it to the slave. "Take that to Stkaa-
Emissary, at once."

The slave abased itself and left. He could have dumped
the note direct to Emissary's beltcomp, but it would have
to travel over the Citadel's datanet. Quantum cryptcom
was secure, supposedly, but the mere transmission of the
message was information, and he had to deny his enemy
all the information he could. It was now his only advantage. A handwritten message was more private.

Of course the Kdatlyno slave who'd brought the food
was Rrit as well, and who knew what it might be reporting
to that execrable Rrit-Conserver even now. He was helpless, completely dependent upon his enemies. Rage got
the better of him, and he kicked over the table, sending
the sliced *pirtitz* flying across the room to stain the delicate tapestry. A servitorb floated over to the mess, ready
with tools for a cleaning slave, but there was no cleaning
slave, and Kchula kicked at it too. *Fools*! How could he
attain greatness when all he had to work with were fools?
That must be dealt with at once. He snapped open his
beltcomp and punched up the command bridge on
Distant Trader. Another piece of data for Rrit-Conserver's
intelligence net, but one that couldn't be avoided.

"Raarrgh-Captain." His subordinate's image floated
over the belt-comp. There was two heartbeats delay for

light speed, then his eyes widened as he saw Kchula's snarling rictus.

"Sire!"

Rage tightened Kchula's throat until he could barely get the words out. "Where . . . are . . . my . . . warriors?"

"Sire, I abase myself! The first *rapsar* capsule jammed in the launch tube. We're clearing it now . . ."

"On all the ships? You try my patience." A new fear shot through Kchula. What if it were not incompetence but betrayal . . . ?

"On *Distant Trader* only. I judged it best not to launch the Heroes without the beasts, sire."

"You judged it best . . . ?" Rage.

Raarrgh-Captain raked his claws over his face. "We stand ready to launch them on your command, sire."

"Fix the launcher! Heroes can't take the Citadel alone. Get the *rapsari* on the ground."

"We are working on it with all speed."

"Work faster!" The assassin had struck by now, perhaps the traitor as well. How long before the Rrit connected it to him? *Not long at all.* "I am vulnerable here!"

Movement behind him. It was Ftzaal-Tzaatz. "You could return to orbit, brother."

"And demonstrate my guilt by running! Are you a fool? There is nowhere to go from orbit. We can't outrun Rrit warships to the edge of the singularity."

Ftzaal's voice stayed calm. "I make the suggestion merely to demonstrate the correctness of your current course of action."

It was insulting to be reassured, but there was nothing he could do about it now. "Is there any word from the traitor?"

"None. There will be soon enough."

"You heard the Patriarch's speech."

"Of course."

"I am opening negotiations with Stkaa Pride now. They have no love of the Rrit now that their conquest plans are thwarted. We need an ally here on the surface."

There was a long pause from Ftzaal while he processed this. "I concur."

Kchula returned his attention to the image on his belt-comp. "How long before the launchers are ready, Raarrgh-Captain?"

"Before your localtime nightfall, sire, at the latest."

"Nightfall! That is far too long."

"Shall I have the Heroes leap without their beasts?"

"Don't toy with me, Captain. Fix the problem."

"As soon as possible, sire."

Alarms began to sound throughout the Citadel, a deep, sonorous booming. Kchula-Tzaatz cringed involuntarily. At best they had found the assassin, at worst the traitor. In either case he was rapidly running out of time.

> *A spy is worth eight-to-the-fourth warriors, a traitor eight-to-the-fifth.*
>
> —Si-Rrit

Two warriors of the *zitalyi* in full battle armor crouched on one knee at the entrance to the Command Lair, weapons ready in their shoulders. Their faces were hidden beneath the blast shields of their helmets, but Second-Son knew that behind them their eyes were alert, searching out threats. Second-Son moved with neither haste nor delay and his manner was calm, as befitted a son of the Patriarch, but he found it difficult to quiet his mind beneath their watchful gaze. The alarms had been shut off, but the tension in the air was palpable. The inner sanctum had been breached, the heir apparent attacked in his own chamber, almost killed. The Patriarch's Guard was disgraced and Guardmaster humiliated. Second-Son rippled his ears at that thought at least. One of the guards noticed, shifted his attention slightly, and Second-Son's momentary pleasure evaporated. The guards could not, of course, know what was in his mind, but Patriarch's Telepath could, and if he *had* looked in Second-Son's mind then those same guards would need only a gesture from Myowr-Guardmaster to kill him on the spot. Would his father order it done? He shuddered. Meerz-Rrit was Patriarch; he would have no choice.

His skin crawled as he went up to them. They did not shoot, although their manner made it clear they would like to shoot something. They waved him into the antechamber. Beyond the inner door he heard voices raised to snarls, muffled but clear.

"They have harmed my son. I will spit their heads on pikes in Hero's Square!"

"He will recover, Patriarch."

"That is not the point, Rrit-Conserver."

"Hrrr. This is the most important point."

There was a pause, then the Patriarch spoke again, slightly calmer. "You are right, of course. Nevertheless I do not intend to let the attempt go unavenged."

Second-Son breathed deeply and entered the Command Lair. Things were not going as planned. He must be calm, remain flexible, wait for his moment. The Command Lair floor was knee deep in a holo of the Citadel, defenses highlighted in red, command units shown in green, combat units in orange, support units in blue. Guardmaster was at a command desk, snarling commands into his comlink. Meerz-Rrit stopped his pacing as Second-Son came in, lips twitching over his fangs, clearly still upset.

"Do you have suspects, Father?" *Do you suspect me?*

"It is not enough to suspect. I must have evidence."

"Evidence. Who would stand to gain by First-Son's death?"

Conserver unfurled his ears. "On first inspection, only you, Black-Stripe."

A thrill of fear ran through Second-Son. "Conserver, you insult me." *He knows!*

"It is a simple fact, not an accusation." Conserver noted Second-Son's carefully suppressed reaction. *So he is involved. But he did not do this alone.*

"Had I designs on my brother I would not require such a devious weapon." *Only the* p'chert *toxin on my* wtsai. Second-Son hoped he wouldn't have to use that weapon here and now. His father, Conserver, and Guardmaster were all consummate warriors. Surprise might gain him the first kill, and the toxin might gain him the second, but that was all he could hope for, and even if he won, the guards would come in . . . If First-Son had died and he slew his father he could claim their fealty and their obedience as Patriarch, but First-Son had not died. "Stkaa Pride." He tried to keep his voice level. "Stkaa-Emissary expected your support and lost everything. He seeks vengeance." *Focus their attention elsewhere.*

Meerz-Rrit turned his paw over. "No, that . . . that *thing* . . . This attempt took preparation, and Stkaa Pride has not had time."

"If not them, then who else has cause for vengeance?"

Conserver narrowed his eyes. "It is not vengeance they seek, it is advantage."

Meerz-Rrit's whiskers twitched. "Your wisdom shows, Conserver. The attack while the assembly was in session was designed to show Rrit Pride as vulnerable before the Great Pride Circle."

"To what end, Father?" Second-Son spread his ears. *Confusion mimics innocence.*

"Perhaps they were planning to declare open *skalazaal* before the assembly, and at the same instant claim first blood. To rob Rrit Pride of *strakh* with all the Great Prides at once, and claim the Citadel and the Patriarchy for themselves." A thrill of fear shot through Second-Son. Did his father know, or was he guessing?

"No, the loss of First-Son would cost us *strakh*, but no more." Rrit-Conserver's voice was sure.

"No pride has taken advantage." Second-Son did his best to sound like he was puzzling out the problem.

Guardmaster stood from his console and turned. "They could not. First-Son did not die."

"But they did not, and could not, know that. Even we did not know his condition until his slave found him."

"The possibility frightens me." Meerz-Rrit lashed his tail. "*Skalazaal* declared and the heir dead immediately afterward. Think of the *strakh* that would accumulate to such a bold stroke!"

"But they did not make the declaration." Conserver stroked his whiskers. "Either some component of their plan was not in place, or the timing is coincidental and there is a deeper game here."

"The game is deep enough already."

Second-Son breathed deep before he spoke. "What game?" *Divert their attention!*

"This is the question." Guardmaster turned his paw over. "Declaring *skalazaal* as the stroke falls is within the bounds of honor. Attack without declaration is not. To claim it now would bring shame and censure."

Second-Son unfurled his ears. "Perhaps the perpetrators want to have someone else blamed for their crime." *Plant the seed of doubt before the evidence starts to grow!*

"Guardmaster." Meerz-Rrit's voice carried decision. "Have Patriarch's Telepath know the minds of our guests. We will find the guilty by the evidence of their own thoughts."

"Most have brought their own Telepaths. Their minds will be shielded."

"This is no obstacle for Patriarch's Telepath."

"It will take considerable time, sire, and the results may be less than reliable."

"Find me the guilty, Myowr-Guardmaster. Give me no more delays."

"As you command, Patriarch."

While they spoke, Rrit-Conserver had closed an ear to listen to his complant, his eyes far away for an instant.

"Patriarch, Ztal-Biologist has completed his investigation of the creature. His findings are ready."

"Excellent. Guardmaster, you know what I want. Seal the Citadel until Telepath's investigation is complete. If the guilty are in my house they will not leave it. Rrit-Conserver, with me."

"As you command."

Outside the Command Lair the guards fell into formation ahead of the Patriarch, clearing the corridors and rooms ahead of him in deadly earnest. Ambush by a second assassin was not impossible, and they were determined the Patriarch not fall victim on their watch. Meerz-Rrit was impassive, the agitation he had displayed so freely in the Command Lair masterfully suppressed in the presence of inferiors. Second-Son excused himself since his father had given him no instructions. He needed time and space to think. The world was collapsing around his ears. He himself would not be subjected to Patriarch's Telepath, but Kchula-Tzaatz would be, sooner or later. When he was, Second-Son's part in the plot would be known at once, and then what? *Exile, castration, death in the Arena.* There were no positive outcomes.

Curse Kchula-Tzaatz! He had promised warriors, a fast coup, bloodless and simple, and the Patriarchy as his own! Had Second-Son refused the offer, reported it, he would have been a hero, at least seen as a dutiful and honorable son. Had the plot worked, this morning the Patriarchy would have been in his grasp, First-Son dead while the Great Pride Circle met, Kchula's Heroes dropping from the sky even as Kchula himself declared the Honor-War. A simple slash with his toxin-edged *wtsai* and his father

would be out of the way, and an order sent, his first as
Patriarch, for Guardmaster's defenders to stand down.
With Kchula throwing his support to Second-Son as his
warriors secured the Citadel, none of the Great Circle
would dispute the new order. And all whom he ruled
would know he was a ruler ready to enforce his edicts with
his own claws.

But the Heroes had not fallen from the sky, and the
assassin had given the game away without even managing to
complete its task. Now what was he? A fugitive, soon to be
an outcast. If he could disappear he might live as something
more, if he could find a place, claim a name, or at least a
function. Not on Kzinhome—no, his ear tattoos marked
him—but on some far outpost. Tzaatz Pride could smuggle
him to Jotok, perhaps. Kchula owed him that much!

His went straight to the Old Tower in the House of
Victory, where the Pride-Patriarchs were quartered. He
was not supposed to have contact with any of Tzaatz
Pride; there was to be no connection between them. He
went anyway, relying on his ear tattoos to take him past
the guards of both Rrit and Tzaatz who stood outside the
quarters. At the entrance to the area reserved for the
Tzaatz delegation he found a closed door and a black-
furred kzin lounging idly on a *prrstet*, idly carving ornate
decorations on the silkwood handle of his variable sword.
The other looked up casually, eyes calmly questioning.
Second-Son found his pose insolent and unfurled his ears
to display his tattoos.

"I must see Kchula-Tzaatz at once."

"He is not available." The other seemed unconcerned
despite the urgency in Second-Son's tone.

"I am Second-Son-of-Meerz-Rrit, and I demand to see him at once."

"I am Ftzaal-Tzaatz-Protector-of-Jotok. I abase myself, sire." Ftzaal-Tzaatz made no such gesture. In other circumstances Second-Son might have insisted that his rank be recognized to the point of challenge. This time he did not. Ftzaal-Tzaatz's belt held no ears; he did not need to advertise his prowess. The Protector-of-Jotok was unmatched in single combat anywhere in the Patriarchy. "Kchula-Tzaatz is not available."

"Where is he?"

"I cannot say." Which meant either he didn't know or wouldn't reveal what he did.

"When will he return?"

"You are not to have contact with Kchula-Tzaatz, traitor. Leave now." Ftzaal-Tzaatz kept carving, not even bothering to look up. Rage swept Second-Son at the insult, but he controlled himself. It was a short-lived fool who provoked points of honor with the Protector-of-Jotok. Instead he turned on his heel and left, tail lashing uncontrollably.

What was Kchula doing? Was he in his quarters after all with that lethal thug guarding the door? Negotiating with some other Great Pride? Fled already to his ship? Desperately gaining control of a badly botched assault landing?

Or was there never to be an assault landing? Was it all an elaborate trap? No, the *rapsar* assassin at least had been inserted. Some plan was in motion, but what it involved was no longer clear.

What was clear was, he had to get out. For now his part

in the coup remained hidden. For now he had room to escape. He went directly to the main boost bay, running now. *How long do I have?*

He arrived out of breath, found the hangar doors shut and mag sealed, guards at the control panel. He ran up to them, ears unfurled, recognized the kzin in charge.

"Dispatcher! I require an orbit rated gravcar, at once."

Dispatcher jumped to his feet and gave a claw-rake salute. That was gratifying, after Ftzaal-Tzaatz's grating arrogance. "I abase myself, sire. The hangar is sealed."

"I can see that. I require the vehicle. Don't delay me."

"Sire!" Dispatcher gave the ritual cringe. "The Citadel is sealed on the Patriarch's explicit order! I cannot in all honor submit!"

"The order does not apply to me."

Relief flooded Dispatcher's features. "I will verify it at once, of course!" He practically dived to the comlink in order to absolve himself of responsibility.

"No!" Running would label him as guilty; to be caught running . . . "I will . . ." He breathed deep. "I will talk to my father myself." Second-Son left the hangar, thinking furiously. There were deep tunnels to the space defense weapons, and more than once he had used them to sneak under the walls, but with the alert the tunnels would be sealed and the positions manned. With the Citadel at battle readiness there was no way out. He knew its secret passages and hideaways in intimate detail, but he had no doubt that Guardmaster knew them at least as well. There was nowhere to hide either.

There was only one answer, though it froze his liver to think of it. He had to stay close to his father, very close.

That way, at least when the critical moment arrived he would be there. He breathed deeply, struggling to calm his mind, hoping that any who might scent his fear would assign it to the unknown danger they all faced.

> *The wise Patriarch keeps his claws sharp by*
> *keeping them sheathed till he needs them.*
> —Si-Rrit

Meerz-Rrit lashed his tail in impatience as he walked. Rrit-Conserver noticed his agitation but said nothing. Ahead of him two paws of *zitalyi* fanned out, securing each corner in the hallway along their path. The infirmary was in the heart of the oldest part of the Citadel, a curious blend of ancient stone and advanced medical technology. In a room not far away First-Son lay unconscious still, his very breath assisted by machines. Ztal-Biologist greeted them, an untidy-looking kzin with white stripes, noble born and with an incisive mind, but no true warrior. He led them to the dissection table where a pair of Whrloo were dissecting the half-melted remains of the creature in an open-topped nitrogen freezer.

"What is this thing?" Meerz-Rrit waved an angry paw at the mass of flesh.

Ztal-Biologist prodded the corpse with a long specimen probe. "It is a Jotoki *rapsar*, a single-purpose genetic construct. This one is an assassin."

Rrit-Conserver raised his ears questioningly. "*Rapsari* have not been used for combat in eight-squared generations."

Ztal-Biologist narrowed his eyes. "There has been no

serious threat to the Line of the Patriarch in eight-squared generations."

"Are you certain of your finding?"

"I abase myself before your knowledge, but within the bounds of my limited understanding there can be no doubt, sire."

"State your evidence, Ztal-Biologist." Meerz-Rrit had no time for questions.

"As you wish, Patriarch." He made the ritual cringe. "With my assistants I have examined the specimen in detail, physically, biologically, and genetically. Physical evidence first. Observe . . ." He gestured at the frozen corpse with the probe. "These structures are hybrid gill/lungs. It can extract oxygen from both air and water. This capability and the water splashed in First-Son's chamber imply that it hid in his bathing pool while it waited for him. This also suggests that its entry path may have been through the Quickwater River Gate into the Central Garden. This is purely conjecture at this point, but there are three *zitalyi* unaccounted for. One has been missing since last night, and his post was on the Quickwater gate." He paused, gestured again with the specimen probe. "Note here the suction disks on its soles and palms, for wall climbing." He used the probe to peel open the shredded abdominal cavity. "Here you can see, it has no digestive system, just a large central organ filled with ready-to-use ATP and proteins. Once activated the creature could live only eight to sixteen days, depending on its activity level." He let the abdominal flaps fall closed again. "Beyond this, its body is clearly designed for swift and silent killing. Its venom is paralytic, and lethal in small doses, based on that produced by the *p'chert* lurker of our own South Continent, much more effective against a kzin than any alien toxin could be. Note the large, set-forward eyes and the aural sonar system based on these large external eardrums. Its skin contains Pierin chromatophores and Jotok scent-camouflage glands, allowing it to blend with its environment both visually and chemically. I believe it has conscious control of its metabolic rate, allowing it to match its infrared signature to its background as well."

Rrit-Conserver nodded. "And the advanced state of decomposition?"

"This was a difficult puzzle to solve. Before its discovery the creature was more than half digested by its own body chemistry. This is no accident, and the mechanism is fascinating. Its cells produce a powerful digestive enzyme that is catalyzed by a second enzyme which in turn is neutralized by metabolic breakdown products and in fact binds to them so they can be excreted through its skin. When respiration or muscular activity ceases there are no more breakdown products. The catalyst builds up in the cells, triggering the enzyme which begins to digest the body. The creature is designed to self-destruct."

"Hrrr. To what end?" Conserver fanned an ear up questioningly.

"Had it succeeded in killing First-Son and returning to the bathing pool, it would have dissolved there and left no evidence. If we take as a base assumption that it would accomplish its mission or die in the attempt, then in general it would leave little or no trace of its passing. Its toxin has also been modified to break down in the body of its victim, leaving only innocuous protein fragments behind. First-Son was fortunate he was discovered quickly."

"We are all fortunate." Some of the emotion had returned to Meerz-Rrit's voice.

"Continuing with the genetic evidence, I have had my techslaves sequence its genetic code, which does not correspond to any creature in the central genetic library. It shares sequences necessary for nucleated cells, bilateral body symmetry, and an internal skeletal structure. These are common to many species on many worlds. However, most of its genome has been tailored to meet its special requirements. In addition to the Jotoki and Pierin components it has features borrowed from . . ."

"Enough!" Meerz-Rrit cut him off. "What is your conclusion?"

"As stated, Patriarch, this is a Jotok-engineered *rapsar*, a biological war machine and in this case a purpose-built assassin. The evidence supports no other interpretation."

"And who sent it?"

"Jotoki gene engineering technology is widespread throughout the Patriarchy. However, this construct displays an incredible degree of sophistication, fully equal, I believe, to those constructed in the Succession Wars when the art was at its peak. I would be surprised if this were made anywhere but Jotok itself."

Meerz-Rrit's lips twitched over his fangs and his ears flattened. "Jotok is the homeworld of Tzaatz Pride."

"Yes, Patriarch."

"Kchula-Tzaatz! I'll see him flayed alive."

Rrit-Conserver raised a paw. "Caution, Patriarch. This is not yet proof of guilt."

Meerz-Rrit spun around to face his advisor, his tail lashing. "What more do you require?"

"This weapon points too clearly at Tzaatz Pride."

"Who else then would use it?"

"Someone who stands to gain by seeing us attack them. We must be certain. Your vengeance is best directed at the guilty, Patriarch."

"Enough!" The Patriarch's mouth relaxed into a fanged smile. "We shall find the guilty. You, slave!" He beckoned a Whrloo biotech.

The Whrloo buzzed into the air, eyestalks lowered in the largest gesture of submission it could make. "I am forrr yourrr serrrviccce, Patrrriarrrch."

"Summon the Great Council to the Command Lair immediately, make sure Patriarch's Telepath is there. Tightbeam Fleet-Commander to ready his ships for combat. I want an assault squadron boosting for Jotok immediately, ready for hyperspace at my command."

"At onccce, Patrrriarrrch!" The Whrloo left, wings blurring.

"Guard-Leader!"

"Command me, Patriarch!" The senior guard raked his claws across his face.

"Extend an invitation for my cherished cousin Kchula-Tzaatz to attend my presence in the Command Lair. If he does not come voluntarily, compel him."

"At once, Patriarch!"

Rrit-Conserver unfurled his ears. "It is a tremendous violation of the traditions to publicly put a Telepath on a Pride-Patriarch." His tone was cautionary.

"It is a violation of protocol to attack my son, undeclared, unannounced. A coward like this deserves no consideration."

"We do not yet know that Tzaatz Pride is the perpetrator, Patriarch. The repercussions in the Great Pride Circle . . ."

"The repercussions of allowing this attack to go unanswered are unacceptable. We will know soon enough who did this. If Kchula-Tzaatz is innocent I will give him a world in redress for our intrusion. If he is guilty, his pelt will hang in the Great Hall tonight."

> *Adversity is the forge of courage.*
> —Kzin-Conserver-of-the-Reign-of-Vstari-Rrit

The assault *rapsar* was huge on Raarrgh-Captain's screen: a multi-legged beast plated with armored scales, a massive head with teeth that could bite through mag armor, and four long, pincer-equipped tentacles sprouting from its neck. A battlesteel troop compartment on its back was made to hold four swords of Heroes. Its reentry bubble bulged where the troop compartment was, and it was this bulge that had caught on a strut in *Distant Trader's* launch tube, tearing the transparent bubble and leaking oxygenated anti-acceleration fluid to boil and freeze in the vacuum, subliming away to nothingness. The beast had survived the accident, but it would die soon, as would the Heroes in the troop compartment. The only way back aboard *Distant Trader* for them was by way of the planet's surface. With the reentry bubble torn, they wouldn't survive the journey. In the screen Jotoki techslaves in vacskins could be seen swarming around with plasma torches, cutting away the snarled monofilament fabric to free the jam in the tight confines of the launch tube.

"How much longer?" It was not the first time he'd snapped the words into the comlink.

"Unknown, Captain. There was some damage to the launch coils. There is a circuit fault. We're tracing it now." The screen view wobbled as Second-Engineer spoke. The display was being remoted from his helmet.

"Work with speed." Raarrgh-Captain spit the words, as if his impatience could materially affect the outcome. "We have no time!"

"At your command, Raarrgh-Captain." The screen flared for a moment as Second-Engineer's claws came in front of the camera in salute.

Raarrgh-Captain cut the connection, his own claws extending and retracting of their own accord. Time was passing quickly, and he was only too aware that the precision timing of the operation had been hopelessly compromised by the accident. There remained a window of opportunity to carry it out; how large that was depended on how much of the rest of the plan had already come into play, and how well Kchula-Tzaatz was able to hold things together in the Patriarch's Citadel. The failure was not his fault—the cargo ships had been modified too quickly into assault carriers; the tests with the reentry bubbles were inadequate and incomplete. Fixing it was his responsibility, however, and Kchula-Tzaatz was unlikely to remember too clearly that it was his own order for speed in the Jotok shipyards that had led to the problem.

The fur on the back of his neck bristled. Kchula might well kill him for his part in the failure, but if the plan did not succeed the Rrit certainly *would* kill him. As commander of the fleet element of the attack, the riches that would fall to him for a successful *skalazaal* against Rrit Pride were immeasurable. At the moment they also seemed poor compensation for the risk he was taking to earn them.

"Your status, Captain?" Ftzaal-Tzaatz's face was in the shipcom cube, looking as controlled as ever, but his gaze was *intense*. The Black Priests were never a calming influence, and Ftzaal's reputation as a killer did not help. He had a way of making one feel like a prey animal.

"We are tracking down a wiring fault."

"You understand time is of the essence."

"Of course, sire." He paused. "May I request a status report from the surface?"

"The Rrit have sealed the Citadel, which means my assassin has struck. The *Ftz'yeer* stand ready. Kchula-Tzaatz waits. I have no word on further developments."

Raarrgh-Captain didn't ripple his ears. Kchula had no choice but to wait. "Has *skalazaal* been declared?"

"I will deliver the challenge scream when you launch. We must be certain it is declared, or the landers will die on the Citadel beam defenses. Pray to the Fanged God the Rrit communications are still functioning."

"Why would they not be?"

"Consider. They must now suspect our landing is impending. If Myowr-Guardmaster were, for example, to stand down his communications center, the declaration might not reach the ears of the Citadel gunners until it was too late."

Raarrgh-Captain laid his ears flat in shock. "Guardmaster is a kzin of substantiated honor! He would not knowingly breach the honor code."

Ftzaal-Tzaatz considered him narrowly for a long moment. *He does not understand the subtleties. It was wise to not inform him of the traitor.* "Myowr-Guardmaster is honor bound to ensure his warriors know of the Honor-War once it has been declared, but that has not happened. The honor code does not expect prescience. He can act as he sees fit before the declaration without dishonor, and if, for example, he orders a communications systems check that renders him incapable of informing his warriors of our declaration until after the beam defenses have destroyed our attack at the atmospheric interface"—he flipped his tail—"this is merely unfortunate, for us. Myowr-Guardmaster will retain both his honor and the Citadel intact."

Raarrgh-Captain's reply was cut off by the comlink. Second-Engineer's face appeared in the holoscreen. "The circuit is corrected, Raarrgh-Captain, and the obstruction is freed."

Raarrgh-Captain snarled in satisfaction. "Clear the area, we launch immediately."

"Yes, Captain."

The view on the screen panned and tilted as Second-Engineer recalled his slaves to the airlock. He was last through, Raarrgh-Captain was pleased to see, making sure everything was done and the area clear before he sealed the lock behind himself. He was a good leader; one day he'd command his own ship. He returned his attention to Ftzaal-Tzaatz.

"Ready to launch on your orders, sire." The formalities must be observed.

"I will make the declaration. Launch immediately."

"At your command." Raarrgh-Captain made a gesture to the deck officer, who snarled something into his com-link. The deck shuddered and the assault *rapsar's* reentry bubble appeared in the screen and streaked away, heading around the curve of Kzinhome's globe, trailing an almost invisible mist of ice crystals from the tear in its side. Raarrgh-Captain roared the *veaccrsarrr,* the ancient salute to those about to die. The deck shuddered again and another reentry bubble appeared, glinting in the light of the Home Sun as it dropped toward the surface. He did not roar the *krrsuk* for victory. Barring grievous accident this one would see the landing, but the odds of them living to reboard *Distant Trader* were small indeed.

> *The hunter waits where he knows prey will come.*
> **—Wisdom of the Conservers**

"The Patriarch desires the attendance of Kchula-Tzaatz." Guard-Leader stood with confidence before the black-furred noble, helmet visor raised. Behind him the armored figures of his section stood, relaxed and alert.

"My brother is not available." Ftzaal-Tzaatz purred the words, watching Guard-Leader carefully for his reaction.

"My orders are to find him and present him to the Patriarch."

Ftzaal shifted his stance slightly, preparing himself. "May the Fanged God guide you to success."

"The Fanged God has guided me here." Guard-Leader

counted the odds. Eight armed *zitalyi* against three Tzaatz retainers and Ftzaal-Tzaatz. The retainers would be brushed aside if it came to a fight. The black killer's reputation was fearsome, but he was overmatched here, and even he was not immune to a beam pistol.

"And now he will guide you elsewhere."

"With respect, honored guest, we must search the Tzaatz quarters before we can leave." Guard-Leader's voice was steady, his eyes fixed on Ftzaal's, making it clear that he would observe the formalities, but that he was not leaving until his mission was complete.

"With respect, Guard-Leader, I cannot allow this violation of Tzaatz Pride sovereign domain."

"I offer the Patriarch's apologies, but with the weight of his command, I must insist." Guard-Leader put his hand to his sidearm.

Ftzaal-Tzaatz screamed and leapt, his variable sword suddenly in his hand. Guard-Leader jerked his beamer up to fire, but there was a sharp pain in his upper arm and nothing happened when he tried to pull the trigger. An instant later he was on the ground, staring up at the Black Priest's slicewire. Behind Ftzaal he saw a *zitalyi* leap, and he started to roll clear so he could attack when the other went down. Ftzaal spun in place, his slicewire blurring, and the *zitalyi* was cut in half, blood and viscera splashing. The black warrior completed his turn and Guard-Leader finished his roll still looking up at his blade. He realized the reason his beamer hadn't fired was that Ftzaal-Tzaatz had amputated his arm.

Ftzaal stood over the prostrate body looking down, his mouth a fanged smile. The battle had taken instants, and the other seven Rrit had died in utter silence. Not a shot had been fired to warn of their fate. "*Zitalyi*." There was contempt in his voice as he toed the body. "I would have expected better."

"Kill me then, black *sthondat*," Guard-Leader snarled his defiance.

Ftzaal made a gesture, and one of his warriors knelt to bind the amputated stump where Guard-Leader's arm had been. "No, you have a job to do for me." He kicked the beamer aside, and the severed arm went with it. "Tzaatz Pride claims this fortress and this world with it. This is *skalazaal*, fang and claw. Take that to Guardmaster." He backed up, keeping his variable sword leveled, meeting the wounded kzin's gaze with his own. "Get up. Go quickly." He gestured, and Guard-Leader backed out, then ran.

Ftzaal turned to his warriors. "Seal us off. *Skalazaal* has been declared. The landers are on the way." He looked to the door to his brother's chambers. Kchula was a coward, unworthy of his name. Nevertheless, he would serve his purpose. *And I am bound by my oath.* Ftzaal let his mouth relax into a fanged smile. They were committed now. That was good. He was tired of waiting. He turned to the *zitalyi* he'd cut in half and knelt to pull off his helmet. Two quick cuts with the force-wire of his variable sword and he had two ears. He wouldn't wear them himself, but no one else would be able to claim his prize.

> *Courage is like love, it must have hope for nourishment.*
>
> —Napoleon Bonaparte

"What's that?" Kefan Brasseur pointed out the window at a series of brilliant streaks across the sky. Behind him Tskombe and Cherenkova were debating the implications of the Patriarch's speech. He had taken little heed of their conversation. They were military, obsessed with the military implications in which he had only passing interest. More importantly, they did not understand the kzinti, did not understand the cultural context the Patriarchy existed in, and that made their speculations mere noise.

Ayla Cherenkova looked up from the point she was making, then came to see herself. "Reentry tracks. Lots of them."

Tskombe joined them. "It looks like an invasion."

She shook her head. "It can't be. We're here to negotiate."

"Who says it's us?"

She shrugged. "Who else could it be?"

"Slave race rebellion. Those have happened before." Brasseur's eyes were big as he watched the lengthening streaks.

Tskombe nodded. "Or some species we've never heard of. The Patriarchy is big."

"And maybe it's the UN and we're just here as an expendable diversion."

Brasseur shook his head. "They wouldn't do that."

Tskombe raised an eyebrow. "Wouldn't they?" Brasseur looked away, realizing he was now the one making judgments without a cultural context.

Cherenkova smiled a wry smile. "Ours is but to do or die."

Alarms sounded in the distance and, segment by

segment, the outer fortress wall and its turrets blinked from burnished copper to the silvery mirror of activated mag armor.

"It is an invasion." Brasseur breathed the words, not quite willing to believe what he was watching.

Cherenkova nodded. "Whoever it is, is going to win."

Brasseur looked at her. "How do you know?"

"There's no defensive fire. Those are all controlled reentries, all on the same trajectory. There's no fireballs, no ships falling out of orbit. "

The researcher shook his head. "Kzinhome is too well defended. The ratcats wouldn't give up without a fight."

She shrugged. "You're watching it happen."

Brasseur nodded. "This is what it must have been like at K'Shai, when the kzinti first came."

"K'Shai?"

"Wunderland. It's what they call Alpha Centauri system."

She nodded and stood silently, watching the glowing streaks reach out for them like long fingers, seeming to accelerate as they grew closer and the parallax changed. As they approached they separated into three groups, each clearly targeted to land close to the Citadel. The Citadel turrets were all operational now, blank mirror balls with only the exit apertures of heavy beamers showing. They traversed slowly as they tracked the incoming ships. *Why aren't they firing?*

"Perhaps it's an exercise, a demonstration for our benefit." Tskombe voiced her thoughts.

"After the Patriarch's speech today? If it's a demonstration it isn't for us."

"What should we do?" Brasseur was worried now. He had seen many duels, but he hadn't seen *battle* before.

Tskombe spread his broad hands. "What can we do? We wait, keep our heads down, stay out of the crossfire."

They watched. With startling suddenness the closest streak resolved itself into a glowing silver wedge streaming incandescent gases. The wedge grew until it was distinguishable as an assault lander, the first in a formation of four, followed by a cluster of smaller objects that could only be infantry drop capsules.

And then they were overhead and gone. Tskombe had a brief glimpse of the ships, stub wings glowing white hot on their leading edges. They were decelerating hard but still supersonic a few hundred meters up. Instinctively he stuck his fingers in his ears, a fraction of a second before the distinctive *wham wham* of their shock waves shook the building. The inner fortress had no mag armor. Tskombe began to wish that it did, but the ancient stones had stood greater tests in their time, unshifted. Across the room Brasseur was holding his head in pain, but Ayla had got her ears covered in time—good reflexes. She was smart and capable, and he was quite sure she could be relied on in a pinch. She looked no older than thirty, and even if she were five years older, then she must be an officer of some ability to have been promoted to command rank so early. Her fitted uniform showed off her lean figure to advantage, and the way her cheeks flushed when she was passionate, as they had in the interview with Meerz-Rrit, the way she pursed her lips when she was thinking, as she was doing now, made his body respond in a way it hadn't since he was a teenager. It was a reaction he concealed carefully. The middle of a mission was not the time to be thinking of seduction. There would be time afterward, perhaps, on the way home in *Crusader*, in the brief interlude before new assignments pulled them light-years apart. Maybe there would be more time, a few weeks perhaps, if they were delayed in debriefing. She raised her head to follow the drama playing out in the sky overhead, and the sun spun gold in a twist of hair sprung loose against the delicate curve of her neck. He resisted the urge to push it back into place, a gesture too intimate for their professional relationship. He hoped there would be even more time than a few weeks.

And still no defensive fire from the ground. He returned his attention to the window and a problem more pressing than repressed desire. In the courtyard far below a group of kzinti were wheeling out some huge wooden contraption, a heavy beam bent backward over a truss support, black torsion bands showing strain.

A catapult? He looked again, certain he was missing something. More kzinti were ripping heavy stones from the garden arrangement; the activity had the look of frantic improvisation. The catapult was literally a museum piece; he had seen it on display in the Hall of Weapons. It made no sense.

He was about to ask Brasseur about that when foot-steps pounded in the hall. The humans wheeled as one to see Yiao-Rrit bound into the room, a brace of weapons clanking on his back, a pile of segmented ceramic armor in his arms.

He dumped the gear on the floor in a loud clatter. "We must leave at once. Arm yourselves."

"What's happening?" Brasseur said it for all of them.

"*Skalazaal*. Tzaatz Pride is attacking." He dumped the pile of armor on the floor.

"Is there danger?"

"You have my guarantee of safe passage; you carry my brother's sigil. This may no longer be sufficient. My life is now your protection, but should that fail you will need to defend yourselves."

He handed beam pistols to Brasseur and Ayla, a magrifle to Tskombe. The weapons were built to kzin scale, and even the sidearms were heavy and awkward. The magrifle was huge even in Tskombe's large hands, Ayla noticed. The drive coils along the meter-long barrel were fat and powerful. They would accelerate its crystal iron projectiles to transsonic speeds in that meter, and those projectiles were big if the size of the magazine was any measure. They'd probably penetrate just about anything, but she didn't want to think about the recoil.

Tskombe was evidently thinking along the same lines. He held the weapon back to Yiao-Rrit.

"This is better in your hands."

The Patriarch's brother waved it away. "The traditions of *skalazaal* forbid me the use of energy weapons."

"This is a projectile weapon."

"The projectile is not launched by my own muscles. It is an energy weapon. Come, time is short." He led them out of the room and down a spiral staircase to the main floor at a run. They trailed him, awkwardly carrying the heavy equipment. An explosion shook the ground and he held up a paw to guide them into another room, spacious and well decorated, but windowless.

"You will be safe here for a time at least. Wait here. Don your armor, learn your weapons. I must learn more; I will return when I have." He bounded into the hallway beyond without waiting for a reply.

Ayla examined her beamer, identified the safety and the trigger. It had sights, but the eye relief was wrong. The grip was too large for her hands and the trigger was out of reach if she held it as it was designed to be held. The best compromise was to treat it as a short rifle, with one hand on the barrel and the other only half-holding the grip, her wrist swiveled far enough forward to activate the trigger. It wasn't a perfect solution, and the barrel would get too hot to hang on to if she had to do a lot of shooting, but it would serve. She considered firing a test shot, then decided against it. She didn't have enough information about the situation to risk it. Instead she helped Brasseur, showing him how to activate and fire his own weapon.

"What's *skalazaal* mean?" She showed him where to put his hands so he wouldn't snap the safety over by accident.

"The literal translation is 'Honor-War.'" He fumbled with the pistol, trying to find a comfortable grip. "It's a formally declared conflict between Great Prides."

"And what's a Great Pride?" She put her armor on while he answered—heavy chestpieces and protective plates for shoulders and arms.

"The major political division of the Patriarchy is along clan lines, prides. Who belongs to a pride is a complex question, and any individual can usually legitimately claim to belong to one of several groups by reason of relatedness, skill set, or accomplishment."

"I see . . ." She didn't. She had taken the smallest of the three armor sets. Even with the adjustment straps cinched all the way up it was loose and heavy, but it was better than nothing.

"A Great Pride is a pride of prides." Brasseur was lecturing as though he were back in front of his class at the university. "Average genetic relatedness within a pride is about point one five to point two, somewhat closer than second cousins, although between any pair of individuals it can go anywhere from basically zero to point five, parent/child or full siblings, or higher with consanguinity. A Great Pride is a group of prides who share a set of common bloodlines and who traditionally exchange mates among themselves. Typically it has an average relatedness of point oh five to point one five."

"So what does this have to do with what's happening?" Tskombe had struggled into his armor. The fit wasn't as bad as it might have been. It must have been built for small kzinti, maybe youngsters.

"It's essentially a feudal system based on bloodlines. Individual kzinti swear loyalty to their subcommander, who swears loyalty to his commander, who swears loyalty to his pride, which takes its identity from a Great Pride, and of course all the Great Prides owe fealty to the Patriarch."

"And the Honor-War?" Ayla hung the Patriarch's sigil back over her chestplate by its blue ribbon. It might yet prove important to display it.

"At any level there can be conflict. Their social system recognizes this and controls it. Between individuals, there is *skatosh*, the challenge duel. Between Great Prides, it's *skalazaal,* and of course there are intermediate forms. There are strict rules of honor as to the forms of combat and the weapons which can be used, as expressed in their traditions."

Ayla hefted her beamer. "I don't think I'll let tradition stop me from using every weapon I can get my hands on."

"Tradition carries the force of law with the kzinti, or more. It doesn't apply to us; we're animals."

"So what does that mean?" Cherenkova's voice carried an edge.

"It means we're caught in the middle of a war, Captain." Tskombe interrupted as he chambered a round into the heavy mag rifle. "It means we're probably going to die."

Tskombe in alien battle armor seemed transformed from man into iconic *warrior,* ready to fight and win or die trying, and his demeanor gave weight to his words. She tightened her jaw and said nothing. Brasseur's face showed fear as the reality sank in, and he looked awkward in his own protective gear. He had been looking at this as an academic exercise, she realized. For him the entire trip was a chance to get closer to his research subject. The thought that his studies might prove lethal had never occurred to him. *How did he survive so long on W'kkai?*

Time began to stretch and conversation lagged among them, the silence interrupted only by the occasional snarled command from the catapult team outside, as they winched down the arm and loaded it. Tskombe, impassive, lay down behind his weapon to cover the entrance. Brasseur paced. Ayla settled herself onto a huge suspended couch, a *prrstet* the kzinti called it, and watched, beamer at the ready. It was so large she had to climb onto it, feeling like Alice in Wonderland. The entire situation had a dreamlike quality to it. There was nothing to do but wait.

The dead are no one's ally.

—Si-Rrit

The Command Lair holo display showed Kzinhome from orbit. Blue trails tracked assault landers and drop troops along their insertion trajectories. Meerz-Rrit paced back and forth as he watched them advance. A yellow target icon glowed around the head of every trail, and around Kzinhome's globe green dots marked space defense systems, mass drivers, and gamma ray laser domes. Green flashed red as the targets came into the engagement horizon of each weapon, indicating it was locked on and ready to cut the attackers from the sky.

All of them useless in *skalazaal*. Meerz-Rrit cursed, and across the room Second-Son watched him warily. The invaders would touch down unhindered by anything but atmospheric friction. The battle would be decided hand to hand. Tzaatz Pride had made its declaration even as they launched their attack.

It was a bold stroke, and it had thrown the Citadel into chaos preparing to receive the coming assault. He had to grant daring to Kchula-Tzaatz, to make such a move while he himself was in the stronghold of the enemy. Kchula had earned himself a fighting death in the arena for that, at least.

Meerz-Rrit snarled under his breath. But it would be death, no question. Where was the *sthondat*?

Guard-Leader should have returned with him by now. He was tempted to com Myowr-Guardmaster to find out, but the leader of the *zitalyi* had bigger things to worry about right now. A good leader gave his subordinates tasks and let them carry them out. Kchula himself was a distraction now anyway. He could not leave the citadel, and despite the boldness of his stroke, he would not win. The Citadel had been built to withstand siege long before energy weapons were invented.

"Second-Son! Citadel defenses, primary display." He kept his voice calm. Second-Son positively stank of fear and needed steadying.

"Yes, sire!" Second-Son manipulated the command console and the display changed to an overhead view of the fortress. Meerz-Rrit had considered sending Second-Son out to lead a force of defenders with the rest of his inner circle, but his son's fear ruled that out.

And he did need someone to run the displays. Let him learn command by his father's side, gain confidence here. He was young yet for leadership, and if he was not all Meerz-Rrit might hope for, he was still blood.

"Zoom on the House of Victory." Time to find out why Kchula was not yet in his presence. Patriarch's Telepath would take his battle plans right out of his mind. *And where is Patriarch's Telepath?*

Second-Son zoomed the display as directed, but his reply was interrupted by a buzzing from the door. A Whrloo flew in.

"Patrrriarrrch'sss Telepath doesss not commme, Patrrriarrch." The Whrloo hovered in front of Meerz-Rrit, eyestalks lowered.

"What?"

"Parrrdon this onnne. He sssennndsss thisss messssage. Kchullla-Tzzzatzzz isss invadinnng and willll trrriummmmph. The traitorrr is Sssecond-Ssson. He hasss donnne allll he cannn nnnowww forrr yourrr linnnne."

It took a moment for the Whrloo's speech to register. "Second-Son!" Kchula-Tzaatz he knew about, but Second-Son! Meerz-Rrit whirled but Second-Son was already in midleap, his scream echoing from the walls of the Command Lair, *wtsai* extended. Meerz-Rrit dropped to the floor, kicking out to disembowel. The surprise left him off balance and the kick merely ripped the skin on Second-Son's flank. It was enough to deflect the *wtsai* though, and rather than plunging into his belly it sliced his thigh. He rolled to his feet, adopted the *v'dak* stance, and saw his opening, but fire burned from the wound up his leg and icy numbness followed it. His vision blurred and he couldn't leap.

Second-Son regained his feet, breathing hard, his father's blood on the edge of his blade. "Feel the sting of the *p'chert*, Meerz-Rrit."

The leg collapsed and Meerz-Rrit fell to the floor, the room darkening before his eyes as the neurotoxin took hold.

"You dishonorable *sthondat*."

"Patriarch now, Father."

"First-Son still lives." Meerz-Rrit spat the words.

"Not for long." Contempt.

Rage swept Meerz-Rrit, and it gave him the strength to leap one last time. Second-Son wasn't ready for it, and his father's impact sent him sprawling, a vicious slash across his chest. In a panic he stabbed out with the *wtsai* but the blade skidded off Meerz-Rrit's own *wtsai*, still on his belt, and then his father's fangs were at his throat. Unable to breathe, he slashed wildly, this time connecting, driving the weapon deep into the soft belly.

Meerz-Rrit gave a strangled cry and collapsed on top of him. With shaking fingers Second-Son pried his father's dead jaws from his throat and struggled from under the corpse. Panting, he stood over the body, exultation warring with horror and fear in his liver. He had done it, claimed his right as Patriarch with his own claws. His father lay dead at his feet, and whatever the future would bring, it was no longer the security he would have known as *zar'ameer* to First-Son. He trembled as the implications of what he had done came over him.

And his father! He knelt by the body, suddenly wishing for a sign of life. Memories of his kittenhood flooded back unbidden. Meerz-Rrit had always been a distant figure to him, burdened as he was by the responsibilities of his office, but he was a presence as constant as the very stones of the Inner Citadel. To have changed that fact of life was . . .

Enough! There was much to do and little time to do it in. But weren't those Meerz-Rrit's own words, when the time for thought gave way to the need for action? The sorrow would not leave his liver. He looked away from the body. First he must camouflage the crime, and then kill First-Son. A moment ago he would have exulted at the thought, driven by jealousy, but now he felt a strange reluctance. Meerz-Rrit's other sons were much younger, still spotted kits at their mother's teats. Only First-Son had always been there in his life, first a model for his behavior, then a foil for his thwarted ambition.

No, he no longer had the desire to see his brother dead, but now he had the *need*. If he wanted to live, Elder-Brother had to die. He flattened his ears. No time now for reflection. He had to act, before anyone discovered his crime and his dishonor. There were guards outside the Command Lair who could enter at any moment. He suddenly became aware that the Whrloo had left, fled during the fight. It was danger and opportunity, witness and scapegoat. He ran out to the corridor.

"Treachery! Meerz-Rrit is dead. Kill that Whrloo!" None of it was even a lie.

"Sire!" At once the *zitalyi* were bounding down the corridor after the hapless slave. Second-Son's mouth relaxed into a fanged smile, and he turned and loped toward the infirmary where First-Son lay.

> *. . . and his Patriarch commanded Chmee to hold the gate. And so when Vstari of the Wild Pride led eight-to-the-fifth Heroes to the fortress and demanded surrender, Chmee refused them.*
> —The Warlord Chmee at the Pillars

The herd grandmother bellowed in rage and Pouncer ran like a scalded kitten across the scorching desert. Behind him the thundering *tuskvor* stretched from horizon to horizon, the dust of their passage rising to form a solid orange wall behind him. Ahead was nothing but sand as far as the eye could see, and it burned his pads as he ran. Fear drove his legs faster and faster but he wasn't gaining

ground. The dry air burned thirst into his throat, and his
eyes watered with the hot wind. The thunder grew inexorably closer, and though he seemed to float between
each step, he was going to be trampled. The grandmother
bellowed again and again, the booming cries deafening,
coming in steady, urgent rhythm. He looked back and saw
her tusks coming for him, and in that instant he tripped,
sailing in slow motion over the sand as time seemed to
contract, stretching the moment into infinity, and then he
was tumbling, rolling, and the herd was overrunning him,
tree trunk legs pounding down to crush him into oblivion.
He lay on his back, helplessly watching as the grandmother's
boulder-sized foot blotted out the sky, coming down like a
drop forge.

She bellowed. The alarms were going off. She bellowed.
His eyes shot open.

He was in the infirmary, in a sleepfield, white walls,
medical instruments, a spray infuser strapped to a shaved
patch on his upper arm. How had he got there? The
alarms kept blaring rhythmically. What was happening?

A vague orange shape in front of him. "Chief Medical
Officer!" His head swam with the effort of speech.

"Sire! You're awake."

"Why are the alarms going off?"

"It isn't clear. There's an attack, Heroes landing."

"The *tuskvor* . . ."

"You've been unconscious. There was a creature, a *rapsar*,
in your chamber."

Gray skin, toxic fangs dripping, claws extended to
kill . . . Had that been him? The memories flooded back
murky and indistinct.

"Where is my father?"

"In the Command Lair."

"Is it the *kz'zeerkti*? I don't hear the lasers." Was it sabotage? A monkey attack was far from the worst possibility. *What was that thing that attacked me?*

"They haven't fired. I don't know why."

Pouncer rolled out of the sleepfield and stood. Immediately the world spun around and he nearly fell. Chief Medical Officer grabbed his arm to steady him and guided him back onto the sleepfield.

"Your body has been cleansed of the neurotoxin but you're still injured. You need rest."

Pouncer shook himself and struggled to stand again. "This is my father's Citadel, and mine. I'm going to defend it."

"Sire, there's nothing you can do . . ."

"I can carry a beamer. I can hold a position."

"Sire . . ."

Pouncer silenced him with a gesture, gathered his concentration and staggered out of the infirmary. He paused in the hallway, leaning against the wall and breathing heavily while his vision cleared. The wounds in his shoulders had been force-healed, but the new flesh still throbbed painfully. His first thought was to join his father in the Command Lair, but he paused. There was nothing useful he could add to the direction Rrit-Conserver and his father were giving the defenders. No, better to find Guardmaster and help him lead the close defense where the Heroes of the *zitalyi* could see him. He was not the warrior his father was, not the diplomat, not the strategist, but he could lead from the front.

Weapons first! He headed for the arena. By the time he reached it his head had cleared and his muscles were responding better. The alarms had shut off, but the citadel was eerily deserted and he saw only one Pierin slave, its exoskin blue with fear as it scuttled to cower beneath a stairwell. Once there it contracted into a ball, its skin roughening as its chromatophores turned gray to match the shadows it hid in. Slaves lacked the liver for battle; that was why they were slaves. Distant, heavy booms shook the structure's foundations, the sonic signature of assault landers, landing at Sea-of-Stars spaceport from the direction. There were no other sounds of battle. Why weren't the defense weapons firing? The arena was empty, but the weapons cabinet recognized him and opened. He grabbed up his mag armor and a beamer, headed for the Patriarch's Gate, putting it on as he ran.

The gate was open, the courtyard vacant. Outside twice-eight-cubed Heroes in Rrit colors were standing in massed rank and column as though on parade. That made no sense. Why weren't the perimeter weapons manned? He arrived panting, found Myowr-Guardmaster marshaling the *zitalyi* with frantic energy.

"Guardmaster! What is happening?"

His mentor turned as he came up, eyes widening. "Sire! No!"

"What is it?"

"Drop your beamer! It's *skalazaal*!"

"What?"

"Tzaatz Pride has declared *skalazaal*. You must use your own strength."

As Guardmaster said it, Pouncer realized that the

zitalyi were carrying variable swords only. That explained the close-ranked formation, the empty guard-posts, the lack of defensive fire. Cursing, he threw the heavy beamer to the ground. He had not thought to bring a variable sword.

"Sire, take this." Guardmaster tossed him his *wtsai*. It was a casual enough gesture, nothing more than practical in face of imminent battle, but Pouncer did not miss the significance of the act. A *wtsai* came with the earning of a name. That Guardmaster had chosen to give it to him now . . .

"I am honored, Myowr-Guardmaster, but I have not earned . . ."

"You will earn it today." Guardmaster's snarl was grim.

A meteor streaked toward him, brilliant even in the daytime sky. Seconds later another followed it, simultaneous with the crack of the first one's sonic boom. In seconds the sky was full of flashes, and Pouncer stopped to watch the display. A flurry of drop troops fell out of the sky opposite the gate, scorched reentry bubbles cracking open as they touched down. They scrambled to secure a perimeter, and moments later an assault lander came in under maximum deceleration, still moving fast enough that its heavy skids dug long grooves in the soil. Its assault ramp blew down even as another came down beside it.

An arrow soared toward the attackers from the battlements behind them, falling far short. A few others followed.

"Hold your fire!" Myowr-Guardmaster's shout was harsh. "Wait till they close."

Pouncer grabbed his arm and pointed. "What in the name of the Fanged God is *that?*"

Something was coming down the lander's assault ramp, huge and reptilian, ponderously armored, flanked by Tzaatz warriors in mag armor, variable swords held ready. Guardmaster's eyes widened and his lips curled away from his fangs. "More *rapsari*, like the thing that attacked you."

"They violate the traditions!"

"Hunting *sherreks* are allowed, and trained *metzrr*, and siege weapons drawn by *zitragor*." Guardmaster's voice was derisive beneath his tension. "Why not these?"

First-Son snorted in disgust. "Tzaatz Pride plays games with its honor before the Great Pride Circle."

"Tomorrow the Great Pride Circle will sit in judgment on Kchula-Tzaatz. Today . . ." Guardmaster nodded toward the immense war beast. Its handlers had turned it to face the Citadel. Behind it a second beast was emerging from the assault lander. ". . . today we fight these."

"This requires a judgment of the Circle immediately! The battle must be stopped." Even as he said it Pouncer realized the gulf between what should be and what was.

"The battle will not be stopped, sire, and the way to ensure victory before the Pride-Patriarchs is to be victorious now." He raised his voice to an angry snarl directed at the waiting *zitalyi* formation. "Hold your positions! Dress the line on the right! They'll come to us soon enough."

As if on cue the beasts began to advance, each one flanked by a phalanx of Tzaatz warriors in battle armor. Smaller *rapsari* were formed up behind the leaders, each still twice the size of a full-grown kzin.

"By the Fanged God . . ." A *zitalyi* beside Pouncer tightened his grip on his variable sword as the enemy formation approached, his voice awed.

"Steady!" Guardmaster snarled the word.

"What are we waiting for?" Pouncer asked.

"We have a surprise for these honorless curs." Guardmaster's voice was hushed. "Wait for it . . ."

The enemy advanced, a solid wall of muscle, armor, and blades. Pouncer could hear the crunch of their footsteps, hear the *rapsari* snarling.

"Wait for it . . ." the moment seemed drawn out forever. Pouncer's claws extended of their own accord as he fought down the urge to scream and leap against the oncoming horde. What was Guardmaster waiting for?

"Nets now!" Guardmaster's voice cut the air like a knife and the netgunners atop the Citadel battlements fired, filling the air with spin-stabilized monofilament nets to entangle the attackers. The salvo ended and Guardmaster paused for a beat, two beats, to let confusion grow in the attacking ranks. "Archers now!" A storm of arrows followed the nets to kill those too entangled to dodge out of the way. "Skirmishers forward!" He swung his variable sword overhead. From the Citadel's battlements leapt swarms of lightly armored *zitalyi*. Their collective scream drowned out the whine of their grav belts; their variable swords glinted as they swept to attack. The advancing Tzaatz ranks were thrown into disarray by the arrow storm, but the Tzaatz had their own archery, insectoid creatures with modified middle legs that cocked and fired the heavy ballistae and repeating crossbows mounted on their backs as fast as their kzinti handlers could feed the arrows into them. A counter-fusillade rose up against the leapers. Immediately behind it Tzaatz grav skirmishers leapt to intercept. The skirmishers were difficult targets in midair, and most of the missiles went wide or glanced off mag-reinforced crystal iron armor, but some struck home and not all the *zitalyi* were alive when the Tzaatz warriors ran into them in midair. There were screams of rage and agony, and the clash of metal on metal. Bodies and body parts fell from the flurry, but the *zitalyi* had leapt from a height and had the momentum advantage. The huge *rapsari* snapped at the closest ones as they landed. The skirmishers' casualties were heavy, but those who survived to land destroyed the cohesion of the attacker's front line in their attack.

"*Zitalyi!* In battle line, *advance!*" The Patriarch's guard stepped off as one at Guardmaster's command, and Pouncer felt a thrill run through him at the sight of the disciplined ranks moving to battle.

"Now we have them!" There was grim satisfaction in Guardmaster's voice. "First-Son, stay by my side."

"As you command, Guardmaster." Pouncer tightened his grip on his *wtsai*.

Ahead of them the first wave of *zitalyi* closed with the disordered Tzaatz at a steady lope. Guardmaster moved between the first and second waves, and Pouncer went with him. The close-ranked formation they were using was a ceremonial anachronism for a race that had practiced space warfare for more generations than could be remembered. A unit trained to use the accurate, lethal, and long-range weapons gifted by technology would have been hopelessly disorganized in the situation, but the Patriarch's Guard were as well drilled in close combat and close-order maneuver as they were in more advanced forms of force application. Pouncer had long thought the

hopelessly obsolete parade-ground evolutions the *zitalyi*
practiced a complete waste of time and effort in an age of
conversion weapons. Now he realized the true worth of
such training, and his liver thrilled as he watched his warriors move as a single body with a single purpose. Sunlight
flashed from their mag armor as snarled commands shot
back and forth. Ahead of them the Tzaatz officers tried
desperately to reorient their shattered formations to
receive the attack, but the surviving Rrit skirmishers were
still fighting hard. As Pouncer watched, one of them leapt
for a leashed trio of small, vicious *rapsari*. He dodged past
their snapping jaws to slice at their handler and all five
went down in a snarling pile of tangled limbs, adding to
the confusion in the enemy ranks.

"First wave, Charge!" Guardmaster roared the words.
The leading *zitalyi* leapt as one, their combined kill
scream echoing from the Citadel walls and drowning out
the sounds of battle. Eight-cubed warriors hit the Tzaatz
battle line at once, carving their way forward with
remorseless efficiency. Scream-snarls and the scent of
blood filled the air, and Pouncer found himself thirsting
for the kill. He became so caught up in the drama unfolding before him that he almost didn't notice the Tzaatz grav
skirmisher who had leapt the struggling front ranks and
touched down in front of him, variable sword raised for
the killing stroke. The slicewire came down and Pouncer
parried instinctively with his *wtsai*, only to see it cut in
half by the molecular-thin, magnetically stiffened blade.
His instincts still saved his life, deflecting the stroke
enough that the slicewire glanced off the mag armor on
his shoulder instead of penetrating the articulation at his

neck. He dropped to the ground and lashed out with a spin kick, connecting with his opponent's elbow. The variable sword went flying and his opponent spun helplessly, robbed of purchase by his still-activated grav belt. Pouncer rolled to his feet and followed up his advantage with a scream and a *g'rrtz* high kick. The Tzaatz warrior's head snapped back and lolled, and his body sagged limply, held up only by its grav belt.

A hand on his shoulder . . . Pouncer wheeled to find Guardmaster standing behind him. "Well done, he would have killed me." All at once he realized the skirmisher had not been trying for him but for the force commander. The Tzaatz were not without courage themselves.

"I just reacted . . ."

"You did well. You have my blood-debt." Guardmaster turned back to the battle before Pouncer could reply, snarling into his comlink. "Greow-Formation-Leader! Flank guards out now!"

On the right a formation of *rapsari* were moving to take the *zitalyi* in the flank. These were reptilian raiders, bipedal on powerful legs with a heavy counterbalancing tail, dagger teeth in well-muscled jaws, taller than a kzin, more heavily built, but still far faster than the lumbering assaulters with the main Tzaatz attack force. They were mag-armored themselves, and their talons were augmented with multiple slicewires. Their riders carried crossbows and in moments they would be enveloping the Rrit line. As Pouncer watched, Greow-Formation-Leader pivoted his unit to face the new threat. The *zitalyi* knelt to receive the charge, slicewires fully extended and canted forward to present the attackers with a fence of blades.

The advancing *rapsari* stopped short: stalemate. For a long moment it looked like the flank attack had been countered, but then a flurry of arrows from the launcher *rapsari* in depth came raining in on the defenders. *Zitalyi* fell where they stood, and Greow himself was cut down by one of the crystal iron missiles. Already the launchers were preparing another salvo. The Tzaatz would destroy the blocking force from a distance, then the raiders would sweep in and wreak havoc with the main Rrit formation. Without thought Pouncer grabbed up his recent opponent's dropped variable sword and leapt to attack. Spinning around he spotted one of his father's commanders. He knew what had to be done.

"Kdar-Leader, Second Formation! With me! Kill the handlers!" Without hesitation he leapt toward the enemy. Attack screams rose behind him and he knew Kdar's Heroes were following. They would succeed, or they would all die in the effort.

His charge took him through the space between Greow-Formation-Leader's left and right forward sections. The Tzaatz couldn't use their ranged weapons when both sides were engaged at close quarters. A few leaps took him to the closest raider as a bolt from the rider's crossbow flashed past him. The beast snapped at him with jaws strong enough to crush him through his armor, but he dodged to one side and struck at the articulation on its knee. Behind him he could hear the attack screams as Greow-Formation-Leader's warriors leapt to attack with him. The *rapsar's* rider stabbed at him and he dodged again. His own blow had glanced off the beast's leg armor, and now it kicked at him with hind claws the length of his forearm. His belly armor saved him from disembowelment, but the force of the blow sent him flying backward, just as another raider's jaws closed on the space were his head had been. A Tzaatz net flew past and wrapped itself around the *rapsar*'s leg. It tripped and fell, crushing its rider, who screamed in agony. The helpless *rapsar* snapped impotently and Pouncer found himself on his back, somehow now amongst the front rank of attacking Greow-Formation-Leader's *zitalyi*. A battle-scarred face in Rrit-liveried armor looked down at him as he rolled to his feet.

"First Sergeant!"

"Command me, sire!"

"Take your four-sword to the right flank. Make them turn, don't let them build momentum."

"At once, sire!" First Sergeant started yelling commands as Pouncer rejoined the battle. The Tzaatz flankers had the advantage of momentum with their beasts, but if Pouncer's small force could keep them disorganized then they couldn't use it.

He was dimly aware of the clash of arms behind him. Myowr-Guardmaster's warriors were heavily engaged against the huge assault *rapsari*, but he could not spare the instant it would have taken to look. Immediately in front of him a raider *rapsar* snapped its jaws and a Rrit warrior died in gurgling agony. Pouncer stepped forward and brought his sword up. The beast crashed down, its severed aorta spraying him with hot blood. Its rider swung at him as he fell, but the blow went wide and on the backswing Pouncer caught him under the shoulder, cleanly amputating his sword arm. He moved to finish his victim, but a blow came out of nowhere and staggered him sideways. One of the reptilian raiders, wounded and out of control, had tripped on him and fallen, crushing him to the ground and pinning him beneath its bulk. He struggled to free himself, fighting to breathe under its crushing weight. A shadow fell across him and he looked up to see a Tzaatz warrior scream snarling in triumph, variable sword upraised to deliver the killing blow. Fear and rage spiked in his system and he lashed out with his one free arm in a desperate attempt to unbalance his attacker. He had no leverage and the variable sword came down. He would have been beheaded, but the Tzaatz's marker ball skidded off the *rapsar*'s armored flank, and the slicewire just glanced off Pouncer's helmet. The Tzaatz screamed and swung again, only to die as a *zitalyi* leapt out of nowhere and ran him through his belly articulation. The body dropped, spilling blood and guts, and then the *zitalyi* was gone again, spinning away to engage another raider-mounted Tzaatz.

Pouncer struggled free of the encumbering body and rolled to his feet, adopting *v'dak* stance, instantly ready for another attack. There was none, and he realized that the flank attack had been stopped. The bodies of warriors and raider *rapsari* alike lay broken in the dirt, and a single wounded raider was running for the forest, shrieking in animal pain and dragging its dead rider in its tangled harness. Of the original twice-eight-squared of Greow-Formation-Leader's force, only a pawful remained standing, a bare half sword. The action had taken only heartbeats. There was no time to rest. *Fear is death. Rage is death.* Pouncer felt only exhaustion, but that too could be fatal.

A crystal iron ballista bolt *thunk*ed into the ground an armspan in front of him. He jumped and turned around, assessing the situation. The Tzaatz missile beasts were again finding the range. To his right Kdar-Leader was deploying his depth elements as flank guards. Farther away on the right flank a group of heavy-bloated, six-legged *rapsari* waddled toward the Citadel walls, guarded by a swarm of raiders and out of arrow range. The mounted flank attack had been meant to cover their advance. The function of the fat waddlers was unclear, but the way was now open to attack them. Pouncer looked around for more *zitalyi* to rally, but they were all fully engaged. The Rrit had nothing left to attack them with. Guardmaster would have to commit his depth formation from reserve or let the attackers reach the walls unchallenged.

A hail of steel balls as large as his head caromed through the remnants of his formation, one of them shattering the corpse of a *rapsar* raider directly in front of Pouncer. One thing was clear, they could not stand long where they were.

"*Zitalyi* to me!" Panting hard, he ran back to where Guardmaster was directing the second wave in its attack against the Tzaatz main body. The Tzaatz had brought forward more of the heavy assault *rapsari*, and the leviathan beasts were simply crushing the opposition before them. The first *zitalyi* wave had made the Tzaatz pay heavily for their advance, and several of the creatures lay dead or mortally wounded, surrounded by the bodies of Tzaatz and Rrit alike, but there were too many of them for the light *zitalyi* forces to stop entirely.

"Guardmaster! Command me."

"Sire!" Guardmaster's relief at seeing Pouncer was evident.

"We stopped their flank attack, but they have more beasts moving to the Citadel on that side." Pouncer panted as he spoke.

"How many Heroes have you left?"

"Just five, including myself."

"And Greow-Formation-Leader?" Guardmaster couldn't keep the concern from his voice.

"Dead in their first salvo. Kdar-Leader's flank guards are covering that side from farther back now, out of range of the Tzaatz arrows."

Myowr-Guardmaster was silent for long moment, surveying the battlefield. When he looked at Pouncer, his face was determined. "You must fall back, sire. We cannot hold them here."

"We will hold them or die."

"We cannot hold them. We can only buy time with our lives."

"A Rrit does not run."

"You foolish kitten, what do you think we're buying time for, if not your escape? You are the Patriarch's son. Now go!" Guardmaster pushed him toward the inner gate, but still Pouncer hesitated. "Go! My duty is to die here. Yours is to live and avenge me."

A lumbering assault *rapsar* came into range, and the outer rank of *zitalyi* leapt for its flanks, variable swords seeking the chinks in its armor. Tzaatz troops jumped from its back to engage them, and the beast reared back, seizing a Rrit in its jaws and crushing the life from him. It tossed its victim aside and snapped again. Another beast moved up behind it, this one smaller, but shooting gouts of sticky toxin from fleshy nozzles on its head to encumber the defenders. The second battle developed in front of them, and Guardmaster snarled combat codes into his comlink, then *"Zitalyi!* Quarter flank left . . . Attack!" The second-wave commanders screamed orders at their troops, and the last Rrit formations began to close with the oncoming Tzaatz. He turned to Pouncer once more, shoving him in the direction of the Citadel. "Go, curse you! I've just ordered the gate closed." He didn't wait for a reply. "You four . . ." He pointed to the survivors of Greow's formation. "Assault line. With me, advance!" Ahead of them the leading *zitalyi* were slashing at the huge war beasts, trying to climb their flanks to kill the handlers who rode behind their serpentine necks.

Pouncer watched him for a long moment, then turned and ran back toward the Patriarch's Gate. To his left the huge waddling *rapsari* had reached the walls with their reptilian bodyguard. He could now see they had huge, suckerlike mouths and concentric rows of rasplike teeth. Several had attached themselves to the Citadel walls, and acrid fumes billowed from their nostrils. As Pouncer passed, the eye-watering scent of powerful acid reached his nose. The creatures were literally eating their way through the cerametal structure of the fortress. A cross-bow bolt bounced off his armor and tore a gash in the back of his hand, but neither the warriors nor their creatures moved to intercept him. He looked behind him to see more *rapsari* charging for the gate, pushing through the defenders who were still hanging on behind him. Showers of arrows arced overhead to suppress the Rrit

archers on the battlements, and behind them more Tzaatz
grav skirmishers leapt to seize the heights. Guardmaster
was buying him time with his life; it would not be much
time. He turned to run again. A double-sword of *zitalyi*
stood at the huge battlesteel gate, the last guards there.
They urged him forward as it ground closed, Tzaatz bolts
buzzing past too close for comfort. He flashed past them
and through the gate just in time.

The ground vibrated as the gate came down and the
seals engaged, and Pouncer paused to catch his breath.
The courtyard was full of arrows stuck point first in the
ground, overshoots aimed at the defenders on the battlements, and more salvoes fell as he watched, a steady,
deadly rain. Close to the wall he was safe, but not for long.
Snarls and the clash of weapons rose above him, and he
looked up reflexively. Tzaatz leapers with grav belts had
gained the battlements. A sundered body in *zitalyi* colors
fell, hitting the ground with the nerve-jarring *crack* of
bones breaking inside rigid armor. The rain of arrows
would slow now. Pouncer took a chance and ran for the
outer bastion that guarded the entrance to the Middle
Citadel. To his right an eight-sword of Tzaatz warriors in
mag armor and grav belts touched down in the courtyard
and fanned out. He ducked into a doorway into the outer
bastion wall. It led to a secondary sector gun position,
abandoned now as unusable in a battle of *skalazaal*.
He slapped a palm against the release, and the heavy
battlesteel blast door slammed closed. It would take time
for the attackers to breach the barrier. For a moment he
considered the heavy laser cannon, positioned to sweep
the walls. The position entirely controlled the approaches

to the Middle Fortress. The targeting system was already up and running, the power banks fully charged. When the attackers came through the gate he could slaughter them with impunity; it would be simple . . .

He pushed the thought away. He was First-Son of the Patriarch. Rrit Pride would not be the ones who broke the traditions. There was a hatchway in the rear of the emplacement, and he ripped it open and dived through. Beyond it was the arterial corridor that ran through the heart of the Outer Fortress defenses. The tunnels to the space defense weapons would be sealed, but if the attackers were concentrating on the gates he might be able to escape over the river wall by jumping into the Quickwater below. He ran down the corridor at a fast lope, down a set of stairs to a tunnel that would take him beneath the outer courtyard and then up another set to the arterial corridor of the outer wall. He dashed down it to the New Tower and up the spiral stairs to the battlements along the top of the outer wall. The mag armor showed mirror silver along the walls. The Citadel's defenses were formidable, but denied the use of its high technology weapons it was vulnerable to envelopment.

A salvo of arrows snapped past his head as he ran onto the battlements. There was a Tzaatz archery unit concealed in the trees a bare bowshot away. He looked at the long drop to the Quickwater below. They wouldn't likely be able to hit him in midair if he leapt, but there was no chance they wouldn't notice. Once in the water he'd be helpless while they closed in on him. Farther down the wall a unit of *zitalyi* fired back with crossbows. Not all of the defenders were carrying the weapons. The first defense alert had been for ground attack, and they had brought heavy beam weapons. The *skalazaal* had taken them by surprise.

That's a lesson for Guardmaster. The next thought followed automatically. *If he survives.* The Tzaatz had used surprise to tremendous effect.

A fusillade of heavy steel balls flew up from below, some slamming hard against the magnetically reinforced cerametal walls, others hitting *zitalyi* defenders and hurling their crushed bodies into the outer courtyard behind them. Pouncer ducked behind a battlement instinctively. *Where did that come from?* He tracked the trajectory back, saw another specialized assault *rapsar* still swaying from the force of the launch, modified mid legs already cranking its back-mounted catapult down for another shot. A gravcar beside it was laden heavy with more of the balls. The traditions of the Honor-War denied all but muscle-driven weapons, and denied the use of slaves, but *rapsari* eluded both restrictions. Tzaatz Pride was treading narrowly on the edge of honor, but though the Conservers might later refine the code to prevent another upstart from toppling their regime with biostructs the way they were toppling the Rrit, no one would be able to dispute the fact of their victory.

No, not victory. The Rrit are not yet fallen. The Citadel defenses were strong, and the Tzaatz were a long way from their homeworld. The *rapsari* were beasts, powerful perhaps, but still only beasts. The battle would be decided claw to claw, and there were no better warriors in the Patriarchy than the *zitalyi*. A swarm of Tzaatz on grav belts leapt up as another catapult *rapsar* swept more defenders from the battlements. The remaining Rrit met them on the points of their variable swords; kill screams and the clash of weapons against armor rose in the air. Two of the enemy landed three leaps from Pouncer, facing him. He drew his own variable sword and extended it, ready to receive them. They leapt again as soon as they had touched down, aided by their gravbelts. Pouncer took *v'dak* stance, twisting sideways to strike as the first one's leap carried him past. The blow glanced off his opponent's back plate, and he pivoted to kick. His foot connected hard and the Tzaatz warrior slid over the ice-slick surface of the cerametal rampart, scrabbling for a purchase. The other attacker slammed into Pouncer from behind, knocking him flat. Pouncer twisted to escape, bringing his weapon up to block the blow he knew was coming. The variable swords connected, the shock hard enough to shatter bone. The other raised his weapon again and brought it down, aiming for Pouncer's vulnerable eyes. Fear and rage warred in Pouncer's liver as he struggled to free himself. *Fear is death,* some distant part of his brain told him. Time seemed to slow down, and he watched as the Tzaatz warrior raised the sword above his head. Pouncer slid his own sword into position, leaving himself open for the killing blow, but as the other brought his sword down he flipped his own blade up in between the gaps in the vulnerable shoulder joint of his opponent's armor. The Tzaatz screamed in agony as his amputated arm fell to the ground. Pouncer kicked himself up and over and drove his sword into the other's face. Without pausing he whirled around to face the first attacker, who had regained his footing a hairsbreadth before tumbling off the wall. Pouncer dropped to *v'scree* stance as two more Tzaatz moved up behind the first. He could not run; with their grav belts they would catch him before he had gone two leaps. Panting hard, he prepared to take them on. They closed in, snarling. He fell back a pace, and something hit his chestplate with a sharp *crack*, glancing off and staggering him backward. He twisted in midfall, kicked out blindly in case his attacker had leapt with his fall, but when he look up again the Tzaatz were gone. One of the catapult *rapsari* had fired wide. His attackers had been thrown off the wall by a barrage of the heavy steel balls. Had he not stepped backward he would have gone with them. A high-pitched whine rose, and he whirled to see a spybot whine past, still on its patrol circuit. *The Command Lair should have those under active control. What is happening down there?*

No time to worry about that now. Below him more Tzaatz troops were coming out of the forest, and along the wall the grav skirmishers were finishing the last of the defenders. It was too late now to escape by the river. Pouncer turned and ran back the way he had come, diving into the tower entrance and half running, half falling down the stairs. His only hope now was to hide in the Citadel until the attack was over. His honor didn't twinge at that course. He knew now that the Citadel was lost. His duty now lay to the Rrit dynasty, and the most important thing he could do was survive.

Where to run? For an instant he considered the House of Victory. Kchula-Tzaatz himself would be there, with just a handful of retainers to guard him. *If I can get to him I can challenge him to* skatosh. *He is old and slow, and when he is dead his forces must surrender. I can end this before it has truly begun.* But Kchula-Tzaatz would have planned for that, and his brother the Black Priest was there, the most accomplished single-combat expert in the Patriarchy. If Pouncer challenged for single combat, Ftzaal-Tzaatz would stand for Kchula, and while Pouncer was confident in his own skills, the Protector of Jotok was legendary.

No, if his duty was to survive he would survive. He headed for the Inner Fortress, aiming for his own chamber and the hidden shelter behind his bathing pool. Twice he crossed open courtyards under the noses of the invaders and their *rapsari*. Twice speed and surprise saw him clear. He gained the Hall of Ancestors without further pursuit, and thought he could hear the sounds of battle closing in around him. From the Hall a corridor led to the side. A dozen leaps down that was his chamber and safety.

He bounded the last length toward it, twisting in midair, touching down with hind claws extended to brake. He skidded sideways, already turned ninety degrees to face down the cross corridor, legs gathered to start running again with a leap as soon he cleared the archway. The water of his bathing pool would break his scent trail, and he would be safe there, for a time. Safe enough while the attack played itself out, safe long enough to plan an escape, to plan revenge for the betrayal Tzaatz Pride had visited upon his line.

The archway slid past and the corridor opened before him. In front of his chamber a full sword of Tzaatz warriors and a pair of *rapsari* raiders. No escape there!

He let his momentum carry him past the opening, aborting the leap. There was a roar from one of the Tzaatz, and a high, keening cry from a *rapsar*. They had seen him. He twisted again, awkwardly, and leapt in the direction he had been going already, his mind calling up a map of the Citadel. Here in the ancient core of the fortress there were many twists and turns, many potential hiding places.

If only he could reach one of them. The sounds of pursuit grew behind him. He turned a corner and ran through a narrow light well in the second tier of the south curtain wall. On the other side he skidded to a stop, turned and ran out again, back to a doorway he'd already passed. Through the door he bounded up a circular staircase to another corridor. Hopefully that would confuse his scent trail enough to throw off the trackers.

He turned off his intended path again to avoid distant footsteps and ran blindly. Snarls and sounds of pursuit rose behind him and he chose the right-hand path at another intersection. Another corner and he found the corridor blocked by an ornate iron gate. He slammed into it painfully hard, using it to stop himself, and wrenched at it. It failed to open. He wrenched again, looking for the locking mechanism, then realized where he was. Beyond the iron gate was an open courtyard, exquisitely manicured hedges, ornate fountains, high stone walls with no windows. This was the Garden of Prret, and the gate would recognize only his father. Even if he could get it to open there was nothing beyond it but the kzinrette quarters. The only exit was the one he was standing in front of. Beyond the gate a couple of kzinretti were lounging on *prrstet* in the sun, not obviously disturbed by the fighting going on around them. Another, more skittish perhaps, was peering from the branches of a tangletree, nothing but her great, liquid eyes visible in the shadows between the leaves.

He wrenched at the gate again, though he knew it was pointless, feeling desperation flood through him as he realized he could go no further. *Fear is death.* The pursuit was growing closer. He turned around to face the oncoming hunters, drawing his captured variable sword and extending the slicewire. There was nowhere left to run, nowhere left to hide, and there were worse fates than to die defending his father's harem. Guardmaster's words came back to him: *You will earn your name today.* It would be a death of honor, and he would make sure the attackers paid in blood for their conquest. There was nothing else he could hope for.

The pursuing warriors caught up quickly, slowing and deploying as they realized their quarry was trapped. If they had netguns it would all be over. He scanned them and saw they had none, but . . . The second *rapsar* had fallen behind, but it came forward again to stand beside its twin. Its handler snapped commands and they moved forward, jaws hanging open to expose razor fangs. They were plated in mag armor themselves, mirror surfaces carefully articulated at the joints, lethal adversaries in close combat.

So they would use the beasts. Unless . . .

"You are cowards!" He spat the words. "You don't dare face me claw to claw."

One of the Tzaatz took a step forward. "So claims the one who ran like a *vatach*!"

"I stand before you now at eight-to-one. Which of you has the liver to make it even odds?"

No doubt they were brave Heroes. Would they be so foolish as to take on a noble trained in single combat? He took up *v'scree* stance. They had not yet seen what he could do. He could take two at once, probably three, perhaps four. There were eight in the sword, plus the *rapsari*. If they all came at once he would die.

"Only because your hole is blocked, *vatach*." The warrior took another pace forward. Pouncer took his measure: big and competent looking, hard muscles rippling under his fur. He wore rank tattoos on his ears, but Pouncer couldn't read the Tzaatz symbology. Was he the sword leader?

"At least I do not scavenge the carrion of beasts. Send on your reptiles so I can take a worthy challenge."

The big kzin's jaws relaxed into a fanged smile. "You will die for your insults."

"At eight to one. This *vatach* trembles to face your heroism."

"I would face the Fanged God and win." The other made a gesture, and the rest of the sword fell back a step. Yes, he was the leader, and his anger was going to lead him to a fatal mistake.

There was a clang behind him and Pouncer's ears jerked back even as he leapt sideways to face a new threat. A tawny flash sped by him: a kzinrette. The gate was standing open now. How had she got through the gate? Had it been unlocked after all? He cursed the lost opportunity under his breath. It was far too late now to run now. He spun back to face his enemy, bringing his sword up and over to block a leap, but the kzinrette had startled the Tzaatz too. For a moment she hesitated, and he recognized the eyes he'd seen peering from the tangletree. "T'suuz!" It was his litter sister, her back carrying the same distinctive stripe pattern that marked his own.

She didn't appear to recognize him, her attention focused on the alert warriors in front of her. They watched her, unsure what to do, and then she bolted through a gap between two of them and disappeared down the corridor and around the corner.

For a moment Pouncer considered bolting himself, through the now open gate. It would be *chrowl* for some of the kzinretti, and no doubt these warriors would find themselves distracted by the wealth of available females. They might even fall to fighting among themselves and give him a chance to escape. He abandoned the thought. If he had got through the gate before the standoff he might have had a slight hope. As it stood now, facing down the enemy a leap away, they would be on him before he could get eight leaps if he turned.

So he must fight, but on his terms. "You don't even deserve the death I would give you." *Let their anger be their counsel.* Pouncer kept his eyes locked on the warrior, alert for the leap he knew would come. The other bared his fangs and gathered himself. *Rage is death*, and the other kzin was very angry. "*Sthondat!*" he spat, with contempt in his voice. His abdominal muscles tightened in anticipation. *Fear is death.* He steadied his grip, aligned the marker ball of his sword with his opponent's nose.

The warrior's scream of rage echoed down the corridor. His sword was drawn back, coming around as he leapt in a two-handed overhead swing that would cleave steel. Pouncer swept his own weapon up to block the blow, deflecting it down and to the side. His attacker's momentum carried him tumbling forward, and Pouncer brought his own sword down, aiming for the weak joint between the neck and carapace plates of the other kzin's armor. A subtle twist of his wrist at the last moment slid the monomolecular slicewire between the articulated grooves and thrust it home, decapitating his opponent. Motion blurred in the corner of his eye, and he yanked the weapon back up in time to block a second attacker whose leap had come a heartbeat behind the first one. The shock of the impact jarred his wrists, spattering the droplets of blood that surface tension stuck to the otherwise invisible wire. The other turned the parry into a spin, coming at him from the other direction and forcing a counterparry. Pouncer managed to get his blade into position to block again, but the force of the attack nearly slammed his own slicewire back into his face.

Again the Tzaatz warrior turned the block into an attack with a fluid twist. *This one is better than the first.* Pouncer fell back a pace to give himself room as he blocked and got in a counterstroke himself. The other blocked it effortlessly and followed up with a strike, feint, strike that pulled Pouncer's guard down. The second strike glanced off his shoulder but the angle wasn't quite right to slide through the gaps in his armor's articulation. Pouncer fell back another pace. *This one is dangerous.*

For a moment the dueling pair faced each other, breathing heavily through gaping fangs. The other's eyes bored into his, pupils dilated almost round. His ears were up and swiveled forward, but his stance was relaxed, and Pouncer realized the extent of his adversary's craft. He had not been goaded to attack by Pouncer's insults. He had expected his aggressive companion to leap, had readied himself and taken advantage of the first warrior's suicidal attack to catch Pouncer with his guard down.

"You are skilled." The other's eyes were locked on his.

"You will not defeat me." Pouncer's breathing was heavy, and he wished he felt the conviction he put into his words.

The other rippled his ears. "You are also alone." He made a gesture to bring the rest of the sword forward.

Pouncer's gaze didn't waver. "You lack honor, *sthondat*." If he could provoke the other to leap . . .

His adversary just rippled his ears again. "Perhaps, but I claim victory." He repeated the gesture, and for the merest fraction of a second Pouncer's eyes flickered from his opponent's gaze to the rest of the sword. Fangs showing and variable swords extended they advanced. He tensed himself, ready to die with honor.

"Chrrrooowwwlll . . ." It was a low, warbling cry, primal in its need, and sexual desire rose in Pouncer. He knew it was death to let his gaze waver from his opponent, but he couldn't help flicking his eyes to the side a second time.

T'suuz! His sister hadn't fled, she had only let the warriors think she had. She was behind them now, crouched low in the mating posture, her invitingly tufted tail raised and flicking back and forth in open invitation. It was not her fertile time, her scent told him that much, but . . .

"Chrrroooowwlll . . ." The sound tugged at deep buried instincts in Pouncer's brain, and he fought to keep his eyes

locked on his opponent. Some of the Tzaatz had turned to watch her, the battle forgotten. Again her tail flicked, and one of them took a step toward her. The warrior facing Pouncer didn't shift his gaze, but Pouncer's expression must have told him what was happening behind him. "Forward, you fools. There will be kzinretti for us all when this is done."

The Tzaatz who had moved first took another step, and that was all it took. Another Tzaatz grabbed at him and he turned and slashed with his variable sword. Another screamed and leapt and in an instant the entire sword was slashing at one another, screams of rage and pain filling the corridor. And suddenly T'suuz had a variable sword and was slicing out the throat of one of the Tzaatz. Pouncer's opponent sensed the danger at his back and lunged forward. Pouncer stepped back to clear and counterstrike, but the move was only a feint, and the other pivoted to leap and strike at T'suuz. She had shifted her attack to one of the *rapsari* and had taken off its hind limbs. Before it hit the floor she was at the second *rapsar*, gutting it with her captured weapon. She had no armor and her back was turned. Pouncer's opponent's pivot-and-strike was going to slice her in half.

Pouncer screamed and leapt. Startled by the scream, the other aborted his pivot, but it was too late. Pouncer's foreclaws were at his face, followed an instant later by the variable sword, driving deep into the neck joints. The blade bit home, and the other died drowning in his own blood. For a moment Pouncer stood there, muscles straining against the sagged weight of his now dead opponent, and then he let the body fall. Breathing hard he screamed the *zal'mchurrr* to consign the spirit of a worthy warrior to the Fanged God's Pride-Circle.

"I've been watching for you. I thought you'd never arrive."

He looked up. T'suuz was speaking, and the enormity of what had just occurred sank in. "You . . . you . . ." Pouncer could not articulate the words. Kzinretti did not fight Heroes, not with the finely trained reflexes she had just shown him, not with *weapons*, not with *deception*.

Not with success outnumbered six to one. But she had done it.

"How did you open the gate?"

She rippled her ears. "I can open that gate. I expected that you would come here. I was waiting for you. I had already unlocked it. You had only to pull the latch."

He looked, saw the simple mechanism he had not seen in his earlier haste. He had allowed himself to be motivated by fear and felt ashamed. That was over with now. "How did you know I would come here?"

"Patriarch's Telepath exerted such influence as he could on the course of the battle."

Pouncer's ears swiveled up and forward. What did that mean? "Patriarch's Telepath—"

"Everything will be made clear later. We have to move now." She ran past him to the still open gate. "Come! This way!"

"But how—"

"There is not time. These will have reported finding you. Come!" Still he stared at her, his disbelief growing. *Report* was not a word of the Female Tongue nor even the Kitten's Tongue but the Hero's Tongue, and kzinretti could not speak the Hero's Tongue. Their brains were not advanced enough. It was a fact. He had learned it.

She grabbed his paw and yanked. "Come!"

He followed her into the Garden of Prret. She paused to close the gate behind them, sliding the heavy locking mechanism home with a solid *thunk*. She turned and ran through the garden and he followed her, past ornate carvings and inviting *prrstet*, heading for the Inner Quarters beyond the Garden. Pouncer found himself strangely uncomfortable. The architecture, stone, the smell, it was still the Citadel, but he hadn't been into the kzinretti's quarters since he had left his mother's teats. Penetrating his father's sanctum was a violation of the most severe dishonor. Only alien slaves were allowed past the gate, to tend the gardens and care for the kzinretti and their kits.

T'suuz led him to an archway that opened into the high-domed vault that was the entrance to the Inner Quarters. A fountain burbled in a pool surrounded by tapestries and cushions. *Prret* reclined, washing themselves, playing idly. Most of the kzinretti ignored them, but one young female flipped her ears up inquisitively at the sight of him. She was barely past kittenhood, with sleek fur and great, limpid eyes. She sidled toward them, tail flipping flirtatiously, *chrowl*ing deep in her throat. It was probably her first fertility, and Pouncer found himself suddenly flooded with the same desire T'suuz's trick had raised in him, only stronger, much stronger. The immediate danger of their position washed away in the urge to mate. Her ripe scent came to him and he took a step forward.

There was a snarling hiss and T'suuz bounded in front of him, facing down the kzinrette. "Mine!" she spat, raking her claws. The kzinrette startled, looking unsure. T'suuz snarled again and advanced on her, fur bristling. The kzinrette looked from T'suuz to Pouncer and back, looked again. T'suuz advanced again and the kzinrette bolted.

Pouncer growled in sudden frustration, found himself looking deep into his sister's eyes.

"Focus! We must not delay. Do you understand?"

"Yes . . ."

"This is your life! If we escape you will be Patriarch. You will have many *prret*. If we linger you will die. Focus!"

"Yes . . ." Pouncer shook himself, the *prret*'s scent still rich in his nostrils, her inviting, chirruping *chrowl* still inciting his desire.

"Come!" He followed. She took him deeper into the Inner Quarters, past bright nurseries and quiet crèches and lavish couching suites. There were other *prret* in their time, other temptations, but Pouncer kept his focus narrowly on following his sister, some distant part of himself amazed at his body's response to fertile females.

A door in a cut stone wall led to a staircase down, another door to a service tunnel. The corridor was dusty, lined with conduits for power, air, water, vacuum, liquid nitrogen, and liquid hydrogen. Its walls were unadorned stone blocks, its floor worn smooth by the feet of generations of servitors. Machinery hummed in the background. It was low and narrow, part of the ancient fortress converted now to a modern purpose. How long since a kzin had trod this way? Maybe never; it was beneath the dignity of a warrior to visit the domain of slaves.

The corridor branched, and branched again, doors

leading off to either side. Pouncer quickly lost his sense of direction but T'suuz took them unerringly forward, through a door into a storage room full of musty equipment of uncertain purpose. Behind a heavy rack a hole had been cut through the stonework to pass a set of conduits. Stones had been pulled from the wall to enlarge the hole just enough to squeeze through. T'suuz wriggled through with ease, her lithe body fitting snuggly through the gap. Pouncer had a harder time, breathing hard and struggling. His hip caught on a projection. She pulled hard and he felt fur ripping, then tumbled through, falling awkwardly to the gritty floor. The corridor he found himself in was of more recent construction, utilitarian sprayed fibercrete, filled with the distant hum of turning machinery. T'suuz led on again, and the hum grew to a roar as they passed through a chamber where the conduits were big enough to stand in. A control panel glowed against one wall. A maintenance hatch set low by the floor led onto a metal mesh catwalk high on the wall in a cavernous hall, too dimly lit for kzinti eyes to see with comfort. Far below, the bulking silvery domes of fusion generators marched in ranked pairs into the murk, and the air vibrated with the essence of their power. At the control wall Kdatlyno technicians were making obeisance to a full four-sword of Tzaatz warriors who were securing the area with snarled shouts, backed up by half a dozen *rapsari*. He did not need T'suuz's cautioning gesture to warn him to silence. They crept along the catwalk, hugging the wall to take the scant cover the shadows there provided.

The catwalk dead-ended, and for a moment Pouncer wondered where they were to go next. T'suuz climbed the

railing, gathered herself and jumped. Involuntarily
Pouncer reached out to grab her back but she was already
gone. But when he looked to find her body shattered on
the floor below he saw her just two leaps away and a leap
down, balancing on a conduit barely large enough to stand
on. She turned to beckon him on but he had already seen
what he had to do and was climbing onto the teetering
rail. He paused for a moment to gather himself, but he
was twice her weight. The railing swayed and he overbalanced, falling forward. He grabbed wildly at nothing and
then he was falling. Instinctively he turned the plunge into
a leap, pushing out hard with his legs in a desperate
attempt to save himself. The floor was a blur far below and
he seemed to hang in midair. All of a sudden the conduit
was in front of him and he twisted to grab at it.

His leap was far from perfect, and the conduit was too
small for him. He landed heavily, sliding forward over the
curved surface. The conduit rang like a gong when his
armor hit it, the noise echoing from the rock walls of the
chamber, and his variable sword fell to smash on the floor
far below. For an endless time he dangled while the
Tzaatz below snarled back and forth, alerted by the sudden
noise. Spotbeams stabbed the darkness, came up to sweep
the catwalk, but somehow missed him as he dangled
there. The beams moved on and he breathed deep, then,
paw by paw, he struggled back to the top. T'suuz watched
him, unable to help from her precarious perch, her eyes
shining green in the darkness. When she saw he was safe
she turned silently and loped down the conduit. Pouncer
followed, still shaking from his near miss. Their route
took them along the conduit to another, then down the

length of the power hall, where another dizzying, dangerous leap took them to a second catwalk and through another hatch.

She has done this before. The route was too complex and her movements too certain for her to be running blindly. Kzinretti could be clever escape artists, he knew, but this spoke of *planning*, and kzinretti were not supposed to be able to plan. Time to worry about that later.

He closed the hatch behind him, grateful to leave the searching Tzaatz warriors behind. They were in another corridor, more of a tunnel, made of old and crumbling bricks. It stank of damp and mildew, and clearly hadn't been used in a long time. Tritium glowlamps were set in the walls, but glowed so feebly as to barely illuminate themselves. How many half-lives had passed since they were installed?

He sniffed the stagnant air cautiously and recognition dawned. "I know this place. This is the Quickwater defense tunnel. It leads from the House of Victory to the old emplacements across the river."

"It leads to freedom. We must hurry." T'suuz started to lead him along the tunnel, then suddenly froze. A sound echoed, scurrying footfalls in the darkness behind them, fast and light. Pouncer froze, ears swiveling up and forward. Beside him his sister activated her variable sword. Something was coming, several somethings. The cadence was too rapid to be a kzin, and padded paws would be quieter. *Rapsar* seekers perhaps, sent to clear the tunnel. Weaponless, Pouncer dropped to attack crouch. When they came, he would be ready.

Execute every act of thy life as though it were thy last.
    —Marcus Aurelius, Emperor of Rome

It seemed like hours had gone by, but by Cherenkova's beltcomp it was just thirty minutes before Yiao-Rrit bounded back into the room, his lips pulled back over his fangs. "The battle is not decided, and it may yet be lost. My duty is now to your defense and safe return. We are leaving the Citadel for the spaceport. Follow me. If I am attacked do not hesitate to use your weapons. The sigil of the Patriarch will not protect you."

He waved them into single file behind him and led them to a narrow side corridor. They moved out, Tskombe first behind the kzin, Cherenkova bringing up the rear. Instinctively she looked behind to cover their backs. The Patriarch's brother was not running but she found she had to trot to keep up to him. Brasseur was soon panting, but Yiao-Rrit did not slack his pace. The sounds of battle were far away, and Ayla began to believe that they were going to get away with it. That hope vanished as they rounded a corner to enter a courtyard through an arched gateway. There were two dozen enemy warriors in there, deployed in battle formation. Surprised and angry snarls greeted their appearance, and the enemy leapt to attack. Instinctively Ayla raised the beamer and opened fire. Her first shot caught a warrior in midleap, overloading the superconductors in his magnetic armor. The silver surface turned copper and she fired again, the second shot exploding the thin metal plate and vaporizing his chest cavity behind it. She dodged sideways and his body landed where she had been standing. If she hadn't been fast and

accurate she would already be dead. There was no time to
dwell on that now. She picked the next closest attacker,
already launching himself at her, and again fired twice.
Her shots went wide and she looked death in the face as
his fangs came for her throat. His weight slammed into
her, throwing her backward hard against wall, but his body
slid lifeless to the floor, the decapitated head rolling away
from her feet. She looked up and saw Yiao-Rrit, variable
sword in midswing. Their eyes met for a split second in
understanding: The humans would engage distant targets,
the kzin would deal with any who got close. She picked
another target and fired. To her left Tskombe was flat on the
ground behind the heavy magrifle, pumping rounds into the
massed attackers. The Tzaatz were brave, and even with
only hand weapons they would have slaughtered the
humans, but the few in the first wave who survived
Tskombe's withering fire were cut down by Yiao-Rrit.

"Go, I'll cover." Tskombe had slowed his rate of fire,
now sending carefully aimed shots into potential Tzaatz
hiding places. The heavy slugs tore through stonewood
and stone with indifferent ease, making it clear to the
enemy that exposure was suicidal. Yiao-Rrit went first,
covering the length of the courtyard in three long bounds.
Cherenkova ran after him and Brasseur, panting, followed. She arrived to find the kzin standing over two
freshly dead creatures, reptilian predators like half-scale
tyrannosaurs with heavy forelimbs. The beasts were plated
in mag armor, and blood splattered red on Yiao-Rrit's
muzzle. More blood seeped from the armor articulation
near his waist, and she could see from the way he moved
that he was badly wounded. No time for that now. She

turned and fired into one of the opposite archways, spalling stone with her beam. Brasseur joined her and started firing too.

"What are those?" She gestured at the reptiles between shots.

Yiao-Rrit growled. "*Rapsari,* specialized genetic constructs. Tzaatz Pride holds Jotok." She wasn't sure what that meant, but she recognized the contempt in the kzin's words.

"Will there be more of them?"

"They have trackers, assaulters, raiders, sniffers, assassins. There will be more."

Across the courtyard Tskombe picked up his heavy weapon and ran. A Tzaatz warrior stood up leveling a huge crossbow. Cherenkova fired, her beam going wide, but close enough to spoil the enemy's aim. The crystal iron bolt embedded itself in the stone wall a handspan behind Tskombe. He turned around in the archway and sprayed rounds to slow the pursuit, and then Yiao-Rrit was bounding down the hall, the humans sprinting after him. Even with his wound he was faster than they were. Behind them snarled shouts rose as the Tzaatz regrouped to follow. On the run Cherenkova checked her weapon's charge: more than half gone. If there was much more fighting to be done they'd be in trouble.

Yiao-Rrit led them into a large room, thick wood beams arching up to the vaulted ceiling, heavy pelts hanging from the wall, dozens of huge swords and battle-axes arranged into elaborate rosettes and serpentines. The kzin went to the vast cut stone fireplace that occupied one end of the room. He stood there staring at it long

enough that Cherenkova began to wonder if he'd
snapped under the pressure, then he reached out and
pulled on a carved projection. A lever cleverly built into
the elaborate mantelwork moved, and the back of the
fireplace slid open, revealing a dark square a meter on a
side. Yiao-Rrit gestured them forward.

"Here—go in, go down. This will take you outside the
Citadel. Avoid armed warriors and follow the trail to the
west, toward the sunset. It will take you to the Hero's
Square. There will be grav-service there. The sigil of the
Patriarch will give you *strakh* enough to get to the Sea-of-
Stars spaceport. Show the sigil to Chuut-Portmaster, and
he will get you aboard a scout ship that can take you to
Crusader at the edge of the singularity."

"What about you?"

"We haven't got room to run enough to break your
scent trail. It will not take the Tzaatz long to find this passage. I will gain you as much time as I can here."

"But—" Brasseur seemed prepared to argue.

Sounds of pursuit rose behind them. "Go!" Yiao-Rrit
grabbed the ambassador and tossed him through the dark
opening as though he were a rag doll. Ayla knew a zero
choice option when she saw it, and she dived through
before the kzin could grab her. She found herself
sprawled on uneven bricks, and Tskombe came piling in
on top of her, whether thrown by Yiao-Rrit or simply
motivated by the oncoming enemy was unknowable. For
a moment they lay there, and she was suddenly acutely
aware of his hard-muscled body against hers. The sudden
scent of his sweat spoke directly to her hindbrain, triggering
reactions that were entirely inappropriate under the

circumstances. She swallowed hard and breathed deep to refocus her thinking, with little success. She was suddenly aware of the pounding of her heartbeat in her ears. The room they had been in was reduced to a square of light. Yiao-Rrit threw the lever back and the plate began to close again. She yanked her hands back instinctively, although they were nowhere near its path. She saw the huge kzin turn and draw his variable sword. Snarls rose in the air, and then the light was gone.

Tskombe picked himself up and she followed. They were at the top of an ancient and musty stairway made of eroded brick. The way down was dimly lit by faintly glowing green globes.

"Let's go." He was already moving down the stairs, picking his way carefully in the barely adequate light. She followed him wordlessly. In other circumstances his summary adoption of command would have rankled. Right here, right now, he was the one who had the ground combat experience, and she wasn't about to argue. Brasseur came behind them. The heavy kzin beamer was an awkward burden on the narrow, uneven stairs, and she tripped twice, twisting an ankle the second time. Pain shot through it every time she put her foot down, but this wasn't the time to stop to nurse it. She gritted her teeth and carried on. The stairs led to a tunnel of the same crumbling brick, the footing still uneven and the damp, musty smell of long abandonment strong in their nostrils. Fortunately their pace down the tunnel was slow enough that her sprain wasn't a factor.

Fortunate so long as there was no pursuit. But the Tzaatz would track them; if kzin noses weren't up to the task, the *rapsar* sniffers would be, and she had no doubt both could move in the dark faster than humans could. How long was the tunnel? If they weren't out of it before the pursuit resumed . . . She didn't finish the thought.

> *Blood is the price of victory, brothers. Now let us make the enemy pay high.*
> —Second-Commander at the
> siege of the Last Fortress

Kdar-Leader stood at the front of his formation, more than three quarters gone now, but they stood shoulder to shoulder, five abreast in the tunnels before the Command Lair, six leaps behind a sealed battlesteel blast door. He breathed deep. It would be their last stand. The enemy would be stopped here or not at all. They had fallen back as the Tzaatz swept through the breaches in the Citadel walls that their beasts had dissolved for them. Their losses had been heavy, but not a single *zitalyi* had turned tail and run; each fallback was controlled, each new position defended until it was no longer tenable, and then abandoned under cover from those who had already taken up the next one. The surface of the Citadel was already in Tzaatz hands, but the tunnels were deep and there were stores there for seasons. If they could hold out, keep the Tzaatz at bay, then help might arrive; one of the other Great Prides would honor their oath of fealty to the Rrit.

If they could hold out. It shouldn't have been a question. The blast doors were designed to shrug off heavy energy weapons, but the Tzaatz had come prepared. Those things, *rapsari* Guardmaster had called them . . .

The battlesteel started to blacken and smoke in the center. In heartbeats the corridor was full of blinding acrid fumes, and the now familiar snouts of the rotund reptilian breachers appeared, oozing a thick, corrosive ichor that ate cerametal like water ate salt. It was imperative to hold fire until the beasts exposed a target . . .

"Crossbows now!" The front rank fired and knelt, the second rank fired over their heads and knelt, then the third and fourth ranks—and that was all the crossbows he had. With rigid self-discipline they turned and filed through the single space left for them between the sword ranks behind, to re-form and reload behind them. The lead swords braced for what they knew was to come. At the door the beast had suffered greviously. It was armored with some kind of plastic, not mag-armored cerametal like the others, lest it dissolve its own protection, and that material was unequal to the impact of thrice-eight crystal iron penetrators fired at point blank range. Its armor hung in tatters from its snout and foreparts, and the bolts had struck deeply. Ichor mixed with blood oozed from the wounds and ate holes in the stone of the corridor, but it was still alive when its handler, invisible behind it, drew it back from the breach it had created. Through the gaps came something small and fast, razor teeth snapping like a *sherrek*: the fast and vicious harrier *rapsar*. More poured through the gap after it, and they launched themselves at the defenders without hesitation. Rrit variable swords flashed and slicewires bit home, but the attackers were hard targets and some got through to the first, the second, even the third rank, and where the razor teeth clamped onto Rrit flesh they did not let go, not even when the creature's body was cut from its head. Defenders fell, and ahead of them Tzaatz crossbows advanced into the gap, their bolts killing those who had not been taken to the ground by the beasts.

Kdar-Leader waited, watching as the Tzaatz advanced, then keyed his com. "Ambush parties, move now, move now." He waited another four heartbeats to give his element leaders time to start moving, then "*Zitalyi*, next position, fall back!"

The lead sword ranks, those who had survived the onslaught, knelt in place and the crossbows fired over their heads, four successive salvos that stopped the Tzaatz in their tracks. Again with commendable discipline the front swords fell back through the empty file in the crossbow ranks, and then the whole formation turned to run back to the next blast door. Behind them a Tzaatz screamed in triumph, rallying his Heroes to pursue, but the voice was cut off in gurgle and attack screams filled the corridor. Kdar-Leader's ambush parties were dropping from ventilator shafts overhead, wreaking havoc and buying him the time he needed to consolidate his defenses for the next engagement. It would cost them their lives, but their deaths would be honorable ones.

How many of the breaching *rapsari* did the Tzaatz possess? He had seen three killed that he was sure of, and this fourth one was surely too badly wounded to continue. It would take them time to bring forward another, but time was something the Tzaatz now had in abundance, and something the Rrit were rapidly running out of. If something drastic didn't happen soon, Kdar-Leader's own death of honor wasn't far away.

Kill them all and take what you want.
                    —Zirrow-Graff at Kdat

Sword-Sergeant loped efficiently down a high vaulted hall full of transparent display cases holding antique armor and weapons. He could not help mentally adding up the value and dividing out the booty that would fall to him. Kchula-Tzaatz would not fail to be generous in return for the great victory he was gaining here. Sword-Sergeant's share was not large, but this was Kzinhome, this was the Citadel of the Patriarch; the wealth here was beyond his wildest imaginings. He would gain a holding and females at least for this, and his home would be full of trophies from this vast storehouse of wealth. Behind him Third-Sword was evidently thinking the same thing, running his fingers over a silver-threaded tapestry of more *strakh* than he could ever hope to display.

"Watch your arc, clear that corner," Sword-Sergeant snarled. He didn't have to repeat himself. All of his warriors knew he would follow the command with his claws if he had to. Third-Sword moved, checking behind the display cases for refugees. Finding none, he raised his tail and rocked the tip back and forth, no threats. The other kzinti of his blade moved past him toward the far end of the hall, where an arched gateway led into a courtyard. Sword-Sergeant watched, alert for any sign of danger. The farthest one reached the wall, gave the no-threats signal.

"Seventh area secure," Sword-Sergeant snarled into his comlink. "Proceeding west."

"Confirmed." Even before the voice crackled in his ears he was giving tail signals to his warriors. Hind-Blade, cover the exit. Fore-Blade, prepare to clear-and-secure forward. The eight kzinti of his unit moved as one, half deploying to defend the archway, the other half lined up behind a pillar, out of the line of sight of the opening. Sword-Sergeant took the lead of Fore-Blade and glanced back to ensure everyone was in position. Crossbow trained on the entrance from behind a display table, Hind-Blade-Leader touched his paw to his forehead—ready.

Sword-Sergeant looked back to *Rapsar*-Trainer, still waiting at the end of the hall, tapped his nose, and gestured to the archway. Sniffer forward.

Rapsar-Trainer came up the hall, a squat reptilian sniffer waddling hard to keep up with him, eyestalks straining forward in eagerness. Sword-Sergeant wrinkled his nose in distaste. The sniffer looked like easy prey, but its scent told him the meat would be foul. He had little more affection for *Rapsar*-Trainer, who was clearly no warrior. Still, the *rapsari* were useful. They had started the day with four sniffers; three had died at the hands of Rrit defenders. Those deaths would have been his own Heroes if the sniffers hadn't been there to lead the way.

The sniffer waddled to the arch, proboscis wiggling for scent, eyestalks wrapping around the corner to check for danger. Color flowed across the chromatophores on its hindquarters, coding what it detected for *Rapsar*-Trainer.

Rapsar-Trainer gave a signal. Low threat left.

Sword-Sergeant acknowledged the signal with a tail flip. More meat for the glory of Tzaatz Pride. He leapt for the doorway, tail streaming behind him for balance, hind claws reaching forward to carry him into a roll as he landed, clearing the way for the rest of Fore-Blade, half a leap behind him. He caught a blur in the corner of his eye, pivoted and swung. His variable sword amputated the head of a statue before he realized his error. Embarrassing. He kicked the statue over to avenge that dishonor, and the intricate mechanism inside fell apart into randomly shaped components. *Strange, but irrelevant*. He turned his attention to the minor danger the sniffer had warned of.

He was in a courtyard garden, full of complicated sculptures and manicured hedges. A crippled kzin on a gravlifted *prrstet* lay by a bed of flowers, with a pair of silent Kdatlyno attendants. He twitched his tail in disgust. The ears of this pathetic specimen were barely worth putting on his belt. He turned to signal Hind-Blade through the arch, then paused to cuff Second-Sword, who was trying to detach a small statue from its base.

"Booty later," he snarled. For a second it looked as though Second-Sword would challenge-leap, but then he looked down and performed the gesture of submission. "I obey, Sword-Sergeant."

"See that you do." He returned his attention to the motionless trio in front of him. "Hind-Blade-Leader, secure the perimeter. I will kill this *sthondat* myself."

He advanced on his victim. Neither he nor the slaves made any move either to fight or to flee, which was somewhat disappointing. As he drew closer the wasted kzin seemed oblivious to his presence. All at once recognition dawned, and a thrill of exultation ran through Sword-Sergeant. "Hind-Blade-Leader! Stop!" This would win him a name! "Defensive formation! Here now!" He keyed his vocom. "Chruul-Commander, we have the telepath!"

He couldn't keep the gloating from his voice. He gestured at the Kdatlyno with his weapon. "You slaves, stand aside. We will take him."

The Kdatlyno didn't move, but the crippled figure on the *prrstet* shifted, turning his blank staring eyes to meet Sword-Sergeant's. In any other context Sword-Sergeant would already have screamed and leapt for such impertinence. Gutting one slave would ensure the other obeyed him in future, but something about the crippled telepath made him hesitate: those eyes, huge and infinitely empty, staring through him, paralyzing in their intensity . . .

He would have backed away, but that would never do in front of his warriors. Instead he repeated his threat. "Stand aside slaves, or I'll . . ." He didn't finish his sentence. The world vanished and he was falling in infinite blackness, his ears filled with his own screaming. Distantly he was aware of his body falling to the ground, but he could only think to end the darkness. Vainly he beat against his skull with his fists for relief, each flash of pain bringing some scrap of grounded reality to his sense-starved mind. It wasn't enough. In desperation he slammed his head against the ground, willing his awareness back to the here and now. The exploding pain of every impact gave just an instant's respite from the despairing emptiness. Not soon enough the quiet fell.

Third-Sword watched in fascinated horror as his screaming leader beat his own brains out on the flagstones of the Puzzle Garden path, unsure of what to do. The answer came an instant later as Telepath's huge, blank eyes focused on him, but by then it was too late to run. He was smarter than Sword-Sergeant, but it still took him several attempts before he managed to drive his *wtsai* through his own braincase.

> *Don't speak to me of honor. Victory is everything.*
> —Vsar-Vsar, the Seven World Scourge

Kchula-Tzaatz looked down from his chamber in the House of Victory at the carnage in the Citadel's Old Courtyard, where the broken bodies of Tzaatz, Rrit and *rapsari* lay where they had fallen in twice-eights. It was truly a great day. The battle had never reached the House of Victory, though it had come close. Some of the Great Pride-Patriarchs had thrown their retinues into the defense of the Citadel, hoping no doubt to curry favor with Meerz-Rrit, but they had been swept aside with the *zitalyi* defenders. A far smaller number had offered their support to Kchula-Tzaatz, but he had refused them all; no need to take on obligations of honor when victory was sure. Stkaa-Emissary's guards stood as an outer cordon to Ftzaal-Tzaatz's elite killers, an obligation Kchula had accepted when he feared the entire plan would come apart. He now would rather not have given such *strakh* to Stkaa-Emissary, but what was done was done. All Stkaa Pride would want from the new ruler of the Patriarchy was support in their monkey war and against Cvail Pride. That was already part of Kchula's plan to unite the Great Prides under him, and since Chmee-Cvail had thrown his warriors in with the Rrit, the deal would simply allow him to use Stkaa Pride for his own vengeance. It was a triviality.

"Victory is ours, brother." Kchula jumped and whirled. He had not heard Ftzaal-Tzaatz come in.

He fought down the urge to snarl in anger at being startled. *My brother's stealth is my tool.* "The Command Lair
is taken then?"

"Ktronaz-Commander just vocommed me."

"I must go there at once."

Ftzaal led a formation of his guard to escort Kchula
through secured areas. There was still fighting going on in
isolated pockets of the Citadel, but the key points had
been taken and the outcome was no longer in doubt. Still-
warm bodies were strewn through the fortress, and once a
pair of Rrit leapt from ambush, variable swords humming,
only to be quickly dispatched by Ftzaal's elite warriors.
Kchula took care to show no fear. Now was the time that
he would cement his rule as the greatest conqueror in the
history of the Patriarchy, but he was still relieved when
they reached the base of the Patriarch's Tower and the
tunnels leading down to the Command Lair.
Aboveground the Tower was a well preserved piece of history, its stones eight-cubed generations old or more;
belowground it was a very up-to-date fortress. The mag-
armored blast doors at the tunnel entrance were proof
against even conversion weapons, but the corrosive juices
of the breaching *rapsari* had eaten large holes through the
thick plates. Kchula wrinkled his nose at the harsh, acidic
scent as they passed. The fighting had been hard, and carbonized beam scars marred the walls near a pile of dead
warriors in Tzaatz livery. At the far end of the corridor a
pair of AI-directed defense turrets had been hacked from
the wall with slicewires. Someone had neglected to turn
them off at the declaration of *skalazaal*, and the cost to the
attackers had been heavy.

Kchula gestured to a retainer, Aide-de-Camp. "Document that." *The evidence will be useful later, if it becomes necessary to erode Rrit honor.*

Aide-de-Camp claw-raked and obeyed, and the remainder of the party continued. Tzaatz warriors had chalked battle codes on the walls as they advanced, indicating enemy positions, cleared rooms, and directions for follow-up forces. Following them they rode a drop tube down seven levels to the Command Lair. The carnage there was incredible, the halls literally slick with blood. The *zitalyi* had made a last stand and the Tzaatz had broken their resistance with swarms of harrier *rapsari*, small, fast and vicious. Twice-eights of the scaly bodies were strewn around the Command Lair, intermingled with the tangled dead of Rrit and Tzaatz. It had been a costly fight, but that was no matter. *Victory is what counts, not the price.*

He waved Aide-de-Camp forward. "See that the dead receive full honors, and that their conquest share goes to their sons and brothers."

"Of course, sire."

It was no more than honor demanded, and Ktronaz-Commander would have seen it done regardless. Issuing the order himself simply asserted his command and reaffirmed his loyalty to his warriors. The word would spread, *Kchula-Tzaatz himself insisted the protocols be followed,* and his *strakh* would rise with those who pledged their fealty to him. Few would stop to consider the price he would pay if he issued the opposite order. *Greet necessity with enthusiasm.* He would have preferred to accrue their shares to himself. *The dead are no one's ally.* He scowled slightly at the requirements of honor.

A moment later he was striding through the doors of the Command Lair, and elation washed away every other emotion. The legendary nexus of Rrit control! He looked around with triumphant glee, ran his hands over the control panels that would issue orders to swing the might of the entire Patriarchy wherever he desired it. This was power! How long had he dreamed of possessing it? The day was his. It remained only to consolidate his triumph.

Across the room Ktronaz-Commander's command group had a temporary command post set up until the more sophisticated Rrit system could be brought under control. Snarls in battle code rose from comsets as Ktronaz-Commander directed the mop-up. Pockets of Rrit *zitalyi* were still fighting fierce rearguard actions around the Citadel. Still, the House of Victory was secure, the nobles of the various Great Prides assured of their safety. More important, the crèches had been taken, the Rrit kittens already executed. There would be no upstart contestants to his rule.

He caught a snatch of transmission, ". . . Sea-of-Stars secure . . ." Ktronaz-Commander looked up, jumped to attention, and saluted.

"Sire, the spaceport is taken." There was blood on Ktronaz-Commander's face. The fighting had been hard. "And we found a gift for you, cowering in a hole in the infirmary." He made a contemptuous gesture to a corner. Kchula followed the motion, saw Second-Son-of-Meerz-Rrit, being watched by two Tzaatz guards.

"Kchula-Tzaatz." Second-Son pushed forward. His escort moved to stop him, but fell back at a gesture from

Ktronaz-Commander. "I have kept my end of the bargain, now it is time for you keep yours."

Kchula looked Second-Son over, his lips curling. The scion of the Rrit did not impress in person. "Your father is dead then?"

"He is." The image of his father's death rose unbidden in Second-Son, and he fought it down. *I have killed before. Why does this haunt me so?*

Kchula looked sharply to Ftzaal-Tzaatz. "Has this been confirmed?"

"His body lies there." Second-Son spoke before Ftzaal could answer, pointed to one of the corpses Kchula had been ignoring. Kchula nudged it over with his toe, saw the Rrit ear tattoos, the distinctive black stripes. Even in death Meerz-Rrit looked regal, and Kchula kicked the body.

"And your brother?"

"Your assassin struck. He did not die at once, but he is surely dead now."

"How do you know?"

"I went to the infirmary to confirm it myself. His body is gone."

"Gone?" Anger flooded Kchula. "I need the *ztrarr*, the proof-before-the-pride-circle. An empty bed is no evidence."

"My pledge was only to kill my father; your assassin was supposed to take care of First-Son. I claim my due." There was arrogance in Second-Son's voice, though he avoided looking at his dead father.

"You would still be Patriarch, is that it?" There was amazement in Kchula's voice, replacing the rage. *There is*

*nothing to be gained by killing this wretch. Let us game
with him instead.*

"You pledged it on your honor." Second-Son's hackles
rose. He had taken humiliation enough for this day. The
price he had paid was high, and he was not going to
denied. His father . . . He could not help looking at the
body, could not stand to look. *What have I done?*

"And so I did." Kchula-Tzaatz let his fangs show, just a
little, enjoying his game. "But if you were to die in challenge duel, perhaps the Patriarchy would fall to me."

Fear shot through Second-Son, though he did his best
not to show it. "You cannot rule. The Patriarchy belongs to
the Rrit."

Kchula looked at his captive, controlling the urge to
have him executed on the spot. *He is my tool, nothing
more. His use is not yet ended.* Still his voice was full of
contempt when he spoke. *This tool will be more useful
wielded in a strong grip.* "Power belongs to the powerful.
Tzaatz troops control the Citadel."

"No Great Pride would stand for it!" Second-Son spoke
with a conviction he didn't feel, seeing the situation spinning out of control.

"But if the Rrit line is ended . . . Someone must rule,
mustn't they? Who will gainsay me if I tell them I am
Patriarch?" Kchula let his mouth gape into a fanged smile,
enjoying the fear that blossomed in Second-Son's eyes.

He means to kill me. Second-Son twisted away from his
guards and leapt for the door, but found himself tripped
up, flat on his back with Ftzaal-Tzaatz's variable sword at
his throat.

"In a hurry to leave, traitor?" Ftzaal's hard eyes locked

on Second-Son's, his lips twitching over his fangs, inviting Second-Son to give him the pleasure of executing him.

"Stand down, Ftzaal." Kchula's voice was firm. "I play with the coward. We shall stand by the honor of the Tzaatz Pride." He looked at his warriors. "You see how the scion of the Rrit upholds the honor of *his* Pride." Reluctantly the black-furred killer retracted his sword's slicewire and stepped back. Second-Son stayed where he was, his scent now so rank with fear he didn't bother to try to hide it, but daring to hope that he might live. Kchula raised a lip in contempt. "Stand up." Second-Son obeyed and Kchula went on. "Tell me you deserve the position I am about to grant you, groveling coward."

"You promised me . . ." The hope in Second-Son kindled.

"And I will not have it said that Tzaatz Pride does less than fulfill its bargains." Kchula took a small case from his carry-cape, withdrew a metal disk from that. "Did you know my brother served the priesthood? Not a High Priest, but the Stalkers-in-the-Night—a priest of death and darkness. Perhaps it is fitting that he bestow you with the sigil of your new office." He tossed the disk to Ftzaal. Second-Son turned to see, felt fear surge anew. It wasn't a sigil of office, it was a . . .

Ftzaal-Tzaatz moved in a blur too fast to see, the disk coming up to slap hard against Second-Son's back. Pain burned in his shoulder as its teeth embedded themselves deep in the muscle, and he fell to his knees as it spread to paralyzing numbness.

"The *zzrou* is filled with *p'chert* toxin." Kchula's purred with satisfaction as he put an ornate medallion around his neck. "It is keyed to this transponder. Do not allow your-self to get too far from me, Patriarch." His voice dripped sarcasm. "And since the transponder monitors my life signs, make yourself concerned with my well-being."

"You *sthondat*!" Rage and humiliation swept over Second-Son as he realized what had been done. The *zzrou* listened constantly for its transponder's signal. If the signal grew too weak, it would start to leak poison into his system. Too much of that for too long and he would die, painfully. It was meant for controlling slaves; to have it used on him was too deep an insult to bear.

Kchula pressed a button on the transponder medallion and the burn intensified, sending Second-Son writhing to the ground in agony. "Respect! Please, Patriarch." His voice was mocking. "We your humble servants deserve that at least!" He let his fangs show again, closed on Second-Son, knelt to whisper in his ear, stabbing the words like daggers. "Listen to me, coward and traitor. I am keeping my bargain in making you Patriarch. Once that is done, Tzaatz honor is satisfied. The Rrit name will be use-ful in taming the Great Prides. Very soon I will have my power consolidated. If you want to reign long after that, you will find ways to remain useful. Do you understand?"

Second-Son's eyes slid to the medallion around Kchula's neck. He remembered his father convulsing as he died, and he shuddered. His voice was weak as he stammered out a barely audible agreement. Kchula stood and cocked a leg, sending a spray of urine into Second-Son's fur. In other circumstances the gesture might have been protective; the scent mark meant to keep other warriors from challenging a ward of the Pride-Patriarch.

Here it was meant purely to humiliate, to convey the message, *You are my property.*

Kchula finished and waved a paw. "Ftzaal, take this excrement from my sight. Summon the High Priests, and see that he's ready for the Naming Ceremony."

"As you command, brother." Ftzaal gestured to his warriors, who dragged Second-Son to his feet and hauled him away. Kchula watched with satisfaction. *The Rrit line is weak, their strength rotted out. They could not have stood against me.* His earlier fears were long vanished. Now to see to the Great Prides. "Aide-de-Camp!"

"Command me, sire!"

"We require a seating of the Great Pride Circle. See that it is arranged immediately. Ftzaal-Tzaatz will direct you."

"At once, sire."

"And see that he ensures the Rrit fleet knows a Rrit will hold the Patriarchy." Aide-de-Camp left on the leap, and Kchula snarled in satisfaction to himself. *That rumor will reach the Great Prides. For the next few days confusion will be my ally.* He turned to survey the scene. "Ktronaz-Commander, report."

"We have achieved all of our major objectives. There is still fighting at Long Reach, but the Rrit cannot stand against our *rapsari*."

"And the Rrit fleet?"

"Fleet-Commander is known to be in orbit, and we have been jamming transmissions since the Heroes leapt. No Rrit ships have interfered with our operations."

"Excellent . . ."

"You are Kchula-Tzaatz." The voice was thin and weak,

and it dared to interrupt him. Kchula whirled to face the speaker, saw a wasted body on a gravlifted *prrstet*, pushed by two impassive Kdatlyno. It bore Rrit ear tattoos. How had such a specimen got past the guards?

"I am Patriarch's Telepath." The living corpse seemed to stare right through him, unseeing eyes huge in his wasted face as he answered the unspoken question. Kchula felt unsettled. The prize of prizes had come straight to his lair. He moved to assert his dominance. "I am Patriarch now." *It is true in all but the final fact.* "Serve me well and you will be rewarded. Serve me poorly and . . ." Kchula let the threat hang in the air.

"I am sworn to serve Meerz-Rrit."

"Meerz-Rrit is dead." Kchula couldn't keep the exultation from his voice as he said it.

"I already know this. I am Patriarch's Telepath."

The way he said it implied that there was no fact Patriarch's Telepath should not be expected to know, but Kchula refused to be impressed. "Then get out of my way until you're sent for."

"I have knowledge for you, Kchula-Tzaatz."

Kchula raised an ear. "Well, what is it then?" Impatience.

"Your line will end."

"What?!" Kchula-Tzaatz rounded on the telepath, his killing leap prevented only by his disbelief at the possibility that such a specimen could offer such insolence.

"Your line will end." Telepath's voice carried no inflection.

"You are Patriarch's Telepath. You will serve me."

"You are not Patriarch."

"I *control* the Patriarch, you fool." Anger. "Second-Son has the teeth of my *zzrou* in his back."

The unseeing eyes didn't blink. "Second-Son is nothing. Zree-Rrit is Patriarch."

"There is no Zree-Rrit. Who are you talking about?"

"I choose not to tell you."

"Insolent cur. I'll have you put to the Hot Needle."

"You have not the ability to torture me."

"Take him!" Kchula's voice was imperious, commanding, but the guards failed to respond. He looked sharply around the room, but his warriors, even Ktronaz-Commander, stood silently as if in suspended animation. Telepath's blind eyes bored into his, and he felt himself incapable of moving. For the first time he felt afraid.

"You have no power over me, Kchula-Tzaatz."

Kchula-Tzaatz breathed deep. This one was dangerous, but he had controlled telepaths before. Even Patriarch's Telepath would fall into line when he understood the new realities. "Where is your *sthondat* extract, addict? How far away are the cravings?"

Patriarch's Telepath ignored him. "Hear me, Kchula-Tzaatz. Meerz-Rrit is dead, and my obligation is over. Your line will end." The crippled kzin slumped forward on his polarizer bed and lay still.

"You impertinent *sthondat*! I'll . . ." Kchula stopped. *My obligation is over? That couldn't mean . . .* He looked at the immobile body. "Medical Officer! Medical Officer!" and a moment later a medium-sized, harried-looking kzin scurried in and prostrated himself.

"Sire! Patriarch!" *Patriarch!* Some of Kchula's anger left at the word. It would yet be true. His entourage were already responding to his new status, and that was good. He pointed at the polarizer bed.

"That's Patriarch's Telepath. Don't let him die." The guards were standing silently watching the body, aware now as they had not been moments before. Ktronaz-Commander's voice rose again the background, issuing orders as if nothing had happened.

Medical Officer moved to the body, assessed the situation in a glance and yelled "Orderly! Stimpacks and the boost kit! Immediately!" He went to work on the body, pumping hard on Telepath's ribcage to stimulate his stopped heart.

Orderly came at the run, ignoring Kchula completely in his rush, dumping the heavy emergency gear and setting it up. Kchula-Tzaatz turned away, swept his gaze across the others in the room. Gradually the murmur of voices returned to the room. Ktronaz-Commander and his staff were directing the mop-up operation, the guards standing ready in the door. Nobody seemed to have noticed the strange interlude. That was good. It would not have done for his underlings to see the fear that Patriarch's Telepath had engendered in him. He raked his claws angrily in the air. Patriarch's Telepath had humiliated him, and then tried to cheat him of both dominance and the invaluable resource he represented. When he was recovered he would be well punished for his insolence. It might be necessary to have his own telepath constantly by his side to protect him from Patriarch's Telepath while still allowing proper use of the greatest mind in the Patriarchy. That thought brought another. Where was Rrit-Conserver? There was another resource worth preserving, but it too came with dangers. How best to exploit it while managing the risk?

He became aware of movement beside him. Medical Officer was on the ground in full prostration.

"Sire." Medical Officer's voice was apologetic.

"Speak." Already Kchula felt himself growing angry. The body on the *prrstet* lay still. Orderly was putting away his equipment.

"He's gone. Sire, I tried . . ."

Kchula cut him off. "Stand."

Medical Officer stood and Kchula-Tzaatz screamed and raked his claws across his face, sending him reeling. "Leave my sight, you incompetent fool, and take that offal with you." He kicked at the *prrstet*, sending it spinning. He looked sharply around the room in case anyone else challenged his position, but none met his eye. It was some time after the Kdatlyno slaves had pushed the body away that he realized he could have vented more of his anger by killing them. Unlike Medical Officer, they were completely expendable.

Alliance is born of necessity.

—Si-Rrit

Pouncer knelt in attack crouch, breathing silently through his mouth, muscles tense, ears up and swiveled forward, nostrils flared, eyes straining to see deeper into the gloom. The noises came nearer: footsteps irregular, heavy breathing, the occasional grunt. The musk of something living rose above wet dank. Beside and behind him T'suuz stood ready with her variable sword. She had wanted to lead the attack, wanted to give him the weapon when he insisted on leading himself, but he was twice her weight and she needed it more than he did.

Three figures emerged, bipedal shadows, not kzin. They must be *rapsari*. He screamed and leapt, taking the first in the chest, his weight slamming the creature back to the floor, and scattering the ones behind it. His claws skidded off ceramic armor, and he reached for the vulnerable throat with his fangs, thirsting for the kill. He was about to snap off the creature's life, when a glint on its chestplate blossomed into recognition. It wore his father's sigil! He jerked his head, and his jaws shut on empty air. In the same instant, he realized that T'suuz would be closing with her variable sword, would dishonor the Rrit name with murder before she saw that the creatures were protected. Without thought he rolled and leapt back at her, catching the edge of her sword against his shoulder carapace. She tumbled back, snarling, and leapt clear to face him, clearly taking him for a threat.

"T'suuz! Stop!"

A beamer bolt flashed overhead and chewed brick shards from the ceiling. Another hit him square in the back, overloading a segment of his mag armor. He felt the burn of the suddenly red hot plate, smelled charred fur. A second hit in the same place would kill him, and he threw himself forward, carrying T'suuz to the ground with him.

"T'suuz, they wear the sigil. They are allies! "

Another salvo of beamer fire went through space they had been standing in a second before, followed by the hypersonic *whamwhamwham* of a magrifle set for bursts, earsplitting in the confines of the corridor. He felt the shockwaves slap against the back of his head. If he had been still standing they'd have killed him. He wrestled with his sister. The kill rage was on her, and she struggled to leap from his grasp, though without the element of surprise, it would have been suicide against the creature's weapon.

"They wear the sigil! Don't strike them!" He fought to keep her down, yelled louder. "Cease fire! I serve the Patriarch."

The firing stopped. "Who are you?" The voice was alien and deep, breathing hard, the words mushy and slurred.

"First-Son-of-Meerz-Rrit." He paused a second. Kzinretti were not normally introduced in formal greeting, but T'suuz was no ordinary kzinrette. Would honoring her identity insult the watchers in the darkness? Which protocol took priority?

They were aliens; first honor must go to his blood. "I stand with the kzinrette T'suuz." In fact he didn't stand, he stayed flat on the damp stones of the floor. He could barely make out the aliens in the dim glow of the tritium lamps. They couldn't see him or he'd already be dead, and he had no intention of silhouetting himself into a target.

"Stand up where we can see you."

"First you must guarantee my safety."

"You are in no position to bargain. We are armed and we will shoot to kill."

"I am your ally and entitled to your trust."

"You attacked us. What guarantee do we have you won't do it again? Stand up now or we shoot!"

"You wear my father's sigil. My honor is your guarantee."

Facing into the blackness, Tskombe raised the magrifle to pump a warning burst into the darkness, wishing he could spot a target. The weapon had elaborate sights, doubtless including thermal imaging, but he didn't know how to use them. A hand pulled the muzzle out of line. Brasseur.

"Don't do it. Don't shoot."

"Back off." Tskombe's bit the words off short, adrenaline pumping through his system. He didn't need the civilian second guessing him.

"No! Trust me."

"This is a military situation, *Ambassador.*" He underlined Brasseur's role. "You're just along for the ride here."

"He is who he says he is. No kzin would lie about that."

"They shave the truth."

"He made a specific claim."

"He nearly took my throat out." Tskombe pumped the magrifle, pushing Brasseur back against the tunnel wall.

"Why didn't he finish the job?" The scholar was pleading as Tskombe raised the weapon again. "He saw your sigil! Listen to me! He's the Patriarch's son. His father just pledged peace between human and kzin. Kill him and you'll start a war."

"There's already a war." Tskombe bit off the words, then raised his voice, screamed challenge in the Hero's Tongue. "Stand now or I shoot!"

Listening, Pouncer considered his options. He could see the alien with its weapon raised, a shadow in the faded light of the tritium lamps. Clearly it could not see him in the darkness pooled on the floor or it would not be ordering him to stand. The only knowledge it had of him was that he had leapt. It didn't seem to know exactly where he was now. That suggested a tactical advantage he might take, but that was of limited use. He could not in honor act against those entitled to his protection, even aliens.

But the creature bore him no such obligation, and after his aborted attack it was ready for vengeance. He was not obligated to stand. He could run, perhaps, take the risk of being shot while doing so if the alien fired again, but in the midst of the Tzaatz attack that would be abandoning his responsibility to offer them protection.

Could the alien's persistent hostility be taken as a refusal to accept protection? He curled his tail in vexation. This was as tangled as one of Rrit-Conserver's ever so hypothetical tests of honorable action! The aliens could refuse protection, but the current misunderstanding was a direct result of his mistaken leap. His obligation would not be discharged until they refused with the full knowledge of the situation.

Silently he motioned for T'suuz to crawl away from him, in case they fired at his voice. He was also required to protect kzinretti in his care; how that applied to a kzinrette who acted like a kzintosh was a question he didn't even want to consider. "I am your ally and I stand above you on the ladder of honor. Climb it with me, give me your guarantee you will not shoot, and I will stand."

There was a long pause, urgent mutterings from the darkness in some guttural, alien tongue, then, "I will fire only in self-defense."

"Done." Pouncer climbed to his feet, being careful to move slowly. Now the question was, would the alien stand by the honor of his pledge. His armor would protect him from the first round, if he were lucky. He stayed where he was, let the alien come closer.

"What are you doing here?" The tallest alien approached, mag rifle raised.

"Tzaatz pride has taken the Citadel. I am marked for death."

"Have you seen Yiao-Rrit?"

"My uncle? No."

Tskombe was silent.

"You must be my father's *kz'zeerkti* ambassadors."

Tskombe nodded and gestured to his companions. "We are. Major Quacy Tskombe, Captain Ayla Cherenkova, Ambassador Kefan Brasseur."

"Do the Tzaatz pursue you?"

"Yes . . ." Tskombe hesitated. "Your uncle put us into this tunnel, and stayed to guard the entrance. He was outnumbered . . ." Tskombe stopped, not wanting to continue.

"I'm sure he was true to the honor of our line." Pouncer kept the emotion from his voice. Yiao-Rrit would not yield while he lived, and the situation at Citadel was such that he would not live long. Yiao-Rrit, Myowr-Guardmaster, how many others had he lost this day? *My father . . .* The thought came unbidden and he pushed it away . . .

"I have no doubt he was. He was a true warrior."

"You wear my father's sigil. You are entitled to my protection, as you were to my uncle's."

Tskombe nodded. "I . . . we . . . appreciate that." He breathed out, only then realizing how tightly he had been holding his weapon.

"Hrrr. You must agree to follow my instructions."

Tskombe paused. "Within reason."

"Acceptable. T'suuz, come forward." His sister emerged warily from the darkness, her variable sword retracted but held ready in her hand.

The alien took a step back, raising the rifle. "You held out on us. She didn't step forward when you did."

"T'suuz is my sister. Kzinretti are not bound by honor."

There was a low growl from behind him, warning. T'suuz was insulted. He still didn't know what to make of her. The correct protocol to introduce her to aliens in the middle of an Honor-War would have eluded Rrit-Conserver. And she *had* remained hidden when honor would have brought her forward. The truth, however unpalatable, was never formal insult.

"What do you know of the situation?" Tskombe saved him from further awkwardness.

"Little. The Citadel is overrun by Tzaatz Pride. This morning I was First-Son-of-Meerz-Rrit. I am now . . ." He hesitated, wondering what new name fate had brought him to, and came up with nothing. "I am now a fugitive." He paused. "What do you know?"

"There was an invasion." Tskombe shrugged. "Yiao-Rrit got us here, told us how to get to the spaceport. We have a battleship waiting for us beyond the singularity."

"I will ensure you get to the spaceport. The *kzintzag* and Lesser Prides will still be loyal to Rrit Pride. Once we are beyond the reach of Tzaatz warriors we will be safe."

"What will you do after that?"

"My fealty is to my father. I will see the usurpers scoured from his Citadel." Pouncer said it with a confidence he didn't feel. "We must go. Time is short." He turned to move down the tunnel.

Brasseur held up a hand though in the dark no one saw him. "A moment, please, to speak to my companions."

"Quickly then." Pouncer was impatient to be moving.

Brasseur motioned Cherenkova and Tskombe closer, and switched to Interspeak. "Be careful. The situation has changed, but the rules of conduct remain the same. He is the Patriarch's son, so our behavior before him is as vital as it was before Yiao-Rrit. Any statement you make must be true, or at least unfalsifiable. Any commitment you make must be carried out regardless of personal cost. If you can't back it up, just don't make it. We represent Earth. If we want to avoid a war we have to show ourselves worthy of being considered equals."

Cherenkova snorted. "I don't consider them my equals."

Brasseur looked at her in annoyance. "Will you pay five billion lives to assert your superiority?"

She looked back at him, keeping the anger out of her voice. "I am sworn to uphold the UN Charter, regardless of personal cost." She held his gaze for long moment in the dim light. "How about you? Are you willing to die to save five billion lives?"

There was a long silence. Tskombe broke it. "Let's go."

T'suuz led. Brasseur noticed that, unable to suppress his fascination even in their dire straits. She seemed more intelligent than any kzinrette he had ever seen; she was certainly the first he had ever seen carry a weapon. There was new information here, knowledge undreamed of. This trip would secure his position as the preeminent kzinologist in Known Space.

A grinding crash echoed down the tunnel from behind

them, followed by distant snarls, weirdly distorted by the length of the tunnel. The Tzaatz had found the secret entrance and were coming after them. He quickened his pace. He would become the preeminent kzinologist in Known Space, if he survived.

At the head of the little column, Pouncer caught up with T'suuz. "We must hurry."

"It's not much farther." The tunnel branched and she turned left.

They came quickly to the end of the tunnel. Rungs set in the wall led to a hatch overhead. It was scaled thick with rust, but the locking mechanism moved in smooth silence in T'suuz's hand. Someone had been maintaining it. Pouncer knew where they were now. As a kit he had often played in the long abandoned fibercrete bunkers that had once been the Citadel's outer defense ring and listened to the heroic stories of the *zitalyi* who guarded the path to Hero's Square. He even knew the hatch they were standing under, and he knew it to be welded shut. Evidently appearance did not match fact.

He touched her shoulder. "You have used this route before." It wasn't a question.

"Many times."

Pouncer narrowed his whiskers in disbelief. "There is a *zitalyi* guard post above here."

"I know."

"How did you evade them these many times?"

She flipped her ears and twitched her tail. "A kzinrette has means of persuading even the elite of the Patriarch's guard. You have much to learn, brother." The hatch cover swung easily upward as she pushed and sunlight filtered down. She motioned him to silence and climbed up. He followed her cautiously, pausing to examine the long rusted welds on the other side of the hatch cover. They were intact; instead the entire frame had been cut out and the joints cleverly concealed. Someone had gone to a great deal of trouble to arrange for this secret exit. He started to speak, then thought better of it. His world had been turned upside down. He needed time to process the new information.

She crept through the overgrown moss that covered the bunker's floor toward the opening that had once been a blast door. Muted snarls rose outside and her tail shot up to signal silence. Pouncer froze. There were Tzaatz warriors just outside. The snarls grew closer, and he caught the scent of *rapsar* raiders. Their escape route was blocked. He started back down the hatch as the enemy drew closer and T'suuz crept hurriedly back.

"There are too many Tzaatz there to seduce. We will have to go back." Seconds later they were back in the ancient tunnel with the hatch closed and locked overhead.

"What's going on?" It was the female human.

T'suuz snarled, frustration in her voice. "The enemy is outside. We must fight our pursuers here, then wait for darkness to get past the guards outside."

"No." Pouncer raised a paw. "There is another way out."

"The other tunnel dead-ends."

Pouncer rippled his ears, glad for once to be the one surprising T'suuz. "You have much to learn, sister." He pushed his way past the humans and led them back down the tunnel at a steady trot. The scrabble of claws on brick echoed down the tunnel toward them, warning that the Tzaatz behind them were still actively hunting them. The tunnel's acoustics made it impossible to estimate how far away the enemy was, but it was certain they were rapidly running out of time. He moved as fast as he dared back to the junction and took the other fork. He was nearly running now, heedless of the sound, and the humans were having trouble keeping up.

Behind them the sounds of pursuit grew louder. Pouncer felt the fight juices building in his bloodstream in anticipation of combat. T'suuz grabbed his arm. "Where are we going?"

"There is an emergency exit." He didn't stop moving. "I don't know when it was put in, many eights of generations ago. Do you know the Sundial Grove?"

"I know it."

"These tunnels were built when siege was a real possibility. The exit is concealed in the root cone of a broadleaf tree in the grove, but it may not work. We must be prepared to fight."

"You have not used it?"

"It can only be used once."

Moments later he was bending over a heavy steel grate in the floor. "Help me move this. Don't fall in." He bent, and T'suuz bent with him, straining as they hauled the heavy cover open as it ground noisily on its hinges. He folded his ears tight against the harsh noise. *Not good to make noise.* It couldn't be helped. The exposed vertical shaft vanished down into echoing darkness.

"Now stand back, cover your ears." She did as she bade him, and saw that the *kz'zeerkti* did too. He groped in the dark for the lever he knew was there, fought down panic when he didn't find it. There! He pulled down on it hard. At first it didn't move, then all off a sudden it lurched down. The locking bars pulled out of the overhead panel and the panel exploded downward. There was a tremendous roar and the tunnel filled with choking dust as tons of gravel poured from above into the shaft at their feet. Pouncer sprang backward, thinking for an instant that the tunnel had collapsed even though he knew better.

The roar stopped, replaced by the *chink* of a few pebbles on stone.

"Up! Quickly! There is little time." He bodily pushed the manrette into the now empty overhead shaft. She began to climb, followed by the other two aliens and T'suuz. He went last, as befitted the only warrior in the little party. There were no glowlamps and the shaft was pitch dark, but halfway up he sensed another hatch in the wall. He groped, found another lever above it, climbed higher and pulled it, muscles straining against metal seized tight with age. It let go all at once and he slammed his knuckles painfully on the stone while tons more gravel cascaded down into the shaft below him. He cursed at the pain, but they were safe from direct pursuit now. Coughing and sneezing at the dust, he climbed higher. Above, the manrette was struggling with the heavy hatch above. For a moment he wondered if he'd miscalculated. It would be difficult, maybe impossible to switch positions in the narrow shaft. If the manrette couldn't open it they'd be entombed. He should have sent T'suuz up first, or at least one of the larger alien males. He could hear the manrette snarling in its strangely musical voice, and the other aliens answering in kind. A rhythmic banging echoed down the shaft, and he cringed, imagining Tzaatz warriors on the surface coming to investigate. The air was thick with dust and the walls were claustrophobically tight in the total darkness. Pouncer fought down hyperventilation. *Fear is death.* But of all deaths to face, entombment and slow suffocation had to be the worst.

No, he had faced the worst death: the absolute void Patriarch's Telepath had thrown him into. He put out his paw, felt the rough stone, listened to the aliens chattering above him. Deep breath in, deep breath out. Here was reality, and he would face what it brought with his mind placid.

Above him ancient hinges groaned and a thin bar of light appeared, vanished, reappeared and grew larger. The hatch fell backward with a thud, and a rush of cool, fresh air flowed into the shaft. Above him T'suuz climbed higher and he climbed after her, blinking in the fading light of sunset. He climbed out into the tangled root arch of an ancient broadleaf tree, big enough that all five of them could shelter beneath it. The humans were shaking themselves and coughing, his sister started grooming the dust from her pelt.

"What was that?" T'suuz gave up her task as he hauled himself out of the shaft. She needed a slave, a bath, and a thorough combing.

"There are two vertical shafts, one up and one down. They are the same length." Pouncer pawed at his own coat, uncomfortably full of grit. "The upper shaft is filled with gravel, supported by the overhead panel. In a siege the attacker will control the ground around the Citadel.

They might find the tunnel exit, but if they do they will see nothing put a shallow pit full of stones. They cannot use it to get into the Citadel. The first lever opens the panel that dumps the gravel from the shaft above to the shaft below, leaving it empty so we can climb free. The second lever dumps more gravel into the shaft after you have left, sealing it off from pursuit."

The shorter human male seemed excited by this. "How long ago was that installed?"

Pouncer turned his paws up. "Long before my time."

"Before space travel?"

"I don't think so. The Citadel is that old, but there is little left of what was built then."

The shorter male was about to say something else when the taller one cut him off. "We need to plan our next move."

"Hrrr . . ." Pouncer turned a paw over introspectively. "My first duty is to see you off-world."

T'suuz cut him off, her tail lashing. "No, your first duty is to survive."

"There is no survival without honor." He turned to face his sister.

"We must go into the jungle." T'suuz's voice was calm and sure.

"What will we find there?" Pouncer was dismissive.

"Where did you think I was leading you? I am of the *czrav*. They will shelter us far from Tzaatz searches."

"You are my sister, the Patriarch's daughter. You are no outcast outlander."

"You are my brother, and the son of my mother, herself a treaty gift to the Patriarch from Mrrsel Pride of the *czrav*. We both carry jungle blood."

"The line of the pride descends through the male."

"Blood descends from every ancestor. Listen, brother! A kzinrette speaks to you in the Hero's Tongue. Tell me what noble pride of Kzinhome carries this in their genes."

Pouncer raised his ears. "How is it that a kzinrette comes to carry these genes at all?"

"These secrets are not mine to reveal. Come to the jungle and you will learn them for yourself."

"What of the aliens?"

"We must leave them here. They will not survive with us."

"They will not survive here." Tension showed in Pouncer's voice. "They wear the sigil. Rrit Pride is sworn to their protection. With the fall of the Citadel they are simply prey, marked for death. We cannot leave them."

"The jungle will be hard enough for kzin. We cannot herd these herbivores."

Pouncer snarled. "Herbivores or not, we are bound by the honor of our pride to protect them."

"May the herbivores have a word?" Kefan Brasseur cut T'suuz off before she could answer, snarling the words like a predator. That surprised Pouncer, who had assumed the larger human would naturally be Speaker for the small band.

"You may, but you must accept my decision without question. Here I speak for the Patriarchy." Even as he said it Pouncer realized that it was probably no longer true.

Brasseur made a passable attempt at the gesture of respect-between-equals. "Your authority is unquestioned, but we do not answer to the Patriarchy. Nor are we slaves, and the MacDonald-Rishshi treaty forbids the hunting of humans save convicted criminals. We are free sentients entitled to the protection of the Patriarchy by the word of Yiao-Rrit. However, we are not required to accept that protection should we choose to forgo it."

The fur bristled at the back of Pouncer's neck. He was not accustomed to having his word questioned by an inferior, let alone an alien herbivore who somehow considered itself his equal. Nevertheless he could see no counter to Brasseur's statement. "I will hear you, *kz'zeerkti*."

Brasseur nodded and continued. "We have no desire to become caught in your conflict. Our only goal was to observe the meeting of the Great Pride Circle at the invitation of the Patriarch, and to negotiate a permanent peace between our species. We have accomplished that, thanks to your father. Our mission now is to return that information to Earth, so that our species may initiate our half of the bargain."

"I acknowledge your concerns, Kefan-Brasseur. However it is unlikely that my father continues to express the will of the Patriarchy. Kchula-Tzaatz will now take up leadership of the Great Pride Circle." *If the Great Prides do not now fall into civil war.* Pouncer kept the thought unvoiced. "What his decree will be, I cannot say." As he said it Pouncer realized what his words meant. The Tzaatz attack was successful and the Citadel had fallen. The thought he had pushed away earlier rushed back unbidden. His father was certainly dead, along with his uncle, his brothers, even Second-Son. He was alone now, without blood allies save T'suuz, and the realization weighed heavy on him.

"Whoever he is, he would be a fool if he did not recognize

us as representatives of Earth." The Brasseur alien was still speaking. "The consequences of any other course of action would be serious. We are not the enemies of anyone here. Unlike you, no one is hunting us. We will go to the spaceport under the protection of your father's sigil."

Pouncer's lips curled away from his fangs. "I will not speak for the wisdom of the Tzaatz. But I cannot allow you to expose yourself to the risk that would entail."

"You cannot forbid us."

"You will become hostages for Tzaatz Pride."

"They will gain nothing and lose much by doing so. This Kchula-Tzaatz will understand this."

"Rrit Pride is sworn to protect your safety. If you insist on presenting yourself to Kchula-Tzaatz, I must go with you."

"No!" T'suuz spat the word, cutting off Brasseur before he could answer. "You and I may be the last of the Rrit line now, and I am a female. You must survive." There was a hidden pain in her words, and Pouncer understood she had come to the same realization he had.

"Then our line will end with honor." Pouncer's snarl was flat, not quite masking the emotions he did not wish to show.

"Kchula-Tzaatz spoke of the conquest of humanity at the Great Pride Circle. I don't see him giving us free passage." Tskombe's voice was calm.

"Our priority has to be to get off the planet." Cherenkova spoke with conviction.

Tskombe shook his head. "That's impossible now. Our options are limited."

Brasseur threw up his arms in frustration. "Sensibly we can only present ourselves to Kchula-Tzaatz, and insist that we be given a shuttle back to *Crusader*. His honor won't allow . . ."

Pouncer cut Brasseur off with a snarl. "Tzaatz Pride has no honor."

Brasseur was about to answer but Tskombe held up a hand. "Are you willing to bet your life on that, Ambassador? Because that's exactly what you're doing."

"Well . . ."

"I am not an expert on Kzin, Ambassador, but this kzin"—he indicated First-Son—"has demonstrated his trustworthiness to me, personally. This Kchula-Tzaatz has not. The power structure has been overturned. We can't take anything not proven for granted."

"Enough!" Pouncer raised his arms for attention, willing himself to relax. "I agree with Major Tskombe." Rrit-Conserver had spoken of the importance of balancing the factions. He was Patriarch here, of this tiny pride of one kzinrette and three aliens, but enforcing his position was proving more complex than he could have imagined. "We will go to Hero's Square and I will find transport to the spaceport. From there we will get you aboard a ship to the singularity. There will be no more talk of presentations to Kchula-Tzaatz."

"Hero's Square is too dangerous." T'suuz had her ears laid flat. "You will be recognized."

"I intend to be. The *kzintzag* owe no fealty to Kchula-Tzaatz. Rrit *strakh* will get us a gravcar."

"The risk is too large to take for herbivores." There was contempt in T'suuz's voice.

"No risk is too large for honor. And we need a vehicle. We cannot walk to the jungle."

Her reply was cut short by the quiet whir of a gravcar. Pouncer held up his paw for silence, looked out through a gap in the root arch, caught just a glimpse of the car through the spreading branches overhead. Another whirred past, flying wing on the first. The Tzaatz were securing the area, and they were still within a stone's throw of the Citadel. The arch of the broadleaf tree's root cone had covered them from the car's sensors, but soon the Tzaatz would come on foot, with sniffers. They needed to be moving, immediately. He looked back in to the suddenly silent group huddled behind him. "We must go. We can discuss strategy in a safer place." Without looking back he slid through the tangled roots and onto the forest floor.

The others followed him and he found the path that would take them through the forest to Hero's Square. Darkness was falling, and the Sundial Grove was peaceful, just a few benches around a clearing in the forest, cushioned in moist grasses. In the center was the ancient stone sundial that gave the place its name. He knew the area like his ears knew his name. Its familiarity was an odd note of comfort in the devastation surrounding him. He stopped at the trail, turned around, looked long and hard at it. It would be a long time before he saw it again, if ever.

> *The courageous may choose the manner of their death; the cowardly have it chosen for them.*
> —Si-Rrit

The maintenance shaft was cramped and dirty, the domain of slaves not kzinti warriors, but warriors did not shirk at discomfort, and Kdar-Leader ignored the grime matted into his coat. It didn't matter; he would not live long enough to see it clean again. What did matter now was to find a death of honor, striking hard at the invaders, making them pay dearly for their victory. Behind him were the remnants of his unit, First Section Commander, a lean, tough and cagey fighter; Gunner, aggressive and smart; Demolitions Expert, stolid and reliable; and Communicator, not even a warrior but ready now to give his life to the honor of the Rrit.

That would happen soon, now that the Tzaatz held the Citadel entire. How many groups of *zitalyi* had escaped to the tunnels as he had was unknown. There had to be a few, because occasionally the sounds of combat still came through the ventilators, weirdly distant and distorted. Equally certain, there were only a few, because he had seen so many die. All of his little band were wounded. Kdar-Leader himself was bleeding badly from a gash where a slicewire had slipped through his armor articulation at the hip. That mattered only in that it would slow him in combat.

A noise echoed ahead of them and he dropped to a crouch, looping his tail to signal the others to silence. It would not be a Tzaatz, because they had shown no liver for the dangers involved in following the *zitalyi* into the very bowels of the Citadel of the Patriarch, but it could very well be one of their despicable creations. It was not Kdar-Leader's place to decide if their employ fell within the technical bounds of the rules of *skalazaal*—that was a question the Conservers would be debating for generations yet—but he knew the smell of cowardice, and the *rapsari* stank of it. They were nothing but mindless flesh machines, built to kill so their masters need not face their enemies claw to claw. Unconsciously his lips twitched away from his fangs in contempt. No true Hero feared death. Everything living died—even the universe would come to an end in some unthinkably distant future. You could only choose how you died, and Kdar-Leader intended to die well.

The noise was not repeated, and after a long, tense wait Kdar-Leader crept forward again. The maintenance tunnel ran lower even than the Command Lair, carrying all the power, data, air, and water that the underground complex needed. Near the Command Lair was a cramped machinery room, and from that room a vertical ventilation shaft that ran straight up to the computer core immediately above the Command Lair. The Tzaatz would have the computer core well protected, of course, but it was unlikely they knew the danger the shaft presented. It was not on the Citadel maps, and they would not know where to look. The tunnel itself was straight and level, but the power had been cut off in the fighting and the darkness was absolute. They had to feel their way along it a pace at a time, whiskers stretched out and quivering. Though he knew where he was going, the darkness was disorienting. That and the white noise coming from the air pumps ahead played tricks on his mind, and sometimes it seemed as if the tunnel was sloping steeply or twisting around on itself. It required iron self-discipline simply to keep moving forward, but he was the leader; he could show no fear.

He sensed the open space as they came to the machinery room, felt along the wall for the ladder that led up to the vent shaft. It got easier when he found it, the rungs providing the stable reference point that the floor had been unable to. Slowly he climbed, and his Heroes climbed after him. At the top a faint patch of light showed. Air flowed past in a quiet, steady rush. They need not fear making noise, so long as nobody spoke or fell. Their scent was a larger concern, but the Citadel had seen its share of blood, rage, and fear today; the Tzaatz shouldn't scent them until it was too late.

And then he was there, peering through a mesh grill into the computer core. Pierin slaves worked there, obedient to their new masters, showing five-armed Tzaatz-liveried Jotoki the workings of the system. A full sword of Tzaatz were on guard. The computer core was one of the most vital objectives in the Citadel and they knew it. But only two of them were truly alert, those at the door, and they were facing the wrong way.

He twitched hunt-signs with his tail to let the others know what he saw, unsure if Gunner behind him could see them in the dim light. It didn't matter; the plan had been set before they entered the maintenance tunnel. He, First Section Commander, and Gunner would take on the Tzaatz while Communicator and Demolitions Expert set the charges that would destroy the computer core and rob the Tzaatz of that invaluable prize. They had relied on stealth up to now, but once he burst through the grating that would be over. Then it would be up to him to spread chaos long enough for the others to clamber up and leap through.

He climbed higher, checking carefully to see how the grating was attached. If it were bolted in place it would be difficult, although he could cut his way in with his variable sword if he had to. Better, though, to leap right through the panel.

His paw pads moved carefully, found clips, tested them. He was in luck: a solid shove would take out the grating, and he would be leaping right behind it. Unconsciously his jaws gaped into a fanged smile and he breathed deeper, faster, priming his body for the combat to come. He twitched his tail again to prepare his comrades . . . four . . . three . . . two . . . one . . .

Leap! And the grating exploded outward as his killscream echoed from the walls. Tzaatz and slaves alike scattered in shock, and as he landed he had already cut in half a Tzaatz who had taken off his mag armor. A second drew his variable sword, but Kdar-Leader cut off his arm before he could bring it around, and his second stroke decapitated his enemy. A second scream and Gunner was beside him, disemboweling a third guard. The panicked slaves were running for the door, preventing the two Tzaatz there from entering the fray. The three still in the room were on their guard now, variable swords drawn and ready. Two of them advanced on Kdar and Gunner while the third circled to take Kdar from the flank. He fell back a pace to cover his side—where was Section Commander? The first swung, then the second and Kdar fell back again as he parried them both. Then another scream and Section Commander was beside him, sword blurring as he waded into the flanking Tzaatz. The other fell back, and Kdar gained back the ground he had given. They had momentum now, and the last Pierin was running out the door on its spidery limbs. The Tzaatz guards there had been pushed halfway down the access corridor by the exodus of slaves, but in heartbeats they would be back in the fray and tip the balance.

"Push them to the door!" Even as he said it Kdar took another pace forward, leading with a thrust, cut, thrust combination that forced his opponent back. At the door the battle would be two on two and the Tzaatz weight of numbers wouldn't matter, not for the time it would take to set the charges at least. Section Commander made a quick lunge and pushed his opponent back a pace, then two, then three. Kdar's opponent was forced to fall back as well or leave his vulnerable side exposed to Section Commander.

One of the guards who was blocked out in the corridor drew his *wtsai* and threw it in one fluid motion. It spun past Kdar's ears in a whirling blur and *thunk*ed into something behind him. There was a gurgling scream. He risked a glance backward and saw Communicator go down, clawing at the blade lodged in his throat. Neither he nor Demolitions Expert had mag armor, which was why they were setting the charges rather than fighting. Motion flashed in the corner of his eye and he raised his arm to block a blow that would have cut him in half if he'd let himself be distracted an instant longer.

"Push!" He screamed the word and all three *zitalyi* stepped into the attack. The Tzaatz fell back, and then suddenly Section Commander was down, blood gushing from his severed sword arm. He was beyond saving, a few heartbeats from death as his dying heart spurted out his life's blood through the arteries in his shoulder, but he swung his other arm around to pull his opponent off his feet. The Tzaatz who had killed him jumped clear, then went down to finish the job. The move left him open to Gunner, who slid his slicewire between the other's articulated shoulder plates, killing him instantly. It was two on two now, and the surviving Tzaatz had been backed to the door. If Section Commander had died an instant earlier the Tzaatz now caught in the corridor would have been able to flank them and the battle would have been over already.

As it was, it was just a matter of time. The alarm must have been raised already; more Tzaatz would come. An image from his kittenhood flashed through his mind, he and his older brother standing off eight of the sons of Kdar-Zraft at once. But then they had been a team, and their adversaries individuals. The Tzaatz would not be so foolish. Those facing him had a coherent guard, matching their strokes and parries to expose neither of them to Kdar or Gunner. It was a standoff, one the Tzaatz thought they would win because they could count on reinforcement, but one that Kdar *knew* he would win, because he did not intend to survive the fight.

He had only to buy enough time for Demolitions Expert. That could not be long now, but even as he realized that, Gunner missed a stroke and overextended. The Tzaatz facing him might have jerked back at the thrust, but instead he slid his slicewire down and underneath, catching Gunner in the gaps of his breastplate articulation. The big warrior went down bubbling blood, and suddenly Kdar had to face two adversaries at once.

He knew how to do that, fall back a space and put his sword into a blurring series of combinations that kept both his opponents fully engaged. Thrust, parry, thrust, parry, thrust, parry. The Tzaatz could not break his guard, but he would tire rapidly—already fatigue was setting in, and when it did he would slow, and when he slowed he would die.

"Expert! Work quickly!" The words nearly cost him his life. The breath they took left an opening, and a slicewire glanced from the front of his breastplate. He fell back another pace, and that was where he had to stand. Any farther and the Tzaatz behind would be into the room and he would die at that instant. His arms felt like lead. The Tzaatz behind licked their chops, sensing his coming exhaustion. He got in a solid blow, felt his sword dig in, saw a chunk of metal flying away from his opponent's shoulder plate. The Tzaatz's mag armor had failed or had never been turned on. There was a weakness there he could exploit, if he could set up an opening . . .

Then suddenly a body filled the space beside him, the Rrit killscream deafening even through his laid-flat ears. It was Demolitions Expert, fresh and full of fight juices. That could only mean the fuses were set. The battle was over, if they could hold out heartbeats longer. The enemy fell back at the new attack, and there was the opening. Kdar swung his variable sword around and brought it down with all his strength, cleaving through the Tzaatz warrior's depowered mag armor as though it weren't there. The move left him open, as he knew it would. It didn't matter. One of the Tzaatz in the corridor had advanced over his comrade's body. Already Demolitions Expert had died, sliced in half by a blow that armor would easily have stopped. The Tzaatz in front of him kept his sword moving, forcing Kdar to stay engaged, while his

companion leapt through the gap Expert had left to take
him from the flank.

It didn't matter. They were too late and he knew it. "I
serve the Rrit!" He screamed the words in triumph as the
second Tzaatz moved in for the kill. The blast slammed
Kdar-Leader into the wall. It was a death of honor.

> *It is easier to seize power than to wield it, easier
> to wield power than to hold it.*
>
> —Si-Rrit

Kchula-Tzaatz admired the view from the Patriarch's
Tower, stretching out his arms to take in the whole of the
plain of Stgrat. "It is mine, Ftzaal." He couldn't keep the
gloating from his voice. In the distance a continuous
stream of cargo landers was falling into Sea-of-Stars
spaceport, almost all of them ferrying in Tzaatz occupation forces. "All mine."

"Now we must hold it, brother." Behind him Ftzaal-
Tzaatz was intently studying an intricate Kdatlyno touch-
sculpture. He kept his voice carefully even.

Kchula whirled to face him. "Hold it? Who will take it
from us?"

"We have shown that Kzinhome can be taken. What
Pride-Patriarch does not now covet our success?"

Kchula twitched his tail. "None will dare stand against
our *rapsari*."

"Our losses in the attack were serious." Ftzaal turned to
face his brother. "We are tremendously vulnerable."

"No! We are victorious!" Kchula-Tzaatz raked the air
with his claws. "The Great Prides do not see the resources

thrown into this conquest. They see only that the Patriarchy itself has fallen to the Tzaatz!"

"A development which is sure to raise their fears."

"None are poised to leap. By the time any are, our position will be consolidated."

"How do we know none are ready to leap? There could be a fleet falling in from the singularity this instant."

"Your role is intelligence, *zar'ameer*." Kchula turned to fix his gaze on his brother. "Have you failed me?"

Ftzaal waved a paw dismissively. "Our resources have been aimed almost exclusively at the Rrit. Any other pride considering such a leap would have concealed their preparations as carefully as we. The Fanged God would be favorable indeed if we were to learn what the Rrit so clearly have not."

"Kitten's fears!"

"It is my function to consider the possible."

"And it is mine to lead the Pride." Kchula turned back to the window. "Today is a day of victory, and the Great Pride Circle is here to witness it. We shall not betray our weakness through overcaution."

"As you wish, brother."

Kchula let Ftzaal's acquiescence hang in the air for a while, watching the distant stream of landers as they decelerated for touchdown, considering how to broach a more delicate subject. His brother was useful, but required careful handling. "We have another matter to consider. Rrit-Conserver."

"He must die." Ftzaal-Tzaatz's voice was suddenly harsh.

Kchula turned to face him. "You are hasty to throw

away the spoils of our victory. We have already lost Patriarch's Telepath. Rrit-Conserver possesses the finest strategic mind in the Patriarchy."

"I remind you that mind is opposed to our own goals."

Kchula raised his ears. "Do you doubt that it could be turned to support them?"

"I am certain it cannot." Again Ftzaal's voice was harsh.

"Why is that?" *And what is his real objection?*

"His loyalty remains with the Rrit." Ftzaal drew his variable sword and took up the resting guard stance, then moved to attack crouch and back, a standard drill of the single combat form.

"He owes fealty to Second-Son, and we control Second-Son."

"He owes fealty to the Patriarchy, and First-Son is the rightful heir."

"First-Son is dead." Kchula snapped the words, as if that could make them true.

"We have not confirmed that, and until we do the question is enough to prevent Rrit-Conserver's honor from binding him to our puppet." Ftzaal-Tzaatz's voice was again neutral and controlled. "Where the road of honor forks, a Hero may take either path with pride."

"First-Son is dead. Dead or a fugitive unworthy of a name, fleeing in cowardice. We will let that be known, and Rrit-Conserver's fealty will fall to us."

Ftzaal turned a paw over, considering. "Until we see his body First-Son is not dead. We may brand him a coward, but until that is proven our words will not suffice to command Rrit-Conserver's honor either."

"Hrrr. Do not give me problems!" Kchula turned away

angrily. *He objects because he feels his position threatened. I must not allow this one to gain too much power, and Rrit-Conserver is an excellent tool for that task.*

"Then do not seek problems out. Rrit-Conserver is a consummate strategist, but he is not the only strategist. Alive he is dangerous, no matter what holds we may put on him. The dead are no one's enemy."

"Don't be a fool. The Great Prides will take taming. The name of Rrit-Conserver will go far to convince them of the legitimacy of our puppet."

"Brother, I must say again, it is too dangerous." Ftzaal changed his practice to left blocks and right blocks, his slicewire hissing as it cut the air.

"What steps must we take to control him?"

"None I can think of will be sufficient."

Kchula's tail lashed unconsciously. "You lack imagination."

"I serve Tzaatz Pride to the best of my ability, brother."

"Do you? Perhaps Rrit-Conserver is more of a threat to your position than to my rule."

Ftzaal-Tzaatz's eyes narrowed. "You mock my honor."

"The enmity of the Black Priests and the Conservers is no secret. Prove me wrong."

"Such proof is impossible." Ftzaal's self-control reasserted itself. "Judge my actions. I am your blood, *zar'ameer* to your rule. My plan has delivered Kzinhome and the Patriarchy into your hands. Decide for yourself my honor and loyalty."

Kchula's whiskers twitched. "And yet you do not wish to see Rrit-Conserver's mind applied in Battle Circle."

"Any plan he gives us will contain a hidden trap. You can depend upon it."

"By so doing he would betray his fealty to the Rrit."

"Only if we can show him the body of First-Son."

"So we will show him that body."

Ftzaal's ears fanned up in concern and he retracted his slicewire, returning his variable sword pommel to his belt. "Such deception treads on the edge of honor, brother."

"And the rest of this has not? I have heard enough!" Kchula raked the air with his claws. "This is not about honor. This is about power."

"Without at least the appearance of honor there is no victory. The power will slip through your grasp."

"Do not try my patience, Ftzaal." Kchula turned and strode out of the room, slamming the heavy door open as he passed.

Ftzaal-Tzaatz watched him go, then after a long moment turned to look out the window as his brother had, watching the stream of landers in-falling to the spaceport. Sea-of-Stars had become the nexus from which Tzaatz power was spreading to seize control. Rarely had such power had been seen in the history of the Patriarchy. Not since Hrrahr-Chruul, eight-cubed generations ago, had a Rrit been overthrown, and Hrrahr-Chruul's dynasty had lasted just three inheritances before Kdar-Rrit rallied the Spinward Prides to reclaim Kzinhome. Three inheritances was just enough time for Kdar's sublight fleet to make the journey from the spinward edge of the Patriarchy to Kzinhome. Loyalty to the Rrit ran strong through the Patriarchy, so strong that if Ftzaal didn't know better he might have thought it etched in the very genes of the species. Not that there weren't already enough alleles that needed to be weeded from the genome. *What price will*

the Patriarchy pay for the Black Priest secret? The
Succession War had been long and bloodly, and the
Dueling Traditions had *not* always been followed. Kdar-
Rrit had ended Hrrahr-Chruul's line, and three other
Great Prides had been destroyed in that conquest. Even
today the descendants of the Spinward warriors held
worlds that had once been another pride's, the spoils of
conquest liberally dispensed by victorious Kdar. The
Patriarchy had been seriously weakened by that conflict,
but it had not mattered then; there had been no other
species to pose the slightest threat to even the weakest
border colony.

Only the slightest quiver of his whiskers betrayed
Ftzaal's concern as his mind quite automatically ran over
the forces at play, assessing potential strategies and calculating possible outcomes. The situation was drastically different today. The dangers that Meerz-Rrit had laid before
the Great Pride Circle were no less real because it was a
Rrit who brought them forward. The Patriarchy was at
critical point in its history, and the ripples of the Tzaatz
conquest would persist for generations to come. Quite
certainly they would outlast the Tzaatz dynasty, however
many inheritances that was. Unconsciously Ftzaal's tail
twitched. Their position was far from solid; the loss of the
Citadel's computer core to *zitalyi* holdouts just one in a
chain of incidents that the Tzaatz had so far been unable
to prevent. Much depended on the next few days. They
had to consolidate their victory immediately, or the other
Great Prides would sense weakness, and then . . . It was
quite possible the Tzaatz dynasty would go down in the
Pride Saga with no inheritances at all.

In the time-before-time Chraz-Rrit-First-Patriarch led his pride against that of Mror-Vdar, and Mror-Vdar commanded the magic of fire and so slew eight-to-the-fifth Rrit warriors in a single heartbeat, and Chraz-Rrit was left alone on the battlefield. He might have fled then, but instead he challenged Mror-Vdar to single combat, claw to claw, fang to fang, with the victor to claim everything and the vanquished to be czrav, to wander prideless forever. So Mror-Vdar laid aside wtsai and wtzal, but he did not lay aside his magic, for no one could see that he kept it. They dueled in the morning, and the Fanged God himself was watching to see who would triumph. And so it happened that Chraz-Rrit's fangs found Mror-Vdar's throat, and to save himself Mror-Vdar used his magic and Chraz-Rrit was burned deep and leapt away. The Fanged God stopped the fight then, and decreed that magic had no place in a duel of honor. Chraz-Rrit was ready to fight on, but Mror-Vdar refused to lay aside his power. Three times the Fanged God commanded him to, and three times he refused, so the Fanged God declared him honorless and czrav and banished Vdar to live in the jungle, and gave victory to Chraz-Rrit. And ever since then kzinti have dueled with their own strength and nothing more.

                                        —The Legend of the Duel

It was usually a pleasant morning's walk down well-worn paths from the Sundial Grove through Darkmoon

Park to Hero's Square for Pouncer. This time the journey had taken all night. The Tzaatz were out in force, and in the face of sophisticated sensors stealth meant getting behind thick, hard cover and staying there. Fortunately the forest was abundant in natural movement, from the broadleaf trees swaying and creaking in the wind to the scurrying of night scavengers small and large. Cover enough for desperate flight, if you were careful. The weak predawn light found Pouncer and his small pride in the shadow of the ancient stone wall that surrounded the Hero's Square. At one time the wall had been the outer defensive bastion of the fortress city that was ruled from the Citadel. Now it was surrounded by dens and shops, the wall itself used as a structural element for the buildings that found themselves next to it. Tzaatz gravcars whirred over the scene, and checkpoints had been set up at the main gates through the ancient fortifications, where Tzaatz guards checked every face passing through and vicious raider *rapsari* snarled and snorted, pulling hard on their harnesses, eager for a command to kill. They watched the activity from a distance, stood aside to allow a gravcarrier loaded with long planks of stonewood to set down beside a crafter's shop on the outside of the wall.

"Don't they ever sleep?" Cherenkova was clearly surprised at the amount of activity so early in the morning.

Brasseur shook his head. "Kzin are crepuscular predators, most active at dusk and dawn. They catnap at midnight and midday. The square will slow down as the sun gets higher."

She nodded. "We have to be out of sight by then."

He shrugged. "I'm sure our Hero there knows what

he's doing." Cherenkova gave him a look. Even now the scholar seemed more interested in the opportunity to observe kzinti cultural interactions up close than in the possibility that they might end the day as guests of honor at a Tzaatz hunt. It turned out to be easy to get into the square; there were simply too few of the invaders to cover every possible entrance. The wall was a tradition rather than a defense, and had been since the kzinti went to space. There were many stairs over it and arches through it, put there over the generations for the convenience of some long-forgotten merchant trader and maintained for the convenience of those who followed him. The little group slipped through a smaller arch, barely more than a tunnel, and quickly lost themselves in the bustle of commerce. As soon as they were in the market district Pouncer obtained several well-worn fur blankets from a wide-eyed trader, who abased himself and tried to convince them to take his best stock when he saw who his customer was. He tried to appear brave, worthy of the honor being bestowed upon him, but even Cherenkova could see his fear clearly.

Pouncer ripped holes in the blankets for vision and the humans wore them over their heads. The furs were hot, uncomfortable and musty, but they served to disguise the humans from casual recognition, and more important, masked their smell from both kzinti and *rapsari* sniffers. They were paid no particular attention. A young kzin with three fur-swaddled aliens and an unleashed kzinrette were far from the strangest thing to be seen in Hero's Square on even an average day, and this was not an average day. There was still the risk that Pouncer himself would be recognized, but it was still too dark for that at any distance.

They made their way in silence through the brightening dawn, twice turning away to avoid Tzaatz patrols with sniffer *rapsari*. As the sun rose, Cherenkova began to worry about the possibility of someone recognizing Pouncer, and a glance traded with Tskombe showed he had the same concern. There was nothing they could do but follow where the kzin led.

Ahead of them Pouncer had the same worry. He knew where he was going, he knew how to get there, but the Tzaatz patrols were making it difficult. Every time he grew close to his goal he was forced in another direction to avoid them. There was no doubt in his mind that he was the primary subject of the Tzaatz search. Kchula-Tzaatz's attack had been wildly successful, but it would be useless if he could not show the heads of all of the Rrit. Pouncer alive was more of a danger to him than the entire Rrit fleet. The *rapsari* sniffers were the primary danger; the smells of the market crowded too close for a kzinti nose to pick out any one scent at any distance at all, but one look at the long, questing proboscises of the sniffers had told him all he needed to know about the function of that particular breed of genetic construct. They would have his scent from the Citadel, from his chambers if nowhere else, and if they picked him up it would be the end of his run.

The sun was nearly over the horizon when he finally found his destination, and at first he didn't recognize it. What had been a poor stall had been markedly improved, the front rebuilt with fine flamewood, a new awning of oiled *posrori* skin, the stalls next door taken over to make room for an enclosed feeding area already half built. Provider had gained *strakh* indeed from the patronage of the Patriarch's son, and wasted no time taking advantage of it.

The old kzin was in the front of his stall, dispensing water to the *vatach* on display there. He took good care of his stock. He turned as Pouncer and his small band arrived at the counter, his eyes widening in instant recognition.

"Sire! Patriarch! You . . . We feared . . . They've been searching for you . . . You must come inside." He glanced over their shoulders to see who might be watching, then beckoned them to the side of his stall, where a door led into a storage area behind the front cages. It was the response Pouncer had hoped for, and he went in, T'suuz and the humans behind him. It was cramped quarters for all of them. *Vatach* and *grashi* scrabbled in their cages, and a preparation board held a pungent array of chopped roots beside a large tub of half-stirred sauce. The air was heavy with animal scents.

"Not Patriarch yet, Provider, not while my father still lives." *And I pray to the Fanged God that he does*. "I thank you for your hospitality. We will not stay long; you are endangering yourself in sheltering us."

Provider made the gesture that meant *irrelevant*. "You will stay as long as you need." He unfurled his ears to show the tattoos of the Rrit. "I commanded a grav tank in the Kdatlyno uprising, and led a full four-sword at Patriarch's Reach, and again at Avenari, where I was wounded." He raised his arm to show a long white streak of fur that grew over a scar on his flank, evidence of some weapon that must have nearly cut him in half. "The Tzaatz will have to kill me to take you from beneath my roof."

Pouncer made the gesture that meant I-am-in-your-debt. "I am honored by your fealty. You have the gratitude of the Rrit, for what that is worth now."

"The thanks of Rrit are priceless in any circumstances. Think no more of it, sire." He held up a paw before Pouncer could speak further. "Here, you must eat; you must be starved. We will make plans later." Provider was already fishing a *vatach* from a cage. Pouncer was hungry enough to eat it whole, but it would not do to insult the prowess of their benefactor, so he carefully beheaded the runner and dipped its body in the sauce. T'suuz, dropping instantly into the part of the trained kzinrette, knelt beside him to be fed. It was a role, he suddenly realized, that she had played her entire life, and with that realization came the understanding of how galling that role must have been for a mind as quick and ambitious as hers. He had a bite of the *vatach*, so as to not insult his host, then gave her the rest. The next he offered to Kefan-Brasseur, who refused it, as did the other humans. Provider brought out some Jotoki popfruits, slave food for his Kdatlyno, and the *kz'zeerkti* ambassadors found them more to their taste.

Many *vatach* later the feasting stopped, and a kzin younger than Pouncer brought water bowls to wash the blood from their paws and jowls. *This is Provider's son,* Pouncer realized, he who hunted beyond the Mooncatchers for wild-caught *grashi*, and no doubt larger game as well. The youngster was only in mid-adolescence, his fur still carrying the faint spot pattern of a kitten, but he carried himself with confidence and his movements had an economy and purposefulness that made him a presence. *There is strength to be found in the lone hunt, strength that cannot be assigned by title or privilege.* It was a truth he knew from his own hunts, but there was a difference between an occasional afternoon's pleasure chase and a lifetime of hunts on which livelihood and life depended. Pouncer, born to rule and trained to that role since birth, found himself in awe of this near-kitten.

And this I cannot express. To be Rrit was to rule. To doubt his own ability to carry out his birthright was impossible, at least publicly. *The best I can do is strive to be worthy of the honor birth has given me.*

"I hesitate to interrupt." Kefan-Brasseur was speaking. "We have to resolve our current predicament as soon as possible."

If Provider was surprised at the alien's speech he did not show it. Nevertheless he addressed his reply to Pouncer. "What are your intentions, sire?"

"These *kz'zeerkti* are under my protection. I must see them safely to their ship at the singularity's edge."

"Have they a ship at the spaceport?"

"No, but Chuut-Portmaster will grant me one."

"The Tzaatz are heavy on the ground there. Sire, it is too dangerous for you to go."

"May we borrow your gravcar?"

"All I have is at your disposal, sire."

"We will go and look." He raised a paw to forestall Provider's objection. "And I give you my word we will do nothing foolish."

Provider's gravcar was old but serviceable. Pouncer
flew because T'suuz could not. The humans sat in the rear,
all three easily fitting in the space meant for two kzin. He
lifted out and rotated for the spaceport. Treetops slid
beneath them. Pouncer kept them low in order to evade
possible detection by Tzaatz patrols, inasmuch as that was
possible. It was not long before the spaceport came into
view. Pouncer swung around to enter the local traffic
landing pattern. T'suuz grabbed his shoulder and pointed.
"Look."

He followed her pointing, saw clustered assault *rapsari*
on the stabilized turf of the boost field. A dozen or more
assault shuttles were down on the field, as well as a pawful of Swiftwing couriers and a flight deck's worth of
transatmospheric fighters. The glint of mag armor highlighted Tzaatz warriors. A steady stream of freight haulers
was falling out of orbit to be marshaled on the ground by
the Tzaatz, and around the perimeter of the spaceport,
weapon carriers stood in defensive positions with others
circling overhead to intercept incoming traffic. The route
off-planet was very firmly in enemy hands. Pouncer guided the gravcar into a tight loop to take them out of the
approach path, hoping they were too far out for the aborted
approach to draw attention. There were a few tense
moments when a Tzaatz patrol seemed to be following
them, but it veered away without incident. Pouncer guided
the car back to Hero's Square and they again took refuge
in Provider's shop.

Inside Pouncer raked the air with his claws in frustration and turned to Tskombe. "If we could gain access to
Chuut-Portmaster we would have a ship for you!"

The human stroked his chin. "Perhaps we could wait until he leaves. Do you know where he lives?"

Brasseur interrupted before Pouncer could answer. "I would be very surprised if he has not been removed from power."

Pouncer turned to face the historian. "He is not of the Rrit; the declaration of *skalazaal* does not apply to him."

Brasseur shrugged. "I know your traditions, but I also know the demands of power. The Tzaatz need control of the spaceport for its cargo handling facilities. They would not leave such an important asset in enemy hands. Tradition demands they leave him at his post, but you can be sure he's not alone in it, and he will not be free to do as you ask."

"Hrrr." Pouncer flicked his tail in annoyance. "You are probably right."

Cherenkova pursed her lips, thinking. "The key question is, will the Tzaatz allow us to leave?"

"We cannot know this."

"Sire, I can find out for you." Provider's son had come in, bringing water. The group turned to the adolescent. "I can bring food to the guards on the perimeter; it will not be seen as unusual. They must have been given instructions. Perhaps they hunt these aliens as game; perhaps they have no interest in them. I will learn the truth."

"No!" Provider snarled at his son, fangs exposed. "Have you no honor? We will not trade the *strakh* of the Rrit for that of the Tzaatz."

The adolescent started to answer but Pouncer held up a hand to stop him. "Your son trades no *strakh*, Provider. His suggestion is clever, and brave. Let him go."

There was a long pause, then Provider signaled his agreement. His son began loading cages of *grashi, vatach,* and other delicacies into the antiquated gravcar. Its rear, Pouncer now noticed, had been modified so it could serve as a mobile market stall, with indentations to hold jars of sauce without slopping. He began to help, carrying cages to speed the loading, and quite quickly the car was ready. The adolescent took the pilot's seat with casual confidence and powered up the polarizers. Pouncer stopped him before he could lift out. "How are you known, youngling?"

The adolescent claw-raked. "I am called Far Hunter, sire."

"Because you travel far to find the best *grashi,* yes? Do you also hunt alone?"

"I do now, sire. When I was younger my father came with me, but his injuries no longer allow it."

"You are young for a name, Far Hunter, but I can see you have earned it. Your father brings honor to your house, and you are well worthy of his inheritance."

"Thank you, sire."

Far Hunter left on his mission, and Pouncer, T'suuz, and the humans waited in Provider's storeroom. Provider himself was kept busy serving customers, and twice Tzaatz ground patrols came by asking after any of Rrit Pride. Provider quite truthfully told them that the Patriarch's heir had visited his shop just two days ago. He played the role masterfully, distracting the searchers with food while he cleverly shifted the conversation without the Tzaatz realizing that he had not quite answered the question they had asked. After the second patrol Provider closed his jars and came back to wait with the fugitives.

Pouncer got up in protest. "We must leave, Provider; we cost you *strakh* with your custom by forcing you to close."

The old kzin gestured for him to sit down. "No, sire, you honor me with your faith in my loyalty. Those Tzaatz *sthondat* ask questions only as an excuse to wolf down my best *vatach*. We will wait here for my son to return."

Tskombe's eyebrows went up. "You're just going to leave your stock unguarded in the front?"

Provider looked at him. "The Tzaatz have no honor, but not even the most craven would stoop to stealing from a public market stall in daylight."

Tskombe nodded, absorbing this, and the little group lapsed into silence, listening to the bustle of the market die down as the sun grew higher. It was some hours later by his beltcomp that Far Hunter returned.

"I visited all the port entrances. It's tightly guarded by Tzaatz and their creatures, and shuttles are coming down to unload more all the time. There were gravtanks and combat cars as well, and Tzaatz warriors checked every vehicle allowed to enter. I asked after Chuut-Portmaster as though we shared *strakh* and was cuffed for my trouble, but I overheard that they search for the *kz'zeerkti*, as well as any of Rrit Pride."

"Then we cannot get the aliens off-planet."

Far Hunter turned his paw over. "The Tzaatz are sloppy and ill disciplined. It would be possible to get in, perhaps."

Pouncer's whiskers twitched. "It is one thing to gain access, but we need a ship, and a pilot."

"I can fly a ship. Given an automanual I can learn to fly a kzinti ship," said Cherenkova.

"Hrrr." Pouncer turned a paw over, considering. "I cannot accompany you off-world. I would be unable to stand for your protection. I can turn that duty over to a loyal Rrit warrior, but not to you."

Cherenkova turned to him. "With respect First-Son-of-Meerz-Rrit, as a passenger on a ship I was piloting there would be little you could do to protect us anyway. We greatly appreciate your loyalty to your uncle's oath, but at some point we must resume responsibility for our own fates. I suggest that point comes when our ship boosts for orbit."

"Hrrr . . ." Pouncer considered this.

"You *kz'zeerkti* wear the Patriarch's sigil," Provider said. "You are welcome to stay in my home until the Tzaatz are gone. The population of kzin will not stand for their dishonor long."

Cherenkova was about to answer, but Tskombe cut her off. "No." The soldier spoke Interspeak to the other humans so the kzinti couldn't understand him. "We have to get back to human space. The Tzaatz are looking for our Hero there because he's the Patriarch's heir, and their victory won't be recognized until they kill him. So why are they also looking for us? Meerz-Rrit has agreed in principle to peace. The only reason Kchula-Tzaatz would want to prevent us from leaving is if he intended to change that. I would bet my career he is planning a war with humanity, at least a continuation of the conquest program. There's obviously pressure for that to happen, and his leadership isn't solid; he can't take the risks Meerz-Rrit was prepared to in the name of peace. Leading a war will help him consolidate his role. The UN needs to know this."

Brasseur nodded. "I think you're right."

"We thank you for your generosity, Provider," Cherenkova answered in the Hero's Tongue, carrying on as though Tskombe's words had made no difference to what she was about to say. "But we must return to our own world as quickly as possible."

"What ship would you fly, Cherenkova-Captain?" Pouncer asked.

"I saw some Swiftwing-class couriers on the field when we landed, fast and long ranged. One of those would be best. I need the documentation to learn to fly it."

"My half brother is Cargo Pilot. I will see what I can do to get you an automanual," Provider said. "Until then we will hide you at my home."

T'suuz said nothing, but her tail lashed. Her disapproval was clear.

They took Provider's gravcar to his home, then he and his son left, the one to reopen their market stall, the other to find his half brother Pilot and perhaps obtain a Swiftwing automanual. Provider's home was spartan but comfortable, located in a forest clearing shared with a couple of similar structures ten or fifteen kilometers from Hero's Square. It was small by kzin standards, ample on a human scale. There were four rooms on one level, built around a central sand-floored den and backed against a layered sedimentary cliff face. The front two rooms were built of thick stonewood timbers; the rear two were actually hollowed out of the cliff. A fireplace in the middle of the den led to a chimney that went up through the rock, although there was no need for it with the approach of the dry season. A loft above the outer rooms provided storage, and it was here that the humans were quartered among anonymous boxes and dusty war trophies from the time when Provider had been Tank Leader. It reminded Cherenkova of her aunt's attic, where she had explored as a little girl and found all kinds of fascinating treasures long discarded by the adults in her life, a keyhole glimpse at her elders' history before she was born. There was something compellingly human about an attic full of forgotten memories, something probably common to any sentient that led a settled existence. She said as much to Brasseur and he smiled.

"Your paradigm is shifting. The UN would have you believe the Kzin are evil predators bent on nothing more than killing. That's just propaganda. They're bound by the rules of life, of evolution, and those are universal. They're built of DNA and amino acids because those are nature's preferred building blocks in a liquid water environment, and those blocks are formed into muscles and skeleton and organs because they are solving the same evolutionary problems we are. They have fears and desires, hopes and dreams just like we do. In those emotions they're closer to us than a dog is, probably closer even than a chimpanzee, because they operate on the same plane of intelligence that we do."

Cherenkova shook her head. "I'm not sure I buy the universal-rules-of-life argument. The Outsiders aren't built of DNA and amino acids."

"The Outsiders are a perfect example. Their biology is as far from ours as it's possible for a biology to be. Their environment is deep space, their blood is liquid helium, their evolutionary history is fundamentally different, and their civilization is eons older. We have almost no touch-points with them—but they still trade for what they need, just like we do, just like Provider does. That's a fundamental constant in any civilization; in fact it's one of the defining characteristics of a civilization."

"That doesn't mean they share our emotions. You can't tell me a kzin understands love in the human sense, just to take an example—much less an Outsider."

"Yes, I can tell you that. They have eyes. You wouldn't argue they don't see the same things we do."

"Eyes are physical structures, emotions aren't."

"Eyes are evolutionary adaptations to an environment bathed in photons. Organisms that live in darkness do not evolve eyes, or lose them if they possess them. With sentient beings that live in groups, the most important part of the environment is the other intelligent sentient beings in the group. Emotions are how we deal with them, and emotions are manifested in the physical structure of our brains. They're no less adapted to our social environment than our eyes are to Sol's spectrum. Watch how Far Hunter takes care of his father, or watch the way he looks at T'suuz. Watch how fiercely loyal T'suuz is to her brother. Were they humans in the same situation their actions would be no different. Sexual attraction ensures that reproduction happens, and sexual love ensures the offspring get the support they need from their parents. Familial love ensures you put your best efforts into helping those who share your genes. That's no less adaptive than color vision or the ability to make tools."

"Maybe so, but Pouncer is risking his life to help us. I appreciate it, but it hardly serves his genetic interests."

"You're a military officer. Wouldn't you risk your life to uphold your honor?"

She nodded. "I've done as much."

"Of course you have. And isn't that *known* to be a hallmark of a good officer? Look at human history. In cultures where legal authority was weak, distant, or absent entirely, a person's reputation was everything. If your word was not your bond, and not *known* to be your bond, you could not be transacted with. That would effectively isolate you from the community, and that could be lethal if you were ever in trouble. Keeping your word regardless of personal cost is adaptive. If your word is known to be conditional, in *any* circumstance, you can't be trusted. The same applies to having a reputation for standing up for yourself, regardless of cost; without it you can be bullied out of what's yours. The kzinti are just an extreme case of that dynamic. I can explain the biological reasons behind that if you like."

Cherenkova shook her head. "I don't think I'm ready to believe my genes are pulling my strings quite so effectively."

"Consider this. Would you run into a burning building to save a friend's child?"

"Any decent human would."

"Notice how you place a positive value on a person's willingness to risk their life to save another." Brasseur smiled, in his element as a lecturer before a class. "Now suppose there were two burning buildings, and you had to choose between running into one to save a single child or the other to save three children. Knowing you couldn't save them all, which do you choose?"

Cherenkova laughed. "Three, of course."

"So three lives are more valuable than one?"

"Yes."

"Now what if the single child were your own? Which would you save?"

She paused, considering the logical trap but unable to avoid it. "My own first, but these are highly artificial situations."

"So three lives aren't more valuable than one when the one is your own child. Answer me this then. How many children would have to be in the second building before you chose *not* to save your own child first?"

And Cherenkova had no answer for that. Brasseur smiled, having won his point. "First-Son-of-Meerz-Rrit would make the same choice, because his emotions are based on the same social and evolutionary realities that yours are." She looked uncomfortable. "Your paradigm is shifting. It's not a bad thing."

On the other side of the loft Tskombe was hefting a wickedly curved scimitar that Pouncer called a *kreera*. It was a one-handed weapon for a kzin, big enough to be a broadsword for him. She watched him carefully as he took a stance and cut the air with the blade. Was he any less a warrior than Yiao-Rrit had been? Were the dynamics that drove his behavior as a leader and an officer, the dynamics that drove her *own* behavior as a leader and an officer, any different from those that drove a kzin to scream and leap to avenge an insult? She wanted to believe that there was some fundamental difference between them. Kzinti *see us as slaves and prey animals*. It had been thirteen years since the destroyer *Astrel* had arrived too late to save the

Midling research expedition from a kzinti raider, and second officer Cherenkova had led the landing party that entered the stripped base camp to find the bloody evidence of kzinti atrocity. They had played games with their prey . . . She shook her head, unable after all this time to scour the unbidden images from her memory. But humans used other humans as slaves, either as explicit chattel as in ancient Rome or more subtly, woven into the social norms as on Plateau or Jinx, or even in the underground flesh markets on Earth, where those unlucky enough to have been born illegally struggled to live without UN registration. Humans had even used other humans as prey animals, and before the kzinti came the UN's restrictions on intra-species violence were enforced not with honor as in *skalazaal* and *skatosh* but through the wholesale drugging of the entire population, lesser measures having proved inadequate to the task.

She settled down on a pile of soft pelted furs made from an animal that Provider called a *frrch*, and thought about it. There was nothing else to do while they waited for Provider and Far Hunter to get back. From her position she could watch out the loft's window for the gravcar's return, Tskombe's mag rifle by her side in case the Tzaatz came first. Pouncer and T'suuz catnapped for most of the afternoon. Her eyes kept straying from her self-appointed task to watch Quacy at his practice, running over his lean, taut muscles as he ran through routines of attack and defense so well practiced they were reflexive. He was so *male*, and he made her very aware of her own femininity. The danger of their position only made the attraction stronger. She had promised herself not to act on it for the sake of the mission, but the mission had changed drastically. *And we may be dead tomorrow.* She realized she was licking her lips as she watched him, and quickly returned her attention to her vigil.

After awhile he came over to watch out the window with her. "I can take over."

She smiled. "I'll stay. I like the view."

He sat down on the furs, sweat glistening on his biceps.

"Why did you join?" He asked the question idly, some time later.

Ayla shrugged. "I always wanted to fly, to be a pilot, to command ships. I dreamed of it since I was little." She paused. "You?"

He shrugged. "Half a sense of duty, half a sense of adventure, half no better plan for my life."

"That's three halves." She laughed.

"If I were smart enough to do math I wouldn't be in the infantry." He smiled and she laughed again at the standard joke. Infantry officers had to be every bit as qualified as pilots just to operate the gear they carried; it was centuries since the complete desiderata for an infanteer were a strong back and a weak mind, but their traditions ran back to the centurions of Rome and beyond. Even today mud and blood, sinew and steel remained their stock in trade.

"Family?" She tried to sound casual.

"My parents and a brother, but . . ."

He trailed off and she nodded. Life among the stars wasn't compatible with close family ties. "I have my parents."

"Siblings?" he asked.

"I had a sister, but she died. Valya was her name."

"I'm sorry."

"We weren't close. She married a wealthy man, permanent lockstep contract. I didn't hear much from her after that. They had a child, but I was based on Plateau by then with my first command. I never met her. They sent a few pictures when she was a baby."

He nodded as well, and the conversation lagged again as they watched out the window. Ayla looked at him again. She could still smell the musk of his sweat and it did things to the back of her brain. *Very, very male.* She smiled to herself. *And not lockstepped.*

While the others were occupied with their private musings, Brasseur roamed Provider's home, even more fascinated by his surroundings than he been by the House of Victory. There was a fifth room to the side of the den—*house* somehow did not seem to be the right word. It was a kitchen of sorts, and two Kdatlyno slaves lived there, making batches of viand sauce according to Provider's recipes, as well as operating a large meat smoker, cleaning up after the game animals caged outside, and generally keeping house. The kitchen was well stocked and full of the smell of the pungent roots and herbs, the thick, leathery *nyalzeri* eggs and barrels of *zitragor* blood that made up the sauces. They must have understood the Hero's Tongue but they refused to be distracted from their work and Brasseur was loath to interfere. He watched them go silently and efficiently about their business, then turned instead to studying the dwelling itself. It was old, very old, but despite its age it was functionally equipped with the technologies of its era: There were power and lighting, data access, hot and cold water, solid-state refrigeration,

shelved books bound in the kzin upside-down style, some
kind of vidwall, and a datadesk. He examined the
stonewood timbers, huge and stained with their age. It
had been built, he speculated, over a thousand years ago,
and from what he could see of the other dwellings in the
clearing it was far from the oldest around. In a human
house that would explain the complete absence of modern
building materials, but the kzinti had had metals and com-
posites for tens of thousands of years before Provider's
home was built. They used natural materials because they
preferred them, and that spoke volumes about their ability
to sustain their planetary ecology in the face of the
demands of their civilization. Part of that was their slow
growth rate, part was that when their population density
got too high they tended to fight each other or leave on
conquests.

And that had larger implications. Millions, maybe
billions of sentients had died over a timespan longer
than human history, entire races brought into slavery in
generations-long conquest wars in order to maintain this
idyllic setting. *What is adaptive for the individual is not
always adaptive for the group.* He settled down to watch
the rain, feeling a familiar disquiet. Any research field that
worked on the timescale and scope of entire civilizations
was bound to give the researcher an acute sense of human
mortality. Being trapped on a hostile and alien world
made Brasseur acutely aware of the inescapable brevity of
his own life.

In the loft Quacy Tskombe was doing another set of
drills with the heavy scimitar while Ayla Cherenkova kept
her vigil from the window. Eventually he tired and came

to sit next to her on the *frrch* skins again. The setting sun threw red highlights into wayward strands of her hair, the same way it had in the window of the House of Victory, in a time that seemed a lifetime ago. Almost without thought he tucked it behind her ear. She turned toward him and their eyes met. Her lips were parted and he could see the rapid pulse in her neck. The house was silent. Pouncer was still napping, and Kefan was downstairs trying to engage T'suuz in some sort of conversation. He leaned toward her and she closed her eyes, and the whine of a gravcar rose in the clearing. He looked up, saw Far Hunter disembarking in the twilight below. He was willing to ignore that, but then Brasseur called them from below, and they had to go downstairs to find out what had happened. He had little enough to tell them beyond the bare fact that Provider was talking to Cargo Pilot and would not be home that evening. By then Pouncer was up and Brasseur started a poetry game with him that they were all drawn into.

Hours later Tskombe arranged his *frrch* blankets, and went to bed, exhausted. *How many hours has it been since I slept?* Far Hunter laid out their sleeping arrangements, and Ayla's own space was on the other side of the room, with Brasseur and two kzinti between them. He was acutely aware of the whole of that distance, as great as the gulf between desire and consummation. He breathed in and out slowly to calm his mind. It was the first time he had allowed himself to relax since the Tzaatz invasion ships had rocked the House of Victory with their sonic booms, some forty hours ago by his beltcomp. Exhaustion quickly pulled him into a deep and dreamless sleep.

Some timeless time later he jolted awake to moonlit darkness, suddenly aware of a *presence* beside him. His fight-or-flight reflex kicked in, but it was Ayla. She held a finger to her lips to warn him to silence, the curves of her body clear in the moonlight filtering through the windows. She slid beneath the fur blanket beside him, reaching out to touch his chest. No pretense of professional distance now. Her touch was electrifying and desire flooded him. She was soft and warm and he pulled her to him, inhaling her scent like a drug. They kissed with desperate urgency and she moved to straddle him, the heat of her body burning against his. This was not seduction, not courtship, but pure chemistry, catalyzed by the danger they had shared, by the knowledge that they might yet die on this hostile planet, four hundred million million kilometers from home. He entered her, saw her bite her lip against a gasp and they began moving in unison in a rhythm as old as the species. She was beautiful, more beautiful than any woman he had ever been with, and his hands found her breasts, swollen and bursting with her fertility and he found all of a sudden that he loved her and he would have wept with the realization but for the need to stay silent, and they climaxed together in a moment that went on and on, while the house slept around them.

Afterward Ayla lay with her cheek on his chest, listening to his heartbeat, her hair spilling softly down over his arm and felt warm and safe in his presence. She was unsure what had prompted her boldness, what had awakened her in the night to come to his bed, but it had been urgent, a desire as strong as her sense of rightness, of closeness, was now. She was in the fertile part of her cycle, she knew, or would have been had she not been on long-term contraception. *It's only hormones, progesterone and estrogen flooding my system, overriding common sense with desire for the strongest male I can find. The stakes have gotten high, and now my brain is manipulating me into behaviors that are effective in propagating my genes to another generation because I might not get another chance.* She breathed in his masculine scent, letting it flood her with warmth. *This feeling now is just oxytocin and endorphins, more hormones released in orgasm to bind me to the alpha male once I've mated him.* It was true, she knew, but the emotions were no less real for the knowledge. She cuddled close against him, allowing herself to feel small against his size. It was a luxury she rarely got in her profession.

She woke before he did and realized she was famished. Sunlight streamed in the window and something smelled excellent downstairs. She climbed down the loft's ladder on oversized rungs to find Brasseur cooking meat and *nyalzeri* eggs on skewers by a smoldering fire in the fireplace. One of the Kdatlyno brought in more firewood as she came up.

"Good morning." The academic moved over to let the Kdatlyno stoke the flames.

"What's that?" She asked the question dubiously, but her mouth salivated at the smell. For a moment she feared having to explain the previous night, but Brasseur either hadn't noticed where she'd slept or was carefully not mentioning it.

"*Zianya*. It's excellent with Provider's sauces."

"Is it safe?"

"I've had it dozens of times. It's better than beef."

"I'll have some." Hunger overrode any other objections. He handed her a skewer, the meat still rare and dripping. The sauce was pungent and hot and she wolfed it down, feeling the nutrients flooding her body.

"God I needed that." She had another skewerful at a slower pace. "Where's our Hero and the others?"

"They went out so they wouldn't have to smell me burning meat. Provider brought back a datacube for you." He pointed to a table. "The Swiftwing automanual."

Her heart surged and, hunger forgotten, she picked it up and plugged it in to her beltcomp. It was kzin standard format, as was the data on it. That would have represented an insurmountable obstacle, but the human's beltcomps had been fitted with both adaptors and software to read them specifically for this mission. She downloaded it to her comp's memory and scanned through it. The translation was uneven and many chunks of symbols and jargon were simply untranslatable, but all the information was there. She could fly this ship, given enough time to learn its systems. And she *would* fly this ship. For the first time since the attack she began to believe she would see Earth again.

Quacy Tskombe was awakened by the smell of fresh-cooked meat and looked up as Ayla plopped down beside him with a dish full of skewered *zianya*. While he ate she loaded the automanual cube into his beltcomp as well. "Here, learn this," she said as he finished and handed it to him. There was a change in the way she moved around him, the way they interacted.

No, there was a change in everything. *Why haven't I noticed how beautiful she is?*

He took it and scanned it. "The automanual. It's good we have it, but why do I have to learn it?"

"Because you're going to be my copilot."

"Can't you fly it yourself?"

"Sure, but if something goes wrong up there I'm going to need all the help I can get. You're rated on assault carriers, so you at least have some heavy polarizer experience. Kefan is only rated on personal fliers."

Tskombe made a face. "If I were smart enough to be a pilot I wouldn't be in the infantry."

Cherenkova laughed. "Flying is easy, it's landing that's hard." She tabbed the screen of his beltcomp. "You can start on page one." Her smile was radiant, and her manner was easy.

He scanned the page, puzzling out the untranslated chunks of the Hero's Tongue. "In an alien language no less." He sat down heavily on the *frrch* skins. "This is going to be delightful."

In truth Tskombe found the process of learning to maneuver in space an interesting challenge and spent the entire day on the automanual's simulator. He had a lot of hours on heavy-grav vehicles and, despite his self-deprecation, had not expected much of a learning curve. In fact the basics of reactionless thrusters close to a planet's surface were not difficult, but making the transition to orbit was another question entirely. Power straight up and the polarizers would run out of reaction as they climbed out of the gravity well. In theory it was possible to drive straight up until you reached escape velocity; in practice the power cost was prohibitive. Instead you had to angle the thrust, take advantage of the planet's rotational energy to get you into orbit. That became increasingly difficult as you moved away from the equator, and the rules for calculating boost angle in spheric coordinates were not simple. Once in space a whole other set of considerations came into play: thrust points, apopromixate, periproximate, intermediate and hybrid orbit adjustments, insertion angles, heat management, atmospheric skip, dealing with thruster failures, power failures, nav system failures. Everything had to be planned well in advance, and the art was a far cry from his experience of slamming assault vehicles down on attack positions, coming in so low the landing skids wound up full of tree branches. Energy management was another unfamiliar issue. More than once he wound up helplessly adrift on a simulation run through one small navigation error growing into a large power deficiency. A Swiftwing had tremendous acceleration and generous reserves for a ship its size, and it was easy to correct mistakes with thrust, but too much thoughtless maneuvering would get you stranded. The autopilot could do it all for you, of course, but in the kind of emergency Ayla would need him for there was no guarantee the autopilot would be operational.

If you even trusted the autopilot in the first place. What slave race did the kzin use to develop their flight control software? How could you trust a system like that to a slave? The opportunities for subtle sabotage were boundless. The penalties for a slave programmer being caught would be severe, of course, but the odds against being caught were long, if you did it right. You could, just for example, disable the hyperdrive in deepspace, or even more effective, have it stay on as a ship came into a stellar singularity . . .

Tskombe shuddered and set up another simulation run. If he learned the Swiftwing's systems well enough, Ayla wouldn't have to use the autopilot.

The Conserver serves the Traditions. The Traditions do not serve the Conserver.
                                        —Kzin-Conserver

The early morning sun peeked anemically through the huge windows that stretched to the arched beams on the ceiling of the Great Hall of the Patriarch. Rrit-Conserver watched carefully from the hidden gallery that had hosted Meerz-Rrit's *kz'zeerkti* envoys just days ago, a lifetime ago for many brave lives now extinguished. The hall was filling rapidly, the floor with the same Pride-Patriarchs who had listened to Meerz-Rrit's speech, the galleries with the nobility of Kzinhome itself, the Lesser Pride leaders whose fealty pledges to the Rrit stretched back to before space travel. This gathering was at Kchula-Tzaatz's direction, as was his attendance. Behind him four Tzaatz guards ensured his outward cooperation, but he ignored them as he watched the assembly carefully, noting who spoke to whom, the motions of the crowd, the expressions, the mood of the hall. *The guards do not control me, because I fight not with my body but with my mind.* Tzaatz Pride had already made a mistake in letting him live. Conservers were oath bound to act with impartiality to preserve the traditions, and perhaps they were counting on that. *But here the traditions have been transgressed, and I am free to act as I see fit to redress that.* Perhaps the Tzaatz would make further mistakes. Below him the burble of voices rose. He made his observations not because he expected to be surprised by what he observed but because at such a critical juncture no piece of information was unimportant. *The situation is fluid. There may yet be advantage here.*

His concentration was interrupted by footsteps at the door, and he turned, nodded in sardonic greeting to the black furred newcomer.

"Ftzaal-Tzaatz. It saddens me to see a warrior of your reputation stain his name in this honorless farce."

"Honorless?" Ftzaal-Tzaatz rippled his ears in amusement. "Tzaatz Pride has observed the traditions. The rules of *skalazaal* apply."

"The Great Pride Circle will not stand for the manner in which Tzaatz Pride has conducted it. Slaves may not be used in battle. Your dishonor is great."

Ftzaal twitched his tail. "My brother has used not slaves but beasts in battle, a practice supported by the oldest traditions."

Rrit-Conserver would not be dissuaded from his point. "And your assassin *beast* struck First-Son-of-Meerz-Rrit before you declared the Honor-War. The Great Pride Circle will banish your brother, and you beside him."

"The Great Prides will wish to avoid the fate of the Rrit. None can stand in *skalazaal* against *rapsari*." *Nor will they know the entire gene construct production capacity of Jotok has been committed to this conquest.* It was the single secret Kchula-Tzaatz guarded most closely. It was at the moment of victory that the Tzaatz were most vulnerable. "They will be happy to find any reason to accept my brother's dominance, and so they will be willing to overlook trivial deviations from the formal standard."

"And you? Why do you accept your brother's dominance?"

Ftzaal-Tzaatz's whiskers twitched. "It is not for the sword to question the paw that wields it."

"There is no Great Pride that would not count itself fortunate to claim the fealty of the Protector of Jotok."

Ftzaal moved to stand beside Rrit-Conserver, looking down on the gathering throng below. "I am bound by blood and honor to Tzaatz Pride. That is a loyalty claim no other pride can make."

In the hall below voices quieted as the successional procession began in ponderous ceremony, first the fearsome Hunt Priests, masked and robed in red, the blades of their ceremonial *wtsai* flashing as they slashed and lunged in ritual combat, symbolically slaying the Fanged God's enemies to make the way safe for the High Priests to follow. Conserver watched them advance, then looked to his captor. "Not even the priesthood?"

Unconsciously Ftzaal's lips twitched away from his fangs. When he spoke his voice was dangerously quiet. "What does a Conserver know of the Black Priests? We shall not speak of this."

Rrit-Conserver kept his reaction under control. *There is depth here, and danger.* In the Patriarchy all black-furred kittens went to the Black Cult, and vanishingly few ever left it. There was more to Ftzaal-Tzaatz than the speed of his blade. Rrit-Conserver filed the point, and went on as if he hadn't noticed it. "Rrit Pride has held the Patriarchy for half-eight-cubed generations, Ftzaal-Tzaatz." Rrit-Conserver's voice was calm, but the intensity of his words carried the emotion his training forbade him to express. "That cannot change. The Great Prides will not allow it. The Guild Prides will not allow it. The Conservers will not allow it."

Below them the Practitioner Cult was advancing, each member laying down a rough-hewn board of sweet-scented *mrooz*, and then returning to the end of the line to collect another from the wood-bearers, their movements fast within the slow moving pageant. The higher cults followed on the ceremonial walkway, in groups of four and in a bewildering array of ceremonial dress, the Star Priests, the Beast Cult, many more than Rrit-Conserver could recognize. Chanting rose as they came, echoing from the stone walls.

"And Tzaatz Pride would not dream of violating such a strong tradition." Ftzaal raised his voice slightly to be heard. "A Rrit shall rule the Patriarchy, and a Rrit shall inherit the Patriarchy." Ftzaal rippled his ears and flipped his tail. "I owe my own fealty to the Rrit through the pledge of Tzaatz Pride. My brother is aware of the due he owes, *skalazaal* notwithstanding. The Tzaatz shall be content to serve as trusted adviser to the Patriarch."

"No one will follow the nursing kitten Kchula-Tzaatz puts at the head of the Great Pride Circle." Rrit-Conserver lashed his tail. "Nor the bastard son of a Rrit daughter he produces to follow him."

"Wise as always, Rrit-Conserver, but we shall not insult the Great Pride Circle by giving them a kitten as leader." There was a roar for silence down below, and the chanting stopped, leaving sudden silence in its wake. They both turned to watch the assembly, and Ftzaal continued with his voice lowered. "The ceremony is about to begin. You consider Tzaatz Pride honorless? Watch and learn the meaning of dishonor!"

The High Priests were advancing now, each borne on a litter carried by four of the black-furred Black Priests, the red sashes over white robes symbolizing the blood-purification rite that was the hallmark of their sect. A dull booming began in the hall—four huge conquest drums behind the dais, each supported a rhythmically dancing drummer. At first the movements were slow, the sound almost inaudible, but it built steadily, rising in tempo and intensity as the drummers moved faster and faster until they drowned out speech and even thought. The huge ceiling beams vibrated to the sound as the drummers worked themselves into a frenzy, each pounding all four paws on the tight-stretched drum skins in complex, ever changing cycles. Suddenly a drumhead ruptured, the high frequency *bang* making Rrit-Conserver's ears ring through the wall of sound. Almost immediately a second drum burst, then the third and the fourth. The drummers lay collapsed and exhausted in the ruined instruments. The silence was total as Kchula-Tzaatz ascended the dais.

"Brothers! Listen to me now!" His voice echoed from the walls. Rrit-Conserver kept his eyes on the crowd. *I must watch the reactions of the Pride Circle. If the Rrit have any allies left I will find them there.*

"Brothers! Yesterday in this hall you heard Meerz-Rrit stain the honor of our entire species. Yesterday our so called Patriarch commanded you all to turn away from the path of conquest which is rightfully yours." Kchula-Tzaatz paused for effect. "Tzaatz Pride alone has not stood for this. The way of the kzinti is the way of conquest. The *kz'zeerkti* cannot stand before the combined might of the Patriarchy. Tzaatz Pride alone has acted to preserve the honor of us all." He held up his arms, tail held high in triumph. "The Honor-War has been declared, fought and won. See what dishonor has brought to Rrit Pride!"

At what was obviously a predetermined moment a Tzaatz guard stepped forward, and thrust a polearm high in the air. Impaled on its end was a messy sphere, tawny orange, stained rust red. Concentrated as he was on the Pride Circle's reactions it took Rrit-Conserver a moment to recognize it.

"Behold the head of Meerz-Rrit." Kchula-Tzaatz was roaring in triumph. Another Tzaatz guard stepped forward, another polearm was raised toward the rafters. "Behold the head of First-Son-of-Meerz-Rrit." Another polearm went up. "The head of Myowr-Guardmaster." Another. "The head of Patriarch's Telepath." Another. Rrit-Conserver turned away, his self-discipline unequal to the sight. The guards moved in front of the door as he stepped toward it. He looked over to his captor, still watching the display with detached interest.

"I would leave this sorry demonstration, Ftzaal-Tzaatz."

The black-furred killer twitched his ears in amusement. "And miss the ascension of the next of the Rrit dynasty. Have you no curiosity?"

"It is Second-Son." Rrit-Conserver's lips twitched "He has betrayed his own blood. Spare me this shameful demonstration."

Ftzaal fanned his ears halfway up, mildly interested. "You seem so sure."

"Your brother would have raised his head after First-Son's had it not been so." He wrinkled his nose, disgusted. "I would leave now, Black Priest."

If the reference to his background stung, Ftzaal-Tzaatz gave no sign. "As you wish." He waved a paw for the guards to stand away from the door. "Escort him to his chambers. He is not to leave them."

The lead guard claw-raked. "As you command, sire." Two of them opened the door and waited for Rrit-Conserver while the other two fell into step behind him. He ignored their presence. Escape was not on his mind. The second head Kchula-Tzaatz had held up had been bloody and mutilated, but he had recognized it. Ztal-Biologist. *First-Son still lives, but they wish him thought dead. There may yet be salvation for the Rrit.*

Back in his austere chamber Rrit-Conserver settled himself on his *prrstet* and began to run through the Eight Variations of honor in his mind. *First variation. Honor flows from integrity, integrity from respect, respect from effort, effort from self-discipline . . .* He felt his breathing slow as he focused himself on the mental exercise. He was well into the seventh variation when the door opened. He did not open his eyes, did not twitch his ears. *Do not seek the information, let it flow to you.* Time flowed without measure. Heavy footsteps sounded, the tang of sweat, the slight musk of female, a male of high dominance, recently mated. He spoke without moving.

"Kchula-Tzaatz."

"You did not stay to see the ascension of the new Patriarch, Rrit-Conserver." The conqueror was in a good mood, his voice purring with satisfaction.

Rrit-Conserver opened his eyes. "There was no need to watch you play with puppets, Kchula-Tzaatz."

"Do I detect a note of disrespect toward our esteemed Patriarch?" Kchula flipped his ears and twitched his tail, amused by his game.

"Second-Son is a traitor to his blood."

"Second-Son?" Kchula rippled his ears in amusement. "His name is Scrral-Rrit now. Have you the proof-before-the-pride-circle of his guilt?"

"I have proof enough for myself." *I saw him in the Command Lair; he was involved in the plot. His hand took his father's life.*

"And this is enough for you to disavow your own sworn loyalties?"

Was it? "Perhaps." *What does honor demand of me now?*

"Perhaps." Kchula rippled his ears. "So seldom do I hear a Conserver unsure of the answer to a question of honor."

"Today is an unusual day."

"Today is a great day in the history of the Patriarchy." Kchula licked his chops, gloating in his voice.

"What is it you wish of me?"

"I am your colleague now, Rrit-Conserver. I am a trusted advisor to our new and noble Patriarch Scrral-Rrit. I wish merely to share your mind in guiding our sire's hand as he assumes his command of the Patriarchy."

Rrit-Conserver twitched his whiskers. "You wish your usurpation legitimized by the name of Rrit-Conserver."

"You question my motives." Kchula flipped his ears in amusement. "My dear Conserver, I am shocked."

"I question your honor, Kchula-Tzaatz."

Kchula's mouth relaxed into a fanged smile; his humor evaporated. "I have been advised to kill you." His ears folded back and his eyes locked onto Rrit-Conserver.

Conserver met the conqueror's gaze with equanimity. "That is probably wise advice."

"You begin to try my patience."

"That holds no relevance to me. If you intend to kill me, leap. If not . . ." He flipped his ears. "I am in the middle of my meditation. I would have peace."

"Tradition makes you immune to challenge."

"You care no more about the Conserver Traditions than you do about the Dueling Traditions. Or any others."

Conserver's voice held contempt and for a long moment Kchula looked as though he would leap. Conserver subtly shifted his position to receive the attack. Kchula was large and strong, but he was used to having others do his killing for him. If he leapt, Conserver's battle discipline would be enough to defeat him. It would be a simple solution—death for the usurper in a fair duel of his own choosing. But Kchula did not leap, precisely because he was used to having others do his killing for him. Conserver considered goading him further, but decided against it. Let the game play out, and see where it leads. *Kchula needs something from me, and need is power.*

"I would have your ears for that insult, Conserver, but you're more use to me alive."

"If you would take my ears for it then it is not an insult but a statement of fact." Conserver waited while Kchula followed the logic chain through. "And what use do you have for me?"

Does he know of the destruction of the computer core?
Kchula unconsciously snapped his jaw at the tenacity of
the *zitalyi;* even now he could not consider the Citadel
cleared of opposition, and every day brought another
strike from deep in the bowels of the fortress. He was losing
strakh before the Great Pride Circle, and that was something he could ill afford. He considered his prisoner for
long heartbeats, weighing options. Rrit-Conserver met his
gaze with equanimity. *I must be open enough that his
mind can engage our problems, but not so open that he
knows how truly vulnerable we are now.* "As you point
out, your support will be invaluable in bringing stability to
the Patriarchy. The sooner the Prides accept the new realities the less damage we will suffer. Squabbling profits no
one. We face larger dangers now, and your mind is an
essential weapon if our species is to survive them."
*Threats will not shift this Conserver; let us see what flat-
tery can do.*

Rrit-Conserver remained impassive. "I am nothing
but dangerous to you alive. You cannot change that,
Kchula."

"And why is that?"

"You seek to convince me I owe my loyalty to Second-
Son-of-Meerz-Rrit. Even if you succeed at this I will owe
no loyalty to you. The mind you desire to put to your uses
will be directed against your rule."

Kchula lashed his tail, annoyed. "You would support a
spineless coward over a warrior of proven skill."

"I am sworn to the Rrit."

"And if this last of the Rrit should die?"

"There are many who share the blood of the Rrit."

"Including Tzaatz Pride."

"Your claim is far from strongest, Kchula."

"And far from weakest. But Second-Son will not die yet, and your fealty belongs to him regardless of your personal feelings."

"Perhaps."

Kchula turned and paced the room, tail lashing. "The question of your survival becomes one of control."

"I am a Conserver. You cannot control me."

"Then I should kill you after all."

Conserver made the gesture that meant *irrelevant*. "I will not serve you, Kchula-Tzaatz. You possess no lever that could so compel me."

"You will serve Scrral-Rrit." Kchula's voice was harsh.

Rrit-Conserver turned a paw over and studied it. *This was the critical moment.* "So long as he proves to be worthy of the honor of the succession." *But Second-Son will not prove worthy.*

Kchula lashed his tail. "That is enough for me. You have the freedom of the Citadel, as tradition demands. I will expect that you too will follow the traditions." He turned and left.

Conserver resumed his meditative posture. *Kchula-Tzaatz is a fool. He believes that I believe First-Son to be dead.* Rrit-Conserver would serve Second-Son, which would satisfy the outward form of honor, and Kchula-Tzaatz would come to believe that he controlled Rrit-Conserver as he controlled Black-Stripe. But Pouncer would return, if he could, when he could. *And on that day, Kchula-Tzaatz will learn that I do not serve him.*

*One must not judge everyone in the world by
their qualities as a soldier, otherwise we should
have no civilization.*
　　　　　　　　—Field Marshal Erwin Rommel

Kefan Brasseur looked through Provider's loft window at
a steady rainfall. Until an opportunity to get a ship arose
they were effectively confined to Provider's home, and
time had started to drag as the initial shock of the assault
and their immediate fear of capture had worn off. Most
days Brasseur spent his time practicing with his pistol and
the magrifle, interspersed with attempts to get T'suuz to
talk with him. They were consistent failures, this last
attempt no more than the others. It was frustrating: A
kzinrette with a behavior set like the one she had displayed during their escape was unheard-of, but now she
showed no interest in anything but food, sleep, and baring
her teeth at anyone who seemed to be bothering her
brother.

He turned away from the window. Cherenkova and
Tskombe were absorbed in their beltcomps. The military
officers were almost as frustrating as T'suuz. True, their
skills were important, but their single-minded obsession
with getting off the planet was blinding them to the privilege they were enjoying as one of only a handful of
humans to arrive on Kzinhome as anything other than a
war trophy. They treated each other with exaggerated
casualness. It was a courtesy they were paying him, perhaps, a cover for what was obviously a strong and growing
sexual relationship. Brasseur sighed. He had long since
grown bored of studying the games humans played with

each other. The stakes were unvaryingly status, dominance, power, and sex, the strategies largely limited to blackmail, bribery, bluff, and betrayal. He had even less interest in playing them than in watching them. It was why he had chosen to study the kzinti. He could spend a lifetime here and never stop learning. T'suuz alone was fascinating.

"You saw her in the tunnel, on the way to Hero's Square." He carried on his train of thought aloud, not really addressing the words to anyone. "She spoke fluently, she fought, she *planned*. Kzinretti don't do that."

Tskombe looked up from a Swiftwing simulation run. "Well, she isn't doing it anymore."

"No one's ever seen an intelligent kzinrette. This is revolutionary, and she won't *talk* to me. She's acting like a pet."

Cherenkova looked up from her own simulation. "I'm sure she has her reasons."

"If only I had more time . . ."

Their conversation was interrupted by a scream snarl from the central den: Pouncer's voice, distorted in rage. The humans looked up to watch him. "My brother has assumed the Patriarchy! My father and my uncle are dead and my own brother has betrayed their blood to the Tzaatz!" He screamed as though tortured, his claws rigidly extended, his mouth a smile of fangs. "They have tamed him with a *zzrou* like a slave animal! He is not Rrit!" There was an inarticulate howl, and then what sounded like a war of wildcats, as the other kzinti snarled words unintelligible through the din.

Brasseur looked at the other two, closed his mouth.

The tension in the air was palpable. He started to speak again, stopped, started. "We need to be leaving," he said. "This is going to get out of control."

From that point forward Brasseur put all his spare time into learning the Swiftwing's systems as well. The courier only took two pilots, but getting into the spaceport would be risky, and they might not all make it. Every day Far Hunter, Provider, and—against everyone's strong objections—a well disguised Pouncer went out to gauge the enemy's strength and intentions. What they learned was not encouraging. The Tzaatz had firm control of the spaceport, and the space defense weapons were fully operational. All the knowledge they could bring on board would be hardly enough. He pored for hours over the details of hyperspace navigation and the mass reader. Hyperdrive had been traded to the inhabitants of the We Made It colony by the Outsiders and stolen from humanity by the kzinti. It was immediately apparent that there were serious gaps in the kzinti knowledge of the system. It required an aware mind to read the mass reader, the primary instrument, for some reason to do with the observer-collapse of quantum wave-functions that was glibly but incompletely explained in the automanual. It was suspected that this was related to the Blind Spot effect, which was a trance state induced by looking directly into hyperspace with the naked eye, another observer-collapse phenomenon. There were those who were immune to the Blind Spot, and those who could not make a mass reader work. The two were correlated, and there was an almost offhand remark that both effects were related to the Telepath's Gift, another thing that was poorly understood but seemed to do with the collapse of quantum wave functions in hyperspace. That was interesting, as was the status of telepaths in kzinti society; he'd already written papers on that subject. Now was not the time, but one day the connection would be worth following up.

"Have you seen the Blind Spot?" he asked Ayla during a break in his study.

"Every pilot tries it once."

"What's it like?"

She shook her head. "You have to see it. Or *not* see it, which is the point. It can't be described."

He asked her what she knew about hyperspace, and her answers were almost verbatim what the kzinti automanual said. Evidently humanity knew little more than the kzinti. Brasseur found that frustrating too. Whoever had paid the Outsiders for the hyperdrive technology should have paid a little more for the science behind it.

Tskombe himself had advanced to singleship tactics, and again the learning curve steepened as he studied intercept curves and evasive maneuvering. At the infantry ranges he was used to, lasers traveled in straight lines and instantaneously hit their target. The hit probabilities were controlled by turret slew rates and target track precision, and the main problem was dealing with camouflage and spoofing. In space lasers dipped into gravity wells, defocused with distance and could take long seconds to reach targets that, at fifty or more gees of acceleration, could significantly alter their velocity vector in that time. As relative velocities became a significant fraction of the speed of light, relativity began to play a part and the math became truly horrendous. The ship's artificial intelligence handled the details of predictive targeting, but it in turn had to be managed to give it the best chance of a successful shot. He began to learn the intricacies of the course funnel and thrust lines, and the simulations grew more complicated. Reactionless thrusters were not truly reactionless, of course, in strict obedience to the second law of thermodynamics, and the performance curves of different drives varied not only with the magnitude and relative direction of the local gravitational gradient but with the relative and absolute motion and rotational velocity of the mass that created the gradient, an effect known as frame dragging. The Swiftwing automanual gave scant coverage to those details, and Ayla downloaded a UNSN space combat text to his beltcomp from hers. The manual called the combined gradient total-spacetime-distortion or TSTD and described it with various derivatives and integrals of four-dimensional spacetime equations. Not only TSTD but its rate of change were important and the text referred to them frequently.

The entire subject began to give him headaches. The humans had decided to sleep and wake on Kzin's twenty-seven-hour-thirty-six-minute day, and the minutiae of space combat began to invade his dreams as he lay beside Ayla after sex. After the desperate urgency of the first night their touches had become gentler, more intimate as they learned each other's bodies. He found lying beside her afterward as rewarding as the act itself, a new experience for him. Despite the danger, Tskombe found he didn't want their time on Kzin to end. It had to, though, and that meant he had to master space combat. The key was to set up conditions where your performance was better than your opponent's, which required understanding not just TSTD and delta TSTD but the relative performance of your own ship and your adversary's as those variables changed. At first it had seemed that the tremendous amount of thrust and power available to a ship gave it almost limitless options in maneuver. As his understanding grew he realized that in any given situation there were at most a handful of possible options, sometimes only one, and any time your opponent had narrowed you down to a single option your course became absolutely predictable and you became an easy target. As he developed a feel for the subject the odds stacked against them became clearer and he began to develop misgivings about the planned escape.

"I don't see how we're going to get away."

Ayla looked up from the simulation she was running and cocked an ear. "Why is that?"

"Kzinhome has twenty-four orbital battle stations, plus all the ground defenses, plus the fleet in orbit, carriers, destroyers, cruisers, battleships even. The Rrit fleet is divided: some of them have fled, some are waiting to see what happens. Maybe they won't shoot at a fleeing ship, or maybe they will. The Tzaatz fleet is up there too, and they'll certainly shoot a fleeing ship. There's a lot of fire-power in the gauntlet we have to run."

Cherenkova nodded. "Our Hero assures us we'll have a valid transponder code."

"And if it doesn't turn out to be valid?"

"If we don't get into orbit, we're in trouble. If we do, it's simple."

"Not so simple. I never made a combat landing without the whole fleet going in first to suppress the space defenses. Landers are sitting ducks in low orbit and reentry. The ground weapons will have us bull's-eyed from the space-port perimeter to the transatmosphere, and from low orbit all the way to synchronous orbit those battle stations are going to have us in their sights."

"My point exactly."

"I don't follow."

"We aren't making a combat landing, we're making an escape. The flight regime is entirely different."

"How so?"

"Because we'll be accelerating the whole way out. Getting to the ground makes you a target because you have to slow down, get stable, slide into the atmosphere and decelerate for touchdown. Every step you become more and more predictable. Going the other way the search sphere gets bigger every second and you gain more freedom of maneuver. Once we're out of the atmosphere we'll have it made."

"We're going to be in range for light-seconds. They'll send interceptors."

"Maybe, maybe not. Far Hunter says a lot of the Rrit fleet has boosted out, gone privateer, basically. The Tzaatz have limited resources up there, and nobody knows who's on what side. Confusion is our ally."

Tskombe nodded. "We have to get a ship first."

"That's your department. You get me in the cockpit, I'll get us home."

Tskombe nodded, though he was troubled by that problem too. His department was not going well. Far

Hunter was now going every morning to the spaceport, bringing fresh *vatach* and *grashi* to the Tzaatz guards, building *strakh* with them. Late in the evening he would return and make additions to the crude model of the spaceport that was growing in the back room, and the group would discuss ways of getting access to a Swiftwing. The Tzaatz guards were sloppy, but there were lots of them, and their *rapsar* sniffers made up for their lack of attention. In terms of a ground combat plan there was really only one option. They had to wait until Provider's half brother Cargo Pilot told them a courier was prepped for launch, then Far Hunter would smuggle them in with a load of game. They would get to the edge of the parking apron, then the kzinti would cover the humans while the humans got on the ship, moving with deliberate stealth, but ready to kill anyone or anything that got in their way, slave or kzin or *rapsar*. They would key in the transponder code that Pilot gave them and take off. The kzin would come back out the way they had come in. Pouncer's obligation would be discharged, the humans would be on their way home, and quite possibly there would be an interstellar war. Tskombe couldn't devote time to that thought. There wasn't enough time to do what had to be done. He went over the basics of fire-and-movement with the others, modifying the tactics to account for the fact that the kzinti would be carrying crossbows. They did some simple drills in the forest, away from Provider's neighbors. There was little other preparation they could make, and the attempt would be a gamble when the time came.

At that, it would not be the first time Quacy Tskombe

had gambled his life; but now that Ayla was sharing his bed and his thoughts the stakes had become much higher. How long had it been since that first night? His beltcomp would tell him, but the length of time was nothing; it was the emotions that counted. They had become, what? Lovers? Partners? The labels didn't really matter. They didn't talk about the future. If they survived the escape attempt the exigencies of military careers would part them as soon as they handed in final reports on their mission. That was nothing new, and they both had kept their previous relationships shallow for that very reason. Now, without either of them having planned it, it was different, and he realized he was falling in love with Captain Ayla Cherenkova. That was a strange thought for him, more than a little disturbing. Quacy Tskombe had led the life of a nomad. The son of an infantry officer himself, he had never spent more than a year in the same place, moving with his father's postings. He had gained entry to the academy at sixteen, and the four years he had spent there were the longest he had ever lived in one place. Sexual relationships for him were matters of convenience. He had learned not to get attached.

So what was different about Ayla Cherenkova, a woman even more focused on her career than he was? Perhaps it was their situation, stranded together on this hostile, alien world. Certainly that was what had brought them together, but she had trembled in his arms on the third day, allowed herself to be vulnerable with him, open the gates to the fear they had both been holding desperately inside. And after that things had changed. There was no awkwardness between them, no question but that they share the same chamber, the same *frrch*-skin bed, no question that they ended the day with sex, and Tskombe found to his amazement that it was not the rush of orgasm that drew him to her but the simple comfort of her touch, her voice, her scent.

He found himself watching her, thinking of their time together when they were home, making plans for their careers that would allow them to be together. In their current situation such thoughts were fragile, and dangerous. He hadn't shared them with her, though he imagined that she was thinking the same thing. Maybe it was how beautiful she looked as she straddled him, because she was beautiful, and grew more so to his eyes every day.

She was sitting cross legged beneath the glowlamps, working on her beltcomp. She looked up and smiled. "We *are* getting out of here."

> *Maintenes vous bien loiaux franchois je vous en pry.*
> *(Stand fast, loyal Frenchmen, I pray you)*
> —Joan of Arc to the citizens of Tournai,
> June 25, 1429

Captain Lars Detringer looked out through the bridge transpax at the distant, brilliant flare that was 61 Ursae Majoris, brighter than the full moon from Earth even at this distance. He bit his lip and considered his options. The diplomatic party had not uplinked a report in days. Accordingly he had sent a query to the kzinti defensive sphere commander. There had been no answer. Then his omnipresent escort of Hunt-class battleships had tight-beamed perfunctory apologies and then vanished into hyperspace. Now the entire kzinti command network seemed to have gone off the air, and what traffic his antennas had managed to snag out of the ether was fragmented. Ships had boosted out of orbit like hornets from a disturbed nest; other ships had appeared around the singularity's edge and fallen in under maximum thrust and in attack formations. If he didn't know better he would say there was a war underway. Except there were none of the sharp electromagnetic bursts that marked the discharge of gamma ray lasers, no sudden peaks in coded traffic that marked fleet-to-fleet engagements, no distress calls from damaged warships.

Detringer turned away from the view and paced. The bridge crew got out the way; they knew better than to disturb the captain in this kind of mood. His concern had grown to worry as the time since the group's last report had stretched out. That report had been very positive, and then . . . nothing. The worry hadn't gone away now that the unusual activity in the system seemed to have quieted down again. There was still no contact with his diplomatic party, and still no answer to his queries on the kzinti command net. He had considerable freedom of action in commanding a capital ship on detached duty, but there were few courses open to him. He couldn't leave and abandon the team on the ground. He couldn't boost into the kzinti singularity without provoking a diplomatic incident, and perhaps a fight against odds that even *Crusader* couldn't handle. He had hyperwaved a report to the UN, but it would be weeks yet before he would get an answer, and the answer was likely to leave the solution to his own discretion.

And the news coming in on hyperwave wasn't reassuring either. In the General Assembly Muro Ravalla's faction was mounting a hard press for power, and Secretary Desjardins was having trouble holding his coalition together in the face of it. Ravalla was a strident voice for preemptive war to "contain the Patriarchy while it was still containable," in his own words, although the rest of his rhetoric left little doubt he would go far beyond containment if given a free hand. Wunderland was continuing its aggressive military buildup, and it wasn't entirely clear if it was aimed at the kzinti or at the UN. Jinx and We Made It and Plateau had formed a Colonial Coalition, and were encouraging other colonies to join as a counterweight to UN hegemony. War within Known Space wasn't impossible, and Detringer didn't want to make the choices that would inevitably force on him.

He spun around to look out at 61 Ursae Majoris again, squinting at it as though he could somehow pick up the invisible pinprick that was Kzinhome, and thereby discover what was going on down there. *Ayla Cherenkova is smart and competent, and she's with a good team. Whatever is happening she'll get a message out somehow, or get here herself.* He had to believe it was true, or there was no point in waiting as he had waited, as he would wait until he got explicit orders to leave. It was a course of action he was unwilling to follow, its only merit being that it was better than any other. He *did* have faith in her; he'd seen what she could do as their careers had paralleled each other over the years. Her colleagues had seemed equally competent, equally qualified. If anyone could handle the situation, whatever that situation was, they could, he was convinced. *Except there are three of them against a world of predators, and something has gone drastically wrong.* If he knew nothing else he knew that. Skill and competence could only take you so far in a situation like that, and then you needed luck, and a lot of it.

There was nothing to do but wait. He turned on his heel and started pacing once more.

> *Alea iacta est*
> *(The die is cast.)*
> —Julius Caesar at the Rubicon

Days later they made their attempt. It was stiflingly hot beneath the *grashi* cages in the back of Provider's gravcar, and the stagnant air mingled their musk with the gingery scent of kzin. Tskombe was lying flat on his back in the vehicle's cargo bed with the board that supported the cages a handspan from his nose, his magrifle digging uncomfortably into his chest, and crushed between T'suuz and Pouncer tight enough that breathing was difficult. The space had been built for just the three humans, and with the two kzinti packed in it was claustrophobic, to say the least. Far Hunter and Provider were flying the gravcar to the spaceport, just another meal run for the hungry Tzaatz who guarded it, or so they hoped. Cargo Pilot had identified a Swiftwing for them, fueled, serviced and now delayed on the ground while the V'rarr Pride delegates it was to take to hyperspace finished some convoluted negotiation with the Tzaatz. While they did that the humans were going to steal their ship. There was a final council of war around Provider's big table, debating the best strategy

to get to the ship. Everyone had thought it was a bad idea
to bring Pouncer; his presence increased the risk of detection, increased the danger if detection did occur, and did
not materially improve their chances of success. Pouncer,
of course, had insisted on coming. His honor demanded
no less than his personal presence for those his pride was
sworn to protect, and now Tskombe muttered subvocal
curses at a species that held honor higher than common
sense. The plan now was that Pouncer would escort them
aboard the Swiftwing and see them away, at which point
Provider would take him and T'suuz over the
Mooncatcher Mountains to the jungle and whatever
refuge they could find there. If any of them survived that
long.

They bumped down, and he heard muted snarls from
above, not quite loud enough for him to follow the conversation, though he recognized Far Hunter's voice. Then the
clang of steel cage bars and the now familiar squeal of
grashi about to be eaten as Far Hunter traded food for
strakh with the Tzaatz perimeter guards. Tskombe tried
not to breathe as the snarls came closer. Was there a
sniffer? Several times he thought he heard something
snuffling, questing after him. But after a time the
thrusters whined and the gravcar lifted off, and very shortly
touched down again. The plastic sheeting that had concealed them was stripped off and he found himself blinking
in the sunlight.

"Quickly." Provider's voice was a muted growl. "This is
as close as we can get."

Pouncer leapt out of the space, and Tskombe rolled
over and followed him awkwardly. Pouncer and the other

kzinti carried crossbows and variable swords; the humans
had the weapons Yiao-Rrit had given them in the Citadel,
a time that already seemed to belong to someone else's
life. Tskombe's magrifle was in a fabric sheath that he carried on his back like a slave's packload. T'suuz and the
humans were all on leashes, a move designed to reduce
suspicion. Humans were almost unheard-of on Kzin, but
the leashes implied they were under kzin control and thus
not dangerous.

At least that was the theory. They had modified their
collars to break away with a tug in an emergency, but
Tskombe still found it galling to be led around by
Provider. Cherenkova's face showed her discomfort plainly,
but Brasseur seemed unfazed. Had he done this before on
W'kkai for his research? Tskombe didn't want to ask. Far
Hunter beckoned and they moved off.

The gravcar had landed in a yard full of freight containers
next to the ship bay where the Swiftwing was grounded,
and a couple of hundred meters away a group of Jotoki
slaves were working to unload a careworn freighter.
Further away a handful of kzinti discussed something with
lashing tails, and the sounds of their snarling conversation
occasionally rose above the thrum of machinery that pervaded the port. Nobody seemed to have noticed them,
and they set off, Far Hunter leading. They traveled in two
groups, Tskombe with Provider and Far Hunter,
Cherenkova and Brasseur with Pouncer and T'suuz. The
humans had communications through their beltcomps if
they needed them. Again the goal was to reduce suspicion. Tzaatz patrols were heavy throughout the port, but
Cargo Pilot's information was that the Swiftwing was

empty. If they made it that far they were safe, or at least safer. If they were caught before then their odds of making it out alive were vanishingly slight.

Almost on cue a pair of *rapsar* raiders came around the corner of the terminal building. The Jotoki immediately prostrated themselves to the Tzaatz riders, and the arguing kzinti stopped to look up. The reptilian raiders sniffed the air while the Tzaatz scanned the area. Tskombe forced himself to relax and walk casually, not even looking in the guard's direction. *How will kzinti know if a human is walking casually?* They wouldn't, most especially not at two hundred meters. Still he couldn't suppress the reflex. They turned a corner, found themselves in a long alley between stacked containers, and he keyed his com.

"Cherenkova, Tskombe, are they following us?"

"Negative. They've moved off around the terminal. We're leaving the gravcar now, staying about a hundred meters behind you."

"Acknowledged." *Even now her voice touches my soul.*

"The Swiftwing is in the next ship bay," Far Hunter said. "On the other side of this yard."

"Let's just keep walking."

They continued in silence past ranked cargo containers, each coded with the dots and commas of the kzinti script. Far Hunter walked just a little distance away—far enough to respond to any attack on Provider and Tskombe, not so far as to be obviously in a defensive posture. It seemed to take forever to thread their way through the storage yard, but then they passed the last container and a parked gravlifter. The Swiftwing was in the center of the ship bay, ramp closed.

And there were the Tzaatz guards again with their *rapsari*. They must have paralleled the group. The leader gestured peremptorily. "You! With the slaves. Come here."

One of the Tzaatz beckoned imperiously and Tskombe felt his whole body tense, but Provider simply moved as the Tzaatz commanded. His voice was a muted snarl. "Their mag armor is off. They are suspicious, no more. No one can see us here. If there is a problem we will take them silently at close range."

"As you command, Father." Far Hunter's voice was calm.

"*Kz'zeerkti*, you are to cover the beasts with your weapon. Fire only if you have to."

"Got it." Tskombe could barely get the words out. Would the Tzaatz smell his fear? Of course they would, but a slave amongst kzinti would be expected to be afraid.

They drew close to the riders. Far Hunter claw-raked, Provider did not.

"How are you known?" The Tzaatz bore rank tattoos on his ears, but Tskombe didn't know how to read them.

"I am Provider, once Tank Leader of the M'nank Conquest to Avenari. This is my son, Far Hunter."

"And what are you doing here?" There was suspicion in the guard's voice.

"I owe my half brother *strakh*, and will gain much shipping this slave off-world."

"Hero's Square is the place for trading, old one."

"My half brother is not coming to the market."

"Hrrr . . ." The Tzaatz paused, considering. "What type of slave is this?"

"*Kz'zeerkti*."

"So I thought." The Tzaatz paused, scrutinizing Tskombe. "Where did you get it?"

"It came to me from a noble who owed me *strakh* for saving his life."

"We are searching for three *kz'zeerkti*. Perhaps this is one of them. You must bring it before Chruul-Commander."

Provider claw-raked. "With respect, I cannot."

"You have no choice." The Tzaatz drew his variable sword to emphasize his point, but before he could extend it Provider had drawn his own and decapitated him. Far Hunter screamed and leapt for the second Tzaatz, but the warrior had backpedaled his mount, and Provider's son found himself latched on to the reptilian creature's throat and underbelly with teeth and claws. The *rapsar* screamed in pain and ripped its assailant loose with its foreclaws. Far Hunter fell to the ground bleeding, and then the Tzaatz turned the raider and spurred it away.

As soon as Provider had moved Tskombe had ripped off the slave collar and backed up three paces, instinctively pulling the mag rifle over his shoulder and stripping the concealing sleeve off it. As the second Tzaatz fled he rolled to the ground and into firing position. *Fire only in emergency*. This certainly counted: if the Tzaatz got away their escape would be compromised. The butt of the weapon found his shoulder as his eye found the scope. *Short bursts*, he reminded himself; the kzin built weapon had a ferocious kick. Breathe out, breathe in and squeeze . . .

The magrifle roared and three crystal iron penetrators blasted through the back of the Tzaatz's unpowered mag armor like tissue paper. The warrior's body exploded in a mist of blood and shattered bone, and the penetrators, barely impeded by the impacts, carried on to decapitate the *rapsar* as well. Two kilometers away a spherical hydrogen storage bubble exploded into a ball of almost invisible blue flames. For long seconds the weapon's echoes reverberated over the noise of the port, and then the dull rumble of the tank's explosion reached them. For another second there was only silence, and then the alarms went off.

There was a paw on his shoulder, pulling him to his feet. His instincts told him to fire but the kzin's grip would not allow it, and then he recognized Provider. "*Kz'zeerkti!* Get on the ship! My son and I will stay here to guide the others to you."

And Tskombe realized he would never again see either of these two enemy aliens who had risked their lives to save him. *What can I say at a moment like this?* Words from his childhood floated back. "*Salaam alychem*"—go with peace, the ancient prayer of Mohammed in his father's rusty Arabic.

"Run!" Provider took the magrifle from him and pushed him toward the Swiftwing. In the distance he could see Tzaatz units responding to the emergency, though none knew yet what the emergency was. He had some time, not much. He ran, arriving forty seconds and three hundred meters later trembling and out of breath, then spent another panicked minute trying to open the cover that protected the ship's ramp release. Finally he got it open, punched the button and the ramp hissed down. He took two more seconds to look for Ayla and Brasseur before he ran in, and then he had to spend another thirty seconds getting the cockpit unsealed. Once inside Tskombe strapped himself in to the oversized acceleration couch fumbling to find the adjustments to bring it close enough to the controls for him to reach them. *Start the checklist, get everything running.* When Ayla got there she'd only have to strap in and boost.

He started running down the items he'd memorized in countless simulation runs. Primary power, on; check power cell level, it was orange which was good; light hydrogen tanks, purged; primary cooling, on and pressurized; tritium deuteride feed—on, wait for the fuel state to stabilize. He looked out the window, saw Provider open fire on a half a dozen *rapsar*-mounted Tzaatz who were moving into the launch bay. *Was he allowed to do that?* No time for the complexities of the honor code. The thirty seconds it took for the fusion reaction to heat up and stabilize seemed to last an eternity. Outside the window the fight was stalemated, both sides forced to cover behind cargo containers, but that would only last until the Tzaatz brought up reinforcements. Thruster power, on; thruster check, forward, rear, port, starboard—all on and all off, positive; transponder on; a glance to check the clearance code symbols scrawled on the back of his hand and too much time to get them entered, and then pray the space defense weapons recognized the code; autopilot—should be on but they wouldn't have time to load the course data, so off. *Where are you, Ayla?* Boarding ramp—leave it open, have to remember to close it when she got on. A crystal iron slug *spang*ed off the transpax, leaving a gray smear and making his hands shake with adrenaline. Weren't the kzinti forbidden the use of such weapons?

What were the rules? Stick with the checklist. Out-com—skip it. In-com—skip it. Navigation—skip that too. Life support—on. A warning light flashed—hull integrity breach, and the loading ramp whined shut to turn it off. It took him an eternal minute to find the override to re-extend it.

Come on, Ayla! He toggled his beltcomp, talked into the microphone. "Cherenkova, this is Tskombe, where the hell are you?"

"There's more Tzaatz in the container yard. We've had to pull back. I can't get to the ship."

"Where are you?"

"Back at the other bay near the gravcar. We can't see Provider or Far Hunter."

"Hang on, I'll bring the ship to you."

Deep breath—*you've done this a thousand times on the simulator.* But this was no simulator, this was an alien starship and he was in the middle of a firefight and that wasn't a simulation either. His pilot, his partner, his lover was out there and he had to get her aboard. *Ground combat is my job, Ayla, you should be flying the ship.*

More slugs rang off the hull. Mag armor! He reached over, flipped the switch, saw the transpax view get dimmer as the high gauss field forced the molecules into some semblance of a polarizer. What else was he forgetting? Flight information displays to atmospheric, what else? No time for anything else. He put his hands on the controls, dialed in power and biased the polarizers backward. The Swiftwing shuddered, and he fed in power and bias together. The courier parted company with the landing apron and lurched into the air. The simulator had never lurched, and Tskombe cut power instinctively, causing the ship to drop like a rock from three meters. In desperation he shoved the power back on, preventing a complete crash, but the ship still hit the ground hard, the forward momentum it had picked up in the short hop sending it skidding over a repair trolley with a sickening crunch. No time to assess the damage; power back on, gently this time, shift thrusters back and swing. The principle was the same as a combat car, but the Swiftwing was tremendously cumbersome. *And they call this a light ship.* He'd always wondered why battleships maneuvered with such ponderous care. Now he knew.

A synthesized kzin voice snarled something in his ear about ground proximity—some warning mode that he could doubtless override if he knew how and had time to do it. For now it was just a distraction. The movement of the courier ship had drawn the attention of the Tzaatz, and now they shifted fire. More crystal iron slugs caromed off the transpax, aimed this time, not stray shots, and a couple of times the panes flickered black as they damped out a visible spectrum laser pulse. He could feel the heat coming off them despite the superconductor film that dumped it to the Swiftwing's frame. A couple more hits and he'd lose a pane, mag armor or not, and that would be the end of that.

So don't take hits, torque the thrusters around, spin the ship so its back is pointing at the enemy, thrusters to full rear, spike the power to emergency and down again. The courier shot forward as though from a mag launcher and he felt his weight surge sickeningly as the artificial gravity compensated. The spin was still on the ship and he quickly brought the thrust back to vertical and guided it higher as it spun toward the perimeter fence. As he came back facing the way he had come he could see the results of his efforts: a container stack sent flying like a giant had kicked it, broken crates strewn two hundred meters. He couldn't see if he'd managed to hit any of the Tzaatz, but the flying cargo must have at least distracted them. At least there was no incoming fire for the moment. He considered trying the trick again, but time was not on his side and the thrusters were an imprecise weapon even in skilled hands, which his most certainly were not.

So get Ayla, get her hands on the controls and get out of here. Wobbling and bouncing, he set a course for the control tower.

"Cherenkova, Tskombe, what's your status?"

"We're still here." Her voice crackled on the com. "Incoming fire has stopped for now. You be careful with that thing."

"I'm doing my best."

"Just don't break it."

Movement on the edge of the spaceport caught his eye. He keyed transmit. "You've got combat cars coming in from the southwest."

"Acknowledged. We're moving farther south now, before the ratcats here get reorganized."

Tskombe threw a worried glance at the incoming dots, four of them, getting big fast. The tower was coming closer, but he'd put a lot of distance between it and him when he'd pulsed the drive. He resisted the impulse to crank on more speed. He lacked the finesse to bring the courier down where he wanted to; he'd have to accept the slow approach if he was going to get close to Ayla.

He looked up. The cars were coming too fast—they'd be there before he was. Blue-white lines lanced across the sky at him, air ionized to plasma by their lasers. No choice then, but take it carefully. He edged up the power, felt the Swiftwing surge forward. His brief flight had taken him over a kilometer and a half across the spaceport. Below slaves and kzinti alike were watching, not yet understanding who was who in the battle now in progress.

Handle the combat cars first. The Swiftwing's AI had a self-defense mode. He hunted the control panel, flipped up a safety cover, slapped the toggle. A series of cannisters chugged into the air, arcing over his head toward the combat cars. Five hundred meters distant they blossomed into silver dust clouds, some of them hitting the ground first, leaving long silver streaks behind them. What was that about? *Do the kzinti consider that a weapon?* No, those were dusters, packed with aluminum microspheres designed to frustrate laser beams. The dust was too fine to disperse quickly in atmosphere; the defense systems were set for space. He slapped another toggle for ground mode and cursed an AI that could pick up threats just by tracking optical flow but couldn't tell if it was in space or on the ground unless you told it. Hydraulics hummed as the turrets swung into position, then incandescent lines stabbed at the incoming combat cars. One fireballed and fell, but the others ducked down, hugging the ground and getting below Tskombe's line of fire. The stricken vehicle hit a liquid oxygen bubble at speed, triggering a fire that splashed white hot, igniting whatever it touched to burn explosively. Below him the onlookers started running for cover, belatedly realizing the danger.

There was a plan. Target the bubbles and wreak absolute havoc. Some would be full of hydrogen, which burned hot but rose too quickly to do much damage, but almost anything would burn in contact with lox. A few ruptured oxygen bubbles would keep the Tzaatz well occupied. Except the AI didn't recognize the bubbles as threats and Tskombe was overloaded with piloting as it was. He had no chance at all of putting the weapons on manual, even if he could figure out how to do that, which was far from certain.

It occurred to him that the enemy were now Tzaatz and not kzinti. *I have shifted my paradigm.* Brasseur would be proud. He pushed the thought away. Just fly, get Ayla on board, get on the weapons and then the enemy would be anyone downrange. He refocused on the control tower, coming up now too quickly, and eased the power back. Not enough. He eased it more, scanned for her hiding place.

"Four hundred meters in front of you." Her voice was clear. She was reading his mind. "Reference the loader bay. We're right there."

He scanned the horizon, found the bay, nudged the controls slightly left to bring it down. The combat cars were still out of sight, down below buildings. They'd have to slow down to maneuver there, and the ship's guns were a match for them. Seconds to go now. He cut power, grounded the ship, skidding sideways into a parked loader and sending the wreckage careening into another one further down. Jotoki cargo slaves were fleeing in every direction, along with a few kzinti overseers who had no idea what was going on. He was a hundred meters from the bay where Ayla was, not great flying but close enough. Loading ramp down. He looked for the switch, remembered he'd already overridden life support to keep it extended.

"Okay, the ramp is down. Go!"

"Coming . . ." She was already running, her breathing heavy in the microphone. A hundred meters—ten seconds for an Olympic sprinter, maybe fifteen for Ayla. "Tanj!" She was panting, and she'd stopped.

"What?"

"We've got ground troops coming in." A hail of crystal iron slugs rang off the hull to underline her words. Tskombe looked around, picked up a two-sword of Tzaatz in battle armor and grav belts, shooting at the ship with mag rifles from behind some cargo haulers.

"Where are you?"

"We're moving south to the control tower, out of the line of fire."

The AI wasn't shooting back. Why not? Some mode somewhere was letting it ignore small targets. "Have they seen you?" He fumbled with the controls while he spoke, trying to change the AI settings.

"I don't think so. They're all focused on you."

Tskombe breathed out. Ayla couldn't run through the firestorm to get on board, but as long as no one saw her she'd be safe. *I should be worried about Kefan, too.* He wasn't, not in the same way. *She is my mate now.* That simple fact made a tremendous difference. He assessed the situation. He was safe enough for a few seconds. The light weapons couldn't hurt the ship, unless the gunners got lucky. He keyed his beltcomp. "Hang tight, I'll take care of them." Even as he said it a warning horn sounded and the damage control panel lit up. They'd hit something external and the computer snarled something about pitch sensors. No time to worry about that; forget the AI, get the guns under manual control and start taking names. It took more time than he had to figure out the command sequences, but he got the bottom turret responding and a targeting graticule on the viewscreen. There would be a way to change the spectral response, pick out moving targets, but there was no time to find it. He swung the graticule around until it intersected the leftmost hauler, fired, traversed to the next one, fired, traversed again, walking the fire through the enemy position, leaving a trail of burning wreckage behind him. The fire slackened, but more slugs rang off the hull. Another caution light came on and the computer snarled another warning.

Most of the two-sword must be dead by now, but the survivors were still shooting, though they stood no chance at all against a starship with mag armor engaged. His weapons were light for a ship, more than heavy for ground combat. *Don't they give up?*

The transpax flared white and went dark, the heat from the blocked laser bolt hitting him like a physical blow. If the mag armor hadn't been on the panes would have blown in and killed him. No hand-carried beamer would do that; the combat cars were on the scene. The AI traversed the top turret and fired at a threat it could understand, and an explosion blossomed two thousand meters away at the edge of the cargo area. *This is getting out of hand.*

Another combat car popped up, fired and dropped down again before the AI could target it. While the top turret was still slewing to track it another popped up and down, this one closer. The only consolation was that the quick exposures were too short for the Tzaatz gunnery systems too, and their beams went wide.

That would change as they worked their way closer. The courier was a big target, and they were small and agile. The closer they got the more accurate they'd be, and the larger the angles his turrets would have to move through to engage them. He was running out of time. Another hail of crystal iron penetrators reminded him that there were still ground troops out there.

So, get the ship as close to Ayla as he dared, shield her with its mass from the small arms, get her on board, and get the hell out of there. He put another series of bolts into the troops around the haulers, slapped the bottom turret back to AI control, and grabbed the controls. The Swiftwing lurched into the air and slid toward the loading bay. He finessed it around, trying to get the ramp pointing toward Ayla and the nose pointing at the enemy. He almost had it when a terrific impact slammed the ship to the ground, the horizon jolting sideways and coming to rest lopsided. The AI snarled about thruster failure and Cherenkova was screaming in his ear. "Tanks! They've got tanks!" An explosion near the loading bay cut her off and when she came back on the air she was coughing. "Kefan just got hit. Go! Quacy! Take off!"

"Get aboard!"

"I can't get to the ship. Just go! They don't know we're here."

He couldn't see the tanks, but another heavy impact rolled the little ship. If he was going to leave it had to be now.

He keyed the transmitter. "I'm not going without you."

"Tanj it, Quacy, Kefan is dead! They're going to kill me shooting at you! Get out of here!"

Another explosion cut her off and he knew she was right. If she was going to survive he had to get the fire away from the immediate area. The Tzaatz had too many forces on the ground now. Still he hesitated a long second, long enough for another tank round to slam the Swiftwing sideways. The damage control panel flashed like a Christmas tree and the computer announced the destruction of the top turret. There was no other option. He slammed the thrust levers to emergency and the acceleration kicked him back hard. The courier spiraled upward, the horizon canting crazily sideways as he fought to compensate for the damaged thruster. His ears popped suddenly and painfully, blinding him with sudden agony. Somewhere there was a stability augmentation mode that would let the computer do it for him, but it was all he could do to keep the ship roughly level. All the training he'd done to learn how to fly an orbital insertion was out the window. This would be a power-wasting direct ascent launch.

The synthesized voice was saying something, distant through his throbbing, ringing ears. Probably important. He listened closer. Pressure warning? What pressure? He felt lightheaded, trying to understand what was going on. Hydraulics? Hydrogen feed? What other pressures were important on a Swiftwing? Coolant? He checked the indicators but they were level. Were they? He peered closer, trying to figure that out should be easy, just a glance, but his head was muzzy and his eyes wouldn't focus. Why was that? The sky outside was turning from blue to purple.

The pain in his ears suddenly made sense. Cabin pressure! He found the toggle for the boarding ramp override, stared at it for a long moment to make sure it was the right one, and flipped it closed. There was a whine behind him and the sudden hiss of air. His ears popped again and he breathed deep. A stupid mistake, and nearly fatal. How high was he? The instrument panel said three five-hundred-twelves and seven sixty-fours in whatever the kzinti units were, the eights and ones figures spinning up too fast to read. High enough that the sky was already fading from purple to black. He breathed deep, feeling better. Hypoxia gave you two minutes before unconsciousness at best.

Dammit, Ayla, you're the pilot. Kzinhome was invisible behind him but its defense systems hadn't chopped him out of the sky so at least the transponder codes must be correct. Outside the stars were bright and hard. He was out of the atmosphere, on his way out of orbit. A Swiftwing did over a hundred gravities reacting against Kzinhome's mass—less with one thruster out of action, but still far more than the four a combat car was capable of. The violent oscillations died down as Kzinhome's mass receded behind him. The TSTD integral was turning from a plane to a point. He breathed deep again and edged the nose down to pick up orbital speed, then started to slide the thrust vector around into line with Kzinhome's rotation vector. Despite the ragged takeoff his power profile wasn't too far out of line. He wasn't about to be stranded in deep space, as long as he didn't make any more mistakes. Skin heating had been right at maximum though. Thank Finagle he hadn't ripped the seals off the loading ramp. He dialed back thrust and called up the navigation screen to set up his boost profile to the singularity's edge. His beltcomp held *Crusader*'s orbital data.

A chime chimed and the com screen lit up to show a kzin in space armor. "Swiftwing eight four two, I am Fourth-Flight Leader. Identify cargo and destination." Fourth-Flight Leader sounded bored, a routine check, but when Tskombe looked at the screen the kzin's eyes widened. He snarled something unintelligible, reached for a control, and the screen went blank again. The kzin had seen an enemy alien in the cockpit, and that was all the identification he needed.

So much for his fears about the transponder codes. Now a fighter pilot somewhere knew who he was. So what to do about that? He looked out the transpax, but of course Fourth Flight was invisible against the hard black, even if they were inside his field of view. They would know where he was, though, and they'd be plotting their intercept this very instant, as well as informing the rest of the kzinti defenses about his location. It would take the fighters some time to close. They had no lasers, but an orbital battle station could vaporize just about anything it could see, and there had to be more than one that had a line of sight to him right now. *Do the Rrit or the Tzaatz control them now?* It didn't matter; either was liable to shoot at a fleeing human in a stolen ship. Adrenaline surged and he yanked the controls hard over, wasting power. There had to be an evasive action mode in the AI.

What was it Ayla had told him? It was hard to get close to a planet, much easier to get away. He hoped fervently that she was right. He shoved the thrusters to emergency again. He had no hope of navigating to rendezvous with *Crusader*, if *Crusader* was even still waiting at the singularity's edge. He had to simply get out of the system and get into hyperspace. He'd have time on the boost to figure out the hyperdrive, if he didn't get shot out of the sky first.

Keep the thrusters on full, and keep a wiggle on the control column to keep the battle stations off target. He didn't even bother trying to bring up the sensor systems to get his single surviving turret ready. Even if he could make predictive targeting work, his weapons lacked the power to be effective against an orbital fortress. Unfortunately the reverse was not true, and the only defense he had was hard maneuver and distance. He might get one of the fighters, if they got close enough, but the AI's close defense routines could do that for him, hopefully. Almost as an afterthought he flipped the defense environment toggle back to space.

A data window appeared, projected holographically on the transpax and covered in combat icons. The huge but visibly shrinking sphere must be Kzinhome; the rest were mysterious. One of the icons blinked, and at the same time he heard the now familiar *chunk chunk chunk* of dusters being launched. Moments later silver spheres blossomed in front of him, getting rapidly bigger as the Swiftwing overtook them. Suddenly one of them flared sun bright as an invisible laser beam blasted aluminum dust into energized ions. He had a single panicked second of adrenaline surge as it exploded past. They *were* shooting at him. Desperately he twitched the controls back and forth in what he hoped was a random and unpredictable pattern. At the same time hydraulics whined and the AI announced it was targeting something. Fourth Flight must be close behind, maybe already launching missiles.

So how far out were the battle stations? It didn't really matter; he had no idea where they were, no idea what tactics to employ if he did know where they were. There was a wide difference between theory and practice, and all he knew was that every second he kept accelerating put them farther behind. The fighters could chase him, might catch him yet with their superior acceleration, but they had limited power reserves. If he could run far enough fast enough they would have to give it up and go home. Then the worry would be warships, cruisers and destroyers on patrol high up in the gravity well. They'd have his course information and they had both the power and the drives to intercept him. If he got caught by as much as a scout ship he'd die; it was that simple.

But Ayla would have known about them, and she would have known how to deal with interception. There was a way to survive the situation.

Ayla . . . Is she even alive? He felt his stomach tighten. He didn't even want to consider the possibility that she might not be. She was with Pouncer, she had the protection of the Rrit, and he had now come to understand fully what that meant. She would not die while the Patriarch's son lived. But Pouncer remained a fugitive on his own world, and his body would only stop the first beam. It was the Tzaatz who were in control of the spaceport, and the operation had gone badly wrong. Had that last tank round killed her, or injured her so badly she couldn't avoid capture? The Tzaatz would search now, and if they caught her they would put her in the hunt park.

In combat all is chaos.
                                                            —Si-Rrit

Crystal iron penetrators stitched the ground around Provider, but none came dangerously close. Two full swords of Tzaatz had arrived almost immediately after the Tskombe-*kz'zeerkti*'s shots had alerted them, but too late to stop the sprinting alien from getting aboard the Swiftwing. The Tzaatz were firing at the ship now, not him, but their use of energy weapons justified his own. He aimed the magrifle and fired, controlled bursts that killed two immediately. The advance stopped as the enemy took cover, but now they knew there was another threat out there. Once they located him it was only a matter of time before he died; the numbers allowed no other result. The smart option would be to take advantage of the confusion and escape.

Honor had other demands. First-Son-of-Meerz-Rrit would have heard the shots and be on his way as quickly as possible. The other humans would need cover fire to get to the ship, and he was the only one who could provide it. He could not leave, but . . .

"Son, find the other humans, guide them here!"

Far Hunter had moved to cover behind a large shipping

container, his crossbow leveled at the Tzaatz but far out of range. "I cannot leave you here!"

Provider half turned to face his son, feeling the kill rage swell in his liver. "By your name I command your obedience! Go!"

"Father—"

Provider locked eyes with his son. "Go!"

There was a final hesitation, then . . . "At once, sire!" Far Hunter left at a sprint and Provider returned to his weapon, sending a burst toward a half sword of Tzaatz skirmishing forward to better fire positions. Sending his son as a guide was a smart decision. Armed with only hand weapons he could not help here, and having him guide in the aliens would save time. It would also keep Far Hunter out of the line of fire, a consideration he did not admit to himself was more important to him even than his honor. Rounds stitched the area around him, none too close. It was still spec fire; they hadn't spotted him yet. That wouldn't last long.

Across the landing bay a Tzaatz showed his head from behind a gravloader. Provider pumped a round into the vehicle drive compartment. Its power cell shorted and the vehicle vanished in a blinding flash, throwing burning wreckage across the bay. One threat gone, regardless of his mag armor. His position wasn't bad: down on the ground, partially covered by the fibercrete footings of some unfinished structure. The sun was high, and thermal sensors would have trouble picking him out against the warm backdrop. How long till First-Son brought the humans? Far Hunter had only left moments ago, but the distance was not large. Far across the spaceport he saw

movement and he took a second to sight on it through the
magrifle's searchscope: a full sword of Tzaatz in gravbelts
deploying in response to the alarms. He didn't waste his
precious few rounds on such difficult targets. The enemy
across the landing bay were the more immediate threat.
More rounds slammed into the courier ship. If the human
managed to get its weapons up and running that would
make a tremendous difference, but could the alien do
that? The courier's drives where whining as it powered up.
At least it was wasting no time.

Provider fired again, this burst knocking a Tzaatz off
his *rapsar*, but his target landed in a roll and bounded to
his feet again. The Tzaatz had their mag armor powered
up now, and the time of easy killing was over. He was
sighted on another Tzaatz but his target dodged behind
cover before he could stabilize the shot. The whine of the
courier's thrusters spiked and vanished into the supersonic,
and an instant later there was a violent *crunch*. He looked
up to see the Swiftwing skidding across the bay, dragging
crushed ground equipment in a shower of sparks, its loading ramp still extended. It lifted again, spun around and
was suddenly gone in a blur. Across the bay containers,
equipment and Tzaatz alike flew through the air in the
wake of the thruster's reaction pulse.

Provider didn't hesitate. The human was gone. It hadn't
seemed the type to embrace the shame of cowardice, but
who could judge the rules of alien honor? Suffice that his
own duty obligation was now discharged. Now he had to
find his son. He emptied the remaining magrifle bolts at a
formation of heavy assault *rapsari* moving across the field
in the distance, then abandoned the weapon and ran into

the forest of containers. Cover, for a time. Far Hunter would be there somewhere, hopefully with First-Son-of-Meerz-Rrit. It was time to go. He moved off at a lope, inhaling deeply to follow his son's familiar scent trail. He covered the ground easily, formulating a plan as he moved. They would meet up, return to the gravcar, leave the way they came, boosting high and fast, without stealth. The Tzaatz would be unlikely to stop a vehicle *leaving* the spaceport; their concern would be directed outward, but if he and his companions were stopped, then fleeing the firefight was all the excuse they needed. The preoccupied Tzaatz would not question that.

He rounded a stack of shipping containers and sniffed left, sniffed right, chose the righthand path. Far Hunter's scent was faint, for he had been moving fast; farther on it would be heavier as his exertion made him sweat. Where was he? Time was short. Another intersection, but before he could assess the scent trail the *slap* of air suddenly ionized by high-powered lasers sent him to cover. The Swiftwing was coming back, its turrets stabbing fire at something he couldn't see. A series of flashes blossomed on its hull and he had sudden knowledge of the nature of its targets, born of the beltful of campaigns he'd fought as Tank Leader. Medium laser hits—the Tzaatz were bringing up combat cars. That was a bad thing.

He heard movement and froze: footfalls, heading fast for the landing bay, enough for three kzin and two aliens. Why were they going in that direction? Surely they'd seen the Swiftwing take flight, and the humans had communications. Was Tskombe-*kz'zeerkti* coming back to the landing bay?

No time for theories; he had to link up with them. He launched himself down the narrow corridor between the racked containers to intercept, came around a corner.

Found himself face to face with four Tzaatz and two harrier *rapsari*, managed to brake before he actually collided with them.

"Halt!" The lead Tzaatz snarled the command by reflex, as startled as Provider was. For a split second he considered running, but the Tzaatz carried beamrifles as well as hand weapons. Did the rules of honor apply with a heavy weapons firefight going on overhead? If he stood his ground the rules would apply, and he could fight. If he ran they would not, and the beamrifles would cut him in half before he'd gone two leaps.

"I halt for no Tzaatz." He snarled the words defiantly, but he had halted. His crossbow was gone and so he drew his variable sword.

"You'll die for that insult, carrion eater." The lead Tzaatz was big, well muscled, his fur laced with white lines that marked battle scars, his belt heavy with the ears of his enemies.

Provider adjusted his stance. "Leap if you dare, *sthondat*. I was a warrior before your father lost his spots."

The Tzaatz flicked his tail. "You'd like me to leap, wouldn't you, old one? You'd like a quick death in combat and some honor for your name—not that you have a name." The contempt in the officer's voice was as clear as it was casual, his voice rich in the guttural undertones of Jotok's counterspinward dialect. "It isn't going to be that easy for you." He paused, sizing up Provider as though he were a game animal. "No, for you it's going to be very hard." He made a gesture to one of the others. "Take him." The Tzaatz warrior raised his weapon.

Provider screamed his challenge and leapt, but the Tzaatz had a netgun and fired before he was halfway to his target. He landed in a ball, tightly wrapped in carbon monofilament. Instinctively he slashed with the variable sword, the molecule-wide slicewire cutting through the tough fibers with ease—but it was awkward, it took time, and they were already on him, a foot smashing into his wrist to disarm him, a beamrifle butt slamming into his head, more blows against his ribcage. He defended himself as best he could but hampered by the net, outnumbered four to one, there was little he could do. The blows rained down unceasingly, stunning him, each impact reducing his ability to avoid the next. Pain flared as bones broke, but the Tzaatz continued their assault. The harrier *rapsari* scented blood, moved closer, long tongues licking over razor sharp triangular teeth, hungering for their piece of the kill. Rage flooded Provider and he grabbed up his fallen variable sword with his good hand, slashing awkwardly through the shredded net. He connected with one attacker, but the slicewire glanced off shiny mag armor without effect. Another blow from behind slammed him to his knees and he rolled painfully. He stabbed upward with the sword, and the low angle let him slide it under the Tzaatz officer's belly plate. The officer died, choking on his own blood, and all semblence of restraint vanished from the rest of the sword, devolved now into a screaming mob, punishing him with blows from all sides. Perhaps the intent had been to take him alive; now their only goal was to kill. A weapon slammed into the back of

Provider's head and he pitched forward to lie motionless, still half covered by the net. One of the harrier *rapsari* sank its teeth into his ankle, sawing at it wildly, but Provider didn't move.

From the edge of the landing bay Far Hunter watched them beating his father as another sword of Tzaatz mounted on *rapsari* raiders arrived on the scene. He had given up searching for First-Son-of-Meerz-Rrit, had realized when the courier came over that the aliens and the Patriarch's heir would no longer be moving toward him. He had turned around to find his father, had spotted him just heartbeats before the Tzaatz had netted him. He had fought down the instant rage that demanded he attack at once; he was no good to his father dead. Honor demanded vengeance, but today was not the day he would have it. Instead he watched the fight, watched as they dragged the lifeless body away like a netted *griltor,* watched until the Tzaatz were out of sight, his claws rigidly extended, ears laid flat, fangs bared.

Only when they were gone did he stand. There was little time if he wanted to escape, but honor came first. Very deliberately he hooked one claw beneath the skin above his right eye, feeling it stab, fresh and sharp. He dragged it slowly, excruciatingly down and across the bridge of his nose, felt his other claws dig in as he did so, continued down to the opposite cheek, tearing the flesh deep enough that he felt bone beneath his claw. Blood welled up in the open wounds and he breathed hard against the pain. The wound would scar—visible evidence of the vengeance oath he swore in snarls through his clenched teeth. Blood dripped down into his right eye and he wiped it away. Neither his blood nor his pain mattered, would ever matter again. The only thing that mattered was that the day would come when he would swim in the blood of the Tzaatz. There would be a search now, and the blood might bring the sniffers, but the spaceport was large and had many places to hide, and he was used to covering his tracks in close country. His lips twitched over his fangs as he waited for the sun to slide to the horizon. Night would bring the first taste of his vengeance to the Tzaatz, but not the last. His tail lashed unconsciously as he laid his plans. No, not the last by far. *Father, you have taught me well.*

> **No plan survives enemy contact.**
> **—Anonymous**

The Swiftwing rocked as another tank round hit it, and a second tank penetrator slammed into the already wrecked storage building behind Ayla, spraying razor shards of fibercrete, knocking her to the ground. She looked up, momentarily dazed. Pouncer and T'suuz had vanished; Brasseur lay sprawled on his side where the concussion of the first impact had thrown him. He stirred feebly—not dead as she had thought, but certainly dying. No time to worry about that now; the kzinti couldn't be far, and they wouldn't leave without her. Kefan needed help, but Tskombe was more important right now. She reached up to key her comlink but the concussion had torn her lapel mike away. She cursed, willing him to do as she had told him, and she sighed in relief as the Swiftwing pitched up and then boosted skyward, shrinking to a silver dot in seconds, leaving behind the double *bang* of a sonic boom.

Incandescent lines stabbed after it from the combat car's lasers, and she held her breath, fearing the sudden fireball that would signal the death of her lover. It didn't come, but she watched the empty patch of sky where the ship had vanished for long seconds after she knew it had to be safely out of range.

There was a momentary silence and a strange feeling came over her. Quacy was gone. Her ticket off-world was gone. She looked down and met Brasseur's gaze, glassy and unfocused. They were in serious trouble, trapped on this alien world and surrounded by heavily armed and now thoroughly enraged enemy carnivores. She shook herself. Time to succumb to that later; first she had to get the hell out of the spaceport. She looked around, spotted the two kzinti behind a cluster of storage drum. She looked around, saw no Tzaatz either, and beckoned them over.

"Where is . . ." Pouncer's voice trailed off. Brasseur looked bad, skin pasty, eyes now rolled up to show only whites, with blood trickling from his mouth and ears.

Pouncer's eyes met hers. "Your companion is dead."

"Not yet he isn't." The words came without thought as another part of her brain took over, running through the steps of combat first aid that she'd trained on a thousand times. *Secure the area, assess the casualty, check airway, check breathing, check circulation.* Already there was a problem because he wasn't breathing anymore and there was no pulse in his neck. *And the area isn't secure either, so who cares?* With head injury and an immobile casualty you have to be aware of spinal trauma. She found herself snarling orders to the others about how to hold him, how to roll him over in one smooth motion to avoid doing further damage, and she tried to hold him steady while she gave mouth-to-mouth resuscitation. That was a risk she'd have to take. And his tongue lolled limply, and you weren't supposed to use your own fingers to clear it in case the casualty bit them off in a sudden seizure, but she did anyway because there was no time and he was dead anyway. She knew it, knew it as soon as they'd rolled him over and she'd seen how the side of his skull was caved in, but she was trained to continue CPR until medical assistance arrived or there was no hope left, and it took a person half an hour to die completely, so she carried on, breath in to inflate his chest, then twelve quick pumps on his ribcage to restart his heart, at least to keep blood moving through his brain, breath, pump, and repeat and repeat and repeat. She knew it was useless because medical assistance wouldn't be arriving and he needed an autodoc immediately, if not a surgeon, and the nearest one of either was light-hours away at the edge of the singularity. She kept on because not to keep on would be to abandon the only other human on the planet and Tskombe had just boosted for Earth without her and she didn't want to think about that.

And he had to do it, and I told him to do it. The end result was that he was gone, and it would have been harder if she was the one on the ship and had been forced to leave him behind. So she kept on, with tears in her eyes though she wasn't crying and it seemed like hours before Pouncer interrupted her, though the alarms were still sounding and so it could only have been minutes.

"Cherenkova-Captain, we must leave now."

When she wiped the tears away they came away red with Brasseur's blood, which was smeared all over her face. She looked down and saw where her pumping had spread the blood from his crushed temple, and she knew that even if she revived him he would need life support that was available nowhere on this alien planet. And she knew that thought was irrelevant because he was far beyond anyone's ability to revive; even if he'd suffered those injuries already inside a fully equipped autodoc he was gone. The living network of neurons that made up the person that was Kefan Brasseur was mangled beyond repair, and there was no power in the universe that could undo that.

And still she didn't want to give up on him for reasons she didn't even want to understand. She stared down at the body as though through a fog. "We can't leave him here."

Pouncer put a heavy, soft paw on her shoulder, a surprisingly human gesture. "He is dead. May your gods find his spirit."

She shook her head. "We can't leave him here."

Pouncer didn't argue further, he just picked up Brasseur's body like he was a rag doll, all caution for spinal injuries forgotten. "The sniffers will follow us easily. We must get back to the gravcar."

"No!" T'suuz spoke the Hero's Tongue for the first time since they'd entered Hero's Square, her snarled words urgent. "The Tzaatz will be there already. We must find another vehicle."

"A combat car."

"A transporter; they will miss a combat car immediately."

"You are wise, sister." Pouncer snarled his agreement. "Can you carry the other monkey?" For a moment Ayla didn't realize he was speaking of her, and then T'suuz was picking her up, putting her on her back, and both kzin were running at a steady lope. T'suuz didn't have the thick mane that Pouncer did, but she had enough fur for Ayla to hang on. *So T'suuz can speak and fight after all. Kefan would have wanted to see that.* She found the rhythm of the kzinrette's lope and let go with one hand to draw her oversized sidearm. Kefan would not see anything any longer. She had spent all the time she could on grief. Now she had to focus on survival, or she wouldn't live much longer herself.

> *The quality of the crate matters little. Success depends upon the man who sits in it.*
> —Manfred von Richthofen

Nothing had changed on the screens, but the situation was deteriorating. Despite the fact that his own survival hung in the balance Quacy Tskombe found it hard to concentrate. Unconsciously his jaw clenched, his stomach knotted tight. He had no choice but to take off. Ayla had said it herself, and she was right. She was an officer, a commander. She knew the risks, knew how to balance them, and there were larger things at stake than a man's love for a woman. The UN needed to know what was happening on Kzinhome, and the mission had to take priority. She was not the first friend he'd lost in combat, not even the first lover.

He pushed his feelings aside. There was no finagled

time to lose focus. There were fighters back there, with pilots who knew the orbital combat game. He couldn't allow himself to be caught. First things first. He hauled out the automanual, punched keys desperately to find out how to read the combat display. He had practiced on it, but not enough to memorize the symbology. Fortunately he was used to the manual by now, if not the actual ship, and he found the relevant manpage quickly.

The triangular icons with the dot in the middle were the fighters, and the transparent green funnels attached to them showed how much they could have changed their velocity vector in the half-second delay speed of light lag imposed on the situation. The Swiftwing was simply the point at the center of the display where the three coordinate system lines met, and the little silver spheres were the battle stations. The huge orange sphere was obviously Kzinhome itself, the smaller orange sphere was a moon— the Hunter's Moon, by the dots-and-commas label floating above its surface; the Traveler's Moon was invisible on the other side of the planet. He touched some keys, and a series of transparent, curved surfaces in red and green appeared around his position: intercept planes. If nothing changed, the fighters would be in a position to shoot when he crossed them.

And they were coming rapidly closer. He didn't have a lot of time. He called up his own course funnel to see what his options were. For a few seconds he thought he might have hope. A slice of his course funnel was blue instead of orange and he thought that might indicate an escape route, but when he looked up the key in the automanual he discovered that it was simply a collision vector warning.

If he chose a course in the light blue slice it would slam him into the moon if he didn't change course again before he entered the dark blue slice. Nothing he could do would move his delta vector out of the intercept plane. The best he could do was crash into the moon and cheat the hunters of their prey.

Unless—unless he could plot his course close to the moon, skim around it and use the gravitational slingshot to pick up velocity. TSTD would be sharper there, giving the advantage to the ship with more muscle. He could pick up a lot of velocity if he cut it fine enough. He'd get catapulted out of the system at some tremendous rate and the fighters would be left far, far behind. If he picked his course right even the warships up in the gravity well would have trouble laying on a vector to intercept. That was the trick he needed. Hope surged and he slid his finger through the air, drawing a new course line, watching his course funnel bend and extend as he set up the lunar pass. The results were astonishing, his velocity on exit getting up to a measurable fraction of light speed. The red shift would make a noticeable difference to the total power flux of any lasers from behind that happened to hit him, and it couldn't help but make things difficult for the gunners.

Except the fighters, of course, would be on his tail and they wouldn't be affected much by relativity. In fact if they followed him through the maneuver they would gain almost as much through the slingshot effect as he did. And when they got in missile range they would blow him out of the sky.

He put the automanual down feeling sick. He was

helpless, with nothing to do but watch the end coming. It was a horrible feeling. Combat on the ground was messier than it was in space, physically demanding, mentally exhausting, lethal in the extreme. Death, when it came, came quickly, but there was always something you could do right up to the last instant; no matter how desperate the situation, how faint the hope, you could keep trying until you died. Unconsciously he touched the claw scars on his arm. During the mop-up on Vega IV a kzin had screamed and leapt. His battle armor had saved him from instant death, but the kzin would have killed him anyway if he hadn't fought back, kept on fighting back as it ripped his combat carapace off piece by piece to get at his vitals, kept on fighting against an enemy who was so clearly going to kill him with strength and reflexes and kill rage that he could not hope to match, kept fighting right up to the instant DeVries had blown its head off with a magrifle. They thought he'd need a new arm but he'd managed to keep the one he was born with. On the ground you could hide, you could run, you could ambush. Ground combat was as much art as science, and still a matter of force of will. Space combat was ruled entirely by cold equations, the remorseless variables of mass, thrust, acceleration, velocity and momentum. Know the initial conditions and you could predict the outcome with the certainty of an introductory physics experiment.

It was not his choice of arena, but here he was, and his only choice was death at the hands of superior pilots in superior craft with superior weapons or deliberate suicide by ramming the moon. He pounded his fist on the oversized armrests of the crash couch in helpless frustration.

Unless . . .

He drew his finger through the display space, trailing the navigation cursur, dialing in acceleration. Unless he could turn this encounter into ground combat after all, or at least some close approximation. He was closing on the moon fast, and if he cut his course right in tight, right down on the deck where a combat car belonged, there might be a brief period when the curve of the moon hid him from his pursuer's view. He moved his finger, pulled the course funnel around until it was skimming the moon's surface and, *yes*, at maximum acceleration he'd have a quarter of the surface between him and the fighters. And if they thought he was doing the gravitational slingshot and he instead threw on the brakes . . .

I'll be on the surface and they'll go right on past at speed and wonder what happened to me.

It was worth a try. It was the only chance he had. The key would be to back off on the acceleration slowly while the fighters had him in view, then jam on deceleration once he was below the horizon. Too much too soon and they'd figure out the game. Too little too late and he wouldn't be able to stop and he'd be on the slingshot to oblivion.

Heart pounding, he set the problem up. For several long minutes it looked like there was no solution. The Swiftwing simply didn't have the thrust to stop the sling-shot effect completely. On the first pass the best he could manage would be an elongated egg of an orbit, and when the accelerating fighters came around the curve of the moon behind him as he slowed down he'd actually be on his way up and away toward the apogee—or whatever the apogee was called for the Hunter's Moon. He'd be a sitting duck. His mind raced, he was running out of time and options.

The answer, when it came, was blindingly simple. He would brake hard on the curve in, right up to perigee, then flip the courier on her back, cant the thrusters *up* and use them to hold his orbit close to the surface. That wouldn't help him land. He'd whip around the moon at low altitude and some tremendous orbital velocity and stay below the horizon while the fighters accelerated past and out toward the edge of the gravity well. The thrusters would hold him in the low point of the orbit while the axis of his orbital egg rotated around the moon's center. Once he had come right the way around he'd put the thrust forward again and decelerate. He couldn't do that forever of course, but if he made a full orbit his pop up and subsequent deceleration would happen with Fourth Flight already past and boosting for the singularity's edge. A fighter's best sensors faced forward; with luck they wouldn't even pick him up. If they didn't they'd have to slow down and change course to catch up with him.

This is the pilot's art. Physics frames the rules, but the game is chess.

Except he was the only piece on his side of the board, and he wouldn't get to trade colors and start again if he lost.

And if I make an orbit and a half *before braking I'll pop up with the fighters on the other side of the moon.* They'd have one chance to pick him up as he came around behind them, but he'd be low and fast, hidden in the ground clutter from pulsed search beams, moving perpendicular to the beam line to render Doppler search useless. Turn off the mag armor and deep radar would see right through him, maybe. It was a chance, it was worth trying.

He set up the course. His inexperience made it take longer than it should have, and he wasn't entirely sure how much margin of error he needed for his high speed spin around the moon. *Cut it close,* his instincts told him, and he cut it as fine as he dared. Better to slam it in trying to get away then let himself be picked off as a Tzaatz pilot's trophy. He almost missed his first critical point trying to correct an error that cut it just *too* close, but he made it and, punched execute. The course icon flashed and the AI growled that it was entering the funnel gate just in time, but there was no discernible change to the progress of the icons. The Swiftwing was dialing back thrust by just over one percent per minute, if he was reading the kzinti panels correctly. Nothing to do now but wait, but no longer passive waiting. He was tempted to take command of his surviving turret and try to shoot down some of Fourth Flight, but decided against it. The AI was a far better gunner than he was, and it still thought the fighters were too far back to make it worth the shot.

So wait, and watch the moon grow larger, and larger, and larger, looming overhead until it filled the transpax and fell toward him at a horrific rate. And then the artificial gravity wrenched at his stomach with sickening force and the lunar surface was a gray blur and he was upside down and the gravity wrenched again as the thrusters shifted vector to keep him tight, tight, tight to the surface as he whipped around. And the dots on the plot board had disappeared and he was behind the moon and fought down the urge to vomit at the vertigo.

This too is the pilot's art. He had ridden assault landers through the atmospheric interface, felt the wrenching jolts and wondered which were maneuvers and which might be hits that would leave them a tumbling wreck, burning through the atmosphere toward a death they'd never feel, and then the final controlled crash of touchdown and the ramp slamming down and he had led his company out to take the control tower or the outer defense line or whatever the objective had been that time. Never had he been anything more than a passenger, and now that made all the difference in nerves and tension. But he had to be in control this time because he was flying below the moon's mountain tops and the AI knew nothing of topography. It was up to him to fly the contours, if there were any, and a miscalculation would leave nothing but another crater in the moon's well scarred surface. How high was he anyway? A thousand meters maybe; apo-whatever was three kilometers, peri-whatever under a hundred meters when the Swiftwing had flipped over to present her thrusters to the stars.

So he kept his eyes glued to the transpax for a bump of gray on the too close horizon that would grow to a mountain in the time it took him to blink, and then twitched the controls left just in time to see gray flash past on either side. And then he was through the crater rim wall and sailing over a vast expanse of emptiness that spoke of the impact of something bigger than Everest in a time before the Earth was born. And three heartbeats later he twitched the column again and he was out the other side.

He flicked his eyes to the course funnel to see if he had to do it again and saw he was already more than halfway around. And the fighters must be in front of him by now. His muscles were rigid and aching but he didn't dare let go, didn't dare relax. He had to remind himself to breathe. It seemed to take forever for his ship icon to crawl around the tiny world. And it occurred to him that he hadn't shut down the transponder and that the fighters might have picked up his signal and be tracking him. They shouldn't be able to pick it up below the curve of the horizon but once he popped out behind them it would be a dead give-away. He didn't dare look away from the gray/black horizon ahead. And then he was starting his second orbit and the enemy icons had vanished from display, though whether that was because they were lost in space ahead of him, accelerating after nothing or because they were tucked in behind him just waiting for him to pop up was unknowable.

A second time the vast crater wall loomed. *An orbit and a half.* This time he was ready for it, the tremendous speed of his passage seeming to slow down as he became accustomed to it. And then it was over and the thrust switched from below to behind as the courier spun on its axis and he was looking backward. He took his hands off the controls, flipped off the transponder, and the surface fell away as he arced high out above it, vulnerable now to detection, if the fighters hadn't been fooled by his trick. No way of knowing that either. At least he was no longer liable to drill a hole in the side of a mountain. He breathed out and waited again, this time for the apo-whatever so the thrusters could bring him into landing orbit. He breathed deep. What else could they pick up? Navigation radar? Data carrier? Mag armor? Shut it all down, then check the manual to see if there was anything else. And then very quickly the moon was coming up again, but this time he wouldn't be skimming the surface. He came in at a low angle, took control back from the AI as the Swiftwing skimmed in, braking hard. He picked out a boulder field, extended the skids and brought the ship down like a combat car. It was a harder landing than he intended and rocks bigger than he was sailed gracefully into the distance in the low gravity. The Swiftwing skidded to a stop. He was down. His heartbeat pounded in his ears and he realized he was shaking.

He took a deep breath, glanced at his beltcomp. It had taken three hours for the entire chase. It had seemed like minutes. Could they pick up his drive emissions? No time to waste figuring it out. He snapped the master power switch to *off*. The cockpit went dark and the whir of the lifesystem faded. He wouldn't boil or suffocate immediately, and now there would be no stray radiation from the drives or anything else giving him away. Not much he could do about his thermal signature, but in the full glare of 61 Ursae Majoris the boulder field would be a hot, noisy image to anyone searching for him. It would be easier to pick him up visually—a glint of that hard bright light from the transpax would be all it would take—but that meant Fourth Flight would have to search visually, and that would be difficult, at best.

And that meant Fourth Flight would have had to track him to the moon. They had to know something had happened. Ships didn't just vanish into the blackness of space, and experienced fighter pilots would know better than he how to exploit a gravity well. There was nothing he could do about that possibility now. He was a rabbit and he'd beaten the foxes to his hole. Now he had to simply wait and wonder if they'd given up and gone away. He watched the harsh gray landscape and the brilliant starscape for a while. For a while he thought he might catch a glimpse of his hunters, see a star moving steadily across the background that would be the sun reflecting from one of the fighters, but with the sun almost right overhead that wasn't going to happen.

He went to the food processor, found it gave out nothing but slabs of raw meat, flash heated to body temperature. It might be his last meal, but he wasn't that hungry yet. So he waited, once again, for a death that might come without warning at any instant. He had done what he could to survive, and waiting was now an active strategy, not a passive acceptance of a hopeless situation. He would stay where he was until he couldn't stay there any longer, until his life support threatened to give out, until the fighters had to give it up for lack of fuel.

Except, he realized, they could put themselves in orbit and use none. But a fighter only carried its pilot, and one kzin could only fly so long before he had to go back to the carrier. Would there be another relay of fighters? How many resources would they devote to searching him out? It was a question impossible to answer. The only solution was, wait as long as he could. How long that was depended on the lifesystem. At least with no active pursuit he could lay a course to rendezvous with *Crusader*. Captain Detringer would be getting worried by now, after two weeks with no contact with his diplomatic team. He would have monitored disturbing transmissions from Kzinhome. He'd know something had gone drastically wrong. His emergency orders were to wait for their return if there was a loss of contact, unless he was actually attacked by superior kzinti forces. There was no time frame specified for how long he was to wait. The captain of a capital ship had considerable latitude in cases like that. Lars Detringer had impressed him as a patient man, but he would have notified the UNSN by now, and perhaps gotten orders to leave. Was he still waiting?

The alternative was to attempt to navigate hyperspace by himself, in a damaged ship with low power reserves, not his first choice option. He got out the automanual to study rendezvous orbits, but found he couldn't concentrate on the words. *Stress reaction. I left Ayla behind.* The thought would not leave his mind, and already he knew he would be returning to Kzinhome to get her. There was simply no other option. He put the automanual down again, looked out at the bleak, lifeless vista through the transpax. He would have lots of time to learn now, if he had any time at all. It began to get warmer. Eventually he'd have to turn the power back on to run the lifesystem, but not yet.

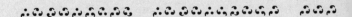

WISDOM OF THE CONSERVERS

The mightiest river is made of raindrops.

Not even the Patriarch commands the sun.

Time makes bones of life as *stlsi* [carrion grubs] make bones of a carcass.

A wise enemy is better than a foolish friend.

Wisdom comes slowly even to the wise.

No slave comes willingly to anger.

All warriors must eat

Ask the experienced, not the learned.

The Fanged God won't protect a fool.

The victor is not weary at the moment of victory.

Never give advice in a crowd.

Truth only hurts when it should.

Speak truly, but speak with care.

The Fanged God sells knowledge for labor and honor for risk.

Hunt in the cool season for the food you need in the hot.

Battle has no time for sorrow.

Wind comes to everyone, but meat only comes to the hunter.

It's not the kill, it's the thrill of the chase.

Good friends are worth the wealth of a world.

Ctervs hide in still water.

A fool will say what he can't understand.

Brothers fight harder than neighbors.

The Pride is no braver than the Patriarch, no wiser than the Conserver.

Ropes trap fools, puzzles trap the wise.

When a fool quotes proverbs the wise [sentient] listen.

The cunning hunter follows the wind to the sun and doubles his tracks.

The rain rains.

Strakh flows to the noble as the rain to the river. Strong in cunning does not mean weak in courage.

The meat lies beneath the fur.

Swimmers [fish] never thirst.

Choose your name wisely, then bring it honor.

Greet necessity with enthusiasm.

Sheath pride and bare honor.

He who drinks the wind shall thirst, he who stalks the stream shall starve.

When honor and shame balance on a needle, who holds the needle?

Lead with action, follow with words.

ა ა ა ა ა ა ა ა

THE HAMMER

A kzintosh is not stronger than a Kdatlyno, not wiser than a Jotok, no more skilled than a Pierin, no more adept than a Whrloo. The honor code is all that separates us from lower animals. To apply the honor code the Conserver must first understand its purpose, that he may serve its goals; second, comprehend its import, that he may well advise his Pride and Patriarch; and third, be without strakh, that he may render dispassionate judgment. There is no more difficult calling than Conserver, and none more worthy.

—Kzin-Conserver-of-the-rule-of-Zrarr-Rrit

In the Citadel's central courtyard a detachment of *rapsar*-raider mounted troops formed up to conduct a clearing patrol. The situation on Kzinhome was stable now, or stable enough at any rate. The Citadel itself was at last secure, or at least the Hunter's Moon had gone around twice since any of the haggard and starving *zitalyi* hold-outs had launched a last suicidal attack from within its walls. Outside the walls . . . Kchula-Tzaatz paced, worried. Outside the walls there were still attacks. The majority of the *kzintzag* and all of Lesser Prides of Kzinhome had accepted his rule with the ascension of Scrral-Rrit to the Patriarchy, and the Pride-Patriarchs and Emissaries had all pledged their fealty to the newly ascended Scrral-Rrit; the cowering *sthondat* was useful to that end at least. The

Rrit Fleet was largely gone, fled with the execrated Fleet Commander, perhaps to operate as privateers, perhaps to pledge fealty to some other Great Pride. If they chose to harry Tzaatz supply lines they could be a problem, but so far that problem had not yet arisen. Tzaatz Pride had much *strakh* right now, and he needed to take advantage of it while he could. The Rrit orbital fortresses were his and, more importantly, the Patriarchal shipyards, and already materials were flowing up-orbit to create his fleet, a fleet to outmatch anything in the Patriarchy. That would take time, but for now no other Great Pride was in a position to attack. His *strakh* now was such that he could demand much. Eventually that would wear thin, and he would have to bring pressure to bear to achieve his aims, squeeze the results he needed from the planet, but by then *rapsar* production on Jotok would have made up the horrific losses they'd suffered in the invasion. The *zitalyi* had fought hard, no question, not just at the Citadel but everywhere. Casualties had been high, among Tzaatz and *rapsari* alike.

Kchula-Tzaatz stopped pacing and looked back down into the courtyard where the patrol was heading out. No, the pacification of Kzinhome was going as well as could be expected. His anxiety was because of a message he had received that morning, short and to the point. The message was from the Circle of Conservers. Kzin-Conserver was coming.

Kzin-Conserver! A figure so powerful and so distant that he was nearly a legend throughout the Patriarchy. His status rivaled that of the High Priest's, but where the priesthood concerned themselves with rarefied ritual, the

Circle of Conservers concerned themselves with the very
practical application of tradition. Ritual could be followed
and forgotten with no impact on life. Tradition had to be
observed, or at least be seen to be observed, and here
even Meerz-Rrit had bowed to Kzin-Conserver. Kchula-
Tzaatz was under no illusions as to the traditions he had
bent in mounting his attack, despite his care in maintaining at least the appearance of adherence. What if
Kzin-Conserver decided that in fact the traditions had
been violated? Unconsciously Kchula's ears laid themselves flat. The thought did not bear thinking.

Already he wondered if perhaps he should have
planned the meeting for a venue other than the Patriarch's
Tower. It was necessary to give the title of Patriarch to the
cringing coward that Ftzaal-Tzaatz had so effectively
turned into a traitor. It was not necessary to yield the
perks of the station, and so he had taken over the
Patriarch's quarters. Already he was making changes.
Meerz-Rrit's taste had been surprisingly spartan for one of
unlimited *strakh*, and, when time allowed, Kchula was
expropriating choice furnishings and decorations from
around the Citadel to adorn his new home. Now it
appeared that might not have been a wise decision, at
least not until his conquest was more secure. Kzin-
Conserver might not appreciate Kchula's temerity in
usurping the Patriarch's quarters. He was nervous, though
he did his best to control it. His expected guest was late
and there was nothing he could do about it.

There was a knock on the door and he almost fell over
himself in his haste to open it. Kzin-Conserver was old
even for a Conserver and grizzled, his ears too wrinkled to

stand upright, his tail spotted and scaly with age, but he carried an unshakeable air of authority. Alone among every sentient on Kzinhome he had nothing whatsoever to fear from Kchula-Tzaatz. The High Priest's approval of Second-Son's ascension to the Patriarchy had been a mere formality. Kzin-Conserver's endorsement of the traditions followed by Tzaatz Pride in their attack was anything but, and there was nothing Kchula-Tzaatz could do if he chose to withhold it. A word from Kzin-Conserver and the Great Prides would turn against him as one, and then the Tzaatz line would end; there was no point in denying the possibility. Conservers were immune to challenge duels, and assassination at this point . . . No, the Great Prides would not swallow it. Indeed, if Kzin-Conserver were to simply die of old age it was likely the Great Prides would turn on him in vengeance for what they would assume was treachery. He had played too close to the edge of honor to get away with anything less than the full endorsement of the Circle of Conservers, and for matters of the Patriarchy that meant everything would stand and fall on Kzin-Conserver's judgment. Prior to the attack he had convinced himself that use of *rapsari* was simply an unconventional extension to the use of more conventional war beasts, a long-standing and accepted practice in the Honor-War. Now it remained to convince everyone else. One of the primary reasons he had spared Rrit-Conserver's life was to lend legitimacy to his conquest and Scrral-Rrit's attainment of the Patriarchy. Those measures seemed thin cover now. Kzin-Conserver had specified that their interview be conducted alone. That was a bad sign.

"You are well I hope, Kzin-Conserver?" Kchula performed a ritual claw-rake to show a respect he did not feel.

The old kzin looked Kchula over through eyes still sharp. "I am as well as can be expected for my age, which is not well at all. I did not choose to attend the Great Pride Circle, despite Meerz-Rrit's invitation. Now I am forced to journey to the Citadel anyway. Your conquest has caused me much distress."

"I act to defend the honor of our race, Conserver."

Kzin-Conserver wrinkled his nose. "You act in the interests of *strakh* and power, Kchula-Tzaatz, let us not pretend otherwise. Meerz-Rrit's decision and the Great Circle's reaction to it are merely convenient for you now. This attack took seasons to mount." The old kzin moved into the room and took a *prrstet*. "You understand there are serious questions of tradition here." His voice was deep and somber.

"I have the assurance of Tzaatz-Conserver that all our actions have been within the accepted interpretation of the traditions. The use of beasts in battle is common in the Tzaatz Pride saga, and well known in the Patriarchy."

"And where is Tzaatz-Conserver?"

"On Jotok, where he belongs, applying the traditions to my own Lesser Prides."

"He belongs by your side, the better to advise you against decisions as rash as this one." Kzin-Conserver held up a paw to forestall Kchula's protest. "I know Tzaatz-Conserver, and I know how he advised you. If he had done otherwise you would not have left him behind."

"We who serve Scrral-Rrit take the advice of Rrit-Conserver now." Kchula tried to divert the conversation.

"You who serve . . ." Kzin-Conserver rippled his ears. "Repeat it often enough, Kchula, and perhaps eventually you will believe yourself. I'm sure what you meant to say is, you who control the Patriarch keep his Conserver far from your council, while you exploit his name for your own purposes."

"Honored Kzin-Conserver . . ."

Kzin-Conserver slashed a paw through the air. "I will not be interrupted. Let me be very clear. The use of genetic constructs is against the Dueling Traditions."

Kchula turned a paw over with exaggerated care. "It is a question of sea or sky."

Kzin-Conserver lashed his tail. "On the contrary, it is a question firmly rooted in stone."

Kchula looked up sharply. *This is a dangerous development.* "This is not what Tzaatz-Conserver has assured me."

"You tread the edge of dishonor, Kchula-Tzaatz. Shall I order Tzaatz-Conserver here and ask him?" Kzin-Conserver watched Kchula stiffen in ill-suppressed fear. "I'll spare you the humiliation. Do you know K'traio-Tzaatz?"

"I do not." Kchula bit the words off short.

"You are more ambitious than scholarly, Kchula-Tzaatz. You would do well to spend more time in your father's Hall of Ancestors. The story of Myceer-Rawr is most enlightening."

"If I may ask you to summarize, honored Conserver?" *Conservers value politeness.*

"I will spare you the details, Kchula, and show you the shape of this little-known story. Ancient Rawr Pride sought the blood of Krowl Pride for an insult three generations old. Myceer-Rawr traded all the *strakh* he commanded for *rapsari* shipped from Jotok by your ancestor, K'traio-Tzaatz. The growth vats have always been a Jotoki specialization. He then invaded, and Krowl Pride retreated, fled into their mountain strongholds on Ktzaa'Whrloo and lured the Rawr after them. The Krowl are born mountain warriors, and they and Myceer-Rawr both knew they could not be defeated in their high fortresses. The *rapsari* were Rawr's answer to that problem, and it was a cunning and innovative one. Rawr sent in the constructs to hunt them out, but those first *rapsari* were modified from work-beasts made for the jungles of Jotok, and they fared badly in the mountains where the air was thin, dry, and cold."

"And so . . . ?"

"Impatience will be your downfall, Kchula-Tzaatz." Kzin-Conserver paused, letting the point sink in. "And so Rawr Pride was defeated, and Krowl Pride gained much of their *strakh*. The question of the use of *rapsari* arose, of course, for while battle beasts are strong in the traditions, these constructs were something else again, undreamt of when the traditions were established. No Great Circle could be convened; in a time long before hyperdrive existed they occurred once in a generation or less. Emissaries might travel half their lives to attend a Circle, and spend the remaining half to bring its rulings back to their worlds. A Patriarch's Voice might never set eyes on the Patriarch in whose name he ruled. Eventually word came here to Kzinhome of what had happened, and Kzin-Conserver of the dynasty of Veascry-Rrit then ruled that the use of *rapsari* by Myceer had followed the Dueling Traditions, because the traditions did not outlaw *rapsari*, but that the traditions must be changed, or genetic constructs would take the place of energy weapons and the Honor-War would become lethal to entire prides, perhaps our entire species." Kzin-Conserver locked eyes with Kchula and stopped. "Do you understand what this means, Kchula?"

"I have never heard of this ruling."

"Hmmph." Kzin-Conserver twitched his whiskers. "It made no change to the outcome of the duel, and so is less well known than others with more dramatic results. Nevertheless it exists, and you will not convince me that Tzaatz-Conserver left you ignorant of it."

He means to judge the Traditions against me! Kchula-Tzaatz stared, watching the disaster unfold in front of him, unable to speak. *Could I kill him?* The certain wrath of the Great Prides would descend on him no less certainly than if Kzin-Conserver announced formal proscription against Tzaatz Pride. Perhaps somehow he could change the presentation, convince them it was accidental, but Kzin-Conserver was still waiting.

"Do you understand what this means, Kchula-Tzaatz?"

"You will judge against the honor of Tzaatz Pride, you cannot . . ." Kchula-Tzaatz was prepared to beg, if he had to.

"What is the responsibility of the Conservers?" Kzin-Conserver cut him off.

"To judge the Traditions."

"No, it is our *function* to judge the Traditions." Conserver's voice hardened. "What is our responsibility?"

The hair at the back of Kchula's neck bristled. *He is questioning me like a kitten.* It was insulting, but there was nothing he could do about it. "To ensure the continuity of the kzinti line."

Kzin-Conserver rippled his ears, satisfied. "I see that Tzaatz-Conserver has been less than completely lax in his guidance. Allow me to shape another story for you." The old kzin lashed his tail. "Why should tradition require that the Patriarchy flow through the Rrit line? The priests tell us the Rrit are the Chosen of the Fanged God, but that bears no meat in a universe where the Fanged God can play only with virtual quantum particles and live only behind an event horizon. Why then? What makes them worthy of the honor?"

What answer does he require of me? There was only one safe reply. "I do not know, Kzin-Conserver."

"Is not heroism and conquest enough for you? You long to take the Patriarchy for yourself, yet you do not know what restrains you from what you desire most." Kchula started to object and Kzin-Conserver waved him down. "No, do not bother to deny it." He gestured to take in their surroundings. "Here in the Patriarch's quarters your ambition is abundantly clear. You have taken all but the name. Why then install this weak puppet Second-Son and call him Scrral-Rrit?"

Kchula's lips curled over his fangs at the reminder that he was still technically subordinate to his puppet. "Tradition demands it."

"Tradition demands it, yes. And more specifically, you

know that if you usurped the Rrit line I would pronounce proscription against you, and every Great Pride in the Patriarchy would be at your throat. Even if I do not pronounce proscription the Great Prides may yet take that leap. But while you tread heavily on tradition in the pursuit of your ambitions you realize that you cannot act with impunity. There are some rules even you will not break, not because you revere them but because you fear the consequences if you are not seen to revere them. It is not just tradition, but tradition backed by force which compels you to do what you would rather not do, yes?"

"Yes." There was no point in denying it.

"So what gives legitimacy to your own position as leader of the mighty Tzaatz Pride? How did you come by this honor?"

Kchula snorted. "I am First-Son-of-Vraat-Tzaatz. I was born to it."

"Honor must be earned, must it not? Why confer great *strakh* on a mewling newborn?" Kzin-Conserver didn't accept the safe answer.

"A Conserver doesn't have to ask such a question. This too is tradition."

"Yes, and where does the legitimacy of the Tzaatz rule on Jotok come from?"

Kchula looked away, not wanting to answer. "Our oath of fealty to the Rrit." *Why else preserve the odious Scrral-Rrit as figurehead? Is this triviality what he is driving at?*

"And so your own position springs from adherence to the same traditions that bind your Pride's fealty to the Rrit."

"What has this to do with the use of *rapsari*?" Despite

his delicate position Kchula could not conceal his impatience.

"You do not yet see, Kchula-Tzaatz, though it is in front of your nose. Tradition does not exist by itself. We Conservers do not enforce obedience to it for no reason. Tradition serves to make predictable what would otherwise be unpredictable. Predictability leads to stability. If tradition did not demand that the First-Son of each generation take leadership of his Great Pride, then all a Pride-Patriarch's sons, and perhaps fealty-pledged warriors, would fight to claim it on his death. Would you rule Tzaatz Pride if Ftzaal-Tzaatz claimed it from you?" Kzin-Conserver waved a dismissive paw. "Your ears would be on his belt, if he bothered to wear them. It would be thus at every succession, and the prize which is Jotok would be destroyed in a pawful of generations. If the traditions did not decree that a Rrit become Patriarch, then the Great Prides would war upon each other constantly. These traditions serve to stabilize our species for the benefit of all. The Dueling Traditions serve to limit the damage of inevitable conflict. *Skatosh* sets the limits on a challenge duel, and prevents the brother of a slain warrior from claiming vengeance if the fight was fair, which also prevents a squabble from becoming a pridewar. *Skalazaal* exists so that when pride-wars occur worlds are not sterilized as Pride-Patriarchs contend for what they might wrest from each other. Every tradition exists for a reason, and the reason is always stability."

"And what does that mean here?"

"You have violated the Dueling Traditions! Tzaatz Pride has used *rapsari* in battle. Think what you have unleashed! Pride-war fought with battle beasts as the wealth of worlds is squandered on their creation, generations of conflict ending inevitably in the destruction of the Patriarchy and the fragmentation of our race. Tradition demands that I pronounce your conduct and your pride honorless, and your conquest without validity, for where tradition is violated other traditions exist to restore stability. Not all the Pride-Patriarchs have left Kzinhome yet; there are enough to form a Great Pride Circle to sit in judgment on you." Kzin-Conserver's tail lashed. "The least penalty the Great Circle will impose upon you will be to pay the blood-price of Meerz-Rrit." Fear shot through Kchula at the words as Kzin-Conserver continued remorselessly. "Blood price for the Patriarch! Do you realize what that will mean? Jotok will be forfeit to the Rrit! And perhaps there will be more. The Great Circle may well choose to end your line. And then, Kchula-Tzaatz, then you should pray to the Fanged God that you die in battle for as much honor as you can trade your life for. If they take you alive you will be given the Ceremonial Death, and it will last for the Traveler's Moon."

Fear froze Kchula-Tzaatz's liver as Kzin-Conserver stared him down. *It cannot come to the Ceremonial Death. I can flee and hide, find another name. I can bribe him . . .* "Honored Kzin-Conserver, do not do this . . ."

"Stop!" Kzin-Conserver slashed his talons through the air, surprisingly fast for one so old. "Do not beg and lower your esteem with me even further than you already have. You are a coward and a bully and unworthy of this house. Your great victory is built on the bodies of warriors whose urine you are unworthy of licking. You fill my nose with the stench of your fear, mighty conqueror. I have told you what might happen. Now I will tell you what *will* happen."

"Please . . ." Kchula felt his heart pounding. *Anything but the Ceremonial Death. I could have him killed . . .* But he could not have Kzin-Conserver killed without bringing down the very fate he was so desperate to avoid, and so he forced himself to stay still, to listen, to gain any advantage he might.

"What will happen. The future is open, there are many possibilities." Some of the contempt had faded from the old kzin's voice, but his eyes bored into Kchula's, demanding attention. "Consider first if I act as my own traditions would have me do. Yes, the Great Prides will leap at your throat if I judge against you, and I myself would find the finest traditions to guide the Hunt Priests in the preparation of your Ceremonial Death. There are exquisite variations long lost to all but those of us who study the ancient ballads. What will happen then? Will the weak and vacillating Scrral-Rrit then seize the Patriarchy by the scruff?" Kzin-Conserver lashed his tail contemptuously. "He is less worthy than you for the position he holds. No. What will happen is that the other Great Prides will become restive. Meerz-Rrit was wise when he spoke of an end to the conquest hunts. The Patriarchy can expand only at great risk now, and the Pride-Patriarchs know it. You have shown them that it is possible to triumph in *skalazaal* even over the Rrit. There will be more Honor-Wars, and they will come soon. Scrral-Rrit will die because no one will follow him, and with the Rrit line ended the Great Prides will war over the spoils of Kzinhome. The Patriarchy will fall, Kchula-Tzaatz."

"There must be another way, esteemed sire." *A way that will see me retain my spoils.*

"Esteemed sire, now?" Kzin-Conserver rippled his ears without humor. "I stand amazed to see humility in the great Kchula-Tzaatz. Yes, there is another way. I can choose to overlook the precedent of Rawr Pride. I can stand before the Great Pride Circle and declare that your conquest was within the boundary of tradition, though barely. I can legitimize your illegitimate, your cowardly, your *carrion-sniffing* attack." He lashed his tail angrily. "You were clever in putting your *zzrou*-tamed Rrit puppet above you, clever in preserving Rrit-Conserver to legitimize his rule, clever in making virtue of your ambition by claiming only loyalty to the honor of our race. You have given me that much to work with. And I *will* work with it, because while it is my function to maintain the traditions, it is my duty to preserve my species, and it is my judgment that to give you the end that you deserve would cause the total collapse of the Patriarchy. Where tradition collides with duty, it is tradition that must change, as it did with Myceer-Rawr. *Skalazaal* may now be conducted with *rapsari*, but Jotok is the source for genetic constructs in the Patriarchy, and I doubt you will be eager to supply your rivals with the means of your overthrow. It will take time for the other Great Prides to develop their own capabilities. The damage is contained for now. May the High Priests beseech the Fanged God that it gets no worse."

"Kzin-Conserver . . . !"

"Enough!" Again Kzin-Conserver lashed his tail and bared his fangs. "I will hear no more from you. You say you take Rrit-Conserver's advice? He will sit on your councils, and so will Scrral-Rrit. I may yet have your pelt, Kchula. Do not test me."

"I shall see it done, honored sire."

Kzin-Conserver waved a paw dismissively. "Now leave my sight before I change my mind for the pleasure of watching the Hunt Priests take you. I would be alone with the view."

Kchula's lips twitched over his fangs, but he turned and left in silence. Kzin-Conserver had thrown him out of his own quarters. *He insults me deliberately, because he has no other option to sate his desire to see me fall.* It had been a humiliating interview, and a frightening one by turns, but the fact was, Kzin-Conserver was reacting exactly as Ftzaal had said he would. *I will live, and my place in the sagas is now secure.* As he realized it, Kzin-Conserver's contempt suddenly meant nothing, and exultation swelled in his liver. Neither the Conservers nor the Priests nor the Great Prides could dare challenge Kchula's victory. He had *won*, and if he must suffer the gratuitous insults of the old fool as the price of victory, it was cheap enough at that.

He went to the Command Lair. No need to let anyone else know of the indignity he had suffered. Kzin-Conserver would leave on his own time, and in the meantime the pacification of Kzinhome required all his attention. The *zitalyi* were a diminishing problem, and the Lesser Prides could be cowed, but the *kzintzag* weren't granting his Heroes the *strakh* they deserved, and that lack of respect could be fatal if left unchecked. Public duels would fix that problem, public duels carefully arranged for Tzaatz victory, with the heads displayed in the center of Hero's Square. His brother and his cadre of killers would be useful for that. Few would challenge the Protector of Jotok deliberately, but with provocation and deception such duels could be arranged. He needed to find Ftzaal to craft a strategy to ensure their victory did not slip through their grasp at the lowest level now that it was secure at the highest.

As he crossed the courtyard beneath the Patriarch's Tower, Ktronaz-Commander intercepted him.

"Sire! We have a problem."

Kchula snarled. *Problems are becoming too common.* "Your warriors' efforts are inadequate, Commander. What have the *zitalyi* curs done this time?"

"It is not the *zitalyi*, it is the *kzintzag*."

"And . . . ?"

"There has been an incident. A patrol commander in Hero's Square demanded his due *strakh* from a trader. The trader leapt in challenge and was slain, cut in half by the commander's variable sword."

"Good." Kchula let his fangs show, grimly satisfied. "The commoners need to learn their place."

"Sire! The trader was popular. The whole market leapt as one upon our patrol! They inflicted heavy losses but they were outnumbered eight-cubed to one. They were torn to pieces, *rapsari* and all."

"Torn to pieces . . ." Kchula's tail lashed. Mass violence was the first step on the road to rebellion. Public duels would not suffice to solve this problem. "I want those involved hunted down and put in the Arena."

"It was the whole market, sire, and none of our Heroes survived! We have no way of identifying the guilty."

"Hrrr . . . The Lesser Prides are responsible for their fealty-bound. Make examples of their Patriarchs."

"Sire! The Great Prides will not allow us. The traditions . . ."

"There is a new tradition." Kchula cut him off. "Most of the Great-Pride-Patriarchs have left already; the rest will not remain long. Our freedom of action can only increase. In the meantime, if you cannot take the Lesser Patriarchs take their sons. The Lesser Prides will serve as an example to both *kzintzag* and the Great Prides. We cannot allow defiance." Kchula's eyes narrowed. "The conquest of Kzinhome is only the first stage, Ktronaz-Commander. It remains to secure the victory."

"At once, sire."

Ktronaz-Commander knew better than to argue. He left at the bound, and Kchula went down to the Command Lair. The corridors had been cleaned of blood and bodies, but the scars of the battle still remained: walls carved with slicewires and embedded with crystal iron ballista bolts. Ftzaal-Tzaatz was already there, and Kchula beckoned him into the privacy field at the back of the room and updated him on the situation.

When he had finished, Ftzaal-Tzaatz furled his ears thoughtfully. "There is more."

"What now?"

"The reason there is defiance among the *kzintzag*. There are rumors that First-Son-of-Meerz-Rrit still lives."

"Tell me."

"We have largely pacified the populace. The Great Prides find it expedient to accept your rule; the Lesser Prides of Kzinhome are afraid to object, openly. The *kzintzag* have less to lose. Resistance is scattered, but it is there. The assaults on our Heroes grow bolder and more frequent. Did Ktronaz-Commander mention that the attackers screamed the name of First-Son-of-Meerz-Rrit as they leapt?"

"He did not."

"He has not developed the information sources that I have. None of his warriors survived to report, but it is true nonetheless. There are those among the *kzintzag* who believe him to be alive."

"Is there truth to them?"

"Who can know? We have not found his body. A courier was stolen from the spaceport. Was he on it?"

Kchula lashed his tail. "It was those cursed *kz'zeerkti* fleeing for their homeworld." *Or so Ktronaz-Commander informs me, but is he correct?* Ktronaz-Commander's rigid worldview made him reliable and predictable, both important traits in a subordinate. It did not make him particularly insightful.

"Yes, but there is a connection. We know the *kz'zeerkti* escaped through a long-abandoned defense tunnel. The scent trail included a kzinrette and a kzintosh, and the eldest Rrit daughter is missing. First-Son is the only member of the Rrit inner circle we haven't accounted for. Perhaps he was with them."

"Perhaps he was not. It could have been any of the *zitalyi*; the Fanged God knows there are enough of them. This fortress has more tunnels than a *grashi* burrow. First-Son might still be in these walls, and the Forbidden Gate wasn't sealed when we found it. Anyone might have been at the palace kzinretti."

"Seals are unnecessary where honor rules." Ftzaal twitched his whiskers. *Not that you understand honor, brother.*

"And a full sword of our Heroes was slain in front of it, and two *rapsari* raiders. Perhaps they got it open before they died."

"And who killed them?"

"*Zitalyi*, who else?"

Ftzaal turned a paw over. "No *zitalyi* would take a kzin-rette from the Citadel. Only the Patriarch's brother would do that, or his son. No, the monkeys escaped with First-Son, of this we can be sure. We know also that the *kz'zeerkti* fled to orbit in that stolen ship. Fighters of the Rrit still in orbit pursued them, but the courier escaped. The human battleship has left the singularity's edge. Did the courier make it there, or did it escape to hyperspace itself? We cannot know, but Meerz-Rrit swore peace with them. They owe him counterfealty. How better to demonstrate it than by saving his son? We must consider the possibility that the monkeys now give him sanctuary on one of their worlds."

"What do animals know of honor? And why would First-Son allow a monkey to fly a ship he was better qual-ified to fly himself?"

"I merely offer possibilities. There are more rumors: that he is in the mountains, that he leads the *zitalyi* hold-outs in raids against us, that he is even now raising support for a counterinvasion with V'ax Pride, or with Churrt Pride, or any number of others. Obviously at most one of these can be true, but it is not the veracity of these rumors that is important but that they exist at all. The *kzintzag* here on Kzinhome will not accept our rule while they believe he lives."

"These rumors will fade, only fools can entertain them. By the Fanged God, we showed them his head!" Kchula snarled.

"We showed them *a* head, and we know it was not his. This too is rumored among the *kzintzag*."

"Someone has broken fealty." Kchula's lips twitched over his fangs. "I want every warrior and every slave involved in that deception killed."

Ftzaal made a dismissive gesture. "There are no such slaves, nor kzinti. I took care of the deception personally, brother, and alone. To do otherwise on such a matter would be to invite obvious and tremendous risk. It is not impossible that I was observed by a slave, but unlikely."

"Then where has this rumor sprung from?"

Ftzaal turned a paw over. "Sheer necessity. Meerz-Rrit was a popular Patriarch, and First-Son well favored to succeed him. This was the expected path of history, the path of tradition and stability. We have upset that, and even those who may yet gain from our conquest fear instead what they might lose. The hope that the status quo might return drives the rumors that First-Son fights us to regain his birthright. Yet for any of these to be true, he must be alive. We showed his head at Second-Son's ascension, and so the first question anyone hearing that he is alive must ask is, 'Did not the Tzaatz spike his head at the Patriarch's Gate?' The rumor that we showed another head *must* exist, for it supports every other rumor, and that in turn supports the hope that is all that stands between the *kzintzag* and their well justified fear that Tzaatz Pride now controls the Patriarchy. It would have existed no matter what the truth. The critical point is, true or not, we do not want these rumors to reach the ears of Kzin-Conserver. He would be motivated to investigate further."

"He's little threat now that he recognizes the necessity of our dominance."

"If *kzintzag* rebellion continues, our dominance will fall into question. Soon the entire planet will know that the head we claimed as First-Son's is not his. We will be accused of our deception, and Kzin-Conserver has latitude enough to pronounce ruling against us even then. You say he supports us because he sees Second-Son as too weak to rule. I doubt he feels the same about First-Son. A genetic scan of the head we posted is evidence enough, and our deception may yet be revealed."

Kchula growled in frustration. The situation was getting too complex. "We will destroy the heads and let the evidence fade. If we're caught we'll assign it to a mistake made in the confusion of battle. We will lose no *strakh*, and if Kzin-Conserver suspects the truth is otherwise, his suspicions are no more than that." He looked at Ftzaal-Tzaatz. "Your estimation of Kzin-Conserver's power of restraint was accurate, if not your estimate of Rrit-Conserver's danger."

Ftzaal made the gesture of obeisance-to-a-compliment. *My brother will yet learn of Rrit-Conserver's danger, but now is not the time to remind him.* "The approach we take to the question of deception is irrelevant, as is the reality that the accusations will in fact be true. The critical point is, there are those will stand to gain by seeing our honor called into question. This accusation will have power, and combined with the rumors already in existence it will give strength to those who oppose us. Kzin-Conserver does not support us, he supports our puppet, Second-Son. Second-Son is the ascended Patriarch now; First-Son has no claim to the Patriarchy but challenge-claim, and we will not allow that to happen. This isn't clear to the *kzintzag*, and as long as they believe otherwise, as long as they *choose* to believe otherwise, our opposition will again gain strength. Did you know that Zraa-Churrt has delayed his departure? Perhaps this is why they say First-Son treats with him for respite. Kdori-Dcrz has also stayed longer than he planned, and there are others. The Great Circle are watching and waiting, and if they sense weakness they will leap. If they sense strength they will rally to our side. These are powerful prides, and we need their support. If we cannot hold Kzinhome we cannot hold the Patriarchy."

"These rumors must be stopped at any cost. The Great Pride Circle must not end with our grip on power in question."

Ftzaal turned a paw over. "The only answer is time. I will see what I can do."

"Unless First-Son reappears. That must not happen."

"The only way to be sure of that is to find his body. If he has fled to the *kz'zeerkti* worlds he is far beyond our reach." Ftzaal-Tzaatz paused, enjoying his brother's growing anxiety. "There is another possibility. A grav transporter was taken during the incident at the space-port. Its wreckage was found yesterday where the Long Range meets the Mooncatchers. I suggest we send tracker teams."

"Show me."

Ftzaal made a gesture to command the AI, and a spinning globe map of Kzinhome appeared in midair. He stabbed it with a foreclaw and it ballooned around his finger, zooming in to show the North Continent, the Great Desert, and the Plain of Stgrat, and the thick chain of mountains separating them. The zoom continued in stages until Ftzaal had a narrow canyon centered in the view. Another gesture and the map graphics were overlaid with satellite imagery. Ftzaal spun the view, zoomed again, and there, skidded onto a scree slope and half crumpled, was a grav transporter, as yet unworn by the elements.

Kchula-Tzaatz keyed his comlink for Ktronaz-Commander, and made the command gesture that would dump the display data to his subordinate's beltcomp.

"Command me, sire!" Not imaginative, but reliable. Ktronaz *was* a good choice for his role.

"Search from these coordinates. First-Son-of-Meerz-Rrit has been there." Kchula spat the words angrily. "Find him, kill him, bring me his head." He broke the link without waiting for an answer and looked at his brother, tail lashing. "We shall correct this *mistake* before I have to explain it to Kzin-Conserver." He turned on his heel and left.

When his brother was gone Ftzaal twitched his whiskers and keyed his own com. "Ktronaz-Commander."

"Sire."

"First-Son will have a kzinrette with him. I want her brought to me, alive at any cost." *And if what I suspect is true, the Black Cult will regret the day they expelled me.* Unconsciously Ftzaal lashed his tail.

*I do not advocate war for its own sake, I do not
hold stock in munitions companies. I am not
doing this for any personal ambition. I am
doing this because it needs to be done. We need
a final solution to the kzin problem.*
                    —Assemblyist Muro Ravalla to the press

Most of Earth was in darkness as Tskombe's shuttle fell
out of *Crusader's* belly and toward the planet. The aurora
borealis drew a brilliant, shimmering circle around the
sixtieth parallel, barely visible from space against the perpetual daylight of the arctic midsummer. Farther south it
was night, with just the faintest hint of sunlight showing
over the planet's eastern limb. The pilots had the cabin
gravity turned off and Tskombe floated easily between
them, delighting in the rare privilege of being in the cockpit for reentry as they chatted jargon back and forth with
approach control. There were cities up there beneath the
aurora—Whitehorse, Reykjavik, Igloolik, Oslo—but it was
impossible to pick them out. To the south it was easier to
identify the geography. The continental coastlines of
North and South America were thick luminous bands, the
interior landmasses densely frosted with light, but individual
cities were harder to find; even the sprawling superglomerate of New York was lost in the larger glow. Darker
patches marked the Rockies, the Great Lakes, the Andes,
and the Amazon Basin as they slid below, and then they
were over the Atlantic, the globe looming noticeably larger
as they spiraled down a great circle twisted into a reentry
helix by their own motion and the Earth's rotation. He
understood the maneuver in theory at least—Ayla had

taught him that—but as he watched the pilots perform the delicate orchestration he was glad he didn't have to conduct it. The sun rose as they came around the planet's curve, the solar terminator slicing Europe and Africa in half. Like the Americas, their night sides were brilliantly outlined in cities, but on the sunlit side the planet seemed uninhabited, no sign of civilization visible to the naked eye from his altitude. Ironic that the planet seemed most alive when most of its inhabitants were asleep. The town he was born in was down there, lost somewhere in the sea of light. He tried to spot it, tracing south from the prominent boot of Italy, but there were too many lights, and not enough time. The only clues to their streaking passage through the edge of the atmosphere were a few gentle accelerations and the steady return of weight. Their path would take them over the southern tip of Africa, and then back up over Southeast Asia to cross the wide Pacific, but the shuttle nosed up to take the reentry friction on her belly and Tskombe strapped into the jump seat behind the pilots with nothing to watch but the flashes of incandescent gas streaming past, shock-heated to thousands of degrees in a fraction of a second by the ship's passage. An hour later they were back in darkness and in the atmosphere, back over land, nose down again, lining up on Long Island's MacArthur Field, though they were still far back over the American desert, empty enough that the cities there formed only a glowing filigree on a black backdrop. Ahead the tracery blended back into the sea of light that made up the east coast superglomerate.

New York, New York! The city-nation, the world capital. How many years had it been since he'd left it behind to discover the stars? They fell lower and the luminous smear broke up into individual lights, buildings and the riding lights of gravcars, locked into endless streams by traffic control. He strained forward, and sooner than he expected the unmistakable skyline of the vast city appeared, gravcars flitting between islands of sculpted office towers reaching for the sky. He wasn't sure what made the City special in the face of the vast, urban sameness that covered the continent. Perhaps it was the port, its piers extending far out to sea, where a thousand bulk carriers a day arrived from around the world, disgorging their myriad cargos to feed the insatiable maw of the four billion humans crowded close on the continent. More likely it was the dense concentration of government and corporate power housed in the core of the city, home to the UN since it began, center of world financial power since a century before that. Part of it was certainly the people, energized with a purpose that seemed to be bestowed simply by living there.

And I left Ayla behind. The thought constricted his throat and ruined the elation of the view. It was the primary credo of the infantry that no one was ever left behind. Regardless of personal risk you brought home your own, alive or dead or in pieces. He had lived it when he held the dropship down on the raid that failed to retake Vega IV until every last soldier in his scattered unit ran, crawled or was dragged back through the perimeter. He had lived that rule when he carried Lieutenant Nikorki out of the disaster at Chara B on his back with her blood soaking his battle vest. She had died, and he'd known she would die, and he took her out anyway, because she was one of his own. *But I didn't live it on Kzinhome, when I left Ayla Cherenkova a hundred meters away and boosted.* It didn't make it better that he'd had to do it to save her life, but it made it worse that she was his lover. *I left her there, but I'll bring her back.* His throat was so tight it was hard to breathe. Tskombe clenched his fists, his fingernails digging into his palms hard enough to draw blood. The pain was good, punishment and reminder at once. *I will bring her back or die trying.*

There was a UNF colonel waiting for him when they grounded, and a completely unnecessary armed escort. Captain Detringer had transmitted his report ahead to UNF Command, but his arrival in person was highly anticipated. The colonel returned his salute and shook his hand as he introduced himself, a name Tskombe promptly forgot, and then they bustled him through the throngs at MacArthur arrivals. A flash of the colonel's ident took them through customs without stopping, and on to a tube car. The ride was under an hour, their destination an anonymous station connected to some anonymous building in midtown Manhattan, a nondescript standard issue government office complex with tattered decor and faded lightpanels. He was given rooms in it, comfortable and more spacious than those he'd had on *Crusader,* but the elevator had a thumb-pad and it wouldn't open for him. He was used to confined quarters, having spent much of his life on ships, but here he found the lack of freedom oppressive. The colonel shook his hand again and left his life forever. An orderly brought food and explained the room controls. Another came to look after the formalities that were a staple of military life, in clearance, medical clearance, transfer acknowledgment, net address update, next-of-kin forms. He was a hero, everyone kept telling him, but they treated him more like a prisoner.

He was thirty or forty floors up, he reckoned, certainly in the government district that surrounded the UN complex. The window gave an uninspiring view of a parking pad full of gravcars and an array of featureless windows on the building across the way. After a while a civilian came to interview him; he too had a name, but in his mind Tskombe just referred to him as *the civilian*, and he was as nondescript as it was possible to be. He was neither heavy nor light, tall nor thin, middle-aged with slightly thinning hair, his face the typical nondescript racial blend of the Flatlander. His jumpsuit was conservative but not expensive, his manner was tense but somehow ineffectual, and Tskombe found his very presence annoying.

"So tell me again what caused the attack?" The civilian's voice was flat and wheedling, asking a question he'd asked before. The interview was hours old, and going nowhere.

Tskombe shrugged. "I haven't told you what caused it. I've told you it's a civil war, I know that much, what they call an Honor-War. Dr. Brasseur could tell you more, much more. We need to get my team back."

"Your report mentioned that Ambassador Brasseur was killed."

"Yes, it did."

"So when you say 'your team' you're referring to Captain Cherenkova only."

Tskombe spoke stiffly. "In the military we recover the bodies of our fallen comrades, if it's at all possible. Perhaps you're unaware of that tradition."

The civilian ignored Tskombe's suggestion. It had become a bit of a game. Tskombe would suggest that they mount a rescue and the civilian would pretend he hadn't heard him do it.

"And you say the Patriarch has been deposed."

Tskombe sighed, resigned to one more time around the circle. "The Patriarch is dead, so far as I know." He laughed mirthlessly. "Long live the Patriarch. We had the beginnings of a peace treaty, a dialogue at least, and he made a speech to the Great Pride Circle forbidding them to attempt conquest against us. Against any race, in fact."

"And you believed him?"

"He's Patriarch. Of course I believed him. Lying to an herbivore would be beneath him. He staked his honor on that speech, in front of every Great Pride in the Patriarchy."

"Perhaps this whole civil war thing was simply staged to lull you into a false sense of security. Something to get our guard down before they attack." The civilian questions trod the thin line between due diligence and actual paranoia.

"Why would our guard go down? I just told you, they're having a civil war. The important thing is we have to get Captain Cherenkova back."

"I'm afraid we have bigger things on our minds at the moment, Major." At least the civilian didn't outright ignore the point this time. "What's your estimate of the size of the attacking force?"

Tskombe controlled the reflex to break the man's nose, breathed deep to keep himself calm. "I've told you already, I have no idea. I saw perhaps a dozen landers go over, with a lot of drop troops coming in. I wasn't everywhere on the planet."

"You're a military man, a commander. You must have a better idea than that."

Tskombe let annoyance creep into his voice. "If I had one, why wouldn't I be giving it to you? Isn't that what I'm paid for? I was a fugitive; do you understand what that means? I spent most of the attack either hiding or running for my life. I didn't have a lot of time to take notes."

"There's no need to display that attitude, Major."

"That's where you're wrong."

"What?"

"There is a need to display this attitude." Tskombe leaned forward, meeting the interrogator's gaze. "There may well be a need to display an attitude that's a lot more problematic. I am not a hostile witness, I am not a prisoner of war, I am an officer of the United Nations Forces and there is absolutely no need for this cross-interrogation. Everything you've asked me today is answered in my written report. They're the same answers I provided in my verbal report to Captain Detringer aboard *Crusader*, and both of those report were hyperwaved here when we cleared the singularity at 61 Ursae Majoris." He pointed to the civilian's datapad. "I'm sure you know what they say, and if there's anything you don't understand, I suggest you read it again. The answers will be the same tomorrow, unless I think of something important between now and then, in which case I will be certain to volunteer it, because that is my job to do so."

"It's my job to help you remember. That's what this interview is about." The civilian sounded defensive.

"Look." Tskombe smiled, trying to defuse the situation. "I appreciate you're doing what you have to, but my colleagues are still on Kzinhome. I need to talk to General Tobin as soon as possible."

"That's not my . . ."

". . . decision. I know. It's his. Just tell him I need to talk to him, and only him. And in the meantime, I would like it if you would get my data into the database, so that I can thumb for the elevator and actually leave this floor and get some fresh air. I am making the assumption that this oversight is simply due to bureaucratic incompetence and not actual malice."

"I'll see what I can do." The civilian's manner was stiff.

Tskombe smiled again, not really meaning it. "I would appreciate that."

The civilian left and Tskombe waited, keyed up and bored at the same time. He took out the Sigil of the Patriarch that Yiao-Rrit had given him, turning it over in his hands. It was heavy, deeply embossed with a figure that might have symbolized a spiral galaxy, or perhaps a multi-bladed weapon. The reverse side was covered in the dots and commas of kzinti script, but not in a style he could read. *Probably the Patriarchal Script.* The Hero's Tongue was a hard language to learn, and one of the hardest parts was the many variations of address, one for superior to inferior, another for inferior to superior, another for conversation between equals, between brothers, between father and son, between more distant relatives, the Patriarchal Form, the Noble Form, the slave command imperatives, and a dozen more subtle variations he had never learned. There were at least twelve scripts, the most common four of which he knew well enough to read. *Kefan could read this.* Except Brasseur was dead on Kzinhome. *I'll bring him back too, if I can.* The Tzaatz had probably eaten him by now, and Tskombe's fists clenched again. *They're wasting my time here with bureaucracy.*

He didn't hear anything further from the civilian, but the next morning the elevator opened to his thumb. He took it to the ground floor, went into the street. He was, as he had suspected, in the UN district. It was hot and humid, high summer in New York, and he took a slidewalk down to the waterfront. It had been a long time since he'd left Earth, with the ink on his commission scroll still damp and a galaxy in front of him to discover. He found a quiet coffee shop and sat down to scan the newsfeeds. If the UN needed him they could get him on his beltcomp. Most of the news was local—crime, sportvents, and scandal in equal measure—but he eventually found a hard news channel. There had been more skirmishes between UNSN ships and kzinti raiders around W'Kaii, and Secretary Desjardins was trying to balance factions in the General Assembly arguing for everything from ignoring the incursions as a colony problem to outright extermination of the kzinti for the continued safety of humanity. Public opinion on the matter was split, a result Tskombe found surprising, until he gave up on the newsfeeds and flipped through the entertainment feeds. Perhaps a quarter of the holos were war stories, where heroic UNF soldiers held off hordes of rapacious kzinti against desperate odds. The remainder were divided between fluffy and humorless comedies, steamy semi-erotica, and the bizarre and confusing productions of the new sensationalist school.

Public opinion was divided on the kzinti, he realized, because the vast majority of Earth's twenty billion had never seen a live kzin. Their impressions were formed by cheap cubies where the kzinti were cardboard cutout villains. It had been centuries since they'd posed any serious threat to Earth, and the opinion any particular individual was likely to express in a poll was built on equal measures of misinformation and indifference and hence little better than a coin flip, which explained the split results. Even the debates by the representatives in the General Assembly had more to do with who would gain from military spending than with any reasonable assessment of the threat the kzinti actually posed.

He looked up from the holocube and watched the crowds streaming by. How many years had it been since he'd last left Earth, last walked Central Park? Enough that he had grown into a soldier and a commander—and Earth, he now realized, had not grown with him. The vibrancy he had remembered seemed nothing more than self-indulgent decadence now, what had seemed sophisticated now looked simply pretentious. The real energy was in the colonies, where people were carving out new worlds for themselves. There was corruption there, fear and greed, deceit and treachery, but at least people still strove for something more. They hadn't allowed themselves to sink into self-satisfied and unquestioning complacency.

A 'caster was bleating on about a dog in Kuala Lumpur who'd gotten stuck in a storm drain. Intercontinental news. He flipped the cube off in disgust and went back to watching out the window, running over the problem of getting Ayla off of Kzinhome. Getting into 61 Ursae Majoris' space would be difficult, actually locating Ayla harder still. *If she's still alive.* The fear wouldn't leave the back of his mind, but he couldn't allow himself to make any other assumption. *She is alive until I find her body.* The situation on Kzinhome would dictate the tactics they would use to find her. Kzinti would be essential on the rescue team, as interpreters, as guides, even as spies, if they had to operate secretly. They would have to be recruited on Wunderland; there were enough of them there, descendants of those left behind when the UN undid the original kzinti conquest. *What is happening there now?* Kchula-Tzaatz was dangerous, but was he still in power? The situation was too fluid to make predictions, and so they would have to go in ready for any eventuality. Two ships at a minimum, disguised as traders with kzinti pilots. Four would be better, plus another diplomatic mission, if the Great Pride Circle would accept one. *What would the best approach be? Tanjit!* He needed Brasseur to help him with this, to outline the best way to handle the kzinti. There was no point in pursuing that line of thought.

He went back to his quarters, slept fitfully, and spent the next day waiting for a promised interview with the civilian that never materialized. By twenty-one o'clock he gave up, took the elevator down to slidewalk level, and let the passing strip take him wherever it was going. He crossed to the high-speed center strip and looked down to the pedestrian level below. Around the UN district the area was pleasant, manicured lawns and gardens, tall and graceful towers built around green courtyards. Even at this hour the slidewalk was crowded, mostly government

functionaries in somber jumpsuits with the occasional
military uniform standing out of the crowd. Overhead
gravcars streamed in nine levels, one for traffic heading to
each of the eight prime compass points and one held clear
for emergency services. Here and there a hoverbot
patrolled, cameras swiveling. He took junctions at random
and the neighborhood changed, the buildings becoming
older and less well maintained. Garish advertisements
floated in the air, cajoling him to eat, to drink, to buy or
sell, either from the storefronts he was passing or from
well-known global chains pushing well-known global
brands.

He came to a junction and got off the slidewalk, went
down to the pedestrian level. The setting midsummer
sun still glinted off the building tops, but it was already
twilight on the ground. He walked south, beyond the
slidewalk, and character of the area changed again. He
was in the midtown gray zone, crowded close against the
south Manhattan seawall—one of the semi-official chunks
that festered in every city where the ARM's near perfect
record of crime suppression failed. Every city had its gray
zones, pockets of crime and poverty occupied by the
human detritus of the well ordered world machine the
UN ran. Sometimes, as in Kowloon, the gray zone borders
were knife sharp, and you could get your throat cut just by
crossing the wrong street. In New York the borders
were vaguer. By some estimates half of Manhattan outside the government district was gray zone. According
to the government there were none in the city at all.
Here by the seawall the neighborhood wasn't pleasant,
but it was reasonably safe while the sun was still up.

Shabby vendors' stalls hawking cheap consumer goods occupied the central strip, separating pedways where rickshaws, rollers, and bikes competed with foot traffic for maneuvering room. The half-burned smells of a dozen cuisines cooked on open grills mingled with the sweaty tang of too many people on a too hot day. Here and there taspers sat slumped against the building walls, staring with stupid, vacant grins at the passersby, their souls lost to the wire. Most were gaunt, a few skeletal, in the last stages of current addiction. Once you knew the incandescent bliss brought on by direct electrical stimulation of your pleasure center nothing else mattered, not even food or water. Only the most extreme hunger would penetrate a tasper's mind to motivate eating, and they never ate enough to sustain life. It was a form of suicide, slow, horrific, and all too often public. The surgery that sank the electrodes into the brain had long been outlawed, but that only created a black market fed by unlicensed meat surgeons and purveyors of hacked autodoc codes. The tasp was too easy a solution for anyone looking for a way out.

"Want something different, soldier?" A heavyset man beckoned him into a doorway while holos of naked women performed lewdly overhead. "Anything you can imagine and a whole lot more you can't."

Tskombe waved him away, moved to the center median, away from the flesh hucksters lining the street. In the intersection a crowd of bounce kids had a grav-grid set up, taking turns to leap and twirl in the reduced gravity to the heavy, pounding beat pouring out of their sound system. The holoshow in the middle was showing a tornado and the kids jumped and spun in it as though it were carrying them away. *But I'm not in Kansas anymore, Toto, and the lions I'm dealing with are anything but cowardly.* The thought came unbidden with the irony of his mood. Surely nothing Dorothy saw in Oz was as strange as the reality Tskombe was looking at now. A couple of the kids had managed to disable a hoverbot and were stripping it for parts, probably for barter. The fertility laws had gone a long way to create the gray zones; the refusal to register unlicensed births created an underclass of non-persons whose very existence was illegal. Unregs were denied official identity, and with it health care, education, jobs, services, police protection, even access to the monetary system, since no ident meant no bank account, which meant you couldn't make a transaction. Perhaps the government thought that if it ignored them they'd disappear, but the unregs persisted in trying to live their lives anyway. Most of them wound up in the gray zones, where they could trade goods to survive. As Tskombe watched, the bounce kids dissected the bot with surgical precision; they'd obviously done it before. Maybe they just wanted its polarizers to expand their grav-grid. Zoners were good at converting junk into tools.

On an impulse he went to a call booth, only to find it stripped as well. He used his beltcomp instead, thumbed for an old friend's directory listing. The name came up, and a once familiar dial string. He paused before he punched it. The last he'd heard from Freeman Salsilik was a wedding invitation; that had been just before the raid on Harfax, his first combat command. He'd gotten the invitation com right before they'd boosted out. The screen flashed dial now? at him. He'd meant to send a letter, even a present, when he got back, but he'd had to send so many letters then, to the families of his soldiers who'd died, who'd been maimed and crippled, it hadn't seemed the right time. He looked at the blinking words. It had been fifteen years since he'd left Earth, fifteen years soldiering on alien worlds, four campaigns and a dozen assault landings, and it had never been the right time. Freeman had stayed on Earth, got married, had children, worked at . . . wherever it was he'd worked. Was he still married? If he'd had children they'd be nearly grown now. The address by the dial string was on Central Park West. Freeman had done well for himself, at least.

And Quacy Tskombe? He was a major now, qualified to be a colonel. The mission to Kzinhome had been a cherry for his record, Marcus Tobin's seal of approval that would confirm his promotion and pave the way to general, expedited. Tobin had graduated from Strike Command to System Defense, and Tskombe, despite being two ranks too low, was on the short list to succeed him. He had twelve medals too, but what was it Napoleon had said about medals? *Men will die for a handful of ribbon.* What he didn't have was a family, and what he no longer had was anything in common with Freeman Salsilik. He thumbed cancel and the dial string vanished. No need for the warm handshake followed by the awkward silence, conversation across a gulf neither of them could hope to cross, reminiscence over events that had long lost meaning to either one. He left the call booth and walked again, past a child urinating in the street while its father pretended to be looking the other way. Fifteen years gone, and what would he have in another fifteen? More, he hoped, than he had now. *Will I have Ayla?* It was a question mark as sharp and painful as a knife blade. New York had nothing to offer anymore. He had to get back to Kzinhome, and the only way to do that was to motivate the UNF bureaucracy to mount a rescue. He turned back the way he had come, ignoring the crowds around him, almost welcoming the anonymous sterility of the UN building's lobby when he reached it. When he got back to his rooms his beltcomp chimed, and he answered it. It was the civilian. General Tobin was arriving from system defense headquarters on the Moon in the morning. He had a half an hour meeting with him before noon. Tskombe spent an hour pressing his uniform, not because the razor creases would make any difference to the course of the interview. He could have thumbed for the night orderly and had it done for him; a major's rank came with privileges. He didn't do that. The orderly would get it autopressed, and auto-pressers never got it quite right. He pressed it himself, as he always had, by hand. He was a soldier, and that was how it was done.

The sun was oppressive the next day, the air heavy and humid. He had felt it only long enough to walk from the tenth-floor skyport to the military gravcar that was waiting for him there, but there was a heat bulletin on the local newsfeed, warning people to stay inside and avoid the sun as much as possible. There would be deaths today, withered struldbrugs and young children in rooms with no climate control, probably some of the taspers he'd seen last night, fried in direct sunlight because they didn't care enough to move to the shade. The urban heat bubble of the East coast megalopolis raised the local temperature as much as ten degrees. On Earth it didn't matter how many problems you solved, how efficient you made your processes, how completely you recycled. The inexorable crush of population guaranteed there would always be another crisis. The fertility laws helped, but the Fertility Board itself was corrupt, and despite the promises made every election to clean it up, somehow each census came in higher than the last one.

It was just a three-minute flight to UNF headquarters. General Tobin had an office there, though he was rarely at it. Tobin was a field commander, stocky and with his broad chest full of medals, iron gray hair cropped close. System defense was the largest and best funded command, and for that reason a highly political post. As a result he preferred to command from the Moon, where the only politicians who could interfere with him were those willing to get on a shuttle. It did little to decrease the frequency of political visitors, he admitted, but he maintained that it improved their quality considerably.

After the pleasantries he got right to the point. "You're not in my chain of command anymore, Major. What's this meeting about?"

Tskombe nodded. "My mission is complete, my report is filed. I'm asking to be returned to your command."

"That's not my decision."

"But your request wouldn't be denied."

"True." Tobin leaned back. "So tell me why you're so eager to get out from under the Security Council."

Tskombe shrugged. "There's nothing more I can do for them. There won't be another diplomatic mission to Kzinhome anytime soon."

"I read your report. It's disturbing. It could mean war. All-out war."

"I hope that can be averted, sir."

"You've heard what Assemblyist Ravalla is saying." It wasn't a question.

"I saw a little on the newsfeeds."

"He's been pounding the war drums hard. It's an election trick, appealing to emotion and making Secretary Desjardins's policies seem weak. Desjardins was relying on the success of your mission more than you might imagine."

"All the more reason for me to get back to active service."

"Quacy." Tobin leaned forward. "I've known you long enough to know that you don't do anything without a plan. What is it you want?"

"Sir, there is another issue . . ."

"I'm listening."

"Sir, Captain Cherenkova is still down on Kzinhome, trapped in the middle of a civil war. We have to get her out of there."

Tobin nodded. "I understand your concern for your comrade, Major, but there are larger things to consider here. I understand from your report that you allied yourself with the son of the deposed Patriarch."

"Yes sir, I did. We did."

"Did you ever stop to consider that you put yourself, and by extension the United Nations and all of the human race, in a very bad position with respect to the new Patriarch?"

"The new Patriarch is also the son of the deposed Patriarch, sir."

"Don't dodge the question, Major."

"I'm not, sir. My point is that we had no basis or ability to make a long-term judgment. It was a tactical situation and our lives were at stake. We had an understanding formed with Meerz-Rrit, with whom we were empowered to negotiate. I should add that that occurred through some very difficult negotiations, and that Captain Cherenkova, Dr. Brasseur, and myself pledged our personal words to cement the bargain. Meerz-Rrit took that understanding and acted to make it happen on the kzinti side based on nothing more than our word that we would do our utmost to see the UN implement its half of the deal. He took considerable personal risk to do that, and in fact that risk, while not a contributing factor in the invasion, has been used by his usurpers to justify his overthrow. We learned all this later. At the time we had no idea who would win, or even who was fighting, and allying ourselves with First-Son-of-Meerz-Rrit was purely a matter of survival. We did not at any time have the opportunity to ally ourselves with the invaders, or with Second-Son-of-Meerz-Rrit, who I assure you is only a figurehead Patriarch. Even if we had had options, to break faith with Meerz-Rrit's heir would have destroyed the credibility we had worked very hard to build up with the Rrit, and I emphasize it would *not* have bought us any new credibility with the Tzaatz. To switch sides would confirm our role as herbivores, without honor, untrustworthy and existing only to be conquered. At least now when we negotiate with Kchula-Tzaatz we can start at the table as warriors who can be relied upon to keep their word at any cost."

"Your arguments are persuasive, Major."

"They are the simple truth sir."

"Nevertheless, you understand, that in purely human terms, your actions have caused quite a disturbance. The General Assembly is already split down the middle on the issue of what to do about the kzinti. The civil war and your alliance with the losing side have brought the issue to a pitch."

"How do you mean?"

"Muro Ravalla is vying to be the next Secretary General. He's riding on the wave of fear this has brought on, and his position is that we need to exterminate the kzinti, once and for all. Immediately."

"He's a fringer, he'll never get in."

"He controls the largest single faction on the floor right now. This crisis over the kzinti has put him dangerously close to a majority. Desjardins is on his way out."

"How?"

"Your little announcement has caused quite a bombshell. Right now it's still under secret discussion in the Security Council, but that's only because Ravalla is waiting for the right moment to leak it to the 'casters. Once it gets out, all hell is going to break loose, mark my words. There will be a confidence vote, and Desjardins is on record saying he'll retire if he doesn't win the next one. When he goes I wouldn't bet against Ravalla winning Secretary General, with a majority behind him as well."

"Sir, I recognize that, but with all respect, we still need to go and get Captain Cherenkova back. We simply can't leave her there; it's not an option."

"It isn't an option I like taking, but that is exactly what we're going to do." He held up a hand to forstall

Tskombe's protest. "We aren't going to abandon her. We are going to go through channels to this Kchula-Tzaatz and ask for them back, very firmly I might add."

"Sir, with respect, that is simply going to fail. The Patriarch is dead, the Patriarchy is in civil war, or might as well be! Who are you going to go through? The Patriarch's Voice on Wunderland? His influence is gone, dissolved; it died with Meerz-Rrit. Are you going to send another diplomatic mission? They'll be eaten! The *only* hope we have of stopping it is to throw our weight behind First-Son-of-Meerz-Rrit, and the way to do *that* is get down on Kzinhome and find Ayla Cherenkova." His voice carried the passion of his feeling. *And how much of my interpretation of the right course of action is based on my desire to get her back? Almost all of it.*

Tobin leaned back, looked Tskombe over. "Quacy, are you personally involved with this woman?"

"She's a fellow officer, sir."

"Skillfully evaded. I'll take that as a confirmation." He leaned forward again. "So you are recommending what, that we send in a squadron, just show up in kzin space in violation of treaty and stage an assault landing?"

"No sir, we go in a freighter, or several, carrying a hand-picked team, with Wunderlander kzinti as guides and interpreters. I'll go myself. Just give me the ship."

"You are seriously advocating dropping a group like that, uninvited by *any* of the factions involved, into the middle of an alien civil war to find Captain Cherenkova and this deposed maybe-Patriarch? Who you left, I might add, in the middle of a firefight. I hate to break it to you son, but she and First-Son-of-Meerz-Rrit are probably dead."

"Sir, it was you who taught me the UNF didn't leave people behind."

"So your primary goal here is the recovery of Captain Cherenkova."

"Yes sir."

Tobin's expression hardened "Your personal feelings are getting in the way of your judgment."

"We can't abandon her sir."

"We aren't abandoning her. Neither are we creating a major diplomatic incident at an extremely delicate time for both the kzinti and ourselves. Am I clear?"

"Yes sir."

"Good." Tobin leaned forward. "I understand it's hard, Quacy. I don't like it any more than you do. You've done a good job in difficult circumstances. I'm putting you down for a citation and recommending your expedited promotion to full colonel. My request to have you transferred back to my command will go out this afternoon and it will be complete before you get back to quarters. In the meantime, you've got four weeks' leave, starting now. Tell the orderly to put the paperwork through when you go out."

"Thank you, sir." There was nothing else to say.

"And Quacy?"

"Yes sir."

The general leaned forward, putting force into his words. "There will be no unauthorized missions here, understood? I want your feet to stay firmly on this little green Earth. Not Kzinhome, not Wunderland, not even a weekend on the Moon, do I make myself clear?" Tobin's gaze was level and unblinking.

"Absolutely, sir."

The general's expression softened. "I understand how hard it is for you, but I have to keep my eye on the bigger picture. There's a very good chance that she's already dead, and if we don't handle this properly a lot more people are going to die as well. We're going to do our best, Quacy. Going in commando style is just too risky."

"I understand, sir." Tskombe saluted and left, keeping his face expressionless.

The gravcar was waiting to carry him back to quarters. Tobin was right, of course, and his decision was the only viable one. There was no hope that Ayla was still alive, and no hope that a rescue mission would be able to locate her even if she was. He had been denying that reality, denying it from the moment the Tzaatz tanks had shown up and he'd been forced to boost with her and Brasseur still on the ground. He put his head in his hands. Ayla was gone.

In the time before time, Ftz'rawr, Patriarch of the Stone Lands, coveted the daughter of Kzall Shraft. Kzall thought Ftz'rawr weak and would not give his daughter, for though Ftz'rawr offered all the iron in the Stone Lands, he had not enough strakh to command a daughter of Shraft Pride. He sought then to win her by challenge, but Zree Shraft fought as her champion, and Ftz'rawr was defeated. Finally Ftz'rawr declared the Honor-War, and eight-to-the-fourth warriors of the Stone Lands descended and slew all of Shraft Pride save Zree Shraft, son of Kzall, who escaped and swore vengeance. Twice-eight times around the seasons Zree Shraft wandered, and no Pride would take him in, for he was death-marked by Ftz'rawr, who had threatened to end the line of any who aided him. And Zree became Zree-Shraft-Who-Walked-Alone and lived his life to fulfill his blood-vow. Ftz'rawr heard of this and was afraid despite his armies and his walls, and so sent Egg-Stealer the grashi to whisper in Zree's ear. Egg-Stealer told Zree Shraft that if he would foreswear kin-vengeance Ftz'rawr would renounce the death-mark, and Zree could claim a place at another Pride's circle. Zree Shraft was cold and tired and hungry and alone, but he took Egg Stealer and told him fiercely, "Tell Ftz'rawr that I will only find warmth in the den he has stolen from me. Tell him that only his blood will slake my thirst and only his death will sate my hunger. Tell that I will not sleep until his ears are on my belt, and tell him I am coming." And Egg-Stealer scurried to Ftz'rawr and told him so, but Ftz'rawr flipped his tail at the news, for he was Great Patriarch now, and had nothing to fear from an outcast. But the Fanged God had seen Zree's pledge, and wanted to see if it was true. So he sent Zree Shraft four tests, of strength, of courage, of wisdom, and of honor, and each of these tests is a tale to itself, which I have no time to tell here. There was one test for each season, and Zree Shraft passed each one in turn, so the Fanged God rewarded him with an army. Zree Shraft led his warriors against Ftz'rawr and the

> *Pride of the Stone Lands was defeated. Zree slew*
> *Ftz'rawr to avenge his father and became Great*
> *Patriarch, and when he died the Fanged God put*
> *him by his side to lead his army, for there was no*
> *other general to equal him.*
>
> —Kitten's Tale: The Legend of
> Zree-Shraft-Who-Walked-Alone

The yearling *zianya* looked around nervously as Ayla Cherenkova watched through a pair of kzinti binoptics, holding one lens to her eye and using it as a telescope because they were too large for her to use both at once. The cluster of new shoots the graceful creature had found was tasty and rich, a rare bonus of nutrition and energy in an area where herd competition made sure that the best of the vegetation was consumed as soon as it appeared. It cropped them eagerly, but the prize didn't come without risk. It was over a hundred meters from the rest of the herd, a dangerous distance from the protection afforded by fifty sets of eyes, ears, and noses. Every few bites it looked up and peered around nervously, fear not quite winning out over hunger in whatever calculus of survival its small brain used to determine the best balance between risk and reward. Evolution had shaped it to make the tradeoff well. It was alive because every single one of its ancestors had made that calculation correctly long enough to reproduce at least once. On average its behavior was exactly optimized for its environment.

Optimal on average, but in this particular instance it had made a disastrously wrong decision. Its genes would not see another generation. Cherenkova could not see

Pouncer, but she knew he was there, creeping paw by paw through the long grass. Closer to the herd the odds were long that he would be spotted before he could leap. Out here the *zianya*'s chances were much slimmer.

There! The long grass rippled and the *zianya* must have heard the rustle. It looked up sharply, wide set eyes scanning for the threat. Pouncer remained invisible, but the prey animal's survival calculations suddenly switched in favor of safety. It turned abruptly and started to trot back to the herd.

Pouncer screamed and leapt, and even at a distance of two hundred meters Cherenkova's blood froze at the sound. The *zianya* startled and froze as well, its head whipping around to see two hundred and fifty kilograms of predator bearing down on it in midleap. Pouncer hadn't been as close as he might have liked, and the herbivore launched itself into a run for its life, bounding so high and fast it seemed to be literally flying, skimming the grass. Like its behavior, its body was optimized for a lifestyle dominated by inexorable predation, with long, powerful legs for instantaneous acceleration and a streamlined rib cage built around a tremendous set of lungs for sustained speed. Pouncer tore after it, his body sinuous and muscular, a streak of orange and black through the long, sunburnt grasses. In the distance the rest of the herd turned as one and took flight. He was no more than ten meters behind the animal, but he was slowly losing ground. A healthy adult *zianya* could run both faster and farther than a kzin could, and with the lead it had started with there was no way Pouncer could catch it. It beelined for its rapidly receding herdmates, and it began to look like it had gotten

away with its gamble. Pouncer was running flat out, but
visibly losing the race.

There was a second blood-curdling scream and T'suuz
burst from cover, almost directly in front of the fleeing
animal. She had positioned herself between the prey and
the herd while her brother stalked it, and now the evolutionary value of cooperative hunting showed itself. The
panicked *zianya* skidded in a desperate effort to turn and
spoil her attack, but it must having been moving twenty
meters a second and was unable to overcome its momentum. Hunter and prey collided with an audible *thump*.
T'suuz tumbled free of the collision and the *zianya* fell in
a cloud of dust, skidding. It was up again and running
almost instantly, but one leg dragged. T'suuz's claws had
found their mark. The skid and the fall had cost it time,
and the injury slowed it. It accelerated away again, no
doubt oblivious to the pain and straining every sinew to
save its life, but Pouncer was hard on its heels now. In desperation it tried to veer away from him but T'suuz had
recovered from her tumble and was cutting across the
chord of its escape circle in anticipation of just that move.
It caught sight of her and dodged back in the other direction, out of options. As it came in front of him again
Pouncer leapt, his claws catching it across the hindquarters, knocking it off balance. It staggered and that was all
it took; another leap and his talons dug into its flanks as he
dragged it down. A high-pitched squeal of agony tore the
air, cut off a second later as T'suuz caught up and sank her
fangs into its throat.

Cherenkova breathed out, suddenly aware of her heart
pounding with adrenaline over the chase, and ran to join

them, suppressing the urge to cheer. It was long over when she got there, the *zianya* bloodly and lifeless. Evolution had made humans into omnivores, efficient hunters who still had to be cautious of the large carnivores who stood at the very top of the food web, and she was overcome by a surge of pity for the poor creature. She looked away as Pouncer began to butcher it with a flaked stone knife to preserve the battery in their single variable sword. T'suuz watched him and licked her bloody muzzle clean. Ayla kept her feelings to herself. There would be meat tonight, the first in four days, and that was what was important.

They saved her the haunches and she roasted them in a fire started with dry grass and sparks struck from a battery pack salvaged from the wreck of the grav transporter they'd stolen at the spaceport. She called it grass, but it wasn't really, just as the glorious plants the kzinti called burstflowers weren't really flowers. Both were excellent examples of parallel evolution. Grass and flowers were latecomers to Earth's biosphere, she knew, but they were good evolutionary answers to the problem of making a living through photosynthesis and had analogs on many worlds. Here the grasses were multi-stranded, like feather dusters, and the flowers had lobes instead of petals, but they still filled the same ecological niche. The grasses burned well enough that she had to be careful not to start a brushfire when she cooked, and they put their own delicate flavor into her meat.

She'd been there long enough to learn how to cook primitive. T'suuz had promised she could lead them to the *czrav*, the primitive Prides who lived in the deep jungle, out of contact with the Patriarchy. How long ago had that been? Long enough that the mountains where they'd abandoned the grav loader were now long out of sight behind them. Now even the wide savannah was ending, sloping down into the river valley that was the entrance to the vast rainforest jungle that stretched south and west a thousand kilometers or more. Long enough that hunger and exposure were becoming routine, long enough for her clothes to stiffen with sweat and dirt and her nose to become used to her own stench. The savannah was infested with gnat-like creatures that swarmed in clouds. They were almost invisible, but gave a tiny, nasty bite that took a long time to heal. As well there was a bigger, buzzing flyer the kzinti called a *v'pren*. *V'pren* got to be as big as her thumb, with jaws to shame an army ant. Their bite took out a sizable chunk of flesh, and between the *v'pren* and the gnats her skin had grown raw and sore. Pouncer had warned her that *v'pren* could kill when they swarmed, and she believed it. There were other dangers too, venomous lizard-things called *mzail mzail*, and the nomadic kzinti hunter prides that Pouncer called the *cvari*. It had surprised Ayla that fifty thousand years after the kzinti had gone to space there were still pockets on Kzinhome that lived wild, hunting with hand-crafted weapons and following the ancient migrations of the savannah's fauna. It had taken only five hundred years from the invention of the steam engine until the last of Earth's aboriginal tribes gave up the hunter-gatherer way of life for the temptations of technology, but it seemed the *cvari* would maintain their lifestyle until the end of time. They carefully avoided the nomads, and Pouncer made her choose hidden locations for her cook fires so they wouldn't be spotted.

Neither of the kzinti seemed to mind her smell too much, although they both made a point of sitting upwind while she cooked. *It can't be more alien than squid.* She'd been living on a diet that alternated *zianya* with hunger and was getting tired of it. Her skin and scalp were dry and itching. That could be just a lack of hygiene or . . . *What vitamins am I missing here?* Her beltcomp told her that a pure protein diet could do that anyway, something to do with the natural acids in the meat, but it didn't tell her what plants on Kzinhome were safe to eat. Of course even *zianya* was not guaranteed to be safe; perhaps the itching was symptomatic of something else, some subtle toxin building up in her system. The *v'pren* seemed to die after biting her; whether the gnat-fliers did as well she couldn't tell. Presumably something in her blood was fundamentally incompatible with their system. *But kzinti eat people.* That was a strangely reassuring thought; it meant eating *zianya* wasn't going to kill her immediately.

Brasseur had said he'd eaten it dozens of times, but that didn't mean it was a survivable diet. *How did he live so long among kzinti?* She had regarded him as an ivory tower academic, not at all well suited to the realities of a dangerous universe, certainly not when compared to combat veterans like herself and Quacy Tskombe. Now she was having to revise that estimate. Wherever she had gone, whatever she had faced, she had the might of the UNSN backing her up. All those years Kefan had spent in the Patriarchy he had only himself. It won him new respect in her eyes. *But it doesn't bring him back to life.*

Nor did that thought help with her own survival. She looked at her *zianya*. Best to stick with what wasn't immediately dangerous, and accept the long-term risks. How long she could survive alone on Kzinhome was an open question, but she wasn't ready to die of acute poisoning just yet. Starvation wasn't an option either, and that thought reminded her of just how hungry she was; four days was a long time with no food. She took a half roasted section of haunch from its improvised spit over the fire and tore into it, the juices running down her chin. The meat was tough but rich and she swallowed hungrily, as much a carnivore as any kzin. Closer to the bone the meat grew too raw and she put it back over the fire to cook further. While she waited she piled a few rocks into a rough inukshuk, the ancient trail markers of the high Arctic Inuit. *Now the people will know I was here.* She'd left one at each night's campsite since they'd left the grav loader in the mountain foothills, a small gesture that somehow affirmed her humanity in her ultimately alien environment.

Pouncer watched her eat for a while, wondering at the monkey alien's food rituals. He appreciated prepared meat, heated meat, spiced meat, even seared meat, skewered and sizzled on red hot plates at a fine house, to be served still steaming while the aromas rose and enriched the air. The preparation of food there was as much a part of the show as the trained dancers on the stage, but this Cherenkova-Captain, she charred the *zianya* like she was trying to sterilize it, and he couldn't understand the purpose of the strange little stone piles she built each evening. Aliens were so . . . alien.

Their camp was concealed in a natural hollow beneath

a small, sandy hillock topped by a lone, wide spreading grove tree. Pouncer stood and leapt to the top to watch the sunset between the younger trunks on its edge. After a time T'suuz came to join him. They lay in silence together, while Pouncer contemplated her. He knew little of kzinretti, but nothing she was corresponded to anything he knew. There was no doubt she was as intelligent as he was, and there was no doubt she deliberately concealed that fact from every other kzintosh but him. That her experience went far beyond the garden of *prret* was obvious, but how she had obtained it was another mystery. There was much to be learned, but so far she had volunteered almost nothing to satisfy his curiosity. The sheer exigencies of escape had precluded any further inquiry since they had crashed the stolen grav loader in some nameless canyon in the Long Range mountains. Survival had become their next concern, and remained their major one, but now there was time. He looked back to the fire where Cherenkova-Captain was slicing the *zianya* haunch into thin strips to preserve it. She would be busy until well after nightfall. He turned to T'suuz.

"So tell me your secrets, sister."

"What secrets?"

"How a kzinrette comes to know of more than food, mating, and kits."

She turned to look at him. "My reason is the equal of yours. Why should I not know as much as you?"

"Hrrr." Pouncer considered that, watching the sky turn velvet black as the stars came out. He turned his palm over to contemplate his talons. "There is more here than raw ability. You are educated and experienced. I am sure it was not Rrit-Conserver who bent your brain every day from dawn to dusk, nor Myowr-Guardmaster who took you into the world to learn sea-sky-and-stone. How did you manage this?"

T'suuz rolled her ears in amusement. "What has a kzin-rette in the Forbidden Garden got but curiosity to satisfy and time to satisfy it with? We are cared for by slaves trained to obey the Hero's Tongue; all are sentients, most of them technical experts in one or more fields. They have access to the entire Citadel and its resources, they can travel anywhere on the planet, beneath the notice of any kzintosh but with the unquestioned authority of the Patriarch's livery. I have walked Hero's Square on a Kdatlyno's leash, traveled South Continent with Pierin slaves as guides. What *kzintzag* or noble would dare question the destination of a slave delivering the Patriarch's daughter? The Female Tongue is enough to control the slave walking me, and even if I must use the Hero's Tongue on occasion, what kzintosh would believe what he'd heard?"

"And how is it that you have reason at all?"

"Do you remember the Test of the Black Priest?"

"Only vaguely. I was very young." Pouncer leaned back, remembering. "I remember being frightened because he was so large. It was the first time I was away from mother, but he was gentle."

"And what was the test?"

"He asked questions, but I don't remember what questions. I do remember I didn't know the answers and had to guess. I don't know how I passed, or how anyone passes at that age."

"You pass by not knowing the answers. For males the test assesses telepathic ability. Those who show latent talent are taken to become telepaths. That's what happened to Elder Brother."

"I am . . ." Pouncer caught himself. "We are the eldest of Meerz-Rrit, sister."

"No, Patriarch's Telepath was eldest, M'ress's first litter. He failed the test and the Black Priests took him and gave him the *sthondat* drug. His litter-sister failed too. For females the tests assess reasoning skills, and again you must not know the answers. Those who reason too well are abandoned at the jungle verge to die. I would have failed myself, but M'ress taught me how to respond, coached me carefully while you slept. It was a tremendous risk for her to train her second daughter, and against the edicts. Had I been caught she might have been given the Hot Needle of Inquiry, and perhaps ruined a plan generations long in the execution."

Pouncer twitched his whiskers in puzzlement. "Who would put a kzinrette to the Hot Needle?"

"The Black Priests would, if they suspected the truth."

"Why?"

"That isn't my secret to tell."

"Then tell me why our mother took the risk."

"Her own training forbade her to, but ours was a difficult birth and she could not bear again. She feared that she would lose us both, and she had the help of the most powerful telepath in the Patriarchy."

"Have you been to the jungle?"

"Once, with our mother to be presented to her Pride."

"Hrrr. I have hunted the jungle verge. It is a dangerous

world. Often hunt parties don't return. The *czrav* must be strong to make their home there."

"The *czrav* are the reason hunt parties don't return, if they manage to survive the other dangers. Their secrets are guarded more closely than mine."

"Hrrr." Pouncer turned a paw over. "The jungle is an unforgiving home."

"It is where we evolved, brother."

"But not where we evolved to." He paused, contemplating. "You are not the only one, of course."

"The only kzinrette with reason? Of course not. I am of Vda line, and all pure daughters of our line possess reason, and one quarter of those of Kcha/Vda whose fathers do not carry the black fur genes and who do carry certain other gene sets. I am one of very few privileged to learn and travel, because I am the Patriarch's daughter, and because Patriarch's Telepath could correct mistakes, should there be one."

"Have there been mistakes?"

"Twice."

"Patriarch's Telepath will make no more corrections." Pouncer paused, considering, remembering his unreasoning fear of the wasted figure on the floating *prrstet*, his anger at the test he believed might have killed him. *I didn't trust him. How little I knew. He was full brother to me.* He looked to the distant horizon as he spoke. "Our brother is certainly dead, sister, and our father. Yiao-Rrit and our other uncles, even Third-Son and the other kits. Second-Son has much to answer for." Unconsciously Pouncer's claws extended. "What was our sister's name, littermate to Patriarch's Telepath?"

"M'rtree."

"M'rtree." Pouncer repeated the name slowly. She had been dead before he was born, convicted of having too much potential, of being a threat to the dominant line. *Had I become Patriarch, how much of this would I have learned? How much did my father know? Almost certainly nothing. Revealing this to the Patriarch would have been too large a risk. Truth is held from those with power. This is an important lesson.* He turned a paw over, extended his claws to look at them. "M'rtree, you too shall have your name avenged."

There was a long silence, then Cherenkova's voice came up the slope, low but urgent. "You two had better come here. We have a problem."

The two kzinti turned and leapt down to the fire beside the human. The problem was a gravcar, high in the sky but coming fast.

Pouncer spat. "The Tzaatz are searching for us. Their full spectrum scanners will have picked up the fire."

Cherenkova nodded. "We need to be out of here."

T'suuz grabbed up the half-roasted meat. "The jungle verge!"

Pouncer didn't answer, just picked up Cherenkova, threw her on his back and started running. On two legs, burdened, he was nowhere near as fast as he had been chasing the *zianya*, but he was still more than fast enough for Ayla, who clung on for dear life. She risked a look back, saw the vehicle coming in at high speed, a second one closing in behind it. There would be others. She had been surprised that the Tzaatz had not pursued them sooner. She couldn't imagine the UNF being so slow on the uptake.

A pulse of heat struck her from behind like a physical blow, as though someone had opened a blast furnace. A second later a line of long grass exploded into fire in front of them. Lasers! The first one must have missed by a hairsbreadth, for her to have felt the heat of the beam like that. Pouncer and T'suuz began to dodge wildly right and left to spoil the gunner's aim, and Cherenkova was uncomfortably reminded of the fate of the fleeing *zianya*. The Tzaatz didn't seem interested in taking prisoners. The dry grass burned fast, forming a wall of fire, but the kzinti simply leapt through it. For an instant the heat was incredible and smoke burned Cherenkova's eyes, but then they were through it and beneath the cover of another grove tree at the jungle's edge. Behind them the whine of polarizers grew and cut off. A gravcar had landed. Another flew overhead, invisible through the thick growth. Pouncer and T'suuz slacked their pace to avoid the thick trunks. Behind them a keening cry echoed: a *rapsar* raider. The Tzaatz behind had dismounted and were giving chase with their beasts. The kzinti stopped for a second to look back.

T'suuz snarled. "Lasers. Honorless *sthondats*. The Conservers will have their testicles."

Pouncer twitched his tail. "We were not the target. They sought to herd us by setting fires."

"Little difference if they'd hit us."

"When honor and shame balance on a needle, who holds the needle?" Pouncer pointed a paw. "We'll go downhill, there will be a river we can follow."

Wordlessly his sister complied, while Cherenkova hung on to his back and wished for a weapon. *I am worse than useless here, a mouth to feed who cannot hunt, the source of the fire that gave away our position, a burden to be carried.* She amounted to a clever pet to the kzinti, nothing more. It was not a comfortable reality for a woman used to starship command, but there was no changing it. *If I'm ever going to get off this world I need to develop my own capabilities.*

The jungle thickened and they slowed again. There were no sounds of pursuit, and she doubted any scanner at any wavelength could effectively penetrate the heavy foliage overhead. They entered the canopy of another grove tree. The trees were well named; the thick central trunk soared to a bushy crown that spread wide and sent runner vines back down to the ground, where they took root to form secondary trunks. Those close to the center were heavy and solid, those on the edges no thicker than her thumb. The tree covered nearly a hectare and the central trunk was better than two meters thick, shaggy with heavy loops of shed bark. The going was easier there, though it was almost completely dark beneath its cover.

A few minutes more brought them to a wide, sluggish stream. T'suuz stopped and regarded it, judging distance. "We can break our trail here."

Pouncer held up a paw. "No. Still water means *ctervs*. We must cross where there is a current, or it is very shallow. We'll go downstream."

They moved on in silence, broken only by the weird calls of jungle animals, some distant, others seeming right on top of them. Twice they disturbed something really big, or so she surmised from the deep, barking alarm call it gave, and the tremendous crashing as whatever it was lumbered away, knocking over small trees. She never actually saw one, and Pouncer seemed undisturbed, so she surmised the animals were herbivores. The largest herbivores were always bigger than the largest predators. She'd learned that somewhere, and it was a calming thought. *Yea though I walk in the shadow of the valley of death I shall fear no evil, because I'm with the two toughest wildcats in the whole tanjed jungle.* Occasionally a gravcar whined overhead. They couldn't hear the trackers behind them, but the Tzaatz had not given up the search. About five hundred meters downstream the river narrowed and quickened into a small rapid, burbling over rocks.

"Here, brother?"

Pouncer sniffed the water carefully. "Here. You take the *kz'zeerkti* across, and give me the haunches. I'll lay a false trail. This burned meat stinks enough they won't notice the monkey scent gone. Keep heading downstream but angle away from the bank. The ground will be easier away from the river."

"Agreed." Cherenkova dismounted from Pouncer's back and declined to get on T'suuz's. There was no need for her to be carried across the river, and she had her pride. A moment later she was debating whether she should have chosen differently as they waded through the murky, knee-deep water with the mud sucking at her boots. She didn't know what a *cterv* was, and she didn't want to find out. The other side of the river was mossy, soft ground, slow going and impossible to avoid leaving tracks on. If the ruse didn't fool the pursuers the Tzaatz would have no trouble at all catching them. T'suuz again offered her back but Cherenkova declined. T'suuz could move no faster than Ayla could on this ground, and the kzinrette's strength was a resource that needed conserving.

They were some distance from the river, moving uphill and onto more solid ground when Pouncer caught up again. Before they could greet him, a kzin screamed in rage and agony behind them. The first was joined by another, and then by a piercing, unearthly cry that could only have been a *rapsar*. The cacophony drowned out the jungle sounds and Cherenkova imagined she could hear splashing water. As quickly as it began the din ended.

Pouncer growled in satisfaction. "They tried to cross still water."

Cherenkova nodded. "The jungle doesn't forgive mistakes."

Pouncer let his fangs show. "They will be out in force at daybreak, and the Tzaatz learn jungle tracking on Jotok. They are unlikely to repeat that error. We must break our trail permanently. We need to find a *myewl* shrub, it will cover our scent."

They listened while he described it, low, with small, smooth leaves, growing in clearings on higher, dryer ground. They found it just as the dim light that filtered through the canopy had faded to the point where Cherenkova could no longer see colors, though perhaps the kzinti still could. They ate the half-cooked *zianya* haunches there, so their powerful odor wouldn't give the sniffers something to work on. The meat was somewhat bedraggled for being dragged through the bush. Cherenkova gagged because it was half raw; the kzinti gagged because it wasn't all raw.

The *myewl* bush was an unremarkable plant, perhaps waist high, and not enough different from any other jungle plant that Cherenkova would have found it on her own. The leaves gave off a faint citrus odor when they were broken. The three rubbed them copiously over their bodies. The juices were slightly astringent and left Cherenkova's skin feeling cleaner than it had since they'd crashed, a welcome side effect. Taking a few steps to pick some more leaves she found a place where the foliage was crushed down. Freshly imprinted in the soft dirt was a four-taloned footprint a meter across. She motioned for Pouncer to come and look.

"*Grlor* predators." He twitched his tail as he said it. "They hunt in packs, usually much deeper in the jungle. These tracks are fresh. We'll stay in the trees."

Cherenkova nodded and swallowed hard. *What do they hunt that's so big they need to cooperate to bring it down?* She didn't want to find out. They took more *myewl* branches in case they needed them again and trudged on in the darkness, Pouncer leading, Cherenkova in the middle, and T'suuz taking up the rear. The night was alive with sound and movement, and Cherenkova found it frightening. At least the *myewl* seemed to stop the tiny gnat-fliers from biting, although they still swarmed densely enough that it was impossible to avoid inhaling them. From time to time gravcars whined overhead but they seemed impotent to spot the fugitives. It didn't surprise Cherenkova. There was so much life and motion in the jungle that whatever sensor readings they got through the triple canopy would be swamped.

Pouncer found another grove tree and they spent the

night in its central trunk. Its rough bark hung in shaggy
loops and made for easy climbing. Five meters up it
branched six ways at once. The branching left a platform
just large enough for all three of them, Cherenkova sand-
wiched between the two kzinti. *I can no longer see them
as enemies.* The absence of anger was a strange feeling.
She remembered her shock at the bloody wreckage of
Midling Station, how she had sworn to avenge the hapless
victims of the kzinti. Shock had become rage, and her
career had changed from an adventure to a crusade: to
save humanity from a voracious alien menace. The rage
had muted over the years, hardened into an implacable
hatred, not hot but cold. She had made it her life's work to
keep the enemy at bay. More years had given her the wisdom to understand that the situation was not so clearcut,
and that humans too were capable of atrocity. She had
made the decision to keep her mind open when she'd
taken the mission to Kzinhome, though her instincts had
screamed against it. Even with that, if someone had told
her she'd be spending the night in an alien jungle between
two man-eating predators she would have laughed. Now
she was glad of it. Despite the heat of the day she cooled
down quickly once they stopped moving, and their fur and
body heat were welcome.

Light didn't filter through the thick canopy until the
sun was well up. Cherenkova awoke to find herself looking at a bright red and green lizard-thing. It was about the
size of her hand and was perched on the bark by her head,
regarding her curiously on extended eye stalks. Closer
inspection revealed an almost invisible coat of fine fur—
not a lizard then, but something else. *Everything here is*

something else. She sat up on one elbow and it vanished in a scurry. Pouncer was gone, but she found T'suuz at the base of the tree. The day was again moving toward sticky hot, and hunger gnawed at her belly as she climbed down. T'suuz had caught a *kz'zeerkti*, the species whose roughly simian appearance led the kzinti to give its name to humanity. She helped T'suuz butcher it into strips, not because she needed the help but because Cherenkova felt she should be doing something to contribute to their collective survival. On closer inspection there were obvious anatomical differences: four digits rather than five, a cross-braced rib cage, ears set too high on its skull for a primate. Still, it had large, lemurlike eyes set in a wrinkled face that looked at once like a baby and a very old man. It had a prehensile tail too, an efficient adaptation to life in the jungle canopy on any planet. The monkey ecological niche and the monkey body plan went hand in hand. *Just as the kzinti approximate the big cats despite a completely different evolutionary track.*

Cooking it was out of the question; even a small fire might alert the searchers overhead. She contemplated it for a while, trying to control an automatic revulsion fortified by a fear of monkey-borne diseases. *But it isn't a monkey, and no disease on this planet has evolved to deal with the human immune system.* Of course neither was her immune system able to recognize Kzinhome's pathogens, but that state of mutual disinterest was good enough for her. In that at least she was lucky. What she ate might be deficient in nutrients or simply poisonous, but she didn't have to fear some devastating jungle illness. She closed her eyes and chewed, gagging down what she could because she needed to keep her strength up. They covered the rest of the meat with crushed *myewl* leaves, to minimize its scent, and then wrapped the resulting bundles in tough grove tree leaves.

Pouncer returned as they finished. Tzaatz tracking teams mounted on *rapsar* raiders were moving down the river, he told them, quartering the area with *rapsar* sniffers. They reapplied *myewl* leaf and pushed on, not on the ground but above it, clambering through the upper reaches of the grove tree to its edge. She had started out with trepidation, sure she couldn't match kzinti climbing ability, but surprisingly she had an advantage in the treetops. T'suuz was well over twice her sixty kilos, Pouncer nearly four times more, and she could climb easily on branches that simply wouldn't hold them. The grove tree was a complex three-dimensional tangle and she found herself climbing higher and ahead, spotting more substantial routes and directing the kzinti to them. *So I have something to offer after all.* It felt good to be useful again. The grove tree went on for half a kilometer or more, and for that distance they would leave no ground spoor at all. The ploy was a calculated risk, trading speed for stealth. It was clever. Whether it was clever enough to fool the jungle-experienced Tzaatz was another question.

There was a clearing at the edge of the grove tree, with another one beyond it. The clearing was coincidentally full of *myewl* shrub. They were on high ground, traveling on a spur that led deeper into the river valley, and both species enjoyed the same soil conditions. They climbed down and took the opportunity to reapply the shrub's leaves. Once up in the next grove tree she felt better leading the way again and rapidly gained confidence in her climbing ability in the web of branches fifteen meters up. She had time now to appreciate the tremendous system of life the tree supported. It was virtually its own ecosystem, supported by the hard green fruits that grew everywhere on the smaller branches. There were several varieties of the lizardish creature she'd woken up to, and dozens of different types of what she labeled *birds* for their bright colors, although their motions seemed closer to bats. Once she saw a long, furry creature with six legs that she dubbed a weasel-snake, and several times she saw groups of *kz'zeerkti* on branches much higher up. The dense web of branches made the grove tree a monkey's paradise.

They had almost come to the tree's central trunk when Pouncer froze, tail erect with the tip cocked forward. She had learned that signal meant *freeze* and she did. T'suuz, some ten meters behind him, froze as well. Very slowly Pouncer pointed down. For a long moment Cherenkova saw nothing, and then movement on the jungle floor caught her eye.

It was a *rapsari* sniffer, small and round bodied, proboscis swinging back and forth as it searched for familiar scents. It had sensed something, but it was confused. It advanced slowly, circling first left, then right. Its handler came behind it, riding one of the reptilian raiders and wearing full mag armor. He snarled something quietly into his comlink. Cherenkova held her breath. A second raider-mounted Tzaatz came up beside the handler. The two conferred momentarily in muted snarls. A gravcar whined overhead. The handler sniffed suspiciously and Cherenkova held her breath. The second Tzaatz looked up, searching the branches. He seemed to be looking right at her and she wanted to scream, her pulse pounding in her ears. It seemed impossible that he didn't see her. Slowly he raised his binoptics to his eyes and started methodically scanning overhead. He hadn't seen her, but he would any second. The *rapsar* sniffer had circled back. Two more Tzaatz moved through her field of view, one of the reptillian raiders grunting. How many were there?

Suddenly she found herself eye to eye with kzinti binoptics. The Tzaatz snarled and pointed right at her and cold fear shot through her system. They were caught, and she was acutely aware that the Tzaatz were under no obligation not to eat her. The sniffer handler looked up and snarled as well. She started to climb away. They hadn't spotted Pouncer or T'suuz. If she could lead the hunters away they might be able to ambush the Tzaatz. At least they wouldn't all be taken together. She looked down to see the warrior raising a crossbow.

There was a scream, suddenly cut off, and the warrior looked away from her. She saw him startle and fire at something she couldn't see, and then a *rapsar* raider ran past without its rider, and both Tzaatz spun their mounts to run. The ground shook under heavy impacts and then *something* appeared out of nowhere and bit the closer Tzaatz in half. It was easily twenty meters long, and amazingly fast for that bulk, long necked and sinuous, like a wingless dragon. The other Tzaatz turned to face it, drawing his variable sword in an act of undeniable courage. Before he could swing at it another of the beasts thundered in and snapped him up, impaling him on half-meter fangs and shaking him like a wolf with a rabbit, decapitating his raider *rapsar* almost accidentally in the process. The other Tzaatz had fled, but distant, heavy footfalls shook the jungle floor, followed by a deep, rumbling call. The *grlor* hunted in packs, Pouncer had said.

She watched in fascination as the beasts devoured their victims. Even a tyrannosaur would have turned tail in front of a *grlor*. The Tzaatz armor and equipment gave them only slight trouble as they tore at the bodies with talonlike foreclaws, digging kzinti meat from its artificial carapace and gulping it down in chunks. The grisly spectacle was over in under a minute. The second beast began to devour the dead *rapsar* raider. The first sniffed, searching back and forth for more prey. It spotted the sniffer, still ambling in circles, and reared back, then struck with speed that would have done credit to a cobra. One second the creature was there, whiffling its proboscis for scent, the next it was gone, and the *grlor* was swallowing. The sniffer hadn't even made a mouthful.

It was smaller game than Cherenkova. How high could that sinuous neck reach? She suddenly realized that her hands hurt from clenching the branches so hard. It took a conscious effort to relax the muscles, and when she did she discovered she was shaking. *Fair enough; this wasn't covered in command school.* She started to climb higher to get out of reach. That was a mistake.

Alerted by the noise of her movement, the first *grlor* looked up, and she found herself staring down into eyes as big as cannonballs and a maw large enough to stand in. Then it struck, its two-meter head smashing through branches as thick as her arm without slowing down. She felt the rush of air as the jaws missed her, but the impact of its attack threw her off the branch she was standing on. Frantically she grabbed out, managed to connect with a higher branch and hang on. For a moment she hung there dangling while the predator contemplated her from below, then, arms trembling, she managed to pull herself up and over the next branch. It wasn't a particularly thick one, and it swayed dangerously under her weight, but she couldn't make herself let go to reach for the next higher one.

The beast seemed to understand she was too high to take, but it hadn't lost interest in her. It stretched its neck up and leaned back, lifting its front legs off the ground and counterbalancing itself with its heavy tail. Its huge head came up, but even at its full height it was a couple of meters too short. That distance gave Cherenkova no confidence at all on her precarious perch. It could easily shake her off it if it tried, and she wondered if it were that smart. At that close range she noticed it was covered in the same fine fur that the tree-scampering lizard-things were, and there were other anatomical similarities as well. Evidently they came in all sizes. She noticed that the jungle noises had stopped, replaced by dead silence. Nothing cared to advertise itself to the *grlor*.

The *grlor* sniffed at her, nosed at branches with its snout, then lowered its forward body but kept its neck stretched up into the grove tree canopy, its curiosity seemingly diverted from Cherenkova. She allowed herself a sigh of relief, then sucked her breath in again. Pouncer! He was still on one of the thicker, lower branches, frozen in place, well within range of the *grlor*'s teeth, and unlike her he could climb no higher. As she watched he slowly reached down for his variable sword. In the distance some creature called, and another answered it. The beast sniffed again, sensing prey close by but confused by the *myewl* scent. Pouncer extended the weapon's slicewire. The hum of the mag-stiffened filament was normally inaudible, but in the total stillness it sounded loud. If Pouncer leapt and struck hard enough he could decapitate it, but his footing was poor, and if he fell the other *grlor* would take him. He was going to try . . .

She couldn't let that happen. Desperately she grabbed one of the grove tree's dense green fruits and threw it at the monster. The fruit bounced off its head, and the *grlor* looked up, its annoyed attention refocused on her. She clambered farther into the grove tree, hoping to draw it away from Pouncer. The huge head snaked after her, smashing through branches and nearly throwing her off again. She grabbed a branch and stopped climbing. The *grlor* seemed to learn from that and bashed against the branches again, shaking her insecure perch wildly. It snapped at her unsuccessfully, then reached up again to the branches. Cherenkova hung on white-knuckled as the beast started tearing away branches with its teeth, a new trick that shook the tree violently.

A kzinti kill scream echoed through the jungle, followed by a deep, rumbling call, and the *grlor* stopped to listen. Its partner, still devouring the *rapsar,* looked up and turned to face the direction the call had come from. The call sounded again. The second *grlor* abandoned its meal and snaked off through the grove tree's trunks, shaking the ground as it ran. The first hesitated, then pulled its neck down from the canopy and took off after the first.

Grlor hunted in packs, and the pack had found better prey.

Cherenkova breathed out, still trembling. She didn't feel sorry for the Tzaatz. *Better them than me.* In the back of her mind she had always wondered how predators as ruthlessly efficient as the kzinti had ever felt the evolutionary pressure required to evolve intelligence and develop weapons. Now she understood. She looked down to Pouncer, who waved her forward. They would carry on. Still shaking she made her way forward to the next grove tree.

The ridge they were following began to slope downward, and they were soon out of grove tree habitat and into a belt of heavy thorn vines that hung in tangled ropes from sparsely distributed trees vaguely reminiscent of palms. The vines were arm-thick cables and the thorns were big enough to make serviceable daggers, but Cherenkova was past wondering at their size. Whatever the *grlor* normally hunted would be a grazer, and a big one. Any plant less well protected would be an easy treat for it. It occurred to her that the vines and the trees might be symbiotes, the trees giving support to the vines, the vines protecting the trees from the grazers. It took them all day to force themselves through the maze toward the river valley floor. Several times Tzaatz gravcars floated over while they crouched under vine thickets, vulnerable there as they were not under the triple canopy, but they got away with it. They seemed to be getting ahead of the search. There was no way a *rapsar*-mounted rider could make it through the thorns, and the Tzaatz seemed loath to dismount.

They stopped for the night by a rivulet and ate the *kz'zeerkti* T'suuz had killed the previous day. The flavor of the *myewl* leaves had seeped into the meat and Cherenkova found it delicious and satisfying even eaten raw. The meat was richer than *zianya*, though tougher, and it made a welcome change.

After they had eaten Pouncer spoke. "You saved my life today, Cherenkova-Captain."

She shook her head. "You and your sister are my only allies on this world. Without you, I would have died long ago."

"Hrrr. This is true, but you have my father's pledge of protection. Now you have my blood debt too." He gave her the kzinti claw-rake salute. She thought it a simple courtesy until she noticed that he had actually drawn blood from his nose, and she found herself at a loss for a response.

He noticed her discomfiture and rippled his ears in humor. "You have much *strakh* with First-Son-of-Meerz-Rrit; this is not a bad thing. There was a time when that was a highly coveted honor." He looked away, and she could sense he was looking to something that existed far beyond the wall of thorns surrounding them. "Someday it will be again."

She slept again between the kzinti, this time finding not only warmth but comfort and reassurance in the contact. Still, she awoke in the middle of the night to find the sky was clear and alive with stars framed by thorn vines. One of them, maybe, would be Sol, barely visible as a fifth magnitude pinprick if she only knew where to look. *Crusader* was up there somewhere too, though probably long gone from kzinti space by now. Even if it were there she could expect no help from that quarter. *Crusader* was forbidden to enter 61 Ursae Majoris's singularity, and even if it did, Lars Detringer had no idea where to find her. More than that, any attempt to rescue her would most probably end with *Crusader*'s destruction. She was expendable—far more expendable than a capital ship, and under the circumstances the UN could make no other choice but to expend her. Had Quacy made it as far as *Crusader*? Had he made it to Earth? He would not abandon her, she knew, but he was only one man, light-years away now, if he was even still alive, and he could never find her where she was. She felt suddenly very alone.

> *The sand will run with my enemy's blood. May the Fanged God find me worthy.*
> —Battle Chant of the Arena Warrior

The Command Lair was quiet. All present were intently watching the wall-sized holo display. Kchula-Tzaatz allowed his mouth to relax into a fanged smile at the scene. It showed not star maps or strategic intelligence but the Patriarch's Arena, where a lone warrior stood surrounded by six dead slashtooth, their blood still fresh in the sand. They looked lethal even in death, heavily muscled, but lean and agile. Around the arena the onlookers roared and slashed the air with their claws. The warrior had defeated the single slashtooth, which was expected, and the pair, which was common. Defeating three at once was an accomplishment. Now he would face four at once, and when it came his death would now be one of honor. The watchers were in a blood frenzy. The camera swung to focus on the crowd, where a sudden circle had formed around a challenge duel. The combatants screamed and leapt, slashing at each other, colliding, falling to roll, then recovering. One of them was injured, and he leapt clear, limping on a bloodied leg. The other screamed and leapt again, but his opponent turned and ran from the arena. The victor roared in triumph, and the circle closed again. There would be more duels in the stands today. The warrior was the son of a Lesser Pride, sentenced to the arena because Tzaatz Heroes had been killed by *kzintzag* on his father's land. It was a good Arena, and it taught a lesson.

The crowd's attention refocused on the Arena floor, and the camera view swung back to the warrior. The four slashtooth had been released, and he was judging his moment. The warrior carried only his *wtsai*, and he was bleeding from a shoulder wound. Kchula looked around the Command Lair to gauge the effect of the display on his own inner circle. Ftzaal-Tzaatz was watching with a critical eye for the Hero's skill; the puppet Scrral-Rrit watched with ill-concealed bloodlust, Rrit-Conserver with studied detachment. Ktronaz-Commander was concentrating on his beltcomp and ignoring the display, no doubt organizing some detail of their occupation. Telepath was lolling in a corner, lost in his own mind, but little more could be expected of that specimen. *I would rather have used* rapsari, *to demonstrate the dominance of Tzaatz Pride*. But *rapsari* were in shorter supply than he was comfortable with. Slashtooth were one of the traditional arena animals, and he would get credit, at least, for following tradition. *Greet necessity with enthusiasm*. The crowd was getting more than a show from the display; they were learning the price of resistance to Tzaatz rule. The Arena had been full every night for the last Hunter's Moon.

In the display the warrior leapt, not allowing the beasts to gather. He connected with the first slashtooth, his hind claws tearing at its neck as it tried to dodge. He let his momentum carry him into a tumble. It had been a good first strike, but he must have hoped to kill the beast at once, and in that he had failed. All four turned, circling to surround him. One of the ones behind him closed to snap, but he must have sensed the attack, for he leapt again at the slashtooth he'd injured, leaving the other's jaws to close on air. This time his claws tore flaps of skin from its forehead, effectively blinding it. Blood spilled and the slashtooth keened in pain. It still wasn't dead, but it was out of the fight, and that was good enough for the warrior's purpose. He was good, very good, both with base skills and the higher strategy necessary to handle a four-to-one fight. The crowd roared its approval. It looked like the warrior would win this round too. He had been trained by the *zitalyi*.

In annoyance Kchula waved a hand, ordering the Command Lair's AI to cut the projection. "Enough entertainment, we need to make progress." No need to watch the defiant warrior win honor in his death. "Ktronaz-Commander, report."

Ktronaz-Commander abased himself, not a good sign. "Our teams continue the search, Patriarch."

"Continue to search?" Kchula stood up, angry. "It's been four days. Are you even sure it was them?" Ktronaz remained abased. It was galling to be forced into such humiliation in front of the assembled Tzaatz war council, but it was better than the alternative, which would be instant execution at the claws of Ftzaal-Tzaatz.

"We cannot be sure until we catch them, Patriarch. The *kz'zeerkti* . . ."

"I have seen the images." Kchula waved a hand at the screen, striding back and forth at the head of the room. The AI interpreted the words and gesture as a command to play the relevant recording. The holo display lit up again, showing gun camera footage from a combat car, blurry and unstable with the car's motion. Two kzinti figures ran through the savannah while laser bolts ignited the grass around them. The larger of the two carried a creature on its back, and if you used your imagination you could suppose it was one of the *kz'zeerkti* aliens. "I need proof."

"Sire, the jungle . . ."

Kchula kicked his subordinate in the ribs to shut him up. "The jungle. I tire of your excuses. Jotok is covered in jungle, Tzaatz warriors are trained in jungle combat. Four days and four nights since you found them, and you haven't so much as a footprint!" He turned on his heel. "And what of these attacks on our Heroes? Are they anything like the scum we just saw? Do the Lesser Prides require stricter lessons?" Kchula didn't wave to the screen to bring up the Arena; he didn't want to see the condemned warrior winning any more honor.

"Rarely, sire. They are rabble among the *kzintzag*, nothing more. They ambush lone warriors. The attacks are isolated, the damage limited. We are asserting control."

"Not quickly enough. They insult our honor. I want reprisals. The Arena is not punishment enough. You will end the line of every scum who opposes us. Fathers and sons, brothers and uncles. Is that clear?"

Ktronaz-Commander claw-raked, as well as he could in his position. "As you command, sire."

"Ftzaal!"

"Yes, brother?" The black-furred kzin had been watching the exchange from the sidelines dispassionately.

"Organize your warriors into hunt parties. Make sure they are protected against the *dangers* of the jungle." Kchula looked at Ktronaz-Commander with contempt. "Kzin-Conserver is returning tomorrow. He knows by now . . ." Kchula paused to substitute words; Rrit-Conserver was in the room. ". . . that we made a mistake in identifying First-Son-of-Meerz-Rrit's body. I do not need the ascension called into question." Across the room Scrral-Rrit, who had been Second-Son, cringed at the suggestion. He was included in the war council by the demands of tradition, but not invited to speak at it.

"I will see it done, brother. I request the use of Telepath in the hunt."

"Take him."

Ftzaal-Tzaatz claw-raked and left, making a peremptory gesture to Telepath as he went to the door. Telepath scurried after him.

"As for you." Kchula spat at his prostrated ground force leader. "You who call yourself Commander, get out of my sight. Send for Stkaa-Emissary."

"As you command." Ktronaz-Commander backed away on his belly, and claw-raked at the door, his ears laid flat.

Kchula watched him go. *He will be angry, and the reprisals will be harsh. The* kzintzag *will learn that consequences of defying the Tzaatz are severe.* His mouth relaxed into a fanged smile.

"So First-Son lives." Rrit-Conserver's voice cut the silence like a *wtsai* blade.

"Not for long." Kchula rounded to face the speaker, fight juices still fresh in him.

"You were not wise to reveal that fact to me, Kchula-Tzaatz."

"Are you going to tell me now that he commands your loyalty above this specimen?" He stabbed a claw at the still silent Scrral-Rrit. "The belief that First-Son was dead was instrumental in securing your support for this sorry *sthondat*'s accession to Patriarch, which is in turn useful in pacifying the Lesser Prides. It is no longer necessary."

"I already knew that, Kchula. Now I may no longer pretend that I don't."

"Know this then. The use I had for you has ended. Find others or face the arena."

"Threats now, Kchula-Tzaatz?"

"You are a fool if you doubt my willingness to do it."

Rrit-Conserver's whiskers twitched. "And insults. You cannot lose further honor with me, Kchula-Tzaatz." It was a simple statement of fact. *I will not conceal my response to the disrespect he throws in my face.* Kchula bristled and looked about to leap. *He is a fool, and a coward. How did he gain power, and how does he retain it?* Ftzaal-Tzaatz was a large part of the answer. No one would challenge-claim Kchula while the Protector of Jotok stood as *zar'ameer.* Why Ftzaal-Tzaatz stood content with that position when he was clearly the superior warrior was less clear. *What is the Black Priest's game?* "Putting a Conserver in the Arena will unite the Great Prides against you in a heartbeat. While First-Son lives your puppet is useless."

Kchula relaxed. "Who knows if First-Son is alive or dead? We have this Patriarch here, so ascended by the High Priests, approved by both Kzin-Conserver and yourself. None of you can now go back on that."

"When First-Son returns none of us will need to. His claim takes priority, and your puppet"—he still did not look at Second-Son—"will not stand up to it."

"He won't have to. First-Son will never get close enough to him to challenge, you can mark my words on that. If he's in the jungle the chances are he's already dead."

"You are overconfident, Kchula-Tzaatz. Your failure is thus inevitable."

"Pah. We don't know if this fleeing *vatach* we seek is even him. Soon enough the issue of the Rrit succession will be irrelevant. Already the Lesser Prides of Kzinhome bow to my command. The Great Prides will follow strong leadership, whoever gives it. Once they are used to my commands issued in Scrral-Rrit's name, they will become used to my commands issued directly. I have mated the Rrit daughter we still have, and she is safe in the Garden of Prret, and our Patriarch will have no sons. My Eldest by her will succeed me, and the Tzaatz line will rule the Patriarchy."

Across the room, the cowed Second-Son looked like even he might leap at that deep insult, but Kchula locked eyes with him, and moved a paw to the pendant that might command the *zzrou* to send poison into his system. The erstwhile Patriarch subsided into humiliated silence.

"And how will you lead the Great Prides anywhere but further pride war and anarchy, Kchula?" asked Rrit-Conserver.

"A strategist like you shouldn't have to wonder, wise Conserver." Kchula said the words with mocking formality. A chime sounded and Kchula touched his command desk. "Watch and learn." Behind him the guards opened the Command Lair doors to admit Stkaa-Emissary. "Where I lead the Patriarchy will follow." He turned to face the newcomer. "Stkaa-Emissary."

"Kchula-Tzaatz." Stkaa-Emissary turned to Scrral-Rrit and performed a perfunctory claw-rake. "Patriarch." He turned to Rrit-Conserver. "Honored Conserver." His courtesies were all appropriate to their recipients by virtue of their own rank and his, but he had addressed Kchula-Tzaatz first, a fact lost on no one in the room.

"Stkaa-Emissary. You gave me fealty when I most needed it." Kchula's eyes were wide, ears swiveled up in focused attention for the other's response. Putting it in those terms assumed the submission of Stkaa Pride to Tzaatz Pride, not yet a reality. *But so I define the power relationship, and dare him to defy it. Let Rrit-Conserver be witness to this.* "Tzaatz Pride honors its obligations. Your reward is the vanguard of the greatest conquest in eight-cubed generations. Are the fleets of Stkaa ready to leap on Earth?"

"If you compel the support of Cvail, and offer your own, we cannot fail."

"The entire Patriarchy will be behind you." Kchula turned to Scrral-Rrit. "Will it not, Patriarch?"

"Yes, yes, of course." It was the function of Scrral-Rrit to confirm the edicts of Kchula-Tzaatz as he was required to. Kchula felt pleasure at that. While he was obeying the letter of tradition in deferring to his puppet, the real power relationship was obvious to all.

"Sire!" Stkaa-Emissary's tail stiffened, his whiskers bristling in the thrill of the hunt. "The Heroes of Stkaa will leap at your command!" Who he addressed the "Sire" to was open to question.

Kchula growled. "We have trifled with the *kz'zeerkti* for too long. Conquest is our destiny."

"Yes, sire! I request permission to leave at once to tell Tzor-Stkaa! We have ships at the ready."

"Granted." Kchula purred deep in his throat. There was no longer any question as to who was being addressed as "Sire." "Tell him to leap on K'Shai as soon as preparations can be completed. Retake your world and reclaim the honor of Stkaa Pride. Our fleet will be behind you, and the fleets of all the Great Prides. We shall stage from K'Shai to Earth itself, and then its colonies will be easy meat. Ch'Aakin and the others we will retake at our leisure"

"I shall send news of our victories." Stkaa-Emissary left at the leap, and Kchula turned to Rrit-Conserver.

"You see now what will happen? The Lesser Prides are quelled by my puppet. Now the Great Prides will be quelled by the thought of spoils, and the need for solidarity in the face of the *kz'zeerkti* enemy. We shall finish this upstart race, and by the time the war is done my own position as the undisputed power in the Patriarchy will be secure. This matter of First-Son-of-Meerz-Rrit is a triviality. If my brother does not kill him the jungle will. Even if he somehow survives his position will be irrelevant."

Rrit-Conserver remained silent.

> *The woods are lovely, dark, and deep*
> *But I have promises to keep,*
> *And miles to go before I sleep.*
> *And miles to go before I sleep.*
>
> —Robert Frost

Was it better to go in person or just make a comcall? Colonel Quacy Tskombe stood in front of the UNF Personnel Command building, considering. He caught a glimpse of his reflection in the call booth glass and looked away. The tabs of his new rank no longer looked new; his face looked decidedly older. He considered the options. Go inside and his presence there would be registered as soon as the cameras saw him, but there was little chance his conversation would be monitored. Make a call and he might well get monitored, but if he didn't, there'd be no connection between him and Jarl—at least, not until later, when someone scanned the call logs. And if he did get monitored, it would be an accident. He hadn't done anything illegal yet. There was no reason for there to be a tag on his ident.

In person is better when you need a favor. But he would be asking Jarl to put himself on the line, and the less implicated he was the better, once Quacy Tskombe vanished and people started trying to figure out how that had happened, once Marcus Tobin in particular started looking. That wasn't a pleasant thought. Tobin was more than his commander, he was his mentor, and a friend. But the UNF was not his future. His future, if he had one, was Ayla Cherenkova, and he was going to get her off Kzinhome or die trying.

Comcall is best, and keep it short. Keeping Jarl safe had to be a priority, if only because the other would be less likely to refuse to help in order to protect himself. Jarl Nance was another old friend, a UN Military College classmate, and a man who, like Freeman Salsilik, he had not seen in years. His name was first on the short list Tskombe had made of people who might be able and inclined to help him, names culled from memory and searched on the 'net. Where Tskombe had chosen the infantry and life among the stars, Jarl, despite a reputation as a daredevil and rule breaker at school, had chosen administration and a career in New York. Now he ran the Transit office for Personnel Command, which gave him a certain amount of indirect power. Tskombe had protected Jarl more than a few times, saved his career from ending before it began over cadet pranks, and now it was time to call in the favor.

He'd spent most of his enforced vacation trying to get approval to go back to Kzinhome to get Ayla off it. It was becoming clear that neither Marcus Tobin nor the military bureaucracy were going to yield on their position. They had, not unreasonably, given her up for dead. The only problem was, Quacy hadn't given up and he wasn't feeling reasonable about it. The mission he wanted was out of the question for the UNF, so he was going to do it himself. To get to Ayla he needed to get to Kzinhome, which meant getting to Wunderland. Those were problems he'd face when he had to; the immediate difficulty was getting off Earth. Jarl might be the solution to that.

So next decision: call on his beltcomp or use a call booth? One less trace if he used a public screen, but they'd be more likely to monitor the call. A harried-looking man came up, jumped in the call booth and started dialing. Tskombe watched as the strain on his face grew tenser as the call went through, and then the man was almost instantly in the middle of a heated debate with whoever was on the other end. It would be a while before he finished; that simplified the decision a lot. He tabbed Jarl's dialstring into his beltcomp and thumbed call. The screen flashed its wait pattern, then Jarl looked out of the screen. He had aged visibly, lost a lot of hair and gained a lot of weight. *Do I look so different after fifteen years?* That wasn't an important question right now.

"Jarl, Quacy Tskombe."

"Quacy!" The face in the screen smiled in recognition. "How are you? Where are you?"

"I'm in New York. Listen, I need a favor."

"Name it." That was the old Jarl, ready for any adventure, and Quacy's hopes rose. If anyone could get him on a ship it would be Jarl.

"I need to get to Wunderland."

"Just thumb your orders over and I'll set you up." Jarl smiled, happy to help an old friend. "We should get together before you go."

"I'd like that, Jarl, but listen, I don't have any orders."

"Well, as soon as you get them . . ."

Tskombe cut him off. "I'm not getting any orders, Jarl. I need to get on a ship."

The other man's eyes widened. "That's illegal."

"I need you to do it."

"You know I can't do that." There was fear in Jarl's eyes now, the friendliness gone.

"It's important. I have to get to Kzinhome, at least to Wunderland so I can find my way from there."

"Quacy! For Finagle's sake! Going off-planet without orders, that's desertion."

"There are lives at stake."

Jarl half turned, as if to see if anyone was watching over his shoulder. "It's not even safe to talk about that kind of thing."

"You owe me, Jarl." Tskombe hadn't wanted to say it. *And when you have to say it there's a problem.*

Jarl looked away. "I . . . I'll do what I can. I can't promise anything."

"Thanks."

"Sure, anything." Jarl smiled again, some semblance of his old self returning. "You know that."

"I know, Jarl." And Tskombe had believed him, right up to that final line, but he knew Jarl was lying now; he had heard the fear in his voice, seen the way his eyes had slid away from the cam as he spoke. There would be no travel documents downloaded to Tskombe's beltcomp, no authentications to clear him through customs and port security, no berth on a ship boosting for Wunderland. He was going to have to find another way, because Jarl was not going to do anything that might be dangerous, no matter what loyalty he owed old friends, not even to level old debts. Fifteen years was too long.

Which was why he was pushing buttons in an office and not commanding a combat team. A commander had to be willing to take risks for those he led or lose the ability to lead. Jarl was not a bad man, but his character did not include risk taking. His stunts in school had been attention getters, risking school discipline but no serious consequences, and when it came down to choosing a career path, he'd chosen the safest he could. Tskombe left the call booth and got back on the slidewalk. Would Jarl turn him in? For a moment the question turned Tskombe's veins to ice water, but then he relaxed. No, that would involve more trouble for him than staying silent. Jarl would just forget the call, deny all knowledge if anyone asked him. That was his way. He'd only take action if he had to do it to save himself.

A cold sweat suddenly beaded on Tskombe's back. And what if Jarl felt he had to do it to protect himself? On a colony world the thought wouldn't have entered his mind, but this was Earth, where personal privacy was centuries out of fashion. What was the statistic? Ten percent of every data channel was dedicated to the ARM for monitoring purposes. He'd kept the call short to lessen the odds of an intercept, but low risk didn't mean zero. So if the ARM already knew and Jarl didn't report him, Jarl would be in serious trouble.

Would he do it? One way to find out, perhaps. He punched redial on his beltcomp, and got a busy screen. He punched disconnect as the system started to ask him if he wanted to queue the call. Jarl was talking to someone.

Was it ARM, or was it coincidence? No way of knowing, but the question wasn't going to go away now. Tskombe leaned against a building wall, thinking. He should have thought this through before hand, should have made a clearer plan. He keyed the screen to replay the call. He muted the audio, watched Jarl's eyes as the conversation progressed. The beltcomp's small display made it hard to see, but it was written there on Jarl's face as he mouthed the promise, in the way his eyes flicked to the dialer by the pad even before he'd rung off. Jarl was looking to his next call, he had already decided he needed to report Tskombe purely to protect himself.

Tskombe cursed low under his breath and looked up. There was a hoverbot there, just floating. It was impossible to say which direction its scanners were facing. Had it been there before? Could the ARM really respond that fast? He looked long and hard at it, and after a long moment it floated away. If it had been following him it wasn't paying attention anymore. Which meant nothing of course. There would be other bots with broad-spectrum zoom cameras higher up. There were cameras in the corridors, cameras on the streets. Earth didn't even have anonymous money, you had to thumb your account for every transaction. He couldn't so much as take a skycab or use a call booth without having it logged. He would be tracked, if anyone felt like tracking him. This was Earth.

He let the slidewalk carry him toward Central Park. He needed a drink, and he needed time to plan, preferably out of sight. The first problem was easy enough to solve. He let the slidewalk carry him along to the next hotel, he didn't catch the chain name but it didn't matter. The lobby was grandiose in marble, polished brass, and crystal, designed to impress, but it was interchangeable with any other designed-to-impress lobby in any other chain hotel in known space. Only the gravitational field told him what planet he was on. Half a millennium of cheap transport and instant communications had homogenized Earth's culture, and since the hyperdrive had become reality, that culture had inexorably permeated the colonies as well.

The hotel bar was classy in the same way, a real live piano player with a real live piano playing light jazz, well-dressed men and expensive women, UN politicos and business players. He bought a drink that claimed to be single malt scotch distilled from pure-strain grain and was priced accordingly, and sat down to think. He had acted hastily in contacting Jarl, and he'd done it without a back-up plan, a serious violation of military planning procedure. He'd been overconfident that a call to a friend would solve his problems, get him a berth on the next shuttle boosting. He was used to the colonies where state control was less total, and used to the front line military, where rules were meant to be broken. Earth was a different ballpark, and just because he still knew his way around Manhattan didn't mean he knew his way around. He'd had nagging doubts about Jarl and had suppressed them. *That is because I've been avoiding the truth about what I'm doing.* He downed half his whiskey at once, taking the burn in his throat as punishment for the ultimate sin of lying to himself. *I am deserting, nothing more, nothing less.* It was a violation of his oath as an officer, his own personal creed of duty and integrity, his self-identification as a commander. It would transform him in an instant from a war hero on his way to a general's bar to a hunted criminal, but it was what he had decided to do, and half-measures would only make him fail at the transformation. *Unacceptable.*

So how much damage had his conversation with Jarl done? Assuming Jarl reported it he would get no more than a slap on the wrist from Marcus Tobin, maybe not even that much. It was unlikely Jarl had the conversation recorded. If the ARM hadn't monitored it at random then there would be no evidence. *Except what I'm carrying here.* He pulled out his beltcomp, called up the recording and erased it, then purged the empty memory. No need to provide that evidence himself. At the same time, he could well have his ident tagged, and that would make getting away in the future a lot more difficult. Flatlanders had too little privacy. He had never noticed that when he'd been a Flatlander himself, nor had he noticed it when he left for space. Only on his return was it clear how tightly the ARM controlled Earth's population. Their badges read *Maintient le droit,* but they said nothing about whose rights were maintained. Outside the gray zones, Earth had a very low crime rate. Petty criminals tended to get caught, major criminals and syndicates simply got the laws changed to redefine whatever they did as legal. Muro Ravalla was widely accused of colluding with an industrialist cabal who siphoned billions out of the defense budget into their own pockets. Ravalla simply stood up and invited his opponents to demonstrate that he'd broken the law, while his faction slipped through amendments that made what he did legal.

Not a helpful thought train. Quacy Tskombe had

already broken the law and he had no political clout to
save him if he got caught. He planned to break it again;
the only question was how. It was clear he wasn't going to
get on a ship with a UNF clearance on his ident. If he was
getting off-planet, he was going to have to find someone
who could make it happen, and that meant finding some
criminals. He sipped his drink, considering. He had a limited amount of time to make that happen, and he had to
be more careful now, just in case Jarl had gotten his ident
tagged. He looked up at the camera bubble in the piano
bar's ceiling. Whatever he was looking for, this wasn't the
place to find it.

He paid for his drink, and took the opportunity to
download his credit balance from his bank to his beltcomp. Money, at least, would not be a factor. Fifteen years
soldiering added up to a lot of accrued pay and bonuses,
with dividends piling up in his investment fund. With so
many years living with the UN forces off-world he'd had
little need to make major purchases. Doing the download
meant assuming the risk that he'd lose the beltcomp and
his savings with it, but it also meant the ARM couldn't
freeze his assets. That wouldn't make much difference on
Earth, where they could tell the financial system not to
accept credit tagged with his ident, but if he could make
it to a colony world he could convert his balance to cash
and spend it without trace. Outside the long summer dusk
was fading slowly. He'd spent longer than he'd thought in
the bar. He avoided the slidewalk, went back down to the
pedestrian level, walked up toward Central Park, looking
for . . . what? He couldn't hope to find a connection to a
smuggling syndicate wandering the streets at random; the

best he could hope to do would be find someone who could point him in the right direction. His skill set wasn't particularly adapted to navigating the underworld.

Another hoverbot whirred overhead, a common enough occurrence, but newly disturbing. Was it looking for him? When he'd been at the academy the accepted truth was that the ARM had a thousand cameras per block in the City. It was hard to know if that was true. Certainly it took the cops only minutes to show up at any crime in progress that could be visually identified as such. Desertion wasn't that kind of crime, but the computers could recognize his face, if anyone told them to look for it, and there were other indicators, like downloading his entire net worth to his beltcomp. *Did Jarl really turn me in?* What could anyone do about it if he did? If Jarl had agreed to get him off-planet then the crime was conspiracy to desert. If he actually tried it then the crime was desertion, but neither of those things had happened. *So why am I feeling so edgy?* If they were tracking him they'd know where he was from his bar transaction, so they might have sent a hoverbot to pinpoint him. On the other hand, hoverbots were everywhere, a fact of life.

Overhead a gravcar broke out of the traffic pattern and headed down toward him. Another common occurrence, but a thrill of fear ran through him. *Why?* The gravcar hadn't been in the eight-layer traffic pattern; it had been underneath it, on the level reserved for emergency vehicles. *Cop!* Instinctively he ducked under the slidewalk and turned to run back the way he'd come. In response a siren wailed and a spotbeam split the gathering darkness. An amplified voice told him to halt, but he ignored it. The spotbeam swung and pinned him, and then he was pelting down the pedestrian way, dodging startled citizens as the gravcar pursued him. Dimly he was aware of the stupidity of trying to outrun a gravcar, of trying to outrun the ARM at all, but as long as he kept moving they couldn't get out of the car and take him.

As long as he kept running . . . but he couldn't run forever. A citizen ahead of him collapsed, and he felt a sting on his neck, followed by spreading numbness. Mercy needles! One wouldn't knock him out, but ten would, and they'd spray until they got him. He started dodging left and right, trying to make himself a difficult target. They wouldn't want to keep hitting bystanders, so make it hard for them. The amplified voice was still telling him to halt, but he ignored it. He needed a plan! First get out of the line of fire. An arched glass doorway led to a shopping arcade and he dodged into it. Behind him the siren blared again, warning people out of the way as the ARM set their gravcar down. The arcade was upscale, selling expensive clothing and unnecessary gadgets from posh storefronts. Tskombe settled down to a steady jog, trying to look like a man in a hurry and not a fugitive. There was a camera ball over the doorway, another at every hall intersection. The ARM dispatcher would have them slaved, tracking his progress and keeping the pursuers updated. A map holo floated over an information booth and he scanned it as he ran past, saw three exits from the arcade. By now the ARM would have them all covered. He was caught. He might as well have let them take him outside. He stopped running, breathing deeply, looked around to assess the situation. A commotion at the doorway he'd come in through warned that the cops were out of their car and in close pursuit. He was running out of options in a hurry.

A blank metal door marked staff only. Maybe it went nowhere; but it was better than nothing. He jogged to it, tugged at it. Locked. He thumbed the pad reflexively but the door ignored him. Not an option. He turned to find a place to hide, and was nearly knocked over as a man in a green maintenance uniform came through the door carrying a heavy box.

"Excuse me."

"My fault." Tskombe smiled, held the door open for him. The man walked on without looking back, and Tskombe went through the door. It closed behind him with a satisfying *thunk*. The cops would miss the maintainer, and it would take them time to round up someone with access. The corridor beyond the door was narrow, bare gray fibercrete with bare gray doors set at fifty-foot intervals, back entrances to the stockrooms of the posh stores, here and there piles of broken packing or discarded sales brochures. To the right it dead-ended; to the left there was a corner, and he jogged in that direction. Around the corner it was another fifty meters to a T junction. There was a camera ball there; if they hadn't tracked him through the service door they knew where he was now. Nothing to be done about that, but it would take them time to respond, and he had to make the most of it. He ran to the junction, evaluated left and right again. More anonymous corridor and blank metal doors, but the wall to the right was worn red brick. The arcade had been built flush with an older building, and this had once been its exterior wall. He ran that way on the theory that it might lead somewhere that the ARM didn't have on their maps; it was the kind of overlap space that tended to get overlooked. He jogged around another corner, found a set of ornate iron stairs leading up. He took them, found a door at the top. It was wooden and ajar, and he went through to find himself in a room full of painting and sculpture, much of it wrapped in plastic, some of it partially packed for shipping. Another door, and he found himself in a pleasant gallery, with artwork nicely displayed on well-lit walls and spotlighted pedestals. Behind a counter a middle-aged woman was looking at him with something between surprise and disapproval.

"Sorry." He smiled disarmingly. "I took a wrong turn. Can I get to the slidewalk from here?"

Wordlessly she pointed, and he followed her finger out to the slidewalk level. On the pedestrian level below three ARM cruisers had landed haphazardly near the arcade entrance beside the unmarked vehicle that had originally spotted him. A gaggle of cops were standing at the arcade entrance, but none was looking in his direction. He stepped onto the slideway and let it carry him away, breathing deeply, looking down so the cameras couldn't see his face. They could still pick up on gait and body structure, but if he didn't walk it would take them awhile to synthesize the track. Safe for the moment, but only for the moment.

His beltcomp buzzed with an incoming call and he answered. Marcus Tobin's face looked out at him. "Quacy, what the hell are you doing?"

"What do you mean, sir?" Tskombe stalled for time.

"What do you think I mean? I have a recorded call here

showing you trying to arrange transport off-world. The ARM are looking for you."

As long as his beltcomp was on net they could track him with it. Tskombe scanned his surroundings. There were some hoverbots up high, but no cruisers. That wouldn't last long, he had to keep the conversation short. "I can't deny that, sir."

"I gave you direct orders . . ." Tobin was angry, as much because his faith had been betrayed as because Tskombe had disobeyed him.

"I appreciate that, sir." What to say to a friend and mentor who he'd just turned into an enemy. "And I'd like to thank you, sir, for all your support over the years . . ." He hesitated. ". . . and friendship."

Tobin's eyes widened as he realized just how serious Tskombe was. "Quacy, don't do this." The anger had left his voice, leaving only concern. "Just let them pick you up, I'll square the paperwork."

It was as close as he'd get to a formal invitation to come back into the fold, no questions asked. A cruiser floated down ahead, scanner head out and twitching back and forth to pick faces from the crowd. They were closing in on him.

"Sir . . . Marcus . . . I'm resigning my commission." Tskombe hesitated again. There was nothing else to say. The UNF wouldn't recognize the resignation, of course; they didn't allow you to leave on a whim. He saw in Tobin's eyes a kind of regret. He understood, though he could not condone. Tskombe punched off the connection, looking around without trying to appear desperate. There was another cruiser behind him; no doubt both were being vectored in by the ARM dispatcher, watching a little red dot on a screen that was Tskombe's beltcomp, localized to a meter or less by network triangulation. He had to cut the signal, but he couldn't just ditch the comp. Its authorization crypts encoded all the money he had in the world. It might have been easier to accept Tobin's offer. Too late for that now; he'd burned his bridges.

A glint by the slidewalk caught his eye: a piece of trash, an aluminized quickmeal wrapper. He scooped it up. It was just big enough to slip the beltcomp into. He wrapped it tight, leaving no gaps. The metal layer should be enough to block the signal. Now he just needed a hole to hide in.

"Hey friend, you want something? Anything you can imagine and a whole lot more you can't." A half familiar voice. Overhead a pair of holographic women gyrated lewdly over mirrored windows. The flesh huckster smiled greasily, beckoning. Tskombe stepped off the slide-walk, finding just what he needed, perhaps.

"How much?"

Greasy laughed. "It depends what you want. Some things come high, but it's all good, friend, it's satisfaction guaranteed. You talk to Moira, she'll set you up."

Shelter for awhile—there wouldn't be any cameras in a brothel. Tskombe went inside. The building was rundown but not overly dirty. Old promotions for sex holos lined the walls, the colors faded and the motion flickery. Heavy, worn half drapes hung from the mirrored windows, allowing in more sunlight than such a place was comfortable with. Behind the desk was an array of newer holo stills, young men and women. Moira was a heavy woman somewhere between forty and four hundred, blond hair hanging to her shoulders. She had been a beauty once, he could see, and was trying too hard to hang on to a glory that was never coming back.

"What's your name?" Unlike the huckster, her smile seemed genuine.

"Quacy."

"Well, Quacy, what can I get you?"

"Just the standard." *Whatever that is.*

"Don't be shy, we're here to make your dreams come true."

He shook his head. "That's all I'm dreaming of."

"You UNF?"

"Sure." Tskombe nodded. There was no point in hiding it.

"Thought so. All the nice girls love a soldier. You do like girls, don't you? Or do you want a boy?"

"A girl is fine." Tskombe half turned. The crowd outside couldn't see through the mirrored windows, but he could see out. Was there a camera watching the door?

"I knew it." Moira seemed pleased with her perceptive powers. "I can always see what people like. And you'll see just *how* nice our girls can love you in a moment. Do you have a favorite hair color?"

"It doesn't matter."

"It's been awhile, hasn't it?" She raised an eyebrow archly. "Well, I won't hold you up with more questions." She reached behind the counter and took an old-fashioned key off a hook. "Trina will take good care of you." She held up the key. "It's five hundred, for half an hour."

"How much for an hour?"

"Eager man." She gave him an arch smile. "It's eight hundred. A discount, and very worth it."

"Fine." He got out his beltcomp, waited for her to set up the transaction for him to thumb.

"Just one little formality first." Moira held out a black pad. "Just put your thumb there." Tskombe hesitated, but they wouldn't be in the business of shopping their customers to the ARM, and he complied, felt a sudden sharp pain in his thumb and yanked it back to see a drop of blood welling out.

Moira smiled apologetically. "Have to make sure you're clean, clean, clean. All our girls are clean, tested every day, and all our clients too. Doesn't that make you feel better? We're a quality establishment." She tapped her fingers on her databoard. "Of course I'm sure you are . . ." The black pad beeped and flashed and she smiled. "Yes, I knew you were. I can always tell, just by looking. Your blood sugar's low, though." She tut-tutted in mock disapproval. "Busy boys need their food. I can have something sent up after if you like. It's an extra fifty."

"Sure, but don't wait; I'll take it as soon as you can get it upstairs."

"Oh yes, keep your energy up. You'll want to be in top form for Trina. She's very good. I'll leave it outside the door."

"Sure." Tskombe waited while she keyed the transaction.

"Okay, thumb it honey." She held out another thumb pad, this one to scan his print to authorize the debit.

A brothel should have ways of ensuring its customers' privacy, but better be sure. "What does the transaction come up as?"

"Oh, it shows as a credit adjustment. Like you'd been

undercharged for something somewhere else and were
making up the difference."

"What store?"

"Now honey, I don't ask your secrets, you shouldn't ask
mine."

"One in this building?"

"No honey, it's in uptown. It'll come through as a bank
adjustment. Don't you go complaining to them that it's a
mistake or everyone will find out where you go for play-
time." It could have been a threat, but she delivered it as
friendly advice. *We have a shared interest in keeping this
secret, so why don't we do that?* He thumbed the pad and
her desk beeped its approval. The bank computers would
register the transaction, and the ARM would have his
ident tagged. In three minutes the cruisers would be
screaming off to uptown and they'd be wondering how he
got there so fast. That might or might not lead to an investigation that would wreck whatever cozy deal Moira had
with whoever it was she'd bribed to cover her transactions,
but that wouldn't happen in the next hour, and what he
needed most was time, to think and to plan. Time he should
have taken beforehand. *Too late now.*

"Room five." Moira handed over an old fashioned key.
"Your hour starts in five minutes. You get another five
minutes grace period at the end. Anything over that and
it's another five hundred. You have to thumb out down
here and it's in the system, so don't think you can sweet-
talk me later. Overtime is overtime." She tapped at her
desk. "Trina knows you're coming."

He went up the stairs, found room five. The key fit the
lock. The room was small and dimly lit, just big enough for

a bed, a sink and a table with a mirror behind it. Trina was there, a petite girl, dark haired, with pale skin, as unusual as he was in Earth's homogenized gene pool. She looked young, barely past adolescence, long legged in black lace stockings and a black bustier that showed off her hourglass figure. She was looking into the mirror, facing away from him, but her eyes met his in the glass, crystal blue, beautiful and fragile in equal measures. Tskombe was momentarily lost for words.

Trina wasn't. She turned around, confident in the power of her sexuality, and came toward him. "Moira told me you were nice." Her breasts were soft against his chest as she looked up at him. "What would you like to do?"

He looked down at her too young face and evaded her, went to sit on the tiny bed. "Nothing, I just need a rest."

She turned to face him. "Don't be shy, I've seen everything, heard everything, done everything. I'm yours for an hour, completely yours." She put her hands behind her neck, showing off her small, firm breasts. "We can do anything you want."

He looked at the ceiling so he didn't have to look at her. "What else did Moira say?"

Trina pointed at a padcomp on the table. "Just that you were nice. We have a code, so I know what to expect."

He looked down, met her gaze. "Really, I just need to rest for an hour."

"Oh, I can help you *relax*." She sauntered forward and straddled his knees. "Let me be nice to you."

She reached for the seal on his jumpsuit but he caught her wrist, hard. "Don't." He said it with more force than he meant to, and suddenly her eyes were big and frightened and it occurred to Tskombe that some of her clientele would not be *nice* at all. He let her go and looked away, speaking more softly. "Just don't."

"Fine, whatever." She stood up and sat on the table with her arms folded tight, fear turned to anger turned to defensiveness. The silence dragged out while Tskombe ran over his escape and his options. There weren't many. With an ARM tag on his ident he was a marked man. He couldn't ride a slidewalk without the cameras picking him up, couldn't buy a sandwich without alerting the transaction computers. He could hide in the gray zones, as he was hiding now, but the only person with less status than an unreg was a fugitive. An unreg could at least show his face in the daylight. They bartered with registered citizens and the citizens took a profit. Fugitives had to barter with the unregs, and what little trickled down to their level didn't buy much of a life. It certainly didn't buy a ticket off-world.

He took a deep breath. He could still get it all back, take the slap on the wrist for the call to Jarl, take the bigger slap that evading the ARM would bring. He could say he was visiting this brothel, didn't want anyone to find out, make it out to be one big mistake. It would wreck his accelerated promotion, but he'd have his life back, his career would be intact.

Except—except he would never get to Wunderland, not even by accident. They'd make sure of that. *And Ayla is still on Kzinhome and I have to get her back.* That was the beginning and the end, and he realized that his old life was already over. He needed a new one, plastic surgery, new retinas, an ironclad forged ident. He needed a hookup, and maybe this girl could help him with that, at least.

He looked up. Trina was looking at the wall with an expression of studied disgust.

"Look, I'm sorry if . . ."

"Whatever." She was still annoyed, insulted perhaps, that he didn't find her irresistible, though he couldn't imagine she actually wanted sex with yet another stranger.

"I really just need a place to be out of sight for awhile. The ARM is looking for me."

She looked at him, looked away, not believing. "Really. Sure. Whatever."

"I need to get a new ident. I need a meat surgeon."

She looked at him again, her voice softer. "You're serious?"

"Dead serious."

"What did you do?"

"It's complicated."

"It always is." She stood up, leaned against the wall. "Look, what you did, it's not my business. I might know someone who can do it. It's expensive."

"I have money."

"Maybe not this much. If it were cheap every unreg in Manhattan would have an ident."

"What's the process?"

"How much you got?"

"Enough."

"*Enough* is not enough."

"You're getting eight hundred for me to sit in your room for an hour. I've got enough. Get me a hookup and I'll get you a nice bonus."

"Moira's getting eight hundred . . ." There was a momentary wash of anger in her face, and then it was gone. She thought for a moment, then nodded. "The process, simple enough. You get your face worked, a new set of eyes, new prints. The best way is, they yank a citizen off the streets, he looks more or less like you. So then he vanishes, you take his place."

"He dies, you mean? Why not just swap eyes and thumbs and let him go?"

"What do you think this is, charity work?" Her voice had a sudden edge. "Maybe death is better than living as an unreg after you've been a citizen, you ever consider that? Anyway, the last thing you need is him yapping to ARM and showing off the bone scars where they grafted your fingers onto his hands. They might not believe him, but they'll haul in whoever he says he was, which is to say *you* for questioning anyway. And guess what? When they find the same set of bone scars on you, you're busted."

"I'm going off-planet, they won't bust me."

"ARM is off-planet."

"They aren't this far off-planet." *Which begs the question of where I go if I come back with Ayla.* "Can it be done without murdering someone?"

"Snag a deader from the hospital, bribe someone to change the records. Costs more and it's riskier. Why bother?"

"Because I don't want to be involved in murder."

She shrugged. "It's your funeral. I'll hook you up. How big a bonus do I get?"

"Eight hundred, barter equivalent. I'll buy whatever you want, Moira won't see any of it."

"Not enough. You got the money to do this thing, you got the money to pay me right."

"Eight hundred is an hour of your time, and it's generous. I don't imagine you're the only one who can hook me up. If you can do it Moira can do it. If she can do it, half the gray zone can."

Her face tensed and she looked away, not answering. After a long pause she spoke, her voice dead and flat. "Fine, eight hundred. I'll find out tonight, maybe. Come back tomorrow. Better reserve your time when you leave." She turned around to face him again. "I'm always booked up."

There was a trace of defiance in her voice and he looked at her. She wanted him to want her, and if he didn't take her he must not want her enough. There was pain there, hidden beneath her ice-slick attitude. She was far too young to be doing what she was doing for a living, far too innocent to speak of expedient kidnap and murder in casual terms. Against his better judgment he asked. "Why do you do this?"

"What?" She rounded on him, suddenly angry. "You mean a nice girl like me? Why do I sell my body to strangers? Is that it?"

He held up his hands. "I didn't—"

"Sure you did. Finagled fool that you are." Her eyes flashed. "What the tanj do you know about me to decide if I'm nice or not?"

"I'm here for the rest of the hour. Neither of us wants sex." She almost flinched at that. "It's conversation. We can sit in silence if you want."

"It would be better." She turned back and faced the

wall, her shoulders tense. The silence dragged out, and twice Tskombe started to speak and thought better of it.

It was Trina who broke the silence. "I'm unregistered." She shrugged angrily, not turning around. "My parents wanted a baby, my mother, she was desperate for her own little baby to love, but she had bad genes, she couldn't get a birthright. Her family had money though, and Dad was UN connected, he could fix things. So he fixed them, he got her a birthright, and they had me. Brilliant."

"What went wrong?"

"My father had enemies, powerful enemies. They found out, of course they found out, and there was a scandal and they yanked her birthright back. Except guess what? She was already pregnant. So she just didn't tell anyone. Why should she? She wanted her baby and they could afford it, I'd never need my own ident, my own money because they'd always be able to pay my way. As for education and medical, well, if you have money you can get those things outside the system. I didn't need an ident. She wanted a baby." Tskombe could hear the tears backing up in her throat.

"So what happened?"

"What do you think happened? You think my father's enemies gave up when they had him down? How long have you been off-planet? They ruined him, destroyed him totally. They bought people, set up deals and then yanked them when he was committed. We lost everything, and then there was a gravcar accident, and we lost him too. That was the end of my mother. She just died inside. I was eight, and I remember it so clearly, even more than my own sadness. I knew daddy would come home, I believed that. He couldn't just be *gone*, you know, so I wasn't really sad because I had that hope. Mom knew better. She just sat by the window, for days and days, didn't eat. We used to have a maid, Jendi, when we had money, and she came over again, for free, to look after me. It was more than sadness that Mother had, there was something wrong with her, some kind of schiz thing, depression. That was her gene problem, why she couldn't get a birthright. She just went down to the beach one day and swam out to sea. They found her a month later way down the coast. She put rocks in her pockets to make sure."

"I'm sorry—"

"You're sorry?" Trina snorted. "What have you got to be sorry about? She wanted me. She wanted me so much, more than anything, enough to break the law. I know she wanted me. She *loved* me. And then she left me, just left me by myself, unregistered. Do you know what it means to have no ident?" Her voice was choked full of long buried hurt. "I'm nothing. Dirt. Even dogs get licenses. She just left me, eight years old. How can you do that to someone you love?"

Tskombe came up behind her, put a hand on her shoulder. The girl stiffened at his touch but didn't move away. Tears welled up in her eyes, and then she was sobbing, silently at first, and then openly. He put his arms around her, feeling awkward, and held her. It seemed that he should say something, but there was nothing to say so he just let her cry.

After a while she looked up, cheeks damp but no longer crying. "I have an aunt, my mother's sister, but she was with the Navy and couldn't come. She sent a card to the funeral, that was all. So Jendi took me home, looked after me, but she had no money either. It got bad with her husband. When I was ten I had to leave. I always know when it's time to go. So what were my options? I ran with a gang and we stole things. I could do it and it didn't matter if I got caught. They feel sorry for you when you're little and cute." She laughed bitterly. "But I'm not little anymore, and an unreg caught stealing, that's a quick ticket to a brain blank."

"So you came here."

"I moved up in the gang. Miksa, he was the leader, he ran the gang, and I was the planner. I always knew the good places, where someone would slip up, when it was safe to move, when the ARM were watching, or one of the other gangs. We did well, and I was Miksa's girl. But he got jealous. Boys don't like girls smarter than they are, and it was time to go again. I was thirteen, that's old enough to sell your body. I'm lucky; I'm pretty enough to work a place like this. Mac and Moira . . ." She looked away. "There are a lot of worse places. They don't beat me up, they don't . . . they don't do a lot of things that places like this do to their girls. I make the customers happy, I do what they want, and I have a place and food and clothing." She looked up at him, searching his eyes for any hint of judgment, of condemnation of her choices. "Look, I don't like starving. It's what I have to do, so I do it." She looked down again, nestled closer against his chest. "It's nice that you didn't just take me. Most men . . ."

He hugged her tighter, not wanting to know what most men did. "It's alright."

"Why didn't you?"

"I'm lockstepped." Not quite true, but explaining everything about Ayla would be too complex, and telling her she was too young would be hurtful.

"Most of them are too."

"Not like I am."

"What's her name?"

"Ayla."

"What's yours?"

"Quacy."

"Quacy." Trina looked at him, looked away again, her eyes very distant. "Ayla's very lucky."

Tskombe nodded. "I hope so."

The padcomp on the table chimed and Trina went over to check it. "Your time's up. You have to thumb out in five minutes or they'll charge you again."

"Are you going to be okay?" The words seemed empty.

She laughed mirthlessly. "Oh, I'll be fine. I know how to survive. You come back tomorrow and I'll have your hookup. A good meat surgeon and a line one keyjock who can get the records fixed. I know who to tab."

"Listen. Thanks."

"Sure." She smiled wanly, shyly. It seemed she was about to say something but she didn't, and Tskombe had to go. There was a handmeal and a bowl of nondescript pudding waiting by the door, not worth the fifty he'd been charged for it, but he wolfed it as he walked. Downstairs he pushed his thumb on Moira's pad to clear his account. She smiled at him. "Was Trina good for you?"

"Yes." He nodded. "Yes, she was. I'd like an appointment with her tomorrow evening."

"Of course!" Moira beamed. "We're happy to see a regular.

Trina's one of our best." She keyed her desk. "You're set for twenty-thirty tomorrow night."

Tskombe went out into the oppressive heat of the evening. The immediate hue and cry of pursuit was gone, and the growing darkness would make it harder for the cameras to pick him up. He'd be safe, for a while, but he still needed to get off the street. He was hungry as well, despite the meal, but he couldn't buy anything without revealing where he was and restarting the chase. That was a sobering thought. He wasn't an unreg, but without being able to access his own money he might as well be. If all went well Trina would have that problem solved by tomorrow night; he could go hungry that long if he had to. In the meantime he still needed to get out of sight, just in case a hoverbot saw him.

A block farther he found a flickering holo over a set of dirty stairs. At the bottom a dented metal door done in chipped black paint. The holo said Deca-Dance, a bounce bar. Good enough to start with, not the kind of place they'd come looking for him. Inside the music was loud. Overhead a dozen cubes showing a dozen channels ranging from sports to cheap sex. He didn't particularly fit the crowd, but that didn't matter for his purposes. On the dance floor slick young toughs jockeyed to get closer to the provocatively dressed women gyrating in the grav field in the center. The women were studiously ignoring them, pretending the only reason they'd come was to dance with their companions. There'd be a fight before the night was out. That was fine by Quacy; he wasn't going to get involved. He found a quiet corner under the sound dampers, by the end of the bar away from the dance floor.

He waved away a waitress before she could take an order. A place like this wouldn't care if he didn't buy anything, so long as he didn't start trouble. No one was going to come looking for him here, that was the main point. He needed to watch, spend some time seeing who might be a connection, who was just a prole. If Trina didn't come through for him he'd have a backup plan already in motion.

It took less than fifteen minutes to prove him wrong— someone *was* looking for him. The lieutenant commander was in Navy dress uniform and he stood out in the dressed-to-shock crowd like a pop flare in the night sky. He drew eyes as he searched the room, drew more as he came across to Tskombe. That was a bad thing, the two misfits together, an invitation to get tumbled. Some of those slick muscles would be users needing their iron, and some of them would be armed. He scanned the crowd, picking up the ones taking a read on the newcomer. For a moment he considered just leaving, but he wasn't about to get busted. The Navy wasn't the ARM, and he was alone, and dress uniform wasn't what you wore to nail a fugitive. The Navy wanted to talk to him; fine, he'd talk to the Navy. The timing didn't make a difference, except to his mood. But when it came right down to it that was the Navy's problem and Tskombe wasn't too worried about that.

"Colonel Tskombe, UNF." Not a question.

And the tumble would happen outside. No sense hurrying into that. "How did you find me?"

"That's classified. Just be glad it's me and not the ARM." The Navy didn't waste words. "I understand you've been trying to get transport to Wunderland out of channel."

Tskombe shrugged. "I was going to leave when you walked in, but I didn't. What doesn't happen isn't a crime."

"I can't imagine you're that naive."

Tskombe snorted. "So what's it going to be? Conduct to the prejudice of good order and discipline?"

"An enthusiastic prosecutor might turn it into treason."

"Aren't you going to quote chapter and paragraph?"

"Is it necessary?"

Tskombe said nothing, let the throbbing music fill the silence.

Navy waved for the waitress. "You're aware you're risking your career." It wasn't a question.

"Not really your problem, is it?"

"I'm interested in the reason."

"Do you know the history?"

"You were on the diplomatic mission to Kzinhome. Your report was interesting reading."

Tskombe turned to face the other man. "Then you know Captain Cherenkova is still there. She may still be alive." He looked the crisp uniform over, put emphasis on his words. "She's one of *your* people."

Navy pursed his lips. "Left behind by *you*. On an alien planet full of predators. Do you believe she's alive?"

"I won't speak for the UNSN, but the UNF does not, Strike Command does not . . ." Tskombe felt his jaw clench, hands unconsciously balling in to fists. ". . . I do not leave people behind." He took a deep breath to calm himself, spoke more slowly. "She was alive when I saw her last, that's enough for me. I'm going back to get her."

"So what do you propose to do? Fly there singlehanded, penetrate the defenses, search the entire planet for her?"

"If I have to." Tskombe turned away to watch the dancers, ending the conversation.

The lieutenant commander leaned on the bar, refusing to let it be over. "And how do you propose to do that?"

"That's my problem, isn't it?"

"On the contrary, delivering combat troops to the objective is very specifically a Navy problem."

Tskombe made a dismissive gesture. "The UN, and through it the Navy, has very specifically declined to accept this problem."

The waitress came over. "Vodka and tomato juice." Navy looked at Tskombe. "And single malt scotch, if I recall?"

"You've been studying."

Navy nodded to the waitress, who tabbed her beltcomp and slid off to collect the drinks. "Can I ask your position on the issue of punitive and preemptive strikes against the kzinti?"

"Who the hell are you, anyway?"

"Lieutenant Commander Khalsa, fleet strategist. That doesn't mean anything, since I'm not here representing the fleet." He gestured for the bartender.

Tskombe looked over the dress uniform. Khalsa wore the torch insignia of naval intelligence. "Had me fooled there." The Navy man also had two combat bars on his service medal ribbon, unusual for a staff officer, but he wore no campaign ribbons. "Where did you see action?"

"That's not really relevant." Khalsa spread his hands.

"Suffice to say that in a very short time you have made yourself some enemies, Colonel, and I am not one of them."

"Does that make you my friend?" Tskombe didn't bother to hide the sarcasm.

"Answer my question and we'll see."

"Preemptive strikes? I think they're a mistake right now."

"Your own report says a militant faction has taken over the Patriarchy."

"My own report also states that the Patriarch of Kzin commanded his . . ." Tskombe groped for the word. Brasseur would know of course, but Brasseur was not here. He fought down the feelings that thought forced to the surface. ". . . his leadership to cease hostilities."

Khalsa nodded. "The Patriarch killed in this palace coup."

"That's the one."

"Just so I understand your position, you think we should leave ourselves vulnerable to the militants who've just taken over the kzinti government because the former leader favored peace." The waitress arrived with their drinks, and Tskombe took his and sipped.

"No, fleet strategist. I think we should very aggressively defend human space and send any ratcats who stick their nose over the line home by the molecule. That isn't the same as a preemptive strike. Maybe war is coming, maybe it isn't. Let's not make it inevitable."

"And why do you feel it isn't already inevitable?"

"I didn't say I felt that way."

"So how do you feel?"

Tskombe drained his scotch. "None of your damn business." It occurred to him to wonder how much his feelings for Ayla were interfering with his judgment. Pouncer had made it clear Kchula-Tzaatz wasn't bound by Meerz-Rrit's pledge. That didn't necessarily mean he would attack, although he'd spoken aggressively at the Great Pride Circle. If Kchula-Tzaatz was already moving to engage human space, preemptive strikes were not only justified but would save human lives, millions of human lives. The only problem was, open war would erase any chance Ayla had of seeing human space alive again. He put the emptied shot glass back on the bar top. *How many lives would I see sacrificed to give her the slightest chance of surviving?* It wasn't a comfortable question for a man sworn to defend his species, but he couldn't deny what he knew in his heart. *I would see worlds die for her.* The answer was made no more comfortable by the knowledge that he would not hesitate to sacrifice himself if that were necessary. "Are we done?"

There as a long silence while Khalsa sipped his drink, lips pursed. "I want you to meet someone."

"I don't." Enough was enough.

"What if that someone could get you to Kzinhome?" Navy was still talking.

Tskombe laughed without humor. "You need something more overt to arrest me. Why bother with entrapment? Just do it."

Khalsa put his drink down. "It's like this, Colonel. You might be useful to me, or you might not. That depends on some decisions you're going to make in the next hour, starting with this one. If you decide to be useful to me, we proceed. If not, I go find another way to accomplish my purpose." He leaned closer. "There are other people taking an interest in you, who see you as a potential threat. We watch them, and that's how I happen to know about your call to Captain Jarl Nance in Personnel. It isn't a matter of concealing your intent, of giving them not enough evidence to hang a charge on. If they decide you're dangerous they aren't going to trump up charges. There won't be a trial or a sentence, you'll just vanish. Permanently. Right now, I'm betting they've decided you're dangerous."

"Why would I be a threat to anyone?"

"Because of your report. There are those who stand to gain through a declaration of general war with the kzinti. Your report is worth gold to them, as long as they can interpret it the way they want to."

"You're speaking of Assemblyist Ravalla."

"I very much doubt you'd find evidence to link him to this group."

"That doesn't mean he isn't linked."

Khalsa cocked his head. "Perceptive."

"The question is, why, if my report is so valuable, they'd want me out of the way."

"Because they can take what you've written and present it as they like. They can hold it up to the world and demonstrate the treacherous nature of the kzinti. 'Look, they killed our ambassadors! Look, they've been planning another invasion! Let's kill them all now!'"

"That's not what my report says."

"Exactly. But it is how it will be presented, so long as they can be sure that you aren't going to contradict them. There's nothing worse to an ideologue than someone pointing out uncomfortable facts. Before you called Jarl Nance you were a question mark, someone to be watched. Now you're a danger, someone to be controlled. I may be reading that wrong. Maybe they'd be just as pleased as I would to see you go to Kzinhome, to provoke the kzinti further, and to die so they can make you a martyr."

"At least everyone involved seems to have a confluence of interest. Why do *you* want me to go to Kzinhome?"

"My group foresees several possibilities. An associate of mine would like to find out what you think on some issues, and that will narrow down the range."

"That's not an answer."

"No, it isn't. For my own reasons I may be willing to get you to Wunderland and connect you there with someone who can get you to Kzinhome. That will have to do for now. Do you want to talk to my associate, or do you want me to leave? I'm not here to impose my company on you."

Tskombe considered that for a while. "I'll talk to him."

Khalsa shook his head. "It's not a him." He thumbed for their drinks and they left the bar. Some of the inhabitants watched them leave, but none followed them. Maybe they sensed danger, maybe Tskombe had overestimated the risk. Unknowable. They took the pedestrian level south to the Southside Terminal, then walked to the shore. Cameras were few and far between in that section of the city, and it was easy to keep in shadow dark enough that the computers wouldn't tag a hit on Tskombe's face. The sea wall that surrounded Manhattan was made of fiber-crete, sloping steeply up fifteen meters from the perimeter to a broad, flat top. It was crested with a five-meter expanse of some dense, rubbery material—the exposed portion of a huge, inflatable dam that could be pumped up to buy the island city another five meters of protection against a storm surge. If the dike failed, the entire island would be under water. Tskombe wondered why anyone ever built on land below sea level, but of course it hadn't started that way. *Cheaper to build a wall than move the city, the first time high tide came into the streets.* And it kept on being cheaper to improve the wall over hundreds of years, as the icecaps shrank and the oceans rose, until the flood defenses were as huge and sophisticated as any medieval fortress, and the ocean surrounded the city like a besieging army, patiently awaiting the inevitable weakeness. Eventually storm and tide would align to overwhelm the seawall, and most of the city on Manhattan Island would be erased forever. Millions would die, but even that tragedy would go unnoticed in the wider devastation such a storm was sure to wreak on the eastern seaboard of North America. A quarter of the world's population lived on land now coveted by the oceans, and every coastal city had its seawall. By the time a storm grew big enough to overwhelm Manhattan's many others would already be gone.

And the world would pause and mourn for a day, and the next day go about its business, because the loss of ten million souls would be made up in a month's Fertility Allotment, and many would secretly thank the weather gods for bringing them a birthright certificate they would otherwise never have seen. It had happened before, to Tampa, to Sydney, to a host of smaller places whose names Tskombe had never known. It would happen again. Earth was a restless planet, and people swarmed in flood zones and fault zones and pyroclastic flow paths for the simple reason that they had to live somewhere, and there were too many people.

On the other side of the sea wall it was just four meters down to the water. Out in the channel vast superfreighters churned past in close order, an endless stream two minutes apart, traffic controlled from the Port Authority. Khalsa scrambled down the far side and threw a small silver ball on a wire into the water. He plugged the other end into his beltcomp.

Tskombe followed him, choosing his footing carefully on the last meter below the tide line where the surface was algae slick. "What are we doing here? I thought I was going to meet someone."

"We're meeting a dolphin. My beltcomp will translate though this transducer."

"A dolphin." Tskombe nodded. _Why did I assume I would be talking to a person?_ Dolphins were evolved to fight in three dimensions and they were the acknowledged masters of space combat maneuver, but the mass and volume required for a dolphin tank was prohibitive on all but battleships and carriers. It wasn't surprising that a fleet strategist would know a dolphin. That didn't explain why it was important for him to talk to one.

Khalsa tapped at his beltcomp and the silver ball gave off a series of high-frequency clicks and buzzes that Tskombe presumed was Cetspeak, the human/dolphin interface language. For a while nothing happened. Khalsa sat down on the dirty fibercrete to wait, heedless of his dress uniform, and Tskombe sat down beside him. _Why dress uniform?_ Because they had to hurry, whoever _they_ were, and they called Khalsa away from some formal function in order to track Tskombe down. They'd moved as soon as they'd known he was moving. Events were moving very fast. Ravalla's group had been watching him already, and Khalsa's group was desperate to make sure they found him first. That didn't explain how quickly the ARM had gotten after him. Maybe Jarl hadn't turned him in; maybe ARM were already watching him too, and they monitored the call because they were monitoring all his calls. *Or more likely ARM is acting on Ravalla's orders.* The cops wouldn't need to know why they had to bring him in, they just had to do it.

There was a splash and a high-pitched, falling whistle, and a second later a bottlenosed dolphin appeared in the dark water, its mouth wide in a permanent, toothy smile that oddly reminded him of Yiao-Rrit. *How would kzinti and dolphins get along?* Both were purely predatory species; they might have a lot in common.

Khalsa did something to his beltcomp. The dolphin clicked and whirred in response and the translator spoke, its voice flat and non-inflected. "Welcome, Tskombe. I am . . . Curvy." The first syllables were a series of rapid and undecipherable clicks, but the last word was a two-tone falling whistle, *cuurrrr-vveeee.* Curvy was the dolphin's name, or at least the human version of it.

"Curvy is the world non-computational chess grandmaster." Khalsa did something else to his beltcomp. "You can speak now, it's set for voice translation."

The dolphin chirped and whistled, then eyed Tskombe while the translator spoke. "Do you play, Colonel?"

"No, I'm afraid I don't."

"That is unfortunate. All tacticians should play chess."

"I am here for a reason . . . ?"

"You are the human who has been to Kzinhome. We have interest in you."

"So I'm told. I imagine dolphins are as interested in keeping the kzinti away as we are."

"No, dolphin interests are not aligned with human interests in the war with Kzin."

"Why not?"

"Kzinti are land predators. They will make humanity into slaves and prey animals. They have neither the motive nor the ability to enslave dolphins. Dolphin tactical teams aid humans because we gain various human assistances. Not least of these is human restraint in the exploitation of fish stocks and of the continental shelf zones. Kzinti live at population densities orders of magnitude lower and do not fish commercially. Kzinti conquest of humanity would bring automatically what we currently must earn, at no risk to ourselves."

"So why are you helping us?"

"We flatter ourselves to believe that dolphin tactical expertise is superior to human in three-dimensional combat arenas. We do not flatter ourselves to believe that the withdrawal of that expertise will lead inevitably to human failure in the coming war."

"In other words, you might as well help us because it makes no difference anyway."

"You are overly cynical, Colonel Tskombe." Tskombe caught his own name in the dolphin's speech beneath the translator's electronic tones. It came out in a click and a three-tone trilling whistle. Click-*zzzwwwiiip*-oooowrwr-wrwaaay. If you listened carefully you could almost imagine it was speaking English. "The kzinti also have no motive to trade with us for dolphin-hand manipulators and other technologies which we cannot make for ourselves. Before the kzinti came, dolphin dive crews had a long history of successful cooperation with sea miners, and before that with fishermen."

"Cooperating with some humans, and against other humans."

"Humans arrange themselves in factions, so it is impossible to do otherwise. Dolphins cooperate with the UN government."

"In order to gain access to certain technologies and protected ocean ecological zones."

"As I stated."

"Which the kzinti would grant you without thought, without even thinking of it as a grant in fact." Tskombe waved a hand at the stinking water. "I was wrong. Dolphins must yearn for kzinti victory."

"Our primary concern is the approach to total war, and all that it implies. Unlike humans, the kzin have not deployed ecocide as a weapon. A war of extermination would inevitably involve laying waste to entire kzinti worlds. The oceans are tremendously vulnerable. We do not want to see them provoked to retaliation."

"So what have I got to do with that?"

"You are the primary contact with the peace faction on Kzinhome. Assemblyist Ravalla has already laid plans to force a confidence vote in the General Assembly. We have predicted this outcome, and it is now unfolding. We predict he will be successful, and if he is successful he will launch a war of extermination. This is not his stated intention, but it is clear in our outcomes matrix that this is his intent."

"I think you're overstating my importance."

"It is not we who overstate your importance. Assemblyist Ravalla has read your report and taken steps to have it revised to better suit his purposes. General Tobin has been pressured to have you reassigned to Plateau in order to ensure you do not interfere with Ravalla's plans. So far he has resisted, but this may not produce overall positive outcomes for you. Ravalla's group would not hesitate to kill you if that became necessary. His position is strong, but not dominant, and his faction may disintegrate once he comes to power, leaving him vulnerable. He plans the war in order to secure his position. If a negotiated peace is developed he will be unable to do that."

"And you think I can stop him?"

"There is a nonzero probability that you can bring home a negotiated peace. This would derail Ravalla's drive to war. The window of opportunity is very small. We have been working to have you assigned to another mission to Kzinhome. Your attempt at precipitous flight forced our hand, and Ravalla's. You are no longer safe on Earth."

Tskombe looked at the dolphin in silence for a long minute. *I should have stayed where I was. I should have trusted Marcus Tobin.* It was too late for that now, and too late also for regrets. "I think you're also overestimating the size of what you call the peace faction on Kzinhome. Meerz-Rrit ordered the Great Pride Circle to cease aggression, and very few of them were pleased with the order. He's dead, and his older son is my contact, and unlike his father he has not pledged peace with us. Even if he had, he isn't in power and in fact he's likely dead by now. I have absolutely no power on Kzinhome."

"Yet you desire to go there."

"My goal in going to Kzinhome is very simply to get my colleague off-planet. In my estimation, much as I dislike giving ammunition to Ravalla's side of the argument, war with the kzinti seems probable at this point."

"Would you be willing to attempt to avert it, if we were to assist you to get to Kzinhome?"

"I'd be willing to try. I can't imagine what I could effectively do."

"We have run a strategic matrix centered on you. The current situation is highly nonlinear. Very small inputs can have dramatic effects on the course of the future."

"Meaning, everyone really does make a difference?" Tskombe's voice was sardonic.

"No." The nuances of sarcasm were beyond the translator's ability and Curvy took the question seriously. "No deliberate choice made by the vast majority of humans alive today can have any impact on the course of events whatsoever. However, you have a unique set of actions available to you. Depending on your choice tree your actions may be key."

"So I can change history?"

"Not you alone. There are many thousands whose immediate choices may radically alter the course of events. These are the individuals we have modeled in our strategic matrix. The impact you have will depend on their choices as well."

"How can you possibly have modeled every person of importance?"

"We cannot. Of course there are actors not modeled who will also have their part to play. Perhaps a technician has inadequately serviced a grav coil, starting a chain of events leading to your death, or saving your life by preventing some other lethality from overtaking you. This is unknowable and incalculable. By definition we can only work with what is both knowable and calculable."

"It isn't easy being an oracle."

"Matrix strategy is necessarily a statistical science. We are guided by Bayes's Theorem to move from what we know to what we don't know. Rudovich's contribution was the extension of Markov chains to construct probability webs such that the outcome space is reasonably constrained. Thus the same choice may lead to positive or negative outcomes depending on the choices of others. Rudovich showed that most choices have zero or small consequence, with the inevitable result that some choices are highly consequential. Timing is also critical, and the interactions are difficult to predict in detail. Nevertheless, it is possible to assign an overall probability to the choice tree of a given individual in terms of positive or negative matrix outcomes."

"And you have done this for me?"

"And many thousands of others."

"Why does *your* choice tree include talking to me then?"

"Your positive outcome correlation is high, assuming you choose to act in the interests of peace."

"That must be true of everyone in your matrix, given

that we are all by definition actors who might make a difference."

"True, although few are individuals who have positive choice correlations as high as yours. More importantly, the choice tree you must follow to achieve your own goals is very close to the choice tree required to minimize the chance of war. We have had you in our master matrix since your assignment to the diplomatic mission, and our matrix data has been sufficient to indicate you are making choices which might well be useful to our larger goals. In addition, you are accessible and potentially subject to influence, as many of our primary actors are not."

"So what do you want me to do?"

"We want you to go to Kzinhome and convince the Patriarch that war is not in his interest."

"That's all?" Tskombe snorted. "I just came back from that mission."

"There is a new Patriarch, as you know." Again Curvy seemed to miss the sarcasm. "In return, we will get you to Wunderland and do what we can to get you all the way to Kzinhome with a kzinti guide."

Tskombe thought about that for minute. *Decision time.* "Your offer is generous, Curvy. I'll take your trip to Kzinhome. I don't expect I'll be able to speak to the Patriarch, and I don't think he'll listen if I do."

"By yourself your success is unlikely. We will be working to influence many choice trees to support our desired results. Positioning you correctly is positively correlated with goal achievement for both you and us. Will you accept our cooperation?"

"I will, of course."

"Excellent. How long will you require to finish your business on Earth? Time is of the essence. The ARM continue their search for you."

"I have no more business on Earth. I can leave anytime."

Curvy whistled and bobbed. "This is very positively correlated with success. Commander Khalsa, arrange the ship."

In response Khalsa tapped keys on his beltcomp, waited a moment, looked up. "It's coming."

Tskombe looked at him. "You're bringing a ship here? Right here?"

Khalsa nodded. "By direct descent. Now that we have you, it's important to get you out of here before the ARM catches up."

Tskombe whistled. He'd learned the direct descent profile when Ayla had taught him how to pilot. Rather than fly a ship into the atmosphere on a braking trajectory you could drop it straight out of orbit on polarizers. The maneuver drastically cut the time spent on reentry, and took about a thousand times as much fuel. He'd been in a few direct descents himself, on assault landings. The profile was used for little else. For a commercial flight the fuel cost would wipe out your cargo profits. Khalsa's group were well organized to have a ship waiting, and they were quite determined to hang on to him now that they had him. He wasn't sure how he felt about that.

"How long before it gets here?"

"Perhaps thirty minutes."

Tskombe nodded. *Thirty minutes to get off-planet, thirty minutes to get away from the corruption and degrada-*

tion and systematic misery of this sorry world. He knew in his heart he would never be back, and he knew he wouldn't miss it. A thought struck him. "I'll be back in thirty minutes."

Khalsa broke in. "Where are you going?"

"I forgot something I have to bring."

"Whatever it is isn't important enough. ARM is still looking for you. You're lucky to have beat them this long."

"I'm going."

Khalsa grabbed his arm. "You don't understand. Our ship just committed to direct descent. This is an unauthorized reentry; if we abort we won't be able to do it again. When it gets here, we're getting on and going. It can't wait around, not five minutes."

"Put it on hold."

Khalsa met his gaze, saw the determination there. He clicked keys on his beltcomp, waited, clicked more keys. "No answer. It must already be into ionization blackout." He looked at Tskombe. "Whatever it is, it's not important enough."

Tskombe shook away the restraining hand. "Believe me, it is exactly that important. I'll be back in thirty minutes." He left at a run, before dolphin or human could say anything else. He ran on the slidewalks, heedless of cameras, his breathing deep and rhythmic, synchronized with the long, steady stride he learned in the infantry school. In fifteen minutes he was at a familiar doorway.

"Hey friend . . ." Tskombe ran past the door hustler and into the brothel before he could start his pitch. Moira was still there.

"Hello, soldier. What can I do for you?"

"Is Trina available?"

"She's got a client." Moira tut-tutted. "But don't worry, your appointment is confirmed for tomorrow evening."

"I need to see her now."

"You can't. Now let's not be troublesome." The words were gentle, but an edge of steel came into Moira's voice that belied her matronly demeanor. A brothel would have problems, now and again, and the madam had to have means of dealing with them. "Let me get you another girl."

Tskombe ignored her and ran up the stairs to room five. The door was closed, and locked when he tried it. Behind him he could hear footsteps on the stairs, Moira and possibly the doorman, doubtless armed. He wouldn't be the first client to make trouble over one of their whores, wouldn't be the last. He slammed his shoulder against the door, but it was steel and didn't budge. He slammed it again and pounded, and then Moira was there, a mercy gun in her hand.

"Stop that, soldier." Her voice was tense. "Or you're going to wake up in an alley with a headache."

"Look, I need to talk to Trina."

"We all need something . . ." She stopped as the door opened to Trina's client.

"What the hell is it?" The man was naked, and visibly annoyed. He was Tskombe's age, but unlike Tskombe he looked it, partially bald with a bulging belly. His glistening, half-erect penis protruded obscenely.

"Excuse the interruption." Moira's voice was warm and soothing. "My friend here was just leaving."

"Trina!" Tskombe called her name without taking his eyes off Moira's.

"What are you doing here?" He flicked his eyes sideways for a second. She was at the door behind the man, naked also.

"I'm going to Wunderland, Trina. No idents required. You can come if you want."

"She can't leave." Moira's voice was flat and emphatic.

Trina ignored her. "When?"

"Right now. I came back to give you the chance. It's up to you. I won't be back tomorrow."

"What's going on?" The doorman had come up the stairs behind Moira.

"She can't leave!" Moira was starting to lose control.

Trina looked at Moira, looked at Tskombe. "I'm going."

"You can't." Moira waved her weapon, her voice shrill. "You, soldier, you've got ten seconds to get out of here and never come back. Trina, get back in your room."

Tskombe kept his eyes on the madam, spoke slowly and firmly. "I'm going to take your advice, and I'm leaving in ten seconds. If Trina comes with me you'll never see us again. If she doesn't, I'll be back in thirty minutes with fifty ARM troopers. Shoot me full of mercy needles and I'll be back in the morning and I won't be happy. Kill me and it won't be the ARM, it'll be half of Strike Command, out of uniform and looking for payback. Take your pick." He locked eyes with Moira, daring her to call his bluff. She raised the gun and he watched her finger tightening on the trigger. For a long moment the tableau held, and then she lowered it again.

"Take her. She's trash anyway." Moira's voice was thick with rage. She turned and stormed down the stairs, sweeping the doorman in front of her.

Tskombe turned to Trina, but his eyes found her client, his face red with anger. "Hey! I paid . . ." Tskombe's fist smacked into the fat man's face with the sound of an axe hitting wood, cutting him off in mid complaint. He staggered back, blood streaming from a broken nose.

"Work it out with Moira."

"Let's go." Trina was already dressed in a black jumpsuit, a small pack over one shoulder. They left the fat man there, walked out through an empty lobby. Tskombe checked his beltcomp. Twenty-three minutes gone, seven to make it down to the flood wall to catch the ship.

"Why did you come for me?"

"Someone had to. Are you always packed and ready to leave?"

"I packed after you left."

"Why did you do that?"

"It was time to go. I always know when it's time to go."

He didn't argue, there wasn't time. There was an ARM cruiser patrolling the slidewalk level, and another one higher up, while a swarm of hoverbots whirred overhead. In his reckless run on the slidewalk level Tskombe had surely been picked up by several cameras.

No sense in wasting time. Tskombe put one hand over an eye, as if he was injured and waved wildly at the nearer cruiser. It was a calculated risk. The cruiser's AI might bust him anyway, but in the dark with half his face covered it wouldn't have much to work on. The cruiser slid over and grounded and the driver got out.

"What's the problem?" The cop reached out.

With combat-trained reflexes Tskombe grabbed the cop's offered hand and pulled, overbalancing him. He stepped back as the man fell forward and rotated his hips, brought his other hand to the man's shoulder in one fluid motion, then used both hands to drive the cop to the ground with his own stiff arm as a lever. The cop grunted in pain and Tskombe dropped down with one knee in the small of his back. Using his left hand to control the trapped arm he grabbed the cop's mercy gun from his holster. The cop's partner was already on her way out of her side of the cruiser and Tskombe locked his eyes on her, bringing the weapon up to his line of sight until the line of the barrel intersected his target. He pulled the trigger and the weapon sprayed slivers of anesthetic. She went down, instantly unconscious as they dissolved in her bloodstream.

The cop under him surged and struggled to get to his feet and Tskombe put a burst into him as well. The heavy body relaxed and he looked up. Two hoverbots were already closing in. They probably hadn't tagged his ident yet, but they were responding to the violent scene and they'd be reporting the situation to their controllers as they moved.

"Get in the cruiser" he yelled, but Trina was already running. He ran after her and dived into the driver's side, slamming the door shut just as a spray of mercy needles splattered against the glass. Ahead of him the other cruiser switched on its patrol lights, flashing red and blue. They were on to him, and with ARM officers down they wouldn't be alone for long. Dispatch would already be vectoring other units on to him. Most gravcars could only fly automatic over the city, but an ARM cruiser would have an override, hopefully already engaged. He punched the cruiser's throttle and polarizers whined as they shot forward. So far so good. They blew past the other cruiser and it pivoted to follow them. Tskombe took them into the bottom of the eastbound traffic level. Traffic was dense and he edged up through it.

"What are we doing?" Trina's voice was remarkably level, given the circumstances.

"Getting out of here, hang on." The other cruiser was in the traffic pattern behind them. There was an intersection ahead and he pulled the cruiser up to the top of the eastbound level on the right-hand side. As they entered the intersection he pulled up and canted the thrust sideways, whipping them around a tight left-hand curve and up into the bottom of the northeast-bound level into the northbound level. He held the thrusters there, dodging through holes in the traffic pattern until they broke out the top of the northbound level and plunged into the bottom of the northwest-bound level, still within the confines of the intersection. They missed a heavy transporter by inches, and a second later there was a heavy, jarring bang as they collided with a building. The cruiser kept flying, though, and then they were into the westbound level, merging again to the southwest-bound level, merging with the heavy flow heading down and across the river. Tskombe looked around but the ARM was nowhere in sight. The main worry was that they'd shut down his controls and take the car on remote, but there would be some confusion in the dispatch center, and it would take them some time to figure out just which car he'd taken. That wouldn't last long, but he only needed a couple of minutes. He scanned the skies.

There! A vertical streak in the sky, like a shooting star in slow motion, falling away from the full moon overhead. He banked the thrusters and pulled the car up, taking it out of the traffic flow and over the city in a ballistic curve. Down below he could see dozens of flashing red and blue lights. The ARM were out in force, on full alert. He concentrated on the glowing line as it plunged to the waterfront, adjusting course to intersect its projected endpoint.

"They're behind us." Trina was looking backward, still sounding calm.

"How close?"

"Maybe a minute."

"They can't do anything until we stop."

"Let's hope not."

He could see the ship now, a rapidly growing cross at the end of its ionization trail, almost directly overhead in its vertical descent trajectory. It was impossible to tell at that distance, but he guessed it would be a courier, the same type of ship as the Swiftwing he'd stolen to escape from Kzinhome, but with the straight-angled lines of human design. He turned his eyes back to the ground, searching along the south Manhattan shoreline for the container terminal. They were less than a minute away. More flashing red and blue lights lifted out of the traffic pattern, rising on intercept trajectories. It was going to be a very close race between the ship, themselves, and the ARM.

The courier ship was just touching down as they came in to land. To shave seconds Tskombe didn't decelerate as they fell toward the rendezvous. That turned out to be a mistake. The cruiser didn't have the power reserves of the combat cars he was used to. He dumped full power to the polarizers at the last instant before touchdown but it wasn't enough to fully arrest their descent. The cruiser hit the top of the seawall hard and slid, plasmet crumpling. An instant later they were airborne again, arcing out over the water. Instinctively he fed power to the polarizers to prevent a second impact but they were wrecked, scrubbed off the bottom of the vehicle when they hit. The water came up hard and they were stopped. There was a second's pause while the vehicle rocked and the spray of their impact rained down around them, and then he felt water swirling around their feet. The car was sinking fast, bubbles already boiling up from the shorting forward batteries. He undid his harness buckle, realizing he didn't remember doing it up in their flight, and then reached over to undo Trina's.

"We're going to have to swim for it."

"I know."

But there was already too much water pressure against the doors to open them, and the windows wouldn't open without power. The river swirled over the front of the canopy as the vehicle nosed down and under. Frantically he kicked at the windows but the transpax didn't yield. The pale moonlight faded and turned murky as they slid beneath the waves and the water boiled up higher inside.

"We're going to drown!" For the first time Trina's voice held an edge of fear.

Tskombe started to say something reassuring, was cut off by a hard *bang* as the overloaded batteries exploded. The shock drove his head against the canopy and when he looked up he felt wetness on his face, whether blood or

water it was now too dark to tell. "We just have to wait for
the pressure to equalize." He managed to keep most of
the panic out of his voice, pushing hard on the door as he
spoke. It might as well have been welded to the frame.
The pressure wouldn't equalize until they were sitting on
the bottom. How far down would that be? They couldn't
be that far from the seawall, but the ship channel was
dredged deep to clear the hulls of the superfreighters.
The seawall sloped at forty-five degrees; every meter away
from the shore meant another meter down. Too far down
and they had no hope of survival. That thought galvanized
him and he slammed his shoulder hard against the door,
but it didn't budge. They were angled steeply forward,
and the water in the foot wells was halfway up his thighs.

"Remember to breathe out all the way up. If you hold
your breath you'll rupture your lungs. You'll have lots of
air." He breathed deep himself, trying to sound calm. "I'll
say ready, and you'll have time for three deep, quick
breaths to get lots of oxygen into your blood, and then I'll
say go. We both open our doors then. Just swim up and
keep breathing out."

"Okay." Trina's voice was calmer, but the fear was still
there. His ears popped painfully. It was totally dark now,
and the pressure was still going up. How far had they
bounced from the seawall top? He tried to think back. It
was ten meters at least, maybe more than twenty. From
ten meters they might make it, from twenty they probably
wouldn't. There was a sharp, metallic *spang* overhead and
his ears unpopped. Reflexively he put his hand up in the
darkness, to discover the gravcar's roof bowed in from the
inexorably building pressure. He shoved against the door

again, but it didn't move. At this depth the water pressure against the door would be measured in tonnes. If the vehicle weren't flooding fast enough to counterbalance some of it, that pressure would have already crushed the passenger compartment like a mealpack under a boot.

How far to the bottom? Even as he thought it they grounded with a jarring thump and tilted backward, the water sloshing around his chest. He expected them to settle to an even keel but they didn't, a second, softer jolt halting their descent still pitched steeply nose down. Why was that? An instant later a grating sound and a lurch told him the reason. They had landed on the steep sloped seawall, slick with mud and algae, and now they were sliding down it. The door was still held closed by the water, but they would slide more slowly than they sank, slowly enough that the pressure would equalize and they could get out. Maybe.

The water was up to his chin when he felt the door give a little. "Trina, ready . . ." He heard her breathe in-and-out, in-and-out as he did it himself. On the last breath he said "Go!" and shoved his shoulder hard against the door. There was a rush of bubbles and the dark water flooded into the tiny remaining airspace. He pushed out hard into the blackness to clear the car so he wouldn't get snagged on anything. His feet found the seawall and he kicked up, breathing out and swimming hard. *How far to the surface?*

Something whip thin and steel strong grabbed him by the arm, wrapping around it tight enough to hurt and pulling hard. He screamed, precious air bubbling free, grabbing at it with his free hand. Another something wrapped itself around that arm and then he was being hauled through the water fast enough that the current sucked his jump boots right off his feet. With strength born of the drowning terror he fought against whatever it was. His foot connected with slick flesh over powerful muscles, but that made no difference at all to whatever had taken him.

Suddenly light blazed and he broke the surface, splashes echoing close, something solid against his belly. Whatever had him by the arms let go and he fell forward, breathed deep and opened his eyes. He wasn't on the surface, he was in a transpax sphere better than two meters across, lit from above and full of air, open to the water at the bottom, a diving bell. Outside it a tooth-grinned face operated a large buttoned control panel. Dolphins! The dolphin was wearing a set of dolphin hands, but used its nose to run the panel. An instant later Trina arrived in another splash, thrust into the bell by the manipulator tentacles of another set of dolphin hands, a dolphin trilling behind her, as it pushed her up the bell's side enough to hang on. A second later it vanished with a splash. *Was that Curvy?* Did she anticipate this outcome in her strategic matrix and have help standing by, or was the dolphin dive crew there anyway? Trina coughed and gasped, shaken but alive. The dolphin controlling the bell nudged a lever with delicate precision. A motor hummed and bubbles began to spill out the bottom of the bell as it rose through the murky water. There were no handholds; the bell was simply a place for dolphins to grab a breath while working on a deep-water site. They were forced to brace themselves awkwardly on the slippery, curved sides on the bell to stop themselves from falling into the water. A large, mechanical shape loomed in the murk and vanished again—some other piece of dolphin hardware, maybe a submarine. It occurred to Tskombe that the dolphin world was one where ARM not only had no control but had almost no knowledge. Their civilization numbered in the millions and occupied three quarters of the planet's surface. What did they do with the technology they bought?

His ears popped again, and overhead light began to filter in from the surface. They seemed to be rising slowly, but their ascent rate would have been enough to kill them both with the bends if they'd been under pressure any longer than a few seconds. *How long were we down? How deep?* He'd never know the answer. *Deep enough that we would have died without the dolphins.* The top of the bell broke the surface and city light flooded through the transpax. The bell's waterline was well above his head, so he couldn't see what direction they were moving, but then his feet touched solid ground, hard and slippery. They were back to the seawall. The bell driver touched the control panel again and they stopped. End of the line. He looked across to Trina, saw her nod in understanding, and ducked back underwater and out of the diving bell. He floundered up the seawall slope, found himself alone.

For a second panic gripped him. *Trina!* But Trina was out on her side and coming up, coughing and cursing. He grabbed her and hauled her up, the fibercrete tearing at his bare feet. The courier was there, its underhull glowing red and radiating palpable heat, actually floating over the water, its boarding ramp extended to the seawall. A big empty bowl had formed in the river beneath it where the polarizers were holding back its weight in water. He ran for the ramp just as the first of the ARM cruisers braked to a stop on the top of the seawall, blinding spotbeams swinging to pinpoint them. An amplified voice demanded that they halt, and an instant later Trina collapsed. Without breaking stride he picked her up and ran. He slipped and fell on the steep, slick surface, tearing flesh while mercy needles spattered where he would have been if he hadn't fallen. He picked her up again and ran for the courier as more ARM cruisers dropped to the seawall top. He was actually on the boarding ramp when a dozen wasp stings stitched across his back. Numbness spread where they hit and he felt his knees going weak. He staggered forward a few more steps and then collapsed, spilling Trina onto the rough-surfaced metal. Everywhere he looked there were blinding spotbeams. He squeezed his eyes shut and crawled up the ramp, trying vainly to roll Trina up the slope. There was a roaring in his ears, and in the distance the sound of barked commands. He couldn't make out what they were saying, and darkness fell.

> *Now Chil the Kite brings home the night*
> *That Mang the Bat sets free.*
> *The herds are shut in byre and hut—*
> *For loosed till dawn are we.*
> *This is the hour of pride and power,*
> *Talon and tush and claw.*
> *O hear the call! Good Hunting, All*
> *That keep the Jungle Law!*
> *—Rudyard Kipling, "Night-Song in the Jungle"*

The jungle had changed as they pressed deeper into it, and Ayla Cherenkova found herself awed. Spire trees soared a hundred meters or more overhead to widespread crowns, their huge trunks buttressed like ancient fortresses. Beneath their canopy it was perpetually twilight, the air humid and rich. The ground was covered in something halfway between moss and fungus. For the most part the undergrowth was scattered and the going was easy. They had followed the valley to its heart until they came to a vast, coiling river and were tracing its course steadily downstream. The Tzaatz had long since given up pursuit. She'd lost track of how long it had been—a month, two months, maybe more. More important, there had been no sign of *grlor* for days. Without grove trees or thorn bushes for cover, she, Pouncer, and T'suuz would be sitting ducks for the predators. There were lesser hunters, still huge and fearsome by Earth standards, but none who would attack two adult kzinti when they had a better option, though they might have made an easy meal of a lone human. She was careful to stay with her guides.

She had lost weight since entering the jungle, but her skin was taut over muscular ripples she hadn't seen since she was a cadet, and she no longer noticed the higher gravity. Her UNSN uniform was gone, rotted and torn until it was unwearable. She'd replaced it with *zianya* skin tanned in a blend of *myewl* juice and resin trapped from the short, bushy *shoom* trees, then sun cured in a clearing and stitched together with sinew. Her boots were holding up well, thankfully, but already she knew how she was going to make their replacements when they finally succumbed to the rugged terrain. *I am adapting to this environment*. She knew now where to look for the fresh *vlrrr* shoots that hid pulp as sweet and thirst quenching as watermelon beneath their tough exteriors, knew how to hide her trail with *myewl* leaf, and knew she had to climb out of the river bottom to a dry sandy ridge to find it. Given any reasonable approximation to a blade she could skin, cut, and fillet a *kz'zeerkti* or one of the rabbit-like *vatach* with skill and efficiency. She could track the larger fauna, like the huge but slow-moving *czvolz*. They were supremely docile, and would be easy meat save for the putrid oils that pervaded their flesh. They, and seemingly they alone, grazed the moss-fungus from the forest floor, and she reckoned it was this that gave them their distinctive stench. Even *grlor* would not touch them, so said Pouncer. She could navigate without a compass, for a short distance anyway, using just the contour lines of the land. The jungle was becoming less an impenetrable tangle and more a world she could move through. She still itched everywhere, still longed for a bath, and she had no illusions that she would ever come to enjoy this lifestyle, but she was surviving, and on Kzinhome that was something.

The river banks had steepened, and she was climbing ahead of the kzinti over a small rise when she froze in her tracks. The jungle still surprised her every day, but not like this. Before her was an immense beast, easily fifty meters long, like a vast, long-necked sausage on tree trunk legs. It was covered in shaggy fur, and long, sharp-looking tusks protruded from its upper jaw, complementing the large horns on its forehead. Its eyes were small in a head the size of a barrel. Adrenaline spiked in her system, and for an instant she feared a predator more fearsome than the *grlor*, but then it munched down a bush, almost in a single bite, and she realized it was an herbivore. Behind it were more of the creatures, most smaller, some larger still, moving placidly amongst the towering trunks. Ayla held her breath. Even the infants were the size of rhinoceros. Here and there five-ton youngsters nursed from brontosaur-sized mothers. The entire herd was moving slowly, taking a bite, meandering a few paces, taking another bite, moving again.

Nursing. That struck Ayla. Despite their primitive, dinosaurlike appearance they were mammalian, or at least pseudomammalian.

"*Tuskvor!*" T'suuz had come up beside her, her voice a hushed snarl. "We lack hunt cloaks."

"We must move back before they see us." Pouncer's voice was equally quiet.

Ayla looked at him. "What will happen if they do?"

"If they sense carnivores nearby they will charge. We will be crushed. They are feeding up before their migration. There may be *grlor* nearby too, hoping to pick off stragglers."

Ayla nodded, swallowing hard. It was difficult to imagine a pack of *grlor* settling for stragglers, but when faced with a herd of *tuskvor* that was what they'd have to do.

One of the *tuskvor* snorted and turned its head in their direction, tossing its tusks. They backed slowly down the hill and backtracked a kilometer before starting a wide detour up onto higher ground.

The going was harder farther from the river, with steep slopes and smaller trees, which meant denser undergrowth. They kept at it. Better to err on the side of caution with a herd of *tuskvor* on the move. They made it high enough that the grove trees started again, and Pouncer killed a *k'ldar*, a larger, forest dwelling cousin of the *zianya*. Cherenkova smoked the meat that was left over and they spent the night in one of the trees, not as comfortable as a shelter built on the ground, but at least they were out of the way of predators.

The next day they came to a vast clearing, an entire valley, kilometers across, waving with the tufted plants that passed for grass on Kzinhome. It seemed as though a piece of the now distant savannah had been transplanted into the heart of the jungle. A forest fire had swept through the area within the last few years, clearing out the canopy. It must have been ferocious to consume the mighty spire trees the way it had. Most had burned completely, only charred remnants remaining, but at intervals tremendous trunks still reached for the sky, dead and gray, like accusing fingers pointed mutely at the lightning god who had destroyed them. Finger-thick saplings clustered here and there. The savannah's victory would be short lived. The fast-growing grass would take what gains it could, but where the river valley gathered enough moisture to support the trees, it was the trees that would ultimately triumph.

In places the ground was still crunchy, and just beneath the surface the soil was ash gray. Cherenkova worried because of the lack of cover, but Pouncer assured her that *grlor* didn't like to hunt in open areas. They crossed it, grateful for the easy going. A small stream rolled down the center of the valley to feed one of the tributaries that in turn fed the main river. They stopped there to rest and eat in the heat of the midday sun. The kzinti napped while Ayla took advantage of the relatively clean water to wash herself and her clothes. She took her time, enjoying the cool luxury of a pool beneath the shade of a cluster of saplings. When she was done she climbed up the bank, and froze.

Six kzinti, loping through the tall grass toward them. They came steadily, unhurried, not concealing themselves. Quickly she woke Pouncer and T'suuz. Pouncer rolled to his feet and put a paw to his variable sword, but T'suuz stopped him "Show no threat. These will be a pride of the *czrav*, bound by blood allegiance to our mother's pride. We will be safe with them."

The newcomers carried journey packs of tanned leather and their bows and *wtzal* hunting spears were well crafted of wood, but the arrow and spearheads glinted with the heavy gray of crystal iron and the colors in their cloaks shimmered and shifted to blend them into the background. Some carried weighted throw nets, others game bags laden with small quarry, but if they were a hunting party they had not caught anything large enough to justify their numbers.

"Hunt cloaks." Pouncer kept his voice low. "Sophisticated for primitives."

T'suuz twitched her tail. "You should know by now that *czrav* are anything but primitive."

The newcomers formed a semicircle. Four of them were female, all lean and muscular, and none of them looked friendly.

"I am Kr-Pathfinder." A leopard-spotted male took a

step forward as he spoke. "You cross Ztrak Pride territory with no border gift." He spat the words, and the warriors behind him were in fighting stances. Pouncer assessed them. *They know the single combat form, or a variant.* A wooden spear was no match for a variable sword, but six to two were not good odds against opponents who knew what they were doing, even with that advantage.

"Apologies." T'suuz claw-raked, speaking before Pouncer could. "I am T'suuz, daughter of M'ress of Mrrsel Pride. This is my brother, First-Son-of-Meerz-Rrit, and the *kz'zeerkti* emissary, Cherenkova-Captain. We meant no trespass, but claim sanctuary by blood allegiance."

Kr-Pathfinder fanned his ears up. "Mrrsel pride. Hrrr. What do you seek sanctuary from?"

Pouncer stepped forward, gesturing T'suuz to stay back. "Tzaatz Pride has declared *skalazaal*. They came with genetically engineered war beasts and have overthrown my father and taken the Citadel of the Patriarch. They seek my ears for their trophy belt."

"Why did you come here?"

"We stole a vehicle and flew it until it was out of power, where the Long Range meets the Mooncatchers. We have been traveling on foot since then, to reach the jungle and Mrrsel Pride." He made the gesture of deference-to-an-equal. "I add to my sister's apologies. We were not aware of the pride boundaries. I offer this kill as border gift." He indicated the dismembered remnants of the previous day's *k'ldar.* "Poor as it is, it comes with the gratitude of the Rrit, and my blood debt to your Pride."

"Hrrrr." Kr-Pathfinder turned a paw over, considering. The other male stepped forward, younger than the first and heavily built. "We will take your malformed *kz'zeerkti* creature. It will make good sport."

Pouncer twitched his tail. "The Cherenkova-Captain is under my protection. It is not prey."

The large kzin slashed the air with his claws. "Kr-Pathfinder, this nameless kitten stretches tradition too far. He trespasses and then claims sanctuary, insults us with burnt meat, prey taken in our own territory! Let us take what is ours."

Kr-Pathfinder held up a paw. "Tradition is tradition. First-Son is under *skalazaal* and his mother's pride is blood-bound to ours. He is entitled to sanctuary, and we must honor that, and honor his protection of his *kz'zeerkti* too. He may stay with us for the Traveler's Moon unharmed."

"Kr-Pathfinder, you cannot be serious!"

"Why would I not be, Sraff-Tracker?" The leader fanned up his ears.

"This kill is an insult." The large kzin spat. "The meat is burned and worthless."

"The kill is nothing. He claims Mrrsel Pride blood, and he has given us blood-debt." The tension between the two went further than the issue at hand. One day they would fight a challenge duel.

"He is a Rrit, a noble and no *czrav* of Mrrsel. As for his blood debt . . ." The warrior spat in contempt. ". . . he is a nameless kitten, half outbred. He holds back the *kz'zeerkti* and the kzinrette too. Let him give us them as border gift and save his *strakh* for the *kzintzag*."

"I am sworn to the protection of the *kz'zeerkti* and my sister both." Pouncer took a step back, casually adopting *v'scree* stance. T'suuz moved sideways, putting herself between Cherenkova and the others. Cherenkova backed up, but there was little point to the maneuver. If it came to a fight Pouncer and T'suuz together couldn't save her, and even if she started running now there was no way she could hope to evade a pride of kzinti on the hunt. If she still had the beamer . . . but she didn't. She could only watch for an opportunity to act, if one came.

"Sraff-Tracker is right." A female stepped forward, firm-muscled, an adolescent just ripening into fertility. She wore decorative ear-bands and stood with cocky self-confidence. "Take away his weapons and I'll fight him claw to claw."

"He has asked sanctuary, C'mell." Kr-Pathfinder's voice took on an edge of snarl. "Tradition demands we give it to him."

How do I respond to the challenge of a female? Pouncer sized her up, could not help noticing her sleek shape and well tufted tail. *As I would any other threat to those I protect. If she leaps, I will kill her.*

"Tradition demands we defend our borders." Sraff-Tracker let his fangs show. His belt was heavy with ears. "He trespasses, insults us with burned meat and empty promises while he keeps both food and female in front of us."

"Do you challenge me?" Kr-Pathfinder laid his ears flat. Perhaps the duel would be right now.

Sraff-Tracker laid his own ears flat too, lips curling up to reveal his fangs. For a long moment the tableau held, but ultimately Sraff-Tracker did not leap.

Kr-Pathfinder turned to Pouncer. "We welcome you as

our guest, First-Son-of-Meerz-Rrit. Will you share meat with us tonight?"

"I am honored, Kr-Pathfinder, and my Pride is honored." Pouncer carefully ignored the female C'mell, who was looking at them with ill-concealed hostility. Aside from her and Sraff-Tracker the remainder of the Ztrak hunters seemed to accept them, warily. That was enough for now.

Kr-Pathfinder swung his tail up and around in a wide circle, the hunt sign for *gather*. Pouncer looked around in momentary confusion, saw four more kzinti appear a good bowshot downstream, another four upstream. Understanding dawned: these were cutoff parties, set to intercept them if they fled in either of the two easy directions. *This was not a chance encounter; we have been well stalked. They set their ambushes close without sound or scent. My sister is right—the czrav are more sophisticated than they appear.*

A third cutoff group appeared over the slope behind them. Pathfinder set a course and the group followed. Cherenkova was pleased to discover she could keep up. She was growing tougher in the jungle. *I have survived so far. I might yet survive this.*

> **Hunger leads the hunt.**
> —Wisdom of the Conservers

Ftzaal-Tzaatz stretched and yawned luxuriously on his portable *prrstet*. He rolled to his feet and walked out of the pop-dome that served as his lair and onto the sunburnt savannah. His was not the largest pop-dome, but unlike anyone else's it was his alone. The afternoon heat soaked into his dark fur, a welcome change from the cool shade in his dome. Gravcars with beam weapons secured a perimeter around a small hillock in the grassland; closer in, his elite *Ftz'yeer* patrolled on raider *rapsari*. He had been on the hunt thrice around the Hunter's Moon, but now his quarry was close, so close he could almost smell it.

He went to a smaller pop-dome beside his command lair. Guards jumped up to claw-rake as he came in, but he focused his attention on the figure who did not, lolling on a narrow pallet. Telepath was moaning incoherently, eyes rolled back in his head, mucus streaming from nose and mouth. He was in an advanced state of *sthondat* withdrawal. Ftzaal had seen the symptoms before. Denied the drug that freed its powers, a telepath's brain punished itself through the pain center. Telepath's skin would be on fire, the agony penetrating to every bone in his body. It was the weakness of telepaths that they needed the drug, that they would dishonor themselves to get it. It was the strength of the Black Priest cult that they controlled the drug, and so controlled the telepaths. That was the way of the world.

Ftzaal knelt by the pathetic figure and shook him roughly. "Telepath. Telepath!" It took him several tries to get a response.

"Please, the *sthondat* . . ." Telepath's head lolled, his eyes opening but refusing to focus.

"Not until you find the *kz'zeerkti* for me."

"Please, no! It dreams of burned meat and boiled roots."

"Can that be worse than the cravings?" Ftzaal held up an infuser, forced Telepath's muzzle around so he faced what he needed so badly.

"Please, I can't tell without the drug. I need it . . ."

"You *can* tell without the drug, and you will. There is only one human on the planet. Yesterday you said it was close."

"No, no not close, it's far away." There was desperation in Telepath's voice.

"Where?"

"I can't feel it. I need the drug. Please . . ."

"No drug until we have it." He leaned close suddenly, snarling in the other's ear. "What are you hiding, Telepath?"

"Nothing, hiding nothing." Telepath convulsed and closed his eyes. The mind-trance was on him, not deeply, but enough for Ftzaal's purposes.

Ftzaal watched him impassively. *There was fear behind the pain. I have found something deep.* "Then where is it?"

"In . . ." Telepath's voice was halting. "In a valley . . . there's grass, a stream. Yesterday the trees were burned, it's with kzinti, many kzinti."

"Many?" *Interesting.* "Is First-Son-of-Meerz-Rrit there?"

No response. Telepath convulsed again, writhing. "You won't escape that easily." Ftzaal leaned forward and pushed the infuser against Telepath's biceps, depressed the plunger, just a fraction. Telepath's eyes shot open, his breath coming in sudden pants. "Oh yes, please more . . ."

"Is First-Son-of-Meerz-Rrit there?"

"Yes . . . yes . . . he and his sister. Please, the drug, the drug, oh please . . ."

"His sister?" Ftzaal's ears fanned up, his voice suddenly sharp.

"No . . . No . . ." Telepath struggled, his eyes flickering open as he tried to master his need for the drug.

"Tell the truth, *sthondat*, or I'll leave you with the cravings another day." Ftzaal withdrew the infuser and Telepath flinched at its absence. "The kzinrette we saw with him. Is it his sister?"

"Yes . . ." The word was agonized. "The *kz'zeerkti* thinks so."

"Good. How far?"

"I don't know, I don't know." Telepath was babbling. "It's traveled . . . the *kz'zeerkti* doesn't know how far, the Traveler's Moon, once, twice around the Traveler's Moon, downstream, or the Hunter's Moon, it doesn't know . . . Everything is burned over . . . Please . . ."

Ftzaal depressed the plunger, watched Telepath's face tense and then relax, and all of a sudden he was asleep and peaceful, a string of drool hanging from his chin.

"Senior Guard!"

"Command me, sire!"

"See that he's cleaned up. When he wakes make sure he eats well. He has earned his keep today."

"At once, sire."

Ftzaal left the pop-dome, went to the larger one that served as his command lair. Its top was shiny black, soaking up sunlight and turning it into power to run the computers and electronics inside. Twice around the Hunter's Moon, that was the right time-frame. Telepath wasn't lying, not in the state he was in. Downstream was the natural direction to go, into the dark heart of the jungle where air and space reconnaissance were useless, where tracking was difficult, where every aspect of the living landscape could become a tool to foil the hunt. The information was interesting: more kzinti, and First-Son's sister. His suspicion had been right. He was on to something bigger than the fleeing First-Son-of-Meerz-Rrit. *And if I am right about what it is then the Black Cult has been wrong.* Telepath had lasted three days without the *sthondat* drug, holding out as long as he could. *He's still hiding something. I need to rake that to the surface. This is my key to return to my devotion. For this they will make me High Priest.* There was his oath to his brother to consider, but time enough for that later.

Time enough for pleasant imaginings later. He walked into the command lair. "*Ftz'yeer* Leader!"

"Command me, sire!"

"Prepare my gravcar, and two full swords of Heroes in support. We'll need sniffers. Leave the raider *rapsari* at home. Once we find them we'll bring in the whole force."

"Beam weapons or variable swords, sire?"

"Variable swords and netguns. We want him alive, and more importantly we want his sister alive." Ftzaal's mouth relaxed into a fanged smile. "The hunt is on!"

Lead not by force but by example.

—Si-Rrit

Pouncer loped down the jungle trail in the middle of the Ztrak Pride hunt party, once more carrying Cherenkova-Captain. He was tired and the alien was heavy, but he would not show weakness before the pride. That morning Kr-Pathfinder had told him that Ztrak Pride's lair was another day's journey downstream, and they had been traveling all day. It couldn't be much farther. The first sign that there was any habitation in the area was a watch platform, set high in a spire tree and well camouflaged. Pouncer would have missed the sentries except they held their weapons high and called a greeting to the returning group. The valley walls steepened to a cliff face, and past the watch platform a faint path led to a staircase, carefully arranged to look as though the rocks that formed it had simply happened to fall into their configuration by accident. They climbed it and found the den complex of Ztrak Pride. It was a natural cavern halfway up the cliff. It would have overlooked the main river, save for the towering spire trees that blocked the view. Except for a large sandy area near the front reserved for the pride circle fire, the entire floor was covered in polished planks of some dense, fine-grained wood that Pouncer didn't recognize. A cold stream ran through the center of the main cavern from somewhere deep in the rock, providing fresh water, and spilled out the front of the cavern in a little waterfall. He was surprised to find the *czrav* had power; warm lights glowed in recesses in the walls. Deeper into the cave were quarters for families and individuals. The raw rock of the ceiling was covered by vast sections of tanned skins, held up by the polished rib and leg bones of some immense creature.

"Tuskvor!" The realization hit him all at once. He turned to Kr-Pathfinder. "You hunt *tuskvor!*"

"Yes." The lean warrior clearly thought it unremarkable.

Only a fool hunts tuskvor. It was standard wisdom, but the *czrav* defied standard wisdom in more than one way. It explained why there had been so many in Kr-Pathfinder's hunting party, and why they had only carried small game. The *vatach* and *ctlort-myror* were simply provisions to feed the hunters while they set up a more worthy kill. A more worthy kill! What did it take to cut a full-grown grandmother from the herd and bring her down? Kr-Pathfinder's hunt party seemed too few for that task.

It was difficult to judge how many lived in the cavern complex. It seemed to run quite deep into the cliff face. The circle of sand around the fire stones was big enough for several hundred to gather to hear a story, although only a few were present when they arrived. Cherenkova-Captain drew interested looks, nothing more. The hunting party dispersed, and Kr-Pathfinder brought them deeper into the den to a large side chamber. The highly polished floor was covered in layers of animal furs; the doorway was through the wide open jaws of what could only be a *grlor* skull. The door was guarded by a still-spotted youngster with a long, curved sword. More furs formed the door, and Kr-Pathfinder pushed them aside and ushered them through. The room was ringed with comfortable *prrstet*. A large, fit-looking kzin looked up from one as they entered, his eyes deep and compelling. Across the room a tiger-striped kzinrette yawned and stretched on another.

Kr-Pathfinder claw-raked. "V'rli-Ztrak."

"Good hunting, Kr-Pathfinder?" It was, to Pouncer's surprise, the female who spoke. The Patriarch was a female! *A mother Patriarch? How different are the social conventions when females think like males? Cherenkova-Captain may have insight here.*

"Good hunting, in a manner of speaking. The high-stream *tuskvor* have already moved; we could gain no more. We have found something more interesting." He motioned to Pouncer, T'suuz, and Cherenkova.

V'rli-Ztrak nodded. "The migration is beginning soon. Are we prepared?"

"We will be ready when the herds move." Kr-Pathfinder made the gesture-of-obeisance. "May I present First-Son-of-Meerz-Rrit; T'suuz, daughter of M'ress of Mrrsel Pride; and Cherenkova-Captain, emissary of the *kz'zeerkti*. They are under *skalazaal* and asked sanctuary under the traditions." The male turned to look at the newcomers, and seemed somehow familiar to Pouncer, something about his eyes . . .

"We are blood-bound to Mrrsel Pride. We honor our obligations. You have done well, Kr-Pathfinder." V'rli twitched her tail and the lean hunter claw-raked and withdrew. She turned her attention to Pouncer's group. "So, who speaks for you?"

"I am Speaker for my companions." Pouncer answered before T'suuz could.

"Sit, relax." V'rli-Ztrak waved them into *prrstet* with her tail. "Quicktail!" Her voice rose.

"Honored Mother!" The youngster who had been by the door appeared.

"Food for our guests!"

"At once!" Quicktail was gone in a flash, proving the worth of his name.

Honored Mother, Pouncer thought to himself. *So this is the form of address for a female Patriarch.* V'rli turned her gaze back to him. "So you are here to tell me that your father has been slain in *skalazaal* with Tzaatz Pride, yes?"

Pouncer controlled his surprise. *How did she learn this, here in the jungle?* "News travels quickly."

"We learn of important things, eventually. We know the Citadel of the Rrit has fallen, and there is a new Patriarch."

Pouncer growled deep in his throat. "Kchula-Tzaatz is not of the Rrit. Whatever he may call himself he is not Patriarch."

"Rrit blood flows in the Tzaatz line, and Kchula has bred the Rrit daughters."

T'suuz's lips curled away from her fangs, in disgust rather than anger. "Just one daughter. I escaped, the rest are too young." She had no desire to be bred by Kchula-Tzaatz.

"Kchula's son will claim the Patriarchy, but he does not," V'rli went on. "It is Scrral-Rrit who leads now."

Pouncer snarled. "My half-brother rules in name only. He is a disgrace to the Rrit line."

V'rli flipped her tail. "Perhaps. It is true that he has no choice. Tzaatz warriors control the Citadel. A Rrit must rule the Patriarchy, so say both the Priesthood and the Conservers. So say both the Great and Lesser Prides, and most importantly, so say the *kzintzag*. Scrral-Rrit gives his name to Kchula-Tzaatz's edicts and legitimacy to his reign. In return Kchula gives him the name of Patriarch and his life. What would you have him do?"

Pouncer's lips curled away from his fangs as anger

flooded through his body. "My brother sells Rrit honor for his worthless pelt!"

"And what of your own honor, you who claim sanctuary with the *czrav* in the jungle?" V'rli-Ztrak's eyes bored into his.

Pouncer's eyes flashed as he met her gaze. Had she been a male he might have challenge leapt at the insult. *How does one deal with matters of honor when females lead Prides.*

Cherenkova-Captain spoke up before he could answer. "First-Son-of-Meerz-Rrit has pledged his life to my protection. I am an alien to your world, and a historical enemy of your species. He has repeatedly risked his life to ensure my safety, simply because I wear his father's sigil. I am no judge of kzinti, but it seems to me First-Son has more than upheld not only his own honor but the Rrit name as well."

V'rli's ears fanned up. "Is this true?"

"It is," Pouncer said. *She questions my integrity to test me. Sheath pride and bare honor.*

V'rli turned her paw over. "Through our blood allegiance to your mother's pride you are entitled to sanctuary here for the time of the Traveler's Moon. What will you do with it?"

"I will rest and recover while the Tzaatz will tire of hunting me, and then we will travel to Mrrsel Pride that I may claim a name there."

"Oh? You have accomplishment enough to claim a name now?"

"I fought in defense of my father's Citadel. I have slain his enemies in single combat and brought honor to the

Rrit name. The commander of my father's *zitalyi* gave me a *wtsai*. Yes, I will claim a name from my mother's pride."

"Why not claim one from us?"

"I have come to you for sanctuary. The Naming Traditions forbid me to."

V'rli-Ztrak turned her paw back again and looked at him. "You are wise as well as accomplished." She flipped her ears and twitched her tail. "Or at least well schooled."

"Rrit-Conserver taught me well."

"And when you have your name and a place in your mother's pride?"

It was a valid question, and one Pouncer had not considered until now. Still, there was only one possible answer. "My brother has taken what was rightfully my father's, and rightfully mine after him. Kchula-Tzaatz has stepped off the road of honor in his conduct of the *skalazaal*. I will earn my vengeance in blood and the Patriarchy in my hands."

V'rli-Ztrak twitched her tail in amusement. "More Tzaatz arrive daily from beyond the singularity, did you know that? The Lesser Prides haven't the liver for rebellion. They are fast becoming Kchula's instruments. The *kzintzag* complain, but they do his bidding. What you are likely to earn is the Ceremonial Death."

"If that is what the Fanged God plans for me I will accept it."

"You could choose to turn away from that path, live here with your mother's pride."

"With respect . . ." Pouncer paused. How to decline such an offer without insult? "With respect, I must follow my own path."

"Even if it leads to death?"

"Then it will be a death of honor."

V'rli met his gaze and held it. Under other circumstances Pouncer might have found it uncomfortable, but now he just met it, firm in his conviction. After a long while she spoke. "May Ferlitz-Telepath know your mind?"

A telepath, here? She tests me further. He could not refuse the request. She read the question on his face and nodded to the silent kzin on the *prrstet*. Pouncer followed her gaze. Ferlitz was sleek and well muscled, as confident as any warrior, and he bore a name. In that, he was unlike any telepath Pouncer had ever seen or heard of, but his eyes . . . Now he knew where he had seen them before: Patriarch's Telepath. "He may."

Ferlitz-Telepath blinked, a long slow blink, and Pouncer's vision flashed. For an instant he imagined he was seeing himself from across the room, and then sensation was gone. Ferlitz turned to V'rli. "He speaks from the liver."

"True courage runs in your blood." V'rli considered, measuring her words. "You will not do this alone."

"I am First-Son-of-Meerz-Rrit. I will lead the Lesser Prides, if they will follow, the *kzintzag* if they will not."

"You are bold as well."

Pouncer made the gesture-of-lesser-abasement. "I am not bold, and I am not eager for death, but I know the Traditions. The Conservers teach 'Choose your name wisely and then bring it honor.' My name is Rrit, though I did not choose it. I am of the Patriarch's line. I will bring it honor."

"Your *half* name is Rrit." V'rli corrected "What name will you choose for yourself?"

Pouncer didn't hesitate. "I will choose Zree."

"Zree-Rrit." V'rli turned a paw over, considering. "Following the legend of Zree-Shraft-Who-Walked-Alone. An unusual choice."

"It is a fitting one, for me."

"Yes." V'rli looked at him speculatively. "Yes, fitting for someone who has lost Pride and birthright together, who finds himself outcast. It is a good name to die with. Will it suit you as well if you are so fortunate as to become Patriarch?"

"I chose it long before the Tzaatz came." Pouncer lowered his ears, reminded of the responsibility he had borne in his father's shadow. "I can imagine no calling more alone than Patriarch."

"The burden of your birthright lies heavy on you."

"Yes." *I was once reluctant to carry this burden. Now that it has been taken from me I find myself all too eager to pick it up.* For a moment he considered taking V'rli's other option. He could claim a name with Mrrsel Pride and live out his life in the jungle; it would be easier, far easier . . . *But that is not the way of honor.*

"There is nothing more important than a name." V'rli looked directly into his eyes.

"Honored Mother!" T'suuz's snarl cut the room before Pouncer could reply. "He needs to know of the Telepath's War."

"Does he?" V'rli-Ztrak's voice held a sudden edge "And why?"

"The lines of Kcha and Vda combine in him and me,

and we are of Rrit blood. We are victory in the long struggle. My brother has proven his courage and honor. You have heard his decision. He needs to know."

"This is dangerous, and against tradition."

T'suuz drew herself up, tail erect. "He has to know his destiny. I am not wrong, V'rli-Ztrak. This our mother taught me, this was the reason she was treaty-gifted to the Patriarch. You *know* this to be true."

V'rli's reply was interrupted by Quicktail, who came in leading a trio of kittens younger than himself, each carrying a platter piled with slabs of spiced *pirtitz,* The pungent aroma filled the room. Quicktail himself carried two platters and presented them to Pouncer and T'suuz. Two of the others gave their burdens to V'rli and Ferlitz-Telepath; the smallest, only half grown and still cute in a big eyed, fuzzy way, gave a smaller platter to Cherenkova. If they were curious about the *kz'zeerkti* they gave no sign.

Quicktail performed the ritual abasement. "Honored Mother, honored guests, may you enjoy your feast." The kittens emulated him, their eyes serious with the burden of their responsibility, and Quicktail led them out again.

There was silence while they all ate, and V'rli considered Pouncer with huge, liquid eyes. When she had finished she turned her paw over, considering. "So you want to know of the Telepath War, First-Son-of-Meerz-Rrit?"

Pouncer twitched his whiskers. "It is perhaps enough to know that there is such a war."

"Perhaps." V'rli turned her paw back and looked at him. "These are dangerous secrets. You must pledge your honor and your life to their preservation."

Pouncer made the sign of blood-debt-fealty. "I will do that."

"And what of your *kz'zeerkti*? Shall it know our secrets too?"

"Cherenkova-Captain has my blood debt, and her species may yet be valuable allies."

"Hrrr." V'rli considered further. "Very well. Do you know the legend of Chraz-Rrit-Star-Sailor?"

"There are many."

"There is only one that matters. It is told that in the time between the wet season and the dry Chraz-Rrit-Star-Sailor won the fortress of K'dar from the Sorcerer Pride. Among his prizes he took the kzinrette P'rerr as his own. His consort V'rere became jealous and betrayed him to his enemies in order to gain his empire for herself, and so Chraz-Rrit was nearly slain in an ambush at Hrar. While he lay wounded the Sorcerer Pride attacked the Citadel, and V'rere too was nearly slain in the defense. The Fanged God became angered that V'rere's ambition had so nearly destroyed the Patriarchy, and so commanded that all kzinretti surrender their reason, so that never again would consort and sire contend against each other. P'rerr wished only to be with Chraz-Rrit and so submitted to the Fanged God's will, but V'rere refused in her pride, and so the Fanged God banished her to the jungle forever. As a reward for her loyalty P'rerr was told that the line of the Patriarchy would forever flow through her."

Pouncer waved a paw dismissively. "This is a kitten's tale."

"Every kitten's tale carries truth in it, or at least wisdom. There is more to this one. It is told that after her banishment jealous V'rere schemed to again be by Chraz-Rrit's side, and so when once more the cool season turned into the hot, and she came into her fertility, she disguised herself as P'rerr. She stole into the Citadel and played with P'rerr and told her stories, and because P'rerr had given her reason to the Fanged God she did not notice that V'rere was disguised as she. When V'rere had P'rerr's trust she gave her the tea of the *zee* flower, and P'rerr fell into a deep and dreamless sleep. In the dead of the night, still disguised, V'rere came to the Patriarch and mated him, and when the hot season again became cool she bore him kits. Knowing she could not maintain her ruse forever, she put her kits beside sleeping P'rerr and stole out into the desert once more. When P'rerr awoke she thought they were hers and suckled them. But Egg-Stealer the *grashi* had been hiding in a burrow in the Patriarch's Garden and saw it all happen, and when V'rere had gone he ran to the Fanged God and told him everything. The Fanged God was enraged at V'rere's trickery and to punish her he commanded the prey animals to leave the jungle, that V'rere would be forced to follow them across the desert and know thirst. Then he commanded the Black Priests to examine every kit of the Patriarch's Line in their fifth time around the seasons, and to banish all who carried the signs of the Line of V'rere. Finally, his anger abated, he turned to Egg-Stealer and thanked him for his warning and granted him a boon. And Egg-Stealer asked that his line become so plentiful that it would never end, and the Fanged God made it so, and this is why the *grashi* flourish in flood and in drought and on every world, why even when the kzinti leave a place the *grashi* remain where they have been."

"This tale is no secret."

"No, but it is the key to knowledge long suppressed by the Priests and the Patriarchy alike."

"And this knowledge is . . . ?"

"The meat lies beneath the fur. The story is ancient but the scent is clear even after all this time. Look at the characters. There are many touchpoints between the last stories of the Old Heroes and the most ancient verses of the Pride Saga. It is certain they speak of the same set of events. Chraz-Rrit-First-Patriarch of the Rrit Pride Saga is Chraz-Rrit-Star-Sailor of the Old Hero Legends; this has long been assumed to be true, and there is much evidence to support it: the Citadel is the same, the story of Chmee at the Pillars, the betrayal of Hromfi, the tale of the Lost Kitten—there are too many parallels for it to be otherwise."

"The Pride Saga contains history; the Legends, these are only stories."

"No, the Pride Saga contains history as those who composed it wanted history remembered. The Legends contain the history that they would rather have seen forgotten."

"You are hardly the first to suggest the Old Hero Legends are another version of the early Rrit Pride Saga. The Conservers debate the point to this day, and there is no proof."

"Absolute proof they are identical is impossible, but also unnecessary. Look instead to the differences. In the Saga the enemy are Jotoki possessed of starships, but in the Legends the enemy are kzinti possessed of magic. In the Saga the protagonists are possessed of technology equal to that of the Jotok, and it speaks on the assumption the listener will understand it. The legends speak only of gods and of magic, and the magic is possessed only by the enemies of the Pride. They wield it and the Heroes must hide; they use it and the Heroes die; a sly Hero steals it; a clever Hero turns it against its masters. Only in the Legend of the Quest is Chraz-Rrit gifted his sword of fire by the servant of the Fanged God. Only in the Legend of the Citadel does Chraz-Rrit give magic to the Pride, and this is the last Legend. And again, in the Pride Saga we kzinti sail the stars to conquer the Jotok, advanced space-craft were a common technology, and the tale-teller speaks to an audience who he assumes will know this, but still Chraz-Rrit is credited with being the first to fly. To have the same kzin to achieve flight be the first to master interstellar travel stretches credulity. And yet, the legends name him Star-Sailor, clearly a unique achievement at the time or he would not have claimed the name, and the legends say he flew with the stolen magic of the Sorcerer Pride."

"You speak well, Honored Mother, but you do not enlighten me as to how you come to speak well."

V'rli raised a paw for patience. "Truth earned is truer than truth given. Do you know the Telepath's Legend?"

"As Father read it to me."

"So compare that tale to mine and tell me how they are the same."

Pouncer twitched an ear in annoyance. "They are as like as any two legends. There are Heroes and their enemies, Patriarchs and priests, fortresses and temples. Something was, and becomes something else, and today it remains the same. With respect, Honored Mother, I don't see the point of this."

"The point, the first point, is the one I have just made. Simply that the Old Hero Legends are based on events from the time of Chraz-Rrit, sometimes the same events we find in the Pride Saga, sometimes from before that time. They have been distorted to present those events in a certain way, and distorted further simply because of their age, but they contain fundamental truths. Accept this as a working hypothesis."

"Accepted."

"The second point is, if those with power at the time these events took place had wanted them remembered they would have included them in a saga, if not the Rrit Saga then a lesser one, to be passed intact from generation to generation in the memories of the Conservers. They did not do this, so we may conclude they did not want these events recorded. However, they were unable to repress them entirely. Not even the Fanged God could forbid tale telling at the pride circle. The best they could do is insert variations that served their interests."

"Hrrr. Perhaps you assume too much. Time inevitably distorts legends, but there is no evidence anyone has distorted them deliberately. Nor do I see any motive."

"Then I will give you both proof and motive. Each legend explains a truth about today in terms of happenings long ago. What truths are explained? Other than the ubiquitousness of the *grashi*, both explain how the Black Priests came to their responsibilities, the one story for kzinretti, the other for telepaths. Both these responsibilities are combined in the Kitten's Test, and the penalties for failing the tests are serious: death for females and *sthondat* addiction and slavery for males."

"I am . . ." Pouncer groped for words. "I am astounded, for many reasons at once." He paused, absorbing what he'd just heard. "Let us return to the legends. You said you would give me proof of their distortion and motive for it."

"The proof of their distortion is simple. What the Black Priests do is cull the species. This is what they do today; the legends tell us they have been doing this since time immemorial. This is something that touches every kitten in every Pride. These facts could not be suppressed. Instead the legends were distorted to justify the practice. The *sthondat* drug is powerful, addictive, and debilitating, yet giving it to still-nursing kits is spoken of as *caring* for them. The execution of precocious females is done to *protect* the species, and both are carried out on the orders of the Fanged God. This is supported by the traditions, by the rituals, by the entire structure of the Priesthood. Any argument, any protest, is automatically cast in heretical terms. Through their control of belief they exert effective control of the entire Patriarchy, save those of us who choose to live outcast."

"Hrrr. I do not see this providing power. Many do not take the existence of the Fanged God as literal truth. Father did not, and I do not. The Priesthood in general and the Black Priests in particular exist at the sufferance of the Patriarchy, not the other way around."

"And yet you follow the traditions."

"I am First-Son-of-Meerz-Rrit. It is expected of me."

"And if you did not meet this expectation?"

"There would be consequences . . ."

"Consequences!" V'rli spat. "It would shake the Patriarchy to its core. If the Patriarch's son flouts tradition, who might not? If the traditions cannot be relied on then no one would be safe. The doubts of one would become the fears of the next. Pride War would be the result, would it not?"

Pouncer twitched his tail in annoyance. "Pride War is already the result, and Kchula-Tzaatz has not been particularly bound by the traditions in his conduct of it."

"But you yourself would not dream of breaking them. And the Great Prides and the *kzintzag* alike adhere to the traditions because the Patriarch does. Some traditions serve the species, like the code of honor, and the Dueling Traditions, but many serve only the priesthood, and the priesthood serves the Black Priests."

Pouncer flipped his ears. "The High Priests do not believe that."

"The High Priests stay in their temples and seek unity with the Fanged God. Perhaps they achieve it, who knows? We say the High Priests are most powerful because they sanctify the ascension of the Patriarch, but this is not power because they cannot choose not to do it. We say the other cults serve the High Priests, but this is like saying you serve your slaves by providing them food and shelter. The Black Priests act for the High Priests in the waking world, and what High Priest even knows what a Black Priest does? A Black Priest comes into a Pride-Patriarch's stronghold and says 'The High Priests have so commanded,' and who can question them? The Black Cult are many things, all of them dark, all of them powerful, and their stranglehold on our species starts with the Kitten's Test. They are the Bearers of Bad Tidings, and what tidings are worse than the news that a promising son will be taken to become Telepath, that a daughter still suckling will be abandoned to the jungle verge? Who in all the Patriarchy does not fear the Black Cult?"

"They are just one order among many, and others are more dangerous."

"You speak of the Hunt Priests. The Black Cult are too stealthy to ripple the drinking pool, but they are the ultimate power in the priesthood. All the orders are pledged to obey the High Priests, but it is the Black Cult that speaks for them. The Hunt Priests do not apply the Hot Needle save at the order of the Black Cult. The puzzle traps of the Conundrum Priests hold their enemies, the Practitioner Priests in every Pride serve as their eyes and ears and noses. They do not often show their power, but they are playing a long game, as are we."

"And this game is?"

"The Longest War."

Pouncer's ears swiveled and he wrinkled his nose, puzzled. "This is a scientific term, the non-random survival of randomly varying individuals. I do not understand how you use it here."

"The phrase has come to be used in a strictly technical sense, but its older meaning is quite literal. We fight the war for control of the kzinti gene line."

Pouncer's ears fanned up. "You jest."

"If I call it the Telepath's War is the meaning clearer? You ask for motive. This is their motive." V'rli's eyes narrowed and she leaned forward. "I will retell the legends from another vantage. We have traced the genes, and we know the kzinti line diverged into two primary streams around the time of the Jotok Conquest, some eight-to-the-fourth generations ago. By far the largest of these is the Kcha line, encompassing every Pride that ever went to space, and almost every Pride still here on Kzinhome. The other, the Vda line, is confined to us, the *czrav* of the central jungles, and yet this tiny, isolated gene pool is eight-squared times more diverse than that of the entire Patriarchy. What does this mean to you?"

"A genetic bottleneck."

"Almost. There are other clues. The Kcha line shows signs of gene manipulation, several episodes of it, all of it ancient, almost certainly the work of the Jotoki."

"They are a slave race. No Jotok would dare such treachery!"

"Not today, but the Jotoki were not always a slave race, and their gene manipulation skills remain unparalleled. Shall I tell you the other clues?"

"Please."

"The largest single phenotypic difference between Kcha and Vda is expressed in brain formation. Kzinretti of Kcha have a third less frontal cortex than kzinretti of Vda. Kzintoshi of Kcha have a less dramatic frontal cortex reduction—but more importantly, they compensate for this by coopting the telempathic centers. As a result telepathy is eight-to-the-fourth times rarer in Kcha than in Vda, and sixteen times less powerful. Most telepaths of Kcha require *sthondat* lymph to awaken their talents. Among the Vda line, few do."

"This is incredible."

"So now I will tell you another story. Eight-to-the-fourth generations ago there were many kzinti lineages resident only on Kzinhome. Some prides mastered technology and went to space, other prides did not advance so quickly, or at all. Those with technology inevitably expanded at the expense of those who did not, either through assimilation, which enhanced the genetic diversity of the assimilators, or through marginalization, which decreased the genetic diversity of the primitives. One of these pre-technological prides embraced the Black Cult rituals. How they originated we can only guess. As with all traditions they served a social purpose; in this case it was either the suppression of female independence or the suppression of telepathic talent. Both might offer threat to an established power structure. The Legend of V'rere suggests the first, the Legend of Telepath suggests the second. Perhaps it was both at once. Whatever the origin, the gene pool was not large, a few pawfuls of prides, and so could evolve rapidly, at least at first, while there was still enough genetic diversity. Later, when the diversity was exhausted, changes would come much more slowly. Over some small number of generations the Black Cult rituals had their desired effect. An inevitable consequence is that they could not advance their culture as rapidly, if only because half the culture was punished for thinking. This group was the Kcha lineage."

"Your reasoning is sound."

"Inevitably the dominant lineages which we combine to label Vda pressed hard against the lineage of Kcha as they began to exploit more and more planetary resources. Equally inevitably the spacefarers made eventual contact with the Jotoki. We can assume the outcome was war, not the Jotok War the Pride Saga speaks of when we enslaved them, but one before that. Some of the legends may refer to this war, or perhaps not; at this distance in time it is impossible to reconstruct the chronology in detail. Jotoki history is nearly erased, but we know they had a starfaring civilization long, long before we did. Their mastery of genetic engineering was complete even then. We have no reason to assume the Vda lineage were any less warriors than we are today. Even with better technology we can expect the Jotoki to have been hard-pressed. How did they deal with this upstart race of carnivores? Not through direct combat; they are a genetically uniform species, which inevitably reduces conflict, especially coalitional conflict. They are not natural warriors."

"How then?"

"They exploited the inherent instability of a fragmented power distribution. They enlisted the Kcha lineage prides to do their fighting for them. Kcha lineage would almost certainly have resisted marginalization or extinction; how much better could they do this with high-technology weapons? The Jotoki introduced genetic modifications to those of the Kcha line, presumably to make them better warriors. This technique was so successful that very quickly the situation was reversed and Kcha had all but exterminated Vda. The Jotoki force-grew entire armies of Kcha warriors and tailored them to suit their purposes. This explains the extremely rapid onset of the genetic bottleneck, which may have been as short as a single generation. It is certain they gave them weapons and the training to use them. This explains the legends describing kzinti armed only with iron weapons against other kzinti possessed of magic; this is Kcha against Vda. It also explains the early verses of the Rrit Pride Saga in which both atmospheric and interstellar flight appear from nowhere in a single generation—gifted to Kcha by the Jotoki."

Pouncer fanned his ears up. "This story is incredible."

"It is well supported by the evidence, for those of us who have cared to look. The Jotoki must have been pleased at their success, but they were ultimately caught in their own trap. Having conquered Kzinhome, the Kcha warriors turned against their Jotoki masters and enslaved them. The Pride Saga tells us Chraz-Rrit-First-Patriarch was a cunning warrior and legendary leader, and this must have been so for him to have succeeded as he did. Nevertheless the social fabric of nomadic hunters was completely unadapted to the task of running an interstellar civilization. Inevitably this led to many problems as primitive beliefs clashed with technological realities. In particular the Black Cult gained access to Jotok genetic engineering skills and made further changes to the Kcha gene line. Which of the changes are due to the Jotoki and which to the Black Cult we can now only surmise. One thing we do know. The black fur gene is double-recessive, and its allele supports both telepathy in kzintosh and high reason in kzinrette. Black fur guarantees their absence. The Black Priests serve their genetic interests when they serve their creed."

"This is proven?"

"The facts are well supported. The link between them . . ." V'rli twitched her tail. "I find the arguments persuasive, but correlation does not demonstrate causation.

The truth is buried in the distant past and will never be known in detail. Regardless, the actions of the Black Priest cult are well known, as is what they would do if they knew the *czrav* secret. The tradition of deep secrecy is ancient in our line."

"But why secrecy and stealth? Telepathy is a great power; it is only the *sthondat* addiction which renders it a burden. What army could stand against you if you knew the minds of its commanders?"

"Telepathy carries its own burdens. Partial adepts are good hunters because they can sense their prey and know which way it will leap before it does. Full adepts cannot hunt because they feel the fear and pain of their prey as if it were their own. The strongest cannot even defend themselves against attack. And then, too, the mind-trance is seductive. Some who enter it never come out. This is the lure of the *sthondat* drug."

"Hrrr." Pouncer turned a paw over, considering.

"No, our way is better. The Patriarchy tolerates us, and we are slowly welding the lines of Vda and Kcha together again, through treaty gifts like your mother and other means. We will inevitably win, as long as we are not interrupted."

Pouncer looked up to meet V'rli's gaze. "You face a new danger then, Honored Mother."

"What is it?"

"The Tzaatz. Ftzaal-Tzaatz is a Black Priest, as well as *zar'ameer* to Kchula. The Black Cult has gained a powerful advantage in Tzaatz Pride's seizure of the Patriarchy."

"We have kept our secrets this long. We will keep them now too."

Off in the distance a *tuskvor* bellowed. Pouncer's ears swiveled reflexively to follow the sound, weirdly distorted by its passage through the caves and chambers of Ztrak Pride's den. "I hope you are right. I hope I have not led them to your den. The Tzaatz will not stop searching until they know I am dead."

> He who has a thousand friends has not a
> friend to spare,
>   And he who has one enemy will meet him
> everywhere.
> —Ali ibn-Abi-Talib, the fourth Caliph (602-661 A.D.)

The courier *Valiant* climbed steadily out of Sol's gravity well. When Tskombe woke up the sun had already shrunk to a quarter of the diameter it showed on Earth. At first he had sat and stared through the navigation blister's transpax, because the only alternative was to lie and stare at the walls of his tiny cabin. He had been too groggy with an overdose of ARM mercy needles to do anything else. It amazed him that he'd made it aboard. Now he sat because the view was spectacular, and because he needed time to think.

Time. It was something he had plenty of now, and little else besides. He'd thrown his career away. Somewhere between calling Jarl and his desperate flight with Trina he had crossed a line that even General Tobin could not erase for him, nor would his commander choose to. He had broken fealty, the ultimate crime, though that would not be what his charge sheet said. In return he had what he wanted now: he was on his way to Wunderland, to

Kzinhome, to find Ayla. On Earth he had allowed that to become a single-minded goal, had taken the refusal of Tobin to allow him to pursue it as a personal affront. Now that he was actually embarked on his mission the odds stacked against its success were becoming increasingly clear.

Footsteps on the ladder behind him. He turned. It was Khalsa.

"Recovered, I hope?" The Navy man was solicitous.

"Recovered physically, at least."

"And mentally?"

"I wonder whether I've made the right choice."

"For the human race, you certainly have. For yourself . . ." Khalsa shrugged. "Only you can answer that."

Not even I can answer that. Not until I know if the gamble was worth it. But even as he thought it he knew he could have taken no other choice, for the simple reason that he would not have been able to live with himself otherwise. It wasn't a rewarding train of thought, given his chances of success. *Time for a new subject.* "So you owe me an explanation."

Khalsa raised an eyebrow. "Yes?"

"Who are you working for."

"Naval Intelligence."

"You told me you weren't representing the Navy."

"Officially I work directly for the Secretary of War."

"And unofficially?"

"I have a certain degree of freedom to operate. The Secretary usually finds it expedient to know little about what we're doing."

"Including the freedom to task a ship to Wunderland?"

Khalsa shook his head. "This flight isn't authorized."

"This flight isn't unauthorized either. I know what it takes to get away from a planet. I've done it. There's been no interception. You had this courier standing by to take me off-planet. That's not arranged on the spur of the moment."

"We've cleared the inner system defensive sphere with bluff and liberal use of an Ultra clearance ident. Direct descent is unusual, but nobody had a reason to stop us. Once everyone on the ground gets all the pieces of the puzzle we may get intercepted after all. Do you feel well enough to talk to Curvy?"

Tskombe raised his eyebrows. "She's here?"

Khalsa nodded. "Curvy is who I work for. This is her ship. I'm her command pilot, among my other duties."

A dolphin with her own ship? Tskombe suppressed his surprise. He had assumed the dolphin worked for Khalsa, a humanocentric mistake. "And who does Curvy work for?"

"Curvy is Senior Strategist for the Secretary of War. In point of actual fact, the ex-Secretary of War."

"*Ex*-Secretary?"

"Muro Ravalla forced the no-confidence vote this morning, well ahead of the schedule we predicted. Secretary General Desjardins is out, and the entire cabinet is being replaced. Which means that you, I, and this ship are now in legal limbo. None of us are going back to Earth for a long time."

"What happens now?"

"That depends on you. Would you like to talk to Curvy?"

"How's Trina?"

"The girl? She's still getting over the mercy needles. She took a lot, and she's half your mass." Khalsa looked annoyed. "You risked a lot to get her on board here."

"It was worth it."

"What is she?"

"She's a street kid, unregistered." Tskombe let Khalsa fill in the implications behind that. "She doesn't have much of a life on Earth."

"A noble gesture to save her from her life." Khalsa smirked sardonically. "What do you plan to do with her here?"

"We'll drop her with the Bureau of Displaced Persons on Wunderland. Get her some care and an education. She'll have a chance at least."

Khalsa pursed his lips. "She's here now, it won't cost us anything. Not that you didn't nearly ruin this operation for the rest of us. You couldn't have been more conspicuous if you tried."

Tskombe shrugged. "I couldn't leave her."

"You still haven't answered my first question."

Tskombe nodded. "I'll talk to Curvy."

He followed Khalsa down the short ladder from the navigation blister. He was surprised the dolphin was on the ship, both because he had thought she was one of the ones who'd rescued himself and Trina from the sinking gravcar, and because there was simply no room for a dolphin tank on a ship the size of *Valiant*. He quickly learned that *Valiant* was the exception. The courier's entire cargo area had been converted to dolphin quarters. Tskombe found it somewhat surprising that the UNSN intelligence held a dolphin in enough esteem to give her unrestricted use of a ship. His next surprise was that Curvy didn't spend all her time in the tank, which only occupied half of the cargo compartment. The other half had the gravity switched off, and she received her guests there. She was wearing a flexprene body suit with grav polarizers built in and tanks and filters designed to keep her skin moist at all times, as well as a set of dolphin hands. In front of her was a command console, its holocube displaying an array of chessmen. The manipulator tentacles on the hands clicked over the databoard and the pieces moved in response.

Tskombe was about to speak, but Khalsa held up a hand for silence. The game was moving almost too fast to follow; a move per second seemed to be the rule. They didn't have long to wait before the black king flashed in defeat and the board reset itself. Curvy was playing white.

She turned to face them, popping and whistling. Her translator spoke, flatly inflected. "Welcome back, Colonel Tskombe."

"Curvy. I assume I have you to thank for the rescue?"

"Indirectly only. The dive crew who intervened are my family pod. They were prepared mostly to assist me in event of emergency. As it was they assisted you."

Tskombe bowed. "I thank you then, for them."

"As I said, dolphins have long cooperated with humans. I have questions for you, Colonel."

"Ask."

"Why did you return for the female?"

"It had to be done."

The dolphin-hand tentacles tapped the console and the

chessboard vanished, replaced by numbers that began flowing through the display cube. "You are more impulsive than we had estimated. The strategic matrix needs updating."

"Does this upset your plans?"

Curvy contemplated the numbers for a long minute, tapped more with her manipulators, considered a three-dimensional graph evolving in time. "The outcome space is shifted to a more extreme domain."

"Meaning?"

"Your correlation coefficient remains essentially the same for both positive and negative outcomes. However, the scale of those outcomes is increased in both directions."

"So I'll win big or lose big."

"The strategic matrix does not apply to your personal outcomes but to our organizational goal outcomes. Making predictions for individuals is difficult and error prone." Curvy's manipulators tapped on her databoard. "Does Captain Cherenkova remain your primary sexual interest?"

"Trina is just a girl."

"I will assume that means yes."

"Yes." *Not that Trina won't be a very desirable woman soon.* But soon was not now, and the least of what drew him to Ayla was her physical beauty.

"Understood. How much additional risk are you willing to undertake to accomplish our mission in parallel with yours?"

"How do you quantify risk? I'll work to prevent a war, if possible. I don't believe that anything I can do will influence the Patriarch significantly."

"Your willingness is the important factor. Remember that your actions do not exist in a vacuum." Curvy's manipulators tapped more. "Thank you, Lieutenant Commander, I believe I have the necessary updates."

It might have been the end of the interview, but Tskombe had questions. "So tell me about strategic matrix theory."

Curvy pivoted in her grav suit. "What do you want to know?"

"I want to know how a dolphin can ask me three questions and make predictions about a future war between the Patriarchy and humanity."

"You must have studied game theory in staff college."

"Some."

"Game theory is to strategic matrices as quantum theory is to statistical mechanics. In game theory each player has a number of strategies to apply to a given situation. Choice is assumed to be constrained to a small number of alternatives. A strategic matrix combines many, many games, each of whose players are constrained to some range of choice. The key is, these choices can then influence the choice set of subsequent iterations of the matrix. In raw form this is a highly exponential problem, making large-scale predictions impossible over any distance in time. Intuitively we know this can't be correct; a society as a whole is far more predictable than any particular individual in that society. In a strategic matrix we use statistical techniques to constrain the global choice set and thereby determine a range of possible futures. As it turns out, and as a few seconds' thought will tell you, most choices made by most individuals have almost no impact on the course of the global future, which inevitably means that a few choices have tremendous impact. With some probability of success we can back-trace outcomes to choices and the individuals who make them. Once we've identified such an individual we can then try to influence their choices to bring about a desirable outcome in the future."

"That's as clear as mud. Do you think you can really predict the course of events on a large scale?"

"It isn't even that hard. All we are doing is quantifying the process." Curvy pivoted in her wet suit to tap keys. *"Ceterum censeo Carthaginem esse delendam.'* Predicting that Rome would go to war with Carthage is straightforward. With two major powers in the Mediterranean any outcome other than war was impossible. History shows us this with exquisite clarity, and in fact the wars continued until one side was destroyed, as such wars do. Not until conversion weapons were a serious factor in war did great powers resolve their differences other than through combats where the goal, if not always the outcome, was the annihilation of the enemy. This change was also predictable, and was predicted even before strategic matrices by those with the vision to see it, due to the effect that conversion weapons had on the outcome sets of those empowered to make decisions that might lead to war."

"Meaning what?"

"In the era of nation-states human leaders proved willing to exterminate millions or tens of millions of the enemy, and to allow a similar fate to befall their own populations in the name of victory, because their personal outcome set was highly positively biased through the war process, becoming negative only in the relatively rare case of total defeat. Conversion weapons brought the same highly negative outcome set to the leaders that the populace had always faced, and they are lethal enough that the leaders' best efforts could not mitigate that change. The growth of United Nations power and its eventual transformation into de facto world government is traceable directly to this, again an unsurprising result given the initial conditions. This is the predictability of large-scale social systems."

"And you can do this with precision now."

"Within limits. The wars between Carthage and Rome were inevitable, and predictable. However, predicting that Carthage would be destroyed in the war launched by Cato the Elder is much more difficult, yet clearly the events are intimately linked. Still we can assess that Cato the Elder was far more likely to influence this event than Caecelius, merchant of Pompeii. A predictive strategic matrix allows the appropriate links to be made, in probabilistic terms, a priori. We can then assess unfolding paths in global choice-space."

Tskombe shook his head. "I find it hard to believe you can make predictions like that with enough accuracy to be useful."

Curvy squeaked and squealed, something that might have been laughter. "Do you invest in the markets, Colonel?"

"Not directly. My money sits in a floating investment fund. The bank invests it for me." *Or it did.* Reflexively he patted his beltcomp, where his total net worth sat in encrypted authentication codes.

"And you pay a fee for this service, yes?"

"One percent of all profit over the market average in a year."

"Why pay the fee when you could invest yourself?"

"I lack the experience and expertise to do it myself. And more importantly, the time."

"So how much better than the market average do you think your fund manager does?"

"I don't know, I've never thought about it."

"I can tell you that without knowing where you bank."

"You mean you don't have those details at your finger-tips?" Mild sarcasm.

Curvy chirped something and the translator said "Untranslateable," then "It works like this. Every day there are some stocks on the exchange that move many percentage points. Up or down does not matter. If you could predict those stocks reliably, you could make a fortune. We assume in market analysis that a priori evidence exists that can be used to make such predictions."

"That's blindingly obvious."

"Of course you can't win every bet. So how much better do you think your good bets have to be than your bad bets to start making money?"

Tskombe shrugged wordlessly.

"One percent. If you can consistently come out one percent ahead on every trading day, consistently reinvesting what you make, you'll triple your money in four months. If you could manage to be just five percent better your wealth would mount so fast than in a year you would own the world."

"That seems impossible."

"Do the math. Compound interest is powerful."

"*Literally* own the world?" Tskombe's voice was heavy with disbelief.

"No, because you would start to own too large a fraction of the market. As your wealth becomes a significant proportion of the market you lose the ability to concentrate your fund base in those high-yield investments. You cannot beat the system when you *are* the system. However, on a smaller scale the principle applies."

"So what does all that mean?"

"It means that market analysis doesn't work. Your fund manager's best efforts are no better than random choice. If he were doing even a tiny fraction of a percent better his results would be phenomenal, and you would be wealthy beyond the wildest dreams of avarice. Every day he has the opportunity to make not fractions of a percent but many percentage points, and yet he fails to do this, despite all the sophisticated predictive tools he employs."

"That can't be true. He only gets paid if he makes money for me."

"True, but it doesn't *cost* him anything if he loses money for you. The situation is asymmetric, to his advantage. He bets with your money, shares the gains, and leaves the losses to you. Suppose he splits every investment both ways. Half his customers will lose and half will win, and he'll collect his pay on the winners. The losers curse his name, but as long as he can replace them with new clients he doesn't need to care."

Tskombe blinked. *I'm talking about the stock market to a dolphin.* "So if I understand you, you're telling me strategic matrices don't work."

Curvy whistled. "Exactly correct in the case of markets.

Everyone is trying to make predictions based on the same information, but once you make a trade based on a prediction you change the market. Since everyone is processing the same information at the same time any advantage you might have is immediately erased. You cannot predict those large market moves that are reactions to events which are by definition unpredictable. If they were predictable, they would have been widely predicted and so any advantage you might have extracted is immediately erased. It is theoretically possible that you could develop a better method of extracting information from the market, and hence retain an advantage, but this is very unlikely, and you would retain your advantage only as long as you could keep your methodology secret, which in practice is impossible, since there exists a large segment of traders who analyze the investment patterns of the rest of the market in order to determine exactly these strategies. Because of the feedback loops formed in this way the market is inherently unstable. In that it's just a mirror of the real world, which is in fact exactly what it's supposed to be."

"So strategic matrices are *your* predictive tool. Why do you spend so much time and effort developing the damn things?"

"There is a fundamental difference. We apply them to the socio-political arena, which does not include feedback loops as large or rapid as those at work in the market. We can in fact make reasonable predictions and expect to be correct, within error bars. The future may evolve along widely different lines, but the lines, at least, can be assessed in advance, the critical path junctions identified, and sometimes we can act to induce events to unfold along one path instead of another, by influencing individuals who in turn can influence events at these critical points." The dolphin paused and seemed to be reflecting on something. "It is of course an error-prone process, and we lack the ability to repeat our experiments."

"You don't inspire much confidence."

"Were you looking for confidence?" If Curvy was human her voice might have been sardonic. "I thought you were looking for Captain Cherenkova." Curvy turned to her console. "If you will excuse me, Colonel, I have much work to do." She looked at her console, manipulator tentacles tapping. "I would enjoy talking with you again, if you like."

Later Tskombe sat in the courier's tiny wardroom with Khalsa. The Navy commander produced coffee in bulbs, pretended not to be offended when Tskombe added synthetic crème de cacao from the food processor.

"I don't understand what you're doing here. You've taken tremendous risks to help me, on Curvy's recommendation, but Curvy herself has no confidence in her strategic matrices. It doesn't make sense."

"Astute observation, but there is another factor."

"Which is?"

Khalsa leaned back and sipped his coffee. "Consider the Second Punic War. Hannibal is outnumbered, undersupplied, outmaneuvered, still he wins battle after battle. He doesn't win by force of numbers, he wins by outthinking his opponents. This is not a statistical fluke; he manages to beat the odds. In the markets, you've heard of Markland Stage?"

"The financier?"

"He started from nothing and made his two percent per day, until he owned too much of the system to keep beating it like that. There are other examples. Henry V of England, Erwin Rommel, Gael Sistorny. There are those who do beat the odds, people who are so far out on the bell curve that the math simply doesn't work for them anymore. Consider: the emergence of Hannibal's military genius could have been predicted, in probabilistic terms at least, given sufficient data. Predicting the specific tactics Scipio Africanus might use in any given battle is much more difficult, but this was exactly what Hannibal excelled at. There are commanders, like Hannibal, like Alexander, like Genghis Khan, who not only win consistently despite the material and numerical superiority of their enemies but who defy statistics as well, a much more difficult feat. How they do it we don't know, maybe they're just extremely lucky. The important thing is, they do it."

"And you think I'm that person?"

"No. Curvy is that person. Strategic matrices are an old tool, but it takes more than tools to make a craftsman. Curvy knows how to use her tools. If she tells me that sending you to Kzinhome will make a difference, I'll send you to Kzinhome."

"Curvy is not a commander."

"Dolphins don't have commanders. They don't form large-scale societies, and they don't fight wars, certainly not as we know them. Nevertheless, Curvy's predictions are accurate. She knows what has to go into a matrix, she knows what has to stay out. She beats the odds, Colonel. If she's betting on you, I'm betting on you."

Tskombe reflected on that for awhile. "Curvy had to

update the matrix. She didn't have all the information. How do you know she has it all now?"

"I don't. Updates are an ongoing process. The amount of information entropy, basically how much we don't know, is computed in the matrix."

"Ever have it happen that new information turns your calculations upside down?"

"Sometimes."

"What do you do then?"

"What else can we do? We recalculate and keep trying to influence events toward positive outcomes."

"Positive in your own definition."

"Of course."

Tskombe shook his head. "I can only imagine you use more forms of influence than tracking down potential deserters to make them an offer they can't refuse."

"Different people respond to different incentives." Khalsa shrugged. "In a case like yours, the decisions likely to lead to positive outcomes for you are aligned with those likely to lead to positive outcomes for us. Sometimes we have to change a target individual's choice set to ensure they make the right choice."

"Change their choice set . . ." Tskombe contemplated the wall, recognizing a euphemism when he heard one, then looked up to meet Khalsa's gaze. "Does the matrix ever tell you to kill someone?"

Khalsa stood up. "I should check our navigation." He left Tskombe to himself.

Tskombe watched him go. Khalsa didn't play by any rules but his own. *An intelligence branch with a certain degree of freedom. He reports to the Secretary of War, but the Secretary doesn't want to know what he's doing so he can deny knowledge later. Now the Secretary of War is being replaced and Khalsa is acting entirely on his own, with no oversight whatsoever. His goals are positive, but this is a dangerous thing in a world that's supposed to be free.* But the UN wasn't a free society; it wasn't even the freest of all societies. That was just what they taught children in social studies class, and when they were taught young they tended to keep believing it on an emotional level, even when the facts they lived with every day were very different. *I believed it myself, until I went away and came back.*

It was a two-day flight to the edge of the singularity and hyperspace. Trina recovered, slowly. She had been hit much harder by the mercy needles than he had, and so managed to absorb the care and attention of Khalsa, Tskombe, and Virenze, *Valiant's* petite but tough copilot. Trina looked tiny and fragile even in the narrow bunk of her closet-sized cabin, and though the effects of the tranquilizers had worn off she still slept a great deal, only picking at the food she was brought. They fell into a routine over her care. It was a surprisingly comfortable arrangement for Tskombe. Khalsa, unlike Curvy, asked no uncomfortable questions either about her, or, so far as Tskombe could tell, of her. Her withdrawal was disturbing at first, but she seemed to need the quiet, if not to recover from the mercy drugs then to recover from the rest of her life. *And fair enough that she should.*

"Why did you come back for me?" she asked him once.

"I couldn't leave you there."

"Why not?" She sounded almost resentful. "There are

thousands like me, millions. What difference does it make?"

"It makes a difference to you."

And she had no answer for that, and when she turned over in her bunk to cry he rubbed her back to comfort her, feeling slightly awkward. There were fine scars there, and no doubt more he couldn't see, both on her skin and in her heart. *Some of her clients wouldn't be nice at all.* He found himself wondering what depravities this woman-child had endured, and shuddered.

Flight in the cramped courier didn't suit Tskombe's style, but his company was congenial enough. The copilot, Virenze, was a dark-haired woman who'd been in the first attack on Atraxa. She was serious and taciturn, obviously competent but not very social, and he imagined Ayla Cherenkova had been like this early in her career, before she had enough rank to allow herself to relax off duty. Her skill as a pilot wasn't in doubt; she'd shot the direct descent profile singlehanded and put the ship down within meters of its target. He found himself spending more time with Curvy. At first it was simply because Trina spent all her time in the observation blister, and the dolphin's hold was the only other space in the ship where he didn't feel cramped, but he found her interesting company. He challenged Curvy to chess, not expecting to win but hoping to learn something in the effort. The games weren't successful; Curvy won so quickly Tskombe never had a chance to learn, and Tskombe posed no challenge at all as an opponent. They switched to go, which whiled away a pleasant day, though Curvy won four games in five, and finally settled on poker, which was an even match. They played for imaginary salmon, which seemed to appeal to the dolphin's sense of humor, especially when she was winning.

They were in the middle of a game when Khalsa came on the in-com. "Passengers to crash stations. We've got trouble."

Tskombe checked to make sure Trina was belted into her acceleration couch in her room, then went up to the cockpit. He got there just as he went weightless, but he was used to being weightless on troop transports. The pilots were pouring everything into the drive polarizers, and cabin gravity was a waste of power. He shouldn't have been there, but they didn't send him away. They were strapped into their command couches, vac suits on but helmets off.

"What's the problem?"

In response Virenze hit keys on the display controls. The starscape spun until a warship floated in it, black on black, streamlined for semi-atmospheric operation, weapons blisters faired into the hull.

"What's that?"

Khalsa made a face. "It's a cruiser, Viking class, and it is coming fast on an intercept course. They'll be in firing range in four hours."

Tskombe nodded. "What do they want?"

"They want you. I've been ordered to stop and hand you over."

"What are you going to do about it?" It was a rhetorical question; Khalsa had already demonstrated he wasn't going to give Tskombe over to his pursuers, though a brief thrill of fear ran through him at the thought that he might be caught this close to escape.

"We can run, and we can pray. We're a fast ship and we're not far from the edge of the singularity, but they're fast too, and we're low on power after that direct descent on Earth."

"You don't mind defying Navy orders?"

"They can't give me orders; they aren't in my chain of command. This isn't the first time we've run clandestine missions the Navy doesn't know about."

The Secretary of War is gone, so you don't have a chain of command. Tskombe kept that thought to himself. "Your high clearance ident isn't enough?"

"I tried it. They still want you. Looks like the new Secretary General has the whole scenario figured out. They don't want you loose."

"Are you sure it's me they want?"

Khalsa laughed. "They'll take me, too. Ravalla's crew has been sparring with us, Curvy and me and the rest of the WarSec team, for a long time now."

"So what are you going to do?"

"Maximum boost until we're at minimum power for the hyperspace jump, then shut it right down and drift, and hope they have a sensor glitch. If they give it up and go home we'll jump and call for help when we hit Wunderland. The Wunderlanders have no love of the UN. They'll send a ship out to get us, and we'll deal with the red tape later."

"Can we fight?"

"We've got two missiles and two light turrets. We haven't got a hope against a cruiser. I have a couple of tricks up my sleeve; maybe they'll make a mistake. I'd rather not start shooting at our own side, but I will if I have to."

Tskombe nodded, watching the display. The cruiser grew gradually larger while Khalsa reworked his intercept data. Tskombe should have gone back to his cabin and strapped in, at least gone back to make sure Trina was okay, but Khalsa didn't order him to do it. He'd grown too accustomed to being in the picture. He thought back to his combat drops, times when he'd had no idea what was going on, which jolt was violent evasive action and which was the hit that was about to kill him. It was a helpless feeling, and he'd always been eager for the hard, unmistakable slam followed by sudden stillness that meant the landing skids had hit the ground. He'd be unstrapped and running even before the landing ramp blew down, leading in the ground assault. His troops thought it was heroism; they'd told him so. In reality it was desperation to get off the shuttle and into a situation where he had some semblance of control over his own fate. *Not that I have any control here.* The thought came unbidden, and he wished Ayla was piloting. He was sure Khalsa was a perfectly competent pilot. He'd never flown with Ayla, but something about her told him she was an ace. *And more important than that, if she were here, we would be together.*

Time seemed to creep and fly at the same time. Virenze had set the mission clock to reach zero when the cruiser was in firing range, and while the last seconds seemed to last forever the previous four hours had simply vanished. There was a distant, hydraulic whine as *Valiant*'s turrets traversed, and a series of faint, almost subaural thuds.

"Dusters out." Virenze's voice was terse. Behind them the cannisters would burst into clouds of finely divided aluminum dust, which would disperse and absorb laser pulses, to a degree, and as long as Khalsa could keep them between *Valiant* and the cruiser. "Missiles?"

Khalsa shook his head. "Wait until he fires first. They may be trying to provoke us into providing an incident."

They waited tensely. The mission clock ticked up positive seconds. The faint thuds of the turrets came again as the ship's AI launched more dusters automatically. Minutes later it did it again, and the cruiser still hadn't fired. Tskombe began to think that perhaps they wouldn't when an alarm sounded, subdued but urgent, and a red icon appeared on the pilot's central plot board.

"Missile launch," Virenze reported. She studied her instruments. "Looks like four contacts."

"Tanjit." Khalsa's expletive showed that he too had hoped there might not be a fight. "Launch screeners, get us a solution for our own missiles." He tapped course commands into his console. "And see if you can get some screeners in their course funnel while you're at it."

Virenze's hands flew over the controls. "Defensive screeners away . . ." She paused. "Missiles are locked; recommend we delay launch until he's closer." She tapped another command. "And he'll be flying through a dozen shot cannisters. I delayed their burst until the last moment. Maybe he won't see them in time."

"Maybe." Khalsa's voice was doubtful. The screener cannisters were loaded with millimeter-sized iridium balls, unlike the fine powder the dusters carried. A missile flying through the ball screen at tens of kilometers per second relative velocity would be shredded if it hit even one. A warship's armor could take more, but they could cause enough damage to be dangerous. If the Navy captain didn't pick up the trap his ship might get taken out of the fight before it had truly started. It was more likely he would pick it up, but at least then he'd have to waste acceleration avoiding it, which would buy *Valiant* a little more time. At this point, though, buying time was just an exercise in delaying the inevitable.

"Their missiles are tracking . . . Drive signature shows B-mark twos." Virenze's voice was taut.

"Lasers to point-defense mode." Khalsa nudged the controls and the cabin gravity surged to compensate, momentarily tugging Tskombe to the floor.

"Screeners bursting in his course funnel . . ." Virenze paused. ". . . Now!" Another pause. "He isn't evading, he's . . . no, he's seen them, he's going outsystem."

Khalsa nodded. "Staying between us and the singularity edge. He's smart enough, that captain."

Tskombe looked out the transpax, feeling there should be some sensation of motion, some sight of the enemy, but there was nothing. The entire battle was being played out on instruments, and they would live or die based on the cryptic readouts.

"He's entering our launch window."

"Launch now." Khalsa's voice was terse, and the deck thudded dully once, then twice, as *Valiant*'s single pair of seekers punched out under maximum acceleration. Two more red icons appeared on the plot board. "We've done all we can."

Suddenly two of the cruiser's missiles vanished from the plot. "Looks like we got two with the screeners, sir." Even as Virenze said it another icon vanished. "Make that three."

"It isn't over yet. He's reloading his launch bay."

"Fourth missile's gotten through." Virenze's voice didn't waver, though Tskombe felt adrenaline rush through his system.

"More screeners, sound collision and override acceleration limits." Khalsa looked over his shoulder at Tskombe. "Get out of here, it's going to get rough." Tskombe turned to go as the pilot firewalled the throttles. Gravity came back as he reached the door, but it was facing backward and not down, and he found himself falling to the cockpit's back wall. His weight built inexorably, until he could barely breathe. There was no question now of getting to the acceleration couch in his cabin. He was going to ride out the battle where he was.

"It's through, sir!" Virenze sounded scared for the first time.

Khalsa's response wasn't audible, but *Valiant* suddenly gyrated, the previously immobile starfield spinning violently, coming to rest again. His weight surged again and he grunted under the stress.

"Still tracking!"

"We're almost to the singularity line."

"How close?"

"Thirty seconds . . . twenty-eight . . ."

"They'll have their missiles set to cripple us before we can jump."

"Twenty-two seconds . . ." Tskombe could hear the tension beneath the calm in Virenze's words.

"Jump now." Khalsa's voice carried sudden decision.

"We're not far enough . . ."

"We'll take the risk. Jump."

"Hyperdrive now." Virenze hit a key, and at the same instant something in the blackness flared searing white, and the transpax went opaque. For a long moment nothing else happened, and then a giant's fist struck *Valiant* and sent her tumbling. Cabin gravity went from eight or nine gees to none, and Tskombe, not strapped in, slammed hard against the cockpit wall, then again against either the floor or the ceiling, he couldn't tell which. Alarms blared loudly, and then were abruptly silenced as the lights went out. Dim emergency lights glowed on the control panel as the pilots threw switches, frantically trying to get the situation under control. Their terse chatter was tense, grew tenser as the extent of the damage became clear. Khalsa began to curse as he tried in vain to get system readings. *Valiant* was dead in space. Tskombe could hear the hiss of escaping air.

"Vacuum leak! Helmets on." Khalsa barked the order. "Quacy, get back to your cabin, I'm sealing the cockpit." Even as he said it the hiss grew to a roar. Tskombe's ears popped, an alarm blared, and the cockpit's blast door began sliding shut. Instinctively he launched himself under it and into the passageway leading back to the wardroom and the hold. The door closed behind him with a solid thunk, and his ears popped again as the pressure rose again. He grabbed a handhold and stopped himself. Had the pilots got their helmets on in time? He flipped himself over to a com panel and keyed the cockpit. The indicators glowed, showing the system was intact, but there was no response from the pilots. He went back to the blast door and checked the pressure indicator. The cockpit pressure read zero. The little leak had become explosive decompression, and the pilots had had seconds at most to get their helmets on. Strapped into their command couches as they were it didn't seem likely that they would have managed it. If that were true the ship was under the cruiser's guns and helpless, or already in hyperspace and pilotless. Tskombe breathed out slowly as the seriousness of the situation came down on him. Neither option was good.

Steel is no stronger than the sinew that wields it.
                                                —Si-Rrit

The sun was a flaming red ball on the horizon from the gravcar, but the valley below was already in shadow. Ftzaal-Tzaatz sniffed the air, stiff with the charred scent of the burned-over trees, though the fire that consumed them had burned out seasons ago. The vehicle touched down, the others sliding in around it to form a perimeter. He nudged Telepath, lolling in the back seat beside him.

"Here?"

"Close . . ." Telepath's eyes fluttered open and he looked around the clearing. "Yes . . ." His eyes closed again. "Yes, they were here."

"How long ago?"

"Several days, I think. The memory is still fresh in the *kz'zeerkti*'s mind, but it has not referenced it."

"Good enough." Ftzaal keyed his comlink. *"Ftz'yeer* Leader! Dismount the *rapsari*. Sniffers forward."

"At once, sire."

The back ramps on the carriers banged down and his *Ftz'yeer* Heroes swarmed out, red and gold glinting on their mag armor. A brace of sniffers surged to the front, proboscises wiggling eagerly. Ftzaal keyed his comlink again. "Quickly. We want to pick up the scent before darkness falls."

He leapt from his own car to the ground. He had a decision to make. They would be proceeding on foot from this point forward. Ktronaz-Commander had already demonstrated that combat cars operating on top of the triple layer canopy were essentially useless for supporting troops on the ground beneath it. Simply tracking their quarry was risky, and not likely to be effective. There were too many places to hide in the jungle, and First-Son-of-Meerz-Rrit had already shown himself to be adept at laying subtle traps for the pursuers.

No, simple pursuit would not work. It would be night hunting then, to fix their quarry while they were sleeping. When they knew First-Son's habits and the paths he followed, ambush teams would be inserted in front of him. Then the pursuit would intensify, sacrificing stealth for speed, to drive their prey into the trap. So the decision was made, no air support. Combat cars whining overhead would only warn him to cover his tracks more carefully.

A deep, booming bellow echoed through the valley, drowning out the other night sounds. Ftzaal froze, his ears swiveling up to home on the sound. *I must use caution. Kzinhome's jungles hold predators more dangerous than feral Jotoki.* Even at the thought, something flashed out of the darkness overhead, snapping. He hit the ground instinctively and looked up, saw gray wings and talons against the night sky: a saberwing. He'd never seen one live, but he'd recognized it immediately. They were a frequent feature in the Legends, powerful sky predators but no match for a kzin. They were probably in its territory. He picked himself up and keyed a warning to the *Ftz'yeer* over his com. It would harass them until they had moved far enough away. For a long moment he watched carefully, but it didn't return. High up he heard its keening call, and then nothing but the quiet rustlings of his warriors around him. He flashed signals with his tail and they moved into formation.

Another bellow rumbled out of the valley below, followed rapidly by a third. The calls echoed and faded, then another set rose. There was something *big* out there. Ftzaal pulled his goggle visor down over his eyes and toggled the spectral response to deep infrared. The muted colors of the moonlit scene jumped into sharp black and white contrast. Here and there blurred white shapes revealed the small night creatures, stalking, hiding, feeding, mating in the fields and the jungle fringes, but the burned-out tree trunks prevented him from seeing more than a few eights of leaps away. Whatever had made that call was far down in the valley, to judge by the echoes. He turned slowly, ears swiveled up, his mouth slightly open to enhance both hearing and sense of smell. There might still be something else . . .

There! A flash of white behind a tree trunk, gone before he could see what it was but big enough to be *something*. The visor let him see what might otherwise be invisible, but it also reduced detail and restricted his field of vision. He pushed it up again, eyes straining to readjust to the darkness. Had it been a kzin? If they had come down too close to their prey then First-Son would already be escaping. Would Telepath have brought them in too close on purpose? He looked suspiciously at the other, but Telepath was looking around with quick, jittery glances, radiating not guilt but nervousness. He didn't like being in the jungle in general, and he didn't like being here in particular.

Enough speculation. Time to move. Ftzaal patted his netgun, found reassurance in the weapon. "Sniffers, over here!" he ordered. "Senior Handler, to me now."

Shapes came out of the darkness, the pudgy sniffer *rapsari* snuffling at the ground. "Command me, sire!"

"Over there." Ftzaal pointed to where he had seen the shape. "Find me a trail."

"At once." Senior Handler's tail flashed signals to his companions, and they moved out in a search wedge. Ftzaal's own tail signaled his sword leaders into formation on either flank and he moved out after the sniffers.

They were not long in finding the track. A stone's throw forward Senior Handler halted the formation and whispered into his com, "Sire, we have kzin scent here."

Ftzaal went to him. His sniffer was waddling in circles, proboscis wrinkling, with faint colors flowing over the chromatophores on its hindquarters. He inhaled deeply. Yes, there it was, faint but clear, the distinctive scent of kzintosh, but strangely muted. There was a something else there, something unfamiliar, that made the scent trail hard to identify. He strained his eyes in the darkness. He was sure he'd seen *something*. He pulled his goggle visor down again, and saw a glow on the ground, where something warm-blooded had stood for some period. Like the scent, the infrared impression was weaker than it should have been for a kzin. The ground was still warm from the heat of the day, not far off body temperature, so the signal would have been weak anyway, merging with the warm background even with the visor's signal processors working to find and enhance significant details. Still, there should have been more . . .

Hunt cloaks dumped body heat to chemical cold packs to mask the wearer's thermal signature, but if their quarry had hunt cloaks then why hadn't they been wearing them on the savannah when Ktronaz-Commander's Heroes had found them? Something else then? *The unknown is dangerous.* He shook off his doubts. The trail was here; it was the best lead they had, and they would follow it. His tail flashed signals for the trail scouts to advance with goggles down. Perhaps what he'd seen wasn't a kzin, perhaps it was, but it was a threat, and they needed to know about it. The hunt party moved out again.

Progress was slow, but Ftzaal didn't mind that, they needed to take their time. The *Ftz'yeer* were experienced jungle fighters, but Kzinhome's jungles were a fiercer environment than those of Jotok. Ktronaz-Commander's troops had come in force and moved fast, but this was an environment where stealth counted for more than firepower. He did not expect to flush First-Son-of-Meerz-Rrit this night, nor the next. They would track him but not let him know he was being tracked, then, when Ftzaal understood his route and his habits, the trap would be set. Before that could happen the *Ftz'yeer* had to understand the jungle, and the way to that goal was through experience. *We will convert the unknown to the known, and make the environment our ally.* There was no hurry, not yet.

Another series of bellows rumbling up from below, definitely closer this time. His comlink buzzed. "Sire, this is First Scout."

"Go ahead."

"I saw something, maybe a kzin, I couldn't tell . . ."

"Confirmed." Could they have come down so close to their quarry the first time? Simple probability argued not. He raised his goggles and looked again to Telepath, saw no deception in his miserable face. "Carry on, stay alert."

Disturbed air overhead, the rush of wings. The saber-wing was over and gone before he caught a glimpse. Shouldn't they be out of its territory by now? Something itched on the back of Ftzaal's neck. The jungle almost seemed to be watching them. Warning instinct, or simply nerves in a new and dangerous environment? *The Ftz'yeer look to me for leadership. I must not show them fear here.* First-Son would not be the last fugitive to run for the jungle. If Tzaatz Pride were to control Kzinhome they would have to learn to live, to search, to fight here too. His tail twitched signals and the small group moved on again.

The Hunter's Moon had slid halfway across the sky and they were deep into the valley. Behind them the smaller Traveler's Moon was starting to rise. The burned-out tree trunks faded away, revealing a wide open meadow and then, abruptly, the living jungle, a distant dark wall edged by giant spire trees. The forest fire had burned over the upslopes, but this meadow, probably a marsh in the wet season, had stopped it from getting into the low ground nearer the river. A signal came back from Senior Handler. The trail had split. There were two kzin in front of them, each now moving in a different direction. Decision time— split his force, or stay together? No decision really, this early. It was tempting to believe they were right on First-Son's tail, that he and his sister would both fall into his hands this very night, but that must have been the think-ing that had cost so many of Ktronaz-Commander's Heroes their lives. *The real hunt will come later, for now we must maximize caution.* He signaled forward for the trackers to advance, together, signaled for the flankers to move into open country formation.

Another cluster of the echoing bellows sounded, these very much closer and something else, a sound like running water, but with sharper notes, like gravel pouring off a conveyer. The sound grew louder, distinct *snap*s rising over the general tumult. The sound was coming from the jungle ahead, and he strained his eyes in the moonlight to see what might be making it. He became aware of some-thing else, a vibration in the ground.

"Sire! Lead Scout! There's something moving in the treeline! Something big."

Ftzaal snapped down his goggle visor and immediately saw large white blobs moving in the tree line, still obscured by dark gray trunks, but *huge*, swaying ponder-ously, and coming toward him. The first one cleared the woods: vast tusks on a head bigger than him, a long neck connected to a body the size of a spacecraft. He stared for a long moment before he understood what he was seeing.

Tuskvor! As with the saberwing, he'd never seen one live, though he recognized them immediately.

"Tuskvor!" Lead Scout had recognized them too.

Ftzaal keyed his comlink. "Halt in position. We'll work our way around them."

It took time to move the hunters around the herd, more time to search the margins of the valley to reacquire the scent trail. Dawn was starting to brighten the eastern sky by the time they'd found it again, running straight along a heavily beaten *tuskvor* trackway. Ftzaal moved them well off the trail at that point, to the heart of a bramblebush thicket where they should, he hoped, be safe enough to rest for the day. They slept in shifts, with half the force always on alert. When afternoon started to turn into twilight Ftzaal allowed himself to relax, slightly. They'd survived a night and a day in the jungle and successfully avoided some of its more dangerous inhabitants. More importantly, the *tuskvor* trail had a single pair of kzinti pawprints, made within the last couple of days. It was a tiny clue, but it was enough. The sniffers were on the right track.

When darkness fell they took up the hunt again, paralleling the trail, moving literally paw by paw to avoid making noise. There was little they could do about their scent, but slow movement generated less of that as well. Every once in a while the sniffer handlers would move in to verify that they were still following the right spoor.

Toward dawn his vocom clicked. "Lead Scout. I see a kzin."

Ftzaal signaled the rest of the patrol to stop and moved forward cautiously. Lead Scout was in good cover, coming up to a bend in the trail. He had his full spectrum visor down, and Ftzaal snapped his into position as well. Lead Scout pointed up, and for a moment Ftzaal couldn't see what he was indicating, and then suddenly the scene snapped into focus. High up in a spire tree there was a platform, artfully built into the branches so as to be almost invisible. Only the radiative heat difference between live and dead wood allowed the visor's systems to pick it out. There was a blur on the platform, only faintly visible, but it could only be one thing: a kzin wearing a hunt cloak. They had found something important.

But there was no need to hurry yet. He snarled an instruction for *Ftz'yeer* Leader to move the patrol back and find a good lair to lay up in, well off the trail. He and Lead Scout worked their way backward into dead ground, then circled cautiously to come at the platform from another angle. From their new position a second platform was visible. As the cold, gray light of dawn began to filter through the triple canopy there was motion. A pair of kzinti arrived on the trackway and scrambled up the spire tree. A few moments later another pair came down and disappeared back into the jungle. Some time later the process was repeated at the second watch platform. The sentries wore hunt cloaks and carried small journeypacks, provisions, perhaps, for a day spent on guard. They must be of the *czrav*, the primitive jungle dwellers the *cvari* hunters had told him about. Telepath had seen many kzinti with First-Son-of-Meerz-Rrit through the *kz'zeerkti's* mind. Their quarry had gone to ground with these primitives. Ftzaal's tail twitched unconsciously. The changing of the guard had the feel of long-established routine, and they weren't doing all that just to protect a fugitive. *The question becomes, what are they guarding?* Finding out would be difficult. To their left was the river, to their right a steep bluff. The platforms were positioned so that anyone advancing along the trackway between them could not avoid being seen. They could perhaps sneak through at night. *Primitives won't have full spectrum goggles, but primitives shouldn't have hunt cloaks either.* They couldn't take the risk; they were going to have to find another way.

Slowly he moved back into cover with First Scout. They made their way back to the patrol lair. Ftzaal gestured for his subcommanders and gave them quick orders. Blade patrols, four each, would move up the bluff and around to reconnoiter that way. The cacophony of jungle noises would help to cover their movement, but they were to use maximum stealth regardless, and take no risk of compromise. There would be more guards; they had only to locate them. Even if they saw First-Son-of-Meerz-Rrit they were not to take action; he had proven himself too adept at eluding pursuit. They would wait until the trap was set; only then would they act.

His subcommanders snarled their assent and left to organize their separate subpatrols, leaving only Ftzaal's personal guard and Telepath behind in the lair. Ftzaal keyed his com to task a high-resolution scan pass by *Distant Trader*. Its optical instruments weren't as good as those in the orbital defense network, but using the Patriarch's assets might invite questions from those still loyal to the Rrit. Using their own ship posed no such dangers, and Raarrgh-Captain could be relied upon to keep it quiet. He was fortunate; the ship's orbit was favorable, and before the sun was halfway up he had the data. He spent the time until noon with his visor down and in display mode, scanning the images through the full spectral range. There was nothing to reveal the presence of anything unusual in the jungle. Even the watch platforms he'd spotted didn't show up, despite their location high up in the canopy. He pulled his visor up and looked around for a moment, as if he could see with his own eyes what his sensors could not. Whatever the *czrav* were hiding, they were hiding it well. He pulled his visor back down and began resurveying the orbital imagery, looking for cutoff points and assault landing zones. Ktronaz-Commander could have a *rapsari* Battle Team assembled in half a day. By then his reconnaissance would be complete enough. The river and the bluff formed a natural channel. Control both ends and nothing trapped inside could escape. If First-Son were there the rules of *skalazaal* applied, but that would make little difference. The primitives might have hunt cloaks, perhaps even variable swords and mag armor, but the dry season was upon them. The stark landscape of the charred valley they had landed in showed that the jungle would burn, and burn hard. Fire would be his primary weapon.

And I need to know if First-Son is there. Telepath had been hiding something, and he had to address that now. *The telepaths have power, if they should ever manage to wield it.* A *tuskvor* snorted from the trackway, close enough to startle him, and he froze. It wouldn't be alone, and even if they somehow survived a charge it would destroy the stealth on which the mission depended. He listened for the bellow that would warn him they had been scented, but they had picked their cover well and the wind was in the other direction. After a moment he relaxed and got out an infuser and an ampoule of *sthondat* extract in preparation for another difficult interrogation. Telepath had become increasingly recalcitrant as the hunt wore on, fueling Ftzaal's suspicions and at the same time obscuring the evidence he needed to prove them. *If such evidence exists.* He could not yet be sure, today he would learn. He held up the infuser. Sthondat *lymph gives us power over the telepaths.* In the face of the ability to know another's mind, it seemed a flimsy tool.

Telepath was sleeping, huddled in a miserable pile. He did not take well to the rigors of the jungle. Ftzaal nudged him awake. "The *kz'zeerkti.* Where is it?"

Telepath looked up blearily, involuntary tremors shaking his limbs. His expression grew vacant for a moment. "It is gone . . ."

"Gone?" Ftzaal's ears swiveled up. "Where . . . ?"

"I . . . I can't say. . . ."

"You can't see its mind?"

"No . . ." Telepath's eyes slid shut, leaving his answer ambiguous. Ftzaal's tail twitched. There was something wrong here. Telepath's reactions weren't quite right. He had seen it before. The *sthondat* slaves were strangely reluctant to share information on other telepaths, and some other subjects. *Why the* kz'zeerkti? *Why now?* Telepath had shown no more than disinterest cowed into obedience until his telepathic trace of the man-monkey had come to the burned-over meadow. *What changed there?* Honor forbade him from lying outright, but a telepath had precious little honor to begin with, and no one knew better than Ftzaal the subtleties of deception and the honor code. He had begun to suspect in the Black Cult that there was something systematic to their intermittent uncooperativeness. He had researched it, documented it and proven his point. *Rebellion*, a subtle and slow one, but one that was progressing all the same. None had taken him seriously, Priest-Master-Zrtra least of all. He had staked his reputation on it, and lost. *Why would they not believe?* Because to believe was to face hard truths that the Cult did not want to acknowledge. Only the effects of the *sthondat* drug made telepaths tractable. If a pure strain line of telepaths arose, a line that had no need of the drug, there would be nothing to stop them from ruling the Patriarchy. It was the role of the Black Cult to prevent that, though no one outside the Black Cult knew that secret. *No one except the telepaths, perhaps.* Ftzaal turned a palm over. *If* sthondat *conditioning failed even once, what secret could we hope to hide from them?*

It was a worrisome question with no good answer. Still, he had his lever of control over this specimen at least. He held up the infuser, pulled Telepath's head around so he could see what he craved. "Do you want this?"

Longing filled Telepath's eyes; his pupils dilating until the irises had all but disappeared. His paws shook, and he opened his mouth and then closed it again. "No . . . no, my powers are fully functional." His voice firmed and he moved his eyes to meet Ftzaal's gaze. "The *kz'zeerkti* is gone. We will find nothing here."

"Nothing?" Ftzaal had the evidence of his own senses:

the watch platforms were there for a reason. What game was Telepath playing? "Are there no kzin minds close?"

"You know it is difficult for me to tell at a distance; our own *Ftz'yeer* are enough to mask other kzinti. The jungle fauna make it more difficult still." Telepath's shaking had subsided. He seemed strangely calm. He looked away, his eyes rolling back as he reached out with a sense Ftzaal could not imagine. "Yes, there are other kzin, *czrav*. They are savages, I am in a kzinti mind now . . ." His face slackened as he absorbed information from the other's awareness. "No . . . he has not seen the *kz'zeerkti*."

"Hrrr." Ftzaal raised the infuser. "Perhaps you need more extract."

"No!" Telepath's eyes snapped open. For an instant fear was written there. "No, no, I could read him clearly. He has not seen the *kz'zeerkti*."

Why the fear? And when did Telepath ever refuse the extract? Something was wrong, Telepath was hiding something. Ftzaal's eyes narrowed.

"Or perhaps, yes, yes, I do need the extract." Telepath's eyes were suddenly full of the familiar need, and Ftzaal relaxed. The *sthondat* slaves hated the drug and what it did to them, but ultimately they could not turn it down. Telepath offered his arm and Ftzaal leaned forward with the infuser, then stopped, looking to meet Telepath's gaze. Why had he refused the first time, why was he asking for it now? His words could not have been better calculated to ease Ftzaal's suspicions. There was a look in his eyes, guilt, caught in the act, but what act? Realization dawned. *Whose mind are you in, Telepath?*

Telepath screamed and leapt. Despite suspicion's warning, Ftzaal had not been expecting the move, and only well-honed reflexes took him out of the path of Telepath's talons. He pivoted automatically and hooked the other's wrist and elbow. Telepath flew forward, facedown, and Ftzaal followed him, twisting the captured arm around and back. It was a move that produced paralyzing pain, but Telepath was long conditioned by *sthondat* withdrawal pains, and he rolled despite the force being applied. Ftzaal felt the bone break, and then Telepath was pivoting to strike again, another kill scream splitting the air. Ftzaal pivoted out of the way again and drew his variable sword in one fluid motion, the slicewire humming out to full extension. As Telepath came past he brought the slicewire down, splitting him open from shoulder to sternum. Telepath's body pitched to the ground, blood gushing to mingle with the jungle mud. Ftzaal stood over the body in *v'scree* stance, variable sword held ready. The *Ftz'yeer* of Ftzaal's personal guard had turned inward in time to see the end of the fight.

Slowly he lowered the variable sword. "First Blade Leader." His snarl was hard edged.

"Command me, sire."

"Bury him immediately. The *czrav* might not have heard the kill scream through the jungle noises. We must not leave scent spoor."

First Blade Leader gestured to the rest of the blade, and they began digging a hole with their *wtsais*. Idly Ftzaal nudged Telepath's body with a toe. Whatever secrets he held he would hold forever now. Had it been the right decision to kill him? In truth he had had no choice; if the sounds of the fight had not already alerted the watchers, they certainly would have if he'd allowed it to go on. *He broke his elbow rather than submit.* Telepath had stood no chance at all in a fight against Ftzaal-Tzaatz-Protector-of-Jotok. He must have known that, and chosen death over betrayal of what he wanted to keep hidden. *He was in my mind. How many times has he done that before?* Telepaths had trouble reading the minds of the black furred; it was the reason black kittens were taken for the Cult. One thing was certain, they were very close to something much bigger than First-Son-of-Meerz-Rrit. *The Black Cult must know of this. First, I need proof.*

His com clicked in his ear—Third Sword Leader.

"What is it?"

"Sire, my Communicator has cut himself on some kind of plant, and it has poisoned him. We have tried to clean the toxin from the wound, but he's getting worse."

"Can you move him?"

"He's already half paralyzed. We need a gravcar or he will die."

This accursed jungle. "Abort your patrol, do what you can for him there. I'll send Medic to you with a carrying party. We can't bring a gravcar this close without compromising ourselves. Uplink your location and I will give you a bearing and coordinates for the extraction point as soon as I get them."

"Understood." The com warbled with a databurst and Third Sword Leader's patrol coordinates appeared in his visor.

Ftzaal met Second Blade Leader's gaze. "Take your Blade and Medic *here*." He stabbed the air with a talon, marking the point on the map display his visor projected for him. "Move quickly, but don't sacrifice stealth."

"As you command, sire." Second Blade Leader claw-raked, gathered his command with a glance and moved out. Ftzaal watched them go. It was almost pointless to send them. He wasn't sure what species of flora Communicator had cut himself on. Kzinhome had many poisonous plants, some of which were actually aggressive, though he was familiar only with what he'd read. It sounded like a fangthorn, and if that was true he had condemned Communicator to death when he had made the decision to have him carried to the extraction point rather than bring a gravcar straight in to his patrol. Fangthorn venom attacked the central nervous system, and if Communicator was already half paralyzed his only hope would be immediate and total blood replacement. *But it is important to be seen to try, even as I refuse to compromise what we have accomplished here just to save a life.* The fangthorn was just one of eight-cubed traps the jungle held from the unwary, and even the best trained Tzaatz knew about them only in theory. *This is not Jotok, this is Kzinhome, and this jungle is so lethal even the primitive* cvari *on the Savannah avoid it, yet these* czrav *live their lives here.*

Ftzaal looked over to where the rest of his guard were still burying Telepath. There would be more lives lost than the two the operation had already claimed. *The jungle holds its secrets close.* Ftzaal let his mouth relax into a fanged snarl. He would prize those secrets out, regardless of the cost.

*And they had hair as the hair of women, and
their teeth were as the teeth of lions.*
—Revelation 9:8

The jungle night was cool with the approach of the dry
season, and Ayla Cherenkova edged herself closer to the
pride circle fire to soak up its welcome heat. The flames
licked up toward the cavern roof at the entrance to Ztrak
Pride's lair. V'rli-Ztrak was in her place of honor on the
Pride Rock, the flickering of firelight and shadow playing
tricks with her tawny skin and tiger stripes, Ferlitz-
Telepath by her side. The two were pair bonded so far as
Cherenkova could tell, though she didn't fully understand
the dynamics of kzinti mating. The females outnumbered
the males by three to one, and the adults tended to cluster
in groups with one to three males and one to six or seven
females. The males always took the same places around
the circle, but the females sometimes went to different
groups. The younger kits stayed with their mothers; the
older ones played and scuffled in the shadows, while the
young adults lay sprawled against each other in compan-
ionable piles, bellies replete with the feast of fresh
alyyzya meat, seasoned with some kind of roasted root
she couldn't identify. It was *hvook raoowh h'een*, tale-
telling-time, and the youngster Quicktail was leading a
poetry game, pulling verses from his audience and then
spinning them back with clever twists, accompanied by
devastating imitations of his seniors. Ayla's command of
the Hero's Tongue wasn't good enough to catch all the
nuances, but the audience loved it, ears rippling and tails
twitching in good humor. Earlier an old warrior named

Greow-something, battle scarred and half lame, had told the tale of the Taking of Fortress Cta'ian, part of an epic cycle that evidently he told every night for three nights on the cusp of the High Hunter's Moon. She had grown to love Tale Telling and the way it brought the Pride together. She felt a sense of belonging there, almost the same as when she had been a little girl, cuddled on her mother's lap while her father told her fairy tales that he made up as he went along. It was a feeling she'd never thought she'd have living quite literally in the lion's den. She was still a long way from home, but for the first time since she'd arrived at 61 Ursae Majoris she felt safe.

And ironically, they had to leave. The Traveler's Moon was at its cusp, and their time of sanctuary was over. Tomorrow they would push deeper into the jungle to find Mrrsel Pride and perhaps more permanent safety. She yawned. She was tired, and tomorrow would be a long day. She was starting to think about going to sleep when there was a commotion at the den mouth. Night-Prowler, one of the young hunters guarding the den that night, came in at the run, interrupting a clever verse. "V'rli-Ztrak! Douse the fire! There are trespassers in the southern valley!"

"How many?" V'rli gave a sign and a pride member leapt to the valve that sent water filtered through the sand above into the deeper den. Embers hissed as the fire began to go out.

"At least twice eight, that we saw. They're riding strange beasts, I've never seen them before. And they've taken Kdtronai-*zar'ameer* from his watch tree."

"What?" V'rli's ears swiveled up and forward, anger suddenly in her voice. "How was he taken?"

"They were stealthy, and we didn't see their approach. They have net guns, and other beasts on leashes. I saw it happen, but it was too late. My brother is shadowing them, carefully. I came to warn the pride."

Pouncer leapt up. "It is the Tzaatz, hunting with *rapsari*. I must leave at once. I am endangering you."

"No." V'rli's voice was firm. "You will do no such thing." She turned her attention back to Night-Prowler. "You have done well."

Pouncer motioned for T'suuz and Cherenkova to come with him. "They're looking for me. I have to go."

"No." V'rli lashed her tail. "This is Ztrak Pride territory. You have asked sanctuary and been given it. You are under our protection now."

"Honored Mother . . ."

"There is no threat, to you or to us. We have not kept our secrets eight-to-the-sixth seasons and more without well established defenses. No doubt the Tzaatz have learned some of the jungle's lesser dangers. Now we will teach them that tracking the *czrav* is the greatest hazard of all." She raised her voice. "Quicktail!"

"Honored Mother!" The spotted youngster came in and claw-raked.

"Go with Night-Prowler. Your job is to find Kdtronai-zar'ameer. You must bring him back." V'rli waved Pouncer as she spoke.

"At once!" Quicktail left at the bound.

"Kr-Pathfinder, hunt leaders, assemble your groups. I want ambush parties, ready to leave immediately." The quiet scene exploded into action, snarled commands filling the air as warriors grabbed weapons and prepared to defend the pride. She turned to one of the older females, heavy in pregnancy. "M'mewr, take the kits to the deep den; Greow-Czatz will go with you." She pointed a paw. "Ferlitz-Telepath, find me their minds."

"At once, V'rli."

Pouncer stepped forward again. "If you will not let me leave, let me fight. Tell me who I should follow."

"And I." T'suuz was standing beside him. Ayla wondered if she too should volunteer. *I will go with Pouncer, and take my chances with him.* It was her only real option. How she would fight effectively against kzinti backed up by *rapsari* was another question.

"The *mazourk* stand ready, Honored Mother." Another kzin interrupted before V'rli could reply.

V'rli twitched her tail. "C'mell, you will lead the *mazourk*. Take Mind-Seer with you."

The young female who'd nearly challenged Pouncer made the gesture-of-abasement-to-a-compliment. "I am honored."

"Lead them well," admonished V'rli. "Hold them back, but be ready. The Tzaatz must not survive."

"I obey." C'mell vanished into the night, snarling orders.

"Honored Mother . . ." Pouncer would not be put aside.

"Your place is at the den mouth, your sister too."

"I can do better than—"

"No!" V'rli cut him off. "You do not know the valley, and we who have lived here do. Someone must guard the den. If you do it you free another warrior to slit Tzaatz throats."

"Hrrr. There is no—"

"*Sssss!* Do not say there is no honor in the task. You guard our kits, *my* kits. The future of our pride is in your hands. It is a great honor. Be worthy of it."

"I obey, Honored Mother."

"May the Fanged God leap with you."

Pouncer and T'suuz left at the bound, and Cherenkova went to follow them, but V'rli stopped her.

"No, *kz'zeerkti*. You come with me."

It was not what she would have chosen to do, but she was a good enough officer to know when it was time to shut up and follow orders. She followed V'rli and Ferlitz-Telepath to an alcove. Beneath a heavy, sand-colored pelt the size of a polar bear's was a quite advanced combat console. V'rli touch the surface, and it lit up to show a three-dimensional map of the valley, icons glowing orange and blue to represent friend and foe.

"Ferlitz-Telepath?" Her snarl was sharp.

"The danger is near . . ." His voice was as distant as his eyes. "They see in the dark . . . hunt with strange creatures . . ."

V'rli's whiskers twitched. "How far?"

"Close . . . In the southern valley . . ." The big kzin slumped to the ground as his mind reached out into the night and V'rli knelt by his side.

"*Kz'zeerkti*, can you run the console?"

Ayla nodded. "I can try. I won't know all its functions."

"We need only map and display. I must watch over Ferlitz and direct his search." She handed Ayla an over-sized headset. "We do not use transponders. You will keep the map updated manually from the wireline vision feeds, and from what Ferlitz gives us. I will command our Heroes. You feed me information when I want it, understood?" V'rli's snarl was urgent.

"Understood." Ayla touched the surface, spun and swiveled the display, moved an icon, just to make sure she could do it. The interface was entirely intuitive, at least for the simple functions. Video feeds from hidden cameras let her survey the battlespace. She slid a finger, ran one of them from thermal through visual to active millimetric radar. The image responded, and she tested the pan and zoom commands to confirm the feeds would do what she needed them to.

"Trees . . . A watch platform . . . They know where we are . . ." Ferlitz was mumbling, sounding far away. "The *mazourk* are moving to the central clearing."

She stabbed the map with a finger. *Central clearing, that can only be . . .* here! She moved an icon to a grid location, but there was a word she didn't recognize.

"Honored Mother! What are *mazourk*?"

"*Tuskvor* riders, our reserves. A *czrav* secret. We won't use them unless we have to."

Tuskvor *riders?* For a moment Ayla thought she'd misheard. *If the* czrav *can tame* tuskvor *they're more formidable than I imagined.* She saw movement in one of the camera views, moved an icon and told V'rli, "Kr-Pathfinder's group is in position on the bluff. No Tzaatz in sight."

"Good, we may yet have time." V'rli snarled into Ferlitz's ears and he echoed her words, ordering Kr-Pathfinder to hold in place. *They are using telepathy instead of vocom, untraceable and unjammable.* It was not just the *mazourk* that made the *czrav* formidable opponents.

"More . . . more to the north . . . with flyers. . . ." Ferlitz sounded feverish now, his reality entirely unconnected with the room his body happened to be in.

"Ferlitz, find me the leader."

"The leader . . ." Ferlitz echoed his instructions weakly. For a long moment he was silent, then his entire body tensed and his voice strengthened. "It is a Black Priest!"

"A Black Priest—this is dangerous."

"Yes . . ." His voice weakened again. "I cannot read him. I need the extract . . ."

"You must not. Not yet."

Ferlitz-Telepath's eyes flickered open. "Give it to me." His snarl was imperious, commanding.

V'rli hesitated, then reached into a hidden niche in the back of the combat console, came away with a small vial of oily fluid. Ferlitz relaxed and she metered drops into his mouth. He licked his lips and was instantly in the trance again, deeper this time.

"He seeks a female . . . and the *kz'zeerkti.*"

V'rli snarled. "He will not find them."

Cherenkova watched her displays, grainy with the thermal gain ramped all the way up. The now familiar shapes of *rapsari* moved in one of them, and she spun the display to map the camera's field of view. "Honored Mother, enemy in the south valley. Looks like scout groups."

"How close?"

How close? How do the czrav *measure distance?* "Almost to the ambush parties."

V'rli lashed her tail. "South ambushes attack now.

Northern ambushes, prepare to move south. *Mazourk,* stand by." Ferlitz echoed her words, barely audible now, his body twitching. The *sthondat* drug was powerful, but it came with costs.

On her screen Cherenkova could see the ambushers screaming and leaping. They cut down the *rapsari* mounts first, then the Tzaatz riders. The *czrav* ambushers were incredibly fast, and as soon as they had struck they vanished again into the jungle. They did not escape unscathed however; not all the bodies they left in their wake belonged to their enemies. Deeper into the image something moved . . .

"More scout parties, covering the first. They know our first positions," Cherenkova reported. V'rli circled her tail in acknowledgment, her attention focused on Ferlitz-Telepath.

"Fire . . ." He seemed delirious. "They are using fire . . ."

"Fire? Where?" V'rli demanded. Even as she did Cherenkova saw her screens flare bright as lasers torched the ground cover.

"South valley again." Ayla kept her voice under control, for her own benefit, not V'rli's. "The cover groups are starting them."

"All teams to the river!"

"No! No, they're watching the river." Cherenkova blurted the words without thinking. V'rli looked up at her sharply.

"How do you know this?"

"They must be; it's the logical tactic. They're searching out the den. Their plan is to burn this side of the valley. They locate us with their search groups, then drive us out with fire. They expect we'll flee to the river for safety from the fire, and that's where *we* will be ambushed."

V'rli looked at her for a long, long moment and Cherenkova did her best to keep her gaze level. *Have I overstepped my position?* Her last ground combat training had been in officer candidate school, and sketchy enough when she got it, just enough to give a naval officer a grounding in the concepts. *I must be right.*

"Yes . . ." Ferlitz-Telepath seemed completely delirious. ". . . the river . . . with net guns."

V'rli leaned close to Ferlitz, her voice sharp in his ear. "All groups, that order is countermanded. Move to the base of the bluff, get on the rocks. Let the fire sweep past." As Ferlitz relayed her words in his trance, her eyes met Ayla's, understanding conveyed in a glance. Ayla had V'rli's respect now, and her trust.

Now to prove worthy of it. Cherenkova kept scanning her screens. Something about the way the covering Tzaatz had withdrawn before the attack . . . Her cameras could see in darkness, but could they? She stabbed a finger into a control icon, twirled it to traverse the image and zoom. Yes . . . "The Tzaatz have spectrum goggles. The fire will blind them."

V'rli looked up from Ferlitz. "That is important to know. We will attack in its wake. Keep me informed."

"As long as I can, Honored Mother." The flames were already licking high in the tinder-dry undergrowth, and even the huge, thick-barked spire trees were beginning to burn. It wouldn't be long before Ayla started losing her sensors; already the heat was flaring the screens, blurring out the details she needed to keep track of the Tzaatz movement. *And what if the Tzaatz are using the smoke and flame for cover themselves?* They could infiltrate past the ambush parties and attack the den itself. Did they know where it was, or did they only know the general area? *We'll find out soon enough.* She fumbled with the interface to damp the camera gain. Cryptic symbols floated in the air, and she stabbed them in sequence to make it happen. One of them worked and the displays cleared.

"They have gravcars . . ." Ferlitz seemed to be struggling, and V'rli put her hands beneath his head so he wouldn't hit it on the hard stone floor.

Ayla switched her displays to the north valley. There were shapes there too, *rapsari* raiders carrying Tzaatz warriors, and the small, vicious harriers leashed in braces of four. Their plan was becoming clear now. Locate the *czrav* and drive them with fire to the waiting trap lines. *Which implies they don't know we have a hidey hole here. The den will be our last stand, but they might not find it.* It was a comforting thought, and true enough beneath the lush jungle cover and at night. Come daybreak, though, the jungle would be burned off, and the den mouth would stand out like a sore thumb as the Tzaatz sifted through the ashes for the bodies of the dead. *But where are the gravcars?*

On her screen the small fires the Tzaatz lasers had started were growing fast. The jungle vegetation was tinderbox dry, and the resinous *shoom* trees burned like blowtorches, fast and hot enough to ignite bigger trees that might otherwise only smolder.

She became aware of the smell of smoke, only now

drifting into the cavern. *This is a real battle*. There was death just outside her door, searching hungrily to come in. Of course she had known it was real, just as she knew that the maneuvering points of light in her plot tank had been real ships, when the cruiser *Amalthea* descended on W'kkai at the vanguard of the fleet. She had known there were real people aboard those other ships, real people who died horribly every time one of those lights went out, but somehow the reality never hit home until she *smelled* the burning when *Amalthea* got hit. She'd never forgotten the burning smell, and for an instant she was back on the cruiser's bridge. Ayla had vented *Amalthea*'s atmosphere to space to save her, condemning forty of her crewmates to death in the same instant. Her attention drifted as a roaring filled her ears. Smoke was the smell of battle for all of history, smoke and blood and fear. *I wonder how real it is to the masses on Earth who rely on us to keep them safe?* The entire concept of war for most of the twenty billion Flatlanders was formed by thirty-second holocasts broadcast to their homes after dinner, smoke free.

"Status!" V'rli's snarl brought her back to reality. A camera view went dark in the same instant and she switched the display to one still live. Movement caught her eye and she panned and zoomed an image. A swarm of harrier *rapsari* were moving up the rocky scree slope beneath the bluff, proving the ground for the armored Tzaatz warriors following them. "Enemy moving toward the den entrance."

V'rli snarled. "We have a surprise for them. Sraff-Tracker, be aware, your moment is coming."

"He . . . is ready . . . he sees them." Ferlitz had trouble

getting the words out. He was slipping deeper into his trance.

Ayla swiveled her cameras. She thought Sraff-Tracker should have been on the scree slope and directly in the path of the harriers, but nothing showed on her displays. Frantically she panned and zoomed all the cameras along the south cliff face, but nothing showed. "Honored Mother! I can't find Sraff-Tracker." *If he's out of position and those creatures get through . . .* She didn't want to think about that.

"Wait, he will show himself." V'rli's voice was calm.

With growing concern Cherenkova watched the enemy advance unobstructed, until they were on her last camera to the south. Another hundred meters and they'd discover the den mouth.

"Honored Mother . . ." Before she could finish there was a deep rumble that shook the cavern. For a split second she feared a cave-in, and the camera she had watching the Tzaatz went dark. She commanded its neighbor to cover as much of its field of view as it could. The screen was full of dust thick enough to obscure the light of the now furious forest fire. *Not explosives. Then what?* No time to find out. She needed to keep her point of view moving; she was the eyes of the whole defense. Still she couldn't help watching the churning dust for a clue as to what had happened.

And then she saw it, as the dust dispersed in the wind kicked up by the fire. The entire scree slope was changed. Both Tzaatz and their *rapsari* were gone without a trace, and at least a hundred meters of jungle with them. Sraff-Tracker was above the bluff, not on the scree slope. *They brought the whole cliff down!* The *czrav* had kept their secrets for longer than humanity had known civilization. Now she was beginning to understand how.

On her screens another group mounted on *rapsari* raiders swept through the jungle behind the now raging fire. To the north the Tzaatz were setting up their stop lines, ambushes laid forward with a solid line of warriors farther back. A gravcar slid through one of the displays skimming over the canopy. *There are the flyers.* There would be spybots there too, though the smoke and flame would render their sensors much less useful. It was strange that the kzinti possessed such high technology but chose to fight each other with hand weapons. *They do it to save their civilization from self-destruction.* And really that was little different from the choices the UN had made for humanity before the kzinti first contact.

Another gravcar floated over. "V'rli, they have air reconnaissance."

"Ignore it. Their sensors can't get through the jungle canopy."

And how is she so sure? But the *czrav* were no strangers to technology or its capabilities, though they chose to use it little, and they had their channels into the heart of the Patriarchy. *No time to wonder. What else can the Tzaatz do with a gravcar?* They could move units, and they could be weapons platforms. Troop movement would require somewhere to land; weapons platforms would be useless over the canopy. The gravcars could watch the river and little else, which was what they were doing. *Why don't they have assault vehicles?* A combat carrier could dump boost and smash through the foliage like an incoming missile, something the lighter gravcars could do only at the risk of tearing off a polarizer and crashing. *Their resources are limited. The Tzaatz have other problems to deal with.* That was good news. A series of deep bellows echoed out of the night. She selected her central camera to check the situation with the reserves. The *tuskvor* were sensing the fire, and getting nervous. How did the *mazourk* control them, and just how good was that control? She could see they would need them to break the attack, and that moment was coming soon. They couldn't afford to have the beasts panic and run before that.

"Ferlitz, tell all the groups, the Tzaatz are moving north behind the fire. Leap on them when they come through."

The telepath echoed V'rli's words, and as he did so Cherenkova imagined she heard them in her own head. *Telepathic leakage. Can the Tzaatz hear his thoughts too?*

"They obey . . ."

There was no time to worry about that. Cherenkova spun her cameras to keep the location plots updated. The Tzaatz were advancing behind the flame front, expecting to kill or capture anyone who came through the fire, but Ztrak Pride knew the ground, knew where to find the low spots the fire couldn't reach. With fur scorched and blackened they held their positions and let the fire sweep over them to take the attackers from behind as they passed, and then vanish into the smoldering wilderness. *There's too much smoke and flame, too many hot spots for thermal vision to function well.* Cherenkova allowed herself a grim smile of satisfaction. *We have turned their weapon against them.* She scanned her displays again, updated the position icons. The forest fire was raging now, beyond anyone's

control, rolling north between the river and the bluff like
a predator consumed with the kill rage. Cherenkova imagined she could feel the heat coming from her screens,
though the cool of the cavern was unchanged. She was in
the safest place she could be for the fire, and she felt awe
at the discipline of both the *czrav* and their enemies at
choosing to continue the fight while it raged around and
over them.

"The south has failed . . . they will come from the north
now . . ." Ferlitz's words were thick now. He was going
deeper into the mind-trance.

Even as he said it Cherenkova saw the northern force
begin to deploy. Another group edged forward over the
scree slope toward Kr-Pathfinder's position. "Honored
Mother . . ."

Scream snarls from the front of the cavern sent adrenaline surging. Pouncer and T'suuz had leapt upon something that had made it to the den. Not all the Tzaatz had
been killed in the avalanche.

"Watch Ferlitz!" V'rli tore off her decorative ear bands
and leapt into the dark to join the battle.

"V'rli! V'rli!" Ayla called, but the kzinrette was gone.
There is a time to ask and a time to act. She jumped over
her console to kneel by Ferlitz-Telepath. "Kr-Pathfinder,
take your group downslope. The Tzaatz are in front of
you." *Will he relay my commands as well?*

He did, though she couldn't hear him do it because of
the screams of rage and pain spilling from the front of the
cavern. Unbidden, her mind's eye called up the image of
the vicious *rapsar* harrier. The Tzaatz had done exactly as
she'd anticipated, used the smoke and flame to get past

her cameras and get into the den mouth. *And if you anticipated it, why didn't you do something?* No time for second guesses. Pouncer, T'suuz, and V'rli were all that stood
between her and death in the dark, and she needed a
weapon.

"No . . ." It was Ferlitz. "Your place is here . . .
Command the battle . . ."

Cherenkova looked at him sharply. His head lolled
back, eyes closed, and his breathing was shallow and
rapid. He seemed to be struggling to stay conscious, even
to stay alive. Watch him, V'rli had said, and he clearly
needed help, but she didn't know what to do.

"No . . . Command the battle . . ."

Was he in *her* mind too? She sat stunned for a second,
and then movement in her displays grabbed her attention.
Command the battle. The northern Tzaatz were advancing toward the wall of flame, and the *czrav* forces were
committed in the south. The den mouth had been found.
If the main force reached it . . .

She looked up, scanned the battle display. *"Mazourk!"*
What are their capabilities? She had never seen a herd
charge, but she could imagine it. "C'mell, the main Tzaatz
force is moving south to the den mouth. Turn north and
charge."

Ferlitz's voice had dropped below audibility, but the
huge beasts in Ayla's display turned ponderously and
began to move north. Ayla switched cameras and waited,
tensely. Would the beasts even broach the margin of
the fire? They were big enough that even that fierce
conflagration should cause little damage, if they were
only exposed for the time it took to crash through it.

And will they be enough to break the Tzaatz advance when they do?

At first the display showed only the lick of the flames, with the Tzaatz force moving into position behind it, and then a shape loomed through the smoke, huge and dark, coming fast. Another appeared behind it, and a third, while the first resolved itself into a *tuskvor* herd-grand-mother, sixty meters long and twenty tall, bellowing in fear and rage, tusks like sharpened battering rams swinging back in forth in search of a target for its fury. It couldn't see between the smoke and the darkness, but its rider would have full-spectrum goggles. A fourth shape lumbered through the wall of fire, and Cherenkova could now see the *mazourk* on a platform on the lead *tuskvor*'s back, guiding it with what looked like a kite bar and harness. It had to be C'mell, though the thermal imagery wasn't fine enough to reveal details of identity, and behind her were eight more of Ztrak Pride, armed with bows. Ahead of the charge the Tzaatz stood for long heartbeats as the *tuskvor* closed the distance to their first outposts. A fifth *tuskvor* emerged from the smoke, and then a sixth. Cherenkova held her breath, waited for the Tzaatz to break and run.

They didn't. Incredibly, as the *tuskvor* reached the first line of blockers they leapt to attack instead, covered by a storm of crossbow bolts and trapnets from the reserves behind. Their heroism was wasted, and the herd charge stormed through their positions without slowing down, leaving broken bodies strewn in its wake. Crystal iron hunting arrows soared from the archers on the *tuskvor*'s platforms but bounced fruitlessly off Tzaatz mag armor.

Undeterred, the *czrav* leapt from their mounts to attack,
killing the few Tzaatz who'd survived with variable swords
and leaving the bodies to the fire that rushed on behind
them. Cherenkova stabbed a finger into her display to
rotate and zoom. The first line had been skirmishers,
lightly armed. The second line was heavier, with raider
rapsari among the trees. As she watched the distance
between the two forces closed and she held her breath in
anticipation of the impact. And then the Tzaatz force
wavered. A *rapsar* raider took a few steps backward, then
turned to run. Other Tzaatz followed it, and then the line
was broken and they were routed, fleeing into the jungle
to save their lives.

Ayla suppressed the urge to cheer. Instead she whispered again in Ferlitz's ear. "C'mell! Split your force, hunt
them down." She snarled the words like a kzin. "Don't let
any of them live." She was unqualified to lead a ground
battle, but she was doing it, and doing it well, and there
was exhilaration in that. She scanned the displays, saw a
few scattered Tzaatz wandering in the dark, spectrum
goggles blinded by the fire, unfamiliar with the terrain,
cut off from their support. "Kr-Pathfinder, take the lead
on the ground. Hunt down the survivors. I'll direct you."

In her camera view Kr-Pathfinder made the tail signal
that meant, "As you command." Cherenkova breathed
out. They had won, barely, and she would live to see
another day. Even as she thought it, she became aware
that the sounds of battle from the front of the den had
vanished, and then there were footsteps in the dark, coming closer.

Only a fool stalks tuskvor.
                    —Wisdom of the Conservers

"Tuskvor!" Ftzaal-Tzaatz hadn't believed the call when he heard it. The *czrav* were putting up tougher resistance than he'd expected, and though the *Ftz'yeer* were seasoned jungle fighters, there had been rumors about what might be found in the jungle, and about what might find you. None of his warriors would show cowardice, but there was no denying some of them were nervous, and there had been a few com calls that night that could be attributed to nothing else. You couldn't see far in the jungle even in daylight. The darkness, the smoke, and the fire all added to the confusion. They were his weapons but . . . *Every blade has two edges.* Priest-Master-Zrtra had taught him that, and his master's teachings had always been wise.

And then he saw for himself the huge shapes looming out of the darkness, bellowing in rage and fear. The fire must have stampeded them. *Why then are they charging through the flames?* No time for that question. His first line was already broken. He had to act now if he wanted to save any of his force.

He keyed his com. "Back to the gravcars. Now! Quickly!"

If they had grav belts they could have escaped, but with little scope to use them in the jungle he'd judged the extra weight not worth the few long-leaps the batteries could provide. The *Ftz'yeer* were well disciplined, wheeling in formation and heading back the way they'd come at a fast trot.

It wasn't fast enough, not nearly. "Run," Ftzaal ordered. "Sword leaders, keep your Heroes together. *Rapsari*, fall back first."

They complied, and he ran himself. He keyed his com again. "Don't run in front of them, angle out of their way."

A few long-leaps would save all their lives now, but you couldn't carry everything for every contingency, and in a different situation the extra weight might be lethal. Everything was a tradeoff. Little comfort to know now what he should have brought then. Ftzaal looked over his shoulder. The herd was swinging to follow them, snapping down the fire-blacked tree stumps, their heads raised high and looking down to see their quarry. They were now no more than a bowshot behind. He could feel the ground shake beneath their pounding footsteps in the brief instants his own feet touched the ground. Make a plan! The *Ftz'yeer* were scattered, but they all had communications, they would respond to his orders. They could make a stand with variable swords, cut the creatures' legs from beneath them, but the mass and momentum of the huge beasts would be just as lethal when they fell. There was nowhere to hide. There was nothing within sprinting distance even close to big enough to stop a *tuskvor*.

What must have been the herd-grandmother was in front, bellowing ferociously. The whole herd would be following her lead. Inspiration! He slapped his comlink between strides, panting deeply as he ran. *"Ftz'yeer!* First sword split right, second sword split left!" *The herd can't chase all of us.* He angled left himself, back down toward the river. If he could make it that far the big spire trees would provide some protection, in case the herd decided that he was the one it would follow. His muscles were burning now, and he had to concentrate on every leap to keep his legs driving him forward. His warriors were vanishing into the darkness, each following his own path now. The call of a *grlor* echoed through the night, not close but not far either, reminding him that fire and *tuskvor* were not the only dangers the jungle night held. *There is vulnerability for each of us alone in the dark, but most will live to regroup.*

"Sword leaders, split your blades." He snarled the words. Verifications crackled back in his ear as his subcommanders passed his commands to their Heroes. He was running with Second Sword, and the warriors on his left and right angled away, and in seconds they were separated in the darkness.

He risked another glance backward, saw gleaming tusks and a huge head extended as a *tuskvor* thundered after him, another one close beside it. *The herd has chosen* me *to follow.* The thought galvanized him, and he ran harder, cutting to one side in the hopes that they might hold a straight course.

The *tuskvor* turned to follow him. The slope steepened, making running in the darkness more treacherous. A single fall would be the end. He breathed deep, dodging left and right. The *tuskvor* were big; a kzin could outmaneuver them, but if he got caught in the herd there would be no hope for survival at all.

His pursuer bellowed, so close that its call shook his belly. Something hit him, sharp pain in his right leg, and he fell. The *tuskvor* had stabbed with its tusk and hit him, but hadn't been quite close enough to run him through.

He skidded, dove sideways, and a foot as big as a tree stump came down beside his head. *I will die here in the herd.* There was no time for fear, for sadness, for panic, for anything but the realization that he was absolutely helpless, and then the huge beasts thundered past, one on each side of him.

There were none behind them. It took long heartbeats before Ftzaal understood that there were only two *tuskvor,* that he would not be ground to mush beneath the herd because the herd was gone. Even as his Swords had split, the *tuskvor* had split to chase them down. *These are not herd animals!* Ahead of him the two who had been pursuing him were turning, one right, one left, ponderous with their momentum. *They are coming back to make sure they killed me.* They'd turned to either side so that, if he'd survived, they would intercept him no matter which way he ran. The realization went through him like an electric shock. *I am being hunted.* Not just hunted, hunted with intelligence and cunning. Bellows rose over the valley slopes, mixed with kzinti kill screams, abruptly cut off. His elite *Ftz'yeer* were being slaughtered.

As he would be, if he stayed where he was. He went to click his goggle visor down, only to realize it had been torn off in his fall. There was only one way to go, and that was to follow his pursuers and stay inside their turning circle. *Tuskvor* had powerful senses of smell, but the valley would be full of kzinti scent by now. *And aren't* tuskvor *supposed to be diurnal?* They would march without rest for days on end during their great seasonal migrations, when they crossed the North Continent from one side to the other, but they weren't migrating now. *Or are they?*

He knew too little about the jungles of Kzinhome. *When I planned my brother's attack I did not anticipate the jungles would become a battlefield.*

One of the *tuskvor* bellowed, and he moved after them, hobbling on his injured leg. He was slower than they were now, but they would take some time to find him again. He staggered and stumbled, fell facefirst into water. He was in a meadow like the one by the burned-out valley, and it *did* become a marsh in the wet season. Even now in its center there were a few puddles. He stayed flat on the ground, crawling deeper into the mud so the water would cover his body and his scent together.

It was unpleasant but it seemed to work. The great beasts circled around and churned by again, slowly this time. They appeared to be searching, vast heads swaying to and fro. They stopped, and he could see them clearly in the moonlight. Low snarls rose in the Hero's Tongue. Some of the *Ftz'yeer* had survived, at least. For a moment hope surged, until he realized where the snarls were coming from. He looked up at the nearer beast, saw a blurred shadow on its back. It could only be a kzin in a hunt cloak. Did they also have wide-spectrum goggles? If they did it was only his fall that had saved him, the cold water masking enough of his thermal signature that the riders had overlooked him, at least the first time. He crawled deeper into the marsh, ignoring the painful throb in his wounded leg. There was much the Tzaatz would have to learn before they could say they controlled Kzinhome.

First he had to survive, and then he could find vengeance.

A Hero may only be judged in how he dies.
                                        —Si-Rrit

Ayla felt along the wall until she found a rock, picked it up and crouched behind her console. If she were lucky, if she took them by surprise, she might kill one Tzaatz before they gutted her. If she were very lucky they would overlook her entirely, but she had little hope for that. To a kzin nose she would be stinking of fear and fight, and the Tzaatz had those nasty reptilian sniffers . . .

The footsteps came closer. She steeled herself for the moment.

It was V'rli-Ztrak who appeared from the darkness. Ayla relaxed, trembling with reaction, though some small part of her brain was actually disappointed that it hadn't come to combat.

"What is the battle status?" V'rli's snarl was rich with fight juices as she scanned her eye over the combat console.

Ayla put down the rock. "Honored Mother, I committed the *mazourk*. The Tzaatz are broken and our Heroes are hunting them down even now."

"Good." V'rli knelt by Ferlitz-Telepath, who was now mumbling inaudibly. She checked him as efficiently as any human paramedic, then looked up to meet Ayla's eyes in the dim light cast by the combat console. "You have done well, *kz'zeerkti*." There was approval in her voice.

Ayla nodded, suddenly feeling the rush of tension release. *We've won.* She would live another day. *Quacy would be proud of me.* All at once she wished she hadn't thought that thought. She missed him horribly. She blinked back tears and blamed them on the smoke, checked her displays again to put her mind on something else. Everywhere she looked the Tzaatz were running, or simply gone.

Pouncer appeared in the darkness behind V'rli. He was carrying a bloodied body, a kzinrette—T'suuz. Pouncer dropped to his knees and the body slid to the floor. He leaned back and howled, long and mournfully. "Honored Mother . . ." He seemed unable to find words. "Honored Mother, my sister is dead."

V'rli put a paw to his shoulder. "She fought well for my pride, Kitten-of-the-Rrit, and so did you."

Pouncer snarled and slashed the air with his talons. "She will have a verse in the Pride Ballad, and I will write in Tzaatz blood."

V'rli lashed her tail. "Your day will come, but not now. The Tzaatz have found the den. We must move the pride."

"No. We have paid in blood for this den. My sister must have her death rite."

"You do not understand. We keep the Long Secret. We work through stealth. The Tzaatz will be back. Or would you have what happened here today happen to every pride of the *czrav*?" There was anger in V'rli's voice. "The migration is beginning. We must move."

"I will stay. My time of sanctuary with you has ended anyway."

"You have earned your place at our pride circle tonight. You must come with us. How many generations have we spent hiding the Telepath's Gift from the Black Priests? The lines of Kcha and Vda are united in you. We need your blood."

Before Pouncer could answer there was noise at the cavern entrance. They went there to find Quicktail, breathing heavily. "We have Kdtronai-*zar'ameer*, Honored Mother. And we have ears!" He held up two sets of Tzaatz trophies, blood still dripping where they'd been severed from their owner, his fangs showing through a wide smile.

V'rli turned to face him. "Where is he?"

"His leg is injured. Night-Prowler is bringing him. I ran ahead to bring the news."

"You have both done well." V'rli turned to face Pouncer again, her voice less harsh. "Your sister brought you here to see you survive. Don't throw away her gift." She turned to Quicktail before he could answer. "Find C'mell, gather the *mazourk*. There is much to do yet. The Tzaatz will return. We must be gone by morning." She looked to the limp, bloody body of the Patriarch's daughter. "And first we must have a death rite, for a Hero."

Quicktail left at the bound. Pouncer's tail lashed and his lips twitched over his fangs. He dropped to all fours and screamed, a long, mournful howl that embodied grief and promised vengeance as it echoed in the chamber. Ayla breathed out shakily. They had won, but the Tzaatz would be back. *This is getting dangerous.*

To see the right and not do it is cowardice.
                                                   —Confucius

The transpax in *Valiant's* cockpit was opaque, and on the other side of it was hyperspace. Quacy Tskombe, fully vac-suited, checked the mass reader carefully, making sure none of the glowing blue lines radiating from the center of the globe were too bright, or too long. They had remoted most of *Valiant*'s instrumentation to Curvy's console, but the mass reader needed a mind to look at it in order to work. It was a skill he'd practiced with Ayla in case *Crusader* had left 61 Ursae Majoris and they'd had to take their stolen Swiftwing through hyperspace themselves. He hadn't needed to then, but the exercise was paying off now. *I am becoming an experienced pilot.* He needed to check it every four hours, which meant suiting up, sealing himself in the companionway and depressurizing it, then entering the damaged cockpit. The first time he'd done it he found his worst fears realized. Both Virenze and Khalsa were strapped into their command couches, dead of explosive decompression. It wasn't a pretty way to die. *I would expect to be numb to violent death by now.* He'd seen enough of it in his career, but he wasn't numb, and though he'd wrapped their bodies in sheets from their staterooms on a subsequent trip he still felt their presence when he entered the cockpit. He owed them his life. If they hadn't fought the ship so well, if Khalsa hadn't risked an early jump to hyperspace, then the cruiser would certainly have destroyed them. No one knew what happened to ships that tried to enter hyperspace too close to a gravitational singularity, except that they never came back. Exactly how close was *too* close was something else that wasn't exactly clear, which is why he checked the mass reader with clockwork regularity, despite the fact that the around-the-clock visits to the cockpit violently disrupted his sleep pattern.

He checked the power readings and the rest of the

ship's vital statistics while he was there. *Valiant* had taken a lot of damage, but he couldn't make repairs until they got out of hyperspace. They had power, they had life support; everything else would have to wait. He hadn't told Trina how close they'd come to dying themselves. He told Curvy, but the dolphin didn't seem too concerned by the prospect of her own death. She mourned the loss of the pilots, though—her friends for many years, he learned— with two days of withdrawn silence. After that she returned to what seemed to be her usual self, and they resumed their poker games. He had never known a dolphin, and she combined a mischievous sense of humor with a strange formality and depth of thought that was occasionally intimidating. Trina had come out of her shell somewhat. She still spent long hours by herself in the navigation blister, although with the transpax opaqued to keep out the Blind Spot the beautiful starscape view was gone. Sometimes she came down and played chess with Curvy. It was progress.

They had settled into a routine by their seventh day in hyperspace. Tskombe spent the bottom watch playing poker. Trina had gone back to her cabin, and he finally left after a long series of hands that saw him lose an entire barrel of imaginary salmon to the dolphin's clever sequence of bluff and counterbluff. He folded his last hand and on a whim went up to the navigation blister, just to avoid having to go back to his cabin. He climbed the ladder, saw someone already there. It was Trina, backdropped by . . . *nothing*. The blackness of space wasn't there, nor was the blankness of opaqued transpax. The walls warped weirdly into each other and into Trina, who seemed to vanish by degrees. He found he couldn't see, found his entire awareness being sucked into the non-seeing blindness which seemed to absorb the world as he watched.

In a panic he looked down, his head swimming. There were things in his visual field, but he was unable to tell where one began and another ended, or in fact put a name to any of them. He held on to the ladder, his tactile sense providing the grounding that vision no longer could. He squeezed his eyes shut and felt his way down the ladder. When he opened them again at the bottom the disorientation was fading, although he still had to feel his way along the wall to stay upright. He groped his way down to the cargo hold. Curvy whistled in surprise as he stumbled in.

"I can't see properly." He fought to keep his voice level. "Something's happened in the navigation bubble. Trina's up there . . ."

"Did you see the transpax?" Curvy's translator made few inflections, but he was well enough acquainted with Cetspeak to sense her immediate concern.

"I don't know, it was strange . . ."

"It is the Blind Spot. I will blank the transpax from here. You must bring her down at once."

Curvy's manipulator tentacles flew over her console, and Tskombe groped his way back to the access ladder. At the top the transpax was a plain opaque gray again, and nothing seemed strange at all. It was hard to even imagine what it had looked like before. Trina was staring blankly and unblinking, her lips slightly parted. For an instant she seemed dead, and then he saw her chest move as she breathed. He picked her up, maneuvering her awkwardly but easily in the zero gravity.

"I saw . . . I saw . . ." She stirred at his touch. Her voice was hushed, barely coherent, and though her eyes were wide and unblinking, she seemed to stare right through him. He carried her back down to the crash couch in the wardroom.

Curvy met him there, the first time the dolphin had ventured out of the hold in the journey. There was barely room for her in the accessway. "How long was she there?"

"I don't know, I just found her."

The dolphin nodded, an incongruously human gesture. "She's in the void trance. It is not dangerous, and it will pass. She unblanked the transpax and saw the Blind Spot."

"That was the Blind Spot I saw?"

"It was."

Tskombe shuddered. "It did things to my mind, like the walls were all being sucked into nothingness."

Curvy chirped and whistled. "Doing things to your mind is what hyperspace does. Hyperdrive requires the continuous collapse of a superposition of the vacuum quantum state. That is something that minds do. Are you familiar with Schrödinger's Cat?"

"No."

"It is a thought experiment in quantum superposition. Its resolution explains why you need a living mind to watch the mass reader. Sometimes singleships don't come out of hyperspace, and one theory is that the pilots have been sucked into void trance and couldn't get out by themselves."

"Have you ever seen the Blind Spot?"

"No. Commander Khalsa and Lieutenant Virenze have tried it. Some are immune, but they were not."

Every pilot tries it once. Ayla had told him that, he remembered now. He could consider himself a pilot now, of sorts. Why had Trina tried it? Maybe she hadn't known what she was doing.

"It was like being dead," she told him a day later. "Like being gone, drifting without thought."

"That's not a good thing."

"Sometimes it is." Her voice was small and she looked away, and he felt his heart tear for the pain she was clearly in. He told himself it was necessary, that she was facing things that before had simply been buried. Still, it was hard to see her so anguished and be unable to do anything about it. She slept as much as she had while recovering from the tranquilizers. Ship routine fell back into its already well developed groove. As watches passed uneventfully Trina slowly came back to herself. She had discovered a voracious appetite for reading, and spent hours in the navigation blister with a datapad on her lap. There was no way to disable the transpax controls there, and Tskombe worried that the call of the Blind Spot might suck her back, but while she seemed at home in the space, she never again unblanked the dome.

The first significant event happened three days later. Curvy was working on some aspect of her strategic matrix and Tskombe was sitting in the wardroom because he was bored of sitting anywhere else, thinking about Ayla because, except when he was playing poker with Curvy, or keeping the ship running, he couldn't think about anything else. Trina came out of her cabin and watched him for a long moment.

"You love her very much, don't you?"

"Ayla, you mean?" He looked at her. "Yes, I do."

She nodded, and sat down to read a book off a datapad. She went through a book or two a day now. The exchange was trivial exchange, but it came back to Tskombe later when something altogether more remarkable occurred, a half day farther out. Trina beat Curvy at chess.

At first Tskombe didn't understand the dolphin when she told him. "I know you sometimes let her win so she can learn."

"That is not what happened this time."

"You can't tell me that an absolute neophyte mastered the game well enough to beat the world non-computational champion in under a week."

"No, I cannot tell you that. There are limitations. She can beat me at speed chess, but not a full game, and it has happened more than once. Watch our next game."

So Tskombe watched them play a game in the hold. If it was a joke, it seemed an unlikely one. The games were quick, with just five minutes on each side of the computer's chess clock, and both players put total focus into the game. Astoundingly Curvy took more of her five minutes than Trina did of hers. Tskombe looked on in amazement as she won three games in a row. He was no chess expert, but Trina's moves looked almost prescient in countering Curvy's attacks. It was when the pair switched to twenty-minute games that Trina faltered. The depth of foresight that she had shown in the quick games evaporated, and even with more time to think her moves seemed much more appropriate to a rank beginner.

It was then that Trina's offhand comment in the ward-room came back to Tskombe. He talked it over with Curvy. "She's developing telepathy, or some sense close to it."

"What do you base that on?"

"She was packed and ready when I came to get her on Earth. She's told me before, she always knows when it's time to move. Now she seems to know what I'm thinking almost before I think it. I had it down to intuition, but it takes more than intuition to win chess games."

Curvy whistled something untranslatable. "That was my thought. I did not want your judgment contaminated by mine."

"What do we do now?"

"We will wait and see what develops. This is an unknown parameter for the matrix."

His curiosity aroused, Tskombe took the dog-eared deck of cards they played poker with and they did some tests. One of them would draw a card and look at it while Trina would try to guess the suit. She managed it something like one third of the time, good enough that it couldn't be random chance. What it was, on the other hand, wasn't entirely clear. At first he was convinced it was telepathy, until he tried a control experiment where Trina tried to guess the cards with no one looking at them. Her hit rate remained constant at around thirty percent. He told Curvy about it.

"Precognition then." The dolphin seemed excited. "Very rare, but there have been cases."

"Then how does she know what people are thinking?"

"It could be ordinary intuition providing a confounding factor."

Tskombe shook his head. "She doesn't beat you with intuition."

"This is a pertinent fact. However, she can only beat me in short games."

"I don't think it's either telepathy or precognition. If she were reading your mind, she'd do better in long games where you had the board position more thought out. Precognition wouldn't do her any good. Knowing a chess master's next move isn't going to help you when they're planning two or three or fourteen moves ahead in the game. Even knowing all of them wouldn't help, if you didn't understand where they were leading."

Curvy chirped and whistled a sound-stream that Tskombe had learned indicated puzzlement. "It could be a wild talent. They are even rarer than precognition, perhaps one in a billion."

"So what is the talent that lets her know what people are thinking and be ready to move at the right time and guess cards and win at chess against the world grandmaster, but only if the games are fast?"

"I cannot guess."

Tskombe pondered. "Maybe she's just lucky."

"She defies the odds too consistently for that."

"What else defines a lucky person?"

"She is adolescent; her brain is going through tremendous changes. This is the developmental period when psi talents start showing up. The Blind Spot has awakened something up in her, triggered something that was ready to blossom. Our statistical sample is large enough to rule out luck. She is developing a psi talent."

"Khalsa told me you study people who consistently beat the odds, even granting them tremendous skill. What if blind luck *is* a talent?"

Curvy had no answer for that, and they left it there.

Trina herself had no insight into whatever it was. She didn't understand how she beat Curvy, or why she was better at quick games than long ones. She didn't know how she knew when it was time to leave at all the critical moments in her childhood when leaving was a matter of survival, didn't know how she guessed the right cards. Curvy's opinion was that she made the right chess moves when it was critical that she do so, less good moves when it was less critical. She didn't so much win the games as stave off defeat long enough to turn it into victory. She was adamant that she didn't know what people were thinking, or what was going to happen; she just acted on her feelings and, more often than not, they turned out to be correct.

The rest of the trip passed uneventfully, and five days later they dropped out of hyperspace on the outskirts of the Centauri system. It was when Tskombe tried to get the cockpit running again that the full extent of the damage the cruiser had done was clear. Both main polarizers were off line, and both out-coms and the transponder were down. The ship's automanual had procedures to use the cabin gravity polarizers for drive. They produced under a gee of thrust, which meant it would take five weeks to reach Wunderland, but that was only an annoyance. The lack of communications wouldn't be a problem; *Valiant* had power and supplies for three months. Once they got into Wunderland's defensive sphere without a transponder they would be intercepted, identified, and rescued, which was good enough. Tskombe wasn't eager to try docking the ship wearing a vac suit in the airless cockpit, and without the main polarizers they couldn't make a surface landing.

That plan fell apart when the cabin polarizers failed three days later. Suddenly *Valiant* was drifting, and they had a problem. Trina helped Tskombe strip down the system, which revealed that the superconductor coils were thawed. The liquid nitrogen pump system checked fine, and the valve indicators showed the system was sealed, but the main reservoir was empty. Calling up the maintenance history showed the tank pressure spiking during the battle, then holding steady until it dropped immediately to zero when the main polarizer superconductors went out. There was battle damage, and a weakened link had given out all at once. The cabin gravity polarizers had been running on what nitrogen was left behind the backcheck valves, until slow leakage left too little to keep the coils cold. The pilots would have caught the problem right away. Tskombe, operating well out of his element, hadn't. His first instinct was to valve over some nitrogen from the fusion reactor, which was on a separate loop and still had pressure, but when they actually opened up the cabin gravity polarizer coils he saw that the superconductors had quenched and burned out. That left the chance of repairing the main polarizers. The drive compartment had been spaced, which wasn't a good sign, and when Tskombe suited up and went in to look he could see they'd been shredded by fragments sprayed from the hull by whatever it was that had hit them. Their bulk had shielded the hyperdrive from immediate destruction, which was, at least in retrospect, a good thing.

Communications now became a major issue. If they couldn't call for help they would starve. They could stretch their supplies somewhat, but without thrust their five-week infall orbit profile turned into fifty-six years. Wearily they stripped down the outcom transmitters, following the automanual's instructions. One had been switched on during the battle and had been fried by the electromagnetic pulse of the cruiser's missile, but the other was putting out a signal. They traced it, found the feed cables intact, but the signal wasn't making it out of the ship. There was an antenna problem, and given the battle damage the likely solution was that the antenna array itself was wrecked. Someone was going to have to go outside and fix it, and that someone was Tskombe. He sighed and looked up at Trina, who was watching him with concern as he worked. *What does it mean for her luck if she wins chess games and guesses cards but dies of slow starvation on a crippled starship?*

He suited up and went into the emergency airlock. Through the tiny transpax window the starfield revolved slowly. The cabin polarizers had tumbled them as they failed, and the ship was spinning fast enough to give an appreciable sense of down, which was out through the airlock. Once he left the ship he would fall into space, untethered. That was a frightening thought, despite a polarizer belt that would let him fly himself back to *Valiant* in free flight. Running out of power was one danger, being struck by the tumbling hull as he maneuvered was another. He took a deep breath. It had to be done. Without at least one antenna functioning there was no communication between the ship and anyone outside it.

He picked up the replacement array he and Curvy had jury rigged in the hold, and put it at his feet so it wouldn't fly around on its short tether when he jumped. Once he got positioned on the hull properly he would try to connect it to the hull mount. He turned around to give Trina the thumbs up through the airlock's internal viewport. He got a thumbs up back, and a brave smile, and then pushed the purge lever. There was a rush of air, quickly fading to silence as the lock pumped down to vacuum.

There was a checklist on the arm of his suit, things to do to verify it was in fact space ready now that the lock was in vacuum. He ran down it. Air feed off, pressure steady for a count of sixty, air feed on, verify air flow, check polarizers, rotation and thrust, verify power, check coolant, check communications. Checklist complete. He was completely unqualified to do this, but it had to be done. *I wasn't qualified to fly a ship off Kzinhome either.* Tskombe unsealed the airlock and pulled the heavy door in and up, balancing himself against the gentle outward acceleration so he wouldn't simply tumble out. Vertigo. The stars were waiting, and it was harder to let go than he thought it would be. He closed his eyes and opened them again, and fell.

He let himself fall for some seconds, then triggered the yaw control to spin him around facing *Valiant*, triggered it the other way again to stop the rotation when he was. The port side of the ship seemed fine, but as it turned slowly beneath him he could see the starboard side was melted and glassy, the ablative armor deeply pitted from the thermal flux of the cruiser's warhead. He applied thrust to stop his fall, taking Curvy's advice to do everything gently. The dolphin would have been a better choice for the job—her three-dimensional instincts and the dexterous power of her dolphin hands would have made the job easy—but Curvy had no vacuum gear.

The antenna mounts were in the sensor bay on the courier's back, halfway between the navigation blister and its sharply angled twin tails. As that part of the ship rotated past Tskombe got an idea of how difficult the job was going to be. The sensor bay doors had been sheared off by the blast, or more accurately, by the tremendous thrust caused by their ablative armor flash-boiling away. The ship's hull in that area was basically intact, but there were no handholds but the lip of the bay itself. The acceleration given by the ship's rotation was gentle, but it was constant, and he would have to hold on with one hand and work with the other. If he slipped he'd fall away again, which wasn't a big deal, but *Valiant*'s rotation made *down* the rear of the ship, and if he hit the tail assembly it could be fatal.

There was no way to match rotation with the ship; he simply had to judge the spin and go for it, like jumping onto a three-dimensional merry-go-round that was already spinning. The airlock, thankfully, was on the ship's side, close to the center of rotation, but more importantly, not exposed to the long axis of the ship's spin. Missing an approach on the way back would be annoying, but not as dangerous as falling from the sensor bay to the tail.

He tried out the thruster controls, spinning, thrusting, spinning again to brake. They were simple enough, but his maneuvers lacked finesse. He was overcontrolling and wasting power. Enough of that—he didn't have it to waste.

Nothing to do but do it. *Trina is a lucky girl. If I don't get the antenna fixed, she won't get rescued.* The thought gave him little comfort, if only because he wasn't convinced of the theory. Still, she had come through the attack without so much as a bruise, which was better than the rest of them. He timed the ship's stately motion, once, twice and . . . thrust, gently but not *too* gently. Better to come in hard than get sliced in half by one of those razor-sharp leading edges. He ignored the looming tail, concentrated on the sensor bay. He had to grab it on the first try; if he failed he had to instantly rotate and thrust back out the way he'd come to get out of the way as the tail came around.

Do it right first and he wouldn't have to handle any problems. The bay came up, faster than he'd expected, and he toggled the polarizer. As he came in he grabbed on hard to some projecting connection inside the bay. An instant later he bumped into the hull and rebounded, but his grip held and he didn't bounce off into space again. A gentle acceleration tried to push him off into space, stronger here than it had been at the airlock. *Down* had changed direction, to point along the ship's back to the huge tail section, stationary now against a starfield rotating with stately majesty. A deep breath, and he was suddenly aware of the pounding of his heart in his ears. Step one complete.

The bay was a mess. The doors had shielded the

equipment inside from the blast, but when they'd been torn off everything projecting through them had been taken with them, both omnidirectional antennas, the long com dish, the radars, everything, torn out by the roots, with cables and components spilling haphazardly into space. He'd gone over the layout with the automanual until he had it memorized, but it still took him awhile to recognize the com array mounts in the mess.

It was immediately obvious he was going to be unable to do the work while holding on to the bay with one hand; it was a two-hand job. Perhaps he could swing upside down and wedge his feet beneath the bay door mounts. He tried it, awkwardly, nearly slipped and fell, but managed to get them secure. *Valiant* wasn't big enough to carry extensive spares. The unit he was attaching now had its gain control section improvised with components stolen from the cockpit and lashed together with his limited electronics expertise and a lot of advice from the automanual. A length of coaxial cable, stripped of its outer shielding, served as the actual antenna. It dangled beneath him by its tether now and he pulled it up.

Attaching it should have been simple, but it wasn't. The sensor bay wasn't very big, and because he had to use it as a foothold he had to half squat, uneasily balanced, and work between his knees. The procedure would have been absolutely impossible under full gravity. He immediately found he couldn't lean his head forward far enough to see clearly what he was doing, so he had to work by touch. The suit gloves were thick enough to make what should have been a simple operation difficult, and the long, whippy antenna length continually got in the way. He dropped it three times just trying to get the threads to line up, and once nearly fell backward, saving himself with a desperate grab. Heart pounding, he steadied himself. There was no way he was going to be able to thread the connector without seeing what he was doing.

Maybe if he held on to the connector with one hand and leaned back . . . The cables looked strong enough to hold his not-so-large weight. He let the antenna go and tried it, gingerly, ready to grab with his free hand if the cable suddenly gave way.

It held. He breathed out, and slowly, carefully pulled the antenna back up and positioned the screw threads. It was still awkward to rotate with the length of the wire whipping around, but he managed to get the first thread mated, and after that it was easier. He took his time, screwing down the mounting a turn at a time. Finally it was threaded as tightly as he could get it by hand. Mission accomplished, time to go back. He stood, dancing carefully around the now mounted antenna, to get himself in position to launch out and away far enough that he could clear the tail while he maneuvered back to the airlock.

Something slipped and all of a sudden he was falling, slowly at first. He twisted, and punched wildly at the polarizer controls. Thrust hit him in the back and something snagged, then tore. He bounced painfully off of the courier's hull, and spun, sliding over the top of the ship. He went right between the tails and fell off into space, spinning wildly with the polarizer still on full thrust. The centrifugal force of his spin made it difficult to operate the controls and it took him some time to get the thruster switched off. Awkwardly, he killed his rotation. *Valiant* was now five hundred meters distant and receding rapidly, so thrust again to come to zero relative and coast. It took a lot of thrust to stop; he'd picked up a lot of momentum from the ship, plus whatever the uncontrolled surge had given him. He was trembling. That had been a near thing, and if he'd hit the tails he would have been injured, and he could have torn the suit. He took a deep breath and steadied himself. He was drifting slowly toward *Valiant*, and they should be able to hear him now.

He keyed the transmitter. "Tskombe to *Valiant*."

Nothing.

"Tskombe to *Valiant*."

Silence. On instinct he reached behind to his service pack to where his suit antenna should be. His hand found only empty space, and remembered the momentary snag he'd felt. The antenna must have caught on some jagged piece of hull, and torn off when he'd hit the polarizers to clear the tail. He adjusted his heading slightly to carry him past the airlock, then hit the polarizers gently to increase his closure rate.

An amber light blinked in the corner of his vision. He turned his head to the suit readouts projected on the visor. Low power. He breathed in and out again. He'd used a fair bit getting the feel of the polarizer, wasted a lot in the fall, and a lot more in killing the momentum he'd picked up from it. Nothing to worry about, he was on his way back. *I just need to nail the approach . . .*

He didn't nail it, though he came heartbreakingly close. He was off a couple of degrees as he came in and overcorrected. He corrected back the other way as the airlock handholds came close, grabbed for them and missed. He drifted past, rotated to line up again, and hit the thruster. There was a second of thrust, and then it cut out. The amber icon flashed to red, and he was still drifting away at perhaps a half a meter per second. *No power.* Cold horror seized him as he realized the situation had switched from risky to fatal in that split second. Desperately he keyed his transmitter again, but there was still no response. Inexorably *Valiant* got farther away. His suit still had power, but the thruster had its own batteries, and they were dead. The suit was good for forty-eight hours, give or take, and he was going to die a slow and lonely death.

Hours later *Valiant* had faded to a pinprick and then finally vanished. Time dragged. He slept and woke, and slept again. Occasionally, and without much hope, he keyed his transmitter. His air was becoming heavy, saturated with CO_2 and his thinking was fuzzy and unclear. *This is what it is to die.* He had nightmares then, about Ayla at the spaceport. She was taken by the kzinti, and when he tried to save her the kzin who nearly killed him at Vega IV screamed and leapt, fangs bared for the killing bite. *I never should have left her.* Sleep blended with delirium and he barely recognized the warship when it occulted a quarter of the sky, black on black, bristling with sensors and turrets, a weapon tube large enough to destroy worlds running down its lower spine. They sent a flitter for him and he wondered if they'd eat him alive. It wasn't until they vented pressure into the hangar and the medics ran in to strip his suit off that he realized it was a human ship. His legs wouldn't support him, and his rescuers held up him.

"Colonel Tskombe?" The man was tall and broad-shouldered, with iron gray hair and beard, and an air of command in his Wunderland-accented English.

"Yes."

The man offered his hand "I'm Captain Cornelius Voortman, and you're aboard the battleship *Oorwinnig*. You're lucky to be alive."

"Thank you, sir." Tskombe took the hand and shook it, doing the expected thing and saying the required words. "Sir, my ship . . ."

"Your dolphin and the girl are safe aboard. We responded as soon as we got their distress call. You are the hero of the day, I understand."

"Commander Khalsa fought the ship, sir."

"And you saved it. My report to the UN will be clear on your role, and on the kzinti's treaty violation in attacking you." Voortman's voice hardened. "The ratcats will pay dearly for this attack."

Kzinti. Tskombe controlled his expression. Whatever story Curvy had told the Free Wunderland Navy didn't involve an illegal flight from Earth and attack by a UNSN cruiser. *They pinned the attack on the kzinti, which is exactly who the Wunderlanders would expect.* It was a logical and necessary move, but it made his position difficult. He spoke carefully. "Sir, this mission . . ." There was no way to explain the situation. ". . . Sir, I would rather you hold back your report."

Not the required words. Voortman stiffened. "May I ask the nature of your mission?"

"It's need-to-know only information in the UNF, sir. Our very presence here is secret." *Would the UN have warned Wunderland to look out for* Valiant? *If it had our reception would have been very different.*

Voortman nodded, relaxing slightly. "I understand your concerns, but I have my duty to carry out. The UN is jealous of Alpha Centauri's independence. We don't need to provoke discord by falsifying reports."

Tskombe nodded. "All I can ask is that you consider that our very presence here is secret within the UN hierarchy. A lot is at stake."

"I'll do that." Voortman bowed, polite but formal. "Your distress call interrupted us in the middle of an exercise. My medics will look after you."

He left and the medics took him to the battleship's small but well-equipped med station. Trina and Curvy were already there. Trina hugged him fiercely; the dolphin chirped and twirled in her suspensor belt and came over to nose him affectionately. They fed him while the medics fussed over him, and finally let him sleep. They didn't get a chance to talk alone.

He didn't get a chance to talk to them in the morning either. On first watch the next ship cycle there was a service for Virenze and Khalsa on the hangar deck, and Tskombe watched impassively as the bodies were ceremoniously loaded into the airlock. Two crewmen in immaculate dress uniform took the sky blue UN flag from the coffins, while Captain Voortman said the eulogy. Tskombe didn't really hear it. *How many times have I said those words myself?* Perhaps it would have meant more if Curvy had said it. The sentiments were heartfelt, but ultimately meaningless. Words would not give life back to the dead. The loudspeaker played some somber bugle call as the heavy

airlock door swung shut. As the mournful trumpet faded
away there was a faint shudder in the deck as the bodies
were jettisoned into space. He saluted at the right time,
and turned to go with Trina and Curvy.

There were no fighters in the hangar deck. Almost all
the available space had been given over to four pairs of
tremendous fusion generators. He asked Captain
Voortman about them idly on the way out.

"Very observant, Colonel." Voortman hesitated, then
seemed to reach a decision. "I am going to exercise my
discretionary power as captain, Colonel Tskombe, and
allow you to see something no one in the UN knows about.
You're about to enjoy the unique privilege of seeing this
ship prove its full capabilities for the first time."

"I'm honored, I'm sure." Tskombe didn't know what
else to say. Voortman took him up to the bridge. Why he
was invited while Trina and Curvy were not he didn't ask.
The bridge itself was spacious, even luxurious, in stark
contrast to *Valiant*'s cramped cockpit, even in comparison
to *Crusader*'s ample control spaces. *Oorwinnig* was a battleship, an expression not only of Alpha Centauri's power
but of the system's pride and independence as well. There
was room in her design for more than lethal functionality.

"See that?" Voortman pointed through the wrap-
around transpax panels to an irregular blob against the
starfield, about the size of the full moon but barely a quarter
as bright. "That's Echo Delta 1272, a trivial chunk of this
system's Kuiper belt, more rock than ice, twenty kilometers
by fifteen, and a thousand kilometers distant. It's been
unremarkable for the last five billion years, but it's about
to become part of history."

"What . . ."

Voortman held up a hand to cut off the question. "Indulge me please, and watch." He turned to an officer behind him. "Weapons free, engage at will."

"Aye, sir."

At first nothing happened, but then Tskombe noticed faint fountains of dust erupting from either end of the asteroid, as though twin meteors had struck it on opposite sides. Faint, but they must have been kilometers big already to be visible at this distance, and they grew as he watched. For long seconds that was all there was, but then the impact zones began to glow red. The red points expanded into circles and their centers ran up the spectrum to white hot and then to actinic blue. The transpax automatically darkened, then darkened again until the body of the asteroid was invisible except where it was incandescent, until Tskombe could feel the heat coming through the screen despite the damping and at a distance of a thousand kilometers. To make its heat tangible at that range, whatever they were hitting ED1272 with had the energy of a small star. He saw red through his eyelids and had to turn away, waited until he felt the heat fade from the side of his face to look back. The transpax had undarkened and there was an expanding orange halo where the asteroid had been, hazy like a streetlight seen through fog, still expanding and fading back to red as he watched.

Conversion weapons. A gigatonne warhead could vaporize an asteroid that big, but a conversion attack was over in a single flash, and the destruction had commenced at most a few seconds after Voortman had given the order. No launcher, no missile was fast enough to cross a thousand kilometers in that time. What he had seen looked like a pair of beam weapon hits, but the energy output! No ship-mounted laser put out a fraction of a percent of the power required to do what he'd just seen done, and the inescapably low energy transport efficiency of laser beams guaranteed that none ever would. Not even the huge fusion generators that had taken over *Oorwinnig*'s hangar deck would provide enough power.

So either this was a carefully staged demonstration or the Wunderlanders had something very new. *And given the complete accident of our presence here, this isn't being staged.*

"We call it the Treatymaker"—Voortman answered his unspoken question—"and it is this ship's primary weapon." The tall Viking smirked. "It's based on a kzinti invention called a charge suppressor. As you'd expect it suppresses electric charges; to be exact it uses a monopole beam to interfere with the mediation particles of the electrostatic force. They use it for climate control, preventing charge separation in the upper atmosphere to keep clouds from forming. It's derived from a Thrintun device, although we suspect it was actually developed by the Tnuctipun, back when life on Earth was limited to algae. They used it as a weapon, at short ranges. As you can see we've made improvements."

"That's . . ." Tskombe groped for words. "That's incredible."

"Impressive little toy, yes?" Voortman smiled in grim satisfaction. "A single beam literally tears matter apart as the atoms repel each other, but the trick is to use two beams, one positive and one negative. That creates a current flow between the contact points. Beam power requirements are tremendous of course, but all of it is delivered to the target and the zone of destruction can be controlled with fine accuracy. Unlike lasers the atmospheric degradation is trivial. Unlike conversion warheads there is no possibility of intercept. Power coupling approaches one hundred percent. It is a tremendously efficient weapon. The ratcats are about to learn a painful lesson."

Tskombe looked at him in shock. "You can't be intending to use it."

Voortman raised an eyebrow. "And why not?"

"It would start another war."

The captain snorted. "The war has already begun, or didn't you notice? Secretary General Ravalla has wasted no time making his intentions clear. Wunderland is offering full cooperation and support, of course. We have our differences with Earth, but we recognize our common enemies."

Ravalla was moving with tremendous speed. *Not a good sign.* Tskombe controlled his reaction. "Do you know how soon the war is going to turn hot?"

"Not long. It will take some time to gather forces, and then we strike, with the full strength of the human race combined. The timing is perfect, with this new weapon coming on line. Wunderland lacks the strength to attack by itself, but Ravalla is a man of action. With the UN beside us, we can rid ourselves of the ratcats once and for all."

Tskombe felt sick in the pit of his stomach. "Using this weapon on a world . . . It would be nothing short of genocide." *Ayla is on Kzinhome.*

The tall man laughed bitterly. "You are a Flatlander, Colonel Tskombe. Your world was never occupied."

"But still . . ."

"Don't pretend to be shocked, you are a soldier." Voortman's voice was hard. "Ten generations of my family have known only war with the kzinti, and there are no records before that because Earth chose to use relativistic weapons to prevent what was happening here from happening there. I lost ancestors then, though I'll never know their names." He turned to look out through the transpax to the still expanding incandescence that had been Echo Delta 1272. "This is war, Colonel. This is *another* war with the goddamned ratcats. My mother was crippled fighting them, my father was killed before I was born." He turned back to face Tskombe, his eyes blazing. "I swear upon the cross that Christ died on my children will grow up in peace, and if I must sterilize a thousand worlds to buy that for them I will consider the price cheap."

"You invite the kzinti to do the same in return. Would you see Wunderland razed?"

"Wunderland has been razed, Colonel, and by humans, not kzinti. Go look at Thor's Crater and then give me a Flatlander's moralizing on genocide. But the kzinti will not have the chance to retaliate. You speak of genocide as if it were a bad thing, Colonel. In fact, genocide is the plan." The captain's words were hard edged with anger. Tskombe had been to Thor's Crater on Wunderland, where metric-ton slugs sent at nearly lightspeed from Earth had punched through the planet's crust with impacts measured in tens of gigatonnes. Millions of

Wunderlanders had died in that attack. Tskombe found it wiser to say nothing.

Voortman was still talking, his voice slightly less intense. "Ironically enough that was when we learned of the charge suppressor. The kzinti used it to clear the impact dust out of the skies and forestall environmental collapse. For that at least we owe them. And now that we have duplicated their technology, they will be repaid for everything." The captain smiled a smile as lethal as any kzin's. "In full."

Beware the hidden blade.

— Si-Rrit

"They are called *czrav*, brother." Ftzaal-Tzaatz looked out windows of the Patriarch's Tower, watching the landers coming and going from the distant spaceport. His thigh still ached where the Chief Surgeon had repaired the wound the *tuskvor* had given him. "And they represent a grave danger."

"A bunch of primitives cowering in the jungle? Don't be a fool." Kchula-Tzaatz reclined on his *prrstet*, stroking the ears of a young kzinrette.

Ftzaal ignored the insult and kept his voice level. "I do not believe they are primitive."

"You just told me they were." Kchula keyed his vocom and spoke into it. "Slave Handler, send food to the Patriarch's tower."

"At once, sire."

"Fresh *zianya*, Ftzaal?" Kchula ran his hand down the kzinrette's sleek flanks, and she purred and nuzzled him in response.

My brother distracts himself with luxuries. Ftzaal lashed his tail in annoyance and went on with his point. "Even the *cvari* nomads who hunt the savannah call them primitive, but they never penetrate the deep jungle. They see the *czrav* only when the *czrav* choose to be seen. I think theirs is a world hidden in the very heart of the Patriarchy, a world we do not control."

"So they hide in the jungle. Let them. We have nothing to fear. We went to the jungle to find First-Son-of-Meerz-Rrit. Both Ktronaz-Commander's experience and your own shows us that, even if it was he who we tracked to the jungle verge, he cannot have survived."

"This is my point, brother. Even the *cvari* who live next to the jungle shun it; only a few of the Lesser Pride nobility will hunt the fringes, more for the honor than the sport. They go well equipped and they do not stay long, and even then the jungle claims enough of them. No one returns from the deep jungle. *No one.* I lost three *Ftz'yeer* just tracking First-Son-of-Meerz-Rrit, plus Telepath, and Ktronaz-Commander's attack force was destroyed."

"Ktronaz-Commander." Kchula snorted. "His competence is marginal."

"He is unimaginative brother, but not incompetent, and my *Ftz'yeer* fared no better." Ftzaal's lips twitched over his fangs. "I hope you are not questioning *my* competence as well."

"No, brother, but . . ."

"But nothing! We can barely survive a night in the jungle with all the equipment we can bring to bear on the problem, and yet the *czrav* live their lives there. First-Son fled there quite deliberately. What does he know that we do not?"

"It is irrelevant. Even if he has found safety with these . . . these *czrav*, what of it? Soon his very existence will be forgotten. It is the Patriarchy that is important. The attacks on our Heroes have dropped drastically, the Lesser Prides of Kzinhome accept our rule, and so do the *kzintzag*. Even the Great Prides bow to my commands now."

"Do they?" Ftzaal-Tzaatz's ears fanned up and forward. "This is a new development."

"They obey without question." Kchula's tail stood straight up in aggressive satisfaction. "Cvail Pride is supporting Stkaa against the *kz'zeerkti*. Stkaa's raiders are already probing the monkey defenses. Vdar Pride's fleet is in hyperspace by now, the rest are not far behind. Throughout the Patriarchy the shipyards are in full production." He slashed at the air with his talons. "A final resolution of the monkey problem is a popular cause. Once more around the seasons and I will leap at their throats with the greatest fleet ever assembled in this galaxy."

"This is an old galaxy, brother, and a big one. The odds do not favor our fleet being the largest in its history."

"Bah. You remind me of that prattling Rrit-Conserver."

"Hrrr." Ftzaal turned a paw over. "Rrit-Conserver should have died the day we took the Citadel. I don't like that he sits at our councils."

"And you claim to be worried about rebellion! Kzin-Conserver has ordered it! What do you think would happen with the *kzintzag* if I denied his order?" Kchula snorted in derision. "That old fool won't last long, and then we can be rid of Rrit-Conserver as well. In the meantime he serves his purpose in legitimizing our rule."

"Scrral-Rrit is sufficient for that purpose, and far easier to control. And had Rrit-Conserver died on the day we struck we could have called it a tragic accident made in the heat of battle. Now we have no such option, and who do you think will take Kzin-Conserver's place if *not* Rrit-Conserver?"

"And what will he do then? First-Son is gone, Scrral-Rrit is ours, and his sister is carrying my kits. Our control is absolute, Ftzaal."

"Except for the *czrav*."

"Do you not tire of that topic?" Kchula snarled the words, getting close to the edge of his temper.

"We are both newcomers to Kzinhome, brother. It does not concern me that I have no knowledge of the *czrav;* it concerns me that even the Lesser Prides and the *kzintzag* know nothing about them. Even among those who live next to them there are few who have ever met a *czrav.* They are called primitives, but primitives do not use hunt cloaks and broad spectrum goggles. A factor we do not control or even understand cannot help but be dangerous, brother."

"We have no evidence they use either."

"I know what I saw."

"In the dark, while dodging a herd charge."

"Ktronaz-Commander's patrols were wiped out to the last one. My own *Ftz'yeer* were hunted down by those *tuskvor.*"

"You were herd charged, it was bad luck. Only a fool hunts *tuskvor,* even nursing kittens on Jotok know this."

"Only a fool believes herding herbivores will hunt on their own. I saw the *czrav riding* the beasts." Ftzaal stood and paced.

"You saw *something*. Even you admit you didn't see clearly."

"You explain it then. This was not a herd charge. Herd animals don't split. We were watched from the moment we set down in that valley, and when we were in too deep to escape we were ambushed. It was a carefully laid trap."

"This is not Jotok. What do you know of Kzinhome's beasts? Your vaunted *Ftz'yeer* were wiped out, and so it must have been a trap, is that it?" Kchula-Tzaatz snorted. "You saw a blur on the beast's back, and it must be a *czrav* with a hunt cloak. They followed you at night, so the riders must have had night goggles. These are speculations, not proof-before-the-pride-circle. What is a fact is I lose more *strakh* with the *kzintzag* every day, and this does not help."

"They vanished without trace. We went back in daylight and they were gone. Does that not arouse your curiosity?"

"Perhaps you killed them all."

"We found no bodies."

"Destroyed by the fire, or perhaps they didn't exist at all."

Ftzaal stopped pacing and rounded on Kchula. "Brother, do not mock me. We found their den, emptied in a single night. There were cables left behind, scraps of equipment. They are not so primitive as we might like to think."

"Maybe not, but they are irrelevant. We have larger game to stalk, Ftzaal." The door chimed and Kchula waved a paw to command the AI to unlock it. "Enter."

"Telepath saw First-Son alive, and with the *czrav*." Ftzaal turned a paw over. *This is a subject more likely to engage my brother's interest.* Four Pierin slaves came in, the first two carrying a trussed and struggling *zianya*. The third carried a long *sk'ceri* knife for the sacrifice, and the fourth carried two bowls, one full of pungent *tunuska* sauce, the other empty to catch the blood.

"First-Son is gone; that is all that matters. He is no longer any threat to my rule." Kchula inhaled deeply to enjoy the strong fear scent of the helpless *zianya*. "As for Telepath, do not remind me of what you have cost me. We require another one."

"We do, but even that carries risk. I feel our control over the telepaths is slipping too."

"On what evidence?" The *sk'ceri* blade rose and fell. There was a single, anguished squeal and then the *zianya's* blood was spilling into the sacrificial bowl.

"Telepath was keeping something from me. He didn't want us to find First-Son. He didn't want us in the jungle at all."

"And now he is dead. Where has your liver gone, Ftzaal? What was not wise was giving you the lead in hunting down First-Son. You have been gone half a season and gained nothing, and I have needed your expertise here. The *kzintzag* ask why we search the jungles if First-Son-of-Meerz-Rrit is not alive. "

"Your puppet is not popular."

"My puppet will soon become as irrelevant as his brother. We will waste no more time pursuing him. We are in midleap on the *kz'zeerkti* and the war will require our full attention." Kchula turned his own attention to the *zianya*. "Let us eat, and look to the future. What's past is past."

There was a blur of motion and suddenly the Pierin with the knife was on the floor, blue circulatory fluid gushing from its split braincase. Ftzaal stood over it in a combat stance, *wtsai* poised to strike again. Kchula blinked, not comprehending for a moment, then saw the blade in the creature's manipulator, oily toxin gleaming on its edge where the *zianya*'s blood had been. The other slaves had shrunk back to the edges of the room, feverishly making gestures of submission to distance themselves from the treachery and its punishment. *Betrayal!* The kill rage flooded through Kchula and he screamed and leapt on the nearest Pierin, ripping open its abdominal segment with his hind claws. The others fled while he tore at the corpse.

By the time his anger was spent a sword of *Ftz'yeer*, summoned by Ftzaal, were on guard outside the Patriarch's quarters, beamrifles held ready. The room was a mess. The slaughtered *zianya*'s blood bowl had been overturned by Kchula's leap and its blood seeped into the floor, mingling with the pungent blue Pierin circulatory fluid that was spattered everywhere along with gobbets of Pierin flesh. By the sauce bowl, Ftzaal sniffed carefully at a thin plastic pouch.

He looked up, undisturbed by Kchula's violent rage, and held the pouch up, pincered carefully between two claws. It was still dripping with the red *tunuska* sauce it had been concealed in. "*P'chert* toxin, kept sealed until the last minute to prevent the sniffers from picking it up. The slave had only to slice it open with the knife to coat the blade, and then strike."

"I could have died." Kchula was trembling, residual

anger mixing with sudden fear at how close the assassination had come to succeeding.

Ftzaal twitched his whiskers. "Evidently you have someone's full attention, brother."

"I want every Pierin in the Citadel executed. *Now!*"

"Shouldn't we wait until we can trace the roots of this plot?"

Kchula looked at his brother for a long moment. "Yes . . . yes we should." His voice was calmer. "Who do you suspect?"

"It is a primary error to speculate in advance of the facts. Pierin is the homeworld of Cvail Pride. I imagine Chmee-Cvail is less than pleased about being ordered to support Tzor-Stkaa in a war he would rather lead himself."

"I will spike his head at Patriarch's Gate!" Kchula's tail lashed angrily.

Ftzaal-Tzaatz held up a paw. "Slower, brother! Let us look before we leap. It may be Chmee-Cvail, it may not. We need evidence first, and I suspect it will point much closer to home. These are not our Pierin, or Cvail Pride's; they belonged to the Rrit, and their loyalty may remain there."

"Scrral-Rrit! He wouldn't dare!" Kchula's hand went to the transponder medallion around his neck. "He wears my *zzrou*. His own life is forfeit if I die."

"Patience. We'll see how tame your tame Patriarch really is." Ftzaal keyed his com. "*Ftz'yeer* Leader!"

"Command me, sire." The voice was not that of his old friend and companion on eight-squared adventures. That *Ftz'yeer* Leader had been trampled by *tuskvor* deep in the jungle, this new one promoted in his place. *My brother doesn't realize the price I have paid for my loyalty. We flow through these roles in our life, and flow through our life until we die.* It was a good rule to remember, but a hard one.

Ftzaal pushed the thought away. "Bring our ever noble Patriarch here. If he resists, compel him."

"At once, sire."

It wasn't long before *Ftz'yeer* Leader brought a half sword of *Ftz'yeer* into the room, pushing Meerz-Rrit's Second-Son in front of them. Scrral-Rrit was bleeding slightly from a talon wound on the side of his face, but otherwise uninjured. He had resisted, but not much.

Ftzaal picked up the *sk'ceri* knife and held it in front of the supposed Patriarch. "What do you know about this?"

"Nothing. Should I?" Scrral-Rrit was nervous and his fear stank in the room.

"We'll see." Ftzaal went to where Kchula was standing, pushed the button on the *zzrou* transponder medallion and held it down. That should have sent *p'chert* toxin flooding from the *zzrou* teeth imbedded in Scrral-Rrit's back. In a heartbeat he would be writhing in agony, in a few breaths he'd be dead.

Scrral-Rrit stayed standing, his head now bowed. He knew he'd been caught. "Please . . ."

"Quiet, *sthondat!*" Ftzaal cuffed him to the floor and turned to *Ftz'yeer* Leader. "Take him and strip him. He has an electronic mimic to replicate the *zzrou* signal. Find it, destroy it, and then learn all he knows."

Ftz'yeer Leader claw-raked. "The Hot Needle of Inquiry, sire?"

"Yes." Ftzaal-Tzaatz spat the word.

Scrral-Rrit looked up from his prostrated position, deep terror suddenly in his eyes. "No! Not the Needle! Please! It wasn't me! It was Rrit-Conserver! It was his plan, his idea, I just . . ."

Ftzaal waved a paw and the *Ftz'yeer* dragged the piteous Patriarch out, still begging. He turned to Kchula. "A faster resolution than I'd hoped, and more simply solved than an invasion of Pierin."

Kchula snarled deep in his throat. "Rrit-Conserver. I should have known."

"He should have died, brother."

"He may yet." Kchula stormed out of the room, leaving Ftzaal to himself. Ftzaal watched him go, then went to the panoramic windows and looked to the northwest, where the jungle lay, horizons away. *What secrets do you hold? I need to learn them.* Kchula would not cooperate, but that was typical of his brother and also of small concern. Eventually events would prove him right, as they had with Rrit-Conserver; he was sure of that. The key was to be prepared when they did, as he had been with Rrit-Conserver. *I might have let my brother die.* Had he done that he would become Pride-Patriarch of Tzaatz Pride, and de facto Patriarch of all. *An unworthy thought for a zar'ameer. Did Rrit-Conserver consider that in his planning?* He must have, he was too deep a thinker to have done otherwise. Despite Kchula's threat, Ftzaal knew he would not kill Conserver; that window of opportunity was long shut. *So what then is Rrit-Conserver's goal?* He could not want Scrral-Rrit to rule in fact as well as name; the damage that would cause the Patriarchy . . . A pawful of Jotok arrived to start cleaning up the mess. Evidently the Pierin thought it wiser to keep a safe distance. They worked as quietly as they could, while Ftzaal ignored them and thought. *Where could the* czrav *have vanished to so quickly? They ride* tuskvor, *could that be the key?* He turned a paw over to contemplate his talons. *I have some tracking to do.*

He who thinks hardest fights easiest.
                                              —Si-Rrit

"Rrit-Conserver!" Kchula-Tzaatz's enraged voice echoed up the narrow staircase. An instant later the door of Rrit-Conserver's austere room burst open.

Rrit-Conserver looked up from his trance-meditation posture. "Kchula-Tzaatz. I am disappointed to see you here. I'd hoped you'd be dead by now."

Kchula snarled, fangs bared. "So you admit your complicity in Scrral-Rrit's plot."

"Complicity is too strong a word." Rrit-Conserver stood and turned slightly, subtly ready to receive an attack. "Second-Son himself saw the advantage of your death; he planned it eagerly. I merely told him how to deal with the threat of the *zzrou.*"

"You betrayed me."

Rrit-Conserver waved a paw. "That would only be possible if I had sworn fealty to you. I am sworn to serve the Rrit."

"You cannot tell me you think that cringing pretender deserves the Patriarchy more than I do."

"What I think doesn't matter. I serve the Rrit, and the Patriarchy descends through the line of the Rrit. You forget that Scrral-Rrit *is* Patriarch, however much he is your puppet. You are the pretender, Kchula-Tzaatz, not he."

"He's a disgrace to his line."

Rrit-Conserver turned a paw over. "For as many generations as the Rrit have held the Patriarchy it has been the role of the Rrit-Conservers to shore up weak leaders. Read your histories. Scrral-Rrit is far from the worst Patriarch our empire has ever seen."

"He used a slave to attack me. *A slave!*" Kchula slashed the air with his claws. "He has violated his honor, and mine!"

"I told him this plan was beneath his honor." Conserver flicked his ears and twitched his tail, wry humor. "He needs stronger counsel in the future, if he has a future." An ear went up in mock concern. "Perhaps you will leap and kill him now for the insult he's given you."

Kchula snarled. *He knows I need that* sthondat. "And what of your own honor? What will Kzin-Conserver say when he hears of this?"

"As a Conserver I can only use violence in personal self-defense. The advice I give my Patriarch is something else entirely. I will take my sire's judgment with confidence."

Even through his rage, Kchula could see how masterfully his adversary had played the game. He probably wasn't even displeased to see Scrral-Rrit punished. "Your death will take days, Conserver," he hissed.

"Then it will take longer than your fall, once the Great Prides learn of it."

And of course Conserver was immune. Kchula screamed in rage and frustration, but he didn't leap. The consequences in front of the Great Circle would be lethal if they discovered he'd violated the Conserver Traditions, and Rrit-Conserver was a deadly adversary in his own right. Instead he turned and stormed out, slamming the door behind him. *Ftzaal-Tzaatz was right. I should have killed him when I had the chance.*

Rrit-Conserver stood for a long moment after he had gone, then got up and began collecting a few belongings. Scrral-Rrit had dishonored himself. It was time to go.

I have seen lands no man has ever seen.
    —Gudridur Thorbjarnarsdottir, first Viking colonist in North America, circa tenth century

The jungle swayed past at a stately pace as Ayla Cherenkova watched from the *tsvasztet* travel platform strapped to the back of a huge *tuskvor* herd grandmother. She had seen the *tuskvor* in the wild, and seen the *tuskvor* riders on her combat displays in the battle at Ztrak Pride's den, but to ride one herself was something else again. To be a part of the huge herd migration was an experience she had trouble believing in even as she had it. They were ten meters off the ground on the back of a beast sixty meters from tusk tip to armored tail, one of a herd of a hundred or more. The *tuskvor* ambled along at maybe ten kilometers per hour, not fast but steady, and they never stopped to eat or sleep. They were covering distance like a wildfire, surging steadily eastward. Occasionally the herd expanded as more *tuskvor* pods joined them, appearing from between the spire trees to follow the ancient migratory track. The migration was its own self-contained world, the *tsvasztet*'s cargo bins laden down with water, provisions and the entire wealth of Ztrak Pride. It had taken just hours to strip the den to bare stone. The *czrav* traveled light, and the Tzaatz would return to find their quarry vanished.

Pride life continued without interruption on the trek, and she recognized that this migration was as ancient to the *czrav* as it was to the *tuskvor* themselves. She shared the *tsvasztet* with Ferlitz-Telepath, V'rli and Pouncer, but they frequently had company. The great beasts could be steered, like ponderous ships on a powerful river. Their *mazourk* handlers would bring one alongside and the kzinti, cat agile, would leap from the journeypad of one *tsvasztet* to another to gossip, to trade, or just to change scenery. A missed jump would mean a ten-meter fall to a certain death, pounded into the ground by the relentless march of the *tuskvor*, but the kzinti leapt with casual indifference to the possibility, and they never missed their landings.

On the second day Kr-Pathfinder and Quicktail had joined them to swap stories of the battle. Quicktail had ears on his belt now, and a new respect from his elders, although he had yet to claim his name. The migration was a place-between, where the normal traditions were suspended, replaced with a whole new set of norms

"How long is the journey?" Cherenkova asked.

Across the platform Pouncer fanned his ears up. It was a question he'd wondered about himself but hadn't raised.

Kr-Pathfinder stretched on his *prrstet* and rolled over to face her. "It depends on the *tuskvor*. Once around the Hunter's Moon, perhaps more."

Ayla nodded. Once around the Hunter's Moon was a month, more or less. It would be a long time to spend on a *tuskvor*'s back. At least she now understood the design philosophy behind the *prrstet* hammock/couches that were kzin-standard furnishing. They served to smooth out the constant jolting of the *tuskvor*'s heavy gait

A pack of *grlor* joined them on the second day and dogged their passage, hoping to pull down a straggler. There were seven or eight in the pack, enough to be dangerous, but the *mazourk* kept the big grandmothers on the outside of the herd and the predators couldn't get close enough to take any of the smaller animals. They tried though, making feint attacks in pairs or threes, their rumbling hunt-calls echoing over the steady, rhythmic thudding of the *tuskvor*'s heavily padded feet. She saw a herd grandmother kill a *grlor* then. The predator had made a feint at one of the juveniles who'd wandered from the center of the herd, then shied away from its mother as she came to rescue her progeny. The distracted *grlor* didn't see the grandmother accelerating around the edge of the herd, and it didn't angle away fast enough. The grandmother swung her massive head and that was all it took. Her tusks stabbed the beast in the flank. It roared in pain and turned to snap at her, but stumbled. The grandmother plowed over it without stopping, leaving it crippled and thrashing in her wake, to be crushed lifeless by the oncoming herd.

Their own grandmother seemed inclined to charge as well, but Ferlitz-Telepath hauled on the *mazourk* harness lines and kept it moving with the main body of *tuskvor*. To Cherenkova's surprise the other predators in the pack ran to their fallen comrade, snapping and roaring with enough vehemence to discourage another grandmother that seemed about to charge them. As the scene disappeared behind her the *grlor* were nosing at the body. *They understand death. They have more intelligence than I thought.* She had been fooled by their reptilian appearance. The *grlor* didn't return until the next afternoon, and they were more circumspect. There were no more attacks.

They left the shade of jungle for the savannah on the fourth day and the *grlor* fell back. The kzinti put up *tuskvor*-skin canopies to keep the sun off the *tsvasztet* and spent most of the day napping. Ayla spent her time reading books on her beltcomp, titles she'd been meaning to read for years and never quite found time for. Widespreading grove trees dotted the sun-baked landscape on the higher ground, their shapes oddly unsettling to her Earth-raised sense of rightness. Here and there she could see other *tuskvor* herds moving in the same direction as theirs. The migration was picking up steam. Rivers appeared in their path, water rushing and splashing as they grew closer and the *tuskvor* ahead broached the current, then the tilt as their own beast came over the bank and the crystal water churned muddy far below to run as thick and dark as chocolate downstream. Far ahead on the horizon the distant line that marked the Long Range Mountains grew inexorably larger.

On the seventh day she began to get bored. The kzinti were content to nap the day away and tell stories in the cooler evenings. She would have liked to be able to move around, but there was no way she could leap from *tuskvor* to *tuskvor* as the kzinti did. Even with skilful maneuvering the *tsvasztet* never got closer than three meters. Her ancestors might have swung happily from tree to tree over similar distances, but Ayla Cherenkova, she decided, was going to make this entire journey on the same *tuskvor* she had started it on. She slept well that night, lulled to sleep by the rhythmic rocking of her mount, with Pouncer's haunch for her pillow. When she awoke the sun was high and warm, but the air was noticeably cooler and drier. They had climbed into the foothills in the darkness, and the Long Range was no longer a distant blur on the horizon. Now the peaks loomed like a jagged fortress wall, and another day would see them into the passes.

The herd had transformed itself too. More pods, hundreds more pods, had joined them in the darkness and the migration had become a vast, roiling river of flesh. The males had joined the herd too, more immense than the largest herd-grandmother, bulking out of the torrent here and there like living islands. Quicktail, who used her to practice his storytelling, told her that at the far end of the migration there would be mating, and the males would fight then for females. That would be a sight to see, from a distance. With the other pods came other prides of *czrav*, and the flow of visitors increased as pride leaders came to pay their respects to V'rli. She thought that Pouncer, deposed son of the Patriarch, might become a center of attention, but except for Czor-Dziit of Dziit Pride, who asked his story and listened while he told it, he seemed to draw no special interest.

While the sun was still low C'mell leapt over to teach Pouncer the art of *mazourk*, guiding the ponderous beasts with the heavy wooden harness bar connected to the network of reins that controlled them. The harness bar, Ayla learned, and in fact the whole travel platform, were built of aromatic *myewl* wood timbers. Evidently the leafy bush could grow to a tree as well, and it served to suppress the scent of predator enough to keep the *tuskvor* from attacking their riders.

"Can I try it?" Ayla asked after the lesson.

C'mell looked questioningly at V'rli, who growled her assent. And Cherenkova took the harness bar under the kzinrette's tutelage. The harness bar levered the harness lines. Pushing forward lowered them to pull the beast's head down and slow it, pulling back raised its head to speed it up, pull left to turn left and right to turn right. In theory it was simple; in practice, it was a lot more difficult. She was barely strong enough to haul the bar back and forth, and it took some understanding of the *tuskvor*'s mood and personality to make it work. Even a kzin couldn't exert enough strength to force a *tuskvor*'s head around against its will, but an even steady pressure would induce it to turn, and its body would eventually follow. Jerking the bar or trying to turn the *tuskvor* too far out of the tide of the migration would make the creature balk, and then it would pull back against the harness hard enough to slam the bar across its guideposts, and break an arm in the process if the *mazourk* weren't quick about getting out of the way. A balky *tuskvor* had to be calmed by gently pulling the harness one way and then the other, convincing it that the pressure it felt was perfectly normal. It took a lot of muscular effort and she began to wish she hadn't asked for the privilege.

C'mell rippled her ears every time the *tuskvor* threw

Cherenkova around. "You look like a *vatach* challenge-leaping a *grlor,*" she said, after a particularly nasty balk. Ayla clenched her jaw and hung on grimly, determined not give up before she'd shown she could handle the basics. She was exhausted and soaked with sweat by the time she was finished. She napped with the pride while the sun was high, and when she woke up she discovered a whole new set of muscles, all of which ached from their unaccustomed use. Fortunately the beasts just followed the herd when left to themselves. On the migration the harness bars were only necessary if you wanted to guide your *tuskvor* next to another one so you could talk to someone. There was no need for her to take regular steering shifts.

The trackway beneath them was pounded into dust, and behind them, where the foothills flattened into the plains, the living river broke up into a network of gray tributaries, fading into invisibility against the backdrop of the jungle verge, now barely visible as a green mist on the horizon. She could see now that the trackway path itself was actually recessed, worn into the landscape after countless generations of migration over this exact route. The migration was an awesome sight, a primeval force of nature, as vast and inexorable as the tides. If a comet were to strike in the middle of it tens of thousands of *tuskvor* would die, incinerated in a fraction of a second, but, she had no doubt, the tens of tens of thousands more who survived would continue inexorably on their genetically programmed course, implacably negotiating the still steaming crater rim, traveling across the scorched, sterilized landscape until they struggled out the other side, indifferent to everything but the compulsion to move east and south with the change of the seasons.

The next day saw them to the Long Range, and the rolling savannah that covered the foothills gave way to alpine forests, and then high meadows dotted with wildflowers. Higher still, the grasses came only in tufts on a landscape built of rock and crags. The way became steep and their *tsvasztet* tilted alarmingly as their *tuskvor* took the grade. For a time Cherenkova feared it would slide free, or she would slide free of it, but the straps held. Frost appeared and the air grew chill, and soon the world was white, with snow-capped mountains rearing above them. The chill became bitter cold, and their waterskins slowly froze solid. Cherenkova slept that night huddled between Pouncer and Quicktail, as warm as any kitten cuddled close to its siblings.

Some time before dawn she awoke to realize that the tilt of the *tsvasztet* had leveled out. She stood up to see the migration forging its way through a glacier-carved pass between two vast, craggy peaks. The Traveler's Moon was overtaking the Hunter's Moon overhead, both nearly full and casting a soft, mystical light that made the entire scene seem unreal. The air was crystal clear, thin enough that breathing was hard, and cold enough to burn her skin, erectile tissue stiffening to raise wispy hairs no longer capable of providing insulation. She rubbed her arms against the goosebumps but didn't dive back to the warmth of her living fur blanket. The stars were out, the Milky Way spilled across the sky as a familiar background to alien constellations that blazed with an intensity she had seen nowhere except a warship's bridge. It was a moment, she realized, that would never occur again in her life, that no other human had ever experienced and, almost certainly, no other human would ever experience again. She watched until she could not watch any longer, until she was shivering uncontrollably, until she could no longer hold her eyes open. By then the *tsvasztet* had tilted downward again as the *tuskvor* found the downgrade, and she slid back between the two kzinti to let their body heat melt the chill from her bones. As a little girl she had dreamed of going to the stars, of seeing sights that no one else had ever seen before, of discovering things that no one else had even imagined might exist. There had been a time when she had nursed an unearthly fear that she might die before she could make that a reality. That fear had long since faded as she earned first her wings and then command rank, acquiring a record that any officer might envy. Still, *this* was something unique, something to tell her grandchildren, if she ever had any, and she fell asleep with the knowledge that she had satisfied a hunger she had almost forgotten she had had.

She dreamed then, of a kill drop, a cliff five thousand feet high, with the *tuskvor* herd surging blindly toward it. Those at the front balked, rearing back, and the herd began to pile up on the cliff's edge. For a moment the vast migration paused, and then the unrelentingly building pressure of the following beasts began to push those at the front forward. A mid-sized adolescent skidded, stumbled and pitched over the edge, bellowing in uncomprehending fear, and then suddenly the river of flesh became a living waterfall, as *tuskvor* after *tuskvor* dropped over the edge to die on the jagged rocks far below. The kzinti leapt from back to back to escape in desperate bounds, but Ayla could not make such leaps, could only watch helplessly as her beast was pushed ever closer to the precipice. She looked across to the next great gray back, a good ten meters away, looked down an equal distance to where walls of flesh pressed together above heavy, trampling feet. It was death if she stayed, and death if she leapt, but if she leapt she would die trying to save herself, and that made all the difference. She gathered herself, and then suddenly Pouncer was there, lifting her like a rag doll and leaping himself, just as their *tuskvor* slipped and fell over the edge. They were airborne for an eternity, and then the kzin landed, claws finding purchase in the thick, tough coat of another herd grandmother, his muscles straining as he fought his way up its back, only to gather himself and leap again, as that beast too stumbled and plunged over the edge. The dream became a nightmare, with Cherenkova hanging on desperately as Pouncer leapt and leapt, tiring steadily but never gaining ground against the tide of the herd. She knew she should let go, should sacrifice herself to allow him to save himself, but her fingers were locked in his mane in a death grip and she couldn't have let go if she tried, and they were both going to die, and then they were airborne again, this time falling as the *tuskvor* they had just landed on pitched forward and over.

And she was floating, falling weightless and surrounded by two-hundred-ton beasts that bellowed in panic and flailed as they fell. And she remembered the first time she was weightless, eighteen years ago now, a cadet pilot in a Rapier trainer on her first familiarization flight, and the instructor had boosted them ballistic and then cut the power and handed her control as they dropped into freefall, just to see what she could do. And she had found at that moment that she could fly. She had dreamed of it all her life, studied hard every night to make the academy, learned the drills by heart, flown the simulators until she could do it blindfolded, dreamed every night of the time she would make it real, but nothing, nothing had prepared her for the feeling of *flying* as she had then, as she was now.

And she was flying, not falling, she had control, and she could save herself, but Pouncer was falling too. She dove then, stooping like a falcon on its prey through air churned violent by the huge thrashing beasts. She dodged flailing tusks, lost sight of him for a moment, then all at once she had caught him. She strained upward then but he was heavy and whatever it was that gave her the buoyancy to fly wasn't powerful enough to arrest his downward momentum, and what she should have done was abandon him but she would not, could not, because he had given his life trying to save her and she could do no less for him, and they plunged down to die together on blood-slick stone amid the shattered bones of the *tuskvor*.

She awoke with a start, and shook her head to rid it of the unsettling images. It was the mountain climber's rule. *Thin air brings strange dreams.* It was one thing to understand where her dream had come from, another to let go of the uncomfortable feelings it gave her. The air was warmer than it had been, and soon 61 Ursae Majoris was rising to show the mountains already receding behind them, the air parched and dusty as they descended to the broad desert plateau opening up in front of them. It would take days to cross it, and already the migration was showing the cost of the march. There were dead *tuskvor* by the wayside, at first rarely, then more often. They were mostly youngsters or small mothers who had entered the migration without the reserves to finish it, occasionally a huge grandmother or male grown too old for the journey. Stragglers tended to be forced to the edges of the migration stream, and when they died the first to arrive were the circling *hrhan*, soaring scavengers with fifteen-meter wingspans and long, snaky necks, who tore at the bodies with razor fangs. Later the *wralarv* would appear, lumbering, shaggy and savage; they looked small in the vastness of the scene, but the smallest of them would have feared nothing from a polar bear. It occurred to her to wonder what it was that drove the *tuskvor* to undertake such an arduous journey. Even the jungle in the dry season was a more forgiving environment than the burning desert.

The sun was high on the second day in the desert when a *tuskvor* slid alongside hers with ponderous grace. Cherenkova was developing an eye for the delicate art of *tuskvor* handling. The *mazourk* was C'mell, and Ayla put down her beltcomp and watched with some envy at the kzinrette's casual skill at her task. A kzintosh leapt from its back to their own travel pad. It took her a moment to recognize him. Sraff-Tracker.

V'rli was lying languidly on her *prrstet*, half napping, half keeping an eye on the harness bars while the *tuskvor* strode along. Pouncer and Ferlitz were gone, having leapt off to socialize early in the morning.

V'rli turned her head. "Sraff-Tracker. Welcome."

Sraff-Tracker made the gesture-of-abasement,

although to Cherenkova's eye it seemed sloppy. "Honored Mother. I come with a question."

V'rli rippled her ears. "I am here with an answer. Perhaps it applies to your question."

"Honored Mother, the Traveler's Moon is well past its cusp."

"That is true, Sraff-Tracker. What is the question?"

"The time of sanctuary is over. Why do we still shelter this outcast and his pet?" He gestured at Cherenkova without looking at her. "We have fulfilled our obligations, and more."

"Pouncer fought with us. His sister died to defend our den. Even the Cherenkova-Captain played its part, and played it well."

Sraff-Tracker snarled. "The *kz'zeerkti*, whatever tricks it can do, it is prey, nothing more. Provisions on some of the *tuskvor* are running low."

"And Pouncer?" If V'rli noted the threat to Cherenkova she ignored it.

"His time of sanctuary is over."

"It was not over when we began the migration. Would you have him jump into the herd now?"

"If we had not taken him in, the Tzaatz would not have come at all." Sraff-Tracker avoided the question.

"Are you saying we should have ignored the tradition of Sanctuary?"

"I am saying that his presence here puts us all at risk."

V'rli snarled. "Did you know a Black Priest led the enemy? He will be seeking more than the heir to the Patriarchy, depend upon it. The world has changed, Sraff-Tracker. The Tzaatz remain a danger."

"Honored Mother! What of tradition? We gave him sanctuary, now that is done. He *must* leave."

"What of honor? Does Ztrak Pride toss out Heroes who fight our fight beside us? His sister died for us, Sraff-Tracker. He has earned his place at our pride circle."

"He has no name!"

"When we reach the high forest den he can take a namequest."

"You must compel him to leave. Tradition demands it."

V'rli let her fangs show. "I will not. Migration began before his sanctuary ended."

"Then I will challenge him and he will die before the sun is down."

"Duels are forbidden on the migration, Sraff-Tracker. That too is tradition."

Sraff-Tracker just snarled, and leapt back to his *tsvasztet*. He climbed from the pad to the platform and snarled something at C'mell, who pulled the harness bar and smoothly guided her *tuskvor* away. V'rli let her eyes slide shut and went back to sleep.

Ayla spent some more time practicing with the harness bar. Their *tuskvor* seemed to be in a particularly uncooperative mood, and she privately named it "Camel." While she grunted and strained to get the recalcitrant animal to go where she wanted it, she thought about Sraff-Tracker's visit. *He represents a danger. Why does he see Pouncer as a threat? Is it C'mell?* She knew little of kzinti mating habits, and she suspected that the rules were very different in a social structure where the kzinretti were more than simple property. She didn't like Sraff-Tracker, hadn't liked him since the day they'd met Tzaatz Pride and he'd decided he'd like to eat her. *So do I warn Pouncer? It should fall to V'rli, but what if she doesn't tell him?* She spent some time mulling that question. She didn't want to get involved in the pride's internal dynamics. *But Pouncer is my ally, and my friend.* She would tell him if V'rli did not.

V'rli made it easy for her. She just told Pouncer, "Sraff-Tracker wants you to leave the Pride."

"Will you support him in this?"

"No."

"Then I will stay, Honored Mother, as long as I and the Cherenkova-Captain are welcome."

V'rli turned a paw over. "You have spilled blood for us, First-Son-of-Meerz-Rrit, and so I stretched the tradition to take you on the migration. You would not have made it to Mrrsel Pride before they had left on their own journey. If you are to stay with Ztrak Pride you will need to complete a namequest."

"I have already decided on my quest, Honored Mother."

"What will you do?"

"I will reclaim the Patriarchy from my traitorous brother and the Tzaatz who stole it for him. I will take back my inheritance."

"You said as much when you first came to us. I thought you might have tempered your desire."

"I am resolved."

V'rli fanned her ears up. "No one here doubts your courage, Pouncer. Do not bring us to doubt your wisdom. Choose another quest, one you can hope to complete."

"I did not choose this quest; Kchula-Tzaatz chose it for me. Honor allows me no other course."

"It is too soon for vengeance. A namequest must be completed alone, and what you speak of requires a campaign."

"And if I alone lead this campaign?"

"You are no longer a kitten, but you are not yet a warrior. Who will follow you?"

"You will, I hope, and where you lead, Ztrak Pride will follow. Perhaps my mother's pride will follow me as well, and where two prides of *czrav* lead perhaps the others will come too. The Tzaatz will have weaknesses, and we will find them and exploit them."

V'rli looked at him for a long time. "Do you know the story of the *krwisatz*?"

"The-pebble-that-trips-pouncer-or-prey. I know it."

"I think you may indeed be *krwisatz*, Pouncer, for Ztrak Pride, for the *czrav*, perhaps for all kzinti, and most of all for yourself." She paused, looking into the bloodred sunset. "Be sure you trip the prey, and not the Pouncer."

It was the first time V'rli had used his familiar name. There was weight in the moment, acceptance with the warning. Even Cherenkova understood the significance there. Pouncer made the gesture-of-obeisance-to-wisdom. "I will heed your advice, Honored Mother."

A *tuskvor* came alongside theirs and a dark shape leapt onto their journeypad—Quicktail. V'rli raised her tail as he clambered onto the platform. "And now my favorite storyteller"—she fanned her ears up— "Tell us a tale, Quicktail. Give us the scent of something worth tracking." She wrapped her tail around her feet.

"This is the story of wise K'ailng . . ." Quicktail began,

settling down in the center of the platform. "Who had traveled far from his homeland, and one day . . ."

The kzinti leaned forward on their *prrstet* as the youngster wove his words into a story. Cherenkova listened too, lying next to Pouncer for warmth against the gathering chill of the desert night. She idly rubbed the fur on his neck, provoking a muted rumble of a purr. It was a comforting action, almost intimate, that the kzin half tolerated and half enjoyed. *Who is the pet here?* She smiled at that thought. Ztrak Pride was becoming his pride, and it was becoming Cherenkova's pride too. V'rli was solidly on their side. In the background the creak of the *tsvasztet* and the occasional grunt of the *tuskvor* were overlaid on the vast rumble of the migration's steady pace, constant, reassuring sounds like the throbbing engines of a ship at sea. Quicktail's story was compelling, but she found herself unable to shake a vague unease. *Sraff-Tracker is dangerous. He doesn't want us in his pride. We're a problem for him, and he isn't going to leave it alone.*

Through birth and death, the Pride lives on.
—Wisdom of the Conservers

The Circle of Conservers was an ancient fortification, built high on a mountain crag jutting vertically up from the warm waters of the Southern Sea. Unlike those of the Citadel of the Patriarch its defenses hadn't been modernized, or even maintained, in the eons since vertical cliffs and deep water were considered strong protections against any foe. The massive walls were still there, and the towers, but the network of defensive tunnels beneath it was long collapsed. The walls had lost their crenellations, the towers' arrow slits had been widened into windows, or filled in entirely. In the courtyard, well tended grasses grew where mighty siege engines had once stood ready to sink the ships of an invader. The massive gates were long gone, leaving only an empty archway, and the untended gatehouses had long since crumbled. The only thing to stop an intruder was the steep, winding trail from sea level to the mountaintop.

Rrit-Conserver paused by the gates, breathing deeply, his limbs sore from a Hunter's Moon of walking, finished by the final climb. The arduous path was obstacle enough, but the real reason for the fortress's decayed defenses was that it had been protected from time immemorial by something much more powerful, tradition. The Conservers maintained the traditions in the Patriarchy, and one of the strongest was that only a Conserver could enter the bastion of their calling. Not even Patriarchs were permitted to violate its sanctity, and with good reason. Only by preserving impartiality could the Conservers be trusted to judge for the benefit of the race. Even the perception of bias would destroy that trust.

Fifth Custodian greeted him at the gate and showed him to his usual quarters, an austere room in what had once been the main keep. He stayed only long enough to drop his scant belongings and groom himself, then hurried to the central. A winding staircase led to a heavy stonewood door bound in iron, behind it a room full of the quiet whir of medical machinery, much of it attached to a wizened figure lying on an instrumented *prrstet*: Kzin-Conserver.

The old kzin looked up as Rrit-Conserver came in, his ears furling up in surprise. "My old friend, what are you doing here?"

Rrit-Conserver made the half-abasement. "I have come to see you, sire. I was worried."

"You should be in the Citadel. These are critical times for the Patriarchy."

"Scrral-Rrit has dishonored himself. I am free of my oath of fealty."

"What did he do?"

"Does it matter?"

"No. Nor am I surprised." Kzin-Conserver's ears relaxed. "You might have advised Kchula-Tzaatz instead."

"Kchula-Tzaatz is as dishonored as Scrral-Rrit, he just hides too well for *ztrarr*. And he will not take my advice."

"Hrrr. I had to force him to put you into their councils. I'd hoped you might provide some balance." The old kzin reclined again, suddenly tired.

"Sire." Rrit-Conserver stepped to the *prrstet*, put a paw on his mentor's shoulder. "How are you?"

"I am dying." Kzin-Conserver struggled to raise his head again. "Which is a welcome thought, when I live like this."

"There are treatments . . ." Rrit-Conserver waved a paw to the medical equipment surrounding them.

"To what end? That I may lie gasping on this *prrstet* and fantasize that I guide that Patriarchy? My life is over. I don't need it anymore."

"You have lived your life well, sire."

"Perhaps. I have abandoned the traditions to hold the Patriarchy together. I am ashamed of that, and also afraid I was still too inflexible."

"You did what you had to for the species. Your decision was balanced."

"In the end it will make little difference. The Patriarchy is dying too."

"No, there is hope yet."

"Hope?" Some of the old fire came back to Kzin-Conserver's voice. "The *kz'zeerkti* are coming, mark my words. Scrral-Rrit is nothing, though we all pretend he is Patriarch to avoid the consequences if he were not. As for Kchula-Tzaatz, the Great Prides will call him leader while they storm to conquest, but when we face the full might of the monkeys they will abandon him. A Traveler's Moon later they'll be at each other's throats." Kzin-Conserver coughed painfully. "We have been a proud race for a long time. I'm glad I won't live to see the end of that."

"We are still a proud race, sire, and First-Son-of-Meerz-Rrit is alive."

"He escaped!" Kzin-Conserver sat upright, reenergized. "I knew that *sthondat* Tzaatz was hiding something. Have you *zatrarr*?"

"No, I knew before that the Tzaatz had not killed him. Now I have the word of a *kzintzag* warrior who helped him escape. He fights the Tzaatz and leads others, and he got a message to me through a slave. His name is Far Hunter."

"Far Hunter. A promising name." Kzin-Conserver relaxed back onto the *prrstet*, breathing heavily after his exertion. "Perhaps there is hope yet." He closed his eyes, speaking slowly. "You will be Kzin-Conserver after me. I have told Senior Custodian."

"I am honored, sire." It was an honor Rrit-Conserver would rather not have had to accept.

"It is a poor gift, in these times. Do your best with it." Kzin-Conserver waved a paw. "Let me rest now. Come back tomorrow." The old kzin's eyes slid closed.

"As you wish." But Rrit-Conserver knew there would be no chance to come back tomorrow and so stayed in silence, his paw on his mentor's shoulder providing what comfort could be given until the end.

They think we don't have weapons? Today we'll show them what a mass driver can do.
—Captain Sael Pollonia at the defense of Luna City (First Man-Kzin War)

Oorwinnig had conducted her test run at the system's edge to hide her capabilities from enemy eyes. Alpha Centauri had lots of kzinti, a decent number of other aliens and more than its fair share of human pirates, freerunners and outlaws who would quite happily sell their species out, so long as the profit margins were high enough. Her tests completed, she plunged back toward the central star. Tskombe did not see Captain Voortman again, and spent the remainder of the voyage with Trina and Curvy. Alpha Cen A itself grew from a dim fourth magnitude star to a burning disk, still small enough to look at directly with the naked eye but putting out as much light as the full moon on Earth. They docked at Tiamat, the largest asteroid of the Serpent Swarm. Tiamat was a potato-shaped mixture of rock and nickel-iron, fifty kilometers by twenty, spun on its long access to generate artificial gravity in the time before humanity gained the grav polarizer. It housed five million humans in its vast warrens, a hundred thousand kzinti, half that many Kdatlyno and Jotok, and a handful of other aliens, all of them the detritus of generations of war. It was the Free Wunderland Navy's major military base, and the economic powerhouse that made the economy of the Centaurus system the showpiece of the UN colonization effort.

Khalsa had planned to land *Valiant* on wide-open Wunderland. Tiamat presented a problem; the sealed world was under even tighter surveillance than Earth. Tskombe was worried about clearing customs, not for himself but for Trina. The UN had a lot of unofficial clout on Tiamat, but they operated in Centaurus System purely as invited guests with no administrative or governmental power, a compromise arrangement arrived at after a long and frequently bloody struggle with the Isolationists and their political arm, the Free Wunderland Party. Even if the ARM on Earth had hyperwaved Tskombe's ident to the Goldskin cops, the Goldskins wouldn't tag it until the UN had cut their way through the jungle of red tape required to get an Earth warrant recognized in the system. Trina's total lack of an ident was a different matter, but as it turned out he needn't have worried about that either. Curvy spoke to the Goldskin running the customs checkpoint, and shortly thereafter an ARM showed up to usher them through the formalities. The UN's left hand didn't know what the right was doing, not yet anyway. They were given senior quarters in the UN section on the one-gee level. The accommodation people shut down the section's swimming pool for Curvy and arranged fresh fish from Tiamat's aquaculture farms. Another ARM, an attractive blonde woman, took Trina to shop for clothes. Tskombe took the opportunity to go for a swim himself, a rare luxury, and he paddled steadily back and forth while Curvy leapt and played amid the darting trout, getting the exercise that she'd been denied in transit and snapping down fresh fish. Eventually they both tired, and Tskombe climbed out of the water to towel himself off.

"I thought we'd be in trouble without Khalsa to grease the wheels."

Curvy came over and nosed herself deftly into her hand-suit. "Khalsa worked on my authority. I have sufficient rank within the UN to command resources as required."

"You do?"

"Yes, of course. I am the UN's senior matrix strategist. My talents are unique, and so they were anxious to secure my services. I am not part of the human hierarchy so they must convince me to work for them. My price, part of my price, has been freedom of movement within human space, facilitated by the UN. Ravalla will want us captured, but his organization is facing many challenges in consolidating power. We are a small detail, and now outside his sphere of direct influence. It will take the bureaucracy a long time to catch up with us here."

Tskombe shook his head. *I knew that, why didn't I make the connection?* "If you have this much influence, why didn't you just request me through normal channels back on earth?"

"We were working to that end through General Tobin.

However, it was a sensitive situation. If WarSec were caught intervening in political affairs it would generate bad matrix outcomes. In general, we therefore avoid it. Still, matrix analysis has indicated that the elevation of Secretary Ravalla to Secretary General will almost certainly lead to war, and perhaps to the revocation of democratic principles on Earth, and ultimately throughout human space. Ravalla's personality profile is dangerous, even for a politician."

"Do you actually believe you can make predictions in that detail?"

"Predictions can be made to an arbitrarily high level of detail, with the probability of correctness falling as an exponential function of specificity." Curvy whistled something that her translator did not translate. "You seek to understand the functional limits within which we can expect to be accurate. We successfully predicted the nature and outcome of the power play that lead to Ravalla's election, within the constraints of our error bars. Admittedly he moved at the earliest possible time. Unfortunately our freedom of action was too limited to allow us to stop it, given the limited amount of warning that our model gave. Launching you to Kzinhome was our best available strategy to prevent war. I have since updated the matrix. The probability lapsed chance of your success is one point four percent."

Tskombe kicked himself to the side of the pool and levered himself out of the water. "That hardly seems worth the effort."

"You do not understand, Colonel Tskombe. To have a one percent influence on the course of history is tremendous power. Most individuals have so little influence as to be irrelevant. You are in a privileged position."

"Privileged with one point four percent." Tskombe thought about that. "And what about the other ninety-eight point six percent?"

"There are a variety of potential outcomes. The most probable is your death on Kzinhome at seventy-six point one percent, followed by your death on approach to Kzinhome, at twelve point nine percent, followed by a variety of outcomes in which you survive but are unable to prevent the war."

Tskombe smirked humorlessly. "At least I've got a better than one point eight chance of living."

"No." Curvy missed the humor. "In a scenario where you survive to see the war start your chances of surviving the conflict are in line with those of all sentients in human or kzinti space, which is to say close to zero. In addition, there are several sub-scenarios in which you are likely to prevent war but are unlikely to survive personally."

Not encouraging. "And what is the chance I'll find Ayla on Kzinhome?"

"Unknown. She was removed from the strategic matrix when you returned from your mission. Probability assessment indicates she is almost certainly dead. If not, her circumstances are so extreme that her role is not quantifiable. Hence we cannot compute outcomes in which she plays a part."

Tskombe fell quiet. Having it put in those stark terms made it clear just how daunting a task he was undertaking. Better, perhaps, to cut his losses while he could. Except, as Curvy had pointed out, if he didn't succeed he was likely to die in a war of mutual annihilation along with almost everyone else. *Damned if you do, damned if you don't.*

Curvy swam away to catch another trout. When she came back, she stuck her head out of the water and whistled again. "Colonel Tskombe, we must discuss Trina and her psi talent."

"Okay."

"You speculated that she was preternaturally lucky."

"Only a theory, with virtually no support."

"I have thought about this in some detail. It is a theory which fits my own experience playing chess with her. In speed chess an amateur has the opportunity to make lucky moves and so win against an expert, because the expert cannot play a deep game. In a standard game the most phenomenal luck will not suffice for victory."

Tskombe nodded. "I've been thinking about that too. Luck has operating parameters."

"Explain please."

"I can kill myself slipping in the shower . . ." Curvy interrupted with an interrogative whistle. Her translator belatedly said "What?" She was unfamiliar with showers, of course, but Tskombe had already started elaborating. "A small fall is potentially fatal, although that's an unlikely outcome. A fall of five meters will probably injure you, I mean a human, unless you are trained to handle it. A fall of thirty meters usually kills, but not invariably. Some lucky individuals have survived falls of ten thousand meters through lucky landings, in deep snow usually. But no one has ever survived a fall from orbit. Reentry is too extreme a regime for luck to play a role."

Curvy whistled, rising and falling "I count myself lucky that I do not belong to a species subject to falls."

Tskombe laughed. *I recognize that whistle . . .* Curvy was making a joke. "We have a long way to fall from where we are now."

Another whistle, this one on a falling note. "Your point is taken, Colonel Tskombe."

"So is yours. So the question is, how far in advance can luck operate?"

"As far as is necessary, it would seem."

"No, it can't be like that. Imagine you had luck, not just because someone has to be on the lucky end of the bell curve and that turns out to be you, but because you had a psi talent that could locally influence events. Did some prehistoric mammal return to the oceans because millions of years in the future you, Curvy, would be born, and being born into an aquatic species would protect you from falls? Impossible, because part of what allowed you to be born in the first place was the evolution of dolphins, including the speculative evolution of genes for a psi talent that makes you lucky. You could not have been born anything but a dolphin; if you weren't, you wouldn't be you. To say otherwise would be to imply that every event in your species history—in all of evolution, in all of the universe—had been scripted simply to bring about your existence."

Curvy clicked. "Such megalomania is a common human conceit."

"Perhaps, but only a conceit in that defying the tremendous odds against your birth doesn't make you special. If you consider the infinitesimal chance of that one particular sperm out of billions combining with one particular egg out of tens of thousands to form you, the odds against your parents even meeting, against their birth, against your grandparents being born and meeting to produce them, it's easy to convince yourself that you *are* special. If a trillion trillion universes ran a trillion trillion times we would not expect to see you born even once. What more evidence of your total uniqueness do you require?"

"You commit the gambler's fallacy. A coin flip may come up heads ten thousand times in a row. The odds that it will come up tails next time remain fifty percent. Of the incomprehensibly huge space of possible evolutionary tracks, some tiny fraction must be followed. We happen to be on the track that has developed, which is no more or less likely than any other track which may have been followed from any given start point, but because we happen to be on this one we are here to discuss our good fortune in existing in the first place, whereas the uncountable legions of potential individuals who remained unborn are perforce unable to discuss their own circumstances. We cannot discuss probabilities post-facto, because events have already transformed them into certainties."

"Yes, but in a very real sense you inherit your parents' luck. Your father didn't drown while fishing at the age of twelve. Your mother wandered between a mother bear and her cubs at eighteen, but the bear didn't attack. All of this luck is required to even get you born."

Again the rising and falling whistle. "While it is possible that my father could have drowned while fishing, I am certain my mother never came between a bear and her cubs."

"You know what I mean, and it goes further. Some anonymous person you will never know fixed a hidden fault in a tube car which therefore didn't crash and kill them both on their honeymoon." Tskombe held up a hand. "Yes, I know they never rode a tube car or had a honeymoon either. The point is, there is an immense, maybe infinite, universe of non-events which are as pivotal as the actual events which do occur."

"Granted."

"So luck has operating parameters. You can be lucky and catch a shuttle by seconds, or lucky and miss a shuttle that's going to crash, or lucky and catch the shuttle and survive the crash. So we can imagine some mechanism that tips the scales one way or another, which implies some form of feedback from future to past, some kind of macro scale collapse of the quantum wave function. But there is a limit. Some things, like attempting reentry in a space suit, luck simply cannot influence. If luck is going to operate on something like that it has to *prevent* you from being in that situation in the first place, but it cannot have an infinite time-horizon either. It can't reach back before you were born to ensure that you *are* born. Neither can it see indefinitely into the future to sculpt events now to suit you then."

Curvy whistled. "Luck is by definition post-facto. To take your example, you don't know if it's lucky to catch the shuttle at the last minute until you land safely at your destination."

"Not even then. Disaster might hit after you land."

"Point taken. Also, the universe of might-have-beens contingent upon your missing the shuttle can, and probably does, include some that are extraordinary and tremendously beneficial. You can never know if any given actual outcome is in fact the most beneficial outcome, although you can speculate."

"So how can you even recognize luck then?"

"In this sense, luck is ultimately unknowable. We can only apply crude statistical measurements. It is unlikely that a person experiences the most fortuitous possible outcome in every circumstance. We can only measure the relative frequency of such outcomes in comparison with another person to arrive at some sense of how lucky they are in fact."

Tskombe nodded. "So there is a limit to both the magnitude of luck's influence on events and the distance in time forward and backward with which luck can exert that influence."

"If there is such a mechanism it must always operate forward in time, although we can only recognize its operation backward in time."

"So what are we saying about Trina? Her life history doesn't seem particularly lucky. At the same time, lots of psi talents develop around adolescence. Perhaps it's just kicking in now."

"That remains speculation. All we can say about Trina is what we have directly observed. She wins at speed chess and defies statistical probability at guessing cards. This may not even be construed as luck."

"What else can it be construed as?"

"Luck is only definable in relationship to positive and negative event outcomes. There is no significant outcome, in terms of her life or well-being, associated with either beating me at speed chess or correctly guessing cards."

"She also survived an attack by a UNF cruiser. By all rights we should all be dead, or prisoners at best."

"Yes, but there is only a single point on that graph. We cannot compute any post-facto probabilities from it. And you and I also survived that attack"

"So what next?"

"With your permission I would like to keep her with me. The graph will grow data points."

Tskombe thought about that. He had thought to deliver Trina to Wunderland's Bureau of Displaced Persons. He had acted on instinct, but now that she was on Tiamat he was going to have to leave her. She was a smart kid, and perhaps also a very lucky one, but the Serpent Swarm was as rough an environment as NYC's gray zones. Curvy had the ability to command resources and could get around on Tiamat. Trina was smart, but her unregistered status had kept her from education after her parents died. Curvy could get that set up, he was sure. It was a good solution.

"Yes," he said. "That's a good idea."

His UNF ident was still valid on Tiamat. He set up an account with the Swarm Central Bank and transferred his electronic cash balance from his beltcomp, breathing a sigh of relief that all his financial eggs were no longer in a basket he had to carry himself. The next step was to board a tube-car heading for Tigertown, the high-gee section of the asteroid where most of its kzinti population lived. He needed transport to Kzinhome. Curvy couldn't supply that because the UNF wouldn't supply that, and a UNF ship wouldn't be welcome anyway. He needed a kzinti ship, and he had to find it himself.

He drew no comment at the Tigertown tube station, though he drew looks. There were a few other humans in the crowd, but no other aliens. There were Jotoki and Kdatlyno on Tiamat, former kzinti slaves, but they didn't choose to associate with their former masters. For the humans who now held the whip hand around Alpha Centauri the dynamic was different. There were seventy five thousand kzinti in Tigertown, more or less, most of the kzinti population on the rock. It was a rough area, less finished than the rest of the station, no slidewalks, bare rock walls with fixtures bolted to them. The air was full of the gingery scent of kzinti, and the corridors bustled with activity. Persleds and cargo floats jostling past auctioneers and rabbit vendors with cages of frightened bunnies, stock long ago imported from Earth by humans. Buyers and sellers haggled over the prices in loud snarls. *Strakh* might have been the medium of exchange on Kzinhome, but on Tiamat the kzinti charged in hard kroner. He followed the main corridors, not quite sure what he was looking for.

What he found was a bar, or whatever it was that kzinti congregated in to eat raw meat and drink alcohol. He went in, saw glassy-surfaced tables and chairs lasered from Tiamat's substance, decorated wall hangings that he hoped weren't made of human skin, swords and weapons displayed on the walls. A few dozen kzinti sat in tight-knit groups, talking in muted snarls or wolfing down large platters of unidentified raw meat. One table held two men and a woman who looked him over coldly, then went back to their business. A large area at the back was roped off and full of sand, and screams and snarls rose over the sound dampers as a pair of kzinti dueled in front of an appreciative crowd. As he drew closer, Tskombe saw that the combatants had bright blue pads fitted that shielded their claws. The crowd was juiced up, fangs exposed and tails whipping back and forth with the action. There would be more duels before the night was over, not all of them in the ring with claws blunted. Past the dueling floor, food and drink service was over-the-counter, more laser-cut stone polished mirror-bright. The proprietor was a big kzin, shaggy-coated and muscular, assisted by a pair of still-spotted adolescents.

The proprietor looked up, saw him and leapt easily over the counter. He met Tskombe halfway across the floor and spoke. "This is not a place for humans." He spoke English with a Swarm Belter accent, thick enough that it took Tskombe a moment to figure out what he'd said.

"I seek a pilot . . ." Tskombe snarled the words in the Hero's Tongue.

"Seek elsewhere." The big kzin's ears had fanned up in surprise when Tskombe spoke his native language, but that wasn't enough to change his mind. He put a softly padded paw on Tskombe's shoulder. Four faint needlepricks warned of the not-quite retracted claws.

Tskombe nodded at the humans, now studiously ignoring him. "They aren't elsewhere."

"Different. Old customers. You will leave now for your own safety." The grip on Tskombe's shoulder tightened and the kzin pushed, gently but firmly, toward the door. There was no point in arguing, or fighting. He left quietly.

Back in the corridor he drew more looks, most of them carefully neutral. Now what? He didn't imagine he would get a warmer welcome elsewhere in Tigertown, but trying to reach a kzinti pilot by working his way through the human underworld would be both more difficult, in that there would be more middlemen to try to work through, and more dangerous, in that the one hand of the UN might find out what the other hand was up to and arrest him. No, he needed to make contact as directly as possible with a kzin, the only problem being that no kzin was likely to talk to him about anything remotely illegal just in case he was setting them up. Come to think of it, no human would either. He was used to his UNF rank and position opening doors for him, but that was because he wasn't used to moving in the underworld.

Time to get used to a new world. Humans could be accepted in Tigertown, the group he'd seen inside clearly were. So now what?

So now wait, get a feel for the area. He found a smoother spot in the rough-hewn rock wall and settled down to watch the crowd go by. Tigertown lacked the extensive vid surveillance of the rest of the asteroid, so no security team would swoop down to get him moving again. It was just a matter of time. He watched the traffic in and out of the bar. The noise swelling out into the corridor grew over time, the general background noise occasionally overridden by some loudly declaimed poetry in the Hero's Tongue. A couple of times screams and snarls told him the dueling floor was in use. Once a small group of kzinti carried out a limp and bloodied body and vanished with it down the corridor. Tskombe couldn't tell if it was alive or dead.

The ARM left the kzinti to police Tigertown themselves, and it seemed they didn't do much of it.

Time dragged and eventually he got up and moved on. He tried to start conversations with various vendors, but none were interested in more than the formalities required to sell their wares. He walked further, learning the lay of the land. The crowds never seemed to thin out. Officially Tiamat ran on Wunderland's twenty-eight-hour day, but a large percentage of the population worked shifts, either for the various military organizations there or the asteroid's nonstop high-technology industries. In turn they drove a demand for continuously available services. Combined with the constant artificial lighting, that made night and day largely abstract concepts. He was going through a corridor past a series of small manufacturers and custom tronshops when a challenge duel broke out in front of him. A ring of spectators formed around the combatants. Tskombe couldn't see past the wall of carnivores. *Discretion is the better part of valor.* Traffic in the corridor was blocked, so he went to one side, put his back against the wall, and waited. Five minutes later the fight was over and traffic resumed as quickly as it had stopped. The victor in the fight was nowhere to be seen. The loser was lying in the middle of the corridor, being ignored by everyone, stepped on by those whose path he happened to be in.

Move on or get involved? *Decision time.* The smart thing would be to move on, no need to wade into a situation he had no understanding of. He started to walk, then thought again. He needed to start somewhere. The injured kzin would at least have to talk to him, and he might be able to provide a lead. *And I can't just leave him there.* He went over to the kzin, helped him to his feet. One leg dragged badly and his arm seemed to be broken. Tskombe took him to a side tunnel, found a quiet spot sitting on a box behind some stacked cargo flats swaddled in quickwrap. The kzin was groggy and gasping for breath, bleeding from a torn ear and with one eye swollen shut.

He shook his head, his one good eye focusing on Tskombe for the first time.

His nostrils flared and his good ear twitched. "The Fanged God has forsaken me in my shame. Now I am helped by an herbivore." He tried to stand and collapsed again. "I think my leg is broken."

"And your arm." Tskombe ran his hands over the bone, wincing in sympathy as he felt the bone grate. The kzin's lips twitched over his fangs, but he remained silent. "What's your name?"

"I have no name. I am nothing."

"Why is that?"

The kzin looked anguished. "Must I explain my disgrace?"

"No, just making conversation. We need to get you some medical attention."

The nameless kzin waved a dismissive paw. "I have no kroner. You are best to leave me, human."

"I have kroner."

"I can't walk."

"So I'll carry you."

The kzin just looked at him, eyes wide in disbelief. He was at least twice Tskombe's mass. His good ear rippled once and his tail twitched. Tskombe smiled. *At least he still had his sense of humor.*

The cargo flats belonged to a tronshop, and there was a floater parked there too. Leaving goods and equipment habitually unattended in a human community would be an invitation to have them stolen. In Tigertown the corridors were lined with all kinds of valuables. The twin drives of honor and shame were enough to keep them safe from kzinti, the claws of their owners served to protect them from thieving *kz'zeerkti*. Few humans were brave enough to risk stealing from a kzin.

Tskombe looked around carefully as he loaded the kzin onto the floater. Nobody seemed to be objecting. He had passed a place with an autodoc a few cross-corridors back, and he pushed his new charge in that direction.

The establishment had a sign that simply read "Healer," in Kzinscript, Dutch, German, English, Interspeak and a sixth language that he didn't recognize. Healer looked dubiously at both Tskombe and the kzin, but the transaction cleared when Tskombe thumbed for it, and Healer unceremoniously loaded the kzin into his autodoc.

"Do you know him?" Healer closed the lid and began scanning the readouts.

"No. There was a fight, and he lost. Everyone else was ignoring him."

"They ignored his shame; it is the most merciful thing. He is honorless, and now *czrav,* an outcast."

"He needed help."

"His honor is not raised by accepting charity from an herbivore." Healer punched some buttons. There was a muted snarl from inside the autodoc that fell to a sigh. Healer had started the anesthetic.

Tskombe showed his teeth. "I'm an omnivore."

"Your honor is not raised by helping a *czrav* either, omnivore."

"I'm not worried about that."

"Hrrr." Healer turned a paw over. "Few *kz'zeerkti* are, I have found." He punched some more buttons, and servos began whining as microsurgical arms started their work. Tskombe strained to see what was happening on the screen, saw enough to know that he didn't want to look further.

"How long will he be in there?"

"The bones must be set and then regrown, and he has internal injuries. Two days at least, perhaps three. Will he be paying?"

Tskombe hesitated, but the injured kzin had told him he had no money. *I knew what I was getting into.* "I'll be paying."

"Five thousand kroner." Healer tapped keys on his console to enter the transaction.

Tskombe thumbed his beltcomp to authorize the payment. "I'm looking for a ship, and a pilot. Do you know where I could find one?"

"Most passengers depart from the down-axis hub."

"I need a small ship that I can hire for myself, and a kzinti pilot."

"I don't know of any." Healer paused, considering. "I perhaps know someone who might."

"I'll leave you my contact information." Tskombe keyed his beltcomp to dump his details alongside the kroner transaction. "Please let me know."

"Hrrr." Healer was concentrating on his control panels. Tskombe watched him for a minute, then left. It seemed like a good time to go.

His altruistic instincts had cost him five thousand kroner, and he had nothing to show for it. He walked further, found nothing promising. The underworld was not his world, the kzinti underworld even less so, and it occurred to him that Trina might be better at navigating it than he would. He pushed the thought away. The underworld was all about making contacts, and he didn't want Trina doing what she'd have to do to make those contacts. Eventually he gave up and took a tube car back to the UN section, tired and frustrated. Trina was back when he arrived, swimming and splashing with Curvy in the pool in a modest one-piece swimsuit. Curvy was lifting and tossing her, as Trina laughed and tried to balance on the dolphin's back, looking in the moment like a little girl without a care in the world. Tskombe smiled, his mood lifting. He had risked a lot to bring her to Alpha Centauri. To see her recapture a moment of her stolen childhood made it worth it.

"Quacy!" She swam over gracefully, sleek as a seal. Curvy leapt, splashed and came up beside her, clicking and whistling. "Did you get us a ship?"

"Not yet." He laughed as she climbed out of the pool. "And it isn't a ship for *us*, it's a ship for *me*."

"You're not leaving me here, are you?" She didn't quite manage to make the question light and offhanded.

"Trina . . ." The words caught in his throat. "Trina, I have to. You can't come to Kzinhome, it's too dangerous."

She didn't say anything, just looked away. He stumbled

on. "We'll get you an ident, you don't need a birthright here. We'll set you up with the Bureau of Displaced Persons, they're set up to look after you. You need to go to school, get your education, get a career." She stayed silent, and he could tell she was fighting back tears. *All she knows is I'm abandoning her, like everyone else in her life.* "Don't worry, I'll come back for you." He said it because there was nothing else he could say.

She gave up and cried then, and he put his arm around her shoulder, the water from her hair soaking through his shirt. She put his head against his chest and he held her, somewhat awkwardly. He was unused to children, not quite sure what was appropriate with one who was almost a woman. The sobs shook her small body, echoing across the pool. Curvy had dived, sensing perhaps that this was a moment to leave the two alone. The overhead lights reflected off the pool's waves to make dappled patterns on the wall and he watched them. Tskombe had made his decision to get her out of the brothel on the spur of the moment, motivated by the confluence of opportunity and conscience. He had planned to deliver her to Wunderland and leave her to a better life while he continued on to Kzinhome, but what Trina needed most wasn't a well-meaning institution, she needed her parents. Failing that she needed a stable adult figure in her life. Tskombe hadn't planned on that role, but it was the one he found himself in.

So he would come back for her, if he could. At the same time Curvy's well computed odds against his success made the commitment seem hollow. It was unlikely that he'd be coming back at all.

"Do you promise?" She looked up at him with big, uncertain eyes.

"Yes, I promise." He felt a lump in his throat as he said it, and he held her close.

The next night he was back in Tigertown. He knew his way around the corridors better now and drew fewer looks. He went to the same kzinti bar as before, saw the same three humans there, and was ejected just as quickly, by a proprietor who was markedly less tolerant than he'd been the first time. He went by Healer's, but Healer was too busy to see him. He sat down at a tube station to think. *Perhaps I'm going about this the wrong way.* It could take him a year to develop the connections he needed. The kzinti had their own thriving sub-economy in Tigertown, and it had to interface with the larger human economy in the Centaraus system. *Maybe the smarter thing to do is just go through a transshipment company, someone who routes supplies to the rock miners.* They'd have existing arrangements with ships, some of which would be flown by kzinti.

He stood up. *That's a much better idea.* Wandering around Tigertown with half a plan and no clue was getting him nowhere fast. He should have realized that sooner. He grabbed the next available tube car and punched for home. He spent the transit time looking up shippers on Tiamat's network through his beltcomp. There were lots. He'd start in the morning.

He knew there was something wrong as soon as the tube car's door hissed open. It wasn't the UN quarters station, and there were three men in ARM uniform waiting for him.

"Colonel Quacy Tskombe?"

"Yes." There was no pointing denying it, they were obviously looking for him, and they'd rerouted his tube car when the computer registered his thumbprint for the fare.

"I'm Sergeant Veers, ARM. You'll need to come with us."

There was no point in resisting either. Unlike New York, where surveillance was pervasive but he could at least run freely, Tiamat allowed no such options. If he bolted they'd just order the vacuum doors sealed and go pick him up. The tube station he'd arrived at was ARM headquarters. They took him in and put him in a cell, one of only two in the section. As the Swarm Belters had steadily pushed the UN out of their affairs, ARM's role on Tiamat had been reduced from effective autocracy over all civilian affairs to a strictly advisory capacity, with the Swarm Goldskins doing the real police work. He asked questions but they gave no answers. That was to be expected, but their diffident manner and discomfort when he asked them told him all he needed to know. They were acting on orders from Earth to arrest him, but they didn't know why. He could use that, maybe.

"Look," he said to Veers through the bars. "I'm not entirely sure what's going on here, but there is a serious mistake."

The other man shrugged. "I have orders to find you and hold you, pending further notice from Earth."

"I'm not surprised you have orders to find me. I think if you'll read them again you'll see that you're supposed to hold my orders from Earth and go and find me so I can read them, not hold me in anticipation of my orders. I'm expecting a mission."

"I know what they said." Veers's voice was dismissive, but he punched keys on his desk. He was checking. Tskombe watched as his eyes flicked over the display. "And they still say that." There was satisfaction in his tone at being proved right.

"Sergeant." Tskombe persisted. "Someone has obviously made a serious bureaucratic error. Check my file and you'll see who you're dealing with."

Veers tapped more keys. "Your file is sealed." He turned to face Tskombe. "Look, I don't know what the problem is, but I do have my orders. They say to hold you and wait for instructions; I'll hold you and wait for instructions. It'll get straightened out one way or another."

Tskombe paused. He'd counted on his impressive war record, culminating in the mission to Kzinhome, to convince the ARM that he'd made a mistake. *Work with what you've got.* "Of course it's sealed. What do you expect of someone conducting classified missions? Now, this problem *will* be corrected." Tskombe used the firm but restrained voice he used on subordinates who'd messed up. "And I'm not going to hold you responsible for carrying out your mistaken orders. I *will* hold you responsible if you don't act to correct them. So you have a choice. Correct the problem yourself and get a commendation for initiative, or hold me here until I miss my mission start and end your career on the spot."

Veers looked uncertain. "I can send a message to Earth."

"What's the turnaround for hyperwave to Earth? Twelve days? That's unacceptable, Sergeant."

"I don't know what you want me to do, sir." The ARM sounded aggrieved, as though the situation was Tskombe's fault. Which was largely correct.

He's calling me sir. That's a good sign. "You can access my immediate superior here on Tiamat."

"What's the ident?"

Tskombe suppressed a smirk as he gave Veers Curvy's comcode. The ARM was almost falling over himself now, to absolve himself of responsibility for someone else's error. *Bureaucracies never change.*

He watched Veers's eyes widen as Curvy's authority status came up on the screen, then widen further as Curvy herself did. He hadn't expected a dolphin. Tskombe couldn't hear the conversation because Veers's desk had switched on its sound damper automatically when it placed the call.

When the call ended he keyed his desk, popping the lock on Tskombe's cell. He was apologetic. "I'm sorry about the confusion, sir."

"Not at all. You were doing your job right. And you're still doing it right, verifying the correctness of your orders. I'll put that in my report." Tskombe left the cell, trying hard not to run. The problem was only temporarily solved. There would be follow-on orders from Earth, probably dealing with both him and Curvy and much more explicit than the first set. Ravalla's team must have issued them as soon as the details of his escape from New York came to light and before the whole situation was clear. Veers would not be fooled twice, and on Tiamat there was nowhere to hide. If he wasn't already gone by then, he'd find himself on a ship back to Earth to face court-martial for desertion. It might be smart to get a ship to Wunderland first, where anti-UN sentiment was even higher than in the Serpent Swarm and the environment was a lot looser. The problem with that idea was that by the time he'd gotten himself, Curvy and Trina to the planet he wouldn't have enough money left to hire a ship all the way to Kzinhome. Something was going to have to happen. They were running out of time.

> The hour of departure has arrived, and we go our ways—I to die, and you to live. Which is better God only knows.
> —Plato, Apology, quoting Socrates

Ayla Cherenkova sat atop the sandstone dome that housed Ztrak Pride's high forest den, watching 61 Ursae Majoris set the sky afire as it slipped toward the red rock spires that marked the western horizon. The forest here was higher and drier than the triple canopy jungle of the eastern den. The high forest den was another cavern complex, set in one of a series of similar domes rising out of the sandy plateau, rounded into almost perfect teardrops by ancient winds, when the forest had not yet claimed this part of the continent from the desert. In the distance a herd of *tuskvor* drank from a small river that snaked lazily along the bottom of a flood-cut ravine. Further up, a big male was moving circumspectly toward the group. Ayla raised her binoptics to scan the herd, but they were doing nothing interesting. She lowered them again and yawned.

The caverns below her were spacious, floored in stonewood over sand. There was plenty to eat. The pride had butchered a few of the *tuskvor* they rode, once they'd cut them out of the main migration stream, yielding hundreds of tons of meat that they cut into slabs and dried in the hot sun atop the dome, where the shade of the tall trees didn't fall. She had been glad to see that Camel, who she'd come to see as *her tuskvor*, escaped the slaughter. She liked to think it was Camel's winning personality that had saved her, although V'rli-Ztrak had spoken disparagingly of her bulging fat pouches. The kzinti liked leaner meat, and when she saw the *tuskvor* butchered she understood why. Even a lean *tuskvor* yielded meat almost too rich to digest this early in the forest season.

She raised the binoptics again. *Tuskvor* fattened themselves in the jungle but they mated in the high forest, their life rhythms governed by the alternating seasons on opposite ends of Kzinhome's central continent. She had learned that from C'mell, who after the *mazourk* lessons had taken it upon herself to teach her the ways of the *czrav*. The huge herd beasts gave birth in the forest too, after a two-year gestation. Mating and birth were vulnerable times when they needed to be away from the *grlor* and the other jungle predators, but the forest didn't provide the huge volumes of lush fodder that the jungle did. The *czrav* moved with them for similar reasons.

By the watercourse the herd was moving closer together, responding to the big male's presence. The vast migration had started to break up as they came out of the deep desert dunes into the western grasslands and up into the forest. The herds now wandered aimlessly in mating groups: a huge mature male, a grandmother or two or three, and a couple of dozen mothers with offspring of varying sizes. The younger males wandered around between the herds, being chased away by the harem keepers if they came too close. They fought each other instead of the big males. The winners got a chance to mature and perhaps hold a harem; the losers died, every time. She'd seen it happen several times now. What was going on in her field of view now was a little more interesting. The full sized males fought the grandmothers for the right to mate with the entire harem that surrounded them. If the male was big enough the grandmother would yield after a little shoving. If not, the struggle would be titanic, with the larger mothers, nearing the end of their own bearing years, joining in to drive off the interloper. As she watched, the male came closer and one of the grandmothers turned to face him. They were evenly matched in size. If a fight transpired it would be sensational.

The male bellowed at the grandmother, but backed off again when she came closer. Cherenkova put the binoptics down again in frustration. Maybe there would be a fight, but it didn't look like it would come before dark. The *tuskvor* mating ritual was fascinating, it was epic, but it was also slow moving and she was rapidly becoming bored with it. After the first frantic days of butchering and feasting and setting up the den, pride life had fallen into a complacent routine. Everyone had something to do except her. She had earned her place in the pride when the Tzaatz attacked, and learned to handle *tuskvor* well enough that C'mell and Quicktail had taken to calling her Cherenkova-*mazourk*. Now those things were past, and once again she felt like a pet. Pouncer had set off on Camel to find Mrrsel Pride's den, his mother's pride, the start of his namequest to gain allies for his cause. It was something he had to do himself, he explained, and it was too dangerous for her to come. She was safe in the den, supposedly, with V'rli-Ztrak standing for her safety, but Sraff-Tracker, in particular, still looked at her like a prey animal. She found it prudent to spend a lot of time outside.

At least avoiding him gave her something to do. She had read hundreds of books on her beltcomp, and its memory held enough to let her read for the rest of her life, but she needed more than that. She needed action, and she wanted to get off the planet. She took to running simulations on the Swiftwing simulator, dreaming of stealing another courier to take her back to human space. The problem with that plan was that it required retracing her steps, and Ztrak Pride wouldn't be leaving the desert until the wet season returned to the jungle. Watching *tuskvor* mate was a good way to pass the time. She was making notes on it, notes on pride life, notes on the flora and fauna of the desert. *I am the reluctant researcher, a kzinologist by circumstance.* Kefan Brasseur would have been pleased.

Chrrowwwlll! The cry was mourning, yearnful, and it yanked Ayla from her reverie. *Chrrowwwlll!* It came again. She had heard it before. *Where?* Aboard the *Fanged Victory*, falling in from *Crusader* to Kzinhome. It was the sound the kzinretti had made in the ritualized mating dance. There was another fact she'd learned from C'mell, though she'd filed the information and forgotten it until the mating call brought it back to mind. The third Hunter's Moon of the year was called the Mating Moon,

and while kzinretti could come into fertility at any time of
year, there was a seasonal synchronization that brought
most of them into heat around that time. She looked up
and saw the Hunter's Moon full above her. Was it the third
time since they'd left the jungle? She couldn't remember.
She'd lost track of how long she'd been on Kzinhome. *Too
long, and no end in sight.*

Chrrowwwlll! Kzinti mating at least would be something different to see. It was getting cooler anyway. She
took a last look at the *tuskvor* herd in the fading light,
where the spurned male was shuffling away from the
group. She stood up and found the path off the dome
down to the den mouth.

The pride circle fire had just been lit, but rather than
the usual good-natured banter that went on as the kzinti
slowly gathered for the first story, it seemed like the entire
pride was already there, watching in intent silence. In the
center of the circle the kzinrette Z'slee was crouched with
her haunches in the air, flicking her well tufted tail back
and forth and howling her need with earsplitting vehemence. The circle was much more structured than it had
been before. The males were in their usual places, alone
or in pairs or threes, but the females were clustered
tighter around them than usual, and they didn't seem to
be moving from group to group. The unmated males had
one segment of the circle by themselves, each of them
alone. Even V'rli was lying close beside Ferlitz-Telepath,
in front of her honored rock rather than on it.

As Cherenkova watched, Z'slee rocked back and forth,
then circled, growling deep in her throat. Ayla recognized
the patterns from the ritual dance on the kzinti battleship

on the trip insystem, but Z'slee's movements were raw and primal, unvarnished by the stylistic interpretation of dance-trainers. She was deep in heat. Ayla found a natural rock shelf by the wall where she could sit and see without getting in the way. Every male had their eyes locked unblinkingly on Z'slee. Instinct told her the mating display could turn violent with no warning, and she didn't want to get caught in the middle. It was deep twilight outside the cave, and the scene was made unreal by the flickering of the pride circle fire. She realized she was holding her breath.

Z'slee was on all fours, crawling with her hind legs stiff toward the unmated males. For the first time Ayla noticed the way the pride circle was organized. V'rli's position was the centerpoint with Ferlitz, and to her right were the highest *strakh* kzinti, the inner circle members first, Kdtronai-*zar'ameer* with V'veen and three other females, Ztrak-Conserver, Kr-Pathfinder, then the senior hunters like Greow-Czatz and M'mewr, and so on all the way around the circle in descending order of status to youths like Quicktail and the young telepath Mind-Seer, who were on V'rli's left. The medium status males tended to be in groups of two or three, and suddenly Cherenkova understood that status equated to mating success. What mattered was the ratio of male status to female status in the group. Higher status males were with higher status females, and more of them. Lower status males wound up with lower status females, but they could pair up to do better together than either could alone. At tale-telling-time the unmated females drifted from group to group and confused the issue, but now they were all with their mothers, and the pattern was clear. They were watching

Z'slee's performance as intently as the males, perhaps judging what they would do when their own fertility arrived.

Z'slee went to Silverstreak, an adolescent not far from the bottom in *strakh*, twitching her tail and chirruping at him invitingly. He watched her intently but didn't move. She came closer, circling to present her haunches, flexing and arching invitingly. Silverstreak licked his chops and looked like he might respond, but then he looked around the circle and seemed to decide not to. After a few minutes Z'slee moved up the line to Wild-Son-of-Hrell-Hromfi and repeated her performance. Wild-Son showed no hesitation, leaping into the circle and grabbing at her, but surprisingly she snapped her tail down and scampered away. He followed her, leaping to catch her. They tumbled in the sand and struggled as he tried to mount her. He succeeded in forcing her onto her belly, but she lowered her haunches when he mounted her, frustrating his attempt to mate. He snarled and bit at her neck, and she *chrowled* again, her cry deep and keening. Every male in the circle stiffened at the sound, and she lashed her head back and forth to keep Wild-Son from getting a grip with his teeth. Where an instant before she had been clearly trying to induce him to mate her, now she was struggling to get away. She managed to get turned around enough to bite him on the muzzle, and he howled in pain. The distraction was enough for her to roll and kick. Unbalanced, he lost his footing and she squirmed away. He leapt again, but she dodged, and while he was recovering she ran to Quicktail and again presented her haunches, tail flipping back and forth, and *chrowl*ing loudly. Quicktail didn't move, but when Wild-Son turned to come back for Z'slee he locked eyes with him and Wild-Son froze, snarling deep in his throat. The tableau held, Wild-Son's tail lashing angrily. He wanted Z'slee, but in her current posture mounting her would leave his back exposed to Quicktail, whose gaze and bared fangs made his own interest clear. Quicktail was younger and smaller than Wild-Son, and Ayla now realized that before the battle in the jungle he had sat below him in pride-circle rank. Now he wore Tzaatz ears on his belt and was credited with the rescue of Kdtronai-*zar'ameer* and since they'd arrived at desert den his *strakh*, and his position in the circle, were much increased.

Z'slee looked back over her shoulder to gauge Quicktail's interest, then slowly, keeping her haunches high, she edged herself out from between the two males. As she turned to pass Wild-Son her hindquarters were exposed to him. He grabbed at her again, and in the same instant Quicktail screamed and leapt, catching the other half-sideways. They went down in a heap of fangs, claws and screamed insults, and Z'slee, tail twitching, went on to Night-Prowler, presenting herself to him as she had to Quicktail. Her plaintive *chrrrowwwll* nearly drowned out the sounds of the fight.

But Night-Prowler didn't move, and Wild-Son and Quicktail tumbled free of each other, each rolling to their feet, breathing hard, each bleeding from half a dozen minor wounds. For a long moment they faced each other, and then Wild-Son leapt. Quicktail stepped sideways and pivoted, lashing out with hind claws as his opponent came past to catch him in his cross-braced ribcage. Wild-Son screamed in pain and rolled. Quicktail leapt after him, only to catch a vicious slash across his muzzle. Blood streamed from the wounds, but then Quicktail was on top and his fangs were at Wild-Son's throat. Wild-Son screamed, kicking out hard to disembowel with his hind claws, but Quicktail arched his back to keep his vitals out of reach without releasing his clenched jaws.

Slowly Wild-Son's struggles subsided. Quicktail shook the limp body with his teeth, like a terrier with a rat, and then released it to fall limp on the floor. Without looking back he turned to Z'slee, still hunched over, twitching her tail for Night-Prowler. Quicktail locked eyes with the other male, breathing hard, blood still streaming from his muzzle, but Night-Prowler didn't move, and his fangs weren't showing. Z'slee looked back at Night-Prowler, tail twitching, then skittered away. Quicktail leapt after her and caught her by the haunches. She struggled, and rolled, but his teeth found the nape of her neck and pulled her over into the mating posture. This time she didn't lower her tail, and when he succeeded in mounting her she raised her haunches higher to give him better access. Quicktail roared at the same instant, his body jerking hard against hers. She screamed, an unearthly sound that made her previous cries seem tame by comparison, and thrashed in his grip, and then they both collapsed.

To Cherenkova's surprise they didn't separate, but stayed tied together at the loins, like wolves, and crawled awkwardly from the center of the circle. The tension bled out of the pride like air from an overinflated balloon. After a long pause V'rli-Ztrak stood and went to the center of the circle.

"Was the fight fair?"

"It was fair, Honored Mother." The pride answered, almost in unison.

"Was it fair, K'dro?" She turned to face the upper-middle-status female beside Hrell-Hromfi, who had just lost her eldest son.

"It was fair, Honored Mother." K'dro's voice was low but level. She lowered her head, clearly grieving.

V'rli furled her ears, satisfied, and went back to her place. Greow-Czatz stood up and began to tell the next saga of the Taking of Fortress Cta'ian, his words breathing life into the ancient story. Wild-Son's body lay where it had fallen. Quicktail and Z'slee were still coupled, the violence of their first mating replaced with amorous licking and nibbles. They lay by Night-Prowler, who moved slightly in front of them to make his protective posture clear. A new coalition had been formed, and Ayla had no doubt that Night-Prowler would be mating Z'slee later in the night. She found she had to consciously relax herself after the intensity of the encounter, but the pride seemed to handle it quite naturally. The tight group postures relaxed, mothers chased after their younger kits, and the unmated females moved from group to group again. It was as if the encounter had never happened.

Hours later Greow-Czatz had finished his story, and Ferlitz-Telepath slipped over to Ayla, who was by then munching on a slice of dried *tuskvor* and caught up in the tale. "We will have the death rite for Wild-Son now. You can watch, but stay back."

"I understand."

The heavier mood of the challenge and mating

returned to the cavern as the pride built the fire up into a roaring pyre. Quicktail rose again to kneel by the body while every member of the pride rose to stand beside them to pay homage to the dead. Some told a short story, some threw a valued possession on the fire, some simply stood in silence. There was a solemnity to the occasion, but also a wild and primitive energy. Some of the story-tellers were excellent, throwing themselves into the roles as they related them, using the play of shadow and flickering firelight to add drama to their words. Around the circle some of the males sparred, sudden, snarling encounters that ended almost as quickly as they began, and Cherenkova found herself unsure if the bouts were serious or playful. At last V'rli rose and stood beside them.

"Wild-Son was brave," she said. "Wild-Son hunted well. He fought hard at the battle in the jungle. He was our blood, and he remains our blood. Now he is dead."

There were snarls and growls from around the circle.

"Quicktail was brave," V'rli continued. "Quicktail was fast, and wise beyond his years. He was loyal and fierce. He was our blood and remains our blood. Now he is dead." She took her *wtsai* from her belt and gave it to Quicktail.

Quicktail took the blade and bent to Wild-Son's body. Two quick cuts and the severed ears were his.

"I am Swift-Claw!" He roared the name as he held the ears up in triumph. "I claim the name here before you all! No one will take it from me." He roared again and the pride roared with him. Two males leapt forward and grabbed the earless body and threw it onto the roaring pyre, where it sizzled and was consumed. The action became a tussle, and suddenly the entire pride was rolling and fighting, male and females together. Some of the fights turned into matings, roars and screams and snarls splitting the night.

Ayla understood now why she had been warned to stay back. *What is the meaning here?* She watched in fascination, making quick notes on her beltcomp. The orgy, if that's what it was, was still going on when she went down into the den to find her *frrch* skins, and sleep.

The next day Quicktail had new respect from the rest of the pride, and both he and Night-Prowler had moved up in the circle, with Z'slee beside them. She saw several more matings while the Mating Moon was high, and she learned the rules of the ritual. The female would choose her suitor, yowling for him, raising her haunches, flipping her tail, but if he responded she'd skitter away to tease another one. Usually the status difference between males was enough that one or the other would abandon the pursuit, but sometimes there would be a fight, short and violent and frequently bloody, although unlike Quicktail's duel with Wild-Son, not usually lethal, a disappointment when the hostile Sraff-Tracker fought Kr-Pathfinder for M'rraow, although at least Ayla had the satisfaction of seeing him lose. The winner would continue chasing the female, who more often than not would already be flipping her tail for a third male. The females always started with lower ranked males and worked their way up the ladder until they could entice no better male to chase them. Mated males tended to have higher status, and they were approached only after a female had courted all the other males. *Why not start at the top and work their way down?*

The higher ranked males already had mates, the highest had several. With mates already and kits to protect they risked more in the mating battles and stood to gain less. A female enticed the lower ranks to prove her desirability to the higher ranks. Bottom up worked for the males too; the higher ranks offloaded the risk of battle to the lower ranks. Quicktail had mated Z'slee first, but Night-Prowler would mate her too, without taking any risk himself. *It's an auction*, she realized, sexualized and ritualized, but nothing more or less. The females wanted the fittest, highest status male they could get to sire their kits; the males proved their worth by fighting and winning, or having enough status that they didn't have to fight. There were other subtleties. Males with their eye on a particular female would turn down another's advances. Females who had borne kits for a male would court their sire first, and often only. Sometimes a female would fight another one who tried to court their male. There were other scuffles, physical and social, that happened away from the pride circle but served to determine who stood where in the mate competition. Cherenkova recognized the patterns. *It's little different from dating up at a bounce bar.* And there was no reason it shouldn't be. Darwinian sexual dynamics were about optimizing the fitness of offspring, and though the details changed, the game remained the same, in any species on any world.

But there were differences in detail. Kzinti pair-bonded sometimes, as Ferlitz-Telepath and V'rli-Ztrak did. Relatedness was important in determining who might mate with who—Quicktail-Swift-Claw and Night-Prowler were half brothers, she learned—and the male coalitions tended to follow blood lines. Once mating was publicly consummated the pair, or trio, would vanish from the pride circle for a more private honeymoon. It was fascinating. *Kefan would be in his element here.* Kzinti mating dynamics where the females were major players in the mating decision were radically different from those of the mainstream where females were simple property. The energy of the mating season threw her own glands into overproduction and she felt sexual desire, not as a passing fancy but as a deep, primal drive, and if screaming her need and raising her haunches would have brought Quacy Tskombe's flesh to hers she would have done it. *And where are you, Quacy?* She didn't want to think of him as dead. *I must find my own place here first, if I'm ever going to get back to you.*

> Oderint dum metuant.
> (Let them hate so long as they fear.)
> —Emperor Caligula

Oorwinnig came out of hyperspace and dropped. She was last in formation, screened by half a dozen cruisers and twice that number of destroyers. Most of her escort were UNF ships. Earth and Wunderland didn't see eye to eye on a lot of issues, but war was something they could agree on, at least since Secretary Ravalla had taken office. It was about time the Flatlanders understood the reality of the kzinti. Captain Cornelius Voortman allowed himself a grim smile.

"Navigation, set course for target, full thrust." He bit the words off, keeping the exultation out of his voice.

This was the mission he'd lived his life to lead. Far below the star Alpha Mensae glowed yellow-orange. Invisible still was Alpha Mensae II, a planet thrice the size of Mars, with an oxygen-nitrogen atmosphere thick enough to breathe. It was a dry world, just a third of its surface covered in shallow seas, and it supported a biosphere consisting largely of jellyfish, algae and lichen. The kzinti had maintained an advanced base there since before humans learned to fly, launching secret raids in the war that ultimately enslaved the Pierin at Zeta Reticuli.

No longer a secret, and not much longer a base. *Oorwinnig* would see to that.

"Course locked in," reported the navigation officer, and the starfield spun and the deck seemed to shift as the cabin gravity compensated for the full push of *Oorwinnig's* massive polarizers. Voortman sat back in his command chair and relaxed. The kzinti had forces in system, but nothing that could deal with his ship. It was unlikely any of the ratcats would even get through the cruiser screen. In a way that was too bad.

"All secure, Captain?" Admiral Mysolin's face appeared in the viscom, his UN gray uniform immaculately pressed. Voortman checked the battleplot, saw the battleship *Atlantic* had come out of hyperspace beside him.

"Yes sir. Forty-five hours to attack position, standard." It was galling to take orders from a Flatlander, but Voortman kept his demeanor carefully professional. There was a larger enemy to think about, and Earth had put more ships into the fleet than Wunderland had.

Mysolin nodded curtly. "Good. Keep me informed." His image vanished and Voortman scowled. The

Flatlanders had nothing like *Oorwinnig* and, despite being the flagship, *Atlantic*'s role was nothing more than close defense of *Oorwinnig*. It was important to remember that. When the time came, the central weapon was Wunderland's.

The scouts and destroyers were twelve hours ahead of *Oorwinnig*, just enough time for the kzinti to have detected their arrival, and for the light units to have assessed their first responses and transmitted the data for the main fleet to pick up on arrival. They were going to have to fight their way in. Hours-long speed-of-light lag would characterize the initial stages of the battle; computerized targeting and countermeasures too fast for merely human reflexes would characterize the endgame. Voortman looked out the transpax at the glowing arch of the Milky Way, four hundred billion stars in a hundred-thousand-light-year disk, spinning on a timescale of millions of years and remotely indifferent to a handful of organic lifeforms struggling over the pitiful two thousand systems contained in the tiny volume of the minor Orion arm that humanity liked to call Known Space. Once the Thrintun Slavers had held an empire that encompassed all that vastness, or so the academics claimed. One day their Tnuctipun slaves had revolted, and the Slaver war had wiped out every sentient being alive in the galaxy at that time. *How long does it take for a species to occupy the whole galaxy? What else might we meet out there?* Both unanswerable questions. He was certain of one thing. Whatever species next occupied the entire galactic volume, it was not going to be kzinti.

The first watch passed uneventfully, though the scout reports said the kzinti were boosting every ship they had to intercept. He carefully monitored the battle board as Mysolin ordered his screening units on counter-intercept missions. Occasionally terse combat reports came in, and they lost a ship in the first encounter, the destroyer *Gloire*, rammed by a scoutship that happened to be close enough to match her infall orbit and fast enough to get past her defensive weapons. *Damn ratcats never surrender.* Extermination was not an answer, it was *the* answer. *Nothing else will stop them.* Anyone who thought differently hadn't seen them fight.

At watch end he handed off the bridge to Kirsch, his able first officer, and went to sleep in his dayroom. Stockpiling sleep was a commander's first duty, because when the battle was joined he might not rest for days. There was always the temptation to stay awake, to watch the battle developing, but the earliest possible kzinti intercept was eighteen hours away. To stay awake now would mean being exhausted at the critical moment, and he couldn't afford that. *A good commander trains his subordinates well enough to trust them.* Kirsch could handle the ship, and would wake him if anything unexpected happened.

And nothing did, though the first main force engagement came in just twelve hours, in the middle of the next top watch. A squadron of kzinti fighters who must have been boosting hard enough to burn out their polarizers blasted through the destroyer screen to take on the cruisers, salvo launching their missiles at some tremendous closing velocity. The UNSN *Vengeance* took the brunt of the attack, lacing the incoming formation with her lasers and evading hard. Her screener cannisters reduced the missiles to so much junk, though a few detonated early to degrade her sensors. None did enough damage to take her out of the battle, and then the fighters, those who might have survived, were through the formation and out the other side, braking hard but out of the fight for another thirty hours, according to the combat computer's best guess. With no missile rounds left the best they could do on their next pass was ram. Voortman was all too aware that they would if they could, but that was a problem for later. Admiral Mysolin was back on the viscom, reorganizing the attack fleet in accordance with the latest intelligence. He had a dolphin tactical team aboard *Atlantic*, and no doubt his deployments were several layers deep in their sophistication. Voortman didn't have a lot of faith in either combat computers or dolphins. As a source of information they were fine. When it came time to position his ship for battle he preferred to trust his own instincts. In this case his instincts disagreed with Mysolin's plan, whatever its source. The admiral sent scoutships back along the fighter's attack course to search out the carrier that must have launched them. A cruiser and four destroyers shaped course behind them to deliver the coup de grace, if and when they found it. At least *Oorwinnig* continued uninterrupted on her maximum acceleration infall to loop around A-M II in attack orbit. In Voortman's mind, there was no need to do anything other than close with the enemy as fast as possible. The kzinti didn't have enough strength in the system to seriously interrupt the human fleet. It was why A-M II was chosen in the first place. It was important that the first test of the charge suppressor weapon be a success.

It's a waste of resources to go hunting for a now fang-less carrier in the vastness of the outer system. Even if they found and destroyed it there would be little advantage compared to the risk posed by the defenses closer in. The human fleet had numbers enough to pursue such luxuries, but war was not about luxury. To Voortman war was about annihilation as Schlieffen had used the word, victory so complete that your enemy could never again pose a threat. It was something Genghis Khan had understood, and perhaps no one since.

But that would come soon enough, and if the fleet was the Admiral's to direct, *Oorwinnig* was his to command. *And then the kzinti will know annihilation, as God struck down the Cities of Sin with fire from heaven.*

There was a lull then, and he went back to his dayroom to grab a nap. Several hours later Kirsch woke him up. A kzinti destroyer squadron, the main enemy force in the system, was boosting to intercept. Unlike the fighters, whose trajectory would take them nowhere near his ship, the destroyers clearly intended to make it past the cruiser screen to cripple the battleships. Com traffic was crackling and Voortman ordered the ship's cameras zoomed to the battle, but the range was too great and there was nothing to see save the occasional brief flash of light. A flash that was over in seconds was a warhead, a flash that lingered was the death of a warship, and almost certainly all aboard her.

Suddenly a face in the viscom, voice and image distorted by the storm of charged particles left behind by the warheads. "They've got a cruiser . . ."

The image vanished, and in the battle view another

flash flared, and slowly faded. Voortman stabbed a finger on the icon and got the dead ship's details. The cruiser *Aurora*, destroyed in action. The kzinti had camouflaged their strength, overloaded the defenses and managed to get a dangerous unit through. The particle storm left by the warheads had replaced the neat trajectory trails on his battle plot with expanding course funnels. He zoomed the view, scanned the threats. *There* . . . One of them was narrower than the others, a ship with more mass and less thrust, a kzinti heavy cruiser. Another warhead winked in the darkness, a large section of the screen went orange. The kzin had launched screeners and then ionized them with a conversion blast to blank out the human sensors. The kzinti captain was covering himself, and he would be somewhere behind the screen, decelerated just enough to let it race in front of him as he closed to firing range. Even a heavy cruiser couldn't stand up to two battleships in a standup fight, but if the ratcat got a missile through their screeners it would do a lot of damage. And if he rammed . . .

Voortman set target lines to stitch the particle cloud and keyed his com. "All turrets, engage at five light-seconds. Countermeasures to free mode. He's going to be coming fast."

"Engagement parameters set." Marxle, the weapons officer, clicked keys.

"Navigation, plot an intercept . . ." The viscom flashed Admiral Mysolin's face, interrupting him. "*Oorwinnig, maintain your course and prepare to fire.*"

"Acknowledged." Voortman ground his teeth. *Why does he waste time with the obvious?* "Navigation, prepare to evade." The Flatlanders were going to take the engagement. *Atlantic* rolled to put her thrust vector ahead of the oncoming warship and boosted hard. On the battle plot her icon slid past *Oorwinnig*, set for the intercept that Voortman wanted for himself. Long minutes dragged past as *Atlantic* positioned herself, and then suddenly a grid of flashes winked in the darkness. The kzin was attacking behind a wall of conversion detonations, trying to saturate *Atlantic's* defenses. More flashes blossomed, then a final, double flash that faded slowly. Had the kzinti gotten through?

"Oorwinnig, you are clear." There was no image to go with the voice, so static torn as to be barely recognizable, but the message was what was important. Voortman felt a mild disappointment. His ship was strong, she could defend herself, and now the battle honors would fall to *Atlantic. Focus on the mission, focus on the enemy.*

Hours ahead the scoutships were already at the planet, skimming down in provocative passes to identify the space defense positions for the oncoming cruisers. Voortman didn't go back to his dayroom, though they were still fourteen hours from attack position. Instead he waited and watched. The distant destroyer screen picked up a few laggard kzinti thrusting in from the edge of the system, too distant to influence the battle in time, too scattered to have any effect when they got there, but screaming and leaping nonetheless. There were no more serious threats; the human fleet could do what they wanted in Alpha Mensae system.

Four hours to attack position. He ordered his engineers to check the weapons systems one last time. The cruisers

closed and targeted the ground based gamma ray lasers
to clear the way for his attack. A-M II had no space
based defenses except the ships that had been in orbit,
and they had already come out to be destroyed by the
in-falling humans. *Oorwinnig* needed to get close to
bring her main armament into play. Next time she could
fight her way in; this time her success was too important
to risk an engagement.

Two hours to attack position. They'd lost another cruiser
and a handful of scouts, and the planet lay open, its
defenses stripped. Voortman paced the bridge impatiently
while Kirsch took over navigation to make sure their
attack orbit was set correctly. They'd have one pass, and
the kzinti would learn a lesson they wouldn't forget. A few
ships boosted from the planet's surface, couriers and cargo
lighters pressed into service as last ditch defenses, but the
orbiting cruisers swatted them down. *Damn ratcats never
give up.*

And then it was time. A-M II had grown from a point
to a disk to a recognizable blue and white sphere. The
kzinti had a major base down there, and quite a few support facilities scattered about the planet. *Oorwinnig*
would end that.

"Target on the horizon, sir." Marxle had the firing solutions plotted, the main spinal mount weapon charged and
ready.

"Fire." Voortman spat the word.

The twin disintegrator beams lanced down to the planet's surface, one positive, one negative. At first the effects
were invisible from orbit, though on the ground the rocks
exploded as suddenly charged atoms repelled each other

with violent force, fountaining monatomic dust hundreds of meters, and then kilometers high. Between the two touchdown points a potential field measured in teravolts developed, and a current began to flow. City-sized sheets of lightning arced between the twin columns of charged atmosphere that marked the beams passage to the ground from space. The ground between the impact points began to heat. The base the kzinti had called Warhead was gone.

"Target destroyed." Marxle's voice was clipped.

"Keep the beams on it."

"But sir . . ."

"Keep the beams on it!" Voortman's words were harsh.

"Yes, sir."

On the ground the disintegrator beams stabbed remorselessly at the planet's surface, and between the impact points the rock began to melt and flow. The effect on the planet's surface was now visible through the bridge transpax, a glowing, boiling cloud already causing a visible bulge in the atmosphere. Subsurface water flash boiled, blowing cubic kilometers of rock into the sky. Anything that lived within a hundred kilometers of the base would be killed by blast and shock.

"Sir, the dust cloud is starting to interfere . . ." Voortman cut the weapon's officer's not-quite-complaint off with a gesture. *Today I wield the fist of God. For you, Vati, I will not falter.*

"Traverse the beams."

"Sir . . ."

"You heard me."

"Yes sir." Marxle clicked keys, slid a finger. *Oorwinnig's* stabilization system had been set up to hold the impact points as steady as possible as the planet spun beneath them. Now that calibration was offset, and the relative motion of the ship and planet caused the beam impact points to slide clear of the roiling dust that had started to block them. They found new rock to chew at, exploding more of the planet's crust into the seething black mass. What had begun as a linear crater became a canyon, torn from the surface by twin pillars of fire from heaven.

"Sir, the superconductors are quenching . . ."

"All available power to cooling." Voortman kept his eyes locked on the planet's image below as his weapon devoured everything it touched. The beams dragged a molten scar across A-M II's larger continent, ten kilometers, twenty, fifty, a hundred, and the boiling dust cloud left in their wake glowed red as it reached into the stratosphere.

"Sir . . ." Now Kirsch too was objecting. A series of shudders rocked the ship and the lights flickered, went down, came back. The tremendous power flux through the disintegrator had overheated the liquid hydrogen that kept it cool, the superconducting coils had quenched, and the tremendous back-current had surged the ship's generators.

"Cooling offline . . ." Marxle's voice held resignation.

"Cease fire. Damage report." Voortman kept his voice under control. The beams had already stopped. His ship would need maintenance, that was certain. *But what matters is that the kzinti will see what I have done and know that God will have no mercy for them.*

The viscom blinked, and Admiral Mysolin was looking at him. "What was that, Captain?"

Voortman saluted. "Sir, I report the enemy base destroyed."

"That and a lot more. Did you have a weapons malfunction?"

"No malfunction. We may have some damage to our superconductors. Our main weapon is offline for now. Repairs are underway."

Mysolin's eyebrows went up. "Is there a reason you maintained fire for as long as you did?"

"With due respect, sir, you are responsible for fleet strategy. I am responsible for fighting my ship."

"And as fleet commander I am now questioning your decision making. I expect an answer, Captain."

Voortman looked at him in silence. *He does not understand.*

"I want to know why you kept firing when the military objective had already been achieved." Mysolin would not be dissuaded from his question.

After a long pause Voortman answered. "Have you read Clausewitz, Admiral?"

"Don't change the subject, Captain."

"I am not, sir. I am explaining my point. Clausewitz said, 'War is diplomacy continued with other means.' I continued firing because the diplomatic objective had not yet been achieved. To destroy a base from orbit, this is trivial. Had I stopped firing that is all we would have done. Instead we have sent the kzinti a message today. We have shown them we have the power to exterminate them. We have shown them that their Judgment is coming. They will fear us now." Captain Voortman smiled a predatory smile. "They will feel our hands on their throats. This was my objective, Admiral. This was Wunderland's objective, regardless of how the UN feels about it. And this is what we have achieved today."

"You have exceeded your orders and your authority and hazarded a major war vessel." Mysolin's voice was cold.

"I have done what was necessary. Sir."

Mysolin looked at him, features cold, but when he spoke it wasn't to Voortman.

"Commander Kirsch!"

"Sir." Kirsch stepped forward.

"Captain Voortman is relieved of command. *Oorwinnig* is your ship. Take her back to Tiamat for repairs."

"Yes, sir."

The image in the viscom vanished, and Voortman wheeled to face his subordinate. "Kirsch! Don't you move a muscle. This is *my* ship. He isn't a Wunderlander. He has no authority here."

Kirsch stepped closer, spoke in low tones. "Sir, perhaps it would be easiest if we went along with the admiral for now. The battle is over, and we do need to go back to Tiamat."

"Don't be foolish, Kirsch."

"Sir . . . Cornelius . . ." Kirsch didn't finish the sentence. He was clearly torn between orders and loyalty. Equally clearly he was going to follow his orders, no matter how unpleasant he found them. Voortman looked around the bridge, met the eyes of his weapons officer, his sensor team. All of them kept their expressions carefully blank. He would find no support there.

Voortman raised his voice. "You have the bridge, Commander Kirsch. Make sure I'm called for the top watch." He stalked off to his dayroom without waiting for an answer. He already knew he wouldn't be called. At Tiamat there would be a court-martial, perhaps. *But I have done what I set out to do, and history will thank me for it.*

Ten thousand kilometers below him the dust cloud left on A-M II's surface continued to rise and spread, blotting the sun from the skies. By the time the planet had gone around its star again it would be enveloped in a gray funeral shroud that would reflect enough light to bring perpetual winter even to its equator. Before enough dust settled to let the sunshine back in again the shallow seas would be frozen to the bottom. The fragile beginnings of life would be completely snuffed out, and the only sign that intelligence had ever visited the planet would be a canyon two hundred kilometers long and eighteen deep.

> *Blood is the strength of the Pride.*
> —Wisdom of the Conservers

The sun was high as Pouncer pulled his *tuskvor* to a halt and surveyed the ground. Mrrsel Pride's den was farther into the canyon lands than Ztrak Pride's, at the far end of a steep walled box canyon, a natural fortification. There would be watchers high on the red cliffs on either side of the canyon entrance. He raised his binoptics and scanned for them but saw nothing. They were well concealed. Best then to leave the *tuskvor* here and advance openly on foot until he was challenged. Mrrsel Pride were his mother's kin. He had kills in battle, and he was First-Son-of-Meerz-Rrit. He could claim his place here, and a name. He needed to do that before he could take on the Tzaatz. The *czrav* prides were a tremendous resource, fanatic fighters, and with their high proportion of natural telepaths, able to communicate and organize beneath the notice of the rest of the Patriarchy, bound as they were to the limitations of the electromagnetic spectrum. More importantly the Telepath War aligned their interests with his. Kchula-Tzaatz himself had shown him how to take the Citadel. Surprise from within, and a small, elite force coming over the wall under the rules of *skalazaal*. The *czrav* would form the elite force, if he could convince them to follow him, and there would still be some in the Citadel who remembered their fealty pledge to the Rrit.

He put his weight on the harness bar to move the *tuskvor*'s head down and waited while the beast slowly yielded to the pressure. Once it was all the way down he tied it off so the beast couldn't wander away, and then dismounted.

He'd expected to be challenged at the canyon entrance, but he wasn't. He moved confidently, but kept his eyes open. It was possible he'd come to the wrong canyon, although Kr-Pathfinder's instructions had been quite clear. There was only one way to find out.

His tail was already twitching with concern by the time he reached the den mouth unchallenged. There were no harnessed *tuskvor*, either outside the canyon or inside it, though their spoor was everywhere. It was possible they had moved, but why? He stood at the empty den mouth and waited for his eyes to adjust to the dimmer light. The charcoal of the pride circle fire was there; this was not the wrong canyon.

"I am First-Son-of-Meerz-Rrit, son of M'ress of Mrrsel Pride!" His call echoed from the distant cavern walls. He listened for a response, ears swiveled up and forward, but none came. "I come to your circle with news from Ztrak Pride." Again there was no answer.

He knelt to look for spoor. Marks in the sandy floor of the cavern, where something heavy had been dragged, many somethings. Cautiously he followed them. The footmarks of kzinti, impressions of *prrstet* pads around the pride circle. Other footmarks, something small and four legged with three clawed toes per foot. Deeper in the cavern was tiled with stone slabs, and the easy spoor vanished. A smear on the stones. He sniffed it. Kzinti blood. The direction of the smear aligned with the drag marks. A bleeding body had been dragged from the den. He found more bloody drag marks. *Many bodies.* With mounting alarm he turned and continued deeper into the cavern. At the entrance to a side passage a flow sculpture of ancient stone was cut in half on an angle, the bottom still standing on its base, the top on the floor beside it. He examined the almost mirror-smooth cut. *A variable sword, but the* czrav *don't use variable swords.* At least, Ztrak Pride didn't, but they used hunt cloaks and other technological impedimenta. They could make variable swords if they wanted to, and perhaps Mrrsel Pride did.

It is unlikely, but not impossible. He didn't want to consider the alternative, and then in an alcove he saw something that removed all doubt. It was a small, scaly body, badly mangled. It took him a moment to recognize it, the source of the three-clawed tracks. *A harrier* rapsar. The Tzaatz had found the den. Sick despair surged in his liver.

Mrrsel Pride, his mother's pride, were dead. He ran then, through rough-hewn passageways and finely appointed chambers, looking for any survivors. Everywhere there were signs of a violent battle, spattered blood, broken furnishings. Nowhere was there even a body. Finally exhausted he staggered to the den entrance and roared, anger welling up in him as the sound echoed from the canyon walls. *Kchula-Tzaatz, you will pay for this.*

And then sick worry spread through him. The Tzaatz could only have found Mrrsel Pride by tracking the migration. They were searching for *him*, and they'd kill everything they found until they were sure he was dead. The blood scent was still fresh; the raid had been only a day ago, at most. Soon they would know that he wasn't among the bodies they'd collected, and they would go looking for another pride. Ztrak Pride, and Cherenkova-Captain . . . He ran out of the canyon to his *tuskvor*. He needed Ztrak Pride now, and now that he had left he would have to win his place there as well. He would rather not have returned nameless to the pride that gave him sanctuary, but he had no option. *It is not just I who need them now. They need me, to warn them of the Tzaatz.* There was no time to waste.

> *Think, if you like, of the distance we have come, but never let your mind run forward faster than your vessel.*
>
> —Captain William Bligh

Quacy Tskombe was watching Trina throw fish for Curvy. It was a game they both loved, and it was like a day

at the marine park for him. Curvy would do a trick, and
Trina would throw her a fish, or two fish, or three fish,
depending on how good she thought it was. Except if
Curvy thought her trick was worth more than she got
she'd leap up and belly flop to splash Trina, who would try
to scramble out of the way, laughing. She never made it,
and she was soaked from the start of the game. The fish
were a lot smaller than the darting trout that still filled the
pool. Curvy was playing for fun, not food, and for Trina.
Curvy didn't have her translator on, so the communication
was entirely nonverbal, but that made the playful care she
gave the girl all the more effective. Swimming was a luxury
Trina hadn't enjoyed since her mother had died, and the
water seemed to cleanse her soul, the layers of tough
defiance dissolving to reveal a carefree girl-child hidden
deep inside. The dolphin was better therapy than any
psychdoc, with a talent for drawing the girl out of herself.
In the safe, restricted environment of the UN quarter,
Trina was slowly healing.

Tskombe sighed and left the pool deck to go back to his
room. It was something that was going to have to stop
soon. The UN support people were still pulling out all the
stops for them on the basis of Curvy's high level ident. He
hadn't heard from Sergeant Veers again, but he knew they
were on borrowed time. Ravalla's group on Earth were
tying up loose ends in the consolidation of power. *One
more day to find a ship, and then we're going to have to
take passage to Wunderland.* That would be a setback,
because the cost of the tickets would eat up enough
money that he'd have to get more before he could hire a
ship, but it had to be done. They couldn't locate in

Munchen either, because they would need to be on a coast somewhere, so Curvy would have salt water. Away from the capital it would be harder to find work. *And my qualifications don't lend themselves to application outside the UNF.* The ability to lead a strike battalion into the attack counted for little in the civilian world.

And Trina would have to go to the Bureau of Displaced Persons. That would be a setback for her as well. Maybe there was a way he could arrange to have Curvy look after her. The Wunderland government should value the dolphin's skills as highly as the UN did. *And maybe that's the answer to the problem.* Curvy was much more marketable than he was, and they could cut a deal. He nodded to himself. He'd book their passage immediately.

He picked up his beltcomp just as it chimed. There was a face in the holocube, a kzin.

At least it wasn't Veers. He keyed *answer*. "Good afternoon."

"You are the human Quacy Tskombe?"

Tskombe nodded. "Do I know you?"

The kzin's image twitched its whiskers. "You took me to Healer, when I was injured. You have my blood debt." The kzin didn't look happy about it.

"You're welcome." Tskombe didn't know what else to say.

"Healer told me you seek a ship with a kzinti pilot."

Tskombe raised his eyebrows. *This might be interesting.* "Yes."

"May I ask why?"

"I need to get to Kzinhome."

The kzin's ears swiveled up and forward. "May I ask why again?"

"Why are you interested in what I'm doing?"

"I might be able to get you in contact with a pilot, to repay my debt to you. I need to understand what you will do with the ship."

Tskombe shrugged. "I was on a diplomatic mission to Kzinhome. The Patriarch was deposed, as you might know, and we were caught in the middle. One of my colleagues is still there, and I want to bring her back."

The kzin's lips twitched over his fangs. "I know of this conflict. I was once Grarl-Rrit-Patriarch's-Voice."

Tskombe's eyebrows went up. "You were?"

No-longer-Grarl-Rrit snarled. "Do you doubt my honor, *kz'zeerkti*?"

"No, please forgive me. I was surprised."

"I was Third-Son-of-Yiao-Rrit, and cousin to the new Patriarch. Scrral-Rrit has dishonored my line, and I am now outcast."

"I am . . . I am sorry."

"Yes. Now I invite the pity of herbivores. My shame is great. Nevertheless, I will not allow myself to owe blood debt to one." The kzin wrinkled his nose. "I find your reasons acceptable. Do you wish me to find you a ship?"

"Please. I would appreciate it."

"It will take some time." The screen went black. For a kzin who had been Patriarch's Voice, No-longer-Grarl-Rrit was not big on formality.

The time it took turned out to be two days, long enough for Tskombe to decide they couldn't delay getting off Tiamat any longer. He was actually in the process of booking tickets when his beltcomp chimed and the kzin appeared, gave him directions to a bar in Tigertown, gave him a time, and told him to go there and wait. Tskombe started to ask who he'd be waiting for, but again the screen went black before he could say anything.

He recognized the place when he got there; it was the same place he'd been thrown out of when he'd started his search for a ship. He took a chair by the bar. It was early yet, and the place was nearly empty. He got a few looks from the kzinti already there and carefully ignored them.

The big kzin who ran the place came over. "You have been told to leave twice already, human." Proprietor's lips twitched over his fangs.

"Grarl-Rrit sent me here. I'm waiting for someone."

"Grarl-Rrit?" Proprietor's ears swiveled up and forward. "Grarl-Rrit is dead." The big kzin spat the words with contempt, but he went away and let Tskombe sit where he was unmolested.

Tskombe considered ordering a drink and thought better of it. Proprietor would let him know if he was breaking a social convention. The method of contact wasn't a question. He was the only human in the place; whoever he was meeting could be watching him right now and he'd be none the wiser. He'd waited long enough to get bored when a large kzin sat down beside him. Proprietor came over and the kzin ordered vodka and ice cream, then turned to Tskombe.

"You are the human the outcast spoke of, yes?"

Tskombe nodded. "I need to get a ship. Grarl . . ." He caught himself. "The kzin who was once known as Grarl-Rrit thought you could help."

The kzin raised an ear. "Who are you?"

"Quacy Tskombe, recently of the UNF."

"Recently . . ." The kzin looked him up and down. "What are you now?"

"Now I'm no one, I need to find someone."

"No one looking for someone. Hrrr." The kzin looked him over again. "You need a pilot, I think. Do you know who I am?"

Tskombe shrugged. "Not a clue."

"So the outcast said nothing?"

"He said to come here and wait."

"And you took his word?"

"I had little choice. I came, and you're here. Who are you?"

"You take risks, taking the word of one like the outcast."

Tskombe nodded. "I judged he was well connected. I didn't ask him to help, he offered."

"He did?" The kzin's ears fanned up. "Why?"

"I helped him, after a fight. He owed me blood debt, he said."

"Hrrr. He retains more honor than his cousin, at least."

Tskombe met the kzin's gaze. "And who are you, exactly?"

"I am known as Night Pilot. I have my own ship."

Tskombe's eyes widened. He'd expected to have to go through more intermediaries. The kzinti dealt directly. "Can I hire you?"

"Perhaps, if you have what I need."

"What do you need?"

"Money. What else?"

"How much?"

"How much do you have?"

"Enough." Tskombe shrugged. "Name your price."

Night Pilot smiled a fanged smile. "One hundred million kroner."

Tskombe snorted. "You're not serious."

"You said name my price. I named it. Perhaps you have not got enough after all."

"Let's not play games here. I'll give you a reasonable fee."

"Then what is your offer?"

Tskombe avoided the question. "Why are you called Night Pilot? Isn't it always night in space?"

"The cargoes I carry must frequently be landed when the drop zone is behind the solar terminator."

"Why?"

Night Pilot turned a paw over. "My clients require the utmost discretion."

"You're a smuggler."

"I am what humans call a freerunner."

"Is there a difference?"

"Hrrr." Night Pilot's lips twitched involuntarily. "I will assume you intend no insult by that. I am a pilot whose clients require discretion and skillful ship command, as you do. I provide that service, and I stand behind both my flight skills and my discretion with my honor. The details of what they ship are no concern of mine. Most independent pilots will not provide such services; few that do are as reliable as I. For this reason I charge premium cargo rates. Does that make it clear? I suspect that the mission you are undertaking will involve considerable risk. My fee must therefore include a risk premium."

Tskombe nodded. "Money I can give you. Do you not seek *strakh* as well?"

Night Pilot twitched his whiskers. "I owe no fealty to the Patriarch or any Great Pride. What use have I for *strakh*?"

And Tskombe could say nothing to that. Kefan Brasseur would have known how to answer, but Kefan was dead. Was Ayla? *Please let her be alive.*

"What cargo are you shipping?"

"It's actually another passenger, a cetacean. The cetacean will require a water tank, which you may consider cargo."

Night Pilot wrinkled his ears. "What is a cetacean?"

"A dolphin, an intelligent marine mammal. This one is a matrix strategist."

"The tank is for a water environment? How large is it?"

"One thousand cubic meters, approximately, half air and half salt water, with several more cubic meters of environmental control equipment and food."

"Hrrr. Mass approximately six hundred tonnes then. I can carry that. And the destination?"

"Kzinhome."

Night Pilot's ears swiveled up in surprise. "You take an extreme risk to travel there unescorted."

"I've been there before." If the kzin was further surprised by that news he kept it to himself. Tskombe went on. "I also need a guide on Kzinhome."

"For what purpose?"

"You have heard there is a new Patriarch."

"Scrral-Rrit. Everyone has heard."

"What do you know of him?"

"Little but that he stains his father's name. The intrigues of the Patriarch's court are of little import here at K'Shai. We are in no rush to replace the Patriarch's Voice."

Tskombe nodded. "I was part of a diplomatic mission to Kzinhome. The new Patriarch took power with the assistance of Tzaatz Pride. In the fighting my colleagues and myself were caught between factions. I managed to escape, but I left someone behind."

"And you wish to rescue him?"

"Her. I hope to."

"And the cetacean?"

"She is a matrix strategist. She will accompany us to the surface."

"No."

"Excuse me?"

"No. I will not transport the cetacean. My reputation stands on my ability to protect my clientele. Environmental considerations demand that the dolphin will remain on the ship. If I am to guide you I cannot also offer protection to the dolphin. Confined as it will be to its tank, it will be helpless if something goes wrong."

"She will not be confined to her tank, she has a set of dolphin hands, and an environmental bodysuit with polarizers. She will be mobile, and her advice will be important."

"This is not a solution on Kzinhome. A water creature will make novel prey, and be unable to defend itself. It will be difficult to protect."

"I'm sure there are other pilots who will take her."

"Then find them." Night Pilot showed his teeth.

Tskombe considered for a moment. *And I will have more freedom to operate if I don't have to worry about*

Curvy. And Curvy will be here to look after Trina.
"Agreed then. The cetacean will remain behind."

"Hrrr." The kzin's fanged smile relaxed. "Now we must discuss the fee."

"I have no idea how much a trip like that should cost. You have the advantage of me. I'll trust your honor to give me a fair price."

"Hrrr." Night Pilot turned a paw over. "Two million kroner for the voyage, both ways, fuel inclusive. Four thousand kroner each day I spend on the ground as your guide."

"You can't be serious. I could get a ticket to Earth for twenty thousand."

"On a passenger ship the cost is split with the other passengers, but there are no passenger runs to Kzinhome. Here you are hiring the entire ship, and myself and my copilot. Earth is just four light-years away; Kzinhome is nearly eight-squared. Fuel is expensive."

Tskombe whistled. "You don't come cheap."

"That price covers my fuel costs, maintenance costs, time, risk, and opportunity costs for the voyage. It is reasonable in the circumstances. We will have to plan carefully for our actions on Kzinhome; it will be dangerous, for both of us."

Tskombe nodded, and tapped his beltcomp, waited for his account readout to display. "I'll give you one million fifty-four thousand kroner, for the ship and for thirty days guiding on Kzinhome."

"Not enough."

Tskombe turned his beltcomp around so the kzin could see the readout. "It's all I have." *Fifteen years accumulated pay and bonuses. I'm taking a tremendous risk here.* His gaze didn't waver from Night Pilot's. *My decision is already made.*

"Hrrr." Night Pilot turned his paw over again, considering. "For this I will take you to Kzinhome, one way, with no time spent guiding."

Tskombe considered. One way meant he had no route home, but he could cross that bridge when he came to it.

"No, that's the whole reason I need a kzinti pilot."

"Hire another kzin to do it for you."

"I can't if I give you everything I've got. Twenty days guiding then."

Night Pilot looked away, calculating. "I cannot afford to let my ship stand idle. Operating expenses do not stop when I do. The price I quote is what my skills and equipment are worth. If I accept your offer I will forgo half my profit, and will have no margin for unexpected fuel costs or repairs. My partner will not agree to this."

"There must be a way."

"Hrrr." Night Pilot considered. "You are flying without cargo, so I will save slightly on fuel. In addition a flight to Kzinhome is attractive, because there is a high probability of finding a lucrative cargo there." He turned a paw over. "I would be willing to take these risks, if my partner agrees." He looked back to Tskombe. "In order to make the risk pay off I must find a cargo as soon as we touch down. I cannot spend time guiding."

"Five days then."

"Hrrr." Night Pilot considered further. "I am sorry, but I cannot." He looked up to meet Tskombe's eyes. "Unless . . ."

"Unless . . . ?"

"My partner can find a cargo while I guide you. You must understand that once my cargo is consigned I will have to leave, no matter how much time I have given you."

"How much time would that be, roughly?"

"I would estimate eight days, roughly, Kzinhome standard. It may vary considerably from that."

Tskombe nodded. "And the minimum time?"

"It will take a minimum of two days to refuel the ship, check systems and prepare to boost again."

"I see." *Eight days is not much time; two days won't be enough.* Tskombe considered the kzin. He wasn't trying to talk up the price, he already knew the full extent of Tskombe's bank account. He was simply laying out his operating parameters so Tskombe could make a decision as to whether his needs would be met by the deal they could strike. "If you get a cargo your return fuel costs are covered. Can we make it a round trip, my flight to coincide with your next cargo flight?"

"The return trip might not be to Alpha Centauri, or even human space."

Tskombe nodded. *And what I need most is to get off of Tiamat, immediately. Everything else can be figured out on Kzinhome.* "I'll take that risk. When can we leave?"

"This is contingent on my partner's agreement. Given that, we can be prepared to boost in twenty-seven hours. Will that suffice?"

Tskombe nodded. "That's fine."

"Do you have anything that needs to be preloaded?"

"Just my personal effects."

"Understood. The ship is *Black Saber*, in bay seventeen at the downaxis hub. I will call you when I have consulted my partner. I do not expect a problem. You should plan to depart in twenty-seven hours."

Night Pilot offered his paw for Tskombe to shake, an oddly human gesture. Tskombe shook it somewhat awkwardly. He felt a strange tension come over him. Everything up to this point had been an obstacle to be overcome. Now he was going to march quite literally into the lion's den. *Ayla, I hope you're there.* Twenty-seven hours, and he would be on his way to Kzinhome. *And what will I do when I arrive?* That was something he hadn't worked out yet, there had been too many more immediate problems to solve first.

He tubed back to their quarters, relieved when the car arrived there and not at ARM headquarters again. The UN on Tiamat still hadn't caught up with his status with the UN on earth. He had one more tube ride to take and he wouldn't have to worry about Sergeant Veers anymore. When he arrived Trina was still in the pool with Curvy. It seemed to Tskombe that she only came out to eat and sleep. Another week or two and he expected she'd be catching trout in her teeth.

"I have a ship!" he announced while Trina swam over and Curvy nosed herself into her handsuit.

Trina beamed. "That's wonderful, when do we leave?" She pulled herself out of the water, sleek and dripping.

"Not we, just me. You have to stay here with Curvy."

"What? No!" Trina was visibly upset.

Curvy trilled. "When last we discussed this I was to accompany you."

"The pilot won't take you. He won't accept responsibility for your safety on Kzinhome."

"What about me?" Trina interjected.

"You can't go because it's too dangerous. We've already discussed this." Tskombe raised his hands to forestall further argument. "Look, this is a good option. We all know it will be dangerous, and it's ultimately my mission. Curvy, you can swing a deal with the Wunderland government and get immunity from the ARM, and that will get you the resources to look after Trina."

"I want to come with you," said Trina.

"Look how well you're doing here with Curvy," he reasoned. "On Wunderland you can—"

Trina cut him off, her voice rising. "You're going for Ayla. You don't even know if she's alive and you're going for her."

"You know that's what I'm here to do."

"Just take me with you, I can help you find her." There was an edge of desperation in her voice. Tskombe was unprepared for her reaction. *She knew this was the plan.*

"I can't." He saw her eyes brimming with tears. "I'll come back for you, I told you that, I promise." The words felt empty even as he said them. The probabilities were he wouldn't be coming back at all.

"You won't be." Trina burst into tears and ran out, nearly tripping on the still dilating pressure door in her haste.

The door contracted again, and Tskombe sighed deeply as he watched it. There was nothing else he could say.

Curvy whistled to break the silence. "This represents a change in plans, Colonel Tskombe. We must make strategy."

He turned to the dolphin, relieved to have a problem he could understand. "I think this is a better option. The situation on Kzinhome is dangerous, and as much as I'd appreciate your advice, you'll be quite literally out of your element. And I'd rather not send Trina to the Bureau of Displaced Persons. They'll look after her, but she needs more than that."

"Let me consider this." Curvy's manipulator tentacles tapped keys on her console. The matrix simulation ran for a few minutes, and then numbers spilled over the screen. Curvy whistled and clicked. "The risk balance is favorable. I concur you may travel alone. Trina's well-being is not a factor in global consideration, although of course I am concerned for her on a personal level."

Tskombe spread his hands. "The pilot won't take you."

"I understand. Nor do I recommend we delay or try to find another pilot. The ARM may rectify their mistake with you at any time, and our efforts will come to nothing. You must leave, and I must stay. The pertinent question concerns what you will do on Kzinhome."

"I haven't figured that out yet."

"I have almost no parameters to build a model with. I expect the situation will be very fluid, which is why I intended to accompany you, in order to construct a more complete strategic matrix as information became available on the ground."

"So in the absence of that, what do I do? I can't search the entire world."

"I would recommend you make contact with the ruling faction controlled by the Tzaatz. You still have the sigil of the new Patriarch's father, which should offer you at least initial immunity from attack. You can negotiate to prevent war, and the entire resources of the Patriarchy will be available to help you find Captain Cherenkova."

"I'm not sure I trust the Tzaatz."

"There is the risk that the ruling faction will be using the threat of war with humanity in order to facilitate their consolidation of power. However, in the absence of a complete model of the situation, I believe this is your best option."

Tskombe nodded. "Not a good option, but the best option." *I knew this was going to be risky when I started.* "How are you going to get to Wunderland?"

"I am not going to Wunderland. I will continue to work for the United Nations. I will be able to exert more effective influence on the course of events within their framework. Despite its independence, Wunderland remains a colony world and is orders of magnitude less powerful than Earth. Also, I would like to retain the freedom to return to the North Pacific. Switching allegiance to Wunderland will make that impossible."

Tskombe's eyebrows went up. *That's the first time Curvy has expressed anything remotely sentimental.* It shouldn't have been surprising. Dolphins were highly social and he could only imagine the sacrifice involved in leaving the oceans to work with a species which was, to them, as alien as the kzinti were to humans. "Listen, we're on borrowed time here. The UN here is treating you well based on your clearance. Once the left hand figures out what the right hand is doing, that will end."

"No, you have been on borrowed time. My position is different. If you will forgive any implied discourtesy, you are easily replaceable in the UN hierarchy. I am not."

"Granted, but you're the one who got me off-world. Ravalla's group is going to see you as the enemy now. It doesn't matter how hard you are to replace if you aren't working for them."

Curvy clicked something and the translator said "Untranslatable," then "I will see to it that they see me as a friend, and more importantly, as an asset."

"You've already deserted from the UN, if not all the way to Wunderland. How are you going to explain that?"

"I will blame Commander Khalsa. Humans are too willing to see dolphins as their tools. Their prejudices will be satisfied, and they will be disposed to believe an answer which seems to serve their purposes."

"And Khalsa's reputation will be ruined."

"Irrelevant. His reputation is of no further use to him."

"His family won't get his pension if they process him with a dishonorable release from the service."

"The Commander had no pensionable relatives. Those he has might suffer a worse fate if my freedom of action is constrained."

"What if that doesn't work?"

"It has already worked. A UNSN fleet is enroute here. I have been asked to serve as Fleet Strategist."

"That's not good news."

"Secretary Ravalla is wasting no time. I have some information which indicates UN and Wunderland forces are already operating together against the kzinti. You are running in front of the storm."

Tskombe nodded. "I can't run until the ship is ready to boost. Then . . ." He spread his hands. They talked some more and played a last round of poker. Tskombe felt a twinge of regret. He had come to like the dolphin, and he realized now that their paths might not cross again. *But I must do what I must do, for her purposes and my own.*

Much later he went up to Trina's small room and knocked on the door. He could hear her sobbing inside. He called her name and got no answer. He stood there awhile, uncertain as to the right course of action. Finally he left. *Let her get it out, and then she'll feel better.*

He slept fitfully and spent the next day packing, using Curvy's UN credit to get the few essentials he'd need for the journey. Trina slept through breakfast and was silent and distant at lunch, but at dinner she had cheered up, chattering happily about some friends she'd met out on the pedmall. She raced through her food and gave him a hug on the way out.

"I'll see you later, check?"

"Check." Her smile was radiant. *It was the right thing to get her off Earth.*

He napped after dinner, set his alarm and woke before it went off. Trina was still out, a disappointment, but maybe it was better that way. One final tube ride, once more not diverted to the ARM. *And now I don't have to worry about that anymore.* Bay seventeen was small and well used, but it looked functional. That was more than could be said for *Black Saber*. He looked with some concern at the ship he'd hired. She had perhaps four times the volume of *Valiant*, and was easily four times older. She was night-black, with her registration in bright yellow on her nose, in both Arabic numerals and the dots and commas of Kzinscript. Umbilicals snaked from her belly: power, data, and more that he couldn't identify. Two heavy hoses were crusted with frost and steaming gently; liquid hydrogen for the attitude jets and liquid oxygen for the life support, he guessed. A smaller hose, heavily shielded and also frosted, was probably for tritium deuteride. The freighter's hull was covered in discolored patches, marking places where laser gouges in the ablative armor had been repaired. The landing skids were worn and still caked with the mud of some distant world. The lasers in her turrets were too big for a ship of her class, her sensor suite seemed patched together from spare parts, and her hyperdrive had been cannibalized from some other vessel, if the change in the hull plating at that section was any indicator. The ship's polarizer nacelles, also cannibalized, bulged out of proportion to her size. She would be fast at least, if she could hold together.

He went up to the bay's observation deck for Trina, but she wasn't there. He'd hoped she'd appear before he had to boost, but it looked like she wasn't going to be. *Not entirely unexpected.* The girl didn't want to be abandoned again, so she was abandoning him first. *I hope at least she has the sense to go back to Curvy.* Night Pilot came down the ramp, two meters of mottled tabby now wearing a tight fitting stretchfab pressurization suit with a fighter pilot's helmet carried easily under one arm. Tskombe didn't have a pressurization suit, and looking from Night Pilot to his battered ship, he wondered if he should have bought one.

"Welcome aboard, Quacy-Tskombe." Night Pilot beckoned him up the passenger ramp. Behind him the ground crew began removing umbilicals. Despite her larger size, *Black Saber*'s passenger space wasn't much bigger than *Valiant*'s. Most of her internal space was given over to cargo. Night Pilot showed Tskombe his cabin, small but adequate for his purposes, and surprisingly clean in view of the generally run-down appearance of the rest of the ship. The kzin ran through a detailed list of procedures to be followed in emergencies ranging from gravity failure to cabin depressurization. Such briefings were standard on any commercial transport, and *Black Saber*'s were not materially different from any of dozens Tskombe had heard before, but Night Pilot delivered the information with such intensity that Tskombe found himself paying close attention. Under the circumstances it was simple prudence. There might be a test later, graded pass/fail, and the penalty for failure would be death. He'd broken the rules on *Valiant* and it had nearly killed him.

After the briefing Night Pilot took him up to the cockpit. There was a creature there, like a five-armed octopus with joints, if you didn't look too close. Each arm had an eye where the limb met the featureless central body, and it sat on a crash couch shaped like a mushroom with five indentations. Two of the limbs were acting as legs to hold it on the couch, the other three as arms to run the controls as it set up the ship.

"This is Contradictory, my partner and copilot." Night Pilot sat in his crash couch and started strapping himself in. The Jotok wasn't wearing a pressurization suit, and Tskombe felt a little relieved at that. It, at least, didn't expect the rattletrap freighter to lose atmosphere as soon as they hit vacuum.

The Jotok bobbed on its supporting limbs and swiveled three eyes at Tskombe. "We are being Contradictory and we are being pleased to meet you." Its voice had an odd whistle to it, like a parrot who'd been trained to speak. The arms facing the instrument panel, and presumably the two eyes attached to them, kept running through the preflight procedure. Tskombe bowed to the alien in return. *It calls itself a we.* Jotok were composite entities, he knew. Each limb began as a free-swimming larva, and it sought out and joined with four others before they all grew to adulthood as a group.

Night Pilot pulled his helmet on and snarled something that Tskombe didn't quite catch, then listened for a reply. He raised the helmet visor and snarled at Contradictory, "We are cleared for our launch window."

Contradictory tapped controls and snarled back, "Prelaunch checklist is being complete in two minutes."

Tskombe raised an eyebrow. The Hero's Tongue was the language of *Black Saber*'s bridge, but its pilots used human measurements. Alpha Centauri system was a crossroads.

Night Pilot's tail lashed slowly as he set up his own displays. Once satisfied he looked back over his shoulder. "Quacy-Tskombe, we will be departing in approximately ten minutes. You should strap in to your crash couch now."

So there would be no opportunity to watch the undocking. It was reasonable, given the situation; he was just a passenger here, but since his experience in the Swiftwing he'd grown fond of being on the bridge. *No more breaking the rules.* He went back into his stateroom and strapped in. No sign of Trina, and now it was too late. He hoped she'd be okay.

For half an hour he lay in his crash couch, staring at the ceiling and not thinking of anything in particular. There were occasional gentle surges as *Black Saber* maneuvered out of the docking bay and into exo-system transfer orbit. Eventually Contradictory came on the in-com and told him he could unstrap.

There was still nothing to do but lie there. Eventually he unbelted himself and went up to the ship's navigation blister to watch the stars. The Milky Way was spread like cream across the center of his field of view and he spent awhile contemplating the millions of civilizations it had seen live and die since its formation. Who could contemplate such an immensity of time and space? No human mind was large enough. Perhaps the Outsiders could. At least they lived on a timescale long enough to follow the starseeds on their eons-long migrations from the galactic core to the rim and back again. *And how long do Outsiders live? And how did they and the starseeds evolve in deep space? What else is waiting for us out there?* He switched off the gravity and let himself float. For thousands of years mankind had dreamed of the stars, and even with the colonization of space and the commercialization of interstellar travel he remained one of a tiny privileged fraction of humanity who would ever see the stars from outside of an atmosphere.

After a while he switched the gravity back on, got out his beltcomp, and called up the newsfeeds while they were still close enough for *Black Saber*'s outcom to talk to Tiamat without speed of light lag becoming a problem. The news wasn't good. Muro Ravalla had publicly signed a defense-of-human-space pact with Wunderland, an obvious first step toward an attack on the Patriarchy. The shipping news announced the departure of no less than one hundred and eighty Earth ships for Wunderland, four entire battle groups. Occasionally he looked up at the stars and smiled despite his concerns. *Curvy knew that was coming, and the fleet left well before the announcement.* It would be hard enough to find Ayla on Kzinhome without a war going on around him. *And I don't know how I'm going to get back to human space when I do.* Night Pilot would take them back for free, if he could find her before Contradictory managed to find a cargo, and if that cargo was going to human space. Unfortunately, the most likely outcome was that *Black Saber* would be long gone before Tskombe had properly started his search. Then he'd be left alone on Kzinhome without *strakh* and without allies, seen as either a slave or an enemy, and in either case liable for the hunt park at the whim of any kzin who crossed his path.

Outcomes. *If Curvy were here she could help me plan. She intends me to prevent a war.* How was that supposed to happen? Contacting the Tzaatz was the plan. He still felt uncomfortable with it. Curvy's strategic matrix didn't require Tskombe's survival, merely the achievement of the intended outcome. So what was he going to do? He needed a contact on the planet, at least.

Inspiration dawned. *Provider!* He could find the old warrior's stall in the market, perhaps. *If he's still there, it's a start, a base of operations. From there I'll have to play it by ear.* Perhaps Provider had Ayla with him, and that would solve all of his problems at once. He closed his eyes, trying to visualize the route Pouncer had led them on in their escape from the Citadel. He hadn't been paying close attention, but years of service in the infantry had trained his mind to pay attention to its surroundings even when he was concentrating on something else. They had come through a low tunnel, on the side of Hero's Square closest to the Citadel. He could get that far easily. The twists and turns of the market were another question, but a few landmarks would be all he needed, and he remembered quite clearly what provider's stall looked like, stout posts of a distinctive yellow wood, the ranked cages of food animals, the sauce jars. Next to that was . . . what? Another stall, selling some kind of electronics. And next to that? He couldn't quite remember.

But there was enough there to work with. If he couldn't find Provider, he could still go to the Tzaatz and negotiate for whatever he could get. He mulled over his options as he went back to watching the stars. *Technology is that which allows miracles to be taken for granted.* The view was no less beautiful for the realization.

Shipboard life soon fell into its familiar routine. Night Pilot and Contradictory stood opposite watches and Quacy found himself spending his copious free time with Night Pilot on his off watches. The kzin was good company, full of interesting stories of his adventures. He was a fourth-generation kit of Tiamat, perfectly fluent in English and Interspeak and several alien tongues as well. He had grown up on *Black Saber*—it had been his father's ship—and he'd learned to fly almost before he could walk. His entire life had been spent freerunning cargos, into and out of situations where the consigners were willing to pay high for a pilot who knew how to fly hard, fight hard, and keep his mouth shut. He'd won Contradictory in a bet with a noble on a kzinti world called Ch'lat, and given his new slave its freedom that night, after the Jotok saved his life when the noble's friends ambushed him on his way back to the ship. Nothing Night Pilot said admitted to any crime in human space, but the lines were there for Tskombe to read between—smuggling at least, possibly piracy. Both captain and ship were capable of it. Beneath her battered exterior *Black Saber* was fast and tough, and Night Pilot owed fealty to no one.

Their sixth day out of Tiamat, Tskombe had trouble sleeping. Eventually he gave up and went down to the cramped galley. Contradictory was there, feeding yellow, double-lobed fruits into his undermouth. They were each the size of a large apple, and so far as Tskombe could see Contradictory was swallowing them whole. He ordered whatever it was that the kitchen made that approximated roasted chicken and sat down to wait while it made it.

Contradictory finished its meal. "You are brave being traveling to Kzinhome, being unowned by any kzin."

Tskombe looked up. "Why is that?"

"You are being eaten of, if a kzin is so choosing."

Tskombe nodded. "I am hoping I won't be."

"We are being presented towards a slave for our time on Kzinhome. It is being possible that this will also being working for you."

Tskombe nodded. *Not a bad idea, if Night Pilot will go for it.* The Jotok's unusual speech pattern raised a question. "How did you come to be called Contradictory?"

The Jotok bobbed up and down. "We are being five self-sections. We think as a group or individually, as each task requires. Each section is possessing a self-symbolic identifier tag, and my name is being simply the sequential conjugation of those tags, being rendered as syllables."

Tskombe raised an eyebrow. "I find it hard to believe that five alien syllables just happen to form an English word."

"They are not being. You will being finding them unpronounceable. When being with other races we choose syllables being phonetically equivalent, being rendered as a pronounceable and relevant word."

"And the relevance of Contradictory?"

"My species is being enslaved to the kzinti since time immemorial, our names being given to us by our masters. I am being a full partner with Night Pilot in this ship. *Black Saber* is possessing of two minds but only one body, and the ship is not being moving if we are not being agreeing on its destination. I am recognizing of the value in my freedom to be disagreeing until a consensus is reached."

"Doesn't that create problems?" Tskombe tried and failed to imagine any kzin brooking disagreement from a slave species copilot.

"No. Consensus is producing toward optimized decisions. This is being part of our value in this partnership."

Tskombe nodded. *Not a problem for Contradictory, who has a five-way vote about every decision he makes, but I wonder how much patience Night Pilot has for the optimization process.* He didn't ask, it wasn't his business. The kzin was living by his honor, and *Black Saber* was a competently crewed ship, which was all that mattered from his point of view. There was a noise, footfalls, and Tskombe looked up, expecting to see Night Pilot. There

was a flash of *something* outside the galley accessway, too
small to be the kzin. *It must have been, but . . .*

He turned to Contradictory. "Did you see that?"

The Jotok bobbed its central body, seemingly unper-
turbed. "It is being human."

The ARM? It made no sense. *Or could the Jotok be
wrong?* He keyed the incom. "Night Pilot?"

"Yes?"

"Are you in the cockpit?"

"It's my watch." The kzin's tone implied there was
nowhere else he'd be on his watch.

"Just checking." Tskombe paused, still absorbing the
facts. "There's another person on the ship."

"It is probably just your manrette." Night Pilot was as
unconcerned as Contradictory.

"My *what*?"

"Your female. She usually comes out for food around
now." Night Pilot sounded irritated at his ignorance.

"My female? I don't have a . . ." A hypothesis occurred.
"Can you come down here? I have a couple of questions."

"Hrrr." There was a pause. Night Pilot didn't like his
passengers interfering with his watch. "Send
Contradictory to take over the cockpit."

Contradictory bobbed in acknowledgment and left,
and Tskombe went to the accessway and called. "Trina!"
He didn't manage to keep the annoyance from his voice.

She came, looking scared and defiant at once. He
didn't look at her, not trusting himself to speak until Night
Pilot arrived. *How did she . . . ?* He would know soon
enough.

"Night Pilot, how did she get on board?"

The kzin wrinkled his nose, puzzled. "The usual way. She arrived several hours before you did. I put her in the other cabin."

"I said one passenger!"

"Yourself and personal effects. This is what I understood." Night Pilot was still confused. "Is she not your female?"

"My female? As in my property?" Understanding dawned. "No, she's not a personal effect, she's a sentient legal entity in her own right." He gave Trina a look. "And she uses her sentience far too well for her own good. And mine."

"Hrrrr." Night Pilot's lips twitched over his fangs. "She told me she was cargo."

"Please don't be mad." Trina looked like she was about to cry. "I heard you and Curvy talking about my luck. If I'm with you, you'll be lucky too." He could hear her trying to convince herself as she said it. She hesitated, looking at her toes. Tskombe had never been upset with her before, and she wasn't sure how to handle it. "I just wanted to make sure you were safe." Her voice was small.

Tskombe took a deep breath. *She didn't want to be abandoned again.* He couldn't bring himself to be angry and turned to Night Pilot. "We have to go back."

"Hrr." Night Pilot paused, choosing his words carefully. "This is possible, but it presents a problem."

"Why is that?"

"You have purchased the use of my ship for the run to Kzinhome, and the fuel load and charges are computed accordingly. We are halfway out of Centauri system now. To decelerate and return to Tiamat means we will be unable to make Kzinhome without refueling. Tritium deuteride is expensive. I mention this only because I understand you will not be able to afford the fuel for another trip. The decision is yours. I will alter course if you order it."

Tskombe just looked at him. The kzin remained impassive. He was right, and there was nothing that could change that. *I could abandon the mission.* Of course he couldn't, so instead he counted to ten, slowly, to get his frustration under control. Trina was going to get her way.

He turned around. "Trina . . ." He still couldn't bring himself to scold her when he saw her eyes. "Where we're going is dangerous. You're going to have to do exactly what you're told, when you're told, no questions asked." He met her too serious gaze and held it. "Understood?"

"Oh yes. I'll do that." Relief flooded her face. "I'll do whatever you say."

"Good." Tskombe nodded. "I've had about all the rebellion I can handle for one day. We'll talk about this later." The kitchen chimed and delivered his approximately-chicken. He left it for Trina and went to his cabin to lie down and think. There was nothing to be done now, but Trina was going to present him with a problem on Kzinhome. *Probably many problems.* Time to think about that later. He put a pillow over his eyes and eventually went to sleep, to dream troubled dreams.

> *When the scent is right, mate.*
> —Wisdom of the Conservers

Darkness was falling as Pouncer's *tuskvor* came to the sandstone dome that was Ztrak Pride's high forest den.

The three-day journey from Mrrsel Pride had taken some of the urgency from Pouncer's drive to warn Ztrak Pride of the danger of the Tzaatz. All day as he rode he had scanned the skies for the glint of gravcars and had seen nothing. The forest was big, but the canopy cover was not absolute as it was in the jungle. Finding a well hidden den by tracking the vast herds of *tuskvor* now aimlessly wandering through the trees would be a difficult task. *Too difficult, I hope, but they found Mrrsel Pride.* He was relieved to see the faint glow of Ztrak's pride circle fire in the den mouth as he came up to it. *That is something that will have to change. The signature may be visible from space.* Reflexively he looked overhead for the fast-moving pinpricks that were ships or satellites. He saw none, but perhaps it wasn't yet dark enough.

He was challenged as he climbed the trail, and Silverstreak greeted him when he answered. He went past, and when he came to the den mouth he could see the pride circle was already gathered for *hvook raoowh h'een*, the fire glowing bright and warm in the middle. *I will wait until the first story is told, and then tell my own tale and give warning.* He took his usual place to V'rli's left in the pride circle, and looked to see who was telling the story. Immediately he froze. *This is not tale-telling-time!* In the center C'mell was crawling on her belly, her tail twitching back and forth in a mesmerizing rhythm. He found he couldn't look away, and then she called. *Chrrroowwwl!* Her deep need clear in the way the sound was torn from her very being. Reflexively he stiffened. The sound spoke directly to his hindbrain, flooding him with desire, and all thoughts of the Tzaatz and the slaughter of Mrrsel Pride were driven from his mind. Some distant part of his brain remembered the last time he'd heard that sound, fleeing for his life ahead of the Tzaatz attack on the Citadel. T'suuz had stopped him then. *Who will interfere if I want her?* He became aware of the rest of the pride circle, every male there with his eyes fixed on C'mell. *What are the rules here?* He had no idea. C'mell *chrowled* again, triggering another avalanche of desire in his system, and he twitched. She was in front of the more senior males on the other side of V'rli, presenting her haunches to Sraff-Tracker.

Sraff-Tracker! The kill rage swept through him. *Rage is death!* He held on to his self-control, barely, though his lips twitched away from his fangs. *Understand the rules first, leap later.* His late arrival had caused a small stir, and C'mell, who was looking backward at Sraff-Tracker, looked around and saw him, her gaze locking with his. She looked back at Sraff-Tracker again and twitched her tail, then leapt with easy grace across the pride circle and landed in front of Pouncer. She lowered her head and turned around, her luscious tail switching back and forth, her ripe female scent enveloping him. *What are the rules?* The entire pride circle was watching him now. In his world kzinretti were mated only by their owners, or those their owners chose to share them with. *How does it work when the kzinretti choose for themselves?* C'mell was inviting him in no uncertain terms. Did anything else matter? As if she were reading his mind she *chrowled* again, and raised her haunches. A fresh wave of her musk came over him, and everything else was forgotten. *When the scent is right, mate!* He moved to mount her.

A killscream echoed through the cavern, and he barely had time to look up as Sraff-Tracker came at his head, hind claws extended to kill. He rolled, not fast enough, but Sraff-Tracker's claws found his shoulder instead of his eyes. Flesh tore, and then he was free and flowing into *v'scree* stance. Sraff-Tracker had rolled with his attack and came back at him. Pouncer bent at the knees to lower his center of gravity, claws extending to slice his adversary's belly, but Sraff-Tracker was pivoting in midair, his hind leg coming around to slam Pouncer's wrist. Pain shot through Pouncer's arm and blood spattered. Sraff-Tracker's other leg straightened and connected hard with the side of Pouncer's head. The impact slammed him to the ground, his head spinning. His vision danced with sparks, but he retained the presence of mind to roll with the fall, so Sraff-Tracker's stabbing fangs closed on empty air instead of his throat. Fight juices flooded his bloodstream as he flipped back to his feet, and he screamed in the kill rage. *Rage is death.* Some distant part of his brain struggled to regain control, but the red rage overcame everything but the need to feel his enemy's flesh tear beneath his talons. He screamed and leapt, knowing it was a mistake, oblivious to the consequences. Sraff-Tracker was on the ground, off balance and recovering from his not quite successful attack. He jerked his arm up protectively up as Pouncer came at him. The motion was late, but the razor edge of his talons still sliced along Pouncer's outstretched arm. Pouncer screamed again, in pain this time as bright arterial blood pumped from the wound. Sraff-Tracker rolled backward and came to his feet a leap and a half away, breathing hard.

"First blood!" Sraff-Tracker's voice was exultant. "I'm going to kill you by slow cuts, kitten."

"Come claim your victory, son-of-*sthondats*." Pouncer spat the words through a fanged smile, claws extended once more in *v'scree* stance. *Rage is death.* His loss of control had cost him blood, and the sliced muscles in his forearm hampered him. *I shall not ignore my teaching again. Guardmaster be with me now.* He settled his feet into position and scanned the area around his opponent, visualized what was behind him. He must not surrender to his emotions here. Muted snarls rose from the watching *czrav*. He was breaking a rule. *What is it?*

Sraff-Tracker dropped to attack crouch, teeth bared, ears instinctively folded flat and back behind his skull. His eyes were narrow with pupils dilated wide with the kill rage, locked on Pouncer, but he did not leap.

His anger wars with his fear. Even as the realization came to him, Sraff-Tracker leapt, his scream echoing in the confines of the chamber. Pouncer twisted sideways to avoid him and brought his claws up to rake at Sraff-Tracker's spine. His wound slowed him, but his claws found the flesh along his adversary's rib cage, ripping deep into muscle and winning a scream of infuriated pain. Sraff-Tracker lashed out and caught Pouncer a glancing blow on the hip but drew more no more blood. The pair separated and again they faced each other across the dueling circle.

"The score evens." Pouncer's voice purred with satisfaction.

In response Sraff-Tracker leapt, though he had not yet recovered attack crouch. The suddenness of his attack caught Pouncer by surprise, and his dodge was too slow.

Sraff-Tracker double kicked at Pouncer's head, his claws connecting with one ear, almost tearing it off. Pouncer snapped around instinctively, his jaws closing on Sraff-Tracker's ankle, but his attacker's momentum carried him away. Sraff-Tracker hit the ground and rolled and Pouncer scrambled clear. Again Sraff-Tracker leapt as soon as he had gained his feet, snapping as he went past. Pouncer had not expected such a fast reversal and dropped flat, feeling the razor edged fangs slice through the hair on his neck.

He is fast, and dangerous. Pouncer leapt to his feet, and again adopted *v'scree* stance. *He gains strength and speed from his anger, but he is skilled too.* Even the veteran Tzaatz warrior who'd nearly killed him at the gate to the Forbidden Garden hadn't been so skilled. *The* czrav *are deadly warriors indeed.* C'mell *chrowled* again, the sound now not even a distraction as he focused all his attention on Sraff-Tracker. On the other side of the circle his opponent had paused to breathe deep. He should attack now, while Sraff-Tracker was tired, but his wound throbbed and his vision swam with his exertion. Sraff-Tracker's talons dripped with his blood. *Fear is death.* Pouncer leapt, his kill scream shaking the walls as he pivoted his hind claws around to launch a *g'rrtz* high kick. With his left he kicked Sraff-Tracker's block to one side, lashing out with his right to connect with his opponent's sternum. Sraff-Tracker stumbled back, overbalanced, and then Pouncer was on him. They went down in a snarling heap. Claws dug deep into Pouncer's belly, the sudden pain overriding his exhaustion. He ignored the damage, using his weight to force Sraff-Tracker down. His jaws found his enemy's shoulder and clamped hard. Sraff-Tracker screamed in rage and pulled away, flesh tearing around Pouncer's fangs.

"C'mell will be mine, and your *kz'zeerkti* will be my mating feast." The big kzin rolled clear, barely able to speak through his fanged snarl. *He wastes energy. Now is the time.* Pouncer screamed and leapt again. Sraff-Tracker pivoted to dodge, but he was slow and Pouncer connected, tearing flesh and driving his opponent to the ground. He screamed again, connected with the lower rib cage. Bone snapped and Sraff-Tracker screamed in pain, thrashing. Pouncer leapt clear, anticipating counterattack, but none came. He flowed again into *v'dak* stance, saw the big kzin writhing and spitting blood. The fractured ribs had lacerated a lung and he was screaming now in pain and fear rather than rage.

Without thought Pouncer leapt again. His jaws snapped and Sraff-Tracker's screams ended in a gurgle as Pouncer's fangs sliced out his throat. *He is dead.* Pouncer found himself trembling with reaction. *He attacked me, now he is dead. The last stroke was mercy.* He looked up, readopted *v'scree* stance as he faced the rest of the Pride. *Rage is death, fear is death. I must clear my mind.* But his mind would not clear. He forced himself to meet the gazes of the pride whose pridemate he had just killed. For a long moment the tableau held, and then it became clear there would be no further attack. He knelt by the still-warm body. *What are the rules here?* After a long moment he leaned back and screamed the *zal'mchurrr* up into the gathering dusk. Sraff-Tracker had fought well, he deserved no less.

Chrrrrowwwl! C'mell's mating call split the night and he stiffened at the sound, sudden desire flushing away the kill rage. She was crouched in front of Kr-Pathfinder now, her haunches raised, flipping her tail for him. Pouncer took a step forward, then another. Kr-Pathfinder didn't move. His gaze was fixed hard on C'mell, but he wasn't showing his fangs. What did that mean? M'mewr was alongside him, her left forepaw over his, and her fangs *were* showing. He came closer, and C'mell began to edge out of the way. As she turned her hindquarters to him a fresh wave of her ripe, fertile scent washed over him, and without thought he leapt for her. She dodged out of the way, but he managed to grab her, rolling her over, the pain from his wounds not registering. He came around on top of her and she struggled madly to get away. With instincts he didn't know he possessed, his teeth found the nape of her neck. Her haunches came up, opening herself to him, and he mounted her. The mating frenzy took him then, his body spasming beyond his conscious control, and he was aware of her raising herself, her body tensing beneath his. He roared, and her mating scream mixed with his to echo off the cavern walls, and in the universe there was nothing for him but C'mell.

He collapsed then, suddenly aware of the silently watching pride. He found to his surprise that he couldn't separate himself from her. Awkwardly they moved out of the center. Pouncer started for his old spot on V'rli's left, but C'mell guided him to lie beside Quicktail, Night-Prowler, and Z'slee. He had been accepted.

V'rli-Ztrak moved to the center of the circle and raised her voice. "Was the fight fair?"

"It was fair, Honored Mother." The voices rose from around the circle.

V'rli folded her ears and lay down again. Quicktail got up in her place and started a poetry game. Pouncer licked C'mell's ears affectionately, seeing in her a new beauty he had not known to exist. His testicles contracted with a slow rhythm, inseminating her in steady pulses, gentle echoes of the ecstasy of their first coupling. She was his C'mell, now and always, and she was going to bear his kits. She purred under his tongue, and then licked his wounds in turn. It was painful, but he was too spent even to grimace. He still had news to tell the pride, but it would wait now. *There will be a death rite for Sraff-Tracker. That will be the time.*

The poetry game lasted half the night, and then there was another story. Finally he and C'mell came apart, to lie close beside each other in the firelight. Eventually the story finished. V'rli rose and went to Sraff-Tracker's body. C'mell nudged him and murmured in his ear, and Pouncer went to kneel beside his recent rival.

V'rli lashed her tail. "Sraff-Tracker was strong. He brought the avalanche down on the Tzaatz in the battle. I remember Sraff-Tracker." She went back to her place and lay down.

Night-Prowler stood and went to the body. "Once I ran with Sraff-Tracker to the river trail to catch a *tuskvor*." He dropped to attack-crouch, as if to leap. "A herd-mother scented us despite the *myewl*, and she charged with her daughters." He stood and spread his arms, to indicate the size and ferocity of the herd. "We fled up a spire tree, but I was slow. Sraff-Tracker pulled me up just in time and saved my life." He stood straight. "I remember Sraff-Tracker."

V'veen rose from her place beside Kdtronai-*zar'ameer*. She walked to the body, removed her ornate ear-bands and tossed them in the fire. Without speaking she turned around to sit down again. The death rite went on, each member of the pride coming in turn to the body while Pouncer held his kneeling position, his head and body held close to the ground

Finally V'rli-Ztrak stood again. "Sraff-Tracker was strong." She said. "Sraff-Tracker was the son of Sraff-Ztrak, a strong Patriarch who led us well. Sraff-Tracker was our blood, and remains our blood. Now he is dead." She waited while the pride growled its approval of the death rite, then turned to Pouncer. "Pouncer was brave," she intoned. "Pouncer came to us for sanctuary and fought with us as a warrior. He has left our circle and returned. Pouncer was our blood and remains our blood. Now he is dead." She drew her *wtsai* from her belt, the blade flashing the light of the roaring fire.

An electric thrill shot through Pouncer at her words and he looked up at her, suddenly ready to fight. *I can defeat V'rli alone, but the whole pride will leap then. Am I to die now?* He had broken a rule by mating C'mell, and now he would pay for it. What he thought was acceptance was merely patience, as the pride waited for the traditions to play out their ancient pattern.

But no, V'rli was offering the weapon to him, handle first. A *wtsai*, symbol of acceptance into adulthood, symbol of acceptance into the pride. Their eyes were on him.

"Does Ztrakr Pride know the legend of Zree-Shraft?"

he asked. *I will be part of this pride; it is important that my name be in their traditions.*

"We do."

He took the weapon and roared until the cavern shook. "I claim the name Zree-Rrit, to follow Zree-Shraft-Who-Walked-Alone in my quest to avenge my father. May the Fanged God test me, I am ready."

"Zree-Rrit, of Mrrsel Pride blood. It is a good name." V'rli's voice was approving. "Your kill was clean, Zree-Rrit. Take the ears."

Pouncer looked at his blade and considered it. *Now is a critical moment. If I am to be Zree-Rrit, if I am to follow the path I have just chosen for myself I must become a leader, and that begins now, in this moment.* What was the right course? He put the edge of the blade against his upper arm and, and in a short, sharp jerk that was harder to make than he thought it would be, drew it past, feeling the razor edge burn into his flesh. Blood welled up, and he slid the weapon into his belt.

"No. I do not claim ears. Sraff-Tracker fought well, let him keep them. With respect, take my blood on your blade as my pledge of fealty to Ztrak Pride."

If the move surprised V'rli she gave no sign. Instead she turned back to the watching hunters. "I show you Zree-Rrit!" And the Pride screamed loud into the night. Pouncer screamed with them. Kr-Pathfinder and Ferlitz-Telepath leapt to throw the body on the pyre, where it sizzled and hissed in the flames. Roars echoed from around the circle, and a scuffle broke out. The tension of the night was about to be released in sparring and feasting and mating.

Pouncer raised his arms. *And now is my moment.*

"Wait! Pridemates!" He waited until he had their attention again. "You sent me from here, and I have traveled to Mrrsel Pride on my namequest. The Tzaatz have killed them all."

Snarls rose, angry this time, and he raised his paws to quell them. "They used *rapsari*, and came in force. This means they have tracked the migration, and they are searching out the prides of the *czrav*. Honored V'rli has taught me of the Telepath War and the story of the line of Vda. Mrrsel Pride's fate will be all of ours, unless we stop the Tzaatz—not just Ztrak Pride but every pride of the *czrav*. The Tzaatz who have stolen my birthright are the Tzaatz who will end the Vda line, *our* line. My mother's blood is your blood. My son's blood will be your blood, and my son will be Patriarch. My war is your war. Fight it with me. The day of the line of Vda has come."

He caught C'mell's eye across the fire, saw her support there. *I am an adult now, accepted into this pride. My place here is secure. If they do not follow me I could accept this as enough.* Even as the thought went through his mind he knew it would not be enough. Tradition demanded that the First-Son-of-the-Rrit should ascend to be Patriarch. Honor demanded that his father be avenged. *If I must fight alone, I will, but I will only win with allies, and everything hangs on this moment.* There was silence as he met the gazes of the assembled pride.

> *It is easy to draw the sword, harder to sheathe it.*
> —Si-Rrit

"What do you mean, destroyed?" There were storm clouds over the Plain of Stgrat, distant lightning flaring in the windows of the Patriarch's tower. The storm they would bring was nothing compared to the rage of Kchula-Tzaatz.

"The *kz'zeerkti* must have had eight-cubed ships at K'Shai, sire." Stkaa-Emissary performed the ritual cringe. "Our Heroes fought bravely, but we weren't prepared for such a force."

"Survivors?"

"A few managed to make it out of the system. Cvail Pride . . ."

"Give me no excuses based on the failings of Cvail!" Kchula rounded on the hapless Emissary, roaring. "I gave you everything you asked for. K'Shai is the gateway to their homeworld. Every Great Pride in the Patriarchy is leaping at your heels and you have failed me!"

"Patriarch. We need your help . . ."

"Enough! Leave my sight!" Kchula-Tzaatz raked his claws in the air, his tail stiff with anger, while Emissary scampered out.

"Calm, brother." Ftzaal-Tzaatz spoke from his *prrstet* where he had watched the whole exchange.

"Calm." Kchula turned to face his brother, still angry. "What do you suggest I do, Black Priest?"

"Evaluate. Why did the humans have so many ships at K'Shai? Did they anticipate our attack?"

"If there is a traitor . . ." Kchula's tail lashed.

Ftzaal turned a paw over. "I tracked First-Son-of-Meerz-Rrit by having Telepath follow the mind of the *kz'zeerkti*. Perhaps it is this *kz'zeerkti* that informs our enemies."

"How could it have access to our plans? How could it transmit them?"

"I merely suggest the possibility."

"You are obsessed with this *kz'zeerkti*, and with First-Son."

"You underestimate these *czrav*. I started my search in the eastern jungles, and when we found them they vanished. We searched for moons and found nothing. The savannah primitives told me the *czrav* vanished every dry season. Finally I thought to track the *tuskvor* migration. We found a den in the high western forests and attacked in force. We outnumbered them eight to one, and they killed half my force! Not one of them surrendered, even the kzinretti screamed and leapt. Kittens barely past suckling fought to the death! I wanted prisoners, they gave me only bodies. There are more of them than we know, brother, and they hold deep secrets."

"They are nothing! It is K'Shai that matters! Give me conquest of the *kz'zeerkti* and First-Son becomes an irrelevancy. Eight-cubed ships! How did they know we were coming?"

"They did not know we were coming. They plan to launch an attack. I believe for the first time they plan conquest."

Kchula stopped pacing to look at his brother. "How do you know that?"

"Because of what happened on Warhead."

"Warhead? What is that?"

"A minor base, a small garrison world. It belonged to Cvail Pride."

"Cvail Pride again. Perhaps this is why they fail to support Stkaa."

"Perhaps. It is irrelevant now. The *kz'zeerkti* raided it and destroyed it."

"Hrrr. They will pay in blood."

"Let me be clear, brother. They did not stop at destroying Cvail Pride's base. They sterilized the world."

"Impossible!"

"Shall I show you the imagery?"

"Don't waste my time. Tell me how they did it."

"I don't know how they did it." Ftzaal turned a paw over. "The weapon they used gashed the crust halfway through to the mantle."

"Impossible!"

"You overuse that word, brother."

"Not even conversion weapons could—"

"And yet something did."

Kchula slashed the air with his claws. "They fight without honor."

"They are animals, what do they know of honor?" Ftzaal twitched his whiskers. "It is what they are capable of that concerns me."

Kchula waved a paw dismissively. "I know how it was done. They used near-lightspeed kinetic missiles, clumsy tools. They did it to K'Shai when we held it, two wars ago, and killed more *kz'zeerkti* than kzinti."

"I take no reassurance in the fact that they will slaughter millions of their own just to ensure our destruction." Ftzaal turned a paw over. "In any event, that does not fit the profile of the attack. They had perhaps eight-squared warships, two battleships and support, enough to deal with the light forces Cvail had there. They fought their way into the system, into close orbit. Kinetic missiles would have to be launched from deep space, and there would be no need to penetrate the system with ships. And again, a scout pilot who escaped said one of the battleships did the damage."

"If they possess such power, why waste it on an insignificant outpost like Warhead?"

"Hrrr." Ftzaal turned a paw over, extended his claws to contemplate them. "This attack was a test run, carried out against an isolated target for the purpose of battle evaluation of this new weapon while their main fleet gathered at K'Shai. The *kz'zeerkti* have not yet put it into mass production. It is experimental, radically so, and therefore expensive, therefore they will have only a few constructed so far, perhaps only the single capital ship. Nevertheless, their test was successful. Cvail Pride, and by extension the Patriarchy, have been dealt a serious blow. We have been given a warning. This will not be the last attack."

"No ship could carry such a weapon."

"And yet it seems one does." The door had slid open before Kchula could reply, revealing a familiar face.

Kchula whirled to face the interloper. "Rrit-Conserver. I thought you'd fled with your tail between your legs. Get out until I send for you."

"I am no longer Rrit-Conserver." The dark-robed kzin hopped onto a *prrstet* and made himself comfortable. "I left because Scrral-Rrit had violated his honor and not through any fear of you, Kchula-Tzaatz. I have returned because I am Kzin-Conserver now, and I will come and go as is my right, and my obligation to the species." The new Kzin-Conserver fanned one ear up. "Or does Tzaatz Pride no longer hold with the traditions?"

He has become Kzin-Conserver! Kchula stood looking at his erstwhile adversary, stunned. *How could I have allowed an enemy to attain such power?* He caught Ftzaal's gaze and knew what he was thinking. *We should have killed him when we had the chance.* "We hold with the traditions of course, Honored Conserver." The words came out late and unconvincing. Across the room, Ftzaal turned to look out the window.

"I heard the last of your conversation." Kzin-Conserver ignored Kchula's sudden discomfiture. "Eight-cubed ships at K'Shai, this new weapon— there will be more bad news from the monkeys. You have stalked the *tuskvor*, Kchula-Tzaatz, and now you have caught the herd-charge. May the Fanged God preserve our species from your folly."

Kchula forced himself to be calm. "If you are Kzin-Conserver, your role is to advise the Patriarch. What advice do you have for me?"

Kzin-Conserver twitched his lips over his fangs. "You are still not Patriarch, Kchula, but I will not waste time pretending that Scrral-Rrit is. There may be a counter-measure to this weapon. First we must learn what it is, in detail. A team must be sent to investigate its effects, to take measurements in this newly melted canyon, and find the wreckage of our own ships to evaluate its function."

Kchula snorted derisively. "This is obvious. Is this the best you can do?"

"This is the only advice I have that you will take. I have other advice, but you will not follow it."

"Don't try my patience, Kzin-Conserver." A note of warning crept into Kchula's voice.

"I tire of your threats, Kchula-Tzaatz. Leap if you mean them, abandon them if you do not. Nevertheless I will advise you as I advised Meerz-Rrit, and you may evaluate for yourself the acceptability of my preferred course of action."

"Out with it!"

"It is simple. Seek peace with the *kz'zeerkti*, while you still can."

"Seek peace! Out of the question."

"I see my judgment was not incorrect."

"Pah! You are a bigger fool that I thought, Conserver. My grip on the Patriarchy depends upon conquest. What will I now tell Stkaa-Emissary? What will I tell the warriors of Cvail? These prides would be locked in *skalazaal* even now had I not grabbed the Patriarchy by the scruff!"

"There are worse fates than *skalazaal* among the Great Prides. Do you remember Meerz-Rrit's speech before the Great Pride Circle? *'We shall not incite other species to our extermination in their own self-defense.'* " Kzin-Conserver laid his ears flat. "We have not seen the last of this new *kz'zeerkti* weapon, and they have not advanced nearly half their strength to Wunderland on a whim. Perhaps even now their fleet is in hyperspace to the edge of our singularity. Kzinhome itself may yet share Warhead's fate."

Kchula turned to his brother. "Ftzaal, tell him what you told me. The weapon is expensive and experimental. They needed a fleet to protect it. They would not dare bring it here."

The Black Priest turned back from the window. "That is my assessment, Kzin-Conserver." He paused. "Still, brother, there is wisdom in what Conserver advises."

Kzin-Conserver raised his tail. "Today the weapon is experimental, but the monkeys will not leave it that way.

I made the mistake myself of underestimating their industrial potential. I will not make that mistake again. When we met them they had left war abandoned for generations. Why were we unable to defeat them then? Two reasons. First, because they are tremendously good at turning other systems into weapons—communications lasers, fusion drives, conversion plants; we learned those lessons the hard way. The second is because there are so many of them. What one innovates eight-to-the-eighth can then produce."

"We have slaves, technology and worlds at our command. I will be the one who finally subjugates the monkeys."

"And if you are? We will meet another race more formidable than humans. Did you know the Puppeteers' ships are invulnerable?"

"No ship is invulnerable."

"Nevertheless, they are. The Puppeteers can manipulate the hull to admit any segment of the spectrum they like, or deny them all. The hull material itself does not ablate at stellar temperatures. Perhaps there is a weakness they keep secret, but does it matter? The Outsiders gifted the *kz'zeerkti* with hyperdrive. What if the Puppeteers give them invulnerable ships too?"

"The *kz'zeerkti* will be our slaves. I swear it by the Fanged God."

"And yet Warhead is destroyed. Stkaa Pride's fleet is in ruins. What will the other Great Prides do when they learn these things?"

"You mock my honor!"

"I state a fact."

"And we will have vengeance for it. We will fight this war in *kz'zeerkti* style. Earth will burn for its temerity and its colonies will be helpless. We will make the survivors of the race our slaves."

"You will violate the traditions!" Kzin-Conserver's voice was stern.

"The conquest of slave races is our oldest tradition."

"So is honor in warfare. How will you burn Earth save with untrammeled use of conversion weapons?"

Kchula's tail lashed angrily. "You have seen the evidence. The monkeys do not trouble themselves with such concerns."

"They are animals, what do they know of the Hero's Way, or of honor? Will you lower yourself to be like them?"

"Bah. We are speaking of the survival of the Patriarchy here. The monkeys must be subjugated."

"You will conquer nothing but ashes. Of what worth are sterile worlds?"

"Do not obstruct my path, Kzin-Conserver. I will do whatever it takes to forge the whole Patriarchy into my sword, and I will strike down any who stand in my way."

"If you violate tradition, I will declare you honorless. The Great Circle will hound you from this fortress and your conquest war will go nowhere."

"Your threat is empty. The Great Circle are behind me in conquest leap."

"Not so much behind you as you might like to think. I have one more piece of news for you. Kdari Pride has just leapt on Vearow Pride."

"What?" Kchula stood up, ears up and tail stiff.

"I thought you might not have heard. *Skalazaal* is still a game of stealth, and neither Pride has anything to gain by letting you know the situation. It seems your leadership hasn't prevented pride-war after all."

"How long have you known about this?"

"Just a Traveler's Moon, since Kdari-Conserver asked me for a fine interpretation of the Dueling Traditions. Today Vearow-Conserver is asking me the same question of interpretation. That will be in response to an unpleasant surprise provided by Kdari Pride. The spoor is clear enough. I expect there will be more direct news of it shortly."

"What was the point you ruled on? Am I vulnerable to it?"

"It is of little consequence now. Suffice to say the precedent set by your *rapsari* left me little choice but to allow Kdari Pride's interpretation."

"Bah. Neither Kdari Pride nor Vearow are of any great consequence."

"You think that is the end of it? There are more ripples in the grass. Another trip around the seasons and half the Patriarchy will be at each other's throats."

"They sap our strength when we could be stripping the meat from the carcass of the *kz'zeerkti*."

"The Pride-Patriarchs listened more closely to Meerz-Rrit than you did, Kchula. They know the danger in attacking the monkeys. They see each other as easier prey now."

"The monkeys are attacking anyway! They are fools."

"Kchula, you are the fool. The monkeys came to nego-tiate peace, and with Meerz-Rrit they had it. You sent their emissaries fleeing into the night with your attack. What result did you expect?"

"How was I to know what negotiations Meerz-Rrit had underway?"

"There was nothing secret about Yiao-Rrit's journey to Earth. The *kz'zeerkti* question was a primary item of discussion for the Great Pride Circle. Had you not been so intent on conquest you might have learned this."

Kchula opened his mouth and closed it, then started pacing. "How the problem occurred is irrelevant. We need to face the *kz'zeerkti* united."

"It is up you to unite them, Kchula."

"I am not Patriarch, Scrral-Rrit is."

Kzin-Conserver rippled his ears. "How quickly we abandon our responsibilities when leadership becomes difficult. Scrral-Rrit remains a puppet. You are the one to make him dance." Across the room Ftzaal-Tzaatz turned once more to look out the window in silence. His tail lashed once and was still.

"What do you suggest?"

"Immediate surrender."

Kchula spat. "And you say *I* lack honor."

"You do lack honor, which is why I recommend surrender to you. Had you the honor of Meerz-Rrit the Great Prides would leap at your command, and the *kz'zeerkti* would be a slave species. Meerz-Rrit would die in battle before accepting defeat. You will merely watch others die in battle in the hopes they might buy you victory. The Great Prides are not following you, Kchula, because they have no faith you will lead them to triumph. They have easier spoils in each other than in a poorly led conquest war."

"I will not surrender."

"Then you must leap at once to avenge Cvail and Stkaa together. It is the only way open now."

"With what? Eight-cubed ships! Not even the Rrit Fleet commands eight-cubed ships!"

"Honor doesn't count ships, Kchula."

"And this new weapon? What do they hope to gain by razing the whole planet? Spoils of rubble and carbon. This makes no sense."

Ftzaal-Tzaatz turned around from the window again. "I think they seek conquest, Conserver."

"No." Kzin-Conserver rose to leave. "We have fought five wars with the *kz'zeerkti*. Each time it was we who leapt against them. This time they have leapt first." He turned a paw over and then turned it back. "Perhaps this is a conquest leap, but I think it is more than that. This is something we have not seen before. They intend to exterminate us. This is total war."

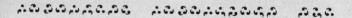

WISDOM OF THE CONSERVERS

Grasp all, seize nothing.

Plan with care, act with courage.

There is nothing impossible to a willing mind.

A scribe is judged by words, a warrior by deeds.

Fair weather follows the storm as night the day.

Rise with the Hunter's Moon and sleep with a full belly.

Hunger leads the hunt.

A poor craftsman carries poor tools.

Lead speech with thought.

Idle time is wasted life.

Even the *grlor* fear the *v'pren*.

If you host a warrior, you host his pride.

Boldness makes Heroes, caution makes warriors, both make victory.

Better wise than strong.

Only the scribe can fill his belly with words.

A puddle is a *strezka's* [beetle's] ocean.

If you want no *kstel* [large slothlike scavenger] in your house, build it with a small door.

If the hunter gnaws bones, what does he bring home to the pride?

The teller's cloak makes no difference to the tale.

The warrior's first victory is over fear.

The best proverb holds no wisdom for a fool.

The Traveler's Moon will be home before the traveler tonight.

A wise Patriarch seeks wise counsel.

Education cures ignorance, but nothing cures a fool.

No sword is sharper than honor.

The noble earns hatred through envy, the outcast through contempt.

Only a fool does not learn from his own mistakes, but it is a wise [sentient] who learns from someone else's.

Test the water with one foot only.

A wise leader serves first his warriors.

Only a fool stalks *tuskvor*.

Anyone can catch *grashi* in mating season.

Rain falls the same on noble and outcast.

Kits are life's reward.

Stalk not the hunter on his home ground.

Sleep is the brother of death.

No thief may steal honor, nor wear it if he did.

When honor and shame balance on a needle, who holds the needle?

He who fights with his mind carries few scars.

∴ ∵ ∴ ∵

THE FURNACE

Here the hammer and anvil wait
While broad shouldered Hephaistos stokes the fire high
Soon the red steel will be forged to the blade
And Achilles will march out to win or to die.
—Unknown

Hero's Square had changed since last time Tskombe saw it. He hadn't had time then to note details, but he remembered it had been bustling with life and commerce. Now even the kzinti seemed subdued, and the slaves scurried from place to place, narrowly focused on their errands to avoid the wrath of their masters. The mood was due to the *rapsar*-mounted Tzaatz patrols, but the patrols themselves weren't acting like triumphant conquerors. Their manner was tense, even nervous, and their tempers short. Their tension translated to the general populace. It made the environment dangerous, and Tskombe wasn't happy about that.

Not that he could do anything about it. He was on a slave's leash, pushing a float cart laden with boxes, and Night Pilot was leading him through stalls and markets. It might have been better if he'd bought a Kdatlyno to do the leading for him, but Night Pilot lacked *strakh* enough on Kzinhome, and he wasn't about to put in the time and effort to earn it. The disguise was effective enough, and though a few inquisitive noses sniffed at the distinctive scent of human, none questioned his presence.

All they had to do was find Provider's *grashi* stall but, unlike the disguise, their search strategy wasn't working. They were systematically quartering Hero's Square, trying to find a landmark that would orient him to the path he'd taken as he'd fled behind Pouncer in what now seemed like another lifetime. It was slow going in the crowd, especially since all of the kzinti and most of the slaves were taller than he was, making it difficult to orient himself. The slaves, at least, gave way without question, but other kzinti had to be given respect and space. For a kzin, Night Pilot was surprisingly calm about the inevitable frustrations the process engendered. Which is to say, Tskombe was reasonably sure he wouldn't simply decide to eat him when they got back to the ship. The upside was that he'd expanded his kzinti vocabulary considerably. He remained unsure of the exact meaning of most of the words, but he was confident they were all obscenities.

And it wasn't as if he'd been paying a lot of attention to the details of their route while they'd been fleeing. Pouncer had been leading the way, he'd just been following, unsure of the situation, concerned only with keeping up and staying concealed. And now they were on perhaps the tenth attempt to find Provider's stall since they'd come through the ancient walls of Hero's Square. There were a limited number of such startpoints. In theory it shouldn't have been hard to find the right one, but the details were blurred in his memory, and he'd already convinced himself that several possibilities were in fact *the* place, only to later rescind that judgment.

A sudden commotion spiked adrenaline through his system. Across the square a Tzaatz patrol on *rapsari* raiders had netgunned a spotted adolescent. He spat curses and clawed at the net as they hauled him away. Tskombe breathed out, trying not to smell afraid. He had missed whatever had triggered the incident. It didn't matter, it hadn't been anything to do with him. Night Pilot tugged his leash, as any kzinti master would do to a recalcitrant slave, and Tskombe gritted his teeth and went back to his search.

There. A stone tunnel, vendors' wooden stalls; were those barrels there before? They could have been moved there later. He looked around, saw a set of stairs running up the side of a crafter's shed.

He turned to Night Pilot. "This is it, we go right here."

Night Pilot's lips twitched over his fangs. "Are you sure?"

"As sure as I can be."

"You have said so before."

"And I've been sure before, and wrong before. I'm doing my best."

Night Pilot just snarled and kept walking. Tskombe led him along a row of stalls, trying hard to verify each decision he made with memory's uncertain record. The sun was going down, and once it did they'd have to go back to the spaceport to spend another night on the ship. He wasn't looking forward to another day of searching, and while they searched for Provider, Contradictory was seeking out a cargo, spending his days talking to the Jotoki slaves of the major shippers for an inside track on a transshipment bid. When *Black Saber* got a cargo, Tskombe would be on his own.

And there it was, a busy stall on a lane branching from the main square. "This is it. Possibly . . ."

"Stay here." It was bad manners to take a slave to a transaction. Night Pilot went up to the stall and Tskombe clicked on the vocom on his beltcomp to listen.

"I am Night Pilot. I search for a *grashi* vendor, Provider-who-was-Tank-Leader."

"He is gone." Tskombe didn't recognize the other's voice over the crowd noise.

"When will he return?"

"He is dead. I am his son, Far Hunter. What service may I give you?" Tskombe breathed out in relief and despair at once. He had found what he was looking for, but Provider was dead. There was the chance that Far Hunter might be able to help him. It was all he could hope for.

"I have a delivery for you." Night Pilot went on.

"What is it?"

"This *kz'zeerkti*." Night Pilot pointed at Tskombe.

Far Hunter's eyes followed the gesture. "Bring it to the back." His snarl showed sudden concern. Night Pilot motioned for Tskombe to come, but he was already moving, relief flooding his system. *At last.*

A minute later Tskombe came into the back of the stall.

"Tskombe-*kz'zeerkti*!" Far Hunter's ears swiveled up. "I never dreamed you would return."

"Far Hunter." Tskombe claw-raked. "I have come back for my companion."

"Of course. You are true to your honor. You fought well at the spaceport."

"As you did." Tskombe took a deep breath. Far Hunter would help him, he was sure of that now.

"Hrrr." Far Hunter's snarl became deeper. "My father was killed by the Tzaatt. I managed to escape with my life. These misbred mongrels squeeze the *kzintzag* while the Lesser Prides do nothing."

"And Pouncer?"

"First-Son-of-Meerz-Rrit is gone. His brother still holds the Patriarchy, in name at least, though he dances for Kchula-Tzaatt."

"Gone where?"

"I don't know. We were separated in the fight, and I couldn't get to them. They stole a gravlifter."

"You were wounded." Tskombe gestured to the thin white lines on Far Hunter's chest that marked fur growing from scar tissue.

"A raider *rapsar*, that day at the spaceport. Since then I have had vengeance, for father and myself." His paw went to the sheaf of ears at his belt and his fangs showed. "I will have more."

"He lost his life helping us. I am sorry . . ." Tskombe found himself at a loss for words.

"He lost his life living up to his name, and the fault is not yours but that of the Tzaatt."

Tskombe nodded. "And my companions, what happened to them?" Unconsciously he held his breath. *This is the key question.*

"I saw them, with Pouncer. The larger one, Kefan-Brasseur, was dead, or very badly injured. I couldn't join them, there were Tzaatt between us. Cherenkova-Captain was alive when I saw her last."

Relief. "Where did they escape to?"

"I don't know. There are rumors that the Tzaatz found the loader abandoned high in the Long Range mountains. There are rumors First-Son fights the Tzaatz. Whether they are true . . ." Far Hunter turned both paws over. "I don't know. None of us who *do* fight the Tzaatz have seen him."

"Far Hunter . . ." Tskombe paused. How to ask for this favor, to an alien enemy who had already paid too high a price to help him? "I need to find Cherenkova-Captain. She is my mate."

"Hrrr. I hunt the Mooncatchers, I know the mountains. I know others who have sources of information. We can find the loader, perhaps, if it is there at all."

"I have to try."

"Of course you do. I need to trap more *grashi*. We will see what we can learn."

"Who will mind your stall?"

"My half-uncle's son trains as my assistant. He is diligent and intelligent, if not yet wise." Far Hunter raised his voice. "Apprentice!"

"Sire!" A young kzintosh appeared from the front section of the stall, his coat still dappled with the spots of youth.

"I will be going hunting, for the Hunter's Moon at least. The stall is yours until I return. Be thrifty, industrious, and courteous. You have the opportunity here to earn much *strakh*, both for our pride and yourself."

The youngster claw-raked. "I will strive to be worthy of your trust, Senior Cousin."

Tskombe turned to Night Pilot. "*Black Saber*'s sensors may be helpful here."

"They can be." Night Pilot turned a paw over. "It will cost fuel. Your retainer is too thin, Tskombe-*kz'zeerkti*."

"Retainer? What is that?" Far Hunter was puzzled.

"It is . . ." Tskombe paused. The word for money in the Hero's Tongue was *k'rna*, a phonetic translation of *kroner*, stolen from Wunderland's North European argot, with its use confined to the kzinti who had to trade with humans. There was another word that meant *exchange token*, but it didn't encompass the nuances of invisible credit that were attached to modern funds. How to explain that to Far Hunter? When it came down to it, money was just a recognized store of value. It was alien on Kzinhome, where value was stored in your status and the universal recognition of it by the entire society. The system of *strakh* worked, so far as he could see, only because kzinti lived and died by their honor. As an economic working fluid it was only a small step up from barter. Electronic funds transfers, digital money, stocks, futures, the miracle of compound interest and all the rest of the working machinery of an advanced economy were impossible to them. A human trader could take over the markets of Hero's Square in a month by streamlining trade, except a human would be eaten first, for insulting a Hero with the suggestion that next month he would have to pay back more than he had borrowed today.

None of which would give any enlightenment to Far Hunter. "It is a form of *strakh*, formalized for exchange purposes," he finished. It was not really an explanation at all, though Far Hunter accepted it at face value.

Far Hunter nodded. "I have *strakh* with my half-uncle,

Cargo Pilot. In turn he will have *strakh* enough at the spaceport for fuel."

Night Pilot's ears fanned up. "A stall vendor has *strakh* to fuel a starship?"

Far Hunter rippled his ears. "My *strakh* does not come from trading *grashi*. I fight the Tzaatz for what they did to my father, but I am not alone. The Rrit governed fairly; the Tzaatz demand too much from us. The Lesser Prides are afraid to act but we of the *kzintzag* have little to lose. We leap in the name of First-Son-of-Meerz-Rrit. A search for Cherenkova-Captain is a search for First-Son. For this purpose I command all the *strakh* on Kzinhome." He smiled to show his fangs. "Tell me how much fuel you need, you will have it."

"This is good. We will need maps too." Night Pilot tapped at his beltcomp. "Coordinates. I can track you on the ground in real-time as you move, and search terrain ahead of you. Our sensors are better than you might think for a ship our size, and I know how to avoid notice from the orbital tracking net."

Tskombe looked at him. "Have you smuggled on Kzinhome before?

Night Pilot rippled his ears. "Smuggling is unknown to kzinti, in the human sense."

"Because it's against the honor code?"

Night Pilot rippled his ears. "Because there are no import or export restrictions in the Patriarchy. What Great Pride would accept such an arbitrary imposition by the Patriarch?"

"So what is your role here then?"

"There are still those who make shipments in secret, to

avoid the oversight of rivals, just for example. In honor, this is not smuggling."

Tskombe shrugged. The difference between the rules of human honor and kzinti honor was as wide as the gulf between barter and a market economy. "So we need maps, survival gear, food and water, transportation to the area, what else?"

"A place to start." Night Pilot turned to Far Hunter. "You said a vehicle was found?"

"It was. There are snippets of information. Kchula-Tzaatz's brother leads raids to distant places, first the jungle, then the desert and the high forests. It is said they search for First-Son."

Tskombe shook his head. "We need something better than that."

"I have friends among the *cvari* savannah hunters. Little escapes them. I will see if I can learn where the grav loader crashed, and we can start there. In the morning I will arrange to have your ship refueled."

Night Pilot twitched his tail. "Where should I aim my sensors?"

Tskombe shrugged. "Can we find out where the Tzaatz have launched these raids?"

"Hrrr." Night Pilot turned a paw over. "I have contacts who will know. In the morning I will ask."

Tskombe nodded. "I'm grateful for your help, Far Hunter."

Far Hunter waved a paw. "It is nothing. My father swore fealty to the Rrit, and I have sworn to serve his memory. You wore the Patriarch's sigil. I am at your service."

"I still have it." Tskombe held up the medallion he had carried a hundred light-years.

"You are true to your own honor, Tskombe-*kz'zeerkti*. We need a toast." Far Hunter raised his voice. "Apprentice! Blood mead for our guests!"

Apprentice appeared with a set of huge flagons and a ceramic decanter and poured a thick, dark red liquid. Tskombe looked at it dubiously, but there was no way to refuse it.

Far Hunter stood up. "To vengeance," he snarled, and Tskombe was about to echo him and drink when Night Pilot stood up.

"To success!"

They looked at him expectantly. *Kzinti toasts are individual.* No matter; it was amazing enough that a custom like toasting existed in any form in another species's culture. He stood up. "To the Rrit!" It seemed the thing to say.

The kzinti snarled in approval and drained their flagons at a gulp. Tskombe drank his as quickly as he could. The mead was heavy, thick, and bitter, and he nearly gagged getting it down. *And to Ayla.*

He sat down, stomach churning and head already swimming. The flagons were two liters at least, and the drink's alcohol content was high. He had never been much of a drinker, and the rest of the night was a blur.

61 Ursae Majoris was high in the sky when he woke up, and painfully bright. He was back in Provider's house, now Far Hunter's, though he couldn't remember getting there. His head was pounding, and he wished for a fistful of

detox pills and the rest of the day to stay in bed. *Not the smartest way to start the mission.* But he couldn't have avoided it. Far Hunter and Night Pilot were his only allies, and he was lucky to have them. Perhaps they wouldn't have been insulted if he'd turned down the toast, but he couldn't have taken the risk.

He dragged himself up to find Trina waiting for him. "Good morning."

"What are you doing here?" The same two silent Kdatlyno were performing their morning cleaning rituals. *It's as if I never left.*

Trina smiled far too cheerily, she was enjoying her adventure. "Night Pilot brought me here. Contradictory is refueling the ship. They're taking off tomorrow."

Tskombe nodded and suppressed the urge to scold her. It wasn't her fault, and though he'd be more comfortable with her safe on the ship, Night Pilot couldn't take responsibility for her forever. Instead he sat, waiting for the room to stop spinning.

"There's some meat here. The kzin in the front gave it to me. The sauces are good. Night Pilot went out with the other one; they said they'd be back this evening."

Tskombe looked at the serving. She was eating with a serrated *skeceri* knife, slicing off chunks of still warm raw meat, dunking them in sauce, and swallowing them almost whole. She'd developed a taste for kzinti cooking, or lack of it, on *Black Saber.* He looked away. His stomach wasn't ready to consider food yet.

Trina saw his look. "There's these eggs, too. Nay-something, they use them raw in the sauce, but I boiled mine." She held one up, a mottled round sphere, fuzzy like a peach. "I can make some for you too." She seemed eager for him to say yes.

"It's pronounced *nyalzeri.*" He avoided her question to avoid disappointing her. "You don't speak the Hero's Tongue, do you?"

She laughed. "No. When would I have learned that?"

He sighed. *She shouldn't be here, and here she is.* "You're going to have to know the basics." He touched his nose. "Nose, *naughl.* Nostril, *raughl.*"

She repeated what he'd said, stumbling over the accent, and they began to run through the language. He taught her only the slave's form, to prevent her from getting herself into trouble. It filled the time. By *hvlazch'pira*—afternoon—she was getting good at the vocabulary, and his appetite had returned enough to eat. Trina boiled him a pair of the eggs while they worked, and then later cooked some of the meat for him. By evening she was stringing together sentences and her accent had improved considerably. She was good at languages. *Or just lucky.* The hypothesis he'd developed with Curvy seemed almost silly now. *But she wins at chess.* So how to test the hypothesis?

He picked up one of the uncooked *nyalzeri* eggs. It was firm rather than hard, like an oversized chicken's egg with a layer of leather over it, resilient up to its breaking point. He looked it over. Trina was looking at the wall, her eyes distant as she memorized verb conjugations. He hefted the egg, calculating, and without warning threw it at her. She turned to face him, her mouth starting to ask a question. The egg grazed her ear and hit the wall with a splat, leaving a small mess behind.

"What did you do that for?" Trina looked at him, wide eyed and aggrieved.

"It was an experiment to see how lucky you are. I'm sorry."

"I guess I am lucky." She smiled, pleased that he'd confirmed her rationale for sneaking aboard *Black Saber*. "No harm done. I'll clean it up."

She hopped up to get a rag, also pleased to demonstrate her usefulness, and Tskombe watched her carefully. *She turned at the exact instant necessary to make the egg miss her.* So what did that prove? What would it have proven if he'd hit her square on the side of the head? The consequences were too trivial either way. If random luck was actually a non-random psi talent then it couldn't be expected to intervene when survival wasn't at stake. He pursed his lips, thinking about it. The heavy *kreera* sword he had practiced with last time he had hidden in Provider's house was hanging on the wall. One good swing would cut Trina in half. *Unless she has preternatural luck.* He looked away. He wasn't convinced enough of the hypothesis to do the experiment.

Far Hunter was back at dusk, looking like the cat that got the canary. "I have the regions the Tzaatz have been operating in. Night Pilot has them too, and his ship will be boosted by midnight. We can leave at once. He will guide us from orbit as we enter the area."

Tskombe nodded, pleased and relieved. Coming to Kzinhome had been the ultimate gamble. So far it was paying off. They began packing Far Hunter's gravcar with pup tents, rappel gear, flash-dried meat rations in foil pouches, emergency supplies. It was the same gravcar that he had taken with Provider to the spaceport, and he wondered how Far Hunter had managed to get it out without being caught.

Trina helped them load as they put the weapons on board. There were variable swords for each of them, a compound bow as tall as he was, a set of edge-weighted throwing nets of almost invisible filaments in graduated sizes. He watched as she heaved a well-worn magrifle into the back of the vehicle, then struggled to lift a case of its rounds. He remembered the competent way Ayla Cherenkova had handled her oversized beamer and looked away. Trina was untrained, unqualified, inexperienced and, so far as combat and survival went, woefully naïve. There was not a weapon there she could be expected to use effectively. He bent over to pick up a box of *grashi* traps. *I hope she really is lucky.* Winning chess games was one thing; taking on an alien planet was another.

The next day Far Hunter's contacts had gotten the locations of all the Tzaatz movements that might conceivably be involved in a hunt for Pouncer, along with the relevant dates. There were a lot of areas. Night Pilot and Contradictory boosted for low orbit and they were soon downlinking a steady stream of high resolution imagery of the areas where they might, potentially, find a clue. The operational areas Far Hunter had identified were hardly pinpoint precise, but they told the story of a steadily expanding search starting from a canyon at the base of the Long Range. *That's where the loader ran out of fuel, if the rumors are true. Black Saber's* sensors gave them multi-spectrum images of the valley, and when the first orbital pass was complete, Tskombe put on a set of data goggles that had belonged to Far Hunter when he was a kitten. They gave him a bird's eye view of the rugged, stony valley floor good enough to resolve individual pebbles. That was a problem. The area was six kilometers long and two wide, and Kzinhome's seasons had changed and changed again since the crash. He'd started with optimism, scanning over the projected terrain images at high speed in the hopes of finding the abandoned loader, the logical search start point for both the Tzaatz and them. He hadn't found it, which might have been because the Tzaatz had hauled it out and might have meant it was never there in the first place because they were searching the wrong valley. He'd gone back at maximum resolution and started again, in the hopes of finding some wreckage, landing skid marks, anything. It was a much slower process. *Black Saber* had the whole valley mapped in high detail under five minutes, but to examine the images closely enough required picking up some long-degraded trace that Ayla might have left. That meant a slow, thorough search for some tiny ambiguous detail, scanning through the imagery at a speed that would have been a walking pace on the ground. He concentrated first on the watercourses. Anyone traveling the wilderness for any distance wouldn't want to get too far from water.

Some hours later he took the goggles off. He had sore eyes and no way of knowing if he'd missed the vital clue, or if it wasn't even in this valley. The enormity of the task he'd undertaken began to sink in. *When Stanley set out to find Livingstone he at least knew to follow the Nile. I have no such guidance.* Still, it was what he had come to do, and he would do it. *The UNF doesn't abandon its own, and I will not abandon Ayla.*

Trina came in with a tray of fire-roasted *grashi* and sauce. He took the dish eagerly, only then aware of how hungry he was. She took the datagoggles in exchange and sat down with them. He'd agreed to let her help with the search when he was done, privately resolving to go over everything she covered himself, just to make sure. She wasn't trained to track and trail, as he was. She could easily miss something subtle, and he wasn't prepared to take that risk.

"Where should I start?" She was experimentally waving her hands in the air, learning the gesture commands that would pan and zoom the image, her head turning left and right as she searched what for her had become a wide valley in the distant mountains. Tskombe looked up at Far Hunter's wall screen, where the image she was seeing was remoted, along with a moving map display that showed the topographic features of the area, with the viewpoint displayed on the main screen highlighted.

"Try here." He pointed to the blue line of the watercourse he'd been searching, and made a sweeping motion with his other hand to command the AI to move the datagoggle viewpoint there.

"Sure." She turned her head left and right, searching, twitching her wrist to advance her viewpoint slowly as she looked. Tskombe turned to his *grashi*. Trina was becoming a good cook.

"What's this?" He looked up from his meal to see what she meant. On the wallscreen she'd outlined a small pile of rocks in the rough shape of a person.

Adrenaline surged and it took him a second to find his voice. "It's an inukshuk."

"What's that?"

"It means 'in the form of a man' in Inuktitut. The original cultures in the high Arctic on Earth used them to mark trails, because there were no easy landmarks there."

"What does it mean?"

Tskombe went up to the image, examining the inukshuk in mingled joy and disbelief. "It means Ayla was there. It means she made it out of the spaceport alive." He noticed something and gestured the image to the right. "There's the remains of a campfire too, just about the right age from the look of it."

Trina took off the datagoggles. "I guess we should go here then. The gravcar is packed."

Tskombe nodded and looked at his beltcomp so she wouldn't catch him staring at her. He'd spent eight hours tediously scanning through the image data for some trace of Ayla, and she'd found exactly what they were looking for almost as soon as she'd put on the goggles. *Luck?* Evolved luck might or might not trouble itself to save her from a face full of egg, but life was about time, and Trina's luck seemed to see no reason to have her waste her life on tedious searching when what she wanted was right there to be found in the dataset.

He nodded. "Yes, we should go here."

Trina was smiling proudly. "I'm good at finding things."

He nodded again and rubbed his sore eyes, wishing his own luck were as good as hers. *But she's here, and I might have spent a month searching that valley and missed the inukshuk.* He smiled to himself. *Luck is a relative term.*

The important thing was, Ayla was out there somewhere. Now all he had to do was go and find her.

> *The greatest commander knows his enemy's thoughts before his enemy thinks them.*
> —Si-Rrit

The Hrungn Valley fell jagged out of the Mooncatcher Mountains to spread into a broad and fertile river basin that opened onto the northern extreme of the vast plain of Stgrat as the Mooncatchers fell away to foothills. From his vantage point Pouncer could see the house of Chiuu Pride, its polished obsidian roof glinting over its rambling vastness in the setting sun, with pennants fluttering from jutting spires. The house was a tangible testament to the pride's wealth and power. Chiuu Pride's fealty to the Rrit was so old it was told of in the legends, and the Hrungn Valley had been theirs for all that time. The cold mountain streams that fed the meandering Hrungn River in its center brought nutrients that fed the soil. In the vast *meeflri* fields surrounding the great house the Kdatlyno slaves were ending their day. At the change of the seasons the *meeflri* would be tall and golden, but now the fields were shorn flat, and the Kdatlyno had spread husk mulch to nourish the tiny seedlings while protecting them from the harsh sun of the dry time. Here and there long feeder trays held last year's crop, the heavy seeds ground fine to make tempting fodder for the wild *melyar* herds that moved through the valley. Hrungn Valley *melyar* raised on *meeflri* was prized throughout the Patriarchy for its rich, delicate meat.

It was an idyllic scene, or should have been. Pouncer's lips twitched over his fangs as he raised his binoptics to his eyes and scanned the valley. Beside the great house was a series of pop-domes, sprouting like excrescences to mar the view from its broad upper windows. A patrol mounted on raider *rapsari* watched by the gate as the Kdatlyno filed past. Farther north another patrol was heading back from their daily vigil over the tungsten mine dug into the rich veins that had formed when tectonic forces thrust the ancient Mooncatchers up from the plain. The Tzaatz were there in force, extracting *strakh* which was not theirs, and Vsar-Chiuu's Eldest and Second-Sons had already died in the arena for insisting on their birth-given rights. Vsar-Chiuu himself, too old now to leap in defense of his own honor, bore the enemy presence in humiliated silence to buy the lives of his surviving kits, while the Tzaatz made free with his lands and holdings. It was wrong. Chiuu Pride gave fealty to the Rrit, and the Rrit in turn were sworn to their protection. Pouncer's tail lashed in anger. His father was dead, and his brother, his honorless, nameless brother, was allowing Kchula-Tzaatz to do this in the Rrit name.

He snarled deep in his throat. *No more.*

His tail twitched commands to the warriors behind him, twice-eight-squared of Ztrak Pride, ready now to follow him to death or victory in the Longest War. Dusk and dawn were the best times for hunt cloaks, when eyes were transitioning to night vision, and the rapid change in ground temperature threw up many targets for thermal scanners. He assessed the ground ahead, judging the route forward. *I must make this raid a success, inflict damage and withdraw with no casualties. The goal now is not to defeat the enemy but to let the Patriarchy know that I am not defeated.* Every one of his party had variable swords, built by the Pride, and most had mag armor, although some disdained it as too bulky and restrictive. *I have changed their customs by my very presence.* He didn't know if that was a good thing or not.

To his left Czor-Dziit of Dziit Pride was watching, and how Pouncer handled himself today would determine if Czor threw Dziit Pride's weight in with Ztrak Pride or led his own campaign. The Tzaatz raids on *czrav* prides in their high forest strongholds had ensured the *czrav* would fight. Whether they would fight with him was another question. To his left Kdtronai-*zar'ameer* moved to cover, watching him from a stone's throw away. It was not only Dziit Pride's faith and fealty that hung on his leadership today.

He moved forward to a gully that led down into the valley. It would be dark in the valley by the time they were there, down in the river bed where the Hrungn's flow had dropped to a trickle in the heat and the burstflower bushes clustered close enough to hide their approach. The most dangerous time was now, when they were exposed on the slopes. Somewhere out there the Tzaatz would have watchers, and they'd already picked up the spoor of *rapsar* patrols that reached up to the valley rim, but the Tzaatz were sloppy, and he had chosen his route with care, over hard, dry rock that wouldn't hold scent. Only bad luck would get them caught before they reached their objective, and if they were they had the strength to fight and flee before the Tzaatz could bring up reinforcements.

He looked back. His warriors were flowing like liquid over the forward slope, their hunt cloaks shimmering into the background whenever they stopped moving. He had trained them well. Czor-Dziit would be impressed. The *czrav* were hard fighters, made tough by their self-imposed exile to the wild lands while the rest of the Patriarchy had grown soft, but they knew little of formations or the tactics of large scale combat, knowledge that Guardmaster had drilled into Pouncer's brain since he'd left his mother's teats. *Guardmaster be with me now.* This was no training scenario, to be stopped and played back afterward for his mentor to show him the mistake that had cost him the battle. This was real, and his first command in front of experienced warriors inclined to be skeptical of his abilities. V'rli-Ztrak had agreed to let him lead the attack on the main enemy camp, even as her own forces closed on the tungsten mine. It was an opportunity he had won with his own claws. The Tzaatz were about to pay for his father's death, and his sister's, for the slaughter of Mrrsel Pride, for the sons of Vsar-Chiuu and their insults to the Lesser Prides. Pouncer snarled. Kchula's debt was heavy. If he could turn today's opportunity into victory the Tzaatz would be paying it for a long time.

A distant whine rose in the distance, and he flashed the tail signal for *freeze*. At once the whole formation went to ground, motionless under their hunt cloaks. The whine grew and a Tzaatz gravcar slid over the ridgeline and then down into the valley. It wasn't patrolling, and it didn't alter course. Pouncer waited until it had settled next to the pop-domes that quartered the Tzaatz, and then started moving again. He was about to signal his forces to move with him when something caught his eye. He dropped to one knee and raised his binoptics, boosting up the zoom to focus on the gravcar. The occupants were dismounting, two Tzaatz guards in full armor and a third with the red-gold sash that carried the Tzaatz sigil. The third had black fur. It could only be Ftzaal-Tzaatz. Pouncer smiled a fanged smile. He had never seen the feared Black Priest before, but his name came up frequently in spy reports. To kill or capture Kchula's brother would transform the raid into a tremendous victory. He waited until the Tzaatz had gone into one of the pop-domes, carefully noting which one it was, then signaled for the advance to continue. In silence his warriors started moving again.

The bottom of the gully was a tangle of rain-tumbled rocks and the going was hard, but its depth and the vegetation that lined it would give them cover right down to the riverbed. It was deep twilight by the time they made it to the Hrungn, and their progress slowed further. The riverbed was rocky, with treacherous footing in the poor light. The ground was easier close to the bank, but the heavy branches of the dusky burstflower bushes made the going no faster. That was a problem. Their attack was supposed to start at midnight, to coordinate with V'rli's at the tungsten mine. He had planned their move to bring them into position just before that time. Cherenkova-Captain had suggested he leave a larger margin in case of delays, and now he saw the wisdom of her suggestion. *Guardmaster would have said the same thing, and I would have listened to him.* He resolved not to make the same mistake again, if he ever got a second chance.

He glanced over to Mind-Seer, who would scan the

minds of the Tzaatz leaders before the attack went in to ensure their surprise was complete, and to give warning of the Tzaatz response before the Tzaatz themselves could coordinate it. Ferlitz-Telepath was with V'rli to do the same job for her attack, and to scan Pouncer's mind to be sure his assault was ready before V'rli committed herself.

Silent communications, completely secure. The entire Patriarchy doesn't have half as many adepts as the czrav, nor half as powerful. Overhead the battle stations would listen in vain for electromagnetic transmission. *The czrav have more power than they ever dreamed.* Ferlitz would warn V'rli if he wasn't in position, but being late on the start line would jeopardize the entire operation. The only answer was to push forward harder. That risked weakening his force through injury before he even got to the objective. A twisted joint was all it took to render a warrior useless in battle, and the treacherous footing offered plenty of opportunity for that.

But I have no option. He pushed the pace, using every last glimmer of vanishing daylight to cover as much ground as possible before darkness slowed them down. He was hot and panting by the time he reached the prominent oxbow bend that marked the closest approach of the river course to the Tzaatz positions. His warriors were spread out in the night behind him. This was where rigorous formation drills paid off. They filed into the assembly point in silence, each taking up a preassigned position. There was no wasted time. As soon as the last one was in, he went to the center to meet his element commanders. C'mell led the blocking party, her honor as his mate. He would have rather seen her safe at the high forest den, but three-quarters of the force were kzinretti. *Czrav* tradition demanded that she lead beside him, and even if it hadn't, C'mell herself would have brooked no such restriction; the kzinretti of the *czrav* were not the pampered pets of his father's forbidden garden. Kdtronai-zar'ameer led the security teams, who would ensure they had no unpleasant surprises from the flanks as they went in to the attack. Muted snarls, and then Kdtronai led his warriors out. The plan called for them to wait to give the security elements time to secure the area, but they didn't have that much time. As soon as Kdtronai's units were away Pouncer nodded to C'mell. Her force, armed with the lethal *czrav* short bows, would set up on the road to the main house, the natural escape route for any Tzaatz who made it out of the pop-domes alive. She would make sure there were no survivors. He looked at Mind-Seer, whose eyes were unfocused as he reached out to the thoughts of their enemies. *Had we brought* sthondat *extract we might even know the Black Priest's mind.* They hadn't, nor would he ask Mind-Seer to use it if they had. Perhaps Mind-Seer would have volunteered to. *Do not dwell on it, it is not an option.* Time stretched out, and then the telepath shook himself and flashed a tail signal to Pouncer. *Clear!*

Pouncer flipped his tail to signal his assault force to follow him and moved off. Every sense was heightened, his eyes picking up details from dark blurs, his ears up and straining forward for any sign that their attack had been detected. His nose twitched in the air, picking up the rank scent of the *rapsari* as well as the sharp odor of Tzaatz urine marks, arrogantly sprayed around Vsar-Chiuu's

stronghold as though the invaders owned it. His mouth
gaped into a fanged smile, ready to rip the throat out of
any who came into his path.

No more!

The metallic odor of blood filled his nose with offensive
suddenness, and he stopped, sniffing to identify the
source, ears swiveling back and forth. There was only the
gentle wind, and the distant scurrying of night creatures.
Time was running out, and he moved on sooner than he
might have, to find a Tzaatz body lying decapitated beside
its gutted *rapsar.* Kdtronai's security team had cleared the
way for him. The pop-domes loomed ahead; loud snarls
and snatches of bad poetry spoke of a raucous celebration
inside. *The enemy enjoy their unearned gains.* Fast tail
signals sent his sub-detachments to their start lines. No
time to waste. He checked his beltcomp. Already V'rli's
force would be leaping on the Tzaatz at the tungsten
mine. He waved his tail in a circle and pointed it forward.
Now! In the same motion he drew his variable sword and
extended the slicewire. One clean swing cut through the
tough skin of the pop-dome. He leapt through the opening, the interior lights painful in his eyes, colliding with a
Tzaatz guzzling from a flagon. He swung instinctively,
though his opponent was just a blur, and suddenly the
Tzaatz was two blurs, falling to the ground in a welter of
blood. *Clear the entryway!* He found another target,
stepped forward and swung again. The Tzaatz had their
armor off, and they were easy meat for his slicewire.
Behind him he could hear attack screams, as the rest of
his force cut their way into the structure.

A blur of motion caught his eye, and he ducked back

instinctively as a thrown *wtsai* whipped past his head to embed itself in one of the dome's support members. He turned to the attack and leapt in one fluid motion. The Tzaatz who'd thrown the weapon rolled back and sideways to evade him, but Pouncer twisted in midair and cut him in half. He pivoted then, scanned for threats. *Ftzaal-Tzaatz is here.* His leap had carried him across the ground floor of the pop-dome. A metal staircase wound up the inside of the dome and he jumped to it, running up behind the rigid slicewire of his variable sword. That action saved his life. Something slammed into the monomolecular filament, nearly tearing the handle out of his hand. The force of the impact made the wire sing, and the vibrations stung his hand. Reflexively he spun the blade around, just in time to deflect a second blow. The enemy weapon was another variable sword, and the enemy was Ftzaal-Tzaatz, it could be no other, white fangs gaping in a black furred face. There had been no kill scream, just the whistle of the slicewire as the Black Priest sprung his ambush. Already he was bringing in another cut, and Pouncer tilted his blade to block it. He spun the wire again, bringing it around to beat Ftzaal's out of line, and then followed up with a killing stroke with enough force to cleave his opponent in half. Ftzaal wore no armor; he was brave to be in the fight at all.

Ftzaal swung again and Pouncer blocked again and countered, then leapt back as the Black Priest turned the move into a feint that drew Pouncer's response into an overextension. Ftzaal's slicewire hissed past his head. *He is not brave but confident. He has no fear because he does not expect to lose.* Pouncer attacked to buy time, and the black-furred killer spun away from the blow, and as he came around launched into a feint, thrust, feint pattern so fast that by the time Pouncer realized what had happened he was dangerously overexposed again, his own blade far out of line as Ftzaal swung over and down to cut through his belly articulation. Pouncer jumped backward, the only defense he had, but even as his slicewire hissed through empty air Ftzaal was leaping forward, pressing his advantage. Out of position and off balance, Pouncer threw his slicewire up in a desperate last ditch block. It was a hair too slow, and Ftzaal's wire slid along his. Sudden pain burned in his right ear; a fraction farther and he would have lost it, and perhaps his head with it. Desperately, he rolled out of the way, throwing his slicewire up to block another attack, but Ftzaal was already in midleap and battered his guard out of the way, simultaneously lashing out with a kick that connected painfully with Pouncer's wrist, knocking his variable sword out of his grasp. Pouncer rolled backward in desperation and Ftzaal's blade slammed into the space he had occupied an instant before, gouging a chunk from the flexible flooring. Pouncer rolled again, this time coming to his feet. He grabbed up a small bowl-table and threw it at his adversary. Ftzaal blocked it easily, the bowl separated from the table stand by his slicewire. Pouncer backed up and found himself against the curved side of the pop-dome. There was nowhere else to go. Ftzaal's snarl gaped wide, showing razor fangs, and he screamed and leapt, his slicewire blurring. Pouncer ducked and tried to leap sideways, but he didn't have enough room and he wasn't going to get clear in time. Ftzaal's slicewire was a blur heading for his vulnerable neck articulation, and then Ftzaal himself was coming at him, the blade somehow coming out of line as the Black Priest was stumbling, falling into the resilient side of the dome to bounce off and tumble, his leap ruined. Pouncer leapt for his variable sword and grabbed it up, pivoting to face his adversary even as Ftzaal recovered his feet in a creditable half roll and came up with his weapon in guard position.

Stalemate again. They watched each other warily, and Pouncer gulped air in hungry gulps. *What made the master swordsman stumble?* Pouncer flicked his eyes from his opponent's shoulder for half a heartbeat, saw nothing, did it again and found the bowl of the bowl-table, rolled to one side now. Ftzaal had landed on it in his leap and lost his footing. Krwisatz, *the pebble-that-trips-pouncer-or-prey. Except today Pouncer is the prey. Learn the lesson there.* Pouncer stepped sideways to clear his touchdown area for his own leap, and Ftzaal's lips twitched over his fangs. He was going to attack again.

Feet pounded on the stairs, and the Black Priest's eyes flicked sideways. The stairway was behind Pouncer, but he could sense his pride-mates stopping at the top, taking stock of the situation. The odds had shifted now.

"I'll take the rest of that ear later, Rrit." Ftzaal snarled the words.

So he has recognized me. Pouncer didn't answer. *Let him eat my silence.* He motioned his comrades forward, but Ftzaal back flipped, slicing open the side of the pop dome while he was still upside down and bursting out through the gap. Without thought Pouncer leapt after him, exultation in his liver. *He is good, but not good enough. C'mell's ambushes will take him.* Then he too was through the slashed dome wall, dropping to an easy crouch, searching for his enemy, his vision still half dark-adapted.

Polarizers whined and a gravcar boosted past, so close the wind blast nearly knocked him over. He looked up to see it vanishing into the night. Ftzaal-Tzaatz. He screamed into the night, a hunter cheated of his prey. For an instant he wished for a gravcar. *But sky mobility is the enemy's strength, not mine.* Gravcars required fuel and maintenance and infrastructure beyond the resources of the *czrav.* His strength was stealth, not speed, the ability to vanish into the countryside in an instant, to travel unde-tected, to appear suddenly and in force, anywhere and everywhere. *I must not fight the Tzaatz on their ground but on my own.*

The sounds of fighting had faded from the shredded pop-domes, replaced by the snarls of his warriors as they scoured the ruins for information. A strange, keening roar split the night, suddenly cut off. C'mell's forces had found the *rapsar* quarters and were slaying the beasts. He ran back to the other pop-domes, got status reports from each of his sub-commanders there. The news was good; no serious injuries, and all the Tzaatz dead in the first attack. He went back to the main pop-dome, confirmed that all was under control there on both floors. On the second level he saw again the severed bowl of the bowl-table. It was ornately carved of flamewood in an alien style, perhaps Jotoki. On impulse he dropped it into a pouch on his combat harness and went back to the ground floor.

The assault team there was still sifting through bodies

for intelligence. He had one more task to do, and then he would melt back into the night. He turned and ran to the main house, snarling the code word to Kdtronai's cut-off teams who held the approaches secure so they would know who he was. He loped up to the door, then rang the great gong that announced visitors. The doors were of heavy stonewood beams bound in iron, once enough to withstand considerable assault. He could have sliced them open in a heartbeat with his variable sword, but he refrained, waiting impatiently while he heard the wards drawn back from the inside. Two impassive Kdatlyno hauled the heavy doors open, and behind them, as Pouncer had hoped, was Vsar-Chiuu.

The old kzin stood ready, his eyes clear, his hand steady as he held *v'scree* stance, variable sword in hand, ready to defend his home and his honor with his life if he had to.

"You kill the Tzaatt. Who are you?" The voice was suspicious, but if Vsar truly distrusted this stranger who had come so abruptly in the night he would never have opened his door voluntarily.

"I am Zree-Rrit-First-Son-of-Meerz-Rrit. I am sworn to your protection." Pouncer claw-raked, one hand on the pommel of his variable sword in case the old kzin attacked while his guard was down.

"First-Son, Zree-Rrit now! Can it be true?" Vsar-Chiuu stepped forward and peered at Pouncer, then relaxed, retracting the blade of his variable sword. "Yes, you have your father's markings. I knew him when he was just a kitten."

"I am his son." Pouncer retracted his own slicewire and

made the gesture of obedience-to-the-Patriarch-in-his-absence, as though bearing his father's coat pattern were a matter of duty and not genetics.

"What you have done here today, there will be repercussions . . ."

"No Tzaatz will take anything of yours again, not while I live."

"And one repercussion may be that you do not live. The Patriarchy has come to dark days." The old kzin wrinkled his nose. "Your father called you Pouncer, as I recall."

"He did, sire."

"I saw you when you were presented to the Circle of Lesser Prides, before you were weaned. You struggled hard, and jumped on his tail when you got free. He had to hold you up with both hands." Vsar-Chiuu rippled his ears. "You seemed worthy of that name then. You seem worthy of his name now."

"I will strive to be." Pouncer checked his beltcomp. "I come to give you a message, to pass on to the Tzaatz when they come. *Skalazaal* is alive, between Rrit and Tzaatz. I will not rest until I have Kchula's head spiked at Hero's Gate."

"Hrrr. It is good to hear that. I will enjoy passing this message."

"I must go now, but we will be watching."

"We." Vsar-Chiuu growled in approval. "You have allies, Zree-Rrit. This is good. You have another ally in Chiuu Pride now. I will do whatever I can do to help you."

"It is safer if you do not. There will be repercussions."

Vsar lashed his tail. "What will the Tzaatz do to me? Take my land and kzinretti? Abuse my slaves? Kill my eldest sons?" He hissed. "They are *sthondats*, and I have little enough to lose. Already my youngest are hidden well, and I am too old to fear death any longer. Fealty runs both ways, Zree-Rrit. I will not have it said Chiuu Pride has forgotten its honor."

"Chiuu Pride's honor is above question. I must go now, but I will come again, sire, and we will talk more." Pouncer claw-raked and went out, collecting Kdtronai's guards as he went. Quicktail had the rest of the assault detachment assembled at the withdrawal point, and Pouncer quickly took the lead and headed back for the assembly area. They met C'mell's warriors there, and though he longed to nuzzle her, to reassure himself that she was really there, really safe, he did not. *This is combat, and I am the leader.* He checked quickly to see that the rest of her party had returned and then led them back into the riverbed. This time they moved in the center of the stream so the water would cover their spoor and scent trail. It was difficult and uncomfortable going and again Pouncer found himself wishing he'd allowed more time. Estimates that had seemed generous looking at a map were proving woefully inadequate now. He pushed the pace as hard as he could, sloshing through the darkness, tripping over underwater stones, falling farther behind with each step. They had to meet up with V'rli's group and be out of the Hrungn before daybreak. The raid wasn't a success until they were all safely away. *We have no margin for error here.* Decision time. If they stayed in the river, the sniffers wouldn't be able to track them, but they would be caught still in the valley when the sun came up. Worse, V'rli's group could not leave without them, and he would endanger the entire pride. If he left the river, they would save time, but the sniffers would pick up their trail. Either way the Tzaatz would find them, and without the element of surprise his light force wouldn't be able to stand up to a *rapsar* attack.

So what to do? He kept moving as he thought. At least the forced pace kept him warm. Despite the heat of the day the night air was chill, and the Hrungn ran cold from its high mountain springs. The valley was rich with the smell of turned earth, and something else, vaguely familiar, jogging his memory. He sniffed, then inhaled deeply to catch the faint scent. *Myewl!* It was more common in the jungle downlands, but it liked dry ground by jungle standards, enough that even here next to the mountains the aromatic plants could find habitat close to the river. The *myewl* leaves would break their scent trail. There would still be ground spoor—a moving force the size of his couldn't help but leave signs for a good tracker to follow—but the Tzaatz relied too much on their sniffers. It was a risk worth taking. He moved out of the river bed, clambering over dry rocks in the darkness, then scrambling over the bank that marked the full river margins in the flood season. Burstflower bushes lined the rivers edge, and he headed upslope, toward the dryer, sandier area that must be ahead. The *myewl* scent grew stronger, and on a low sandy hill he came into a clump of it. He gave the tail sign for *gather*, and watched again as his well disciplined force filed into their preassigned places in the night-defensive formation. The *czrav* were all seasoned hunters, and didn't need to be told the significance of the *myewl*. With *wtsai* and claws they stripped the leaves from the branches, crushing them to spread the juice over themselves. It took time, but when they moved out they were moving faster. Pouncer breathed a little easier, but still pushed the pace. Soon their path would turn up, and the steepness of the valley wall would slow them down again. They had to make time while they could. In the distance riding lights winked in the sky, gravcars falling into the stronghold of Chiuu Pride. *The Tzaatz are arrogant, and they give themselves away.* Ftzaal-Tzaatz would have summoned trackers, and the gravcars would sweep the valley with their sensors. It was too late for that. The background clutter of large animals and wind-rocked branches would be enough to confuse them. The Tzaatz would have to track them on the ground, over a trail made difficult by the river and the *myewl*, and they could track on the ground no faster than Pouncer could move ahead of them. They were safe. He kept moving quickly, though his warriors were visibly tiring, and his own muscles complained loudly at the unaccustomed strain. They were safe, but there were still deadlines to meet. He did not want to keep V'rli waiting at the rendezvous.

The eastern sky was growing brighter when they arrived in the grove of broadleaf trees where the *tuskvor* were tethered. V'rli's group was already there in defensive positions. She met him as they came in.

"Any injuries?" Her tone asked the unspoken question. *Any killed?*

"None." Pride won through the exhaustion and he held himself as a warrior should. He had made it, in and back, and brought all of his first command with him. "The *rapsari* are dead, and all the Tzaatz save one."

"Just one?"

"It was the Black Priest, Ftzaal-Tzaatz. I fought him myself."

V'rli's ears swiveled up. "He is dangerous." Her eyes went to Pouncer's ear, now bound in *myewl* to hide the bloodscent. "He wounded you."

"It is minor, Honored Mother. We should go."

"We should." Czor-Dziit had joined them. "You have won a great victory here, Zree-Rrit."

"Ztrak Pride's victory, I think. I made mistakes, sire."

"Mistakes are inevitable. What matters is how you handle yourself when they occur. You handled yourself well. On your next raid Dziit Pride will share your victory too."

"I am honored, sire."

"No, I am honored, Zree-Rrit." Czor-Dziit claw-raked, and V'rli gave the tail signal for *mount*. Around the grove the *mazourk* leapt up to their travel platforms to take the tiller bars, and the raiders of Ztrak leapt behind them. It would be three more days through mountain, desert and grasslands to the high forest den, but they had ears now, and the battle behind them. *Tuskvor* grunted and stirred. Morale was high. V'rli rode the first *tuskvor* out of the grove and Pouncer rode the last. Already his raiders were snarling back and forth, weaving the story of the raid into a whole that the entire Pride would share. It would become part of the Pride Ballad soon enough. Pouncer stood to the back of the platform, not joining in the levity, looking back over the *tuskvor*'s heavily swaying tail. *I have started something today which I can no longer turn back.* There will be war between *czrav* and Tzaatz. He took out the severed bowl-table. On closer examination he could see the indentations made for serving ladles. It was meant to hold blood sauce for feasting. He turned it over to examine the almost polished surface where Ftzaal-Tzaatz's slicewire had cut through it with little more resistance than if it had been air. *Krwisatz. Will you trip pouncer or prey?* They had won this engagement, but the war was far from over. *What unseen factor might yet turn victory into defeat?*

We swim the same sea as the sharks.
                              —Dolphin saying

Curvy whistled to herself as she tapped on her console, the manipulator tentacles of her dolphin hands snaking expertly over the keys in response to brain impulses picked up by tiny coils of superconductor in the control cap she wore. Zwweee(click)wurrrtrrrtrrr answered her from across the dolphin tank, and Curvy chirped happily at the reminder that she was no longer alone. Dolphins prefer to be gregarious, and she had spent too much time with only human company.

Few dolphins chose to work with the UNF for just that reason. It was one thing to be on a dive team for some human mining corporation in Earth's oceans, to work and play with friends and family, and listen to the ancient rhythms of the ocean. It was something else to leave the oceans for the uncomfortable environment of space, to be reliant on another species even for food. It was unnatural, but it was necessary. If the cetacean world was to have any influence over their own oceans, some dolphins had to work with the humans, even to the extent of helping them fight their wars.

And so she was on the UNSN battleship *Crusader*, at the core of a fleet five hundred strong, plotting strategy as they boosted for the world the kzinti called W'kkai. She punched execute to run her strategic matrix, a complex condensation of a hundred thousand factors that might affect the battle to come. She had carefully designed it to winnow out the courses of action required to optimize the chances of getting the desired results. Not *her* desired results, which would have seen peace between Man and Kzin; that option had been foreclosed. Secretary Ravalla had come to power faster than she had thought possible, or to be more technically accurate, at a date ahead of 97.3% of the range of possible dates computed by her previous calculations, although he had only achieved a minority government (33.4% probable and thus not much of a surprise). Given that combination of outcomes it was highly probable (85%) that Ravalla would move immediately to war, but the total probability of all three events was less than one percent. Events had landed on an outlier, and the results were disastrous. War was in progress, and the best course of action now was to ensure that the UN won it, quickly. If the Patriarchy reacted as her models predicted, a long war would lead to an inevitable escalation that would see planets razed, Earth most certainly included. That was an outcome to be avoided at any cost.

Of course a short war also had a high probability of that outcome. Curvy dove to snap up a trout while her simulation ran. The prognostics weren't positive, but life continued. Zwweee(click)wurrrrtrrrtrrr dove with her and for a moment they swam in synchrony, bathed in the flickering light from one tank wall where the entire fleet's com channels were displayed, so the dolphins could follow battles in real time. She ducked under him and rubbed her beak and melon along his belly, an affectionate tease. He rolled and chirped and then they leapt, as well as they could in the not-quite-big enough tank. Later they would mate; for now there was the simulation run.

The computer beeped and flashed, and together they went to look at the results. Battle tactics in three dimensions. The humans had an overwhelming fleet compared to what intelligence said they would find at W'kkai. It would be a straightforward battle; their losses would be light. The real battle would come later, when the kzinti set out to take back what was theirs. The Patriarchy was big, exactly how big nobody knew for sure. She had models, with upper and lower bounds, and the alarming thing was that the upper bounds were so much larger than the humans were willing to believe. The elements of kzinti social structure were an important factor, incompletely known. Perhaps it had been a mistake to influence events to allow Dr. Brasseur to be sent to Kzinhome. The a priori probability of his death had been low, and the social data he might have come home with would have greatly enhanced the models. Instead, they had lost not only the additional data he would have brought back, but his insight into the data they already had.

Curvy trilled, concerned at what she saw on her screen. Zwweee(click)wurrrrtrrrtrrr clicked in concurrence, and dumped his own data to her screen. Victory at W'kkai was not an issue. The consequences of that victory were less encouraging. The best possible solution was to target Kzinhome itself as soon as possible. If that could be done successfully there was a high probability the remainder of the Patriarchy would fall apart without offering serious threat to Earth. Kzinhome was heavily defended though. Her first campaign concept had involved attacking it almost immediately, but that plan revolved around the unprecedented combat power of the Wunderlanders' Treatymaker, and that was now out of action for the foreseeable future.

And of course it was beyond the capacity of the Ravalla faction to delay their attack until the human forces were fully ready. They would forfeit their political position if they reneged on their aggressive rhetoric now that they were in power. The negative outcome spaces downstream of that position seemed to have no impact on the faction's decision making. The best they could do now was attack the Patriarchy's weaker worlds, gain experience for the human fleet, and hopefully draw some of the protection away from Kzinhome itself. It was not the most optimal plan she could imagine, it was simply the best one under the circumstances.

Her consort slid beneath and rubbed her belly with amorous insistence, and concern dissolved in the mating flash. They dove together with bodies intertwined, losing the cares of known space in love play for a few blissful minutes. She wriggled as he entered her, delighted at his touch, his company, his essential dolphin-ness. She had forgotten how much she missed her own kind. Dolphins had their priorities straight. If humans would only spend more time mating and less time scheming, the galaxy would be a better place.

*You will find nothing there but the dark heart of
the jungle, and if you somehow survive its beasts
and fevers, it will seize you, it will seduce you, and
you will never return.*
　　　　—Major Wes Wrightson, Gambia, 1818

The high noon glare of 61 Ursae Majoris baked rivers of
sweat from Quacy Tskombe's brow. He wiped it away and
examined the stone circle of a campfire and the inukshuk
beside it. There were scattered bones nearby, remnants of
one of the graceful *zianya* herbivores that populated the
rolling savannah. In tracking Ayla they had found six
campsites with inukshuk scattered across the grasslands
between the mountains and the jungle. It was Far Hunter
who read the land and divined the direction the fugitives
had most likely taken in their flight, but it was Trina who
had found all six campsites. Certainly they had missed
many more, but they had the trail, and that was what
mattered. Trina's formidible luck was no longer something
he questioned but something he counted on. When she
and Far Hunter agreed on the direction to travel he took
their advice without question. His own tracking skills were
unnecessary, and, though he didn't like to admit it, far out-
classed. Even he could have found this campsite, though.
A grass fire had swept through the area a season ago,
leaving a large charred circle easily visible from the air, a
logical place to look for a campsite. Ayla's cook fire must
have gotten out of control.

　　He looked up to the forbidding green wall where the
jungle began, just a few hundred meters away now. The
trail they had followed pointed straight to the jungle, and

he remembered T'suuz telling Pouncer that they would find shelter in there.

"Far Hunter!" he called. The kzin was examining the ground on the other side of the gravcar. "What is a *czrav*?"

"A jungle primitive. Even the savannah *cvari* see them rarely. Why do you ask?"

"Pouncer said he would find shelter there." It was really T'suuz who had, but Tskombe had learned that Far Hunter would not believe him if he said T'suuz said anything of import. Kzinretti were not supposed to be that smart.

"Poor shelter there. The *czrav* are dangerous, and they are not even the greatest of the jungle's dangers. I have hunted the jungle verge. Few who go deeper ever come out again."

"It seems that's where they went."

Far Hunter furled his ears. "My hope is dwindling, Tskombe-*kz'zeerkti*, for your cause and for mine."

"Hey, look at this!" Trina called, interrupting.

Human and kzin went to look and found long scars in the center of the burned area where soil had melted into dark glass.

Tskombe pursed his lips. "Laser beams." Ayla's cooking fire hadn't been the cause of the burned area after all.

"Hrrrr. The Tzaatz found them and attacked with energy weapons. They have no honor."

Tskombe looked at him. "I've seen kzinti kill each other with more than hand weapons."

Far Hunter snarled, showing his fangs. "Of course, but not in a pride war, or a duel. There are traditions."

Tskombe nodded, feeling sick at heart. Three runners

on foot, against at least a gravcar with heavy weapons. The chances of survival were not good. They followed the slashes of glassified dirt to the jungle verge, found an area where trees had ruptured when the beams flash boiled the moisture in their boles. Splinters of wood had sprayed like grenade shrapnel to imbed themselves in nearby trunks. The damage continued some little distance into the tree-line, enough to suggest that perhaps the runners had gotten away. On the other hand, there was no wreckage in the area, no sign they had fought back successfully. Tskombe resolved to keep looking anyway. He had not come so far to give up, even if Ayla was already dead.

Far Hunter was sniffing the ground farther into the forest. "There is no sign of a trail."

"There wouldn't be, at this distance in time. We haven't found anything we can track yet."

"Hrrrr."

Trina moved deeper into the woods and Far Hunter looked up sharply. "Do not go further."

She turned around. "Why not?"

Far Hunter bared his fangs. "The jungle is a dangerous place. You can be lost within a few paces, and prey within a few more."

She stepped back, looking worried. Tskombe turned back to the open savannah. "I think we should search from the gravcar. We can cover more ground that way."

Far Hunter twitched his whiskers. "Agreed."

It was harder than he thought it would be. From the air the jungle was a vast, green maze split by the muddy, serpentine coils of the river. It was impenetrable from below, its secrets well hidden from above. After the second day

of searching from the gravcar they lost *Black Saber* when
Contradictory landed a contract to take a cargo to a world
called Reessliu. It was a round trip contract, by way of
Ktzaa'Whrloo, so at least the freerunner would be back,
eventually. *Black Saber*'s instruments were no help in a
ground search conducted beneath jungle canopy, but
once Tskombe found Ayla he wanted to take her back
immediately. *But that is not what's going to happen.*
There were no guarantees. Night Pilot gave them an estimated time of return, and that was all. *Black Saber* went
where her cargos took her, and the Patriarchy was a big
place. *Getting back to human space has now become as
large a problem as finding Ayla.*

Time to think about that later. And as *later* became *now*
he continued to push the problem back. The days grew
noticeably shorter and the first rains of the wet season
began without a single clue emerging from their search.
At night they camped on the relative safety of the savannah, by day they flew down the newly swollen tributaries
of the river. It was a search strategy dictated as much by
necessity as planning. Far Hunter's theory was that, if the
fugitives had survived, they would have followed the river
downstream. That theory meshed conveniently with the
fact that the river banks were the only part of the jungle
floor they could actually see. There were cool, clear pools
in the smaller tributaries, inviting in the heat of the day,
but Far Hunter warned them against entering still water.

They found nothing, and continued to find nothing.
One day after another fruitless search it occurred to
Tskombe that he'd lost track of time. It had been what, a
month? Two months? They returned to their camp on the

savannah to eat a *zianya* that Far Hunter had caught. Trina and Tskombe roasted their portion on the same cook fire that Ayla had set, a season or more ago. It made him feel connected to her, as though she were alive. *And she is alive, I have to believe that*. The jungle was large, the search could take years. Patience was the key.

And still the next day, in his heart he believed that today might be the day they found her. It was not, nor was the next. The Hunter's Moon made its way through its phases, chased around the sky by the smaller, faster Traveler's Moon. The wet season was well upon them. Every day brought larger storms, and the languid river began to run faster, hastened by its myriad overflowing tributaries. The danger of standing water was replaced by the hazard of its powerful current, but there was less drive to swim. The constant rainfall was cooling the parched jungle, and the desiccated vegetation began to swell and blossom. Tskombe found himself changing too, adapting to the environment. He could recognize hidden threats, in the fangthorn and the trapvine, he knew the tracks of the *alyyzya* and, though he'd never seen one, the fearsome *grlor*. His dark complexion was burnt almost black by the relentless sun. Trina had changed too. He had already seen the little girl behind the abused adolescent emerge in her time on Tiamat, and now the little girl was growing, maturing into a confident young woman. Unlike him she wasn't adapting to the jungle, her luck forbade it. If she needed to drink there was a clean stream nearby, if she wandered too close to a trapvine it turned out to have already caught its dinner. Her confidence was the misplaced confidence of youth, that nothing bad could happen to *her*. Except her case it turned out to be correct.

Her luck was failing though, in the search for Ayla. *But good luck for her is not good luck for me. Perhaps her fates have arranged for her to have this interlude, to heal away from the humans who have done her the most harm, kept safe by good fortune alone in this lethal environment.* Certainly Far Hunter was good for her. The kzin had taken an almost paternal interest in her, as a human might in a lost raccoon baby. He teased her gently and taught her little hunting tricks. She teased him back and learned to groom his pelt, a fair exchange. It reminded Tskombe of the earlier relationship she had forged with Curvy. *And where is Curvy now?* Earth, human space, Muro Ravalla and the threat of war, all these things seemed impossibly distant, completely unconnected with the daily round of their life. Even Ayla seemed distant, despite being the focus of his quest. Only in his dreams did she seem real, calling out to him, urging him not to give up on her. By day there was only the jungle, vast and alive, taunting him with its impenetrable secrets.

On their sixtieth or six hundredth flight Trina was flying under Far Hunter's tutelage, another round of the life lessons he insisted on teaching her. Tskombe kept his attention focused down, swept his eyes up and down the wide river, as the triple canopy unrolled beneath them, looking for something, anything.

And there was *something*. He gestured *down*, and Trina slid the gravcar down into the burned-over valley he'd spotted and landed on a thin layer of grass growing over still-charred ground. The jungle air was thick and humid, full of the scent of life. The morning had seen marching thunderstorms flood rain from the sky while fist sized hailstones rang off the gravcar's canopy like strakkaker fire, but now 61 Ursae Majoris burned down mercilessly from a clear blue sky, and the soaked ground steamed tendrils of water vapor up to join the next storm cycle. Tskombe climbed out, already drenched in sweat, and looked around at the sparse forest of burnt trunks.

Far Hunter leapt out. "What have you seen?"

"Just that this area is burnt over."

"You suspect more laser fire?"

"Or a cook fire. What else do we have to go on?"

Far Hunter knelt to examine the soil. "This fire is too old, it happened several years ago at least." He pointed. "See how the shoots have pushed through the charred layer and grown? The tree trunks have faded to gray."

Tskombe nodded, sighing heavily. "Another false alarm. Where do we go from here?"

The kzin fanned his ears up as he surveyed the landscape. "Not so fast. It is still likely they would be following the river. Jungle navigation is hard. This tributary branch would have been their easiest choice. This burned area is easy going too. They may have come through here and left sign that has lasted in the char."

"That way." Trina pointed downslope from the cockpit. "I think that way." Tskombe nodded and they got back in. Far Hunter took over the controls, flying slowly a few meters up, looking for clues. Tskombe had them fly through the center of the burned area, hoping to find stones arranged to hold a cook fire, or better yet another inukshuk, but there was nothing. A rushing stream ran through the center of the valley, running brisk with the morning's rain. Tskombe felt a mounting despair, for the first time since they had started the jungle hunt.

"We're searching for a needle in a haystack."

Haystack translated as *grass pile* in the Hero's Tongue, and Far Hunter looked puzzled. "Why would you expect to find a needle there?"

"Well, you wouldn't expect to, that's the point."

"Then why look?"

"Well, because you need to find the needle."

"Needles are trivial possessions. Why not just get another one?"

"Well, you would normally." Tskombe laughed, his mood improving slightly. "What I mean is, we're wasting our time here."

Far Hunter put a paw to his nose, where four parallel lines of white fur marked the scars from the blood oath he had sworn. "Hrrr. I am pledged to take vengeance on the Tzaatz for my father's death, and my fealty belongs to the Rrit. I have no time in my life which is not bent to this task." He took his paw away and unfurled his ears as he contemplated Tskombe. "Have you some priority higher than your search for your mate?"

And when you put it like that . . . Tskombe shook his head. "No. No I don't."

Far Hunter growled in deep satisfaction. "Then it is settled. We will search on." He spun the gravcar for another pass up the valley from the river.

"Look over there." Trina pointed. "Something's different."

They followed her finger. The valley fell into the river bed, cutting through a steep bluff that the river itself had etched eons earlier. Along the river bank the area between the water and the bluff was burnt over as well, the blackened and denuded spire trees reaching for the sky like the twisted pillars of some dark cathedral, but the burn was darker, the edges sharper, unrelieved by the sprigs of green that softened the harshness of the fire ravaged valley.

"Yes." Far Hunter slid the gravcar down to the ground at the border between the two areas and got out again, crouching to examine the ground cover, standing again to inspect a tree. "This was another fire. It burned between the bluff and the river, and stopped when it reached the old burn." He moved to examine a spire trunk as Tskombe and Trina got out to follow him. "The trunks are still sooty, the ground crust is intact. This fire happened at the start of this dry season."

"Lasers?"

"Hrrr. We must search to know. Perhaps . . ."

They got back in the gravcar and patrolled up the river in silence, Far Hunter zigzagging the car slowly. The fire had burned hot, and even the stones were carbonized funereal black. The area was probably safer than the rest of the jungle, but Tskombe still kept a careful eye out for danger. Days earlier they had seen the footprints of a *grlor* pack, but big herbivores could find no food here, and so they and the big carnivores that preyed on them would avoid the area. Still the blackened, dead landscape *felt* dangerous. *That's a good thing, it will keep us alert in our search.* Tskombe leaned forward in his seat, straining to pick up some shape that didn't belong, but there was nothing but the unending blackness. As the day wore on

the ground stopped steaming as the unrelenting sun
baked the moisture from it and heat waves began to ripple the stagnant air instead. By midafternoon they were
powerful enough to make the more distant of the burned
trunks appear to twist and warp. The strip between the
bluff and the river was a kilometer wide and seemed to go
on forever. Tskombe counted himself lucky. If they had
just ten or twenty square kilometers to search a meter at
a time, their haystack had gotten a lot smaller. *If* they were
in the right place. *If not I no longer have anything of value
except time*.

They came to a rockslide where the whole face of the
bluff had given way, chunks of rock as big as houses torn
from the cliff in a slide that stretched two hundred
meters. The rocks were fire blackened too, but still sharp
edged. The fall had happened before the fire, but it was
recent. It might even have occurred during it, perhaps
triggered by the heat.

Trina pointed. "Look there."

He looked. It was a bone, sticking out from beneath a
massive boulder, bleached white by rain and sun in stark
contrast with the blackened landscape. They set down and
got out to examine it.

Up close they could see it was a tibia. The foot was gone,
along with the fibula. Far Hunter examined it closely,
sniffed at it.

"It is kzinti."

"Are you sure?"

"Yes. A male."

"Is it Pouncer?" Tskombe felt a sudden dread. If it
were Pouncer then the odds were high Ayla was under the

slide as well. His throat tightened as he pushed the thought away.

"We cannot know." Far Hunter looked up. "This area is important. We must search it thoroughly."

They did, on foot, clambering over the semi-stable slide. Tskombe thought they would get filthy with soot, but what remained on the rocks after the heavy rains was baked onto their surfaces and didn't come off that easily. They found nothing else on the slide, but Tskombe did find what looked like a steep trail leading up the face of the bluff. They followed it and found a cave mouth on a ledge. It would have been invisible from below. Inside was a large, sand-floored cavern and signs of a large bonfire. Other signs of inhabitation were plentiful.

"This is a *czrav* den." For the first time ever Far Hunter sounded apprehensive. "We must not stay here."

"Why not?"

"The *czrav* . . . Few have ever seen one, fewer still live to tell of it."

"Pouncer thought he would find sanctuary with them."

"If he has, he is lucky. They are ferocious warriors, unwelcoming of strangers. We are transgressing on their territory. We must leave and make a proper border gift at the edge of their territory."

"It looks like they have already left."

"They are migratory, but they will return."

"Where do they migrate to?"

"No one knows."

"When will they be back?"

"I cannot say."

"So we're supposed to wait at the edge of their territory for some indefinite period of time."

"This is the tradition. It is important that we follow it."

Tskombe nodded. "We might as well look around while we're here, to see if we can find any proof that Pouncer did arrive here."

Far Hunter hesitated, the war between courage and fear plain in his expression. "Yes. We must be fast."

Trina had been exploring deeper in the cavern. "I found an inukshuk," she said.

Near the round fire place was a large rock, its surface worn smooth. Beside it, neatly piled, was another manlike stone sculpture. Tskombe breathed out. Ayla had been here, literally in the lion's den. Its presence showed she had stayed some time, which in turn meant Pouncer must have been with her, to extend his protection to her, and T'suuz, to make whatever connection she had to these frightening alien primitives. *She made it this far. Now where did she go from here?*

> **So in war the way is to avoid what is strong and strike at what is weak.**
>
> —Sun Tzu

Ayla Cherenkova stood in the den mouth, watching the setting sun paint the sky in rich tones of red and orange, its last rays turning the towering cumulus cloud to the west into jagged spires, like predatory fangs set to devour heavens. Below the sandstone dome of the den four *tuskvor* turned south at their *mazourk*'s urging, another deep patrol heading over the mountains to raid the

Tzaatz. It was frustrating to watch them go and have to stay behind. She was, after all, a warrior, and the *czrav* were her tribe now, her *pride*. Her instinct was to hunt with them, raid with them, to build the bonds of trust and respect that warriors built together. Pouncer had denied it of her and, though that was frustrating, his word was law. There was no question that Pouncer was leading the pride now, Patriarch in all but name. He was close to becoming Great Patriarch of the *czrav*. Dziit Pride followed him, and Fvaar Pride, and others were lending support, if not yet fealty. That would come soon, as *czrav* victories gained momentum. The slaughter of Mrrsel Pride by the Tzaatz had galvanized the *czrav* prides and turned them against eons of self-imposed isolation. Ztrak Pride had made the decision to send only its nursing mothers and kits back to the jungle on the countermigration, not to their own jungle den, compromised as it was by the Tzaatz, but to that of Mrrsel Pride, along with the few straggling Mrrsel survivors who'd been away when the Tzaatz had come to kill them. For them it was simply logical, but many other *czrav* prides had made the decision to stay in the high forest over the next migration as well, laying in provisions to last over the barren season, simply because they could better launch raids against the Tzaatz from there. Several hundred balky *tuskvor* had been held back from the countermigration to carry the raiders from their high forest bases into the mountains, to descend on Tzaatz positions in the foothills at the northern edge of the Plain of Stgrat. They were a force to be reckoned with.

Ayla picked up a rock and idly threw it over the cliff, watching it vanish. The *czrav* were ferocious warriors.

Even though raids were forbidden to her she was still part of the struggle. She was a commander, trained in the organizational skills and tactical finesse the *czrav* needed to turn their embryonic rebellion into a victory. The plan of attack Pouncer was now leading was Ayla's, a strategy crafted from ten thousand human years of human conflict. The *czrav* lacked the strength to stand in a face-to-face fight against Tzaatz *rapsari*, but they didn't need to. Instead they had moved fast and deep into enemy territory, struck hard and vanished again like ghosts. The Tzaatz had responded at first with large-scale sweeps, but they lacked the *czrav* standard of fieldcraft, and their unwieldy formations were too big to move fast enough to catch the night raiders. With the failure of that strategy they had begun garrisoning themselves, staying in larger groups and sticking to their fortifications, and that had the effect of isolating them from the Lesser Prides they purported to rule. Tzaatz authority in the northern plains was thoroughly undermined. A *czrav* raiding party pressed hard by Tzaatz gravcars could find shelter with any smallholder now, and the Lesser Prides were beginning to lend food, shelter and weapons, and most importantly information. All of Ztrak Pride carried variable swords now, and Pouncer drilled them relentlessly in the group combat form. It was guerrilla war, nothing less. They fought dirty, and they fought to win, and it was working, at least locally. The future was less certain. To be more than an annoyance to the Tzaatz, Pouncer would have to take the Citadel of the Patriarch. That would require facing the Tzaatz head on, there was no other way.

She had become closer to the young leader through the

process, but there was more to their relationship than that. Pouncer still relied heavily on the advice of V'rli, on Kdtronai, on Kr-Pathfinder, but she was different. She still wore the Sigil of the Patriarch around her neck, the magical talisman that let her live in the lion's den in perfect safety. If Pouncer were to die, his protection would die with him, and so her loyalty was absolute in a way that theirs was not, despite the bonds of blood and honor. Ayla herself had total faith in the commitment of the *czrav* warriors to him. She saw how they reacted to his presence, how even Pride-Patriarchs tried to emulate him in every way. Pouncer never expressed anything less than complete trust in them himself, but he had been betrayed by his own brother, and she knew that faith was a jealously guarded commodity for him.

She watched the *tuskvor* grow small on the horizon, vanishing as 61 Ursae Majoris slipped beneath the horizon and the velvet night enveloped the forest. They moved according to her plan, but she wanted a position on the raids herself. *Pouncer was right to deny that of me.* It was an uncomfortable reality to accept. She was small and weak next to the kzinti, her reflexes slow, her senses dull. She would be nothing but a liability in an engagement restricted to muscle-powered weapons. She could, perhaps, claim that she was not bound by the rules of *skalazaal*, that the weapons she could carry would make her invaluable in combat, but she did not push the point. She was accepted now in the tribe, if not as a kzin, then as a worthy ally and a member of an unconquered species. To suggest anything that might put that status into question, much less something that smacked of questionable honor, was unthinkable. To be recognized as equal to even the smallest and weakest kzin was important. Ayla had no desire to be seen as a member of a slave species. *Or as prey*. The thought rose unbidden, and her hand went to the sigil around her neck.

Still, I can do more. She turned away from the den mouth as the sun sank below the horizon and the warm wind began to cool. *I can bring the future forward.* The hunt-cloth cover that camouflaged its opening fell into place behind her and she made her way to the deeper level where Pouncer kept his command post.

He was there by himself, working on a screen, planning the future of the campaign. He drove himself harder than anyone. During the day he trained the warriors, and at night he trained their leaders, and after they had all gone to sleep he planned strategy and organized the next attack. He insisted on leading every raid he could. The strain was not showing on him yet, but privately Ayla wondered if he had the reserves necessary to keep up the pace for what was destined to be a long, hard fight.

He looked up as she came in. She didn't hesitate. "Pouncer. I want to be on the next raid."

He blinked. "Cherenkova-Captain, you have already heard my reasoning on that issue."

"I have more reasons you should let me."

Pouncer fanned his ears up. "I will listen."

"You are attacking the Tzaatz now, doing damage. Have you a plan to finalize the victory?"

"It is too early yet to consider victory. We must first show the *kzintzag* that we can fight effectively."

"No, it is never too early to start planning how you're going to win. I can help you with that."

"I rely on your strategic skills, Cherenkova-Captain. It is your physical prowess that gives me pause. You are too vulnerable, and too valuable to risk."

"I have killed kzinti in combat."

"Strength and reflex are not factors in space combat."

"I have killed them in person, side by side with your uncle at the Citadel."

"With energy weapons."

"The weapons issue is beside the point. I am a trained strategist, but I can apply my strategy better if I lead while I do it."

"Hrrr." Pouncer turned a paw over, considering. "What would you do with your strategic thinking, if I gave you free rein?"

"I would establish a forward base in the Long Range and from there I would launch raids against Tzaatz positions down the eastern plains."

"That is a long journey from here, much longer than the direct route to the Plain of Stgrat. What will you accomplish there?"

"They'll be forced to respond to us. The terrain in the mountains is tremendously difficult. They will have to commit more forces to the area in an attempt to flush us out. The Citadel is the center of power on Kzinhome, and we will turn their attention away from it. Also, by moving the center of our attacks to a different area we will prevent them from isolating our exact location, and we'll appear to be increasing our strength to the Lesser Prides and the *kzintzag*. Weather conditions are difficult in the Long

Range, which favors us too. We remain vulnerable to space reconnaissance."

"We know the orbital parameters of the fortresses. So long as we move with the *tuskvor* they cannot track us."

"They'll learn that trick and we will follow the fate of Mrrsel Pride." Ayla leaned forward. "Give me a small force, let me show what I can do with it."

"An independent force. It is a clever idea, whoever leads it. What else do you suggest?"

"We need to form an alliance with other Great Prides, somehow."

Pouncer rippled his ears. "You are losing your reason. If I had access to a ship you would already be on your homeworld."

"It's vital. Eventually we have to take the Citadel. Kchula-Tzaatz respects the rules of *skalazaal* now because we are little more than a thorn in his side, but when we launch the final attack he's going to be faced with the loss of everything. Do you trust his honor not to use energy weapons then, even space weapons?"

"Hrrr." Pouncer turned a paw over. "You are correct."

"We *must* have the Great Prides watching, and in a position to intervene if necessary. If they have ships in orbit, Kchula will be constrained."

"There are Great Prides who will side with me, perhaps." Pouncer thought back to the time he had put in memorizing the Pride Leaders, their strengths and weaknesses, their alliances and interests. Tzaatz Pride had its rivals, Churrt Pride for one. *Now that information is becoming useful.* "How will we achieve this, with no ship and no access to a spaceport?"

"It will take time, but it can be done. We need to plan to send an emissary to any Great Pride you think will lend its support."

"Perhaps only to one, if its Pride-Patriarch has enough influence. He will be able to bring others with him."

"You have one in mind?"

"Zraa-Churrt, of Churrt Pride. But who to send as emissary?"

"You yourself would be the best choice."

"I cannot leave, you know that. It cannot be a *czrav* either, Zraa-Churrt may take that as an insult."

"Or a *kz'zeerkti*, for the same reason." Cherenkova smiled sardonically. *Now I'm planning to get a kzin off-world before I go myself. I've committed myself to Pouncer's victory.* "Vsar-Chiuu perhaps?"

"Perhaps, but he is old. I will think on this awhile."

"Send a message to Kzin-Conserver too. Declare *skalazaal* formally through him. We can't give the Tzaatz any room to break the rules."

Pouncer cocked an ear and regarded her curiously. "You have learned a lot about my world, Cherenkova-Captain."

"It is my job to know my enemy. I have learned all I can about the Tzaatz from this distance. Let me lead warriors and I will learn more."

Pouncer considered, then. "No. You are too important to risk."

She shook her head, frustrated. "I'm no more important than any other warrior here."

"You forget I am still sworn to your safety."

"You have saved my life many times now. I discharge you from your obligation."

"The only thing that will absolve me of my responsibility is your safe departure from my world."

"And I believe that the best thing I can do to ensure my own safety is to ensure your swift victory against the Tzaatz."

"Cherenkova-Captain, I respect your skills, I am lucky to have you as an ally, and proud to have you as a friend, but I cannot allow it. You are *kz'zeerkti*, not kzinti. No kzin will follow you as leader, however wise your strategies."

"Send V'rli with me. They will follow her, and she is smart enough to listen to what I have to say, and to improve on it."

"V'rli is honored mother, she cannot leave her pride."

"You are Patriarch now, in all but name. She will go if you tell her to."

For a second Pouncer's lips curled up to show his teeth. "I will claim no Patriarchy but the one I was born to." There was a hard edge in his snarl.

"Then let me fight with you for what is yours. Let me be *zar'ameer*."

Pouncer's ears flared up. "You are not my brother. You are not even kzinti."

"Your brother has betrayed you, but you are right, I am not kzinti. I alone on this planet can have not the slightest hope of becoming Patriarch. I alone will never covet your position, not even for an instant. My only goal is to leave your world to go back to my own, and I can only achieve it when you are Patriarch. We have a perfect alignment of interests, and no conflicts at all. Not even C'mell can claim that."

"C'mell." Pouncer wrinkled his nose. "Another recalcitrant female. She should be back in the jungle with Mrrsel Pride."

"She chooses to be by your side."

"She is heavy with my kits. She takes too much on herself."

"She is free to choose her own path. Some things even the Patriarch cannot command."

Pouncer looked up at her sharply. *Those are Guardmaster's words, when I desired to overreach myself. Is he speaking through her?* Cherenkova met his gaze with her own, giving no sign she knew the deeper significance of what she said. "Hrrrr." He turned a paw over. "You are persistent, Cherenkova-Captain. I am not surprised your species wins wars."

"Here's your chance to use that talent for your advantage. You're needed here now, to prepare the forces that will gather, to make sure the *tuskvor* are armored, that variable swords are produced, to train warriors to the combat forms. You can't go on every raid, and Tzaatz attention needs to be diverted away from our preparations. Let me be your sword."

"A *kz'zeerkti zar'ameer.*" Pouncer rippled his ears. "If nothing else it will stand out in the Pride Ballad. You win, Cherenkova-Captain. I will give you a force, one large enough to make an impact. I'll expect to see you win with it."

"I won't disappoint you." She claw-raked, as tradition demanded, and left. *I came to him to unconvinced my own idea would work. I'm leaving inspired to ensure its success. He is a natural leader, and he'll make a good*

Patriarch. Whether that was good for humanity was another question. She found herself surprisingly unconcerned with the answer to that question.

Pouncer meant what he said about a force big enough to make an impact. A Hunter's Moon later she rode out on a *tsvasztet* atop a huge herd-grandmother at the front of a column of two dozen *tuskvor* and over two hundred kzinti warriors, well provisioned and equipped to operate independently. As the den receded into the distance and the high forest gave way to the open grasslands, she felt the familiar, half welcome tension that she always felt at the start of an operation. There was the awareness that lives depended on her, as well as military success. There was always the potential for failure. Blood would be shed before she was done, perhaps including her own. It was a sobering thought, but she felt *alive*. She was no longer a hanger-on, no longer the outsider. She was a war leader at the head of her warriors, taking them into battle, and it didn't matter that those who followed her had once been her sworn enemies.

Her force was hand-picked, almost entirely kzinretti from Ztrak, Dziit and Fvaar Prides, all combat experienced, all volunteers. She had trained them with Pouncer's assistance and within the limits of time available and taken only the best. The very best she had made into her personal guard, a reluctant bow to the reality of her physical vulnerability when faced with kzinti in hand-to-hand combat. Her bodyguard were all from Mrrsel Pride, away on a hunt when the Tzaatz struck. All had lost kits in the attack, and all were sworn to blood vengeance. K'lakri, the kzinrette who led them, became her chief lieutenant.

Cherenkova herself carried a beamrifle, her single privilege as an alien.

There were Tzaatz fliers from time to time, and she knew that higher up the cameras on the orbital fortresses searched for them day and night, but the *tuskvor* skin canopies over their *tsvasztet* would defeat all but the closest inspections. She had computed the orbital periods of the fortresses on her beltcomp, to ensure that everyone was under cover when they flew over, and the Tzaatz knew too little about the rhythms of Kzinhome's seasons to know the significance of *tuskvor* moving south at this time of year. The beasts themselves knew better, and they were balky. Their migration urge had passed, but they wanted to be in the jungle fattening up for the next one, and they needed constant urging from their *mazourk* to stay on course. *The* mazourk *will tire quickly, we need to rotate them. That's something that we haven't yet addressed.* There were many things they hadn't addressed, an impromptu war could be fought no other way. Victory would go to the side which was the least disorganized, the least misled about the other's intentions. So far she was on the right side, but the Tzaatz had resources that the *czrav* didn't. The balance could tip at any moment.

It was a twelve-day ride to her chosen base area, through a pass in the jagged peaks where the Mooncatchers met the Long Range and into the foothills at the edge of the Plain of Stgrat on the other side. It took another three days to find a den that was well hidden from both air and ground, and defendable with the limited force they possessed. The prevailing winds were from behind them, and she realized that the Plain of Stgrat should have been in the rain shadow of the mountains, while the desert should have been rainforest, at least close to the mountains. It was a minor mystery, until K'lakri explained the use of charge suppressors for climate modification. The chain of suppressors prevented water vapor from nucleating into clouds and raindrops as the winds were forced to rise and cool against the mountain chain. Instead the moisture had to rise higher before it could condense, forming the almost permanent cloud deck that trailed from the mountains out over the plain of Stgrat. The extension of the cloud-forming cycle allowed the vital moisture to slip over the mountains to nourish the plain beyond them at the expense of the windward desert. *And it protects me from orbiting eyes.*

On a reconnaissance with her elite guard on the fourth day she found a suppressor site high on a nameless peak. It was solar powered, its fibercrete mountings so old and worn they looked like natural stone. Cherenkova didn't approach too closely. Presumably the charge suppressor was focused wide, without enough beam power to disintegrate something so solid as herself, but she didn't want to learn the hard way that that presumption was wrong. From their vantage point they could see the wide sweep of the desert to the north, and the fertile green plains to the south. She had a sudden realization, the reason the *tuskvor* migrated through the desert. *The kzinti have been doing this for thousands of years, weather engineering on a vast scale. They have turned the climatic patterns of this whole region upside down. The* tuskvor *once migrated through jungle and plain all the way from one side of the continent to the other. Now the plains are desert and the jungle reduced to high forest. This project has been going on so long the* tuskvor *have evolved to cycle through desert for half their lives.* She looked at K'lakri with new respect. *They have been civilized since before humanity tamed fire.*

It was not the first time she had come to that understanding since she arrived on Kzinhome, it would probably not be the last. After a time they moved off to continue learning the ground around their new location. Academic interest could come later. For now she had a war to wage.

> *Who shares my vengeance today shares my blood, and who shares my blood is my brother.*
> —Hri-Rrit at the Black Tower

"Zree-Rrit?" Kchula-Tzaatz looked down through the orbital fortress's command bay windows at the majestic curvature of Kzinhome. "Who is this Zree-Rrit?"

Ftzaal-Tzaatz's attention didn't waver from the sword battle drill he was practicing. "I told you before, brother, that a Rrit leads these attacks. I believe it to be First-Son."

"You saw a striped pelt in the dark, seasons ago. This signifies nothing."

"The Rrit markings are distinctive, and I have studied First-Son. It was him. Vsar-Chiuu said the Rrit had returned."

"Vsar-Chiuu. We should have made an example of him."

"That would have alienated the Lesser Prides even faster." Ftzaal executed a perfect side-front-side parry combination in slow time, his eyes locked on his reflection overlaid in the command bay window as though it were an opponent.

Kchula growled. "I will not disbelieve you, Ftzaal. Still it signifies nothing. Whoever it is must be destroyed."

"Of course, but there is a deeper game here. This messenger from Kzin-Conserver that *skalazaal* has been declared. This constrains us."

Kchula ignored the point. "*Skalazaal* already exists, if this is indeed the Rrit. We are no more constrained than before."

"It exists by no less than three traditions, through inheritance from his father, by his own scream-and-leap, by formal declaration. Why declare it again by Conserver-law?" Ftzaal paused, concentrating on the transition from guard-stance to attack-stance before continuing. "It is so that we *know* the Rrit has survived, because we could deny the other traditions by avoiding the knowledge of his survival. And more importantly so Kzin-Conserver knows, and the rest of the Great Prides."

"Kzin-Conserver." Kchula spat. "What need has he of this knowledge?" Kchula looked out at the fortress docking bay where a badly damaged Hunt-class battleship was being stripped to its frame. *Patriarch's Talon* had been the pride of the Rrit fleet until he had taken the Patriarchy and the fleet had scattered to the stars to raid the commerce of Tzaatz allies. Stkaa Pride had laid a trap and caught the battleship, and managed to cripple her. Now she was back where she had started, this time as a war prize. Two heavy cruisers floated nearby, each severely battle-scarred and in desperate need of heavy mainte-nance. They would wait while the stripped hulk took priority. Kchula growled to himself. Patriarch's Talon, *you will be my sword of vengeance*.

"Zree-Rrit needs him to know." Ftzaal pivoted and executed a complex reverse block. "His forces are light, he has no space power. We could destroy him overnight if we were not bound by the traditions. I have been ruthless in my search, brother." Ftzaal completed a thrust, block, thrust combination that ended with him reversed one-hundred-and-eighty degrees. His eyes met Kchula's. "I have come down on the jungle and the high forest like the Fanged God's fist." His voice was harsh, snarling the words. "And yet he has eluded me, save when *he* chooses to attack. And he *is* attacking now, not fleeing, not cowering in the jungle. Now he chooses to formally declare his presence, constraining us and challenging at the same time. His *strakh* with the Northern Lesser Prides grows, and ours falls." Ftzaal whirled, his slicewire whistling through the air. "This new declaration shows that he is looking to the time when he will rally the Great Prides against us. He is a danger that needs to be ended. Now."

"Why have we not already done so then?"

Ftzaal sniffed. "You would not give me the resources, brother, in the time when we could claim not to know we were bound by the traditions. Now Zree-Rrit has made it explicit and we must tread more carefully."

"I have given you every resource I could spare."

"And I have located five *czrav* prides, one in the jungle, four in the high forest, and destroyed them all. I have not been idle, brother. But there are eight-squared or eight-cubed *czrav* prides. Maybe more, no one knows. If you want Zree-Rrit destroyed I must have more power, especially now. The *czrav* won't be so easy to eliminate under the traditions."

"Resources." Kchula paused, contemplating the world turning slowly beneath him. The battle station was in a polar orbit, and South Continent was giving way to North Continent in his field of view. The Plain of Stgrat was clearly visible, stretching wide and green between the ocean to the south and the mountain ranges and deserts that bordered it to the north and west. To the east it was dark, and on the night side of the terminator a sprinkling of lights marked population centers. On the day side there was little to indicate that the world was inhabited at all.

And down there, somewhere, are my enemies. And not only down on the planet's surface. Kchula turned to face his brother. "While you deal with five prides of primitives the humans have destroyed five worlds. Six now, with the loss of Vz'vzmeer. *Skalazaal* is epidemic, Kdari Pride wars with Vearow, Stkaa Pride wars with Cvail and now Varalz has leapt on Sceee, and who knows how many more I don't yet know about? Half the Rrit fleet is out raiding our allies. The Patriarchy is falling apart, Ftzaal, and you ask for more forces for your private hunt!"

Ftzaal stood motionless in leaping-stance, his variable sword extended and canted to guard his body, his other arm stretched backward as a counterbalance. "First-Son-of-Meerz-Rrit is a greater danger to your rule. You said yourself you wanted him destroyed. I am merely telling you what it will take to accomplish your goal."

Kchula growled deep in his throat. "We have less than perfect control over a few Lesser Prides. The *kz'zeerkti* are razing whole planets!"

Ftzaal moved fluidly from leaping-stance to guard-stance and then back, repeating the motion until it was perfect. Only then did he break concentration to speak. "Which is why you have ordered our ships back to Jotok."

"Jotok is our power base. We can't risk losing it to the *kz'zeerkti*, or to another pride."

"Without ships you limit my ability to hunt out this Zree-Rrit."

"You have reconnaissance enough from this fortress and its brothers."

"Which move on fixed orbits, and the *czrav* have shown they know when they are being watched. I need tactical surprise, and more warriors, and mobility for those, and more *rapsari*."

"Use cargo haulers to move your forces. Use them in your search as well."

"They lack a warship's instrumentation." Ftzaal leapt and whirled, his blade splitting the air, until his slicewire stopped a handsbreadth from his brother's nose. Kchula didn't flinch. He was accustomed to his brother's battle drills. "The *czrav* attack from a new direction, did you know that? From a new stronghold, so my spies tell me. It is claimed a *kz'zeerkti* leads the attacks."

Kchula spat. "Impossible!"

"Impossible?" Ftzaal retracted his slicewire and hung his variable sword on his belt. "First-Son fled into the jungle with a *kz'zeerkti*. Now one fights with him. How is this impossible?"

"No kzin would follow an alien."

"There are stranger things. It is said this new army is composed of kzinretti."

"Shall I say impossible again, Ftzaal?" Kchula snorted. "Give me evidence or leave me in peace."

"Evidence. There is none, where none of our warriors survive their attacks. These are rumors, but they are unique rumors, which inclines me to believe them. They are at least worth the effort of verification."

"Then verify them."

"I need more resources!"

"Where shall I get them, Ftzaal?" Kchula lashed his tail. "From the defenses of our homeworld?"

"If necessary. Jotok is less important now. We have done the impossible, brother, we have dethroned the Rrit. If you want the victory to last you will make peace with the *kz'zeerkti* at whatever price they demand, and concentrate everything here. These *czrav* spread rebellion like a contagion. Let the Great Prides fight each other, so long as they don't come here."

"Make peace." Kchula snorted in contempt. "You have been listening to Kzin-Conserver-who-was-Rrit-Conserver."

"Conservers are known for their wisdom, brother. We do not have to like his advice to heed it."

"Making peace smells of dishonor."

"Don't talk to me of dishonor," Ftzaal snarled, suddenly angry. "This campaign has cut close enough to the edge of principle already, close enough that we left Tzaatz-Conserver on Jotok. What would *he* counsel you?" Ftzaal slashed the air with his sword. "Make peace with the *kz'zeerkti* to free your hand to consolidate what we have here on Kzinhome. Whether this Zree-Rrit is First-Son does not matter, whether he is even Rrit doesn't matter.

What matters is, he claims the name, and the *kzintzag* believe him, and so do the Lesser Prides. They believe him because they desire, more than anything, for it to be true, because they suffer under our rule and they loathe our puppet. They will follow Zree-Rrit, whoever he is, all the way to the gates of your Citadel, and they will take off your head to present it to him."

"Leaving honor aside, if I do not lead the Great Prides in conquest they will not follow me."

"They are not following you now! The Patriarchy has become nothing but factions warring over spoils while the monkeys carry out the systematic annihilation of our species. Make peace and give me what I need to kill Zree-Rrit! Make peace and save us all!"

"Victory will reunite the Great Prides, and the monkeys will be destroyed."

"With what will you achieve victory, brother? The Rrit fleet is scattered, our own is committed to Jotok, and inadequate to defend even that against the monkeys' power. Stkaa Pride is butchered, and Cvail will enjoy their victory only until the *kz'zeerkti* bring forward their world destroyer. The others, they give you a few token ships while they plot conquest on their brothers, those who have not already leapt in *skalazaal*. To defeat the *kz'zeerkti* you need an organized fleet, but before the Great Prides will give you that fleet you must defeat the *kz'zeerkti*!"

"And yet you want me to siphon from my meager reserves so that you can hunt primitives."

"Zree-Rrit is First-Son, make no mistake, and he seeks your ears, brother."

Kchula lashed his tail. "So what if this Zree-Rrit is

First-Son? They will never take the Citadel. He's as bound by *skalazaal* as we are. Even we did it only because we had *rapsari*, and we are the only ones who can make them."

"*Rapsari* are not the only advantage to be found in battle. Shall I tell you a secret, brother, a Black Priest secret?"

"What is it?" Kchula leaned forward. His brother rarely even mentioned his time with the Bearers of Ill Tiding.

"An army of kzinretti, a Rrit who rides with the *czrav*, warriors elusive beyond easy understanding. These things are not unanticipated by the Black Cult."

"So?"

"So they go hand in hand with other things that make this threat more dangerous than you might realize."

Kchula waved a paw dismissively. "This isn't a secret, it's a riddle."

"I cannot say more without violating my oath."

"Your oath." Kchula twitched his tail in annoyance. "What fealty do you owe to Priest-Master-Zrtra now?"

"It is my own honor I owe fealty to, not him. I hold my loyalty to you to the same standard, brother." He paused, assessing his brother. "Else I might be Pride-Patriarch."

Kchula's tail stiffened. "Do you threaten me, Ftzaal?"

"I state a fact." The variable sword blurred and suddenly the slicewire was at Kchula's throat. "Could you stand against me if I challenged?"

Treachery! My own brother! Fear flooded Kchula's system. "No, no of course not, Ftzaal."

Ftzaal held the slicewire where it was for a long moment, his eyes locked on Kchula's, and then he retracted the blade. "Do not insult my honor again, brother. The fact that you are alive is testimony to its depth."

Kchula turned away, breathing deep to conceal his anger. "Which gives me no information on your riddle."

"Take me at my word. You are at more risk from these primitives than you are from the entire *kz'zeerkti* fleet and the rest of the Great Pride Circle combined."

Kchula sat heavily on a *prrstet*. "Fine. What is it you want?"

"Ships in orbit to start, half a dozen scouts."

"It is done."

"Jotok's *rapsar* production returned to full capacity, with the beasts sent here for my use."

"You ask a lot."

"I am saving your empire, and perhaps your life."

"That too then. What else?"

"Trained warriors, of course, and another telepath. Two would be better."

"I have asked your priesthood for another telepath. So far they decline my request."

"This is most crucial."

"They are your order, not mine. Perhaps you should ask them yourself."

Ftzaal snorted. "They will grant one to you long before they grant one to me. Our last Telepath's death at my hands is likely the reason they are slow to respond already."

"Hrrr." Kchula wrinkled his nose. "What did you do there, Ftzaal, to make them detest you so?"

"I held up a mirror and showed them the truth."

"And yet you would go back if you could?"

"I cannot. My oath to you is binding."

Kchula waved a dismissive paw. "I could release you. What would you do if you had a choice?"

"The Black Priest discipline is . . ." Ftzaal paused, choosing his words carefully. ". . . compelling." He turned to look away. "I still could not go back, they would not have me." He retracted his variable sword and turned a paw over to contemplate his extended claws. "Not yet."

Not yet? Kchula raised his ears. *My brother contains depths, dangerous depths, though his loyalty is useful.* "Do you believe in the literal truth of the Fanged God?"

"The Fanged God is for the High Priests to know. I believe in the literal truth of power."

"And yet you are content to give me rulership."

"There is more power in the Black Cult's discipline than you will know if you rule as Patriarch for eight-to-the-fourth seasons, brother." Ftzaal turned back to face Kchula, and his eyes shone, bright and intense. "That is something they couldn't take when they cast me out."

Kchula shifted, uncomfortable with the topic. "Hrrr. Enough philosophy. What else do you require?"

"That is all for now. The telepath is vital. I must have at least one."

"I will do what I can."

"It is First-Son's *kz'zeerkti* that is key here. With a telepath I can track it. It is the unknown factor. I need to rake out its story, one way or another. For the rest of them—make peace while we still can, let us secure our back before we look to new conquest."

"The *kz'zeerkti*." Kchula lashed his tail. "They are less a menace than you imagine. I shall tell you a secret too, Ftzaal, one less mysterious than yours."

Ftzaal unfurled his ears. "What is it?"

"See this ship?" He pointed to the gutted *Patriarch's Talon* floating outside the dock. "We are converting it. The *kz'zeerkti* are powerful, but they have a weakness in that almost all of them still live on their original world."

"What use is this if we lack the strength to conquer that world? Even the Rrit fleet couldn't penetrate their system defenses."

"Conquer their world, no, we cannot do that." Kchula showed his fangs. "But we can destroy it."

Ftzaal laid his ears back, shocked. "Destroy it? How?"

"It is a *kz'zeerkti* innovation, so it is simple poetry that we shall finish them with it. Relativistic weapons, kinetic impactors arriving close to lightspeed." Kchula raked his claws through the air. "I will strip their world to its core."

Ftzaal stared at his brother for long heartbeat, aghast. "Have you lost your reason, brother? This is not the fine edge of honor, this is unthinkable! What of the traditions? Are we to become like them?"

"Don't bother me more with tradition, Ftzaal." Kchula snorted. "This is about species survival. The monkeys have shown us the way. Now we will follow where they lead. I will scorch their homeworld, and their other worlds will be my conquest prizes. The *kz'zeerkti* will be a slave race, for once and for all. We need only protect our systems long enough to give us time to strike." He turned to face his brother. "As for Zree-Rrit, I'll give you everything you want, including your telepath. You get me what I want. Bring me Zree-Rrit's head."

*Trade what you have for what you want, trade
what you want for what you need.*
                                        —Jotoki maxim

"We are being within orbital parameters. Fuel state is
being positive. Ktzaa'Whrloo approach control is being
contacted on this watch. Initiating transfer from inbound
to parking orbit." Contradictory stood on three armlegs
while the other two flipped switches on *Black Saber*'s control
board. Outside the ship's cramped cockpit the starfield
flipped itself over as the Jotok aligned her thrusters to
take them into orbit. Ktzaa'Whrloo hung overhead like a
ripe popfruit. The ancient seat of Krowl Pride was a dusky
red world orbiting a bright orange star.

"Cargo reception?" Night Pilot strapped himself in to
his crash couch, ready to take over the watch.

"We have been contacting of our client and cargo
reception coordinates are arranged. We are being expecting normal ground handling times."

"Hrrr. Is the cargo secure for reentry?"

"It is being so. We are being reverifying of it at soon."
Contradictory clicked more keys. "Ship is being secured
for atmospheric interface."

"What is our descent profile?"

"It is being normal atmospheric braked descent with
minimum thrusters assist."

"Hrrr. Good, we'll save some wear on the thrusters."
Night Pilot checked his screens for the approach. "I have
confirmation that we are in atmospheric configuration."
He clicked keys. "I have confirmation that our approach
path is clear to preset coordinates." He clicked more keys.

"I have confirmation that we can relaunch immediately once we're unloaded." He paused. "Refueling?"

"Refueling is being on orbit at Ktzaa'Whrloo main transfer station after reorbit. We are being confirmed that client Sklar-Overseer has being arranged for fuel at there."

"Also good." Night Pilot nearly purred in satisfaction. *Black Saber* would make a handsome profit this run. A light flashed. "Priority message." His ears fanned up and he made a gesture to command the ship's AI to put it on screen.

". . . all ships, be aware. *Kz'zeerkti* scouts have been detected deep in system, orbital parameters to follow. Krowl Pride warcraft are intercepting now. Verarz-Krowl commands nonessential ships in system to proceed beyond the singularity and wait until the invaders have been repulsed. Be prepared to aid survivors and to fight if necessary. Marshaling orbits to follow. Be aware more enemy ships may be in system and undetected. Message repeats . . ."

Night Pilot made a gesture to cut the transmission, then tapped his console to bring up the enemy's positions and the commanded escape orbits. His nostrils flared when he saw them. "By the Fanged God, they are deep. How did they get so far in system without being picked up?"

Contradictory whirled, bringing the two armlegs that had been typing down to stand on as he brought two of the ones he'd been standing on up to replace them. "I am being concerned about more forces."

"Hrrr. Yes . . . This situation could devolve. The

kz'zeerkti are sly. They had so many ships at K'Shai. Now we know the reason."

"We are being assessing that we should be aborting of the approach."

"No. We deliver our cargo."

"The humans are being coming in force." Contradictory added a third arm to the two constructing intercept profiles with the flight computer. "They are being destroying twice-eight worlds now. If we are being caught our lives are being ended."

"Honor demands we fulfill our bargain."

"We are being unconcerned with matters of honor."

"Then be concerned with your reputation." Night Pilot flipped his tail in annoyance. "We have no choice but to deliver if we want to carry cargo to this world again."

"You are being unpersuasive. The humans are being ensuring no cargo are being carried here by any ships at ever."

"I do not have to persuade you. I am Captain, I have only to decide."

Contradictory brought up a holo. "Please be viewing of intercept profiles. Human ships are being in intercepting range at departure timing of us."

Night Pilot growled. "We are landing."

Contradictory swiveled three eyes at the kzin. "Are you being forgetting of incident of Meerowsk?"

The kzin wrinkled his nose. "I have not forgotten."

"Your life is being saved by us there. Your life is also being saved by us at Ansrarw."

"I know this."

"Please being allowing of us to again being saving of your life at Ktzaa'Whrloo."

Night Pilot gave his copilot a look. "Have I complained about your argumentativeness recently?"

"You are being complaining constantly. This is why we are being Contradictory as our name."

"Hrrr. We deliver our cargo." Contradictory put a fourth limb up to construct intercept scenarios, balancing on the one armleg remaining. Night Pilot bowed to the inevitable. "We will be fast."

Fast meant a more aggressive approach profile, and a subsequent increase in fuel usage. On reentry Night Pilot pushed the skin temperature to the limit to get the most out of atmospheric braking. Fast meant heavy muscle work for both of them, unloading the motley cargo of *cznip* spice and fabricator cells that Sklar-Overseer was importing from Reessliu beneath the nose of the Krowl hierarchy, loading up the sealed crates, contents unknown, they would carry to Sklar-Overseer's contact on Kzinhome. The Whrloo slaves were diligent workers, but their small size meant they needed grav manipulators to unload the heavy crates and bales, and they were slow about it. In the end the need for speed meant that Night Pilot and Contradictory moved more than half the cargo themselves. Fast meant that, with muscles aching and not enough sleep they preflighted *Black Saber* and took off with a landing gear fault that really should have been fixed on the ground. There was no time to repair it if they wanted to avoid getting caught in the developing battle.

Through the whole process Contradictory kept one eye on his databoard, slaved from the cockpit with updated intercept scenarios. Krowl battle control in one of the orbital fortresses kept them updated on the progress of the *kz'zeerkti* fleet. The news wasn't good. The human scoutships had been followed by a wave of cruisers, falling in from the edge of the singularity and then, once the cruisers were established in attack orbits, the heavy battle units had emerged from hyperspace. The pattern was clear by now, repeated in system after system. The humans would arrive without warning and in overwhelming force. The scouts would identify the defenses and the cruiser screen behind them would deal with minor outposts in the system and any kzinti ships attempting to escape. The battleships would close with the planet and engage its orbital defenses to allow the carriers to get into low orbit to launch their transatmospheric fighters and bombers. By then the battleships would be engaging the ground defenses, and under fighter cover the bombers would get in through the weak spots, usually far from the main bases, get low to protect themselves beneath the horizon and then, at the last moment, pop up to launch salvos of conversion warheads. The warheads would streak in, hugging the terrain, sequenced so that the detonation of the first would degrade sensors and defenses to clear the way for the next. By the time the last had gone off the bombers would already be out of the atmosphere, redocking with their carrier after a single orbit.

And that was what was starting to happen at Ktzaa'Whrloo. In none of their other attacks had the humans attempted to assault ships or secure the planet. They got in, destroyed everything and got out before the Patriarchy could react. Night Pilot thought that dishonorable. Contradictory thought it irrelevant, and concerned itself with the cruiser screen. It was tightening already, and with the scoutships far in advance of the cruisers in the screen would have plenty of time to change their velocity vectors to intercept anything the scouts picked up trying to escape.

Refueling in orbit presented a sudden problem. Priority went to warcraft boosting to meet the humans high up in the gravity well, and Sklar-Overseer lacked the *strakh* to get them advanced in the priority sequence, or at least he lacked the willingness to use his *strakh* to do it. The human scouts were braking hard now, already into the inner system, and there had been skirmishes between kzinti and human craft. Time was running out, and the seriousness of the situation was apparent. Krowl Pride didn't have the forces to resist the humans. The battle station was in chaos, warriors with nerves on edge making impossible demands on panicked slaves. Service Master, in charge of the fueling bays, was short and to the point. "You will be fueled when the combat ships have been fueled, not before." Night Pilot, frustrated to the edge of his temper, bared his fangs and resisted the urge to scream and leap. There was nothing to be gained by it, and it might even delay them further.

"We are being attempting to be rectifying of the delay." Contradictory was wearing slave livery, necessary protective camouflage in the Patriarchy. It set out, while Night Pilot took advantage of the time and the atmosphere in the fueling bay to work on the balky landing gear retractor. The problem turned out to be a broken piston sealing ring. He was able to get a replacement from the station's stores, but actually installing it was a delicate, finicky task better suited to Contradictory's fine manipulation skills. He settled down to a repair session that mixed frustration and obscenity in equal measure, trying to get piston, sleeve and sealing ring to stay together long enough for him to finish the assembly with only two hands to do the job with.

For the eighth time the assembly fell apart as he tried to slide the sleeve into place. He resisted the urge to hurl it across the bay and looked up to find Contradictory, back already. "We are being fueling immediately."

"Hrrr." Night Pilot growled, relieved that the problem was solved, annoyed that his partner had succeeded where he had failed. "How did you arrange this?"

"Techslave Fueling Controller is being Jotoki, we are negotiating with them directly. We are being having in addition to being first fueling priority the guarantee of tanks being capacity filled."

"Excellent."

"We are being indebted to the Fueling Controller, who is therefore to being embarked."

Night Pilot's ears stiffened. "Slave theft is beneath our honor." His voice held an edge.

"It is being irrelevant. Service Master is being now dead in a challenge duel. It is being also unlikely he is being predeceasing of this battle station of significant time length."

"Hrrr. I still don't like it."

"It is being our function in this partnership to being performed of necessary tasks which you are being finding difficult. We are now being saving of your life at

Ktzaa'Whrloo. We are being asking that you are remembering of this at similar circumstances."

Night Pilot waved a paw. "Yes, yes. Help me get this piston assembled."

Contradictory did it on the first try. Night Pilot growled to himself in annoyance and considered eating their new passenger when it arrived. He hadn't had fresh meat in a long time, but mostly he enjoyed the thought because it would upset Contradictory.

Contradictory, oblivious, was already directing Whrloo techslaves to connect the fueling hoses. Night Pilot lashed his tail and went aboard *Black Saber* to plot their boost course. They would launch on a retrograde orbit. That would cost them power overall, but because the human ships were all trying to match velocities with the planet it would give them some additional closing speed, reducing the human's engagement times and giving them a distinct lead in a running fight. With full tanks they could afford to use the tactic.

The tactical situation update from battle command was not encouraging. The human cruisers were intercepting any ship that tried to make it out of the system. The situation on the battle station was hardly better. He growled and started plotting alternate escape routes, in case they got surprised on their planned course. He was interrupted by Contradictory who catapulted himself into the cockpit and began strapping in.

"We are now being ready to leave. Docking control is being giving clearance for bay door release."

"Our tanks are not full."

"Fueling lines are being disconnected. Our tanks are

being as filled as they are being filled." It clicked keys and Night Pilot felt his ears pop. "Loading ramp is being closed, cabin is being pressurized."

"What about our passenger?"

"Techslave Fueling Controller is being killed. Veefrawi-Captain of heavy cruiser *Pride of Conquest* is being objecting to his ship being fueled subsequent to us. Veefrawi-Captain is being arriving at shortly to being discussing this with yourself. We are being fortunately warned by newly appointed Fueling Controller." Contradictory clicked keys and indicators flashed as the Whrloo ground crew cleared the fuel lines and vacated the bay.

Night Pilot opened his mouth, closed it. "We are boosting. Now."

Contradictory clicked keys. "I am being agreeing with you."

"Hrrrr. There is always a first time."

"I am being requesting docking control departure clearance at now." Contradictory keyed his com and snarled into it. Night Pilot unconsciously furled his ears, betraying his worry. If Veefrawi-Captain thought to go to docking control first they might not get it. There was a short, tense wait before docking control authorized their departure. Then they had to wait again while the fueling bay was pumped down to vacuum. He watched the external pressure, alert for it to stop dropping. That would be a very bad sign.

Finally the immense bay doors began to swing open. He rotated thrusters and nudged the throttles forward. *Black Saber* rose and glided forward, accelerating as

Night Pilot dialed in more thrust. They were through the doors before they were halfway open. Did he imagine an outraged face in the fueling bay observation window? *It no longer matters.* Once they hit space, he shoved the throttles to their limits. The deck surged as he spun their acceleration vector to bring them into their retrograde escape orbit. Satisfied they were within parameters, he turned the precomputed boost profile over to the AI. He looked over to his copilot, who was busily running through the post-launch checklist with the computer.

"We are done." He breathed out, his ears relaxing at last.

Contradictory spun on its undermouth, swiveling eyes at Night Pilot in sequence. "We are being one more time saving of your life."

"Hrrr. You have more blood debt from me than I have blood."

If the Jotok was pleased with the answer it gave no sign. *Black Saber* was well away from Ktzaa'Whrloo and boosting hard for the singularity's edge when they picked up the scoutship, a couple of light-seconds away and closing at nearly two five-hundred-and-twelfths of lightspeed. The scoutship was decelerating to slingshot past the planet, and as soon as they detected it, Night Pilot changed their thrust vector perpendicular to the scout. It would make a missile shot harder, and it would serve to determine if the scout had detected them as well.

A minute later they had an answer. The scoutship changed its vector to intersect theirs. Evidently it had decided *Black Saber* was easy enough game to take on without diverting a cruiser to intercept. Night Pilot cursed as the icon moved in his plot display. He punched up the intercept planes and course funnels for each ship. The results were not encouraging. They couldn't evade completely. They would have to fight.

The big kzin spun the navigation plot. "Compute intercept course and fire dusters."

Contradictory swung the targeting cursor and set up a protective screen pattern. Scoutships didn't usually mount combat lasers, but dusters were cheap and there was no need to take chances. A series of tremors shook the ship as the turrets traversed and fired. "Dusters are being launched. Missiles?"

"Hrrr. No. Missiles are expensive. We will live or die, and the scoutship will be past and unable to attack again. If we die we gain nothing by killing it. If we live we might need our missiles later."

Contradictory clicked keys. "You are being unthinking like a kzin."

Night Pilot growled. "I have been sharing life support with you for too long."

"Being also locked with predictive targeting are interceptors."

"Excellent. Now we wait."

But there was no wait. A horn sounded and a new icon appeared in the plot display. Contradictory tapped firing commands. "Missile detected. Interceptors are being launched." The countermissiles streaked away and the transpax dimmed to cut the actinic blue light of their unshielded fusion cores. It brightened again as the missiles vanished to points of light, fast moving stars that twinkled and vanished. "Firing screeners." Long moments later the transpax dimmed again as one of the interceptors detonated. On the plot board the incoming missile icon vanished.

And then they were past. Somewhere in the blackness there might be more missiles, or clouds of screener balls that might shred *Black Saber* so fast they wouldn't even know they were dying until they were already dead. What tricks the enemy had already played they couldn't know, but now nothing could catch them. Night Pilot rotated their thrust vector to make their course less predictable, eyes fixed on the plot display for the sudden blink of a warning icon. None appeared. After a time they both relaxed. They weren't out of the system yet, but the higher they got in the gravity well the less chance they had of being intercepted again, and with their retrograde orbit the closing velocities would only increase, making it that much harder for the humans to achieve kills.

Of course the next human ship they were likely to meet would be a cruiser armed with heavy lasers. Time would tell.

Eventually Contradictory unstrapped. Combat was over, for now at least, and *Black Saber*'s systems needed the mate's attention. It pivoted on its undermouth while Night Pilot recorrected their course to compensate for the violent maneuvering they'd done. Night Pilot returned his attention to his instruments, keeping an eye on the combat display just in case there were any more surprises. The long com crackled with traffic, reporting brief, savage engagements as the *kz'zeerkti* scouts swept in and past Ktzaa'Whrloo. At first the reports were short, calm and concise, painting a picture of a well organized defense, but as the main human force closed and engaged they became fragmented and tense, occasionally desperate and all too frequently cut off in mid-transmission. He picked up reports from *Pride of Conquest* as the heavy cruiser set course for the main human battle fleet at maximum thrust and cut her way through the enemy destroyer screen behind an almost solid wall of missiles and laser fire, destroying five *kz'zeerkti* in the process. It was a heroic achievement, but it earned nothing but the right to take on the human battleships, whose huge spinal mount lasers gutted her before she could get into range. Night Pilot heard Veefrawi-Captain himself at the end. His ship was crippled, every compartment spaced. He was setting course to ram one of the enemy battleships. Whether he succeeded or not was unknowable; there were no more transmissions from *Pride of Conquest*.

At first it was mostly ships involved in the fight. Then the orbital defenses came up, sending targeting messages and damage reports that told a story of overwhelming enemy firepower. Contradictory's prediction of the lifespan of the orbital fortress they'd refueled at proved correct. Service Master and Fueling Controller had lost little in dying before the battle. Ground defenses came up, reporting contacts, and then, in voices ranging from shock to outrage, conversion weapon strikes. Inevitably they too fell silent. Night Pilot felt ill as he scanned through the channels for a signal. For a long time there was nothing, and then finally a faint voice, badly garbled by its passage through an ionosphere roiled by the energies of total mass conversion. It was a secondary command base, badly damaged but still functioning. Cha'at-Commander's surviving forces were deployed to defend against ground attack when it came, ready to fight to the death. So far they had seen no landers.

Night Pilot zoomed his combat display all the way out. The ship's AI had identified human units by their own transmissions, unreadably scrambled but usable for triangulation, and now arrogantly frequent in victory. The in-falling fleet had converged on Ktzaa'Whrloo and was on its way outsystem again. The scoutships had simply used the planet as a gravitational slingshot as they sped past to pick targets for the heavy units, but even the battleships had gone no lower than semi-synchronous orbit. Only the carriers had grazed the atmosphere and now, their attack craft recovered, they too were boosting for the system's edge. Cha'at-Commander would see no landers. The *kz'zeerkti* had not come to conquer, only to destroy.

Night Pilot shuddered involuntarily. He had heard of the human tactics but it was another thing to watch them carried out. Cha'at-Commander didn't understand he was waiting in vain for an honorable enemy to close for the finish fight. Perhaps he refused to understand, but Night Pilot did, only too clearly now. *They are* v'pren. The thought was chilling. *They are* v'pren *in the feeding swarm, and the Fanged God help any who fall into their path.*

Contradictory came in, swiveling eyes. "Ship systems are being secure. We are being undamaged."

"Good. We were fortunate."

"Where are we being going now?"

"Hrrr. Kzinhome, for now. We still have a cargo to deliver. If the Tskombe-*kz'zeerkti* has found its mate it will return with us to human space, and it may prove wise both to have *kz'zeerkti* passengers and to find our way to human space again. If the *kz'zeerkti* hasn't found its mate, Kzinhome is probably the safest place to wait, and we can leave with full tanks if we can strike a contract with Far Hunter."

Contradictory popped open an access panel to check the cockpit coolant levels. "I am being agreeing. This war is not being good for trade. We are not being desiring of being getting caught at the middle again."

Night Pilot watched him work for a minute, pleased with himself. Any decision Contradictory didn't argue with was probably a good one.

Stiffen your resolve, ready your sword and let battle be joined, with victory to the swift and strong. It is not bravery which drives us now but fealty, for we avenge our fallen fathers who died to save our lives. I will not have you follow me if you fear the enemy, I will not have you follow me if you are unwilling to make that selfsame sacrifice. I will only lead those who know in their blood that our cause is just, and with the Fanged God's judgment behind us, know that we will prevail, that we will conquer, that we will take back what is ours."

—Skrullai-Weeow
before the Battle of the High Pass

It was warm in the inner chamber of Ztrak Pride's western den, and Pouncer inhaled deeply to calm himself. The air smelled faintly of the scentwood paneling cut from the high forest far overhead. That aroma was overlaid with other scents, the odor of kzinti bodies, *tuskvor* flesh from the just completed Midwinter Bloodfeast, the earthy smell of the ancient rock itself. The Pride-Patriarchs gathered there had gorged heavy after the travails of another migration and the further journey to Ztrak Pride. They had come early from the jungle for this meeting, taking the first *tuskvor* and leaving their prides behind to travel with the main migration. Ztrak Pride itself was still split, the young and nursing mothers who had gone back to the jungle for the wet season not yet returned. *But C'mell is here.* He was glad of that; her presence gave him strength, even as he worried over her continued participation in raids against the Tzaatz. *At least that worry is gone, for awhile at least.* She was too busy with the kits now to raid, though she still went out to hunt. His kits would have her spirit, and that too was a good thing.

The pride leaders gathered into the circle. The festivities were over. Now it was time to forge the future. By the time the bulk of the *czrav* had returned, their plan of attack, if there was to be a plan of attack, would be complete. Pouncer looked out at the circle of battle scarred faces in the chamber, experienced warriors and leaders with ears heavy on their belts. Every one had been a Pride-Patriarch or Honored Mother longer than he had been alive. *And yet I am to lead them now. What would my father have done?*

He stood up and caught C'mell watching him from the shadows, both kits held to her teats to nurse. *My father would lead, with courage and wisdom. He would seek the best counsel, lay his plans with cunning and execute them with skill.* What he didn't know was *how* Meerz-Rrit would have made it happen. C'mell lowered one ear to him, their secret greeting, and slipped into the darkness, back up into the den. She had a faith in him he wished he felt in himself.

Show confidence, that above all. He had made his plans carefully, if not with cunning, and he could execute them with determination, if not skill. *I have been trained by Guardmaster, the best warrior in the Patriarchy, and advised by Cherenkova-Captain, a subtle strategist even for a kz'zeerkti.* Neither of them were there now to guide him. He would stand or fall on his own.

The assembly had quieted when he stood, and he took the time to look each of the Pride-Patriarchs in the eye. *My father taught me that.* He raised his arms, tail erect. "Honored Cousins. We are gathered here in war council—"

A tall, well muscled warrior stood up and banged his long *wtzal* hunting spear for attention. "You are not Great Patriarch! You are not even Pride-Patriarch." His voice was challenging. "What claim do you have to stand at this circle and call us honored cousins?"

Pouncer turned to face the interrupter. "I am Zree-Rrit, First-Son-of-Meerz-Rrit, and I am Patriarch of the Patriarchy. This is my claim." *Zree-Rrit; even after all this time it still feels strange to say.*

The warrior snorted. "And I am Sraa-Vroo of Vroo Pride of the *czrav*, and I do not accept the leadership of the Patriarchy. Nor do my honored cousins, nor do the *czrav* prides they lead. This is our way, and this has always been our way. You are not of the *czrav*, certainly not a

Pride-Patriarch of the *czrav*. You have no right to be here."

Pouncer felt his claws extend reflexively at the challenge, but kept himself calm. "I am of *czrav* blood, through M'ress of Mrrsel Pride. Some of the *czrav* prides have chosen to follow me. I hope you will as well when you hear what I will present today, honored Sraa-Vroo." It was difficult to control his anger at the deliberately insulting challenge, but it was important to remain true to courtesy-between-equals. *Sheathe pride and bare honor.*

"Follow you?" Sraa-Vroo rippled his ears and spat in contempt. "Honor demands my attendance at the High Circle. It does not demand I listen to a spot-furred kitten."

Rage jolted Pouncer like a physical thing and his teeth bared of their own accord. He could feel his body making ready to leap. *Rage is death.* He breathed deep. *If I am to achieve what I need to here I must not leap.* He found himself incapable of answering, but V'rli-Ztrak waved her tail. "He speaks in my place, and my pride stands with him."

Sraa-Vroo turned to her. "If he speaks in your place, why are you here then? Doesn't the Honored Mother care to lead her own pride?"

V'rli snarled, fangs suddenly bared, and she crouched to leap. Pouncer held his arms up again to interrupt, suddenly calm, as though his own anger had transferred itself to her. "This is unnecessary. I will take less of your time than a challenge duel will, and impose less of a cost. Hear me and decide for yourself what you will do."

"I will listen." Sraa-Vroo sat down, reluctantly, not taking his eyes from V'rli and with his lips still raised to show his fangs. V'rli sat down as well and Pouncer breathed out.

I have passed the first test. There was no time to rest on his small victory.

"Honored Cousins, I am First-Son-of-Meerz-Rrit, rightful Patriarch. The Tzaatz have stolen what was mine, and for that reason I am sworn to blood vengeance against them." He paused, again meeting every gaze in the chamber. "None of this need concern you. The *czrav* have lived since the time before time beneath the notice of the Patriarchy, and beneath the notice of the Black Cult. You may choose to continue that life, so long as the Tzaatz allow it. Those who follow me . . ." He nodded to V'rli and Czor-Dziit and V'reow who led the remnants of Mrrsel Pride. ". . . are committed to a different path."

"And in following you they have brought destruction upon us all," Sraa-Vroo snarled. "Entire prides have been wiped out. We are *czrav*, we carry the Long Secret. We have no business making war on the Patriarchy, whoever happens to rule it."

Pouncer's lips came away from his fangs. "I *am* the Long Secret. I am of *czrav* blood and the Patriarchal line, the genetic welding of Kcha and Vda."

"So you claim."

"So he is," V'rli said. "We have done the gene scans."

Sraa-Vroo waved a dismissive paw. "And still we have no business making war on the Patriarchy. You have sworn blood vengeance against the Tzaatz. I grant you are true to your honor, but we have no need to join your *skalazaal*. But I am sure this Kchula-Tzaatz will accept a treaty-gifted daughter of the *czrav*. We can weld the Patriarchal line with ours through him, without bloodshed and without risk to our dens and kits."

"Kchula-Tzaatz is not of the Patriarchal line!" Pouncer snarled the words.

"But his line will rule the Patriarchy."

"No!" V'rli stood. "Meerz-Rrit exemplified all we want to preserve of the Kcha line. Kchula-Tzaatz is all we want to breed out! His brother carries the mind-blank gene set. Could we choose a worse genome to mate?"

"We have welded other lines. Half the Lesser Prides carry our blood."

"And the Black Priests cull their kits! If we want to win the Longest War we must win it at the top. There is nothing so important to our victory as the Patriarchal line!"

"So we shall wait a few generations, and give the black-fur gene time to be diluted in Kchula's descendants. Since when has the Longest War been a matter of haste?"

"Since the Tzaatz deposed the Rrit! You said it yourself! How many of our prides has the Black Priest destroyed now? Where do you think he will stop?"

"So we give him what he seeks and he will stop. Send him Zree-Rrit and save us our blood."

"You tread on my honor," V'rli spat.

"You tread on our traditions, our ways, our secrets and our very lives. How many *czrav* will die so you can protect this Rrit?"

Pouncer stood before V'rli could answer. "You think the Black Priest hunts me? Yes, he does. But do you think he will stop when he finds me? No, he will not."

Sraa-Vroo snorted. "I do not know what Ftzaal-Tzaatz will do, and neither do you. Call Ferlitz-Telepath and have him know the Black Priest's mind and we will find out."

V'rli snarled. "You know he cannot know a mind that carries the mind-blank gene."

"Give him the *sthondat* extract then, and that obstacle can be overcome."

V'rli slashed the air with her claws. "If you want to see a telepath take *sthondat*, ask one of your own. I will not ask it of mine."

"And yet you ask me to risk my pride in an Honor-War that is not mine."

"You are free to decline, Sraa-Vroo, and free to leave this circle if you wish, as is everyone here." Pouncer looked around the assembly. "I will make my proposal to those who stay."

"Oh, I will stay, for amusement if nothing else," Sraa-Vroo riposted.

"Hrrr." *He is staying, and he is silenced, for now.* Pouncer raised his arms for attention again and continued where he had left off. "Honored Cousins, there are those of you who follow me now, and those who do not. For myself, I did not choose this path, it was chosen for me and I have no alternative but to take it to its end. I will lead those who will follow me to reclaim my birthright, and yours. For us, victory will mean victory in the Longest War, and defeat will mean extermination. Make no mistake, the cost will be high in *czrav* blood, and victory is not assured. I can offer nothing for your fealty except my own blood debt. With the support of Ztrak Pride and Dziit Pride and Mrrsel Pride I have shown what can be done, but that is not enough for final victory. Our strength depends on our unity, nothing else will give us success. For that reason I have decided . . ." He paused again, assessing his audience, making them wait on his words. "I have decided that if I do not have the support of every one of you here I will not press this campaign. Together we can win, together I believe we *will* win. Separate, it is better that we do not try. I will not see the *czrav* bloodline destroyed piecemeal. If I do not have your unanimous support, I will fight my own war, alone." He paused again. "The decision is yours, Honored Cousins. I will leave you to make it."

He turned and walked out into the darkened den passage, as snarls exploded behind him.

". . . final victory . . ."

". . . what of the risk?"

". . . the Tzaatz . . ."

". . . just a kitten . . ."

". . . natural leader . . ."

The last voice was Czor-Dziit's, and though his opinion was not news it made Pouncer feel proud to realize that he had won the respect of that seasoned warrior. *I have done my best. Now the Fanged God will guide my course.* The voices faded behind him as he climbed up to the chambers of the outer den. The air was cooler there, the scents less intense. He went to the quarters he shared with C'mell. They were austere by any standard, but he felt at home there with her, comfortable in a way the Citadel had never been with its relentless crush of history. *And yet I will be returning there, or dying in the attempt.* It was a thought he did not want to think, and he turned his attention to C'mell. She was there, reclined on the *frrch*-skin *prrstet*, the kits piled up against her asleep, bellies plump, tails curled around their noses. He knelt and nuzzled them. Male and female, Whitepaws and W'neee, they were heavily spotted as *czrav* kits were, but already he could see the pattern in their fur that would become the distinctive Rrit striping when they came of age. They stirred but did not wake, and he lay down to nuzzle C'mell as well, taking strength from the contact of her firm flank. She swished her tail lazily and rubbed her whiskers on his chin.

"What did they say?"

"They are deciding now."

"What will they say?"

"I don't know."

"The full brother of Patriarch's Telepath doesn't know?" She rippled her ears. "What do you *think* they will say?"

"Sraa-Vroo is opposed. He is respected, others may side with him."

She turned a paw over, considering. "It may not be a bad thing if he does. The Tzaatz are powerful. We risk a great deal by attacking them."

"It is the path I must follow."

"And I must follow you, but stealth is the *czrav* way." There was worry in her eyes.

"If we win we will never have to hide again."

"And the same if we lose." She nuzzled him and they lay together in silence.

One of his lieutenants came to the entrance, Swift-Claw who had been Quicktail. "Pardon me, sire."

Reluctantly Pouncer looked up from his mate. "What is it?"

"Our *mazourk* have returned from the jungle with the mothers and kits. They have brought an outsider."

"An outsider?" Pouncer's ears fanned up. "Is there a reason he hasn't been killed?"

"Sire, he carries your father's sigil! And he brings *kz'zeerkti* with him."

"Cherenkova-Captain? She is leading the raids to the south."

"No, sire! There are two *kz'zeerkti*, strange ones. I thought it best . . ."

"You were right." Pouncer jumped up, trading one last glance with C'mell. "Take me there." As he went out Whitepaws stirred in his sleep, and C'mell ran a rough tongue over the kitten to settle him.

The afternoon sun was sending its rays slanting through the treetops, and Pouncer blinked as he emerged from the den. Twice-eight *tuskvor* milled beneath the den mouth, grunting as *mazourk* supervised the unloading of the laden *tsvasztet*. M'mewr was ushering the mothers and kits up the rocky trail to the den. The pride was whole again, and that was a good thing. Those who had stayed over the change of the seasons to fight were spilling out of the den. Snarling and purring rose as long-separated mates were reunited and old friends traded greetings. Soon the mating season would begin once more, continuing the cycle of generations. A *tuskvor* bellowed and another answered. Swift-Claw led him down the mounting ledge, where a lone kzin waited, apart from the turmoil of the returning migration. His muzzle bore four narrow stripes of white fur, the scar sign of a blood oath, and more white on his chest, sign of battle injury. It took Pouncer a moment to recognize him.

"I know you . . . Far Hunter! How did you come here?

Welcome! How is your father?" The questions spilled out.

The other claw-raked. "My father is dead, sire. Killed by the Tzaatz as we helped the *kz'zeerkti* to escape." He stepped aside to show two smaller figures. "I have brought you these."

This time recognition was instantaneous. "Tskombe-*kz'zeerkti*! Welcome! I should have expected it would be you. And which one is this?"

Tskombe smiled, carefully not showing teeth. "This is Trina, First-Son."

"I am Zree-Rrit now, much has changed. Why have you come back?"

"To bring Captain Cherenkova home again."

"Your loyalty is impressive."

"Is she here?" Even Pouncer could hear the eagerness in Tskombe's voice.

"She was here. Now she leads our advance base in raids against the Tzaatz."

"Raids against . . ." Tskombe's puzzlement showed. "She leads *kzinti* raids, you mean?"

"You *kz'zeerkti* are skilled and subtle planners. She has proven her worth as a warrior."

Tskombe opened his mouth, closed it again. "When can I see her?"

"Now that the *tuskvor* are back we will be sending her supplies and reinforcements, this coming Hunter's Moon, or the next. You can go with them."

The human breathed deep. It was not the answer he was hoping for, but he accepted it. *More waiting.* Pouncer noticed his reaction. "She has a telepath with her, Mind-Seer. We can let her know you are here."

"I would like that very much." Tskombe smiled. *I am getting closer to her, and I know she's alive.* "It's good to see you again, First . . ." He caught himself. "Zree-Rrit."

"To you, I am always Pouncer." He gestured for the newcomers to follow him. "Far Hunter, you have sworn a blood oath."

"To avenge my father." The rangy kzin gestured to the ears on his belt. "I have killed many Tzaatz, in Hero's Square and other places."

"You do justice to his memory."

Far Hunter riffled a paw through the ears. "I hope to have *strakh* enough here to claim a name at your circle . . ." He hesitated, then went on. "And your sister, if she is still unmated."

"Hrrr." Pouncer looked away. "You can have any name you choose. But my sister . . ." He paused. "My sister is dead too, killed by the Tzaatz."

Far Hunter was silent, but his lips twitched over his fangs. The moment stretched uncomfortably long, and Trina reflexively edged herself closer to Tskombe.

"They will pay in blood." Far Hunter snarled the words under his breath.

"They will pay higher than you imagine. Right now the *czrav* High Circle are meeting to discuss the future. If they agree, I will lead an army against Kchula-Tzaatz."

"And if they do not?"

"Then you and I will fight our own war." Pouncer looked to the horizon, then back to Far Hunter. "But vengeance will wait for a full belly tonight. You must be hungry from the journey." Pouncer gestured to one of the

youngsters who was unloading a *tuskvor*. "Sharp Ears! Get
a fresh kill for our new arrivals."

"At once, sire!" The youngster left on the bound.

Pouncer led the three up to the top of the sandstone
dome to talk and admire the view. The experience seemed
not-right somehow, the peaceful scene at odds with the
gravity of the events unfolding around it. *Above me the
Tzaatz search me out from the orbital fortresses, below me
the Pride Leaders are debating my future and my fate, and
here in the middle I am feasting old companions as if nothing else mattered.* He looked to Far Hunter "Tell me how
you came to join the migration."

"Hrrr." The *kzintzag* warrior turned a paw over. "This
kz'zeerkti appeared at my stall and led me on an impossible
quest. This other one"—he indicated Trina—"is a tracker
of outlandish ability. We found the old jungle den of Ztrak
Pride, and then found Ztrak border markers, where we
waited with a border gift until M'mewr arrived and
accepted it."

Pouncer raised his ears, confused. "But that den is
abandoned."

"Abandoned, but the border we chose was the one with
Mrrsel Pride. M'mewr led a hunting party there, and
found us. They would have killed us on the spot, but
Tskombe-*kz'zeerkti* still carries your father's sigil. She recognized it as the same as the one Cherenkova-Captain
wears."

Pouncer rippled his ears. "You three have performed a
feat of tracking the Tzaatz have been unable to duplicate."

"Hrrr. The Tzaatz lack patience. They still overfly the
jungle with gravcars, but they fear to walk in it. We

camped on the jungle verge and went to the border marker to wait every day for the entire wet season, and into the dry again."

Sharp Ears arrived then, with another youngster, carrying a dressed and gutted *zianya* not devoured at the Bloodfeast gorging. Although he was still replete Pouncer shared a haunch with Far Hunter, and was surprised when the humans ate their portions raw. *Everything is in flux.* Eventually the protocols of greeting and feasting had been satisfied and they sat as the sun went down, trading stories of recent events. Beneath them the hustle and bustle of the migration faded as the Pride went down into the den. Soon it was tale-telling-time, and Pouncer took them down to be introduced to the pride.

And still the High Circle remained in their sealed assembly in the chamber below. Pouncer found it hard to concentrate on the stories the *tuskvor* travelers were telling of the newcomer. Finally, at general insistence, Far Hunter stood to tell the tale of their search and their arrival. He called Trina up with him to act the *kz'zeerkti* roles, and Pouncer took the opportunity to speak to Tskombe.

"Come, and talk with me. I have been missing my *kz'zeerkti* advisor."

They slipped out into the darkness and walked and talked, taking the high trail back up to the top of the sandstone dome and bringing each other up to date on the events since they had parted. At the top they sat on the smooth rocks, and Pouncer described his campaign as it had unfolded so far while Tskombe listened. *He is becoming an experienced tactician.*

Tskombe nodded as he listened. "You have done a lot."

"Not as much as we need to do. Our raids here are just pinpricks. The *czrav* are ferocious warriors, but even with every pride behind me it will be a close fight. We must fight a single, decisive battle, but Cherenkova-Captain has identified a problem. If we force such an engagement the Tzaatz may transgress their honor."

"Meaning what?"

"They may employ weapons prohibited in *skalazaal*. They will not do it if they are certain of victory, with Kzin-Conserver watching, but if they start to lose . . ." Pouncer trailed off. It was a problem he had avoided mentioning to anyone except Ayla; he hadn't wanted to dissuade the *czrav* leaders from supporting him. That didn't solve the problem though.

"So what can prevent them from doing that?"

"Hrrr. I need the Great Pride Circle to bear witness to the battle, with armed ships in orbit willing to intervene if the rules are broken."

"How is that arranged?"

Pouncer rippled his ears and twitched his tail. "It is not to be arranged. A Great Pride Circle is not convened lightly, or in haste. Even in my father's day they were planned far in advance. Now half the Great Prides are locked in Honor-War themselves, and the rest are fighting your species." Pouncer paused and looked away to the far horizon.

"I didn't know it had gone so far. We didn't have much news in the jungle den." An image of *Oorwinnig* flashed before Tskombe's mind's eye, and the destruction it had wrought on ED1272. *Muro Ravalla has his war.* Bile welled up in his throat at the thought. *How many will die for his vision of power?*

"I have agents now, even in the Citadel. It is true, Tskombe-*kz'zeerkti*. You and I are enemies now."

"No." Tskombe shook his head. "We are not enemies. You risked your life for me. What can I do for you?"

"Advise me as Cherenkova-Captain did. The Pride Leaders are deciding now which path to take. If they follow me, where should I lead them?"

"The only place you can lead them is to the Citadel, and the Patriarchy."

"Hrrrr. I may be leading them all to destruction."

"There are no guarantees in war. Once you start one, you can't control it."

"Some things are more likely than others. We can win, perhaps, if the fight is fair. If it isn't, if the Tzaatz break tradition, we will be destroyed."

"What do you need to ensure that, short of a Great Pride Circle?"

"I need support. I need witnesses while the battle takes place, witnesses powerful enough that Kchula will not dare violate the rules. There are Great Prides who oppose him. I am still First-Son-of-Meerz-Rrit. If several of them put warships in orbit, we would be safe."

"Will they do it?"

"Perhaps, if I ask. I will have *strakh* with them, if I could reach them, but the Tzaatz guard the spaceports too tightly now."

Tskombe smiled, being careful to keep his teeth from showing. "I know where I can get a starship."

Pouncer's ears swiveled up. "Tell me."

"I came here with a freerunner named Night Pilot. He's back in orbit after a trip, and now he's waiting for me. Far Hunter has arranged fuel for him, and can arrange more. He can take your emissary to the Great Prides."

"Hrrr. This is good fortune. Can you contact him?"

Tskombe held up his beltcomp. "I have the codes right here, and his orbital data." He tapped the small screen. "He will be overhead . . ." Tskombe tried to do the conversion math in his head and came up with a rough answer. ". . . overhead at midnight. He can come down by direct descent if we need him to."

"We will have to be careful in contacting him, and in bringing him down. Ftzaal-Tzaatz is actively hunting for us, and the orbital fortresses are always watching and listening."

Tskombe nodded. "Night Pilot knows how to get in and out without being seen."

"Hrrr. I will still have to choose an emissary." Pouncer looked up at the sky, now flecked with stars. Some of the pinpoints moved, satellites or ships or docks or fortresses. *Once upon a time only stars filled the sky.* "If the Pride Leaders decide to follow where I lead."

Tskombe nodded. Perhaps it would be better for him if they didn't. He had *Black Saber* in orbit, and Night Pilot was actively eager to have *kz'zeerkti* passengers on board for his passage back to Known Space and out of the way of the United Nations' onslaught on the Patriarchy. He was almost in contact with Ayla. *Best, perhaps, if we just get her and go.* That thought had no honor. *I owe blood debt to this kzin, who risked his life for me, blood debt to Far Hunter, who lost his father for me. I cannot do less than honor my obligation.* All he could offer Pouncer was *Black Saber.* He would offer it.

Much later they walked back down and Pouncer laid out his plans. Tskombe nodded as he listened. *He is bold, I'll give him that.* He was amazed to learn the sheer size of the *czrav* population, but perhaps he shouldn't have been. They had half a continent to hide in. The *czrav* had won the support of the Northern Lesser Prides, and slowly extended their base of support south into the Plain of Stgrat. That gave them a safe corridor, where *czrav* agents could count on the support of the *kzintzag* and the nobility together. They had freedom of movement in those areas. The weakness of the *czrav* was the fierce independence that kept them from combining their power even as they worked toward their common goals.

Pouncer stopped at the lip of the den to look out into the night. "But if they will follow me, no force on this planet can stand against them."

"Will they follow you?"

"They are debating that now." Pouncer tried to keep the tension from his voice. *Everything depends on this moment.* The return of Tskombe-*kz'zeerkti* could only be a good omen; the availability of a ship at this moment could not have been better timed. *But I still need to choose an emissary.*

In the den Far Hunter was still relating the tale of their search to the now rapt audience around the pride circle fire. He was a natural storyteller, as good as Swift Claw if less practiced. Inspiration dawned. *Yes!* He is not of the *czrav*, he speaks well, he will be acceptable to the Great Pride-Patriarchs. *I will send him, if he will go.*

A paw on his shoulder, V'rli-Ztrak. She was bleeding badly from a slash that ran from her neck to her arm.

He reached out to her. "You have been . . ." She cut him off with a raised hand.

"The wound is nothing. Sraa-Vroo challenge-leapt and I killed him. He did not know the single combat form." She paused. "The *czrav* are behind you, Zree-Rrit, every pride. We will take our destiny back from the Patriarchy."

Pouncer found himself wordless. It was his moment of triumph, but he didn't feel triumphant. *I have taken on a vast responsibility.* He looked over to where Tskombe-*kz'zeerkti* had joined Far Hunter and Trina in the center of the pride circle. *I must not fail.*

There followed a time of frenetic preparation. Agents were sent out to gain information on the state of the Citadel defenses, patrols dispatched to reconnoiter routes and lay up points for the march of the building army. *Czrav* manufacturing was sophisticated, but not geared for large scale production, and so necessary equipment had to be stolen from the enemy, mag armor for warriors and *tuskvor* both, and variable swords, grav belts, combat computers and more. Far Hunter traveled south with a raid, to stay behind and rendezvous with *Black Saber* for his mission to Churrt Pride and beyond. Pouncer found himself missing the presence of the Cherenkova-Captain, but Tskombe stepped almost unconsciously into that role, bringing his greater ground combat experience to bear. The list of details he carried in his head was tremendous, and every day the plan was refined. *These* kz'zeerkti *are formidable planners.* Good planning was essential; there

was very little time. Their attack was set for the next High
Hunter's Moon, and already it had half waned from its last
peak. *I must strike while I can, while the* czrav *are
behind me, while the Tzaatz do not suspect my full
strength, while the Lesser Prides and the* kzintzag *still
support us.* The experienced warriors of Ztrak and Dziit
and Mrrsel Prides became the leadership who trained the
others in his tactics. He pushed his followers without
mercy, himself harder still. Every day more prides arrived
from the migration, and the increasingly crowded *tuskvor*
needed to be managed and fed.

I have unleashed something I can no longer control. He
was riding the storm, guiding it as he could, but helpless
to prevent its advance. It would carry him to the Citadel,
and to victory or death. He had no time to think about
that, there was too much to accomplish first.

> *Honor demands vengeance.*
> —Creed of the Fanged God

The lighter floated out into the docking frame, thrusting
gently onto a rendezvous trajectory. Overhead Kzinhome
revolved and steadied against a backdrop of stars.
Raarrgh-Captain let the pilot fly while he looked out the
window at his new command. Once *Patriarch's Talon* had
been a battleship, armed and armored for the Long Hunt.
Now it was a stripped hulk, the only thing left her power-
plants and her massive polarizers. The rest of her hull had
been replaced with an open framework that held her new
arsenal. It lacked the sophistication of the spinal-mount
gamma ray laser and the secondary turrets and the racks

of seeker missiles that had once made her a force to be reckoned with, but it was more lethal by far. *Patriarch's Talon* now carried launch racks full of simple tungsten spheres half the height of a kzin, wrapped in a thin shell of low albedo coating. With three-quarters of her hull cut away, the battleship's drives could push her at unheard-of accelerations, and when she was traveling so close to the speed of light that time dilation was the primary targeting factor, she would release those masses to travel on their own. They had no guidance, no warheads, no ability to locate and track a target, or even to maneuver. All they could do was travel as straight as a laser beam until they hit their target or missed it. For any space combat Raarrgh-Captain had ever fought they would be absolutely useless. Even moving at seven-eights-over-eight-squared times the speed of light, any ship not already crippled could elude them. In fact, the limitations on the ex-battleship's own sensors and guidance systems meant that they were likely to miss even a target dead in space, given the tremendous lead distance required to align her velocity vector on the target at such speeds. *Patriarch's Talon* had once been a weapon of power and precision. Now she couldn't hope to hit anything smaller than a planet.

Of course, that was exactly the plan, and a projectile of that much mass arriving at just under the speed of light would punch a crater to a planet's core. A pawful of them would sterilize a world, and it was that task, and that task alone, that *Patriarch's Talon* had been stripped for. In days his ship would be ready. It couldn't happen soon enough. There would be more suffering, more slaughtered kits by *kz'zeerkti* before he could bring his weapon to bear. Every day brought new reports of colonies wiped out to the last kzin; even long established and well defended worlds were being invested and burned from orbit. The *kz'zeerkti* had seemingly unlimited resources and their fleets were unstoppable, but they had not been in space long as a species, and they had a fatal weakness that the more established kzinti did not. Their colonies were few and lightly populated, all still at least partially reliant on their homeworld. Eliminate that and their campaign must inevitably collapse. Penetrating the heavy defenses of Sol system would be impossible for a ship, or even a fleet, but *Patriarch's Talon* no longer had to get close to strike.

And so Raarrgh-Captain would take his new warship deep into human space, to the borderland of Sol, and with alignment and timing precise to the edge of measurement he would accelerate to his hellish attack velocity and launch his war load at Earth. It was an unheard-of measure and it stood against the Traditions, against the Way of the Hunter, against honor itself to vandalize a living world like that. He would have been justified if he refused the mission, even justified if he renounced his fealty to Tzaatz Pride over such orders. He had considered both those options long and hard. It was true, as he had told Ftzaal-Tzaatz when the Black Priest had issued his orders, that the kzinti had never, in all their Conquests, used even conversion weapons on a world, let alone something like this. But it was also true, as Ftzaal had replied, that the kzinti had never before been faced not only with defeat but extermination. The *kz'zeerkti* had shown no scruples in their attacks on kzinti-held worlds, assaults designed not for conquest but for annihilation. The monkey war was no longer about spoils and status, it was about species survival, and that changed everything.

Changed everything except the fact of final victory. That would remain a kzinti honor. His mouth relaxed into a fanged smile.

> *Cleopatra: Sink Rome, and their tongues rot that speak against us! A charge we bear i' the war, and, as the president of my kingdom, will appear there for a man. Speak not against it, I will not stay behind.*
> —William Shakespeare, Antony and Cleopatra,
> Act III, Scene VII

Ayla Cherenkova wasn't fast enough to run with the kzinti she commanded, so they carried her into battle instead. Her sedan chair was borne by eight kzinretti, her elite guard, each sworn to defend her to the death. It had room for her maps and planning charts, primitive tools long superseded by combat consoles, but they needed no power source. On a rack overhead was the heavy kzinti beamrifle that she was allowed to use because she was neither kzin nor slave, though if she ever had to use it, it would mean that her plans had failed badly. There was also room for Mind-Seer, her telepath, though he marched on his own except in battle, and beside the beamrifle were a series of small vials of *sthondat* lymph, should Mind-Seer ever need them in emergency. So far he hadn't; the *czrav* attacks had all gone perfectly, and his natural talent had been enough to know the minds of their enemies and pass Cherenkova's orders to her warriors.

And they were *her* warriors. Ayla smiled at that. Even among her volunteer kzinretti there had been some doubts at first, but now there was no more question about her ability to plan, to command and to lead. They would hit an installation, kill all the Tzaatz and take not just the ears but the bodies before vanishing into the night again. It was a tactic she had developed herself, aimed at striking fear into her enemies. The Tzaatz had a name for them now, *pazpuweejw*—the death shadows, the malevolent phantoms who haunted the ancient Kitten's Tales. She liked that name; it meant that her tactics were working.

She stuck her head out the side of the chair as they came to a rise. "K'lakri, stop here."

"As you command."

The bearers put her down, and Cherenkova picked up her beamrifle and got out of the chair. With just her belt-comp she didn't have all the functionality of a combat console but she could move around. Mind-Seer came up beside her.

"I have news from the den, Cherenkova-Captain."

"What is it?"

"The Tskombe-*kz'zeerkti* has returned for you."

"Quacy? He's back?" It took a moment for the news to sink in, and joy flooded her system. All at once she longed to hold him and be held, to touch him, at least to talk to him. Tears came to her eyes unbidden and she wiped them away. *Time for this later. You have a battle to win.* Still she couldn't help smiling. She was due to return to the den soon anyway. Her force had been fighting thrice around the Hunter's Moon and they needed a rest. *Quacy! It will be good, so good to see him.*

She turned to Mind-Seer. "Tell them I'm glad. Tell them, tell *him* I'll see him soon."

Mind-Seer closed his eyes and muttered to himself as he reached out with his mind for that of Ferlitz-Telepath. Ayla watched him, somewhat in awe, as she always was, of the Telepath's Gift. He opened them a moment later. The message had been sent.

And now focus on the battle. She came up to the hill, slid up on her belly and raised her binoptics to scan the target. It was a rare-earth mine, worked by Kdatlyno, recently confiscated from the minor pride of Vaasc by the Tzaatz as punishment for withholding tribute. It was possible the Vaasc had really done that—the Lesser Prides were growing steadily more rebellious as the limits of Tzaatz control became clear—but it was more likely that Kchula-Tzaatz wanted the mine's output to feed his fleet construction program and its wealth for himself.

And ultimately it didn't matter. Another part of Cherenkova's overall campaign plan was that the Tzaatz themselves would be punished every time they tried to exert control in the northwestern prideholdings. With every heavy-handed move Kchula made, with every rapier-swift reprisal she mounted against them, the forces of the *czrav* gained credence with those who lived in the shadow of the Long Range. Vaasc Pride were not yet allies of Pouncer's, but soon they would be, as other Lesser Prides had already pledged fealty to the resurgent First-Son-of-Meerz-Rrit.

She scanned the scene. The mine head was in a valley half full of tailings, and it slanted deep into the planet's crust to ferret out the scant pockets of rare-earth metals.

The Tzaatz had a heavy guard mounted. A few of them had taken to carrying beam weapons as well, a disturbing trend she could do little about. Pouncer refused to countenance the *czrav* taking similar steps, and though he allowed her to carry her own weapon for last-ditch self-defense, he probably would have rather she didn't.

She scanned the valley. There were a lot of Tzaatz, but guard duty was a boring and unrewarding task that quickly took the edge off even the best troops. More importantly, she couldn't see her *pazpuweejw* though she knew they were there, infiltrated into their attack positions like the shadows they took their name from.

Mind-Seer came up beside her, looking faraway as he reached out with his mind. "The attack is ready."

Ayla nodded, not so much to acknowledge his words as to confirm them to herself. She felt the familiar pre-battle tension growing in her.

"Are we safe? Do the Tzaatz suspect?"

"Meat . . . the mating . . . distant home . . . The sentries are unaware. . . ."

"Good. Tell V'levian to advance."

Again Mind-Seer's eyes unfocused. "She moves now."

Ayla swung her binoptics to focus on the closest Tzaatz guardpost, three of them on raider *rapsari* at the access road that led to the mine complex. For a moment there was nothing, and then she saw a blur of motion, and the guards and their beasts were down.

"Tell M'telv to go."

"Yes . . ." His eyes closed briefly, then shot open. "There are hunters! Coming fast!"

"Alert!" It was K'lakri, running up the slope at the same

instant. "The Tzaatz are coming." Ayla whirled around to see her guard commander pointing skyward. There was a high pitched whine, growing rapidly louder . . . "Gravcars!" Ayla shouted. "Back to the rally point." A swarm of assault vehicles were dropping out of the sky onto their position.

Too close for coincidence. It took Ayla half a second to assess the situation. "They know we're here. Mind-Seer, order the attack aborted, V'levian and M'telv are to withdraw to the rally point under their own command. K'lakri, we're withdrawing now. They might not have us spotted yet."

"As you command." K'lakri flashed tail signals to her warriors while Ayla scrambled back to her sedan chair, but by the time they got there it was too late. The first three gravcars slammed down not a hundred meters away, Tzaatz pouring down the ramps. There were no *rapsari,* at least, and at K'lakri's order her *pazpuweejw* elite guard screamed and leapt as the enemy closed, carving left and right with variable swords. They weren't as strong as males, but they were faster. Their sex helped; the Tzaatz were slow to understand that the females were attacking them, and they cut down half the Tzaatz in under a minute. She grabbed her beamrifle and looked for targets.

But already the weapons on the cars that hadn't landed were firing as they made a low pass, pulled up and swung around to come back down. Netguns! Four of her bodyguard were caught and struggling, the rest diving for cover, though there was little enough on the rocky slope. Mind-Seer drew his own variable sword and leapt for a Tzaatz warrior. None of them carried weapons that could engage the cars; all they could do was fall back. Another wave of assault vehicles dropped out of the sky, slamming down in the gravel on the hill. Ayla ran for a small ravine, slid down into it in a shower of stones. Her force needed its commander, and for that she had to survive. She looked around wildly for Mind-Seer but couldn't see him, or anyone. Heart thumping wildly, she belly crawled under a low bush. Hopefully the Tzaatz wouldn't be looking for a human. If they found her they might think her a slave. That would be a good thing, as long as they didn't choose to eat her right then and there. She looked at the beamrifle in her hand. They might not eat her, *if* they didn't find her with a weapon. *But I won't abandon my weapon, and I won't pretend to be a slave to buy my own safety.* She would hide, but if they came for her she would shoot her way out or die trying. Minutes dragged by like hours, and her breathing stabilized. She could hear the Tzaatz moving about on the hilltop, snarling back and forth as they secured the area. They seemed to have missed her little gully, but there would be scent trail, and they might have some of their odious *rapsar* sniffers with them. She pictured the terrain and assessed options. She needed to get a plan together to get her captured warriors back.

Screams of rage and pain came from the hillcrest, two voices, too inarticulate for her to make out the words, but she understood what was happening. Her *pazpuweejw* were being interrogated. Anger swelled through her and she gripped her beamrifle. She had her rescue plan, and it was right here, right now. She scrambled up the slope she had slid down, came face to face with a surprised Tzaatz and pulled the trigger. His mag armor was depowered and

his chest exploded as the beam hit him. She dropped
behind his still steaming corpse for cover and started picking targets, pulling the trigger and moving on. For about
fifteen seconds she had the advantage with firepower and
confusion on her side, and then they spotted her. The
Tzaatz warriors weren't cowards, and they screamed and
leapt without regard for their own safety. She snapped the
weapon to multifire and swept it across her front, hitting
at least three in mid leap, sending the rest diving for cover
amid a spray of shrapnel from rocks exploded by beams
that missed. She saw one of her *pazpuweejw* claw her way
out of a net and move to free another. A Tzaatz leapt to
stop them and she snapped off a shot, catching him in the
face. The body dropped, headless, and the two kzinretti
vanished over the hillcrest. *They will free the others while
I cover them, and the Kzinrette Secret will be safe.* There
was silence while she watched, and again the minutes
dragged, then rock clicked on rock to her left flank. She
spun, saw a flash of movement and fired, catching a
Tzaatz in midleap. His mag armor was on, but her weapon
was still on multifire and the beams shredded him. She
whirled back to cover her front again but nothing else was
moving. Impasse. She became aware of pain, looked down
to see that the beamrifle's charge pack had burned a hole
in her shirt sleeve and sizzled the skin beneath. The indicator was way down. She'd gone through over half a
charge already.

*And I have to move or they'll get me from both flanks
next time.* If they managed that the game would be over.
Had all her captured warriors escaped? A killscream sounded
from above and cut off with a gurgle. That suggested that

they had, and the Tzaatz were paying in blood to follow them. It was time to leave. Carefully she slid back down the ravine, then moved across the slope under the cover of some low shrubs, hoping to work her way back up. A gravcar whined over, searching, and she jerked her weapon up to fire. It hadn't spotted her, a miracle on the sparse terrain, and she let it pass. A beamrifle would do little to a combat vehicle anyway. She was running out of options. If she'd been smart she would have headed back for the rally point, and she listened for the voice in her mind that would be Mind-Seer, feeding her information, but there was nothing. *Is he even alive?* An unanswerable question. More rock on rock. She swung the rifle again, but there was nothing there. *Think fast, monkey.* They would stalk her, but as long as she didn't let them box her in she'd have the initiative. For that she had to keep moving. So that was the plan, fire, fall back, wear them down. Keep to the bushes where they'd have trouble picking her up from the air. They might get her in the end, but she'd make them pay.

She checked the skies for gravcars, spotted one, hanging five hundred meters away, spotted another. They knew generally where she was, and they were waiting for her to break cover. She slid backward carefully, keeping the bushes between them and herself as a screen. They would have sensors that could pick her up, if she exposed herself, but most sensors had limited fields of view. She lay down carefully and waited. There was a small knoll another ten meters back, and she crept around behind it, then slid forward to the crest, put the weapon on her shoulder, clicking it off multifire to conserve what charge she had left.

Unbidden, her mind's eye conjured a view of the scene at Midling base. *They* ate *the survivors*. She couldn't let that happen to her. *So concentrate, watch for targets, keep thinking ahead.*

She didn't have long to wait. A Tzaatz moved into her field of view, stopped, and crouched. He was carrying a netgun, and as he scanned the area in front of him he flashed tail signals to those following him. *Why aren't they using energy weapons?* They might have thought she was kzinti, but even so she'd broken the rules first. *And they have my scent trail by now. They know who they're looking for.* The gravcars could rake the whole ravine without exposing anyone to her fire. So she would find the answer to that question later; for now she would just be thankful. A second Tzaatz moved up some five meters to the left of the first and knelt, and the first got up to advance again. Ayla shot him right there, firing twice to make sure his mag armor was defeated, then swung the sights to the second and shot him as well. There were snarls and crashes behind them, but she was already sliding back down the knoll, turning to run back another tactical bound. The terrain favored her in a hit and run defense. *At least here I'm buying time for the others to escape.*

Fifty meters back she spotted a small pile of rocks and a larger slab, just enough room for her to nestle down between them and ambush again. *Two each time, there can't be that many.* They were coming too quickly, typical ratcats. *If they slowed down enough to set an ambush behind me I'd be done for.*

Noises to her front. She scanned left, scanned right, saw nothing. They *were* slowing down, she'd proven herself too deadly with the beamrifle. Even Heroes didn't want to die if they didn't have to. More noises, and it seemed she should have spotted the trackers by now. . . .

A blood curdling scream came from behind her. She rolled, tried to bring the rifle around, but it was too late and a black blur hit her. She saw a taloned claw as big as a pie plate coming down, and then pain exploded, and her world went dark.

Sheathe pride and bare honor.
                    —Conserver wisdom

Scrral-Rrit, Black-Stripe, Second-Son-of-Meerz-Rrit, none of the names seemed right, and the kzin who bore them sat contemplating a puzzle sculpture in the Citadel's Puzzle Garden. In the distance he could hear the burbling of the chaotic water clock at the center of the garden's hedge maze. As the clock's flows shifted in volume and turbulence its sound changed. Sometimes it rushed and splashed and gurgled so you could hear it anywhere along the hedge maze border, sometimes it simply trickled and dripped, and even if you found your way to its base you couldn't hear it at all.

I have no name. It would have been better if it were true. Even if none of the names he was called by applied, there was the name he had given himself, though he never spoke it aloud and would have preferred never to think it either. *Slave-of-the-Zzrou.* The teeth of the poison carrier no longer pained the way they once had, and he would have preferred that reality were different too. They had grown into his flesh, become a part of him, though he could never forget they were there. Pain and death were always just an instant away, to be delivered at the whim of Kchula-Tzaatz. He tried to avoid the conqueror and his savage temper as much as possible. That had become easier lately. His importance to the Tzaatz rule had dwindled, but that was not a good thing either. When his usefulness ended he would become a liability, and death lay down that road too.

Across the Puzzle Garden a robed figure was contemplating another puzzle sculpture. As he watched, the figure moved a segment and then rotated the sculpture on its base until it stopped with a sharp *click*, clearly audible even at that distance. Rrit-Conserver. *No, Kzin-Conserver now*. There were differences in the roles, it was important to remember them. There were few in the Citadel who had the patience to even attempt the Higher Sculptures, crafted by the legendary Conundrum Priest Kassriss, eight-squared or more generations ago. Fully half of his sculptures were still unsolved, and those remaining were the hardest. It was quite possible that Kzin-Conserver might solve one, something that hadn't happened in living memory.

Scrral-Rrit approached and waited. If nothing else, the absolute humiliation of his situation had taught him patience. He waited while the shadows grew long and the light faded, while Kzin-Conserver considered the puzzle, occasionally walking around it, peering into it as though he could somehow divine its inner mechanisms through sufficient staring. Eventually he turned a protruding element and was rewarded with another click. Seemingly satisfied, he turned to face his visitor.

"Scrral-Rrit. You are attentive today."

"I would seek your counsel, Conserver."

Kzin-Conserver's ears swiveled up. "On what?"

"On my future."

"Your future is beyond my scope."

"Then advise me on my present."

"And what is wrong with your present?"

So here it is. He didn't want to say it, and he found he could not meet Conserver's gaze. *Sheath pride and bare honor.* He took a deep breath. "I am ashamed, Kzin-Conserver."

"As you should be, Black-Stripe." Conserver's voice was not harsh, but his words stung sharper than the *zzrou's p'chert* toxin.

"I did not . . . I did not wish this."

"And yet you chose it."

"Aaaiii!" Scrral-Rrit looked skyward, as if beseeching the Fanged God to end his misery. "I didn't know what I was choosing!"

"And what would you change? Would you again be your father's son, your brother's *zar'ameer?* Do you dream of what might have been if you had not chosen to listen the promises of Kchula-Tzaatz?"

"My own humiliation is nothing. The Patriarchy is destroying itself. I am Patriarch, if only in name. I must do something."

Kzin-Conserver turned a paw over, considering. *Such selflessness in Black-Stripe. Is it genuine?* There was no deception in the miserable kzin's eyes. *Perhaps it is.* He looked to the tiny spots that dotted Scrral-Rrit's pelt, white fur growing from pinpoints of scar tissue, the marks of the Hot Needle of Inquiry. It was rare to escape the refined agonies of the Hunt Priest's ritual untransformed. *Perhaps he has learned from his ordeal.* He chose his words carefully. "The Patriarchy is old, it has survived many trials. It will survive this too." *In some form.* He didn't add the reservation.

Scrral-Rrit furled his ears tight. "It may not survive this. The *kz'zeerkti* are savage. The Great Prides will not defeat them unless they unite."

"This is true."

"What should I do then?

"If I give you advice, will you take it?."

"I will take it, Conserver. I was ambitious, and proud. I envied my brother. Now look at me. I will never outlive the shame of the *zzrou*. The Hot Needle . . ." He shuddered. "I can never undo what I have done to my father and my brother. I can never undo what I have done to myself. Perhaps I can undo what I have done to the Patriarchy."

"Time's arrow flies only forward."

"You told me once, a wise Patriarch seeks wise counsel. Counsel me and I will listen."

"My advice is this. Wait patiently. You are not without power. Use it carefully, when the opportunity comes."

"Power?" Scrral-Rrit wrinkled his nose. "What power do I have? I do not even command myself. Kchula punishes me on a whim. He could kill me just as easily." Reflexively he touched his shoulder blade where the *zzrou* waited. He controlled another shudder. "I do not dare face the Needle again." He sat down heavily on a bench by the sculpture.

"No!" Kzin-Conserver barked the words. "Stand up, Son-of-the-Rrit." Reflexively Second-Son stood. Kzin-Conserver spoke, fast and firmly. "You are always in command of yourself. If you want to take pride in yourself, act with honor. Make your decisions based on what is right. Carry them out without regard to the consequence."

"What of—"

"No! That is the beginning and the end. You asked my advice, now you have it."

"This is not advice! How can I reclaim the Patriarchy? How can I stop the war?"

"That is not up to you anymore, nor is it up to me."

"You are telling me to do nothing!"

"No, I am telling you to act with honor. Honor is not judged by the size of the action but by its rightness."

"But . . ."

"No!" Rrit-Conserver slashed the air with his paws. "You overreached yourself when you aspired to be Patriarch. If you wanted to influence the course of the Patriarchy you should have studied hard, worked as your brother did and become his *zar'ameer*. It is too late for you to play that role. You have made your choices. Now play the role you have chosen with honor. Do not over-reach yourself again."

"I . . ." Scrral-Rrit seemed about to shrink, then pulled himself straight. "I will do as you say, Conserver."

"Good."

Scrral-Rrit left and Kzin-Conserver watched him go. *He has the desire now, but does he have the strength?* The answer would become clear in the fullness of time. Kzin-Conserver returned his attention to the puzzle sculpture.

The latest move had revealed an inscription, a quotation from the teachings of Meerli. The bronze cylinder that bore the words was scarcely tarnished, in marked contrast to the rest of the statue. It had been a long time since anyone had found this configuration of the puzzle; perhaps no one ever had. It was a clue, but a subtle one. He recited it to himself, bringing up the larger text it was taken from in his mind. The exercise refreshed his memory on the meaning of Meerli's wisdom, as it was intended to. *This lesson has been here for generations waiting to be learned, despite the many eyes that have searched for it.* That was a lesson in itself. *What other lessons has life hidden around me, waiting for me to find the correct way of viewing them?*

Cultivate your allies, lest your enemies do.
                                              —Si-Rrit

Far Hunter took a deep breath, primarily to control his shivering. Zraa-Churrt's Patriarchal Hall was cold, and when he breathed out again his exhalations condensed into fog. He had experienced this level of cold before, hunting high in the Mooncatchers for premium game for his father's stall, but he had not expected to find it inside and his thin robe was not protection enough against the chill air.

"Advance, Rrit-Emissary." Zraa-Churrt himself was not cold. He was large, made larger by his heavy white pelt, eight-cubed-generations adapted to life on the frigid ice-world that was his Patriarchal seat. Carbon dioxide froze at Vraaal's poles in the winter, and even here at the equator the ice never melted. Only in the salty oceans was water a liquid, and life on the land, such as it was, depended entirely on the ocean food web for subsistence.

For a moment Far Hunter hesitated, still unused to his new title, and then he walked down the long hall to Zraa-Churrt's dais. *Night Pilot should be doing this.* The freerunner was older and more experienced and would doubtless present himself better than Far-Hunter-Rrit-Emissary could. But Night Pilot *was* a freerunner, and an Emissary had to be fealty-bound to the lord for whom he spoke. Night Pilot had refused to even enter Zraa-Churrt's hall, because of the requirement that he prostrate himself at the door.

He claw-raked when he reached the dais. Zraa-Churrt unfurled his ears. "So you are Speaker for First-Son-of-Meerz-Rrit?"

"I am, sire. Thank you for your time in this audience." He spoke carefully, watching his tenses. Pouncer had carefully schooled him on the proper forms of address and respect. They were complex, as one might expect. He was a low-ranked emissary speaking to a high-ranked noble, but representing a higher-ranked noble. As if that were not complex enough, Pouncer's status as the deposed-rightful-Patriarch-unrecognized-in-favor-of-his-younger-brother added another layer of formalism that had to be understood and adhered to.

"Sit." Zraa-Churrt gestured to a *prrstet.* "What may this humble pride do for you?"

"Zree-Rrit seeks to regain the Patriarchy, rightfully his by birth. He asks you to honor your fealty pledge to his father."

"We honor the pledge without hesitation." Zraa-Churrt leaned forward. "*How* we honor the pledge is the question. What does Zree-Rrit want?"

"Ships in orbit at Kzinhome, to see that the traditions are followed in the *skalazaal.*"

Zraa-Churrt's ears went up. "Is that all?"

"That is all, sire."

"Hrrr." The Patriarch turned a paw over. "Are you aware of the progress of the *kz'zeerkti* war?"

"My pilot was nearly caught in one of their attacks before he came to Kzinhome."

"They are overwhelming. All the ships I command would not stop them if they chose to destroy *my* world." He looked away for long moments, then looked back to his guest. "How many ships would Zree-Rrit require?"

"As many as you can send. More is better. The Tzaatz must understand there will be consequences if they violate the traditions."

"You are bold in your questioning of Tzaatz honor."

Far Hunter spat, suddenly angry. "I have seen Tzaatz honor. I watched them beat my father to death while he was trapped in a net. I have seen them throw the First-Sons of the Lesser Prides of Kzinhome into the arena on manufactured pretexts. I have seen them strip smallholders of all they own for less insult than I just offered." His lips came away from his fangs and he felt his claws extend, even as a part of his brain fought for self-control. *This is not the way of the diplomat.* "The truth is never insult."

"Truth." Zraa-Churrt turned a paw over and contemplated it. "Have you the proof-before-the-pride-circle?"

"Proof?" *Can he not see?* Far Hunter touched his nose

and the four white scar streaks he'd gouged with his own claws. "These scars are my blood oath, sworn when I saw my father die. I will not rest while Kchula-Tzaatz lives."

"The blood oath. I have heard of this rite."

And all at once Far Hunter understood. *They do not have the same blood oath ritual, because they cannot see white scar-fur on their pelts.*

"I can prove nothing standing before you, Pride-Patriarch. Come to Kzinhome yourself. Have Churrt-Conserver ask Kzin-Conserver, or simply watch. The evidence is everywhere."

"I cannot come myself and abandon my holdings here. The *kz'zeerkti* are coming. Meerz-Rrit was right about that, at least. We have convinced them of the need to destroy us, and they are doing it."

"Send ships then, sire!"

"And I would not be surprised to see ships of another Great Pride at my singularity either." Zraa-Churrt went on as if he hadn't heard. "*Skalazaal* is becoming more frequent even as we should be uniting before our common enemy."

"Sire, lend your support to Zree-Rrit! He can unite the Patriarchy as his brother cannot, as Kchula-Tzaatz has not. We need you."

Zraa-Churrt returned his attention to Far Hunter. "It is distasteful, what Kchula-Tzaatz has done with the Patriarchy, Rrit-Emissary." Zraa-Churrt wrinkled his nose. "I stayed past the end of the Great Pride Circle to see what would happen. I was not encouraged when I left." He paused, thinking, while Far Hunter dared not breathe.

"Yes. I will send ships to Kzinhome. Not many . . ." He raised a warning paw. ". . . but perhaps enough."

The young Lady K'ab'al Xoc endures the blood-letting ritual, her flesh pierced with stingray spines to summon the Vision Serpent and sanctify the throne ascension of Itmanaaj B'alam, Shield Jaguar II.
   —Mayan glyph inscription, lintels 24, 25, and 26, structure 23 at the ruins of Yaxchilan

Ayla Cherenkova woke, bleary eyed, to the thin, gray light of dawn filtering down from the tiny window far above in the tower over her cell. She stretched and looked to the scores she'd scratched on the stone wall, groped around for the pebble she used to make them, and added another. There were forty now, forty days since she was captured, more or less. She hadn't thought to make them at first, before she'd realized that she might be there for a very long time indeed. She was naked and it was cold outside of the pile of straw they gave her to sleep in, but she made herself get up and do her daily exercise routine: pushups, wide, narrow, and hands together; situps and side crunches; isometrics for the major muscle groups; chinups using the door frame; jogging in place for four thousand paces. At least she had enough room to exercise. The cell was built to kzinti scale, and with kzinti regard for claustro-phobia, which made it generous by human standards. She'd lived in tighter quarters on ship. She was sweating by the end of her routine and dried herself down with the hay and went through her morning ablutions. It was a ritual designed to save her sanity through discipline. It would buy her some time at least, before her mind snapped from confinement.

The sanitary facilities were primitive: a bucket of water for drinking and washing, an empty bucket for body wastes. She'd read nightmares about prisoners forced to live for months in their own filth in dungeons like this, but her captors were meticulous about keeping her clean. Her straw bedding was changed daily, and both buckets with every meal, by the same two Kdatlyno slaves who brought her food. She couldn't imagine it was through any concern for her well-being. The kzinti probably couldn't stand the smell of less hygenic conditions. She had, in the short time before they put her in her cell, begun to discern a hierarchy of sorts among the slave species. Any slave could hold any role, but the Kdatlyno seemed to draw the bulk of the menial tasks. The insectoid Whrloo seemed to have more supervisory roles, while the Pierin worked as personal servants and the Jotok took care of more technical jobs. Twice she had seen slaves of other species in the distance, one a looming shadow, the other small and quick, but had no idea what they did or where they came from, or even what they were called.

It was funny the things your mind considered when it had unlimited time to itself. For a while she had obsessed about what might happen next, and scenario after scenario involving the hunt park ran through her head. Now she was simply resigned to indefinite waiting in her cell until something happened. *Resigned to wait, yes, but not resigned to my fate. When an opportunity to escape comes up I have to take it, and if they put me in a hunt park, I'm going to take a few of the bastards with me.* There was a degree of desperate optimism in her thoughts that wouldn't allow her to contemplate the odds against her survival in any of those situations. As bad as it was, she was probably far safer as a prisoner of the Tzaatz than she was trying to survive on Kzinhome alone, and while she'd fight her hardest in the hunt park, she would be a cornered rabbit biting at the fox.

Pouncer was out there, and Pouncer wouldn't abandon her, but neither did he have the strength to storm the Citadel, and there was no guarantee he'd win when he tried. And Quacy! Was she only imagining what Mind-Seer had said, that he had come to Kzinhome for her? She hadn't touched him, seen him, heard him; it seemed much more likely to be a fiction invented by her subconscious to encourage her to hold on to her sanity until she could get out.

The keys jangled and the ancient lock snapped open, though it was early for the morning meal. She looked up as the heavy door swung in and one of the Kdatlyno looked in, gesturing for her to come out with long spindly arms, its silver knee and elbow horns glinting in the dim light against its tough, leathery skin. It seemed cramped in the kzin-sized doorway. A Kdatlyno would probably win a duel with a kzin, and she had to wonder how they'd been conquered, and how they stayed conquered.

The Kdatlyno ushered her down a stone flagged hallway to another room. She didn't like the looks of it: iron chains hung from the walls, and a large table of dark wood was in the center. A large, black-furred kzin was working with something on a long bench against the wall.

He turned around as she came in and the slave closed the door behind her.

"I am Ftzaal-Tzaatz." The kzin held up what looked to be a long, silver skewer.

"Good for you." There was a reflex to cringe, to cover her nakedness, but she resisted it and stood straight. *He isn't human anyway. Make him respect you for courage and you'll do better.*

"My new Telepath tells me your mind is closed to him." For the first time Ayla noticed another kzin, this one lying on a mat on the floor in what seemed to be a drug-induced stupor. "Why is this?"

"I don't know, why don't you tell me." Defiance wouldn't help, but it would keep her morale up. She noticed two more black-furred kzin, standing impassively in the shadows. *Will they eat me?* The thought was somehow more terrifying than the simple fact that she might die.

"Then I will enlighten you." Ftzaal was watching her intently. "There are three possibilities. One is simply that what Telepath says is true. Another is that someone is shielding your mind for you. The third is that Telepath can in fact read your mind and refuses to tell me what is in it."

"I can't help you with that."

"That is too bad. At first I believed that Telepath might be deceiving me." He looked at the prostrate figure. "I have worked diligently with him the last Hunter's Moon, and I no longer think this is possible. Telepath has become increasingly eager to know your mind, as I have encouraged him."

Cherenkova looked from the black kzin to the slumped

figure, uncomfortable with the stress he'd put on the word *encouraged*.

"That leaves the other two options." Ftzaal-Tzaatz continued. "I suspect the second is most likely true; your species is not noted for its telepathic prowess. Someone is protecting your mind. The question is, why?"

"I don't know. Why don't you find whoever that is and ask them."

The kzin ignored her barb. "I am going to ask you. You are about to face the Hot Needle of Inquiry. Be proud, this is a privilege rarely accorded to slaves."

"I'm not a slave, and neither is my species."

Ftzaal-Tzaatz flipped his ears, mildly amused. "I can tell you'll provide good sport in the hunt park."

"I'll have your pelt if you try it."

Ftzaal held up the skewer. "The Hot Needle is a technique perfected by the Hunt Priests, who are justifiably feared by the *kzintzag* for their skill in applying it. Unfortunately, it would be beneath the honor of a Hunt Priest to squander his talents on a lower animal, and so you will have to be content with my own inexpert attempt." The bench behind him held an array of similar skewers, some delicately small, some as large as climbing pitons.

"I don't have any information for you."

"That is unfortunate, because information is the goal of the Hot Needle. The beauty of the technique is that, while the pain is excruciating, there is no chance that the subject will die prematurely."

"Perish the thought." Ayla put all the spirit she had into it, but couldn't keep a quaver out of her voice.

"*Kz'zeerkti* anatomy is different, of course, but similar enough to ours that I think there will be only a few modifications necessary. I have read the references gained during the monkey wars. Your pain threshold is lower than ours, so care must be taken to prevent you from losing consciousness." Ftzaal swished his tail. "Acolytes!"

The two waiting black kzinti moved. She shrank back despite her decision not to flinch. They grabbed her impersonally, with enough strength that even attempting to struggle was impossible. A second later she was face down on the table, and the kzinti were strapping her ankles to the lower corners. Her arms were splayed wide and secured as well, as though she was about to be crucified, which might yet turn out to be true. The straps were designed for kzinti, and they had trouble cinching them tight enough to hold her securely, but when they were done she wasn't going anywhere.

"The needle cauterizes the flesh it penetrates." Ftzaal was still talking. "There is no chance of infection."

Infection? That was worrying, not because Kzinhome's microbes had shown any interest in her but because it implied she'd be there long enough that they had to take special precautions. Reflexively she struggled against her bonds, but she couldn't move. Ftzaal went to the bench and flipped switches. Intense blue flames leapt up, and in their light she could see that the array of skewers was arranged so their points and shafts would be heated red hot while their wooden handles stayed cool. Fear shot through her system. *I could give it up now, tell him I'll tell him everything and spin him plausible lies.* It would buy her time while he verified the truth, and perhaps he would never find out. She found she couldn't take her eyes off the skewers, their shafts already beginning to glow. For the first time she began to understand that he intended to break her. At the same time her fear fueled her defiance. Ftzaal had been serious when he said the Hot Needle was an honor. He was treating her as he would a warrior, a testimony to the damage she had inflicted on the Tzaatz. If she surrendered she would lose that hard won respect, she would become a slave in his eyes. As a warrior she could deal with him as an equal, as a slave she would probably wind up in a hunt park. Her survival depended on her resistance.

She could smell the hot metal now, and Ftzaal took a long, hot needle by its wooden handle and brought it to her. He brought his paw down on her right hip, and she could feel the radiated heat against her skin. She struggled and managed to generate enough movement that he couldn't slide the needle in with the precision he wanted.

"First Acolyte, take her leg. Second Acolyte, hold her waist." Ftzaal's commands were calm. Her small and temporary victory hadn't ruffled him at all. She felt their paws seizing her like velvet vises, with the faintest pressure of their needlelike claws on her skin to warn her of the consequences of further struggle. She felt Ftzaal's grip again, pulling the flesh out below her hip to make a target for the needle. First and Second Acolytes tightened their grip until she couldn't move at all, and Ftzaal put the needle through, slowly and deliberately. The pain, when it came, was excruciating and she screamed despite her resolve not to, muscles convulsing against the restraints. The point bit into the wooden surface and she was pinned there like a butterfly on a card. Slowly, too slowly, the pain faded to a pulsing throb.

"Now her lower limb." Again the acolytes immobilized her more completely than the straps could, exposing her right calf. Ftzaal selected another needle. Again she felt the heat as he brought it close, and then pain, sudden and burning, lanced through her as he slid it remorselessly into the muscle. She was ready for it this time, and screamed through gritted teeth as her muscles convulsed hard, but the black acolytes held her motionless.

She had expected the pain to come with questions, to be applied to punish resistance and withdrawn as a reward for cooperation. Ftzaal simply picked up another needle. She noticed his ears were folded tight against the volume of her cries. *At least he's suffering too.* Cherenkova took dark satisfaction in that thought, and resolved to scream as loud as she could. To her surprise Ftzaal ordered the straps removed from her ankles; they were no longer necessary. The strap was taken off her right wrist as well, and they positioned her right hand in front of her face. Ftzaal chose a shorter, more slender skewer to violate her here. *Why aren't they asking questions?* Again she screamed, her throat growing hoarse. She felt herself trembling, her body reacting with adrenaline and the need to fight or flee, but she could do neither.

More needles, smaller ones this time, staking her hand down through the web of her thumb and between her knuckle joints. Her hand became a single hot spot of pain and she could not help looking at it, bright dots of blood around the dimpled flesh where the needles stabbed in, and the disturbingly appetizing smell of her own flesh fried by the heat. She tugged frantically against the restraints still on her other arm, desperately motivated to pull out the impaling metal, to nurse her injuries, but the strap was unyielding, nor would the acolytes have allowed her an instant's respite had she somehow managed to pull it free. Ftzaal switched to the other side, and that hand was also released, positioned, and run through with the cruel steel needles, this time by her side, forcing her elbow awkwardly up into the air. The horrifying process continued, slowly and inexorably. Her left leg was drawn up until it was underneath her, skewers pinned through the sole of her foot between her metatarsals.

And still no questions. She was eager for them now, eager to be cooperative, if only they would remove the searing needles from her flesh. There was a roaring in her ears as waves of pain coursed through her body. Tiny needles slid under her fingernails, under her toenails; a larger one through the cartilage of her upper ear nailed her head to the wooden tabletop, leaving her staring permanently at her right hand. Her breath came in gasps and she felt dizzy. She let her eyes flutter closed to let the relentless pain carry her into unconsciousness and peace, but if she relaxed her body the needles in her hip and calf would tear out. She would have thought herself beyond caring about that, but her body's self-defensive reflex wouldn't allow it.

And all of a sudden she realized the subtle genius of the torture she was being put through. Enough pain would push any sentient being into unconsciousness, but by making her position deliberately awkward the Hot Needle of Inquiry forced her to stay awake to maintain it, and therefore fight the relentless pain. The asymmetry guaranteed that her mind would find nowhere to escape, short of final capitulation to her captors, or death, if she was that lucky. That was why there were no questions. The only goal of this stage of the inquisition was to break her, utterly, in the shortest possible time.

After what seemed like hours Ftzaal-Tzaatz finished. By then Ayla was beyond screaming, beyond resisting, each new penetration of her flesh barely registering against the burning agony which had enveloped her body. There were hundreds of needles, she'd lost track of them all, and it didn't matter anyway. She still had not begged for mercy, but only because she knew it would not come. Perhaps Ftzaal interpreted that as stubborn defiance, but if he did that didn't matter either.

He left, for a time, and she suffered while he was gone, straining to maintain the position that brought the least pain. He returned eventually, the time interval long enough that she grew to want sleep, but sleep was impossible. Strangely she didn't feel hungry, though she must have missed several meals. Her world space was strangely ethereal, as though she were drugged, and even the pain had somehow transformed itself into something else.

"Now, *kz'zeerkti*, we will discuss First-Son-of-Meerz-Rrit."

"I have no information for you."

"You lead raids for him. You lead kzinretti smart enough to plan and fight. I need to know about this."

"I am fighting for myself." *And if he's asking, then my kzinretti all got away.* It was a small victory. It lent her courage for what she knew would come. *I can win other victories here.*

"Hrrr." Ftzaal touched one of the needles in her arm, and the slight motion freshened the dulled pain back to agony. She gasped, eyes watering. "You are stubborn."

"I have nothing to tell you." The words came around deep breaths as she fought to control herself.

"Then tell me of his sister. She wasn't like other kzinretti, was she? She spoke and planned like a male."

"If you know, why ask me?"

"I need confirmation."

"His sister is dead." Ayla took some satisfaction in disappointing her captor.

"You didn't answer my question."

"I don't have any other information for you."

The Black Priest considered her at length. "Why do you maintain fealty to First-Son-of-Meerz-Rrit? You are *kz'zeerkti* and he is kzinti. War has come again; our species are enemies."

"I have my own honor to maintain."

"You hold your pledge to an enemy alien higher than loyalty to your species? I don't believe that." Again he touched a needle and she gasped.

"Believe what you want. I'll stand by my pledge." *How much more of this can I take?*

"Hrrr. Did you know your fleets are sterilizing kzinti worlds?"

"I had heard something like that."

"And this makes no difference to you?"

"I have my own war to fight. Against you, and your brother."

Ftzaal ran a soft paw over the handles of the rows of needles that skewered her left side from collar bone to thigh, provoking another scream. "My brother has an interesting mind. He is less bound by honor than most kzinti, even as you seem to hold yourself to a higher standard than the average *kz'zeerkti*."

Ayla remained silent. It took effort to answer, and she needed every ounce of strength to hold her position and withstand the new pain. The tiniest deviation from perfect stillness was excruciating, and she breathed in and out in short gasps in order to minimize the movement of her rib cage.

"This doesn't interest you?" She could hear the mocking tones in Ftzaal's voice. "It will interest you to know he has violated the Hunt Traditions, although I will add, not without severe provocation. Do you remember the razing of K'Shai, the world you call Wunderland?"

"It was . . ." The words hurt and Ayla took time to breathe before continuing. ". . . before my time."

"But you know of it, yes?"

"I've been to Thor's Crater." Pause, breath. "And others."

"Hrrr. You are a savage species. The galaxy has more to fear from you than us, but we are sentients too. We can learn what you teach us, and you have taught us much. The use of fusion drives as weapons, for example, and interstellar communications lasers. Those were the first lessons. We have learned the use of relativistic weapons too, and how easy it is to destroy a world if you don't desire to conquer it later."

A sudden thrill of adrenaline shot through Ayla, momentarily overriding the pain. "You haven't . . ."

"Yes, we have." Ftzaal's mouth relaxed into a fanged smile. "Even now our attack ship is in hyperspace to your singularity with enough lightspeed impactors on board to flay your homeworld bare. My brother intends to end this war."

"You wouldn't do that. Tradition won't allow it." Even as she said them Ayla's words rang hollow in her own ears. Kefan Brasseur had taught her the power of tradition in *kzinti* affairs, but her own experience told her that power was not absolute. The Tzaatz especially were prone to bend ideals to expediency.

"Is it any different than what humans are doing to kzinti worlds right now? Our traditions demand that we conquer, not destroy, but honor demands vengeance." He paused letting it sink in. "I have a bargain to offer you, Cherenkova-Captain. It is a generous one, in the circumstances."

"I don't want it."

"You may not want it yet, but you will soon. I disagree with my brother's methods, and I disagree with his assessment of priorities. I see no need to destroy your species when we could do so much more with you in partnership. My interest lies entirely in First-Son-of-Meerz-Rrit, and the Telepath War and the line of Vda."

"I don't know what you're talking about." The words hurt to say.

Ftzaal rippled his ear. "Yes, you do. I also know about it, in some detail. I know how they have hidden from the Black Cult for so many generations. It is unfortunate for them they have chosen to throw their lot in with First-Son; before that the priesthood had little idea they existed.

I had my own suspicions. The telepath gene has not gone extinct in eight-to-the-fourth generations of vigilant culling, nor have the genes of the reasoning kzinrette. There had to be a natural reservoir somewhere. Even I did not suspect the full truth, though in retrospect it seems so clear. Where else could such a line exist but on Kzinhome? Where else on Kzinhome but in the jungles, among the *czrav* who live beneath the notice of the Patriarchy? Such facts as I could divine I raised to Priest-Master-Zrtra, but the Priest-Master would not hear them, nor would the Black High Circle."

"How frustrating for you."

"Perhaps, but that time is over. The Black Cult will not be able to deny the evidence I present to them, and they will thank me for exterminating in a season what they could not since the time before time. I will rule the High Circle, if I can keep my incompetent brother from destroying the Patriarchy beforehand."

"At least we agree on something." She spat the words, and the defiance cost in waves of pain.

Ftzaal rippled his ears, amused. "I think we will agree on a bargain very shortly. Here is what I offer. Tell me where to find First-Son-of-Meerz-Rrit and I will tell you the launch coordinates and trajectory information for the ship that will destroy your world. Nothing less will save your world, Cherenkova-Captain. In addition, I will send you back to your Earth in a fast courier. You, and you alone, can save your species."

Ayla remained silent, gritting her teeth. *Billions of lives are at stake.* How could she know he was telling the truth? How could she be sure he would keep his end of

the bargain if he was? *He is kzinti, his honor is his life.*
She had learned that honor could be a slippery concept,
even among kzinti. *But he is more than kzinti, he is a*
warrior. She didn't want to believe it because she didn't
want to face the choice she was now facing, but she knew
in her heart of hearts that Ftzaal-Tzaatz was telling the
truth. Earth would be destroyed if they weren't given the
information necessary to intercept the impactors, and
Ftzaal-Tzaatz would give her that information and send
her home to give warning if she gave him what he was
asking for. *But I cannot betray Pouncer.* The pain didn't
make it any easier to think.

Ftzaal held up another red hot needle, looking over her
body as if deciding where to place it. "This is a generous
offer, Cherenkova-Captain. I will give you some time to
consider it." For a long moment he waited while she
breathed in and out, trying not to anticipate the pain she
knew her lack of cooperation was about to bring. Finally
he put the needle down in front of her close enough that
she could feel the heat of the glowing shaft on her face. It
was a warning that there was more to come if she didn't
make the right decision. He turned to the acolytes.
"Watch her. Make sure she remains alive."

"As you command, sire." Ayla barely registered the
words; the pain was reasserting itself over her consciousness. She was still coherent enough to be startled when,
seconds later, Ftzaal opened his robe and urinated on her,
the hot stream splashing over her body, burning where it
ran over the needle wounds. In spite of herself she gasped
in pain anew, fighting the urge to struggle that would only
make it hurt more. *He is scent-marking me, to let the others*

know I'm his property. It was a protective gesture, to keep the acolytes from becoming careless with his prize, but she found it degrading anyway. *This means he will be gone longer than before, perhaps much longer.* Sleep deprivation and hunger would soon start to erode her will to resist, even her will to survive. Ftzaal left and the acolytes faded into the darkness, leaving her alone with her torture. She would not weep, but her eyes were bright with tears. She could only wait for it to be over. Some timeless time later, in the twilight world of consciousness enforced over sleep by pain, she thought she saw a herd of *tuskvor* surging over a kill drop, as she had dreamed a lifetime ago coming over the high mountain passes on the *czrav* migration, only this time it was not Pouncer but Quacy Tskombe who leapt to save her, and this time she could not fly to save them both.

> *The greatest illusion is the illusion of control.*
> —Kzin-Conserver-of-the-reign-of-Vstari-Rrit

The broadleaf trees gave pleasant shade to the Sundial Grove. Kzin-Conserver sat on the grass beside a bench, performing the Eight Variations of Honor in his mind. The tranquillity of spirit he had felt in his days as Rrit-Conserver was increasingly eluding him. *I am a slave to events, and events are not tranquil.* He controlled his breathing, and focused on the discipline.

"Kzin-Conserver." It was Ftzaal-Tzaatz. Kzin-Conserver abandoned the sixth variation, took a moment to steady his mind before opening his eyes to greet the Black Priest.

"I would walk with you, Conserver."

"As you wish." Kzin-Conserver rose and together they headed on the path that led from the grove back to the Citadel. A Tzaatt patrol mounted on *rapsar* raiders went past, and Ftzaal said nothing until they were alone again.

"We still fight the Honor-War we declared when we took this fortress. First-Son-of-Meerz-Rrit has become a formidable enemy."

"For a time I think you thought you had won your honor-duel."

"My brother was convinced. I was not."

"And now?"

Ftzaal turned a paw over. "The storm is gathering. I can sense it. Now it is my brother who is unconvinced." He paused. "You favor the Rrit in this."

"Second-Son is Rrit as well. You mean that I favor Zree-Rrit over the puppet of the Tzaatt."

"Of course."

"When I was Rrit-Conserver, I favored the Rrit over the Tzaatt, and yes, First-Son over Second-Son for reasons of both tradition and character. Now it is not my place to favor one side or the other. I only pass judgment on adherence to the Traditions, and give guidance to the other Senior Conservers."

"And give advice to the Patriarch."

"When he asks for it."

"Scrral-Rrit has changed since the Hot Needle."

Conserver rippled his ears. "I have noticed."

"Hrrr." Ftzaal's tail lashed. "He is still unworthy of the title he bears."

"His future carries the stain of his past."

"And despite your neutrality you favor his brother in this challenge."

"I favor no one, which does not mean I have no judgment. Zree-Rrit has shown himself honorable so far. He is the elder brother and so entitled by blood to be Patriarch. For these and other reasons I believe he will serve the Patriarchy better than his brother."

And my brother. Ftzaal started to say it and didn't. He remained silent until they reached the bank of the Quickwater. On the other bank the Citadel wall rose straight up, its coppery surface glinting in the light of high noon. They turned to parallel it. "There are ships in orbit now. Churrt Pride and Vdar Pride and Dcrz Pride, and others."

"I have heard."

"They tell my brother they have come in case the *kz'zeerkti* come, to defend Kzinhome."

"And you believe differently?"

"I do not believe Zraa-Churrt would dishonor himself with untruth. They are here for the reason they have given. I believe there is a further truth. They have come to bear witness to *skalazaal.*"

"Perhaps. You have overstepped the traditions, though no one has proof-before-the-pride-circle. The Great Prides fear this more than anything." Kzin-Conserver looked to the fields beyond the Citadel's northern wall, where a formation of lumbering assault *rapsari* were going through their paces. "You are expecting a battle. Your forces are growing stronger every day."

"I have committed everything I can to the defense of this fortress. This is the critical point. My brother believes we must protect Jotok, but it is here we will stand or fall."

"Against the *kz'zeerkti* or against First-Son?"

"Against both." Ftzaal paused again. "If First-Son comes here, he will die. If he does not come here . . ." Ftzaal's lips twitched away from his fangs. "I will rake out his hiding place soon."

"You have put his *kz'zeerkti* female to the Hot Needle."

Ftzaal's ears swiveled up. "You have good ears to have heard that."

"When you are Kzin-Conserver you hear many things. I have also heard the *kz'zeerkti* are in hyperspace to our singularity. I have not heard how your brother intends to deal with them."

"He has given command to Ktronaz-Commander."

They walked in silence for awhile, then stopped to watch a squad of Kdatlyno who were setting long metal spikes in a freshly dug defensive ditch. Kzin-Conserver turned to the Black Priest. "Why do you follow your brother?"

"I am his *zar'ameer.*"

"Even when he violates the traditions?"

Ftzaal started to speak, stopped, started again. "It is not for the sword to question the paw that wields it." His voice held an edge.

"You had a question for me."

Ftzaal shook himself angrily. "No. I have answered it for myself." The Black Priest turned and walked back the way he had come.

Kzin-Conserver watched him go. *Events are beyond his control now, and his brother's, and mine.* He looked up at the sky, where the ships of eight Great Prides were circling invisibly, defense against the *kz'zeerkti* fleet which would inevitably arrive to scour Kzinhome, defense against the temptation for Kchula-Tzaatz to use energy weapons against Pouncer in his War-of-Honor. Each of those Great Prides would be pursuing its own interests too, interests that were now starting to tear the Patriarchy apart. Stability, that sacred goal of the Circle of Conservers, was long gone. *I have failed in my responsibility.* It didn't help that he knew there was no way he could have succeeded. It was too late by far to save the Patriarchy he had been born into; perhaps it was too late to save it in any form at all. He thought back to the last Great Pride Circle. Stability had seemed so close then. At the time he had no idea how violently the apparent path of history would be diverted. *The storm is gathering, and this time I know it. The question is, when will it strike?*

> *Seize the critical moment and the battle is yours.*
> —Si-Rrit

It was time. Pouncer climbed aboard the *tsvasztet* strapped to the huge herd-grandmother. Ferlitz-Telepath was already there, and Tskombe-*kz'zeerkti* and the Trina manrette, and Swift-Claw, Z'slee and Night-Prowler, acting now as his personal bodyguards. He looked across to the other beasts, where V'rli had Ztrak Pride marshaled, and where Czor-Dziit led Dziit Pride. The other *czrav* prides were farther back in the herd; the honor of the fore went to those who had fought with him the longest.

But they are all here! The *czrav* army was eight-to-the-sixth strong, eight-cubed prides and sub-prides, half eight-to-the-fifth *tuskvor*, the beasts armored and armed, articulated assault ladders on their necks and heavy weapons on their backs so they could serve as living siege towers at the walls of the Citadel of the Patriarch. His Heroes were trained to a standard even Guardmaster would be proud of, confident and ready for battle. He looked up into the darkening sky, streaked bloodred as the last rays of sunset lit the clouds from the western horizon. *And they will have blood themselves, soon enough.* Up there were Kzinhome's orbital fortresses, capable of wiping out his entire force in heartbeats. *Today is the supreme gamble.* The Tzaatz knew something was happening; his spies had told him that. The Great Prides were watching overhead. Skalazaal *will be declared and open for all to witness.* Kzin-Conserver who had been Rrit-Conserver would ensure that it was. Kchula-Tzaatz might yet decide to wipe out the threat to his rule with lances of fire from space. He would not do it with impunity.

And he will not do it yet. The weather was overcast and they would move at night. The Tzaatz did not know of the force assembled against them, would not know until it was too late. *Or so I hope.* The Telepaths had searched the minds of their enemies for knowledge of the coming onslaught, but even they could not see everything. There were too many risks in an operation this size, too many loose ends to control them all.

Another kzin climbed aboard, a kzinrette. *C'mell!*

"You should not be here!" He spoke before she could.

"I should not be anywhere else." She leapt easily to the front of the travel platform, moved to the tiller bar where Night-Prowler was. The other silently gave way to her.

"Where are the kits?"

"They are with M'mewr." Expertly C'mell unhooked the tiller bar from its restraints and tightened up the harness lines. Their *tuskvor* snorted in response to the pressure but didn't balk.

"They need their mother. C'mell . . ." he started to reason.

"And their father." She waved a paw. "Who will make sure you are safe if I don't?" She pulled the bar back to raise the beast's head. It grunted and started to move. "And now it is too late for me to leave."

Their beast lumbered forward and he started to argue. Already the other *tuskvor* were starting to move with them, the vast herd reacting like a single living organism, gathering momentum. C'mell pulled on the bar to haul the huge head around to set their direction. South! To the mountains and down through the passes, through the northern valleys and into the Plain of Stgrat, to the heart of the Patriarchy, to the Citadel, to battle and to destiny.

I am committed. Pouncer abandoned his argument. Around him the herd picked up speed. The great beast swayed beneath him. There was no need to give any other order. That quickly the plan was in motion. He moved to the side of the travel platform and looked out into the gathering darkness. Strangely, he felt as if a great weight had been lifted from his shoulders. *Now we travel, and my work is done until the battle begins.* Those he had trained were now acting on their own, carrying out the well prepared plan. He looked to the back of the *tsvasztet* where Battle Captain of Ccree Pride hunched over the combat console with headphones on. Ccree Pride's experts had isolated the Tzaatz command bands. Even without breaking the enemy crypting they would be able to identify enemy units, and with the consoles carried on every command *tuskvor*, they would be able to triangulate and know their positions. The *czrav* had vocom too, but they wouldn't use it until the final stages of the battle, when the total security of telepathy was less important than the speed and flexibility of direct vocom. On top of dens scattered through the high forest, jammers would be switching on to delicately confound the ground scanners on the orbital fortresses, while overhead *Black Saber's* sensors watched the Tzaatz forces for the first sign that the *czrav* advance had been detected. Inevitably it *would* be discovered, despite deception and camouflage and countermeasures. It was impossible to move such a vast force in stealth, but with luck and the Fanged God's favor they would be through the bottleneck of the mountain passes and into the Plain of Stgrat by then, where it would be much harder for the Tzaatz to mount a defense.

On the other side of the travel platform Quacy Tskombe paced, worried. The only way they were going to get Ayla back from the Tzaatz was to take the Citadel, he knew that. *But what will they do with her when the attack starts?* They could kill her on a whim, or as a last-second vengeance for their defeat. *Or the attack could fail.*

He turned to Ferlitz-Telepath, unable to keep himself from asking the question again. "How is Ayla?"

Tolerantly Ferlitz looked away, closed his eyes, concentrating. Tskombe saw the pain cross his face and flinched. After a time Ferlitz looked at him again. "She is still alive, still in pain."

"Can you tell her we're coming?"

"It is still too far, and too large a risk if she knows."

Tskombe breathed in, breathed out. "I know, I know." He looked out into the gathering darkness, listening to the relentless rumble of the *czrav* army's advance. *Hang on, Ayla, I'm coming.* Trina came to stand beside him. *Now she is the one who comforts me.* He sat down on the *prrstet* and concentrated on the next phase of the advance. Morning should see them at the northern foothills, the following evening should see them starting the ascent through the passes. The passes were the critical point, and they needed to get through them in darkness.

"Ferlitz, how are our guides?"

Again the telepath closed his eyes, this time reaching for the minds of the scouts pre-positioned along the planned route, and along alternate routes as well in case something forced them to change plans. This time he was lost in the mind-trance for a long time, sometimes muttering to himself. Tskombe himself got flashes of images, a high mountain meadow still sunlit as the lower elevations were not, a river crossing seen from a nearby hill, a camouflaged hiding place beneath a burstflower bush. *Ferlitz is sharing what the scouts see.* Along with the images came a sense of rightness and safety. So far there were no ambushes. *But we have only begun.* It would take three days to ride from the passes to the Citadel, and it was certain battle would be joined before they got there.

The night passed uneventfully. There was a rotation set up between them, so someone would always be awake to watch the combat console, but he and Pouncer weren't part of it. They would alternate, unless there was a battle, in which case the kzin would lead and Tskombe would make sure he got the information he needed. Quacy was surprised to have so much of Pouncer's trust so quickly, but it seemed he was simply stepping into Ayla's shoes as *kz'zeerkti zar'ameer. She has done a lot here.* His thoughts returned to her again unbidden, and he pushed them away. *She needs me to be strong now, to do my job to get her out.* Eventually exhaustion overcame him and he slept, rocked asleep by the steady swaying of their *tuskvor.* Fitful dreams made his slumber far from restful, but it was welcome all the same.

Dawn found them in the foothills, as expected, and there was no sign the Tzaatz had noticed their presence, either in the telepathically gathered reports of the scouts or in the imagery downlinked from *Black Saber.* Tskombe grew tense as the sun rose in a cloudless sky, leaving them vulnerable to the sensors of the orbital fortresses and the Tzaatz ships in orbit, but they continued on their way unmolested. The interference the *czrav* were beaming skyward was subtle, so as not to give the game away. It was possible to laser-jam the optical sensors as well, but that too-obvious measure had to wait until the battle was joined. The vast *tuskvor* herd was too big to simply escape notice, but the camouflaged *tsvasztet* on their backs might, and the Tzaatz didn't know enough about the beast's migratory patterns to realize how unusual their movement south was at this time of year. Darkness came again and they were climbing into the passes. *A few more hours is all we need.* Tskombe managed to avoid asking Ferlitz-Telepath about Ayla again. The Gifted kzin was spending nearly all his time in the mind-trance now, relaying messages, checking on the advance scouts, searching out the minds of Tzaatz commanders, still too far away to read clearly.

We should have brought another telepath. He had known that from the beginning, but every commander in the force needed a telepath to communicate with his or her command, and even among the *czrav* there weren't enough to go around. The air grew cooler as they climbed through the passes, and by midnight the lead elements were on their way down again. The Plain of Stgrat lay open before them. *We're through.* For the first time since they'd started he allowed himself to relax, and he slept again, dead to the world.

He was awakened by Trina shaking him. "Hey! They've started fighting."

He rolled off the *prrstet.* War seemed was no different from peace; the rumble of the herd went on unchanged. *But that will change soon.* He went back to the combat console, where Pouncer was conferring with Battle Captain.

Pouncer looked up. "The scouts found a Tzaatz *rapsar* patrol. I tasked V'rli with eliminating it."

"Results?"

"We will know soon."

Tskombe studied the display. The advance of the *czrav* army was a red tide across the map, the last elements still pouring through the passes of the Long Range, the lead elements spreading out into a broad frontal advance. A blue icon marked the Tzaatz patrol, no doubt from the garrison at Skragga Pride's ancestral estate. Advance elements of Ztrak Pride were already assigned to deal with that garrison, but now they were chasing down the patrol.

"I'm getting code bursts." Battle Captain's voice was tight. "They don't seem to be getting an answer."

"Hrrr. We need our surprise to last longer."

Ferlitz-Telepath, still deep in the mind-trance, stirred. "Blood . . . they leap . . ." After a moment his eyes flickered open. "V'rli reports success. We have no losses."

There was a collective release of tension. *The first obstacle is clear.* Tskombe knew better than to relax. *We were lucky. It will get harder.* He looked to Trina, who seemed to be fascinated by the entire venture. *Will her luck keep her safe?* He no longer doubted she had it, he only wondered if it would last.

His beltcomp said an hour had passed when Pouncer ordered the main force to stop. V'rli's unit advanced by itself to take on the Tzaatz garrison that stood guard over Skragga Pride. Ferlitz-Telepath watched the battle through the minds of the combatants, and again he shared the images with Tskombe. *Two Tzaatz guards on rapsar raiders, bored and tired, the rest of the garrison asleep. Suddenly a huge shape looms from the darkness, a tuskvor, the ground shaking beneath its footfalls. Sudden fear, the rapsari bucking and turning to run, a huge head swinging down, tusks spreading gore, and the herd moves through, pop-domes crushed underfoot, fear and confusion, dark shapes with variable swords dropping from the flanks of the tuskvor to slice out the lifeblood of anything they find, a rapsar sniffer running in panic, a huge foot coming down, and angry bellows echoing from the distant valley walls.*

That quickly it was over. Victory in the darkness; the Tzaatz hadn't known what hit them.

"I have an uplink signal." Battle Captain's words were clipped.

"What? Where?" Pouncer scanned the combat display. A blue icon appeared, deeper into Skragga Pride territory.

Tskombe shook his head. "The scouts missed an outpost."

Pouncer's tail lashed. "Battle Captain, jam the signal. Ferlitz, relay that to V'rli. Have her destroy it at once."

Battle Captain's paws flew over his board, isolating the signal for jamming. "There is a downlink." He paused while he checked readouts. "Our surprise advantage is gone."

"We knew we'd lose it soon." Still, Tskombe was disappointed. They had a long way to go, and now the Tzaatz would have days to prepare their defenses. Ztrak Pride closed on the previously unknown enemy and destroyed them too, and he dared hope that the message from the doomed outpost might get lost between the orbital fortress and the Citadel. Pouncer ordered the advance resumed as the first rays of dawn shone over the eastern horizon. *Days blend into each other in combat, I'd forgotten that.* How many other lessons would he have to learn anew? Hopefully not many. *And none critical.* He couldn't resist asking Ferlitz how Ayla was again, though he knew the Tzaatz would not execute her, if that's what they were going to do, until the last possible moment. He got the same answer as before. *She's alive, that's all that matters.*

In the early light of dawn the army was an impressive

sight, the herd spread out from horizon to horizon in battle array. In the high forest the trees were taller than the *tuskvor* and it had been impossible to gain a sense of the immensity of this vast, living fleet. C'mell and Swift-Claw traded places on the tiller bar. Night-Prowler prepared dried meat while Z'slee checked her weapon yet another time. Life on their cramped, moving world continued unaffected by the violence and death at the front of the formation, kilometers in front of them. *Our turn will come soon enough.*

The sun was barely up when the first gravcar came over. It came fast and high, well out of range of any hand weapons. It zoomed over the length and breadth of the herd and then vanished again without slowing down. *At least they didn't start shooting.* Tskombe had little trust in the restraint of the Tzaatz, if only because he had little himself. *If I saw this herd coming toward me I would use every weapon I could lay hands on.*

Battle Captain immediately started reporting crypted transmissions from the gravcar and identifying enemy positions by their answers. The orbital fortresses started downlinking, probably sending imagery.

Tskombe smiled, imagining the consternation in the Patriarch's Tower. "Jammers to full," he ordered. *Kchula-Tzaatz must have known something was coming.* It seemed unlikely that he could have understood the scale until he saw it. *The question now is, what will the response be?*

The response wasn't long in coming. A phalanx of gravcars came in low and fast. As they swept over arrows rained from their back compartments, fired by Tzaatz warriors who crouched low to take advantage of the cover of their sides. Tskombe held his breath as they swooped in and ducked behind the *tsvasztet*'s side. He needn't have bothered; the gravcars were moving too fast for effective shooting and all the arrows went wide.

The Tzaatz learned from that and the next pass was slower, the fire more accurate, but the *czrav* were prepared, and heavy ballista rounds arced into the air from the back of *tsvasztet* specially modified to carry them. It seemed a waste of effort—no weapon driven by spring tension could throw a projectile hard enough to penetrate cerametal—but to his surprise one of the gravcars was suddenly yanked from the air, as though an invisible giant had swatted it down.

"Nets." Pouncer had followed his gaze. "Monomolecular filament nets trailing the leader rounds. The other ends are attached to boulders."

As Tskombe watched, another ballista fired and caught a car, and this time he could see the heavy stones yanked hard from the back of the *tsvasztet*, though he still couldn't see the monofilament. The sudden load was too much for the gravcar's polarizers and it pitched forward, its own momentum driving it into the ground. It tumbled and broke up on impact, but warriors from the next *tuskvor* in line still leapt to the ground to see what they could kill.

The gravcars circled wide after that, but staying out of ballista range put them out of effective arrow range as well. It was a standoff.

"It was the Cherenkova-Captain's idea." Pouncer's ears were up and forward as he watched the duel, and Tskombe noticed anew that half of the left one was missing. *He is battle-scarred.* Tskombe looked forward, past where C'mell was again steering their *tuskvor.* The gravcars flew off in that direction. *So far so good, and the Tzaatz aren't using energy weapons.*

Dziit Pride overran another Tzaatz garrison later that day with little more effort than it had taken Ztrak Pride the previous night. *Black Saber* downlinked imagery showing their route. It was surprisingly empty of resistance, but that anomaly was explained when he sent down the area around the Citadel. The Tzaatz had decided to make their stand there, using the natural defenses of the river backed by the fortress. The imagery was full of ranked assault *rapsari,* some almost the size of *tuskvor.* The difficult wooded areas were patrolled by raiders and packs of the vicious harriers. *So the battle will be joined there.* Darkness fell with little further action, though gravcars continued to circle and harass them. The night grew cold beneath ice-hard stars and he tried unsuccessfully to sleep on the steadily rocking *prrstet.* He could hear Pouncer working with Ferlitz to identify the thoughts of enemy commanders. There was consternation and even fear among the Tzaatz, but mostly there was confidence, and Tskombe had the uneasy realization that the Tzaatz telepaths would also be searching out his mind to learn Pouncer's battle plans. The *czrav* telepaths back in the dens should have been blocking his thoughts, but he called up Beethoven's Sixth Symphony in his mind anyway. It would help him relax and make it hard for the enemy to learn the *czrav* strategy in case the blocking didn't work.

From Ferlitz they learned that Ftzaal-Tzaatz had taken

personal command of the battle. The knowledge was the source of the confidence with which the Tzaatz awaited the attackers, but by the time sleep finally claimed Tskombe, Ferlitz hadn't managed to read the Black Priest's thoughts. A judicious dose of *sthondat* extract had failed to help, though it had put Ferlitz deeply into the mind-trance. Morning arrived, seemingly an eyeblink later. Dawn was bloodred as 61 Ursae Majoris climbed over the eastern horizon, and there was something else, a scent in the air like wood smoke. Instinctively his hand went to his side where his respirator should have been hanging. A long forgotten voice from the Infantry School spoke in his head. *In the event of a gas attack you will have nine seconds to don the respirator.* The inhaled dose of cycloserasine necessary to kill a warm blooded being was so low you could count the molecules individually, and if you could actually smell its warm, inviting odor you would be dead before your next breath if you hadn't already injected the antidote. *What do the rules of honor say about war gases?* He held his breath but he wasn't wearing UN battle armor and he had no respirator and he recognized the ridiculousness of an act that might extend his life another forty seconds. The herd surged forward indifferently and no one else on the *tsvasztet* died in twitching convulsions. He breathed out and breathed in, and another red glow beyond dawn on the horizon warned of the true nature of the threat. The grasslands were burning ahead of them. The Tzaatz had set the savannah on fire to disrupt the herd.

"Even now the Tzaatz tread the edge of honor." Pouncer had come up beside him, leaning forward to assess the red glow. It stretched across the horizon, reflected from the clouds overhead.

"As long as they don't cross the line." Tskombe paused. "How are we going to deal with that?"

"Hrrr. Ferlitz-Telepath has known the minds of our route scouts. There are places the fire has died down. *Tuskvor* can cross fire, if it is not too serious."

"No." Tskombe shook his head. "The Tzaatz will use lasers from orbit to restart the fire in our path, no matter which path we take."

"What do you suggest then?"

"Counterburning. We start our own fires along the route we want, burn everything we can, and advance over the ashes." Tskombe looked to the sky. "*Black Saber* can do that for us." He paused, realizing the dangers inherent in his strategy. "And then we pray for rain."

Pouncer turned a paw over, considering. "I concur." He turned to Battle Captain. "You heard?"

"Yes, sire."

"Give the order to *Black Saber*. We remain on the primary route."

"As you command." Battle Captain keyed his console and spoke into it, then looked up. "Sire? *Black Saber* is targeting now. Night Pilot sends a message."

Pouncer fanned his ears up. "What is it."

"Scoutships falling in from the singularity. The *kz'zeerkti* fleet has arrived."

"Hrrr." He traded a glance with Tskombe. "We may yet die at the moment of victory."

"I can talk to them, get them to wait until we can finish our battle. They might even land troops to support us."

"No!" Pouncer slashed his claws in the air. "This is *skalazaal.* I will not give the Tzaatz excuse to accuse me of using a prey species in battle. You may talk to them after we win, not before."

Tskombe looked at him. *Prey species* . . . He let the point go, mentally calculating drop time from the singularity's edge. *We'll only get one chance to win.* After that the human fleet would attack in their now well rehearsed pattern, and the globe shaking detonations of conversion warheads would erase civilization on Kzinhome. *And I will die, and Ayla* . . . That was a thought he didn't want to think.

A brilliant blue-green line stabbed out of the sky ahead of them, the colors almost too pure to be real, the visible signature of an invisible gamma ray laser beam fired from orbit, powerful enough to strip the electrons from the oxygen and nitrogen in its path to produce the ionization glow. Dirt fountained where the beam touched the ground, ringed by flame and followed half a second later by a thunderclap report as the superheated column of ions shocked the quiet air around it. Tskombe blinked, the dazzling afterimage of the laser burned onto his retina. For an instant he thought Night Pilot had misunderstood and *Black Saber* was firing on them, but no mere freighter could mount weapons that could hit like that from orbit. The beams were the main armament of an orbital fortress. The Tzaatz had grown impatient. The dry savannah crackled as the fire took hold and the flames rose up. More beams stabbed downward and the flames grew and merged, until they were a wall of fire ten meters high. He swallowed hard. A direct hit by one of those beams would vaporize a *tuskvor*, and the Tzaatz could, if they chose, drag their target lines through the vast herd as easily as a child could fingerpaint. Thick black smoke swirled up, choking him and stinging his eyes, and their *tuskvor* bellowed. Others answered it throughout the herd as C'mell struggled with the tiller bar and snarled a stream of unintelligible curses as she tried to keep the beast on course. The Tzaatz might have hoped to stop the herd with the vast grass fires set ahead of its advance; now they were trying to destroy it outright by setting the fires all around them. *They're getting closer to the edge of honor. We have them scared.* That was a less reassuring thought than it might have been.

More beams stabbed down and the fires grew around them. Any other herd animal would have panicked and stampeded, but the Tzaatz hadn't reckoned with the power of the *tuskvor*'s migration instinct. The heat grew intense, even high up on the *tsvasztet*, but the advance continued, the booming bellows of the herd rising up over the crackle of flame. Their own *tuskvor* snorted and bucked as it charged through a wall of flame that roared up in front of them like a living thing bent on consuming them whole. Tskombe threw himself flat on the floor of the *tsvasztet* and held his breath while flame licked around their sides, and then they were through. C'mell, her fur singed black in patches, was still hanging on to the tiller bar while Pouncer, Z'slee and Swift-Claw had leapt to extinguish half a dozen minor fires that had started on the *tsvasztet* itself. Something big crashed into the platform and it jolted sideways, almost spilling him to the burning ground. Another *tuskvor*, blinded by flames and bellowing in pain, had collided with theirs. The *tsvasztet* on its back was an inferno, and as he watched a kzin leapt from it, his fur burning hard enough to turn him into a living fireball. The kzin landed hard, and badly, rolling and screaming in pain, an unearthly wail that penetrated straight to Tskombe's hindbrain. The injured *tuskvor* lurched back the other way and fell sideways, crushing the critically wounded warrior and cutting off the sound. The massive beast thrashed its limbs, bellowing as the fire swept around it, but it wasn't going to be getting up. Tskombe grabbed the rail of the *tsvasztet* and looked around, breathed out in relief to see the surging armada emerge from the smoke and flames, despite the new gaps in the ranks.

He suddenly became aware of an absence. *Trina!* He looked around frantically and didn't see her. *Her luck has failed.* He cursed himself for relying on such an ephemeral shield as statistical improbability, his throat tightening in response to feelings he couldn't afford to show in battle.

Two hands, and she was clambering over the edge of the travel platform. His eyes met hers, traveled over the edge to where a burned-through securing line was retied. If she hadn't done that, the whole platform might have slid off the *tuskvor*'s back on the next severe jolt. His gaze went back to hers, gratitude expressed with a glance. On the horizon ahead more flames glowed as the counter fires set by *Black Saber*'s beams surged against the firestorm ignited by the Tzaatz. A vast wall of smoke stretched up into the sky, the convection triggering cumulus clouds which built higher and higher as they rode inexorably toward a scene that looked like some medieval version of the gates of hell. The beam strikes from heaven stopped as suddenly as they had begun.

"Tell Vlorz Pride to shift to the northern route. They will come down on the far side of the Quickwater. Dziit Pride is to move to the reserve position." Pouncer was beside Ferlitz, again commanding the battle, ignoring the danger they had just come through

Tskombe searched the skies, knowing with an old soldier's instincts that the pause was only the harbinger of another form of attack. Within minutes a squadron of gravcars swept over in close formation. These were armed with heavier, longer-ranged ballista. They concentrated their fire on a single *tuskvor*. Most of the shafts bounced off its mag-armored flanks, but a few found their way into gaps in the articulation. The huge beast bellowed in pain and fell, writhing, crushing its *tsvasztet* and throwing its occupants to the ground. Some of the scurrying figures escaped, perhaps to be picked up by a following *tuskvor*; some were struck down as the *tuskvor* shuddered through its death agony. Answering bolts flew up from the *czrav*, dragging down more attackers with their monofilament nets, but the Tzaatz were willing to fight now, as they had not been before, and the battle broke up into a dozen or more skirmishes. The fighting lasted an hour and cost them four *tuskvor* that Quacy could see, many more that he could not, according to the reports flowing in through Ferlitz-Telepath.

More gravcars appeared, combat carriers and tanks with polarizers too powerful to be overloaded with the boulder laden nets, and the rain of arrows intensified. Tskombe could only watch, powerless as *tuskvor* after *tuskvor* inexorably fell. The rules of honor would have allowed him to carry an energy weapon, and a magrifle like the one he had carried in the escape from the Citadel so long ago would serve admirably to engage the gravcars, but he didn't have one. Neither the Tzaatz nor the orbiting ships that served as witness to the conduct of the Honor-war would know the fire came from an alien exempt from the rules, and he had no wish to provide the enemy with an excuse to bring their vastly superior firepower to bear. The advance swept on, but the gaps in the ranks were getting larger. Ferlitz-Telepath was in the mind-trance continually now. Pouncer consulted Battle Captain's plot board, updated now with intelligence Ferlitz had gleaned from the minds of the enemy commanders.

"Tell Kralar Pride there are positions in front of him. He is to engage and fall back, pin them in place. The remainder of the force is to follow Vlorz Pride."

Ferlitz echoed the words in a whisper. The entire force changed course now, following the northern route now being swept by Vlorz Pride, avoiding a series of *rapsar*-reinforced defensive positions that Ferlitz had discovered in the minds of the warriors waiting to spring the trap. The trap would be inverted now: the forces the Tzaatz had committed to ambush would be tied down and useless for the main defense of the Citadel.

Something flashed overhead, and Tskombe looked up in time to see a gravcar. Trina turned at the same instant and a crystal iron ballista shaft flew past her ear. Tskombe had a momentary flashback to the time he'd thrown the *nyalzeri* egg at her. Behind her, Ferlitz-Telepath was on his back, very still, pinned to the floor with the shaft through his temple. He would know no more minds. Tskombe saw Trina's eyes widen with fear at what had nearly happened, and he went to her, took her to the front of the travel platform to look forward.

Behind them Pouncer knelt by the body, going through the motions of emergency first aid, but there was no hope. He looked up in despair. *My communications are severed at the critical moment.* The advancing army was changing formation, and vulnerable in that moment without his direction. The Tzaatz would be reacting to the change, and he needed to know the minds of their commanders. He lashed his tail, angry at himself. *I was a fool to take just one telepath.* But keeping two for himself would have meant depriving one of his other commanders of one, a decision that could be equally dangerous in a different set of circumstances.

He looked around at his army, saw the orders he needed to issue. *There is one way.* He went to Ferlitz-Telepath's travelpack, drew out a small, clear vial full of black, oily fluid. *The sthondat extract. I am full brother to Patriarch's Telepath. The Gift is latent in my genes.* He opened the vial. The extract smelled bitter, and Pouncer contemplated it a long time as the battle around him seemed to slow down, time compressing until the moment contained only the vial and himself and the decision he was about to make. *I cannot be Patriarch if I am a slave to the extract.* The telepaths of the *czrav* managed to avoid addiction through sparing use of the drug, usually. *But I am not a telepath. I will need more, much more.* There was danger there, and he remembered his brother's wasted body on its gravlifted *prrstet*. Death was a better fate than *sthondat* addiction. He looked up to survey the advancing *tuskvor*. *I have come so far, am I to lose in this moment?* He looked back to the vial, its acrid smell penetrating the back of his brain, harsh and yet somehow alluring. *This moment is the reason Patriarch's Telepath tested me. Did he foresee it somehow? I passed his test through self-discipline. I can pass this test the same way.* Rrit-Conserver had taught that self-discipline was the fundamental underpinning of all that made a warrior. Now it was time to prove himself worthy of the training he had been given. He tipped the vial backward, felt the liquid slide onto his tongue. Immediately he began to feel strange, more aware of his heartbeat, a curious tingle, not unpleasant, began in his paw pads. It became difficult to focus his vision, and he felt his knees buckling. He gripped the railing of the *tsvasztet,* trying to hold himself up. *I must not lose myself to the mind-trance.* Blackness enveloped him, the same ultimate emptiness that had nearly cost him his sanity when Patriarch's Telepath had tested him in the Citadel's puzzle garden. His grip loosened on the rail and it fell away in extreme slow motion. Reality slipped away with it and the fear again rose in him, counterbalanced by the kill rage, and the universe was dark and empty and he was utterly alone in it.

> *Any fool knows victory requires you to concentrate all effort at the point of decision. It is the art of the commander to know where the point of decision will be.*
>
> —Si-Rrit

"As you command, sire." Ktronaz-Commander toggled

the display and the Command Lair's strategic display of
the Father Sun's singularity vanished, replaced by a waist-
deep terrain holo of the Plain of Stgrat, the data relayed
live from eight-cubed sources and integrated to show the
best possible real-time map of the unfolding advance. He
stood back with Kzin-Conserver and Scrral-Rrit to give
Kchula-Tzaatz and his guest an unobstructed view.

Zraa-Churrt leaned close to the highlighted dots that
marked the enemy. "What are these beasts they ride?"

"*Tuskvor.*" Kchula-Tzaatz spat the word.

Zraa-Churrt's ears went up, pink fans against his white
fur. "*Tuskvor*? I thought they were untamable."

"Evidently the *czrav* have found a way. It is irrelevant.
They will not stand against *rapsari*."

"Their force seems formidable."

"These rabble do not concern me." Kchula slashed his
claw across the tiny images of *tuskvor* that populated the
plain. "I will wipe them aside."

"Your confidence is commendable." Zraa-Churrt
paused, considering the map. "I hope you will not tell me
this citadel is impregnable. You proved yourself it could
be taken."

"With *rapsari*. Nothing else would have done the job.
No other pride in the Patriarchy has an eighth of the
growth vat capacity I command on Jotok, not a sixteenth.
These herd beasts are big, but they are herbivores, not
meant for fighting. When they meet my main defense
force this advance will falter and die."

"And yet you still set the savannah on fire with energy
weapons."

"My brother is a skilled warrior. If he can win without

fighting he will. It is within the traditions." Kchula turned to Kzin-Conserver, who was impassively watching the exchange. "Is it not?"

"It is." Kzin-Conserver kept his voice carefully neutral. "Although barely."

"No. This attack is of no consequence." Kchula made a gesture that dismissed Kzin-Conserver's reservation and the holo at once. "My concern is the *kz'zeerkti*. Ktronaz!" Another gesture from the commander recalled the presentation of the Father Star and its environs out to the singularity's edge. The cryptic symbology of intercept planes, course funnels, orbit curves and spacetime gradients filled the representation. "The monkeys must be destroyed, once and for all."

"My fleet is here to defend the Patriarchy, as are those of my brothers."

"Hrrr. It is a pity you could not have brought more ships."

The white pelted kzin turned a paw over. "My own worlds need defending too."

"Of course, Zraa-Churrt. Your fealty will be rewarded."

"Perhaps."

Kchula looked sharply at the Pride-Patriarch, who returned it calmly. *He is insufficiently submissive. When this mess is done with he will need to be taught a lesson.* "Ktronaz-Commander, are your plans complete?"

"As we discussed, sire. There are no significant changes."

"Excellent. Prepare your defensive orders."

Ktronaz made the gesture-of-obeisance and took control of the display again to plot his battle.

"And Ftzaal-Tzaatz is commanding the ground war against these *czrav*?" Zraa-Churrt asked the question offhandedly.

"He does."

"Why isn't he with Ktronaz-Commander then?"

"He leads his *Ftz'yeer* personally."

"I see." Zraa-Churrt turned a paw over. "Shall we return to the others?"

Kchula made a gesture and his guards opened the door to lead the way up from the Command Lair to the Patriarch's Hall where the other Great-Pride-Patriarchs were waiting. The Hall's huge, arching space with its massive ceiling beams was as impressive as it had always been, but now it was echoing and empty, far too large for the eight-and-half-eight Pride-Patriarchs gathered there to speak to him. Not a quorum of the Great Circle, but enough that he could not hope to evade their eyes in anything he did. It was frustrating. The banners draped on the walls, woven with stories of Rrit triumph, seemed to mock his achievements. *But I am the first to take this hall from the Rrit.* The huge, silent conquest drums waited patiently for their drummers to dance to his victories, the ranks of carved *prrstet* in exotic fabrics begged to be filled with his fealty bound nobles. *When I have defeated the* kz'zeerkti *I will proclaim a feast to my greatness.* He looked at the faces watching him now. They were carefully neutral. *They are not my allies but my rivals. I must bend them to my use here.*

He considered ascending the dais, but decided not to, moving instead to a round table toward the back of the hall. *Let them think I see them as equals.* Scrral-Rrit and

Kzin-Conserver took *prrstet* to either side of him. They were both simple obstacles to his plans now, but neither could be removed easily.

"Brothers," he began. "The *kz'zeerkti* are coming. By sunrise tomorrow the battle will be won or lost."

Kdori-Dcrz fanned his ears up. "What of the challenger, Zree-Rrit?"

"Kchula-Tzaatz feels he is of no consequence," Zraa-Churrt answered before Kchula could.

"Why is that?"

"Ftzaal-Tzaatz commands the battle." Again Zraa-Churrt answered.

"Hrrr." Kdori-Dcrz folded his ears again. "In this case perhaps the challenger *is* of no consequence." He looked to Kchula. "Tell us of the *kz'zeerkti.*"

"They are a threat, but we have the power to defeat them here, and we will. Ktronaz-Commander is plotting his intercepts as we speak. We will meet them high in the singularity. Your fleets will follow mine to intercept. Their strategy relies on their carriers, and they will be the priority for attack. We will ignore the covering forces, they are only a distraction, and if any battleships come in range of Kzinhome the orbital fortresses will deal with them."

Kdori-Dcrz stood. "With respect, brother, and I think I speak for all present, I put forward that it would be better to meet them close in, backed by the weapons of your orbital fortresses."

Kchula snarled and let his fangs show. "Do you question my orders?"

"Those were orders?" Mtell-Mtell unfurled his ears. "I

thought you merely advised the Patriarch." He gestured to Scrral-Rrit.

Kchula opened his mouth to snarl in rage, closed it again. *I cannot antagonize the Pride-Patriarchs.* Instead he looked at Scrral-Rrit. "Patriarch, do you so order?" He fingered the medallion controlling his puppet's *zzrou*.

"I do." Scrral-Rrit looked more humiliated by having to issue the command than he did by having Kchula do it for him.

Kchula looked back to Zraa-Churrt. *Let him argue that.* "Will that suffice, honored brother?"

He expected agreement, but instead Zraa-Churrt turned to Kzin-Conserver. "Conserver, I request a ruling."

Kchula whirled to face this new interruption as Kzin-Conserver replied. "On what point?"

"My brothers and I are here to defend the Patriarchy. In the circumstances we are also witnesses here to *skalazaal*. Does our obligation to protect Kzinhome require that we abandon our positions at the Patriarch's command, and so abandon our obligation to bear witness?"

"Hrrr." Rrit-Conserver turned a paw over, considering carefully. "Yes, with exceptions."

"And these exceptions are?"

"It is the role of the Patriarch to ensure that *skalazaal* is declared and open, and to ensure that the traditions are followed." Kzin-Conserver spoke carefully. *I am treading a narrow path of honor here. I must be impartial regardless of my personal preferences.* "In this case it is the Patriarch himself who is challenged, and further he is challenged by his brother, whose claim supersedes his own despite the accession of the High Priests. The Patriarch cannot be considered to be able to give fair judgment in this case. Responsibility as witness then falls on the Great Pride Circle."

On the other side of the table Mtell-Mtell twitched his whiskers from side to side. "Who we Pride-Patriarchs represent here."

"Yes." Conserver made the gesture-of-peer-acknowledgment. "The claims of fealty and responsibility are now of equal weight. Compromise is demanded."

"Another judgment, Conserver?" asked Zraa-Churrt.

"Of course."

"Is a defense mounted close in-system compromise enough?"

Kzin-Conserver turned a paw over. "It is."

Kchula controlled the urge to scream and leap in frustration. "But . . ."

Kzin-Conserver held up a paw. "I have ruled, Kchula-Tzaatz."

Kchula lapsed into silence, fuming. *But I have lost little here, in failing to get the Great Pride fleets out of sight of the ground battle. Ftzaal would be unlikely to use a free hand even if I won it for him, nor will it change the outcome. It is the kz'zeerkti who are the danger.* He looked to the ceiling and contemplated the heavy chandeliers as though they held some clue as to how the battleground far above was developing. A close-in defense backed by the orbital fortresses made sense, but it ran the risk of allowing the enemy to launch their fighters and bombers into Kzinhome's atmosphere. Once they were in and low they would be almost impossible to intercept, and the Citadel of the Patriarch was a primary target, although he might survive the attack in the well protected Command Lair. His lips twitched away from his fangs. *I should have scourged their world the moment I had the power to command it.* Now he could only wait to see if the monkeys would raze Kzinhome first.

> I have known the glory of the universe, and all its horrors.
> —Patriarch's Telepath

The universe was black and empty and expanding and at the edge of it there was an awareness. Without body or senses Pouncer reached for it, *stretching* himself and found himself looking back at a body collapsed on the floor of the pitching *tsvasztet*, a kzintosh, powerfully muscled but limp and motionless. *He is dying.* Unimaginable grief swept over him, the pang of loss, and then the *tuskvor* balked and he turned back to the tiller bar, steering the beast with savage intent, flooded now with the desire to revenge a lost mate, and he realized that the body was his own and the awareness he had found was C'mell's, and she had thought that she'd lost him. He tried to speak to her and could not, but she felt him respond to his own awareness, first with surprise, then with relief and understanding, and he *knew* her in a way that he had not before, even in the close intimacy of mating, and he could have stayed there with her forever but he could not. The universe was expanding and there were other awarenesses, Battle Captain, Night-Prowler, the strangely different mind of Tskombe-*kz'zeerkti* and the Trina manrette, the faint, unforthcoming glow of their *tuskvor*, other kzinti, other creatures, jamming into his mind in a growing torrent of hope and fear, desire and rage, hunger and thirst and satiation. He tried to shut them out but found he could not, the torrent expanded beyond his ability to control, and he felt his own awareness eroding, torn away in the onrushing flow like a sapling in a storm.

He had a purpose, to direct the battle. How to find a stranger you've never met in a crowd? *This is the burden Patriarch's Telepath bore.* Time seemed to have no meaning as he jumped from awareness to awareness. Familiar emotion keyed recognition, here a commander, here a Pride-Patriarch, here a telepath, and he had half the battle won. He gave images to the telepath, a map of the battle unfolding as he saw it and then he moved on, secure in the knowledge that the information would be given to the telepath's commander. A harder task now, finding the minds of his enemies, waiting farther out in ambush. He found them too, surrounded by the small, vicious points of consciousness that could only be *rapsari*. Again he leapt from mind to mind, slower this time, taking the time to search out plans and tactics. He saw the battlefield through eight-to-the-fourth pairs of enemy eyes, saw how they had shaped it, prepared positions and traps for his force, and again he reached for the *czrav* telepath and gave him a revision of his initial plan, launching spoiling attacks to protect his own flank as he ordered his vast, living armada around in a sweeping turn to take the enemy where they were weakest. His force responded, and as the situation changed he sent more orders to respond ahead of the enemy. *How much time has this taken?* He had no way of knowing until he thought to tap the time sense of one of his Pride-Patriarchs, and realized that it was taking a long time indeed, and they were closing hard on the Citadel gates. The Tzaatz were in confusion, trying to move forces already being overrun by *tuskvor*. He sensed their fear, and the exultation of the *czrav* who sliced out their lives. He sensed their pain and confusion as death overtook them, and sorrow at their loss swept over him. *This is the strength and weakness of the Telepath's Gift, the needle balance between the power to kill with ease and the cost of the pain of death.* In *knowing* his enemy as he was, he was *becoming* them, and that intimacy made the immediacy of their death a terrible thing. *Am I this strong?* It was within his power to call off the attack. *Not every necessary thing is easy.* He steeled himself and went on, resolving to end it as soon as possible.

His advance guard were engaging more Tzaatz now, pinning their units in place, denying them the ability to respond to his main assault as it swept closer to the citadel. It was going well, so far, and he again revised his instructions to his commanders. *But we have yet to meet the heavy* rapsari. The raiders and harriers the Tzaatz outposts used were easy game for *tuskvor*-mounted Heroes, but the true test would come before the citadel gate, where the beasts clustered close and heavy siege weapons waited. He stretched his mind there, to gauge the defenses and the readiness of the defenders, and there he found not a mind but a place where a mind should be, a black hole in the universe.

It took him a long time to recognize it for what it was. The Black Priest! Ftzaal-Tzaatz was insulated from the world of observer quantum wave collapse by the Black Fur gene, which made his awareness unavailable to Pouncer, but he was there, waiting for him, he could sense that much at least. *He is alive, he is aware, there must be a way to reach him.* He concentrated, directed all his energy at it, felt his own awareness burning away with the effort of the attempt, but nothing he could do would penetrate the barrier. *The Black Fur gene is powerful.* More *sthondat* extract would let him know Ftzaal's mind. *But I cannot lose myself in the mind-trance. If only I could touch him . . .* Physical contact would strengthen the bond, let him break through the Black Priests' barriers, but that was impossible. Already he could feel the drug's effects fading, and the desire for more, to rekindle the *vision*, was strong, strong within him. The Citadel gates were coming up. *How much time has passed?* He fought the craving, fought as well to return himself to awareness, to open his eyes so he could lead his assaulters to the walls of his father's fortress, as he must. He entered a twilight zone then, between the two universes and then found another awareness, in terrible pain. It was different somehow, a *kz'zeerkti*. Cherenkova-Captain! *She suffers the Hot Needle!* Her pain swept over him, consuming him like a swarm of *v'pren* and from far, far away he heard himself howling in response.

And the world returned like a sudden bath of ice water, and he found himself lying on the floor of the *tsvasztet*, Swift-Claw kneeling over him with concern. Sounds of battle rose, kzinti kill screams mixed with the deep, booming bellows of enraged *tuskvor* and the keening cries of *rapsari*.

He staggered to the front of the *tsvasztet* where C'mell still had the tiller bar. They were surging past Hero's Square, entering the forest of broadleaf trees that separated it from the Citadel, and the *rapsar* assaulters were waiting for them there. As he watched, a pair of them appeared and attacked a *tuskvor* immediately in front of him. They were half its size, but vicious, with pincer tentacles that slashed and stabbed, seeking the vulnerable flesh beneath the *tuskvor*'s armor. The *tuskvor* bellowed in pain and the Ztrak Pride warriors on its back leapt with grav belts and variable swords to attack the Tzaatz infantry who rode the *rapsari*. The *rapsar* keened and tore at the *tuskvor*'s neck. Blood began to fountain to the ground as the *tuskvor* struggled, thrashing its huge tail and trying to bring its tusks to bear on its antagonist. The other beast snatched a *czrav* Hero in midleap, crushing his life out and casting him aside. The *tuskvor* went down with a crash that shook the ground and snapped ancient broadleaf trunks to the ground. A volley of steel balls from a Tzaatz launcher *rapsar* deeper in the woods came over, one of them tearing the canopy and half the *tsvasztet* railing off of Pouncer's *tuskvor*, coming so close to him that he felt the wind of its passage. He toggled the vocom on his beltcomp and spoke into it, the battle picture he'd gained in the mind-trance still fresh in his memory. "Ztrak Pride, close and attack. Dziit Pride, right flank from reserve, take the north walls, clear the way for the assault prides." *The need for stealth is gone now, and the Tzaatz won't have time to break the crypting.* "Support prides into position. Ccarri Pride, lead the others to secure the perimeter."

The mind-trance was still strong enough on him that he *felt* his warriors responding to his commands, even as the confirmations crackled over the vocom channel. The battle had broken up into swirling knots of violence, the cohesion of both attack and defense broken by the close country. A pair of resin-spraying assaulters lumbered out of the trees, gouting noxious goo from their forehead nozzles. C'mell hauled on the tiller and their *tuskvor* bellowed and balked. She yanked the releases, letting the control lines run free, and the angered *tuskvor* swung its horns at the nearer assaulter, ripping its side open. It collapsed in a stew of its own ichor, twitching. The *tuskvor* lurched and jabbed at the second one, missing. The assaulter came closer, under the *tuskvor*'s long, powerful neck, spraying wildly. A gobbet of the sticky poison hit Pouncer on the arm, burning where it touched, and drying to a thick resin almost at once, but there wasn't enough there to incapacitate him. The *rapsar* keened and their *tuskvor* ran over it, crushing it underfoot without slowing down, but the attack had already taken its toll. The *tuskvor*'s neck and forebody were covered in the goo, and it bellowed in rage and pain. C'mell struggled hard to reel in the lines she'd let loose to regain control over the beast, but the resin had hopelessly snarled them. The *tuskvor* spotted another *rapsar*, this one a catapulter, and it bellowed and charged. The damaged *tsvasztet* lurched and slid backward as the catapulter cut loose a salvo of steel balls.

Pouncer grabbed for support. "Grav belts!"

The balls flew past and several smacked the *tuskvor* in the chest hard enough that Pouncer heard the bones break even over the din of the battle. The *tuskvor* bellowed again but kept moving. One of the balls tore away the *mazourk's* station, and panic filled him for an instant when he didn't see C'mell there. He looked wildly around, saw her behind him, closing the last buckle on her grav belt. She tossed him his own and he quickly snapped it around his waist even as the *tsvasztet* lurched again, its forward securing lines torn loose. He leapt for the still-stable back section as the *tuskvor* reached the fleeing catapulter, goring it and throwing its handlers to the ground to scramble out of the way before their now lifeless creation toppled on top of them. The violent motion parted the last restraining rope, and the front half of the travel platform slid off its back and splintered on the ground as the *tuskvor* stabbed at the corpse again and again. Another *tuskvor* blundered past with its *tsvasztet* on fire, this one crushing the *rapsar* handlers who'd managed to escape. Ferlitz-Telepath's travelpack was there, and he reached inside for the remaining two vials of *sthondat* extract. Already he was craving the power of the mind-trance. *I am not addicted, I will only use them if I need them.* Even as he thought it the impulse seized him to throw them away, to remove even the temptation to start down the path of Patriarch's Telepath. Their injured *tuskvor* staggered forward and the *tsvasztet* lurched dangerously. Reflexively he slid the vials into his hunt pouch and drew his variable sword as a two-sword of *rapsar* raiders appeared before them, their riders firing crystal iron crossbow bolts. Pouncer saw Battle Captain go down, a bolt through his neck. He looked around, counting his small band. Night-Prowler was nowhere to be seen. *But*

C'mell is still here. That fact was more important than he ever could have imagined. *Pray the Fanged God she is still here at the end of this.*

The raiders circled, waiting for their prey to go down, and then a fresh shower of arrows rained down from nowhere. Pouncer looked up and saw the walls of the Citadel looming over them, mirror bright with mag armor engaged, with Tzaatz archers firing from the battlements. Here and there other *tuskvor* had made it to the walls, standing to their broad chests in the Quickwater. Their *mazourk* had hauled their necks high to act as assault ladders for the Heroes swarming up them. Further back, siege engines mounted on the backs of other *tuskvor* pumped ballista shafts and showers of catapult stone at the enemy to clear the way for the attackers.

"Leap!" Pouncer roared and leapt himself, just as their *tuskvor* collapsed half on the bank, half into the Quickwater, and the back half of the *tsvasztet* tore off to sink in the current. His grav belt surged as he arced for the parapet. A Tzaatz was waiting for him there, but he parried the first attack with his variable sword, then cut the attacker in half with a well timed counterswing. Pain flared in his mind as his opponent died, the echoes of the mind-trance spiking his death agony into Pouncer's awareness. The distraction nearly cost him his life, but he *saw*, in a single brilliant flash, the second Tzaatz, felt his developing attack and the rage in his killscream. He pivoted, slicewire blurring, and the other was dead and falling over the edge.

Shapes landed beside him. The two *kz'zeerkti*. *Where are the others?* There was no time to worry about that.

"Tskombe-*kz'zeerkti*! Your mate! Go to that tower!" He pointed to Forgotten Tower, overshadowing the Puzzle Garden, where he could sense the dulled awareness of the tortured Cherenkova-Captain. "Go down the stairs, all the way. At the bottom there is a corridor with cells. At the end there is a chamber. She is there!"

Tskombe nodded in acknowledgment. Pouncer had changed since his recovery from the *sthondat* drug. He was more distant, more commanding, and the depth in his eyes was frightening. *What does he see there?* He followed the pointing talon to the distant tower, locking it into his memory. All along the wall *czrav* warriors were gaining the battlements, and a storm of arrows came up from the courtyards and the inner curtain wall. He looked to Trina and swallowed hard. It wasn't the first time he'd faced death in combat; it *was* the first time he'd brought a teenage girl with him. *But I couldn't leave her, and she's lucky . . .* He would need luck himself, and lots of it. He grabbed her hand and they leapt for the tower, grav belts whining as they arced toward it.

Pouncer watched them go, and more shapes landed beside him, C'mell and Z'slee, he knew without looking. In the courtyard below them the Tzaatz were bringing up another siege *rapsar* with powerful secondary legs meant to cock and fire the heavy ballista mounted on its back. Behind him Ztrak Pride had secured the outer north wall and Dziit Pride were leaping in to reinforce them. The attackers had taken heavy losses, and their hold on the battlements was precarious. If the *rapsar* below came into action it could cost them that tentative victory. He reached out with his mind, felt again the presence-of-absence that was the Black Priest. *He is close.* He found another mind, nearby, *Ftz'yeer* Leader waiting in ambush in the Citadel's central courtyard, ready to lead his elite force out on his master's command, to crush any *czrav* penetration of the inner sanctuary. He knew beyond doubt that Ftzaal-Tzaatz was directing the defenders now. Behind him he sensed his own forces, the vast array now embroiled in lethal combat with the *rapsari*. *We need reinforcement or we will lose the battle here and now.*

He keyed his beltcomp. "Assault prides, leap to the north wall. Support prides, saturation fire from the east across the Quickwater." Below him the Tzaatz were bringing their launcher creature to bear. He screamed and leapt, and the two kzinretti screamed and leapt with him. As he touched down a sword of Tzaatz leapt at them. *I will earn victory here, or a death of honor.*

> *Seize what your enemy desires and he will conform to your wishes.*
>
> —Sun Tzu

There was little arrow fire as Tskombe jumped for the tower, and he and Trina touched down unmolested. The tower was old, its stones worn smooth by the ages, and a tightly coiled spiral stairway ran down it. He led the way down. It coiled down to the left, as tower stairs did on Earth. *And on Earth that's done so that right-handed attackers fighting up the stairs have their sword arm hampered against the inner wall.* It occurred to him to wonder if kzinti had a preferred hand, and then he had an answer as a warrior screamed and leapt in front of him, variable

sword held in the left hand with maximum freedom of
motion. He parried the blow awkwardly with his right
hand, then thumbed the retractor until his slice wire was
dagger short. He ducked the next attack and stabbed it
down, getting the tip into the shoulder articulation. The
hit wasn't crippling, but his opponent fell back, bleeding,
and dropped his weapon. Tskombe reextended the slice
wire and swung, this time getting the edge inside the
Tzaatz's belly articulation and gutting him. *So the spiral is
no help, but being on the high ground is always an advantage.* He leapt over the body, nearly slipping in fresh
spilled blood and continued down.

Thirty seconds later something was wrong. *Pouncer
said a corridor*, but he was in a garden, aromatic and well
manicured hedges and complex sculptures. A panicked
Jotok ran past, arm/legs undulating, but he could see no
other way down. He breathed deep while Trina caught up.

"Which way?" she asked.

He looked left and right, then inspiration struck. "You
tell me."

She nodded, and without hesitation ran across the
garden. On the other side was an open archway, and
another set of stairs spiraling down. *Trina's luck.* He took
the lead again and found a corridor two flights underground, musty with the damp of ages. *But Pouncer said
cells.* This corridor ran straight, with occasional arches
leading to cross corridors. Trina ran and Tskombe followed her, trying to keep track of the twists and turns so
they could find their way out again. *I'm trusting her luck
so why bother?* Because her luck wasn't his luck, he
realized. The image of her turning just in time to avoid

the ballista shaft that went on to kill Ferlitz-Telepath
was burned in his mind.

They took stairs spiraling down again. It was an old part
of the fortress, the walls made of huge stones. At the bottom was another corridor, this one with cells, and at the
end of it a chamber. A kill scream paralyzed him and he
turned to see a black blur in midleap. Instinctively he
swung the variable sword and his attacker was cut in half.
The body parts slammed into Tskombe and knocked him
over, covering him in gouting blood. Another scream split
the air and a second black-furred kzin flew through the
space he had been standing in. He struggled to his feet
shakily. *He had no mag armor.* If the kzin had been wearing any, strength and mass alone would have made the
match a short one.

He wiped blood from his eyes, saw the second attacker
impaled through the forehead on a long, wicked looking
skewer stuck into one of the large wooden support posts
that held up the ceiling. Trina was standing in front of him
looking shocked. There was smeared blood on the kzin's
feet and it took half a second to put the picture together.
*He leapt at Trina even as I killed his companion, and got
blood on his feet and slipped, hit the skewer and died.*
Trina's expression told of horror and he followed her gaze.
He saw a human figure staked to a heavy table with cruel
steel spikes. It took him longer to realize it was a woman,
and he did not want to think it was Ayla, but it was. She
was naked, her body twisted into an unnatural position by
the skewers. Coagulated blood caked around the larger
wounds, and her hair was matted. He knew from Ferlitz
that she had been there three days, at least. Her eyes were

closed, her breathing steady, but he could tell she was not asleep. Her face looked strangely relaxed, as though she had somehow come to terms with the constant, excruciating pain.

"Ayla!" He was afraid to touch her. If she moved the skewers might tear out. She didn't respond.

"*Ayla!*" Her eyes fluttered.

"Ayla, it's me."

"Quacy?" Her eyes wouldn't focus at first. "Quacy, am I dreaming?" Her voice was distant and dreamy.

"No, I'm here, I'm real." He put his hand on her shoulder tentatively, as though even that contact might do her further injury.

"Oh Quacy." She looked up at him, moving just her eyes because of the way she was pinned down. The reality of his presence brought her mind back from wherever it had fled from the pain, and she shuddered. "Oh Quacy it hurts."

"It won't hurt much longer. Just hang on." He tried to be gentle getting the skewers out, but it was impossible; they were driven deep into the wooden table top and had to be worked loose. "Trina, help me."

Trina moved around to Ayla's head to pull out the smaller needles that pinned her hand to the board.

"Valya?" Ayla was staring at Trina with an odd expression. "Now I know I'm dreaming."

Trina stopped, her expression frozen. "What did you call me?"

Ayla's eyes refocused. "I'm sorry . . . Valya, my sister . . . you look like her."

Trina was staring, eyes round. "Valya was my mother."

Tskombe let go of the skewer he was working on, understanding arriving with sudden shock. He looked from one face to the other, saw the family resemblance in the shape of the nose, the chin and the high cheekbones. Suddenly he remembered how familiar Trina had seemed when he first met her. *And lucky Trina has come fifty light-years through two wars to find her only living relative.* It made sense now.

And there was still a war on. "Come on, we have no time." He pulled hard on another skewer.

"Quacy . . ." She gasped in pain as the skewer let go and pulled free. "There's a ship aimed at earth, lightspeed weapons . . ."

"We don't have to worry about that now. First we're going to get you somewhere safe."

She shook her head violently, a motion that must have caused considerable pain. "No, we have to stop it. The black-furred kzin, he knows the coordinates."

"One of these two?" He gestured to the bodies.

"No, another one. Ftzaal-Tzaatz."

"Is he the one who did this to you?"

"Yes." She groaned as another skewer came free, fresh blood oozing from the crusted wound.

The Tzaatz will pay for this. Tskombe smiled grimly as he worked another needle loose. The flesh seemed to be cauterized where the needles had gone in. *They put them in hot.* Anger flooded him. *Oh yes, they will pay.* Each tug caused her new pain, but Ayla gritted her teeth and bore it stoically.

Noises in the corridor. He grabbed up the variable sword and turned to face a mag armored kzin coming into the room at the bound, four more behind him.

"Kr-Pathfinder!" He lowered the variable sword, relief flooding over him.

"Tskombe-*kz'zeerkti*. We must leave, now."

Tskombe nodded. "Help me get her free."

Pathfinder gave tail signals, and a pair of *czrav* warriors moved to secure the room's other entrance. Then he grabbed the larger skewers that pinned Ayla's thighs and calves and yanked. Ayla screamed then, but she didn't cry, as Tskombe and Trina and Pathfinder pulled the needles from her body. The tears didn't come until the last skewer was gone and she collapsed, unable even to sit up. She tried, struggling, and when she couldn't she looked down at the horrific damage done to her body and wept, and Tskombe lifted her and carried her out of the chamber of horrors that she thought she'd die in.

Pathfinder snarled. "She is lucky to be alive."

Ayla breathed in and out, self-control reasserting itself. *I am still an officer.* Still she had to fight down a wave of nausea as she saw what had been done to her. "They've ruined me, Quacy."

"Don't worry, it's nothing an autodoc won't fix." He tried to be gentle as he carried her, but there was still a battle going on, and speed was critical. He took a moment to kiss her though, gently at first because he was afraid he might hurt her, and then hard because he loved her and had lost her and wanted her to know that he'd never let her go again. And then they had to go, so he carried her up the spiral staircase into the light. He found himself in the same garden as before, but on the other side of the tower. *Pouncer's instructions were right, I should have gone right around the tower on the outside.* But he hadn't and who knew how fate would have woven events if they'd taken the easy way. Trina's luck worked in mysterious ways.

"We have to get the black-furred one." Ayla was breathless, still trembling in his arms. "Ftzaal-Tzaatz."

"Oh we will." He clenched his jaw grimly. Sounds of combat rose over the Citadel walls.

Kr-Pathfinder dropped to attack-crouch, searching for hidden dangers in the ornate garden. He made tail signals, commanding his half-sword into defensive positions, then keyed his vocom. "Sire, we have the Cherenkova-Captain and the other *kz'zeerkti.*"

Tskombe looked at him, only then realizing that the big kzin's appearance was not coincidence but plan. *Pouncer is winning here.* He found that somehow surprising, and he realized he had never allowed himself to think in terms of final victory, even as he planned for it. *Because to win I had to have Ayla, and now I do.*

A crystal iron crossbow bolt embedded itself in the tower's stonework with an audible *spang*, a handsbreadth from his head. One of Kr-Pathfinder's sword wheeled and fired an arrow back, knocking a Tzaatz warrior from the battlements. Other Tzaatz appeared. *And now I have her, we've got to get out of here while we still can.*

> **Scream and leap.**
> —**The Dueling Traditions**

Ftzaal-Tzaatz watched the battle unfold from the security of the Patriarch's Tower. Far below Heroes contended with sinew and steel, fighting for every last stone of the Citadel. The *czrav* forces had made it over the north wall and penetrated as far as the Middle Fortress. That was as it should be. He turned to the semi-comatose form drooling on the *prrstet* beside him, one of two telepaths he had managed to extract from the Black High Circle.

"Where is First-Son-of-Meerz-Rrit now?" He almost purred the words.

The telepath's eyes rolled back in his head. "He is . . . he is rallying warriors to storm the Hall of the Patriarch."

"Is he still in the mind-trance?"

"No . . . Not in the trance . . . but still aware . . . aware of mind space . . ."

"Excellent." Ftzaal turned his palm over. "It is time to put the bait in the trap." He looked again to the unfolding battle and keyed his viscom. A holo appeared, showing the Command Lair where Kchula-Tzaatz watched the battle with his entourage.

"Brother." Kchula's voice came over the voice link.

"The battle threatens you. I have created a secure area in the Patriarch's Great Hall. You must move there with your staff."

"From the Command Lair?" Kchula's voice was incredulous. "If they can get me here, how is the Great Hall safer?"

"Because I so command it to be safer." Ftzaal snapped the words testily. "There is a secret way to the Command Lair. They may use it."

"I will go then." Kchula broke the carrier.

Ftzaal returned his attention to the battle unfolding beneath him. *My brother serves his purpose at last. The*

Rrit still feels the effects of the sthondat. *He will sense* Kchula *and go to him.* His claws extended of their own accord. *And when he does I will capture him, and test a theory.* He keyed his com again.

"Assault *rapsar* parties, move now. Citadel defense, fall back. The trap is set, *Ftz'yeer*, stand by for my word. Remember I want him alive."

"As you command, sire . . ." "As you command, sire . . ." The voices cracked back. Outside in the forests eight-cubed assault *rapsari* began moving to cut off and encircle the *czrav*. They had Ftzaal's other telepath with them to shield their minds from the *czrav*. Their presence would be a complete surprise. Neither the *czrav* nor the Rrit would escape him today. Unconsciously, his jaw relaxed into a fanged smile. *I will go there myself to see the Rrit taken.* He turned to the telepath beside him. "In a moment you will cease shielding my brother's presence. We will show this leader-of-*czrav* what he is really up against."

Eat today or be hungry tomorrow.
—Dolphin saying

Crusader fell in toward the Traveler's Moon, and Curvy watched on her battleplot as the two fleets closed. The kzinti weren't climbing up to meet the UN force high in the gravity well, as they usually did. Instead they were waiting for the UN ships to close. Their battle plan was clear. They would let their orbital fortresses engage the human fleet while their battleships and other heavy units maneuvered for close combat, accepting high casualties to get at the carriers that were the heart of the UN attack plan. Still, she could see advantage to be gained. The kzinti were deployed in battle groups, and it was clear from their motions that they were not well coordinated. They were probably acting independently, and if the human force could split them and engage them separately they could keep their casualties to a minimum. She keyed data into her console. Projections on her strategic matrix ranged from twenty-five to fifty percent casualties for the UN force, a heavy toll for ultimate victory. Kzinhome was well guarded, but there were no outcome spaces that did not result in UN success, so the only problem was how to minimize the losses.

There was a higher level problem, which was the response that the rest of the Patriarchy would mount to the destruction of their homeworld. It was a large empire, its full extent still unknown, though it would probably collapse with its central authority removed. What might happen after that was worrisome. The UN had demonstrated how easy it was to devastate a world. Her strategic matrix showed a nearly ninety percent probability of kzinti retaliation in kind, with a thirty percent probability that they were already mounting an exterminating attack. That probability had dropped somewhat when she'd seen how many major kzinti combat units were committed to the defense of their homeworld, but it was still far from zero. A fleet attack was only one way of razing a world, and not even the most efficient. The UN had proven that too.

She nosed her way to the bottom of the tank to snap down a salmon, and then swam over to nudge Zwweee(click)wurrrrtrrrtrrr from his nap. They mated in an amorous flurry, and then she let languor overtake her and she half-napped while he watched the unfolding battle. They worked in split watches now. *Even with the end of worlds at hand life's pulse goes on uninterrupted.* They would destroy Kzinhome and the universe would continue. There was no sense in regretting what she couldn't control.

To see is not to understand.
—Patriarch's Telepath

The Tzaatz screamed and leapt, and Pouncer's variable sword was already in the trajectory of his leap, canted just so. The Tzaatz died, decapitated as Pouncer's slicewire found the gaps in the neck articulation of his armor. In mind space Pouncer felt him die, and the sudden terminal pain flooded his awareness. He shook off the sudden paralysis, then froze again as he felt a disturbance in mind space. The *sthondat* extract had worn off to the point he could no longer know *thought,* only *presence,* but this presence was special. *Kchula-Tzaatz! He is in my father's hall.* He looked around to assess the battle, saw the Heroes of Ztrak Pride, much diminished, had secured the House of Victory. He was already in position to attack. *We can take the Great Hall and end this here.*

He raised his voice. "Ztrak Pride, with me, skirmish order. Advance!"

His warriors leapt to obey, and he could not help but purr at the crisp discipline of his command, even as he appreciated the gravity of their task. His forces held the entire north wall now, and his furthest advance scouts were as far south as the Inner Keep. *I will win this yet.* He looked to C'mell, leading his left forward four-sword now, and to Swift-Claw, leading his right forward. *We have lost so many. . . .* He would not falter now, so close to victory. Their deaths would not be in vain.

"C'mell, take your four-sword to secure the rear of the Hall. Don't let anyone escape that way."

"As you command." Her reply was clipped, as professional as any *zitalyi*. *I cannot show her favor.*

"Sire, we have the Cherenkova-Captain and the other *kz'zeerkti.*" It was Kr-Pathfinder, his voice confident.

"Acknowledged. Move to the Great Hall of the Patriarch. We are securing it now."

"As you command."

They advanced against trivial resistance. The Tzaatz forces seemed to be falling apart. It was almost too easy, and he reached out into mind space to detect a trap. There were potentials, to be sure . . . *More* sthondat *would let me know their thoughts, know their intentions.* He pushed the thought away. *I cannot allow myself to become addicted.* He would have to make do with what he had.

They gained the entrance to the Great Hall, rushed up the ancient stone stairs into the vaulted antechamber. Tzaatz grav skirmishers still leapt overhead and arrows fell sporadically, but resistance seemed to be dying down already. He could *sense* Kchula-Tzaatz inside. *And my brother!* He contained his eagerness to confront them in favor of caution and security. *I owe it to my warriors not to squander their lives.* He sent a sword forward to secure the entrance, and they reported it clear.

He advanced another sword and followed it. The hall

was large, full of hiding places. Clearing it would take time. As he moved forward he was struck by the changes that had taken place since the last time he had entered its familiar confines. *I have lost my father, become a warrior, taken a name, found a mate, fathered kits of my own, forged an army and led it here. . . .* Meerz-Rrit would be proud of him, and there was both joy and sorrow in that realization.

Kill screams echoed, cutting off his reverie, and at the same instant mind space was flooded with new awareness, eight-cubed bright spots of awareness, close. *Ambush!* With the realization came the knowledge that he had been tricked, that the Tzaatz had shielded their numbers from him in mind space, had encouraged him to overconfidence and overextension. *Red and gold mag armor.* The elite *Ftz'yeer* were leaping to the attack. At the same time voices flooded the com channel

"Sire! *Rapsari* to our north, eight-squared . . ."

"Sire! We need reinforcement . . ."

A flash in mind space, lumbering *rapsari* in wedge formation, closing in on the prides who held the perimeters. They were built like raiders but quadrupedal and bigger, much bigger. *They made these to kill* tuskvor. In that instant he realized how long the Tzaatz had been anticipating his attack. *They have kept their own secrets well.* In the vision the wedge slammed into his perimeter guard like an in-falling comet, fangs slicing *tuskvor* flesh, and then a Tzaatz screamed and leapt and he nearly died as he pulled his variable sword in line to block the blow.

"Ztrak Pride! To me, defensive circle now!" He screamed the command, and blocked again as the *Ftz'yeer*

swung overhand. His warriors responded, and he anticipated another attack, feinted low and then sliced his
opponent's belly open when he fell for it. There was no
time to celebrate the victory—two more Tzaatz leapt to
attack him. He parried one and dodged the second, and
then had to fall back to the forming defensive circle. *The*
sthondat *extract aids my anticipation.* He *felt* another
attacker closing from the flank, pivot turned and cut him
in half almost without effort, and then he was in the circle.
Something *popped* and he ducked in time to avoid a
monofilament net that flew over his head to entangle the
czrav warrior beside him. He turned and hooked his
slicewire into the mesh and brought it up, ripping the net
open, but the distraction left him vulnerable, and the
Tzaatz he had just blocked whipped his slicewire up and
under Pouncer's sword arm. Pouncer leapt vertically and
the slicewire cut empty air instead of amputating his arm
from the armpit up. He swung as he came down and
decapitated the Tzaatz from above, spinning in midair to
gut the second one even as he screamed and leapt.
Victory, for a heartbeat, but more netguns were firing and
the tight defensive circle of *czrav* was disintegrating. A
mind flash showed *tuskvor* in lakes of blood, his support
prides fighting for their lives as the Tzaatz cut the Citadel
off with eights and eight-squareds of *rapsari*.

We will live or die in the next moments. The *czrav*
beside him went down and he slipped sideways and
brought his slicewire up to gut the *Ftz'yeer* who'd overextended himself to gain the kill. *These* Ftz'yeer *are too
good.* In the raiding campaign he had grown used to the
low standard of battle discipline in the Tzaatz rank and

file, but Ftzaal-Tzaatz's elite were as good as any *czrav*, and here with the advantage of surprise and numbers they were going to win. His defensive circle was starting to collapse under the pressure. More netguns popped, and he risked a glance backward to see a quarter of his force struggling under the monofilament mesh. *They mean to take us alive.* That was bad, that meant the Ceremonial Death. . . .

No time to consider it. He stepped forward, feinted, blocked and slashed downward, and a Tzaatz fell at his feet gushing blood. *They will not take me alive. . . .* He stepped back again. The defensive circle was getting smaller. His death of honor would come soon. Flashes of pain and fear struck him in mind space. His force was being slaughtered. The Tzaatz had laid their trap well. *But I can save what I can.* The prides outside the Citadel walls could escape, if they could disengage from the *rapsari*. It would be a shameful retreat, but the shame would be his, and he would not have to endure it long. His warriors would survive, with their honor intact. *Sometimes honor demands that we accept shame.* He keyed his vocom to give the order.

"*Ftz'yeer*! Hold!" The voice rose over the din of battle, and Pouncer looked up, surprised. The kzin who gave the order was standing by the high-arched entrance to the main hall, broad shouldered in red-and-gold armor. The circle of Tzaatz drew back, and Pouncer looked around the antechamber. He had a pitiful pawful of warriors left, standing back-to-back and watching warily for any renewal of attack. They were outnumbered four-to-one at least, the outcome of the battle, this part of it anyway, was in little doubt. *Why did they stop?* He reached out with mind awareness but sensed only the presence of his enemies.

"Zree-Rrit-First-Son-of-Meerz-Rrit, show yourself." The Tzaatz leader's eyes searched the circle, searching. "An honor truce has been commanded."

Honor truce? Why? He stepped forward. "I am Zree-Rrit."

The Tzaatz made the gesture-of-respect-to-an-enemy. "I am *Ftz'yeer* Leader. Come with me."

Warily, Pouncer followed him into the Great Hall, his warriors coming after him. *Could it be a trap, even with the Pride-Patriarchs watching?* It seemed unlikely; the Tzaatz had victory within their grasp without the need for trickery. Inside the vaulted chamber he understood the reason for the sudden truce. C'mell was there, her four-sword deployed to guard a small group of kzinti in noble's robes.

"Look what I have caught for you, Zree-Rrit." C'mell's tail stood straight with pride and pleasure as she met his eye. She made the gesture of mate-fealty and pointed. In the center of the ring of slicewires was Kchula-Tzaatz. There were others at the front of the hall, Zraa-Churrt and the Pride-Patriarchs he had asked to come bear witness to the traditions, his traitorous brother Scrral-Rrit—and Rrit-Conserver! *No, he is Kzin-Conserver now.* He resisted the urge to greet his old mentor. *There will be time for that later.* He looked to C'mell and returned the gesture. She must have infiltrated her small force into the Great Hall and taken the Tzaatz leader by surprise. *She has forced Kchula to the truce and saved us all.* There were sporadic sounds of battle from outside the hall, but they quickly faded. *Skalazaal* was over. Now it was time for *skatosh*.

The Pride-Patriarchs were watching, and Kzin-Conserver himself. *I must be true to the finest point of honor.* He stepped forward, drawing his variable sword, waving C'mell's warriors out of the way so he could stand before his enemy face to face. "Kchula-Tzaatz. For the death of my father, for the usurpation of my birthright, for the dishonor you have brought this house and the Patriarchy, I challenge you to single combat." *Fear in Kchula's mind.* His mind-awareness was increasing again; it seemed to come and recede in gradually diminishing waves. Pouncer dropped into attack crouch. *He is old and fat. I will finish this here.* He shot a glance at Scrral-Rrit. *And I will deal with my traitorous brother later.*

There was a commotion at the entrance to the hall, a wedge of *Ftz'yeer* entered, and a black-furred kzin. Ftzaal-Tzaatz dismissed his bodyguard and drew his variable sword. "I stand for my brother." The black killer stepped forward, extending the slicewire of his variable sword. "Leap if you dare, Rrit."

Pouncer had turned to face the newcomer, and he screamed and leapt, his own slicewire blurring around to catch Ftzaal before he could take a defensive stance, but Ftzaal turned sideways and brought his blade up and blocked the blow effortlessly. Pouncer fell back before Ftzaal could counterstrike, but Ftzaal followed, delivering a swift left-right combination that Pouncer wasn't ready for, nearly breaking his guard. Pouncer flexed his knees to bring his center of gravity lower and present a smaller target, hiding behind his own blade as though it were a sapling. There was a split second while Ftzaal flowed into a lower stance to match him, and in that instant Pouncer kicked out with his forward leg, hoping to connect with his opponent's knee and break it. Ftzaal was ready though, and pivoted slightly, catching Pouncer's heel with his own and hooking it forward. Pouncer sprawled to the ground. *I've been trapped.* Even as he had that awareness he was rolling to get out of the way of the killing blow he knew was coming. Ftzaal's blade came down a handsbreath from his head. Pouncer knocked it clear and rolled again, flipping back to his feet, and the pair faced each other, eyes locked. *I have the mind gift, what is he thinking?* But Ftzaal's awareness was muted to his mind sense even this close, and Pouncer couldn't *see* enough to give warning of the Black Priest's next move. *The black fur gene is at work.*

Ftzaal screamed and leapt, swinging overhand and Pouncer moved to block the blow, but it was a feint and the real threat was Ftzaal's hind claws, coming around to rake at his face now that Pouncer's slicewire was out of line. Instinctively he jerked back, although his armor would have protected him from any serious damage. As he did so Ftzaal brought his blade around and down, aiming for Pouncer's neck articulation. *Double feint!* In desperation Pouncer twisted sideways. The motion saved his life as the monomolecular filament cut into the grooves that protected his neck but didn't penetrate all the way. He didn't get a chance to reflect on his luck. Ftzaal had used the momentum of his swing to carry him into a spin, swinging again as he came around. Pouncer blocked awkwardly and fell back, and again they faced each other.

Ftzaal was breathing deeply and evenly through bared

fangs. "I want you alive. Put down your sword and I pledge my honor to your life."

"I came here to win or die. Pledge your honor to your own life." Pouncer turned the last word into a scream and leapt, feinting high, slashing low. Ftzaal blocked and spun sideways as Pouncer touched down and turned, his hind claws tearing strips from the lavish carpeting as he stopped his forward momentum with sheer muscle, crouching low to keep himself from tumbling. He slashed again, and his opponent jumped back to avoid the unexpected strike.

"You are skilled, Rrit. I may actually wear your ears."

"You'll have to collect them first, Ftzaal." Pouncer spat the words with a confidence he didn't feel. *He is better than me and he knows it.* With more *sthondat* drug he could know even Ftzaal's mind well enough to anticipate his moves, but he didn't have the option of taking it now. *And dare I face the addiction? Could I bring myself to kill him with our minds connected? Sthondat* was seductive, but he had seen what it had done to his brother. *I don't want to share Patriarch's Telepath's fate.*

And he didn't have the option to take more now anyway. *When in doubt, attack.* Guardmaster's words came back to him. He screamed and leapt again, swinging his variable sword up and around to catch Ftzaal on his weak side. His opponent pivoted to block the blow, and Pouncer went past, lashing out with his hind claws at the Tzaatz's hip to knock him sideways. The ploy worked, but his claws skidded off Ftzaal's armor. His adversary staggered but didn't fall, and still managed to get in a counterblow as Pouncer came past. The slicewire bounced off the back of

Pouncer's helmet. There was little chance it would have hit a weak spot with enough force to penetrate from that angle, but the blow served as a warning. *Never leave an opening.* The first mistake would be the last when facing the Protector of Jotok in single combat.

He rolled again as he landed, then flattened himself to the ground as Ftzaal's slicewire blurred over his head. He had a split second's respite to scramble clear as Ftzaal brought the swing around to cut him in half from above. He dodged back and forth, flat on his back as a flurry of blows rained down around him, then finally managed to get his slicewire into position to block. He caught the edge of Ftzaal's weapon and managed to flip it out of line, but from the floor he lacked the angle necessary to exploit the advantage, and Ftzaal just stepped back out of range, flipping his ears in amusement. Pouncer rolled to his feet, breathing hard. Ftzaal was relaxed and unruffled. *He is toying with me.* It was a sobering realization. Pouncer was putting every sinew into the fight. Ftzaal-Tzaatz was not even trying hard. The black-furred killer would end the fight when and how he chose and there was nothing Pouncer could do about it. *I too have more power here than I am using; my troops control the Citadel.* He pushed the thought away as honorless. He had chosen *skatosh* to finish Kchula-Tzaatz because he needed to set an example for his followers, needed to demonstrate that he was the kind of Patriarch who fought his own fights. His warriors would come if he called them despite the traditions that said they should not, their loyalty was that strong. It would save his life if he did, but he would lose their respect. He could never rule effectively without their support, and the

Patriarchy needed a strong Patriarch now more than ever. *No, if my destiny is to die here I will die here, but I will not show cowardice to my followers.*

Ftzaal circled him slowly, forcing him to turn to keep his guard toward his enemy. *When in doubt, attack,* but he was tired now, and his opponent was still fresh, and Guardmaster had also cautioned that attack must come from a position of strength. *I am allowing him to set the conditions of battle here, fighting his fight. I need to change that, force him to fight my fight.* The problem was, Pouncer's fight was Ftzaal's fight, the single combat form, and Ftzaal was better at it. Nor was he liable to be sucked into the kill rage with a few insults.

Ftzaal lunged forward, slicewire cutting the air, and Pouncer blocked and stepped back. Ftzaal snapped his weapon vertical, avoiding the block and then bringing it down again to slice through Pouncer's arm articulation. Pouncer turned and rolled backward, the only option he had to save himself, and again Ftzaal rippled his ears. "Let me know when you're ready to die, Rrit."

Pouncer didn't waste breath on a reply. *Make a decision fast, time is running out.* He flicked his eyes around his father's hall, seeking anything he could turn to his advantage, but there was nothing. *So if you can't fight your own fight, at least choose a fight that isn't his either.* His eye came over the crimson Patriarchal banners hanging down the carved stone walls and inspiration struck. He screamed and leapt, not at Ftzaal but past him, retracting his slicewire as he did. Ftzaal swung as he went by, but the distance was too large for him to connect, and then Pouncer was at the drapery, claws extended to catch the fabric. It sagged as it took his weight and for a moment he thought it would collapse, but it was heavy woven *hsahk*, firmly bolted to the vaulted roof, and it held. He scrambled up it, his claws tearing slashes into the precious fabric as he went.

"So the Rrit runs like a *vatach*." Ftzaal was enjoying himself. "And you think this is how a Patriarch fights?"

Again Pouncer didn't bother to answer. At the top of the drapery he drew his variable sword again and extended it to full length. Leaning backward he leapt to grab one of the thick stonewood ceiling beams. On his way past he swung the sword, arm fully extended, to cut the support chain of one of the room's huge, ancient chandeliers. The chain parted and the chandelier fell as he grabbed at the beam with his other hand, claws digging in. He pivoted his hind claws around to get purchase, and then levered himself onto the beam. The chandelier crashed to the floor, spraying gemstones from their fittings, but Ftzaal-Tzaatz had managed to dodge out of the way before it hit. *His reflexes are incredible.* Already the Tzaatz had understood that Pouncer was not fleeing but changing the ground rules, and he was leaping to climb another drapery, choosing one far enough away that he too would be up in the ceiling beams before Pouncer could scramble over to cut it loose beneath him. Ftzaal's reflexes would be an asset in a battle fought in such an awkward and precarious environment, but most of the single combat form would be inapplicable. The assembly below watched, awestruck. Pouncer swung his slicewire through the beam beneath him. The timber popped loudly as it was severed and ancient strains suddenly relieved. He felt it give slightly beneath him, but the two cut faces pressed against each other kept it from collapsing completely. *Now I have a trap, if I can lure him into it.* A second cut would drop a section of timber to fall to the floor, and if Pouncer could get Ftzaal to stand between himself and the first cut, when he made the second cut the Tzaatz would fall with it.

But he couldn't make it that obvious. His mind awareness surged slightly, perhaps in reaction to the intense emotion of the encounter, and through it he *knew* Ftzaal, *felt* his intention to kill him and his complete confidence that he would succeed in it. It was a frightening mind to face. *Fear is death.* He leapt from beam to beam toward his opponent, who had finished his climb.

"You will not escape me, Rrit." Ftzaal leapt as well, so they were on the same beam, now facing each other. There would be little opportunity for maneuver here. Confined as they were to the linear space of the beam, they would fight a battle of finesse with the variable sword, with the added tactic of trying to unbalance the other fighter into a fatal plunge to the stone floor below.

Pouncer slashed the beam beneath him, backed up, slashed again so a thick chunk of stonewood crashed to the ground. The remaining segments of the beam sagged, now supported only at one end. Too many beams cut would bring the whole roof down. *And that too may be a strategy, if I have to employ it.* It would be a last resort.

"You think that gap will stop me?" Ftzaal spat, angry now as he had not been before. He had expected an easier kill. Pouncer backed up further. *Let him think I am afraid. He will grow careless.*

Ftzaal screamed and leapt the gap, landing with perfect footing and coming up into attack stance, feinting down and swinging high. Pouncer let his guard drop with the feint, but not so much that he left himself vulnerable to the swing. *I knew he was going to do that.* Pouncer flowed into *v'dak* stance, and smoothly blocked two more blows. *I am gaining something from mind awareness.* It was not enough to win, but perhaps enough to survive.

Ftzaal fell back, and Pouncer took the opportunity to cut the support chain for one of the decorative tapestries hanging from the ceiling. It fell with deep rustle of heavy fabric and nearly enveloped Ftzaal where he stood. As it was, he had to leap backward, nearly losing his balance in the process. The black kzin's fangs showed white in a wide gaped smile. *He is angry, and rage is death.* Pouncer began to think he might win. He held his ground a long moment, waiting for the wild killing leap, but it didn't come. The Tzaatz was too smart a warrior to let hot anger interfere with cold intent. He advanced and Pouncer fell back, a pace at a time, all the way to the wall. There was a wide ledge there, where the beams joined the walls and roof. When he got close to it Pouncer turned and leapt. He had hoped the sudden move would give him room to maneuver, but Ftzaal had anticipated it and leapt with him. Pouncer pivoted as he landed, nearly overbalancing, and found Ftzaal's slicewire already coming for his head. He got a partial block in, enough to deflect the blow, and the weapon slashed chunks of ancient stone from the wall to clatter down into the hall below. Pouncer retreated again as Ftzaal feinted low, feinted high and then swung in the middle, but again mind awareness gave him enough warning to keep his guard where it needed to be when the killing slash came. He fell back until he came to the next crossbeam, the one he had cut. *Now we spring the trap.* He swung hard, overhand, connected and swung again, beating Ftzaal's guard down through sheer force. It was a short term strategy that would lead to exhaustion without any other result if he kept it up, but it bought him the second's respite he needed to leap backward onto the beam. The position he held was precarious and difficult to guard, but he stayed there long enough for Ftzaal to recover and swing at his ankles. *Let him think I have made a mistake, and he will expect me to correct it.* He blocked the blow, then leapt down the beam, leaving the way clear for Ftzaal to mount it and follow him. He turned again, adopted *v'scree* stance in time to see his opponent take the same position. Ftzaal advanced, slowly and deliberately. When he got within striking distance Pouncer began to withdraw. He flicked his eyes to the beam with each backward step, trying to pick up the almost invisible cut he'd already made.

There! He backed up farther, taking each step carefully, as Ftzaal continued to press his guard. The thick timber sagged slightly as Ftzaal approached the cut, less than perfectly stable. Would Ftzaal notice? Pouncer feinted forward to make sure he didn't, which turned out to be a mistake. Ftzaal easily parried the quick thrust and slash then countered with his own attack, taking advantage of Pouncer's overextended position at the end of his slash to beat his slicewire out of line and then thrust for the kill. Pouncer backed up again, but Ftzaal pressed him hard, his slicewire again slamming Pouncer's out of line to expose him for the finish. Pouncer nearly lost his variable sword with the impact, and overbalanced dangerously, nearly falling. He forgot about his trap and concentrated on survival, regaining his balance just in time to get his slicewire back in line to block another swing. For an instant it looked like he'd gotten away with it, teetering precariously but still on the beam, but then Ftzaal slammed his free fist into Pouncer's shoulder, toppling him. He lashed out to save himself, his variable sword flying off into space as he tried to regain his balance. He fell and for a long instant his vision was full of the hard stone floor far below. He grabbed wildly and managed to get his claws into the side of the beam. Wood fibers tore into long scratch marks, then held, and he was dangling. His variable sword shattered on the ground, and for a heartbeat he flashed back to the instant he'd leapt after T'suuz, high on the conduits in the Citadel's power hall on the day of the Tzaatz invasion.

Ftzaal-Tzaatz came and stood above him, looking down. "You fought well, Rrit. Not well enough." Ftzaal raised his slicewire for the killing blow. In desperation, Pouncer brought his hind claws up and braced them against the beam, then leapt into space as Ftzaal brought his variable sword down. He had swung with enough force to cleave through armor articulation, and deprived of its intended target his swing carried on, cutting through the thick stonewood beam as though it wasn't there. The section he was standing on was between Pouncer's first cut and his own. No longer supported at either end it fell. Ftzaal leapt up to grab one of the remaining beam sections, but he hadn't expected the fall and his leap was slow.

He managed to connect with one set of claws but he held on to his variable sword with the other. His claws cut long grooves in the dense wood as Pouncer's had, but with only one paw there wasn't enough purchase to entirely support his weight. They pulled out and he too fell.

Pouncer twisted in midair to land on his feet. His leap aimed for one of the huge conquest drums—its taut drumhead was the only thing in the room that might serve to break his fall. He hit it and the drumhead burst with a deafening *boom*. He hit the floor beneath it hard on all fours, joints collapsing to absorb the impact. His chin hit the ground, snapping his head back and making the world spin. He stood, steadying himself on the drum's rim and tried to get the scene to focus.

All eyes were on him, *czrav* and Tzaatz alike. Ftzaal-Tzaatz had not been so lucky in his fall. His body lay bent and broken over the fallen beam section. Ears ringing, Pouncer staggered from the wreckage of the conquest drum and went to his recent adversary, kneeling to pick up the Black Priest's finely carved variable sword. The slicewire was still extended, and he turned to the head of the hall. The fall had hurt and he was exhausted and disoriented, shaking now in reaction to the fight juices. It took a long moment to realize that he had won. He tightened his grip on the variable sword. *I will not falter now.*

"Kchula!" Pouncer bared his fangs and found a sudden, deep anger welling up that made it difficult to speak coherently. "Your brother is dead. Stand your ground." *Rage is death*, a tiny voice said in the back of his mind, but he found it too easy to ignore.

Kchula-Tzaatz rippled his ears and raised a beamrifle from under his cloak. "It was amusing to watch you fight my brother. I'm going to enjoy killing you, kitten."

He brought the weapon to his shoulder and triggered the aim dot, swung it to target Pouncer. The silence in the room was complete; even breathing seemed to have stopped. None of the *czrav* were close enough to intervene, and Pouncer couldn't move fast enough to get out of the line of fire before Kchula could shoot.

"You have no honor, Kchula." Pouncer spat the words, hoping the insult would goad him to leap, but in mind space he saw Kchula's intention to kill form, the command to pull the trigger welling up in his forebrain. The split second's warning might have saved him, if he had anywhere he could dodge, but he didn't and with his eyes he saw his own death arriving in the mirror-bright bore lens of the beamrifle.

There was a piercing scream and suddenly the welding of mind-picture and sight dissolved as a tawny shape flew through the air. Scrral-Rrit-Second-Son had leapt at Kchula, his *wtsai* extended to kill. Kchula whirled and fired but the beam went wide, spraying shards of ancient stone from the wall, and then Scrral-Rrit was on him, driving the primitive weapon up through the gap between breast armor and belly articulation, up beneath Kchula's ribcage to slice organs and sever arteries. Kchula screamed in pain, falling backward under the attack with arms flailing, and the beamrifle went flying. Scrral-Rrit withdrew the weapon as blood geysered from the wound, then stabbed again, this time up and under Kchula's chin, driving it up into his braincase.

The flailing stopped, and at that instant Second-Son screamed, his back arching as though he'd been scourged, every muscle in his body tensing. He stayed like that for long heartbeats, then pitched forward, face down in his victim's still oozing blood.

The zzrou! "Brother!" Pouncer leapt to Second-Son's side and slashed his robe open with one claw swipe. The *zzrou* was there, a dull octagon on his brother's shoulder. He tore it loose, ripping flesh as its teeth came free. It was a reflexive act, and it would have emptied the *zzrou*'s poisonous contents into his brother's body, had it not already done so itself when triggered by the cessation of Kchula-Tzaatz's heart. *P'chert* toxin dripped, oily and acrid, and Second-Son was gasping on the floor.

"Bring a Healer!" Zree-Rrit's command brooked no hesitation, but when he turned back to face the dying puppet-Patriarch, Pouncer's voice was soft. "Breathe deep, brother, help is coming."

But Second-Son's breaths came quick and shallow, his eyes glazing as his eyelids fluttered. "There is no time . . . I have paid for my dishonor."

"A Healer, now!" Pouncer lashed out the order, and Medical Officer of the Tzaatz was running forward, slaves and kzinti alike scattering before him, but Second-Son's eyes were already shut, and his breathing had stopped. *P'chert* toxin was swift.

"You have earned your name at last." Pouncer cradled Second-Son's head in his lap, the universe reduced to the still-warm body before him, the last of his family. The *sthondat*-induced mind awareness was strengthened by the physical contact, and he felt the last glimmer of his brother's consciousness dwindle and fade, until all that was left was an overwhelming emptiness.

Medical Officer arrived and dropped his crash bag, slapping a spray infuser against Scrral-Rrit's chest and starting the elaborate dance of resuscitation. Pouncer stood and moved back, knowing it was too late. *P'chert* toxin attacked the central nervous system, destroying the cell proteins at the synaptic gap. The countertoxin could prevent the damage from occurring, at the cost of doing some of its own. It could not reverse it once it had occurred. Medical Officer would try of course, the oath of his craft demanded nothing less, but he and Pouncer and everyone watching knew he would not succeed.

Pouncer stood back to give him room anyway, looking at the silent body. *My brother is dead, he isn't coming back.* Some things even the Patriarch could not command. *I am alone now.*

"No, you will never be alone again." It was a familiar voice. He looked up and saw C'mell, her armor smeared with Tzaatz blood.

"How did you . . . ?"

"The *sthondat* works both ways. Your thoughts leak, to those sensitive enough to respond." She nuzzled him. "You are safe, my Hero, and you are Patriarch."

Her physical touch triggered a flood of emotion, and he saw himself through her eyes, felt her love as physical thing, but mind awareness was receding again, further this time as the effects of the drug wore off. He felt his deep connection to his mate growing indistinct. *How can I live in a universe so dark, having seen the light?* The instinct was to get more, immediately, to not only prevent the fading of mind awareness but enhance it to its ultimate capacity. *This is the* sthondat *addiction*. The realization didn't help, the pull was strong. *But* sthondat *drug cripples too*. He remembered Patriarch's Telepath's emaciated body lying on its gravlifted *prrstet*. *This blade cuts two ways. The Patriarchy needs a strong Patriarch. I cannot be slave to the drug and rule*. He stood to face the room. More *czrav* were filing in, disarming the Tzaatz who were still there. The struggle was over. It was hard to know what to do next.

"Patriarch!" Czor-Dziit abased himself at the entrance as he came in with thrice-eight battle-scarred warriors behind him.

"Patriarch!" Zraa-Churrt did as well. "Patriarch . . ." "Patriarch . . ." One by one the assembly made their obeisance.

"Enough." Pouncer held his paws up for silence. "Stand, all of you! You who have seen fit to fight with me, those who stood by Rrit Pride in its darkest hour, you all are worthy enough to stand with me. As we have shared battle, we will share victory."

"Patriarch!" Czor-Dziit's voice showed his amazement, but he stood, and the others stood with him. There was a commotion at the back, snarls rose. Tskombe-*kz'zeerkti* and Kr-Pathfinder with his half-sword, and the manrette Trina.

Pouncer raised his voice. "Let them through!" Tskombe was carrying Cherenkova-Captain, and Pouncer felt anger when he saw her condition. *They have given her the Hot Needle*.

"Where is Ftzaal-Tzaatz?" There was urgency in Tskombe's voice.

Pouncer pointed to the body. "He is dead." Beneath his dark complexion Tskombe paled, a signal Pouncer had learned meant there was a serious problem. He swiveled his ears up. "Why, do you need him alive?"

"The Tzaatz have launched a vengeance strike on Earth. He's the one who knows the launch coordinates."

"Hrrr." Pouncer turned a paw over. "Your species and mine are at war now, Tskombe-*kz'zeerkti*. Your fleet is falling in to the attack even now."

"If either race is going to survive we need to stop this."

"I agree." Pouncer looked to the black furred corpse. "Do any other Tzaatz know the coordinates?"

Tskombe spread his hands. "Someone must. Kchula-Tzaatz would, perhaps."

"He is dead too."

Tskombe was silent, and Pouncer became aware of the entire assembly watching him. *I am Patriarch now, and I need to lead.* There was little time before the humans arrived to destroy his world. *I may be the last Patriarch ever. Kchula has given me a gift with this revenge strike. I can use it to bargain for my world, if I can get the launch data.* There would be other Tzaatz who knew the information, the technicians who had set up the attack profile at the Patriarch's Dock in orbit, but he wouldn't be able to find them before the human fleet arrived. Earth would die, and Kzinhome would die before it.

Unless . . . He remembered a rumor about Patriarch's Telepath. *I am his full brother.* How much of his Gift did he share? His paw went to his hunt pouch, felt the two vials of *sthondat* extract there. *I cannot rule as a slave to the drug.* He could not rule if the Patriarchy was destroyed either. There was no time, and no choice. He drew out a vial and drained its bitter black fluid in a single gulp.

Immediately the mind-trance came on him full strength, familiar now, but with none of the gradual onset of the previous time. He felt C'mell's love, Tskombe's concern, Cherenkova's pain, the loyalty of Kr-Pathfinder and V'rli and Czor-Dziit and the *czrav*, the fear of the slaves who cowered around the Citadel while their masters contended for its rulership. The blackness of mind space was absolute, but he forced himself to open his eyes, not surprised to find himself on the floor. *I must not show myself to be owned by this.* He stood shakily and turned, walking with deliberate steps to the black-furred corpse over a floor that seemed to pulse and writhe with the thoughts of the onlookers. He knelt, grateful that he had to walk only a short distance, and gazed into Ftzaal-Tzaatz's glazed-over eyes, still open from the moment of his dying, touching him on the shoulder. *It was said Patriarch's Telepath could know the minds of the recently dead.* He closed his own eyes and concentrated, seeking out the tiny, dying spark of awareness that had been the most feared warrior in the Patriarchy, trying to block out the overwhelming strength of the other minds around. He found it, finally, behind the darkness of the black fur gene, and nearly lost in the blinding light of impending death. The awareness stirred at his intrusion, and pain became dawning recognition.

You fought well, Rrit Kitten. You will be a good Patriarch.

May the Fanged God welcome your soul, Protector of Jotok.

And *there* was the information he sought, a battleship stripped to its frame, launched to destroy the *kz'zeerkti* homeworld with relativistic impactors, and *there* the coordinates and trajectory data, and the launch time, and with it the knowledge the *kz'zeerkti* had little time left. He focused on the knowledge, infused it, welded it to his own awareness until it was a part of him, until the awareness that had been Ftzaal-Tzaatz faded at last and went dark. For a moment he drifted in the same emptiness that Patriarch's Telepath had known, and then the surrounding minds came surging back at him, flooding out his own thoughts, his own sense of self diluted by the wash of *otherness*. It was frightening, exhilarating, danger and joy at once. *This too is the* sthondat *drug's danger. I must never take it again, never.* He opened his eyes, momentarily disoriented by the sudden return of external reality. Ftzaal's body lay before him, seeming somehow shrunken. He pitched his head back and roared the *zal'mchurrr* to consign a worthy warrior to the Fanged God's pride circle. The scream had the effect of clearing the other minds from his, and when he stood to face the room they were at enough of a distance that he could keep them at bay.

"Did you get it?" Tskombe-*kz'zeerkti* was watching him anxiously.

"I have it. Now we must deal with your compatriot's fleet."

Only the dead have seen the end of war.

—Plato

Quacy Tskombe swallowed hard. The Citadel's Battle

Room was set to show the close space defense zone of Kzinhome. The ships of the Tzaatz and the various Great Prides who had come to lend their strength to the Patriarchy were boosting out beyond the orbit of the Hunter's Moon. UN Scoutships had skirmished with kzinti destroyers higher up in the gravity well and had fared poorly. Kzinhome was far better defended than any target they'd taken on before this, but now the human cruiser screen was closing for battle. The green icons that marked kzinti forces were well deployed to intercept the incoming fleet, and they presented a formidible force. It was the size of the UN fleet that gave Tskombe pause. The ranked green icons filled a globe over a meter across at the display's scale. There were hundreds of ships, more firepower than had ever been assembled in one place in known space, to his certain knowledge.

And they are coming to destroy this world and every-thing on it. He had no illusions about the intent of the fleet. Looking at the armada as it was laid out in the plot tank he had no illusions about their ability to do it either.

Unless I can convince them otherwise. He looked to Ayla, sleeping now on a gravlifted *prrstet* under a sedative from his medkit, with Trina looking after her. The girl was gazing with childlike concern and adoration at the woman who was her last link to her mother. Ayla wasn't in danger, yet, but she was weak and in pain and grievously injured, and she needed medical attention that she could only get aboard a hospital ship. He thought back to his escape from Earth. If he hadn't fled, hadn't deserted, he wouldn't be here for her now, but he was painfully aware of the reception he was likely to receive in contacting the fleet. *Maybe they haven't uploaded my file.* It was a faint hope. It would have been better if Ayla could have made the transmission. Her record was unblemished

But she couldn't. It was up to him. He looked across to Pouncer, who would speak after him, and nodded. Pouncer made the gesture that commanded the room's AI to transmit. There was a pause for speed-of-light lag, and then the Pierin slave who ran the equipment raised a manipulator to tell him he could begin.

He took a deep breath. "This is Colonel Quacy Tskombe of the United Nations Special Mission to Kzinhome. I am here with the Patriarch of Kzin and I have a negotiated peace settlement here in my hands."

He counted ten seconds slowly, the turnaround time, then another endless minute. The UN would be getting the right person on the line. The display showed a face, gray haired and severe. "This is Admiral Mysolin. Who are you?"

Tskombe repeated himself, waited the ten seconds. The admiral looked offscreen for a second, said something with the audio cut off, then came back online.

"Colonel, I have no information on your mission. Can you verify who you are?"

"You'll have to check with New York."

Ten seconds. Mysolin smirked. "Colonel, you and I both know that's not going to happen. I understand you're in an uncomfortable position planetside, but I've just fought my way across Known Space against fanatic resistance and paid my way into this system in blood."

"We don't have time to argue. Admiral, I have important information for you. You have to stop your attack."

Ten seconds. Mysolin was using the time, checking something on his screen while he waited for Quacy's signal to arrive. "I have your file here, Colonel." His eyebrows went up. "You're a fugitive, according to this, and I'm in no mood to discuss the situation. I'm here with overwhelming firepower and a set of very specific orders from the Secretary General. You say you have information for me then give it to me, and then I'm going to finish what I've started here."

Tskombe looked over at Pouncer. "Admiral, let me put this in the barest possible terms. The kzinti have launched a revenge strike with enough lightspeed impactors to reliquefy Earth's crust. I have here the only kzin who knows the launch coordinates and trajectory data, which represent the only chance we have of getting ahead of those rocks and carrying out an intercept. Press home your attack and your victory is going to be a moot point for twenty billion people."

Ten seconds. Mysolin's face hardened. "I hope you don't expect me to respond to threats, Colonel."

Tskombe felt his blood freeze. *They aren't going to stop* . . . "Sir . . . Sir, you have to believe me."

Ten seconds. "I don't have to believe you, and I see no compelling reason that I should. You're a deserter, and from all outward appearances a traitor. You may be just a simulation on a kzinti computer. Whatever you are, you're on the wrong side of this war. I'm sorry about that, but that isn't going to change what's about to happen here."

"Sir, I can understand your hesitation." Tskombe tried to keep his growing desperation out of his voice. "I can verify that there's a ceasefire in effect. Take your fleet into a parking orbit and issue defensive orders. You'll be left alone."

Ten seconds. Tskombe felt his heart pounding and tried to keep his breathing under control. Finally Mysolin spoke. "And give them time to set up for us?"

"Sir. You said it yourself, you've got overwhelming fire-power. You might not be aware but there's a civil war down here, they're in no position to stop you. What have you got to lose?"

Ten seconds. "I have ships to lose, and lives. Now I'm done talking here. I'm sorry for your predicament, Colonel." Mysolin made a chopping gesture and his image vanished.

Tskombe slumped. The UN would raze Kzinhome now. The Command Lair was well protected. It wasn't impossible that they might survive the attack, but civilization on the planet would be destroyed, and three humans were not likely to survive long in that environment. He looked across to Trina, who was looking worried. *She's finally run out of luck.*

Pouncer turned a paw over and moved to the primary battle console. "I am Patriarch now. I will direct the defense. We may yet prevail, Tskombe-*kz'zeerkti*" His voice was level as he spoke, but his eyes were on the icon array of the human fleet, and Tskombe could tell he didn't favor their chances.

Nor do I, but we'll go down fighting. It occurred to him that with that thought he had finally crossed the line from deserter to traitor, not that it would make any difference soon. He looked across to Ayla. *So I haven't saved her, but at least she knows I didn't abandon her.* Battered as she was she still looked beautiful, and he knew he could have made no other choice.

The viscom flashed with an incoming signal, and a face appeared. Admiral Mysolin again. His expression was sour. "Colonel Tskombe, on the advice of my Senior Strategist, I'm going to put my fleet in parking orbit. We will not attack unless attacked. I want the trajectory information for those impactors. We're going to verify your story. Let me promise you this. I have your communications triangulated. If this turns out to be some kind of ruse, and we wind up taking this planet by force after all, you will not survive. Am I clear on that?"

"Sir. I'm on your side. I'm going to switch channels now and make sure the kzinti fleet knows the program. I'll be back on the air in three minutes with the information."

The display split and another image appeared, with a long snout and a broad, toothy grin. Curvy. She whistled and chirped, and her translator spoke. "You have done well, Quacy Tskombe. I look forward to poker. You owe me many salmon."

Mysolin looked annoyed at the interruption. "Three minutes. I'll be waiting."

Tskombe nodded and then made room for Pouncer on the transmission dais. Pouncer strode up, confident in his command, the look Tskombe had first seen in his eyes when he came out of the mind-trance had deepened. *He has mastered the* sthondat *extract*, Tskombe realized. *He is Zree-Rrit now in every way. He's going to make a formidable Patriarch.* Pouncer made the gesture that ordered the AI to switch to the General Command channel and strode into position. "Heroes of Kzinhome, this is Zree-Rrit-Son-of-Meerz-Rrit, Patriarch of Kzin. A peace-with-honor has been negotiated. The *kz'zeerkti* ships will adopt parking orbits and will not be intercepted while in those orbits. Fire weapons only in self-defense. End transmission." He slashed a paw in the air, commanding the AI to terminate the link.

Tskombe raised an eyebrow. "Aren't you going to wait for acknowledgment?"

Zree-Rrit's lips twitched over his fangs. "I am Patriarch. They will obey."

Tskombe nodded, slowly breathing out the accumulated tension in the room. "Right."

He met Ayla's gaze. She had woken up and watched the final exchange. He went to her, felt the warmth of her presence, took her hand carefully so as not to hurt her, sat with her and Trina on the *prrstet*.

Ayla smiled up at him. "What happens now?"

"Now, Cherenkova-Captain." Zree-Rrit answered before Tskombe could. He fanned his ears up, his tail relaxed, secure within the absolute authority of his command. "Now, we forge peace on the anvil of war."

> *Peace cannot be kept by force; it can only be achieved by understanding.*
> —Albert Einstein

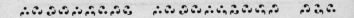

IT'S HOWLING TIME IN KNOWN SPACE!

THE MAN-KZIN WARS
CREATED BY LARRY NIVEN

THE MAN-KZIN WARS
0-671-72076-7 • $6.99

THE BEST OF ALL POSSIBLE WARS
0-671-87879-4 • $6.99

MAN-KZIN WARS IX
0-7434-7145-8 • $7.99

MAN-KZIN WARS X: THE WUNDER WAR
0-7434-3619-9 • $21.00 (HC)
0-7434-9894-1 • $7.99

MAN-KZIN WARS XI
1-4165-0906-2 • $22.00

NOVELS:
DESTINY'S FORGE by Paul Chafe
1-4165-2071-6 • $25.00

LES FILS D'ABRAHAM

MAREK HALTER

LES FILS
D'ABRAHAM

LAFFONT

© Éditions Robert Laffont, S.A., Paris, 1989

ISBN 2-266-03711-0

A ma mère,
Perl Halter, poétesse yiddish,
dont l'œuvre s'inscrit dans la langue
d'un peuple assassiné,
pour m'avoir transmis
son amour des mots.

1

ISRAËL

RENDEZ-VOUS À JÉRUSALEM

Mars 1961

A petits coups de volant, Hugo Halter bouscule sa voiture dans les virages qui enlacent la colline, balançant devant lui, à contre-ciel, l'une ou l'autre des apparitions de Jérusalem. C'est la quatrième fois de la semaine qu'il fait le voyage et, toujours le même vertige au cœur, il guette l'instant où la ville se déploiera enfin devant lui — si nette, si précise au bout de l'ultime ligne droite.

Il jette un regard à sa femme Sigrid, qui paraît accablée de chaleur et plutôt indifférente au paysage. Il roule encore quelques instants, passe un carrefour désert et, comme s'il voulait ne rien perdre de ce moment béni, vient se garer doucement sur l'aire de dégagement qui domine les pentes du village arabe d'Abou Gosh, couvertes du duvet des jeunes arbustes. Là, il coupe le moteur, ouvre la portière sur le spectacle des lointaines murailles crénelées de pierres blanches et grises, luisantes dans le soleil et, s'éloignant de quelques pas :

— Viens voir, Sigrid... On dirait une aquarelle...

Sigrid ne bougeant pas, il se tourne vers elle et, la paume de ses mains levée, répète :

— Viens... Viens donc voir... Jamais, je crois, je ne m'en lasserai.

— Il fait plus frais ici, répond-elle.

Et moqueuse, elle referme la portière.

Déçu, il s'assied sur une borne, serrant ses bras maigres contre le corps, comme pour se protéger. Et il reste de longues minutes ainsi, immobile, ébahi, cherchant pour la énième fois à situer la vallée du Cédron ; puis la source du Gibon ; puis encore l'obscur foyer de cette lumière si vive qui, comme chaque fois qu'il revient ici, l'aveugle, le ravit — en même temps qu'elle lui fait un peu peur.

Bien avant Jérusalem, se répète-t-il, il y avait ici Salem, où le roi Mulki Sedek a, un jour, accueilli Abraham. Le mont Morya et sa grande roche plate, destinée aux sacrifices, où David concevra l'idée d'élever un Temple à l'Éternel. Il y a eu le Temple de Salomon, détruit par Nabuchodonosor, reconstruit par Ezra, abattu par Antiochus Épiphanes, à nouveau élevé par les Asmonéens, démoli encore par Pompée, rebâti par Hérode jusqu'à ce que Titus, tout près de nous...

Tant de mots... Tant de noms... Toute cette histoire légendaire et mythique dont il ne se lasse décidément pas d'invoquer les héros... Au fond, Sigrid n'a pas tort... Comment partagerait-elle cette ivresse ? Comment goûterait-elle, avec lui, autant que lui, le parfum de cette poussière dont il n'est pas un grain qui ne soit chargé d'esprit, de mémoire ? Hugo en est là de ses réflexions. Il cligne drôlement les yeux, fronce ses sourcils gris tant la lumière est forte. Il a l'air d'un banal touriste, jouissant en silence et en secret d'un panorama unique au monde. Et c'est alors que, un peu plus bas, au détour d'un virage, dans un nuage de poussière qui semble sur le point de voiler un instant le soleil, surgit un camion militaire.

« Étrange, se dit-il... Cette route déserte... Au cœur d'un jour de shabbat... »

Il n'a pas le temps d'en dire plus ni de s'interroger davantage. Car, une fois le camion parvenu à sa hauteur, un bruit qu'il connaît bien couvre le vrombissement du moteur.

— *Rebono shel olam* ! Mon Dieu ! gémit-il, en se

jetant à plat ventre et en cherchant machinalement le pistolet qu'il n'a pas.

Ce bruit assourdissant, c'est celui d'une arme automatique qui, dissimulée derrière la bâche, est en train d'arroser la voiture, puis la borne où il était assis, puis à nouveau la voiture. Quand il relève la tête et se redresse, il ne voit déjà plus qu'un amas de tôles tordues, criblées de trous. Et quant à Sigrid, elle est là, toujours là — mais à demi étendue sur le siège, la tête coincée sous le volant.

« Mon Dieu, répète-t-il... Mon Dieu... », tandis qu'il se précipite. Une autre rafale. Une autre encore. Une déflagration, un choc, à l'instant où, ivre de douleur, suffoquant, il tente d'ouvrir à toute force la portière disloquée. La violence de l'explosion l'a projeté en arrière, sur le bas-côté, juste à côté de la borne où il était assis un instant plus tôt. Tout est allé très vite. Il a juste eu le temps d'apercevoir la bouche ouverte, les yeux exorbités de Sigrid. Puis l'image de ces vieux Juifs, en caftan, le châle de prière sur la tête, qu'il avait surpris, un jour de soleil comme celui-ci, dans l'obscurité d'une synagogue... Puis l'incendie de l'imprimerie familiale à Berlin et, à Varsovie, le visage de son grand-oncle Abraham... Il entendra à peine le gémissement des sirènes, le grincement des pneus autour de lui, les exclamations en hébreu au-dessus de sa tête.

« Quand le mort repose, murmure-t-il entre ses dents... Quand le mort repose, laisse reposer sa mémoire... »

Les yeux clos, la bouche pleine de sang, le ventre, les cuisses, la tête douloureuse, il voit une tache sombre dans un ciel sans force.

On se penche sur lui. Il essaie de se débattre. Peut-être veut-il même dire un mot, prononcer un vague nom. Hélas, son corps n'est plus au rendez-vous.

Paris, avril 1961

Que sais-je de Hugo en ce jour de printemps où un télégramme de mon autre cousin, Mordekhaï, du kibboutz Dafné, m'apprend sa mort ? J'en sais ce que nous savons tous, dans la famille. C'est le plus secret d'entre nous. Celui dont la vie — et maintenant la mort — sont frappées au sceau du plus grand mystère. Il a depuis toujours, et pour nous tous, cette inégalable aura des hommes de l'ombre et des héros.

La première image qui m'en revient (mais est-ce vraiment une image ? n'est-ce pas déjà un souvenir ? une légende ?) remonte à Varsovie, dans les années d'extrême tourmente. J'ai trois ans. C'est le jour de mon anniversaire — le dernier, mais je ne le sais pas encore, que célébrera la famille au complet. Hugo, fuyant l'Allemagne, débarque chez nous à l'improviste. Ployant sous un volumineux sac à dos, maigre, mal rasé, il fait taire sur-le-champ la fête autour de moi. On croirait un roi mage. Ou un père Noël fourbu, traqué, vaguement inquiétant. Dans son sac ni cadeaux ni friandises, mais ces paroles si graves :

— Les Allemands, souffle-t-il d'un air d'infinie lassitude, seront bientôt à Varsovie. Les Juifs doivent quitter la Pologne. Il n'y a pas de temps à perdre...

Mon père proteste. Ma mère s'exclame qu'une famille ne peut fuir ainsi, tout abandonner. Mon oncle David tente de railler, de prendre les choses à la légère — je l'imagine, avec son air de sage et sa barbe rassurante, expliquant que Hitler ne peut rompre si vite les accords signés à Munich ; qu'il ne faut pas exagérer la cruauté des persécutions nazies ; qu'elles ne sont pas plus terribles que les pogromes tsaristes et que les pogromes — malheur à nous ! — les Juifs ne connaissent que trop... Et moi je me mets à pleurer, oh oui ! tellement pleurer de cet anniversaire perdu, de ce gâteau auquel personne ne touche, de ces menaces terribles que mon âme d'enfant sent poindre à l'horizon ; et, tandis que mon père m'adresse un regard grondeur, c'est le cousin Hugo qui me prend dans ses bras. Sa barbe me picote la joue. Je vois, sur le revers de sa vareuse, une traînée de poussière qui me fait penser tout à coup : « Cousin Hugo a fait une bien longue route et je suis dans ses bras. » Et c'est alors que, l'index levé, il prononce ces mots à jamais gravés en moi :

— Tu vois ces Juifs, Marek ? S'ils ne changent pas, ils mourront...

Il dort chez nous, cette nuit-là. Et les deux nuits suivantes. Puis il nous quitte comme il est venu, son sac sur le dos. J'entends dire autour de moi que le grand-père Abraham lui a offert ses économies pour qu'il puisse s'embarquer sur un cargo vers l'Amérique.

Des années plus tard, au soir du premier Kippour de l'après-guerre, l'ombre de Hugo revient. Nous sommes, mes parents et moi, au nombre des survivants du massacre. Nous sommes les orphelins d'un peuple décimé. Et nous voici à Lodz, en compagnie de quelques amis, dans une petite pièce faisant office de synagogue où traîne encore l'odeur de la mort. Mon père, depuis quelques mois, emploie tout son temps à retrouver la trace de ce qui demeure de la famille. Il occupe ses soirées à rédiger des annonces qu'il expédie à la presse yiddish, partout dans le monde. Il trie les réponses, les classe, écrit lui-même à des destinataires dont il ignore s'ils sont encore en vie. Et voici que ce soir-là, au cœur donc de l'été 1946, il reçoit, de New York, une lettre de Hugo.

Nous y apprenons que notre mystérieux cousin, après cette fameuse nuit d'anniversaire à Varsovie, traverse la Pologne embouteillée par des dizaines de milliers de réfugiés en marche et des convois militaires, échappe dix fois à la police en quête d'espions allemands, invente mille stratagèmes pour emprunter trains ou camions réquisitionnés par l'armée et parvient enfin à Gdynia où, avec les économies du grand-père Abraham, il achète un billet de passage, à fond de cale, près des machines, sur le *Stefan Batory,* l'un des derniers paquebots à faire le voyage d'Amérique.

Ce qu'il devient alors ? A quoi il occupe les jours, les années qui commencent ? J'ai la lettre ici, sous les yeux — bavarde et énigmatique à la fois, comme il était toujours. Et le plus simple est, je crois, de lui laisser la parole :

« Je suis arrivé à New York au début du mois de septembre 39. L'organisation humanitaire Joint m'aida à trouver un logement et Jacob Kastof, un ami d'Abraham, me procura une place de metteur en pages à l'imprimerie du quotidien yiddish *Forward,* au 175, East Broadway, à Brooklyn, qui, en ce temps-là, était encore un quartier juif.

« Malgré un pouvoir que beaucoup d'entre eux ignoraient, les Juifs américains ne furent pas plus attentifs à mon témoignage que les Juifs polonais. La Pologne était déjà occupée. Les nouvelles qui nous en parvenaient avaient de quoi nous angoisser. *Forward* publia même un article sur l'existence d'un camp de concentration près de Lublin. Mais le journal lui-même ne croyait pas à la menace. Personne, je dis bien personne, n'imaginait possible la destruction des Juifs d'Europe. Et c'est en 1943 seulement qu'une autre revue consacrera sa couverture à notre martyre. 1943 ? Quelques jours après la destruction du ghetto de Varsovie...

« Pour l'heure, je suis accablé. Désespéré. Je me demande même si je n'aurais pas dû rester à Berlin et, mourir pour mourir, le faire chez moi, parmi les miens.

14

Mais le désespoir est le souci du cœur et je décide de sauver mon âme. Je me retire dans un " shtibl ", une petite synagogue à Brooklyn où pendant de longues semaines, je prie, prie et prie encore — adjurant l'Éternel, Dieu d'Israël, de ne pas abandonner Son peuple, de lui ouvrir les yeux sur le danger, de faire comprendre au monde insouciant et aveugle qu'il dort sous un volcan dont la lave prendra bientôt l'aspect de millions de formes humaines...

« Oui, pendant quatre semaines, je n'ai cessé de penser à vous, là-bas, à Varsovie, qui rêviez sous un ciel couvert d'écailles de poisson mort. Ce ciel, je le savais, allait tomber sur la terre, la recouvrant d'immondices et la plongeant dans la nuit. Ne souriez pas, mes amis. Ne vous moquez pas de ma piètre littérature. Je suis un homme de l'ombre, pas un écrivain — et j'essaye simplement de raconter...

« Malheur... Solitude... Sentiment d'être seul, atrocement seul, à prêcher dans le désert, plaider pour le néant... Je passe tout mon temps libre à écrire aux journaux, à harceler les personnalités politiques. En septembre 1941, je réussis même à rencontrer le rabbin Stephen Wise, l'un des dirigeants les plus fameux du judaïsme américain, et son adjoint Nahum Goldman. Je leur raconte ce qui se passe en Europe, ce que j'ai vu en Allemagne, ce que je sais de la déportation des Juifs polonais. J'explique qu'il ne s'agit plus d'un pogrome, que ce n'est plus une banale haine — mais que ces hommes exécutent un véritable " travail " qui consiste à nous éliminer de la surface de la terre... Ils m'écoutent tous deux avec beaucoup d'attention. Mais vous imaginez ma tristesse et ma colère quand, quelques jours plus tard, j'entends le même Nahum Goldman déclarer à la radio : " Le problème des communautés juives européennes se pose davantage en termes de secours qu'en termes politiques. "

« En attendant, les manifestations contre l'engagement des États-Unis se poursuivent. Le fameux Charles Lindberg, celui-là même qui, le premier, traversa l'Atlantique en avion, accuse publiquement les Juifs de pousser l'Amérique à la guerre. Certains journaux, parmi les plus honorables, reprochent aux Juifs leur mauvaise grâce à s'assimiler... En Amérique ! la patrie des minorités !... De plus en plus désespéré, je songe même à me suicider...

« Heureusement pour nous tous, le Japon attaque l'Amérique. Oui, j'affirme que le 6 décembre 1941, à Pearl Harbour, les Japonais ont sauvé le monde. Car, croyez-en un homme qui vivait aux États-Unis en ces temps-là : sans cette humiliation militaire l'Amérique n'entrait pas en guerre. Pour ma part, j'exulte. Je respire enfin. Et, dès la fin 41, je suis l'un des premiers à me porter volontaire pour aller combattre les nazis. Je suis au Maroc. Puis en Tunisie où le général Omar Bradley réclame un interprète d'allemand et où je participe à la libération de Hammam Lif...

« Vous croyez connaître la guerre ? Vous ne la connaissez pas du côté de ceux qui tuent. A Hammam Lif, pour la première fois de ma vie, il m'a fallu tuer. Tuer des nazis, il est vrai, mais des êtres vivants, tout de même. Et j'avais aussi très peur de mourir. Je me revois avançant, avec le 11e corps d'armée, le long de la plage, sous le feu de l'artillerie ennemie placée sur les hauteurs de Bou Kornine. Je tire et je crie. Je crois que je crie très fort. Et je crois que c'est ce cri qui m'a sauvé. Il m'a sauvé de ma peur. Comme jamais auparavant, j'ai senti que j'étais un être vivant dans un monde grouillant de vie et que je n'avais d'autre devoir, d'autre but que de vivre. Coûte que coûte. Innocents, coupables, rien ne comptait plus, que la vie. A la fin de la journée, la ville et, bien sûr, le palais du bey de Tunis étaient libérés. Quelques centaines de soldats et officiers allemands, membres de l'Afrika Korps, hébétés, attendaient sur la place centrale d'être interrogés. Me croirez-vous ? Je n'éprouvais aucune haine à leur égard. Pour moi, ils appartenaient à un monde mort et j'avais hâte de retrouver les vivants.

« Le soir venu, parmi la foule qui se déversait sur les plages pour contempler les chars allemands, immobilisés dans les sables, un homme m'a béni. Musulman,

16

chrétien, juif ? Je ne sais. Mais brusquement, je me suis souvenu que c'était samedi, jour de shabbath, et que Hammam Lif comptait une communauté nombreuse. Je choisis au hasard un vieillard et lui demande le chemin de la synagogue. Surpris par mon uniforme, il dit en anglais : " *Jew ?* " Je fais oui de la tête et, pointant le doigt sur sa poitrine, je demande à mon tour : " *Jew ?* " Pour seule réponse, il me prie de le suivre.

« Le jour, en Afrique, tombe brutalement, sans transition — et nous nous retrouvâmes bientôt, mon guide et moi, dans une petite cour déjà plongée dans l'obscurité, où il me sembla entendre une mélodie de mon enfance. Ému, je poussai une porte qui s'ouvrit sur une pièce carrée, basse de plafond où une famille était réunie autour d'une table. A l'évidence, c'était une famille arabe. Mon guide, qui s'appelait Salem, parla d'ailleurs en arabe. Et le maître de maison, lorsqu'il m'accueillit, présentait la parfaite image de cette hospitalité orientale dont il m'a souvent été donné, par la suite, d'apprécier l'incomparable qualité. Or savez-vous ce qu'il advint ? Les enfants s'approchèrent de moi. Les femmes se mirent à nettoyer la table. On me présenta un verre de vin. Des voisins arrivèrent. La pièce fut bientôt pleine. Quelqu'un se mit à chanter. La foule reprit en chœur. Et que croyez-vous qu'ils chantaient, ces Arabes de Hammam Lif ? *Al Irá Avdi Jakob* — " Ne crains pas, mon serviteur Jacob ".

« Un homme à la barbe blanche et rare comme celles des Chinois de Chinatown à New York m'adressa la parole en hébreu. C'était le père de mon hôte et il me demanda, en me montrant la radio posée sur un petit guéridon incrusté d'ivoire et de nacre, si je voulais connaître les nouvelles. On entendit d'abord des bruits de parasites. Puis des voix incertaines. Puis un grand vacarme de langues, d'accents qui se chevauchaient. Et puis enfin, dans un anglais à la prononciation lente et claire, une voix qui annonçait la destruction du ghetto de Varsovie.

« " Qu'y a-t-il ? " demanda le grand-père, en voyant ma stupeur, mon chagrin, mes sanglots. Les yeux dans

le vague, je ne savais que répéter : " Varsovie...
ghetto... ma famille... " Je murmurai le nom des miens,
vos prénoms, cher Salomon, chère Perl. Je répétais,
mais dans un grand désordre, ce que je vous avais dit,
lors de cette fameuse nuit... Le vieil homme comprit. Il
dit quelques mots en arabe. Et, tandis que de grosses
larmes coulaient aussi sur ses joues, les femmes se
mirent l'une à hurler à la mort, l'autre à se couvrir le
visage, la troisième à se déchirer la poitrine. J'étais à
Hammam Lif. Devant ces Juifs extravagants qui ressem-
blaient à s'y méprendre à des Arabes et qui pleuraient
ma famille de Varsovie, je fus soudain envahi du plus
inattendu des sentiments. Ce fut comme un basculement
en moi. Ou comme une révélation. Ce fut comme si un
invisible ressort se détendait brusquement. Je venais de
comprendre que le judaïsme ne s'arrêtait pas au pied
des murs du ghetto de Varsovie. Et malgré les morts,
malgré la disparition du monde auquel j'appartenais, je
ressentis une sorte de joie sauvage, cruelle, unique,
miraculeuse... Pour la première fois depuis ma fuite de
Berlin, j'étais sûr, oui sûr, que Hitler avait perdu la
guerre. Du moins sa guerre contre les Juifs.

« " L'homme porte son destin attaché au cou ",
disent les Arabes. Je portais, moi, mes chers cousins, la
vieille sacoche de cuir dont vous vous souvenez peut-
être et où j'avais glissé, cette fameuse nuit, les quelques
pages du livre familial que le grand-père Abraham, à
votre insu à tous mais en grande cérémonie, avait tenu à
me remettre. Cette sacoche — et son précieux
contenu —, je ne m'en dessaisirais plus. Chargé de
mémoire, comme d'autres ont charge d'âme, je savais
que j'étais le témoin, que dis-je ? le porte-flambeau et le
prophète de notre entière lignée. Jamais, tout au long
de ces années, ne me fit défaut cette conviction : je
retournerais à Berlin, je reverrais Varsovie...

« Pour l'heure, il me restait une année à passer à
Tunis. J'y connus quelques filles. Des étreintes rapides,
furtives, comme pour tuer le temps, tromper l'inquiétude ou la mort. Je m'y fis aussi des amis — car " un ami
fidèle, dit l'Écclésiaste, est une tour forte et qui l'a

trouvé, a trouvé un trésor ". L'un d'eux, Marwan Assadi, avait un fils du nom de Hidar, qui était alors âgé d'une quinzaine d'années et dont l'intelligence, le charme peut-être et la grâce me faisaient parfois penser : " On dirait le fils que je n'ai pas eu et que peut-être je n'aurai jamais. " Hidar était arabe. Nous n'étions d'accord sur rien. Nous passions des nuits entières à discuter de cette Palestine qui n'avait jamais existé, lui expliquais-je, que dans les rêves absurdes d'Hadrien et, bien plus tard, des Britanniques — et où je ne me lassais pas de reconnaître, moi, la terre qui depuis deux mille ans attend le retour d'Abraham. Mais enfin, je l'aimais. Et il était, je vous le répète, comme un fils ou un jeune frère.

« En juillet 1944, j'arrive à Palerme. Un mois plus tard, je pose le pied sur la côte française, aux abords d'une petite ville du nom de Saint-Raphaël. Je traverse la France au pas de course. Je me retrouve dans les Ardennes, officier de liaison d'un maréchal de fière allure. Je suis à Strasbourg sous les bombes, dans le fracas des mitrailleuses — trouvant néanmoins le temps de visiter la cathédrale, d'arpenter l'ancien quartier juif, de me promener sur les quais Finckwiller, avec, dans le cœur et la tête, quelques-uns des feuillets que m'a confiés Abraham. Ces pages, je les ai relues maintes fois dans les tranchées. Elles racontent l'histoire de notre famille, l'aventure de Gabriel, fils d'Aron, les débuts de l'imprimerie. Et à Strasbourg donc, voulant tout vérifier, tout revivre, voulant revoir cette " Montagne Verte " où, voici plus de cinq siècles, notre Gabriel apprenait le métier d'imprimeur dans l'atelier même de maître Gutenberg, je réquisitionne une jeep.

« Las ! Je m'égare dans les dédales de la guerre autant que dans ma mémoire. Un détachement de l'armée allemande me surprend à une vingtaine de kilomètres de la ville. Ma jeep est prise sous le feu allemand. Contraint de l'abandonner, blessé à l'épaule et au ventre, je me mets à courir à travers champs pour rejoindre les lignes alliées. Je saigne comme un bœuf. Je suis au bord de m'effondrer, de défaillir. Et c'est alors qu'une voiture, roulant à vive allure dans la direction du Rhin, me renverse. C'est Sigrid... Sigrid Furchmuller... En visite à Strasbourg chez une amie, elle a été surprise par l'avancée des forces françaises et tente, désespérément elle aussi, de retourner chez elle. Je ne me souviens pas très bien de la suite. Sigrid, paraît-il, n'était pas très intéressée par ma personne. Mais, la voiture ne démarrant pas et la guerre aiguisant le réflexe de survie, elle pensa, non sans raison, que soigner un officier américain pouvait lui être utile. Si les Alliés arrivaient d'abord, elle était en train de sauver l'un des leurs ; si c'étaient les Allemands... Ce furent les Alliés, bien sûr. Sigrid me sauva la vie. Je témoignai, en retour, pour elle et sa famille. L'année suivante, elle me suit aux États-Unis, se convertit au judaïsme — et me voilà marié à une Allemande, fille d'un général nazi.

« " J'oublie de vous dire que le sang de ma blessure avait effacé l'encre des feuillets d'Abraham que je portais dans ma sacoche. J'avais eu la vie sauve, mais au prix de la mémoire. Je renouais avec le monde des vivants, mais en rompant avec celui des morts. Faut-il y voir un symbole ? C'est Sigrid, la jeune et belle épouse dont je me sentais si coupable, qui me persuada d'entreprendre la reconquête de cette histoire effacée.

« " Publie des appels dans la presse, me dit-elle, écris aux organisations internationales, à l'Office des réfugiés, à la Croix-Rouge, au Joint, à l'UNWRA... Chaque réponse que tu recevras sera comme un miracle, et ta fièvre baissera. "

« Sigrid avait raison. Mieux : elle devint une sorte d'intendante de cette mémoire en lambeaux — écrivant aux uns, relançant les autres, m'inspirant une lettre à celui-ci, une réponse à celui-là. La guerre était finie. Le nazisme était vaincu. Il me restait — il *nous* restait — à craindre cette autre source de malheur que les Juifs appellent l'oubli. Étrange que ce soit à moi, Hugo, le moins pieux des Halter, peut-être le moins juif, qu'incombe le devoir de renouer les fils. Tout est là, de nouveau. Sur mon cœur. Dans un petit carnet qui, déjà, en quelques pages, rassemble des siècles d'histoire. »

Quinze ans plus tard, en 1961, troisième et dernière séquence. Notre cousin s'est, officiellement du moins, installé en Amérique. Il est devenu metteur en pages à l'imprimerie du *Forward*, le quotidien américain de langue yiddish — ce qui, pour un homme de sa culture, reste un emploi curieusement modeste. Nous avons eu vent, de loin en loin, à travers les cartes postales qu'il nous adressait parfois, d'étranges et lointains voyages. A Beyrouth, par exemple. Au Caire. A Prague. Au Yémen. Un ami de mes parents affirme même l'avoir rencontré un jour à Francfort. Il portait une moustache, des lunettes d'écaille, il avait les cheveux teints en noir, un air de banquier ou de transitaire international — mais, pas de doute, c'était bien lui, il était attablé au fond de l'arrière-salle d'une brasserie et il était en grande discussion avec Israël Beer, qui passait en ce temps-là pour un proche conseiller de Ben Gourion. Pourquoi ces ruses ? Ces déguisements ? Pourquoi tous ces mystères ? Et pourquoi, surtout, Hugo ne trouvait-il jamais le temps de passer par Paris pour nous rendre visite ? Ces questions exaspéraient mes parents. Elles finissaient moi-même par me hanter. Jusqu'au jour où, en 1961, donc, l'énigmatique cousin vint enfin nous rendre visite. C'était la veille de Pâque. Ma mère était occupée à préparer le repas du Seder. Et le voilà qui, sans crier gare, flanqué de cette Sigrid que nous ne connaissions pas encore, sonne à la porte. Il semble à son aise. A peine vieilli. Les joues tout juste un peu creusées. Sa chevelure blonde un rien dégarnie. Mais à l'aise, oui. Heureux de pouvoir échanger quelques mots de yiddish avec nous. Et rivalisant avec mon père dans l'ordre de cette mémoire qu'ils ont l'un comme l'autre, au même moment, et sans la moindre concertation, décidé de reconstituer. Qu'a-t-il vraiment en tête, ce jour-là ? Qui est vraiment cet homme à l'allure d'intellectuel que je revois, appuyé sur le rebord de la fenêtre, ses longues jambes élégamment tendues et croisées devant lui ? Que cache cette drôle de voix de basse qui imprime des accents si modernes à la langue du ghetto et qui me renvoie irrésistiblement à ce jeune homme blond et déterminé qui m'avait pris dans ses bras un soir de janvier 1939, au cœur du ghetto ? Hugo est là. Il parle. Il nous a même présenté Sigrid, cette épouse qui, à distance, nous intriguait si fort. « Voici Sigrid, a-t-il dit... ma femme... la fille d'un général de l'ex-Wehrmacht. » Je revois ladite Sigrid, mince, blonde, vêtue d'un tailleur gris, de coupe masculine. Elle a un chemisier de soie blanche. Des escarpins en lézard qui mettent en valeur la finesse de ses chevilles. Elle sourit. S'adresse à ma mère. Plaisante. Bref Hugo et sa femme sont tout proches. Eux que nous soupçonnions de bouder, de snober la famille partagent en toute simplicité notre modeste dîner. Et pourtant rien n'y fait : on les sent, *je* les sens plus lointains qu'ils n'ont jamais été. Est-ce pour cela que leur mort, quelques semaines plus tard, en Israël même, sur les hauteurs d'Abou Gosh, m'apparaît à la fois épouvantable et « dans l'ordre » ? Quelque chose dans ces deux visages, ces silhouettes et ces destins qui les exempte du sort commun...

Peut-être faut-il que j'ajoute, pour être tout à fait complet, que c'est à nous, les Halter de Paris, que Mordekhaï envoie, juste après son télégramme, les effets personnels de Hugo. Pourquoi nous ? Je l'ignore. Mais toujours est-il que nous arrivent un matin le passeport, le portefeuille, le chéquier, les clés du mort — ainsi que ce fameux petit carnet où il avait entrepris de reconstituer et consigner notre commune mémoire familiale. Émotion de mon père. Ivresse de cette coïncidence. Je le revois le soir, le dimanche, plongé dans ce mince carnet, pelliculé de noir, où il retrouve des noms qu'il connaît, d'autres qu'il a oubliés, d'autres encore qui sont comme les pièces manquantes d'un puzzle dont il avait fini par désespérer de jamais achever le montage.

— Curieuse affaire que l'histoire de notre livre familial, me dit-il un soir, après dîner. Il a pris son volume au fil des siècles et il ne lui a pas fallu cinq ans pour se réduire aux dimensions d'un mince carnet d'adresses.

Et puis, un autre soir, sur un ton déterminé, presque brutal, que nous ne lui connaissions pas :

— Nous allons ensemble, grâce au carnet de Hugo, renouer enfin tous les fils d'Abraham.

Mon père est un homme simple et bon. Il est imprimeur, fils et petit-fils d'imprimeur et ainsi depuis des générations. Il aime passionnément ce rôle d'intercesseur entre le monde des signes et celui de la lecture. Lorsqu'il compose sur sa linotype le texte d'un article ou d'un livre, il lui arrive d'en modifier un mot, de rétablir la syntaxe d'une phrase. Et je crois que c'est là le pire « forfait » dont se soit jamais rendu coupable ce vieux Juif de principes et de vertu, dont l'entière existence semblait devoir s'écouler au rythme de ces menues corrections. C'est dire combien m'étonne cette détermination soudaine. Ainsi que le spectacle de ce modeste scribe devenant tout à coup le plus acharné, le plus furieux des archéologues de la mémoire. Mon père explorateur du passé ! Habité d'une mission si glorieuse ! Mon père architecte fervent de cette invisible maison qu'est la mémoire juive ! Ma mère et moi découvrons un homme nouveau. Et je n'oublierai jamais ma stupeur quand, une nuit, en entrant par surprise dans la petite mansarde où, les nuits d'insomnie, il aimait se réfugier, je le vois devant un grand panneau noirci de noms, certains rayés, d'autres soulignés, tel un comptable d'une entreprise en faillite essayant de retrouver ce qui demeure d'une richesse ancienne. Je découvre ce visage si déroutant, celui d'un homme exalté, possédé, travaillé par des sentiments contradictoires que je ne comprends pas mais qui me font dire — d'un air de fils soumis dont je ne suis pas davantage coutumier :

— Oui, père, nous ferons ensemble ce chemin... Ensemble nous saisirons le témoin que nous passe le cousin Hugo.

2

NEW YORK-TEL-AVIV

SIDNEY ET MORDEKHAI

Juin 1961

C'est à Winnipeg, au Canada, où il est venu rendre visite à son père, que Sidney, notre cousin américain et le frère de Mordekhaï, apprend la mort de Hugo. Important, pour lui, ce voyage à Winnipeg. Sa famille, en effet, n'a jamais vraiment accepté son mariage avec Marjory. Elle est passionnée, certes, par le judaïsme. Elle observe, mieux qu'une vraie juive, tous les rites et cérémonies juifs. Mais enfin elle n'est pas juive. Elle est irlandaise catholique. Et l'introduction dans la famille d'une « goï », d'une étrangère, est ressentie comme une trahison, une sorte de scandale.

— Et Ruth, la Moabite, a coutume de dire Sidney, n'est-elle pas à l'origine de la lignée du roi David ?

— L'histoire ne se répète pas, répond invariablement son père.

— Comment se fait-il alors, renchérit-il, que tu en appelles à la Loi pour me condamner et que tu récuses la Tradition pour m'absoudre.

Dialogue de sourds, bien sûr. Insurmontable malentendu. D'un côté, le vieux Samuel, frère cadet d'Abraham, fils de l'ancienne morale du ghetto, qui, malgré ce quart de siècle passé dans le Nouveau Monde, n'a jamais vraiment quitté Varsovie. De l'autre, un jeune Juif de quarante ans, roux comme un Écossais, solide comme un joueur de rugby, pour qui judaïsme rime avec modernisme et tradition avec adaptation. Américain jusqu'au bout des ongles, il croit au bonheur, au progrès. Et s'il est ici, à Winnipeg, s'il a quitté New York, sa clinique et ses malades, c'est que Marjory attend un nouvel enfant et qu'il veut que cet enfant naisse dans l'harmonie familiale retrouvée. Les choses se sont si mal passées pour le petit Richard, il y a sept ans ! Il a été si malheureux quand son père a refusé d'assister à la circoncision ! Et il a tellement envie, cette fois-ci, que le scénario soit différent ! A présent l'enfant est né. C'est une ravissante petite fille qu'on a décidé d'appeler Marilyn. Le vieux Samuel est content. Ses relations avec Marjory sont devenues presque courtoises. Et tout va pour le mieux lorsque arrive le télégramme de Mordekhaï.

Il faut savoir que, de tous les Halter, Sidney est probablement, à ce moment-là, celui qui se sent le plus proche de Hugo. Il l'a connu pendant la guerre, à New York. Il n'a, alors, que dix-neuf ans. Il ne s'intéresse qu'à ses études de médecine. Mais il est toute de suite fasciné par ce cousin venu d'ailleurs qui apparaît à ses coreligionnaires comme un mélange de provocateur et d'oiseau de mauvais augure. Il le croit, lui. Il sait que ce prédicateur froid est le seul à voir juste quand il brosse, de l'Europe nazifiée, ce tableau apocalyptique. Et il n'est pas rare alors de les retrouver tous les deux, le conspirateur et son jeune disciple, errant, à la nuit tombée, entre Washington Square et la 9ᵉ Rue.

A la Libération, ils se sont perdus de vue. Hugo a repris sa vie de nomade et de cassandre, tandis que lui, Sidney, est peu à peu devenu la parfaite illustration de l'*american way of life*. Et ce, jusqu'à ce jour d'octobre 1960 (à quelques semaines, autrement dit, de son séjour au Canada) où l'énigmatique cousin ressurgit dans sa vie. Ils se sont retrouvés, comme à la grande époque, au White Horse Tavern, Downtown. Hugo a son éternelle allure de proscrit, d'homme traqué. Mais avec, dans le regard, une anxiété nouvelle qui fait grande impression au jeune médecin.

Il a besoin, explique-t-il, de trois cent mille dollars.

Une banque a accepté de les lui prêter, mais il a besoin d'une caution... Sidney peut-il être cette caution ? Peut-il, au nom des liens sacrés qui les unissent, lui rendre ce service ? Sidney, ému mais effarouché, refuse. Il est prêt, comme il le fait souvent, à « marcher » dans une cause humanitaire. Mais il aime les causes claires, les affaires transparentes, il se méfie de ces mystères où semble se complaire son cousin. Pourquoi ces dollars ? A quel usage les destine-t-il ? Comment, quand les remboursera-t-il ? Il n'est pas très fier de ses réponses ni de ses arrière-pensées. Mais enfin, Marjory... Le futur bébé... Ce parfait *american boy* qu'il s'est tant appliqué à devenir... Il sent trop d'implications inavouées dans la requête de Hugo pour prendre le risque de le suivre...

Curieusement d'ailleurs, Hugo ne semble ni surpris ni fâché de sa réticence. Il semble s'y attendre. Le comprendre peut-être. Et le voici qui, changeant de ton, à voix soudain plus basse comme s'il lui confiait un secret, enchaîne : « Tu es ici, à New York, le seul représentant de notre famille... Peux-tu, s'il m'arrive quelque chose, veiller à ce que l'on m'enterre dans le cimetière de Jérusalem ? » Humour ? Provocation ? Pressentiment peut-être ? Sidney, sur le moment, feint de trouver la phrase absurde. Il part d'un de ces petits rires qui semblent vouloir dire : « Allons ! allons ! cher cousin, ne joue pas à cela avec moi... Mais enfin, si tu y tiens... » Et ce n'est qu'aujourd'hui, à Winnipeg, le télégramme de Mordekhaï sous les yeux, qu'il mesure le sens de tout cela — et l'ampleur de son aveuglement.

Un mot à Marjory... Un conciliabule avec son père... Une nuit mélancolique auprès de son bébé... Sa décision est prise : les obsèques sont bien entendu passées ; mais il se doit d'y aller ; il doit à son cousin, comme promis, l'hommage de sa vigilance ; d'autant qu'il y a quelque chose d'étrange dans cette histoire... Oui, il ne peut s'empêcher de repenser, toute la nuit, toute la journée qui suit, à cette conversation qui, après coup, lui semble si atrocement prémonitoire. Ce qu'il va faire à Tel-Aviv ? Il n'en sait rien. Mais il ira.

C'est par une belle et chaude matinée de juillet qu'il débarque à l'aéroport de Lod où l'attend Mordekhaï. Les deux frères s'aiment bien. Ils se retrouvent de loin en loin, à Tel-Aviv ou New York. Ils partagent une même passion pour l'Histoire, quoiqu'ils n'en retiennent pas toujours les mêmes leçons. Bizarrement, pourtant, ils sont aussi dissemblables que possible. L'Américain est grand. Il a les cheveux roux tirés en arrière sur un front haut, des gestes précis de sportif. Il a les yeux noirs, pétillants de malice. Un sourire charmeur dans une barbe très courte, soigneusement entretenue. L'Israélien est plutôt petit. Il a le visage mobile, le regard agrandi par des lunettes, plissé par la myopie. Il parle sans cesse de « son » kibboutz et affecte volontiers un ton, une allure de paysan. A les voir installés tous deux dans le hall de l'hôtel Dan, au milieu des touristes et des officiers israéliens, impossible de deviner qu'ils sont l'un comme l'autre, au même titre l'un que l'autre, les héritiers et neveux d'Abraham Halter.

Tout de suite, dans la voiture, l'Israélien a affranchi son frère. Il lui a tout raconté... L'attentat... Les cadavres criblés de balles... L'enquête policière qui n'a mené à rien... Les obsèques, la veille, dans une petite tombe du cimetière du mont du Repos, à Jérusalem... La cérémonie si triste... La compagnie si peu nombreuse... Lui, Mordekhaï... Sa femme... Un ou deux vieux Juifs venus d'on ne sait où... Un écrivain arabe de Nazareth... Deux types qu'il n'avait jamais vus qui avaient l'air de flics ou de mouchards... Oui, oui, tout s'est passé dans les règles... Non, non, il n'a rien remarqué d'anormal... Bien sûr, il va le conduire au cimetière... C'est si gentil à lui d'être venu ! Ce pauvre cousin Hugo était, au fond, si seul.

Sidney a écouté sans rien dire, avec une attention extrême. Il a répondu que, non, il ne voulait pas revoir les lieux... que, oui, il voulait aller se recueillir sur la tombe... Et puis, sans révéler encore le détail de son histoire, il a expliqué qu'il « savait » quelque chose... Peut-être important, peut-être pas... Une conversation... Juste une conversation, mais qui peut intéresser la police... Est-ce que Mordekhaï peut arranger cela ? Est-ce qu'il connaît quelqu'un à qui il puisse faire son récit ?

Mordekhaï, intrigué, lui a dit qu'il connaît en effet quelqu'un... Pas très bien, mais il le connaît... C'est l'homme qui, au ministère de la Défense, suit le dossier Hugo... Il est venu deux ou trois fois l'interroger... Le passé du mort semble les intriguer... Ses amitiés arabes... Cet attentat si bizarre, tout près de Jérusalem... Sidney souhaite-t-il qu'on le contacte ? Si, si, c'est très simple... Les choses sont si faciles en Israël... Sans attendre la réponse, Mordekhaï s'est levé. Il est allé au téléphone et revient au bout d'une minute en disant d'un ton très naturel : « Il s'appelle Benjamin Ben Eliezer et il sera là dans une heure. On l'attend ? »... Oui, on l'attend. Echangeant, pour tuer le temps, les propos aimables et badins que tiennent deux frères lorsque, après une longue séparation, ils se retrouvent enfin.

— Toi aussi, tu as eu un fils, commence Sidney. Parle-moi de ton fils !

— Arié ? Il est l'âme de mon âme... La chair de ma chair... Surtout imagine sa chance : il est né, ici, sur cette terre... Alors que nous... Enfin, moi...

— Et ton kibboutz ? Comment va ton kibboutz ? On dit, chez nous, aux États-Unis, que le moral n'y est plus tout à fait... Que ce n'est déjà plus l'héroïsme des tout débuts et que...

— Shtouiot ! Bêtises ! Cessez donc d'élucubrer et de vous faire du souci pour nous ! La seule inquiétude que nous avons est militaire : ce sont les incursions de plus en plus fréquentes des terroristes venus de Syrie et du Liban.

— Quand y retournes-tu ?

— Demain, après notre visite au cimetière.

La conversation continue longtemps sur ce ton, faussement badine et, en réalité, terriblement « lourde ». Ombre de la mort. Spectre de Hugo. Sidney, songe Mordekhaï, en a trop dit ou pas assez.

Quel est ce nouveau détail qu'il veut révéler aux enquêteurs ? Pourquoi ces mystères ? Cette gêne ? A un moment, et tandis qu'il s'est lancé dans un récit lyrique des performances du kibboutz Dafné, Sidney le coupe pour demander :

— Que sont devenus les effets personnels de Hugo ?

— Je les ai envoyés à Salomon, à Paris...

Puis, d'un air rêveur :

— Salomon ? Il m'a adressé une lettre, un jour... Il y a longtemps... Je ne me souviens pas d'y avoir répondu... Tu le connais ?

— Oui, bien sûr. Nous nous écrivons quelquefois, il est d'ailleurs venu au kibboutz.

Puis encore, après un nouveau silence et sur un ton de plus en plus embarrassé :

— Avons-nous aussi de la famille à Moscou ?

— Oui.

— Tu la connais ?

— Non.

— Ce Khrouchtchev m'intéresse. Il semble décidé à changer, en Russie, l'ordre des choses. Il reconnaît les crimes de Staline. Mais on dit qu'il n'aime pas plus les Juifs que lui...

Mordekhaï se penche légèrement et plisse les yeux. Il n'a pas entendu la fin de la phrase, un groupe de touristes descendant à grand bruit la volée de marches qui, entre les jets d'eau, mène au salon.

Sidney répète :

— On dit que Krouchtchev n'aime pas plus les Juifs que Staline.

Et, élevant la voix :

— Pourquoi les Juifs restent-ils en URSS ?

— Parce qu'ils aiment le KGB ! répond Mordekhaï en riant. Mais voici Benjamin. Je t'avais dit : une heure ! Vois comme les Israéliens sont ponctuels !

L'homme qui s'approche est jeune. Plus jeune qu'eux... Il a trente ans à peine, un sourire timide, il est tout de gris habillé et n'a vraiment pas l'air d'un baroudeur ou d'un agent. Il parle doucement, d'une voix neutre :

— Le terrorisme sera bientôt le principal moyen d'accès à la presse, à la radio, à la télévision ; une possibilité d'action sans pareille dans les zones sanctuarisées par l'arme nucléaire ; un effet pervers du progrès technique ; l'un des enjeux de l'affrontement entre super-puissances...

Content de son effet et manifestement heureux de s'étendre sur un sujet qu'il connaît bien, il enchaîne :

— Le terrorisme bénéficiera surtout du mauvais rapport qualité-prix des guerres conventionnelles... Au fond, ce n'est rien d'autre qu'un nouveau langage diplomatique ; il suffit de savoir le déchiffrer correctement et de préférence à temps...

Sidney est surpris par le personnage. Il s'attendait à rencontrer une sorte de flic à l'américaine... Un inspecteur... Un incorruptible... Et il se trouve en face d'un expert, d'un érudit qui lui parle de tout ça comme si c'étaient les règles d'une nouvelle science de la guerre. C'est donc d'une voix moins assurée qu'il demande :

— A votre avis, que prétendaient nous dire les terroristes, en tuant notre cousin Hugo ?

— La police n'a encore rien trouvé de précis... Elle penche pour un attentat aveugle comme tous ceux commis jusqu'ici en Israël. Pourtant la personnalité complexe de votre cousin, ses liens avec certains dirigeants nationalistes arabes et, en particulier, son amitié avec un Tunisien qui a vécu dernièrement à Moscou, Hidar Assadi, agent de liaison entre les Soviétiques et la direction du MNA, le Mouvement nationaliste arabe, pourraient être aussi à l'origine de l'attentat.

Puis, se penchant vers Sidney :

— Mais votre frère m'a dit que vous saviez des choses, vous aussi. Sur son passé... Ses amitiés arabes... Toute information supplémentaire pourrait considérablement faciliter l'enquête.

— Oui... Non, fait Sidney, un peu gêné.

— Ce sont des choses sur sa vie pendant la guerre ? Après la guerre ?

— Après la guerre... Oui c'est ça, après la guerre... Hugo a épousé une Allemande...

— Oui, nous savons cela...

— La fille d'un général nazi, tout de même...

— Nous savons cela, répète l'Israélien avec une pointe d'impatience dans la voix. Ce n'est certes pas pour ça que vous êtes venu spécialement en Israël vous recueillir sur sa tombe...

— Mettons que c'est par mauvaise conscience...

— Le repentir et les bonnes actions sont les boucliers qui nous préservent de la colère du Ciel, dit Benjamin. Mais dites-m'en plus : pourquoi cette mauvaise conscience ?

Sidney, de plus en plus embarrassé, commence, sous l'œil sidéré de son frère :

— Au mois d'octobre de l'année passée, Hugo m'a demandé une garantie pour un prêt de trois cent mille dollars...

— Trois cent mille dollars ! C'est une somme considérable, dit Benjamin. Et vous la lui avez refusée ?

— Oui. Mais ce n'est pas tout...

— Ah !

— Il m'a aussi demandé de veiller, s'il mourait, à ce qu'il soit enterré en Israël, à Jérusalem.

— Il ne vous a rien dit d'autre ?

— Rien.

— Vous saviez qu'il était menacé ?

— Non, bien sûr. J'ai cru à une boutade.

— Qu'avez-vous fait donc ?

— J'ai éclaté de rire.

Benjamin ôte ses lunettes et, après quelques secondes de réflexion, reprend :

— Vous a-t-il dit quelle était la banque disposée à lui accorder le prêt ?

— Non.

— Il vous a bien dit « si je meurs » ?

— Non, il a dit exactement : « S'il m'arrivait quelque chose. »

Benjamin paraît de plus en plus pensif. Puis, après un silence et comme s'il était déçu de ne pas en apprendre davantage :

— Rien d'autre vraiment ? Vous êtes sûr de m'avoir tout dit ?

— Sûr.

Il s'apprête à prendre congé. Mordekhaï qui, depuis le début de la conversation, se tenait coi intervient à son tour :

— Le carnet... Etes-vous au courant du carnet ?

— Quel carnet ? demande le policier en se rasseyant.

— Un petit carnet d'adresses qui se trouvait sur Hugo le jour du meurtre et que j'ai envoyé, avec ses autres effets, à notre cousin de Paris.

Dire que le policier est intéressé serait peu dire. Il presse Mordekhaï de questions. L'interroge sur la forme de l'objet... Sa taille... Le nombre de noms qui y figuraient... S'il a eu, avant de l'expédier, la curiosité de le feuilleter... S'il se souvient de ce nom-ci... De celui-là... De ce troisième... S'il est possible de le récupérer... De le consulter... Où l'on peut joindre ce Salomon Halter... Comment... S'il acceptera de coopérer avec les services secrets israéliens... Que les policiers sont impardonnables d'avoir laissé échapper pareille pièce... Mais enfin grâce à vous, grâce à cette rencontre...

Comme la vie est étrange ! Mordekhaï avait le sentiment d'amener, avec son frère Sidney, la plus précieuse des informations. Et le voilà, lui, au centre de la curiosité du redoutable Ben Eliezer !

Cimetière. Entre les hauts cyprès, pointant vers le ciel, la lumière indécise du matin enveloppe le mont du Repos. Calme infini. Paix. L'air est merveilleusement transparent et Sidney peut admirer le paysage à ses pieds : le kibboutz Kiryat Anavim dans la vallée de l'Ayalon, et une succession de taches vertes, sur soixante-dix kilomètres vers l'ouest jusqu'à la mer.

Le secteur ashkénaze du cimetière est pris en tenailles entre celui des Juifs de Boukhara et celui des Juifs du Yémen. Placées côte à côte, les pierres tombales de Hugo et de Sigrid sont d'un blanc presque aveuglant et portent une inscription gravée en hébreu. Sidney ne peut s'empêcher de suivre les lettres du doigt. Le nom de son cousin... Son nom... Toute cette énigme autour de cette mort... Les pierres tombales à perte de vue... Qui sait si les pierres ne vont pas s'entrouvrir ? Si la résurrection de tous ces morts n'est pas pour aujourd'hui ? Sottises, bien sûr... Imaginations indécentes... Décidément, il n'aime pas beaucoup les cimetières et l'éternité ne lui sied guère.

Planté devant la tombe de Hugo, il se demande ce qu'il doit faire. Prier ? Réciter la Hachkaba ? Dire le Kaddish ? Mordekhaï voit son hésitation :

— Tu n'es pas obligé de prier. L'important, c'est d'être ici. Ici on ne meurt jamais...

— Jamais ?

— Pendant la guerre, j'étais avec la Brigade juive en Italie. Et, en passant par Capo di Bove, sous les bombes, parmi les cadavres des soldats américains, j'ai découvert une guinguette appelée « Qui non si muore mai »... « Ici on ne meurt jamais »... Depuis, chaque fois que je suis angoissé, je me souviens de la guinguette de Capo di Bove et cela me rassure.

— J'ignorais que tu te trouvais en Italie pendant la guerre... Au fond, tu aurais pu y rencontrer Hugo...

— Il n'y est pas resté assez longtemps. On l'a vite envoyé en France...

— Tu faisais donc partie du fameux groupe des Vengeurs ?

— Non. Tuer les nazis après la victoire n'allait pas ressusciter les morts. Traduire les nazis devant la justice pouvait contribuer, en revanche, à l'éducation des vivants...

— Moi, je suis pour la loi du talion, réplique Sidney avec vivacité. Les nazis ne comprennent rien d'autre... De même, aujourd'hui, les terroristes... On m'a dit que l'oncle Abraham voulait parler aux nazis dans le ghetto de Varsovie...

— Comme toi, j'admire notre aïeul... Mais on ne parle pas à ceux pour qui la vie n'est pas sacrée...

33

Sidney laisse son regard errer entre les monuments funéraires et les cyprès. Puis, passant une dernière fois de la tombe de Hugo au visage de Mordekhaï :

— Tu ne crois donc pas qu'il faudrait le venger ?

Mordekhaï hésite puis cite un proverbe grec où il est à peu près dit que les dieux de la vengeance agissent en silence.

Les deux frères quittent le mont du Repos sur cette promesse et Sidney lâche un ultime regard en arrière. Est-il en train d'abandonner Hugo — ou s'apprête-t-il, au contraire, à le pister et le rejoindre ?

3

MOSCOU

LES COUSINS SOVIÉTIQUES

Septembre 1961

La cousine Rachel apprit la mort de Hugo plusieurs mois après le drame.

En ce jour de Roch Hachanah 5721, elle écoute de la musique à la radio. Mi-attentive, mi-absente, elle ouvre placards et tiroirs et commence à disposer les objets nécessaires à la fête. Tandis qu'elle s'affaire ainsi, sa fille Olga fait irruption dans la modeste cuisine en brandissant une lettre dont la seule existence a, pour une famille juive de Moscou, quelque chose d'incroyable :

— Maman ! Maman ! Ça vient de Paris !

— De Paris ? s'étonne Rachel tandis qu'elle s'essuie les mains dans son tablier et cherche fébrilement — mais en vain — ses lunettes.

— Ouvre, ordonne-t-elle.

— Je l'ai déjà ouverte, mais je ne sais par quel bout la prendre !... On dirait de l'hébreu... Ou peut-être du yiddish...

— Du yiddish ?

Rachel fixe Olga, qui ne sait si elle doit rire ou s'inquiéter, et lui retire l'enveloppe des mains. Toujours sans lunettes, elle demande à sa fille de lui lire l'adresse. C'est bien elle, oui... Sauf qu'il est écrit Rachel Halter, son nom de jeune fille. Est-ce pour cela que la lettre a, d'après le cachet de la poste, mis six mois à arriver ?

De plus en plus excitées, la mère et la fille se précipitent l'une derrière l'autre vers le bout du couloir, là où travaille Aron, l'époux, le père. Elles le trouvent entouré de livres qui tapissent les murs de son bureau sans fenêtres. Il est occupé, comme tous les jours à la même heure, à préparer le cours d'antiquité gréco-romaine qu'il donne depuis dix ans au département d'histoire de l'université de Moscou.

Rachel lui tend l'objet.

— C'est du yiddish, dit-elle... Ça vient de Paris...

Aron retire la feuille de l'enveloppe et s'exclame :

— Elle est de ton cousin... Salomon Halter...

Puis d'une voix sourde, presque cassée par l'émotion, il commence à lire à voix haute.

Rachel l'écoute en silence, avidement. Puis attend qu'il ait résumé le contenu à l'intention d'Olga qui ignore le yiddish. Alors, elle soupire :

— Tant d'années... Tant d'années...

La vérité est qu'elle se sent vieille, tout à coup, de mille souffrances, de mille blessures. Elle revoit Salomon tout jeune... La famille... Le ghetto... Ces flammes qu'elle n'a pas connues mais qui la hantent tout de même... Et puis à nouveau Salomon.

— Oui, Salomon, reprend-elle, l'œil rêveur... Le petit Salomon... Le fils de l'oncle Abraham... Il devait avoir vingt ans quand j'ai quitté la Pologne, en 1930... Je me souviens très bien de l'oncle Abraham et de son imprimerie de la rue Nowolupje...

Puis, la main sur le bras d'Olga :

— Chez lui, les tracts révolutionnaires, on les imprimait aussi en yiddish... Ton père et toi vous n'êtes jamais allés à Varsovie, vous ne pouvez pas savoir... L'oncle Abraham a bien été le seul à ne pas chercher à me retenir quand j'ai voulu partir pour l'Union soviétique... Il m'a simplement dit, en me voyant faire mes valises : « Le bonheur, c'est comme l'écho. On l'entend, mais on ne le voit jamais... »

Le carillon de l'horloge de la tour du Sauveur, au Kremlin, sonne huit heures. Aron ramasse ses papiers. Boucle sa serviette :

— Au revoir, dit-il... Je dois aller...

— Ne rentre pas trop tard, répond sa femme : les enfants viennent dîner ce soir...

Et lui, sur le pas de la porte :

— Mais oui... La tradition n'exige-t-elle pas que nous soyons tous réunis ?

Les Lerner habitent à l'angle de la rue Kazakov et de la rue Tchkalov, à deux pas de chez l'académicien Sakharov, un appartement réservé aux scientifiques, au quatrième étage d'une maison du début du siècle. Aron Lerner est un homme sec au visage osseux, marqué aux commissures. Il a passé la cinquantaine. Sa famille, venue de Lituanie, s'est installée à Moscou plus d'un siècle auparavant. Et c'est donc là qu'il a rencontré et épousé Rachel Halter — cette toute jeune Juive originaire de Varsovie qui vint, avec beaucoup d'autres, rejoindre la patrie du socialisme et participer à la Révolution, à la construction du socialisme. En vérité, elle a vite déchanté et serait bien repartie pour la Pologne si sa découverte subite des traditions observées depuis toujours par ses parents et son amour pour Aron n'avaient remplacé en elle sa ferveur révolutionnaire.

Aron, lui, n'a jamais adhéré au Parti. Fâcheux pour sa carrière universitaire. Mais au moins en a-t-il profité pour rester à l'abri des épurations successives. Toutes les semaines, la *Literaturnaya Gazeta* fait l'éloge d'historiens dont l'absence de rigueur est patente — alors que l'excellent auteur d'une *République athénienne à l'époque de Périclès* et d'un *L'Art grec et Karl Marx* continue de végéter dans l'indifférence quasi totale. Il se protège de l'amertume par une manière d'ironie à l'égard de lui-même. Si bien qu'il offre, au bout du compte, l'étrange spectacle d'un homme à la fois désabusé et passionné, cynique et pourtant juvénile.

Dire qu'il est attaché au judaïsme serait exagéré. Il a bien parlé yiddish dans sa lointaine enfance. Mais Athènes lui est depuis longtemps devenue plus chère que Jérusalem. Et si la persécution par Staline des écrivains et des poètes juifs l'a bien évidemment heurté, si elle lui a mieux fait comprendre l'attachement de son épouse à cette tradition, cette culture martyrisées, il sait pertinemment que c'est l'humaniste en lui, plus que le Juif, qu'elle a ému et choqué.

Ses enfants ? Sacha, vingt-neuf ans et Olga, vingt-quatre, sont deux jeunes gens semblables à tous les jeunes gens de Moscou. L'un est un brillant étudiant du département des langues étrangères, l'autre fait sa médecine. Comme la majorité des Soviétiques, ils critiquent parfois l'État socialiste. Et ils sont assez attachés à leur mère pour subir de bonne grâce ce qu'ils appellent ses « superstitions ». Sur le fond, cependant, ils aiment l'URSS. Ils croient fermement qu'on y vit mieux qu'ailleurs. Olga est une jeune femme insouciante et « nature » qui ne pose pas trop de problèmes à son père ; Sacha, par contre, se montre à la fois secret et ambitieux. Il est doué, c'est sûr. Plein de talents. Mais il a quelque chose en lui qui inquiète le vieil homme. Comment être sûr qu'il se comportera avec loyauté dans un monde où les loups donnent l'exemple ?

Il fait froid tout à coup. Aron, qui approche du métro, presse le pas et rajuste son cache-nez. La lettre de Paris l'a troublé. C'est, quand il y pense, leur tout premier contact avec l'étranger depuis la guerre. Serait-il possible que les choses changent sous Khrouchtchev ? Il songe que dix ans plus tôt, un message venu d'Occident aurait été confisqué d'emblée. Il en est là de ses pensées quand, dans son dos, une voix crie :

— Aron Lazarevitch Lerner ! Aron Lazarevitch !

Il tourne la tête. C'est Vassili Slepakov, un collègue de l'université, qui le rattrape en trottinant.

— Aron Lazarevitch ! répète l'homme essoufflé. Je te suis, je t'appelle, mais tu n'entends rien... Qu'y a-t-il ? De mauvaises nouvelles ?

— Pourquoi, Vassili Petrovitch ? Pourquoi aurais-je de mauvaises nouvelles ?

— On dit que Rachel a reçu une lettre de Paris.

— Eh bien... Je vois que les nouvelles vont vite...

— Ici, tout se sait, mon ami... Surtout quand on a le même facteur !

Les deux hommes marchent un moment côte à côte,

silencieux, évitant soigneusement les ornières creusées dans la chaussée par de récents travaux de voirie. Aron n'a pas très envie de parler à Vassili de la lettre de Paris. Il sait combien la moindre confidence, la moindre indiscrétion peuvent être fatales... Mais l'autre ne le lâche pas et, arrivé devant la station de métro « Lermontovskaya », il le tire par la manche et lui demande d'un air cauteleux :

— As-tu vu ton fils récemment ?

— Sacha ? Bien sûr... Tout à l'heure, quand j'ai quitté la maison, il dormait encore... Pourquoi cette question, Vassili Petrovitch ?

Vassili feint de réfléchir, et pesant son effet, dit :

— Parce que je l'ai vu, ton fils... Pas plus tard qu'hier soir... Et sais-tu avec qui ? Des hommes du KGB, mon cher... Oui, rue Gorki... Il montait dans une grande Tchaïka noire.

— Tu es sûr, Vassili Petrovitch ? Des hommes du KGB ?

— Allons, Aron Lazarevitch, nous sommes tous les deux de trop vieux Soviétiques pour ne pas les reconnaître au premier coup d'œil... L'imperméable kaki... Un air de ruse et de mauvais coup... Et puis cette arrogance...

Aron ne répondant rien, il toussote ; et, sur un ton faussement détaché, reprend :

— Mais si Sacha ne t'a rien dit, c'est qu'il n'y a rien à dire. Voilà... Oublie tout ça...

Aron, on l'imagine, fera tout sauf oublier. L'image de son fils encadré par deux Kagébistes l'accompagne toute la journée. Peut-être Vassili s'est-il trompé... Peut-être un malentendu... Une erreur de personne... Le soir venu, lorsqu'il rentre à la maison et trouve la table mise, les bougies allumées, il en a presque oublié que c'est Roch Hachanah... Un jour sacré... Le jour de l'an... C'est à peine si l'idée l'effleure que ces simples bougies allumées sur une nappe blanche représentent à Moscou un danger réel... A peine s'il songe qu'on peut être, pour moins que cela, dénoncé comme un adepte d'une religion cachée ou, pis, comme un agent sioniste...

Croisant un voisin dans l'escalier, il ne prend même plus, comme chaque année, la précaution de dire que c'est son anniversaire de mariage... Quand arrive l'heure, pour Rachel, d'appeler les enfants à venir à table, il n'a pas un regard pour Olga qui a pourtant sa natte des grands soirs ; il écoute à peine Sacha s'extasiant, comme chaque année, sur les zakouskis que sa mère a dénichés Dieu sait où, en faisant la queue dans toutes les boutiques du quartier ; quand arrive la fin de la cérémonie et que toute la famille s'est copieusement régalée de ces belles et saintes histoires qu'on ne raconte vraiment qu'à la lueur des chandelles, il n'y tient plus et, repoussant son assiette, interroge son fils :

— Dis donc, Sacha, que faisais-tu, hier soir, rue Gorki, avec deux agents du KGB ?

Sacha, loin de se troubler, le regarde droit dans les yeux et, comme s'il cherchait à le narguer, vide consciencieusement son verre avant de demander à son tour :

— Comment le sais-tu ?

Et le père de répondre, en soutenant son regard :

— Ici, tout se sait.

Silence. Stupeur autour de la table. Rachel, au bord des larmes, qui implore son fils d'en dire davantage...

— Ne te fâche pas... Je comptais vous en parler tranquillement dimanche...

— Eh bien, parlons-en aujourd'hui !

— Bon, bon, ne vous inquiétez pas... je vais tout vous dire, bien sûr.

Sur quoi, il raconte comment le KGB, cherchant des experts pour le « Comité de Solidarité avec les peuples d'Afrique et d'Asie » a enquêté au département des langues étrangères de l'université. On leur a parlé de ses succès en perse et en arabe. On a certifié la qualité de ses sentiments prolétariens. Et ces messieurs sont venus le voir un beau matin pour lui offrir le poste de directeur de section. « C'est quelque chose qui ne se refuse pas, n'est-ce pas ? Des voyages... Une vie passionnante... Un idéal... Rassurez-vous, je ne suis pas un mouchard… C'est tellement merveilleux de se consacrer ainsi aux peuples en voie de développement… »

Le ton du jeune homme a changé. Il est émouvant, avec son enthousiasme. Et on le croirait presque. Son explication a détendu l'atmosphère lorsque Olga, mi-grave, mi-taquine, lui lance :

— Au fond, tu vas aider les Arabes à combattre Israël !

Sacha la foudroie du regard et, comme s'il voulait faire payer son audace à l'impudente, lui répond d'un ton sec :

— Tu peux parler, toi qui sors avec un Arabe !

C'en est trop pour Rachel et Aron qui se tournent alors vers leur fille, exigeant une explication.

— Oui… c'est vrai… bredouille-t-elle, en se tortillant sur sa chaise… Mais c'est un Tunisien… Il fait un stage dans un laboratoire de la faculté de médecine… Un garçon brillant, je vous assure… Il s'appelle Hidar… Hidar Assadi… C'est vrai qu'il n'aime pas Israël… Il dit que c'est une terre arabe… Mais je vous jure qu'il n'est pas antisémite…

Puis, reprenant son souffle, et comme si c'était le maître argument qui allait à la fois la disculper et rasséréner ses parents :

— Figurez-vous qu'il était même très ami, à Tunis, avec un cousin de Maman !

— Un cousin à moi ? s'exclame Rachel.

— Oui, maman… Son nom était Hugo Halter… Un officier de l'armée américaine, basé à Tunis. C'était en 1943, en pleine guerre… Je n'ai jamais osé vous en parler, mais c'est vrai…

— Hugo Halter, répète Rachel… Hugo Halter…

Puis, se tournant vers son époux :

— Aron ! où est la lettre de Paris ? S'il te plaît, donne-nous cette lettre…

Olga la dévisage, comme si elle ne comprenait pas :

— Ça alors ! Je n'avais pas fait le rapprochement !

Sacha fronce les sourcils :

— Quelle lettre ? De quoi parlez-vous ?

Quant à Aron qui, lui, a dans la poche le message de

Salomon, il prend aussitôt la mesure de l'hallucinante coïncidence. Olga et l'Arabe... L'Arabe et Hugo... Comme la vie est étrange... comme cette histoire est folle... Rachel fond en larmes. Olga reste hébétée. Sacha rapproche sa chaise de celle de sa mère et, avec un bon sourire compréhensif, cherche à la rassurer. Lui est perdu dans ses pensées. Il revoit les images du temps jadis. Et puis il observe ses enfants, longuement, l'un après l'autre.

« Je m'appelle Aron Lerner, songe-t-il... Des siècles et des siècles de mémoire... Toute la mémoire d'Abraham... Et voici la chair de ma chair, et voici le sang de mon sang : tous deux livrés aux adversaires les plus acharnés de ce que je n'ose appeler mon peuple... Tous deux, oui, avec leur candeur, leur inexpérience, leur jeunesse abjurant le saint souvenir. »

Aron Lerner aura grand-peine à s'endormir ce soir-là. Grand-peine aussi à chasser les spectres qui l'assaillent. En un seul jour, ses deux enfants. En une nuit, ces deux présages.

4

BUENOS AIRES

DONA REGINA

Décembre 1961

La dernière de la famille à apprendre la mort de Hugo est Dona Regina, à Buenos Aires. La nouvelle lui arrive, elle aussi, par une lettre de son frère Salomon. Pour la vieille femme, cette mort prouve, une fois de plus, qu'Israël n'est pas ce pays miracle dont parlent les sionistes et qui garantit la vie et la sécurité à tout Juif.

Dona Regina est venue en Argentine en 1918, fuyant la police tsariste. Et, malgré ses quarante-trois ans passés sur les rives du Rio de la Plata, elle est restée fidèle à son idéal de jeunesse : elle est communiste et l'Union soviétique demeure son modèle. Buenos Aires ? Elle a appris à aimer Buenos Aires. Elle a vu se développer cette métropole de huit millions d'habitants, quadrillée comme New York par des avenues et des rues qui, en Amérique, se noient dans la mer et qui, ici, s'enlisent dans la poussière de la pampa. Mais son cœur, oui, bat à l'unisson de ses « camarades » soviétiques.

La mort de Hugo l'affecte plus qu'elle ne l'aurait imaginé. N'était-il pas le fils de l'oncle Joseph ? le neveu de son propre père ? Et n'est-il pas scandaleux que des choses pareilles arrivent, de nos jours, à Jérusalem, s'il vous plaît ? « La victoire de Stalingrad n'a servi à rien, dit-elle à Don Israël son mari, si l'on continue de tuer des Juifs de par le monde. » Elle sait qu'en disant cela elle est au bord du blasphème. Mais tant pis ! Elle le dit !

Dona Regina n'a pas peur des contradictions. Elle est d'une nature expansive et aime dire ce qu'elle pense. Au diable la logique !

A plus de soixante ans, elle a quelque chose de bourru qui interdit de l'imaginer en jeune fille gracieuse. En hiver, elle manie les aiguilles à tricoter avec une férocité digne de la lutte contre l'ennemi de classe. Il n'y a pas une activité qu'elle ne s'estime en mesure de mener à bien sans l'aide d'autrui. Ainsi, elle ne va jamais chez le coiffeur. Devant sa glace, elle est tout naturellement à la fois le coiffeur et la cliente. Elle ramène ses cheveux sur le front, au ras de ses yeux noirs et ronds et se fait la conversation. Toujours en mouvement, toujours occupée, elle se donne beaucoup de peine pour cacher, sous une apparence de sévérité, la tendresse qui l'anime.

Depuis leur arrivée de Pologne, Dona Regina et son mari, cordonnier de son état, n'ont plus quitté leur modeste maison avec patio, au fond de l'avenue San Martin, un quartier populaire où chacun sait tout sur tous les autres. Les nuits chaudes et humides, entre septembre et mars, on s'assied devant sa porte, les mains sur les genoux, échangeant avec les voisins des nouvelles sans importance ou écoutant religieusement les tangos de Carlos Gardel.

Don Israël est un petit homme rigolard, qui habite un immense pantalon retenu aux aisselles par des bretelles de couleur. Il a deux passions : Staline et les dominos. Staline mort, il ne lui reste plus que les dominos. Encore qu'une réunion de cellule peut, à elle seule, lui faire manquer de temps à autre une de ces parties acharnées qui l'opposent chaque jour, du soir au matin, à des amis qui, comme lui, sont des Argentins d'adoption. Ils s'expriment tous en yiddish. Et, avec leurs trois quotidiens, leurs revues, leurs cafés et leurs théâtres, ils vivent à Buenos Aires comme autrefois à Varsovie.

Dona Regina ne voit guère son mari et depuis le mariage de ses deux fils, elle se sent délaissée. Seule sa petite-fille, Anna-Maria, une jolie brune de quinze ans, vient lui rendre visite et égayer sa solitude. Anna-Maria va encore au lycée. Mais, comme sa grand-mère, elle veut déjà changer le monde, bâtir le socialisme etc. Elle n'est pas à proprement parler communiste. Mais elle milite dans la jeunesse péroniste, se dit persuadée que seule une révolution « justicialiste » saura faire disparaître l'antisémitisme. N'est-ce pas le fruit de l'inégalité sociale ? N'est-ce pas la colère des pauvres qui est déviée par les riches sur le bouc émissaire juif ?

Ce jour-là, Anna-Maria arrive à point. Dona Regina l'entraîne aussitôt à la cuisine, l'installe, verse du potage dans une assiette creuse à fleurs bleues et ordonne :

— Mange !

Puis elle s'assied en face de sa petite-fille et, sans plus de préambule, lui raconte la mort de son lointain cousin.

— Tu le connaissais ? demande Anna-Maria.

Dona Regina soupire :

— Je connaissais son existence. Tu sais, avant la guerre, on s'écrivait beaucoup dans la famille… On était au courant de tout… De chaque mariage, de chaque décès, de chaque déplacement… On n'était jamais seul, même si on était éloigné de la famille par des milliers de kilomètres. Quand on était heureux, on partageait avec elle son bonheur… En cas de besoin, on demandait de l'aide. Mais Hugo, oui, je savais qui c'était… Il était des nôtres, vois-tu… Va savoir si ce n'est pas cela qu'on a voulu lui faire payer…

Puis, voyant que l'assiette de sa petite-fille est vide :

— Mais tu ne manges pas !

— Mais si… Tu vois bien !

— Mon potage n'est pas bon ? Quand on grandit, il faut manger !

Voyant que sa petite fille n'a décidément plus faim, elle hausse les épaules et range sa casserole.

— Et maintenant ? demande Anna-Maria.

— Maintenant ?

Dona Regina la regarde sans bien comprendre :

— Ah, maintenant ? Eh bien il ne nous reste presque plus de famille. Quelques membres éparpillés çà et là à travers le monde… Des survivants… Une pêche sans noyau, ça se défait…

— Et ton frère ?

— Salomon ? Lui, il m'écrit encore. Il tient même un registre des survivants... Mais à quoi bon ? La famille la plus proche peut se compter sur les doigts d'une main, quant aux autres...

Et brusquement :

— Tu as entendu la nouvelle ? Il paraît qu'une bombe a endommagé le bâtiment du journal *La Prensa*.

— Ah, fait Anna-Maria d'un air sceptique et vaguement dégoûté... Comment le sais-tu ?

— Je l'ai entendu à la radio.

— Encore de la provoc ! s'écrie la jeune fille. L'armée va accuser les péronistes. Depuis l'éviction de Peron et son départ en exil, elle cherche à nous éliminer, nous les militants, les dirigeants des organisations populaires...

Elle a dit cela du ton bravache qu'elle suppose être celui des grands révolutionnaires professionnels selon ses rêves. Puis, en regardant sa montre :

— Zut ! Zut ! Je suis en retard ! Nous avons justement une réunion à La Bocca, près du Vieux-Port...

— Fais quand même attention, dit Dona Regina avec une moue complice.

Mais l'enfant est déjà dehors, courant vers sa réunion et songeant une dernière fois, avant de se perdre dans la nuit, à ce cousin assassiné qui la fait déjà tant rêver. Quel dommage, songe-t-elle, de ne pas l'avoir connu !

Paris, janvier 1967

C'est à la fin de l'année 1961 que Benjamin Ben Eliezer nous rendit visite à Paris. L'ambassade avait téléphoné. Elle avait annoncé à ma mère qu'un diplomate israélien de passage souhaitait rencontrer mon père. Pourquoi ? La voix, au bout du fil, était restée évasive. Il fallait être là, voilà tout. Recevoir le diplomate. Et, dans la mesure du possible, répondre à ses questions. Mon père, quand il apprit la nouvelle, ne parut pas outre mesure étonné. Et, à ma grande surprise, il nous dit qu'il attendait cet homme, qu'il le recevrait volontiers.

Quand Benjamin Ben Eliezer vint, le lendemain ou le surlendemain, il fut reçu courtoisement. Mais de manière plus surprenante encore, mon père refusa de lui communiquer le fameux carnet qu'il venait chercher. « Nous en avons besoin, disait l'homme. Les noms qui y figurent peuvent aider l'enquête sur la mort de Hugo. » Mais par un étrange réflexe de méfiance, parce qu'il ne voulait pas, nous disait-il, voir notre nom mêlé à une affaire « pas nette », sans doute aussi pour des raisons plus obscures qui ne devaient m'apparaître que plus tard, mon père hochait la tête, répétait que ce carnet n'avait pas d'importance, que c'était un objet de famille et que, d'ailleurs, il l'avait égaré. Mon père n'était pas un homme de décision. La seule qu'il eût jamais prise avait été de demander ma mère en mariage. Aussi, cette brusque volonté de préserver, fût-ce au mépris d'une enquête et de l'indispensable recherche de la vérité, la mémoire et peut-être le secret du défunt, m'émut-elle profondément. Benjamin Ben Eliezer revint à la charge plusieurs jours de suite. Mon père était intraitable. Et l'autre finit par s'en aller, découragé et assez furieux. Pour ma part, cette insistance de l'un m'intriguait tout autant que le refus de l'autre. Qu'y avait-il dans ce carnet? Pourquoi cet acharnement des deux côtés? Pourquoi mon père, encore une fois, s'accrochait-il à ce petit objet noir qui, du coup, m'apparaissait nimbé du plus capiteux mystère? Toutes les tentatives que je fis pour en savoir un peu plus se soldèrent par un échec. Et, les années passant, toute cette ténébreuse histoire s'éloignant peu à peu dans le temps, je finis par m'en désintéresser tout à fait.

Est-ce à dire que je cessai de penser à Hugo? Non. Car c'est aussi l'époque où j'ai commencé de mener mon combat pour la paix. J'allai aux États-Unis, en Union soviétique, en Israël, dans les pays arabes. Partout je tenais le même langage. Partout, je me faisais le chantre des antiques valeurs prophétiques de la Parole et de la Loi face aux déferlements nouveaux de la violence et de la haine. Or il arrivait cette chose extraordinaire que, partout aussi, on me parlait de... Hugo! « Vous me faites penser à Hugo », me disait-on dans toutes les langues. « Vous parlez comme Hugo »... « Vous êtes aussi irréaliste que votre cousin Hugo »... Partout, oui, il semblait m'avoir précédé. Partout, je rencontrais son souvenir ou son fantôme. C'était comme un père ou un frère dont l'ombre portée était là, toujours là — quelque initiative que je prenne, quelque discours que je tienne. En sorte que, au lieu de m'éloigner de lui, l'écoulement des années et le tracé de mon propre destin ne faisaient paradoxalement — et sans que je prenne encore, bien sûr, toute la mesure de la chose — que m'en rapprocher davantage.

Parallèlement, d'ailleurs, venait s'interposer sans cesse l'ombre, elle bien vivante, d'un autre homme,

Hidar Assadi. A lui aussi j'avais l'étrange impression, à chaque pas ou presque, de me cogner. Non pas qu'il militât dans le même sens que moi ou qu'il partageât cet exigeant souci de la paix qui était alors le mien. Mais il semblait mener une sorte d'*enquête* sur la mort de mon cousin. Que cherchait-il au juste ? Travaillait-il pour les Soviétiques ? Les Palestiniens ? Le fait, en tout cas, était là. Les responsables arabes me parlaient de lui. Les colombes israéliennes. Les cousins soviétiques. Olga, bien sûr. Quand je me rendais à Moscou, il était en Orient. Quand j'étais à Beyrouth, il rentrait à Moscou. Ce jeu de cache-cache m'exaspérait, mais m'intriguait aussi beaucoup.

J'ajoute enfin que Dona Regina, ma tante argentine, me fit, lors d'un bref séjour à Buenos Aires, en 1964, une révélation tout à fait extraordinaire. Hugo, me dit-elle, était dans sa jeunesse un bien bel homme. Pas une femme qui ne tressaillît à sa vue. Pas une qu'il ne réussît, quand il s'y employait, à séduire. Au point que ma mère elle-même, oui ma propre mère, lui avait été fiancée. C'est lui qui l'avait, selon ma tante, présentée à son cousin Salomon. Et celui-ci avait profité des fréquents voyages de Hugo à Berlin pour la demander en mariage. Une histoire banale, en somme, mais qui me trouble au-delà du raisonnable. Ainsi donc, me disais-je, Hugo aurait pu être mon père... Vraiment mon père... Cette idée m'envahit peu à peu, devint une obsession. Et c'est ainsi que ce personnage dont la mort, les derniers jours, la vie même, s'enfuyaient petit à petit dans le lointain et la brume devenait, à mes yeux, un être fabuleux qui m'accompagnait presque partout. L'enquête policière était au point mort. Là-bas, à Tel-Aviv, un obscur fonctionnaire avait probablement dû classer le dossier avec l'une de ces mentions administratives qui sont comme une seconde pierre tombale. Dans ma tête à moi, il vivait. Et sans que je prenne encore le soin d'en deviner ou chercher la raison, il me devenait, au fil du temps, le plus familier des compagnons.

5

BEYROUTH

HIDAR ASSADI

Février 1967

C'est une année où le beau temps a été particulièrement précoce à Beyrouth. Hidar se réjouit d'être à nouveau là. Il est heureux de retrouver les tons bleutés et safranés de l'Orient, son soleil blanc, ses odeurs épaisses étalées comme des nappes et les appels à la prière des muezzins. Son bonheur, pourtant, est assombri par sa séparation avec Olga qu'il a dû laisser à Moscou. Nous sommes en 1967. Leur liaison dure déjà depuis plus de dix ans. Cette femme exquise est sa joie en même temps que sa mauvaise conscience. Quoi de plus exaltant que de se contempler dans un œil amoureux ? Quoi de comparable au bien-être que procure la libre disposition d'une chair laiteuse, pudique et facile à la fois, qui semble souvent même prendre plaisir aux douces tortures qu'il lui inflige. Où est-elle ? A quoi pense-t-elle ? Comment vit-elle cette liaison ? Elle semble accepter la situation d'un cœur léger. Mais il lui arrive de déceler dans le regard gris de la jeune femme une pointe d'amertume, toute proche de la réprobation. Olga n'est pas une « kulturnyi tchelovek », une « personne de culture ». Elle est naturelle, spontanée, presque ingénue. Et elle parvient mal à dissimuler sa déception, sa mélancolie. Chaque fois qu'il revient à Moscou, il se précipite chez ses parents, rue Kazakov et chaque fois, elle a l'air de l'attendre. Il ne doute pas qu'elle ait d'autres amants. Mais au moins est-il certain qu'elle tient à lui plus qu'à quiconque. Lors de son dernier séjour, ils se sont rarement trouvés en tête-à-tête. Chez lui, à l'hôpital ou dans ses réunions politiques, il y avait toujours foule autour d'eux. Et la veille de son départ, alors qu'il espérait tant passer la nuit avec elle, une dispute a réduit le projet à néant. Une fois de plus il s'agissait d'Israël. Israël et le judaïsme ne sont-ils pas devenus leur thème de conversation principal ? La pierre d'achoppement de leur relation ? Hidar, ce soir-là, lui reprochait son soudain intérêt pour ses origines. Il ne comprenait pas pourquoi elle qui, jusque-là, refoulait si consciencieusement ses origines, était en train d'y revenir ? Le ton avait monté. Et la soirée était gâchée.

La vérité c'est que les Juifs, depuis toujours, fascinent Hidar. Il se souvient de ses amis Sultan, à Tunis, et de la Grande Synagogue qu'ils lui avaient fait un jour visiter. A les voir vivre, il avait l'impression d'avoir affaire à un peuple de frères, tous sortis du même homme et formant une même chair. Les musulmans eux-mêmes ne se disent-ils pas fils d'Abraham ? Oui mais cette filiation unique semble nourrir chez les Juifs une étrange solidarité et d'extraordinaires réseaux d'entraide. Et puis il y a leur permanence. Loin de disparaître, tels les peuples de Grèce et d'Italie, de Lacédémone, d'Athènes ou de Rome, venus longtemps après, ils subsistent toujours. La Loi à laquelle ils sont attachés, les textes et les rites qu'ils pratiquent les ont tenus debout. Pérennité irritante pour les autres. Déconcertante. Pour Hidar les Juifs sont simultanément les hommes les plus transparents et les plus opaques. Tout le monde peut connaître leur histoire, leurs mœurs, leurs rêves et leurs désirs, sans comprendre, toutefois, le mystère de leur durée. Qui sait si ce n'est pas elle, cette durée, qui, plus encore que leur supposé amour de l'argent, suscite l'hostilité des nations ?

Antisémite, Hidar ? Il a lu Shakespeare et Balzac, Dostoïevski et Dickens, les historiens romains, le Coran et Marx. Il connaît tous ces textes qui n'en finissent pas de délirer à propos du vieux Juif sordide et crochu allant chercher son or dans les immondices de l'humanité. Et la vérité oblige à dire qu'il n'est pas toujours insensible ni sourd à ce discours. Les Juifs provoquent en lui des sentiments qu'il sait contradictoires mais qui, pourtant, se nourrissent mutuellement : l'admiration et l'envie, le désir et la haine... Hidar, cela dit, se défend contre l'emprise d'une idéologie qu'il sait pernicieuse. N'est-elle pas responsable du sionisme ? Pire : l'antisémitisme n'est-il pas son alibi, sa nourriture quotidienne ? Au fond de lui-même, il n'est pas loin de croire que l'intérêt d'Olga pour Israël et le judaïsme date de la fameuse lettre venue de Paris... Bien sûr, il a été sot de parler à Olga. Mais comment aurait-il pu deviner que Hugo était le cousin de sa mère et qu'il allait être tué un jour pour rien, sur une route israélienne ? Son père, Marwan, disait : « Ce qui arrive sans qu'on le fasse venir, c'est le destin... Mektoub. » Mais le destin n'explique pas tout.

Hidar essaye pour la énième fois de comprendre ce qui s'est réellement passé. Il aimait Hugo sincèrement. Et, même quand il n'approuvait pas ses initiatives, l'enthousiasme de son ami était si contagieux qu'il finissait toujours par l'aider. Quand, en 1960, Hidar céda une fois encore à la demande de son ami, il savait, il pressentait, qu'il se mettait en danger. Pourquoi, alors, accepta-t-il ? Succomba-t-il à nouveau au charme du Juif ? Crût-il que serait conjuré le danger qu'il prévoyait ! Ou désirait-il secrètement la mort de son ami ? Hugo est mort depuis six ans déjà et cette question le travaille encore.

Hugo, en ce temps-là, cherchait un contact avec la direction du MNA. Fort du soutien du conseiller personnel de David Ben Gourion, Israël Beer, il voulait persuader les Palestiniens d'accepter un dialogue avec leurs adversaires. En présentant Hugo à ses amis, lors d'une réunion à Beyrouth, Hidar savait qu'il lui faisait prendre un très gros risque. D'abord du côté soviétique, pour qui le MNA devait être soutenu non pas en vue d'un dialogue avec Israël, mais comme un outil de pression au Proche-Orient. Et ensuite du côté palestinien, où toute forme de dialogue avec Israël était une trahison à la cause arabe. Pour les premiers comme pour les seconds, le fait qu'un Juif pro-israélien puisse rencontrer les dirigeants du MNA et le dire un jour publiquement pouvait justifier sa mort.

Hidar a toujours su que la faute la plus pernicieuse est celle dont on ignore qu'elle est une faute ; mais plus dangereuse encore est celle que l'on prend pour un acte de vertu. Il se rend compte à présent qu'il ne connaissait pas vraiment les activités de Hugo. Pourquoi voulait-il tant cette rencontre ? Que s'est-il dit, au juste, dans cette mystérieuse maison de Beyrouth, près de l'aéroport ? Ensuite, dans les jours, les semaines qui ont suivi ? Sa seule certitude, c'est que les services israéliens enquêtent sur la mort de son ami et que, sans rien connaître apparemment de ces rencontres secrètes, ils l'imputent vaguement à leur amitié. Cette idée l'inquiète. Car si elle est juste, alors lui, Hidar Assadi, était aussi visé par l'attentat contre Hugo.

Il se souvient brusquement de l'explosion de sa voiture voici quelques mois à Beyrouth. Explosion à ce jour inexplicable et qui aurait pu lui coûter la vie si, au dernier moment, il n'avait décidé de se rendre à l'hôtel à pied. Voulait-on le tuer ou juste le menacer ? Peu importe ! Celui qui a exécuté Hugo le tient à l'œil. Si seulement il savait sa nationalité : Soviétique ? Palestinien ? C'est pour en avoir le cœur net que, ce matin, pour la millième fois, il a décidé de profiter d'une réunion de direction du MNA pour en parler carrément, ouvertement à ses amis.

Mais voici que, tel un amoureux qui, à l'heure du rendez-vous, tremble, prend peur et cherche une diversion, un délai, une excuse peut-être, Hidar, au fur et à mesure qu'il approche de l'hôtel Alcazar, où se tient la réunion, juge son projet stupide et dangereux. Et si l'un des membres présents était mêlé à l'histoire ? Et si, en parlant, il se découvrait et s'exposait ? Trouble. Tergiversation. Quand il arrive à l'Alcazar et qu'il embrasse tour à tour Georges Habbache, Waddi Haddad, Abdel Karim Hamad et Ahmed Yamani, réunis dans un salon ovale et sans fenêtres, rempli de poufs et de lourds tapis persans, sa décision est prise : il préfère encore ne rien dire. Tant pis pour l'honneur ! Stavroguine, son personnage favori, n'a-t-il pas réclamé pour lui et ses lointains descendants le « droit au déshonneur » ?

Hidar Assadi est un homme raffiné. Il a gardé de ses études de sociologie à la Sorbonne, puis à l'Université américaine de Beyrouth (où il a connu Georges Habbache et Waddi Haddad) une vraie culture bourgeoise. Mais il est aussi un redoutable guerrier de l'ombre. Un agent aux intuitions aiguisées par de longues années de clandestinité et il sait, aujourd'hui, en entrant dans ce salon, qu'il est en danger et qu'un mot, un seul mot de trop peut lui être fatal. Ses amis ? Oui, ses amis... Mais qui peuvent, d'une seconde à l'autre, devenir ses plus féroces adversaires... Pas un mot, non... Méfiance absolue... Un geste machinal pour s'assurer que son colt est bien là, à sa place, dans la poche intérieure du blouson... N'étaient la démarche un peu trop raide que lui donne sa jambe gauche atrophiée depuis l'enfance à la suite d'une attaque de poliomyélite, il pourrait presque faire une entrée impressionnante.

La réunion durera deux heures, l'avertit-on d'emblée. Un peu court, certes, vu la qualité des participants. Mais Habbache part à Damas et a demandé que l'on veuille bien aller très vite. Waddi Haddad, venu la veille d'Aden où il a établi, pour les futurs feddayins, un camp de guérilla urbaine, commence par féliciter Hidar : les armes que celui-ci vient d'obtenir de la Tchécoslovaquie et de la Bulgarie, sur ordre de Moscou, sont parfaites. Puis il évoque les activités des trois groupes de guérilleros apparentés au MNA : « les Héros du retour », « la Jeunesse de la vengeance » et le Front de Libération de la Palestine. Et puis enfin, mine de rien, il lui lance une pique à propos de ses fréquentations juives.

Hidar frissonne. Il connaît les tendances policières de Waddi, son efficacité, son absence de scrupules. Il choisit de riposter — et de le faire la tête haute :

— Il faut connaître les Juifs... Il faut connaître leur histoire, leur organisation communautaire et les moyens qu'ils ont utilisés pour créer un État... Pendant la guerre, Staline conseillait aux Soviétiques d'apprendre la langue des Allemands, leur histoire et leur culture. On ne peut gagner une guerre contre quelqu'un qu'on ne connaît pas.

Georges Habbache approuve. Passant, d'un mouvement familier, son pouce droit sur sa moustache, il dit :

— Hidar a raison. Il serait bon que nos militants apprennent l'hébreu. C'est dans la presse israélienne qu'ils apprendront, mieux qu'ailleurs, ce qui se passe à Tel-Aviv...

— Il faut aller plus loin, surenchérit alors Hidar. Il faut copier l'organisation du mouvement sioniste d'avant-guerre, ses congrès, ses collectes, son parlement, sa direction, son armée et ses commandos de choc... ce qui était bon pour eux peut être bon pour nous... Je crois qu'il est temps pour vous de quitter le MNA et de créer un mouvement purement palestinien.

Georges Habbache estime l'idée bonne. Abdul Karim Hamad prématurée, mais intéressante. Après quelques minutes de débat, on s'accroche sur une hypothèse moyenne : créer, très vite, un groupe spécial « Région Palestine ». Hidar n'en voulait pas davantage. Et tout habité de ce merveilleux sentiment de puissance que donne une manipulation réussie et qu'il connaît fort bien, il ne peut réprimer un léger sourire de triomphe.

— Tu penses à quelque chose ? lui demande Waddi Haddad, soudain méfiant.

Jamais Hidar n'a senti, dans une de leurs réunions, une telle défiance, une telle tension. L'idée l'effleure tout à coup que ces hommes sont ses ennemis... Que son assassin pourrait même, allez savoir, se trouver parmi eux... Il chasse cette idée, décide de congédier de ses pensées l'encombrant fantôme de Hugo. Et la discussion reprend, comme si de rien n'était, sur l'attitude à avoir vis-à-vis de l'utilisation de combattants non arabes dans la lutte contre le sionisme. Deux questions qui ne trouveront pas de réponse unanime et dont l'examen est donc remis à plus tard.

A la tombée du jour, Hidar retrouvera sa table habituelle, à la terrasse du café « La Grotte aux pigeons », d'où il peut contempler la mer. La mer vue de Tel-Aviv est-elle la même ? Connaîtra-t-il un jour Tel-Aviv ? Jaffa ? Haïfa ? En soupirant, il commande un arak. Il a rendez-vous avec son contact à l'ambassade d'URSS et a un peu de temps à tuer. Waddi Haddad a dit que la guerre entre les Arabes et Israël est imminente. Que voulait-il dire ? D'où venait son information ? Il sait que l'URSS prépare l'armée de Nasser à la guerre, mais il sait aussi que les spécialistes soviétiques jugent l'Égypte incapable d'affronter avec succès un adversaire parfaitement entraîné et maîtrisant les techniques de la guerre les plus sophistiquées.

Le brusque appel du muezzin à « El-Leil », la dernière prière de la journée, le fait sursauter. Un coup d'œil sur sa montre pour constater que son contact est en retard. Et tandis que les vagues, comme essoufflées par l'ascension de la rive, retombent une à une à la mer, il pense à nouveau à Olga. Doute et désir. Inquiétude et nostalgie. Il aime Olga, oui. Quand la reverra-t-il ?

6

ISRAËL

LA GUERRE

5 mai 1967

Mordekhaï conduit prudemment. La route de Dafné à Hagesharim est inégale. Elle se faufile entre des rochers et grimpe au milieu de chênes plusieurs fois millénaires, pour redescendre ensuite en ligne droite vers des lacs artificiels.

Arié s'impatiente :

— Plus vite, papa, plus vite !

— Rien ne sert de courir, mon fils, répond Mordekhaï en riant.

— Mais le match, papa, le match !...

Arié est un gamin au teint mat et aux cheveux bruns, et, malgré ses quatorze ans, déjà bâti en homme. Il appartient à l'équipe de football du kibboutz qui doit affronter celle de Hagesharim. Ayant raté l'autobus qu'ont pris ses coéquipiers, il a convaincu son père de le conduire au stade dans sa vieille camionnette Ford. Toujours en retard, Arié ! Et, en même temps, toujours si impatient !

Mordekhaï a mis la radio en se disant que ça le calmerait. On entend les Beatles... Les Rolling Stones... Des vieux tubes de l'année passée... Et puis, brusquement, plus rien. Mordekhaï peste déjà contre l'électricien du kibboutz qui a mal réparé l'engin lorsqu'une voix sourde, un peu dramatique, qui n'est manifestement plus celle du charmant disc-jockey de tout à l'heure, annonce : « Esther est malade, elle attend au kibboutz », puis : « David attend son père »... « David attend son père... »

— Qu'est-ce que c'est que ces conneries ? s'exclame le jeune homme. Ils sont devenus fous !

— C'est la guerre, Arié.

— La guerre ?

Arié regarde son père et voit que son visage a, en effet, changé de couleur.

— Oui, ce sont des messages codés... On mobilise, vois-tu... Tout le monde...

— Et toi ?

— Moi aussi.

— Et le match ?

— Après la guerre, mon fils, après la guerre...

Au premier carrefour, Mordekhaï rebrousse chemin.

Arié, alors grave :

— Tu vas te battre, papa ?

— Oui, te dis-je... comme tout le monde...

— Mais...

Mordekhaï devine l'extrême confusion des sentiments de son fils. Mais l'œil fixé sur le macadam, sa tête déjà ailleurs et le cœur battant à tout rompre, il n'a ni le désir ni la force d'en dire plus.

— N'aie pas peur, jette-t-il simplement. « Qui non si muore mai. »

— Qu'est-ce que ça veut dire ?

— C'est de l'italien. Ça veut dire : « Ici, on ne meurt plus. »

— Où, ici ?

— En Israël.

— Mais, qu'est-ce que tu racontes ? dit-il.

Et il se met à pleurer.

La route qui relie Quiryat Shemona au Mont Hermon que Mordekhaï doit traverser est déjà embouteillée. Par autobus, dans des camions laitiers, dans des camionnettes de blanchisseurs ou de boulangers, dans des fourgons découverts, des voitures particulières, d'antiques tacots, les membres des kibboutzim du plateau du Golan, alertés sur leur lieu de travail, dans les champs, les forêts et les viviers, répondent à l'appel.

Depuis plusieurs semaines, des clameurs de guerre retentissent aux frontières. On n'entend partout que des imprécations contre l'État juif, cet « ennemi du genre humain ». A la surprise des Égyptiens eux-mêmes, le président Nasser a massé ses troupes à la lisière du Neguev, expulsé les Casques bleus de la bande de Gaza et de Sharm el-Sheikh, fermé le détroit de Tiran à la navigation israélienne. La Syrie a mis ses troupes en alerte et le représentant des Palestiniens, Ahmed Chou-Keiry, a promis à une foule en délire, massée sur la grand-place de Gaza, de jeter tous les Juifs à la mer.

Certes, ce n'est pas la première fois que les Arabes s'agitent. Et à l'heure où Mordekhaï et le petit Arié entendent le mystérieux appel radio, des informations contradictoires circulent encore quant aux objectifs réels de cette mobilisation. En diaspora, pourtant, on est inquiet. Plus inquiet peut-être qu'en Israël. Peut-être parce qu'on sait d'expérience qu'entre deux versions d'un danger c'est presque toujours la pire qui l'emporte. Peut-être aussi parce que la presse occidentale s'est complue depuis des semaines dans les analyses les plus alarmistes. Commentaires TV apocalyptiques... Pages entières dans les journaux où l'on démontre à l'envi combien le rapport de forces est défavorable à l'État juif... Cartes du Proche-Orient, où l'on souligne son tragique encerclement... Sidney, ce matin-là, n'en mène pas large. Assis sur le lit défait avec, ouvert devant lui, le énième article du *New York Times* démontrant que Tsahal ne résistera jamais à une attaque simultanée de toutes les forces arabes, il se sent terriblement impuissant.

— Dis papa, demande Richard qui vient d'entrer dans la pièce et qui est déjà au courant des nouvelles, pas vrai que l'Amérique ne laissera pas mourir Israël ?

— Je ne sais pas, mon fils, lui répond-il... Tu te rappelles ce que je t'ai expliqué un jour ? L'Amérique n'a pas fait grand-chose pendant la guerre pour les Juifs de Pologne.

— Mais, papa, nous aussi on est américains maintenant. On ne va pas laisser Israël perdre la guerre !

— Je compte beaucoup plus sur l'armée d'Israël que sur nous, Dick...

Richard s'apprête à répondre quand le téléphone sonne.

Comme dans toutes les maisons juives, depuis deux semaines, le téléphone ne cesse de sonner chez Sidney. Les frères, les oncles et les cousins du Canada, de Californie, appellent pour s'encourager mutuellement ou, le plus souvent, pour partager et commenter une information diffusée à la télévision ou lue dans la presse. Même les plus indifférents, les plus assimilés, commencent à avoir peur. Et là c'est Larry, son frère cadet de Los Angeles, qui vient d'apprendre que deux sous-marins soviétiques ont franchi le Bosphore en direction de la Méditerranée.

Sidney répond aux uns. Aux autres. Les nouvelles les plus fantaisistes se mêlent aux plus sérieuses. On discute. On s'affole. Jusqu'à ce que, n'y tenant plus, il décide de se rendre au Consulat. Des centaines de Juifs américains sont déjà là qui, comme lui, savent que du sort de l'État juif dépend leur propre destin — et qui, du coup, se portent volontaires pour aller combattre dans les rangs de Tsahal. Ils sont tous là. Jeunes et vieux. Grands et petits. Beaux jeunes gens au physique sportif dont on devine déjà les soldats qu'ils feront — ou hommes d'affaires au physique plus enveloppé qui rêvent eux aussi d'en découdre. Sidney est du nombre. Il sait que son devoir est de se porter au secours de cet État si fragile dont son père lui disait autrefois qu'il serait le refuge des Juifs et qu'il s'agit pourtant, maintenant, d'aller défendre. Défendre l'État refuge ! Soutenir ce pays qui était supposé soutenir, lui, tous les Juifs du monde ! C'est le cœur à la fois léger et terriblement anxieux que, de retour chez lui, il appelle Mordekhaï pour l'informer de sa décision.

Une fois rentré, une double surprise l'attend. C'est d'abord Marjory qui, affolée, apparemment trop émue pour prononcer un mot, l'entraîne jusqu'à la chambre de Marilyn. C'est une jolie pièce toute simple, aux rideaux tirés, meublée d'une petite table, d'un coffre à jouets, d'un guéridon et d'un spot rose qui éclaire des dessins d'enfant punaisés sur les murs. Marilyn dort. Mais elle a les lèvres blêmes, de la sueur qui perle sur son visage. Et quand Sidney s'approche d'elle pour l'embrasser, il s'aperçoit qu'elle a le front brûlant.

Marjory, baissant la voix :

— Richard a participé à une collecte pour Tsahal et il est resté dormir chez un camarade. Marilyn, elle, voulait partir pour Israël... J'ai eu beau lui dire que c'était impossible, qu'une petite fille de six ans ne pouvait pas faire un vrai soldat, sa déception a été énorme. Elle a passé deux heures à pleurer. Elle vient juste de s'endormir.

Et puis, deuxième surprise : allumant la télévision, Sidney tombe sur le maréchal Grechko, chef d'état-major soviétique, qui menace Israël d'une intervention militaire. Marilyn... Israël... Tout cela se mêle dans sa pauvre tête... Sidney, pour la première fois depuis longtemps, se surprend à tourner autour de la question que ses ancêtres, depuis des siècles, posaient inlassablement : qu'est-ce, au juste, qu'être juif ?

7

MOSCOU

GUERRE DANS LA FAMILLE

Mai 1967

Retransmis à la télévision soviétique, le discours de Grechko met Rachel Lerner hors d'elle.

— Comment peut-il mentir ainsi! Qui croira que trois millions de Juifs menacent cent millions d'Arabes! Je réentends Hitler annonçant que cinq cent mille Juifs allemands menaçaient soixante millions d'Aryens. En finirons-nous donc jamais? L'histoire est-elle vouée à recommencer — toujours, inlassablement, de la même façon?

C'est dimanche. La famille est réunie, au grand complet, rue Kazakov. Olga, bien sûr... Mais aussi Sacha, son épouse Sonia et leurs deux enfants... Rachel, en bonne grand-mère, a préparé le thé, disposé quelques gâteaux sur un plateau. Mais sa colère est si vive, sa nervosité si grande, qu'elle en fait déborder les tasses...

— Allons, Rachel, calme-toi, murmure Aron... Tu sais bien que de t'énerver ainsi ne te vaut rien...

— Comment veux-tu ne pas s'énerver? Comment peux-tu toi-même rester comme ça, impassible? Tu as vu? Tu as entendu ce qu'il a dit?

Sacha ricane :

— Maman est incroyable. Pour elle tout ce que font les Juifs est sacré. Demain les Israéliens construiront des camps de concentration pour les Arabes et elle nous dira qu'il s'agit de jardins d'enfants... C'est grotesque...

Aron se lève d'un bond. Ses yeux — signe de grande colère — ont viré au noir. Et la commissure de ses lèvres s'est creusée un peu plus.

— Comment peux-tu parler ainsi à ta mère ? Et où as-tu appris ce discours ? En écoutant les gens de ton espèce, on en deviendrait presque sioniste...

— Eh bien vas-y, répond le jeune homme de plus en plus insolent... Mais si, vas-y puisque tu en rêves... L'Union soviétique n'a pas besoin de citoyens comme toi.

Aron est devenu blême. Il tremble de la tête aux pieds. Il a les yeux tout embués de larmes.

— Mon pauvre enfant, lance-t-il d'une voix soudain plus sourde... Qu'es-tu donc devenu ? Réalises-tu ce que tu dis ? Tu parles comme un adjudant ou un kapo... Ignores-tu que ta mère est venue ici pour participer à la Révolution ? Tu m'entends : La Ré-vo-lu-tion ! Elle espérait le bonheur pour tous... La société sans classes... Elle voulait vous voir, ta sœur et toi, vivre un jour dans la société de nos rêves... Résultat ? Tu connais le résultat...

Et puis, comme Sacha ne répond rien :

— Tu veux qu'on parte en Israël ? Pourquoi donc ? Parce que nous te gênons ? Parce que ce que nous avons fait, ce dont nous avons rêvé, vous fait honte aujourd'hui ? Ah ! mon fils... Je pleure de te voir ainsi, mêlé à ces gens, arriviste comme eux, corrompu demain...

Rachel semble, en quelques minutes, avoir vieilli de dix ans. Elle s'efforce en vain de s'interposer entre les deux hommes, de les faire taire. Elle tente, sans trop y croire, de leur parler des voisins, des mouchards, du danger qu'il y a à parler de ces choses...

— Laisse-les crier, dit Olga presque aussi bouleversée qu'elle. Peut-être apprendra-t-on enfin ce que Sacha a dans le ventre...

— Toi et tes Arabes, fait Sacha d'une voix devenue dangereusement calme... Veux-tu que je dise à nos parents tout ce que je sais...

Puis, haussant les épaules et se tournant vers ses

enfants, Natacha et Boris, qui commencent à pleurer :

— Venez, gologubtchikis... Venez, mes petits pigeons... On s'en va...

Sonia fait un pas vers Aron, s'arrête. Les enfants font le geste d'aller l'embrasser, se tournent vers leur père, s'arrêtent aussi. Aron les regarde avec tristesse. Il sait qu'à cet instant quelque chose s'est cassé dans l'ordre non écrit qui régissait jusque-là la vie de la famille.

Rachel ne dormira pas cette nuit-là. Vers trois heures du matin, épuisée, à bout de nerfs, elle se lèvera et, sur la pointe des pieds, ira jusqu'au salon. Un livre... Un autre... Quel est le livre qui saurait apaiser cette épouvantable sensation d'angoisse que lui a donnée son fils ? Le matin venu, elle se souvient qu'un collègue de son mari, Vassili Slepakov, doit se rendre bientôt en Argentine pour un congrès sur les Indiens de l'époque précolombienne. Et s'il acceptait de rendre visite à la famille ? S'il se chargeait d'une mission ? L'idée, Dieu sait pourquoi, la rassure et l'exalte. Elle cherche du papier. Un stylo. Et commence à rédiger, dans ce yiddish qu'elle manie si mal, une longue lettre à Dona Regina. Elle ne connaît pas Regina. Ni son mari. Ni, d'ailleurs, aucun de ses cousins d'Amérique, d'Israël et de France. Six ans ont passé depuis la mort de Hugo. Mais elle y repense tout à coup en se disant qu'ils sont tous, aux quatre coins du monde, les cousins de Hugo. Cette idée l'amuse. Puis l'apaise. Elle lui donne, soudain, un sentiment de puissance et de joie dont elle avait, depuis bien des années, oublié la saveur.

8

MOSCOU

LA LETTRE DE RACHEL LERNER

6 mai 1967

Chère famille,

Je ne vous connais pas, mais vous êtes mes cousins et vous êtes aussi les seuls Juifs dont je connaisse l'existence à l'étranger. Nos frères en Israël sont en danger et j'ai besoin de partager mon angoisse avec ceux qui la ressentent comme moi et pour les mêmes raisons que moi. Mon mari, Aron, qui enseigne l'antiquité gréco-romaine à l'Université, aime citer Sophocle disant que les parents sont les seuls témoins capables de partager les souffrances d'un parent. Je suis sûre que nous aussi, nous ne pouvons, en ce moment, compter que sur nos parents.

Ici, la presse, la télévision, la radio font sans cesse de la propagande anti-israélienne. Avec quelques amis, nous avons créé un cercle d'étude de l'hébreu. Aron l'ignore. Je pense qu'il s'y serait opposé. L'ami chez qui nous nous réunissons, une fois par semaine, a fait sensation, à son travail, en se déclarant favorable à Israël. Presque toutes ses fréquentations l'ont immédiatement traité en paria. Elles se sont détournées de lui comme on se détournait, jadis, des lépreux. Quelques personnes fidèles et courageuses, des Russes ou des Juifs, continuent à le rencontrer, chez lui, presque chaque soir. Mais c'est bien téméraire. Les méchantes langues du KGB surveillent continuellement sa porte.

65

Des micros enregistrent sûrement ses moindres paroles. Les invités n'ont donc rien d'autre à faire qu'à boire et ils boivent à la santé d'Israël. Je suis, bien sûr, au nombre de ces invités.

L'antisémitisme n'a jamais disparu en Union soviétique. Mais il a pris des formes toujours différentes. Ainsi à l'époque de Staline il y avait des Juifs parmi les policiers et le pouvoir avait le culot de se servir de cela pour nous faire porter la responsabilité de la Terreur. Aujourd'hui nous savons bien ce qu'était la folie de cet homme. Cette folie-là a liquidé toute une culture : la culture yiddish. Combien de fois je me suis demandé ce qui nous a donné la force de nous battre ! De tout risquer ! Je ne peux trouver de réponse à cette question. Je ne la cherche même pas. Après la déception de mes vingt ans, j'ai voulu retrouver la tradition juive, comme on s'accroche à un radeau. J'ai été aussitôt entraînée dans les rapides, poussée par la force du courant, me heurtant contre les pierres mais suffoquant de joie devant ce sentiment éprouvé pour la première fois : celui d'une vraie liberté !

Voulez-vous, mes chers cousins, que je vous en dise plus ? Ce réveil juif s'est manifesté d'abord comme une forme de protestation. Le sentiment national a également joué un rôle important. Car l'antisémitisme du gouvernement est devenu plus actif à partir de l'année 1948, à la naissance de l'État d'Israël. Les attaques de la propagande contre Israël, grossières et monstrueuses, dans leur haine et leur hypocrisie, nous offensèrent et nous indignèrent. Et c'est pourquoi, entre nous et le pays dans lequel nous vivions, il y a eu une sorte de divorce. Un exemple : quand je voyais les menaces, toujours grandissantes, que faisait peser l'Union soviétique sur Israël, j'imaginais la possibilité d'une guerre et la peu enviable situation qui serait celle d'Aron, officier de réserve étant conduit malgré lui à se battre contre Israël et à tuer ces Juifs qui avaient survécu miraculeusement à l'entreprise des nazis. C'était là, pour moi, une perspective absolument effroyable. Je voulais que nous puissions être parmi les défenseurs d'Israël plutôt que les complices, même involontaires, de ses ennemis.

Pour mon fils Sacha cette question ne se pose pas : il est soviétique et communiste. Ma fille, Olga, est en train de changer. Depuis la mort de notre cousin Hugo, tué par un commando palestinien sur une route d'Israël (vous avez appris la nouvelle, je suppose ?), son intérêt pour Israël et l'histoire juive va grandissant. L'ami d'Olga est un Arabe. Il s'appelle Hidar. Je ne sais pas ce qu'il fait. Mais il est souvent au Proche-Orient. Naguère, il a connu Hugo, en Tunisie. D'après les quelques réflexions de Hidar, j'ai cru comprendre qu'ils étaient liés. La politique, je suppose... Toujours la politique... Hugo œuvrait-il pour la paix ? Organisait-il des rencontres entre les Arabes et les Juifs ? C'est une attitude digne d'estime mais qui, dans ce monde d'abus, de violences et d'iniquités est aussi dangereuse que la guerre.

Si seulement on nous laissait partir pour aider nos frères en Israël !

La création de l'État d'Israël nous a certes causé des problèmes, mais, après les massacres que nous avons subis, elle nous a aussi rendu notre dignité.

Un collègue d'Aron se rend à un congrès à Buenos Aires. Je lui demanderai d'emporter cette lettre. Le fera-t-il ? Je le crois. Il s'appelle Vassili Slepakov. Il n'est pas juif. C'est un honnête homme. Je sais que Regina et son mari sont communistes et qu'ils ont fui la Pologne à l'époque de la contre-révolution. Je le dirai à Vassili Slepakov. Il sera ainsi, je l'espère, tranquillisé.

Si vous pouvez prévenir notre cousin israélien, Mordekhaï, de notre solidarité, je vous en serais reconnaissante.

J'espère que nous nous verrons tous un jour. A Jérusalem.

Rachel Lerner (Halter).

9

BUENOS AIRES

UNE VISITE AVORTÉE

Mai 1967

A peine est-elle informée de la visite de Vassili Slepakov que Dona Regina donne les signes de la plus vive excitation. Un professeur! Et soviétique! Quelle meilleure preuve qu'il y a des savants en Union soviétique! Qu'ils sont libres de leurs mouvements! Que la propagande impérialiste est, là aussi, un tissu de mensonges! Ceux qui, jusque dans sa propre famille, parlent du pays des Soviets comme d'une vaste prison vont en être pour leurs frais. Dona Regina exulte, oui. Elle est au moins aussi émue que pour une veille de Pâque. Et lorsque Dona Regina est émue, Dieu sait si cela se voit!

Pour l'heure elle s'active comme une petite abeille, en prévision de l'événement. Nettoyage à fond de la maison. Dépoussiérage du grand portrait de Staline qui trône dans le vestibule. Révision accélérée de quelques classiques qu'il conviendra de citer le moment venu. Don Israël lui-même n'échappe pas à la remise en ordre et se voit convié à changer de pantalon, à astiquer ses bretelles, à apprendre quelques mots de russe. L'essentiel de la partie se jouant néanmoins en cuisine où la chère matrone s'emploie, deux jours durant, à préparer ses meilleurs gâteaux.

— Qui va manger tous les gâteaux que tu prépares, grand-maman? s'inquiète gentiment Anna-Maria. Le

Soviétique ne vient que pour t'apporter une lettre de Moscou...

— Ce n'est rien, répond-elle sans se démonter. Je lui ferai un paquet pour la cousine Rachel...

— Parce que tu penses que les Soviétiques n'ont rien à manger ? renchérit la jeune fille d'un air faussement ingénu et en sachant fort bien qu'elle va la piquer au vif.

— Ah non ! Ça, c'est de la propagande antisoviétique. Je t'interdis de dire cela...

Le grand jour arrive. La famille au complet est réunie pour accueillir le visiteur. Don Israël a ses nouvelles bretelles. Dona Regina une robe de taffetas rouge, pleine de frou-frous et de dentelles qu'elle n'a pas portée depuis des années et où elle est si engoncée qu'elle a peine à respirer. Ses gâteaux sont dans les plats. Sa maison tout entière respire la fête et l'encaustique. Et l'absurde, c'est que... Slepakov ne vient pas mais, à sa place, un banal coursier de l'ambassade porteur de la fameuse lettre. Ô honte ! Ô désespoir ! Dona Regina ose à peine regarder ses enfants en face. Don Israël part se réfugier dans sa chambre, convaincu que c'est contre lui que toute l'affaire va se retourner. Et les gâteaux reprennent le chemin de la cuisine.

— Cela ne fait rien, dit Dona Regina... Nous les mangerons à sa place... Nous sommes assez bien pour ça, vous ne trouvez pas...

Et pour sauver sinon l'honneur, du moins la face, elle rappelle son mari, lui tend la lettre en lui demandant de la traduire. Et, retrouvant soudain un terrain familier, se met à commenter « la ligne politique » des cousins soviétiques.

— Je ne comprends vraiment pas notre cousine Rachel. Pourquoi ne pourrait-on pas être prosoviétique et pro-israélien à la fois ? Nous, par exemple...

— Mais, justement, vous n'êtes pas en Union soviétique ! dit Anna-Maria en souriant et en privant la grand-mère de tout son « effet ».

Marcos qui ne manque jamais l'occasion de prendre sa fille en défaut dans l'espoir qu'elle abandonne ses engagements révolutionnaires :

— Toi, tu es de gauche et tu es antisoviétique. Révolutionnaire et péroniste. Avec tes copains, vous êtes antisionistes et tu trembles pour Israël...

— Ne te fatigue pas, papa. Tu n'entends rien à la contradiction dialectique. Quant à Israël, c'est plus compliqué... C'est un fait qu'il possède un prolétariat puissant, qui maintient la lutte des classe, tandis que les pays qui le menacent sont réellement réactionnaires, mais...

Dona Regina revient avec une théière et des tasses :

— L'URSS réactionnaire ? Tu ne sais plus ce que tu dis, ma petite... J'y étais, moi, pendant la Révolution, en Union soviétique. Avant, c'était la misère. Et je les ai vues, de mes yeux, les transformations révolutionnaires apportées à l'existence des gens...

Martin est, comme toujours, à la fois amusé et irrité de voir que, dans cette famille, personne n'écoute vraiment personne. Pour changer de conversation il annonce une nouvelle qui lui tient à cœur :

— Le cousin Mordekhaï, du kibboutz Dafné, viendra sans doute, lui, l'année prochaine pour enseigner l'hébreu à l'école Sholem Aleikhem...

— S'il survit à la guerre, remarque Miguel, son frère cadet.

— Ne dis pas de bêtises, dit Dona Regina en crachant trois fois par terre pour conjurer le sort.

Il se fait un silence.

— Bon, dit Miguel, ce n'est pas tout : qui se chargera de photocopier la lettre de Rachel et de l'envoyer au reste de la famille ainsi qu'elle nous demande de le faire ?

Paris, juin 1967

C'est la fin de la journée. Je suis dans ma voiture, coincé dans un embouteillage. La radio annonce une sensible montée de la tension autour du conflit au Proche-Orient. Le président des États-Unis, Lyndon Johnson, a décidé l'envoi d'un porte-avions en mer Rouge tandis que deux nouveaux sous-marins soviétiques ont franchi le Bosphore en direction de la Méditerranée. La guerre semble imminente. Les divisions égyptiennes avancent dans le Sinaï. Israël mobilise. Les chefs d'État arabes multiplient les déclarations belliqueuses et Ahmed Choukeiry, le leader des Palestiniens, promet de jeter les Juifs à la mer — tout au moins, ceux qui survivraient à l'offensive arabe. La guerre ! Des explosions, des flammes, des cris, des cadavres : j'ai l'impression que mon cauchemar n'en finira donc jamais et que ma génération n'est pas quitte, encore, de l'étrange tribut qu'elle doit à la tragédie, à l'horreur. Si cette guerre éclate, quelle sera ma position ? Je n'ai rien contre les Arabes. Je ne nourris, cela va sans dire, aucune espèce d'hostilité à leur égard et les appels de muezzins à Kokand, en Asie centrale soviétique où nous nous sommes réfugiés, mes parents et moi, après notre fuite de Varsovie, me les ont rendus, infiniment et à jamais, proches. Mais je ne peux accepter l'idée de la destruction d'Israël. Je ne peux concevoir que tant d'efforts, tant d'espérances, une telle renaissance après tant d'épreuves, soient ainsi annihilés. Je n'ai pas connu la guerre d'Espagne. Je suis né trop tard pour cela. Mais si je vibre toujours aux récits que j'en lis, ce n'est pas seulement pour les montagnes arides de Ronda, et les bruns brûlés de Tolède, la Juderia à Cordoue et les poèmes d'Antonio Machado : c'est aussi — surtout — à cause de la solidarité que la République espagnole a suscitée à travers le monde. Des dizaines de milliers d'hommes et de femmes qui n'avaient jamais auparavant visité l'Espagne vinrent mourir pour elle. Quarante ans après la Shoah, la survie d'Israël ne vaut-elle pas le même élan fraternel ?

Reste, pour le moment, ma foi dans les vertus de la parole et de l'explication. Ne suffit-il pas de faire pression sur les uns et sur les autres pour qu'ils cessent de se combattre ? Pour qu'ils se reconnaissent ? Et pour que nous fassions, donc, l'économie d'une telle épreuve ? Plein de ferveur et d'impatience, je rameute des proches et des moins proches qui partagent au moins mon souci. Le soir même, nous sommes près de soixante-dix dans mon atelier. Et nous discutons à perte de vue des moyens d'expliquer l'embrasement partout annoncé. Le hasard ayant voulu que je reçoive, quelques heures plus tôt, une photocopie de la lettre de Rachel en provenance de Moscou via Buenos Aires, j'en donne la lecture à mes amis avant de les quitter. Nous avons tous la tête politique et c'est d'un débat proprement politique que nous sortons. La peur que nous ressentons n'en est pas moins celle, terriblement affective et sentimentale, de membres d'une même famille, appartenant à la même culture, tributaires de la même mémoire.

Le lendemain, je me rends près de mes parents pour recueillir leur sentiment.

— Je comprends Rachel, dit mon père après avoir lu la lettre. Si j'étais plus jeune, je m'engagerais pour Israël.

— Mais on n'a pas besoin de nous, là-bas, lui fais-je remarquer. Israël a une armée puissante et organisée. Nous ne ferions qu'y mettre la pagaille.

— Peu importe… Tu ne peux pas comprendre…

Quand, en 1939, Hugo nous a mis en garde contre le danger nazi, nous ne l'avons pas cru. Quand il nous a recommandé de partir ou de nous organiser pour le combat, nous n'avons fait ni l'un ni l'autre. Tu connais la suite...

— Mais, père, les Juifs en Israël sont organisés et les Arabes ne sont pas des nazis...

— Ils parlent comme des nazis... Tu as entendu Choukeiry et Nasser ? On n'évoque pas le feu devant un homme qui vient d'échapper à un incendie...

Mon père retire de sa poche le petit carnet de Hugo qui ne l'a pas quitté depuis six ans.

— Je commence à recomposer l'histoire.

Et puis comme je fais le geste de lui prendre le carnet des mains :

— Non, non... Tu sais bien... Ce carnet est mon affaire...

Puis :

— Je dois m'en aller... On m'attend à l'imprimerie... Mais écoute donc les nouvelles...

Il met la radio. Et, à cet instant précis, comme par un fait exprès, arrive un speaker qui, sur un ton inhabituellement grave, annonce :

— La guerre vient d'éclater entre Israël et les pays arabes.

10

LIBAN

LE CHOUF

5 juin 1967

La vieille Mercedes file le long des pistes infestées de nids-de-poules dans les montagnes violettes et tristes du Chouf. C'est un paysage violent et désolé, terriblement austère. On est le 5 juin, à l'aube. Et pour la première fois de sa longue et tumultueuse vie, Hidar se rend dans le fief des Druzes où il a rendez-vous avec l'émir Kamal Joumblatt en personne — ce patriarche mirifique qui collectionne, dit-on, les secrets et les ruses.

A une dizaine de kilomètres de Moukhtara, où habite la famille Joumblatt, il est arrêté par cinq Druzes armés jusqu'aux dents, qui exigent de voir ses papiers. Puis par d'autres. Et par d'autres encore. Au quatrième barrage, Hidar doit s'expliquer : Kamal Joumblatt l'attend, il est en train de prendre du retard. Et ce n'est qu'après de longs palabres, doublés d'une interminable inspection, qu'ils le laissent enfin passer et accéder au saint des saints.

Là, Kamal Joumblatt règne. Il trône dans son fief, au milieu des siens. Roi dont chaque sujet est la couronne, il connaît les mille dangers qui naissent de la gloire. Il sait les jalousies qui couvent quand un homme est obéi, redouté, ou même aimé. Il mesure avec gourmandise la fureur impuissante de ses ennemis. L'émir a toujours choisi le moment et le lieu pour changer d'adversaire ou d'allié. Avec son port altier, son air de grand seigneur

74

défiant les siècles et leur tumulte, dans cette vaste demeure de pierres roses qui tient du repaire et du palais, du nid d'aigle et du dédale resplendissant, il fait à Hidar la plus forte des impressions.

« Autre chose que Habbache ou Waddi Haddad », se dit-il tandis que le vieux chef, aux manières de lettré et de soldat, lui propose de l'arak (qu'il accepte) et du hasch (qu'il décline).

— Comment les choses se présentent-elles à Moscou ? interroge à brûle-pourpoint l'émir.

— Bien… Très bien même…

— Brejnev s'installe ?

— Oui, fait prudemment Hidar.

— Il a mis Gretchko à la tête de l'armée et Andropov à la tête du KGB. Ça, je comprends. En revanche, je ne comprends pas pourquoi il pousse Nasser à la guerre… J'ai rencontré l'autre jour, à Nicosie, l'ambassadeur soviétique à Tel-Aviv, Tchoubakine, qui a tenté de me persuader qu'en cas de guerre, Israël serait battu, et en vingt-quatre heures.

— Il exagère…

— Il manipule !

Kamal Joumblatt éclate de rire. Un rire sec, comme le cri d'un oiseau de proie. Puis, d'un geste de la main, il fait apporter un narguilé et l'odeur du hasch enveloppe agréablement les deux hommes. Kamal tire quelques bouffées avant de montrer la vallée, d'un geste large de la main.

— Le plus prodigieux des paysages, n'est-ce pas ? C'était l'avis de Gustave Flaubert. Vous avez lu Gustave Flaubert ? Vous savez qu'il a visité le Liban en 1850 ? Croyez-moi, il s'y connaissait en paysages.

Hidar, un peu surpris du tour que prend l'entretien, tourne la tête vers son hôte. Il rencontre un regard dur et amusé. Il juge le moment venu d'entrer dans le vif du sujet :

— Si vous receviez une invitation du Comité de Solidarité avec les Peuples d'Afrique et d'Asie, accepteriez-vous de vous rendre à Moscou ?

— On vous a chargé de m'inviter ?

— On m'a chargé de vous poser la question.

Au loin, se fait entendre l'appel de muezzin. Kamal Joumblatt, sans répondre, se lève :

— Je voudrais vous présenter quelqu'un.

En l'attendant, Hidar admire une nouvelle fois le lever du soleil derrière la chaîne de montagnes, et le jeu subtil des couleurs sur les protubérances rocheuses. Il n'entend pas Kamal Joumblatt revenir.

— Je vous présente Samirah, l'entend-il dire. C'est une jeune Palestinienne, prête à tout. Elle sera parfaite pour vos actions. Présentez-la donc à vos amis...

Hidar regarde la fille dont l'uniforme kaki laisse deviner un corps gracieux. Ses yeux noirs brillent d'une surprenante intensité.

— Elle va à Beyrouth... Pourriez-vous l'emmener ?

Et, sans attendre la réponse :

— J'ai demandé qu'on nous prépare à manger. L'air de la montagne donne faim et vous n'avez pas pris votre petit déjeuner.

Sur quoi Samirah les quitte sans avoir prononcé un seul mot.

— Drôle de fille, remarque Hidar.

— Forte fille, répond Joumblatt.

Et, faisant pivoter son fauteuil pour mieux observer Hidar :

— Et vous, ça va ?

— Oui, bien sûr. Pourquoi ?

— Vous avez retrouvé le meurtrier de votre ami tué en Israël ?

La question est si surprenante, que Hidar en perd, sur le moment, le sens de la réplique.

— Quand on ne sait pas protéger un ami, on perd de son influence ; quand on ne sait pas le venger, on perd ses amis, ajoute Joumblatt d'une voix douce. Je crains qu'il ne soit mort pour rien, votre ami...

— Ah ? fait Hidar.

Puis, jugeant que le vieil homme en prend un peu trop à son aise et qu'il ne serait pas mauvais de le déstabiliser à son tour :

— Et votre fils Walid... Comment va-t-il ?

Deux serviteurs apportent une table basse qu'ils posent entre Hidar et le vieux Joumblatt. Trois autres commencent à servir. Kamal Joumblatt déchire une pita toute chaude et en trempe un morceau dans une assiette pleine de houmous. Et c'est alors seulement que, en prenant bien son temps, il répond :

— Mon fils Walid va bien, merci. Il court les filles et il boit. Il lui manque un peu de culture. Un aigle doit pouvoir survoler la vallée.

— Ne le sait-il pas ?

— Peut-être. Mais il ne sait pas apprécier la beauté de la vallée.

Et, en se penchant légèrement vers son interlocuteur.

— On attrape les oiseaux avec les oiseaux. Il y a un homme qui connaît bien les activités de Hugo Halter. C'était en quelque sorte son Arabe de confiance... Il s'appelle Jemil el-Okby. C'est un médecin, directeur de l'hôpital de Gaza. Je parierais un narguilé en or que ce médecin-là a une idée bien précise sur la mort de votre ami juif.

Un homme armé surgit. Kamal Joumblatt demeure parfaitement placide. L'homme s'approche, baise la main du Patriarche et lui chuchote quelques mots à l'oreille. L'émir se lève alors.

— Venez écouter la radio, dit-il à Hidar, tandis qu'arrivent d'autres hommes, tous armés.

En un clin d'œil, tout ce monde se rassemble à l'intérieur de la maison, dans une grande salle, au sol dallé de marbre gris. A la radio, Oum Kalsoum psalmodie : « Égorge les Juifs ! Égorge ! » Puis, soudain, la voix de Nasser retentit : « Le monde a les yeux sur nous dans notre glorieuse guerre contre l'agression impérialiste israélienne sur le sol de notre patrie... Notre guerre sainte pour récupérer les droits de la Nation arabe... Reconquérir le pays volé de Palestine... La victoire est pour demain... »

« L'imbécile », pense Hidar.

Paris, novembre 1967

Israël, comme chacun sait, gagna la guerre en six jours et je perdis, moi, mon père juste une semaine plus tard. Trop d'émotions ? Une angoisse insoutenable venue soudain s'ajouter à toute une vie d'angoisse ? C'est probable. Toujours est-il que son cœur a lâché et qu'il n'a pas survécu bien longtemps à la grande peur du peuple juif.

Combien de fois ai-je essayé de décrire sa mort ? Combien de fois me suis-je efforcé, en songe ou en pensée, de me la remémorer et représenter ? Je n'y suis jamais parvenu. Je ne faisais, chaque fois, que décrire « la » mort, mille fois évoquée par d'autres. Je ne parvenais qu'à ajouter ma note, ma version, à ce grand roman collectif et abstrait qu'est la mort générique des humains. Alors qu'il s'agissait de ce mort-ci. Ce mort unique, bien précis. Et que ce mort c'était mon père. La mort de mon père ? Un événement très simple et très complexe, classique et pourtant indicible dont je ne saurais, à ce stade du récit, donner meilleure relation que celle du pur procès-verbal.

C'est ma mère qui m'a alerté. C'était la fin d'une de ces journées d'été parisien, si chaudes au soleil, si froides à l'ombre, dont il n'avait cessé de dire, toute la semaine, qu'elles ne lui valaient rien de bon. Le trafic, dans les rues, était plus lent que d'habitude. Les hommes moins aimables. Le bloc où nous habitions, près d'une porte de Paris, semblait plus abandonné que jamais. Et moi, quand j'ai gravi l'escalier et ouvert la porte, quand j'ai crié, comme je faisais chaque jour, ces mots allègres et alertes dont je pensais qu'ils égayaient mes parents, je ne me doutais bien entendu de rien. L'entrée à peine éclairée débouchait sur une pièce étrangement illuminée. Ma mère se tenait dans le passage, à contre-jour. Sans un mot, le visage impassible, elle m'a précédé dans la chambre à coucher. En passant, sans un mot moi non plus, et comme si je m'obstinais à ne pas vouloir comprendre, j'ai corrigé l'alignement sur le mur d'un tableau mal accroché. Mon père était là. Immobile. Allongé sur le dos. Et il n'a pas réagi à mon arrivée. « Crise cardiaque », a chuchoté un homme qui était auprès de lui et refermait une mallette lorsque je suis entré. J'ai compris que c'était le médecin. J'ai compris aussi que c'était grave. Sans un mot, non, sans même regarder son visage, j'ai réalisé que la mort était là. Moi qui la connaissais à peine je l'ai aussitôt reconnue. Elle emplissait la chambre. Elle bouleversait ses perspectives. Elle infestait et dénaturait jusqu'à l'air qu'on y respirait.

Mon père était pâle. Il fixait le plafond. Je levai les yeux moi aussi et remarquai, je ne sais pourquoi, quelques taches de rouille dues à la vapeur. « Il faudrait repeindre l'appartement », dis-je machinalement. Mon père me regarda et sourit. Ses lèvres remuèrent sans bruit. Puis deux mots en sortirent : « Et maintenant ? »

Que répondre à un père qui meurt et qui vous dit : « Et maintenant ? » Je n'ai pas voulu répondre. J'ai pensé qu'il ne *fallait* pas que je réponde. Car je savais qu'il ne mourrait pas tant qu'il n'aurait pas la réponse. Et pourtant, j'ai dit : « Tu verras, tout ira bien. » Et j'ai aussitôt regretté cette phrase inutile et banale. Hélas, c'était trop tard. La phrase était dite. Et je me sentais, pour l'avoir dite, déjà responsable de la mort de mon père.

Sur le coup rien ne s'est produit. L'homme qui devait être le médecin était planté derrière moi, à ma droite, sa mallette à la main. Je me demandais ce qu'il faisait encore là. Ma mère se tenait elle aussi près de moi, mais à ma gauche. Elle regardait. Elle souriait. Mon père nous regardait et souriait aussi. Et puis, il a levé la main. Doucement d'abord, avec difficulté. Puis d'un geste si impérieux que j'ai suivi son mouvement. Il désignait la commode, en face du lit, où était posé le carnet d'Hugo.

Je dis : « Le carnet ? » Il a hoché la tête et laissé retomber sa main. Du regard j'embrasse cette pièce qui longtemps avait été ma propre chambre. Un tableau gris que j'ai peint à notre arrivée à Paris occupait une partie du mur au-dessus de la commode. A côté du tableau il y avait ma photo. La seule photographie qui restait de moi, avant la guerre. Sur la commode même se trouvaient d'autres photos. Celle de ma mère, jeune, belle. Puis une autre : mon père, ma mère et moi, squelettique à la fin de la guerre. Mais à côté des photos il y avait donc le carnet — que je pris et lui apportai.

Du regard, il me remercia. Puis posant ses doigts pâles sur l'objet comme s'il voulait le protéger ou le sanctifier, il commença :

— Continue, mon fils. Oui, continue. Nous les Halter avons toujours été les gardiens des registres...

Comme je le comprenais à peine, je dus me pencher pour l'entendre continuer :

— Nous sommes si peu nombreux, n'est-ce pas... Il ne faut jamais abandonner un Juif... Même mort...

Puis, plus bas encore, et reprenant son souffle à grand-peine :

— Six ans ont passé depuis la mort de Hugo. Dans la vie, six ans c'est beaucoup. Pour la mémoire ce n'est même pas une seconde...

Brusquement son débit devint normal. Sa voix cessa de trembler. Je crus même déceler quelques couleurs sur ses joues creuses :

— Continue à chercher, mon fils. Et quand tu auras trouvé, fais-en un livre. Souviens-toi : l'Histoire est écrite pour raconter, pas pour prouver.

Du coup, le voyant mieux, j'eus envie d'en savoir plus. Je le questionnai sur son refus de collaborer avec

Benjamin Ben Eliezer. Sur sa volonté de garder ce carnet pour lui seul.

— Ton secret est ton esclave, me répondit-il. Mais si tu le laisses échapper il deviendra ton maître.

— Ton maître ? dis-je, interloqué.

Mais, étrangement, il en resta là. Sa voix mourut dans sa gorge. Son regard se figea. Sa main, dans la mienne, devint lourde. Je la posai doucement sur le bras. Et observai à nouveau, longuement, la chambre morte autour de moi.

Nous passâmes la nuit, ma mère et moi, à veiller le corps. Au petit matin elle s'assoupit. Et moi, à ce moment-là, je ressortis le petit carnet que j'avais, sans trop y songer, mis dans ma poche. Je venais de comprendre que, entre cette guerre des Six Jours et cette agonie si brève, j'avais, moi, perdu mon adolescence.

Si je devais généraliser, je dirais que ces jours qui précédèrent et suivirent les six jours de la guerre marquèrent comme jamais l'histoire moderne du peuple juif.

La peur que les Juifs ont alors ressentie était la première grande peur depuis la Shoa. Ainsi donc, malgré les camps de la mort, malgré leur défaite et malgré leur souvenir, on pouvait, encore et toujours, nous menacer d'extermination : la génération d'après-guerre, qui avait cru à la normalité, venait brutalement, et sans aucun préparatif, de découvrir dans le fracas des armes et l'enchevêtrement des images télévisées, son insoutenable précarité. La nouvelle conscience juive sera marquée par cette découverte-là.

Pour nous, les Halter, cette prise de conscience, ce sentiment de fragilité de l'homme juif dans le monde contemporain dataient de l'assassinat de Hugo. Mais, du coup, l'expérience familiale devenait comme le signe, le pressentiment d'une expérience plus globale. La mort de Hugo et la guerre des Six Jours se confondaient. La quête de la paix à laquelle je consacrais de plus en plus de mon temps se mêlait à mon enquête sur les causes, les mystères, les circonstances de la mort d'un cousin. Tout cela se croisait, se brouillait, se répondait, sans que je susse, parfois, sur quelle piste j'errais, dans le cadre de quelle recherche. Six ans après sa mort je me retrouvais en tout cas, et à nouveau, sur ses traces. Mais muni, cette fois, d'un carnet, d'un testament paternel, d'une farouche volonté d'aboutir — ainsi que des leçons d'une guerre dont je ne parvenais pas à croire, je le répète, qu'elles fussent contingentes et gratuites.

11

NEW YORK

UNE AVENTURE DE SIDNEY

20 juillet 1969

Les rapports de Marjory et Sidney sont au beau fixe.
S'il a pu arriver à la jeune femme de marquer quelque
réserve à l'endroit du judaïsme de son mari c'est
maintenant bien fini. Elle connaît les fêtes juives, leur
signification, leurs rites. Elle est de ces femmes qui, par
amour, se sont pliées corps et âme à ce qu'elles
supposent des secrets désirs de leur époux. Au point que
c'est à présent sa famille à elle — son père James, son
frère George, ses oncles, ses tantes — qui s'inquiète et
lui reproche son « enjuivement ».

— Jésus n'était-il pas juif ? s'obstine-t-elle à leur
opposer ? Et les apôtres ?

Mais rien n'y fait. Chacune de leurs rencontres tourne
au débat passionné. D'un côté, on évoque l'abandon de
Jésus par les Juifs ; de l'autre, l'attitude de Ponce Pilate ;
là, on fait flèche de tout bois, et notamment des
territoires occupés ; ici, avec un mélange de candeur et
de rouerie militante, on objecte : « Occupés...
occupés... occupés par qui, au juste » ? Et Sidney voit,
non sans inquiétude, sa jeune femme, et donc ses
enfants (Richard, mais aussi la petite Marilyn) s'éloigner petit à petit de l'une des sources de leur vie. Ne
sait-il pas gré à Marjory de cet hommage qu'elle lui
rend ? Oui et non. Il se surprend parfois à songer qu'elle
aliène peut-être aussi une part de son mystère et de sa

séduction. Pis, il se demande si ce n'est pas cette étrangeté, cette obscure rébellion de l'être qui le séduisaient le plus en elle. Mais enfin, tout cela reste implicite, tout juste avoué et formulé. Et Sidney demeure un époux exemplaire, attaché à son foyer qui, s'il rit parfois de bon cœur aux blagues de carabins de ses collègues, a toujours refusé d'imiter leurs aventures extra-conjugales. « Seuls les morts n'ont pas d'aventures », dit toujours son frère Larry. « OK, lui répond-il... Mais il faut croire, alors, que je suis mort d'amour. »

Arrive l'été 1969. Marjory séjourne avec les enfants dans le Vermont, chez ses parents. Sidney est resté à New York. Il mène une vie de célibataire paisible. Et le voici qui, un soir de juillet, aux alentours de cinq heures, quitte l'hôpital. Il fait beau. Il descend Madison à sa gauche jusqu'à la 59ᵉ Rue, oblique à droite devant l'hôtel Plaza et, porté par la foule, dévale allégrement la Cinquième Avenue. A la hauteur de la 53ᵉ Rue, l'immense oriflamme du musée d'Art moderne lui fait soudain regretter de n'y avoir pas mis les pieds depuis, au moins, deux ans ; et, sans trop savoir comment, mené par la délicieuse insouciance que dégage ce début d'été, il se retrouve dans le hall du musée, prend un billet et se laisse conduire par le flux des visiteurs jusqu'à ce monde de couleurs et de lignes qui le rend toujours si heureux. Un tableau. Un autre. Un autre encore. Toute une ronde de formes qu'il aime bien voir « en bloc », sans trop les distinguer — comme un gigantesque bain de beauté aux unités indistinctes et rêveuses. Et ce jusqu'au moment où, parvenu sans y prendre garde dans les salles du troisième étage, il entend une voix près de lui qui murmure :

— Guernica... Vous ne reconnaissez pas Guernica ?

Non, bien sûr, il ne « voyait » pas Guernica. Mais, à sa place, des visages difformes... Le cheval... La lampe... Et puis, comme dans les récits de Hugo, le bombardement de Varsovie, les cris des Juifs fuyant les synagogues en flammes, les pleurs des mères cherchant dans le néant, à la lueur des lampes à pétrole, les corps de leurs enfants ensevelis... Et encore ce cheval, tué au coin d'une rue par l'éclat d'une bombe et dépecé par une foule affamée...

— C'est fort comme la mort, continue la voix, avec un léger accent oriental qu'il n'avait pas tout de suite remarqué...

— Comme la mort, oui, sans doute... Encore que, de cette mort-là...

Quand il se retourne, il voit une silhouette élancée, serrée dans un tailleur gris clair, puis un regard, un sourire, un regard souriant...

— Touriste? demande-t-il, parce qu'il faut bien demander quelque chose...

— Pas tout à fait... J'ai grandi à Detroit, mais je vis depuis des années à Beyrouth.

— Ah?... fait-il, un peu surpris d'un ton aussi direct.

— Et vous, continue-t-elle... La peinture? Vous aimez la peinture?

— Oui, je crois...

— Moi, je suis passionnée d'art. Quand je viens à New York, je ne rate pas une exposition. Mon mari a une collection d'icônes anciennes... Mais aussi des Klee... Des Kandinsky... Vous connaissez?

— Oui, fait-il de la tête.

— Vous aimez?

— Oui... Bien sûr. Mais je préfère Rothko, Sol Lewitt...

— Vous collectionnez?

— Un peu... Il faut beaucoup de moyens...

Regard amusé de la femme qui se lance dans un discours sur l'art, l'argent, les collections. Mais Sidney ne l'entend plus. Il regarde, fasciné, ces lèvres charnues, parfaitement dessinées, qui s'entrouvrent régulièrement pour laisser échapper une voix dont la seule sonorité l'exalte. La femme, tout à coup, s'arrête — comme si elle était contrariée :

— Mais je vous importune, dit-elle... Veuillez m'en excuser... J'aime tant parler de ces choses...

Sortant de son rêve, Sidney dit alors :

— Mais pas du tout... Vous ne m'importunez pas...

Je réfléchissais... Je suis réellement content de bavarder avec vous...

Et, preuve de son intérêt :

— Où habitez-vous, à New York ?

— Au Westbury, entre Madison et la 69e...

— Ce n'est pas loin de chez moi, remarque-t-il, à nouveau rêveur. Vous aimez marcher ?

— Beaucoup.

Elle a dit « beaucoup » avec un petit rire de gorge ouvertement séducteur et coquin qui lui a fait regretter, sur l'instant, son audace. Avisant, sur Madison, à la hauteur de la 62e Rue, quelques tables d'un café posées sur le trottoir, il songe que c'est la providence qui les a disposées là et propose d'y faire une petite halte.

— Comment vous appelez-vous ? demande-t-il, à peine installé.

— Leïla. Leïla Chehab.

— Vous êtes arabe ?

— Oui. Libanaise. Chrétienne. Mon grand-père est né à Haïfa. Vous savez, en Palestine ? Il a connu ma grand-mère à Beyrouth. En 1947, mes parents ont émigré aux Etats-Unis. J'avais sept ans. Ils se sont installés à Detroit. Mon père travaillait chez Ford...

La présentation de Leïla surprend Sidney. Cette phrase, peut-être innocente : « Il est né à Haïfa, vous savez, en Palestine ? » sonne comme une déclaration de guerre.

— Moi, je suis juif, enchaîne-t-il, d'un ton de défi. Mes grands-parents ont fui les persécutions en Pologne, en 1832. Ils se sont installés à Winnipeg, au Canada. Leurs cousins ont, à la même époque, émigré en Palestine. Leurs enfants ont créé un kibboutz — Dafné — en Galilée...

Leïla sourit, comme si elle voulait lui signifier qu'elle le comprend :

— Mon grand-père racontait qu'à Staton Street, où il habitait — tout près de Hadar, les Champs-Élysées de Haïfa — il y avait beaucoup de Juifs et qu'il entretenait avec eux des relations cordiales. Je connaissais moi-même des enfants juifs à Beyrouth. Tamara, l'une de mes meilleures amies, était juive. Mais en 1947, la Palestine a cessé d'être une terre arabe... Tamara a gagné une patrie, moi, j'ai perdu la mienne.

Leïla parle doucement, sans passion. Plus trace de la moindre coquetterie, de la moindre rêverie féminine. Sidney s'exclame :

— Mais que dites-vous là ? Votre amie Tamara était libanaise, comme vous. En 1947, il y a eu un partage de la Palestine. Un partage juste, entre deux États : juif et arabe. Les Juifs ont accepté le leur, les Arabes non. Avec l'espoir de chasser les Juifs et de récupérer tout le territoire...

Cette fois, les yeux de Leïla lancent des flammes :

— Vous oubliez Deïr Yassin ! Le massacre de tout un village arabe par les sionistes ! Deux cent cinquante-quatre personnes, femmes et enfants compris ! Les Arabes de Haïfa ont eu peur et ont quitté la ville...

— Votre famille avait quitté Haïfa avant 1947.

— C'est vrai. N'empêche que je me sens proche de cette terre, la terre de mes ancêtres.

Et, rapprochant son visage de celui de cet inconnu, si aimable tout à l'heure, et qu'un mur d'incompréhension semble maintenant séparer du sien :

— J'ai maintenant vingt-neuf ans et depuis 1947, l'année d'affliction nationale pour la Palestine, je n'ai célébré aucun de mes anniversaires.

— Mais vous êtes dangereuse ! Vous êtes une vraie fanatique !

Leurs visages se touchent presque, à présent. Elle esquisse le geste de le gifler. Il lui saisit la main. Ils restent ainsi un court instant, sous le regard amusé des passants. Et, brusquement, sans que ni l'un ni l'autre ne sachent vraiment pourquoi, leurs lèvres se touchent. Sidney sent une morsure et un goût de sang dans la bouche :

— Vous êtes folle !

— Pardon, fait Leïla, en dégageant la main. Il ne fallait pas me provoquer. La Palestine est un sujet sacré pour moi.

Sidney paye les consommations en silence, tout en se

tamponnant les lèvres avec une petite serviette en papier…

— Vous êtes vraiment folle, peste-t-il.

Leïla ne dit rien. Elle ramasse son sac et, d'un geste rapide, remet ses cheveux en place. Que va faire Sidney ? Que *doit*-il faire ? Leïla, debout, décide pour lui :

— Vous voulez toujours m'accompagner ?

Ils parcourent, toujours silencieux, les quelques blocs qui les séparent du Westbury. Quand ils atteignent enfin la 69ᵉ Rue, le jour est tout à fait tombé. Il fait presque frais tout à coup.

Devant l'hôtel, ils s'arrêtent. Sidney consulte sa montre :

— Shit ! s'exclame-t-il. Et devant le regard interrogateur de Leïla : J'ai complètement oublié : la télévision retransmet aujourd'hui, en direct, l'arrivée des premiers hommes sur la lune…

— Eh bien, c'est parfait ; pourquoi ne viendrez-vous pas la regarder dans ma chambre ?

La chambre du Westbury. Ses laques jaunes et brunes. Sa moquette épaisse. Sa salle de bains de marbre gris tout imprégnée du parfum de la jeune femme. Son grand lit où, un peu emprunté, Sidney est venu s'asseoir.

« Comme dans un film », se dit-il, tandis que le sol lunaire et ses cratères apparaissent sur l'écran et que la main blanche de Leïla se pose sur sa poitrine, ses lèvres sur ses lèvres puis son ventre contre son ventre. Deux minutes plus tard, le module se pose, dans un halo de poussière grise. Et Sidney, fasciné, découvre les seins, le ventre, les cuisses fuselées de la jeune femme qui s'offre à lui. Est-ce cette émotion-ci ? celle-là ? Le premier homme à poser le pied sur la Lune ? La première femme à poser le sien dans le fragile équilibre qu'était sa vie ? Il ne peut s'empêcher de pousser un cri d'émotion :

— Ouaouh !

Leïla éclate d'un rire léger, perlé, tendre. Lui, sans quitter l'écran des yeux, murmure quelques mots dont il pensait avoir désappris le sens. Là-bas, sur la Lune commence un fantastique ballet. Un homme flotte autour d'un module blanc. Un autre le rejoint. On entend leurs voix. On touche presque leurs visages. Neil A. Armstrong et le colonel Aldrin échangent des propos sans importance avec la base de Houston. Quelle aventure ! Enfin, les deux hommes en scaphandre plantent sur le sol lunaire la bannière étoilée. Et pendant ce temps, oui, un autre homme ici-bas, sur la modeste planète terre, part à la conquête d'un autre monde inconnu.

Le reste de la nuit, ils parlent encore d'Israël et de la Palestine. Toujours pas d'accord, non. Mais à mesure que s'aggrave leur désaccord, grandit aussi leur désir.

— Je quitte New York dans quelques heures, dira Leïla doucement quand les premières lueurs du jour se refléteront dans les vitres. Pourquoi ne viendriez-vous pas, un jour, à Beyrouth ? C'est une ville si charmeuse... Et moi... Moi, je serais heureuse de vous revoir.

Sidney opine, bien sûr. Il viendra, oui, il viendra à Beyrouth. Sans savoir qu'il vient peut-être de sceller son destin.

Sdé Boker, août 1969

— Vous voulez que je vous parle de votre cousin Hugo, me demande Ben Gourion. Je ne le connaissais pas très bien, vous savez... Il est venu me voir à plusieurs reprises... Chaque fois, pour me proposer des rencontres avec des Arabes. Il en connaissait quelques-uns... Des leaders... Je crois bien que je ne l'ai pas vu depuis 1959... Il m'avait été présenté par mon conseiller Israël Beer.

La scène se passe donc en août 1969, deux ans après la guerre des Six Jours. Je suis allé voir le vieux chef dans son kibboutz de Sdé Boker, au cœur du désert du Néguev, sur la route de Beersheva-Eilat. Il est installé là depuis sa retraite politique, et habite une simple baraque de bois, gardée par une sentinelle.

Il a un visage large et jovial, auréolé de touffes de cheveux blancs. Il est vêtu d'un pantalon et d'un blazer kaki qui semblent dater de l'époque de la Hagana. Il évoque des souvenirs lointains. Des visages d'autrefois. Parfois, il me donne le sentiment d'avoir oublié ma présence. Parfois, au contraire, il revient vers moi et, à propos de telle ou telle question d'actualité, réagit avec une intelligence, une ouverture d'esprit peu communes.

— Vous voulez que je vous parle de votre cousin Hugo, reprend-il... Hugo, oui... Hugo... Je le vois encore, le corps sec et les yeux brillants. Il me rappelait

90

les jeunes idéalistes des années 30... Vous savez, les membres de Brit-Shalom, l'Alliance pour la Paix... Judah Magnes... Martin Buber... Eux aussi croyaient à la vertu de la parole... Ils espéraient pouvoir créer un État en dialoguant avec les Arabes... Je le pensais aussi... Mais moi, je n'ai pas attendu ce dialogue pour couler les fondations du pays...

» C'est grâce à eux, vous savez, que j'ai pu rencontrer le grand leader palestinien Moussa Alami... C'était... C'était... C'était, il me semble, en août 1934. Et j'ai aussi parlé avec Georges Antonius, en avril 1936... A l'époque, Antonius était le théoricien le plus connu du nationalisme arabe... Nous nous sommes rencontrés... Nous nous sommes parlé... Et cela n'a rien donné... Votre Hugo, lui, avait des projets précis...

— Des projets ?

— Des projets ? répète Ben Gourion en me fixant bizarrement. De quoi parlions-nous donc ?

— Des projets de Hugo.

— Nous parlions polonais ?

Ben Gourion, né en Pologne quatre-vingts ans plus tôt, est, à l'évidence, déjà ailleurs. Le garde me fait des grands signes et s'approche doucement de nous. Il m'explique qu'il est tard et que le médecin interdit au vieil homme de veiller aussi longtemps.

Quand je me lève pour partir, Ben Gourion ne bouge pas de sa chaise. Il dort, le visage figé dans un relief aussi antique que celui de cette vallée qui borde le kibboutz et où, loin des immeubles résidentiels, il a choisi de vivre le reste de ses rêves.

12

BUENOS AIRES

UN AMOUR PRÉCOCE

Septembre 1969

Mordekhaï arrive à Buenos Aires au printemps 1969. En Israël c'est déjà l'automne. Seul, Arié, son fils, l'accompagne. Sarah, sa femme, un peu souffrante, est restée au kibboutz, en compagnie de Dina, leur fille, âgée de sept ans. La direction de l'école Sholem Aleïkhem a mis à sa disposition un petit appartement, propre mais humide, rue Montevideo, au coin de la rue Cangallo. A Buenos Aires, l'humidité est partout ; on enferme le sucre dans des boîtes métalliques pour éviter qu'il ne se transforme en sirop.

Comme tous les visiteurs, Mordekhaï est d'abord surpris par les dimensions de la ville. Puis par celles, d'un autre ordre, mais tout aussi impressionnantes, de la communauté juive. Il la trouve plus proche, par la langue et les mœurs, des communautés disparues de Pologne et de Russie que de l'*american way of life*. Mais c'est surtout son importance, sa vitalité qui le frappent.

Arié, de son côté, se sent à la fois exalté et perdu... Tandis que son père prend ses classes en main, il se promène jusqu'à la fatigue. De préférence d'un pas pressé afin qu'on ne le prenne pas pour un étranger. Il parcourt ainsi le quai du Rio de la Plata, la fameuse avenue Corrientes, l'avenue du 9 de Julio et la place de la Republica où, comme sur la place de la Concorde à Paris, se dresse un obélisque. Le jeune garçon observe, admire, écoute. S'il ne se sentait pas si seul, s'il parlait quelques mots d'espagnol, il serait parfaitement heureux.

Dès le lendemain de leur arrivée, Dona Regina organise un dîner en leur honneur. Toute la famille est là. Plus quelques amis bien choisis. « Des sionistes, dit-elle à son mari, d'un air mi-entendu, mi-méprisant... Pour faire plaisir aux cousins venus d'Israël. »

Arié, qui ne comprend pas un mot de yiddish, s'ennuie ferme. Il rêve. Observe les uns et les autres. S'enivre doucement de cette langue inconnue et qui, à la lettre, ne lui dit rien. Et ce, jusqu'à l'arrivée d'Anna-Maria. Ce sont d'abord ses yeux qu'il remarque. Des yeux noirs, brillants, ironiques. Très grands. Puis un corsage blanc légèrement entrouvert. Puis le dessin d'une épaule, la naissance du cou, une pointe d'arrogance dans la cambrure du dos.

— Je te présente ma petite-fille, Anna-Maria, lui dit Dona Regina. N'est-ce pas qu'elle est belle ?

— Comme si c'était ça, l'important ! s'exclame l'intéressée, agacée.

Arié rougit. Anna-Maria s'en aperçoit et lui lance, en souriant :

— Tu parles espagnol ?

Comme il fait non de la tête, c'est en anglais qu'elle engage la conversation.

— Je suis Anna-Maria... C'est toi, le fils de Mordekhaï, le kibboutznik ? Je ne te voyais pas comme ça...

— Comment « comme ça » ?

— Je t'imaginais plus paysan.

Arié éclate de rire, pense, ainsi, reprendre l'avantage ; mais rougit à nouveau quand la jeune femme poursuit :

— Tu n'es pas mal quand même, tu sais.

Et s'asseyant à côté de lui :

— Tu aimes le tango ?

— Depuis que je suis à Buenos Aires, je n'entends que ça...

— Mais encore ?

— Je crois que je l'aime...

— Tu veux voir une boîte à tango ?

— Mais...

— Tu as peut-être peur de rater cette délicieuse carpe farcie... Grand-mère dit que c'est la carpe « comme-seuls-les-Halter-de-Varsovie-savent-la-faire »...

Arié, piqué, se lève. Debout, il domine Anna-Maria d'une tête. Il n'a que seize ans et elle en a dix-sept, mais il paraît soudain plus adulte, plus mûr.

— Je vais faire visiter Buenos Aires *by night* à notre petit cousin, annonce la jeune fille.

Dona Regina proteste :

— Comment ! Partir sans manger ? Traîner dans les rues à cette heure-ci ?

Et, grondeuse :

— Laisse donc ce gamin tranquille...

— Que dit ma tante ? demande le « gamin ».

Anna-Maria traduit. Arié marque le coup : il déteste qu'on le traite en enfant et particulièrement devant une jeune fille. Aussi bombe-t-il le torse et rejette-t-il sa mèche en arrière de l'air le plus crâne qu'il peut.

— Allez, petite, *vamos,* dit-il à Anna-Maria, sous l'œil sidéré de Mordekhaï.

Une demi-heure plus tard les deux jeunes gens entrent dans une immense salle enfumée, bourrée de monde, dont Anna-Maria a dit : « C'est l'endroit le plus sympa de la ville. » Au plafond, les pales d'un ventilateur géant bercent des guirlandes de papier crépon rouge et rose. Au mur, un paysage naïf au pastel adoucit la lumière crue des projecteurs. Sur une colonne, au milieu de la salle, Carlos Gardel, roi du tango, sourit au-dessus d'un nœud papillon à pois blancs. Et derrière le bar, une affiche représentant une chanteuse penchée sur un micro indique *Gran concurso de tango.*

Anna-Maria trouve une place. Ils s'assoient. Sur l'estrade, dans un halo orange, une chanteuse, trop vieille et un peu grasse, interprète *Adios Muchachos* tandis que son accompagnateur disparaît derrière un immense piano ; on ne voit que ses pieds qui rebondissent, en mesure, sur les pédales.

— Ça te plaît ? demande Anna-Maria.

Abasourdi par le bruit, la fumée, Arié ne répond pas.

— Tu aimes ? redemande Anna-Maria, en se penchant légèrement vers lui.

— Oui, dit-il.

Et sur sa lancée :

— Tu me plais.

Anna-Maria le toise, comme s'il avait dit quelque chose de parfaitement inconvenant :

— Tu vas un peu vite, tu ne trouves pas ? N'oublie pas que nous sommes cousins.

— Très lointains...

— C'est comme ça qu'on fait au kibboutz ?

— Tu as une drôle d'idée du kibboutz...

— Ch..., taisez-vous, fait un *criollo,* assis à une table voisine.

— Il a raison, renchérit un homme à lunettes. Écoutez ou sortez.

Une voix chante :

« Je soupire pour toi, Buenos Aires
  Sous le soleil d'autres cieux... »

— Sortons, dit Arié.

Dehors, les enseignes lumineuses des *Ciné Novedades, Ciné Continuado, Pizzerias* et autres, se reflètent sur l'asphalte mouillé.

— Tu t'intéresses à la politique ? demande Anna-Maria, à brûle-pourpoint.

— A la politique ? Chez nous, tout le monde s'intéresse à la politique... Notre vie en dépend.

— En Israël, OK. Mais ailleurs ? Est-ce que tu sais, par exemple, qui est le président de l'Argentine ?

— Non.

— Un général. Il s'appelle Ongania. Tu vois que tu ne t'intéresses pas à la politique !

— Et toi, tu sais qui est le Premier ministre d'Israël ?

— Non.

— Une femme. Golda Meïr. Tu vois que toi non plus, tu ne...

Anna-Maria ne le laisse pas finir. Elle part d'un grand rire complice en lui donnant un coup de coude dans les côtes. Et, de nouveau, sans transition, demande :

— As-tu connu notre cousin Hugo ?

— Non, mais j'en ai entendu parler. Il a fait la guerre en Europe contre les nazis... Il s'est battu, lui... pas comme les autres Juifs de Pologne et d'ailleurs...

— Mais la révolte du ghetto de Varsovie... Le grand-père Abraham...

— Une minorité.

La voix d'Arié se fait passionnée :

— Les Juifs doivent apprendre à se battre, comme tout le monde, pour leur pays, leur dignité... Maintenant qu'Israël existe, les Juifs n'iront plus comme des moutons à l'abattoir...

Anna-Maria s'est arrêtée — sans explication, d'un seul coup, comme quelqu'un que vient de frapper une évidence longtemps inaperçue. Dans la faible lumière d'un réverbère, Arié remarque son visage fermé :

— Tu ne parles que des Juifs, dit-elle, les Juifs et encore les Juifs... Et les autres ? Ici, en Argentine, des millions d'hommes vivent dans des *villas miserias*... Des milliers d'autres sont emprisonnés pour délit d'opinion... Tu penses quelquefois à eux ? Et à ceux qui meurent de faim dans d'autres pays d'Amérique latine ?

— Et toi, tu es vraiment sûre d'y penser plus que moi ?

— Bien entendu. Non seulement je pense à eux, mais je vais me *battre* pour eux.

— Pourquoi ?

— Parce que... parce que je suis un être humain. Peut-être aussi parce que je suis juive...

— Si tu veux te battre, viens en Israël. Des filles comme toi, on en a besoin.

— Et qui se battra ici ?

— Les Argentins.

— Mais moi, je suis argentine !

— Et qui se battra pour Israël ?

Arié est partagé entre la colère et l'admiration. Il trouve Anna-Maria bornée mais très belle. Beaucoup plus belle que toutes les filles du kibboutz Dafné et même de Hagecharim. Il s'approche. La regarde. Croit, dans son regard, deviner un consentement. S'approche encore. L'embrasse. Et arrive ce qui devait arriver : une belle, une grande, une gigantesque gifle qui interrompt net son élan. Humilié comme jamais, le jeune homme reste une seconde immobile les bras ballants — puis tourne les talons et s'enfuit en courant.

Arrivé sur le quai du Rio de la Plata, il s'arrête, un peu essoufflé et s'assied sur un banc. Il suit un moment les bruits de la circulation, les chuintements des pneus, les klaxons, le lointain appel des bateaux et il se dit qu'il n'aime pas Buenos Aires. Non, il n'aime décidément pas cette ville qui ne dort jamais. Et il meurt d'envie, tout à coup, de retourner en Galilée dans son kibboutz chéri. Il remarque un gros cafard et le suit du regard jusqu'à la balustrade du pont.

— Alors, kibboutznik, fâché ?

C'est Anna-Maria. Comment l'a-t-elle trouvé ?

— Je t'ai suivi, tout simplement. Tu permets ?

Elle s'assied à côté de lui ; et aussitôt, comme si elle reprenait le fil d'une conversation banalement interrompue :

— Mes amis me poussent à entrer dans la clandestinité. Qu'en penses-tu ?

A quoi joue-t-elle ? Veut-elle, par cette confidence, effacer l'incident ? lui manifester sa confiance ? l'impressionner ? Arié, en tout cas, tombe dans le panneau et, oubliant, comme par enchantement, chagrin, humiliation, nostalgie, répète :

— Clandestinité ? Comment ça : clandestinité ? Tu veux devenir terroriste ?

Anna-Maria sent à nouveau tout l'ascendant qu'elle exerce sur cet adolescent charmant mais mal dégrossi, dont l'horizon n'a jamais dépassé les frontières du kibboutz Dafné :

— Non, combattante !

Et, grande dame à la limite de la morgue :

— Je ne sais pas pourquoi je te raconte ça : tu ne t'intéresses pas à la justice dans le monde, ni à la guerre du Vietnam, tu ne sais rien de l'Amérique latine, tu ne connais pas le Che ni la répression militaire, tu... Pour toi, il n'y a au monde qu'Israël !

— Ce n'est pas vrai, proteste Arié qui, sous le choc, retrouve un peu de son assurance. Je m'intéresse à la justice dans le monde et Israël en fait partie. Mais tuer comme on a tué notre cousin Hugo ou d'innocents passagers d'un Boeing israélien à l'aéroport de Zurich, ce n'est pas le meilleur moyen de faire avancer la justice.

Anna-Maria sursaute : trois cafards escaladent paisiblement, à la queue leu leu, le pied du banc. Arié les chasse d'un revers de la main. Anna-Maria se lève. Lui se lève à son tour. Et d'un geste naturel, ayant perdu toute réserve mais aussi toute gaucherie, il la serre dans ses bras et l'embrasse longuement.

Paris, septembre 1969

— Hugo, je ne le connaissais pas très bien. Je connaissais surtout la famille de sa femme et, en particulier, son frère, un certain Hans Furchmuller. Nous avons fait nos études ensemble. Il est médecin et dirige actuellement un hôpital à Berlin-Est. C'est lui qui, à l'époque, a donné mon nom et mon numéro de téléphone à Hugo.

La femme qui me parle ainsi est âgée d'une soixantaine d'années et en la regardant, je pense avec un rien de nostalgie combien elle a dû être belle. Elle s'appelle Ursula von Thadden et elle couvre pour le quotidien munichois *Suddeutsche Zeitung* un colloque international sur les droits de l'homme en URSS, qui se tient à Paris et auquel je participe. C'est en entendant son nom que je me suis souvenu de l'avoir lu dans le carnet d'adresses d'Hugo.

— Il est venu en Allemagne à plusieurs reprises, avec sa femme, poursuit Ursula von Thadden. Je travaillais à l'époque à Bonn. C'était au printemps 1960. Hugo voulait rencontrer le chancelier Adenauer. Il disait que l'Allemagne était responsable de la vie et de la sécurité des enfants dont elle avait massacré les parents. Il pensait que Konrad Adenauer, qui avait d'excellentes relations aussi bien avec Israël qu'avec les pays arabes, pouvait aider à l'instauration de la paix au Proche-

Orient. En promettant de financer un projet de développement régional, une sorte de Plan Marshall nouvelle manière. Hugo était un homme passionné et tenace. Les obstacles ne lui faisaient pas peur. Les contradicteurs l'irritaient, mais il était trop sociable pour le manifester. Je crois qu'il a rencontré le chancelier, mais ayant été obligée de retourner à Munich, je n'ai pas suivi ses démarches jusqu'à la fin.

A quoi ressemblait-il, je demande. S'il avait l'air inquiet ? Traqué ? S'il donnait le sentiment d'être en danger, de se savoir entouré d'ennemis ? Ça, mon interlocutrice n'en sait rien. Elle a beau chercher, elle ne sait pas. Tout ce qu'elle peut me dire c'est qu'il était, à l'époque, follement séduisant.

— Oh ! n'allez rien supposer, s'excuse-t-elle... J'étais liée à sa femme, vous dis-je... Et puis ces petits jeux n'étaient déjà plus de mon âge... Mais il est vrai qu'on ne pouvait pas le voir sans être impressionné par le magnétisme qu'il dégageait. Un regard pénétrant, insistant... Une bouche légèrement ironique, presque amère, à la façon de ces hommes qui ont tout vu, tout connu, mais qui n'en gardent pas moins comme une nostalgie d'idéal... La chevelure abondante, peu coiffée... Les gestes précis... Des mains que remarquaient toujours les femmes... Et puis cet air d'éternel voyageur qu'on avait peine à imaginer installé, enraciné, marié même...

Ursula von Thadden s'arrête, consciente d'en dire peut-être un peu trop — et de trop montrer, surtout, l'effet que, presque dix ans plus tard, continue de lui faire cette évocation. Elle pouffe. Bredouille quelques propos légers. Et, prétextant le colloque qui reprend, me plante là — sans m'avoir, il faut bien le dire, appris grand-chose que je ne connusse.

13

MOSCOU

HIDAR ET OLGA

Septembre 1969

— Mais vous êtes complètement fou ! Nous sommes sur un projet audacieux qui, s'il réussit, changera la face du Proche-Orient et vous prenez le risque de gâcher tout cela pour un voyage d'agrément ?

L'homme qui parle ainsi à Hidar Assadi s'appelle Victor Tchebrikov. C'est l'un des dirigeants du Comité de Solidarité avec les Peuples d'Asie et d'Afrique. Et son pouvoir lui vient surtout de l'amitié qui le lie au chef du KGB, Youri Andropov.

Le bureau où se trouvent les deux hommes, au troisième étage d'un immeuble moderne de la rue Kropotkine, est une pièce vaste et sombre. La grande baie, qui perce tout un pan de mur, est cachée par une tenture opaque, décorée de fleurs ocre. Un rayon de soleil tardif s'infiltre entre deux rideaux et joue sur le cadre en verre du portrait de Lénine.

Hidar déplace légèrement sa chaise et répond avec le sourire :

— Il ne s'agit pas d'un voyage d'agrément, Victor Alexandrovitch, mais de travail. J'ai été chargé d'une mission et je l'accomplis, me semble-t-il, à la grande satisfaction de nos supérieurs. La venue d'Olga Lerner à Beyrouth ne pourra que troubler nos adversaires. Vous savez très bien que depuis un an, les services américains et israéliens ne me quittent plus d'une semelle. Si nous

101

voulons réussir notre opération en Jordanie, il faut que je retourne au Proche-Orient. Et venir avec une femme...

— Une juive... corrige Victor Tchebrikov.

— Précisément !

— Comment cela : précisément ?

— Les services israéliens réagiront exactement comme vous et le doute s'installera dans leur esprit. Ils me soupçonnent, je le sais. Mais ils n'ont aucune certitude et, a fortiori, aucune preuve. Je reconnais que je tiens à la personne d'Olga Lerner, mais si je vous demande aujourd'hui de lui obtenir un visa de sortie, c'est que j'ai impérativement besoin d'elle...

Un homme comme Victor Tchebrikov n'est pas de ceux que l'on convainc. Tout au plus transmettra-t-il. Et, de fait, le voici qui prend une feuille de papier, une plume et entreprend de résumer par écrit les arguments d'Hidar. Quand il a terminé, il lève la tête vers son visiteur :

— Quant à votre rapport sur « le terrorisme médiatique », il a été jugé fort intéressant en haut lieu. Sacha Aronovitch vous en a-t-il parlé ? Vous passez tout votre temps chez ses parents, rue Kazakov...

— Vous êtes bien informé.

— J'espère que ce n'est pas un secret.

— Non, bien sûr, mais Sacha Lerner et moi...

— Vous n'êtes pas en bons termes...

Victor Tchebrikov sourit, satisfait :

— Vous n'avez pas tort. Sacha Aronovitch était le seul à s'opposer à votre projet. Il ne croit pas les Arabes capables de le réaliser.

Et, tendant la main à Hidar :

— J'espère pour vous qu'il se trompe. Car vos amis, à Beyrouth, sont déjà au courant. A votre prochaine rencontre, ils vous présenteront le projet comme s'il était le leur... C'est ce que vous vouliez, n'est-ce pas ?

En retrouvant la rue, Hidar Assadi est plutôt content de lui. Son rapport a été apprécié. Son idée approuvée. Et la promesse faite à Olga va pouvoir enfin se réaliser : ils iront ensemble au Liban. Hidar n'ignore pas les risques d'un tel voyage. Il sait surtout que, à la frontière d'Israël, Olga peut avoir des réactions tout à fait imprévisibles. Mais il chasse son inquiétude ; s'oblige à allonger le pas ; lève ostensiblement la tête pour contempler la façade ancienne des maisons de cette rue qu'il aime tant et qui, au début du siècle, s'appelait encore la rue de la Vierge Immaculée ; s'arrête un moment, comme il le fait toujours, pour rendre un muet hommage à Tolstoï, devant l'Hôtel de Denis Davidoff ; et, le cœur en fête, prend la direction de la Moskowa.

Olga l'attend près du pont Borodinski.

— Alors ? demande-t-elle, en se jetant à son cou.

— Ça marchera... Nous aurons cette année un automne ensoleillé...

Il la prend par le bras et ils traversent le pont en silence.

— J'ai promis à mes parents de passer les voir avant le dîner, fait Olga. Veux-tu venir avec moi, dis ?

— Tes parents ne m'aiment pas beaucoup. Ils pensent que tu gâches ta vie pour moi... Ta mère surtout... Elle voit, derrière moi, cent millions d'Arabes qui la menacent...

— Qu'est-ce que tu racontes ? Elle sait que tu es tunisien et que tu n'as rien à voir avec le conflit du Proche-Orient...

Hidar s'arrête et observe son amante. Elle a bien changé, songe-t-il. En quoi ? Il ne saurait le dire. Mais il sent ce changement. C'est comme une maturité nouvelle. Un apaisement. Un accomplissement. C'est comme une proximité charnelle qui s'impose à lui, à elle, chaque fois qu'ils se revoient et à l'instant même des retrouvailles.

Olga approche son visage du sien et, en l'espace d'un éclair, il se voit dans les yeux bleu-gris.

— D'accord, d'accord, dit-il... Je viens avec toi... Mais prenons un taxi, veux-tu ? Je n'ai pas le courage de traverser Moscou à pied...

Par chance, une voiture passe — ornée d'un damier noir sur la carrosserie. Un taxi ! Ils s'y installent gaiement. Direction la maison des Lerner — où ils arrivent après dix minutes d'une course tranquille dans les avenues désertes de Moscou.

A la surprise de Hidar, Rachel Lerner a l'air heureuse de le revoir. Aussitôt, elle prépare le thé.

— Alors ? demande Rachel, quand tout le monde est assis autour de la table. Alors ? répète-t-elle en s'adressant à Hidar.

— Que voulez-vous savoir, Rachel Davidovna ?

Rachel fait, avec sa tête, quelques mouvements de balançoire.

— Je sais que nous ne sommes pas d'accord, Hidar... Je sais... Lorsqu'il s'agit d'Israël, nous sommes même des adversaires, mais vous, vous allez en Orient et moi pas... Je risque même d'être obligée, un de ces jours, de faire le voyage dans le sens inverse, en Sibérie...

Elle sourit gravement. Soupire. Et, approchant son visage tout près de celui de Hidar :

— Je voudrais que vous me parliez du Liban, de l'Égypte... Comment voit-on Israël là-bas ? Prépare-t-on la guerre ? Y a-t-il une chance de préserver la paix ? Parlez, je vous en prie...

Devant tant de franchise, de naïveté, Hidar se sent soudain désemparé.

— Je veux bien vous raconter ce que j'ai vu au Liban, mais je tiens d'abord à vous rassurer, Rachel Davidovna ; je ne suis nullement favorable à la destruction d'Israël. Quant à la politique, laissons-la de côté, voulez-vous. Nous allons nous disputer.

Sur quoi, il se met à raconter Beyrouth et les camps palestiniens, le Mont Liban et le Caire, le Nil et les Pyramides...

Rachel, Aron et Olga écoutent, fascinés, comme s'il s'agissait des Mille et Une Nuits. Quand Hidar a terminé, Rachel soupire :

— Vous êtes pour nous comme cette « branche de Palestine » dans le poème de Lermontov...

Puis, rajustant son châle et fixant son vis-à-vis, droit dans les yeux :

— A propos, comment était Hugo ?

Hida se raidit :

— Hugo... Pourquoi Hugo ? J'étais très jeune quand je l'ai connu...

— Mais encore ?

— Pourquoi cet intérêt pour un homme que vous n'avez jamais connu, Rachel Davidovna ?

— Parce qu'il représente, je crois, un pont... Un pont entre le monde d'hier et celui qui est en train de naître... Un pont aussi...

Rachel cherche ses mots :

— ... entre deux abîmes, entre la guerre et le terrorisme... Mais vous ne pouvez pas comprendre.

— Pourquoi ne pourrais-je pas comprendre, Rachel Davidovna ?

Rachel se lève, traverse la pièce à tout petits pas et, arrivée à la fenêtre, se retourne :

— Parce que tant bien que mal, votre monde à vous n'a jamais cessé d'exister... Celui de votre culture, de vos rêves. Tandis que nous... Notre culture a été déracinée par les nazis... Et quant à nos rêves ils ont été saccagés par...

— Par Staline ? achève Hidar, avec une pointe d'ironie dans la voix.

Rachel fait oui de la tête et revient à sa place.

— Vous rendez-vous compte, poursuit-il, que Staline est mort depuis seize ans !

Puis, s'adressant à Aron :

— Vous, Aron Lazarevitch, que pensez-vous de la théorie des « ponts » de votre femme ? Et cette référence constante au grand-père Abraham... Dans un monde qui bouge sans cesse, ne croyez-vous pas que c'est un brin ridicule ?

Aron Lerner sourit, se passe la main sur des cheveux soigneusement plaqués et, d'un ton presque gêné, comme s'il sollicitait d'avance l'indulgence ou le pardon :

— Vous ne pouvez pas comprendre... Nous parlions hier encore avec notre voisin, l'académicien S... Quand d'un monde ancien il ne subsiste rien, ce qui revient et surgit, c'est ce furieux désir d'ancêtres...

Puis, plus résolu et se levant tout à coup — signe que le débat, pour lui, est clos :

— Sachez-le, Hidar : « omnia risus, omnia pulvis, et omnia nihil sunt »... tout est dérision, tout est poussière et tout n'est rien.

— Tu n'aurais pas dû provoquer mon père, fera Olga quand elle se retrouvera, seule avec son amant, dans l'ombre de la rue.

— Pourquoi ?

— Mon père est un faux cynique. D'une certaine manière, cela l'a sauvé à l'époque des grandes purges à l'Université. Mais il en a gardé, comment te dire ? une inguérissable mélancolie... Il faut que tu comprennes que, parce que tu n'es pas soviétique, tu peux te permettre des choses que lui ne peut pas affirmer sans risques. Vous ne vivez pas de la même manière. Tu peux voyager, par exemple, à ta guise et...

— ... Et avec toi, *milaya,* enchaîne Hidar d'un ton câlin — avant de l'entraîner en direction du restaurant Bakou, rue Gorki...

14

NEW YORK

SIDNEY :
UNE RENCONTRE PROVIDENTIELLE

Septembre 1969

Sidney a l'impression de tourner en rond. Sa courte
« aventure » avec Leïla l'a beaucoup plus marqué qu'il
ne veut le reconnaître. Depuis « le jour où l'homme a
marché sur la lune », il se sent tendu, nerveux.

Marjory, le voyant préoccupé, se donne beaucoup de
mal pour lui faire plaisir, le séduire. Mais au lieu de s'en
réjouir, Sidney en est irrité. Et s'en voulant de son
impatience, il devient plus irritable encore. Comme
cette situation l'accable ! Comme il aimerait pouvoir
s'en ouvrir à quelqu'un ! Mais à qui ? Comment se
confier à tous ces vrais ou faux amis dont il refusait, hier
encore, d'écouter les confidences.

En quittant l'hôpital, par cette claire journée de
septembre, il se heurte à Jérémie Cohen.

— Sidney ! s'exclame celui-ci en sautillant sur un
pied ! Non mais dis-moi, espèce de cinglé : tu m'as
écrasé l'orteil ! Tu me paies un verre pour te rache-
ter ?...

Jérémie Cohen et Sidney se connaissent depuis des
années. Ils ont même fait une partie de leurs études
ensemble et depuis qu'ils sont installés, ils ont participé
ensemble à mille actions de médecins pour le tiers
monde, contre la faim, contre la torture... Jérémie est le
meilleur anesthésiste de l'hôpital, mais Marjory le
trouve bizarre et ses collègues le considèrent comme un

phénomène. Il habite Soho, au 350 Broadway, entre Broom et Spring Street, dans un immeuble délabré, sentant l'urine, où des « hassidim » font commerce d'appareils photographiques importés d'Extrême-Orient et où il occupe, en vérité, un loft superbe.

— Belle journée, hein, fait-il. L'automne s'annonce divin. On va au Plazza ?

Entièrement recouvert de cuir noir, l' « Oak Bar » de l'hôtel Plazza bénéficie depuis la sortie des *Plus belles années de notre vie* d'une notoriété dont les habitués se seraient bien passés.

— Je préfère le Polo-bar du Westbury... C'est plus près... dit Sidney machinalement.

— Va pour le Westbury, fait Jérémie — qui entreprend aussitôt, tout en marchant, de raconter sa dernière conquête à Sidney :

— Tu ne vas pas me croire, mon vieux, mais pendant trois mois j'ai été amoureux fou de Sophie, la petite économe de l'hôpital...

— La Française ?

— Oui ! Nous faisions l'amour partout, dans les dépôts, sur les paniers à linge, au milieu des caisses de médicaments. Je ne sais pas comment son mari l'a su... Mais il est venu me trouver un jour et m'a solennellement déclaré qu'il me remettait sa femme ainsi que sa bénédiction. Et du coup, tu sais ce qui s'est passé ? J'ai compris que je n'aimais pas Sophie et je me suis senti aussi libre et léger que l'air.

Et, prenant son ami par les épaules :

— Voilà ! On est arrivés. Oublions ma chaussure, Sid, et mon orteil aussi, je t'offre le champagne pour fêter ma première heure de liberté depuis trois mois !

— Champagne ! commande-t-il, en se laissant tomber dans un large fauteuil de cuir rouge.

Et, dès qu'ils sont servis :

— A nos amours !

Puis, changeant de sujet :

— Figure-toi que je viens de recevoir une invitation à donner quelques conférences à l'Université américaine de Beyrouth. Qu'en dis-tu ?

Sidney sursaute et renverse son verre :

— Pardon...

— Ce n'est rien, ça porte bonheur et ça ne tache pas, fait Jérémie en épongeant la veste avec une serviette.

— Alors, tu vas partir ? demanda Sidney, en se remettant de la surprise.

— Comment cela, si je vais partir ? Je n'en sais rien... Mais qu'est-ce que tu as à me regarder comme ça ? Tu as l'air bizarre...

Et, vidant son verre :

— Je suis sûr que tu as une « affaire »... Je te connais ! Quand on était à l'université, je devinais tout, rien qu'à regarder ton visage. Tu te souviens de la petite Mexicaine que tu as connue au Salvador quand nous y sommes allés après le tremblement de terre ? Elle me plaisait bien, mais c'est toi qu'elle a préféré...

Sidney sourit, flatté :

— Ne parlons pas de ça...

— Et pourquoi pas ? Tu crois peut-être qu'on est là pour parler de l'avenir du monde, de la guerre au Vietnam et de l'assassinat de Sharon Tate ? Ah ! sacré vieux farceur...

— Ce n'est pas ça, répond Sidney en se grattant la barbe. Tu sais bien : pour les Juifs, la famille, les enfants, la fidélité, tout ça, sont des valeurs intangibles.

— OK, épargne-moi le portrait-robot du Juif éternel ; être juif, ce n'est pas toujours une preuve d'intelligence. Combien d'Einstein y a-t-il parmi nos enfants ? Aujourd'hui, on fait ou l'amour ou de la recherche. Einstein tenait les deux fronts... C'était son génie.

— Si ce n'est que cela être génial, alors nous le sommes tous les deux.

Ils éclatent de rire.

— C'est comme ça que je t'aime, Sid !

Jérémie tape sur la cuisse de son ami et commande une autre bouteille de champagne. Puis, rapprochant son visage :

— Raconte !

— Bon, c'est vrai, il y a longtemps que ça ne m'était pas arrivé...

Quand le récit est terminé, Jérémie se laisse aller dans son fauteuil, offre un cigare à Sidney, qui refuse, en choisit un qu'il allume, puis déclare :

— Eh bien, mon vieux ! Je crois que tu vas partir à Beyrouth.

— Qu'est-ce que tu racontes ?

— Je n'ai jamais été aussi sérieux. Ton histoire est belle, bien plus belle que mes aventures avec l'économe de l'hôpital ou les serveuses de chez Wolff. Une histoire comme celle-là, on ne l'interrompt pas en plein milieu.

— Mais comment pourrai-je expliquer...

— Tu n'auras rien à expliquer. Tu seras invité à donner des conférences à l'Université américaine de Beyrouth, à ma place. Tout le monde sait que les Juifs aiment les voyages.

15

OLGA À BEYROUTH

Octobre 1969

Quitter l'URSS, Olga n'aurait jamais cru qu'une telle aventure fût possible. A l'aéroport de Cheremetievo, malgré l'arrogance de la police et la bousculade des passagers, tour à tour excités ou inertes, tout s'est bien passé. Ou presque. En effet, elle venait à peine de passer le contrôle d'identité qu'un homme d'une vingtaine d'années, à la voix impérieuse, se disant policier en civil, a exigé de voir à nouveau son passeport. L'homme s'est emparé du document et, sans autre commentaire, a disparu derrière une porte, à l'autre bout de l'aéroport. Olga a pris peur. Elle s'est vue refoulée, arrêtée. D'instinct, elle s'est coulée dans la peau d'un coupable ; a revu en pensée, et en un dixième de seconde, tous les menus crimes qu'elle avait ou aurait pu commettre ; elle a eu honte, presque aussitôt, de cette réaction stupide, mais enfin elle l'a eue. Et c'est au bout de vingt minutes d'une attente longue comme une interminable douleur qu'elle a enfin récupéré son passeport des mains de Hidar à qui un officier l'a remis sans un mot d'excuse. Cet incident, en soi mineur, l'a pourtant beaucoup troublée. La colère et l'angoisse ne l'ont plus quittée de tout le voyage. Et ce n'est qu'à l'escale de Londres qu'elle s'est enfin ressaisie et que, dans un de ces mouvements d'affection dont elle est coutumière, elle a chuchoté à l'oreille de Hidar quel-

111

ques mots câlins et osés — du type de ceux qu'il lui est arrivé de lire, par-dessus son épaule, dans les romans d'espionnage qu'il rapporte parfois de ses voyages.

Bref, les voici à Beyrouth, Hidar l'avait promis : le soleil est au rendez-vous, ainsi que cette gaieté dolente dont elle a toujours imaginé qu'elle est l'apanage de l'Orient. Pas très différent de l'aéroport de Cheremetievo, celui de Khaldé est également assiégé par une foule de gens. Porteurs... Badauds... Voyageurs éberlués que la préoccupation de retrouver leurs bagages, au milieu d'une immense pagaille, rend moroses... Femmes en maraude... Soldats... Individus louches aux allures de terroristes et de tueurs. Très à son aise, Hidar fend la foule ; écarte du geste mendiants et importuns ; avise un taxi ; négocie le prix ! et demande au chauffeur, un jeune homme en maillot de corps qui conduit une Mercedes climatisée, de les conduire à l'hôtel Saint-Georges par la corniche, le long de la mer. Intrigué par ce couple étrange, qui s'exprime dans une langue absolument inconnue de lui, le jeune homme ne cesse de leur poser des questions, tantôt en français, tantôt en anglais, auxquelles Hidar réplique par monosyllabes avec une évidente mauvaise volonté. Et ce jusqu'à ce que, trop occupé à observer ces braves clients dans son rétroviseur, il rate un virage, dérape et emboutisse un chariot rempli de cages à poules. La querelle du chauffeur et du propriétaire du chariot — fortement encouragée par une foule curieuse et nerveuse — durera près d'une heure. Assez pour que nos deux voyageurs n'arrivent à l'hôtel qu'à la tombée du jour...

Un homme y attend déjà Hidar. Olga le prend d'abord pour un mendiant. Ou, au moins, un vague coursier. Mais, à la manière dont Hidar s'adresse à lui, elle comprend que l'homme est porteur d'un message important. Palabres... Front soucieux de Hidar qui prend l'air du Monsieur à qui on vient d'annoncer une nouvelle catastrophique...

La chambre est si belle... La vue sur les lumières du port si romanesque... Eh bien non ! Il n'y a pas de roman qui tienne :

112

— Mes collègues du Comité pour la Paix se réunissent demain matin. Ils me prient de les rejoindre.

Olga se lève d'un bond :

— Comment demain ? Tu vas me quitter dès le lendemain de notre arrivée !

— Non, *milaya,* non... Une heure ou deux... Peut-être moins... Tu verras : je partirai très tôt... Tu dormiras encore... Tu ne t'en apercevras même pas...

Hidar, du reste, est sincèrement contrarié. Ne comptait-il pas consacrer ces deux premiers jours à faire découvrir Beyrouth à Olga ? Et n'y a-t-il pas, surtout, quelque chose d'inquiétant dans cette soudaine précipitation ?

— Oui, *milaya,* continue-t-il, comme s'il voulait se convaincre lui-même... Pardonne-moi pour ce contretemps... Je te promets d'être là à ton réveil...

— Si j'arrive à dormir !... Maintenant que je sais !...

— *Milaya...* répète Hidar avant de l'enlacer et de la pousser, à reculons, vers le grand lit à baldaquin qui fait face à la mer...

La réunion se tient au siège du FPLP, sur la corniche Mazraa. Sur les murs du bureau de Georges Habbache des posters de Guevara côtoient des portraits de Lénine et une immense carte de la Palestine où le nom d'Israël ne figure pas.

Parmi les participants, deux nouveaux : Ghassan Kanafani, un poète au visage pensif et pâle, et puis Bassam Abou Sharif, un garçon de taille moyenne, brun et vif, dont Hidar a entendu dire qu'il est le responsable des « actions spéciales ».

— Et Hawatmeh ? demande-t-il en s'asseyant. J'ai entendu dire qu'il avait quitté le mouvement.

— Il a voulu créer un groupe à lui, répond Habbache. Qu'Allah le protège ! Mais le moment venu, il sera avec nous...

— Et El Fath ?

— Abou Iyad passera tout à l'heure.

On sert du café turc. On s'observe un moment en

113

silence. Et, au bout de quelques minutes, Waddi Haddad vient se mettre à côté de Hidar :

— Que dit-on, à Moscou, de la mort de Hô Chi-Min ?

— C'est un deuil national.

— Pour nous aussi c'est un choc !

Et, en fixant Hidar de ses yeux noirs sans éclat :

— Et que pensent les Soviétiques de l'opération jordanienne ?

— Ils sont d'accord, répond Hidar sans ciller. Mais à l'expresse condition que tout se déroule selon les plans que nous avons établis et que j'ai présentés hier à Moscou.

— Ils nous promettent quoi ?

— Les armes et les informations.

— Les informations, fait doucement Ghassan Kanafani, nous les avons...

— Il n'y a pas que ça, poursuit Hidar feignant de n'avoir pas entendu. Ils nous offrent aussi des garanties contre une éventuelle intervention des États-Unis ou d'autres pays arabes.

Ghassan Kanafani élève la voix :

— Pour les pays arabes, nous n'avons pas besoin de l'Union soviétique... Pour les États-Unis, c'est différent... Nixon et Kissinger ne laisseront pas facilement tomber leur allié Hussein... Mais...

Le sourire satisfait de Habbache, visiblement content de l'intervention du poète, irrite Hidar :

— Commenceriez-vous à douter, par hasard ?

— De nous, non, répond Kanafani.

Hidar fait à nouveau semblant de n'avoir pas entendu.

— Les Syriens vous aideront, poursuit-il. Ils ont reçu des ordres. Dès l'annonce de l'offensive contre le Palais Royal à Amman, les chars syriens fonceront sur Irbid...

— Et Moscou ?

— Brejnev adressera à Nixon une mise en garde contre toute intervention de la 6e flotte... Mais il faut le savoir : les Soviétiques ne vous laisseront pas beaucoup de temps.

— Combien ? demande sèchement Waddi Haddad.

114

Il est en treillis militaire et porte une casquette kaki qui cache son crâne dégarni.

— Une semaine au plus.

— Ça suffira.

C'est Jael el-Ardja qui, cette fois, a pris la parole. Sa présence a surpris Hidar. Natif de Beit Jallah, près de Bethléem, il habite à présent à Lima, au Pérou, et représente le Front en Amérique latine. Que fait-il là ? Qu'est-ce que l'Amérique latine a à voir avec le règlement de comptes jordano-palestinien qui se prépare ?

— C'est moi qui lui ai demandé de venir, intervient Waddi Haddad, comme s'il avait lu dans ses pensées. Il a, lui aussi, un projet intéressant. Et j'ai pensé qu'il serait bon qu'il nous en parle.

Tous les regards se tournent vers Jael el-Ardja qui explique alors comment le Front a décidé l'assassinat de David Ben Gourion lors de son voyage à Buenos Aires. Ben Gourion, certes, n'est plus qu'un simple citoyen. Mais n'incarne-t-il pas toujours, aux yeux du monde, l'État juif ? et, donc, le sionisme ? Le projet, de fait, est au point. On a même trouvé les exécutants : un certain Ismaël Souhail, et un militant gauchiste suédois. Qu'en pense la compagnie ?

— J'en pense que vous êtes complètement fous ! s'exclame Hidar sans laisser aux autres le temps de réagir.

— Et pourquoi ? demande Haddad.

— Parce que l'opinion publique dans le monde ne comprendra pas l'exécution d'un vieillard pendant un voyage privé en Argentine.

— Mais l'opinion israélienne, elle, le comprendra très bien !

Hidar prend sa voix la plus posée :

— Vous êtes des combattants révolutionnaires, non des assassins et vous devez gagner une double bataille : celle contre Israël et celle contre les médias. Avec ce projet fou, vous perdrez les deux...

115

Waddi Haddad grimace :

— Tu penses vraiment que parce que tu viens de Moscou tu sais, tu comprends tout !

Le ton monte. Habbache intervient. Puis Jael el-Ardja. Puis Ghassan Kanafani qui, cette fois-ci, se retrouve du côté de Hidar, mais n'arrive pas à se faire entendre. Seul l'arrivée d'Abou Iyad réussit à détendre l'atmosphère. Les salutations et les embrassades durent plusieurs bonnes minutes. Le numéro deux d'El Fath, avec sa chemisette blanche à col ouvert, son paquet de cigarettes dans la pochette, ses cheveux soigneusement coiffés, ressemble à un brave professeur de collège, égaré parmi les comploteurs. Et une sorte d'accord tacite se fait pour laisser cette épineuse affaire Ben Gourion à la discrétion et responsabilité des camarades latino-américains.

— C'est bien ainsi, fait alors Habbache en balayant sa moustache de son geste familier...

Puis, se penchant vers Hidar, comme pour partager un secret :

— Il paraît qu'elle est belle...

— C'est vrai.

— Etait-il bien prudent de l'amener à Beyrouth ?

Hidar sourit de toutes ses dents :

— Tu connais le proverbe arabe. « Pour bien aimer une vivante, il faut l'aimer comme si elle devait mourir demain. »

— Je parle de ta sécurité à toi.

— Olga représente mon meilleur alibi.

Comment faire sentir à ce butor que ses remarques l'agacent ? Comment leur faire comprendre à tous qu'avant d'être un danger, un alibi ou Dieu sait quoi, Olga est *d'abord* la femme qu'il aime — et que cela, qu'ils le veuillent ou non, le regarde lui, et lui seulement ? Agacé, mais ne voulant pas le montrer, et préférant ignorer le vilain sourire mielleux de son interlocuteur, il décide de poser *la* question qui le préoccupe depuis une heure :

— Pourquoi cette réunion aujourd'hui ?

— Waddi Haddad y tenait. Il a un projet spectaculaire… Un événement qui précédera la prise d'Amman… Il voulait nous en parler d'urgence…

— Peux-tu en dire un peu plus ?

— C'est une histoire de détournement d'avions. Mais je préfère qu'il nous en parle lui-même.

Hidar sourit, brusquement rassuré. Ainsi donc, c'était cela ! Les camarades soviétiques ont bien travaillé et l'information est passée…

Waddi Haddad s'approche à ce moment-là, une tasse de café à la main.

— Vous parlez de l'amie de Hidar ?

— Non, répond Hidar, nous parlions de toi.

Waddi prend une chaise et s'assied :

— Moi, je ne présente aucun intérêt, tandis que ton amie… Je voulais te prévenir…

— Prévenir de quoi ?

— Je comprends ta stratégie… Les services secrets sionistes seront peut-être déroutés… Mais toi, tu risques d'avoir des problèmes…

— J'ai pleine confiance en Olga.

— Tu as tort. Je te l'ai déjà dit : on ne pactise pas avec l'ennemi.

— Mais je ne combats pas les Juifs !

— Si, bien sûr. Les sionistes à travers le monde représentent le vivier d'Israël. Tous les Juifs sont sionistes, ou presque. Même ceux qui ne le savent pas encore.

— Tu veux donc combattre les Juifs du monde entier ?

— Pourquoi pas ?… A ce jeu-là aussi, nous serions gagnants. Ne sommes-nous pas plus nombreux ?

Il se lève en riant, repose sa tasse sur le bureau et, avec un geste vague de la main qui semble vouloir dire « après tout, c'est ton affaire, j'ai bien tort de te faire la leçon et de me soucier de ton sort », entreprend d'exposer le « projet spectaculaire » dont vient de parler Habbache.

— Qu'en penses-tu ? demande-t-il à Hidar.

— Très bonne idée, dit celui-ci en réprimant un sourire de triomphe. Nous inaugurerons ainsi l'ère du terrorisme médiatique. Quel coup de génie si nous parvenons à faire que les télévisions deviennent enfin les véhicules obligés des causes révolutionnaires !

— J'aime ta formule, grommelle Habbache. Est-ce que je me trompe ou est-ce que le « terrorisme médiatique » n'est pas la guerre la moins chère et la plus payante ?

Voyant tout le monde se lever, Hidar hausse la voix :

— Encore un mot, avant de nous quitter : pas de violence inutile, pas de ségrégation. N'oublions pas que des millions d'hommes et de femmes observent nos faits et gestes.

Et s'adressant à Waddi Haddad :

— N'oublie pas non plus Samirah, c'est une fille courageuse. Est-ce qu'elle ne l'a pas prouvé, l'autre semaine, en détournant à Rome le Boeing de la TWA ?

— J'y pense, fait Waddi, songeur... J'y pense... Mais il faut d'abord la sortir de Syrie... Les Syriens ne veulent pas la relâcher... Quelle idée d'avoir posé le Boeing à Damas ?

— Eh bien, occupe-t'en, tranche Hidar. C'est ton affaire. Je veux voir cette fille libre — et à Beyrouth.

A son retour, il trouve Olga levée depuis longtemps. Et, contre toute attente, de bonne humeur.

— J'ai trouvé ce livre dans un tiroir, dit-elle, en montrant la Bible. Je ne l'avais jamais lu... C'est passionnant, tu sais ?...

— Et c'est ce qui te rend si heureuse ?

— Oui, pourquoi ?

— Je suis étonné, voilà tout.

— Étonné qu'on admire ce qui est admirable ? Écoute donc ce verset !

« Le Juste sera dans la joie, à la vue de la vengeance ;
Il baignera ses pieds dans le sang des méchants. »

— C'est effrayant, n'est-ce pas ? Je me demande qui a écrit cela...

— Dieu.

— Ne ris pas, Hidar.

118

— Je ne ris pas.

Elle s'approche de lui, le livre à la main. L'ouvre au hasard sur le Cantique des Cantiques. Et lit :

> *« Mon bien-aimé est blanc et vermeil ;*
> *Il se distingue entre dix mille,*
> *Sa tête est de l'or pur,*
> *Ses boucles sont flottantes,*
> *Noires comme le corbeau. »*

— C'est, en effet, un joli verset, et tu l'as fort bien choisi, dit Hidar en posant ses lèvres sur celles d'Olga. Mais, pour ta première venue ici, ne vaudrait-il pas mieux visiter la ville plutôt que les pages, certes belles, mais poussiéreuses, d'un livre du passé ?

— Mais ces pages parlent du Liban ! Écoute encore :

> *« Ton cou est comme une tour d'ivoire ;*
> *Tes yeux sont comme les étangs de Hesbon,*
> *Près de la porte de Bath-Rabbim ;*
> *Ton nez est comme la tour du Liban,*
> *Qui regarde du côté de Damas... »*

Chère Olga ! Chère chérie ! Elle est si belle quand elle lit ! Si belle, sous le casque d'or de sa natte blonde ! Et c'est si étrange de l'entendre parler, en effet, du Liban, de Damas — qui sait si, dans une minute, elle ne va pas trouver un verset où il sera question de Habbache, Waddi Haddad et Samirah ? Comme chaque fois qu'une femme lui fait un peu pitié, Hidar est pris d'une de ces furieuses volontés de meurtrir qu'elles prennent en général pour du désir. Il lui retire le livre des mains. Empoigne la belle natte. Lui tire la tête en arrière comme s'il voulait lui déboîter la gorge. Et, la déshabillant à peine, négligeant de se dévêtir lui-même au-delà du strict nécessaire, se force brutalement un chemin entre les deux cuisses bien tendues...

Ils passeront le reste de la journée dans la rue. Olga est gaie. Elle récite à tout bout de champ le verset du Cantique des Cantiques sur le « bien-aimé blanc et vermeil ». Ils visitent la place des Canons, aux arbres fatigués. Traversent la fameuse rue Bab Edriss et son marché aux fleurs. Le quartier d'Al Hamra avec ses cinémas, ses galeries et ses magasins européens, arrache à Olga des cris passionnés. Pas une boutique qui ne l'émerveille. Pas un café où elle n'ait envie d'entrer pour y picorer des douceurs. A proximité d'un vaste parc s'étendant sur les pentes du promontoire du Râs Beyrouth, ils s'arrêtent enfin, épuisés.

— Si on se reposait un peu, « mon bien-aimé aux boucles noires comme le corbeau » ? dit Olga en se laissant tomber sur le gazon.

— Non, *milaya,* répond Hidar. C'est l'Université américaine de Beyrouth...

— Une université américaine à Beyrouth !

— Enfin, « américaine », façon de parler... Elle a été construite il y a un siècle par une mission presbytérienne américaine...

« Façon de parler » ou pas, l'idée enchante manifestement la jeune femme qui, retrouvant toute son énergie, décide d'aller y voir de plus près. Le hall est plein d'étudiants. Ce ne sont partout que clameurs, cris, interpellations joyeuses dans toutes les langues.

— Allons regarder, dit-elle en montrant à son ami un grand panneau d'affichage devant lequel se presse une foule de jeunes gens.

Puis, surexcitée, en désignant une petite affiche du doigt :

— Lis... Oh ! oui lis... Est-ce que ce n'est pas extraordinaire ?

Hidar lit et ce qu'il lit lui semble en effet tout à fait extravagant : « 22 septembre 1969. Grand amphithéâtre de la Faculté de Médecine. Conférence du Docteur Sidney Halter, de Manhattan Eye, Ear and Throat Hospital (New York). »

16

BEYROUTH

LE JEU DU HASARD

Octobre 1969

Quel ennui, s'est dit Sidney lorsque, chez le concierge de l'hôtel Saint-Georges, il a trouvé le petit mot que lui avait laissé Olga ! Déjà ce séjour lui pesait. Il le « sentait » de moins en moins. N'avait-il pas dû annuler sa participation promise à un voyage en Éthiopie ? N'avait-il pas dû renoncer à la grande conférence médicale de Francfort ? Et puis mentir à Marjory n'avait pas été si facile non plus… Images de la jeune femme… Images des deux enfants… Remords… Mauvaise conscience… Au moins ce voyage avait-il le mérite d'éloigner le théâtre de la faute et il ne cessait de se répéter, depuis son arrivée, les mots rassurants de Jérémie : « Beyrouth est si loin, personne ne saura jamais rien car personne, là-bas, ne te connaît. » Or, patatras ! Voici qu'il se retrouve avec une parente sur les bras. Il aurait été heureux de la rencontrer, cette parente, dans d'autres circonstances. Mais pas là ! Pas ainsi ! Pas dans cette effroyable situation où le sentiment de sa culpabilité l'accompagne à chaque seconde. Cela fait deux jours qu'il a trouvé le fameux mot. Et il ne peut plus faire un pas, entrer dans un lieu public, il ne peut plus, comme aujourd'hui, s'asseoir par exemple à la terrasse de cette Grotte aux Pigeons, où Leïla lui a fixé rendez-vous, sans se dire que la cousine va surgir, le héler, l'accoster et… il préfère ne pas imaginer la suite.

Aime-t-il Beyrouth au moins ? Hum... Ce n'est pas sûr. Depuis qu'il est ici, il a vu la misère de certains quartiers, les nuées d'enfants qui se jettent sur les passants pour obtenir une pièce, les estropiés, les vieillards demandant l'aumône. Ce matin même, non loin de la Grande Mosquée qu'il voulait visiter, il a croisé un groupe de touristes américains, les a observés, et il s'est dit qu'il enviait leur détachement, leur joie, leur désinvolture. « Il n'y a que les Américains, a-t-il pensé, pour évoluer avec tant d'aisance au milieu de gens sales, affamés, malheureux. Au fond, ce sont de vrais optimistes... Je dois être, moi, une sorte d'atrabilaire... » Bref, il avait toutes les raisons d'être chagrin lorsqu'il est arrivé à la Grotte aux Pigeons et il s'est même surpris à souhaiter, le temps d'un éclair, que Leïla ne vînt pas au rendez-vous, qu'un mystérieux obstacle se soit interposé entre eux. Mais elle était là, bien sûr. Assise à l'ombre d'un parasol. En la voyant, il n'a pas pu retenir son émotion. Il n'a pas pu ne pas se dire que c'était la plus belle femme du monde. Et c'est finalement elle qui, lorsqu'il s'est approché et qu'il a voulu l'embrasser, l'a repoussé :

— Pas ici, Sidney, pas en public... Nous sommes en Orient... Allons à votre hôtel.

— Vous ne voulez pas dîner ?

— On se fera monter quelque chose dans votre chambre. J'ai peur, Sidney... Mon mari m'a paru bizarre, ce matin. Il a fait quelques remarques sur mon voyage aux États-Unis... Mon mari est extrêmement puissant ici.

Sidney a sursauté :

— Vous avez peur de votre mari ou vous avez peur d'être vue avec un sioniste ?

— Ne dites pas de bêtises...

Elle a effleuré rapidement sa main de ses doigts pâles :

— Je suis heureuse que vous soyez là, mais vous devez comprendre... Ici, tout le monde connaît mon mari. Comme pour vous, dans votre hôpital de New York.

Ils allaient partir, quand une voix, au fort accent slave, s'est écriée en anglais :

— Mais oui ! C'est lui ! Bon Dieu, c'est le cousin Sidney !

Leïla, un peu surprise, a levé vers Sidney un regard interrogateur. Et Sidney terriblement embarrassé a répondu quelque chose comme :

— Ne vous inquiétez pas, je crois que c'est la fille de ma cousine soviétique.

Et, de fait, Olga était déjà près d'eux. Elle s'est étonnée d'avoir « une aussi belle cousine » ; il a répondu, d'un ton sec, que ce n'était pas sa cousine mais une simple « amie libanaise ». Elle lui a raconté comment elle avait fait tous les hôtels de la ville, avant de le localiser au Saint-Georges ; il a observé que « oui, c'était là que venaient souvent les journalistes, les touristes, les hommes d'affaires américains ». Elle s'est extasiée de l'avoir reconnu là, tout de suite, sans hésiter une seule seconde, alors qu'elle ne connaissait qu'une photo de lui — et encore une vieille photo, datant de quinze ou vingt ans, que Rachel, sa mère, avait gardée dans leur album ! Et lui a dit que oui, c'était curieux... le miracle des familles sans doute... la voix muette du sang... lui aussi l'avait repérée, sans même une photo ou rien du tout — à cause d'une ressemblance, simplement, d'une familiarité obscure mais évidente... Et lorsque, enfin, prenant son cousin par le bras, elle a minaudé : « Ne partez pas, je vous en prie, venez prendre de l'arak avec nous... Je voudrais vous présenter Hidar... Mon ami... » Il a consulté Leïla du regard, a feint de ne pas voir son désarroi et, piégé jusqu'au bout, s'est entendu consentir : « Bon... bon... rien qu'un petit moment, alors. » Sidney, maintenant, s'est levé. Il est à la table d'Olga. Et se trouve donc, par la force des choses, face à Hidar Assadi.

Hidar est surpris par ce Juif d'un mètre quatre-vingt-dix, blond et roux. Mais la présence de Leïla l'étonne plus encore. Que fait la femme du puissant Michel

Chehab, magnat de la presse, au bras de ce sioniste ?
Pour une fois, il ne maudit pas le hasard.

Olga, elle, est heureuse comme une enfant :

— Mes parents ne me croiront jamais ! Ils avaient si
peur pour moi ! Vous comprenez, une Juive dans un
pays arabe... Et voilà que je rencontre le cousin Sidney,
de New York, et que nous prenons ensemble de l'arak,
dans le plus fameux café de Beyrouth. N'est-ce pas
extraordinaire ?

— Vous êtes ici pour longtemps ? demande Hidar à
Sidney.

Sidney se cale dans sa chaise, mal à l'aise :

— Pour quelques jours encore... J'ai accepté une
invitation de l'Université américaine...

— Je sais, nous avons vu votre nom sur un tableau de
service. Vous êtes venu seul ?

L'accent de Hidar en anglais est rocailleux, mi-arabe,
mi-russe.

— Oui, fait Sidney, de plus en plus gêné. Nous
venons d'avoir une fille et ma femme ne pouvait
m'accompagner...

Il jette un regard à Leïla et sent le rouge lui monter au
visage. Il avale le contenu du verre que le garçon vient
de poser sur la table devant lui et demande :

— Et vous ?

— Je suis ici avec Olga.

— Oui, mais êtes-vous marié ?

— Avec Olga ?

— Oui, avec Olga.

— Non, pas vraiment...

— Je croyais qu'en Union soviétique, on était très
strict sur ce chapitre.

— On dit tout et le contraire de tout à propos de
l'Union soviétique...

Il y eut un silence, comme si cet échange rapide avait
épuisé tous les sujets de conversation possibles. C'est
Sidney qui le rompt :

— Quel est exactement votre nom ?

— Hidar Assadi.

— Assadi... Assadi... Pouvez-vous l'épeler ?

— Pourquoi ?

— Parce que ce nom me rappelle quelque chose...

— Tu as peut-être vu le nom de Hidar dans la presse, intervient Olga. Il est très important dans le Comité de Solidarité avec les peuples d'Afrique et d'Asie où travaille Sacha. Tu sais, Sacha — mon frère... Hidar, lui, voyage beaucoup, organise des conférences...

Hidar pose gentiment sa main sur la bouche d'Olga et dit :

— Elle exagère.

Mais Sidney qui passe et repasse les doigts dans ses cheveux roux semble ailleurs :

— Assadi... Assadi... Ne seriez-vous pas tunisien, par hasard ?

— Oui, pourquoi ?

Sidney rayonne :

— Alors, vous êtes certainement cet Hidar Assadi dont parlait le cousin Hugo !

Deux hommes, assis à la table voisine, se retournent comme s'ils avaient suivi la conversation. Pour gagner du temps, Hidar avale une gorgée du liquide laiteux. Olga répond à sa place :

— Oui, bien sûr. Ils étaient amis. Sauf que Hidar avait treize ou quatorze ans, à l'époque...

— Vous ne l'avez jamais revu ? demande Sidney.

— Non, fait Hidar, en reposant son verre vide. Mais j'ai été très peiné à l'annonce de sa mort.

— De son assassinat !

Hidar sourit d'un air paternel, ce qui a le don d'irriter Sidney.

— Assassinat ou non, le résultat est malheureusement le même.

— Mais ce sont vos amis qui l'ont tué !

Sidney sent la colère monter en lui. Cet homme à la belle tête crépue lui déplaît. Il se demande ce qu'Olga fait avec lui.

Hidar fait signe au garçon, commande une nouvelle tournée et répond doucement :

— Non, monsieur Sidney Halter, ce ne sont pas *mes amis* qui ont tué Hugo. Je pourrais même affirmer le contraire : ceux qui ont tué Hugo appartiennent au clan de mes ennemis.

Et d'une voix qui se veut neutre :

— Mais vous avez un frère en Israël, n'est-ce pas ?

— Comment le savez-vous ?

— Par la mère d'Olga, Rachel Lerner. Elle est très attachée à tout ce qui est la famille...

Hidar arrête d'un geste le garçon qui va s'éloigner et lui tend un billet de cent livres. Sidney veut protester, mais Hidar s'est déjà levé :

— Laissez... Cela me fait plaisir...

Et, en tendant la main à Sidney :

— J'espère que nous nous reverrons avant votre départ.

— Volontiers, répond Sidney.

Et, se souvenant de Benjamin Ben Eliezer, risque :

— Si vous pouviez, avant mon départ, me parler un peu de Hugo, j'en serais très heureux. Ce cousin m'a depuis toujours fasciné.

Hidar hésite une seconde :

— Je vais essayer, mais je crains de vous décevoir. J'ai connu Hugo il y a plus de vingt-cinq ans. C'était un ami de mon père. Vous trouverez peut-être plus d'informations dans la famille de sa femme. L'avez-vous connue ?

— Non. Notre famille a refusé de la recevoir.

— Pourquoi ?

— C'est idiot... Mais il faut comprendre... c'était au lendemain de la guerre et elle était la fille d'un général nazi...

— Ce n'est pas une tache indélébile, fit Hidar. Sigrid était une femme bien...

Sidney sursaute :

— Vous la connaissiez donc ?

— J'en ai entendu parler...

Et, se levant à nouveau :

— Cette fois, il faut vraiment qu'on parte.

Il tend la main à Sidney.

— Je comprends, dit Sidney, en retenant la main de Hidar. Nous aussi, nous devons partir... Mais... Olga n'avait pas tort, un Juif ne rencontre pas tous les jours une cousine soviétique dans un pays arabe. Aujourd'hui, nos familles sont éclatées, comme un de ces vases anciens qu'on peut admirer ici, au musée de Beyrouth, dans la salle des trésors de Byblos... Pour ressouder une famille, il faut une colle bien forte. Hugo, je crois, disposait d'une ténacité suffisante. Mais le désir ne suffit pas, il faut aussi retrouver les morceaux...

Beyrouth, 6 octobre 1969

Lendemain, donc, de cette rencontre Sidney-Olga. Pourquoi suis-je, à mon tour, là? Que viens-je réellement faire? Et qu'est-ce qui l'emporte en moi de l'infatigable pèlerin de la paix venant, pour la énième fois, consulter, nouer des contacts, poursuivre un interminable dialogue avec les chefs palestiniens — ou du fils de Salomon venant honorer une promesse sacrée et profiter de ces contacts pour retrouver la trace du cousin Hugo? La vérité est que je ne le sais pas très bien moi-même et que, comme chaque fois, j'ai peine à démêler en moi ce qui ressortit à l'une ou l'autre préoccupation. Je suis là en tout cas. Je débarque à Khaldé en début d'après-midi. Même mélange de douaniers débordés, de voyageurs en *galabiah* et turbans blancs, attendant l'avion pour Koweït, d'enfants en pleurs et de cages bourrées de volailles affolées. Et, au milieu de ce capharnaüm, un homme qui gesticule dans ma direction puis se fraye un chemin vers moi :

— Marek Halter? Je suis votre oncle séfarade, Jacob. L'oncle de votre cousine Gloria d'Argentine. Elle m'a prévenu de votre arrivée.

L'oncle Jacob m'a réservé une chambre à l'hôtel Alcazar. « C'est juste à côté de l'hôtel Saint-Georges, a-t-il dit d'un ton fier, et c'est moins cher. » Il m'y conduit en taxi. M'y installe. Donne un pourboire au portier.

Ferme la porte à clé. Attend un moment encore, comme aux aguets. Puis s'approche de moi et murmure tel un conspirateur :

— Savez-vous que le cousin Sidney est là ?

— Comment cela, le cousin Sidney ?

— Oui, notre cousin d'Amérique... Regardez plutôt...

En ouvrant le journal qu'il avait dans la poche à la page des « nouvelles du jour », il me montre un entrefilet soigneusement entouré d'un trait de bic bleu :

— Lisez... Mais lisez donc... C'est lui... Sidney Halter... Il a fait sa conférence hier soir... Trop tard, hein ! Vous auriez adoré l'écouter.

Puis, se rengorgeant et ménageant bien ses effets :

— Et puis, ce n'est pas tout... Il y a notre cousine Olga aussi... Vous savez bien, Olga... La fille de Rachel Lerner... Non, non, ils ne sont pas venus ensemble... Hasard, je vous dis... Pur et simple hasard... Mais elle était hier à la conférence et je les ai vus tous les deux ensemble... Je leur ai parlé de votre venue bien sûr... Sidney n'a pas été plus content que ça, notez bien... Préoccupé, je dirais... A moins que ce soit la réserve censément américaine... mais bon... J'ai tout arrangé... Taratata, je lui ai dit... C'est pas tous les jours la fête... On va se boire un arak après-demain soir à la terrasse du Saint-Georges avec le cousin français Marek...

Merci à l'oncle Jacob. Félicitations pour sa diligence. Un léger sourire intérieur, aussi, à l'idée de ces parents inconnus qui attendaient ce séjour à Beyrouth pour m'être révélés. L'essentiel pourtant n'est pas là. Si je suis venu ici c'est pour des raisons autrement plus sérieuses. Et c'est l'esprit ailleurs, d'un ton probablement détaché, que je réponds : « Oui, oncle Jacob, je me réjouis de ce verre » — avant de me jeter sur mon téléphone et de commencer, incontinent, mon enquête.

J'avais, en arrivant, quelques introductions. Quelques amitiés. Un écrivain français m'a recommandé à Marwan Dajani, un homme d'affaires palestinien, proprié-

129

taire du Strand Building, un énorme complexe commercial du quartier chic de Hamraa où Arafat et ses amis viennent régulièrement. Je m'y rends. La réceptionniste m'oriente vers une porte devant laquelle des feddayin armés filtrent les visiteurs. C'est le bureau de Marwan. Mobilier moderne. Téléphones. Secrétaires hyper-sexy. Marwan incarne, avec une visible satisfaction, l'image du businessman compétent et dynamique.

— Arafat et Abou Iyad seront ici demain, dit-il. Téléphonez-moi dans la matinée, je vous dirai quand vous pourrez passer.

Sur quoi, il appelle le bureau de Georges Habbache, discute un instant en arabe et me dit sans raccrocher :

— Habbache, lui, est parti pour Bagdad. En attendant son retour, Kanafani va vous recevoir...

Va pour Kanafani qui me reçoit dans le bureau même de Habbache. Préliminaires... Arak... Politesses en tout genre... Après un bref échange sur les mérites comparés des poésies française et arabe, nous entrons dans le vif du sujet :

— La révolution arabe peut éclater n'importe où ailleurs qu'en Palestine, commence-t-il. Mais la Palestine est son ferment.

— Vous voulez dire en Jordanie ?

— C'est à envisager.

Ghassan Kanafani est plein de contradictions. Et, pour cette raison peut-être, plus intéressant et plus attachant que ses camarades. Poète, il aime les mots. Mais, militant, il s'en méfie et leur préfère l'action.

— Le verbe n'est-il pas action ?

Il ne le croit pas, il ne croit donc pas aux vertus d'un dialogue avec les Israéliens. Pour lui, parler avec les Israéliens équivaudrait à les reconnaître. Et de cette reconnaissance, il ne veut à aucun prix. Ce qu'il pense de mes démarches dans ce cas ? « On ne sait jamais... Continuez toujours... Des fois que les Israéliens abandonnent le sionisme. » La vérité est qu'il préfère les Juifs aux Israéliens. Eux sont loin. Ils habitent à Moscou, Buenos Aires, New York, tandis que les Israéliens...

130

— Je vous ramène à l'hôtel ? propose-t-il quand il juge m'avoir tout dit.

Puis, ironique :

— A moins que vous n'ayez peur...

— De quoi aurais-je peur ?

— Je ne sais pas... Ma voiture est vieille et ses freins incertains...

— Et puis ?

— Et puis vous avez peut-être peur des terroristes ?

— Parce que vous êtes un terroriste ?

Il éclate de rire :

— Non, vous avez raison... Je suis un résistant... Un résistant à l'oppression impérialiste...

— Quelle oppression impérialiste ?

— Celle d'Israël.

— En tuant des innocents ?

— Pourquoi des innocents ?

Pensant le troubler, ou au moins le désarçonner, je lui raconte alors la mort de Hugo.

— Hugo Halter, répète-t-il, pensif... Hugo Halter... C'était certainement un malentendu... Que voulez-vous : quand on fait la guerre, il y a des balles perdues...

— Je vois que vous connaissez cette histoire... Dites-moi donc ce que vous savez.

Ghassan Kanafani sourit imperceptiblement :

— Tout cela est si loin maintenant... Je vous ai dit que c'est un malentendu...

Puis, comme j'insiste :

— Bon... Je vais vous donner une piste... Et vous verrez, du même coup, comme nous sommes bien renseignés... Vous avez des cousins Lerner... Si, si, ne faites pas cette tête... Nos dossiers sont à jour, vous savez... Eh bien la jeune Olga Lerner est ici... Oui, j'ai bien dit ici, à Beyrouth... Et l'extraordinaire, imaginez-vous, c'est qu'elle a un bon ami qui s'appelle Hidar Assadi et qui, lui, en sait long sur votre affaire...

Hidar Assadi... Bien sûr... Toujours les mêmes ! Ne faisait-il pas partie, donc, des intimes ou des contacts de Hugo ?

131

— Vous connaissez ce voyou ? me demandera l'oncle Jacob lorsque nous nous retrouverons.

— Quel voyou ?

— Celui qui vous a déposé à l'hôtel. Je le connais, vous savez... Ils veulent détruire Israël, mais ils vont détruire le Liban, vous verrez... J'espère seulement qu'ils ne vous feront pas de mal. Faites très attention...

— Ne vous inquiétez pas, cher oncle, lui dis-je en riant.

Et moi qui, le matin même, m'étais si peu intéressé à ses histoires de cousins miraculeusement rassemblés à Beyrouth, je le presse à présent de questions, lui demande comment était Sidney ; à quoi ressemble Olga ; avec qui elle était ; s'il a vu son compagnon ; et à ma grande surprise, je lui demande de bien vouloir avancer à aujourd'hui le rendez-vous familial du Saint-Georges.

17

BUENOS AIRES

UN AMOUR PRÉCOCE (suite)

Octobre 1969

— Je viens de recevoir une lettre de mon oncle Jacob, annonce Gloria au dîner. Il a accueilli notre cousin français. Tout va pour le mieux.

— Que fait le cousin à Beyrouth ? demande Anna-Maria.

— L'oncle ne le dit pas. Il dit seulement qu'il essaye de l'empêcher de « faire des bêtises ».

Anna-Maria éclate de rire :

— Les bêtises pour ton vieil oncle, c'est la politique ou l'amour. Alors de quoi s'agit-il ? Et à quoi ressemble le cousin français ? L'amour ? La politique ?

En parlant, elle frôle de son genou, sous la table, le genou d'Arié.

— Que sais-tu à ton âge de la politique et de l'amour ? lui demande ironiquement Martin.

— Je sais beaucoup de choses, papa... Je sais par exemple que toi, tu es et contre l'amour et contre la politique... Je me trompe ?

Sans l'avoir voulu, elle a élevé la voix. Personne plus que son père n'arrive à la mettre en colère.

— Pour l'amour, tu es trop jeune, lui répond-il ; quant à la politique, nous connaissons les résultats de son action. Auschwitz, Hiroshima, le goulag, ça ne te dit rien ?

Les yeux d'Anna-Maria deviennent plus noirs encore :

133

— Ce sont les horreurs du passé. Nous, nous luttons justement pour que cela ne se reproduise plus jamais...

— En tuant les gens ?

— En tuant les assassins.

— Qui décide qu'on est un assassin ?

— Certainement pas les petits-bourgeois comme toi !

La discussion, de badine, est devenue presque violente. Anna-Maria, furieuse, repousse sa chaise.

— On ne peut jamais manger tranquillement ici, crie-t-elle avec cette formidable mauvaise foi qu'elle a toujours dans ces cas-là et qu'elle n'est pas très loin de tenir pour une forme de l'esprit « dialectique ».

— Tu vois à quoi mène ce genre de discussions, fait Gloria à Martin, tandis que leur fille prend son manteau et s'apprête à sortir.

— Je l'accompagne, dit Arié en se levant à son tour et en se précipitant sur ses talons.

— Tu as fini de me courir après, gémit-elle, quand, à la hauteur de la rue Rodriguez Péna, il la rattrape.

— Pardon... Je ne savais pas que tu voulais être seule...

Anna-Maria fait encore quelques pas en direction de l'avenue Corrientes, avant de se retourner :

— Tu vas rester planté là jusqu'à ton retour en Israël ?

Arié s'approche :

— Je croyais...

— Tu n'as rien à croire...

L'avenue Corrientes est une grande avenue très animée, bordée de cafés et de magasins en tout genre où Arié s'attarde parfois quand, de l'école, il rentre à pied à la maison.

— Je suis content d'être ici avec toi, dit-il à mi-voix...

Puis, voyant qu'elle ne répond rien mais qu'elle a l'air plus calme :

— Dis-moi : je ne voudrais pas t'énerver, mais tu ne trouves pas que tu es dure avec ton père ?

— Tu ne vas tout de même pas prendre la défense de cé petit-bourgeois !

134

— Pourquoi pas, s'il a raison…

— Il a tort !

Ils font encore quelques pas et s'arrêtent à nouveau pour laisser passer le flot des voitures sur l'avenue 9 de Julio.

— Tu as dit tout à l'heure, que pour toi…

— Quoi pour moi ?

— L'amour et la politique sont les seules choses qui donnent un sens à la vie…

— Oui, je l'ai dit.

Et, en l'embrassant du bout des lèvres :

— Pour l'amour, vous, les Israéliens, vous êtes forts. Mais pour la politique, zéro. Vous pensez qu'en défendant votre État, vous réglez les problèmes de l'humanité.

— Ne reparlons pas de ça, je t'en prie… Tu sais bien que tu ne connais pas Israël ! Tu penses que les Israéliens ne manifestent pas contre la guerre du Vietnam, comme toi ici, à Buenos Aires ? Tu crois que nous ne savons pas que les gens meurent de faim dans les favelas du Brésil ?

— Va donc ! Vous ne savez même pas protéger les Juifs qui viennent vous rendre visite !

— Tu parles de Hugo ?

— Oui, Hugo que tu admires tant !…

Le feu est passé au vert et une foule de piétons les entraîne en direction de l'élégante rue Florida. Anna-Maria s'arrête et, comme si elle s'éveillait d'un rêve, consulte soudain sa montre :

— Zut et zut et zut… Elle est arrêtée !

Et s'adressant à Arié :

— Tu as l'heure ?

— Oui, dix heures dix.

— Dix heures dix ? Mon Dieu ! c'est épouvantable ! Je ne savais pas qu'il était si tard… Rentrons… Rentrons vite, je t'en prie…

— Pourquoi si vite ? Il est encore très tôt…

— Mais non ! Viens… Ne pose pas de questions… Je t'expliquerai plus tard… Je t'en supplie…

Et de fait, ils n'ont pas parcouru plus de cent mètres

au milieu de cette foule incroyablement dense qui se presse sur le trottoir, ils n'ont pas échangé plus de deux ou trois phrases, qu'ils entendent une déflagration terrible. Les vitres des magasins alentour volent en éclats. La foule est prise de folie. En une seconde, la panique y creuse des vagues contraires, des tourbillons irrésistibles. Les klaxons se mettent à hurler. Les enfants à pleurer. Les sirènes des voitures de police et des ambulances à retentir dans le lointain.

— Que se passe-t-il ? Que se passe-t-il ? demandent les gens autour d'eux...

— Une bombe ! dit quelqu'un.

— Une bombe ! répète la foule.

— Oui, une bombe d'une puissance incroyable qui a éclaté devant l'ambassade des Etats-Unis, rue Sarmiento... Il y a deux morts... Non, dix... Non, cent...

Arié, abasourdi, suit Anna-Maria comme un automate :

— Où m'emmènes-tu ? Dis-moi, où m'emmènes-tu ? Où allons-nous ?

Anna-Maria, hagarde elle aussi, échevelée, semble ne pas entendre. Elle court. Elle vole. Et ce n'est que place Lavalle, loin de la foule des grands boulevards, devant une vieille maison coloniale au portail de bois sculpté, qu'elle consent à s'arrêter.

— Ah, oui ! fait-elle, comme si elle s'apercevait seulement de la présence du jeune garçon à ses côtés... Tu es là... Bon. Ne bouge pas... Je dois entrer ici... Je reviens tout de suite... N'aie pas peur...

Arié attend quelques minutes, devant le portail, comme elle le lui a demandé. Puis, curieux, traverse la rue pour mieux voir. Des lumières se sont allumées au premier étage. Il distingue plusieurs personnes pénétrant dans une pièce. Il lui semble reconnaître, au milieu de ces gens, Anna-Maria gesticulant avec violence. Que font-ils ? Se disputent-ils ? Arié en est à déchiffrer cet étrange théâtre d'ombres lorsque la sirène d'une voiture de police retentit dans l'avenue voisine. L'obscurité se fait instantanément dans l'appartement. Guidé par son instinct, il s'éloigne légèrement et se dissimule dans

136

l'ombre d'un autre portail abrité sous un porche. La voiture de la police est là. Elle s'arrête juste devant la maison face à laquelle il se tenait il y a un instant. Des policiers — ils sont cinq — disparaissent aussitôt dans l'embrasure de la porte. On entend une cavalcade. Des appels. Des ordres. Arié voit un groupe de jeunes gens qui sortent par une porte latérale. Les policiers qui ressortent deux secondes plus tard, à leur suite. Cavalcade à nouveau. Coups de feu. Un cri. Un juron.

— Anna-Maria ! appelle-t-il doucement à l'instant où le groupe passe à sa hauteur.

Anna-Maria l'entend. S'arrête un dixième de seconde. Le voit. Fait un pas de côté, dans l'ombre du porche où il est caché. Et comme dans cette scène qu'il a maintes fois vue au cinéma, il serre la jeune fille contre lui et l'embrasse longuement tandis que les « policia militar » se lancent à la poursuite des jeunes gens. Un coup de revolver. Un autre. Une voiture qui démarre, suivie d'une seconde. Quand, enfin, il desserre son étreinte, la rue est déserte.

— Maintenant, on peut partir, dit-il calmement.

Mais, c'est seulement lorsqu'ils se mêlent à la foule de l'avenue Corrientes qu'Anna-Maria se détend :

— Merci, dit-elle. Tu as été formidable...

Puis, après quelques pas, retrouvant cette soif étrange que seule l'action assouvit :

— Maintenant, il faut vérifier que personne ne s'est fait prendre.

Et, comme son jeune cousin l'interroge du regard :

— Eh oui ! Nous aussi, tu vois, nous sommes en guerre...

Arié fait un bond !

— Ainsi donc, c'était vous !

— Oui, bien sûr, c'était nous...

— Nous, on fait la guerre quand il n'y a plus d'autre moyen... « B'ein Breïra », dit mon père, tandis que vous...

— Nous c'est pareil, Arié. C'est la même chose...

Le visage mat d'Arié rougit d'émotion. Ses yeux se plissent, il élève la voix :

137

— Comment peux-tu dire cela ! C'est de la démence ! C'est ignoble !

— Ne crie pas... Calme-toi... Les gens vont nous entendre...

Arié s'approche tout près d'elle et lui siffle dans le visage :

— Quand on est en guerre, on est en face de soldats armés. Vous, vous tuez des gens désarmés. Des passants. Peut-être vos propres amis... Comment peux-tu soutenir des actes aussi irresponsables ?

Il en pleure presque. Il ne sait trop si c'est de rage, d'effroi, d'amour — ou bien des trois...

— Calme-toi, répète Anna-Maria. J'ai bien vu que tu ne comprenais rien à la politique.

Elle essaye de garder le même ton décidé mais le cœur n'y est pas. Elle aussi est bouleversée. Ses grands yeux noirs ont perdu leur étincelle d'ironie. Et elle marche à présent d'un pas nerveux, saccadé.

— Comment peux-tu défendre une telle chose, répète Arié derrière elle. Oui, comment ?

Anna-Maria ne répond pas. A la hauteur du théâtre municipal San Martin, elle lui dit simplement — sans oser le regarder en face :

— Maintenant tu peux rentrer.

— Et toi ?

— J'ai encore un rendez-vous.

— Du même genre que celui de tout à l'heure ?

Elle fait non de la tête et sourit tristement :

— J'ai promis à une amie communiste de passer la voir. Il y aura quelques Cubains, Soviétiques...

— Comment ça, des communistes ? C'est bien ce que je dis : les mêmes gens que tout à l'heure...

— Mais non ! Les communistes, ici, s'entendent très bien avec les militaires... Ils font même de très bonnes affaires ensemble.

— Mais... N'aident-ils pas la guérilla ?

Anna-Maria passe tendrement la main dans la noire tignasse d'Arié :

— Je t'ai bien dit que tu ne connaissais rien en politique. Va, on se verra demain...

138

— Je pensais...

Arié s'appuie contre un arbre et la regarde droit dans les yeux, avec une insolence qu'elle ne lui a jamais connue :

— Qu'y a-t-il ? demande-t-elle.

— Je voudrais t'accompagner.

— Eh bien oui, après tout, si tu veux...

Deux pièces au quatrième étage. De la fumée de cigarette. Un spot qui éclaire à peine un tableau du peintre communiste argentin Castanina. Des hommes, des femmes, la plupart jeunes, discutant un verre à la main.

— Mais c'est Anna-Maria ! s'exclame une fille rondelette, à lunettes. Qui est ce jeune homme ?

— Mon cousin.

— Bienvenue au cousin d'Anna-Maria, dit-elle dans un grand sourire.

Elle sort de la poche de son jean un paquet de cigarettes, en allume une et dit tout bas, sur un ton de fausse confidence :

-— La discussion était vraiment passionnante. Ces Soviétiques sont des hommes admirables. Un pays qui produit de tels hommes, bravo !

18

BEYROUTH

LA QUÊTE DU PASSÉ

Octobre 1969

Ces deux rencontres, coup sur coup, ont bien évidemment troublé Sidney. Olga d'abord à la Grotte aux Pigeons. Puis le cousin français, deux jours plus tard, au Saint-Georges. Comment cela est-il possible ? Quel est ce destin capable de réunir trois survivants éparpillés à travers le monde, d'une seule et même famille juive sur cette terre hostile qu'est Beyrouth ?

Si Olga, avec sa gaieté et sa spontanéité naturelle, l'a tout à fait séduit, il se méfie, en revanche, de Hidar qui en sait manifestement plus qu'il ne veut l'admettre sur les dernières années de Hugo. Quant à Marek, il l'a sans doute trouvé sympathique, même s'il refuse sa démarche. Il ne croit pas en l'efficacité de la parole face au déferlement de la violence. Vouloir parler à tout prix de paix avec des terroristes qui ne pensent qu'à tuer lui paraît l'expression d'une inconscience d'autant moins pardonnable qu'elle est lourde de dangers. Vous me rappelez Hugo, lui a-t-il dit. Pourquoi ? Il n'aurait su l'expliquer exactement. C'était juste une intuition. Mais c'était assez pour marquer entre eux cette *distance* qui interdit les complicités véritables. « Faire la paix en parlant... » ricane-t-il encore, seul dans sa chambre après leur départ à tous... « Et pourquoi pas, tant qu'on y est, gagner la guerre en parlant ? Si cela pouvait marcher, on n'aurait plus besoin d'envoyer des GI's au Vietnam, on y enverrait des phraseurs... » Il trouve cette idée fort drôle, se déshabille, prend sa douche et repense à nouveau aux événements des derniers jours. « Incroyable, se répète-t-il... Oui, incroyable... La vie est vraiment ironie. » Et comme s'il lui fallait absolument raconter à quelqu'un la vie « inouïe » qui est la sienne, il décide tout à coup d'appeler Jérémie Cohen.

— Alors comment va l'amour ? s'écrie celui-ci quand il l'a au bout du fil. C'est gentil de me téléphoner... Quelle surprise !

— Devine qui j'ai rencontré aujourd'hui à Beyrouth ?

— Pas Marjory. Je l'ai vue tout à l'heure sur Madison, avec ta fille. Très mignonne.

— C'est vrai ? Comment vont-elles ?

— Très bien. Mais je présume que ce n'est pas pour ça que tu m'appelles. Alors, qui as-tu rencontré ?

— Ma cousine de Moscou et mon cousin de Paris.

— Vous aviez un conseil de famille ?

— Il n'y a pas de quoi rigoler, Jérémie !

— Pourquoi, c'était si triste ?

— Disons que ça m'a compliqué la vie pour Leïla... Tu vois ce que je veux dire : comme discrétion, on a fait mieux !

— OK, mon pote... Tu arrangeras ça demain, tu sais bien...

— Oui, mais il y a autre chose.

— Vas-y !

— Tu te souviens de mon cousin Hugo ?

— Non, mais tu m'en as parlé. Celui qui s'est fait tuer en Israël ?

— Exact.

— Tu l'as rencontré à Beyrouth ?

— Jérémie !

— Bon, bon... Mais accouche ! Qu'est-ce qui t'arrive avec ton fichu cousin Hugo ?

— Écoute... C'est difficile à expliquer... Mais j'ai

vu ces cousins... On avait mille choses à se dire... Et alors que cette histoire est déjà vieille de huit ans, c'est quand même d'elle qu'on a parlé le plus... Tu ne trouves pas ça étrange?

— Les histoires de famille, tu sais...

— Non, non, ce n'est pas une histoire de famille comme les autres! Car voici le plus curieux: on a eu beau parler, échanger chacun nos informations, ça ne nous a menés à rien. Moi, par exemple, au lieu d'obtenir des réponses, j'ai eu l'impression de buter sur mes propres questions...

— Ouais...

— Je vais peut-être te paraître abscons. Mais on dirait que Hugo, chargé par le grand-père de veiller sur le Livre, a, par sa mystérieuse disparition, dépossédé la famille de la connaissance de sa propre histoire, suscitant chez tous une égale frustration du passé. Ou bien, si tu préfères: c'est comme dans les romans d'Agatha Christie où l'on n'est pas apaisé avant le dénouement du mystère; Hugo, tué, a transformé tous ses cousins et cousines en détectives à la recherche d'indices contre l'oubli.

Sidney n'a pas tort. Car à l'instant même où il expose son trouble à Jérémie, je campe, moi, à la pâtisserie Pierrot, rue Georges-Picot, non loin de l'hôtel Alcazar où, parmi les secrétaires des ambassades toutes proches qui avalent leurs gâteaux au miel en papotant, je discute avec... Hidar. Enfin. Importante, cette rencontre avec Hidar. De toute évidence, lui se méfie de moi. Suis-je membre des services secrets israéliens, américains ou français, cela il ne le sait pas. Mais il est persuadé que je suis l'un des trois. Quelle raison pourrait pousser un jeune homme qui n'était ni israélien ni arabe dans pareil bourbier? Encore que Hugo... C'est fou, me dit-il lui aussi, combien je lui rappelle Hugo. Non pas physiquement. Mais à ma manière de parler, de regarder, d'agir, et justement à mon accent. Est-ce qu'un même homme peut ainsi revenir en plusieurs incarnations ? me demande-t-il en riant. Pour moi, en tout cas, la rencontre est, je le répète, importante car cet Hidar, je le sens, sait des choses. Il est dépositaire d'une part, au moins, du secret. Et puisque le destin, en la personne de ma cousine Olga, l'a mis sur mon chemin...

Pour le mettre en confiance, je commence par lui parler du carnet de Hugo.

— Un carnet d'adresses ?

— Oui, une sorte de carnet d'adresses.

— Et mon nom y figure ?

— Votre nom y figure.

— Avec d'autres ?

— Avec d'autres.

Hidar s'accoude lourdement sur la table, manquant la déséquilibrer et me fixe de ses yeux noirs, presque bridés :

— Et avez-vous retrouvé tous les gens qui figurent dans le carnet ?

Le ton trop appuyé me met sur mes gardes. Je prends un moment pour répondre.

— Presque...

— Pourquoi presque ?

— Parce que...

— Cela veut dire pas tous ?

— En effet.

Hidar se détend :

— C'est une histoire inouïe. Si vous aviez le carnet avec vous, je pourrais peut-être vous aider à situer les noms que vous ne connaissez pas...

Je souris...

— Non ! Ce carnet est la seule source de notre savoir familial. Je préfère ne pas le faire circuler.

Et comme Hidar fronce les sourcils, se sentant ostensiblement attaqué, j'ajoute :

— Je suis persuadé, quant à moi, que vous connaissez les raisons de sa mort et que vous ne voulez ou ne pouvez pas les révéler.

Hidar sursaute :

— De quoi parlez-vous ?

— Pardonnez ma franchise. Mais je répète : vous savez des choses que je ne sais pas et...

— Je ne vois pas ce qui vous permet de dire ça.

— Un sentiment, juste un sentiment.

— Eh bien, franchise pour franchise, je voudrais vous dire que je n'aime ni les voyants ni les prophètes...

Puis, après un silence et en me saisissant par l'épaule :

— J'aimais beaucoup Hugo. C'était le meilleur ami de mon père. Et c'est grâce à sa générosité que j'ai pu commencer mes études...

— Vous l'avez donc revu après la guerre ?

Hidar paraît méditer. Un sourire plisse ses lèvres.

— Je vous l'ai dit : vous me rappelez Hugo. Lui aussi avait cette sorte de franchise agressive et cependant, amicale. C'est quelqu'un qui croyait au pouvoir de la vérité.

Puis, encore :

— Je vous assure qu'avec son carnet vous avez beaucoup plus d'informations que moi qui l'ai connu !

Et changeant de sujet :

— Je sais que vous connaissez beaucoup de monde. Comment est Golda Meïr ? Vous l'avez rencontrée ? Et Moshé Dayan ?

Mais il se fait tard et les jours sont courts en septembre. Brusquement, la lumière jaillit des néons. Éblouis, nous fermons les yeux et les rouvrons en même temps dans un grand éclat de rire.

— Pour les contacts entre les Israéliens et les Palestiniens, vous pouvez compter sur moi, dit Hidar presque solennellement. A Moscou, on est intéressé. Il n'y a sans doute pas d'autres solutions au conflit.

A ce moment, on frappe avec insistance contre la vitre de la pâtisserie, Hidar se lève. C'est Olga.

— Bonjour, cousin, dit-elle en sautant à mon cou.

Et, à Hidar :

— Je commençais à m'impatienter.

Elle contemple le plateau chargé de gâteaux et s'exclame :

144

— Merci de n'avoir pas tout mangé !

En rentrant à l'hôtel, j'appelle ma mère pour lui faire part de ma rencontre et pour lui demander, aussi, d'aller récupérer chez moi le carnet de Hugo et de le déposer dans un coffre à la banque.

Beyrouth, octobre 1969

— Hugo était votre cousin ? Alors, pardonnez-moi ma franchise : je ne vous félicite pas.

Le rabbin Ben Moussa pointe vers moi sa barbe, comme un oiseau son bec. Il trépigne de colère :

— Il est écrit dans Pirkeï Avot : « Soyez sur vos gardes dans vos rapports avec les puissants car c'est dans leur intérêt qu'ils se rendent accessibles. » Votre cousin était bien trop heureux de parvenir à les fréquenter pour s'apercevoir du danger. Et pis : du danger qu'il faisait courir à son prochain. Car écoutez bien cela : pour atteindre les grands de ce monde, il utilisait des gens, des *humbles,* sans songer au péril où il les mettait. Je vous le dis : Hugo Halter était un fou dangereux.

La scène se passe dans une petite synagogue de Beyrouth-Est. Une salle obscure avec quelques bancs et une armoire qui abrite les Rouleaux de la Loi.

— Tenez… Un exemple… Pour contacter Kamal Joumblatt, continue le rabbin Ben Moussa, Hugo s'est servi d'un marchand juif, David Stara, qui alimentait en farine les boulangeries du Shouff. Eh bien, comme il a rencontré par la suite les Frangié et les Gemayel, les Druzes ont cru qu'il espionnait pour le compte des chrétiens, et à qui en ont-ils voulu ? A Stara !

— Et alors ?

— Et alors, on a retrouvé le pauvre Stara égorgé dans les environs de Moukhtara.

— Et pour vous, c'est Hugo le responsable ?

— Ce n'est pas sûr que oui et ce n'est pas sûr que non. On a volé de l'argent à David Stara, mais cela ne veut rien dire. Sa mort est là. Hugo, lui, a pu continuer à parader avec les puissants tandis que le pauvre Stara n'est plus de ce monde.

— Hugo a été tué lui aussi.

Le rabbin Ben Moussa, manifestement, l'ignore.

— Tué ? Tué où ?

— En Israël, au cours d'un attentat palestinien.

D'un geste rapide, il frôle les poils de sa barbe et, aussitôt, cite un psaume : « Ils avaient tendu un filet sous mes pas, mon âme se courbait ; ils avaient creusé un fossé devant moi : ils y sont tombés. »

Puis, en me raccompagnant à la porte :

— Hugo est mort, alors n'en parlons plus. Respectons le commandement : « Quand le mort repose, laisse reposer sa mémoire. » Mais attention, jeune homme : il n'y a pas de saints... Il n'y a pas de héros... ici-bas, dans la vallée de larmes et de misères, la perfection n'est pas... et vous auriez grand tort d'idéaliser ce cousin jusqu'à en faire un de nos prophètes... Voilà ce que j'ai voulu vous dire.

19

BEYROUTH-NEW YORK

LE RETOUR À NEW YORK

Novembre 1969

Sidney quitte Beyrouth, le cœur barbouillé d'angoisse. Il est devenu un homme divisé. Le corps de Leïla commence à lui manquer avant même les adieux et il se demande avec inquiétude comment il va pouvoir reprendre une liaison normale avec son épouse. De plus, cette rencontre familiale si inattendue n'a fait que le troubler. Ce qu'Olga lui a dit de ses parents, de leur vie, de leur volonté de partir pour Israël et de leurs rapports difficiles avec Sacha lui semble dramatique. La course pathétique de Salomon à la recherche du passé et sa mort avant de l'avoir retrouvé, tout cela le bouleverse. Le carnet d'adresses de Hugo l'intrigue et quant aux mystérieux préparatifs des Palestiniens dont j'ai eu vent et dont je lui ai — peut-être à tort — parlé, ils lui font peur. Peur pour Israël. Peur pour le monde. Peur pour Mordekhaï, là-bas en Galilée, dans son kibboutz de Dafné.

Sidney ne croit pas que ces organisations terroristes palestiniennes puissent jamais s'orienter vers la paix. Il sait, bien sûr, que si je vois tous ces hommes c'est pour la bonne cause. Il sait que c'est dans l'espoir d'arriver un jour à la paix, fût-ce en leur concédant le droit à un État indépendant à côté d'Israël. Mais est-ce que tous ces efforts en valent la peine ? La force militaire d'Israël n'est-elle pas la meilleure, la seule garantie de survie ?

Sidney est convaincu que si la paix vient un jour ce sera le triomphe, non de la morale, mais de l'intérêt bien compris de diverses puissances. Et c'est, selon lui, une perspective bien lointaine. En attendant ? En attendant il faut gagner du temps, c'est-à-dire aider Israël à se défendre et à se développer. Juste avant son départ il a été impressionné par une manifestation d'étudiants palestiniens à l'université américaine. Sympathiques, de prime abord... Envie de les défendre, de les aimer... En les voyant remplir le campus avec leurs drapeaux et leurs chants, il a pensé instantanément aux jeunes sionistes d'avant la naissance de l'État d'Israël... Mais pourquoi a-t-il fallu que ceux auxquels il a parlé soient partis dans des diatribes antijuives ? Pourquoi cette jeune fille, si belle avec ses yeux gris, ses nattes brunes, ses formes provocantes, lui a-t-elle expliqué que l'holocauste est une invention des sionistes ? Pourquoi faut-il, pour réclamer le droit à un État, dénier aux Juifs le droit au leur ? Pis : le droit à un passé, à *leur* passé ?

Arrive l'heure du dîner. C'est le meilleur moment du voyage en avion. Comme à l'hôpital. Les deux seuls endroits où il fait bon se laisser prendre en charge. Il demande un whisky à l'hôtesse. Voyant que son voisin préfère le champagne, il regrette aussitôt son choix. Mais un orgueil imbécile lui interdisant de changer sa commande, il vide son verre qu'il trouve particulièrement amer. Il attend ensuite que l'hôtesse le débarrasse du plateau et que le commandant finisse d'assener des informations sans importance. Quand, enfin, le haut-parleur se tait, il s'étire voluptueusement sur son siège et tente de chasser Beyrouth de son esprit...

— Vous êtes de New York ? lui demande brusquement son voisin.

— Oui, répond Sidney à contrecœur.

— Vous étiez à Beyrouth en visite ou pour le travail ?

— Pour le travail.

L'homme se mouche soigneusement et s'excuse :

— Je suis enrhumé.

Puis :

— Quel travail ?

— Conférences à l'Université américaine...

— Vous êtes professeur ?

— Non, je suis médecin.

L'homme parle anglais avec un accent arabe fort prononcé. Sidney l'observe un moment. Il a le front dégarni, les yeux légèrement globuleux, la taille corpulente, de la sueur sur le visage.

— Vous êtes libanais ? demande à son tour Sidney.

— Non, péruvien.

— Ah bon. Mais avant ?

L'homme éclate de rire.

— Avant quoi ?

Sidney ne répond pas. Il n'a pas envie de poursuivre et s'en veut déjà de cet « avant ». Mais son voisin, lui, tient visiblement à lier connaissance :

— Je vis à Lima, depuis plusieurs années. Mais vous avez raison, je ne suis pas péruvien.

— Alors, vous êtes arabe.

— Comment l'avez-vous deviné ?

— A votre accent.

— Oui, je suis arabe. Mais arabe de quel pays ?

— Je ne sais pas.

Cet aveu d'ignorance paraît clore la conversation et Sidney profite du silence retrouvé pour s'assoupir. Mais non ! L'autre revient à la charge :

— Connaissez-vous Bethléem ?

— Hum...

— Je suis originaire de Beït Jallah, près de Bethléem.

— Ah ?

— Oui.

L'homme de Bethléem tend cérémonieusement la main :

— Je m'appelle Jael el-Ardja.

— Et moi, Sidney Halter.

— Juif ?

— Juif.

— Vous aimez Israël ?

— Évidemment !

— Colonie américaine !

— Eh oui...

Sidney fait tout pour fuir le débat. Mais l'autre semble en veine de confidence :

— Remarquez, j'admire les Juifs. Ils sont les seuls à avoir eu assez de génie pour récrire l'histoire.

— Quelle histoire ?

— Celle de la dernière guerre. L'invention des chambres à gaz, par exemple, leur a permis de monter et de réussir une gigantesque fraude politique et financière dont le principal bénéficiaire est Israël et le sionisme international.

Cette fois, Sidney sursaute. Il s'apprête à répondre mais une secousse puis la voix du commandement, qui demande « pour cause de turbulences » d'attacher les ceintures, l'en empêchent. Pour la seconde fois en quarante-huit heures, il rencontre chez des Arabes cette étrange volonté de négation : non par sympathie pour le criminel mais par antipathie pour la victime...

Mais Jael el-Ardja reprend. Malgré son anti-américanisme, il aime séjourner en Amérique. Et sur le chemin de Lima, il ne manque jamais de s'arrêter à New York où il descend au Méridien. Est-ce que Sidney connaît le Méridien ? Le Hilton ? Bien sûr, ce n'est pas pareil quand on est soi-même américain...

— Je serais content de vous revoir, conclut-il à la fin du voyage.

— Je vous ai pourtant dit que je suis juif...

— Mes meilleurs amis sont juifs...

Et, brusquement :

— Connaissez-vous Ben Gourion ?

— Oui, bien sûr.

— Personnellement ?

— Oh non, je n'ai pas cette chance...

— Il paraît qu'il doit bientôt se rendre en Amérique latine. J'aurai peut-être, moi, la chance de le rencontrer.

— Oui ? fait Sidney.

Il a l'impression que son voisin lui jette un regard ironique mais le sommeil le gagne et il s'endort enfin.

Le New York qu'il retrouve est paralysé par une énorme manifestation contre la guerre du Vietnam. La presse américaine parle d'une journée historique. Les organisateurs, d'un « succès sans précédent ». La radio du taxi, qui avance péniblement dans les embouteillages, annonce un grand discours du président Nixon pour le 3 novembre. Marjory attend à la maison. Elle a acheté des fleurs, préparé le gâteau au fromage qu'il préfère.

— Ton frère Larry et sa femme sont à New York, annonce-t-elle. Je les ai invités à venir fêter ton retour. Il y aura aussi ton cousin David et sa nouvelle « girlfriend ». Elle travaille à l'ONU. Il paraît que c'est une brave fille...

Comme on est loin de Beyrouth !

20

BUENOS AIRES

L'AMOUR PRÉCOCE (fin)

Novembre 1969

C'est un beau dimanche d'hiver, très chaud, comme il y en a parfois à Buenos Aires. Dona Regina a dû remplacer le bouillon rituel par un gaspacho espagnol qui a l'avantage de se manger froid. Don Israël arbore sur son maillot de corps deux larges bretelles rouges et s'expose avec volupté au courant d'air provoqué par les hélices d'un antique ventilateur bourdonnant sans répit sur la commode. La famille est réunie pour souhaiter l'anniversaire d'Arié. Dix-sept ans, ça se fête !

Anna-Maria, comme à son habitude, taquine sa grand-mère. Martin la gronde. Anna-Maria lui répond. Martin se fâche et pour changer de sujet lance à la compagnie :

— Gloria a reçu hier une seconde lettre de son oncle du Liban. Imaginez-vous qu'il a fait connaissance avec le cousin Sidney de New York et la cousine Olga de Moscou.

— Olga, la sœur de Sacha ? demande Dona Regina.

— Oui.

— Le communiste ?

— C'est ça.

— Décidément, la famille nous envahit, remarque Anna-Maria.

Arié sursaute :

— Merci pour la famille !

Son espagnol s'améliore tous les jours. Et son accent devient de plus en plus celui de Buenos Aires, l'accent « porteño », reconnaissable entre tous.

— Ne sois pas susceptible, dit la jeune fille en lui pinçant le bout du nez.

Mais Gloria leur lit déjà la lettre. Et, une fois la lecture faite, tout le monde se met à parler à la fois. Don Israël s'étonne de cette brusque floraison familiale. Anna-Maria ironise sur « l'hostilité primaire » de l'oncle Jacob envers les Palestiniens. Et Arié, qui connaît Sidney, se demande ce qu'il fait à Beyrouth. Mais, le plus touché, visiblement, par le contenu de la lettre de l'oncle Jacob, est encore Mordekhaï.

— Qu'est-ce que tu as, papa ? demande Arié.

Mordekhaï, qui est demeuré silencieux depuis le début du repas, plisse les yeux.

— Hidar, Hidar Assadi... dit-il ému. Cet Hidar dont parle l'oncle de Gloria n'est-il pas celui-là même qui, encore presque enfant, a connu Hugo à Tunis ?

— Le cousin Hugo qui s'est fait tuer en Israël ? demande Martin.

— Oui. Le père de Hidar et lui étaient très amis pendant la guerre. Et j'ai cru comprendre... Oui, on m'a dit, en Israël, que Hidar connaissait sans doute les assassins de Hugo.

L'information apportée par Mordekhaï occupe tout le reste de l'après-midi. Des amis de Dona Regina venus pour le thé participent bruyamment au débat. On parle aussi du conflit israélo-arabe, de la Varsovie d'avant-guerre, de la fuite du temps. Don Israël, qui aime les blagues, en raconte quelques-unes. Anna-Maria, au bout d'un moment, s'approche d'Arié :

— Je dois partir, lui dit-elle.

Il croit percevoir dans sa voix une sourde inquiétude.

— Je t'accompagne.

N'a-t-il pas été assez ferme ? Assez mâle résolu ? Sa jolie cousine, inflexible, secoue la tête :

— Non.

— C'est une réunion secrète ?

— Très secrète.

— Je te revois ?

— Je t'appellerai.

Dona Regina les regarde depuis une minute avec un mélange d'indulgence et de curiosité :

— Alors, les jeunes, vous complotez ?

Anna-Maria se lève :

— J'ai un rendez-vous.

— Tu rentres tard ?

— Je ne sais pas encore.

— Ah, ces jeunes... soupire Dona Regina...

Et, à la cantonade :

— Le bel âge, n'est-ce pas ? Moi, quand j'avais vingt ans...

La réunion a lieu rue Chacabuco, dans un vaste appartement loué récemment par le mouvement. C'est un appartement bourgeois, très simplement meublé et les fleurs bordeaux qui courent sur les lourds rideaux se retrouvent à l'identique sur tous les tissus d'ameublement. Seul un poster de Che Guevara témoigne des convictions des nouveaux occupants. Les responsables des FAR (Forces armées péronistes) et des Montoneros (Jeunesses péronistes) s'y réunissent depuis quelques jours pour coordonner leurs actions.

Quand Anna-Maria entre, ils sont tous déjà là. Sauf le poète Julio Feldman qui doit venir en compagnie d'un nouveau fournisseur d'armes. De fait, les deux hommes arrivent quelques minutes plus tard. Julio est un grand jeune homme aux yeux bruns, à la moustache grisonnante. Son compagnon a le teint basané, de grosses lunettes fumées qui cachent mal un regard globuleux et, très affairé, il ne cesse de parler à l'oreille d'un Julio très pâle et discrètement attentif.

Mario qui est apparemment le « leader » du groupe, commence :

— La lutte que nous menons n'est pas facile. Et elle le sera de moins en moins. Après la série d'attentats que nous préparons, on peut prédire une terrible répression.

Il regarde autour de lui :

— Aussi, ceux qui veulent abandonner le peuvent encore.

— Il n'est pas question d'abandonner, Mario, fait Julio en lançant un coup d'œil craintif en direction de son compagnon aux lunettes fumées. Nous n'allons pas compromettre notre lutte à cause de la faiblesse ou de la lâcheté de tel ou tel.

— Vous avez peur d'une dénonciation ? demande quelqu'un.

Julio, l'air sombre, ne répond d'abord pas. Tout le monde est suspendu à ses lèvres :

— Je n'ai pas peur d'une dénonciation, dit-il enfin, mais de la faiblesse humaine… D'une naturelle faiblesse humaine… Il y a des gens qui préfèrent être lâches que malheureux…

— Allons, poète !

Mario pose sa main sur l'épaule de Julio :

— Il ne s'agit ni de lâcheté ni de malheur. Se battre pour une société meilleure est un bonheur et tout le monde n'a pas cette chance. Mais il faut reconnaître que cette lutte est difficile. Alors, autant prévenir…

— Il n'y a pas de bonheur qui tienne, insiste Julio. Ce que nous faisons est un devoir. Et si nous sommes là, c'est que nous en acceptons le risque.

— Ça va ! Ça va ! s'écrie un petit bonhomme grassouillet dans le fond de la pièce. Nous n'avons pas de temps à perdre en parlotes !

— En parlotes ? demande Mario, en rejetant d'un mouvement de tête les cheveux qui cachaient son regard. Un révolutionnaire n'est pas un tueur. Quand il accepte de poser une bombe, il doit savoir pourquoi et le faire en toute conscience…

— Et moi, l'interrompt le petit gros en s'approchant, je ne suis pas d'accord. Mais pas d'accord du tout… Il y a le temps pour la théorie et le temps pour l'action. La théorie c'était hier… Julio nous a amené le « compañero » palestinien… Qu'il fasse état de ses propositions.

L'homme aux lunettes fumées s'agite légèrement, comme s'il allait parler. Mais, après réflexion, il se tasse sur lui-même, glisse les mains dans ses poches et attend

156

placidement comme si la question posée concernait un autre que lui. Julio répond à sa place :

— Le compañero Jael nous a fourni quatre caisses de bâtons de dynamite, cinquante-deux revolvers et un millier de cartouches.

— Qu'est-ce que nous donnons en échange ? demande Mario.

— Nous nous sommes engagés à rembourser tous les frais occasionnés par le transport d'armes.

— Et qui paiera les armes ?

Julio se frotte le front à plusieurs reprises, geste familier qu'il oppose toujours aux situations embarrassantes.

— Des « compañeros » palestiniens luttent contre l'impérialisme au Proche-Orient. Leur représentant en Amérique latine, Jael el-Ardja, est avec nous ce soir. Mais la lutte anti-impérialiste est aujourd'hui planétaire... Ils ont donc besoin... comment dire ?... d'un relais en Amérique latine. Nous serons ce relais.

— Comment cela ? demande Anna-Maria qui n'a pas encore pris la parole. Devrons-nous plastiquer l'ambassadeur d'Israël ?

Mouvement parmi les présents. Julio se frotte le front à nouveau et dit :

— Non, nos amis palestiniens ne nous demandent pas ça. Il s'agit de contrecarrer la propagande sioniste... Faire connaître les positions révolutionnaires arabes...

— Et moi, interrompt le petit gros, je proteste... Je proteste de toutes mes forces... Je veux... Je veux qu'on dise franchement aux compañeros du Proche-Orient que nous les soutenons, que nous sommes prêts s'il le faut à aller dans les camps palestiniens en Jordanie pour les entraîner — mais que l'action internationale d'un révolutionnaire argentin ne peut pas se limiter à une propagande anti-israélienne. Surtout que, en Israël, existe aussi un prolétariat qui lutte, une gauche qui partage nos idées...

Il reprend son souffle et lâche :

— Que le diable l'emporte, compañeros ! C'est stupide ce que vous nous proposez ! Votre attitude n'est pas du tout révolutionnaire !

Mario intervient brutalement :

— Cesse de gueuler, Roberto ! Tu voulais de l'action et pas de théories ? Alors, sache que pour l'action nous avons besoin d'armes, que pour les armes il faut payer et que pour payer... D'ailleurs, va au diable ! Tu ne fais que m'embrouiller...

La discussion se prolonge. Le Palestinien n'a pas ouvert la bouche mais tout le monde a compris que si l'on veut des armes, il faut en payer le prix...

Pendant toute la discussion, Anna-Maria a pensé à Arié et cette pensée l'a rendue malheureuse. Julio, le poète, a-t-il deviné son tourment ? Avant de la quitter, il lui conseille d'un ton amical mais ferme :

— A ce stade de notre action, tu ferais mieux de lâcher ton cousin israélien. Sauf si tu décides de nous abandonner... Tu ne peux concilier les deux.

— Et si j'abandonne l'action ?

Julio la regarde longuement et son sourire devient mauvais :

— Tu sais bien que personne n'a le droit d'abandonner la cause.

« Pauvre Arié », pense Anna-Maria.

Tel-Aviv, mai 1970

La veille de la fête de Chavouot, je débarque d'un 747 d'Air France à l'aéroport de Lod où, prévenu par ma mère, le cousin Mordekhaï m'attend. Il y a plus de deux ans que je ne suis pas venu en Israël et le simple fait de revoir des lettres hébraïques au fronton d'un bâtiment me procure une émotion merveilleuse.

C'est la première fois que je vois le cousin Mordekhaï. Lors de mon dernier voyage, il n'a pas pu venir à Tel-Aviv et, mon séjour étant très court, je n'ai pas eu le temps non plus de lui rendre visite dans son kibboutz de Galilée. Suis-je content de le voir ? Oui et non. Ce voyage-ci, comme le précédent, est motivé par mon combat pour la paix. Après avoir rencontré à Beyrouth presque tous les dirigeants palestiniens, y compris Arafat, je suis venu en parler aux dirigeants israéliens. Et il est clair que, pour cela, je me serais bien volontiers passé de ce bruyant cousin. Ah ! les initiatives de ma mère ! Cette manie qu'elle a de tenir la famille entière au courant de nos moindres faits et gestes ! Comprendra-t-elle un jour qu'on peut aimer sa maison sans en chevaucher le toit ? Grâce au ciel, Mordekhaï me plaît tout de suite. Plein de faconde et cependant capable de gravité, il correspond au personnage mythique du kibboutznik : il a les préoccupations d'un intellectuel et vit comme un paysan. Rentré depuis peu, il est encore tout excité par son séjour à l'autre bout du monde. Il me parle de Dona Regina. De la « petite » Anna-Maria. Mais la situation en Israël fournit le fond de la conversation. Je connais peu de pays au monde où la politique passionne autant chaque citoyen.

— Es-tu au courant de l'affaire Goldmann ? me demande-t-il comme nous entrons dans Tel-Aviv.

Puis, devant mon air interloqué :

— Ah bon, tu ne sais pas ? Je te raconterai quand nous serons à l'hôtel. Au fait, quel hôtel as-tu réservé ?

— L'hôtel Bazel.

— Pourquoi pas Dan ? Sidney y descend.

— Parce que Dan est trop cher pour moi.

L'hôtel Bazel, comme l'hôtel Dan, se trouve dans la rue Hayarkon, le long de la mer. C'est un hôtel de cinq étages, neuf et propre, mais sans vue sur la plage. Je dépose ma valise et nous allons manger au coin de la rue Frichman.

— Alors, cette affaire Goldmann ? demandé-je dès que nous sommes installés à la terrasse d'un petit restaurant oriental.

Mordekhaï ajuste ses lunettes comme pour mieux enregistrer ma réaction et annonce :

— Abdel Nasser a invité Nahum Goldmann au Caire.

Je ne partage pas son enthousiasme.

— Ce genre de rencontres, on ne les annonce que lorsqu'elles ont eu lieu.

Mordekhaï hausse les épaules comme s'il voulait s'excuser d'avoir transmis la nouvelle :

— Tu penses que c'est raté ?

— Je le pense, en effet.

— Golda a l'air d'accord avec toi. Elle lui refuse sa bénédiction.

Mordekhaï semble étonné par le refus de Golda Meïr de donner sa caution à Nahum Goldmann. Mais moi, ce qui me surprend, c'est que le président du Congrès juif mondial, titulaire de trois passeports, ait eu besoin de l'autorisation du gouvernement israélien pour se rendre au Caire. A moins qu'il ne prétende y représenter officiellement Israël.

— Goldmann, dis-je, est une personnalité juive attachante. Sa rencontre avec Nasser aurait, sans doute, créé l'événement. Je pense pourtant que les Égyptiens qui ne font pas la guerre aux Juifs mais aux Israéliens, ont intérêt à parler avec leurs adversaires :

— Les Israéliens ne sont-ils pas des Juifs ?

— Oui, mais des Juifs israéliens.

J'éclate de rire.

— Que t'arrive-t-il ? demande Mordekhaï, surpris.

— Je viens de me rendre compte que je te répète ce que j'ai dit voici exactement trois jours à un diplomate égyptien à Paris.

— T'a-t-il invité au Caire ?

— Oui.

— Et tu as l'intention de t'y rendre !

— Oui.

— Alors, pourquoi reprocher son voyage à Goldmann ?

— Parce que je n'irai pas au Caire en tant que partie prenante ! Je ne pourrai être qu'un modeste intermédiaire, une passerelle éventuelle entre des ennemis qui devront un jour se rencontrer s'ils veulent aboutir à la paix...

— Passerelle, dis-tu ? C'est drôle, tu parles comme Hugo... Hugo aussi se voulait une passerelle...

Vingt-quatre heures plus tard, je me présente chez le directeur du cabinet du Premier ministre. Il m'écoute. Me prie d'attendre. Revient au bout d'un moment. « Golda, dit-il, a gardé un bon souvenir de votre dernière dispute. Elle vous attend. »

Golda est là, oui. Forte, carrée, derrière un grand bureau, paraissant ne faire qu'un avec le meuble. Elle sourit, écrase sa cigarette, se lève et, la main tendue, dit simplement :

— Je suis contente de vous revoir...

Quel extraordinaire changement chez cette femme ! Deux ans plus tôt, j'avais rencontré une vieille femme malade qu'il fallait soutenir et ménager. Je la retrouve

solide comme un rocher du désert, volontaire, détermi-
née, grillant cigarette sur cigarette. Je le lui dis. Je me
demande, à haute voix, si l'exercice du pouvoir ne serait
pas le plus puissant des toniques. Nous philosophons un
peu. Nous jouons à parler yiddish. A échanger quelques
mots sans importance. Et ces préliminaires passés, elle
me demande enfin ce qui m'amène en Israël. Je parle
calmement maintenant. Posément. Je sais que le moindre de mes mots sera lourd de sens et d'équivoque. Et je
propose donc cette rencontre entre un diplomate israélien et le président égyptien Gamal Abdel Nasser qui
pourrait, à mes yeux, préparer un voyage de ce dernier à
Jérusalem.

— Vous êtes fou ! s'exclame-t-elle alors. Complètement fou !

Et comme je plaide que c'est avec ce genre de folie
que l'on rompt parfois l'ordre du monde, comme
j'insiste que ce genre d'idées semblent toujours « insen-
sées » avant, mais s'imposent, lorsqu'elles ont réussi,
avec la force de l'évidence, elle m'observe d'un œil
rêveur et laisse tomber :

— C'est drôle... Vous me faites penser à votre cousin
Hugo... Il était bien votre cousin, n'est-ce pas ? Après
tout, pourquoi pas... Oui, pourquoi pas ?

Puis elle éclate de rire, comme si elle voulait éviter de
donner trop de poids à ce qu'elle va dire :

— Vous avez déjà parlé de votre idée à un responsable égyptien ?

— Oui, à Mohammed Hassan el-Toukhami, l'adjoint
à la présidence du Conseil des Ministres. C'est un
« officier libre ». Il a participé avec Nasser à la révolution contre le roi Farouk. Je l'ai rencontré à Paris.

— Bien sûr, murmure-t-elle, après un nouveau
silence qui me semble durer une éternité, je ne peux
vous demander de me donner des garanties. Mais
j'espère que vous comprenez à quel point il m'est
difficile de me lancer dans une aventure pareille.

Puis, comme je lui réponds qu'Israël n'a rien à perdre
mais tout à gagner, en prouvant sa volonté de saisir la
moindre chance de dialogue, et comme, non sans

162

malice, je lui fais surtout observer que tout le monde, depuis mon arrivée, me parle de cette « opération Goldmann » dont l'échec semble lui être personnellement attribué :

— Votre ami égyptien parlait sérieusement d'un voyage israélien au Caire ?

— Tout à fait !

Elle se fait silencieuse encore une fois, et répond :

— Personnellement, je n'ai rien contre... Tout ce qui peut faire avancer la paix est important... Depuis que je suis responsable de cet État et de tous les Juifs qui y vivent, je ne pense qu'à cela, croyez-moi... Mais je ne peux m'engager seule. Notre gouvernement est un gouvernement d'union nationale. Si votre entreprise réussit, le gouvernement sautera. Cela m'est égal, mais je ne voudrais pas qu'il saute pour rien... Je voudrais être sûre que nous ayons quelques chances de succès... Je vais réunir quelques amis du cabinet... Revenez me voir demain à dix-sept heures, à mon bureau de Tel-Aviv...

Elle se lève :

— Pouvez-vous inscrire le nom du diplomate égyptien ?

Puis, me tendant la main :

— Bonne chance...

— Bonne chance à vous aussi...

J'ai vingt-quatre heures devant moi. Vingt-quatre heures à tuer. Je ne comprends pas comment on peut tuer la chose la plus précieuse que l'on ait jamais reçue : le temps. Mais enfin, c'est bien cela que je dois faire. Je rentre donc à l'hôtel et consulte la liste de noms israéliens et arabes que je me suis faite d'après le carnet de Hugo. Beaucoup d'entre eux sont déjà barrés : disparus ou n'ayant pas grand-chose à raconter. D'autres ne me disent rien. D'autres encore me semblent si mystérieux que je les devine, d'avance, indéchiffrables. Et mon regard s'arrête, Dieu sait pourquoi, sur le nom d'un certain docteur Jemil el-Okby, à Gaza. Pourquoi ce nom m'arrête-t-il ? Encore une fois, je ne le sais pas. Mais une brusque intuition me dit qu'il y a quelque chose à chercher de ce côté-là. Quatre-vingts kilomètres... Cent soixante aller et retour... Pas trop difficile à faire en un après-midi, même sur une route encombrée — et je décide d'y aller. Mai est le meilleur mois pour visiter Israël. La lumière est transparente, le soleil blond dans un ciel bleu, et il ne fait pas trop chaud. Jusqu'à Yavné, la route s'enroule autour des vignobles. Puis, les vignobles laissent place aux plantations d'orangers. Je vais tranquillement, sans me presser, prenant même le temps de m'arrêter ici, de méditer là, d'invoquer un peu plus loin la sainte mémoire de Yohanan ben Zakaï qui, prévoyant la destruction de Jérusalem et demandant à Titus le droit de fonder son école abandonne les insurgés, pour que le judaïsme survive ! Tourner le dos aux Juifs de chair pour que soit sauvée la Bible, fondé le premier livre du Talmud ! Quel choix ! Quel atroce, tragique dilemme ! J'en suis là de mes réflexions quand j'arrive aux portes de Gaza. Une patrouille israélienne me demande mes papiers. Je gare la voiture sur la grand-place, près de la Mosquée. Un vent léger chasse la poussière vers le bas de la place, légèrement en pente, en direction du marché. C'est l'heure de la sieste et pourtant, il y a foule. Je suis aussitôt entouré par des hommes qui appartiennent presque tous à un camp de réfugiés palestiniens, collé à la ville. Je demande :

— L'hôpital ?

Ils parlent tous en même temps, mais personne ne répond. Légèrement en retrait, deux soldats israéliens nous observent. Un homme se détache enfin, plutôt jeune, en chemise blanche, jean et sandales :

— Pourquoi l'hôpital ? demande-t-il en anglais.

— Je cherche le docteur Jemil el-Okby.

Sans un regard pour les autres, il me fait signe de le suivre. Nous faisons quelques dizaines de mètres en silence, entrons dans un café au sol de terre battue et nous nous asseyons sur des tabourets bas, près d'une petite table en bois, placée à côté d'une ouverture faisant office de fenêtre.

— Café ?

Je fais signe que oui.

164

— Vous connaissez Jemil ? demande-t-il après qu'on a posé devant nous deux tasses remplies du liquide noir.

— Non, dis-je. C'était un ami de mon cousin Hugo.

Le garçon tressaille :

— Juste avant la guerre, quelqu'un est venu le voir... Lui aussi de la part de ce Hugo...

Et, me regardant droit dans les yeux :

— Qui est Hugo ?

Cette fois, c'est moi qui suis surpris. Qui a bien pu se réclamer de Hugo ? Qui est passé ici, comme d'habitude, avant moi ? Poser la question, c'est y répondre.

— L'homme qui cherchait Jemil était grand, plutôt beau, avec une jambe raide ?

— Exact... Comment le savez-vous ? C'est aussi un de vos amis ?

— Si on veut... C'est un Tunisien... Hidar Assadi... Et Jemil, où est-il ?

— Vous ne savez pas ?

— Non.

Il repose délicatement sur la table la tasse qu'il portait à ses lèvres :

— Mort à la prise de Gaza... Tué dans sa voiture... Un obus... Il se rendait à l'hôpital...

J'encaisse, et demande :

— Et le Tunisien ? L'homme qui est venu le voir juste avant la guerre ? Lui a-t-il parlé ?

— Je ne sais pas... Je crois...

— Avait-il de la famille ?

— Qui ça ?

— Jemil.

— Non, il était originaire de Tunis. Il est venu ici en 1959 ou 60, je ne sais pas très bien. Il voulait travailler à l'hôpital, aider les réfugiés...

— Vous le connaissiez ?

— Oui, bien sûr. Tout le monde le connaissait...

— Le connaissiez-vous personnellement, lui, son histoire, sa famille ?

L'homme hausse les épaules :

— Non... Mais c'était quelqu'un de bien.

Manifestement il n'a pas tout dit. Je n'en tirerai plus

grand-chose, je le vois bien. Quel dommage de toucher ainsi au but et de le voir, ce but, se dérober ! Découragé, un peu triste, je ne peux m'empêcher de penser qu'il y a comme un charme malin qui s'acharne contre moi et mon enquête. Et le soir venu, rentré à l'hôtel, je barre sur ma liste le nom de Jemil el-Okby.

Le lendemain, fatigué et préoccupé, je reviens, longtemps avant l'heure du rendez-vous, autour de la Kirya. Dix fois, vingt fois j'entre et sors du café qui fait l'angle d'Ibn Gvirol et de Kaplan. Et c'est avec un quart d'heure d'avance que je me présente enfin au bureau de Golda Meïr. Vingt minutes passent encore. Je vois sortir le général Dayan. Et cinq minutes plus tard, Golda Meïr me reçoit, toute souriante ;

— Mes amis sont d'accord, dit-elle... Nous avons confiance en vous... Je voudrais seulement que vous me rendiez compte, à moi directement, de la suite des événements...

Elle ajoute :

— J'espère que vous réussirez. Pour nous... Pour les Arabes... Pour nous tous...

Comment exprimer la joie qui est la mienne lorsque je sors du petit bureau ? Je cours. Non : je vole. Je me sens littéralement des ailes. Et s'il n'y avait pas cette exigence de secret, je brûlerais de crier mon bonheur alentour. Rentré à l'hôtel, dans le hall, je me heurte à Mordekhaï et à un jeune homme brun qui l'accompagne.

— Mon fils Arié... Je voulais te le présenter avant notre retour au kibboutz.

Et, me prenant par le bras, non sans s'apercevoir que j'ai manifestement l'esprit ailleurs.

— J'espère que nous ne te dérangeons pas...

— Non, pas du tout, dis-je, je suis content de vous revoir...

— As-tu un moment pour prendre un verre ?

Une fois installés à la terrasse de notre restaurant « habituel », il me demande d'un air malin :

— Alors ?

Je le regarde, étonné.

— Tu étais chez Golda, n'est-ce pas ?

— Comment le sais-tu ?

— J'ai un ami, Benjamin Ben Eliezer... C'est son travail, comment te dire, de savoir. Tu vas donc en Égypte ?

— Oui.

— Golda est d'accord ?

— Oui.

— Alors, c'est gagné ! s'exclame-t-il en me secouant la main.

Et moi je prends conscience que rien n'est gagné du tout et que l'essentiel reste à faire. Ne suis-je pas semblable à ce marieur qui a passé des heures et des heures à essayer de convaincre un pauvre paysan de marier sa fille avec le fils de Rothschild, qui y a usé tout son talent, toute son expérience, toute sa persuasion, qui a finalement obtenu, à force d'arguments, l'acceptation du paysan et qui conclut alors :

— Bon, il ne me reste plus qu'à convaincre Rothschild...

21

NEW YORK

SI DIEU LE VEUT

Octobre 1969

Le Trinity College est situé à l'angle de la 91ᵉ Rue et
de la Columbus Avenue. C'est un immense carré en
briques rouges, parcouru de longs couloirs bordés de
bancs en bois, aussi durs que ceux de pénitents. Richard
aime l'atmosphère, Old England, de son école qui est
aussi la plus ancienne école new-yorkaise. Il s'amuse de
la plaque un peu moisie qui orne le hall d'entrée et qui
désigne l'établissement par son nom d'origine : « The
Episcopal Charity School, 1794. » Aujourd'hui, c'est
une école de riches et, malgré son nom et sa tradition,
plus de la moitié de ses élèves sont juifs.

Richard y a deux amis, très proches — John Kinsey et
Alexandre Seaver — qui sont tous deux goyim et qui
font partie de la même équipe de football. Le Trinity
College est réservé aux garçons. L'amitié y remplace
l'amour. Et s'il arrive à Richard de rencontrer parfois
des filles au Green Bar, à un bloc de l'école, la vérité
oblige à dire qu'elles ne l'intéressent pas beaucoup. Les
études, les jeux, le sport et les amis suffisent amplement
à occuper son temps et à remplir ses pensées.

A la fin d'un après-midi d'octobre 1969, par une
journée ensoleillée mais froide, Richard et ses deux
camarades, en sortant de l'école, sont attirés par un
attroupement sur la Columbus Avenue. C'est l'heure de
plus forte fièvre quand, à New York, tout paraît

s'accélérer ; les hommes, le trafic, le temps. Une violence diffuse émane de la foule. Ce ne sont partout que rafales de klaxon, sirènes de voitures de police et d'ambulances. Les gens vont, viennent, se heurtent et se cognent les uns aux autres dans une sorte de mouvement sans fin, sans ordre, sans direction. Richard aime cela. Il aime cette atmosphère électrique. Et c'est tout naturellement qu'il s'approche donc du groupe.

Une demi-douzaine de jeunes gens barbus sont là. Ils ont la tête couverte de chapeaux noirs d'où sortent des papillotes. Deux petites boucles qui se balancent devant les oreilles. Et ils sont en train de persuader un élève de la classe terminale de Trinity College de mettre les *Tefilline*.

Les *Tefilline* (ou phylactères), Richard sait vaguement ce que c'est. Il en a vu dans la synagogue de son grand-père à Winnipeg. Il se souvient comment les Juifs les enroulent sur leur bras gauche avant la prière. Ce sont deux écrins carrés, faits de cuir teint en noir et munis de lanières noircies sur un côté. Les lanières servent à fixer les écrins. Et c'est par ce « ligotage » quotidien que, d'après son grand-père, le fidèle vivifie et justifie sa foi. « Mettre les *Tefilline,* c'est graver Son nom sur soi », disait-il. Et l'opération leur a toujours paru, de fait, aussi mystérieuse que sacrée.

En attendant, c'est l'élève de terminale qui semble bien mal à l'aise. Il se tortille devant les jeunes barbus. On voit qu'il ne veut pas les froisser, mais qu'il préférerait être à mille lieux d'ici.

— Je suis pressé, bégaye-t-il. On m'attend à la maison…

— Ça ne prendra que cinq minutes, le tranquillise l'un des religieux.

A proximité, au bord du trottoir, stationne une camionnette blanche. Sur son flanc est écrit — en anglais et en yiddish ce simple mot : « Lubavitch ».

— Je suis pressé…, redit gauchement l'élève du Trinity College.

A force de répéter qu'il est pressé, il devient presque comique et la foule rit de bon cœur.

— Tu es bien juif, n'est-ce pas? demande le religieux, d'une voix douce.

— Bien sûr, je suis juif... Mais...

— Tu n'as pas honte de l'être?

— Non... Mais...

— Tu sais que pour être juif, il faut respecter les *Mitzvot,* les bonnes actions?

— Je les respecte.

— C'est bien, mais il faut aussi respecter la *Mitzva* envers l'Éternel...

Alexandre Seaver tire Richard par la manche :

— Viens, j'ai froid. Ça risque d'être long...

Alexandre Seaver est un grand garçon brun, au regard étonné et clair. Il habite à deux blocs de l'école, au coin de Central Park West et de la 93e Rue.

— Et si on faisait escale chez moi? demande-t-il.

Ses deux amis le suivent sans commentaires. Car ils savent que c'est chez lui que l'on prend le meilleur goûter et que les fins d'après-midi y sont généralement les plus douces.

— Je croyais que les Juifs n'étaient pas prosélytes... commence John, une fois installé dans la chambre d'Alexandre, tapissée de lithos de Warhol.

John est fils de pasteur et, des trois, à la fois le plus petit et le plus impertinent.

— C'est vrai, reconnaît Richard. Mais il ne s'agissait pas pour ce jeune religieux de convertir des chrétiens, mais de ramener à la religion quelques Juifs.

— Et quand il se trompe? Quand il s'adresse à un chrétien?

— C'est la raison pour laquelle ils demandent d'abord si la personne est juive ou non...

— As-tu déjà été accosté par eux?

— Non, jamais.

Alexandre allume la télévision. Les cris exaltés d'une jeune femme, qui vient de gagner cinq mille dollars à un jeu télévisé, remplissent la pièce. Alexandre, excédé, coupe le son. Et il ne reste sur l'écran qu'un visage grimaçant de joie, une bouche grande ouverte, un corps en quasi-convulsion.

— Dis-donc, reprend-il : et si tu acceptais de mettre ces *Tefilline,* ces lacets, en disant, après coup, que tu n'es pas juif ? Je serais curieux de voir la réaction de ces illuminés !

— Tu n'as qu'à le faire.

— Mais non ! Toi, ce serait plus normal ! Et plus drôle ! Car tu es juif tout en ne l'étant pas — c'est bien ce que tu nous as expliqué, pas vrai ?

— Chiche !

Une semaine s'écoule. Tous les jours, en sortant du collège, les trois amis cherchent, en vain, les Lubavitch et la camionnette, qu'ils ont surnommée le « *Mitzva* mobile ». Et ce n'est qu'une quinzaine de jours plus tard, alors qu'ils ont presque oublié leur projet, qu'ils retrouvent les Lubavitch à proximité du Trinity College. Ils sont deux cette fois-ci. Comble de malchance, il pleut légèrement et c'est à grand-peine qu'ils arrivent à attirer l'attention des passants. Joie quand ils reconnaissent Richard et ses amis... Visages illuminés... Sentiment, manifeste, d'être en terrain connu... Richard qui s'en aperçoit et qui en ressent du remords ralentit le pas. Mais John et Alexandre le poussent en avant :

— Tu ne vas pas te dégonfler, hein ?

L'un des deux Lubavitch, un garçon robuste, avec une barbe en éventail et un caftan noir mouillé sur une chemise blanche, se précipite à la rencontre de Richard :

— Tu es bien juif ?

— C'est ça, oui.

— Et tu as déjà mis les *Tefilline ?*

— Non.

— Mais c'est la *Mitzva* suprême pour tout Juif !

— Je sais.

— Comment t'appelles-tu ?

— Richard, Richard Halter.

Le barbu sourit :

— Moi, c'est Mendel Fogelman.

Il n'a que quelques années de plus que Richard et semble, au fond, assez sympathique.

— Il pleut, continue-t-il. Voulez-vous entrer dans notre camionnette ? Nous y serons à l'abri.

— La pluie ne me gêne pas, bredouille Richard.

L'homme a-t-il compris le manège ? Toujours est-il que, d'une voix chantante, entraînante, comme celle des conteurs orientaux, il commence d'expliquer la signification des *Tefilline* :

— Les *Tefilline* sont une *Mitzva* de nos jours très négligée. Pourtant peu de rites sont aussi riches, peu recèlent ce pouvoir d'édification et de sanctification...

Une foule s'est agglutinée autour d'eux. Visiblement, Mendel Fogelman aime parler en public. Il lève les bras, branle du chef, s'avance, recule, s'avance encore, feint de prendre à témoin les gens qui l'écoutent :

— Quand Rabbi Nahman ben Isaac demanda à Rabbi Hiya bar Abin : « Que contiennent les *Tefilline* du Maître de l'Univers ? », ce dernier répondit par ce verset : « Qui est comme ton peuple Israël, nation unique sur la terre ? » ; et, à la question : « L'Éternel, béni soit Son nom, se glorifie-t-il des louanges d'Israël ? » il répondit : « Oui, car l'Éternel, béni soit Son nom, dit à Israël : " Vous m'avez conféré un caractère unique, en proclamant : 'Écoute, Israël, le Seigneur est notre Dieu, le Seigneur est Un !' Et moi, en retour, je vous accorde un caractère unique : 'Qui est comme ton peuple, Israël ?'... " »

La pluie a cessé et un timide rayon de soleil se faufile entre deux nuages gris. Mendel Fogelman baisse une dernière fois les bras et sourit à Richard :

— Alors, vous avez compris ? Les *Teffiline,* c'est comme un anneau de mariage entre l'Éternel, béni soit Son nom, et l'homme. Quoi de plus beau que de se lier à la Beauté ? Quoi de plus fort que de s'associer avec la Justice ?

Puis, s'approchant du jeune homme qui sent l'odeur moisie de sa redingote mouillée :

— On attache d'abord les *Tefilline chel yad,* les phylactères du bras... Puis les *Tefilline chel roch,* les phylactères de la tête... Car ainsi se manifeste la préséance de l'acte, de la pratique, sur la méditation et la théorie. N'est-il pas écrit : « Tout ce que l'Éternel, béni soit-Il, a dit, nous le ferons et nous le comprendrons ? » C'est en accomplissant les commandements que nous en pénétrons véritablement le sens...

Là-dessus, il s'interrompt. Regarde Richard droit dans les yeux. Celui-ci le regarde aussi. Découvre qu'il a les yeux verts. Se dit : « Tiens, comme c'est curieux, ce garçon a de beaux yeux verts. » Et quand le Lubavitch lui fait : « Alors ? », il tourne légèrement la tête, distingue, comme dans un rêve, ses deux amis qui lui sourient et, tel un somnambule, ne sachant très bien ce qu'il dit ou ce qu'il fait, s'entend répondre :

— D'accord.

C'est le soir, à présent. Allongé sur son lit, Richard n'arrive pas à s'endormir. Il lui semble que la lueur des réverbères traverse, avec plus de netteté que d'ordinaire, les persiennes de sa chambre. Il n'est pas fier de lui. Ah ! que non, il n'est pas fier de lui. Il a suivi toutes les indications de Mendel Fogelman. Il a enfilé les *Teffiline* et, en enroulant la lanière autour de son médius, comme un anneau de mariage, il a récité ce verset qui l'a tant impressionné : « Je te fiance à Moi à jamais. Je te fiance à Moi pour la Justice et le Droit, par la grâce et la miséricorde. Je te fiance à Moi par la fidélité et toi, tu connaîtras le Seigneur. » Il se revoit si troublé. Si respectueux tout à coup. Il se revoit subjugué par le rite, la voix du Lubavitch. Et puis il revoit l'étonnement de Mendel Fogelman quand, après la cérémonie, il lui a annoncé qu'il n'était pas Juif. Il s'attendait, en disant cela, à un scandale, un coup de colère. Or il n'a reçu qu'un regard triste doublé d'un sourire désolé. Et de cela aussi il se sent navré et honteux.

Il attend l'aube pour s'endormir et quand sa mère le réveille, il a l'impression de n'avoir par dormi du tout. Il prend une douche. Avale un café. Téléphone, de sa chambre, aux renseignements pour demander le numéro des Lubavitch à Brooklyn. Va-t-il y trouver

173

Mendel Fogelman ? Non, car, à Brooklyn, on lui dit qu'il n'est plus là, qu'il est parti pour Boston. Et ce n'est qu'au bout d'une semaine qu'il réussira enfin à joindre le jeune religieux. Mendel Fogelman écoutera en silence la confession de Richard. Puis citera les Proverbes : « Celui qui cache ses transgressions ne prospère point, mais celui qui les avoue et les délaisse obtient la miséricorde. » Et c'est ainsi qu'ils se rencontrent, deux jours plus tard, un dimanche matin, devant l'hôtel Plaza : « Nous traverserons Central Park à pied », avait dit Fogelman. Et Richard est venu au rendez-vous tremblant et impressionné...

Il fait froid ce matin-là. Le parc, cette énorme nappe de verdure que l'on dirait enfermée dans un carcan de béton et d'acier, se reflète dans la palette des *Nymphéas* de Monet. Toute la gamme des verts, des bleus, des bruns, des gris et des rouille y caresse le regard. Et dans les allées, fermées à la circulation et sillonnées par la police montée, des centaines de New-Yorkais font tranquillement leur jogging. Mendel Fogelman porte son habituel chapeau noir et sa redingote usée. Il a la même barbe, peut-être un peu plus ordonnée. Il est gai et ne semble pas en vouloir à Richard.

— Tu sais ce qu'est le Hassid ? demande-t-il à brûle-pourpoint.

— Non.

— Et qui était Baal-Chem-Tov ?

— Non.

Ses yeux, mi-clos, laissent paraître le début d'un étonnement.

— Baal-Chem-Tov naquit en l'an 5458 après la création du monde par l'Éternel, béni soit-Il... En 1698 de notre ère...

La voix de Mendel Fogelman a repris d'un seul coup son rythme incantatoire. Son corps se balance. Ses yeux se ferment tout à fait.

— C'était après les grands massacres par les Cosaques de Bogdan Khmelnitski... Des millions de Juifs d'Europe centrale et de l'Est vivaient dans de petits villages miséreux. Les enfants en bas âge travaillaient

174

durement. Ils n'avaient guère le temps de fréquenter les écoles. Aussi, des centaines de milliers de Juifs se mirent-ils bientôt en marge de la connaissance...

Mendel Fogelman lève les bras au ciel, comme s'il allait s'envoler :

— Connaissance... Connaissance... Pour les Juifs c'est le devoir suprême. Car il est écrit : « Avant tout, étudiez ! Quels que soient les motifs qui vous animent d'abord, vous aimerez bientôt l'étude pour elle-même. » Alors, Baal-Chem-Tov vint. Il vit que les Juifs étaient désespérés et tenta de leur redonner la foi. Il leur dit que ce qui est agréable à l'Éternel, c'est l'intention et non la connaissance elle-même ; il leur dit que, parfois, un chant sincère, un cri rempli de piété approchent plus sûrement la volonté du Maître de l'Univers que la lecture insensible des Textes, fût-elle théâtrale et belle. Et les pauvres se mirent à danser...

Près de Bow Bridge qui surplombe le lac, Mendel Fogelman s'immobilise puis, à la grande surprise de Richard, se met à danser les mains en l'air, la tête légèrement inclinée en avant et les yeux toujours clos. Les gens, autour d'eux, s'arrêtent. Ils ont l'air stupéfaits du spectacle. Et Richard, à dire vrai, se sent terriblement gêné.

Très vite, pourtant, il s'aperçoit que les badauds le sont beaucoup moins que lui. Ils ne rient pas. Ils ne se moquent pas. Mais leurs regards sont emplis d'un visible respect. La danse de Mendel Fogelman n'est pas un jeu, non. C'est un rite. Une cérémonie. C'est une communion avec l'Éternel. Au fur et à mesure qu'il tournoie sur lui-même, que son corps devient plus léger, plus aérien, il se met à ressembler aux oiseaux qui tournent au-dessus du lac. Séduit par la scène, emporté par le rythme de la danse, Richard se met à la ponctuer en tapant dans ses mains. La foule suit son exemple. Un guitariste, surgi on ne sait d'où, se joint au mouvement. Une mélodie juive, entendue il y a longtemps chez son grand-père à Winnipeg, jaillit des cordes, et, entraîné par une mystérieuse nostalgie d'ancêtres ainsi que par les évolutions de plus en plus rapides de Mendel Fogelman, il se met lui aussi à danser.

Quand, plus tard, ils se retrouveront, tous deux, essoufflés, sur un banc du Shakespeare Garden, en face de l'American Museum of National History, Mendel Fogelman dira simplement, comme si cela allait de soi :

— Dimanche prochain, nous irons chez le rabbi de Lubavitch, à Brooklyn.

22

FRANCFORT

SUR LES TRACES DE HUGO

Septembre 1970

En un an, Sidney n'a revu Leïla qu'une seule fois, à la
fin du mois de mai, lorsque, en route pour Mexico où
elle devait rejoindre son mari, la belle Arabe s'est
arrêtée deux jours à New York. Prétextant un congrès,
Sidney l'a emmenée à Washington. Ils sont restés
enfermés, au Four Seasons Hotel, sans songer à sortir
pour admirer les arbres en fleurs ou se promener dans
les ruelles animées de Georgetown. Leïla se proclamait
toujours anti-israélienne et Sidney avait toujours autant
envie d'elle.

Au début du mois, l'armée américaine avait envahi le
Cambodge et, contrairement à ses amis, et particulièrement Jérémie Cohen, Sidney n'a pas trouvé cela
d'emblée choquant : « Du jour où le Cambodge a
accepté de servir de base pour le Vietminh, il est, de
fait, entré en guerre », disait-il... Et s'il reconnaissait
que cette guerre était « moche » (la presse en apportait
tous les jours la preuve) il demandait à qui voulait
l'entendre si l'on avait jamais vu une « jolie guerre ».
Ce n'est que deux semaines plus tard quand David, le
fils de son frère Larry, fut mobilisé et envoyé au
Vietnam qu'il changea d'opinion. Bien que demeuré
hostile au régime en place à Hanoï, il en venait à
éprouver des doutes sur le sens de l'engagement américain. Cela provoqua quelques heurts supplémentaires

177

avec Leïla, inconditionnelle de la « révolution » vietnamienne. Leurs divergences politiques, ce faisant, paraissaient augmenter d'autant le désir qu'ils ressentaient l'un pour l'autre.

Après le départ de Leïla, la vie à New York lui parut si fade qu'il accepta brusquement, et à la grande surprise de Marjory, de se rendre à un congrès médical à Francfort. L'invitation traînait sur son bureau depuis des mois. Il s'agissait du Congrès annuel de la chirurgie ophtalmologique qu'il avait manqué l'année précédente à cause de ce voyage à Beyrouth. Et l'idée d'y assister cette année lui paraissait à la fois exaltante et troublante.

Francfort donc, 3 septembre 1970. Il descend, comme prévu, à l'Intercontinental. Dans le hall, particulièrement animé, sous un énorme lustre, deux hôtesses blondes accueillent les congressistes avec une efficacité souriante. Comme aux États-Unis, chacun reçoit un badge avec son nom, le programme des débats et un guide de la ville.

On est samedi matin. Le congrès ne commence vraiment que ce soir. Remarquant dans le guide l'adresse de plusieurs synagogues, Sidney décide d'en visiter une. La plus proche est celle de la Freiherr von Stein Strasse ? Parfait. Va pour la plus proche. L'immeuble est gardé par quelques policiers en uniforme. Et Sidney est effrayé de constater que trente-cinq ans après la guerre, il faut encore, dans le pays du nazisme, protéger les Juifs. Dans l'entrée, Sidney rencontre un groupe de croyants qui bavardent après l'office du Shabbat. Il y a là des jeunes gens, mais aussi quelques personnes âgées. Pour la première fois en Allemagne, Sidney s'adresse à des Juifs dans son mauvais yiddish :

— Pourquoi vivez-vous encore ici ?

Les vieux sourient, embarrassés, et l'interrogent à leur tour. Ils veulent savoir d'où il vient, ce qu'il fait à Francfort, ce qu'il compte y faire. Mais ils ne répondent pas à sa question.

Un homme le rejoint sur le seuil :

— Il faut les comprendre, dit-il. Ils sont tous

178

malades... Malades dans leur tête. Ils vivent en Allemagne, mais ils en éprouvent de la honte. Pour la plupart d'entre eux, ce pays n'est pas celui de leurs pères, c'est la patrie de leurs bourreaux.

Le soir, après la lecture de quelques discours inauguraux, Sidney prend place à une table de l'immense restaurant de l'hôtel, avec sept autres congressistes de différentes nationalités. A sa gauche, se trouve le rabbin Lewinson, le grand rabbin de Baden et de Hambourg et son épouse, ophtalmologue à Heidelberg. Né en Allemagne, exilé en 1933 aux États-Unis et revenu en Allemagne sous l'uniforme américain, le rabbin Lewinson confirme le diagnostic du jeune homme de la synagogue :

— Oui, c'est vrai, les Juifs qui vivent actuellement en Allemagne sont malades, mais je souhaite qu'ils restent en Allemagne. Pour priver au moins Hitler de cette ultime et essentielle victoire : une Allemagne *judenrein* !

— C'est une remarque pertinente ! remarque un homme d'une soixantaine d'années, aux cheveux blancs, séparés soigneusement par une raie et assis à la droite de Sidney.

Sidney tourne la tête et l'homme lui sourit amicalement en montrant du doigt son badge : « Hans Furchmuller, RDA. »

Sidney a tout de suite le sentiment d'avoir déjà entendu ce nom quelque part.

— Vous venez d'Allemagne de l'Est ? demande-t-il.

— Oui, j'habite Berlin...

— Je croyais qu'il était difficile aux Allemands de l'Est de venir à l'Ouest...

— Pas pour des congrès scientifiques.

Puis, en se penchant vers Sidney :

— En réalité, je suis là à cause de vous.

Et, voyant l'étonnement du médecin juif :

— J'ai vu votre nom sur la liste des participants au Congrès, alors j'ai demandé à mes supérieurs de m'y déléguer aussi...

Il se lève cérémonieusement et se présente :

— Docteur Hans Furchmuller, le beau-frère de votre cousin Hugo.

Les conversations à table se sont tues et un jeune médecin français lève spontanément son verre :

— Buvons à cette rencontre familiale !

Puis, voyant l'air embarrassé de Sidney, il demande :

— Ai-je commis un impair ?

— Non, répond Sidney. Mais Hugo Halter a été tué voici quelques années lors d'un attentat en Israël.

— Attentat terroriste ? demande le rabbin Lewinson.

— Oui.

Un silence accueille cette révélation. On présente le dessert mais personne n'ose plus y toucher maintenant. Hans Furchmuller intervient alors :

— Avez-vous connu ma sœur ?

— Non.

— Et Hugo, l'avez-vous rencontré ?

— Je l'ai peu connu et, pourtant, sa mort m'a beaucoup affecté.

Hans Furchmuller le regarde. Hoche la tête, pensif. Et comme s'il avait une illumination, soudain :

— Si vous n'êtes pas trop fatigué par le voyage, nous pourrions prendre une bière dans un bar et parler ensemble d'Hugo...

C'est ainsi que, dans un vieux café de la vieille ville rempli de bruit et d'odeurs rances, Sidney apprend deux ou trois petites choses qu'il ignorait sur son cousin.

Le docteur Hans Furchmuller lui parle d'abord de lui-même. Il est l'aîné d'une famille de quatre enfants. Lui, mobilisé en 1941, a été envoyé sur le front de l'Est. Son frère aîné, Peter, a été tué en Yougoslavie et son cadet, Wilfrid, est aujourd'hui pharmacien à Kiel. A la fin de la guerre, Hans a été blessé à Berlin. Il y a été soigné et y a connu une fille qu'il a épousée. Pas très heureux de vivre sous un régime communiste. Pas trop malheureux non plus. Le directeur d'un hôpital n'est-il pas, naturellement, un privilégié ? Les membres de sa famille ne viennent-ils pas, à tour de rôle, lui rendre visite ? C'est ainsi, d'ailleurs, qu'il a revu, en 1959, à la veille de Noël, sa sœur Sigrid accompagnée de son époux. Bonne impression dudit époux. Sympathie, estime immédiates. Admiration pour cette culture, cet extraordinaire souci de la paix. « N'a-t-il pas su, malgré les incompréhensions et les haines, nouer d'excellents rapports avec les Israéliens et les Arabes ? N'a-t-il pas le mérite, immense, d'avoir su dépasser les frontières de sa race, de son peuple, de sa mémoire ? » Hans Furchmuller, de fait, ne traîne pas : il présente son nouvel ami à un certain Wolfgang Knopff, qui travaillait, à l'époque, au HVA, le Haupt Verwaltung Aufklärung et qui était probablement un agent. Knopff s'intéresse à Hugo. Il apprécie ses tentatives. Il l'encourage à poursuivre son effort et lui signale un jour la présence à Francfort d'Israël Beer, important conseiller de Ben Gourion, et un homme de grande envergure ». Ne fallait-il pas l'approcher ? Le mettre en contact avec des amis arabes ? Hugo suit, semble-t-il, le conseil de Knopff. Il négocie avec Israël Beer. Et il est aussi surpris que lui, Furchmuller, quand, deux ans plus tard, il apprend par la presse l'arrestation en Israël de ce même Israël Beer, accusé d'espionnage au profit de l'URSS !

Quelle étrange histoire ! songe Sidney. Quel effroyable embrouillamini ! Furchmuller continuera, jusqu'à la fin de la soirée, à broder sur les mêmes motifs, à détailler les portraits croisés de Hugo, de Beer, de Sigrid. Naïf ? Roublard ? Le médecin allemand est-il en train de l'informer ou de le tromper ? De le mettre sur la bonne ou sur une fausse piste ? Que veut-il savoir au juste ? Pourquoi a-t-il présenté Hugo à ce Knopff ? Pourquoi aujourd'hui, pourquoi dix ans après, désirait-il le rencontrer, lui, Sidney ? Voulait-il connaître l'état de l'enquête policière ? Savoir ce que la police, la famille ont découvert ? Et la mort de son cousin avait-elle un arrière-plan plus compliqué qu'il ne l'avait jusqu'alors imaginé ? Ces questions le poursuivront toute la nuit. En sorte qu'au petit matin, sitôt son déjeuner avalé, il décide d'appeler Benjamin Ben Eliezer en Israël.

Celui-ci paraît moins troublé par ce récit que Sidney ne s'y attendait. Il confirmera les informations de Hans Furchmuller concernant le conseiller de David Ben Gourion, Israël Beer, arrêté trois jours à peine après la mort de Hugo et de Sigrid. Mais il se gardera d'établir, dans l'état actuel de ses informations, la moindre relation entre ces morts et la trahison d'Israël Beer. A moins que...

— Oui, à moins que, répète-t-il, brusquement, à l'autre bout du fil... J'ai peut-être une idée... Restez-vous quelque temps à Francfort ?

— Non, fait Sidney. Je pars le 6 septembre par le vol TWA pour New York.

— Je vous appellerai là-bas, dans ce cas, dit Benjamin.

Le dimanche 6 septembre, comme prévu, Sidney quitte l'Allemagne. Il a acheté quelques cadeaux à l'aéroport. Fait provision de journaux. Il s'est confortablement installé dans son siège, de la classe « Ambassador ». Il a feuilleté le *Time* et *Newsweek*. Bu une coupe de champagne. Et c'est alors qu'il est distrait de sa lecture par le passage brusque de deux hommes en direction de la première classe. Il entend des cris et voit un troisième homme, plutôt petit, brun, assis à deux rangs devant lui, se lever et braquer sur les passagers un énorme revolver.

— Ne bougez pas ! crie-t-il.

On entend des pleurs d'enfants dans la classe économique. Un bruit de bagarre en première. Un hurlement hystérique ici. Un homme qui proteste. Un autre qui s'indigne. Un coup de crosse au premier. Une menace au second. L'avion plonge. Quelques paquets tombent par terre et le haut-parleur se met à grésiller :

— Mesdames, messieurs, nous vous demandons votre attention, s'il vous plaît. Veuillez attacher vos ceintures...

La voix est tranquille, l'anglais correct :

— Votre nouveau commandant de bord vous parle.

Le Front Populaire pour la Libération de la Palestine, qui a pris en main la direction de ce vol de la TWA, demande à tous les passagers de respecter les instructions suivantes...

L'avion se stabilise. Sidney regarde ses voisins, un couple de Pakistanais qui n'osent ni bouger ni respirer.

— Restez assis et gardez votre calme, poursuit la voix. Pour votre propre sécurité, placez vos mains sur vos têtes. Ne faites aucun mouvement qui pourrait mettre en danger votre vie ou celle des autres passagers de l'avion...

C'est alors seulement que Sidney prend la mesure de la situation : un détournement ! « Il ne manquait plus que cela », se dit-il et, comme ses voisins, il met les mains sur sa tête.

New York, septembre 1970

Début septembre, peu de temps avant le Roch Hachanah, je me rends à nouveau à New York. Ayant découvert dans le carnet de Hugo, à la lettre T, à côté du mot « taxi », le nom de Benny Mendelson et son numéro de téléphone, je l'ai appelé de Paris et lui ai demandé de m'attendre à la sortie du hall d'Air-France à l'aéroport J. F. Kennedy.

Je suis impatient de le rencontrer. Impatient de retrouver cette nouvelle « trace », cette nouvelle « piste ». Encore que quelque chose me dise, par avance, que je serai à nouveau déçu. J'ai hâte aussi de revoir New York, la seule ville au monde où le présent est déjà le passé et où le passé est tellement dépassé qu'on le relègue à la périphérie, dans ces quartiers-musées que l'on dirait voués à conserver la mémoire de la ville. Le Washington Square de Henry James, d'Edith Wharton et de Dos Passos avec ses maisons de briques rouges et son effervescence bon enfant... Le « village », avec ses rues qui ont encore des noms, un commencement, une fin et des maisons importées du vieux continent... Chelsea... Little Italy, ses cafés avec terrasse, ses capucinos... Lower East Side, ses synagogues, ses magasins de « shmates »... China Town, pour les orphelins de l'Asie... Soho pour ceux qui confondent la bohème de Puccini avec la vie d'artiste... Et puis l'*autre* cité, bien sûr — celle qui grimpe toujours plus haut dans le ciel, le repoussant sans cesse, déchirant les nuages, forçant son bleu, donnant à l'homme de plus en plus de clarté, de plus en plus de liberté, mais aussi de plus en plus d'angoisse... Et puis encore, contre l'angoisse justement, cherchant à toute force à en exorciser le poids, toutes ces minuscules églises, ces temples, ces synagogues comme incrustés dans les blocs luisants et glacés des gratte-ciel — étranges collages urbains ! corps étrangers à cette ville que l'on dirait bâtie sans eux, contre eux ! Imaginez la Loire dans le Grand Canyon ! la place de la Concorde au cœur du désert du Neguev ! New York, suprême artifice... Et si New York était la Babylone moderne ? Si elle était en passe de réussir là où la cité biblique a échoué ? La chance, le génie de New York : avoir su et voulu couler tous les accents du monde dans le moule d'une seule et même langue...

New York, donc. Je débarque vers midi. Il fait beau. Le chauffeur de taxi est là. C'est un homme chauve, corpulent, qui brandit une pancarte avec mon nom et qui, sitôt sur l'autoroute, engage lui-même la conversation :

— D'où venez-vous ? demande-t-il avec un fort accent yiddish.

— De Paris.

— Et avant ?

J'éclate de rire. Je lui parle de Varsovie, de la Pologne, de l'Argentine, du reste. Il me dit qu'il connaît la Russie. Que ses parents viennent d'Odessa. Il me redemande mon nom, puisque le sien est là, affiché sur le tableau de bord.

— Halter, lui dis-je, guettant sur son visage l'émotion, le frémissement au moins que ce nom doit susciter.

— J'ai connu un Halter, dit-il, en tournant légèrement vers moi son visage mal rasé. Il travaillait au *Forward*.

— Hugo, je sais, oui... C'était un cousin... Voulez-vous me parler de lui ?

Et voilà le brave homme qui, pas plus étonné que cela, ne cherchant à savoir ni comment ni pourquoi je « sais » qu'il a connu mon cousin, se met à raconter.

— Je travaillais souvent avec les gens du *Forward*. Ils m'appelaient pour toutes sortes de petites courses. Je stationnais juste en face du building. Aujourd'hui, c'est un temple chinois. Les choses vont si vite de notre temps. Mais à l'époque, parole que c'était le siège d'un foutu journal yiddish. C'est comme ça, en tout cas, que j'ai transporté votre cousin. C'était un homme gentil, prévenant, mais sa femme... Ah sa femme ! Dans le taxi, vous comprenez, les gens font pas attention au chauffeur. Ils parlent... Ils se laissent aller... Ils se disputent... Ils se chamaillent... Sans parler de ces choses qu'ils font des fois, quand ils croient qu'on les voit pas... Enfin là, c'était pas ça... La femme de votre cousin avait un accent allemand, comme celui de Henry Kissinger... Elle dominait complètement son mari et je suis sûr que votre cousin faisait exactement ce qu'elle voulait... Oh ! je me trompe jamais, moi, vous savez ! A force d'interroger les gens, on devient un petit Sigmund. Vous savez de qui je parle ? Hein, vous savez ? C'était l'un des nôtres, lui aussi, pas vrai ? Pour moi donc, l'espèce masculine se partage entre les hommes et les maris. Votre cousin, lui, était un mari. Alors là, complètement.

— Vous vous souvenez de l'objet de leur conversation ?

— Pensez-vous ! C'était il y a longtemps. Je me souviens seulement de leur comportement, du ton sur lequel ils se parlaient.

Et, en se tournant à nouveau vers moi :

— Vous ne les connaissiez pas ?

— Presque pas.

— Alors, je regrette de ne pas pouvoir vous donner plus de précisions. Je présume qu'ils sont morts, hein ? J'ai deviné, n'est-ce pas ? Vous voyez : un petit Sigmund ! Et voilà : vous êtes arrivé. Ça fait quinze dollars et cinquante *cents*.

23

ISRAËL

ARIÉ

Septembre 1970

Depuis qu'il est rentré au kibboutz, Arié n'a presque pas desserré les lèvres. Et aux questions de ses amis qu'intéresse son séjour en Argentine, il répond par monosyllabes, grognements, moues évasives. Anna-Maria ne lui a-t-elle pas froidement annoncé qu'elle ne l'aimait plus ? N'est-ce pas les mots eux-mêmes qui, dès lors, sont porteurs de fausseté, de mensonge ? Arié a retiré sa confiance au langage comme on se fâche avec un ami.

— Il faudrait peut-être l'emmener à l'hôpital de Kyriat Shemona et le montrer à un spécialiste, suggère de temps en temps sa mère.

Mais Mordekhaï éclate de rire :

— Allons, Sarah ! As-tu déjà oublié ce que c'est que l'amour ? Ce n'est pas un médecin qu'il lui faut, mais une fille.

— Mordekhaï !...

— Ne te fâche pas, Sarah... Ne te fâche pas... La sagesse populaire a tout dit là-dessus... Il faut du temps, voilà tout... Le temps voilà la clé... Tu le sais bien : « Un temps pour tuer et un temps pour guérir... un temps pour aimer et un temps pour haïr... »

— C'est dans la Bible, Mordekhaï.

— Je sais. La Bible, c'est la vie...

— Comment cela, « la Bible c'est la vie » ? Tu es devenu religieux, maintenant ?

— Tu n'as rien compris, mon amie… La Bible n'est pas religion, la Bible c'est…

— Je n'ai peut-être rien compris… Mais je sais au moins une chose : c'est que le petit souffre et qu'il faut l'aider… Qu'est-ce que tu proposes pour ça ?

Le pauvre Mordekhaï n'a, hélas, pas grand-chose à proposer. Pas de remède miracle. Et il ne trouve rien de mieux à faire que d'emmener le jeune garçon à Tel-Aviv accueillir le « cousin venu de Paris ». Ne suis-je pas le plus « exotique » des cousins ? Le plus nourri de mémoire, de projets politiques propres à le fasciner ? N'ai-je pas l'avantage, surtout, de bien connaître et Anna-Maria, et l'Argentine, et les terroristes ? Morde-khaï, malheureusement, ne me dit rien. Et trop occupé de moi-même, de mes stratégies et de mes rêves, je ne prends ni le temps, ni la peine de prêter attention au jeune garçon. En sorte que, sur le chemin du retour, la déception s'ajoutant au chagrin, et l'humiliation à la déception, son mutisme, loin de disparaître, est devenu quasi hostile.

Mordekhaï a pris la route qui longe la mer, via Haïfa et Akko. Près de la station d'essence, à l'entrée d'Akko, quelques soldats et soldates sont là, qui font du stop.

— On en prend un ? demande Mordekhaï à son fils qui, de plus en plus boudeur, ne daigne pas répondre.

Puis, stoppant dans un grand crissement de pneus et après que l'une des soldates a couru jusqu'à eux : « Allez, allez, montez… Si vous allez à Kyriat Shemona, c'est la providence qui nous envoie ! »

La fille s'appelle Judith. Judith Ben Aharon. Ses parents sont arrivés du Yémen juste après la proclamation de l'indépendance d'Israël, lors de l' « opération Tapis Volant ». « Sur les ailes de l'aigle, dit le prophète, je vous ai ramenés vers moi »… « Sur les ailes des avions israéliens, dit Judith, ma famille a été ramenée en Terre sainte. »

Mordekhaï observe cette étrange prophétesse dans son rétroviseur. Il la trouve étonnamment jolie, avec sa natte brune, ses yeux noirs, son visage hâlé, sa poitrine bien moulée dans la vareuse militaire.

— Dans une semaine, dit-il, Arié sera aussi sous l'uniforme.

— C'est vrai ? demande la fille.

— C'est vrai, grommelle Arié sans la regarder.

A Nahariya, Mordekhaï emprunte la route de Sasa. Là, ils aperçoivent enfin, à leur droite, le mont Meron. Le soleil, qui avait, un moment, semblé s'être figé et qui les éblouissait dangereusement, commence sa descente rapide derrière le mont Hermon, laissant sur le sommet enneigé quelques taches couleur de sang.

— C'est beau, dit Judith. Je n'ai jamais vu le Hermon de près.

Mordekhaï lui sourit, de plus en plus séduit. Arié lève aussi les yeux, rencontre dans le rétroviseur le regard de la jeune fille — mais, se rappelant tout à coup le visage d'Anna-Maria, tourne la tête et grogne à nouveau.

— Venez nous voir au kibboutz Dafné, lance à tout hasard Mordekhaï, au moment où il la dépose.

Mais la jeune fille l'entend à peine. Et après un dernier coup d'œil au fils qui conserve les yeux obstinément baissés, elle salue distraitement le père et s'en va vers Kyriat Shemona.

Quelques semaines plus tard, c'est le grand jour. Arié est toujours aussi triste. Toujours aussi silencieux. Ce sont toujours les mêmes images, les mêmes regrets, qu'il ressasse. Mais voici qu'est arrivé le moment de partir pour l'armée.

La Ford à nouveau. Mordekhaï au volant. Son fils à côté de lui. La route ensoleillée. Les nuages de poussière derrière eux. Les soldats auto-stoppeurs qui, nonchalamment, leur font signe. Et puis à mi-chemin, tout près du village de Tel Kedesh, une circulation qui se fait un peu trop dense pour l'endroit. Que se passe-t-il ? Un accident ? Un embouteillage ? Quelque chose de plus grave, de plus inhabituel encore ?

— Il y a quelque chose, grommelle Mordekhaï avec cette espèce d' « instinct des catastrophes » dont il aime bien dire qu'il est le propre des pionniers...

A peine a-t-il terminé sa phrase qu'on entend des sirènes de police toutes proches. Des klaxons. Et puis, à la radio, une interruption brutale aux chansons qu'ils écoutent depuis une heure :

— « Aujourd'hui, dix minutes avant midi, trois obus de bazooka ont atteint un autobus qui transportait des écoliers sur la route de Tel Kedesh à Baram, le long de la frontière libanaise. Sept enfants ont été tués, vingt et un blessés. Le conducteur de l'autobus de la compagnie Eged, Rami Yarkoni, de Safed, et l'institutrice Deborah Ben Aharon, de Kyriat Shemona ont succombé à leurs blessures... »

Quelques centaines de mètres plus loin, la route est barrée et la police dévie la circulation vers Ramot Naftali. Mordekhaï suit le flot des voitures. Mais, dès qu'il le peut, il tourne à droite, reprend la route de Tel Kedesh en sens inverse et se retrouve ainsi, sans l'avoir voulu ni prévu, à la hauteur de l'autobus endommagé. Ambulances. Voitures de police. Foule de parents en larmes. Cris, gémissements des curieux et des témoins du drame.

— Circulez ! circulez ! crie un policier au bord de la crise de nerfs.

— Je ne peux pas, dit Mordekhaï, la route est coupée.

— Alors, attendez... Non, circulez... Enfin bon : restez là... On va vous la dégager, cette route... Pour l'instant, y a rien d'autre à faire qu'à attendre et fermer sa gueule !

Mordekhaï et Arié, bloqués en effet, sortent de la voiture et s'approchent de la carcasse de l'autobus.

— Les amis d'Anna-Maria... peste Arié.

— Que dis-tu ? demande Mordekhaï.

Il retire ses lunettes et d'un revers de la main essuie les larmes qui lui embuent les yeux.

— Je dis que ce sont les amis d'Anna-Maria, répète Arié.

— De qui parles-tu ?

— Des salauds qui ont fait cela... Les terroristes...

Et brusquement :

— Regarde, papa, c'est Judith !

La jeune Yéménite est là en effet, perdue dans la foule, tel un bel oiseau noir aux ailes cassées, immobilisée dans un geste de désespoir. Arié s'approche d'elle et la prend aux épaules. Elle se retourne, surprise. Et leurs regards se croisent comme quelques jours plus tôt dans le rétroviseur de la vieille Ford. Cette fois, Arié ne détourne pas la tête.

Le premier Shabbat après la mobilisation, Arié reviendra inopinément au kibboutz. Ses parents sont à la maison. Son père lit en se balançant sur une vieille chaise cannée, sa mère donne à manger à Dina, sa petite sœur.

— Que se passe-t-il ? s'écrie-t-elle en le voyant.

— Tout va bien, maman, ne t'inquiète pas. J'avais besoin de voir papa.

— Tu aurais pu téléphoner.

— C'est vrai... Mais c'est personnel... Il fallait que je voie papa... que je lui parle d'homme à homme.

— Bon, bon, fait Sarah, vexée, je m'en vais...

Puis, un radieux sourire aux lèvres :

— Mais au fait, tu parles maintenant ! Regarde, Mordekhaï, il a retrouvé sa langue !

Sur quoi, elle prend la petite Dina par la main. Et, la mine faussement grondeuse, laisse les deux hommes en tête à tête.

— Alors ? dit Mordekhaï.

— Alors, j'ai une chose à te demander.

— Je t'écoute, mon fils.

— Est-ce que je pourrais travailler avec Benjamin ?

Mordekhaï répète, surpris :

— Travailler avec Benjamin ?

— Oui, Benjamin, ton ami. Il fait partie du Mossad, n'est-ce pas ?

— C'est à peu près cela.

— Eh bien voilà, je voudrais travailler avec lui.

Et, comme Mordekhaï le fixe d'un air de plus en plus sidéré :

— Ce ne sont pas les soldats, ni les policiers qui pourront prévenir des attentats tels que ceux qui ont coûté la vie à ton cousin Hugo ou à la mère de Judith... Contre les terroristes, il faut employer d'autres moyens. Les terroristes qui nous combattent ne cantonnent pas seulement au Liban. Ils sont en Europe, ils sont en Argentine... Ce sont des jeunes comme moi... Je les connais...

Mordekhaï n'a jamais vu son fils dans cet état. Il n'a jamais vu, dans ses yeux, cette lueur mauvaise, presque perverse. A quoi pense-t-il ? A qui ? Pourquoi cet accent de reproche, presque de haine ? Et d'où lui vient cet étrange appétit de vengeance qu'il croit discerner dans ses mots ? Le jeune homme, de fait, continue :

— Est-ce que tu sais, papa, qu'Anna-Maria est une terroriste. Est-ce que tu sais que ses amis posent des bombes ? Tu vois, tu ne le sais pas ! La majorité des terroristes sont comme ça. Certains y croient vraiment. C'est pour cela qu'ils sont dangereux...

Et, prenant son père par le bras, comme s'il se ressouvenait tout à coup de sa présence :

— Tu parleras à Benjamin, dis ? Je crois que je saurai combattre ces salauds.

Chose promise, chose due. Le 6 septembre 1970, Arié reçoit l'ordre de se présenter au ministère de la Défense à Tel-Aviv. A l'accueil, un soldat l'attend et l'invite à le suivre. Le bureau exigu de Benjamin Ben Eliezer se trouve au troisième étage, au bout d'un long couloir. Sur la table, plusieurs téléphones. Au plafond, un énorme ventilateur. Benjamin porte son éternel costume gris et ses grosses lunettes en écaille. Il invite le jeune homme à s'asseoir et lui demande de raconter ce qu'il sait des activités d'Anna-Maria et de ses amis. Quand Arié a terminé, il se lève :

— Tu es ici dans un bureau de l' « Aman », qui est une abréviation de Agaf Modiin (Service de renseignements de l'armée). Ton père m'a parlé de ton désir de travailler dans les services de renseignements. Ce n'est pas impossible, mais il faut que tu finisses d'abord la première année de ton service militaire. Tu parles arabe ?

— Oui.

— Bien ?

— Je crois.

Le téléphone sonne. Benjamin s'excuse et soulève le récepteur. Le second téléphone retentit, il le décroche aussi et demande de patienter. Une oreille au premier. Une autre au second. En vingt secondes, tout est dit :

— Viens avec moi, Arié... Dans la salle des télex... Deux avions viennent d'être détournés par les Palestiniens... Un El Al et un TWA...

24

BEYROUTH

SEPTEMBRE NOIR

Septembre 1970

En ce début de septembre 1970, Hidar séjourne à nouveau à Beyrouth. Il est seul cette fois. Il a fini par promettre à Olga le mariage. Il l'a fait sincèrement, d'ailleurs. En pleine connaissance de cause. Sachant parfaitement que sa décision, une fois connue, sera critiquée aussi bien par les Soviétiques que par les Arabes. Mais enfin, pour le moment Olga n'est pas là. Et il est seul donc, en face de ses tourments.

Ce qui le préoccupe, c'est l' « Opération Jordanie ». Il en a défendu le principe à Moscou et se sent responsable de son succès. Cette opération, plusieurs fois repoussée, va enfin se réaliser ! Et pour la suivre de plus près, il s'est installé dans un studio au-dessus de l'appartement que Waddi Haddad a aménagé au troisième étage du Kataraji Building. Une opération aussi importante que celle de Jordanie ne peut être sérieusement suivie de la Centrale, sur la colline Mazraa, dans un va-et-vient incessant de journalistes et de feddayin. Waddi Haddad, lui, est depuis une semaine déjà en Jordanie, faisant la navette entre le camp de Wahdat et Amman. Et c'est Ghassan Kanafani et Bassam Abou Sharif qui assurent la permanence à la Centrale.

Oui, le Tunisien est inquiet. L'opération Ben Gourion a capoté. Le commando qui devait partir pour Buenos Aires de Copenhague a été surpris par la police, en train d'emballer les armes, au domicile d'une jeune peintre arabe. En outre, il y a tout juste deux mois, Haddad lui-même a échappé, par miracle, à un mystérieux tir d'obus qui a ravagé son salon, atteint sa chambre à coucher et blessé sa femme et son fils. En soi, l'échec de l'attentat contre Ben Gourion a plutôt réjoui Hidar. Mais pas la découverte aussi rapide du commando. Ni cet attentat contre un appartement dont personne, sauf les plus proches amis de Haddad, ne connaissait l'adresse. A croire que les Israéliens sont parfaitement renseignés. Mieux : infiltrés jusque dans les instances dirigeantes du Front. Cette conclusion, il n'est certainement pas seul, il le sait bien, à la tirer. Et il sait aussi qu'elle ne peut, à terme, que semer la méfiance entre eux tous et aboutir à de sanglants règlements de comptes.

Bref, ce 6 septembre, jour J, Hidar se tient dans son repaire. C'est un deux-pièces-cuisine tout blanc. Une table en teck, quelques chaises et un canapé en constituent le mobilier. Sur la table il y a trois téléphones noirs, avec leurs batteries de fils. Sur le rebord de la fenêtre, caché par une persienne, le télex. L'atmosphère est tendue. Il fait chaud. Le gros ventilateur ne parvient qu'à faire voleter les feuilles de papier, posées près des téléphones. La chemise en soie de Habbache est tachée de sueur. Ghassan Kanafani s'éponge nerveusement le front. Personne ne dit mot.

A 14 h 5, enfin, le télex se met à bourdonner et, presque en même temps, le téléphone à sonner. Kanafani décroche :

— Ça y est ! s'écrie-t-il. Samirah et Patrick ont détourné l'avion d'El Al.

Hidar essaie de sourire, mais son visage tendu par l'angoisse ne laisse paraître qu'une faible grimace. Comme tout le monde, il attend la suite.

14 h 12. Le télex et le téléphone s'ébranlent en même temps. Un feddayin arrache la dépêche qui vient de tomber. On annonce de Francfort le détournement d'un Boeing 707 de la compagnie américaine TWA, qui transportait 140 passagers vers New York.

14 h 27. Ça y est, le DC 8 de la Swissair, qui allait de Zurich à New York, vient lui aussi d'être arraisonné. Pour la première fois, Hidar et ses amis laissent un peu de leur joie éclater. On se lève. On danse presque. Bassam Abou Sharif débouche une bouteille de champagne. Habbache prend Kanafani dans ses bras. Les embrassades succèdent aux félicitations.

Mais voici qu'il est 15 h 3. Les trois téléphones sonnent tous ensemble. Kanafani décroche :

— Quoi ? demande-t-il.

Puis :

— Non… Ce n'est pas possible…

Il ne comprend visiblement pas ce qu'on lui dit. Ou mieux : il ne peut, ne *veut* pas comprendre. Quand Hidar s'approche de lui, il est tout pâle et semble sur le point de défaillir :

— L'avion d'El Al vient de se poser à Londres, dit-il simplement.

Habbache sursaute :

— A Londres ! Ce n'est pas possible, voyons !

Mais Kanafani fait un geste d'impuissance :

— Patrick a été mortellement blessé par les gardes sionistes. Samirah a été désarmée. Tous deux sont actuellement entre les mains de Scotland Yard…

Et, parcourant le paquet de dépêches qui tombent maintenant à un rythme de plus en plus rapide :

— Si les autres réussissent, ce sera quand même une victoire…

— Il faut qu'ils réussissent ! siffle Habbache entre ses dents.

Hidar arrache à Kanafani l'un des télex :

— Les avions de la Swissair et de la TWA viennent d'entrer en contact avec la tour de contrôle de Beyrouth.

— Et les autres dépêches ? demande Habbache.

— Elles disent la même chose. Il semble que les avions se dirigent actuellement sur Bagdad.

Silence dans la pièce. Chacun retient son souffle. Bassam Abou Sharif, pour tuer le temps, va préparer un peu de café. La tension est à son comble quand le

196

téléphone, qui s'était tu, recommence à sonner. Hidar sursaute.

— Ça doit être Amsterdam, dit Ghassan Kanafani.

— Mais oui, fait Hidar en décrochant, j'en avais presque oublié Amsterdam.

Une voix lointaine, venue d'Amsterdam en effet, annonce le détournement d'un Jumbo-Jet de la Pan Am, qui effectuait la liaison Bruxelles-New York.

Le large visage de Habbache s'illumine. Il prend Hidar par les épaules :

— Nous sommes en train de réussir, Hidar ! Nous allons secouer le monde et le forcer de tenir compte de la Palestine ! Ce sera notre guerre des Six Jours...

Il commence à faire sombre. Le café a refroidi. Mais Bassam Abou Sharif le sert quand même. Et il règne maintenant dans la pièce un climat, sinon d'euphorie, du moins d'optimisme et d'enthousiasme. A 20 h 50 enfin, Waddi Haddad téléphone d'Amman pour annoncer l'atterrissage réussi de l'appareil de la TWA à l' « aéroport de la Révolution » où se trouve déjà l'avion de la Swissair.

— Le Jumbo-Jet, en revanche, ne pourra jamais atterrir ici. La piste est trop courte.

— Fais-le poser à Amman, conseille Habbache.

— Impossible. Nous tenons la ville, mais les blindés du Roi contrôlent l'aéroport... Je rappelle à minuit.

A l'heure dite, nouvel appel. Ce n'est que deux heures plus tard qu'un représentant du Front au Caire téléphone pour dire que le Jumbo-Jet s'est posé à 1 h 21 à l'aéroport du Caire et que, après avoir évacué tous les passagers et l'équipage, les feddayin l'ont fait sauter.

— Voilà ! fait Hidar. La première manche est gagnée. Demain, le monde entier n'aura d'yeux que pour nous.

Et Habbache :

— Voyons d'abord comment ils réagiront à notre ultimatum. Il faut vite demander la libération de Samirah.

Puis, comme s'il tenait à donner la preuve de son extrême sérénité :

— Et maintenant, je vous conseille d'aller dormir. La journée de demain sera longue.

Le lendemain, quand Hidar descend à la permanence, on lui remet un message de Habbache lui demandant de passer à la Centrale. Une extraordinaire effervescence y règne. Dans la cour, dans les étages, les feddayin pavoisent. Les journaux sont favorables. Tous, ou presque, estiment que les preneurs d'otages usent du seul moyen à leur disposition pour attirer l'attention. Le communiqué du Front figure partout, en bonne place. Et le fait est que, jamais, on n'avait tant imprimé les mots Palestine et Palestiniens.

Hidar se fraie un chemin au milieu des feddayin en armes, des journalistes, des photographes et des équipes de télévision. Il repousse du pied un câble. Bouscule un cameraman. Manque se battre avec un autre. Et, après avoir poussé une porte derrière laquelle Kanafani répond aux questions de la télévision japonaise, il arrive devant le bureau de Georges Habbache, que gardent deux feddayin arborant chacun une Kalachnikov.

Habbache est assis. Il fait face à un jeune homme brun, à moustaches, prématurément grisonnant. Bassam Abou Sharif, debout derrière lui, présente :

— C'est un camarade argentin... L'un des dirigeants des fameux Montoneros...

Le jeune homme se lève :

— Julio Feldman.

— Enchanté, dit Hidar en anglais, tout en serrant la main tendue.

— Je disais au docteur Habbache, dit Feldman, que les Palestiniens viennent de donner une grande leçon au monde. Ce monde qui dort tranquillement sur un lit fait d'injustices, vous l'avez enfin réveillé.

— Julio Feldman est un grand poète, précise Habbache avec une pointe de moquerie dans la voix... Son mouvement est prêt à nous aider.

Puis, prenant Hidar par le bras et l'entraînant vers la fenêtre.

— J'ai parcouru la liste des passagers de l'avion que

198

nous avons détourné. Bassam te la donnera tout à l'heure. Tu risques d'avoir une surprise.

— Une surprise ?

— Oui, une surprise. Mais ne t'énerve pas. N'oublie pas qu'un homme surpris est un homme à moitié pris. Je te téléphonerai d'Amman. En attendant, appelle Moscou pour connaître leur réaction...

Embrassades. Adieux. Fausses protestations d'amitié. Quand Habbache quittera la pièce, Hidar s'approchera de Bassam Abou Sharif qui discute encore avec l'Argentin, et lui demandera la liste des passagers de l'avion détourné vers la Jordanie. Hidar a compris très vite à qui Habbache faisait allusion : parmi les passagers de la TWA, il y a bien entendu Sidney.

25

JORDANIE

DANS LE DÉSERT DE ZARKA

Septembre 1970

Il fait chaud. L'air est immobile. Les portes de l'avion grandes ouvertes ne laissent entrer dans la carlingue aucun courant d'air, aucune brise. A travers un hublot, que les rayons du soleil matinal prennent pour miroir, Sidney n'aperçoit qu'une étendue de sable jaune. Parfois, quelques hommes en armes apparaissent dans son champ de mire, comme sur la scène d'un théâtre, pour disparaître aussitôt derrière les coulisses. Devant lui, une femme aux cheveux défaits, sur lesquels quelques épingles pendent lamentablement, tente de calmer un enfant qui, depuis plus d'une heure déjà, crie à gorge déployée. Le commandant Caroll Woods, un homme d'une cinquantaine d'années, au dos légèrement voûté, repasse pour la troisième fois entre les rangées sans prononcer un mot, comme s'il pensait que sa seule présence rassurera les passagers.

A côté de Sidney, le rabbin Jonathan David, de Brooklyn, a tranquillement sorti un châle de prière d'une sacoche de toile grise, s'en est couvert la tête et murmure :

— Combien précieuse est Ta grâce ô Dieu ! Les fils de l'homme s'abritent à l'ombre de Tes ailes...

Puis, d'un geste mesuré, il sort les phylactères. Les enroule sur son avant-bras gauche. Se tourne vers Jérusalem, tout proche. Et dit la *chaharith*, la prière du matin.

200

Une rafale de mitraillette vient pourtant l'interrompre et fait sursauter Sidney. L'enfant sur la banquette avant se remet à crier de plus belle. Sidney regarde à travers le hublot : au loin, sur le fond bleu du firmament, quelques chars sombres, aux couleurs jordaniennes, se placent en position de combat.

Le rabbin Jonathan David reprend :

— Toi, que la miséricorde apaise et que la prière fléchit, laisse-Toi apaiser et fléchir par une génération malheureuse car il n'y a point de secours.

Sidney regarde le rabbin avec envie et admiration. Il ne connaît apparemment ni angoisses ni états d'âme. Comme le grand-oncle Abraham, là-bas, dans le ghetto de Varsovie ? Oui, exactement. Comme Abraham. Lui aussi se sentait protégé. Cela ne l'a pas préservé de la mort, mais lui a, au moins, épargné la peur. Et Sidney, à sa propre surprise, couvre sa tête d'un mouchoir et joint sa voix à celle du rabbin :

— Écoute, Israël, l'Éternel est notre Dieu, l'Éternel est Un !

Il revoit l'avion, la veille au soir, brutalement posé sur la piste d'un aérodrome inconnu, éclairé par des phares de voitures. Il revoit les trois hommes armés qui sont alors montés à bord. L'un d'entre eux, jeune, souriant, une chemise kaki largement ouverte sur une poitrine bronzée, informe les passagers dans un anglais correct que l'avion se trouve désormais entre les mains du Front Populaire de Libération de la Palestine. Il promet aux gens qu'ils seront bien traités. Mais ajoute qu'ils ne seront pas libérés tant que l'Angleterre, la RFA, la Suisse et Israël n'auront pas remis en liberté les combattants palestiniens détenus dans les prisons de ces différents pays.

La nuit, ensuite, a été particulièrement froide. Sidney a sorti un pull de sa sacoche, mis sa veste ; et, toujours tremblotant, il a enfilé la veste rayée de son pyjama en flanelle.

— Vous le faites exprès ? lui a demandé le rabbin Jonathan David, après avoir rangé son châle de prière et ses phylactères.

— Exprès ?

— Oui, votre veste de pyjama...

Et comme Sidney ne comprend pas :

— Avec votre visage fatigué, votre barbe mal tail-lée et votre pyjama rayé, vous faites penser à un déporté...

Et, hochant tristement la tête :

— Mais vous n'avez peut-être pas tort. Ce qui nous arrive procède de la même démarche que ce qui est arrivé à la génération de nos parents en Europe, voici à peine trente ans...

Oui, il revoit tout ça. Repense à tout ça. Il mesure, surtout, l'absurdité de la situation. Lui, Sidney Halter... Médecin tout ce qu'il y a de plus ordinaire... Lui, l'époux de Marjory, le père de Richard et de Marilyn, bloqué là, en plein désert, comme dans un film ou un roman... Ce genre de mésaventure n'arrive jamais qu'aux autres, se disait-il jusqu'à présent... Eh bien, non... Voilà... Ça lui est arrivé à lui... Et la vérité c'est qu'il n'en revient toujours pas...

A présent la nuit est finie. Le soleil s'est tout à fait levé et la chaleur est déjà étouffante. Sidney est en manches de chemise. Il a soif.

— Pouvez-vous me donner un peu d'eau ? demande-t-il à une hôtesse qui passe.

— Je vous en apporte un verre, mais il faudra dorénavant économiser l'eau. Nous ne savons pas combien de temps nous resterons ici... Le désert, vous comprenez...

Après avoir bu son verre, Sidney somnole un peu. Il a le temps de s'étonner de la phénoménale capacité d'adaptation des hommes. Une nouvelle fois, il repense au grand-oncle Abraham et au ghetto de Varsovie. Il revoit même, Dieu sait pourquoi, ce pauvre Hugo le jour de leur dernière rencontre, quand il est venu à New York, le taper de ces fameux 300 000 dollars. Et puis il finit par s'endormir.

C'est le haut-parleur qui le réveille. Il a peine, d'abord, à se rappeler où il est. Plusieurs feddayin se tiennent à l'avant de l'avion. Le jeune Palestinien, qu'il connaît déjà, énumère au micro des noms de passagers.

— Que se passe-t-il ? demande-t-il au rabbin Jonathan David.

— Le terroriste lit la liste des passagers qui seront emmenés à Amman.

— Ils seront libérés ?

— Il ne le dit pas...

Dès que le Palestinien a fini d'égrener les noms et les nationalités des voyageurs concernés, un tumulte assourdissant remplit la carlingue. Les passagers dont les noms ont été prononcés rassemblent leurs bagages. Certains d'entre eux s'inquiètent de leur destination. Ceux qui restent se mettent à écrire fébrilement des messages pour leurs familles avec l'espoir que ceux qui partent parviendront à les transmettre. Les enfants crient, les tablettes claquent et Sidney pense, encore une fois, au ghetto de Varsovie. Troublé par cette comparaison démesurée, il écrit, lui aussi, un bout de lettre aux siens, et prie une jeune femme, au nombre des passagers « libérés », de le poster à Amman.

Tout doucement, l'avion se vide. Ceux qui restent marquent leur stupeur en gardant le silence. Sidney voit à travers le hublot quelques camions chargés d'hommes, de femmes et d'enfants, quitter la piste en direction des chars jordaniens. Il les suit du regard jusqu'à ce qu'il ne reste d'eux qu'un épais nuage de poussière. Quand il se retourne, le rabbin Jonathan David, prie à nouveau :

— « Ô Éternel, secours-nous, que le Roi nous exauce au jour où nous L'invoquons. »

Une femme s'approche. Elle est petite, ses cheveux gris sont tirés en arrière et ses lunettes, accrochées à une cordelette rouge, se balancent sur sa grosse poitrine.

— Je m'appelle Sarah Malka, dit-elle. De North Bergen, New Jersey.

— Enchantée, répond la femme du rabbin.

— N'avez-vous pas remarqué, demande Sarah Malka, que ceux qui sont restés sont presque tous juifs ?

— Non, fait le rabbin.

— Mais si, mais si, dit-elle en triturant nerveusement la grosse bague verte qu'elle porte à l'auriculaire gauche, j'ai fait le tour de l'avion ; derrière, à quelques rangées de vous, il y a Mme Beeber, de Brooklyn et le rabbin Drillman et aussi M. Benjamin Finstin, de Whiteston, New York...

— Mais moi, je ne suis pas juive, proteste une fille en minijupe. Si on ne retient ici que les Juifs, il faudrait qu'ils me libèrent !

Le rabbin Jonathan David tente de la calmer :

— Allons, allons ! Je suis sûr que vous n'êtes pas la seule « goï » dans l'avion. Faites un tour pour vous en assurer.

Sidney sourit. Puis, il se lève pour se dégourdir les jambes. La chaleur est de plus en plus étouffante. Le soleil brûle le duralumin de la carlingue. Et il faut attendre la fin de la journée, puis la nuit, pour que la température redevienne à peu près supportable.

Le lendemain, la situation n'a toujours pas évolué. Par contre, les toilettes sont de plus en plus sales et l'eau vient à manquer. Mais le pire, c'est l'incertitude, le manque d'informations, l'angoisse. Les hommes ruminent. Des femmes, de plus en plus nombreuses, craquent et ont des crises de nerfs. Le commandant leur distribue des calmants. L'équipage tente de les apaiser. Mais en vain. L'attente devient, d'heure en heure, plus intolérable, plus lourde.

Vers 11 heures, nouvelle visite des feddayin. Celui qui parle anglais a une seconde liste de noms. Il les égrène sur le même ton monocorde que la première fois. Sidney est du nombre. Et sans rien savoir de ce qu'on lui veut, sans poser la moindre question, il obéit et se lève.

— Avec les bagages ? demande-t-il.

— Non. Sans les bagages.

Il ressent un picotement dans la gorge, la peau sous sa barbe qui se contracte. Mais il se lève et s'apprête à suivre le commando. En arrivant à la porte, il est frappé de plein fouet par une lumière si forte qu'il doit fermer les yeux et trébuche sur la première marche de l'échelle.

Il est sur la piste maintenant. Une quinzaine de passagers parmi lesquels un homme à la barbe noire, une calotte sur la tête, attendent résignés la suite des

204

événements. Sidney découvre avec étonnement, juste devant l'avion de la TWA, un autre appareil, suisse. Autour des deux avions, une centaine de feddayin armés montent la garde. Un peu en retrait sont alignées une douzaine de nids de mitrailleuses ainsi que plusieurs jeeps armées de mitraillettes lourdes, et une ambulance du Croissant rouge palestinien.

L'atmosphère est tendue. Les feddayin — dont l'un porte sur sa veste de treillis l'insigne de la Swissair — conservent le doigt sur la détente de leurs armes. Le petit groupe de passagers paraît écrasé par l'ombre du Boeing. Sidney, bien sûr, est en nage.

— Ils vont nous fusiller ? demande la jeune femme en minijupe.

Ce n'est qu'au bout d'un moment — qui semble à Sidney aussi long que la traversée du désert — qu'une jeune Palestinienne s'approche du groupe :

— Des journalistes vont vous interviewer. Mais que ce soit clair : pas de messages personnels, pas de discours, ni de proclamations. Sachez que la vie de tous les passagers est entre vos mains.

Elle fait ensuite signe aux feddayin de s'éloigner des avions. Ils la suivent sur la piste en terre battue, craquelée par l'effet de la chaleur. Sidney remarque que le commandant de bord porte l'insigne du Front Populaire pour la Libération de la Palestine épinglé sur sa chemise blanche, sale et froissée. Puis il aperçoit les pieds nus d'une des hôtesses de la TWA et se souvient d'une phrase du Talmud que son père citait souvent : « Quand les hommes ne respectent pas la Loi, ils se dévorent vivants. »

Quelques minutes plus tard, les journalistes arrivent. Les feddayin les placent à bonne distance du petit groupe de passagers. Drôle de conférence de presse ! Les journalistes, comme les voyageurs, doivent employer des haut-parleurs pour se faire entendre.

— Comment allez-vous ? crie un journaliste.

Le chef de cabine du DC 8 de la Swissair répond dans un anglais marqué par un fort accent suisse :

— Nos gardes sont très gentils. Ils font tout ce qu'ils

peuvent pour nous. Les conditions d'hygiène à bord sont cependant inacceptables. Les toilettes ne peuvent plus être utilisées. Nous avons de quoi manger, mais plus rien à boire...

Pas de photos. Pas d'interventions intempestives. Juste ce soleil torride. Cette douleur à la tête, qui gagne. Cette impression, persistante, de cauchemar et d'horreur. Sidney se sent si mal qu'il n'est, à dire vrai, pas fâché du tout quand arrive l'instant de remonter dans l'appareil. Au moment, pourtant, où il s'apprête à grimper à l'échelle, un Palestinien d'une quarantaine d'années, en uniforme kaki, au front dégarni et à la moustache noire, l'interpelle :

— Vous êtes bien Sidney Halter ?

— Oui.

— Vous avez beaucoup de bagages ?

— Non, une sacoche...

— Alors, prenez-la et revenez. Je vous emmène à Amman.

26

BEYROUTH

LA DISPARITION DE SIDNEY

Septembre 1970

Depuis que les téléscripteurs ont fait tomber les premières dépêches annonçant au monde le détournement simultané des avions d'El Al, de la TWA et de la Swissair, Hidar Assadi est sur le qui-vive. Cette « opération Jordanie » est son opération. Pourtant, il n'en a aucunement le contrôle et ne peut en modifier le cours. Spectateur d'une pièce qu'il a imaginée et qui, à présent, se déroule sans lui, il est un peu l'otage des otages de Zarka et court donc après les informations de la Centrale, sur la colline de Mazraa, à la permanence dans le Kataragii Building.

Le 9 septembre, à 11 h 30, il apprend le détournement du DC 10 de la BOAC, qui relie Bahrein à Londres. Cette nouvelle opération de détournement a été décidée avec son consentement : les Britanniques refusant de libérer Samirah et nul citoyen britannique ne figurant parmi les otages de Zarka, il fallait se donner rapidement une véritable monnaie d'échange. Cependant, les événements ne s'enchaînent pas aussi rapidement qu'il l'avait prévu et voulu. Les négociations pour la libération des otages en échange des prisonniers palestiniens en Suisse, Angleterre, Allemagne et Israël traînent en longueur et quant à l'offensive militaire déclenchée contre le roi de Jordanie, elle semble piétiner. Le temps donné par Moscou pour réussir est en train de s'écouler et Hidar, impuissant, se ronge les sangs à Beyrouth. « N'allez surtout pas en Jordanie, lui a dit son contact à l'ambassade d'URSS... il ne faut pas qu'un homme lié à Moscou soit vu parmi les Palestiniens à Zarka ou dans les camps des environs d'Amman. » Moyennant quoi il en est là — désespérément inactif et anxieux. C'est un appel de Moscou qui le réveille. Olga à l'appareil... Ce coup de téléphone le sidère. Personne, sauf quelques responsables soviétiques haut placés, ne pouvait connaître son numéro à Beyrouth. Et en effet, Olga lui avoue en minaudant l'avoir obtenu de son frère Sacha. Que celui-ci communique un numéro de téléphone secret, même à sa propre sœur, est incompréhensible ! Sauf s'il voulait ainsi lui nuire. La nouvelle annoncée par Olga confirme cette hypothèse : Rachel Halter, ayant appris par sa fille que le cousin Sidney de New York était un spécialiste des maladies des yeux et qu'il utilisait des traitements peu connus en Union soviétique contre le glaucome, a appelé les États-Unis pour lui demander conseil et a appris son enlèvement.

— Son enlèvement ? s'exclame Hidar. Je sais qu'il voyageait à bord de l'un des avions détournés par la résistance palestinienne...

— Pas du tout...

— Que dis-tu ?

Olga parle plus fort :

— Je dis : pas du tout... Sidney se trouvait, en effet, dans l'avion de la TWA, détourné par les terroristes, mais il n'y est plus...

Hidar s'impatiente :

— Sois plus précise, *milaya*. Je t'en prie.

— Je te dis ce que m'a raconté maman. La femme de Sidney a reçu un coup de fil d'Amman, d'une passagère de la TWA, libérée par les Palestiniens et à qui Sidney aurait confié une lettre.

— Que dit la lettre ?

— Ne crie pas, Hidar. Je t'entends très bien ! Je ne sais pas ce que dit la lettre. Mais il paraît que tous les passagers ont déjà été libérés sauf les passagers juifs...

— Et Sidney est parmi eux ?

— Justement, non. Un responsable terroriste serait venu le chercher à l'avion juste après la conférence de presse organisée par les Palestiniens. Et depuis, personne ne l'a revu...

Cette affaire déplaît profondément à Hidar. D'abord parce qu'il n'aime pas cette idée d'une discrimination à l'encontre des otages juifs. Mais, ensuite, parce qu'il a beau n'avoir aucune sympathie particulière pour ce Sidney, sa disparition le gêne. Mieux, elle l'inquiète. Car il ne peut s'empêcher de penser qu'elle le vise lui, Hidar, comme déjà on avait cherché à l'atteindre en tuant Hugo. Il se souvient de la remarque de Kamal Joumblatt : « Quand on ne sait pas protéger un ami, on perd de son influence ; quand on ne sait pas le venger, on perd ses amis. » Et, pour la énième fois, il s'interroge sur la mystérieuse haine qu'un dirigeant du Front semble lui porter.

Après quoi, il prend une douche, s'habille et descend à la permanence. Ghassan Kanafani est déjà là. L'un des feddayin préposés au télex leur apporte des cafés et Kanafani lui tend les dépêches. La première annonce une démarche de l'Irak auprès du FPLP pour obtenir la libération des passagers des avions détournés. La seconde fait état de la déclaration du président américain, Richard Nixon, dans laquelle celui-ci promet solennellement d'obtenir la liberté de tous les otages, sans distinction de nationalité, de race ou de religion...

— Les cons ! peste Hidar.

— De qui parles-tu ? demande Ghassan.

— Je parle de nos amis. Ils devaient organiser un événement médiatique propre, sans bavures et gagner ainsi la sympathie du monde. Au lieu de cela, ils apportent sur un plateau d'argent des arguments, médiatiques justement, au président américain. Celui-ci a beau jeu de les accuser d'antisémitisme ! Il a même l'air d'avoir raison...

— Ils n'ont certainement pas pu faire autrement, fait Kanafani doucement, sans lâcher Hidar des yeux. Israël n'est sensible qu'à la menace exercée contre les

Juifs. Et c'est Israël qui retient le plus grand nombre de nos camarades.

Hidar se fâche :

— Mais de quoi parles-tu ? Tu sais aussi bien que moi que cette opération n'avait pas pour but la libération de nos camarades, mais la conquête de l'opinion publique internationale et la prise du pouvoir à Amman.

— Et nos camarades ?

— En réalisant nos deux objectifs, on obtenait automatiquement leur libération.

Hidar fait quelques pas dans la pièce, nerveusement, en fléchissant chaque fois sur sa jambe malade et, posant les dépêches sur la table à côté du téléphone, il se plante devant Kanafani :

— Pourquoi me regardes-tu comme ça ?

Le visage de Kanafani se détend :

— J'aime bien ta manière de poser les questions. A la russe. Tu es le seul Arabe, à ma connaissance, qui s'exprime comme un personnage de Dostoïevski.

— Ce n'est pas pour ça que tu me regardes de cette façon depuis mon arrivée, tout de même !

— C'est vrai... C'est vrai... Mais disons que j'essaie de comprendre pourquoi Waddi Haddad te déteste autant...

Voilà... Nous y sommes... Hidar vient enfin de voir confirmé ce qu'il soupçonne depuis longtemps : quelqu'un essaie de le compromettre, de faire planer sur lui, parmi les dirigeants du Front, une suspicion obscure. Et ce quelqu'un c'est Haddad.

— Oui... ! dit-il, sans se troubler. Et quelle est, selon toi, la raison de sa haine ?

— Tes amitiés juives.

— Et pourquoi me dis-tu, toi, tout cela ?

Kanafani ne répond pas tout de suite. Il s'assied sur la table, regarde un moment les trois téléphones, se relève, s'approche du téléscripteur, arrache une dépêche, la parcourt des yeux et se tournant vers Hidar, la lit :

— La direction du FPLP à Zarka accorde un nou-

veau délai de soixante-douze heures aux pays déten-
teurs de prisonniers palestiniens...

Puis, en se rapprochant de Hidar :

— Je te dis tout cela parce que je te comprends. Je
ne connais pas de Juifs personnellement, mais je connais leurs écrivains...

La confidence de Kanafani fait plaisir à Hidar. Il
recule pourtant d'un pas : l'odeur de la mousse à raser
du Palestinien l'incommode. L'autre, prenant ce
retrait pour une marque d'hostilité, hausse les épaules
et quitte la pièce.

Hidar, après son départ, essaiera à plusieurs
reprises de joindre au téléphone Haddad et Habbache
en Jordanie. En vain. Vers 6 heures de l'après-midi, il
reçoit une enveloppe apportée par un garçonnet. Dans
l'enveloppe il y a une feuille de papier quadrillé avec
cette simple phrase : « Les oiseaux ont peur des
vagues. » C'est le message convenu avec son contact à
l'ambassade soviétique à Beyrouth. Il quitte à son
tour la pièce et se rend sans tarder à la Grotte aux
Pigeons.

Dès la terrasse, il reconnaît le crâne chauve du chef
des services secrets soviétiques au Proche-Orient.
L'homme est accoudé à une table près de la balustrade et contemple la mer. Hidar s'assied à la table
voisine et commande de l'arak.

— Il fait beau, dit-il en anglais, en se tournant vers
l'homme.

— Ça dépend pour qui, fait celui-ci... Moi je
trouve qu'il fait trop chaud.

Et, s'assurant que personne ne les écoute :

— Nos amis pensent que l'opération dure trop
longtemps.

— On m'a donné une semaine.

— Telle qu'elle est partie, cette opération dépas-
sera la semaine et peut-être la suivante. Les passagers... Ils doivent être libérés. L'opinion publique
commence à protester. Il s'agit de la liberté de la

navigation aérienne. Nos amis ne peuvent la remettre en question. Nous avons des engagements internationaux.

Deux mouettes filent au-dessus de leurs têtes. Elles se jettent à l'eau en criant.

— Il faudrait que j'aille sur place, dit Hidar. Je n'arrive pas à contacter mes amis par téléphone.

L'homme tourne vers lui deux yeux bleus menaçants :

— Pas question ! Vous m'avez compris : pas question ! Si vous êtes repéré, nous serons accusés d'avoir monté l'opération. Débrouillez-vous pour faire passer le message autrement.

Sur quoi il se lève. Pose un billet sur la table. Scrute les quelques groupes de consommateurs présents sur la terrasse. Et lâche, sans presque desserrer les lèvres :

— Dans une semaine, le 17, ici, à la même heure.

Puis, d'une voix plus forte — comme s'il parlait à la cantonade :

— J'ai été ravi de faire votre connaissance, monsieur. Et j'espère vous revoir bientôt. J'espère aussi que vos problèmes seront alors résolus...

Hidar le regarde sortir, attend un moment et se lève à son tour.

Devant l'entrée du café, il cherche des yeux un taxi. N'en voit pas. Il fixe la route, où défilent les voitures. Et soudain, une petite Morris surgit, qu'il voit déboîter et se diriger sur lui en klaxonnant. Instinctivement, il fait un saut en arrière. La voiture le frôle et se fige dans un grincement de pneus sur le trottoir. Cris des autres automobilistes... Insultes... Puis son nom, hurlé par une voix féminine... Relevant la tête, il voit Leïla Chehab surgir de la petite voiture et courir à sa rencontre.

— Vous m'avez fait peur, dit-il simplement en guise de bonjour.

— Je suis désolée, répond Leïla. Mais j'espérais vous trouver là. Je vous ai cherché partout. Il fallait que je vous voie.

Sa voix est légèrement tremblante. Elle porte une robe légère en soie blanche, qui moule parfaitement son corps et Hidar ne peut s'empêcher de la trouver désirable.

— Sidney... dit-elle. Vous avez entendu, pour Sidney...

Et, comme si elle n'était pas sûre qu'il ait compris :

— Vous vous souvenez ? Sidney, mon ami américain... Le médecin... Le cousin de votre amie russe... Nous nous sommes rencontrés ici même, à la Grotte aux Pigeons...

— Oui, oui, je me souviens. Il se trouvait en effet dans l'avion de la TWA.

Leïla l'interrompt :

— Mais non !... Je veux dire : oui, bien sûr ! Il se trouvait dans l'avion de la TWA... Mais la radio vient d'annoncer qu'il a été enlevé par des inconnus... Plus de nouvelles de lui depuis deux jours... Il n'est plus parmi les otages...

Et comme son interlocuteur ne répond rien :

— Je vous cherchais... Je vous cherchais... Vous êtes le seul à pouvoir m'aider... Il faut le retrouver ! Vous m'entendez : le retrouver !

— Pourquoi moi ? demanda Hidar, brusquement calmé.

Une voiture s'arrête à ce moment-là. Une Chevrolet. Deux couples en sortent en riant. Ils observent un moment Hidar et Leïla, font une remarque inaudible et pénètrent dans le café.

— Parce que, dit Leïla, vous le connaissez. Parce que vous travaillez avec le FPLP. Parce que vous représentez les Soviétiques...

Hidar pâlit et s'arrache à la prise de la jeune femme.

— Que racontez-vous là ?

— Mon mari me l'a dit...

Elle pose sur Hidar ses grands yeux noirs embués de larmes et ajoute doucement :

— Mon mari est bien renseigné.

Hidar hésite une seconde puis, avec un sourire forcé :

— Je m'en occuperai...

— Je vous en supplie...

27

TEL-AVIV

ARIÉ DANS LA TOURMENTE

Septembre 1970

Arié a l'impression de vivre les jours les plus importants de sa vie. Depuis le moment où les premières dépêches sont tombées, il est devenu l'ombre de Benjamin. Pris dans le tourbillon des événements, réceptionnant les télex, les faisant porter à Dayan et à Ygal Alon, celui-ci ne s'est pas avisé, ou a fait mine de ne pas s'aviser, de la présence constante du jeune homme à ses côtés. Ce n'est que tard dans la soirée, après qu'ils ont recueilli le témoignage de l'agent de sécurité israélien d'El Al qui a maîtrisé la terroriste palestinienne, qu'il se tourne vers Arié et demande :

— Comment vas-tu rentrer à cette heure-ci à la base ?

Arié, à la vérité, n'y a pas encore songé.

— Bon, bon, je vais prévenir tes supérieurs que tu restes à Tel-Aviv, puis nous mangerons quelque chose. Tu dois mourir de faim.

Quand ils se retrouvent dans le petit restaurant près de la Maison des Journalistes, rue Lessin, où Benjamin a manifestement ses habitudes, Arié remarque que son patron a noué sa cravate, qu'il s'est soigneusement recoiffé et qu'il ressemble de nouveau à un parfait fonctionnaire accompagnant un parent venu d'un lointain kibboutz.

— Pourquoi me regardes-tu comme ça ? demande-t-il.

— Parce que tu changes tellement, tellement... Je t'ai vu tout à l'heure au ministère, sans veste, sans cravate, affairé.

— En effet, oui. Quand je travaille, je m'oublie un peu...

Et, en essuyant ses lunettes :

— Mon père a fui l'Allemagne et le nazisme en 1935. Il a traversé clandestinement plusieurs frontières et mis plus de cinq mois à rejoindre la Palestine. Mais, quand il est arrivé à Haïfa, il portait un costume, qu'il avait lavé et repassé lui-même pendant la traversée, et une cravate. « Il ne faut jamais se laisser aller... disait-il, par respect pour autrui. »

Malgré l'heure tardive, le petit restaurant où ils s'intallent déborde de monde. Sur le bar en formica un ventilateur tourne, sans raison. La radio transmet de la musique arabe. Une jeune serveuse brune se faufile gracieusement entre les tables, les assiettes à la main.

— Elle te plaît ? demande Benjamin, visiblement mal à l'aise dans ce genre de conversation, mais voulant se montrer cordial avec le fils de son ami.

— Non, fait Arié. Elle me fait penser à Judith.

Et il relate sa rencontre avec la jeune Yéménite... leur regard... rien qu'un regard, oui, le jour de l'attentat de Baram... Et il conclut :

— C'est pour ça que je voulais travailler avec toi !

Benjamin sourit mais ne dit rien. Le repas terminé, il annonce :

— J'ai demandé à Myriam, ma secrétaire, de te réserver une chambre dans un hôtel, pas loin d'ici, rue Ibn Gvirol. Moi, je dois retourner au bureau. Le monde continue de tourner...

C'est ainsi donc, aux côtés de Benjamin Ben Eliezer, qu'Arié suivra les événements de Jordanie. Il sera informé heure par heure, minute par minute, de la suite des événements tant à Zarka que dans les camps autour d'Amman ou à Amman même. Imaginait-il ainsi l'univers des services secrets ? Oui et non. Ce qu'il découvre ressemble plutôt aux bureaux d'une banale entreprise. Mais que d'informations en même temps ! Quelle quantité de nouvelles inouïes ! En portant les dépêches d'une pièce à l'autre et en s'attardant parfois à écouter les conversations, Arié apprend ce que la presse ne divulgue jamais : qu'Ygal Alon vient par exemple de rencontrer longuement le roi Hussein à Akaba, mais que Dayan ne considère pas le petit roi comme l'interlocuteur idéal. Myriam, la secrétaire de Benjamin, une grande femme d'une quarantaine d'années, aux cheveux noirs tirés en chignon et aux grands yeux verts en amande, s'amuse de son enthousiasme :

— Je pensais que les jeunes d'aujourd'hui ne s'intéressaient qu'au rock et aux surprises-parties...

Le 12 septembre au matin, les dépêches annoncent la libération des otages et la destruction par les Palestiniens des trois avions détournés. Il ne reste plus, aux mains des ravisseurs, que les 56 otages d'origine juive.

— La première faute commise depuis le début de l'opération, dit Benjamin en apprenant la nouvelle.

Et, voyant l'étonnement d'Arié :

— Les Palestiniens ont entrepris une double offensive : médiatique et militaire. L'offensive médiatique était destinée à gagner la sympathie de l'opinion publique et elle était bien évidemment essentielle au succès de l'offensive proprement militaire contre Hussein. S'ils apparaissent aux yeux du monde comme des racistes, établissant une distinction entre les hommes de différentes religions, de différentes origines, alors...

Benjamin, comme pour mieux le convaincre, l'envoie au deuxième étage, service informatique, chercher les noms de ces 56 Juifs retenus par les Palestiniens en Jordanie.

Quand Arié lui apporte la liste, il la parcourt rapidement. Mais au lieu de se réjouir, au lieu de se répéter que le commandement palestinien a commis une erreur et que c'est la chance d'Israël, il blêmit et s'écrie :

— Que le diable les emporte ! Qu'est-ce qu'ils ont fait de Sidney ?

— Sidney ?

— Oui, le frère de ton père… Sidney Halter.

— Qu'est-ce qu'il a à voir avec le détournement ?

— Il se trouvait parmi les passagers de la TWA et il ne figure plus sur la liste des passagers retenus.

Après quoi, sans plus prêter attention à Arié, il décroche le téléphone, compose un numéro, donne un ou deux ordres brefs dont Arié ne comprend tout à coup plus le sens. Puis, se rasseyant :

— Attendons les nouvelles.

— Benjamin ? Pour Sidney… tu savais depuis le début ?

— Oui.

— Comment ?

— Nous avions la liste des passagers des avions détournés.

— Alors, pourquoi ne m'as-tu rien dit ?

— Pourquoi t'aurais-je dit quoi que ce soit ?

— Mais c'est mon oncle !

Et, gêné de son emportement :

— Les Arabes disent : « Celui qui a une seule goutte de votre sang ne manque pas de s'intéresser à vous. »

Les deux hommes se taisent. Benjamin, pour passer le temps, essuie comme d'habitude ses lunettes et Arié regarde le ventilateur brasser l'air du bureau. Quand le téléphone sonne, ils sursautent en même temps. Benjamin décroche, écoute un moment et peste :

— Mon Dieu ! Sidney a été enlevé par Waddi Haddad.

— Mais pourquoi ?

— Bonne question !

Arié se lève alors :

— Je peux prévenir mon père ?

Benjamin, après une seconde ou deux d'hésitation :

— Attends deux jours.

Deux jours après, c'est tout le paysage qui a basculé.

Les Palestiniens ont occupé Irbid. Le roi Hussein a quitté Amman. Le service de renseignement de l'armée s'est transformé en une véritable ruche. Arié croise dans le couloir le général Dayan, les généraux Sharon et Bar Lev, des ministres religieux, des officiers gradés, de simples soldats. Benjamin va de réunion en réunion. De briefing en briefing. Mais les heures, les jours ont beau passer — on ne sait toujours rien de Sidney.

Le gouvernement américain s'est officiellement ému. La Croix-Rouge internationale s'est adressée à la Centrale palestinienne. Les médias se mobilisent. La télévision montre, tous les jours, son portrait. Et il n'est pas jusqu'à la famille qui, en la personne de Mordekhaï, n'entre dans la danse. Arié lui a parlé plusieurs fois. Marjory elle-même, inquiète, l'a déjà appelé de New York. Et quand il arrive à Tel-Aviv, le 16 septembre, en fin de matinée, tout ébranlé, comme accablé par le choc, il faut toute l'éloquence de Benjamin pour le convaincre que les choses vont s'arranger... Que Sidney n'est pas bien loin... Que cet enlèvement, d'ailleurs, visait quelqu'un d'autre à travers lui... Quel autre ? Hidar Assadi, bien sûr. Le représentant officieux des Soviétiques auprès des organisations palestiniennes. Qui sait, même, si cette disparition ne serait pas secrètement liée à l'assassinat d'Hugo Halter ?

Dans la journée du 17 septembre, les événements s'accélèrent. Le roi Hussein, se sentant menacé par l'offensive des Palestiniens à l'intérieur et des Syriens à l'extérieur de ses frontières, appelle au secours les Américains. Les services secrets israéliens captent sa conversation avec Henry Kissinger. Lequel contacte aussitôt Itzhak Rabin, ambassadeur d'Israël à Washington, qui organise un rendez-vous téléphonique entre le secrétaire d'État américain et le Premier ministre israélien Golda Meïr qui se trouve par hasard être, à ce moment-là, au Hilton de New York. L'Américain veut la promesse d'une intervention israélienne pour sauver le roi de Jordanie. Golda Meïr demande vingt-quatre heures de réflexion et prévient Jérusalem.

— C'est une vraie guerre psychologique, remarque Benjamin en épluchant les dépêches.

— Pour faire peur aux Palestiniens ? demande Arié.

— Non. Pour impressionner les Soviétiques.

— Et Sidney ?

— Toujours rien. Mais nous avons appris qu'Hidar Assadi séjourne actuellement à Beyrouth. Il vient de rencontrer le deuxième secrétaire de l'ambassade soviétique, qui n'est autre que le chef des services secrets d'URSS pour le Proche-Orient.

Et, en ôtant ses lunettes :

— J'ai bien l'impression qu'en enlevant Sidney, Waddi Haddad a commis sa seconde faute.

28

BUENOS AIRES

LES DOUTES D'UNE TERRORISTE

Septembre 1970

Anna-Maria et Mario quittent la ville par la route du Nord. Mario conduit. Anna-Maria est assise tout près de lui et retient difficilement son exaltation. Elle aime quitter Buenos Aires, affronter la pampa, la route sans fin. Elle aime cet asphalte craquelé, bosselé, lézardé, traversé de vagues de sable où la voiture part en embardée. Aujourd'hui les crevasses débordent d'eau de pluie. La route est terriblement glissante. Mais son bonheur est identique. Et c'est le cœur incroyablement léger qu'elle aborde la centaine de kilomètres qui la sépare de Belen de Escobar, où doit se tenir la réunion. « Une réunion importante », a dit Mario. Pardi, oui, elle en a conscience — et pour rien au monde elle n'aurait renoncé à ce voyage.

La vérité est que, depuis le départ d'Arié, elle s'est entièrement donnée au travail clandestin. Elle a passé un mois dans un camp d'entraînement, près de Cordoba, et elle connaît à présent le maniement de toutes les sortes d'armes que la guérilla reçoit des pays du Pacte de Varsovie. Elle sait distinguer le fusil Kalachnikov AK-47 du modèle AKM, légèrement modifié. Elle sait démonter la mitraillette hongroise, munie d'une crosse de métal 156 pliante, mais elle lui préfère sa version tchèque, la VZ-58, beaucoup plus légère, avec une crosse en fibre de verre. Elle a même appris à lancer

220

des grenades et son moniteur l'a initiée au maniement des V 40, les grenades hollandaises à fragmentation, plus légères et « plus maniables » pour une femme. Elle a participé à des opérations mineures. Et, presque toujours, en dépit de l'opposition de ses camarades, elle se promène armée d'un pistolet 9 mm égyptien, baptisé le TO Kagypt. « On ne m'aura pas vivante », répète-t-elle à tout bout de champ — à la façon d'un enfant qui s'émerveille de prononcer une énormité.

Dix kilomètres après Buenos Aires, le couple tombe sur un barrage. Les policiers arrêtent les voitures sur deux files et Mario doit freiner derrière une grosse Chevrolet immatriculée à Mendoza.

— Holà, où allez-vous ?

— A Rosario.

— Vos papiers !

Le policier, grand type costaud au visage très jeune, examine la carte d'identité de Mario, puis celle d'Anna-Maria. Il les montre ensuite à son compagnon, un petit joufflu, lui aussi très jeune, et les leur rend comme à regret :

— Pourquoi arrêtez-vous les voitures ? demande Anna-Maria.

Les deux policiers se regardent. C'est le grand qui répond :

— Vous savez, señorita, il n'y a pas que des touristes qui prennent cette route. Malheureusement, nous avons aussi en Argentine des bandits et des terroristes.

— Vous en avez déjà arrêté ici ?

— Oui, cela nous arrive. Allez, filez !

— *Gracias.*

Mario contourne la grosse Chevrolet dont le chauffeur est en train de vider le coffre et reprend la route. Ils roulent un moment, en silence, entre des pâturages clôturés par des barbelés.

— Qu'est-ce qui t'a pris de questionner le flic ? proteste Mario. Tu te crois en reportage...

Anna-Maria éclate de rire. Un peu trop fort...

— Il n'y a pas de quoi rire ! Imagine que les flics aient fouillé la voiture et qu'ils aient mis la main sur les tracts.

Et puis ton revolver... Tu imagines leur tronche s'ils étaient tombés sur ton revolver !

Mario est fou de fureur. Et, jetant un coup d'œil à sa montre, il grommelle :

— Les camarades ont certainement déjà commencé la réunion. Julio doit rendre compte de son voyage à Beyrouth...

Car c'est bien vrai : tout le monde chez les Montoneros attend depuis plusieurs jours le retour de Julio Feldman. On veut savoir... On veut comprendre... Le détournement simultané de quatre avions par les Palestiniens a provoqué l'enthousiasme et l'annonce de la prise par les feddayin d'Irbid et de Zarka a été accueillie par une véritable explosion de joie. Les Palestiniens ne participent-ils pas à la lutte commune contre l'impérialisme ? Ne donnent-ils pas un magnifique exemple à tous les peuples en lutte de par le monde ? Anna-Maria a bien essayé de faire des réserves. En apprenant cette histoire de ségrégation entre otages juifs et non juifs, elle a bien émis quelques doutes sur les qualités révolutionnaires des camarades palestiniens. « Il est plus facile de critiquer à Buenos Aires que de se battre à Amman », lui a-t-on fait remarquer. Moyennant quoi elle s'est tue et se retrouve aujourd'hui sur cette route de Belen de Escobar.

Mario et la jeune femme arrivent sur le lieu du rendez-vous à la tombée du jour. Il ne pleut plus. Une étoile est apparue entre les nuages. Mario gare l'automobile devant une sorte de manoir anglais. Et tous deux sortent — plutôt soulagés de se dégourdir enfin les jambes.

— Bonne mère ! Vous voilà enfin...

Anna-Maria reconnaît tout de suite le petit bonhomme qui court à leur rencontre.

— Roberto ! fait-elle sur le ton de quelqu'un retrouvant un ami d'enfance...

— Oui, répond Roberto, tout essoufflé... On commençait à être inquiet. Avec tous ces barrages de police, tu comprends... On ne sait pas ce qui peut se passer...

Et de les mener à grandes enjambées, entre des

pelouses soigneusement entretenues, jusqu'au perron de la maison.

— Belle maison ! s'exclame Mario.

— Oui, un *casco*... une véritable maison de maîtres... elle appartient aux parents de l'un de nos camarades...

Une belle porte en bronze... Un long couloir tapissé, tout au long, de gravures équestres... Un hall couvert de papier à fleurs et décoré de portraits d'ancêtres... Un feu qui brûle dans une cheminée de pierre blanche. N'était la vingtaine de jeunes gens réunis là — certains assis sur des fauteuils en cuir patiné, d'autres sur des chaises en bois foncé, d'autres encore debout, un verre à la main — on pourrait réellement se croire dans l'une de ces vénérables demeures appartenant à de non moins vénérables vieillards, jouissant à perte de vue d'un immémorial patrimoine.

— Holà ! On n'attendait que vous ! dit Julio en accueillant les nouveaux arrivants.

Et se tournant vers les autres :

— Nous sommes, enfin, au complet. On peut commencer.

Pendant plus d'une heure, il raconte Beyrouth, ses discussions avec Habbache, Kanafani, Abou Sharif. Leur enthousiasme et leur intelligence. Leur internationalisme.

— Pour le FPLP, expose-t-il, la lutte contre Israël n'est que le premier pas vers la révolution socialiste arabe...

— Et que vont-ils faire des Israéliens ? l'interrompt Anna-Maria.

— Les Israéliens auront leur place dans une fédération socialiste du Proche-Orient.

— En tant qu'Israéliens ?

— En tant que minorité religieuse...

— Religieuse ! s'écrie Roberto de sa voix haut perchée. Bon Dieu de bon Dieu ! Et que vont-ils faire des Juifs non religieux ?

Julio commence à perdre patience :

— Mais pourquoi toujours juger un événement

223

selon les Juifs ? Le monde ne commence pas et ne s'arrête pas avec eux !

— C'est vrai, admet Roberto. Mais c'est souvent à la manière dont on se conduit avec eux que l'on peut juger du reste : l'humanisme d'un mouvement, par exemple.

Mario se lève d'un bond et s'écrie, en rejetant d'une main ses cheveux en arrière :

— Qui parle d'humanisme ?

— Alors de quoi parle-t-on ? demande doucement Anna-Maria.

Tout ce qui a été dit jusqu'à présent lui déplaît. Plus elle y pense, moins elle croit à une révolution qui passerait par l'enlèvement d'hommes et de femmes innocents.

— Que dis-tu ? lui demande Mario.

— Je ne dis rien, je me demandais seulement combien il y avait de Juifs dans les avions détournés.

— Une soixantaine environ, répondit Julio.

— Tous sionistes ?

— Tous sionistes !

Il y a un mouvement dans la pièce. Une grande fille maigre, aux cheveux roux attachés en queue-de-cheval, grogne :

— Quelle importance !...

Le regard noir d'Anna-Maria devient plus grand, plus dur :

— Quelle importance, dis-tu, Juanita ? La vie humaine n'a donc aucune importance ? Alors, pourquoi luttes-tu ? Pour peupler le monde de cadavres ?...

Julio lève les bras au ciel et fait quelques gestes désordonnés :

— Calmez-vous, calmez-vous.

Anna-Maria ne se calme pas. Elle crie de plus belle. Sanglote. S'emporte contre les camarades. Boude. Quand, le lendemain, elle apprend que, parmi ces soixante supposés sionistes, se trouve son propre cousin, elle frise la crise de nerfs. Et il faudra toute l'ardeur, toute la ferveur de ses camarades pour la ramener dans le droit chemin.

— Tu as tort de te mettre dans cet état, lui dira

224

Roberto en la prenant dans ses bras. Tu sais bien que nous dépendons sur le plan logistique des Palestiniens...

— Alors, notre seule conscience c'est la logistique ?

— Au diable, la théorie ! Je suis d'accord avec toi mais nous sommes là non pas pour parler d'Israël et des Palestiniens, mais pour faire la révolution en Argentine. Nous préparons un grand coup... Un très grand coup... Et nous avons besoin de toi.

Paris, septembre 1970

Le détournement des avions par les Palestiniens faisait depuis plus d'une semaine déjà « la une » des journaux français, quand nous fûmes informés de la présence du cousin américain parmi les otages. Ma mère l'apprit par l'intermédiaire d'un poète yiddish, de passage à Paris, ami du père de Sidney à Winnipeg. Le lendemain, elle téléphona à Mordekhaï à Dafné, qui lui confirma la nouvelle. Cette disparition d'un membre de la famille, tout juste trente années après qu'elle eut été déracinée, martyrisée et pour une bonne part décimée, la mit en vérité hors d'elle :

— Voilà de quoi ils sont capables, « tes » Palestiniens, me dit-elle. Et tu veux faire la paix avec eux ?

Je connaissais mal Sidney. Je ne l'avais rencontré que trois fois à Beyrouth et sa disparition ne m'avait pas ému plus que la détention des autres otages juifs. Mais l'événement avait, je me rendais bien compte, une conséquence annexe : il sonnait le glas de mon espoir dans cette rencontre israélo-égyptienne que Golda Meïr m'avait chargé de fomenter. La colère de ma mère, cela dit, était contagieuse. Ce grand rouquin était après tout un cousin. Il se réclamait de la même histoire que moi, se référait à la même mémoire et se reconnaissait dans les mêmes photos de Juifs barbus de la fin du siècle. J'ajoute que je ne voyais aucune cause, aucun combat

226

au monde qui justifiât de prendre des hommes en otages. Et que ces otages soient juifs, qu'une génération après l'Holocauste, on s'en prenne encore à eux, ne faisait, à mes yeux, que redoubler le scandale.

Aujourd'hui, au moment précis où j'écris ces lignes, ma famille la plus proche n'existe plus. Ni mes parents, ni la tante Regina, ni les cousins Mordekhaï et Sidney, ni les Lerner... Et pourtant, au fur et à mesure que le temps passe, mon attachement à leur souvenir grandit. Je les revois parfois en compagnie du cousin Hugo, si distincts les uns des autres, mais puisant tous leur mémoire à la même source que mon père, son père, le père de son père, et ainsi de suite. Et une vague de nostalgie m'emporte et m'éloigne de mon récit. Paradoxalement, plus j'avance dans cette histoire familiale, plus mon désir d'ancêtres s'amplifie. Plus ce désir augmente, plus l'objet du désir s'éloigne. Bientôt, entre lui et moi, s'étendra un interminable désert.

Mais n'allons pas trop vite. Pour l'instant, nous ne sommes qu'en septembre 1970, pendant les événements de Jordanie et sans nouvelles de Sidney. Le hasard a voulu qu'à ce moment-là Vladimir Volossatov, le troisième secrétaire de l'ambassade d'URSS à Paris, me téléphonât. Nous étions en contact depuis quelques années déjà. Il s'intéressait au Proche-Orient et parlait arabe. Je le rencontrais de temps à autre pour lui soutirer des informations sur la politique soviétique. Lui, pour me questionner sur Israël et ses dirigeants. Cette fois-ci, j'étais heureux de pouvoir lui parler de Sidney.

Vladimir Volossatov estima cette disparition « navrante ». Et il me proposa un rendez-vous pour « reparler de tout cela, à tête reposée ». Dans son langage, cela voulait dire : « après un complément d'informations ».

Nous nous rencontrâmes le lendemain, au café Cluny, à l'angle des boulevards Saint-Germain et Saint-Michel, au premier étage :

— J'ai des nouvelles pour vous, me dit-il d'emblée, avec son accent rocailleux. Votre cousin est vivant. Il est dans les mains de Waddi Haddad.

Vladimir Volossatov s'installa confortablement sur la banquette, en face de moi, et ajouta en russe, comme pour lui-même :

— Waddi Haddad... Quel idiot...

Puis, voyant ma surprise :

— C'est une appréciation toute personnelle. L'important, c'est que votre cousin soit libéré.

— Le sera-t-il ?

— Oui, bientôt.

— Par Haddad ?

— Non, par El Fath.

— El Fath ? Mais l'Union soviétique ne soutient-elle pas le Front Populaire ?

— Ça va changer, dit Vladimir Volossatov d'un ton définitif avant de passer la commande.

Quand le garçon posa sur la table un whisky pour le Soviétique et un lait chaud pour moi, il se pencha vers moi :

— Votre famille a de la constance, remarqua-t-il : toujours mêlée aux affaires du Proche-Orient.

— Oui, ça dure depuis des siècles.

— Non, je parle de maintenant. Il y avait votre cousin Hugo ; puis vous ; et, à présent, votre cousin Sidney.

Entendre le Soviétique prononcer le nom de Hugo me déconcerta :

— Vous connaissiez Hugo ?

Le visage osseux de Vladimir Volossatov s'épanouit dans un sourire :

— Je l'ai rencontré à plusieurs reprises. A des conférences internationales du Mouvement de la Paix.

— Vous ne m'en avez jamais parlé...

Vladimir Volossatov vida son verre de whisky d'un trait, comme s'il s'agissait d'un verre de vodka, et, sans plus se faire prier, me brossa de Hugo un portrait qui correspondait assez bien au souvenir que j'en avais gardé. Après quoi, il me parla de la volonté de paix de l'Union soviétique et de l' « idéalisme juif » mal compris dans son pays. Puis, sans transition, il m'avoua que sa femme, Véra, était à moitié juive.

« Par son père », précisa-t-il. Et, comme pour s'excuser :

— Mon beau-père pensait que cela ne comptait pas.

— Pour Hitler, ça comptait, dis-je.

— C'est vrai. Il fut déporté par les nazis.

Nous restâmes un moment silencieux. Un rayon de soleil balayait la banquette en skaï rouge et obligeait Volossatov à fermer les yeux.

— Du soleil, dit-il, ça fait du bien.

— Pourquoi pensez-vous que Hugo a été tué ? demandai-je à brûle-pourpoint.

Volossatov haussa les épaules :

— Un hasard, peut-être. Les terroristes ne choisissent pas toujours leurs victimes. Des ennemis, peut-être...

— En avait-il ?

— Tout le monde en a. Pas vous ?

Il se frotta les yeux, encore incommodé par le soleil qui, pourtant, avait commencé de disparaître ; puis, jetant un regard sur son bracelet montre :

— Je suis déjà en retard. Il faudra qu'on reprenne un rendez-vous. Je voudrais que vous me parliez de Golda. De ses rapports avec Dayan...

Il se leva, posa sa main large sur mon épaule et, d'un ton solennel, déclara :

— L'Union soviétique n'est nullement impliquée dans la mort de votre cousin Hugo.

Et, me laissant déconcerté par cette affirmation, il quitta le Cluny.

29

JORDANIE

COMME UN CHIEN...

Septembre 1970

La voiture glisse dans un nuage de poussière. Les essuie-glaces, dans un va-et-vient grinçant, tentent vainement de dégager la vitre. L'homme venu chercher Sidney à l'avion est assis près de lui et somnole. Le chauffeur s'agrippe au volant, comme son voisin à la mitraillette. Du premier, Sidney ne voit qu'une nuque grasse, parsemée de touffes de poils noirs. Du second, il peut observer un profil très jeune, un nez court, une moustache naissante et un menton déterminé. Ils croisent un convoi de camions, traînant des plates-formes porte-chars, puis une Land-Rover bourrée de militaires.

Sidney trouve la situation absurde. Le destin a choisi pour lui un avion qui allait être détourné et maintenant des inconnus l'emmènent Dieu sait où.

Est-on informé, à New York, de son enlèvement? Il pense à Marjory, à Richard, à Marilyn. Il pense aussi à son père et à Leïla. Leïla, sait-elle ce qui m'arrive? Comment réagit-elle? Sidney n'arrive pas à comprendre pourquoi les Palestiniens s'intéressent à lui. Tout particulièrement à lui. A cause de Hugo? L'idée, à peine formulée, lui semble absurde. Va-t-il, maintenant, se gonfler ainsi d'importance? Se mettre sur le même plan que le prestigieux cousin?

Il aurait tant aimé poser quelques questions! Parler avec ses ravisseurs! Il aurait tant souhaité leur expliquer, comprendre... Mais l'homme assis à côté de lui ronfle doucement et le jeune n'a pas l'air engageant.

Sidney repense à Marjory : il n'y a jamais eu de réelle complicité entre eux. Richard, en grandissant, lui échappe et devient un peu étranger. Quant à Marilyn, elle est encore trop petite — mais ici, en Jordanie, elle lui paraît soudain si proche.

Il fait chaud. Les corps dégagent une chaleur acide. La voiture bringuebale tandis que le soleil est devenu violet. Enfin, Sidney voit une flèche indiquant Amman et les pistes de l'aérodrome de la capitale jordanienne.

Banlieue d'Amman. Un édifice en pierre, blanchi à la chaux et construit sur une colline escarpée. La pièce où on l'interroge loge au bout d'un long couloir. Elle est spacieuse. Un vieux poste de radio et quelques photos de famille sur une commode en teck foncé rappellent encore d'anciens propriétaires. Un jeune homme élégant est assis derrière une table, couverte d'une toile cirée à petits carreaux rouges, sur laquelle repose une bouteille contenant seulement un mégot de cigarette. Trois feddayin armés occupent la pièce. Deux pour surveiller la porte et le troisième devant la fenêtre à travers laquelle leur parvient, atténué, l'appel des muezzins.

Les feddayin ont vidé ses poches. Tout ce qu'ils lui ont pris est étalé sur un plateau en plastique vert, posé sur la table : quelques dollars, sa montre, son stylo, son passeport, son carnet d'adresses, ses cartes de crédit.

— Vous avez de la famille en Israël ? dit le jeune homme dans un anglais parfait.

— Oui, reconnaît Sidney.

— Des amis ?

— Oui.

Le jeune homme hoche la tête comme si cette réponse représentait l'aveu d'un crime et fait signe aux deux feddayin près de la porte d'emmener le prisonnier.

La pièce où Sidney est maintenant enfermé équivaut à un carré d'un mètre quatre-vingts de côté. Il s'agit d'un débarras sans fenêtres, situé à l'autre extrémité du couloir. Sidney s'assied sur le lit de camp qui occupe la moitié de l'espace et lève la tête : l'unique ampoule se balance piteusement au bout d'un fil électrique.

Il pense au K. du *Procès* de Kafka qu'il a vu au cinéma. Ne surtout pas perdre l'équilibre mental. Ni l'espoir. Il se lève, observe les murs, puis la porte. Tout est lisse, sans faille, comme un galet. Il se rassied, quelque peu découragé. Qui pourrait le retrouver ici ? Il pense à nouveau à tout ce qui lui est arrivé depuis la mort de Hugo ; sa rencontre avec Mordekhaï et Benjamin Ben Eliezer, son aventure avec Leïla... C'est vrai que l'on ne va jamais aussi loin que lorsqu'on ne sait pas où l'on va. Si seulement il avait disposé d'un crayon et d'un bout de papier. Il a remarqué que la maison est dépourvue de téléphone.

Il a envie d'aller aux toilettes. Il doit frapper longtemps à la porte avant qu'elle ne s'ouvre. Un barbu pointe sur lui un revolver d'un gros calibre.

— Je dois aller aux toilettes, dit Sidney.

— *Go*, dit le barbu en indiquant le chemin.

En face de l'escalier, entre la pièce où les feddayin l'ont interrogé et celle où il est enfermé, il y a une salle de bains. La baignoire rouillée n'a pas servi depuis longtemps. La lumière du jour pénètre à travers une fente qui subsiste entre les carreaux de plâtre murant la fenêtre.

— *Quick* ! dit le barbu en claquant la porte.

Vite, un crayon, du papier... Sidney fait le tour de l'endroit. Il ne découvre rien avec quoi écrire un message. Au-dessus du lavabo il remarque une petite armoire vide. Il l'ausculte plus attentivement et découvre une lame de rasoir. Le temps presse. Sa décision est prise. Il s'entaille la paume de la main et, à l'aide d'une paille, amenée sous la baignoire par une colonne de fourmis, il écrit avec son sang sur le carton de support du paquet de papier hygiénique : « Je vous en prie, aidez-moi ! Mon nom est Sidney Halter. Je suis un otage retenu au deuxième étage de cet immeuble. » Il gribouille aussi son numéro de téléphone à New York et, après réflexion, y ajoute celui de Leïla à Beyrouth. Il a juste eu le temps de glisser le carton dans la fente quand la porte s'ouvre brutalement sous la poussée de son geôlier.

— Fini ? demande celui-ci. Alors, go !

Tous les jours, peu de temps après un modeste déjeuner fait d'un potage et d'une pita, le barbu l'emmène à travers le couloir devant le jeune homme élégant et poli qui lui repose, d'une voix composée, les mêmes questions auxquelles il donne toujours les mêmes réponses. Après quoi, le jeune homme hoche la tête en signe de désapprobation et fait ramener Sidney dans son cagibi.

Le quatrième ou cinquième jour, peu après 17 heures, un bruit de balles traverse les murs de sa cellule, suivi par celui de l'artillerie, lui-même accompagné d'explosions d'obus. Sidney lève machinalement les bras pour se protéger et devient soudain la proie d'une sorte de rire nerveux. Il ne sait pas contre qui, au juste, il doit se protéger — mais enfin, il se protège, s'assied sur le rebord du lit et se met à compter le nombre des éclats visibles sur les murs. Il se trompe dans le compte, recommence, se trompe encore, il pense à Jérémie Cohen, l'anesthésiste, celui à cause de qui il est parti à Beyrouth... Comme c'est curieux ! comme c'est absurde ! Il y a un mois à peine il aurait dit : celui *grâce* à qui il a découvert Beyrouth. Ses splendeurs, ses bonheurs ! Et là... Ce désarroi... On doit être à la fin du Shabbat, se dit-il. Aussi commence-t-il à réciter le psaume : « Celui qui demeure sous la sauvegarde du Très Haut est abrité à l'ombre du Tout Puissant... » Mais, à sa grande honte, il cherche vainement la suite, recommence à compter les éclats de bombes, tente de deviner qui attaque qui et pourquoi — avant de s'endormir, épuisé.

Au petit matin, quand le barbu l'emmènera, à travers le couloir, jusqu'à son interrogatoire quotidien, il découvrira un trou béant dans le mur des toilettes. Un trou d'obus, se dit-il. Oui, un trou d'obus. Et il se souvient brusquement de la suite de la prière de la clôture du Shabbat : « Tu es mon refuge, ma citadelle, mon Dieu en qui je me confie. »

— Que dis-tu ? demande le barbu.

— Je prie.

Malgré le vacarme de l'artillerie lourde, ponctué par le crépitement de fusils-mitrailleurs, malgré tous ces chocs répétés qui secouent la maison et font vibrer les vitres en mesure, le jeune homme élégant reste impassible.

— Que se passe-t-il ? demande Sidney.

— On se bat depuis quatre jours, répond le jeune homme.

De la pièce voisine on entend un discours retransmis à la radio. Voyant Sidney dresser l'oreille, le jeune homme lâche :

— Le roi Hussein.

— Que dit-il ?

— Je ne sais pas. Ce qu'il dit ou ne dit pas, moi je m'en fiche...

— Mais vos combattants meurent...

— Nous, vous savez, nous aimons mourir.

Mais brusquement, c'est lui qui pose les questions :

— Votre frère israélien a un fils, n'est-ce pas ?

— Oui, en effet.

— Il s'appelle Arié et travaille avec Benjamin Ben Eliezer dans les services secrets de l'armée ?

Sidney a peine à dissimuler sa surprise :

— Je connais, en effet, Benjamin Ben Eliezer, mais je ne sais pas où il travaille. Quant à mon neveu, il accomplit actuellement son service militaire...

— Vous ne savez donc rien de leurs activités ?

— Non.

Le jeune homme se lève doucement et d'un pas dansant s'approche de Sidney. Il est mince, et plus petit que l'Américain.

— Et que faisiez-vous à Beyrouth avec Hidar Assadi ?

— Hidar, comment ?

Sidney a complètement — et réellement — oublié le compagnon de sa cousine Olga.

— Vous vous moquez de moi ?

— Comment ?

Une gifle part. Sidney s'apprête à répondre mais se retient. Il sait que ce serait un suicide et remplace donc sa colère par la pitié. Son corps se tasse. Il baisse les yeux. Courbe doucement l'échine. Et voilà que les feddayin derrière la porte, le voyant ainsi ramassé, croient qu'il va riposter et s'emparent brutalement de lui avant de l'assommer.

Sidney se réveille dans sa cellule, allongé sur un lit. Son crâne lui fait mal. Tous ses muscles sont douloureux. Sa mâchoire même lui semble lourde tout à coup, comme massive. « De la pitié, se dit-il. J'ai eu de la pitié pour ces hommes. Je me suis conduit comme ces ancêtres qui, cravachés par des princes, dans les villages polonais d'avant-guerre, ne répondaient que par le plus passif des mépris. Ils éprouvaient réellement du mépris, ces ancêtres. Ils se sentaient cent fois supérieurs à ces brutes qui devaient employer la violence pour s'affirmer. Curieux de reproduire ainsi les pensées, le comportement, les réactions de ses aïeux... »

Il s'assied sur le lit, non sans difficulté. Il a le dos courbé. Les genoux tout fragiles. Il tremble comme sous l'effet d'une fièvre et pense à la vanité de cette vie dont personne ne comprend le sens — à la vanité, plus grande encore, de cette mort dont la signification est interdite aux vivants. « Quelqu'un trouvera-t-il mon message ? Quelqu'un me viendra-t-il en aide ? Quelle joie, quel apaisement j'éprouverais, se dit Sidney, à pouvoir m'exclamer : Seigneur, ayez pitié de moi ! Mais à qui ferais-je cette prière, moi qui ne vais presque jamais à la synagogue ? » Pour la première fois, l'idée effleure Sidney que son fils n'a peut-être pas tout à fait tort de retourner à la religion.

Il pense encore à son père, à sa femme, à ses enfants. Souvenir de la première nuit passée avec Leïla. La figure si petite, si étrange de Hidar Assadi. Et, par-dessus tout, la vision de Park Avenue sous un ciel infini... Sa main droite s'est involontairement crispée. Il laisse aller tout son corps en arrière et reste un long moment, allongé ainsi, le regard fixé sur l'ampoule électrique qui se balance au-dessus de lui.

Brusquement, la canonnade reprend. Hurlement des sirènes. Crépitement des mitrailleuses. Des coups de feu, tout près, presque de l'autre côté du mur. Des cris. Tel un homme qui se noie et qui s'accroche à la plus humble bouée, il reprend soudain espoir. « Et si quelqu'un avait trouvé son message ? » Il se lève avec difficulté et s'approche de la porte. Sa tête lui fait toujours mal. Il entend des cris en arabe, des coups de feu, encore des cris. Et puis soudain, la porte s'ouvre avec fracas, le repoussant sur le lit. Quand il se relève, il voit deux corps ensanglantés sur le seuil. Espoir... Cette porte désormais ouverte... Ces deux corps immobiles qu'il enjambe... Il s'approche de la cage d'escalier et, ne voyant personne, commence à descendre. Il est déjà au rez-de-chaussée quand il entend quelqu'un au-dessus de lui l'appeler en anglais :

— Monsieur ! Monsieur ! Ne courez pas ! Nous sommes venus vous délivrer !...

Et une autre voix, un peu plus jeune :

— Attendez, monsieur ! Attendez, monsieur, on arrive !...

Fou de bonheur, Sidney regarde dans la direction des voix et ne remarque pas, derrière lui, arriver deux feddayin — dont son gardien barbu.

— Attention ! lui crie-t-on du haut de l'escalier.

— Chien de Juif ! hurle le barbu en avançant, revolver au poing.

Sidney se précipite dans l'escalier mais l'un des deux hommes l'a attrapé par la cheville. Il tombe, les bras en ailerons. Les deux feddayin sont sur lui. Il entend la rafale de mitraillette et sent, presque en même temps, une violente douleur à la hanche.

— Chien de Juif ! répète le barbu.

Mais les yeux de Sidney se voilent déjà. Il lui semble entendre une rumeur étouffée, très lointaine. Pour la dernière fois, il revoit Marjory et les enfants. Hugo aussi. Et puis son corps se détend, il esquisse un geste d'indifférence et dit : « Comme un chien... »

30

BEYROUTH

LE RETOURNEMENT

Septembre 1970

Le rendez-vous d'Hidar avec son contact à l'ambassade a été avancé de plusieurs jours. A Amman, les événements ne se déroulent pas selon le plan prévu. Une centaine de chars syriens T 55, de fabrication soviétique, ont pénétré en Jordanie mais se sont arrêtés à Irbid, tandis que le roi Hussein a lancé une offensive foudroyante contre les Palestiniens massés autour de sa capitale.

Le message de l'ambassade arrive le vendredi 18 septembre, à 10 heures du matin. Il fixe la rencontre à 14 heures le jour même. Hidar est nerveux. Il sent un picotement désagréable au creux de l'estomac, comme chaque fois qu'il a l'intuition d'un événement contrariant. Il aimerait bien appeler quelqu'un, histoire d'échanger quelques mots. Mais qui appeler ? Quel ami ? Il n'a pas d'amis à Beyrouth et décide de sortir.

Beyrouth est une ville qui n'invite guère à la promenade solitaire. A Hamra ou au carrefour Bab-Edress, on se heurte vite aux portefaix, aux mendiants ou aux inlassables palabreurs qui encombrent les trottoirs. La chaussée, elle, est occupée par les voitures et le hurlement des avertisseurs finit par vous étourdir. Hidar, comme chaque fois qu'il se sent un peu perdu, regrette l'absence d'Olga.

Un peu après 13 heures, soit avec près d'une heure

d'avance, il se présente à la Grotte aux Pigeons. Le soleil est au plus haut. La chaleur, torride. Près de la balustrade qui domine la mer, un guide raconte à un groupe de touristes français l'histoire de la ville. Le café est suffisamment vide pour qu'il trouve sans grand mal une place à l'ombre. Il commande un arak. Le boit à toutes petites gorgées. Et, vidant en quelque sorte son esprit de tout ce qui pourrait l'accabler, écoute d'une oreille distraite les explications du guide :

— Les origines de Beyrouth remontent au début de la navigation. Son nom dérive de Beroth qui, en cananéen-phénicien, voulait dire « Puits ». Le nombre de ses ressources en eau lui valut cette appellation...

Une dame blonde, pas très jeune, mais encore jolie, note fébrilement dans un petit calepin jaune. Elle sent le regard d'Hidar lui sourire et, comme le guide poursuit, continue elle aussi de plus belle :

— Les scribes des lettres de Tell el-Armana, cité fondée par le pharaon-poète Akhenaton et son épouse Néfertiti, remplaçaient parfois le nom de Beroth par l'idéogramme cruciforme signifiant « Puits »...

La dame blonde interrompt, une fois encore, sa transcription pour le regarder à son tour — sourire... Clin d'œil... Intelligence muette et subtile invitation... La dame a rougi. Hidar lui a ostensiblement offert son profil le plus flatteur. Tout à son manège, il n'a pas remarqué le faux touriste en veston clair et à la calvitie ravageuse qui a pris place à la table près de lui :

— Vous vous amusez ?

Hidar sursaute.

— Continuez à regarder les touristes, conseille l'homme. Avec ce genre de guide, on apprend toujours quelque chose...

Mais le petit groupe se déplace déjà. Hidar entend encore le guide expliquer que « Beyrouth pouvait, dans l'Antiquité, se comparer à Athènes et à Alexandrie et qu'au Ve siècle avant notre ère, une école de droit y dispensait la science des lois suivant un enseignement systématique »... Et puis il sent à nouveau l'angoisse qui l'envahit.

— J'ai eu Tchebrikov au téléphone, dit maintenant le Soviétique. Un accord avec l'Oncle Sam est intervenu. Il faut arrêter tout. D'urgence.

— Tout ?

— Oui, tout. C'est un ordre.

Hidar regarde une mouette plonger dans l'eau. Il la trouve belle. Il a l'impression d'être entraîné par elle vers les abîmes. Dieu sait pourquoi il voit aussi, tout à coup, les seins d'Olga — très blancs, très laiteux, offerts à son désir.

— Prenez contact avec El Fath, poursuit encore le bonhomme. Vous y avez quelques amis. Chargez-les d'arrêter la guerre et de libérer les otages...

— Nous changeons d'alliance ?

— Oui. Vous pouvez leur promettre ce qui vous paraît nécessaire. Nous honorerons toutes vos promesses. Il faut que les Palestiniens comprennent aussi que vous avez un pouvoir...

L'homme qui, jusqu'à présent, a parlé sans le regarder, comme dans le vide, tourne alors la tête vers lui et le scrute un bon moment à travers ses deux fentes bleues.

— Vous avez de la chance, lâche-t-il enfin.

— De la chance ? Pourquoi ?

— Chez nous, on estime que l'échec de l'opération vous incombe.

— Mais on n'a pas échoué...

L'autre le fait taire d'un geste de la main et passe la commande au garçon qui vient d'arriver :

— Un thé à la menthe, s'il vous plaît.

Et, se tournant à nouveau vers Hidar :

— L'opération a duré trop longtemps.

— Les Syriens sont à Irbid...

— Ils vont repartir.

— Les Irakiens...

— Ils ne bougeront pas.

Il se tait : le garçon revient avec le thé à la menthe.

— L'Oncle Sam exige par ailleurs la libération immédiate du médecin juif.

Et, après avoir bu deux gorgées de thé :

239

— Par contre, pour Kamal Joumblatt, vous aviez raison. En devenant ministre de l'Intérieur, il a légalisé le Parti... Chez nous, on dit que c'est grâce à vous...

Il vide la tasse de thé et, sans attendre ni objections ni éventuels commentaires, se lève :

— Bonne chance... Tout est désormais entre vos mains...

Sur quoi il pose un billet sur la table et, sans se retourner, se dirige vers la sortie.

Quelques minutes plus tard, Hidar fait de même. Il s'attarde un instant devant le café pour contempler Beyrouth et son amoncellement de constructions ocre, blanches et grises. Et puis, haussant les épaules comme pour chasser une idée fâcheuse, il hèle un taxi et s'en va.

Par où commencer ? Le rythme incantatoire d'une chanson arabe, à la radio, l'empêche de bien réfléchir. Il fait chaud. Humide. L'heure est à la sieste. Le taxi suit une rue tropicale, sans promeneurs, où l'éclat blanchâtre de la chaussée brûlante n'est troublé que par l'ombre des portefaix. « La première chose à faire, se dit-il, c'est de déménager... Ne pas être à la portée du Front. » Et, avant même cela, passer à la permanence et consulter les dépêches... Après quoi il montera dans son studio et préparera sa valise. Il vérifie qu'il n'a rien oublié, sidéré de son propre calme. Téléphone à l'hôtel Saint-Georges pour réserver une chambre. Ensuite seulement, il compose le numéro d'El Fath. Abou Iyad étant absent, il laisse un message, demandant qu'il le rappelle au Saint-Georges et quitte enfin le Katараji Building.

Il rencontre Abou Iyad le jour même. Arafat, retour d'Amman, le lendemain. Le leader d'El Fath comprendra vite la proposition de Hidar. Il sait que s'il ne reprend pas en main les opérations de Jordanie, l'OLP lui échappera pour toujours. Ce n'était pas « sa » guerre, dit-il à Hidar. En sorte que puisque lui, Hidar, semble disposé à renoncer...

Le soir même, Hidar prévient l'ambassade. Le lendemain, les forces irakiennes, stationnées en Jordanie,

240

transfèrent un armement lourd aux commandos d'El Fath, renforcés par quelques milliers de Palestiniens venus de Syrie. Et, dans l'après-midi du mardi 22 septembre, Hidar reçoit la visite de Ghassan Kanafani. Ils s'assoient sur la terrasse, face à la mer.

— Moscou a changé d'alliance ? demande le Palestinien sans préambule, en posant sur la table en fer, peinte en blanc comme dans certains bistrots parisiens, un télex d'agence.

Le Tunisien en connaît par avance le contenu. Mais de le lire lui donne le temps d'engager la conversation.

« L'action conjuguée de Washington et de Moscou a rétabli la position du roi Hussein », titre la dépêche. Diable... Diable... Les choses vont plus vite que je ne pensais.

Puis, à voix haute, cette fois, en vertu du bon vieux principe qui veut que la meilleure des défenses soit encore et toujours l'attaque :

— Et les otages ? Tu veux bien me parler des otages !

— Certains ont été libérés par El Fath, d'autres transférés par le Front vers le nord.

— Et le médecin américain ?

Kanafani paraît gêné. Il demande :

— Tu as vu ce qui se passe à Amman ? C'est une ville morte. Sa population est décimée. Les survivants sont à l'agonie. Les destructions revêtent une telle envergure qu'il semble bien qu'aucune maison n'ait été épargnée. Alors, dans tout ça, un otage de plus ou de moins...

Le visage de Ghassan Kanafani est parcouru d'un bref tremblement. Son front haut est couvert de sueur. Ses grands yeux noirs fixent la mer. Il tourne brusquement la tête vers Hidar :

— J'ai eu Waddi au téléphone. De l'hôtel Jordan qui domine la ville et d'où il m'appelait, on pouvait voir paraît-il de très nombreuses fumées noires s'élever vers le ciel. D'autres incendies étaient visibles aussi du côté du Djebel Hussein et à Wahdad qui abritent des camps de réfugiés palestiniens. On ignore le nombre des victimes. Mais Waddi affirme que les morts et les blessés se comptent par milliers...

— Littérature, littérature, le coupe Hidar, agacé, avant d'ajouter : Tu parles comme ces écrivains dont les livres sont remplis de remords. Ils n'ont qu'un défaut, vois-tu : n'avoir jamais tué personne. Car la guerre est terrible, c'est vrai. Ne le savais-tu pas ?

Kanafani se courbe encore un peu. Il est presque voûté, maintenant — tant le poids de la situation l'accable.

— Un révolutionnaire n'est pas un criminel, dit-il à mi-voix... C'est un homme qui tue, oui... Mais qui tue pour sauver la vie...

Puis, se redressant et lançant à son vis-à-vis un regard tout à coup accusateur :

— Tu savais qu'El Fath allait négocier avec Hussein ?

— Oui. Pour sauver ce qu'on pouvait encore sauver. Pour sauver la vie, comme tu dis. Et pour libérer aussi les otages... A propos d'otages, tu ne m'as toujours pas répondu au sujet de l'Américain.

Kanafani tourne à nouveau la tête vers la mer et du bout des lèvres, comme s'il parlait aux mouettes, laisse simplement tomber :

— Il a été tué.

— Tué ?

Hidar s'est levé d'un bond. Son visage, son regard, sont devenus d'une dureté impressionnante :

— Tu veux dire que vous l'avez tué ?

— Non, non, ce n'est pas cela. Waddi Haddad l'avait enfermé dans la banlieue d'Amman pour l'interroger sur ses rapports avec un des dirigeants des services secrets israéliens...

— Et avec moi, n'est-ce pas ?

Ghassan ne répond pas.

— Avec moi ? répète Hidar en le prenant par le bras. Dis-le, espèce de salaud... Hein, dis-le vite...

— C'est une histoire idiote, proteste Ghassan... Un commando d'El Fath a voulu le libérer... Il y a eu un malentendu... Un échange de coups de feu... Ton Américain a voulu s'enfuir... Quelqu'un a tiré... Il est mort...

— Mais la mort ne se manie pas comme un téléphone ! Quand on se trompe de numéro, le téléphone, lui, n'est pas désintégré...

Après quoi, il dégage son bras et se lève à son tour. Son fin visage de poète égaré en politique paraît dur lui aussi — dur et étrangement fatigué.

— N'oublie pas, glisse-t-il encore, que c'est toi qui as voulu cette opération...

— Oui, mais elle devait seulement rappeler au monde le drame palestinien. Les otages devaient être rendus aussitôt...

Deux couples assis plus loin se sont retournés pour écouter et derrière les vitres qui séparent la terrasse du hall de l'hôtel, les garçons suivent la scène avec curiosité. Kanafani s'en aperçoit le premier et se rassied en grommelant :

— Va au diable avec tes scrupules. C'est vrai que personne n'a jamais compris tes faiblesses pour cette famille de Juifs...

L'annonce de la mort de Sidney bouleverse effectivement Hidar. Il n'a pas de sympathie particulière pour cet Américain roux et barbu. Et pourtant... Est-ce parce qu'il s'agit d'un cousin d'Hugo ? Parce qu'il ne parvient pas à effacer Hugo de sa mémoire ? Est-ce parce qu'il voit dans la mort de cet homme un pressentiment d'autre chose ? Toujours est-il qu'il passe le reste de la journée à flâner autour de Beyrouth, entre le port et les plages de Khaldé, le long de la corniche. Il a peur de rentrer à l'hôtel, de se retrouver seul à écouter les nouvelles... « Je suis humain, trop humain, se dit-il. Quand on veut soigner le monde, il faut savoir soigner sa conscience... »

Il entre dans un café, commande à nouveau de l'arak. Voyant un téléphone posé sur le bar, il s'en approche tel un somnambule et sans vraiment savoir à qui téléphoner. Il se souvient de Leïla. Annoncer la nouvelle à Leïla ? Leïla, à sa grande surprise, la connaît déjà, cette nouvelle. Mais il est content de lui parler. Elle, apparemment, aussi. Et ils se donnent rendez-vous le soir même à la terrasse de l'hôtel Saint-Georges.

Le soir venu, Leïla est là. Elle a le visage défait mais elle reste belle. La nuit est belle également. La baie, incroyablement lumineuse. Tout, dans l'air autour d'eux, invite à l'abandon. Quelle est cette émotion qui l'étreint ? Et ce désir ? D'où vient ce soudain besoin de poser un baiser sur les paupières brûlantes de la jeune femme ? Hidar, sidéré, comprend qu'il la désire. Pis : il comprend qu'elle aussi, pour éprouvée qu'elle soit par la mort de son amant, lui porte un irrépressible désir. La mer est là, toute proche. Le bruit des vagues les berce déjà. Leïla, la tête sur son épaule, râle doucement. Et lui, tout aussi doucement, passe ses doigts sur la bouleversante tache pâle, sur le bleu-noir du ciel, qu'est son visage en larmes. Entendent-ils le bruit des pneus sur le gravier ? Puis son nom, prononcé au loin par une voix familière ? Il s'écarte de Leïla, se retourne. Le maître d'hôtel s'avance vers lui, suivi d'une silhouette massive.

— Monsieur Assadi, dit-il en s'effaçant le plus servilement qu'il peut devant un homme gras aux lèvres minces, aux yeux mi-clos et au long nez bourgeonnant.

L'homme tend sa main blanche et baguée vers Leïla et, d'une voix métallique, en français, annonce simplement :

— Je viens chercher ma femme.

Paris, octobre 1970

Ma mère a pleuré. Et je ne sais pas pourquoi, cela m'a irrité. Peut-être savais-je qu'en pleurant un défunt, on pleure sur soi-même. Peut-être devinais-je, derrière ces larmes incongrues, la prophétie de sa propre mort. Elle avait pleuré en tout cas. Oui, elle portait le deuil de Sidney, comme quelqu'un de très très proche. Et elle avait même écrit un poème qui commençait, je m'en souviens, par cette phrase : « Recueille mes larmes et ma réprobation, mon Dieu… »

Vladimir Volossatov, à peu près à la même époque, me téléphona une dernière fois. Il était déjà navré, n'est-ce pas, par la disparition de mon cousin. Eh bien, sa mort l'attristait. « C'est un terrible malentendu, disait-il, avec son inimitable accent russe. Un commando d'El Fath veut libérer votre cousin. Celui-ci ne comprend pas et s'enfuit… le destin ! Oui, mon cher, le destin ! » Pour l'heure, il tenait à me dire adieu. Car il rentrait définitivement à Moscou. « Eh oui, cher ami, tout a une fin… Je dois quitter Paris, c'est si triste. » Et puis, avant de raccrocher, cette dernière phrase dont je me demande jusqu'à aujourd'hui s'il la prononça par calcul, étourderie ou bonté : « A propos, je me suis renseigné pour votre autre cousin… Hugo, n'est-ce pas… Il faut chercher la raison de sa mort du côté d'Israël Beer… Dites-le à vos amis israéliens… Ils comprendront. »

Cette révélation me surprit tant sur le moment que j'appelai aussitôt Benjamin Ben Eliezer. « Curieux, me dit-il après que je lui eus raconté ma conversation. Israël Beer, l'ancien conseiller de Ben Gourion, était, en effet, un espion soviétique... Votre cousin Sidney m'en avait parlé aussi après sa rencontre avec le frère de Sigrid, le docteur Furchmuller, à Francfort. Curieux... Et maintenant, votre ami Volossatov... Les services secrets soviétiques... Curieux... » Benjamin promit d'approfondir son enquête et de me tenir au courant. Puis, il me passa Arié, le fils de Mordekhaï, si visiblement fier de me montrer qu'il travaillait avec lui.

— Je me marierai aussitôt mon service militaire terminé, m'annonça-t-il. J'espère que tu viendras. Le mariage aura lieu au kibboutz...

31

ISRAËL

L'ENQUÊTE D'ARIÉ

Octobre 1970

Le soleil s'attarde un moment sur le sommet des montagnes. Puis, alangui, comme exténué, il chute quelque part dans la plaine et le kibboutz Dafné disparaît d'un coup dans les ténèbres. Un système d'horlogerie met aussitôt en marche, comme chaque soir, le grand générateur central. Les lumières scintillent. Dans les allées d'abord. Autour des hangars et au sommet du château d'eau ensuite. Et puis enfin, dans les maisons. Après quoi, les membres du kibboutz, sachant que l'heure est venue, prennent tous le chemin du réfectoire.

— Tu aurais dû mettre un pull, dit Sarah à Arié. Ici, ce n'est pas comme à Tel-Aviv... C'est le nord...

Puis :

— C'est bien que tu sois revenu pour les fêtes. Cette année, nous avons construit une énorme *Soukka*. Les enfants sont heureux. Ta sœur Dina ne veut manger nulle part ailleurs. Tu veux venir ?

— Non, répondit-il avec un gentil sourire, je préfère qu'on aille au réfectoire. J'ai à parler à papa...

Mordekhaï, intrigué, regarde son fils. Mais la pénombre l'empêche de voir autre chose que son profil. Et toute la famille arrive, à la queue leu leu, dans un réfectoire qui sent bon le concombre, la friture et le café.

Les kibboutzniks, comme il se doit, saluent l'enfant prodigue. Ils disent que l'uniforme lui va bien : qu'il a belle et bonne mine ; ils l'interrogent sur sa vie sous les drapeaux et le considèrent bizarrement comme s'il était déjà un héros.

— Quoi de neuf au kibboutz ? demande-t-il à son père, quand ils se retrouvent enfin seuls, installés à l'une des tables.

— Comme d'habitude... Quelques infiltrations des feddayin de l'autre côté de la frontière... Pas de morts, mais quelques bêtes égorgées... On a également racheté un nouveau tracteur... Et puis il y a les nouveau-nés... Voilà... Comme d'habitude, te dis-je... Mais toi ? Tu as un problème... Tu voulais me dire quelque chose ?

— Oui, mais pas ici.

Après le dîner, Arié prend un gros pull, son père une canadienne et ils vont s'asseoir, tous les deux, sur des chaises longues devant leur baraque de bois. Au loin, dans le noir, des touffes d'étincelles situent les villages des deux côtés de la frontière. C'est Mordekhaï qui commence :

— Tu fais donc ton service auprès de Benjamin ?

— Oui, c'est cela... J'ai suivi de près ces histoires de détournement d'avions et puis l'enlèvement de Sidney...

— Tu sais quelque chose ?

Arié poursuit, comme s'il n'avait pas entendu :

— Le cousin français nous a téléphoné. Enfin : il a téléphoné à Benjamin. Un diplomate soviétique lui aurait conseillé de regarder du côté d'Israël Beer pour dénicher le mobile de l'assassinat de Hugo...

— Attends, fait Mordekhaï. Pas si vite. Pourquoi me parles-tu de Hugo quand je te demande pour Sidney ?

— Parce que nous en sommes tous convaincus : si on arrive à comprendre les raisons de la mort de l'un, on comprendra peut-être aussi l'énigme de l'assassinat de l'autre.

Et, se penchant vers son père avec dans le regard, dans la moue aussi et dans le maintien, une expression de gravité qu'il ne lui connaissait pas :

— As-tu connu cet Israël Beer ?

— Je l'ai rencontré une fois, je crois... A un congrès du Parti Travailliste. C'était... C'était en 1959, je crois.

— Comment était-il ?

— Je me souviens de traits un peu mongols, d'une grosse moustache noire et de rires bruyants.

— Penses-tu qu'il ait vraiment trahi ?

— Qui sait ? Dans un livre qu'il a rédigé en prison, il explique que s'il a agi de la sorte, c'est parce qu'il était persuadé que la sécurité d'Israël passait par un rapprochement avec le camp socialiste.

— Mais de là à livrer des documents !

— Il a toujours prétendu avoir pratiqué l'autocensure sur les informations qu'il communiquait. Mais pourquoi t'intéresses-tu à lui ?

— A cause de ses rapports avec Hugo.

— Avec Hugo ?

— Oui. Il t'en a parlé ?

— Non, pas vraiment. Je sais qu'ils se connaissaient. Hugo voulait un rendez-vous avec Ben Gourion. C'est Israël Beer qui, la première fois, a dû le recevoir.

— Il y a un dossier concernant Israël Beer dans les archives de l'Aman, mais Benjamin ne veut pas me le laisser consulter. Je crois qu'il n'a pas vraiment confiance en moi. Il me trouve trop jeune.

On entend le cri d'un oiseau de proie tout proche et les chiens se mettent à hurler.

— Qu'est-ce que c'est ? demande le jeune homme soudain sur le qui-vive.

— Rien, rien... De toute façon, nous avons doublé la garde.

Puis, après un silence, le regard perdu dans les étoiles :

— Tu sais que demain, c'est Simhat Thora.

— Tu deviens religieux, papa ?

— Non... Nostalgique seulement. Je me souviens, à Winnipeg... C'était une belle fête, tu sais... On sortait de leurs armoires tous les rouleaux de la Loi... On se mettait à danser... Les enfants recevaient plein de sucreries...

Long silence à nouveau. Douce quiétude de la

pénombre. Chaleur de cette proximité retrouvée. Un père et un fils côte à côte, en communion avec la nuit. C'est le fils, cette fois, qui murmure :

— Tu as téléphoné à la veuve ?

— La veuve ?

— A Marjory... La veuve de l'oncle Sidney...

— Oui. Elle attend le rapatriement du corps. La Croix-Rouge s'en occupe. Richard, son fils, veut un enterrement à Jérusalem...

— Comme Hugo, donc ?

— Oui, c'est drôle, comme Hugo...

Mordekhaï n'a pas le temps d'en dire plus. Car, à cet instant précis, des hurlements de chiens déchirent le silence de la nuit. Puis des cris provenant de la basse-cour. Des pas rapides sur le gravier.

— Qui va là ? fait-il, l'oreille brusquement à l'affût, les muscles tendus, la voix assourdie par l'angoisse.

— Jacob Oren. Prenez vos armes et filez vers le château d'eau. On a repéré un groupe de feddayin. Ils progressent vers le kibboutz.

Toutes les lumières s'éteignent d'un coup. Seul le faisceau d'un projecteur s'agite en haut du château d'eau, fouillant les environs.

— Tu as une arme ? chuchote Mordekhaï à son fils, tandis que pliés en deux, ils courent vers la maison.

— Oui, une mitraillette. Je l'ai posée sur l'armoire.

Une seconde plus tard, armés tous les deux, ils courent vers le château d'eau, croisent dans les allées des hommes allant chacun vers son lieu de rendez-vous. Pas un mot. Pas un cri. Seulement un bruit de pas couvert par les hurlements des chiens. C'est comme un menuet admirablement réglé, cent et cent fois répété et qui s'exécuterait à la perfection.

Arrivés près du château d'eau, ils retrouvent quatre autres personnes.

— Nous sommes au complet, fait Jacob Oren, un homme robuste, court sur pattes dont Mordekhaï ne peut s'empêcher d'observer que la situation a métamorphosé, mieux que le maintien, le ton et, jusqu'à la voix...

— Allez, allez, suivez-moi ! reprend-il avec cette autorité insoupçonnée de paysan soldat.

Les six hommes dépassent le hangar. Et, au moment d'atteindre le muret d'enceinte, surélevé de barbelés, ils entendent des coups de feu... Une sirène... Une rafale sur le mur... Une autre... Arié, sans réfléchir tire. Une fois... Deux fois... Et on entend un cri, tout près... Un cri horrible, entre le rugissement et le miaulement — suivi, presque aussitôt, d'aboiements de chiens redoublés.

— Je crois que j'ai touché quelqu'un, dit-il d'une voix blanche...

— On va voir, fait Mordekhaï.

— Non, non, ordonne Jacob Oren. Ne bougez surtout pas. C'est trop risqué.

La fusillade s'éloigne. Arié remarque une étoile filante et se détend. Les réverbères dans les allées se rallument tandis que deux hélicoptères passent, en bourdonnant, au-dessus d'eux.

— Ils ont fait vite, dit Jacob Oren qui suit, la tête en l'air, les clignotants des hélicoptères en train de s'éloigner.

Puis :

— Maintenant, on peut aller voir...

Près du muret d'enceinte, à l'endroit même où Arié a tiré il n'y a plus qu'une mitraillette de fabrication soviétique et une kefiah ensanglantée. Où est l'homme ? Où est l'ombre ? Disparu... Volatilisé... Les recherches, reprises à l'aube, ne donnèrent rien de plus et le commandant de la garnison voisine, venu visiter le kibboutz, concluera que le feddayin a été blessé mais qu'il a utilisé la kefiah pour éponger sa blessure et que ses camarades ont réussi à le transporter.

Arié, au fond de lui-même, aime autant ça. C'est la première fois qu'il tire sur un homme et s'il est fier de n'avoir pas manqué de courage et d'avoir atteint sa cible, il n'est pas fâché que le Palestinien blessé ait réussi à prendre le large. Le feddayin, à sa place, n'aurait pas eu de ces scrupules ? Il se serait fait un plaisir, comme dans l'attentat contre l'autobus, de lui faire sauter la tête ? Possible. Mais l'idée de tuer un homme lui est intolérable...

De retour à Tel-Aviv, après les fêtes, il demande presque aussitôt à parler à Benjamin.

— Je voudrais m'occuper du dossier Hidar Assadi.

Benjamin le regarde, amusé :

— Quelqu'un s'en occupe déjà, tu sais ? On ne t'a pas attendu...

— Je crois que moi, je pourrai faire mieux.

— Le présomptueux devient raisin sec avant d'avoir été raisin mûr...

Et tandis qu'Arié prend l'air buté de celui qui ne sortira pas de la pièce tant qu'il n'aura pas satisfaction, Benjamin ajoute, comme à regret :

— Cela dit, tu connais le mot de Talleyrand : « On ne croit qu'en ceux qui croient en eux. »

— Qui est-ce, Talleyrand ?

— Tu vois que tu as encore beaucoup à apprendre ! Talleyrand était un diplomate français qui, grâce à son intelligence et à ses intrigues, a su traverser, en demeurant au pouvoir, la Révolution, l'Empire, la Restauration, le règne de Louis-Philippe. Disons qu'il avait... un don prodigieux de prévision !

Il s'apprête à ajouter quelque chose quand le téléphone sonne. « Bonjour... Comment ça va... » Quelques propos anodins... Une ou deux politesses dont il n'est guère coutumier... Et, plaquant le combiné contre sa cuisse, il demande au jeune homme, sur un ton cette fois sans réplique, de bien vouloir sortir et le laisser seul.

— On t'a mis à la porte, « haboub » ? dit en riant Myriam quand elle le voit, tout dépité, quitter le bureau. C'est comme ça ici, quand ça devient trop secret, on expulse les enfants...

— D'ici un an ou deux, je serai le maître des secrets, répond l' « enfant », mi-moqueur, mi-sérieux.

— On n'est jamais vraiment maître d'un secret, rétorque-t-elle à son tour — sur un ton plein de sous-entendus.

252

Après le déjeuner, Arié réapparaît et trouve dans le bureau de Benjamin un homme petit, aux bras très longs et à l'épaisse chevelure grisonnante.

— Zvika, dit Benjamin, en le présentant. Il te mettra au courant des activités d'Hidar Assadi. Il te montrera aussi le dossier d'Israël Beer. A partir de maintenant, tu pénètres dans le domaine « top secret ».

Et comme le jeune homme le regarde d'un air éberlué, paraissant ne pas comprendre :

— Tu m'as bien dit que tu voulais t'occuper du dossier Assadi ? Eh bien voilà. J'ai réfléchi et je suis d'accord. D'ici un an où deux, Zvika te passera complètement « l'affaire ».

Puis, coupant court à tous remerciements et effusions :

— Je te laisse maintenant avec lui. Bonne chance !

Zvika Amihay, que l'on appelle « le Bulgare » parce qu'il est né en Bulgarie, est un homme réservé. Redouté, aussi. Il a survécu à la déportation et est arrivé en Israël quelques jours seulement après la proclamation de l'Indépendance. Descendant avec Arié au deuxième étage, il disparaît quelques minutes derrière une porte blindée et en ressort avec deux dossiers. Sans un mot, sans la moindre explication ni commentaire, il entre avec son jeune compagnon dans un bureau minuscule et pose les dossiers sur la table :

— Je viendrai les reprendre à six heures. A six heures précises. Tu as trois heures pour les étudier. On en reparlera après.

C'est un bureau petit, humide et presque vide. Une table faite d'une planche et de deux tréteaux... Une carte d'Israël sur le mur... Une chaise... Et puis le dossier du fameux Israël Beer... Arié a le cœur qui bat. Les mains moites. Les doigts qui tremblent. Par où commencer ? Les fiches ? Les témoignages ? Les minutes du procès ? Les différentes « synthèses », de plus en plus affinées, qui se succèdent le long des années ? Israël Beer a toujours prétendu, par exemple, avoir été élève à l'École des Officiers de Wiener Neustadt, en Autriche. Or voici le témoignage du responsable du centre d'entraînement clandestin des forces spéciales de la Haganah qui se souvient avoir eu une bien étrange surprise en recevant, en 1938, le « légendaire » Israël Beer : celui-ci ne connaissait quasiment pas le maniement des armes. De même, voici une lettre de Jean Miksha, ancien volontaire tchèque dans les Brigades Internationales où Israël Beer est censé avoir passé deux années : n'écrit-il pas, après un entretien d'une heure, à Paris, en présence de l'attaché militaire de l'ambassade d'Israël, qu'il est à peu près persuadé de n'avoir jamais rencontré Beer auparavant ? Arié est si passionné par ces histoires, si troublé par ces contradictions, qu'il ne voit pas le temps passer. Quand il consulte sa montre, il est déjà six heures moins vingt et il ne lui reste plus que vingt minutes pour parcourir le dossier Assadi. Il l'ouvre précipitamment. Des photocopies tombent par terre et s'éparpillent. En les ramassant, il remarque un mince paquet de feuilles remplies de noms et de numéros de téléphone et maintenues par un gros trombone. Les regardant de plus près il s'aperçoit qu'il s'agit ni plus ni moins que de la photocopie du carnet d'adresses de Hugo. Le nom de son père est là... L'adresse et le téléphone de Sidney à New York... Ceux de Salomon à Paris... Tant et tant d'autres... Jusqu'à la lettre « H » où, à côté d'un nom mal rayé qui pourrait être « Hidberg » ou « Hilberg », figure le nom de Hidar, lui-même suivi d'un chiffre qui ne ressemble plus à un numéro de téléphone et qui est le chiffre 300 000.

300 000... 300 000... Et si cela voulait dire 300 000 dollars ? Si c'était le montant de la somme que Hugo avait tenté d'emprunter à une banque américaine et pour laquelle Sidney lui avait refusé sa garantie ?

Arié est tout à coup sûr d'avoir découvert quelque chose d'important. Il en est si exalté qu'oubliant et Zvika et les dossiers, il se précipite pour annoncer la nouvelle à Benjamin. Et, en ouvrant la porte, se heurte au Bulgare.

32

MOSCOU

LA PRISE DU KREMLIN

Février 1971

Aron Lerner a appris la mort de Sidney en lisant la
Pravda. Dans un long article où l'auteur exalte les
éminents services rendus à la cause de la paix par
l'URSS dans le conflit jordano-palestinien, il était aussi
incidemment question de la mort du médecin américain,
Sidney Halter, enlevé par « un commando d'extrémistes, faisant le jeu de l'impérialisme israélien ». Aron
ne connaît ni de près ni de loin ce cousin de sa femme.
Mais, comme tous les héros de cette histoire, comme
tous ces Juifs et toutes ces Juives dispersés à travers le
monde, il a le sentiment, confus quoique insistant,
d'avoir perdu un proche parent. « L'homme meurt
autant de fois qu'il perd l'un des siens… » N'est-ce pas
l'une des meilleures maximes de Publius Valerius Publicola, ce fondateur de la République romaine à qui le
professeur d'antiquités gréco-latines vient de consacrer
un cours à l'université ?

Quant à Rachel, sa réaction a été à la fois très simple
et très étrange. « Six millions et deux morts », a-t-elle
simplement dit après avoir lu l'article qu'Aron lui a
montré. Pour elle, cela ne fait pas de doute : ses cousins
Hugo et Sidney ont été tués parce que juifs : et ils sont
venus, ainsi, accroître de leurs noms le martyrologe de
l'holocauste. Il y a un an, Aron eût protesté. Il eût tenté
de démontrer à sa femme l'absurdité choquante d'une

telle affirmation. Mais aujourd'hui, il ne sait plus... Il a vu les caricatures antisémites dans *Ogoniok* et *Les Nouvelles de Moscou*... Il a entendu les appels à la destruction d'Israël proférés par des « camarades palestiniens » invités à l'université et applaudis chaleureusement par l'assistance... Et il est bien obligé d'admettre que le meurtre politique d'un Juif est rarement le fait du hasard, qu'il procède toujours, peu ou prou, d'une démarche exterminatrice.

La vérité c'est que l'événement l'a probablement éloigné un peu plus encore de son fils Sacha qu'il voyait déjà fort peu depuis leur querelle de la guerre des Six Jours. Mais qu'il l'a rapproché, en revanche, du petit « groupe sioniste » fréquenté, depuis trois ans, par sa femme. Il y a là un journaliste, Zaredski, un ancien officier aussi sévère que courtois qui, chaque année, le jour anniversaire de la victoire, arbore trois rangées de décorations et de médailles. Il y a aussi un ingénieur, Levine, homme doux et effacé. Et puis un professeur de littérature russe, Slepak, qui connaît Pouchkine par cœur... Chaque membre de ce groupe a demandé l'autorisation de partir pour Israël. Et, en représailles, tous ont été aussitôt licenciés et, depuis, ils vivent tant bien que mal grâce à de petits travaux « au noir ». Levine conduit un taxi. Zaredski fait de petits travaux de maçonnerie. Les moins débrouillards subsistent grâce à l'aide de leurs familles et amis. Aron les trouve idéalistes et pathétiques. Mais tellement plus intéressants que ses collègues de l'université ! Tellement plus libres ! Tellement plus humains aussi ! Suivre leur exemple ? Non, bien sûr... Il n'en est pas encore là... L'Union soviétique demeure, malgré tout, sa patrie. Mais enfin plus le temps passe, et plus le cas de ces hommes, de ces femmes, le passionne et le hante.

C'est deux ou trois jours après l'article de la *Pravda* que Hidar Assadi, le compagnon de sa fille, regagne Moscou. Il a changé, Hidar. Ses cheveux crépus ont blanchi. Son pas s'est encore alourdi. Son bras gauche est dans le plâtre et, à la grande surprise d'Aron et de Rachel, il n'a, cette fois, aucune histoire à raconter, aucun événement à commenter. Par contre, et c'est peut-être plus étrange encore, il est devenu plus prévenant. Il s'intéresse à leur vie, à leur santé et arrive tous les jours les bras chargés de menus cadeaux.

Un soir, il leur annonce son mariage avec Olga. Ce n'est pas, cette fois, une surprise. Et Rachel et Aron s'étaient, depuis longtemps, préparés — et résignés — à cette nouvelle. Beaux joueurs, ils décident même de « faire les choses convenablement » et de profiter du congé de la Nouvelle Année pour fêter l'événement. On convie les amis « sionistes » de Madame. Les collègues d'université de Monsieur. Hidar invite la direction du Comité de solidarité avec les peuples d'Asie et d'Afrique, ainsi que quelques ambassadeurs arabes. Et, quant à Olga, elle se contente du service de pédiatrie de l'hôpital où elle travaille. Mélange détonant, bien entendu ! Baroque au possible ! Le soir venu, Rachel ne sait où donner de la tête. Elle est à la cuisine, dans le salon, dans le bureau d'Aron, dans la chambre à coucher, bref partout où il y a des invités et il y en a partout. Aux uns, elle propose des gâteaux qu'elle a confectionnés elle-même. Aux autres elle sert de la vodka et du « kwass ». Avec les troisièmes elle fait l'élégante et engage des conversations. Et avec tous enfin, elle « veille au grain » en suivant de très près les rencontres susceptibles de mal tourner. En fait, tout va pour le mieux. Un ami d'Olga a même apporté un accordéon sur lequel le refuznik Zaredski entonne une chanson de la dernière guerre, laquelle est reprise par le kagébiste Tchebrikov, à la grande joie de Hidar. Et c'est à ce moment qu'arrive Sacha flanqué d'un journaliste des *Nouvelles de Moscou,* Matveï Fedorovotch Egorov, qui semble déjà ivre. Sacha explique :

— Nous venons de fêter le départ d'un ami, commence-t-il, nommé consul à Bucarest...

Et, regardant autour de lui :

— Mais que vois-je ? Maman a invité toute sa bande de cosmopolites...

257

Aron, qui l'a entendu, le fusille du regard. Et venant tout près, grommelle entre ses dents :

— C'est le mariage de ta sœur, Sacha. Ne l'oublie pas. D'autant que...

Il ne termine pas sa phrase. Car des rires et des applaudissements, derrière lui, l'interrompent. Il se retourne. Et au milieu d'un cercle de convives qui tapent joyeusement des mains, il voit le vieil ingénieur Levine, devenu chauffeur de taxi, qui exécute une danse cosaque autour d'Olga.

— Mais c'est le Juif Levine, fait Egorov, l'ami de Sacha.

Les rires, à la seconde même, s'arrêtent. On entend encore quelques gloussements. Quelques toux embarrassées. Et puis le silence se fait tandis que Levine s'avance :

— Je suis juif, dit-il en s'adressant à Egorov. Et toi ?

— Moi, je suis russe ! répond l'autre en se tapant fièrement du poing sur la poitrine.

— Tu n'es pas russe, réplique calmement Levine. Tu n'es que de la merde. Sous les tsars, tu aurais participé aux pogromes dans « L'Union de l'Archange Michel » et en 1917, les bolcheviques t'auraient fusillé.

— Arrêtez, arrêtez ! Je vous en prie, supplie Rachel qui sent que l'affaire tourne mal.

Mais Egorov ne l'écoute pas :

— C'est moi, un communiste, que les bolcheviques auraient fusillé ?

— Oui, toi et tes semblables. Tu n'es pas un vrai communiste et si tu as dans ta poche la carte du parti, c'est par hasard ou par faveur. C'est chez les nazis que tu aurais dû être inscrit...

— Attends, espèce de sale youpin ! crie Egorov, blême de rage.

Et tandis que Rachel et Olga tentent de les séparer, Aron saisit Sacha par le bras :

— Fais débarrasser le plancher à cette ordure... Et tout de suite...

Sacha regarde son père comme s'il le voyait pour la

première fois et, sans un mot, prend Egorov par les épaules et l'entraîne vers la sortie.

Le lendemain matin, Aron annoncera à Rachel son intention de déposer une demande de visa pour Israël. La surprise de Rachel sera si grande qu'elle ne saura, sur l'instant, quoi répondre. Ce n'est qu'une demi-heure plus tard, lorsque, dans une cuisine remplie de vaisselle sale, de bouteilles vides et de mégots, Aron vient l'aider à préparer le petit déjeuner qu'elle demande timidement :

— C'est vrai ?

Aron fait oui de la tête. Rachel, le visage baigné de larmes, le regarde et l'embrasse.

L'hiver 1971 s'annonce difficile. Le mois de janvier est froid, venteux. Les queues, aux magasins, de plus en plus longues. Aron, après voir déposé sa demande de visa pour Israël, s'attendait tous les jours à être renvoyé de l'université. Ses nouveaux amis viennent à présent chez lui, rue Kazakov, et ils restent tard dans la nuit à discuter littérature ou politique.

Un soir du mois de février, alors qu'ils sont quelques-uns à plaisanter autour d'une tasse de thé, on sonne à la porte. Aron va ouvrir avec, déjà, dans la démarche, la résignation du futur bagnard. Mais c'est Levine qui, sans prononcer un mot, salue Aron d'un signe de tête et, après avoir vérifié d'un coup d'œil que son bureau est bien vide, lui fait signe d'y entrer et de fermer derrière eux la porte à clé. Il a manifestement quelque chose d'important à lui dire et redoute les écoutes. Et, de fait, le voici qui, d'un geste fébrile, prend une feuille de papier sur la table de travail et debout, sans prendre le temps de s'asseoir, écrit : « Je suis en taxi et sûr de ne pas avoir été suivi. Affaire urgente et très importante. Demain matin, à 11 heures, nous allons occuper la salle d'accueil du Présidium du Soviet Suprême de l'URSS. »

Devant l'air stupéfait d'Aron, il continue toujours sur la même feuille : « Sans nous faire remarquer, un par un, nous allons pénétrer dans l'immeuble qui se trouve sur la place Rouge et nous allons décréter une grève de la faim. Nous ne quitterons pas les lieux tant que le Président ne nous aura pas reçus. Objectif : notre liberté d'émigration en Israël. »

Puis, posant son stylo, il regarde Aron fixement. Et comme l'autre sourit, l'air un peu sceptique, il déchire une autre feuille de papier et poursuit : « Je comprends votre réaction. Il n'y a encore jamais rien eu de tel dans toute l'histoire de l'URSS. Ce sera la première grève de ce genre, mais peut-être pas la dernière. Ils vont certainement nous arrêter. Les peines seront lourdes. Dix ans, au moins. Mais c'est encore mieux que de rester là, à attendre. Notre arrestation va soulever une tempête dans le monde. Serez-vous des nôtres ? »

Levine leva à nouveau les yeux sur Aron. Celui-ci avait l'impression de vivre un rêve. Il fut pris de panique. Tout allait trop vite. Pourquoi lui ? Il y a des dizaines de milliers d'autres Juifs qui veulent émigrer en Israël ! Dix ans de Goulag c'était autrement plus grave que de rester à Moscou sans travail. Mais pouvait-il refuser ? Il observa Levine. Celui-ci n'avait l'air ni d'un fou ni d'un héros. C'était juste un ingénieur devenu chauffeur de taxi. Et Aron pensa qu'Homère avait tort de dire que « sur la terre, il n'y avait rien de plus faible que l'homme ». D'une main qu'il contrôle mal, il prend le crayon de Levine et écrit seulement : « Qui vient avec nous ? »

Levine sourit et inscrit quelques noms, ceux des nouveaux amis d'Aron, des hommes droits et honnêtes.

— D'accord, écrit alors Aron, stupéfait lui-même de sa décision. Quand ?

— Demain, 11 heures, écrit Levine. Prenez le métro et descendez à la station Bibliothèque Lénine. Ensuite, rejoignez notre lieu de rendez-vous à pied.

Aron fait oui de la tête. Levine lui tapote amicalement l'épaule, frotte une allumette et enflamme les feuilles de papier qu'il dépose ensuite dans le cendrier et réduit avec le pouce en cendre et en poussière. Puis, doucement, cherchant à passer inaperçu des invités, il s'en va comme il était venu : sans un mot, sans un bruit. Quand Aron regagnera la pièce, il fera signe à Rachel de ne pas poser de question. Et ce n'est qu'après le départ de leurs amis qu'il prend un bloc de papier, un stylo et résume, par écrit, le plus clairement possible, la situation. Rachel relit son texte deux fois ; et sans se donner, elle non plus, le temps de réfléchir, ajoute simplement : « Je viens avec toi. »

Cette nuit-là, Aron dort très mal. Il a des cauchemars et se réveille à plusieurs reprises. Vers 4 heures du matin, il a l'impression d'entendre quelqu'un pousser la porte de l'entrée. Il va vérifier, constate que la porte est bien verrouillée, et s'enferme dans son bureau. Là, il feuillette la pile de livres en désordre sur la table, lit un poème de Ion de Chios, parcourt une page d'Eschyle, s'attarde sur une scène de l'*Antigone* de Sophocle : « Je sais bien que je pourrai ; c'était inévitable... Si je péris avant le temps, je regarde la mort comme un bienfait. Quand on vit au milieu des maux, comment n'aurait-on pas avantage à mourir ? » Et, pour la première fois de sa vie, il se demande si l'Ecclésiaste, qui dit presque la même chose, ne lui est pas, au fond, plus proche.

L'entrée de la salle d'accueil du Présidium du Soviet Suprême de l'URSS est imposante. Carrée, massive, ornée de moulures dorées. Les portes de chêne sont lourdes, parées d'énormes poignées de cuivre. Devant les portes, des policiers en manteau noir, le visage rougi par le froid, semblent voués à une interminable faction. Dehors, il neige et, malgré l'heure matinale, la foule se presse déjà. Aron et Rachel sont là. Ils se heurtent à Slepak, le professeur de littérature russe qui salue Aron d'un signe de tête et retient Rachel par la manche :

— Vous ne devriez pas rester là, chuchote-t-il. Une seule personne par famille. Ce n'est pas la peine de se retrouver tous en prison...

Aron, jugeant la réaction de Slepak sensée, embrasse Rachel et lui demande de rentrer à la maison. Après quoi, fermant instinctivement les yeux comme s'il sautait dans le vide, il pénètre à l'intérieur. C'est une grande salle tout en marbre, bordée de bancs tapissés de cuir noir avec, au bout, de méchants guichets percés dans une demi-cloison vitrée derrière lesquels on aperçoit les têtes de quelques fonctionnaires. A gauche des guichets, une queue s'est déjà formée. Des dizaines d'invalides appuyés sur des béquilles, des femmes accompagnées d'enfants en bas âge, des paysans mal vêtus, des vieillards, s'observent, se surveillent et, à mi-voix, se racontent leurs misères. Tout à fait à droite, le long du mur opposé, se tiennent les Juifs. Aron, rapidement, les compte. Ils sont vingt-deux. Vingt hommes et deux femmes. Il y a parmi eux Levine et Zaredski. Il y a aussi Ivanov, un demi-Juif qui, par respect pour la mémoire de sa mère morte en déportation, a voulu se joindre à eux. Et puis il y a Slepak qui, se détachant du groupe, se dirige vers l'un des guichets et passe une feuille de papier au fonctionnaire. Celui-ci lit. Relit. Son visage exprime un immense étonnement. Il dit quelque chose à Levine. Relit une nouvelle fois le papier comme si le sens lui en échappait. Et il saisit enfin le téléphone tandis que Slepak, sourire aux lèvres, revient vers ses camarades.

— J'ai dit, leur annonce-t-il, que tant que le Président Podgorny ne nous aura pas reçus, nous resterons ici.

La tension dans la salle est, bien entendu, montée aux extrêmes. Plus personne ne bouge. Plus personne ne parle. Les fonctionnaires, sidérés, observent les Juifs à travers la vitre. Un homme, en civil, mais à l'allure militaire, regarde Aron fixement de dessous sa chapka à poil ras et, se voyant observé à son tour, feint l'indifférence. Un autre, qui porte la même chapka à poil ras, prend rapidement quelques photos. Et puis, tout d'un coup, de manière tout à fait incompréhensible, la vie reprend ; la foule se presse à nouveau ; la queue devant les guichets devient aussi longue que tout à l'heure ; et alors que les vingt-deux Juifs restent regroupés à droite des guichets, dans une indifférence générale, le petit ballet de la misère reprend son rythme et ses droits.

Les heures passent. Le jour tombe. Aron commence à avoir faim. Il est surtout très fatigué. La salle, maintenant, commence à se vider. Et il ne reste bientôt à l'intérieur que les policiers et les Juifs. Un fonctionnaire malingre s'approche. Il prend bien soin que ses pas, comme au théâtre, résonnent sur les dalles de marbre. Et sans regarder personne, se parlant comme à lui-même, mais assez haut pour que les vingt-deux Juifs l'entendent, lance :

— C'est l'heure de fermer. Je vous prie de quitter la salle.

Constatant que personne ne bouge, ni les Juifs, ni les policiers, il ajoute :

— Le service de nettoyage peut commencer le ménage.

Cinq femmes, en blouse bleue et fichu sur la tête, apparaissent alors. Indifférentes à ce qui se passe dans la salle d'accueil du Présidium du Soviet Suprême, elles posent les seaux sur le sol, commencent à faire gicler l'eau et, sans même lever les yeux, se mettent à l'ouvrage de façon mécanique, méthodique.

Aron regarde fasciné les cinq silhouettes courbées, poussant devant elles avec leurs serpillières leur eau sale. Quand l'eau atteint ses pieds, il lève les jambes. Ses compagnons font de même. Les cinq femmes reviennent avec les seaux, épongent l'eau sale et, sans un regard pour les vingt-deux Juifs assis les jambes en l'air, le long du mur, finissent par s'en aller. Tout se passe comme dans une pièce de Sophocle. Entrée en scène, tour à tour, devant le même décor, des personnages principaux, du chœur, des messagers, des personnages muets... Et, comme pour confirmer le sentiment d'Aron, un fonctionnaire silencieux émerge des coulisses, se dirige vers les fenêtres et baisse les stores. Les grands lustres baroques prennent soudain tout leur éclat... tragique !

Un homme petit, brun, en costume et cravate noirs, pénètre alors dans la salle. Il est accompagné de deux individus qui se tiennent respectueusement derrière lui. « L'un des acteurs principaux », se dit Aron. L'homme s'arrête en face des vingt-deux Juifs, les dévisage l'un après l'autre de ses yeux bridés de Tatare et se présente :

— Toutchine. Chancelier adjoint du Bureau du Président du Présidium du Soviet Suprême de l'URSS, Nikolaï Viktorovitch Podgorny.

Et d'une voix sans réplique :

— J'exige la libération immédiate des lieux.

— Nous ne partirons pas, dit Levine.

Et d'un coup, tout le monde se met à parler à la fois :

— Nous ne partirons pas tant qu'on ne nous accordera pas le droit d'émigrer en Israël ! Vous pouvez nous arrêter ! Nous ne partirons pas !...

Toutchine paraît surpris et presque amusé par l'attitude si déraisonnable du petit groupe. Il lève la main et demande le silence :

— Vous vous rendez compte de ce que vous faites ? Vous occupez un bâtiment de l'État. Nos lois ne plaisantent pas avec ce genre de chose. Est-ce clair ? La sentence sera sévère.

Et, se tournant ostensiblement vers la masse compacte des policiers qui barrent les issues, il ajoute :

— Je vous offre de quitter les lieux sans incident. C'est votre dernière chance. La loi soviétique est sans merci pour ses ennemis.

— Nous ne sommes pas des ennemis, dit Aron. Nous sommes des Soviétiques, comme vous, mais nous exigeons le respect de nos droits...

L'homme paraît cette fois agacé. Il fait un geste brusque de la main gauche, comme s'il chassait une mouche et lâche :

— Le tribunal établira ce que vous êtes, ennemis ou amis. Pour moi, cela suffit !

Après quoi, tournant les talons, il ordonne que l'on, éteigne les lumières.

— Maintenant ils vont nous embarquer, dit l'un.

— Ils n'ont qu'à nous faire sortir de force, dit une seconde voix dans l'obscurité.

— On récoltera au moins un an, remarque un troisième.

— Si vous récoltez un an, vous aurez de la chance. Je

264

dirais plutôt dix, répond le second. Ils mettront le paquet pour décourager tous les autres.

— Ils ne vont tout de même pas nous fusiller! dit la femme qui s'attendait aùparavant à douze mois de prison.

— Ils feront ce qu'ils voudront... répond Levine.

— Mais non, dit Slepak, ce n'est pas comme sous Staline... On aura nos dix ans de camp. C'est suffisant, croyez-moi.

Puis, il y a un silence. Les Juifs se serrent plus près les uns des autres. Ils sentent dans l'obscurité la lourde présence de la police.

— Juifs, j'ai un transistor, dit Levine au bout d'un moment.

— Peut-on capter l'étranger? demande Aron.

— Essayons.

On entend un grésillement, des fragments de musique, des mots dans des langues étrangères, des voix qui se succèdent, à nouveau de la musique et, enfin, une voix lointaine en russe :

— D'après les correspondants... Moscou... un groupe de Juifs auxquels... droit d'émigration en Israël... occupait ce matin l'immeuble de... soviétique... grève de la faim... A l'heure actuelle, l'immeuble est cerné par la police et l'armée... Le monde entier... attention... l'évolution de cette lutte désespérée... Les 22 hommes et femmes représentent des centaines de milliers... Juifs soviétiques... en vain... depuis des années... faire respecter leurs... on apprend de sources bien informées...

Le brouillage couvre complètement la voix.

— Ils savent! s'écrie Slepak. Nous ne sommes pas seuls!

— Je n'ai plus peur, fait Zaredski.

— « Shema Israël », dit doucement Levine.

Une femme s'est mise à pleurer. Et Aron, emporté par une exaltation soudaine, récite :

— « Entre tant de merveilles du monde, la grande merveille, c'est l'homme. »

— Professeur Lerner, fait alors une voix toute jeune près de lui. Professeur Lerner...

— Oui.

— Je suis Volodia... Je suis... l'un de vos élèves.

— Volodia ? Volodia comment ?

— Volodia Blumstein.

— Volodia, c'est vrai... Je ne t'ai pas reconnu, fait Aron en cherchant dans l'obscurité la main du jeune homme.

— J'étais derrière le professeur Zaredski. Je n'osais pas m'approcher de vous, monsieur le Professeur, mais...

— Oui, Volodia...

— Je me souviens qu'un jour, après votre cours, nous étions quelques étudiants juifs... Vous nous aviez dit que vous étiez contre le sionisme... Alors, pourquoi maintenant...

— C'est vrai, fait Aron simplement. J'ai changé.

Et il raconte Hugo, Sidney, Sophocle et l'Ecclésiaste. Il parle longtemps. Très longtemps. Le petit groupe l'écoute en silence. « Quand les nuages sont pleins de pluie, récite-t-il, ils la répandent sur la terre ; et si un arbre tombe, au midi ou au nord, il reste à la place où il est tombé... »

A cet instant, les lustres s'illuminent. La lumière soudaine surprend les grévistes. Aron cligne les yeux et consulte sa montre : il est 5 heures du matin. Le carillon du Kremlin le confirme aussitôt.

— Regardez ! dit Levine.

Au centre de la salle vide se tient Toutchine, entouré de ses deux gardes. Près des portes et des fenêtres, la police veille.

— Écoutez-moi bien, fait Toutchine d'un ton triomphant. Je suis chargé de vous transmettre ceci...

Il s'arrête, comme pour mieux savourer l'effet de ses paroles, et annonce :

— Votre requête est acceptée.

Aron en a le souffle coupé. Slepak regarde Levine, incrédule. Ce dernier fait un pas en avant :

— Vous voulez dire que nous pourrons émigrer en Israël ?

266

— Attendez... Attendez...

Toutchine fait un geste de la main :

— Une décision venue de haut ordonne la création d'une commission gouvernementale chargée de l'émigration en Israël. Et vous êtes invités tous les vingt-deux à la première séance de cette commission.

— Et on nous laissera aller en Israël ? demande Volodia.

Toutchine hésite :

— Je pense que oui. Rentrez maintenant chez vous. Le 1er mars, revenez pour la réunion de la commission.

— Et les autres ? Tous ceux qui veulent émigrer en Israël ? demande Slepak.

— La commission sera là pour les entendre.

Levine fait un pas encore vers Toutchine :

— Et qu'est-ce qui nous dit que vous ne cherchez pas à nous tromper ?

Toutchine paraît surpris par la question. Il semble chercher autour de lui un renfort à ses affirmations. Son regard se fige un moment sur la masse des policiers devant les portes. Brusquement, il se tourne vers Levine :

— La preuve que vous pouvez avoir confiance c'est qu'on vous laisse en liberté ! Et puis tout de même, n'avez-vous pas la parole du Président du Présidium du Soviet Suprême de l'URSS, Nikolaï Viktorovitch Podgorny ?

— Alors, les Juifs ? demande Ivanov. On fait confiance à sa parole ?

Toutchine ébauche un geste vers la sortie. La masse des policiers s'ouvre. Aron avance le premier.

33

MOSCOU

LE GRAND RETOUR

Mai 1971

Aron Lerner et ses amis ont été surpris par une victoire trop facile, trop rapide. Le brusque libéralisme des autorités ne cachait-il pas une ruse ? une nouvelle vague de persécutions ? La sortie du petit groupe de refuzniks, sous les projecteurs de la police et les flashs des photographes de la presse étrangère, avait certes redonné courage aux Juifs soviétiques dans leur ensemble. Mais que cachait, encore une fois, une telle mansuétude ? et ne fallait-il pas s'en inquiéter avant que de s'en réjouir ?

La Commission promise par Toutchine s'est réunie le 1er mars. Les vingt-deux Juifs y ont été conviés et tout s'est passé à peu près convenablement. Les membres de la Commission les ont interrogés sur les raisons de leur volonté de départ. Ils ont répondu. De part et d'autre, on a visiblement fait un effort de compréhension. Et le Président de la Commission, un certain Ghevtchenko, a conclu la séance en promettant des visas pour le printemps et en souhaitant bon voyage à leurs heureux bénéficiaires.

Les choses, pourtant, se sont vite gâtées. La presse soviétique a lancé très peu de temps après une grande campagne pour la préservation des valeurs et de la culture russes. Les caricatures de la *Pravda* et des *Izvestias* présentent les ennemis du socialisme, les

« cosmopolites », sous les traits de « Juifs » eux-mêmes affublés de longs nez et de barbes pointues, se sont multipliées. Il s'est même trouvé des caricaturistes pour, de crainte de n'être pas compris, ajouter sur leurs personnages une peu équivoque étoile de David. Et c'est dans ce climat terriblement dégradé qu'est convoquée fin avril, à l'université, une réunion de professeurs et d'assistants à laquelle Aron Lerner se rend — non sans une certaine appréhension.

Ce n'est certes pas la première réunion de ce genre. Et Aron a l'habitude de ces responsables du Parti fustigeant les « cosmopolites » et demandant au corps enseignant une vigilance accrue. Mais on murmure cette fois-ci que le secrétaire général de la section du Parti de la faculté d'histoire, Ivan Vassillevitch Evguénine, va se lancer dans une diatribe particulièrement violente. Mieux : qu'il va annoncer une offensive radicale contre « les ennemis du peuple qui ont réussi à s'infiltrer dans l'Université même, en y semant la mauvaise graine ».

Le discours du camarade Evguénine dépasse, de fait, en ignominie tout ce qu'on pouvait redouter. Tout y passe. Tous les pires poncifs. Toutes les plus effroyables calomnies. Jusqu'à ce que, à bout d'argument, et presque de souffle, il sorte de sa poche un papier quadrillé et commence à égrener les noms des professeurs et des assistants d'origine juive. Sa besogne terminée, il leur demande de prendre place sur un long banc de bois, placé à la droite de l'assistance. Les interpellés hésitent. Se regardent les uns les autres. Mais une longue habitude d'obéissance — ne sont-ils pas, pour la plupart, membres du Parti communiste ? — fait qu'après quelques secondes de flottement ils obtempèrent. Seul Aron demande :

— Puis-je savoir pourquoi le camarade Ivan Vassillevitch Evguénine nous demande de nous asseoir sur ce banc ? Serait-ce un procès ? Dans ce cas, je demande à être présenté devant la justice de mon pays ; au moins là, on me signifiera mon délit.

Les Juifs, qui n'ont pas encore atteint le banc,

s'arrêtent indécis. Le visage poupin d'Evguénine devient cramoisi :

— Nous ne sommes pas dans une salle de justice, fait-il, mais dans un amphithéâtre d'université. Il nous incombe de discuter des méthodes d'enseignement...

— Soit, répond Aron. Dans ce cas, que nous reproche-t-on ?

— Justement : vos méthodes d'enseignement.

Un instant, Aron Lerner demeure songeur. Il comprend qu'Evguénine est ivre et qu'il ira sans doute au bout de l'infamie. Ne voulant pas se désolidariser des autres Juifs, il décide de les rejoindre sur le banc. Puis commence la comédie. Un à un les « bons » communistes montent à la tribune. Ce sont des hommes, des femmes honorables. Des professeurs de qualité. Ce sont des gens qu'Aron connaît depuis des années, qu'il côtoie, qu'il aime bien. Et aucun, du reste, ne prononce le mot juif. Mais tous, comme pris de folie, se succèdent pour dénoncer ces « sionistes », ces « gens sans réelle patrie », ces « vagabonds sans passeport », pis, ces « mauvais maîtres ». A Léon Rabinovitch, on reproche d'avoir trop insisté sur la politique paysanne de Lénine et ses réformes dans le cadre de la NEP et pas assez sur le Congrès des Peuples d'Afrique et d'Asie, en 1922, à Bakou. A Tenquiz Abouladzé, d'avoir dans un cours sur la poésie soviétique contemporaine, évoqué le suicide de Maïakovski. On exhume un cours d'Aron Lerner sur Platon, dans lequel il se demandait si, en affirmant qu'il existe un système social parfait, Platon n'a pas ouvert la porte à une cohorte de faux Messie...

Aron, qui se contenait jusque-là, n'y tient plus et se lève d'un bond :

— La délation est un moyen d'information méprisable ! crie-t-il. Mais si vous le trouvez digne de vous, alors transmettez au moins l'information en entier...

— Le professeur Lerner n'a pas la parole, dit Evguénine.

— Je suis ici, à l'Université, depuis plus longtemps que vous. Je parlerai tant que cela me semblera utile au service de la vérité...

La tension est brusquement montée dans la salle. Quelques pupitres claquent. Quelques murmures se font entendre. Et Vassili Slepakov, tout tremblant, se lève :

— Objection, camarade Evguénine ! Je pense que nous pourrions au contraire écouter le professeur Lerner. Il a peut-être quelque chose à dire pour sa défense...

— Camarade Slepakov, répond le stalinien de plus en plus rouge et bouffi. Nous ne sommes pas ici au Palais de Justice. Il n'y a ni accusé, ni accusateur. Mais notre pays est assailli par des idéologies antisoviétiques. Et l'université doit être — c'est le camarade Brejnev qui l'a dit, lors du dernier Plénum de notre Parti — à l'avant-garde de la lutte contre tout déviationnisme.

Aron s'apprête à répondre à nouveau. Mais Fedor Rabinovitch, un petit homme dont le crâne dégarni semble rivaliser de misère avec le menton couvert de poils, le prend de vitesse :

— Le camarade Ivan Evguénine n'a pas tout à fait tort, fait-il d'une voix déformée, comme s'il s'exprimait dans un haut-parleur. Peut-être avons-nous commis des imprudences. On s'adresse à des étudiants et, parfois, on s'emporte... Mais de là à nous accuser de déviationnisme !

Aron n'en croit pas ses oreilles. Il regarde Fedor Rabinovitch. Faut-il le secouer ? Lui rappeler sa dignité d'homme ? Mais déjà un autre professeur juif, Boris Zolataïen, entame son autocritique sous l'œil ravi d'Ivan Evguénine. Puis un troisième... Un quatrième... Jusqu'à ce que Tenquiz Abouladzé, dont c'est le tour de parler, se lève brusquement et laisse tomber ses lunettes, les ramasse d'un geste fébrile et commence à fouiller dans ses poches. Sourires dans la salle. Quolibets. Airs gênés. Mais Tenquiz Abouladzé brandit déjà son passeport en direction de la tribune :

— Camarades ! crie-t-il, d'une voix coupée par l'émotion. Camarades ! Je suis géorgien !

On entend des rires, cette fois, dans la salle. Des exclamations. Des franches plaisanteries. Les hommes assis à la tribune échangent des notes, vite griffonnées. Evguénine, de plus en plus ravi de la tournure des événements, se penche en avant :

— Mais oui, camarade Abouladzé, mais oui ! Approchez donc, s'il vous plaît, et montrez-moi cela.

Abouladzé fait un pas vers la tribune, répétant comme un automate :

— Oui, oui, je suis géorgien... Mon passeport, mon passeport le prouve...

Evguénine fronce le sourcil et regarde attentivement le passeport du pauvre Abouladzé. « Hum... Hum... », fait-il en le retournant dans tous les sens comme pour s'assurer qu'il n'est pas faux et en le tendant, pour finir, à ses camarades à la tribune. La salle retient son souffle. Le passeport ayant fait le tour de la table, revient vers Evguénine qui le rend à Abouladzé.

— Oui, c'est vrai, dit-il d'une voix faussement autoritaire. Vous pouvez retourner dans la salle.

Abouladzé reprend son bien, manque à nouveau de tomber et court se rasseoir dans la dernière rangée de l'amphithéâtre sous la risée et les huées d'une assistance à nouveau déchaînée. Et c'est à ce moment-là que Vassili Petrovitch Slepakov se lève d'un pas feutré et s'approche de la tribune.

Ivan Evguénine, surpris, le suit du regard. L'assistance se tait à nouveau. On connaît Slepakov. On le respecte. Professeur émérite, il est l'un des plus anciens membres du Parti à l'Université et son dernier livre sur *Les Causes de la Deuxième Guerre mondiale* lui a valu les félicitations du Président du Soviet Suprême. Lorsqu'il arrive au pied de la tribune et qu'il se tourne vers l'amphithéâtre, tout le monde retient son souffle :

— Chers collègues, commence-t-il.

— Le camarade Slepakov n'a pas la parole, interrompt Evguénine d'un ton tout de même moins assuré.

Mais Slepakov ne le regarde même pas et poursuit :

— Nous sommes dans l'amphithéâtre où je donne habituellement mes cours. Aussi est-ce le professeur d'histoire contemporaine qui vous parle — celle qui se fait parfois devant nous, avec nous...

Ménageant son effet, il se tait à nouveau, s'essuie les lèvres avec un mouchoir et, après l'avoir rangé dans la poche intérieure de son veston, reprend :

— Alors, permettez-moi d'espérer que ce que nous avons vécu ici depuis une heure, ne sera jamais consigné dans un livre d'histoire. Car nos enfants, les Soviétiques de demain, en auraient honte. Et nous-mêmes, en vieillissant...

Il passe les doigts dans ses cheveux blancs :

— Je suis un vieux communiste, continue-t-il, d'une voix tremblante d'émotion, et je voudrais le demeurer. Je vous demande donc, chers camarades, d'arrêter immédiatement cette mascarade !

Evguénine se dresse comme poussé par un ressort, et pointe vers Slepakov un doigt accusateur :

— Mais de quel droit ? De quoi se mêle-t-il...

La rage manifestement l'étouffe.

— Camarades, poursuit encore Slepakov, en l'ignorant superbement. Que ceux qui sont d'accord pour interrompre cette réunion lèvent la main.

Un murmure traverse la salle. Puis un commencement de tumulte, né au dernier rang de l'amphithéâtre, qui envahit les gradins pour s'arrêter sur le banc occupé par les Juifs. Aron lève la main. Deux professeurs d'antiquité slave, assis au dernier rang, lèvent à leur tour la main. D'autres... D'autres encore... Jusqu'à ce que tous les participants à cette étrange réunion (sauf le « Géorgien » Abouladzé) se retrouvent la main en l'air.

Le silence, du coup, est revenu. C'est comme une forêt de mains qui se dressent face à la tribune, avec quelque chose de menaçant. Ivan Vassillevitch Evguénine, debout, incrédule, contemple la salle :

— Comment vous, camarades ?... Tous... Au secours des ennemis de l'Union soviétique ?

Il frémit, il *tremble* d'indignation :

— Eh bien, puisque vous demandez tous la suspension de la réunion, je la suspends. Elle reprendra d'ici quelques jours. Vous en serez avisés...

Après quoi, il descend de la tribune et se dirige, d'un pas légèrement vacillant, vers la sortie. Les professeurs, après son départ, se regardent, se toisent les uns les autres. Comment ont-ils pu ? Comment ont-ils osé ? Le ciel ne va-t-il pas leur tomber sur la tête ? Et pareille rébellion leur sera-t-elle pardonnée ? La gêne, de fait, le dispute à la fierté. Et c'est comme un malaise sourd, mal défini, qui succède à leur audace.

— Merci, Vassili, dit Aron, en s'approchant de Slepakov. Merci. Tu as illustré la fameuse sentence de Publius Valerius Publicola qu'il vaut mieux se fier à son courage qu'à la fortune...

Mais il est le seul à venir. Le seul à oser féliciter le rebelle qui, de son côté, ne répond rien et sourit tristement, visiblement épuisé. Aron lui presse la main :

— A bientôt, Vassili... Tu t'es conduit en ami...

— Non, dit Slepakov. J'ai essayé de me conduire en homme.

Le lendemain soir, quand Olga vient dîner chez ses parents, rue Kazakov, elle est déjà au courant :

— Alors, papa, le soûlard Evguénine a voulu t'envoyer à la potence !

— Pourquoi le soûlard ?

— Parce que tout le monde sait qu'il boit comme un trou !

— Ah ! Vous êtes encore sur cette histoire, grogne Rachel qui arrive de la cuisine... Tu ne veux pas plutôt nous dire où est Hidar ?

— Si, bien sûr, répond la jeune femme. Il avait une réunion au Comité de solidarité, mais il m'a promis de ne pas être trop en retard.

Puis, se tournant vers son père :

— J'ai rencontré, en venant ici, l'académicien Sakharov. Il se plaint de ne plus avoir de tes nouvelles. Je lui ai raconté la séance à l'université. Il en était scandalisé et m'a promis de le faire savoir.

Olga, malgré le temps qui passe, n'a pas beaucoup changé. Elle a toujours d'aussi grands yeux. Une taille aussi bien prise. Elle a toujours ce « port de reine » qui, au temps de leurs fiançailles, faisait rêver Hidar. Seuls ses cheveux blonds ont légèrement terni. Ce qui lui permet de dire : « Je vieillis » avec l'exquise coquetterie de celles qui savent qu'il n'en est rien. Mais pour le reste, elle ne change pas, non. Elle reste la même pétulante jeune femme. Et il n'est pas jusqu'à Victor Alexandrovitch Tchebrikov, dont l'influence ne cesse de grandir à Moscou, qui, l'autre soir encore, complimentait Hidar sur le savoir-faire et la séduction de sa femme. Ne lui arrive-t-il pas, lors de réunions officielles, de faire des remarques iconoclastes sur la bureaucratie soviétique ? Oui, mais venant d'une belle fille blonde, ces blasphèmes provoquent rires, indulgences, pour ne pas dire applaudissements. Et le fait est que s'il n'y avait pas cette sourde inquiétude au sujet de ses parents et de leur départ possible pour Israël, elle serait la plus heureuse des Moscovites. Elle continue à travailler à l'hôpital. Mais elle attend avec impatience le prochain voyage à Beyrouth, promis par Hidar, et conserve du premier, deux ans plus tôt, le plus doux des souvenirs.

> « *Mon bien-aimé est blanc et vermeil*
> *Il se distingue entre dix mille*
> *Sa tête est de l'or pur ; ses boucles sont flottantes,*
> *Noires comme le corbeau... »*

— Que dis-tu ? s'étonne Rachel, qui l'entend chantonner entre ses dents.
— Rien, je récitais *Le Cantique des Cantiques*.
— En anglais !
— Je l'ai appris dans une Bible anglaise, que j'ai trouvée dans un hôtel.
— Il faut apprendre l'hébreu, ma fille, c'est la langue de nos ancêtres...
— Oui, ma mère, oui... Sais-tu que c'est surtout, pour moi, la parole même de l'amour et que, en anglais, en yiddish, peu importe, il me suffit de la prononcer pour...
Elle n'a pas fini sa phrase qu'on sonne à la porte. C'est le bien-aimé en personne, aux boucles un peu

moins flottantes et moins noires — mais qu'elle n'embrasse pas moins avec sa fougue coutumière.

— Alors, Aron Lazarevitch, dit-il en repoussant gentiment sa « milaya », vous l'avez échappé belle ! Le cadavre de Staline bouge encore !

— Vous êtes déjà au courant ? s'étonne Aron.

— Moscou est un petit village où chacun a une âme de commère. Mais racontez-moi donc en détail ce qui s'est réellement passé ?

Aron hausse ses maigres épaules :

— Slepakov s'est bien conduit...

— Ne soyez pas modeste, Aron Lazarevitch. D'après ce qu'on dit, vous n'étiez pas mal non plus.

— Moi, je n'avais rien à perdre. Slepakov si... Mais passons plutôt à table.

A table, la conversation reprend :

— Le potage est délicieux, fait Hidar. Mais, dites-moi : j'ai parlé de cette réunion avec Tchebrikov et figurez-vous qu'il a trouvé cette initiative d'Evguénine déplacée. Que pensez-vous de ça, Aron Lazarevitch ?

— Je m'en réjouis !

— A la bonne heure ! Mais savez-vous maintenant ce que Tchebrikov m'a appris ?

— Allez-y...

— Il a ordonné une enquête et devinez ce qu'il a découvert ?

— Allons, Hidar, ne nous fais pas languir, fait Olga en lui taquinant les cheveux.

Hidar termine son potage, s'essuie les lèvres du revers de la main et dit, d'une voix basse, en regardant un à un tous les convives :

— Eh bien ce que Tchebrikov a découvert c'est que l'initiateur de cette infâme réunion n'était autre que Sacha Lerner.

— Sacha ! s'exclame Rachel en laissant tomber sa cuiller.

— Vous êtes sûr ? demande Aron d'un air soudain égaré.

Hidar fait oui de la tête.

— Mais pourquoi aurait-il fait cela ? fait Aron.

— Peut-être pour vous empêcher de partir... Peut-être aussi pour se protéger... Allez savoir s'il ne voulait pas prouver ainsi qu'il n'était pour rien dans l'initiative de ses parents... Qui sait, oui... « La vérité d'un homme, c'est d'abord ce qu'il cache. »

Hidar n'a pas besoin d'en dire plus. Ni Aron de poser d'autres questions. Le dîner s'achève dans un silence lugubre, à peine entrecoupé de propos faussement badins ou de plaisanteries vraiment forcées. La nuit venue, les Lerner auront peine à trouver le sommeil. Ils se lèveront tour à tour pour aller l'un feuilleter sa Bible ; l'autre, écrire, une fois encore, à la cousine d'Argentine. A l'aube, Aron se rase de près, prend une douche, s'habille et sort tout doucement en prenant bien garde de ne pas réveiller une Rachel qui, les yeux mi-clos, feignant un sommeil profond, l'observe avec attendrissement.

Le carillon de la Tour du Sauveur au Kremlin vient de sonner six heures. La journée s'annonce brumeuse, mais pas froide et l'air sent le printemps. Aron prend la rue Tchkalov qui, malgré l'heure matinale, est déjà animée. Il passe devant le métro Komskaya, qui déverse ses foules d'hommes endormis sur le trottoir. Évite de justesse une Ziss officielle. Et prend la direction de la place Taganskaya où, devant quelques rares magasins, des camions déchargent la marchandise du matin. A 7 heures pile, il arrive au pied d'un bâtiment sombre de six étages, rue Maïakovski. Il lève la tête. Derrière les fenêtres, ça et là, des rideaux s'écartent. Des visages apparaissent. Aron traverse la rue et s'appuie contre un arbre sachant que, de là où il est, il peut observer la porte d'entrée. Et c'est alors qu'il voit Sonia, la femme de Sacha, avec ses deux enfants Natacha et Boris. Puis, presque aussitôt, Sacha lui-même qui s'arrête sur le perron et scrute longuement les environs comme s'il attendait une voiture... Il y a bien longtemps qu'il n'a pas vu son fils, se dit-il. Il le trouve voûté, un peu vieilli. Il est trop loin pour bien distinguer son visage ; mais comme il ne porte pas de chapeau, il voit que son front s'est allongé, que ses cheveux blonds se sont raréfiés.

« Mon fils Absalon, récite-t-il, mon fils. Que ne suis-je à ta place... » et il traverse la rue.

Sacha aperçoit son père quand celui-ci est déjà au pied du perron. Il se crispe, fait un pas en arrière et avance la main qui ne tient pas la serviette, comme pour se protéger. Aron, sans s'émouvoir le moins du monde, monte doucement les quelques marches et fixe le visage troublé de son fils.

— Que... que veux-tu ?... demande celui-ci d'une voix tremblante.

— Rien, fait Aron posément... Rien... Je voulais juste te dire bonjour.

Et, avant que Sacha ne réagisse, il le prend dans ses bras et l'embrasse.

34

BUENOS AIRES

ARGENTINA, ARGENTINA

Août 1972

C'est par le plus grand des hasards que dona Regina apprend la mort de Sidney. Plus d'un an a passé. C'est un dimanche d'août particulièrement chaud et humide. Dona Regina et don Israël, comme la plupart des habitants de ce quartier populaire de l'avenue San Martin, sont assis devant la porte de leur petite maison à attendre la brise venue de la mer. Une radio qu'un voisin a posée sur le trottoir diffuse un tango de Gardel. Et la vieille commère lit une étude sur Septembre Noir, parue dans le *Freiheit,* le mensuel communiste, en yiddish, où l'auteur accuse la CIA d'avoir manipulé des tueurs palestiniens pour disqualifier la révolution arabe aux yeux de l'opinion publique américaine.

— Encore un Halter de moins, fait-elle, pour tout commentaire.

— L'ange de la mort tue et s'en va sanctifié, ajoute don Israël qui, dans ce genre de circonstances, cherche toujours quelque chose d'intelligent à dire.

— Ton ange prend de drôles d'apparences depuis trente ans, répond-elle avec un profond soupir — avant de se replonger dans la suite de sa lecture...

Puis, voyant du coin de l'œil son époux se lever, s'étirer et remonter ses pantalons :

— Mais où vas-tu, maintenant, avec cette chaleur ?

— Qui t'a dit que j'allais quelque part ?

Dona Regina prend son air le plus exaspéré :

— Parce que je te connais et que je sais que tu vas quelque part...

La bouche édentée de don Israël se fige dans un sourire forcé :

— Eh bien, tu as deviné, je vais faire ma partie de dominos.

Après quoi il tire deux ou trois fois sur ses bretelles, comme s'il attendait une réaction et reste planté devant elle pendant un long moment. Puis, ne la voyant pas réagir, il répète :

— Bon... Je dis que je vais faire ma partie de dominos...

Et comme son auguste épouse ne réagit décidément pas et retourne une fois encore à son journal, il hausse les épaules et s'en va tristement.

La vérité c'est que dona Regina est, ce jour-là, bien soucieuse. Il y a Martin, son aîné, dont elle attend, sans trop l'espérer, la visite. Miguel, le plus jeune, qui, lui, ne vient plus du tout. Il y a ce fichu mari avec qui elle ne peut parler de rien et qui préfère noyer ses soucis dans des parties de dominos. Et puis il y a, enfin et surtout, l'avenir d'Anna-Maria qui ne cesse de la tourmenter. Sa petite-fille a abandonné maintenant ses études. Elle disparaît continuellement sans laisser d'adresse ni de trace. Et il y a même eu, voilà un mois, la visite de cet officier de police, un grand gaillard basané qui l'a courtoisement mais fermement interrogée pendant une heure sur les amitiés et les déplacements de sa petite-fille sans lui donner les raisons de ce brusque intérêt... Anna-Maria, elle le sent bien, fait des choses peu catholiques — même si elle est à cent lieues d'imaginer l'ampleur des dégâts et de son engagement.

Ce dimanche, notamment, tandis qu'elle est là, devant sa porte de l'avenue San Martin, à égrener chagrins et souvenirs, la pauvre femme mourrait sur place si elle avait ne serait-ce que le pressentiment de ce qu'est en train de faire son exquise petite-fille...

Nous sommes en août 1972, donc. L'organisation de la jeune fille milite pour le retour de Peron. Mario et Julio sont même allés rencontrer le vieux leader en Espagne. Mais voici que le massacre de seize guérilleros emprisonnés à la base aéronavale de Trelew, a ravivé les passions et que la direction du mouvement a décidé des représailles. Ces hommes sont des chiens, disent-ils. Il faut les traiter comme des chiens. Moyennant quoi la fine équipe a décrété une expédition punitive à Tres Lomos, à l'orée de la pampa. Pourquoi Tres Lomos ? Parce qu'il y a là, camouflé en Institut d'études de l'Armée de terre, un véritable centre de tortures et qu'il a été décidé d'exécuter son chef, un certain Miguel Pelado dont Julio s'est procuré la photo.

Ils sont cinq, ce matin-là, dans la vieille Packard de Mario. Julio conduit. A côté de lui est assise Juanita, une fille qu'Anna-Maria ne connaît pas mais qu'on lui a présentée comme une terroriste confirmée et que Julio tenait à emmener car la présence de deux femmes, disait-il, déjouerait la suspicion éventuelle de la police. Anna-Maria est assise entre Mario et Roberto. Et elle ne se sent pas vraiment différente de ce qu'elle pouvait être au temps de ses premières parties de campagne avec ses premiers « novios ».

La voiture roule doucement, telle une banale voiture de tourisme. Il fait beau. Le soleil, immense, brille sur un ciel sans nuages. Anna-Maria aime la pampa. Elle goûte, comme chaque fois, cet espace sans bornes et sans frontières, ni fluide comme l'océan, ni mouvant comme le désert, mais solide et bon comme la terre. Rouler dans la pampa c'est l'aventure. C'est l'éternité. La route dans la pampa entraîne, tel le chant des sirènes. Et Anna-Maria qui va, avec ses camarades, exécuter Miguel Pelado, ne peut s'empêcher d'être bercée par des pensées poétiques et mélancoliques.

A un moment, alors qu'elle est en pleine rêverie, la voiture fait une embardée et la jeune fille manque glisser de son siège : Julio vient d'éviter de justesse un camion qui ralentissait pour quitter la route et prendre le Rio Salado.

— Doucement ! a crié Mario. Tu risques de nous tuer avant qu'on ne tue l'autre salopard.

Et elle s'entend répondre :

— Je t'en prie, Mario, ne parle pas comme ça.

— Pourquoi ? s'étonne-t-il, en rejetant ses cheveux en arrière.

— Parce que nous ne sommes pas forcés d'insulter, *en plus,* le malheureux que nous allons tuer.

— Comment, « le malheureux » ? Toi, quand tu descends un tortionnaire, tu ne te réjouis pas ?

— Non... Pas vraiment... Je regrette surtout qu'il y ait des tortionnaires à descendre.

La conversation continue quelques minutes sur ce ton. On traverse un village ocre surplombé par une admirable église baroque. On passe un ruisseau boueux qui coupe la route. Puis un pont à demi détruit. Puis un petit chemin poussiéreux que Julio présente comme un « raccourci ». Roberto et Juanita chantent :

> *« Depuis qu'il est parti, triste je vis*
> *Le petit chemin ami, moi aussi je pars.*
> *Depuis qu'il est parti, il n'est pas revenu*
> *Je veux suivre ses pas, le petit chemin adieu ! »*

Bref, tout va pour le mieux et l'équipée pourrait presque tourner, oui, à la banale partie de plaisir lorsque survient la « tuile ». Juste au moment de remonter sur la grande route, Julio s'écrie :

— Attention, les gars ! un barrage !

— Bon. Restez calmes.

Puis, voyant que, de toute façon, il est trop tard pour reculer :

— On va bien trouver le moyen d'enfiler ces fils de pute !

Les « fils de pute » sont déjà au milieu de la chaussée, qui leur font signe de s'arrêter. Dès que la Packard s'immobilise, une dizaine d'entre eux la cernent, pointant sur Julio leurs mitraillettes.

— Où allez-vous ? D'où venez-vous ? Sortez de la voiture ! Papiers !

Julio, très calme, ouvre la portière et descend mais les soldats sont déjà en position de combat et quand il met la main dans sa poche pour prendre sa carte d'identité, lèvent leurs armes comme un seul homme.

— Restez tranquilles, faites semblant de dormir, murmure Mario tandis qu'un officier s'approche de Julio et lui prend ses papiers.

— Julio Feldman, fait-il. Je crois connaître votre nom...

— Peut-être, je suis poète.

— Poète? Ce n'est pas un métier, ça, poète... Et vos amis? Ils sont poètes aussi, vos amis?

— Étudiants, oui... Jeunes écrivains... Nous formons un cercle littéraire...

— Vous publiez un journal?

Julio rit :

— Nous n'en avons pas les moyens.

— Je me fiche de vos moyens... Montrez les papiers de cette bande de bâtards!

Et, en se tournant vers la voiture :

— Toi, là, par exemple... La fille à la place du mort... Viens donc me montrer à quoi tu ressembles...

— Fils de pute, grommelle Mario pendant que Juanita ouvre la portière. Ils vont nous faire sortir un par un. S'ils regardent sous les sièges, nous sommes foutus. Continuons de dormir...

— Montre ta carte d'identité, dit Julio à Juanita.

L'officier sourit. Ce côté macho ne lui déplaît pas. Il regarde distraitement la carte d'identité de la jeune femme; plus attentivement l'échancrure de son chemisier. Et comme s'il lui venait une nouvelle idée, demande d'une voix traînante :

— Et vos autres amis? Pourquoi ils descendent pas?

— Ils dorment. Vous voulez que j'essaie de les réveiller?

L'officier observe Julio puis Juanita... Juanita puis Julio... Cela dure une ou deux bonnes minutes... Et puis tout à coup, sans qu'on sache pourquoi ni comment, fait signe à ses hommes de baisser leurs mitraillettes et, tendant aux deux jeunes gens leurs pièces d'identité, fait d'une voix redevenue dolente :

— *Bueno,* reprenez vos papiers ! *Buen viaje*...

Julio et Juanita, sidérés mais ne demandant pas leur reste, regagnent la voiture. Julio a les mains moites. Le cœur qui bat la chamade. Ses longs cheveux noirs sont collés par la peur et la sueur. Est-ce l'émotion qui le rend maladroit ? Ses fichus doigts qui tremblent trop ? Toujours est-il que lorsqu'il tourne la clé de contact, le moteur tousse et cale. Il essaie à nouveau : rien. S'affole : toujours rien. Les soldats, amusés, s'approchent. L'officier de tout à l'heure, se penchant à travers la vitre ouverte, commente de la même voix traînante :

— Le moteur est noyé, *señor* ! Il fallait passer en première avant de mettre en marche...

Et tandis que Julio remercie et, de plus en plus maladroit, manœuvre le levier de vitesse :

— Mais, au fait... Dites-moi... Vous êtes vraiment le poète Julio Feldman ?

— Oui, bien sûr...

— Poète Julio Feldman, répète-t-il, songeur. Ce nom me dit quelque chose... Peut-être que j'aimerais quand même réveiller vos amis...

Sa voix est devenue soudain plus brève, presque menaçante :

— Je voudrais aussi visiter votre voiture... Sortez tous, s'il vous plaît...

Et toujours à travers la vitre ouverte, il passe la main derrière la tête de Julio pour, sans plus de ménagement, secouer Mario. A cet instant précis, une explosion ébranle la voiture ; Anna-Maria a juste le temps d'être assourdie par la détonation et de sentir l'odeur de poudre, tandis que l'officier, rejeté en arrière, va s'affaler sur le macadam. Mario, son revolver à la main, hurle déjà à pleins poumons :

— Démarre ! Fonce ! Fonce, je te dis, ou je tire dans le tas !

Comme un automate, Julio suit cette fois le conseil du flic : il passe la première, tourne la clé et la voiture fait un bond en avant. Le moteur, pourtant, cale à nouveau.

Il recommence. Et ce n'est qu'à la seconde fois que la voiture démarre — zigzaguant à toute vitesse pour éviter les balles qui, maintenant, sifflent autour d'eux.

— Couchez-vous ! crie Mario en déchargeant, à travers la lunette arrière, son colt en direction des policiers.

Mais Julio a pris son virage. Et une colline referme déjà la route derrière eux.

La voiture tangue d'un côté à l'autre de la route en lacets. Mario remet le revolver sur le siège et pose la main sur la cuisse d'Anna-Maria, toute tremblante, qui aura besoin de deux bonnes heures pour retrouver son calme. Enfin, Julio ralentit. Mario retire sa main de la cuisse d'Anna-Maria. Celle-ci, en remuant la jambe, bute sur un objet tombé sous ses pieds : elle le prend, découvre avec horreur que c'est la casquette de l'officier et pique une nouvelle crise de nerfs.

— Ça va, ça va, fait Mario, de nouveau agressif, tu ne vas quand même pas en faire toute une histoire...

Et comme Anna-Maria, secouée de sanglots, est incapable de répondre :

— Tu penses qu'il aurait mieux valu se laisser arrêter ?

— Laisse-la tranquille, Julio.

Et, après un nouveau virage, pesant manifestement ses mots :

— Je ne sais pas ce que pense Anna-Maria mais je dis, moi, que tu as été trop rapide...

Cette fois, Mario explose :

— Trop rapide ? Tu dis trop rapide ? Mais tu sais quoi, pauvre con ? Tu sais que c'est toi le responsable ? Tu voulais être malin, hein ! Impressionner quelques flics argentins ! Poète... Monsieur est poète... « Je suis le poète Julio Feldman »... Non mais, je t'en foutrai, moi, des poètes...

Et s'adressant aux autres qui ne pipent mot :

— J'espère au moins que vous admettez que, à partir du moment où le flic voulait inspecter la voiture, je n'avais d'autre choix que de tirer... Vous croyez que je suis fier, peut-être, d'avoir tué un homme ? Même si cet homme est un flic ? Soyez donc heureux d'être en vie... Le reste, oubliez-le !

Il attend quelques secondes encore avant d'ajouter, un ton en dessous :

— Si vous pouvez...

A la tombée du jour, ils arrivent enfin à Tres Lomos, un village effacé et boueux que Roberto connaît un peu, pour avoir, une semaine plus tôt, fait les repérages nécessaires. A la fin de la journée, Miguel Pelado, le tortionnaire, a l'habitude de traverser la place, au milieu de laquelle se trouve une fontaine, pour se rendre à l'église. C'est une bâtisse penchée, de style colonial, où Anna-Maria se dit qu'on pourrait tourner un très beau film.

— Maintenant, il ne faut plus faire de conneries, dit Juanita qui s'était tue jusque-là.

Elle fouille sous le siège, en sort un revolver, vérifie le chargeur et relève le cran de sécurité. En professionnelle.

— Range la voiture à côté de la camionnette de la blanchisserie, dit Roberto à Julio. C'est moi qui l'ai placée là, la semaine passée. Elle nous cachera un peu. Deux voitures l'une à côté de l'autre, c'est déjà un parking. Avance encore... Voilà... Maintenant, gare-toi parallèlement au chemin qui mène à l'église. Voilà... maintenant, recule un peu pour pouvoir démarrer aussitôt l'objectif atteint. Évite la flaque d'eau... Bravo... Que le diable m'emporte, c'est très bien ! Maintenant, ouvrez les fenêtres du côté de l'église et ne vous faites surtout pas remarquer...

Roberto dégage alors, toujours de dessous le siège, une mitraillette tchèque VZ 58 et Anna-Maria son revolver égyptien 9 mm.

— Il ne faut pas le rater, hein ! dit Juanita parce qu'il faut bien dire quelque chose...

— Il sera seul ? demande Anna-Maria.

— Non, fait Roberto, mais tu n'es pas seule non plus.

Puis silence. Bruit de fond du village qui se prepare à

la nuit. Une charrette à deux roues, tirée par un âne malingre, qui s'attarde un long moment devant l'église.

— J'espère qu'elle partira à temps, grommelle Roberto avant de se taire à nouveau.

Le temps coule au compte-gouttes. L'angoisse aussi. Est-ce cela un attentat ? se demande Anna-Maria. Même chez les Palestiniens cela se passe comme ça ? Pas de héros, ni d'héroïsme. Plus de précision que d'audace, plus de calcul que de courage. La technique d'un expert-comptable scrupuleux plus que d'un guérillero. Rien qu'une trouille permanente et grelotter de froid pendant des heures dans une vieille bagnole en stationnement. Et tout cela pourquoi ? Pour pouvoir tuer un pauvre mec n'ayant d'autre ambition que de torturer ses semblables. Pour qui ? Pour Juan Peron qui doit, selon toute probabilité, revenir bientôt en Argentine et qui est bien le seul, croit-elle, à pouvoir instaurer la paix sociale et réintroduire dans la vie du pays un peu plus de justice. Elle en est là de sa rêverie quand Roberto l'interrompt et s'écrie :

— Attention ! camarades. Les voilà !

Elle voit un homme en uniforme noir, plutôt petit, plutôt gras, qui avance d'un pas indécis vers l'église avec ses quatre gorilles derrière lui.

— Que le Diable m'emporte ! peste alors Roberto. La charrette...

La charrette a bougé en effet. Dans un grincement de roues, elle s'est mise entre la Packard et l'homme en uniforme. Miguel Pelado, heureusement, avance encore un peu, revient dans le champ de tir et s'arrête une seconde, près de la fontaine, pour caresser la tête d'un bambin.

— Prêts ? demande Roberto d'une voix étouffée par l'émotion.

Comme personne ne répond et qu'ils semblent tous tétanisés par le spectacle de l'homme en train de caresser la tête de cet enfant, il répète, plus nerveux encore :

— Prêts ? Bon dieu de bon dieu, vous êtes prêts ?

Mais Miguel Pelado s'est remis en marche. Lentement. Souverainement. D'un pas de sénateur ou de notable. Lorsqu'il arrive à quelques mètres de l'église, il se retourne soudain et semble regarder vers la voiture. C'est alors que Roberto, sans plus de sommation, crie :

— Feu !

Les cinq jeunes gens tirent en même temps. L'homme se tourne vers la Packard, étonné. On le voit s'affaisser doucement, comme dans un film projeté au ralenti. On voit deux gorilles tomber presque en même temps, mais plus rapidement, plus lourdement, comme s'ils appartenaient à un autre film. Puis le troisième qui s'étale dans une flaque d'eau, éclaboussant la route. Anna-Maria tire, tire encore. Le quatrième garde du corps vacille. Les malheureux ont à peine le temps de sortir leurs armes, des soldats de sortir en courant sur le perron d'un bâtiment en bois, repeint en vert, qui se trouve du côté opposé à l'église — Roberto donne déjà l'ordre de repli ; Julio tourne la clé ; le moteur, cette fois, se met en marche du premier coup ; la voiture s'élance sur la route.

New York, septembre 1971

C'était un beau dimanche pour un mois de septembre. Exceptionnellement, les prévisions météorologiques s'étaient révélées justes : New York jouissait, cette année, d'un été indien. Mon chauffeur de taxi, un Juif soviétique, travaillant pour le compte d'un Juif israélien, tous deux installés depuis peu aux Etats-Unis, traversa sans se presser la ville presque déserte, puis le pont de Brooklyn, et s'engouffra dans le Eastern Parkway dont j'ai toujours adoré la large chaussée bordée de chaque côté par des allées de gazon et des arbres. Des pavillons en parpaing de style anglais ou hollandais, plutôt bas, et qui juraient avec la largeur de l'avenue, affichaient leurs étranges enseignes : Kingdom Hall of Jehovah's Witness, Calvari Evangelistic, Universal Temple Church, The Church of God and Prosperity — et ce jusqu'au numéro 770 où se pressait une foule d'hommes en caftan et en larges chapeaux noirs qui paraissaient surgir de ma plus lointaine mémoire.

— Il fallait me dire que vous alliez chez le Lubavitch, me glissa le chauffeur d'un ton de reproche.

Le rabbi de Lubavitch était — est toujours — une autorité aux États-Unis. Des hommes politiques, des ministres, des stars de cinéma et de la télévision, juifs ou non, attendent parfois des mois pour être reçus. J'avais

289

eu la chance, moi, qu'un ami, lui-même proche du Lubavitch de Los Angeles, intervienne en ma faveur. Et j'avais réussi, de la sorte, à avoir un rendez-vous assez vite. Le nom de cet homme ne figurait pas, je le précise, dans le fameux carnet noir. Mais je me souvenais du récit de Hugo, de sa retraite religieuse à Brooklyn, juste avant la guerre et quelque chose me disait que je pourrais bien récolter là quelques informations inédites. Peut-être s'y mêlait-il aussi de la curiosité. Et puis, je connaissais l'aventure de Richard, le fils de Sidney...

À peine fus-je descendu du taxi qu'un jeune homme me saisit par la manche ;

— Ah ! vous voilà... J'ai vu votre photo dans le journal... Je m'appelle Mendel Fogelman. Je connais très bien votre cousin Richard... On m'a demandé de vous accueillir. Et, plus officiel : Le Rabbi vous attend.

— Et toute cette foule ?

Mendel Fogelman leva les bras au ciel :

— Tous les Juifs ont besoin du Rabbi...

— Pour régler des conflits ?

— Ah non ! Les conflits entre les hommes sont arbitrés par les tribunaux rabbiniques. Le Rabbi ne traite que des problèmes entre l'homme et l'Éternel, béni soit-Il...

— Je croyais que pour parler à Dieu, les Juifs n'avaient pas besoin d'intermédiaire...

Mendel Fogelman fit un geste d'impatience, comme si je lui posais une question absurde et, éludant la réponse, me dit :

— Le Rabbi reçoit tous les dimanches, à 11 heures. Ses bedeaux offrent à chaque visiteur un dollar. Mais vous, vous serez reçu avant...

Puis captant je ne sais quel signal de l'un des gardiens devant la porte d'entrée, il me lança en yiddish, langue officielle des Lubavitch :

— *Mir zenen graït,* nous sommes prêts. Suivez-moi...

Et, fendant la foule :

— *Rebés gast !* L'invité du Rabbi ! Laissez passer ! L'invité du rabbi !

Et, toujours en yiddish :

— *Rebés gast !*

La foule s'ouvrit en effet et nous nous retrouvâmes très rapidement sur le perron, devant la porte du pavillon. Mendel Fogelman frappa et la porte s'ouvrit devant un barbu sans âge, ses papillotes au vent.

— C'est l'invité du Rabbi, répéta-t-il pour la énième fois.

Nous pénétrâmes dans un petit vestibule, où quelques Juifs se balançaient d'avant en arrière au rythme d'une prière. Je sortis une *kipa* de ma poche, la mit sur la tête. A gauche, au fond du vestibule, se trouvait un escalier sur lequel deux enfants jouaient avec une poupée. A droite, une minuscule pièce aux rideaux tirés. Un homme petit, au visage auréolé d'une barbe blanche s'y tenait immobile.

— Bonjour, Rabbi, dis-je en m'approchant.

— Bonjour, répondit-il d'une voix chantante.

Puis, levant un doigt, tel un trait pâle dans la pénombre :

— Vous ne m'avez pas envoyé votre livre.

Le ton n'était pas celui d'un reproche, mais d'une simple constatation.

— Je n'imaginais pas, Rabbi, qu'il pût vous intéresser...

Et, brusquement, en français :

— Vous auriez même pu me l'envoyer en français. Je connais votre pays.

Après quoi, il se tut, comme si le sujet était déjà épuisé. Avant de reprendre, à nouveau en yiddish :

— Vous connaissez le *Habad* ?

— Oui, mon grand-père Abraham était un Hassid.

— Pourquoi dites-vous « était » ?

— Parce qu'il est mort dans la révolte du ghetto de Varsovie.

— Mais vous, vous êtes là...

— Oui, seulement, je ne suis pas un Hassid.

— Alors, je comprends pourquoi vous dites « était ».

Le second sujet étant épuisé, il se tut à nouveau. Et c'est moi qui abordai celui qui me tenait réellement à cœur.

291

Oui, il se souvenait de Hugo, c'était un grand jeune homme blond, arrivé de Pologne la rage au cœur et qui vint, un jour, quelques mois avant la guerre, voir son prédécesseur, le Rabbi Joseph-Isaac Schneersohn. Il l'avait fortement impressionné, ça il pouvait me le garantir. Le désespoir de ce jeune homme, ses cris de détresse en faveur du judaïsme européen ne pouvaient trouver chez le Lubavitch que compréhension et aide. S'il l'avait revu après la guerre? Oui... Quelquefois... Mon cousin n'était pas un mystique... Ah! ça non, ce n'était pas un mystique... Mais il y avait en lui une exigence... Une soif... Une fidélité aussi...

Le Rabbi balaya sa barbe de ses doigts fins, hocha la tête et ajouta à voix soudain plus basse :

— Votre cousin ressemblait à David et a souffert comme Job...

Puis, après un silence que je faillis interpréter comme un congé :

— Je vais vous raconter une chose que vous ignorez, j'en suis sûr...

— Oui ?

— C'est un secret... Un grand secret... Mais je crois le moment venu... Il y a si longtemps, après tout... Voulez-vous connaître un très grand secret ?

— Mais oui, Rabbi !

— Eh bien voilà. Je sais combien ce que je vais vous dire troublera le Juif que vous êtes : Saviez-vous que Hugo avait un enfant ?

— Un enfant ?

— Oui... Il avait un fils... La mère est morte en couches. Mais le fils, lui, est né. Le Rabbi Joseph-Isaac Schneersohn a suivi toute l'affaire de très près. C'est lui qui a fait circoncire le petit, qui lui a trouvé une nurse. C'est lui qui, à l'âge de quatre ans, l'a mis à l'école, au Heder... Et puis, il y a eu le destin...

— Le destin ?

— Comment appeler la chose autrement ? Un jour, le petit traversa la rue... Une voiture... Comme il est dit : « Pleure doucement sur le mort, car il a trouvé le repos... »

292

Une larme perla dans l'œil clair du Rabbi.

— L'événement a eu lieu après la guerre. Mais votre cousin ne l'a pas su tout de suite. Il était encore à l'hôpital, il a connu une Allemande qui lui avait, paraît-il, sauvé la vie. Ça, vous le saviez, n'est-ce pas ? Guéri, il est venu chercher son fils. Et alors...

Le Rabbi se couvrit les yeux de sa main menue, comme s'il voulait échapper à une vision insoutenable et murmura :

— Mais celui qui va périr n'étend-il pas les mains ? Celui qui est dans le malheur n'implore-t-il pas du secours ?...

Puis, découvrant ses yeux, il dit simplement :

— Job.

Après quoi, il poursuivit d'une voix fatiguée :

— Nous avons essayé de le secourir. Cet enfant, vous comprenez, était la chair de sa chair... Il l'a peu connu, peu vu... La guerre, vous comprenez... Ce temps de troubles, de hantises... Mais c'était sa chair, n'est-ce pas ? Son sang... Et la chose est arrivée juste au moment où il pensait pouvoir souffler, poser un instant son fardeau... Il avait payé son tribut à l'héroïsme, vous comprenez... Il avait assez servi la cause, la gloire de son peuple... Et c'était juste le moment où il pensait avoir enfin le droit de goûter à ce fils, de l'aimer... C'est à ce moment qu'il est mort, vous voyez... N'est-ce pas que c'est le destin ? Avec l'aide de l'Éternel, béni soit-Il, votre cousin a retrouvé l'équilibre. Mais je crois, moi, qu'il s'est marié avec la fille d'un général nazi pour exorciser la haine qui l'habitait et qu'il a repris, au Proche-Orient, son bâton de pèlerin pour apaiser la révolte qui le rongeait.

Le Rabbi se tut un moment, puis sourit soudain et s'avança vers la porte : l'audience était terminée ; elle n'avait duré que sept minutes ; mais quand je revins dans le vestibule, les bedeaux du Rabbi attendaient déjà les visiteurs.

Mendel Fogelman me fit passer par un couloir encombré d'un lavabo et me fit sortir dans la rue. Une fois sur le trottoir, il me fixa de ses yeux verts et dit :

— Le Rabbi se souvient de tous les visages, de toutes les misères... Le Rabbi est le Juste parmi les Justes...

Il parlait encore, mais je ne l'écoutais pas : le récit du Rabbi m'avait, on l'imagine, profondément troublé.

35

ISRAËL

LE KIPPOUR 1973

Septembre 1973

Ce sont les fêtes de Roch Hachanah, Arié a choisi de regagner le kibboutz. Dans l'autobus qui escalade les collines de Haute-Galilée, ombragées d'eucalytus, il songe soudain à Anna-Maria. Pourquoi ne lui avoir jamais écrit ? Après tout, Anna-Maria est sa cousine. Et, sans elle, son séjour à Buenos Aires eût été insupportable. Benjamin Ben Eliezer l'a questionné à plusieurs reprises sur ses activités ainsi que sur les rapports entre les Montoneros et les Palestiniens. Arié en savait très peu. Et le peu qu'il en a raconté il le regrette aujourd'hui. Cela ne pouvait que porter préjudice à sa jolie cousine.

Dans le dossier d'Hugo, dont il s'occupe à présent, beaucoup de questions demeurent sans réponse. Mais le dossier d'Hidar en revanche, dont il a aussi hérité, commence à s'éclaircir. Personnage intéressant, ce Hidar ! Il commence à s'y attacher. Il aimerait pouvoir le suivre de près pendant quelques mois, comprendre sa démarche, le rencontrer peut-être. Non pas que le Tunisien ait voulu la mort d'Hugo ou celle de Sidney. Mais il est persuadé qu'involontairement, il en est responsable. Qu'est-ce qu'il peut bien ressentir, à partir de là, en compagnie d'Olga, la cousine des deux hommes assassinés ? On dit la jeune femme de plus en plus attachée à la mémoire familiale. Il voit mal Hidar s'accommoder de cet attachement.

Arié a, par ailleurs, fait la connaissance des Lerner. Ceux-ci ont fini, en effet, par obtenir leur visa. Avec Levine Zaredski, Blumstein, Slepak, d'autres, ils ont été, un beau matin, convoqués à l'OVIR ; reçus par une fonctionnaire du ministère de l'Intérieur ; et se sont retrouvés, un mois plus tard, un soir, à l'aéroport de Cheremetievo, en partance pour Israël. A leur arrivée à Tel-Aviv, ils ont été assaillis par les journalistes et les photographes. Puis quasiment enlevés par le représentant du ministère des Affaires étrangères. L'Agence juive leur a obtenu un appartement à Jérusalem et, depuis peu, Aron donne un cours sur l'hellénisme à l'Université hébraïque. Arié, donc, les a rencontrés. Il a été un peu surpris. Il ne s'imaginait pas ainsi les refuzniks. Malgré leur comportement spécifiquement soviétique, ils se sont sentis aussitôt chez eux en Israël. Ils reconnaissaient le moindre lieu, se souvenaient du moindre événement. Comme si tout Juif portait, dès sa naissance, gravées dans sa mémoire la topographie, les images de la Terre Sainte.

Mordekhaï les a, en tout cas, invités pour les fêtes au kibboutz. Judith, qui a déjà terminé son service militaire et étudie au Technium de Haïfa, doit venir elle aussi. Cette pensée réjouit Arié. Depuis plus de deux ans qu'ils se connaissent, ils n'ont encore jamais partagé la même couche. Et pourtant, ils sont chaque fois heureux, émus de se retrouver. Le jeune homme a maintenant une amie à Tel-Aviv, Shoshana. C'est une belle fille brune, à la peau très blanche et aux hanches trop fortes. Elle est infirmière à l'hôpital Bellisson, à Petah Tikva, et a un petit studio près de l'hôpital où ils se rejoignent souvent. Sans passion, mais avec une amicale tendresse, ils font abondamment l'amour. Arié parle à Shoshana de Judith et Shoshana lit à Arié les lettres de son fiancé Amos, jeune chirurgien parti pour un an travailler dans un hôpital de San Francisco.

Bref, tout cela pour dire qu'Arié, en ce jour de Roch Hachanah, revient à la maison. La station d'autobus se trouve à quelques centaines de mètres du kibboutz et il n'est pas mécontent de pouvoir les parcourir à pied. Ce long voyage lui a engourdi les jambes et il a hâte de respirer profondément l'air de l'altitude. Le jour s'éteint, un vent sec souffle, apportant une odeur de bouse brûlée et d'herbe fraîche. Dans le campement arabe, dans la vallée, les chiens aboient. Une rangée serrée de figuiers de barbarie cache la clôture du kibboutz.

Les parents d'Arié l'attendent. Dina, la petite sœur, lui saute au cou. Et quant aux Lerner, ils sont déjà arrivés, installés par Mordekhaï dans la maison d'hôte, entre la tour d'eau et le vivier. Judith a laissé un message. Elle annonce sa venue pour le lendemain. Elle veut passer la soirée du Jour de l'An avec son père, à Kyriat Shemona. Arié est-il déçu ? Il aurait aimé qu'elle fût là. Et malgré l'air réjoui de ses parents, il en ressent une vraie tristesse. « Tant pis », se dit-il, tandis que, de conserve avec ses parents, il se dirige vers le réfectoire, non sans s'arrêter en chemin pour récupérer les Lerner à la maison d'hôte. Arié s'étonne de leur parfaite connaissance de l'hébreu. Rachel répond en riant que c'est un « hébreu des catacombes » qu'elle a appris dans la clandestinité. Et toute la famille d'entrer dans la belle salle à manger aux nappes, murs et rideaux blancs où, de table en table, on se souhaite : « *Lechana Tova Tikkathev Veté'Hatahem.* »

Mordekhaï verse du vin et dit le kiddouch. Puis, tout le monde déguste une tranche de pomme trempée dans du miel, en formulant le vœu : « Que cette année qui commence soit pour nous agréable et douce. » On boit encore à la paix et on sert enfin le repas. Les cousins moscovites paraissent émerveillés. Arié les trouve agréables, plaisants, intelligents, mais on ne sait pas trop quoi leur dire, ni quoi leur demander. La vie des Juifs en Union soviétique ? Connu. Archiconnu. Leurs problèmes, leur lutte ont été décrits mille fois dans la presse. Et il ne reste plus, à leur endroit, il faut bien le dire, un grain de curiosité. Quand, au dessert, les « kibboutzniks » se mettent à chanter en chœur, Rachel se met à pleurer. Mordekhaï, lui, sourit, essuie ses lunettes et, se penchant légèrement vers sa cousine, récite doucement : « Ainsi parle le Seigneur ; retiens les sanglots de ta voix, les larmes de tes yeux, car il y a récompense pour tes actions. » Et Rachel, au lieu de se consoler, éclate en véritables sanglots :

— Quelque chose ne va pas ? demande Shalom, le mécanicien.

— La cousine soviétique se languit de ses enfants, dit Sarah.

— Où sont-ils ?

— A Moscou.

— Ils reviendront, dit le mécanicien, avec assurance, ils reviendront. Tout Juif, à un moment ou à un autre, revient au pays.

Ce n'est que le lendemain après-midi que Judith arrive à Dafné. Sa peau satinée et ses grands yeux d'un noir d'olivier, aux reflets bleus et violets, sont du meilleur effet sur les jeunes garçons du kibboutz. Émotion. Agitation. Réactions de coqs et de paons. Et, chez les filles, commentaires acidulés et remarques sous cape. Arié, lui, est très fier. Judith n'est-elle pas son amie ? Et à défaut d'être *à* lui, n'est-elle pas ici *pour* lui ? Il tente de se souvenir des sentiments qui l'habitaient lors de sa relation avec Anna-Maria. L'aimait-il ? Peut-être... Mais il s'étonne tout de même de la facilité avec laquelle l'image de l'une efface l'image de l'autre. Et pour l'heure, il est tout à son bonheur de ces divines retrouvailles. L'ennui, bien entendu, c'est qu'il n'ose toujours pas l'imaginer sa maîtresse et qu'il doit lui offrir une chambre dans la maison d'hôte, au-dessus de celle des Lerner tandis qu'il demeure, lui, comme d'habitude, chez ses parents, dans leur maison en bois. Le lendemain, pourtant, aussitôt après le petit déjeuner, il entraîne la jeune fille sur le chemin de Tel Dan.

C'est une belle matinée. Les lourdes branches des chênes millénaires filtrent les rayons du soleil et les roches calcaires les renvoient, tels des miroirs, en éclairant, par le bas, les troncs épais. Judith et Arié ne disent rien. Ils rient. Ils s'enchantent de tout et de rien : le pépiement aigu d'un oisillon, une rangée inattendue de casueinos, égarée dans cette réserve naturelle, un petit renard gris qui s'arrête sur leur chemin pour les observer d'un regard surpris avant de disparaître dans les buissons. Ils rient même, comme des enfants, d'un caillou que l'un d'eux heurte en marchant et qui roule depuis la colline jusqu'à la source du Dan. Ils descendent à la source. Badinent encore. Batifolent. Ils finissent par se baigner, habillés d'abord, puis, riant de plus belle, à demi et complètement nus. Est-ce la couleur du soleil qui les échauffe ? Sa chaleur sur les peaux mouillées ? Est-ce ce sentiment de liberté qu'ils n'ont, ni l'un ni l'autre, jamais connu et qui les rend soudain comme seuls au monde ? Regards pudiques... Puis plus osés... Puis carrément appuyés... Corps qui se rapprochent... Peaux qui se caressent... Miracle, toujours le même, et cependant toujours bouleversant, de deux bouches qui se conjoignent... C'est là, au bord de l'eau que, pour la première fois, Judith et Arié font l'amour. Et là que le jeune homme achèvera réellement le deuil de son attachement pour Anna-Maria.

Judith restera au kibboutz jusqu'au Kippour. A la grande surprise d'Arié, elle sympathisera avec les Lerner, passant parfois plus de temps avec eux qu'avec lui. La cousine Rachel lui raconte Moscou, Judith lui répète les histoires de son père au Yémen. Et Aron Lerner sourit, en regardant ces deux Juives échanger ainsi leur histoire, leur mémoire.

A deux jours du Kippour, Shalom, le mécanicien, qui participe à une patrouille de gardes-frontière druzes, rapporte le témoignage de l'un d'eux sur une concentration anormale de chars syriens sur le Golan. Information confirmée le soir même par la radio israélienne. Puis par la télé qui parle aussi d'une activité inhabituelle du côté égyptien. Qu'en dit Benjamin Ben Eliezer ? Il n'est malheureusement pas là quand Arié essaie de lui téléphoner. Et Myriam répond, comme à l'accoutumée, par un rire amical aux questions angoissées d'Arié.

— Ne t'inquiète pas, on ne fera pas la guerre sans toi, « Haboub »...

Est-ce une impression ? Un effet de sa propre nervosité ? Il sent tout de même une pointe d'inquiétude dans sa voix quand elle ajoute que Golda Meïr réunit le jour même quelques ministres et généraux dans son bureau et que Benjamin doit revenir exceptionnellement au travail le matin du Kippour.

— Tu sais bien, « Haboub », nous vivons au pays des miracles...

Et, enfin, avant de raccrocher et de lui souhaiter une bonne et heureuse année :

— Les chauffeurs d'autobus de la compagnie Egged sont réquisitionnés... On ne sait jamais... Aussi, tu pourras revenir me voir rapidement...

Le jour du Kippour, tout s'arrête en Israël. Les rues, les routes se vident. La radio, la télévision se taisent. Et cette absence de bruits et de mouvements introduit dans le pays une angoisse sourde, imperceptible. Est-ce pour cela que les Anciens baptisaient la semaine séparant le Jour de l'An du Jour du Grand Pardon : « Yamim Noraïm », les Jours Terribles ? Seules, alors, les synagogues résonnent de prières. Et quant aux non-croyants, nombreux en Israël, ils respectent ce jour parmi les jours et restent chez eux à lire ou à se reposer.

Le kibboutz Dafné, comme tout Israël, est donc plongé cette année-là dans le silence et la solitude de la nuit du Kippour. Les Lerner sont assis sur des chaises longues devant la maison de Mordekhaï dont le perron est à peine éclairé. Aron raconte une fois de plus l'occupation du Soviet Suprême. Puis, le « procès » à l'Université de Moscou. Il omet le rôle joué dans cette affaire par Sacha. Mais, après tout, c'est son fils et il n'a pas attendu le jour du Kippour pour lui pardonner ! Mordekhaï et Sarah sont assis, eux, sur un banc, et écoutent le récit avec un intérêt poli. Arié et Judith se tiennent un peu plus bas, sur les marches. Une brise légère amène jusqu'à eux une odeur un peu folle de pain. Dieu est là... Tout près... Et puis, soudain, le téléphone sonne. Arié s'approche de l'ampoule, consulte sa montre : il est 22 heures. Il entre dans la maison où une bougie, à la mémoire de six millions de morts, est allumée et prudemment, d'un geste empreint de remords et de superstition, soulève le combiné. C'est Myriam, la secrétaire de Benjamin qui commence :

— Fini le Kippour, « Haboub », dit-elle en riant.

Mais Arié sent dans sa voix une légère tension.

— Tous ceux qui travaillent à l'Amman doivent rentrer à Tel-Aviv immédiatement.

— C'est la guerre ?

— Quelle guerre ? On a tout simplement besoin de toi. Trouve-toi rapidement un moyen de locomotion. Sinon mets-toi en marche. La route est longue. Benjamin t'attend à la première heure...

Arié, après avoir raccroché, reste un moment à contempler l'appareil comme s'il en attendait une explication. Puis, tel un automate, il se dirige vers la sortie. Et c'est à ce moment qu'il voit dans l'embrasure de la porte, en train de le guetter, ses parents, les Lerner et Judith.

— Vous avez entendu ? demande-t-il.

— Non, fait son père, en frottant ses lunettes avec un pan de son pull... Mais je crois que j'ai compris...

Ils entendent des pas sur le gravier.

— Qui est là ? demanda Mordekhaï.

— Shlomo.

— Où vas-tu ?

— Je vais chercher ma Vespa. Je dois retourner sur le Golan.

— Le soir du Kippour ?

— Le soir du Kippour... Il paraît qu'il y a urgence...

D'autres pas résonnent dans l'allée. Le kibboutz reste plongé dans la pénombre et le recueillement, mais on sent la tension monter, on entend des portes claquer, le bruit d'un moteur solitaire.

— Ça se passe toujours comme ça ? demande Aron.

— Toujours? Non. C'est la première fois, le Jour du Kippour, répond Mordekhaï, la voix nouée.

— Ah! fait le professeur, comme s'il venait de poser une question indiscrète.

Puis, prenant sa femme par le bras :

> « Ah! Mes chers matelots, seuls entre mes amis
> Fidèles à votre devoir,
> Voyez quel ouragan soufflant s'est déchaîné
> Et tourbillonne encore autour de moi. »

— De qui est-ce? demande Mordekhaï.

— Sophocle, répond-il.

Et s'adressant à Arié :

— Crois-tu que l'on m'engagera si je me présente au Centre de recrutement. Je sais manier les armes...

— Chez nous, il n'y a pas de Centre de recrutement, fait le jeune homme, légèrement sentencieux. Tout citoyen est soldat et chacun sait exactement, en cas de mobilisation, où aller.

— Alors, c'est la mobilisation?

— Non, je ne crois pas. Autrement, tout le kibboutz aurait déjà été réveillé. Par contre, je me demande comment arriver à Tel-Aviv...

Des chiens se mettent brusquement à aboyer dans la vallée.

— Je vais téléphoner à mon père à Kyriat Shemona, dit Judith.

A nouveau, des pas résonnent sur le gravier.

— Qui est là?

— Jacob Oren. Il se passe quelque chose... Vous êtes au courant?

— On me convoque à Tel-Aviv, dit Arié.

— Tu veux un « tremp » ?

— Comment ça? Les autobus marchent?

— Non, c'est mon frère Ivry... Il est venu pour les Fêtes... Il est rappelé d'urgence chez lui à Haïfa... Il a une petite Fiat...

— Va pour Haïfa. De là je me débrouillerai...

302

— Je vais avec toi, crie Judith. Peut-être Ivry pourra-t-il me lâcher en route…

Quand le bruit de leurs pas s'éloignent, Rachel, toujours accrochée au bras d'Aron, dit, sans savoir pourquoi, presque en chuchotant, comme une prière : « Shalom, paix. » Et son vœu se perd dans la nuit.

36

ISRAËL

LE KIPPOUR 1973 (suite et fin)

Septembre 1973

La voiture d'Ivry file à toute allure. La route est complètement déserte. Ce vide, cette absence de toute vie donnent au paysage nocturne un air d'irréalité, presque d'inexistence. Ce n'est pas un hasard si le Dieu de la Bible a chargé l'homme de donner un nom aux bêtes et aux plantes, songe Arié : sans le regard que l'homme pose sur eux il n'est pas sûr qu'ils existeraient.

Ivry est médecin à la Sécurité sociale de Haïfa. Il parle peu et cela plaît bien à Arié. Un mot par-ci. Un mot par-là. Un « au revoir » à Judith quand il la dépose à Kyriat Shemona. Une phrase bougonne lorsque, mettant en marche la radio, il la trouve désespérément muette, sans même un appel codé à la mobilisation. Après quoi, il ne dit plus rien jusqu'à Akko. La route simplement. La voiture sur la route. D'autres, beaucoup d'autres voitures qui, d'Akko à Haïfa, les croisent en silence et leur font des appels de phare, comme pour montrer qu'elles partagent le même épouvantable secret. Quel secret ? La guerre, pardi ! Cette guerre à laquelle il n'a, jusqu'alors, jamais participé, et que son père, lui, a déjà fait trois fois : la Guerre d'Indépendance, en 1948 ; la campagne de Suez, en 1956 ; la Guerre des Six Jours enfin. Il sait que c'est absurde, que la guerre n'est pas, loin s'en faut, la plus belle des aventures. Mais c'est une aventure tout de même. Et

l'exaltation, la peur, la jalousie peut-être aussi s'entre-
mêlent dans sa conscience pour former le plus déroutant
des cocktails.

C'est à 2 heures du matin qu'ils arrivent à Haïfa. La
ville dort. Le Mont Carmel, à peine plus noir que le ciel,
se fond dans le firmament. Seuls les environs du port
sont vaguement animés.

— Tu veux que je te laisse ici ? demande Ivry.

— Non, je préfère que tu avances un peu. Jusqu'à
l'entrée de l'autoroute de Tel-Aviv... J'aurai plus de
chance de trouver un lift...

— Tu risques d'attendre longtemps, remarque obli-
geamment Ivry...

— Allah est grand ! lance-t-il en souriant et en se
félicitant intérieurement de cette petite audace de
vocabulaire.

De fait, l'attente sera longue. La route restera vide,
désespérément vide, pendant des heures. Puis, plusieurs
voitures passeront, mais à toute allure, sans s'arrêter. Et
Arié commence à être découragé quand à quelques
mètres de lui, sur une aire de dégagement, freine une
grosse Chevrolet. Il est déjà 5 heures du matin et
l'horizon commence à pâlir.

— Tel-Aviv ? demande Arié.

— Monte, fait l'homme simplement.

Puis, une fois en route :

— Pourquoi vas-tu à Tel-Aviv, le matin du Kippour ?

— Vous ne savez pas ? s'étonne Arié.

— Je ne sais pas quoi ?

— Que c'est la guerre !

— Et toi, comment le sais-tu ?

Arié se méfie brusquement :

— Bof ! Des bruits... De vagues bruits...

L'homme sourit mais ne répond rien. Et ce n'est
qu'une demi-heure plus tard, en passant devant un
écriteau indiquant Césarée qu'il se présentera. Yossef
Almogui... ministre du Travail... Réveillé il y a deux
heures, chez lui, à Haïfa, il se rend à Tel-Aviv pour une
réunion exceptionnelle du cabinet chez Golda Meïr...
Mais voici le siège de l'Amman... Illuminé comme

jamais… Merci monsieur le Ministre… Au revoir, jeune homme… A l'intérieur l'agitation est grande. Des officiers, en manches de chemise et le visage grave, se bousculent dans les couloirs, échangeant des propos brefs et faisant claquer les portes. Arié ne reconnaît rien ni personne. Et s'il n'y avait pas Myriam, au téléphone, il se demanderait dans quel étrange endroit il est tombé.

— Ah ! Te voilà, « Haboub », dit-elle pour une fois pas trop sarcastique : tu en as mis du temps…

Arié en est encore à chercher sa réponse quand la porte du bureau de Benjamin s'ouvre brutalement et qu'il le voit sortir derrière le chef des services de renseignements de l'armée, le général Eli Zeira, lui-même suivi des généraux Yitzhak Hoffi, commandant de la région nord, et Shmuel Gonen, commandant de la région sud. Benjamin, quand il passe devant son jeune protégé, s'arrête une seconde, lui fait un pauvre sourire et une petite tape affectueuse sur la joue.

— Qui est-ce ? demande Gonen, intrigué.

— Le fils d'un de mes meilleurs amis, Arié Halter. Il travaille ici avec moi…

— Halter ? demande le général.

Et, regardant Arié :

— Halter… Halter… Serais-tu parent de Hugo Halter, par hasard ?

— C'est un cousin, dit Arié. Il a été…

— Je sais… Une triste histoire… Je l'aimais bien…

A quoi Arié, sautant sur l'occasion, répond avec un esprit d'à propos peu commun :

— Général, général ! Je mène justement une enquête sur la mort de mon cousin. Pourrai-je vous interroger, à l'occasion ?

— Crois-tu que ce soit le moment ? grogne Gonen. Puis se ravisant : Oh ! Et puis, après tout… Tu n'as qu'à venir avec moi, tout à l'heure, à Beercheva, nous en parlerons en route.

Myriam, qui n'a rien perdu de la scène, ne peut s'empêcher de dire en riant :

— Tu ne perds pas le nord, « Haboub » !

Après quoi elle met Arié au courant des derniers

événements. Selon Benjamin, l'attaque des Égyptiens au Sud et des Syriens au Nord est désormais imminente. Selon d'autres — comme le général Zeira — l'attaque est improbable et la concentration de leurs troupes surtout destinée à exercer une pression psychologique. Pour les troisièmes, une mobilisation générale serait politiquement ruineuse car comme en 1967, elle donnerait d'Israël l'image d'un pays fauteur de guerre ; pourquoi ne pas attendre et laisser les Arabes tirer les premiers ? D'autres enfin — à commencer par Moshé Dayan — proposent une mobilisation partielle qui aurait l'avantage du compromis : Israël mobiliserait une force importante mais défensive...

Arié l'écoute. Oh ! oui, il l'écoute avec une telle ferveur, une telle intensité ! Jamais il n'avait à ce point mesuré la précarité du destin d'Israël. A 9 h 30, tandis que Myriam achève son exposé, Benjamin revient à son bureau. Plus soucieux que jamais. Et seul.

— Où est le général Gonen ? demande Arié.

— Parti pour Beercheva... Par avion... Pourquoi ?

Et, voyant la déception d'Arié, il prend l'air de l'homme à qui revient brusquement à l'esprit une vérité désagréable, grommelle des propos apaisants du genre : « Allons... allons... tu auras d'autres occasions d'interroger Shmuel Gonen sur Hugo. » Et, délaissant le pauvre Arié, il se tourne vers l'émissaire du général Zeira qui lui apporte les derniers renseignements et les plus récentes photos du Golan et du Sinaï. A l'évidence, la guerre est proche. Et la mobilisation pour aujourd'hui.

Convoqué à nouveau par le chef de l'état-major, le général Gonen revient à Tel-Aviv à 12 h 30, en voiture. En l'apprenant, Arié se précipite. Et au moment précis où Shmuel Gonen ressort, accompagné de Benjamin, du bâtiment voisin, il se jette littéralement dans ses jambes :

— C'est bien toi, le cousin de Hugo Halter ?

Et, ouvrant la portière de la voiture qui l'attend :

— Monte... Moi aussi, je peux avoir besoin de jeunes gens comme toi...

Arié regarde Benjamin, qui fait oui de la tête et c'est ainsi qu'il quitte Tel-Aviv dans la voiture d'un des principaux responsables de l'état-major.

Beercheva, la capitale du Neguev, se trouve à cent dix kilomètres de Tel-Aviv. Malgré le Jour de Grand Pardon, la route est animée : des camionnettes, des estafettes, des camions et même quelques autobus embarquent aux carrefours des hommes venus en hâte et visiblement pas vêtus pour la guerre. La mobilisation est en cours.

— L'attaque est pour 18 heures, dit Gonen.

— Et si l'ennemi avançait l'attaque d'une ou deux heures ? demande Arié.

Les traits lourds du général se crispent :

— Dans ce cas, que Dieu nous protège !

Puis, plongé dans une méditation dont il ne souhaite apparemment partager le secret avec quiconque, il se laisse doucement bercer par les ressorts de la voiture. Quand, au bout de cinq minutes, il se tourne vers Arié, son visage ne porte plus la moindre trace d'émotion. Et c'est avec un certain entrain qu'il l'interroge sur ses liens exacts avec Hugo et qu'il lui dit : « Après tout, puisque nous y sommes, voilà ce que je sais de votre cousin. »

Il l'a connu en 1953, il y a juste vingt ans, chez Ben Gourion. Ils ont sympathisé et se sont revus lors des visites suivantes de Hugo en Israël. Ce qu'il aimait en lui ? Son côté talmudiste... Sa capacité à traduire en termes contemporains les éléments bibliques pour mieux comprendre le monde moderne... Il le faisait penser à Justus de Tibériade... Son idéalisme était naïf mais rafraîchissant... Un propos de lui ? Son comportement ? Il se souvient d'une remarque qui l'avait à l'époque surpris. C'était en 1960... Ils avaient été tous deux invités chez Israël Beer, le conseiller de Ben Gourion... En sortant, ils avaient fait quelques pas et Hugo lui avait demandé, à brûle-pourpoint, s'il avait confiance en cet hôte qu'ils venaient juste de quitter. La question, à ce moment-là, ne s'imposait pas. Mais un an plus tard, quand Israël Beer a été arrêté pour espionnage, il était difficile de ne pas songer à cette prémonitoire observation. Hugo, hélas, était déjà mort. Tué deux jours auparavant...

Arié brûle d'en savoir plus. Les questions, les objections se pressent sur ses lèvres. Mais la voiture atteint déjà les faubourgs de Beercheva. Et là, ô surprise ! Il se souvenait d'un village desséché, tout en terre glaise, construit autour d'un marché de chameaux, tenu par des Bédouins. Et il est dans une ville moderne. Urbanisée à souhait. Avec de grandes avenues, bordées d'arbres et d'immeubles. Shmuel Gonen, du coup, semble se ficher royalement de Hugo et des Halter. Redevenu nerveux, presque brutal, il regarde sa montre, décroche le téléphone et demande la communication avec le général Mendler, à Rifidim, dans le Sinaï. Au bout de deux longues minutes, la liaison est établie :

— Albert ! crie-t-il. Ordre de quitter immédiatement les bases arrière et de foncer vers le canal. Ne plus attendre l'attaque des Égyptiens...

— Trop tard ! entend-on dans le récepteur. Ils ont déjà attaqué. Le bombardement a commencé.

L'attaque se révélera une fausse alerte. Et les quatre formations d'avions égyptiens qui ont survolé les installations israéliennes de Sharm el-Sheikh, à l'extrême pointe méridionale du Sinaï, seront obligées de rebrousser chemin devant la contre-offensive des vedettes ancrées à proximité du détroit de Tiran. Mais les nouvelles ne sont pas bonnes pour autant. La ligne Bar-Lev établie le long du canal de Suez a été enfoncée en plusieurs endroits. Huit mille fantassins ont pris pied sur la rive du Sinaï. Une vingtaine de bataillons égyptiens ont réussi à être héliportés derrière les avant-postes israéliens, à proximité des voies de communication. Et l'aviation israélienne, mobilisée sur le Golan où l'avance de milliers de chars syriens menace les centres vitaux du pays, n'est pas là pour les déloger.

Après avoir réuni, et confronté, toutes les informations, le général Gonen — toujours flanqué d'Arié, qui ne le lâche plus d'une semelle — réunit ses officiers autour d'une carte du Sinaï :

— L'objectif des Égyptiens est clair, dit-il. La traver-

sée du canal, la conquête de Sharm el-Sheikh, sur la mer
Rouge et les cols de Mitla et de Guidi. Et, montrant
avec une baguette les lieux cités :

— Ils essaieront d'atteindre ces objectifs en vingt-
quatre heures. S'ils réussissent, la route d'Israël leur
sera ouverte. Sinon, ils tenteront d'établir une ligne de
défense de notre côté du canal, en y installant les
rampes de missiles sol-air.

Puis, se tournant vers les officiers :

— Il faut reprendre rapidement contact avec nos
fortins sur le canal... Celui de Lakekan, au bord du
grand lac Amer... Celui d'Orkal, dans les marais au
nord... Il faut faire avancer nos forces pour freiner
l'avance des Égyptiens...

Mais il ne peut terminer son exposé car les informations reçues par radio évoluent d'heure en heure. Tel
fortin, qu'il convenait de défendre il y a une minute, est
tombé aux mains des Égyptiens. Tel autre, qu'on croyait
perdu, est parfaitement sous contrôle. Exaspéré de tous
ces rapports contradictoires qui se succèdent de plus en
plus rapidement, il finit par jeter sa baguette et par
dire :

— Les objectifs des Égyptiens sont ceux que je viens
d'énumérer. A nous de nous débrouiller pour qu'ils ne
soient pas atteints.

Et, à l'adresse de son aide de camp :

— Fais préparer un avion. Je pars au PC d'Oum
Kheshiba. Préviens les généraux Sharon et Brenne.

C'est ainsi qu'Arié se retrouve à minuit, à la fin du
Kippour, à trente-cinq kilomètres du canal, près du col
de Guidi. C'est le moment précis de l'attaque du PC
israélien par un commando égyptien héliporté. Et en
descendant de l'avion, il doit parcourir sous les balles
une centaine de mètres avant de se mettre à l'abri
derrière une colline de sable où une jeep attend. C'est la
première fois qu'il vient dans le Sinaï. Le bleu de la nuit
qui se reflète dans le sable ocre le surprend et
l'enchante. La bataille ? Elle sera courte. La pleine lune
a permis à l'artillerie israélienne de débusquer rapidement le commando couleur de sable. Et le peloton des

310

vieux centurions, dirigés par le général Sharon qui, conformément aux ordres, a rejoint le PC d'Oum Kheshiba, a pu prendre à revers les Égyptiens. A 3 heures du matin, l'attaque est repoussée. Le général Brenne arrive à Oum Kheshiba à l'aube. Le général Dayan quelques minutes après 9 heures.

— Il faut se replier sur les lignes des cols, dit-il. On ne peut risquer la vie de nos soldats...

Gonen n'est pas d'accord. Abandonner ainsi une grande partie du Sinaï lui paraît absurde et risqué. Arié suit la discussion comme à travers une brume. Il n'a pas dormi depuis deux jours et sombre dans un profond sommeil. Il ne se réveillera qu'à la tombée du jour pour apprendre la contre-offensive décidée par Gonen sur le front sud et pour l'entendre s'inquiéter, surtout, de ce que l'on ne peut plus joindre par radio le fortin Milano.

— Il faut évacuer *tous* les fortins, crie-t-il... Tous, vous m'entendez... C'est la seule façon de bombarder le canal.

Et, comme la radio du fortin Milano ne répond décidément pas :

— Prends un half-track, Yossi, dit-il à un jeune capitaine blond. Trouve-toi deux volontaires pour t'accompagner et file. Il est possible que vous rencontriez les occupants du fortin quelque part en route. Évacuation immédiate !

Un soldat lève la main. Puis Arié qui se redresse d'un bond :

— J'y vais aussi, dit-il. Vous permettez, mon général ?

Gonen l'observe d'un air sévère, comme s'il cherchait à deviner ses arrière-pensées et, haussant les épaules, finit par lâcher :

— Eh bien, soit... Va !

Il arrive ce que Gonen a prévu. Le half-track réussit à se faufiler entre deux colonnes de chars égyptiens. Il contourne Tasa, prend la route de Balouza et, à l'aube, surprend les rescapés du fortin Milano, une trentaine d'hommes valides et six blessés, dans les environs de Kantara. Brèves embrassades. Chargement des blessés dans le véhicule. Détermination de la marche à suivre et de l'itinéraire à emprunter. La route de l'aller risque d'être coupée, à présent? Soit. Il ne reste qu'à tenter de traverser Kantara en priant l'Éternel pour que cette ville fantôme ne soit pas encore investie par l'ennemi.

— Je connais Kantara, dit Yossi. Si vous avez un pépin, rendez-vous au bout de la ville dans l'enclave du cimetière chrétien. C'est indiqué...

Le pépin, de fait, ne tardera guère. Dès l'entrée de la ville, la petite troupe aperçoit sur sa gauche des monceaux de glaise rougeâtre, fraîchement remuée. Puis, en venant un peu plus près, des centaines d'hommes en train d'élever une sorte de mur de terre. On dirait un pullulement de fourmis blanches. Ce sont comme des essaims de bras invisibles qui rejettent sans fin des pelletées de terre. Les éviter? La seule solution est de passer derrière le bosquet, à droite de l'entrée de la ville. Sauf qu'au moment de le faire, on entend quelqu'un qui crie en arabe :

— Hé là! Qu'est-ce que c'est?

— Les Égyptiens! répond Arié, en arabe lui aussi.

Il se fait un silence et, au bout de quelques secondes :

— Tu n'as pas l'accent égyptien...

Puis, une autre voix — mi-inquiète, mi-haineuse :

— Ce sont des Juifs! Ce sont des Juifs!

Une fusée éclairante monte vers le ciel. Yossi crie quelque chose comme « dispersez-vous! ». On entend des coups de feu. Une balle, puis une autre qui passent en sifflant au-dessus des têtes. Arié se met à courir, en se retournant de temps à autre, comme un petit renard gris qu'ils avaient vu avec Judith dans la réserve naturelle de Tel Dan. « Je ne veux pas mourir, se dit-il. Je ne veux pas tomber. » Au moment d'atteindre un long mur gris qui lui semble comme un havre, il se retourne une dernière fois tandis que des balles craquent, tout autour de lui, contre la pierre.

— Le cimetière est de l'autre côté, dit quelqu'un dans l'obscurité.

Il s'accroche alors à une pierre du mur, mais glisse et s'écorche un genou. Il recommence, s'accroche de plus belle. Mais glisse à nouveau. Ou plutôt non : il ne glisse pas, mais sent deux brûlures étranges à la cuisse gauche et se voit incapable d'aller plus loin : sa jambe est devenue aussi lourde que si un poids invisible y avait été suspendu. « Non, je ne veux pas mourir », répète-t-il en rassemblant ses dernières forces. Il prend sa jambe gauche dans sa main droite, la fait passer par-dessus le mur et, à bout de souffle, sentant un liquide chaud qui lui coule le long des jambes, se laisse choir sur les tombes.

— Ça va ? demande Yossi, tombé à ses côtés.

— Ça va, mais je suis blessé.

— Tiens bon, on transmet notre position au PC.

— Où est le half-track ?

— Giora le conduisait. Il a réussi à passer.

— J'ai mal, gémit Arié.

— Approche. Je vais te serrer la cuisse avec ma ceinture. Voilà...

Arié s'accroche à Yossi et se lève. Il parcourt ainsi quelques centaines de mètres. Puis un kilomètre. Un autre. Chaque pas renforce la douleur, lui obscurcit un peu plus la vue. Mais il marche mécaniquement. Il répète et répète encore : « Je ne veux pas mourir... Je ne veux pas tomber... » Au lever du jour il respire avec difficulté. Le bleu de la nuit se mélange, comme sur une palette, au blanc rose de l'aurore. Il vacille. Il va tomber. Deux de ses compagnons s'agenouillent, s'enveloppent de leur châle de prière et disent la prière du matin. Et puis, brusquement, un bruit lointain effleure ses oreilles. Un vent léger l'éteint aussitôt. Mais le bruit revient, têtu, insistant...

— Des chars, Yossi ! Ce sont des chars !

Et quelques minutes plus tard, en effet, quatre centurions surgissent d'une colline de sable. Puis des tanks. Des mains qui s'agitent au-dessus de la tourelle. Un miracle ! Arié s'évanouit en croyant à un miracle.

Il sera opéré à l'hôpital Bellisson, à Petah-Tikva, chez son amie Shoshana. Grâce à elle et avec elle, il suivra jour après jour l'évolution de cette drôle de guerre qui se soldera, le 28 octobre, par une poignée de main entre un général israélien et un général égyptien. Le collaborateur de Benjamin Ben Eliezer verra dans cette poignée de main le début d'un processus de paix qui, s'il vient à se confirmer, fera de cette guerre du Kippour une guerre pas tout à fait inutile. Judith aussi viendra lui rendre visite. Sa mère également qui lui donnera des nouvelles de Mordekhaï, blessé dans la région de Kuneitra et hospitalisé, lui, à Tibériade. Grave ?

— Non, pas grave, lui dit-elle non sans une gêne dans le regard. Nous ne tarderons plus à nous retrouver tous à Dafné.

Le 2 novembre, il quitte enfin l'hôpital. Il marche encore avec une canne. Benjamin l'attend dans une voiture.

— On passe à l'Aman ? demande-t-il.

— Non, fait Benjamin. Je t'emmène d'abord au kibboutz. Ton père est mort.

37

BUENOS AIRES

ANNA-MARIA :
RETOUR À LA CLANDESTINITÉ

Mai, 1974

Anna-Maria a beau s'essayer à dire, après Gide : « Famille je vous hais », les morts successives et violentes des cousins de son père finissent par l'affliger. Mario et Julio estimaient inintéressante la guerre du Kippour puisqu'ils n'y voyaient qu'un banal affrontement entre deux laquais de l'impérialisme yankee. Elle connaît des Israéliens. Elle a côtoyé Mordekhaï, le kibboutznik. Elle a aimé Arié. Et peu lui importe qu'ils fussent complices ou victimes de l'impérialisme : que l'un soit blessé et que l'autre soit mort, ce sont des nouvelles qu'elle ne peut accueillir avec indifférence. De surcroît, la sanglante expérience qu'elle a pu faire, avec la guérilla et au sein de celle-ci, a eu beau l'éveiller au monde — elle n'a pas été concluante. Et le fait est qu'en ce début d'année 74, elle ne croit plus vraiment à la Révolution ni à cette société socialiste, communiste ou justicialiste, dans laquelle tout un chacun serait heureux, libre et égal. Les choses peuvent changer, elle le sait. On trouvera bien encore quelques lumières pour éclairer l'obscurité. Et peut-être sa pauvre lutte, aussi absurde, désespérée, folle qu'elle ait été, contribuera-t-elle, au bout du compte, au bonheur des autres. Nul doute pour le moment qu'elle ait contribué à la victoire de Campara et au retour de Peron. Le premier geste de

Campara, une fois élu, n'a-t-il pas été, comme les Montoneros l'avaient exigé, le rétablissement des relations diplomatiques avec Cuba ? Puis la proclamation d'une amnistie « ample et généreuse » ? Tout cela fait que, à la grande joie de ses parents et de dona Regina, Anna-Maria rentre enfin à la maison, reprend ses études à l'université et s'éloigne progressivement d'un combat qui tend à lui apparaître à la fois, et paradoxalement, vain et victorieux. Ses études recommencent de l'accaparer. Ses lectures aussi. Elle dévore Borgès notamment. Et que l'auteur d'*Alef* pût dire : « L'un de mes pays est Israël qui nous a donné la Bible » l'émeut au-delà de tout. Elle lit aussi Unamuno, Emerson, Joyce. Et dona Regina, la voyant penchée sur ses livres, se dit que Martin a peut-être, enfin, récupéré sa fille.

Mais si le terrorisme de gauche a perdu de sa combativité, le terrorisme de droite, surgi du fond des casernes, des commissariats de police et des « villes misères » réoccupe le terrain que l'autre a laissé vacant. On assassine des militants syndicalistes. Des hommes politiques. Des intellectuels. Il ne se passe pas un jour sans que l'on trouve un cadavre dans les eaux troubles du Rio de la Plata. Et si les gens comme Anna-Maria ont abandonné le terrorisme de gauche, ce n'est certainement pas pour accepter le terrorisme fasciste. Pourquoi Peron laisse-t-il faire ? Voilà ce qu'entre deux pages d'*Ulysse* et de *Finnegan's Wake* elle a le plus de mal à comprendre.

— Tu es une gourde ! lui dit Mario, un soir où, pour évoquer le bon temps d'autrefois, ils dînent dans un restaurant de la rue Florida, Peron laisse faire parce que cela l'arrange.

— Mais le péronisme... Le justicialisme...

— C'est du passé. Peron n'est plus Peron. C'est une vieille poupée manipulée par des fascistes. Il faut faire quelque chose... Nous ne pouvons pas laisser agir ces canailles...

Et, baissant la voix :

— Nous avons besoin de toi, Anna-Maria...

316

Et, après un silence :
— J'ai besoin de toi...

Les longs cheveux châtains de Mario lui cachent, comme d'habitude, un œil et une partie du visage. L'autre œil, profondément vert, la regarde avec une insistance où elle ne sait trop ce qui l'emporte de la conviction militante ou du reste...

— Tu ne veux pas faire un tour, demande-t-il en réclamant l'addition. Je t'en prie...

Un tour ? Oui... Pourquoi pas... Cela n'engage pas à grand-chose... Et Mario est si séduisant quand il regarde de cette façon — avec cet œil de tueur câlin qu'il avait le jour de Tres Lomos. Les voilà côte à côte dans les allées mal éclairées de Palermo. Il lui passe la main dans les cheveux. Elle recule. Il lui prend le bras. Elle laisse faire. Dans les voitures en stationnement des couples s'embrassent. On entend des feulements, des grognements sourds. Le vent charrie des bouffées d'odeurs puissantes. Elle tremble, frémit, se presse tout à coup contre lui.

— Tu as froid ? demande Mario.

Anna-Maria ne répond pas. Et quand une voiture passe, longue, à faible allure, vitres ouvertes sur une musique et un parfum de tabac blond, elle l'enlace carrément et l'embrasse à pleine bouche.

— Je suis restée avec toi un an, dit doucement Anna-Maria. Nous avons vécu dans la clandestinité. Nous ne nous aimions pas, mais nous vivions pour la révolution. C'était entre Tucuman et Mendoza, te souviens-tu ? Là-bas, nous étions devenus peu à peu des militaires et nous ne savions plus ce que pensaient les civils, ni même ce qu'ils désiraient.

Puis, après un nouveau baiser, plus gourmand, goulu que le premier :

— Je ne te l'ai pas dit, à l'époque. Mais je ne me sentais pas à l'aise. Pourquoi tuions-nous ? Pourquoi risquions-nous de nous faire tuer ? Pour faire comme le Che ? Le Che voulait apporter la révolution à des gens qui ne comprenaient même pas ce qu'il leur disait. Lui, un Blanc, disait aux Indiens, pour qui il était le prototype du colonisateur, qu'il leur apportait une idée de la liberté. Il a disparu avec elle… Comprends-tu ce que je te dis ? Peu à peu, je me suis détachée… Un jour, je suis partie…

— Tu reviendras…

Anna-Maria s'arrête et, dans l'obscurité, tente de saisir le regard de Mario :

— Tu ne comprends pas, Mario. Je me suis découvert un intérêt pour cette vie-là. Je suis lasse de vouloir la changer…

— Il ne s'agit plus de la changer, mais de la défendre… Et puis…

Mario s'est remis à marcher.

— Et puis, quoi ? demande Anna-Maria en lui prenant le bras.

Il se retourne :

— Et puis merde : je t'aime !…

L'arrivée, deux jours plus tard, d'Anna-Maria est accueillie par des exclamations amicales. Compliments à Mario pour l'avoir ramenée au sein de la famille. Clameurs. Plaisanteries grasses. La salle de conférences du quotidien des Montoneros *Noticias* est pleine de gens qu'elle ne connaît pas. Mais il reste tout de même encore quelques visages familiers.

— Bienvenue, dit Julio dans un nuage de cigarette. Tu arrives au bon moment : les choses bougent dans le monde…

— Ah ! fait-elle.

— Comment ça, « ah ! », grimace l'ancien jeune homme dont la moustache grisonne de plus en plus. Au Portugal, c'est la révolution. En Amérique, c'est la désagrégation. Tu as quand même suivi dans la presse le scandale du Watergate, non ?

— Commencez pas la discussion, intervient Mario. Nous nous sommes réunis aujourd'hui pour préparer le 1er Mai.

Ce 1er mai 1974, à Buenos Aires, s'annonce grandiose. Depuis 6 heures du matin, des voitures haut-parleurs parcourent les rues en braillant leurs appels : « *Todos Plaza de Mayo !* Tous place de Mai ! » A la radio, des reporters décrivent à mots haletants le passage des cortèges venant des banlieues : « la Matanza, Lomos de Zamora, Avellaneda, Vincente Lopez, San Martin... »

Mario est venu chercher Anna-Maria vers 8 heures. Dans la rue, sur les trottoirs, des groupes déjà nombreux hurlent des airs patriotiques et les orchestres rivalisent dans l'interprétation de tangos déchirants.

Anna-Maria et Mario se laissent porter par la foule. Ils remarquent des camions militaires aux carrefours et les rideaux tirés sur les magasins ou les cafés. Et quand ils veulent prendre le métro, l'entrée en est barrée par une grille métallique.

— Les cons ! rouspète Anna-Maria. Arrêter le métro un jour de manif !

Prise au jeu, elle commence à s'énerver pour de bon. Comme jadis. Comme à la grande époque.

— On va être en retard, répète-t-elle pour la centième fois.

— *Calla, señorita !* grommelle un grand barbu qui porte une fillette sur ses épaules. Peron ne parlera pas avant 15 heures.

— Nous, nous avons rendez-vous à 13 heures ! répond Anna-Maria.

— Alors, vous n'y serez pas, dit le barbu.

— Mais pourquoi n'avancez-vous pas ? demande une grosse dame, derrière eux.

Le barbu, genre M. Je-sais-tout, explique :

— Les gorilles de la CGT fouillent tout le monde, señora. Ils contrôlent les pancartes et les banderoles.

— Qu'on fouille les gens, d'accord, intervient un homme maigre, habillé d'une veste en peau de chèvre. Il ne faut pas que les gens amènent leurs pétards, mais les banderoles...

— La CGT a décidé des mots d'ordre et des slogans. Elle ne veut pas que les Montoneros diffusent les leurs...

Des dizaines et des dizaines de manifestations s'entre-mêlent dans la tête d'Anna-Maria. Cris, banderoles, nuages, cortèges, discours. Et puis toute cette comédie de ceux qui savent, de ceux qui espèrent et de ceux, la majorité, qui suivent sans espérer ni savoir. Le temps passe. Anna-Maria commence à se demander ce qu'elle fait dans cette foule. Mario, la sentant tendue, l'attire vers lui :

— Je suis heureux que tu sois là.

Et la voyant prête à répondre :

— Non, ne dis rien, je t'en prie...

Pas très loin, un groupe d'écoliers chantent un vieil hymne péroniste :

> *La jeunesse*
> *Marche aujourd'hui*
> *Parce qu'elle doit accomplir sa mission*
> *D'un pas décidé et sûr*
> *Elle a le cœur embrasé*
> *Par la flamme lumineuse de Peron.* »

Ils avancent encore de quelques mètres. Mario trouve une coulée dans le sur-place de la foule et tire Anna-Maria par la main, laissant derrière eux le barbu et la petite fille. Sur la gauche, on scande : « Peron, la Patria Socialista. » Devant, un autre groupe comprimé sous une pancarte « CGT obras sanitarias » répond : « Peron, la Patria Peronista. »

Deux types énormes, avec des brassards CGT, les fouillent de la tête aux pieds avant de les laisser passer. La place est bleu-blanc-bleu, comme le ciel, si lumineux. Deux portraits géants cachent la façade du Palais présidentiel : Peron et Isabel, sa seconde femme. Au pied du Palais, la foule est compacte, tel un mur de béton parsemé de cailloux et de grains de sable. Au fond de la place, elle semble plus jeune, plus remuante. Entre les deux, un espace où grouillent des militaires et les gorilles du service d'ordre.

Mario est métamorphosé. Les cris, les chants, comme chaque fois, l'enivrent.

— Tu vas voir ce que tu vas voir, chuchote-t-il à l'oreille d'Anna-Maria. Nous allons tenter de rejoindre les compagnons...

La foule s'est mise brusquement à scander : « Peron ! Peron ! » Ceux qui arrivent derrière Anna-Maria et Mario les poussent inexorablement vers le centre de la place, dans le no man's land sans qu'ils puissent s'y opposer.

— Merde, merde ! peste Mario.

— Pe-ron ! Pe-ron ! Pe-ron !

Soudain, au balcon, apparaissent quelques silhouettes. Les slogans contraires s'entremêlent. Anna-Maria crie aussi. Mais les haut-parleurs grésillent déjà, s'amplifient d'un bruit incertain et, enfin, une voix tremblante se fait entendre :

— *Compañeros !*

La foule bouge, avance, recule :

— Pe-ron ! Pe-ron ! Pe-ron !

Peron lève les bras et les cris s'éteignent lentement jusqu'au silence. Alors, derrière Anna-Maria, les jeunes se mettent à clamer :

— *No queremos carnaval, assemblea popular !* Nous ne voulons pas de carnaval, nous voulons une assemblée populaire !

Peron garde les bras tendus vers la foule qui, doucement, s'ouvre, comme un lourd portail, vers le fond de la place où flotte une énorme banderole blanche avec une inscription en rouge : « Montoneros présents ! ».

A côté d'Anna-Maria, une jeune créole sort un foulard blanc et avec un bâton de rouge à lèvres écrit le mot : « Montoneros. » Comme par enchantement, des milliers de ces foulards s'agitent au-dessus de la foule.

— *Compañeros*, dit la voix formidable des haut-parleurs, *compañeros*, il y a vingt ans, de ce même balcon, par un beau jour comme celui-ci, je me suis adressé pour la première fois aux travailleurs argentins. Je vous avais alors recommandé de consolider vos organisations : des temps difficiles approchaient.

Devant, la foule reprend : « Pe-ron ! Pe-ron ! »

Derrière, des dizaines de milliers de gorges braillent :

321

« *Que se passe-t-il, que se passe-t-il?*
Que se passe-t-il, général?
Le gouvernement populaire est plein de gorilles
On veut en finir, on veut en finir
Avec la bureaucratie syndicale. »

— Silence, *hijos de putas!* crie une femme forte devant Anna-Maria.

Des bouteilles de Coca volent au-dessus de sa tête, filtrant au passage des éclats de soleil.

— *Compañeros,* reprend Peron et les haut-parleurs, lancés à pleine puissance, amplifient encore son chevrotement : je ne m'étais trompé ni sur l'appréciation des jours à venir, ni sur l'organisation syndicale qui a pu se maintenir pendant ces vingt années, n'en déplaise aux imbéciles qui crient là-bas, au fond !

La foule crie :

— « Pe-ron ! Pe-ron ! »

Le barbu à la petite fille repasse devant Mario et Anna-Maria :

— Ça va mal finir, dit-il, je m'en vais ! Pour la petite !

De ses deux mains, la fillette s'accroche au front de son père. Elle paraît terrorisée.

Peron :

— Je disais que pendant ces vingt ans, les organisations syndicales étaient restées inébranlables et aujourd'hui, voilà que quelques meneurs imberbes prétendent avoir plus de mérites que ceux qui ont lutté pendant tout ce temps !

« *Que se passe-t-il?*
Que se passe-t-il?
Que se passe-t-il, général? »

continuent à crier les jeunes, du fond de la place.

Nouveau vol de bouteilles. Mario pousse Anna-Maria en direction de la rue Defensa, mais un barrage CGT les renvoie vers les Montoneros. Au premier rang, ils aperçoivent Julio.

Peron :

— *Compañeros !*

— Viens avec nous, général, reviens au péronisme, crient les jeunes.

Peron :

— *Compañeros !* Neuf ans de suite, nous nous sommes réunis sur cette même place et pendant neuf ans nous avons tous été d'accord dans notre lutte pour réaliser les aspirations du peuple argentin. Et voilà maintenant, après ces vingt ans, que certains ne sont pas d'accord avec ce que nous avons fait.

— Ne déconne pas, Peron ! Reviens au péronisme !

— *Compañeros !*

— Pe-ron ! Pe-ron !

Les soldats casqués, le doigt sur la détente de leurs fusils, prennent position dans le no man's land où pleuvent maintenant des bouteilles. Mario et Anna-Maria rejoignent peu à peu la foule des Montoneros. Ils ne voient plus ce qui se passe devant. Soudain, un mot d'ordre court dans les rangs, répété de l'un à l'autre, s'amplifiant, déferlant : « *Vamos !* » La foule hésite un moment, vacille, puis, brusquement, bascule.

> « *D'accord ! D'accord, général !*
> *Reste avec tes gorilles !*
> *Es el pueblo el que se va !*
> *C'est le peuple qui s'en va !* »

Anna-Maria et Mario se retrouvent côte à côte, avec Julio.

— Vous voyez, dit-il en souriant, vous voyez, ça bouge ! Peron s'est fait avoir par les fascistes argentins et la CIA ! Mais ils nous le paieront !

Et, se tournant vers Anna-Maria :

— Je suis content que tu sois revenue. Nous retournons dans la clandestinité...

38

TEL-AVIV

L'ENQUÊTE D'ARIÉ (2)

Août 1974

C'est une petite brochure encadrée de noir, sur son bureau, qui attire son attention. Arié s'en saisit. Elle est publiée par l'état-major de l'armée et il s'agit tout simplement de la liste des soldats tués ou disparus pendant la guerre du Kippour.

Il saisit la feuille doucement. Le téléphone sonne, mais il n'y prête pas attention. Cette brochure l'intéresse beaucoup trop. Elle est rugueuse, grise, bordée de noir. Elle le fait penser à la pierre posée sur la tombe de son père dans le petit cimetière du kibboutz en Galilée. Légère en apparence et, pourtant, si lourde à déplacer.

« Un homme égale une pierre », se dit-il. « Ou plutôt non : un homme égale une lettre, une inscription gravée sur une pierre. Comme la Loi… Comme la mémoire… » Qui lui a raconté que la Thora est composée de six cent mille lettres ? Soit, selon la tradition, le nombre exact de Juifs arrivés dans le pays de Canaan ? Il ne s'en souvient pas. Ce qu'il sait, par contre, c'est que d'après le Talmud, si une seule lettre devait manquer au Livre, celui-ci perdrait du même coup son caractère sacré.

Mais pourquoi ce jeu d'images, cette pensée vagabonde, dès qu'il s'agit de son père. Arié se lève et fait quelques pas dans ce bureau exigu, mais dont il est si fier. Il se rassied, contemple un moment la photo de Mordekhaï posée sur la table ; ses bons yeux de myope, grossis par le verre des lunettes et ouvre à nouveau la brochure : 2 522 noms, avec, à la lettre H, le nom de Mordekhaï.

Incroyable, toutes les lettres qu'il a reçues. Il ne soupçonnait pas que Mordekhaï eût autant d'amis. Il ne savait pas qu'il avait encore tant de famille. La lettre qu'Aron Lerner a envoyée, après l'enterrement auquel il a assisté, l'a irritée. Cette volonté de généraliser tout le temps ! de faire de la morale ! du sionisme à tout prix !... Il terminait sa lettre par une citation :

« *Innombrables, hélas ! les peines que j'endure !*
Quand ce peuple autour de moi souffre,
Mon esprit se sent désarmé
Devant le Mal... Les germes meurent.
Dans cette illustre terre... »

— C'est du Sophocle, dit Benjamin à qui Arié montre la lettre.
— Alors, Sophocle faisait aussi du sionisme ! a répliqué Arié, agacé.

La lettre de Richard, fils de Sidney, l'a étonnée pour une autre raison. Il ne savait pas que celui-ci fût aussi religieux. Sa lettre est bourrée de citations du Talmud et de rabbins illustres. Et aussi, pleine d'appels à la vengeance.

« *Répands Ta fureur sur les nations*
Qui ne Te connaissent pas.
Et sur les royaumes qui n'invoquent pas Ton nom.
Éternel, Dieu des armées, relève-nous ! »

Drôle de famille, décidément. Toutes les qualités et tous les défauts d'un peuple, déposés dans une seule maison !

Dina, la sœur d'Arié, vient d'avoir ses douze ans. On ne les a pas fêtés à cause du deuil que sa mère veut respecter à tout prix. Arié pense pourtant qu'elle récupère rapidement. Son bon sens paysan l'aide à accepter plus facilement la mort. Arié, lui, ne boite plus et pense sérieusement à se remettre au football. Il a cessé de fréquenter Shoshana dont le fiancé est revenu après son stage à San Francisco. En revanche, il se rend à présent toutes les semaines à Haïfa, pour voir Judith. A moins qu'elle ne lui rende visite à Tel-Aviv. Il ne fait plus l'amour qu'avec elle et attend la fin de l'année de deuil pour célébrer leur mariage. Il en a parlé à Myriam qui, après l'avoir écouté, a éclaté de rire :

— Pourquoi te marier, « Haboub » ? Moi, j'ai envie de divorcer...

Et, plus explicite :

— Le mariage est comme une place assiégée, ceux qui sont dehors veulent y entrer et ceux qui sont dedans veulent en sortir.

Dona Regina aussi a fait parvenir une lettre à Arié. Une longue lettre en yiddish que Rachel Lerner a traduite en hébreu. La vieille tante pleurait Mordekhaï et annonçait la mort toute récente de don Israël, son mari : « Une génération s'en va, une autre vient et la terre subsiste toujours... » D'Anna-Maria, elle disait seulement qu'elle était revenue après l'élection de Peron, qu'elle allait bien, qu'elle était toujours belle, qu'elle s'était remise aux études, mais qu'elle était à nouveau repartie... « Encore de la clandestinité, de la guérilla, s'est dit Arié. Ou de la révolution... »

De fait, la guerre du Kippour l'a conforté dans sa décision de poursuivre ses activités au sein des services secrets. Seul moyen de combattre le terrorisme... Seul moyen de prévenir les guerres... Quant à l'enquête sur la mort de Hugo, elle progresse. Arié a même l'impression d'avoir découvert une pièce importante du puzzle. Elle concerne Israël Beer, ce conseiller de Ben Gourion, accusé d'espionnage en faveur de l'URSS et chez qui Hugo se rendait chaque fois qu'il était en Israël. Le témoignage du général Gonen lui avait donné l'idée de revoir le dossier du procès. Une fiche y était consacrée à ses voyages en RFA et à ses visites dans les bases allemandes de l'état-major européen de l'OTAN. L'auteur de la note avait ajouté, au crayon rouge, une remarque personnelle, mais dont il n'avait tiré aucune conclusion : qu'il était facile à tout visiteur à Berlin-Ouest de se rendre à Berlin-Est. Remarque non seulement judicieuse, mais importante. Comment se faisait-il donc que le dossier ne comportait pas la liste des lieux et des personnes à Berlin-Est, visités éventuellement par Israël Beer ?

Au milieu du mois de mai 1960, par exemple, Israël Beer avait séjourné à Mönchengladbach, chez Reinhard Gehlen, ancien de l'Abwehr et chef des Services spéciaux de la RFA. D'après le dossier, celui-ci n'ignorait pas les séjours de Beer à Berlin-Est mais les expliquait par des négociations secrètes entre Israël et les Soviétiques. Recevant chez lui le conseiller de Ben Gourion, l'Allemand aurait espéré apprendre quelque chose sur ces négociations, ignorées alors de tous. Cette explication ne paraît pas très logique. Gehlen savait, mieux que personne, que les contacts entre Israël et les Soviétiques n'avaient jamais été vraiment rompus. Et que Berlin n'était pas l'endroit le plus discret pour ce genre de relations qui, du reste, se poursuivaient aussi bien à Bucarest qu'à Vienne. A Sofia qu'à Paris. Alors, pourquoi, dans ce cas, Reinhard Gehlen recevait-il chez lui Israël Beer ? Pour pouvoir répondre à cette question, il fallait découvrir les interlocuteurs de Beer en RDA. « Dis-moi qui sont tes amis et je te dirai qui tu es. » Ce vieux proverbe s'appliquait merveilleusement à cette affaire.

A la question concernant, justement, ces voyages à Berlin-Est, si totalement contraires aux recommandations formelles des services israéliens, Israël Beer avait répondu, lors de ses interrogatoires, qu'ils étaient motivés par une simple curiosité ainsi que par le désir de revoir quelques vieux amis. Il se faisait que parmi eux se trouvait le docteur Hans Furchmuller. Nom innocent aux yeux d'Israël Harell, à l'époque chef du Mossad. Mais Arié, lui, sait que ce médecin de Berlin-Est n'était autre que le beau-frère de Hugo. Et qu'il avait présenté son beau-frère, selon ce qu'il avait dit lui-même à Sidney, à un certain Wolfgang Knopff de la HVA, les services spéciaux de la RDA. Le général Gehlen n'était donc pas spécialement intéressé par les négociations israélo-soviétiques, mais plutôt, par les agissements des services est-allemands et leurs contacts avec l'étranger. Explication qui va de soi, selon Arié.

Mais quel était le véritable rôle du beau-frère de Hugo, le docteur Hans Furchmuller ? Était-il un simple et innocent intermédiaire ou un agent actif, et pourquoi pas de haut rang ? Quel rôle a bien pu jouer Sigrid, la femme de Hugo, dans cette affaire ? Et si les tueurs ne visaient qu'elle sur la route de Tel-Aviv à Jérusalem ? Qui sait... Il devenait clair pour Arié qu'il faudrait rapidement établir un dossier sur la famille Furchmuller.

— Bon travail, remarque Benjamin après qu'Arié lui a exposé ses découvertes.

Benjamin, l'un des rares à avoir prévu l'attaque des armées arabes, est monté en grade. Mais malgré sa promotion, il n'a pas changé de bureau. Il loge toujours au troisième étage et le même gros ventilateur, couleur kaki, fixé au plafond, brasse en bourdonnant le même air chaud et humide. D'un geste lent, qui n'a pas changé non plus et dont Arié se dit, en un éclair, que c'est le même geste que Mordekhaï, il enlève ses lunettes et regarde curieusement le jeune homme :

— Mais as-tu des nouvelles de Hidar ?

— D'après le récit de Sidney, observe Arié, il devait bien connaître Sigrid. Peut-être aussi, son frère...

— Je ne parle pas de Hidar par rapport à l'affaire Hugo, l'interrompt Benjamin.

Sa voix devient officielle :

— D'autres attentats se préparent. Il serait important de connaître le rôle de l'Union soviétique dans leur organisation et leur exécution. Hidar est maintenant proche d'Arafat, mais il y a longtemps qu'il n'a pas mis le pied à Beyrouth. Il nous faut savoir pourquoi...

Rome, août 1974

Pourquoi ne suis-je pas allé le voir plus tôt ? Pourquoi ne lui ai-je pas au moins téléphoné ou écrit ? Son nom figurait bien dans le carnet de Hugo. Et je me suis trouvé, toutes ces dernières années, à plusieurs reprises à Rome. Mais voilà : le destin est comme la tortue d'Eschyle, il finit toujours par la rattraper. Je n'ai donc rencontré le père Roberto Cerutti que treize ans après la mort de Hugo, le 9 août 1974.

Le père Roberto Cerutti est une personnalité importante au Vatican. Il dirige la radio du Saint-Siège qui diffuse dans le monde entier et qui emploie plus de trois cents personnes. Son nom est souvent cité dans la presse parmi les rares personnes ayant une réelle influence sur le Pape. Il m'a fixé rendez-vous à 8 heures du matin, devant la tour Léon XIII, qui abrite Radio-Vatican.

Pour Rome, c'est extrêmement tôt, mais la via di Porta Angelica est déjà embouteillée. La vie, ici, commence au petit matin. Le taxi me laisse devant la porte Sainte-Anne ; ce qui m'oblige à retraverser à pied tout le Vatican. Du coup, je me hâte et je gravis au pas de charge les collines de l'État pour arriver devant la tour Léon XIII avec quinze minutes de retard.

Le père n'a pas l'air fâché. C'est un homme grand, sec et son visage, comme ciselé dans la cire, est auréolé de cheveux blancs et posé sur un col romain gris, seul indice avec, il est vrai, une petite croix argentée sur le revers de son veston, de son appartenance à l'Église. Il est jésuite. Suivant l'accord passé entre le Saint-Siège et la Compagnie, Radio-Vatican lui a été confiée et les trois directeurs qui l'assistent sont tous des héritiers de saint Ignace de Loyola. Il me salue, donc. Me prie de le suivre. Ce n'est qu'après m'avoir offert un fauteuil en cuir noir dans son bureau dont les fenêtres donnent sur les jardins du Vatican, qu'il me dit dans un français chantant :

— Ainsi, vous êtes le cousin de Hugo Halter... Que son âme repose en paix.

Après quoi, il pose les coudes sur la vaste table dont le plateau de bois massif est étrangement vide et me fixe de ses yeux bleus :

— Je me suis souvent demandé pourquoi vous ne veniez pas me voir. Je savais que vous faisiez une enquête sur la mort de votre cousin. Comment je l'ai appris ? Par un article dans la presse italienne. Les Israéliens, eux, m'ont rendu visite. Un certain Benjamin Ben Eliezer, un homme cultivé. Hidar Assadi, aussi, le mari de votre cousine soviétique. Un personnage curieux, secret. Mais je suppose que vous les connaissez tous. Ils m'ont interrogé sur mes relations avec le défunt. Ils cherchaient, comme vous, les raisons de sa mort. Alors, où en êtes-vous ?

Est-ce l'atmosphère feutrée de ce vaste bureau blanc, presque vide ? Ce paysage entre ombre et lumière que je vois par la fenêtre ? Est-ce cet homme calme, solide, à l'attitude amicale, presque paternelle ? Ou tout simplement la fatigue du voyage, l'angoisse coutumière, le besoin de communiquer ? Toujours est-il que je me sens en veine de confidence. Je parle. Je raconte à Cerutti mon père et son désir d'ancêtres, la mort de Sidney — qu'il connaît déjà —, mon questionnement sur le judaïsme et Israël, l'oppressant silence de Dieu... Je parle de mon interrogation non pas tant sur les raisons de la mort de Hugo que sur le personnage lui-même...

Quand il juge que j'ai terminé, il m'enveloppe d'un

regard chaleureux, étonnant dans ce visage ascétique, et s'abandonne dans son fauteuil :

— On se trompe souvent en estimant trop haut la valeur d'autrui ; on se trompe rarement en l'estimant trop bas. Je crois, moi, qu'il faut un juste milieu. Vous aviez trop idéalisé votre cousin. Vous l'avez chargé de toutes les qualités et, surtout, de tous vos rêves. Tant que vous ne lui aurez pas accordé le droit à la faute, à la faiblesse, et pourquoi pas au péché, vous n'arriverez pas à le comprendre. Ni à découvrir les raisons de son assassinat.

La voix du père Roberto Cerutti devient plus sourde, comme voilée par le souvenir :

— Je le voyais souvent, dit-il. Et je l'avoue, j'attendais parfois ses visites. J'aimais sa passion, j'aimais ses questions et j'admirais aussi ses remarques. Il n'était pas plus intelligent qu'un autre, ni plus pertinent, mais il était d'une rare simplicité. Cette simplicité dont parle le Christ, qui devrait être une qualité naturelle mais qui a si souvent besoin d'études pour s'acquérir... Hugo Halter désirait la paix au Proche-Orient et selon lui elle passait par l'entente, la compréhension et la paix entre les trois religions monothéistes, c'est-à-dire entre les Fils d'Abraham. C'est pour cela qu'il est venu me voir un jour de l'année 1959, je crois, recommandé par un ami commun, un jésuite français. Pour soutenir sa thèse, il me cita ce jour-là une parabole du Talmud qui m'impressionna : « Après avoir créé la Terre et le Ciel, Dieu a divisé toute la beauté et toute la splendeur de sa création en dix parts égales. Il accorda neuf parts de beauté et de splendeur à Jérusalem, et seulement une part au reste du monde. Dieu divisa, de même, en dix parts toute la souffrance et toute l'affliction du monde. Il accorda neuf parts de souffrance et d'affliction à Jérusalem et seulement une part au reste du monde. » Hugo croyait que tant qu'on n'aurait pas réussi à ramener la paix à Jérusalem entre Chrétiens et Juifs d'abord, puis avec les Musulmans, le monde allait souffrir... Une belle idée. J'en ai parlé à Sa Sainteté qui l'a approuvée...

Le père Roberto Cerutti continue à parler de sa voix chaude. Il cite les Évangiles, la Bible et même un poète arabe, le Cheikh Mohayîd-dîn Ibn Arabi : « Mon cœur est devenu capable de toutes les formes : il est un pâturage pour les gazelles, un couvent pour les moines chrétiens, et un temple pour les idoles, et la Kaabah du pèlerin, et les Tables de la Thora et le Livre du Coran... »

J'écoute son long monologue en silence, j'admire ses connaissances, la fluidité de sa pensée et je me demande si ce sont bien les propos de Hugo qu'il me rapporte ou s'il partage avec moi ses propres réflexions. Aujourd'hui, je crois surtout que le père Roberto Cerutti est semblable à tous les hommes : il s'intéresse aux autres dans la mesure où il s'accorde à eux.

On frappe à la porte. Un jeune prêtre apporte quelques dépêches. Le père Cerutti les parcourt des yeux et m'annonce :

— Richard Nixon a démissionné hier soir de ses fonctions de Président des États-Unis. Il faut que je prépare un commentaire.

Et, en se levant :

— Voulez-vous que nous dînions ce soir ?

39

MOSCOU-BEYROUTH

LES ANGOISSES DU TROISIÈME TYPE

Octobre 1974

C'est deux ans seulement après le départ de ses parents qu'Olga a commencé de réellement ressentir le poids de leur absence. Oh, bien sûr, elle ne s'est pas séparée d'eux de gaieté de cœur, mais elle n'avait jamais cru cette séparation vraiment définitive. Elle entretenait l'illusion de leur retour prochain et conservait le souvenir de leurs multiples départs précédents pour des congrès scientifiques à l'intérieur de l'Union soviétique. Léningrad… Bakou… Tachkent… Alma-Alta… N'en étaient-ils pas toujours revenus? Ne les avait-elle pas chaque fois retrouvés. Cette fois, hélas, il y a la durée : deux années entières ; et puis il y a surtout ce gigantesque espace qui sépare l'Union soviétique de l'Occident auquel appartient Israël…

Alors, Hidar a beau être toujours aussi amoureux. Leur appartement, avenue de la Paix, a beau être plaisant et joliment décoré. Elle a beau être satisfaite de son travail, des réceptions auxquelles elle est conviée, voire des mille et un privilèges auxquels la position — et les relations — de son époux lui donnent droit. Il lui manque quelque chose. Et elle ne parvient pas à être tout à fait heureuse. De quel nom désigner cette nostalgie qui l'emplit chaque fois qu'elle vient à songer à ces douces soirées familiales, à ces fêtes, à ces disputes ? Souvent, le soir, quand elle se sent désœuvrée, ses pas la mènent sans qu'elle y songe jusqu'à la rue Kazakov. Et elle reste longtemps là, immobile, dans la nuit — à se laisser envahir par les douces images du passé.

Un matin d'octobre 1974, elle sort, comme à son habitude et arrive en bas de son immeuble, plongée dans des images surgies de l'enfance, prise dans le souvenir des odeurs et des sensations anciennes. Elle entend à peine la voix, tout près d'elle, qui l'appelle par son nom.

— Olienka ! Olienka ! refait la voix.

C'est Maria Petrenko-Podïapolskaïa, son amie, épouse d'un membre de l'Académie des Sciences, lui-même ami d'Aron, qui la saisit maintenant par le bras :

— A quoi songes-tu ? Tu marches comme une vraie somnambule...

— Rien... Je pensais à mes parents...

— Justement, comment vont-ils ?

Puis, sans attendre la réponse — peut-être parce qu'elle sait bien que les lettres d'Israël sont rares, qu'elles sont distribuées au compte-gouttes et que la censure veille —, elle poursuit, plus enjouée :

— Je vais prendre le thé chez les Sakharov. Veux-tu m'accompagner ?

Et les deux femmes de se diriger, bras dessus bras dessous, vers le 48 *bis* rue Tchkalov où habite le célèbre académicien. L'ascenseur étant en panne, elles gravissent les six étages à pied. Et quand elles sonnent à la porte, première surprise : personne ne répond. On entend bien, à l'intérieur, des bruits et des altercations. Mais elles ont beau frapper, sonner, frapper encore, personne ne se décide à ouvrir.

— Attends-moi ici, dit Maria. Je descends téléphoner.

Quelques minutes plus tard, elle revient tout essoufflée. Elle a bien composé le numéro des Sakharov depuis la cabine proche de l'immeuble. Mais nouvelle surprise : personne n'a décroché.

Dans l'appartement même, les voix se sont tues. Plus un bruit. Plus un murmure. Les voix qu'on entendait tout à l'heure étaient-elles le fruit de leur imagination ?

334

Venaient-elles de l'étage supérieur? Tout cela est bizarre. Le couple avait bien parlé d'un thé. On était clairement convenus de l'heure. Et ce silence est, décidément, bien incompréhensible. De plus en plus intriguées, les deux femmes décident de retéléphoner. Dans la rue, Maria fait remarquer à Olga que, contrairement à l'habitude, personne ne fait les cent pas devant l'immeuble et ce détail leur paraît, à toutes deux, plus troublant, plus inquiétant encore. Comble de malchance : c'est le téléphone de la cabine qui, cette fois, ne fonctionne plus et il leur faut faire une bonne centaine de mètres, jusqu'à la Yaouza, pour trouver une autre cabine. Les Sakharov ne répondant toujours pas, Maria décide cette fois d'alerter les amis. En sorte que, à leur retour, il y a déjà plusieurs personnes, plus inquiètes les unes que les autres, en faction devant l'immeuble. On remonte à la queue leu leu. On sonne à nouveau. Et là, miracle : la porte s'ouvre. C'est Elena Bonner, et Andreï Sakharov apparaît, en train de s'affairer autour du téléphone dont les fils ont été coupés. Que s'est-il passé ? Eh bien voilà, explique-t-il. On a sonné une première fois à la porte. Croyant que c'était Maria, il a ouvert. Et ont alors surgi des hommes armés qui se sont présentés comme membres de l'organisation palestinienne Septembre Noir. Ces hommes, au nombre de cinq, ont exigé de lui qu'il renie sa déclaration en faveur d'Israël du début de la Guerre du Kippour. Ils ont menacé, s'il ne le faisait pas, de le tuer, lui et ses proches. Et seuls les coups de sonnette de Maria, un peu plus tard, à 16 heures pile, ont réussi à leur faire peur : ils ont contraint le savant et sa femme au silence en les menaçant de leurs armes et en les conduisant de force dans la pièce du fond ; après quoi, ils ont attendu que Maria et Olga descendent pour quitter l'immeuble à leur tour — aussi discrètement qu'ils étaient arrivés.

Quelle histoire ! songe Olga. Quel effrayant concours de circonstances ! Et d'où vient que la police, aussitôt alertée par le groupe d'amis, ait réagi aussi mollement ? Hidar, quand elle lui pose la question, trouve sa

« milaya » bien naïve. Enfin : il lui dit qu'il la trouve naïve — car dans son for intérieur, il juge lui aussi l'histoire inquiétante. Qui en veut donc à Andreï Dmitrievitch ? Ce type d'action de commando n'a-t-il pas pour unique effet de discréditer la cause palestinienne à un mois du voyage d'Arafat à l'ONU ? Et, de plus, comment ne pas voir dans cette façon d'opérer, sans le prévenir, dans un domaine — le Proche-Orient — qui, de principe, est le sien, un secret désir de l'humilier ? Cet événement, à quelques semaines d'un prochain départ pour Beyrouth, ne peut que le contrarier.

D'autant que ce voyage ne sera pas facile, il le sait. Les dirigeants du Front n'ont pas apprécié le rapprochement entre l'URSS et El Fath. Georges Habbache a tenu des propos amers à son endroit. Waddi Haddad, pourtant brouillé avec Habbache, a, paraît-il, juré sa perte. Et quand à Ghassan Kanafani qui avait compris, lui, l'intérêt stratégique de ce retournement, il a été tué par une bombe placée dans sa voiture. Le Front a accusé les Israéliens. Les Israéliens, les Jordaniens. Les Jordaniens, Waddi Haddad. Mais Hidar sait bien, lui, que ce sont les Jordaniens qui ont raison : la reconnaissance implicite d'Israël par un homme comme Kanafani était intolérable et mettait en péril la politique du refus, établie et défendue par Haddad. Il reste Bassam Abou Charif ? Oui. Mais Arafat et Abou Iyad l'acceptent moins par amour que par intérêt ; et nombreux sont, du reste, les dirigeants d'El Fath qui continuent de se méfier de lui. A tout cela s'ajoute enfin que le Liban est au bord de la guerre civile et que l'homme fort des Phalanges chrétiennes, Michel Chehab, le mari de Leïla, semble s'être préparé au pire. Malgré cette confusion, malgré tous ces dangers, Hidar ne peut cependant plus reculer le moment du départ. Arafat doit se rendre le 13 novembre à New York, pour participer à l'Assemblée générale de l'ONU. Et Tchebrikov l'a chargé, lui, Hidar, de préparer ce voyage.

Cette fois, d'ailleurs, c'est Tchebrikov lui-même qui a suggéré d'emmener Olga à Beyrouth. Il estime que sa présence auprès de Hidar, quatre ans plus tôt, s'est finalement révélée bénéfique. Le Tunisien s'en réjouit, bien sûr. Mais quelque chose, au fond, l'angoisse. Les difficultés qui l'attendent à Beyrouth... Celles qu'il prévoit et celles qu'il pressent... Cette affaire de faux Arabes chez Andreï Sakharov... Bref, Hidar, cet après-midi-là, est bien embarrassé et, ne sachant trop ce qu'il doit dire ou ne pas dire à sa chère petite Olga, il allume une cigarette. Il s'est mis à fumer depuis peu. Il ne sait pas bien comment cela lui est venu. Peut-être à cause d'un briquet, cadeau d'un jeune étudiant algérien de l'université Patrice Lumumba. C'est un briquet grossier, fabriqué avec une mèche d'étoupe. Mais il l'aime bien et c'est pour l'essayer qu'il a acheté son premier paquet. Toujours est-il donc qu'il allume sa cigarette, aspire une bouffée de fumée et demande, sans préambule :

— As-tu vu ton frère, dernièrement ?
— Non, fait Olga. Pourquoi ?

Hidar hésite :

— Je ne sais pas... Je me demandais seulement si...
— Si Sacha n'était pas dans le coup ?

Hidar s'approche d'elle et relève la mèche de ses cheveux blonds, qui cache son œil droit :

— Allons, Milaya, si on mangeait quelque chose ?

Cette fois-ci Olga a été déçue par Beyrouth. Il pleuvait des cordes. Tout ce qui chatoyait, brillait, étincelait, lui paraissait tout à coup terne. Et le Râs-Beyrouth, entre le port et les plages de Khaldé, qu'elle voit par la porte-fenêtre de sa chambre d'hôtel, était battu par la brume.

Le lendemain, la pluie cesse. Des rafales de vent tiède emportent les nuages vers la mer, dégageant la montagne qui se dresse soudain — si proche, si présente, avec ses pinèdes, ses terrasses, ses villages aux tuiles rouges, et, dans le lointain, au nord, la nef longuement enneigée du Sannin. Olga, alors, reprend sa bonne humeur. Refusant le guide que Hidar lui propose pour lui faire visiter les environs pendant qu'il sera occupé à la Centrale d'El Fath, elle va se promener seule. Et c'est ainsi qu'elle arrive, un peu fatiguée, autour de midi, dans la rue Bechara el-Khoury qui longe une forêt de pins.

Elle s'apprête à abandonner sa promenade et à héler un taxi quand elle voit sortir d'une demeure à l'imposant perron de marbre quelqu'un qu'elle a l'impression de connaître. C'est une femme aux cheveux noirs qui porte un léger manteau gris, serré à la taille. Elle s'éloigne : Olga se rapproche. Elle accélère le pas : Olga accélère aussi et, au bout de quelques instants, finit par la rattraper. Mais bien sûr ! Là, de plus près, arrêtée près de la petite Morris dont elle cherche fébrilement les clés, elle la reconnaît fort bien :

— Vous vous souvenez de moi ? demande-t-elle en anglais. Je suis Olga, la cousine moscovite de votre ami, Sidney Halter.

La femme a un geste de recul, pince drôlement les lèvres et laisse passer sur son visage un air d'étonnement peut-être mêlé d'un peu de peur. Olga recule elle aussi. Elle est sur le point de passer son chemin quand la jeune femme, semblant se raviser, ordonne :

— Montez !

Puis, après avoir démarré :

— Oui, oui... C'est extraordinaire. Je vous reconnais moi aussi... Je dois faire une course : pourquoi ne pas parler en roulant ?

La voiture rejoint une large artère encombrée de voitures et de bruits de klaxon.

— Oui, je me souviens de vous, reprend la femme. C'était il y a quatre ans... Votre ami...

Elle s'interrompt :

— Mais sans doute êtes-vous mariés, à présent ?

— Oui.

La voiture stoppe :

— Pouvez-vous m'attendre cinq minutes ?

— Bien sûr !

Olga regarde autour d'elle. Elles se sont garées juste en face d'une église. C'est une construction blanc et rose, avec une pancarte où l'on peut lire : « Notre-Dame-des-Anges ». Devant, deux vieux mendiants tendent la main.

— Vous attendez Mme Chehab ? demande un homme en costume clair, qui la fait sursauter plus que de raison.

— Oui, hésite-t-elle... Oui, j'attends Leïla Chehab.

— Vous êtes une de ses amies ?

— Pas vraiment... Je suis une touriste... Nous nous sommes connues il y a quatre ans, par hasard...

— Ah bon, fait l'homme, comme si l'explication lui suffisait. La voici...

Leïla paraît contrariée en le voyant :

— Bonjour Béchir, fait-elle du bout des lèvres, tu peux nous laisser.

Puis, engageant sa petite Morris sur la chaussée, entre deux grosses Mercedes, elle demande à Olga :

— A quel hôtel êtes-vous descendue ?

— Au Saint-Georges.

— Je vous dépose.

Elles roulent à nouveau en silence. Ce n'est qu'arrivées devant l'hôtel que Leïla tourne pour la première fois la tête vers sa voisine. Ses grands yeux noirs, aux reflets violets, sont pleins de larmes.

— Pardonnez-moi... Je ne pourrai pas vous revoir... Mon mari me fait suivre partout... Il est très puissant...

— Mais...

D'un geste léger, elle la fait taire :

— Au revoir.

Puis, au moment où Olga s'apprête à la quitter, ces derniers mots presque en chuchotant :

— Je l'aimais... Je l'aimais vraiment.

Cette rencontre inattendue, ce parcours en voiture, ces silences, ces mystères, cet aveu enfin lui laissent une sensation pénible. Elle a, sans trop savoir pourquoi, l'absolue certitude d'avoir croisé un être en danger. A qui s'en ouvrir ? A Hidar, bien sûr. Mais Hidar n'est pas encore de retour. Alors elle hésite un moment entre la chambre et la terrasse de l'hôtel face à la mer et, voyant que le ciel est toujours dégagé, elle opte pour la terrasse. Elle n'est pas assise depuis une minute qu'un homme, petit et corpulent, prend, sans plus de cérémonie, place en face d'elle :

— Je m'appelle Michel Chehab. Je suis le mari de Leïla.

— Oui, fait Olga, à la fois stupéfaite et inexplicablement terrorisée.

L'homme a le visage lourd, un nez empâté, un regard sans couleur :

— Vous êtes bien Mme Assadi ?

— C'est cela, oui.

— Vous buvez quelque chose ?

— Un thé.

L'homme appelle le garçon, attend ensuite qu'il s'éloigne et demande :

— Vous connaissiez bien ce Sidney Halter ?

— Vaguement, oui... C'était un parent...

— Vous saviez que c'était l'amant de ma femme ?

La brutalité de la question la stupéfie davantage encore et, cette fois, la désarçonne :

— Oui, fait-elle, d'une voix hésitante... Enfin, non...

— Pourtant, vous les avez vus ensemble ?

— Ils se connaissaient... Voilà, c'est ça : je savais qu'ils se connaissaient.

L'homme se tait à nouveau, attendant que le garçon serve les boissons commandées et reprend :

— Savez-vous que votre mari est responsable de la mort de votre cousin ?

Stupéfaction d'Olga... Incrédulité... Un regard de défi et de haine à ce gros salopard qui, content de l'effet produit par ses paroles, commence à expliquer, avec force détails, le rôle de Hidar dans l'élaboration du détournement des avions vers Zarka en 1970...

— Vous vous trompez, fait Olga d'une voix mal assurée.

— Je ne me trompe jamais, madame, répond l'homme avec un sourire suffisant.

Et, après avoir allumé une cigarette :

— Et maintenant : savez-vous que votre mari a été lui aussi l'amant de ma femme ?

340

Là, Olga se lève d'un bond.

— Vous mentez ! Je ne sais pas pourquoi j'écoute vos élucubrations. Vous êtes un être malfaisant, monsieur Michel Chehab.

Puis, elle quitte la terrasse sous le regard amusé des clients et des garçons.

Quand Hidar arrive, vers 5 heures de l'après-midi, il la trouve allongée sur le lit, feignant de s'intéresser à la Bible. Mais la foi, cette fois-ci, n'est manifestement pas au rendez-vous.

— Pardonne-moi, « Milaya », dit-il, la réunion a été longue ; et, crois-moi, elle n'a pas été facile.

Il enlève sa veste et s'installe près de sa femme sur le lit :

— Je n'ai pas que des amis, à Beyrouth...

— Je l'ai remarqué, grommelle Olga.

Le visage mat de Hidar se contracte. On dirait un oiseau aux aguets :

— As-tu rencontré quelqu'un ?

— Oui, fait Olga, d'un ton qui se veut aussi neutre que possible : ta maîtresse.

Paris, mai 1977

Roberto Cerutti, le jésuite, directeur général de Radio-Vatican, a fini par devenir mon ami. Chaque fois que je vais à Rome, je lui téléphone et nous tentons de nous voir. M'a-t-il appris quelque chose de neuf sur Hugo ? C'est difficile à dire. Ce qui est clair, en revanche — et étrange — c'est que sa tendresse pour mon cousin tient moins aux qualités qu'il lui aurait reconnues qu'à ses défauts, ses faiblesses : « inconstant, influençable, capable d'abandons et de lâcheté », mais ayant toujours à l'esprit la notion du bien et du mal. C'est son angoisse et ses remords, sa volonté de réparer ses fautes et de combattre ses défauts à travers la quête pathétique, désespérée d'un peu plus de justice, d'un peu plus de fraternité et de compréhension entre les hommes qui ont séduit le vieux jésuite.

Pour le reste, a-t-il des soupçons ? Oui, il en avait. Mais bizarrement, il n'a jamais interrogé Hugo. Celui-ci aurait très bien pu travailler pour un service secret. Peut-être pour deux. Pourquoi pas pour trois à la fois ? Il était dominé par sa femme mais il en avait connu certainement beaucoup d'autres. Ses idées cependant étaient justes et sincère, sa lutte. Ce qui aurait perdu Hugo ce n'est donc pas sa lâcheté, mais sa sincérité.

Curieuse relation que celle du jésuite Roberto Cerutti et du Juif du ghetto, Hugo Halter. Je tente en vain de la comprendre, de la mieux cerner. L'ecclésiastique voyait-il en Hugo le Juif, son frère, que la foi de Jésus unissait à lui ou, au contraire, se considérait-il comme un chrétien que sa foi en Jésus séparait ? La judaïcité de Hugo jouait-elle un rôle dans leur amitié ? J'ai appris par la suite qu'ils avaient organisé, au début de l'année 1960, à Rome, un séminaire judéo-chrétien dont le père Cerutti ne m'a jamais parlé. Plusieurs ecclésiastiques et rabbins y avaient participé. Ils avaient même, paraît-il, prévu un voyage à Jérusalem, qui ne s'était jamais réalisé. On m'a aussi parlé d'autres projets communs mais sans que je découvre en quoi ils consistaient au juste. A ma question, le père Cerutti se contente de citer : « Béni soit le Seigneur, le Dieu d'Israël, de ce qu'Il a visité et racheté Son peuple... » « C'est ainsi qu'Il manifeste Sa miséricorde envers nos pères et se souvient de Sa sainte alliance selon le serment par lequel avait juré à Abraham, notre père... » Vous croyez que c'est la Thora ! Eh bien, non, ce n'est pas la Thora, c'est saint Luc, I, 68, 72, 73.

Ce soir-là, après le dîner, le père Cerutti retourne à la radio et je l'accompagne donc. Et c'est ensemble que nous apprenons le plus important bouleversement de l'histoire d'Israël depuis sa création : le Parti travailliste, au gouvernement depuis 1947, a perdu les élections au profit du Likoud. L'ancien chef de l'Irgoun, Menahem Begin, devient Premier ministre. Menahem Begin, celui dont David Ben Gourion a dit : « S'il arrive un jour au pouvoir, il mènera le pays à sa perte ! »

A partir de là, les événements s'accélèrent. Quelques jours plus tard, à Paris, je reçois un coup de téléphone de Mohamed Hassan el-Toukhami qui m'annonce une invitation urgente du président Sadate. Le lendemain, je suis au Caire. Et c'est plein d'émotion, convaincu que cette rencontre sera décisive que j'arrive, accompagné de Mohamed Hassan el-Toukhami, chez le Président égyptien, dans sa maison située entre l'hôtel Sheraton et les Pyramides. Anouar el-Sadate doit, le lendemain, prononcer un discours devant l'Assemblée Populaire. « Un discours important », me dit-il d'emblée, en plissant dans un sourire ses bons yeux de paysan élevé, comme il aime le rappeler, sur les bords du Nil.

— Vous savez comment on fait en politique? me demande-t-il, après qu'un serviteur en galabiya bleue a posé le plateau avec le café sur la table. On saute sur un cheval au galop et on dit aux autres : « Rattrapez-moi si vous pouvez! » Eh bien moi, c'est une fusée que je vais enfourcher, et vous allez voir tous ces vieux politiciens hors d'haleine me courir après, en me suppliant de les laisser reprendre souffle!

Et, après un court silence accompagné d'un sourire malicieux :

— Je tenais à ce que vous soyez là à cette occasion. Vous serez surpris...

Sur le moment, je ne comprends pas bien ce qu'il veut dire. Le lendemain, pourtant, j'écoute, comme il le souhaitait, son discours à la télévision. Et là, tous ses mots de la veille — cheval, fusée, surprise... — deviennent soudain très clairs :

— Je suis prêt à aller au bout du monde pour épargner la vie d'un seul de mes fils, annonce-t-il. Je suis prêt à aller au diable. Je suis prêt à aller au bout de la terre... Je suis même prêt à me rendre en Israël...

L'Assemblée éclate en applaudissements. J'applaudis moi-même. Le rêve va-t-il se réaliser? Le rêve d'Hugo... Le mien... Deux jours plus tard, je rentre à Paris plein de confiance. Et c'est à Paris, donc, que j'apprends la réponse de Begin : « Nous, les Israéliens, nous vous tendons la main... Faisons la paix... » Exaltation. Sérénité. Bonheur. Et puis, tout de même, cet imperceptible regret : là, sur mon écran de télévision, à l'aéroport de Lod Ben Gourion, surimprimés aux visages de Begin, Dayan, Golda Meïr, Perès, Rabine, Sadate, Mohamed Hassan el-Toukhami, tous debout devant le Boeing blanc du Président égyptien, les visages familiers de Hugo, Sidney, Mordekhaï, mon père, qui n'apparaîtront plus, eux, que dans les pages de mon livre.

344

Mon livre, donc. Cette étrange entreprise menée depuis *La Mémoire d'Abraham* et poursuivie ici. Dans la *Mémoire*, je disais toute la difficulté que j'avais à décrire des Juifs malhonnêtes, violents, injustes, intolérants. Non pas qu'ils n'existassent pas. Mais tant de livres leur avaient été déjà consacrés, les transformant en marques indélébiles, en caricatures dont chaque Juif est constamment menacé. N'empêche. J'ai essayé. J'ai compris, très vite, que l'on ne peut reconstituer l'histoire d'un troupeau en ignorant ses brebis galeuses. Ni vanter les mérites d'un antidote sans décrire le pouvoir des microbes. Au fond, la recherche familiale, la conception de cet arbre généalogique qui se dessine au fur et à mesure des pages, avec ses fourches, ses branches, ses ramures, avec son écorce et son feuillage, avec son essence, sa sève, sa résine, avec ses nœuds, ses frondaisons aussi et ses fruits éventuels et, même, avec ses rongeurs, ses chenilles et ses parasites de toutes sortes, qu'est-ce sinon la libération d'un certain nombre de fantasmes qui apparaissent dans le récit de multiples visages et que la littérature aide simplement à reconstituer et ordonner ? Et, de ce point de vue, ne pourrais-je pas dire que Mordekhaï, Olga, Sidney et même Sacha, c'est moi, encore moi, rien que moi ? Ce Sacha dont je désapprouve les actes, ne fait-il pas partie de ce moi dont j'ai honte mais qui demeure en moi ? Et Hugo ? Ce cousin lointain et anonyme, projeté, malgré lui, dans ce panthéon des figures dramatiques ? A quoi correspond ma recherche ? Pourquoi vouloir absolument élucider sa mort, retracer son itinéraire, donner de la chair aux simples noms figurant dans son carnet d'adresses ? Par fidélité au vœu de mon père ou par espoir d'arracher de son vivant, à travers lui, ma propre vie à l'oubli ? Tout — je veux dire toute ma vie, toute ma mémoire et, d'une certaine façon, tout ce livre — logeait, au fond, dans son carnet. Mon père l'avait dit, d'ailleurs : il *contenait* réellement toute notre histoire familiale de ces dernières années. Cette histoire, il fallait seulement la libérer de derrière les colonnes de noms et de numéros, comme la sculpture d'un bloc de granit !

Dans une entreprise — un *livre* — de cette nature, l'auteur est finalement dans la situation d'un projectionniste qui ferait passer deux films à la fois : celui des événements qui ont marqué l'Histoire et celui des destins, des aventures individuelles. Parfois les deux se superposent : Arié et la guerre du Kippour ou Sidney et le détournement des avions vers Zarka... Parfois, ils se projettent sur deux écrans indépendants, sans que l'un modifie l'autre : l'octroi du prix Nobel de la Paix à Andreï Sakharov n'avait pas influé sur la vie de Sacha, ni la mort de Ben Gourion sur la vie d'Arié, ni la démission de Nixon sur celle du fils de Sidney. Le pouvoir du projectionniste réside dans la possibilité de ralentir le film, de l'accélérer au contraire ou, simplement, d'en arrêter un des deux. Comment fait-il ? En fonction de quels critères se décide-t-il ? Je me demande si, au fond, ce n'est pas un *troisième* film qui décide : celui de l'auteur et de son autobiographie.

C'est ici qu'il faut que je parle d'un événement survenu à cette époque et qui ne fut pas, c'est le moins que l'on puisse dire ! sans influence et sur ma vie et sur le cours du récit : la mort de ma mère. Je ne sais quel sentiment d'urgence me fit arriver chez elle, ce matin-là, bien plus tôt que nous n'en étions convenus. La veille au soir, elle était pâle... Ses mains tremblaient bizarrement. Un médecin avait ordonné des analyses et je devais l'accompagner au laboratoire.

Je sonnai sans obtenir de réponse, sonnai à nouveau, frappai. Rien. Si : au bout d'un moment, un soupir — très faible, très lointain que je ne fus même pas sûr d'avoir distinctement entendu. Je me penchai alors. Regardai par le trou de la serrure. Et vis ma mère, à terre, s'efforçant d'arriver jusqu'à la porte. Je frappai à nouveau, éperdu de douleur et de peur. Je frappai bêtement. Sans raison. Seulement pour lui dire que j'étais là, que c'était moi, qu'il ne fallait pas s'inquiéter, que j'étais tout près d'elle. Elle gémissait de plus en plus fort, tentait elle aussi d'appeler, peut-être même de me répondre, de me rassurer à son tour. Mais elle ne pouvait décidément pas se hisser jusqu'à la hauteur de la poignée. Des ouvriers turcs, qui travaillaient dans l'immeuble, vinrent à la rescousse. Nous essayâmes ensemble mais en vain, de défoncer la porte. Et l'affolement gagnant, la terreur aussi, un ignoble, insupportable sentiment d'impuissance m'envahit. Une voisine suggéra d'appeler les pompiers qui arrivèrent cinq minutes plus tard et, passant par la fenêtre, déposèrent ma mère sur son lit et nous ouvrirent la porte.

La mort était là. Je la reconnus tout de suite. Elle avait l'odeur de mon enfance, sous les bombes de Varsovie. Ou celle, exactement la même, que j'avais humée, quelques années plus tôt, dans la pièce où était couché mon père. Ma mère ne remuait plus. Elle gémissait à peine. Elle était entrée dans une sorte de coma. A la clinique où je la fis transporter le diagnostic fut quasi immédiat : hémorragie interne, cirrhose hépatique, vraisemblablement due à une jaunisse mal ou pas soignée durant la guerre. Trois mois... Trois mois d'angoisse... Trois mois d'espoir... Et, au bout de ces trois mois, la mort enfin... J'étais désormais orphelin. Entre la mort et moi, il n'y avait plus rien, personne, aucune barrière. J'étais comme un réserviste arrivant d'un coup en première ligne. Cette impression, tout le monde l'a ressentie ou la ressentira un jour. Mon cas, cependant, était plus complexe. En perdant ma mère, je perdais aussi le dernier maillon de la chaîne familiale, le dernier témoin d'un monde qui n'était plus et d'une langue qui se mourait ; ma langue maternelle, le yiddish. J'étais deux fois orphelin : de mes parents, de ma mémoire.

Mon héritage : quelques souvenirs personnels ; un album de photos, jaunies par le temps ; des poèmes de ma mère ; la reproduction de la première page de la Bible, publiée par mes ancêtres voici cinq siècles en Italie, à Soncino ; le carton des documents recueillis par mon père ; et puis le carnet de Hugo. C'était beaucoup et c'était peu : juste assez pour oublier et pour commencer la difficile reconquête de la mémoire. J'ai choisi la seconde voie et me suis lancé de plus belle dans cette rude entreprise. Ce fut le début de six années de travail, de recherche, de doute et de joie à la vue de ces milliers de signes, surgis sur le papier, *La Mémoire d'Abraham*. Et puis ces quatre autres années occupées à retrouver la trace des Lerner, d'Arié et de Judith, des Halter des États-Unis, d'Olga, de dona Regina et d'Anna-Maria, mes semblables, mes cousins et les héros, donc, de *Les Fils d'Abraham*.

40

BUENOS AIRES

ANNA-MARIA :
LE RETOUR AUX SOURCES

Février 1978

Peron est mort. La junte militaire a pris le pouvoir. La répression en Argentine s'est faite plus violente, plus brutale. Et la direction des Montoneros, pourchassée par la police et par l'armée, en est réduite à changer continuellement de lieu de résidence et de centre. Tantôt ils sont dans la pampa littorale d'Entre Rios, entre le Brésil et le Paraguay. Tantôt dans la Cordillère des Andes, à proximité de la frontière bolivienne. Tantôt encore ailleurs, plus loin, plus discrets et secrets — même si les tueurs d'AAA, l'Alliance Anticommuniste Argentine, restent constamment à leurs trousses.

Anna-Maria est, comme ses camarades, devenue d'une prudence extrême. Cheveux roux. Larges robes créoles. Parfois, elle met des lunettes soi-disant correctrices qui la rendent méconnaissable. Et la voici un matin, chaud et humide, de ce mois de février 1978, en compagnie de Mario, à la Plata, à plus de cent kilomètres de la capitale, venant déposer un paquet de tracts chez le père Mendoza, un jeune prêtre généreux, hostile aux militaires. La proximité de Buenos Aires lui a donné une brusque envie de revoir la ville, de se promener avenue Corrientes, de sentir le moisi du Rio de la Plata et, *last but not least,* de réentendre, une fois au moins, l'accent rocailleux de dona Regina... La dissuader ? Mario, sachant qu'il n'y réussira pas, décide de l'accompagner. Ils ont pris l'autobus. Ils sont restés près d'une heure dans l'une de ces grosses carcasses abîmées, bosselées, mais tout entières bigarrées, peinturlurées, surchargées de festons, de volutes et de fioritures qui ne respectent aucun code de la route et que les militaires, du coup, hésitent à contrôler. Et ils se sont arrêtés, enfin, à trois blocs de l'avenue San-Martin. Il est midi. Le soleil est haut et chaud. Dans cette partie de l'avenue pratiquement déserte, sans voitures, on vit volontiers la fenêtre ouverte. Et, de la maison voisine de celle de dona Regina, coule la voix de Suzanna Rinaldi :

> *« Viens*
> *Assieds-toi près de moi*
> *Les hommes étouffent*
> *Dans cette folie, mon frère*
> *Faut-il se taire ? »*

— C'est ici ? fait Mario, d'un air de conspirateur.

— Hum ! fait Anna-Maria en posant un doigt sur ses lèvres comme si le moindre bruit pouvait les compromettre.

C'est ici, oui. La maison n'a pas changé. La porte, comme autrefois, n'est pas fermée à clef. Trois ans ont passé. Et pourtant rien n'a bougé. Sauf peut-être ce silence... Cette tristesse diffuse... Cette pénombre inhabituelle dans le salon où, d'emblée, elle remarque un corps allongé sur le canapé.

— Grand-mère... dit-elle doucement.

La grand-mère ouvre les yeux. Les referme comme si elle se rendormait. Les ouvre à nouveau. Elle regarde les intrus d'un air à la fois incrédule et niais. Et puis, sans crier gare, comme si elles s'étaient quittées la veille, elle se relève d'un coup, s'écrie :

— Mais c'est ma petite-fille !

Et, sans poser de question, sans s'en étonner plus que cela, elle embrasse Anna-Maria, serre la main de Mario et met aussitôt la table.

— C'est ma petite-fille, répète-t-elle... C'est ma petite-fille. Vois-tu, je m'occupe... Je fais un peu de ménage... Je prépare à manger pour le cas où l'un d'entre vous viendrait déjeuner à l'improviste... Ce matin, j'ai préparé de la carpe farcie... Tu aimes toujours la carpe farcie, n'est-ce pas ? Je t'attendais... Cela fait si longtemps que je t'attends...

— Et don Israël ?

— Don Israël ? Lui, je ne l'attends plus...

— Comment cela ?

— Voyons ! Tu ne sais pas ! Ton grand-père est mort, ma petite-fille... Oh ! Oui, il est bien mort...

Et, après avoir posé les assiettes, les couverts et le plat sur la table, elle s'assied à son tour, fixe les jeunes gens de ses yeux ronds qui brillent étrangement dans l'obscurité et poursuit d'une voix lasse :

— Il est resté alité pendant presque deux ans. Il mourait, il mourait et il n'arrivait pas à mourir. Deux ans, ma petite fille... Sais-tu ce que c'est deux ans ? Car tu te souviens de don Israël, n'est-ce pas ? Toujours en mouvement, gai, nerveux, incapable de tenir en place... Il m'en faisait voir de toutes les couleurs mais je l'aimais bien... Ah ! si tu l'avais vu, au fond de son lit ! Tout silencieux, tout paralysé ! Plus un mot, plus un geste, rien. Il ne lui restait plus que son regard. Pendant ces deux ans, il a fallu que je l'essuie, que je le lave, que je le fasse manger, que je lui mette des suppositoires... Tu ne peux pas savoir... Pendant deux ans, je lui ai lu le journal... Pendant deux ans, je ne savais même pas s'il m'entendait... Don Israël, tu te rends compte !... Parfois, il me semblait qu'il avait pitié, qu'il me suppliait de l'aider à mourir. Mais comment aurais-je pu ? Tu as connu le vieux docteur Longer ? Il était très gentil. Au début, il venait souvent. Pas pour don Israël : il n'y avait plus rien à faire pour lui ; mais pour me tenir un peu compagnie. Je lui préparais du thé au citron et des petits gâteaux, ceux que tu préfères. Nous parlions de tout et de rien. Et il repartait en hochant la tête : « Vous avez beaucoup de courage, dona Regina. » Une fois, je dormais sur une chaise... Car pendant tout ce temps-là j'ai dormi là, sur cette chaise... Une fois donc, je me réveille en sursaut, il me semble que don Israël m'appelle… Il me semble qu'il me demande quelque chose… Enfin, je prends tous les somnifères qui restent, je les mets dans une enveloppe, je les écrase avec un marteau, je mélange la poudre dans de l'eau avec du sucre, mais quand je me suis approchée de lui avec le verre, il dormait. Je n'ai pas eu le courage de le réveiller pour l'aider à mourir… Enfin… Deux années horribles !

Un matin, avant d'ouvrir les yeux, j'ai su. Je me sentais libérée. C'est vrai : il s'était éteint pendant que je dormais et je me sentais libérée… Maintenant, je suis seule et c'est triste. Avant, j'aimais bien être seule de temps en temps. Mais aujourd'hui, je n'ai plus que cette solitude. Pas de projets. Pas de maintenant. Et même, je commence à perdre des souvenirs. Tu sais, j'ai retrouvé une photo du mariage de Martin, ton père. Je te la chercherai. Tu ne l'as pas vu depuis longtemps, ton père, hein ? Il se fait du mauvais sang à ton sujet. Il a beaucoup changé, tu verras. Il ressemble de plus en plus à mon père, ton arrière-grand-père, Abraham, l'imprimeur. Je me rappelle encore l'odeur de l'encre qu'il rapportait à la maison. Mon père m'avait écrit la première semaine de l'occupation de Varsovie. J'avais répondu une longue lettre. J'avais aussi envoyé un paquet. La lettre est revenue trois ans plus tard, pas le paquet. Tu veux voir l'enveloppe ? Regarde : le nom et l'adresse sont exacts, Abraham Halter, rue Nowolipje, 51, Varsovie, Pologne, et ils ont marqué « Inconnu » ! C'est le dernier souvenir que j'ai de mon père. Inconnu ! Le poisson t'a plu ? Et à ton ami aussi ? Bien, alors j'apporte du thé et des petits gâteaux ?

Quand elle revient de la cuisine, elle reprend :

— Et tes parents… Il faut que je te raconte tes parents… Ne va surtout pas les voir. Ce serait dangereux pour toi et pour eux. Les militaires sont partout… Sais-tu qu'ils viennent d'enlever deux religieuses françaises… Mais, au fond, je ne sais pas pourquoi je te parle de ça. Chacun a son petit paquet de misère et plus on vieillit, plus il est gros. C'est peut-être pour ça que les vieux marchent courbés ? Tu sais, toute mort est terrible. Encore si on pouvait la préparer, comme on prépare un bon repas. Mais c'est toujours une surprise. Elle n'arrive jamais quand on l'attend. Qui aurait dit que don Israël, vif comme il était, une vraie truite dans une rivière, allait pourrir pendant deux ans ? Et pourtant, tu vois, je suis vieille, je suis seule et si je mourais personne ne pleurerait bien longtemps. Mais voilà : je n'ai pas envie de mourir. Mon frère Salomon est mort, mon frère David est mort, le cousin Sidney a été tué, comme le cousin Hugo. Le cousin Mordekhaï a péri, lui, pendant la guerre... Tu sais, Mordekhaï, le kibboutznik, le père d'Arié... Je suis la dernière à me souvenir.

Et, après un nouveau silence :

— C'est quand même gentil d'être venue me voir. Maintenant, file. Et même si tu ne te souviens pas, tu dois vivre.

Elle se tait cette fois vraiment, comme un disque arrivé au bout de son dernier sillon. En quittant l'avenue San-Martin, Anna-Maria ne peut réprimer ni son chagrin ni ses larmes.

Réunion extraordinaire, une semaine plus tard, à Cordoba, dans une maison délabrée, qui a appartenu à un curé « disparu » et qui est noyée parmi les cabanes misérables des sans-travail. Une grande salle nue, aux fauteuils éventrés et aux lustres baroques des années vingt. Un énorme Christ en bois taillé à la hache par les Indiens des Andes, qui domine l'ensemble. Des murs craquelés qui, dans la lumière jaunâtre du lustre, laissent deviner un blanchissement récent. Une soixantaine de personnes sont déjà là quand arrivent Mario et Anna-Maria. Et parmi elles, en faction devant la porte, les deux gardes du corps de Julio, Manuel et Halcon. Ce sont deux hommes entre deux âges, au physique de gorille. Deux « spécialistes » de l'action militaire qui raconteront tout à l'heure comment ils se sont procuré des pistolets, non à balles, mais à dards qui, utilisés avec une forte dose de poison, permettent de liquider en douceur les tortionnaires. Et rien qu'à les voir, à les entendre, on comprendrait que l'organisation n'est plus ce qu'elle était et qu'avec la clandestinité, la radicalité, voire le professionnalisme, c'est toute la ferveur joyeuse des premières années qui s'est perdue en cours de route.

Julio commence par expliquer la raison de cette réunion extraordinaire. Il parle avec la hâte d'un prédicateur auquel l'on n'aurait accordé qu'un temps limité pour prononcer son sermon. « Dans quelques mois, explique-t-il, ce sera le *Mundial,* la Coupe du monde de Football. Des journalistes du monde entier viendront à Buenos Aires et les Argentins, comme vous savez, aiment le football. Alors, pouce ! personne ne nous suivra sur le chemin de la violence ! Nous allons donc proposer une trêve et montrer que les Montoneros aiment aussi le football...

— Que le diable m'emporte, chuchote Roberto à l'oreille d'Anna-Maria. C'est un bien curieux langage : la révolution mise hors jeu par le ballon rond...

Juanita, dont le visage, toujours aussi blême, s'est creusé avec les années, fait observer qu'une campagne de boycott a été lancée à l'étranger par des amis de la démocratie argentine et qu'il ne faut peut-être pas contrecarrer leur action de réprobation.

Julio fait un geste d'impatience :

— Je sais, oui... Le cousin d'Anna-Maria... C'est lui et ses amis qui, à Paris, ont eu cette satanée idée... Mais je ne marche pas... Nous ne sommes d'accord sur rien... N'a-t-il pas écrit que nous sommes devenus de petits chefs militaires... ?

Ricanements dans l'assistance. Il poursuit :

— Il est pour la parole et contre l'action. Certains de nos camarades ici présents savent ce que la parole coûte aujourd'hui, dans ce pays.

Puis après les avoir tous regardés un à un :

— Alors, tout le monde est pour la trêve ?

Outre les membres de la direction, il y a là une foule de militants de base — ceux qu'Anna-Maria ne connaît pas — qui ne peuvent se payer le luxe ni de discuter ni de penser. La motion est donc approuvée à l'unanimité.

Julio parlera encore une bonne heure. Mais Anna-Maria ne l'écoute plus. Cette réunion lui paraît superflue. Elle sait que les vraies décisions ont été déjà prises depuis longtemps. Et que les cadres réunis ici ne sont chargés que de les entériner. Ni débat ni contestation. Elle demande l'heure à Mario. Il est presque minuit. Voyant un fauteuil vide, à la gauche de Julio, elle s'y laisse tomber et décide de suivre de là le reste des discussions. Quels drôles de gens ! se dit-elle. Quelle singulière équipe, vraiment ! Il y a de tout, dans cette salle. Les chefs historiques comme Julio, puis Mario, Roberto, Juanita. Un noyau de jeunes conspirateurs, appartenant à la génération suivante et formés sur le tas à l'école de la guérilla. Quelques vieux péronistes. Des intellectuels épris de justice. Des syndicalistes. Quelques paumés. Et aussi quelques cadres dépêchés de Cuba... Elle en est à s'interroger sur le mystérieux ciment qui parvient à souder des hommes aussi dissemblables quand la porte s'ouvre. Elle se lève pour mieux voir : c'est Carlos, le tout-puissant et redouté secrétaire général de l'organisation, qui rentre du Mexique et qui, avec sa haute taille, un peu voûtée, ses gestes lents, sa voix métallique, sa manière distante de saluer, ses ordres brefs, transforme instantanément l'atmosphère jusque-là chaleureuse qui régnait dans la salle. Il parle du Mundial. Reprend la proposition de trêve de Julio. Il évoque aussi les « *compañeros* palestiniens », « notre idéal commun », les « armes qu'ils nous envoient », « tout ce que le Mouvement leur doit »... La routine, quoi ! La rengaine ! Juste ce qu'il faut pour bercer une Anna-Maria épuisée par les mille kilomètres qu'elle a dû faire en autobus pour assister à la réunion. Elle commence à s'assoupir quand, brusquement, elle entend prononcer deux noms qui lui sont familiers : Nehemia Mozenblum et Mikhael Sander... Tiens !... Pourquoi Carlos parle-t-il du président de la DAIA, la Délégation des associations israélites d'Argentine ? Et pourquoi de ce gentil rabbin qui dirige le séminaire rabbinique latino-américain de Buenos Aires ?

— De quoi parlent-ils ? demande-t-elle à une grosse fille assise sur le rebord du fauteuil...

— De deux inconnus... Deux types à éliminer pour

que la logistique de la cellule révolutionnaire fonctionne à nouveau.

La fille a répondu comme un robot, mécaniquement. Sans réfléchir. Sans émotion visible non plus. Anna-Maria connaît ce langage. Elle ne l'a que trop pratiqué elle-même. Mais quelque chose fait que là, tout à coup, cela ne passe plus. Est-ce ce mot « deux inconnus », qui lui rappelle le mot « inconnu » qu'avaient utilisé les nazis pour parler de l'arrière-grand-père Abraham et qui lui trotte dans la tête depuis sa visite chez dona Regina ? Est-ce la présence de ce Christ étrange, revu par les Indiens des Andes ? Toujours est-il que, pour la première fois dans ce type d'assemblée, elle sent une sourde révolte qui monte en elle, une folle envie de protester :

— Attends ! Attends ! s'exclame-t-elle.

Toutes les têtes se tournent vers elle.

— Si je t'ai bien compris, nous allons proposer aux militaires une trêve et déclarer aux Juifs la guerre !

Carlos baisse légèrement la tête et écarte les jambes à la façon d'un boxeur qui encaisse et va riposter :

— Je pensais que, chez nous, l'intérêt général passait avant nos attaches tribales.

— Attaches tribales ? demande Anna-Maria dont le visage est devenu livide.

Elle fait un pas vers Carlos :

— Mais tu es cinglé !... Complètement cinglé... Ce sont donc des attaches tribales qui me font dire que tuer des Juifs parce que Juifs est un acte antisémite ?

Carlos se redresse. Visiblement, il a peine lui aussi à rester calme :

— Je crois que tu ferais bien de te taire, dit-il doucement.

Puis, martelant bien ses mots :

— Nous devons une aide aux Palestiniens, c'est clair. S'ils nous demandent d'exécuter deux hommes à la solde des Yankees, nous le ferons. Nous l'aurions fait, même s'ils étaient musulmans.

Et, en s'adressant à la salle :

— La décision est prise. Il nous reste à prendre les

ultimes dispositions : choisir des armes qui n'ont pas encore servi et dont la police n'a pas de trace, trouver deux voitures, etc.

— Bravo ! fait Anna-Maria en s'approchant de lui... Oui, bravo ! répète-t-elle.

Et, en levant le poing droit :

— Vive Marx ! Vive Lénine ! Vive Staline ! Vive le Che !

Et comme les visages de ses compagnons marquent le plus parfait étonnement :

— Vous pensez que je suis folle, hein ? Les Palestiniens nous demandent de tuer des Juifs... Nous le ferons. Demain les Soviétiques nous demanderont de tuer des Chinois : nous le ferons. Après-demain, les Chinois nous demanderont de tuer les Vietnamiens : nous le ferons encore...

Sa voix se fait plus rauque :

— Et puis vous verrez ! On ne va pas en rester là ! On va prêter main-forte aux Khmers rouges pour massacrer leur peuple. Aux Syriens pour liquider les gens d'El-Fath. Aux services de l'OLP, pour nos amis du Front Populaire...

— Assez ! coupe Julio.

— Je t'en prie, supplie Mario... Je t'en prie...

Mais leurs mots, leurs abjurations ne font que la rendre plus furieuse encore. Et, toujours face à Carlos, à quelques millimètres de son visage, elle lui souffle d'une voix où ne reste plus que la haine la plus totale :

— Quand tout ça sera fini, camarade, il restera encore Anna-Maria... Ou plutôt non : je te connais et tel que je te connais, ça pourrait bien être par moi que tu commences. C'est vrai, camarade, tu vas me liquider aussi ! Trois Juifs c'est toujours mieux que deux, tu ne trouves pas ?

L'aube s'est levée maintenant. Elle est enveloppée de brouillard, mais enfin elle s'est levée. Et Anna-Maria, Mario et Roberto roulent à grande vitesse vers Buenos Aires.

357

— Tu n'aurais pas dû... dit Mario. Tu savais que ton intervention ne pourrait que heurter Carlos, l'enfermer dans sa décision. Et puis, et puis...

Il fait fonctionner les essuie-glaces comme pour chasser la rosée du matin ou, qui sait ? une idée noire. Et, d'une voix plus sourde, il continue :

— Maintenant, tu es en danger...

Anna-Maria ne répond rien.

— Que le diable m'emporte ! ponctue Roberto. Mario a raison...

Et tournant sa bonne tête ronde vers la jeune fille :

— Tu ne t'en rends pas compte ?

Anna-Maria ne répond toujours pas. On dirait qu'après avoir tant parlé, il ne lui reste plus de mots pour se défendre ou se sauver. C'est seulement à l'arrivée à Buenos Aires qu'elle dira d'une voix neutre :

— Vous me laisserez chez ma grand-mère, s'il vous plaît.

41

BUENOS AIRES

ANNA-MARIA :
LE RETOUR AUX SOURCES (2)

Février 1978

Quand arrive Anna-Maria, dona Regina ne dort pas. On croirait même qu'elle ne s'est pas couchée, qu'elle attendait sa petite-fille. Et ce matin-là, dans la lumière du jour qui se lève, on lit mieux que jamais sur son visage les marques des dernières épreuves. C'est une peau tannée, ravinée. C'est un visage ratatiné qui n'a plus gardé de son passé qu'un regard à la fois agressif et bon, dur et amusé, sous une frange de cheveux complètement blanchis.

— Tu arrives bien, dit-elle, comme si, vraiment, elle l'attendait. J'ai préparé le thé et les petits gâteaux. Après les avoir goûtés, tu pourras te reposer... Dans la chambre de Miguel, au-dessus de la cordonnerie de don Israël, tu te souviens ?

Et comme si elle poursuivait on ne sait quel monologue intérieur :

— J'ai tout gardé comme c'était... Je n'ai rien changé... Tant qu'on peut... Tant qu'ils nous laissent tranquilles...

— Qui ça, « ils » ?

— Les hommes, la mort...

La chambre de Miguel n'a pas changé, en effet. Une table, deux chaises en bois, un lit couvert d'une lourde couverture à carreaux. Et sur le mur, la reproduction des Soleils de Van Gogh, maintenue par quatre punaises que l'humidité commence à rouiller. Anna-Maria s'allonge sur le lit. Elle sent une légère odeur de poussière. Et, défaite par la fatigue, s'effondre. Combien de temps dort-elle ? Quand elle s'éveille, il fait déjà nuit. Elle descend dans la salle à manger. Et dona Regina, en la voyant, se précipite à nouveau dans la cuisine :

— Pauvre fille, maintenant tu dois avoir faim... En attendant que je te réchauffe le dîner, regarde les photos que je t'ai préparées. Elles sont sur la table. Celui à la barbe blanche, c'est mon père, Abraham. Juste à côté, ce sont les photos de Salomon, d'Hugo, de Mordekhaï... Le petit garçon, c'est Sidney... Son père m'a envoyé cette photo il y a plus de trente ans, de Winnipeg... Regarde aussi la grande, couleur sépia... Tu y verras au moins une cinquantaine de personnes... Les Halter... Enfin : les Halter déportés. Aucun n'a survécu. Que veux-tu, ce n'est pas facile d'être juif...

Et toujours sans poser de questions, sans songer à se demander le pourquoi, le comment, de cette visite elle sert en effet son dîner en poursuivant son monologue.

Au dessert, Anna-Maria demande un bloc de papier, un stylo et remonte dans sa chambre. Elle allume la lampe sans abat-jour, posée sur la table, essuie d'un revers de la main la poussière qui s'est accumulée avec les années. Et, d'un trait, sans réfléchir ni se reprendre, couche sur le papier une longue, très longue lettre dont elle s'avise, en l'écrivant, qu'elle était déjà, depuis un temps infini, toute composée dans sa tête. Cette lettre s'adresse au directeur du quotidien *Clarin*. Elle est naïve, parfois chaotique, comme est, cette nuit-là, l'esprit de son auteur. En voici l'essentiel :

« Une lettre d'une " terroriste " à un journal populaire, ce n'est pas tout à fait habituel. Mais nous ne vivons malheureusement pas dans un pays habituel. L'État de droit a laissé place à un champ de bataille moyenâgeux. Chaque maître a sa troupe, sa prison, ses tortionnaires et sa justice. Comment croyez-vous que des jeunes qui rêvent, comme moi, d'une société démocratique, puissent y survivre ? En se taisant, en s'exilant ou en prenant un revolver. Le mien, le 9 mm

TO Kagypt, vous le trouverez joint à cette lettre. Je m'imagine que vous ne recevez pas souvent ce genre de paquet, mais je vous le dis : à une société inhabituelle correspondent des méthodes inhabituelles.

« On m'accusera de tous les crimes. Le seul que je reconnaisse, c'est d'avoir été présente quand, au mois de mars 1972, un officier de police a été blessé sur la route de Tres Lomos. Encore que j'aie appris depuis, que le drôle s'en est tiré — ce dont, croyez-le bien, je me félicite de tout mon cœur. Quant à l'exécution du tortionnaire Miguel Pelado, il méritait ce châtiment. Le nombre d'innocents qu'il a torturés ou fait mourir dans des souffrances atroces le met dans la catégorie des criminels contre l'humanité. Eichman avait trouvé un État pour le juger. Pelado, malheureusement, n'a trouvé que quelques jeunes justiciers.

« Je puis pourtant vous assurer que je n'ai jamais ressenti une quelconque fierté à posséder de revolver. Au contraire. Unamuno, Emerson, Joyce me sont, sinon plus proches, du moins plus chers. Mais peut-on se réfugier dans les livres quand des hommes et des femmes, parmi les meilleurs, se font enlever ? Quand on retrouve ensuite leurs corps dans le Rio de la Plata ? Si j'avais eu l'âge de combattre dans un pays d'Europe occupé par les nazis, je me serais engagée dans la Résistance. Ayant l'âge de combattre dans un pays occupé par son fascisme intérieur, je n'aurais eu aucun respect de moi-même si je ne m'étais, avec lui, engagée dans une lutte à mort.

« Mais ce qui m'amène aujourd'hui à vous écrire, c'est la volonté de sauver deux vies. Et si je n'adresse pas cette missive à la police, c'est que je n'ai aucune confiance dans une police dont le travail consiste moins à protéger les citoyens qu'à les faire taire ou disparaître. Je sais que cette lettre, une fois connue, ne me mettra pas à l'abri ni de sa vindicte ni de celle de mes anciens amis. Mais mes amis ont failli à l'idéal de la justice. Et je ne me reconnais plus grand-chose de commun avec eux. Je ne veux pas d'une politique du crime. Je hais l'idée d'une stratégie du meurtre. Cette stratégie, elle vient de commettre, à mes yeux en tout cas, son premier vrai faux pas : celui qui la fait verser dans l'antisémitisme pur et simple.

« Petite-fille d'une femme qui s'est réfugiée en Argentine pour échapper à l'antisémitisme polonais, arrière-petite-fille d'Abraham, imprimeur à Varsovie qui, le premier jour de la révolte du ghetto, s'est jeté avec une grenade sur un char allemand pour tenter d'opposer à la barbarie triomphante la simple force de son refus, je ne peux décemment permettre l'assassinat de deux représentants de la communauté juive simplement parce qu'ils sont juifs.

« Les deux hommes qui doivent être assassinés sont Nehemia Rozenblum, le président de la DAIA et le rabbin Michael Sander, directeur du séminaire rabbinique latino-américain à Buenos Aires. Ils doivent être abattus très prochainement. Les préparatifs sont avancés. Il faut tout faire, vous m'entendez, tout pour empêcher que ce projet ne vienne à terme. Je sais qu'en écrivant cela je me condamne et que mes anciens amis me considéreront comme traître. Je n'y peux rien. Je ne trahis personne puisque je reste fidèle au contraire à ce qu'il y a de plus sacré en moi ; leur démence contre ma mémoire. Je n'ai pas eu à beaucoup chercher pour trouver où étaient mon choix, ma fidélité, ma vérité.

« Je précise, afin que les choses soient bien claires, que je suis jeune encore et que j'ai une furieuse envie de vivre. Mais j'ai toujours mis au-dessus de tout la notion de justice. J'ai rêvé de la justice pour tous et de tous pour la justice. Je ne peux renier ce rêve. Et quel que soit le prix à payer pour cela, je suis prête à le payer. »

Écrire tout cela l'a épuisée. Il lui a fallu peser chaque mot, écouter chaque syllabe au plus secret d'elle-même. Il lui a fallu se représenter tous les risques qu'elle prenait, la voie où elle s'engageait, l'issue prévisible de tout ça. Harassée, nauséeuse, elle pose ses avant-bras sur la table, y blottit sa tête et s'assoupit. Au réveil, elle relit la lettre qu'elle ne trouve ni assez claire ni assez persuasive. Mais elle n'a pas le courage de recommencer — et la poste.

Publiée deux jours plus tard, dans *Clarin,* elle fera bien entendu sensation. Largement commentée en Argentine, reproduite dans la presse mondiale, elle aura pour premier effet que la police, l'armée, les tueurs de l'AAA se mettent à la recherche de son auteur. On interroge ses parents. On inquiète dona Regina. On moleste tel ou tel de ses amis. Mais à quelques mois du Mundial, le pouvoir n'ose pas provoquer trop ouvertement l'opinion. Et Anna-Maria reste introuvable.

Un mois plus tard, Mario se présentera chez dona Regina. Il désire savoir si elle a des nouvelles de sa petite-fille. Méfiante, la vieille dona lui répond qu'elle n'en a pas.

— Alors, si elle vous téléphone, bredouille-t-il, découragez-la de venir ici. Dites-lui aussi de ne visiter aucun *compañero*. Il la dénoncerait. Ils ont tous reçu l'ordre...

Mario relève d'un geste embarrassé les cheveux qui lui cachent la vue et ajoute plus doucement, d'un ton hésitant :

— Dites-lui aussi... Dites-lui que sa lettre était belle... Dites-lui aussi... Dites-lui...

Dona Regina l'interrompt :

— Je lui dirai... Je lui dirai... Ne t'en fais pas — elle comprendra.

42

ISRAËL

UN MARIAGE AU KIBBOUTZ

Juillet 1979

Cette année-là, l'été fut particulièrement chaud. Le khamsin n'en finissait pas de souffler et les enfants du kibboutz couraient pieds nus sur les pelouses desséchées, pourtant arrosées en permanence par les mouvements circulaires des jets d'eau. Les adultes, employés dans les champs, les viviers, les étables et les ateliers, attendaient avec impatience le déclin du soleil et un souffle de vent frais venu du Hermon.

Un nouvel attentat, fin juin, à Kyriat Shemona, avait fait monter la tension à la frontière toute proche et la presse avait envisagé une possible action militaire contre les terroristes installés au Liban. Mais, à Dafné, on ne s'intéresse qu'au mariage du fils de Mordekhaï avec une juive yéménite. Dans le réfectoire, sous les énormes ventilateurs qui brassent l'air brûlant et les odeurs de cuisine, ce mariage fournit le fond de toutes les conversations. Une liaison entre un Ashkénaze et une Yéménite durera-t-elle ? Arié invitera-t-il son ancienne amie, l'infirmière Soshana ? Cette belle Judith, lui connaît-on d'autres aventures ? Etc. L'Assemblée générale du kibboutz a décidé, en souvenir de l'un de ses fondateurs disparu pendant la guerre du Kippour, de donner un vif éclat à ce jour du dimanche 14 juillet où le mariage doit être célébré. D'habitude, on en célèbre plusieurs à la fois, dans la même journée. Pour Arié, on décide de faire exception. Des invitations sont lancées par centaines aux kibboutzim de la région, aux familles et aux amis de la ville, aux dirigeants du mouvement kibboutzik, aux parents à l'étranger, aux Arabes de Ghajar, le village voisin. On demande même à Yossi, le coiffeur pour dames de Kyriat Shemona, de venir exceptionnellement au kibboutz le samedi matin. Et l'agitation est telle que, malgré son énergie intarissable, Shlomo, le mécanicien, responsable des activités culturelles, soirées dansantes et autres conférences, ne sait plus où donner de la tête. Il faut accorder le piano que les enfants ont détraqué, récupérer l'accordéon prêté pour une fête au Mochav Chear Yshuv, monter une estrade sur le gazon devant la Maison de la Culture, Briefer Haïka, autrement nommée la Pavlova à cause de son passé de danseuse, aider Jacob Oren, le secrétaire général, à préparer des discours qui ne soient pas trop pompeux. Sans parler de toutes ces chambres à préparer pour les membres de la famille dont on annonce l'arrivée : Judith, bien sûr — mais aussi son père, des cousins, Richard, Martin qui arrive de Buenos Aires, d'autres beaucoup d'autres... C'est le vendredi après-midi qu'arrive le héros de la fête. Sa mère a eu beau le prévenir au téléphone, il lui est difficile de croire que tout ce remueménage est pour lui. Dès le lever du soleil, le kibboutz s'affaire. Les portes claquent. Une horde d'enfants déferlent sur les pelouses. On essaie les instruments de musique, la sono. A l'exception d'une équipe réduite, nécessaire dans les étables, et d'une autre, plus nombreuse, qui a en charge la sécurité, tout le monde se prépare pour le mariage. Arié tente de se rendre utile. Il voudrait dresser les tables, installer le buffet. Il fait un tour jusqu'à l'estrade où Shlomo règne sur une dizaine de décorateurs amateurs. Mais nulle part, on ne veut de lui. « Le fiancé doit se réserver pour sa fiancée », lui dit-on. Moyennant quoi il ne réussit qu'à porter une caisse de jus d'orange du camion jusqu'à la cuisine. Arrive le rabbin Natanson de Kyriat Shemona. Le vieil homme est coiffé, malgré le soleil, d'un chapeau de feutre noir. Il interroge longuement Arié sur ses connaissances judaïques, inscrit, à l'aide d'un bout de crayon bleu, dans un calepin usé, le prénom de son père et de celui de Judith. Il s'assure qu'il a bien préparé les anneaux nuptiaux, relit soigneusement la « Kethouba » et prend note, dans son calepin toujours, des noms des deux témoins. Épuisé par tant d'efforts, il réclame un lieu pour se reposer avant la cérémonie. Arié le dirige vers la maison de ses parents. Sur le seuil, le rabbin s'arrête, lève son visage pâle et ses yeux humides vers Arié et demande d'une voix chevrotante :

— Jamais été à la synagogue, hein ?

Et, avant qu'Arié ne trouve une réponse, il ajoute :

— Bien sûr, il n'y a pas de synagogue, ici, au kibboutz, hein ? Tous des mécréants ? C'est bien de vouloir se marier selon la tradition de nos pères Abraham, Jacob et Isaac. Cela prouve que les cendres de l'oubli n'ont pas encore étouffé en toi l'étincelle juive...

Et, soudain rassurant :

— Tu seras béni. Tu le seras. Car depuis qu'il a créé le monde, l'Éternel ne célèbre que les mariages...

Un peu après 19 heures, les premiers invités commencent à arriver. Ils sont vite un millier. Les hommes portent des chemises blanches et des pantalons de toile noire ou bleue. Les femmes des robes de couleurs vives, plus coquettes les unes que les autres. On se montre du doigt les personnalités qui se sont déplacées : le général Dayan, qui a connu Mordekhaï pendant la guerre d'indépendance. Shimon Peres, secrétaire général du Parti travailliste, considérant probablement que le kibboutz Dafné appartient à sa mouvance politique. Plusieurs généraux. Quelques officiers haut placés. Quand le rabbin Natanson, juste avant qu'Arié ne remette l'alliance à Judith, prononce la prière : « Sois béni, Éternel, qui sanctifie Israël, Ton peuple, par le dais nuptial et la consécration du mariage », il y a quelques gloussements dans la foule tandis que Sarah, elle, éclate en sanglots. Mais la liesse reprend avec le spectacle qui suit et avec, surtout, les sketches particulièrement drôles qui dérident jusqu'à Benjamin Ben Eliezer. A la fin de la journée, les personnalités parties, Shlomo branchera la sono et le réfectoire se transformera en une piste de danse — la famille « restreinte » se réunissant autour d'une table, chargée de gâteaux et de boissons, pour pouvoir, enfin à l'aise, commenter cette belle journée.

— Te voilà marié, fait Aron Lerner en s'asseyant.

Puis, levant son verre au bonheur des nouveaux époux :

— Puissiez-vous vivre, chers Arié et Judith, dans un monde sans guerre !

Et, toujours intarissable :

> « *Viendra-t-elle, viendra-t-elle*
> *La dernière de ces années interminables*
> *Sans répit ramenant sur moi*
> *Douleurs et fureurs de la guerre... »*

Voyant le visage de sa mère se figer dans un douloureux souvenir, Arié l'arrête :

— Laissons la guerre et la paix et voyons ce qui se passe au pays du tango...

Il se tourne vers le cousin argentin qui paraît encore éprouvé par son long voyage mais qui grommelle tout de même quelques mots incompréhensibles, dans un mélange d'espagnol et de yiddish. Puis vers Richard qui est resté pendant toute la cérémonie enfermé dans un silence hostile et qui, enlevant brusquement sa redingote noire et son large chapeau bordé de fourrure qui, dans le kibboutz laïc, a fait sensation, vérifie d'une main si sa calotte est bien en place et lance dans un yiddish que le cousin argentin ne comprend qu'à demi :

— On ne fait pas la paix avec Amalek, on le combat.

Il se penche alors au-dessus de la table, débéboucle d'un geste rapide ses longues papillotes, les place derrière les oreilles et récite d'une voix chantante :

« Souviens-toi de ce que te fit Amalek pendant la route, lors de votre sortie d'Égypte... » « Lorsque l'Éternel, ton Dieu, après t'avoir délivré de tous les ennemis qui t'entourent, t'accordera du repos dans le pays que l'Éternel, ton Dieu, te donne en héritage et en propriété, tu effaceras la mémoire d'Amalek de sous les cieux : ne l'oublie point. »

Il regarde autour de lui et levant son index vers le ciel, répète :

« Ne l'oublie point… »

Sarah fait un geste d'impatience :

— Nous reparlerons de tout cela plus tard, dit-elle en souriant.

— Mais non, mais non… insiste Richard. Le professeur a bien parlé de paix ? Je voudrais bien savoir avec qui et sur quels territoires ? L'Éternel…

— Laissons l'Éternel en paix, propose Aron.

Judith, soucieuse de faire diversion, demande de son ton le plus « mondain » :

— Avez-vous des nouvelles de votre fille Olga ?

Aron repose son verre sur la table avant de la regarder et de lui répondre :

— Oui, dit-il, Olga a eu un fils…

— Mazel Tov ! fait Arié.

— Merci, dit Aron. J'ai reçu une lettre il y a environ deux semaines. Elle parle des voyages de Hidar, son mari. Il était allé, paraît-il, à nouveau au Proche-Orient, mais, cette fois-ci, à Bagdad. Olga espère pouvoir l'accompagner lors de sa prochaine visite à Beyrouth…

Arié tressaille :

— Tu ne m'as pas parlé de cette lettre !

Mais Richard lève déjà la main pour annoncer son intervention :

— Voilà où nous en sommes ! s'écrie-t-il. Les Juifs vont dans le pays d'Amalek…

— Hidar n'est pas juif, remarque Judith.

— Oui, mais votre cousine l'est !

Un tango retentit, longue plainte déchirante. Les couples sur la piste s'enlacent. Judith se lève, avec ce sourire un peu timide des jolies femmes qui ne sont pas absolument sûres de leur beauté. Au bruissement léger de sa robe blanche, ornée de mousse, dans tout l'éclat de ses épaules brunes et de ses cheveux noirs, elle contourne la table, sous le regard admiratif des hommes debout le long du mur et qui suivent le bal. Elle s'approche ainsi d'Arié qu'elle invite à danser :

— Tu n'aurais pas dû, lui reproche-t-il en la serrant dans ses bras. J'ai peur de les laisser seuls.

— Ils ne s'entre-tueront pas...

Judith rit et ajoute :

— Ce sont tous des Juifs...

— La guerre des Juifs, tu connais ?

Et après un moment de silence :

— Le cousin Martin semble préoccupé, tu ne crois pas ?

— Peut-être est-il jaloux... Tu as été l'amant de sa fille, n'est-ce pas ?

Judith se blottit contre lui. Mais il la repousse gentiment :

— Je suis tout de même inquiet, ils ont fait des milliers de kilomètres pour assister à notre mariage... Nous n'avons pas le droit de les laisser s'entre-déchirer...

— C'est *notre* mariage, proteste Judith en suivant à contrecœur Arié qui la traîne par la main.

A ce moment, Benjamin Ben Eliezer, qui a raccompagné le général Dayan à l'aéroport de Roch Pina, revient. Habituellement pâle, il a le teint vif aujourd'hui.

— C'est vous, Martin ? dit-il au cousin argentin. Vous êtes exactement tel qu'Arié vous a décrit. Comment va votre fille, Anna-Maria ?

Martin émet un soupir pesant :

— Vous avez certainement lu sa lettre à la presse ?

— Oui, les journaux israéliens en ont reproduit des extraits. Et où est-elle maintenant ?

Martin hausse tristement les épaules :

— Je n'en sais rien... Je ne l'ai pas vue depuis longtemps... La violence, les supplices, la torture, j'espère que tout cela se terminera bientôt...

Richard s'appuie à nouveau sur la table qui grince et pointe son doigt vers Martin :

— Ta fille, la terroriste, n'y est pas pour quelque chose, hein, dans toute cette violence ?

Martin fronce les sourcils :

— Que veux-tu dire ?

— C'est simple, répond Richard, Rabbi Hillel disait :
« Parce que tu as noyé, tu as été noyé, et ceux qui t'ont
noyé seront noyés à leur tour. »

Martin se redresse, les yeux remplis d'une expression
étrange :

— Tu compares Anna-Maria aux tortionnaires de la
junte militaire ? Les victimes aux bourreaux ? C'est
comme si tu comparais les combattants du ghetto de
Varsovie aux criminels nazis !

Richard prend une de ses papillotes entre ses doigts
potelés et cite à nouveau :

— Rabbi Ajabyà, fils de Mahalalel, disait : « Réflé-
chis et tu éviteras le péché. »

Le ton, plus que le contenu de sa phrase, irrite
Martin. Son visage se durcit. Il cherche visiblement une
réponse appropriée, quand Richard reprend, toujours
de la même voix chantante :

— Moi, je compare ? C'est toi qui compares. Moi, je
dis que les uns étaient des résistants et les autres des
terroristes. Et je dis que ces terroristes sont complices
des assassins de mon père !

Sa dernière phrase tombe avec une violence extrême.
Benjamin Ben Eliezer tousse. Aron Lerner fait remarquer qu'il commence à se faire tard et Sarah dit que
toute réjouissance a une fin. Arié fait signe à Judith et
ils se lèvent pour donner congé aux invités, quand,
soudain, Martin se dresse de toute sa taille et, enjoi-
gnant à tout le monde de rester assis :

— Ah ! C'est donc ainsi ! Tu accuses ma fille de la
mort de ton père ?

Richard, alors, se lève aussi. Son chapeau roule par
terre, il le ramasse, chasse d'un revers de main la
poussière qui le macule et se le remet sur la tête. Il
paraît, du coup, plus imposant :

— Je n'accuse pas ta fille, affirme-t-il. De quel droit
l'accuserais-je ? Rabbi Yosé ne disait-il pas : « N'accepte pas d'être juge unique, il n'est qu'un seul juge
unique : l'Éternel » ? Je dis seulement que tous ceux qui

aident les terroristes palestiniens sont responsables de la mort de mon père.

Mais Martin n'écoute pas :

— Ma fille vient de sauver la vie de deux personnes, de deux Juifs ! crie-t-il.

Et faisant, vers Richard, un geste de connivence :

— Je n'aime pas les religieux. Ils n'ont aucun discernement !

Richard enfile sa redingote et, menaçant, fait un pas vers Martin. Sarah s'interpose :

— Pour l'amour de l'Éternel !

C'est à ce moment que le flot de la musique dansante est interrompu par la *Hatikva*, l'hymne d'Isarël. Tout le monde se lève. La foule chante :

> « *Tant qu'au fond de nos cœurs*
> *Une âme juive vibrera*
> *Et en avant vers l'Orient*
> *Notre regard sur Sion est fixé....* »

Aron enchaîne :

> *Notre espoir n'est pas perdu*
> *Espoir de deux mille ans*
> *Être un peuple libre dans notre pays,*
> *Pays de Sion, Jérusalem...* »

Arié lui fait écho, puis Martin, puis Richard...

> « *Notre espoir n'est pas perdu*
> *Espoir de deux mille ans...* »

L'hymne achevé, Jacob Oren monte sur une chaise et lève son verre :

— Je lève le dernier verre à la vie ! Longue vie aux jeunes mariés, longue vie à tout le peuple d'Israël !

— Amen, murmure Richard.

— Amen, répète Martin.

Paris, juillet 1979

Le mariage d'Arié et de Judith m'avait mis de bonne humeur. J'avais été particulièrement heureux, notamment, de retrouver, à cette occasion, quelques membres de la famille. Comme mon père aurait été fier de les voir ainsi rassemblés! J'appréhendais pourtant ces retrouvailles familiales. Un même arbre ne peut-il porter des fruits sains et des fruits secs? N'étais-je pas dans la situation, terriblement risquée, d'un créateur craignant que ses personnages ne lui échappent et ne le déçoivent? Mais non! Ma famille était bel et bien conforme à l'image que je m'en étais faite. Elle était bien à l'image du peuple juif lui-même. Et il n'était pas jusqu'à l'empoignade entre Martin et Richard qui ne s'insérât parfaitement dans cette saga que je tentais, depuis des années, de mettre en scène. Toutes les tendances du judaïsme s'y affrontaient. Tous ses rameaux s'y retrouvaient. Et cela, oui, me rassurait.

Parallèlement à cela, la cause de la paix progressait. Sadate et Begin venaient de signer un traité à Washington. Ne fallait-il pas retourner à Beyrouth? Presser les Palestiniens de suivre leur exemple? Je revoyais Sidney et Hidar, Olga et Hugo, je revoyais Mordekhaï et Arié sur la terrasse d'un café, près de l'hôtel Basel à Tel-Aviv, et maintenant le mariage... Pour eux tous, en souvenir de Kanafani aussi, il fallait essayer. Continuer à lutter. Lutter : une tentation et une nostalgie pour les hommes de ma génération. Trop jeunes pour avoir fait la guerre contre les nazis... Trop vieux pour avoir eu l'enfance insouciante de mes amis de la génération suivante... Juste l'âge de la mauvaise conscience... L'inquiétude... Cette quête éperdue de justes causes, d'amour, de fraternité... Et puis ces angoisses et ces rêves, que j'ai tenté d'exorciser dans la reconquête d'une mémoire familiale, en même temps que dans la recherche d'une solution au conflit israélo-arabe... Deux aventures si proches... Si étrangement voisines et concurrentes. J'ai échoué dans la seconde. Je suis toujours dans la première. Rabbi Tarphône disait dans ce *Traité des Principes* que le cousin Richard aimait tant citer : « Tu n'es pas obligé d'achever l'œuvre mais tu n'es pas libre de t'en désintéresser. »

43

BEYROUTH

AVANT LE SIÈGE

Octobre 1981

Il y a eu l'enterrement de Waddi Haddad. Plusieurs centaines de milliers de personnes manifestèrent leur douleur au cours de funérailles grandioses organisées le 28 mai 1978 à Bagdad. Et c'est Arafat lui-même qui a insisté pour que ce soit lui, Hidar, qui accompagne Abou Iyad à la cérémonie. Image d'union et de réconciliation. Le petit peuple palestinien n'aurait pas compris que la discorde, le conflit ne désarment pas devant la mort. Haddad n'est plus : ses amis devaient tous, et ensemble, lui rendre hommage ; et l'unanimité qui ne s'est pas faite dans la vie et dans le combat c'est là, par les larmes, le pathos, la tristesse des visages, la récitation des sourates qu'il convenait de la retrouver.

Il y a eu, dans le même temps, la grande explication, les yeux dans les yeux, du Tunisien avec Olga. Serments... Promesses... Justifications... Mises en garde... Hidar connaît mieux que personne cette éternelle musique de l'âme et il en a merveilleusement interprété quelques-uns des grands classiques. Il a dit les raisons des détournements d'avion, vers Zarka, en 1970. Son rôle dans l'opération. Les conditions dans lesquelles Sidney a péri. Il s'est expliqué, surtout, sur cette affaire Leïla et a, comme il se doit, demandé humblement pardon pour cette faiblesse passagère et sans conséquence. Les deux époux, du coup, se sont juré un amour sans faille. Ni l'un ni l'autre ne se le serait avoué : mais l'épreuve, suivie de la mise au point, a eu le paradoxal effet de renforcer leurs liens. Ils ont parlé. Pleuré. Ils ont même conçu un enfant né huit mois plus tard, le 3 avril 1979 et que, en souvenir du père de Hidar, ils ont appelé Marwan.

La situation politique de Hidar ? Un bonheur ne venant jamais seul, le Tunisien a incontestablement tiré profit de la promotion de Tchebrikov, protégé d'Andropov, chargé de superviser les contacts avec les mouvements révolutionnaires à travers le monde, et qui l'a tout de suite choisi comme adjoint. Certes Hidar n'a jamais beaucoup aimé la vie de bureau, les réunions quotidiennes et les comptes rendus hebdomadaires. Il n'aime pas non plus ces rencontres désormais obligatoires avec Sacha Lerner, responsable de l'information au sein du Comité de solidarité avec les peuples d'Afrique et d'Asie. Et il ne peut s'empêcher de rencontrer chez le frère d'Olga une certaine fausseté naturelle, faite d'un mélange d'obséquiosité et d'arrogance qu'il a tendance à définir comme juive et qui lui fait profondément horreur. Mais enfin, à ces réserves près, il est heureux et n'est pas fâché d'interrompre enfin le cours de sa vie d'éternel nomade.

Au début de décembre 1981, cependant, il a ressenti les premières atteintes d'un mal trop russe pour qu'il ne le connaisse bien : la nostalgie. C'est l'époque de l'année où Moscou est pluvieux et triste. Dans les caniveaux, il reste encore, çà et là, un peu de la neige tombée fin novembre. Ce sont de petits tas sales qui s'amenuisent de jour en jour, au gré des pluies, mais vous polluent l'âme. Et Hidar a commencé de se dire que le soleil, les saveurs, les couleurs, le bruit, le mouvement, l'odeur, les images les plus lointaines de l'Orient lui manquaient cruellement. On est le 7 décembre. Il a été convoqué au siège du KGB, 2, place Dzerjinski. Ce n'est pas la première fois qu'il s'y rend mais c'est la première fois qu'il le fait seul, sans son ami Tchebrikov. Il pénètre dans le vieux bâtiment rococo qui, sous le tsar Nicolas II, abritait une compagnie d'assurances. Un officier en uniforme l'accompagne au cinquième et dernier étage, là où, il ne l'ignore pas, siège le centre des actions à l'étranger. A chaque palier, devant l'ascenseur, se tient un vague agent, nonchalant et modestement armé. Et Hidar, comme chaque fois, ne peut s'empêcher d'être surpris par une si faible protection. Longs couloirs déserts. Portes en bois mystérieuses. Éclairages tamisés, propices à tous les complots. Il n'est pas là depuis deux minutes qu'une des portes s'ouvre et qu'apparaît un homme chauve, aux petits yeux rouges, protégés par un minuscule binocle. L'homme l'accueille sans un mot, retourne à son immense bureau, dominé par deux portails sur fond or, celui de Lénine et celui de Brejnev. Puis, d'un geste qui se veut bienveillant, il encourage son visiteur à prendre place sur l'unique chaise posée devant lui.

— Je suis content de faire votre connaissance, dit-il en exhibant une rangée de petites dents jaunies par le tabac.

Après quoi, de la même voix graillonneuse qui fait songer à un moteur qu'on aurait oublié de graisser, il expose les dernières nouvelles venues d'Israël à travers une taupe installée depuis de nombreuses années dans les services de renseignements de Tsahal. Il s'agit d'un rapport concernant les voyages du colonel Benjamin Ben Eliezer à Jounieh, au Liban, où il a rencontré des responsables chrétiens. Le rapport mentionne aussi la visite des responsables chrétiens à Jérusalem. Il s'agit d'une délégation composée du vieux Camille Chamoun, de son fils Dany, de Béchir Gemayel, chef des Phalanges, et de son bras droit Émile Farah. Tout ce beau monde serait arrivé à Jérusalem, le 27 novembre, par un hélicoptère qui se serait posé, en pleine nuit, sur le toit de la Knesseth, le parlement israélien.

Tout cela, Hidar le savait déjà, par Tchebrikov. Mais il vient d'en découvrir la source et cette nouvelle inattendue le réjouit. Il trouve en effet amusant qu'un espion soviétique sévisse dans l'ombre de Benjamin Ben Eliezer, son vieil adversaire, acharné, depuis tant d'années, à contrecarrer ses initiatives au Proche-Orient.

La voix de l'homme aux yeux rouges grince à nouveau :

— Le 12 janvier 1982, le général Sharon, ministre israélien de la Défense, se rendra à Beyrouth. Il prévoit d'y établir, en compagnie de Béchir Gemayel, les plans d'une invasion du Liban.

Pourquoi lui dit-il tout cela ? parce qu'il a mission, à partir de là, d'élaborer avec les dirigeants palestiniens une stratégie de riposte. Mieux : il est chargé de favoriser, en échange de livraisons d'armes et d'une aide diplomatique, la réintroduction de l'Union soviétique dans la région. Il pourra compter, dans sa tâche, sur l'assistance d'un certain nombre d'agents locaux. Mais aussi sur l'aide des services spéciaux syriens. La mission est délicate, avertit-il. Elle ne pouvait être confiée qu'à un homme extrêmement sûr. Et c'est pourquoi on a, tout naturellement, pensé à lui...

Hidar arrive à Beyrouth, à l'aéroport de Khaldé, presque désert, le 10 décembre 1981, à 15 h 40. Une vieille Chevrolet américaine stationne au bout de la piste. Bassam Abou Charif l'attend.

— Tu es venu me chercher seul, sans protection ? demande-t-il en l'embrassant.

— Il ne peut plus rien m'arriver, répond Bassam, en ricanant et en montrant du doigt son visage défiguré.

Puis, devant l'air légèrement horrifié de Hidar :

— Ce n'est pas joli joli n'est-ce pas ? Que veux-tu : une bombe envoyée par la poste qui m'a explosé entre les mains. C'est comme pour Kanafani... Nos amis accusent les Israéliens, les Israéliens les Jordaniens et les Jordaniens Abou Nidal... Va savoir où est la vérité. Ce que je sais, moi, pour l'instant, c'est qu'il faut que je me réhabitue à ma nouvelle gueule.

Les deux hommes montent en voiture. Le chauffeur, un jeune feddayin en tenue de combat, démarre en trombe, sans se retourner. Et la Chevrolet arrive vite dans ce Beyrouth de fureur et de bruit qui ressemble si peu, tout à coup, au pur joyau d'Orient fleurant bon l'odeur des beignets, le parfum d'épices et de bonheur qu'il avait, avec Olga, si joyeusement humé. Ce ne sont partout que ruines. Champs labourés d'obus. Destructions. Désolations. Et, dans le lointain, une rumeur de canonnade qui fait sursauter Hidar.

— C'est comme ça tout le temps, dit Bassam en posant amicalement la main sur le genou de son compagnon. Ça vient des environs du musée, dans la rue de Damas là où les milices chiites tentent de repousser l'armée libanaise...

La voiture prend la direction de la corniche. Mais, tout de suite, après le stade, elle oblique dans la rue Mar Elias. C'était autrefois un quartier animé, plein de vie. Il paraît maintenant délaissé, ravagé. Ce ne sont partout que maisons éventrées, carcasses de camions, voitures criblées de balles et aux pneus crevés, abandonnées au bord du trottoir. La Chevrolet, après quelques minutes d'un véritable gymkhana entre les épaves et les ruines, pénètre enfin dans une cour et s'arrête. C'est une bâtisse à peu près intacte dont les murs et les fenêtres sont protégés par des plaques de métal et des remparts en parpaings maçonnés. Plusieurs hommes armés sont là. D'autres quittent la maison. Une sorte d'officier s'avance et vient à leur rencontre :

— Tu vas rencontrer Abou Iyad, dit Bassam, puis on t'emmènera à l'hôtel.

— Au Saint-Georges ?

Bassam le regarde avec ce mélange d'ironie et de tendresse qu'on a pour un enfant qui prétend enfermer la lune dans un seau d'eau :

— Comment, le Saint-Georges ? Ce quartier n'existe presque plus...

Et, l'entraînant dans l'escalier :

— Tu logeras à l'hôtel Alexandre, à Beyrouth-Est, du côté chrétien. Tu pourras ainsi examiner, dès demain matin, le terrain d'atterrissage du général Sharon, près de Jounieh, ainsi que la maison où doit avoir lieu la rencontre avec Béchir Gemayel.

Ils sont déjà au troisième étage et Bassam l'introduit dans une pièce spacieuse mais sombre où crépite une machine à écrire. Abou Iyad est là, qui lui tend les bras, lui offre rituellement du thé et commente avec lui les tout derniers épisodes de l'interminable bataille de Beyrouth. Le soir venu, on se quitte. Les amis palestiniens lui affectent deux anges gardiens. L'un est un Palestinien d'une cinquantaine d'années, un peu gras, au front dégarni et à l'œil légèrement globuleux. L'autre, d'une quinzaine d'années plus jeune, tout petit bonhomme au verbe rapide et au geste précipité, est apparemment un chrétien libanais. Le Palestinien se nomme Jael el-Ardja ; le Libanais Joseph Houbeika.

— Avec ces deux-là, tu ne seras pas perdu à Beyrouth, lui dit Bassam.

Et Joseph Houbeika, quand ils ont pris place dans la grosse Renault, propre et bien entretenue, qu'on a mise à leur disposition :

— Ne t'en fais pas. Je connais la route comme ma poche. Je pourrais t'y conduire les yeux fermés.

Paris, décembre 1981

Ma tante Regina ne me téléphonait jamais. Aussi fus-je certain, dès que j'entendis sa voix, que quelque chose de très grave venait de se produire.

— Que se passe-t-il ? demandai-je.

— Oh ! fit-elle d'une voix étouffée par la distance et les larmes. Anna-Maria a été enlevée.

— Anna-Maria ? Comment ça ? Quand ?

— Hier... Tout le monde en avait après elle, la pauvre petite ! Ses anciens amis, la police, les fascistes... Je l'ai cachée au domicile de la veuve du docteur Longer. Tu te souviens de lui, hein ? Je croyais que personne ne penserait à la chercher chez une vieille Juive. Mais voilà...

— Voilà quoi ?

— Hier matin, Mario, son ami, est venu. Lui non plus ne savait pas où elle se cachait. Il était dans tous ses états, Mario. Il était venu pour me dire que les « compañeros » avaient découvert la cache d'Anna-Maria et l'avaient dénoncée aux fascistes. Je n'ai même pas eu le temps de faire une crise cardiaque. Je lui ai dit : Viens ! Mais imagine-toi qu'il n'y avait pas un taxi libre dans toute la ville. Nous avons été obligés de prendre le « subté », le métro. Quand nous sommes arrivés avenue Pueyredon où habite la veuve Longer, quatre malabars en civil poussaient Anna-Maria dans

380

une Ford noire. Elle se débattait, la pauvre petite ! Comme elle se débattait ! Mais personne n'intervenait. Ici, tout le monde a peur. Je me suis mise à crier. Trop tard. Martin est allé à la police qui a promis de s'en occuper. Mais Mario dit que seule la pression de l'étranger pourrait encore sauver Anna-Maria, ma petite-fille. Alors, je te téléphone.

Dona Regina se tut. Je n'entendis plus que ses sanglots. Que lui répondre ? Comment la rassurer ? Quoi lui promettre surtout ? Je restai moi aussi silencieux, réfléchissant à toute vitesse :

— C'est terrible, dis-je enfin... C'est terrible...

Ce qui était terrible, c'était cette disparition. Mais c'était aussi que ma vieille tante, la seule survivante de la génération d'Abraham, la seule à avoir été épargnée par le déferlement du fascisme en Europe, soit rattrapée, elle aussi, par le fascisme argentin. Je restai de longues secondes à regarder au plafond. Incapable de faire le moindre geste. De prendre la moindre décision. De prononcer, même, le moindre mot. Éduqué dans une certaine idée du bien et du mal, j'avais fait mienne une espérance insensée : que la lumière triomphe de l'opacité du mal, que le genre humain aille de progrès en progrès. Vaincu, le nazisme disparaîtrait — ce nazisme au nom duquel deux soldats m'avaient saisi un jour et avaient lancé à ma mère : « Dites-nous où se cache votre mari et nous vous rendrons votre fils ! » Je ne savais pas, en ce temps-là, que l'ombre masquerait pour toujours la lumière, que le nazisme s'était incrusté en chacun de nous, que la vie avait perdu sa valeur absolue pour ne devenir qu'une monnaie d'échange. A présent, je le saisis. J'étais en train de le comprendre, là, au téléphone, en parlant avec la vieille dona Regina. L'idée me répugnait, mais laissait aussi une chance : « s'ils avaient voulu tuer Anna-Maria, ils l'auraient déjà fait », me dis-je. Et, aussitôt terminé mon échange avec ma tante, je me mis à téléphoner. J'appelai d'une manière fébrile, en chargeant chaque appel de tout le poids de mon espoir et de ma foi. La Présidence de la République française... Le Président de la Commission du Sénat américain... Le Président du Parlement européen... Des hommes politiques... Des ambassadeurs... Des amis qui connaissaient des hommes politiques... Des personnalités influentes en Amérique latine... Des amis d'amis... A 2 heures du matin, épuisé, je me retrouvai à nouveau seul. Ne sachant pas quoi faire de plus. Impuissant? Oui, impuissant. Honteusement, scandaleusement impuissant. Je sentais le temps s'écouler : j'avais envie de l'arrêter. Je sentais l'angoisse monter : j'avais envie de crier. A l'aube, n'y tenant plus, je me mis à ma table de travail, balayai d'un revers de la main les dizaines de feuillets noircis, annotés, plusieurs fois corrigés et rédigeai un appel en faveur d'Anna-Maria. Il parut deux jours plus tard en France, puis aux États-Unis. Avais-je su faire partager ma rage ? Avais-je eu assez de force de persuasion, assez de talent pour le faire comprendre ? Évidemment non. Car le 7 avril 1982, deux jours après le début de la guerre des Malouines, je reçus un coup de téléphone de mon cousin Martin, de Buenos Aires. C'est un homme brisé qui me parle. Un homme hoquetant, sanglotant, dont j'ai peine à comprendre, sur l'instant, ce qu'il me dit. Le corps de sa fille, me raconte-t-il, a été déposé, pendant la nuit, devant la porte de dona Regina. Celle-ci a eu un malaise et se trouve à l'hôpital.

Comment dire mon désarroi à cette nouvelle ? Mélange de stupeur, d'horreur, de haut-le-cœur. Incrédulité aussi. Sentiment que c'est impossible, que ce genre de tragédie n'arrive qu'aux autres. Et puis une espèce de nausée à l'idée de ce livre absurde qui me semble si léger, tout à coup, si vain, face à la mort d'une jeune fille. Le lendemain, ma décision était prise : je me rendais chez mon éditeur pour lui annoncer que je renonçais à achever ces Fils d'Abraham. Il tenta de me fléchir, bien sûr. Il m'expliqua que ne pas partager une histoire d'homme avec les hommes, c'est trahir l'humanité. Rien, pourtant, n'y fit. Dès mon retour à la maison, je me mis à ranger dans des cartons, mes notes, mes fiches, mes photos. Parfois un mot, une phrase, un paragraphe attiraient mon attention et je me surprenais à me lire avec curiosité, étonnement, amitié. Qui a dit qu'« on n'est pas obligé d'achever l'œuvre mais qu'on n'est pas libre de s'en désintéresser ». Je me sentais comme un automate, en tout cas. Étranger à moi-même, à mon entreprise, à ma mémoire. C'est dans cet état, la gorge, les yeux, le corps et la tête pleine de sanglots que j'appris, une semaine plus tard, la mort de dona Regina.

44

BEYROUTH

AVANT LE SIÈGE (2)

Décembre 1981

Le soleil se lève juste. Il est bien rond. Bien blanc. Il
fait encore frais, mais l'hôtel et la rue sont déjà pleins
d'hommes affairés ou de miliciens armés. Au loin, le
canon gronde. A la table voisine, un moine maronite qui
prend son café leur demande l'heure. Et, comme il les
voit répondre, il s'enhardit à leur demander d'où ils
viennent. Le nom de Houbeïka lui dit quelque chose.
L'accent de Hidar le trahit. Aussi se présente-t-il lui
aussi. C'est un chrétien habitant Tunis. Son œil vide, là,
à gauche, c'est un éclat d'obus qui l'a rendu aveugle. Il
parle de la guerre et de la misère. Il accuse les
Palestiniens et les Syriens qui ont enseveli des milliers
de chrétiens sous les décombres de Zahlé. Des illuminés, des estropiés, des religieux de toutes sortes ne
manquent pas en Orient et Hidar en a l'habitude.
Pourtant, ce moine-ci dont la voix semble sortie d'un
autre corps et les paroles venues d'un autre temps,
l'impressionne vivement ; et c'est pourquoi il décide
d'abréger son petit déjeuner et de prendre aussitôt la
route.

L'odeur de cendre froide d'un incendie éteint durant
la nuit au bout de la rue Achrafieh, flotte encore dans
l'air. Il respire bien fort cette odeur de ville en guerre,
mise à sac, livrée aux flammes et aux tueurs. Et c'est
vrai que, fouillant du regard la foule tumultueuse, si

384

familière et pourtant si distincte, ces hommes agités et ces femmes inquiètes aux visages pâles, impudemment ravivés d'un trait de crayon noir autour des yeux, il a peine à ne pas se sentir incroyablement étranger. Quelqu'un avec qui partager ce vertige, cette distance ? Il ne rencontre qu'un regard complice : celui d'un vieux boutiquier juif avec sa calotte ridicule sur son crâne ratatiné. Et c'est plein d'amertume qu'il monte dans sa voiture et prend la route.

Pendant le voyage il reste pensif, laissant Jael el-Ardja raconter les splendeurs de l'Amérique latine à Joseph Houbeïka, qui n'a jamais quitté le Liban. A dix-huit kilomètres de Beyrouth, quelques centaines de mètres après la flèche indiquant le chemin menant à Antoura par Ghadir, la route fait un brusque coude vers la droite et Hidar découvre Jounieh. Mais Joseph, qui conduit, n'emprunte pas ce chemin. Il prend, à gauche, une petite route qui longe le village, aboutit rapidement à un champ à la terre desséchée et arrête la voiture.

— C'est ici, dit-il, que l'hélicoptère se posera.

Et, montrant en contrebas le toit d'un bâtiment :

— C'est le couvent de Sarba. Au-dessous, au bord de la mer, en descendant quelques gradins, se trouve un ancien caveau où la réunion aura lieu. Venez !

Sur le chemin du retour, Jael el-Ardja paraîtra agité, presque fiévreux. Visiblement, l'idée d'avoir à sa merci, en même temps et à la fois, le ministre de la Défense israélien et le chef des Phalanges, l'excite et le comble de joie. Cette joie impudique irrite Hidar et lui donne soudain l'envie d'humilier cet imbécile. Il demande :

— Pourquoi l'attentat contre Ben Gourion a-t-il raté ?

Le Palestinien ne se démonte pas.

— Bonne question, dit-il, en se tournant vers Hidar qui, pour des raisons de sécurité, est assis sur la banquette arrière. Je me la suis posée aussi. Au début, j'ai pensé qu'il y avait un traître parmi les dirigeants du Front. Et je me suis même dit, tu me pardonneras ma franchise, que ce traître pouvait être toi. Aujourd'hui, je crois m'être trahi moi-même, bêtement, dans un avion, en parlant à un médecin juif.

Il hausse ses épaules dans un geste de fatalité.

— Cela devait certainement se passer ainsi. Ce qui est écrit est écrit.

— Un médecin juif ? insiste Hidar.

— Eh oui ! J'avais oublié que les Juifs étaient prompts à la déduction et qu'ils étaient tous sionistes. J'avais demandé à ce médecin s'il connaissait Ben Gourion. Je lui avais aussi parlé de Lima, et, comme la presse avait annoncé le voyage de Ben Gourion au Pérou, il a dû établir un rapprochement et aura prévenu le Mossad. Les Juifs sont très forts en calcul.

— Tu accordes aux Juifs plus d'intelligence qu'ils n'en ont, observe Joseph. Cela dit, tu t'es conduit comme un con.

— Peut-être, fait Jael el-Ardja. Mais le destin a rétabli les choses. Il est dit dans le Coran que l'homme porte son destin attaché au cou. Ce médecin a été tué à Zarka.

Hidar sursaute et doit faire un effort pour retrouver son calme.

— Tu étais à Zarka ? demande-t-il.

— Ah non ! Je ne suis pour rien dans la mort de ce Juif. Le destin s'en est chargé.

Et, se tournant vers Joseph :

— N'est-ce pas chez vous, les chrétiens, que l'on dit : « Va où tu veux, meurs où tu dois » ?

La voiture, pendant ce temps, est arrivée à Beyrouth. Et Hidar ne tarde plus à être rendu au lieu de la réunion. Une vingtaine de personnes sont là. C'est la même pièce que celle où Hidar a rencontré, le jour de son arrivée, Abou Iyad. Ils sont tous là, autour de trois tables couvertes de nappes blanches. Certains boivent du vin ; d'autres de l'orangeade ; il y a de la pita, des salades orientales ; quelques-uns se délectent de gâteaux aux amandes, à la pistache et au miel. Les deux portes-fenêtres étant bouchées avec des sacs de sable, la pièce est éclairée par quatre spots puissants. Il y a là Abou

Iyad, un peu empâté, Abou Jihad, le chef militaire du Fath, Abou Abbas, l'air réjoui, Bassam Abou Charif caché derrière ses lunettes noires. Et bien d'autres que Hidar ne connaît pas.

Le Tunisien souffre de sa jambe. Sa chaussure orthopédique l'incommode. Il s'assied près de la porte et reste un long moment, planté là, à regarder de loin ses camarades. Que lui arrive-t-il ? Il sent un douloureux travail qui s'accomplit en lui. C'est comme des doutes. Une incertitude obscure. Cette réunion lui en rappelle une autre, presque semblable, douze ans plus tôt, avant l'opération en Jordanie. Cette opération qui avait coûté la vie à des dizaines de milliers de personnes — dont le cousin d'Olga... Hidar remarque, sous une carte géante de la Palestine, Jael el-Ardja en conversation avec Abou Abbas. Il les voit rire, se servir du vin. Il repense à ce Sidney dont la mort le fait souffrir et lui fait honte. Il repense à Hugo et à l'énigme impénétrée de son assassinat. Ne dit-on pas, chez les Arabes, qu'on ne répète pas l'appel des muezzins pour les sourds ? Il sait, lui, ne pas avoir droit au doute. Il a été envoyé en mission par les Soviétiques, chargé d'une tâche complexe et doit tout faire pour qu'elle s'accomplisse... Loin du sentiment ! Au diable les états d'âme !

Deux feddayins, pendant qu'il réfléchissait, ont débarrassé les tables. Une vieille femme a apporté, sur un plateau en plastique noir décoré de grosses fleurs rouges, une vingtaine de tasses blanches, remplies de café, et la réunion a vraiment commencé.

— Alors ? a demandé Abou Iyad, en se tournant vers lui.

Ses joues rondes, son front dégarni et le col de sa chemise blanche ouvert sous un pull gris lui donnent l'air d'un quelconque acheteur d'agrumes.

— Nous avons visité les lieux, reconnaît Hidar. Un attentat est envisageable, même si nous ne connaissons pas les précautions prises par les chrétiens. Cependant...

Son visage se durcit. Il devient blême et martèle la fin de sa phrase :

387

— Je suis résolument contre.

La voix de Jael el-Ardja semble sur le point d'exploser :

— Absurde !

— Pas si absurde que ça, répond Hidar calmement. La ruse de qui est sans ruse, c'est la patience.

Il explique longuement sa position. Les Israéliens vont envahir le Liban vers le mois de mai ou dans le courant du mois de juin. Les renseignements reçus à Moscou, de source sûre, l'attestent. L'objectif de cette invasion sera de détruire toutes les bases palestiniennes dans le pays. Il est donc urgent pour les Palestiniens de préparer leur défense. Tuer Sharon n'arrêtera pas la guerre, mais la précipitera. La mort de deux hommes réunis pour parler de la paix n'empêchera pas l'intervention des Hébreux mais la justifiera aux yeux du monde. Quant à Gémayel, sa mort ne peut que provoquer une vendetta sanglante qui plongera le pays dans une guerre fratricide et, là encore, ne pourra que profiter à Israël et à la Syrie. Bref, il propose de préparer, dès à présent, les feddayins à la résistance urbaine. Moscou leur fournira l'armement nécessaire et il suffira, alors, de laisser les Israéliens s'embourber. Si Beyrouth devient un nouveau Stalingrad, les Chrétiens, avec ou sans Béchir Gémayel, ne s'engageront pas dans la bataille. Certains par prudence, d'autres par peur...

Un silence gêné accueille ces paroles. Tous le regardent, stupéfaits, peinés ou soupçonneux.

— C'est une plaisanterie, dit Abou Abbas d'une voix sourde.

Et Jael el-Ardja :

— Nous ne sommes pas des diplomates mais des soldats. Si nous nous mettons à juger et à discuter de tout, il n'y aura plus rien de sacré.

Il regarde fixement Hidar et frappant du poing sur la table :

— Rien de sacré ! Ni la Palestine, ni Beit Jalla !

Cette sortie, si déplacée qu'elle paraisse, n'en correspond pas moins à ce que tous ressentent.

— Notre rôle, c'est de libérer la Palestine et non pas

de défendre les intérêts de l'Union soviétique ou même de la Syrie, reprend Abou Abbas. C'est notre devoir. Le général Sharon a les mains couvertes de notre sang...

Cet Abou Abbas, avec sa moustache tombante à la cosaque et son pathos ridicule, devient bien agaçant. Aussi est-ce à Jael el-Ardja qu'Hidar préfère s'adresser :

— Si tu veux te battre, tu en auras bientôt l'occasion.

Et, en regardant à la ronde :

— Pensez-vous être en mesure d'affronter l'armée israélienne ? Avez-vous une stratégie ? des armes ? Si c'est ce que vous pensez, alors mon opinion et mon aide ne vous serviront à rien. Tuez donc Sharon et Inch Allah !

Il fait le geste de se lever, puis se ravise :

— N'oubliez pas que vous n'avez ni missiles antiaériens, ni...

Il ne finit pas sa phrase car tout le monde s'est mis à parler à la fois. Un feddayin barbu, aux lunettes fines, l'air d'un intellectuel plutôt que d'un guerrier, et qui est le responsable militaire d'El-Fath pour la ville de Beyrouth, se lève et, ouvrant les bras comme un prêcheur s'adressant à ses paroissiens, demande à Hidar de bien vouloir se rasseoir :

— Je respecte ton opinion, dit-il. Mais j'aurais aimé...

On l'écoute avec attention :

— Nous aurions aimé que tu précises ta stratégie. Que tu nous dises plus clairement quelle serait l'aide soviétique en cas de siège de Beyrouth.

La réunion se prolongera tard dans la nuit. Au moment de se quitter, Bassam fait valoir que traverser la ville en pleine nuit est dangereux. Aussi propose-t-il à Hidar un matelas dans la pièce à côté. Mais le Tunisien a besoin d'air. Il descend dans la cour, remplie de sacs de sable et où des hommes en armes font fonction de vigiles. Il fait quelques pas pour se dégourdir les jambes. A gauche, l'ombre ; à droite, le sol luisant de pluie qui brille à la lumière de la lune. Il s'apprête à remonter lorsqu'il sent qu'on lui touche l'épaule. Il se retourne et reconnaît Jael el-Ardja.

— Je sais qu'on me tient pour un sale type, fait celui-ci doucement, et peu m'importe... Je ne veux connaître que ceux que j'aime et quand j'aime quelqu'un, je lui suis fidèle. Oui, j'ai deux ou trois amis parmi lesquels je suis prêt à te ranger : les autres, vois-tu, je m'en fous. Presque tout le monde est nuisible, surtout les femmes...

Il a un geste de mépris. Et touchant à nouveau l'épaule d'Hidar :

— Crois-moi, si tu tiens à la vie, ne fais pas tout ce qu'on te dit à Moscou ou ailleurs... Mais tu ne me comprends pas...

— Mais si, je te comprends, fait Hidar, un peu gêné.

Et tandis que l'envahit une inquiétude diffuse, et dont il a aussitôt honte, Jael conclut — en approchant son visage tout près du sien :

— Non, tu ne comprends pas... Ce que pense le chameau n'est pas ce qui est dans la tête du chamelier... Je t'aime bien parce que tu es intelligent et que tu as su préserver, j'en suis sûr, un peu de la naïveté de ton enfance. Mais c'est justement cette naïveté-là qui risque de te perdre. J'ai connu, il y a longtemps, quelqu'un comme toi. Un enfant, lui aussi. Un naïf. Eh bien tu vois, c'est terrible : on m'a demandé, un beau matin, de le liquider. Qui « on » ? Disons tes patrons. Oui, voilà : tes chefs, tes amis. Ça s'est passé sur la route de Jérusalem. Mais lui n'était pas mon ami. C'était un Juif.

Paris, mai 1984

Plus de vingt ans après la mort de Hugo, j'ai encore l'impression de poser mes pas dans les siens. Et c'est ainsi que, sitôt achevée la rédaction du chapitre « Beyrouth avant le siège », j'ai reçu une lettre de Bassam Abou Charif, m'invitant à Tunis où, après l'évacuation des Palestiniens du Liban, leur Centrale s'était installée.

Car résumons : le 6 juin 1982, en représailles à l'assassinat du diplomate israélien Yaacov Bar Simon-Tov, à Londres, l'armée israélienne, comme Hidar l'avait prévu, envahit le Liban.

Le 23 août de la même année, Béchir Gemayel devenait le 13e Président du Liban. A peine deux jours plus tard, une force multinationale d'interposition réunissant les Français, les Américains, les Italiens et les Anglais se déployait à Beyrouth, dont l'armée israélienne faisait le siège depuis deux mois. Cette force d'interposition devait aider à l'embarquement d'Arafat et de ses troupes vers Tunis. Le 14 septembre, Béchir Gemayel était enseveli sous les décombres du quartier général des Phalangistes, à Ashrafieh, victime d'une bombe syrienne. Le 16 septembre, un groupe de Phalangistes dirigé par Eli Houbeïka, le frère de Joseph, organisait un massacre dans les camps palestiniens de Sabra et Chatila. Une commission d'enquête fut aussitôt constituée en Israël. Elle publia son rapport le 7 février

391

1983. Celui-ci confirmait que le massacre avait été commis par les Phalangistes, mais accusait le ministre de la Défense d'Israël, le général Sharon, d'avoir mésestimé l'éventualité de représailles contre la population des camps de réfugiés en y laissant pénétrer les Phalanges. Le général Sharon démissionna. Le général Joshua Saguy, chef de l'Aman, le service de renseignements de l'armée israélienne, fut démis de ses fonctions : le rapport que Benjamin Ben Eliezer avait établi, avec l'aide d'Arié, sur la stratégie conçue par Hidar Assadi et approuvée par les Palestiniens, leurs prévisions quant aux massacres que les Israéliens ne pourraient pas empêcher, n'avaient même pas été examinés et encore moins pris en compte. Le 3 avril 1984, enfin, Chafic Wazzam, le Premier ministre libanais, accueillait officiellement, et avec beaucoup de déférence, l'envoyé spécial du gouvernement soviétique Karen Brutens.

J'arrivai, moi, à Tunis le 4 mai 1984, très tôt le matin. L'aéroport d'El-Aouïna n'avait rien à voir avec ceux du Caire et de Beyrouth. C'était un aéroport intime, familial, rappelant ces aéroports provinciaux dans les toutes petites villes de Milwaukee. Seul le parfum différait. Ici triomphait le jasmin, que des vendeurs de dix ans proposaient aux voyageurs. Les fleurs étaient enfermées dans un corset de fil à coudre pour qu'elles ne s'éparpillent pas.

Un jeune Tunisien brandissait un carton sur lequel était inscrit mon nom. Il s'appelait Salem et était envoyé par Bassam Abou Charif. Il me déposa à l'hôtel Africa-Méridien, avenue Bourguiba, et s'éclipsa aussitôt. Un petit mot de Bassam me conviait à un déjeuner dans un restaurant, à quelques kilomètres de Tunis. On viendrait me chercher en voiture. Et, en attendant, je n'avais pas autre chose à faire que de déambuler dans la direction de la medina au milieu d'une foule partagée entre l'insolence et la bonne humeur.

Me souvenant de la lettre de Hugo, je décidai de jouer à marcher sur ses traces. Je regrettais de ne pas avoir pensé à emporter son carnet avec moi, au moins à recopier tous les noms arabes qui s'y trouvaient. Mais enfin, j'avais tout de même ma mémoire. Et puis mon instinct qui me disait que je touchais peut-être au but et qu'en marchant, en me laissant aller, je découvrirais quelque chose.

Une voiture vint me chercher à l'heure prévue. La Marsa, à deux kilomètres de Sidi-Bou-Saïd, est un village touristique, édifié à l'emplacement de Mégara. « C'était à Mégara, faubourg de Carthage, dans les jardins d'Hamilcar... » En l'occurrence, c'est Bassam Abou Charif qui m'y attendait — seul à une table basse, chargée de salades, sous les portiques du Café Saf Saf, près de la mosquée. Dans la cour, une étonnante machine élévatrice en bois, actionnée par un chameau qui tournait inlassablement autour d'un puits, recueillait l'eau dans des cruches en terre fixées à une roue.

— Tant d'années ! s'exclama Bassam en anglais, en me serrant la main.

Il avait énormément changé. Son visage, opéré après l'attentat, avait perdu sa finesse. Des lunettes cachaient ses yeux. Il avait grossi. Et pourtant, son sourire était toujours le même, engageant, fraternel.

— Alors, la paix c'est pour quand ? me demanda-t-il.

— J'espérais que tu me le dirais...

Un serveur nous apporta du thé à la menthe.

— Les dirigeants israéliens n'ont toujours pas l'air décidés... reprit-il.

Je l'interrompis :

— Écoute, laissons la propagande de côté. Tu le sais aussi bien que moi, quatre cent mille Israéliens sont descendus dans la rue pour protester contre la guerre du Liban. Les manifestants représentent à eux seuls dix pour cent de la population du pays. Ils seront deux millions pour réclamer les négociations avec vous, si Arafat annonce publiquement la reconnaissance d'Israël, l'arrêt des actions terroristes et l'abrogation de votre Charte qui prévoit la disparition de l'État juif.

— Attends, attends, fit Bassam en souriant. Tu vas trop vite.

— Trop vite ? Tous ces morts ne te suffisent donc pas ? Et toi, regarde-toi...

— Ne parlons pas de moi, veux-tu ? On ne fera pas la paix rien que pour moi...

— Non, mais on la fera sûrement pour que d'autres ne connaissent pas ton sort.

— Et tu penses que les Israéliens ont déjà tout fait pour favoriser la paix ?

— Non. Mais j'ai assez critiqué leur immobilisme, leur manque d'imagination, pour me permettre de dénoncer le vôtre.

Il se détendit brusquement. Un sourire familier éclaira son masque :

— Alors, calmons-nous. Je ne t'ai pas demandé de venir à Tunis pour me disputer avec toi...

Il pensait, en fait, comme moi, que les Palestiniens devaient préciser leurs objectifs. Il comprenait la crainte des Israéliens. Aussi avait-il préparé un texte qu'il voulait me lire avant de le rendre public.

C'était un document courageux qui proposait aux Israéliens des négociations directes. Mais il n'évoquait ni l'arrêt du terrorisme, ni l'abrogation de la Charte. Je le lui fis remarquer.

— Mais si nous acceptions des négociations avec les Israéliens, c'est que la Charte ne compte plus !

— Alors, dis-le ! Et le terrorisme ? Que dis-tu du terrorisme ?

— Ça ne dépend pas que d'Arafat !

— Alors, à quoi servira ton texte ?

Nous discutâmes longtemps. Il prit des notes. Il m'expliqua, non sans raison, qu'un document qui me satisferait tout à fait ne pourrait être publié avant longtemps. Et puis il exprima le désir que je reste à Tunis deux jours de plus pour rencontrer Arafat dont le voyage à Bagdad s'était prolongé. Je déclinai son invitation en arguant que mon livre m'attendait à Paris. Il m'interrogea sur son contenu et parut très surpris que j'y parle de lui. Il m'affirma n'avoir jamais entendu le nom de Hugo. Nous évoquâmes Kanafani et notre rencontre de novembre 1969, à Beyrouth.

— *A long time ago, a long time ago,* répéta-t-il, songeur.

394

— Et les choses n'ont toujours pas évolué, ajoutai-je.

— Je m'y emploie pourtant, dit-il, en posant la main sur mon bras.

— Tu n'as pas peur ?

— De quoi aurais-je peur ?

Il leva les mains comme s'il allait y cueillir son visage :

— Peur de perdre encore une fois la face ?

Et, content de son jeu de mots, il éclata de rire.

J'arrivai en taxi à Hammam-Lif, vers 5 heures de l'après-midi. La foule bigarrée se déversait, par vagues, sur les plages. Je demandai à un passant le chemin de la synagogue. C'était un vieil Arabe barbu dont le large caftan blanc cachait la maigreur. Il se proposa de m'y emmener. Le bâtiment marqué d'une étoile à six branches se trouvait à l'angle de la rue du Théâtre et de la rue d'Alger. Des planches en bois condamnaient l'entrée et les fenêtres. Le vieil Arabe avait l'air désolé :

— Il n'y a plus de Juifs à Hammam-Lif, expliqua-t-il.

— Plus du tout ?

Il réfléchit un moment et son visage s'illumina. Si, si... En cherchant bien... Il y en avait peut-être un... Un infirme... Oh ! on ne sait pas grand-chose de lui, sinon qu'il a les jambes paralysées, qu'il s'appelle Samuel et qu'il habite là, avenue Bou Kornine, au fond d'une impasse obscure.

Nous y allâmes. Mon guide frappa à une fenêtre fermée. Une tête apparut. C'était lui, Samuel. Visiblement, il dormait. Apprenant la raison de ma visite, il promit de nous rejoindre au café Benayed, à deux pas de chez lui, près de l'hôtel Zéfir et arriva en effet une quinzaine de minutes plus tard, traînant ses jambes inertes à l'aide de deux béquilles. Il me raconta son histoire. Tunis... L'accident... Pourquoi il n'avait pas eu le courage de suivre sa famille en Israël... Son père, vieux et malade, qui ne voulait mourir nulle part ailleurs qu'ici à Hammam-Lif.

— Son nom ?

— Taïeb.

Je fus étonné de ne pas être surpris. Mais ne savais-je pas, depuis mon arrivée, que je m'introduirais, à un moment ou à un autre, dans le récit d'Hugo ? Samuel se souvenait parfaitement de mon cousin. Son père aurait pu me donner plus de détails, mais j'étais arrivé six mois trop tard... En revanche, il se souvenait très bien que Hugo avait des amis arabes. Un médecin, Jemil el-Okby, par exemple... Assadi, aussi. Le vieux Marwan Assadi, très actif dans le Néodestour, le parti de Bourguiba, et dont la famille s'était dispersée... Hidar, son fils, venait de temps en temps se recueillir sur la tombe de son père. Hugo, de même, était revenu après la guerre et il envoyait toujours des vœux pour la Nouvelle Année juive, depuis New York. Samuel était triste d'apprendre sa mort. Mais la mort ne l'impressionnait plus : il vivait avec elle depuis trop longtemps. Il me cita l'Ecclésiaste : « Quel avantage revient-il à l'homme de toute la peine qu'il se donne au soleil ? Une génération s'en va, une autre vient et la terre subsiste toujours. »

Il se leva. J'avais interrompu sa sieste. Il allait se recoucher. Mais, au moment où il avança ses béquilles, son visage s'anima et donna tous les signes de la plus extrême surprise :

— Regardez, dit-il, à mi-voix... C'est lui... C'est le fils Assadi...

Je me levai à mon tour. Et, sidéré, n'en croyant pas mes yeux, je reconnus en effet Hidar qui traversait la rue et venait lui aussi de m'apercevoir.

— Que faites-vous ici ? demanda-t-il sans chercher à dissimuler sa surprise.

Et aussitôt, de l'air cynique et malin de celui à qui on ne la fait pas :

— Hugo, hein ?

Son visage d'oiseau était bruni ; ses cheveux me parurent presque blancs ; et je le trouvai plus beau qu'à Beyrouth.

— Vous, les Juifs, vous êtes un drôle de peuple, me dit-il. Vous ne cessez jamais d'interpeller votre passé.

— Et vous ? N'êtes-vous pas ici à cause du passé ?

— Oui. Je suis venu rendre hommage à la mémoire de mon père. Mais je n'interroge pas les morts. Ce qu'il a fait ou ce qu'il aurait pu faire ne m'intéresse pas.

Il aperçut Samuel et, d'un air un peu méprisant, le salua. Puis, se tournant à nouveau vers moi :

— Vous restez à Hammam-Lif ?

— Non, je rentre à Tunis.

— Vous êtes en voiture ?

— Non.

Il leva les bras au ciel, d'un geste indéfini qui pouvait être de bienvenue autant que de fatalité et dit :

— Alors, venez, je vous emmène.

45

NEW YORK-MOSCOU-TEL-AVIV

« ACHILLE LAURO »

Octobre, 1985

Depuis la disparition de Sidney, Jérémie Cohen est envahi par la mauvaise conscience. Il a beau se dire qu'il n'est pour rien dans ce voyage à Francfort, que l'avion de la TWA, détourné par les Palestiniens, n'allait même pas à Beyrouth et que le terrorisme fait de toute façon partie du destin que l'on rencontre, à chaque pas, sur son chemin, il se sent responsable, en partie du moins, de sa mort.

Est-ce pour cela qu'il voit si souvent Marjory ? Et Richard ? Est-ce la raison, surtout, qui fait qu'il s'est lui-même assagi, troquant sa vie de libertin contre une charmante « Dorothy », d'une vingtaine d'années plus jeune que lui, qui est comme un fabuleux miroir devant lequel il gomme ses propres rides et ses cheveux blancs ? Elle aurait pu être très belle avec des hanches moins larges et un regard plus subtil. Mais il est heureux avec elle et songe sérieusement à l'épouser.

On est au début du mois de mai 1985. New York sent le printemps. En quittant l'hôpital, Jérémie traverse, de sa démarche dansante, la Troisième Avenue, puis Lexington et, en arrivant à Park Avenue, il oblique à gauche. Malgré la brûlure de la sciatique qui lui torture, depuis quelque temps, la hanche, il a une furieuse envie de marcher. L'après-midi est chaud. Mais une petite brise fraîche, venue de la mer, lui caresse agréablement le visage. Décidément, le mois de mai à New York est fait pour la promenade ! Dans la 59e Rue, il prend la direction de Central Park. En face de l'hôtel Plazza, au milieu d'une foule de curieux, deux chanteurs de folk-song pincent les cordes de leurs guitares. Le Central Park South est rempli de flâneurs et ses narines exercées sentent même l'odeur de la bouse de cheval : les premiers touristes qui font leurs balades en calèche !

En descendant la Cinquième Avenue, il s'arrête devant la vitrine de la librairie Doubleday, note que le dernier livre de Judith Krantz est paru et se demande s'il ne va pas finir par héler un taxi. Oui ? Non ? Tout bien pesé, non. Il a besoin de réfléchir. Dorothy lui a, en effet, annoncé la veille qu'elle était enceinte et il a toujours aimé réfléchir en marchant. Près de Rockefeller Center, il s'arrête à nouveau, mais cette fois devant le Centre de Tourisme italien. Il aime l'Italie. Florence... Rome... Naples... Les fresques de Pompéi... Pourquoi ne pas offrir une croisière à Dorothy avant son accouchement ? De fait, il pousse la porte. Une brochure parmi d'autres, rangée sur un présentoir, vante les croisières autour de la Méditerranée. Il la parcourt et s'arrête sur un itinéraire : Gênes, Naples, Alexandrie, Port-Saïd, Achdod, Pyrée... Naples et Israël réunis, n'est-ce pas le rêve ? N'est-ce pas, surtout, ce qu'il cherchait ? Il s'enquiert des prix, des dates de départ, de mille autres détails. Et l'idée le séduit si fort qu'il se demande même, en sortant, s'il ne devrait pas songer à associer à ce voyage Marjory et sa fille Marilyn. Dorothy les aime tant !

Cette fois, il prend un taxi. Le chauffeur, certainement un Juif russe, écoute une émission en yiddish. Lui, parcourt une nouvelle fois la brochure. Et s'ils prenaient le bateau à Naples ? S'ils prenaient le temps de visiter Pompéi ? Et s'ils en profitaient pour descendre à Achdod et découvrir Israël ? A sa grande honte, Jérémie Cohen n'a jamais visité l'État juif !

En arrivant chez lui, son siège est fait. Son plan de voyage est prêt. Ils partiront le 5 octobre. Et l'enfant naîtra à leur retour. Le pied marin et l'âme juive : que rêver de mieux ?

En apprenant la nouvelle, Dorothy lui saute au cou.

— Comment s'appelle le bateau, Dick ? demande-t-elle, à la fin du dîner.

— L'*Achille Lauro*.

— *Achille Lauro* ? interroge Viktor Alexandrovitch Tchebrikov.

On est le 3 octobre 1985. Hidar Assadi lui a demandé au téléphone un rendez-vous d'urgence et il est arrivé à son bureau, rue Kropotkine, directement de l'aéroport.

— Pourquoi précisément l'*Achille Lauro* ? redemande Tchebrikov.

Hidar hausse les épaules. Son visage est tanné par le soleil de Tunisie. Dans le bureau, à la baie toujours cachée par une tenture, il fait lourd et il ouvre le bouton du col de sa chemise :

— Un hasard, répond-il. Depuis longtemps, Abou Abbas cherchait un moyen d'introduire quelques feddayins en Israël. Non pas dans les villages frontaliers, mais au centre même du pays. Jaël el-Ardja, qui était chargé de préparer l'opération, a pensé que la manière la plus simple était de mêler le commando aux centaines de touristes qui font le tour de la Méditerranée et visitent la Terre Sainte. Arafat était contre, moi aussi. Peut-être pas pour les mêmes raisons, mais peu importe. Et c'est ainsi que le projet *Achille Lauro* a été remplacé par une opération à Larnaca qui, le 25 septembre, a coûté la vie à trois agents israéliens. La suite, vous la connaissez : les Israéliens ont prétendu qu'il ne s'agissait pas de simples touristes et, en représailles, ont bombardé, il y a deux jours, les Q.G. de l'OLP à Tunis.

Tchebrikov allume une cigarette :

— Vous en voulez une ?

— Non, j'ai arrêté.

— Bon, continuez ! Je vous écoute !

— Vous comprenez, Viktor Alexandrovitch : après le bombardement israélien, nos amis palestiniens sont surexcités. Agir les démange et l'opération *Achille Lauro* revient, du coup, à l'ordre du jour. Le commando recruté par Abou Abbas est toujours là. Leurs cabines sur le bateau sont réservées...

— Mais vous ne m'avez toujours pas dit votre opinion ?

— A vrai dire, j'ai peur... Je crains des bavures. Jael el-Ardja n'a pas la baraka. Quant à Abou Abbas, il est complètement irresponsable et je ne lui fais pas confiance dans le choix du commando...

Viktor Tchebrikov écrase sa cigarette à moitié consumée dans un cendrier en argent massif et lève les yeux sur Hidar :

— J'espère que vous vous rendez bien compte que la mort de touristes innocents sera dramatique pour l'image de la Centrale palestinienne...

Hidar acquiesce d'un hochement de tête. Nerveux, Tchebrikov prend une nouvelle cigarette :

— Peut-on encore annuler l'opération ?

— Impossible. Tout le monde est pour. Le bateau part dans deux jours et le commando est déjà sur place.

Viktor Tchebrikov fronce les sourcils. Il cherche des allumettes, les trouve, allume la cigarette et l'écrase aussitôt :

— Je ne vois qu'une seule solution, dit-il.

Hidar se raidit, un sourire figé sur le visage :

— Vous allez embarquer sur l'*Achille Lauro* et contrôler de près les agissements du commando.

— Et... balbutie Hidar. Et le billet ? Et les détails ?

— Aucun problème. Je fais prévenir notre agent à Gênes.

— A Gênes, dis-tu ?

Benjamin Ben Eliezer cligne spasmodiquement des yeux. Ce qu'Arié lui apprend le laisse perplexe : plusieurs terroristes palestiniens sont arrivés à Gênes. D'après les informations non encore confirmées, des armes convoyées de Tunis à Gênes, dans une Renault rouge, sont parvenues sur le ferry *Habbib*. Étant donné qu'il n'y a aucun objectif israélien dans ce port italien, les Palestiniens visent autre chose. Mais quoi ?

— Je ne vois qu'un scénario... dit Arié à qui une double paternité avait fait perdre un peu de sa juvénilité. J'ai fait vérifier la provenance et la destination de tous les bateaux amarrés à Gênes. Un seul doit, au cours de sa croisière, faire escale en Israël. C'est un paquebot italien, l'*Achille Lauro*.

— As-tu consulté la liste des passagers ?

— Pour l'instant, rien sur la liste de ceux qui embarquent à Gênes. Une cabine a été réservée au nom de quatre hommes dont l'identité ne me paraît pas crédible. Et sais-tu qui a acheté leurs billets ? Ahel Oz, le chef militaire du FLP, affilié à la Centrale d'Arafat !

Benjamin Ben Eliezer siffle doucement entre ses dents :

— Quelle erreur !

Et, après un silence :

— Au moins, grâce à lui, la situation est claire. Les Palestiniens veulent répondre au bombardement de Tunis par un attentat à Achdod. J'espère seulement qu'il n'y aura pas d'Israéliens à bord. Nous cueillerons toute cette jolie équipe à son arrivée en Israël.

Il appuie sur le bouton de l'interphone et demande à Myriam d'entrer. La porte s'ouvre presque aussitôt. Voyant Arié, Myriam ne peut s'empêcher de le taquiner :

— Alors, Haboub, il paraît que Judith est à nouveau enceinte ? Tu tiens vraiment à accomplir la promesse que l'Eternel a faite à Abraham ?

Elle rit, contente de son bon mot. Puis, devant le regard sévère de Benjamin, lui tend un télex :

— Tout chaud. Il vient d'arriver.

Benjamin parcourt le document et le passe à Arié sans commentaire. Le télex dit que le patron du KGB à Gênes, un certain Renzo Antonioni, fait des pieds et des mains pour obtenir une cabine single sur l'*Achille Lauro,* qui affiche complet.

Benjamin et Arié se regardent aussi surpris l'un que l'autre.

402

— Qu'est-ce que ça veut dire ? demande le premier en reprenant le télex.

— Cela veut dire qu'une foule de gens s'intéresse à ce vieux bateau. Car enfin, ce billet, Renzo Chose... ne l'a certainement pas pris pour lui-même. Sa tête est trop connue. Je vais essayer de me procurer la photo du nouveau passager. On est obligé d'en fournir deux à la signature du contrat avec la compagnie maritime...

— Fais vite. Le bateau part demain...

— Je l'aurai demain matin, répond Arié déjà dans le couloir.

Le lendemain, à 8 heures du matin, il est déjà chez Benjamin qui scrute d'un œil gourmand la photocopie qu'il a posée devant lui sur la table :

— Ce n'est pas possible ! s'exclame-t-il.

Et son regard, après avoir effleuré Arié, prend, pour revenir au document, l'expression d'étonnement et de détermination qu'il a eue, voici quinze ans, à l'annonce de l'enlèvement de Sidney :

— Décidément, il se passe quelque chose, dit-il. Si je ne me trompe pas, il s'agit de Hidar Assadi !

— Et ce n'est pas tout, fait Arié en secouant sa tête bouclée et en brandissant d'un air de triomphe quelques feuillets dactylographiés... J'ai aussi la liste des passagers qui embarqueront sur l'*Achille Lauro* à Naples.

— Alors ?

— Alors, il y a un groupe d'Américains ; et, parmi eux, imagine-toi : Marjory Halter, la veuve de Sidney, et sa fille Marilyn !

— Drôle de famille ! ne peut s'empêcher de grommeler Benjamin. Toujours fourrée partout. Toujours là quand...

Mais il préfère se taire et revenir à des considérations plus terre à terre :

— Hidar les connaît-il ?

— Je ne crois pas. Mais il connaît leur nom.

— Et Marjory connaît-elle Hidar ?

— Non plus. Elle, ne connaît en revanche même pas son nom.

— Bon... Bon... C'est tout ? Ou tu as encore une bonne nouvelle à m'annoncer ?

— Il y a aussi un couple d'Israéliens qui a embarqué ce matin à Gênes. D'une manière imprévue. Deux jeunes enseignants qui ont décidé au dernier moment de regagner Israël en bateau.

— Tes Israéliens, ce sont des vrais ? demanda Benjamin, avec un sourire blasé.

— Oui, j'ai vérifié.

— Il faut les prévenir.

— Trop tard. A l'heure qu'il est, le bateau manœuvre déjà. Mais j'ai pris mes dispositions.

Benjamin fronce les sourcils et l'interroge du regard.

— J'ai fait réserver une cabine, à partir de Naples, au nom d'Angus Murdoch et dans une heure, j'aurai un passeport britannique.

Et devant l'étonnement de son patron :

— Angus Wilson et Iris Murdoch... Je les admire tous les deux. J'ai pensé à tout : Marjory et Marilyn ne m'ont pas vu depuis longtemps et tel que j'apparaîtrai, elles ne me remettront jamais.

Il sort de sa poche une moustache noire bien fournie et se la colle sous le nez. Puis il chausse une paire de lunettes cerclées de métal blanc.

— Toi, tu me reconnais ?

Puis, après avoir enlevé son déguisement.

— Hidar Assadi ne m'a jamais vu, même s'il n'ignore pas mon existence. Je pars au début de l'après-midi. Je me débrouillerai pour te tenir au courant. Cette nuit, j'ai eu le temps de bien étudier le dossier et je possède déjà la topographie du bateau par cœur. Le commandant, Gerardo de Rosa, est un vieux Napolitain. Si ça devait tourner mal, je pense qu'il m'aiderait. Mais mon plan repose justement sur l'espoir, une fois en mer, d'un contact avec Assadi. Je me méfie de mes cousines qui seraient trop heureuses de me rencontrer et se mettraient à parler, à raconter ma vie, la leur, etc. Quant aux terroristes, en apprenant qui je suis, ils risquent de s'affoler et d'essayer de me descendre. Hidar Assadi, par contre, est mon meilleur allié. Tu connais sa « ligne » depuis toujours ! S'il s'embarque personnellement, c'est qu'il veut prévenir des bavures, éviter des actes irréversibles. Il sait que ce serait mortel pour l'image de ses protégés.

Benjamin Ben Eliezer a ôté ses lunettes et, les yeux mi-clos, écoute sans interrompre, sans poser de questions. Partage-t-il réellement l'analyse d'Arié ? Cède-t-il à son enthousiasme ? Se laisse-t-il entraîner par l'émotion qui anime son tout jeune collaborateur ? En tout cas, il y croit et n'envisage, de fait, aucune solution alternative. Il ouvre le tiroir de son bureau et prend une feuille de papier sur laquelle il inscrit un nom et un numéro de téléphone :

— Permets-moi de te donner un conseil, dit-il. Aussitôt arrivé sur le bateau, consacre la première journée à observer. Ne te presse pas.

Et, en lui présentant la feuille de papier :

— Apprends par cœur ce nom et ce numéro de téléphone. Puisque tu es britannique, cet homme sera ton associé. Tous les deux, vous dirigez une petite entreprise informatique, Infor-Service, à Oxford. Téléphone-lui deux fois par jour, à huit heures du matin et à sept heures du soir, à un quart d'heure près.

— Et maintenant, conclut-il en se levant, bon voyage et bonne chance...

46

« ACHILLE LAURO »

LA CROISIÈRE

Pleine mer, octobre 1985

— Dorothy, ma chère, je ne sais vraiment pas comment m'habiller pour la réception du commandant ce soir. Imagine-toi que j'ai décommandé le coiffeur. Je n'avais pas le courage... D'ailleurs, je suis sûre que je ne mourrai pas de laisser voir quelques millimètres de cheveux gris, pour une fois. Quand tu auras l'âge des cheveux gris, ne commets pas la sottise de les teindre. C'est un martyre quotidien...

Marjory jette un coup d'œil à travers le hublot. Elle est heureuse. Heureuse de la croisière. Heureuse d'avoir quitté New York. Heureuse que Jérémie Cohen et Dorothy aient pensé à la distraire et à lui faire oublier, au moins pour l'anniversaire de la disparition de Sidney, le vide de sa vie quotidienne. Les gens, de surcroît, sont gais. On les dirait purifiés de leurs malheurs, de leurs préoccupations, de leurs petitesses. Ils se donnent aux jeux les plus éphémères, aux plaisirs les plus gratuits, comme si la vie sur le bateau, coupée du reste du monde, devait durer toujours. La traditionnelle réception de bienvenue donnée par le commandant de bord a mobilisé toutes les imaginations et occupé toutes les conversations depuis le départ de Naples, voici deux jours.

— Non, non, répond-elle dans le téléphone... Je ne rêvais pas... Je regardais la mer. Tu vas mettre ta robe verte ? Et pourquoi pas ton ensemble argenté ?... Ah, voilà Marilyn ! Je te laisse...

Raccrochant brusquement le téléphone, elle saisit le poignet de sa fille :

— Où étais-tu encore ?

Marilyn grimace :

— Laisse-moi, tu me fais mal !

Elle la lâche, oui. Mais fronce les sourcils et insiste d'une voix radoucie :

— Où étais-tu ? Je te cherchais partout...

Et comme la petite ne répond pas :

— Mais enfin, enlève ton walkman et cesse de t'agiter !

A seize ans, la fille de Sidney est plutôt jolie, encore un peu boulotte mais d'une vivacité rafraîchissante. Sa chevelure rousse et bouclée attire l'attention. Ses éclats de rire forcent la sympathie. Et elle sait déjà, comme personne, s'amuser des jeunes gens qui lui font la cour, passer de l'un à l'autre sans vergogne ou bien les fuir tous pour aller se trémousser seule sur la piste de danse du salon Arazzi. La conduite de sa fille désespère un peu Marjory. « Comment peut-on suivre sérieusement des études, lui dit-elle, quand les doigts sont constamment occupés à rouler une cigarette de hasch et les oreilles à écouter un walkman ? » Cependant Marilyn reste attachante. Elle fait tout et le contraire de tout avec une telle innocence qu'elle désarme toutes les colères.

— Tu m'avais pourtant promis de travailler, dit-elle d'un ton de reproche déjà lassé. Et depuis deux jours, tu n'as même pas ouvert un livre. Si ton père était là...

— On n'aurait pas fait cette croisière ! répond la petite en éclatant de rire.

Mais voyant le visage de sa mère se crisper, elle ajoute :

— Ne te fâche pas. Je travaillerai demain...

— Demain, nous serons à Alexandrie !

— Alors, après-demain.

Sur quoi, elle éclate à nouveau de son rire communicatif et disparaît dans la coursive qui mène au pont du Lido et à la piscine.

Il y a plus de soixante-dix Américains à bord de l'*Achille Lauro*. La majorité viennent du New Jersey. Il y a parmi eux quelques jeunes et un hémiplégique sur sa chaise roulante, plutôt sympathique. Mais Marilyn préfère la compagnie d'un jeune couple d'Israéliens qui descend à Achdod. Et, surtout, celle d'Italiens plus gais et plus insouciants que ses compatriotes. Elle a un faible pour l'un d'eux, le chef-mécanicien, Giovanni Badini, qui est peut-être deux fois plus âgé qu'elle. Ne le repérant pas au bord de la piscine, elle s'apprête à grimper sur le pont du commandant quand Jérémie Cohen, allongé sur une chaise longue, l'arrête :

— Tu as tort de courir après un homme, laisse-le courir après toi...

Marilyn fait une grimace :

— Oh ! vous m'emmerdez !

Et, s'en voulant de la grossièreté de sa réaction, elle s'assied sur l'accoudoir de la chaise longue qui vient de se libérer à côté de Jérémie.

— Je m'étonne que vous ne me demandiez pas si je l'aime...

— Pourquoi, ta mère te le demande ?

— Oh ! Ma mère ?

— Qu'est-ce qu'elle a de si terrible, ta mère ?

— Rien.

— N'oublie pas que tu n'as que seize ans...

— Ne jouez pas au papa, Dick !

Et elle s'éloigne en lui lançant :

— Bye, nous nous verrons à la réception. Mon Italien y sera. Aimeriez-vous que je vous le présente ?

A 19 h 30, une longue file d'hommes et de femmes endimanchés attend au salon Scarabéo, comme devant l'entrée d'un théâtre à succès de Broadway. Tout le spectacle consiste à serrer la main du commandant. Des stewards passent le champagne. Les conversations s'engagent :

— Jérémie n'est toujours pas là, fait remarquer Marjory à Marilyn.

— C'est à cause de Dorothy, réplique-t-elle. Elle est toujours en retard.

Marjory est en beauté. Elle porte une robe longue noire, très décolletée, serrée à la taille par une large ceinture de strass.

— Tu as du succès, fait sa fille, en pouffant. Les hommes te regardent. On verra qui d'entre eux sera le plus courageux. Tiens : voilà le premier...

En effet, un homme de taille moyenne quitte son tabouret de bar et s'avance, un verre à la main, vers Marjory :

— Vous êtes américaine ? demande-t-il en anglais, avec un fort accent moyen-oriental.

Et, sans attendre la réponse, il se présente :

— Je m'appelle Antonio Ramirez. Je suis péruvien. Connaissez-vous le Pérou ? Lima ? La vallée de Cuzco ? La civilisation des Incas ? Je vous ai remarquée de loin et je voulais vous dire que vous êtes...

— Très belle, conclut Marilyn à sa place.

— C'est votre jeune sœur ? demande l'homme, galamment.

Elle sourit, gênée :

— Non, c'est ma fille.

L'œil vif, légèrement globuleux, d'Antonio Ramirez feint l'étonnement :

— Ce n'est pas possible ! Mais vous êtes un prodige !

Et aussitôt, penchant légèrement son visage et sa moustache vers le prodige :

— Puis-je savoir votre nom ?

— Oui, bien sûr. Marjory.

— Un prénom délicieux...

La file avance lentement. Jérémie et Dorothy arrivent enfin. Antonio Ramirez s'excuse, exprime son espoir de revoir Marjory très vite et se place discrètement à la fin de la file.

— Qui est-ce ? demande Dorothy.

— Un des admirateurs de maman, dit Marilyn.

— L'homme sur la chaise roulante, qui salue en ce moment le commandant s'appelle Léon Klinghoffer, fait Jérémie. Sa femme est une de mes patientes...

— Vraiment ! s'exclame Marjory par politesse.

Mais, au fur et à mesure que la file avance, Marilyn

devient plus tendue : « son » Italien, Giovanni Badini, véritable doublure lumière de Robert de Niro, se tient, tout de blanc vêtu, aux côtés du commandant et ne semble guère faire attention à elle. Flot des passagers. Couloirs couverts de tapis. Salon Arazzi où un orchestre anglais et une chanteuse polonaise exécutent un tango argentin. Couples enlacés évoluant sur la piste. Marilyn boude toujours et, faisant, de son regard le plus dédaigneux, le tour du salon, s'exclame brusquement :

— Regardez ! Regardez ! L'homme là-bas, sous les balcons, est-ce qu'il ne ressemble pas au cousin Arié ?

Marjory suit le doigt de sa fille :

— C'est vrai, dit-elle, il lui ressemble. Sauf qu'Arié... Arié, il me semble, n'a ni moustache ni lunettes... Par contre, les quatre garçons debout, juste à côté de celui qui ressemble à Arié...

— Et alors ?

— On dirait... on dirait des drôles de types...

— Ne sois pas sotte ! D'ailleurs, l'un d'entre eux, celui avec les cheveux bouclés, est plutôt joli garçon...

Jérémie, sentant que la conversation risque encore de dégénérer, se lève et boutonne sa veste :

— Ce n'est pas le lieu pour se disputer mais pour danser.

Et il tend la main à Marjory. Au moment où il l'entraîne sur la piste, il croise le regard ironique d'un homme au visage d'oiseau et aux cheveux crépus, presque blancs, assis tout seul près de l'orchestre.

47

« ACHILLE LAURO »

LA CROISIÈRE (2)

Pleine mer, octobre 1985

Le 7 octobre, le lendemain de la réception offerte par le commandant, Marjory est réveillée à l'aube par des bruits de voix dans le couloir et un fort balancement du navire. Elle se lève, tâtonne un peu et écarte le rideau. Malgré le brouillard matinal, elle voit, toutes proches, les lumières d'Alexandrie... L'ombre de la ville. Le quai... Elle entend, surtout, ces cris et ces appels en arabe qui entrent soudain dans la cabine.

— Nous arrivons en Égypte, dit-elle à Marilyn.

— Laisse-moi dormir, gémit la jeune fille... Quelle idée d'arriver dans un pays à six heures du matin !

Elle se lève tout de même. Tire sur le tee-shirt troué qu'elle porte en guise de chemise de nuit !

— Comment vas-tu, maman ?

— Mal, j'ai une migraine épouvantable.

— Prends de la bufferin, alors...

Puis bâillant encore :

— Tu as trop dansé avec ton Péruvien, hier...

Marjory hausse les épaules :

— Deux fois... Ce Ramirez était plutôt gentil, tu sais.

Un haut-parleur couvre le bruit du port : « Les passagers sont priés, après le petit déjeuner, de se présenter au foyer d'information pour le débarquement. Tous ceux qui n'ont pas encore acheté leur billet d'excursion pour Le Caire et les Pyramides doivent s'adresser immédiatement à la direction de la croisière... »

— Je crois que je n'irai pas, dit Marjory. Je ne me sens pas très bien...

— Et les Pyramides, maman ?

— Tant pis pour les Pyramides. Mais toi ? Tu n'as pas besoin de moi...

— Oh... Je ne sais pas encore ce que je vais faire... Ça dépend de Giovanni.

— Mais que lui trouves-tu ?

— Il est quand même mieux que ton señor Ramirez !

— Dis donc ! Sois respectueuse avec ta mère ! La grande différence c'est que moi, je ne couche pas avec Ramirez !

Marjory s'en veut de s'être ainsi emportée. Et elle ne peut s'empêcher de penser à Sidney qui, chaque fois qu'elle se mettait en colère, citait *Les Proverbes* : « Celui qui est lent à la colère vaut mieux qu'un héros. » Mais c'est ainsi. Sa fille a le don de la mettre hors d'elle. Et puis il y a sa pauvre tête qui la fait trop souffrir.

Marilyn heureusement s'approche d'elle, s'assied au pied du lit et avec l'exquise délicatesse qu'elle peut parfois avoir, dit :

— Je suis désolée, maman... Je crois que je vais rester aussi... Les Pyramides, elles ne seront jamais aussi belles que dans *Les Dix Commandements* de Cecil B. de Mille...

Et elle pouffe de rire, enfin complètement réveillée.

La plupart des passagers ont débarqué à Alexandrie et l'*Achille Lauro* a repris la mer. Il longe à présent la côte égyptienne dans la direction de Port-Saïd. Le bateau est tout vide. Sur sept cent quarante voyageurs, il n'en reste plus qu'environ cent cinquante. Il se dégage une bizarre impression de tristesse de fin des vacances. Et lorsque Marjory fait un tour sur le pont du Lido, elle est toute déçue de ne pas y trouver le Péruvien ! Elle erre dans ces espaces soudain presque déserts... Échange quelques propos sans importance avec Léon

Klinghoffer, immobilisé sur sa chaise roulante... Elle retourne dans sa cabine d'où elle ne ressort que vers midi et demi pour se rendre à la salle à manger où le maître d'hôtel a dû rassembler les rescapés dans un coin, tout au fond de l'immense pièce. Déjeuner... Marilyn installée avec trois Autrichiens et un couple d'Américains... Propos vains, faussement badins... Toujours ce vide, cette pointe de mélancolie... Le haut-parleur qui retransmet en sourdine l'air de *La Traviata*... Et puis, tout à coup, parfaitement inattendu et inopportun, un cri... Une plainte... Un autre cri... Et puis, comble d'étrangeté, quelques détonations qui font se tourner toutes les têtes... Deux hommes sont là, à l'entrée, mitraillette au poing, qui observent les passagers et qui, sans un mot, traversent la pièce et sautent sur une table vide. Le premier a la tête bouclée, le visage tendu, il brandit un pistolet, a deux grenades attachées à la ceinture et agite son arme en hurlant :

— Debout ! Tous debout ! Rassemblement au milieu de la salle ! Vite ! Vite ! Asseyez-vous par terre, les mains derrière la nuque !

Il lâche une rafale de mitraillette au plafond, comme pour signifier que l'affaire est sérieuse. Et c'est alors que Marjory reconnaît deux des quatre jeunes qu'elle croyait arabes, à la soirée du commandant. Les deux terroristes changent de table — l'un se tenant à présent derrière les passagers accroupis, l'autre devant.

— Ils sont complètement fous ! grommelle Marilyn, accroupie à côté de sa mère.

Puis, avec un petit rire étouffé :

— Ils ne vont pas nous tuer, hein, maman !

Mais le jeune terroriste continue à hurler :

— Nous sommes des combattants palestiniens ! Le bateau est entre nos mains ! Le commandant se trouve sous bonne garde. Nous avons placé des explosifs dans la salle des machines ! Si l'un d'entre vous essaye de contrarier nos plans, il sera immédiatement abattu...

Comme pour donner corps à la menace quelqu'un, sur le pont, tire une nouvelle rafale. Et on entend la voix du commandant qui, dans le haut-parleur, remplace *La Traviata* :

— C'est le commandant Gerardo de Rosa qui vous parle. Gardez votre calme. Le bateau vient d'être détourné par des terroristes palestiniens. Ils promettent de ne rien faire contre les passagers. Ils exigent, en échange, la libération de cinquante prisonniers en Israël, dont Samir Kantari.

Un grésillement... Un coup de feu... La voix du commandant se tait... On entend les machines ralentir... Le plancher vibrer plus fort... Un troisième terroriste arrive, qui annonce que le navire a changé de cap et se dirige maintenant vers le port syrien de Tartous. On fait alors monter le groupe jusqu'au salon Arazzi. Et voilà les cent cinquante hommes et femmes, terrorisés et incrédules qui s'alignent comme des bestiaux sur la piste où, il y a un jour à peine, ils ont si joliment dansé. Marjory a de nouveau la migraine. Elle pense une fois de plus à Sidney et au calvaire qu'il a enduré, là-bas, à Zarka. Elle se prend la tête dans les mains et la serre avec force comme si elle pouvait en extraire la douleur. Puis, découragée, elle enveloppe Marilyn dans ses bras et sanglote sur son épaule.

A la tombée du jour, un terroriste apporte un carton rempli de sandwichs. La soirée passe. La nuit vient. Loin de s'atténuer, le sentiment d'attente, d'incompréhension, d'horreur, ne fait qu'aller croissant. Les gens sont là. Apeurés. Interdits. On entend ici un sanglot. Un peu plus loin une plainte. Seul Léon Klinghoffer, silencieux sur sa chaise roulante, fixe le terroriste assis sur une marche de l'escalier, deux grenades posées à côté de lui.

— J'ai peur, dit Marilyn.

— Pose ta tête sur mes genoux et tente de dormir, fait Marjory en caressant sa tignasse rousse.

Au petit matin, l'un des terroristes viendra avec une liste de passagers qu'il lira à haute voix. Onze Américains... Six Britanniques... Deux Autrichiens... Suivez-moi... Tous sur le pont... Une rafale de mitraillette tirée dans les fenêtres ponctue l'ordre donné. Une Autrichienne d'un certain âge, qui se lève en s'appuyant sur une canne, a une petite crise de nerfs. Un autre se met à hurler. Mais il ne faut pas plus de quelques minutes pour que les dix-neuf passagers se retrouvent tous sur le pont.

La voix du commandant se fait à nouveau entendre :

— Votre commandant Gerardo de Rosa vous parle. Nous sommes au large du port syrien de Tartous. Les terroristes sont en train de négocier par radio avec les autorités...

— Tiens ! il n'est pas mort, fait Marilyn.

— As-tu remarqué, dit en chuchotant Marjory, que tous ceux qu'ils ont fait sortir sont des Juifs ?

— Et les Autrichiens ?

— Ils les ont certainement pris pour des Juifs à cause de leur nom.

Le terroriste hurle en tirant en l'air :

— Silence !

Le soleil est au plus haut maintenant. Le terroriste qui, visiblement, a chaud lui aussi, permet au petit groupe de se déplacer légèrement pour retrouver un peu d'ombre. Deux vedettes armées arrivent à ce moment-là. Marjory voit un homme lever un porte-voix. Un terroriste lui répond, celui qui les garde et qui a visiblement envie de les impressionner, traduit que les Palestiniens exigent la libération de cinquante-deux de leurs camarades du camp de Naharia, en Israël, ainsi que la présence d'un bateau de la Croix-Rouge avec, à son bord, les ambassadeurs américain, britannique, italien et allemand accrédités à Damas. Faute de quoi ils feront tout sauter. Il ne traduit pas la réponse des Syriens, mais Marjory entend répéter, à plusieurs reprises, le mot « Port-Saïd ». Et quand le terroriste, depuis le pont du commandant, leur répond à nouveau, le gardien traduit sèchement :

— C'est un ultimatum. Nous allons frapper à 15 heures.

Un nuage passe. Une pluie fine et tiède arrose le pont. Le terroriste déplace le groupe vers le devant du navire. Marjory serre plus fort Marilyn contre elle. Elle n'arrive plus à rassembler ni ses pensées ni ses souvenirs. Elle ne ressent même plus la peur. Le bruit d'une détonation la fait frémir : c'est une des vedettes syriennes qui a tiré un coup de semonce. Puis le bruit des machines : c'est l'*Achille Lauro* qui reprend la haute mer. Le terroriste échange encore quelques phrases brèves en arabe dans le talkie-walkie. Il attend une réponse. Et ordonne au petit groupe de retourner au salon Arazzi où des sandwichs et des boissons les attendent. C'est à ce moment-là que Marjory s'aperçoit de l'absence de Léon Klinghoffer. Elle voit sa femme, s'approche d'elle.

— Oui, dit-elle, très pâle... Je suis inquiète pour mon mari... Les terroristes l'ont, à l'aide d'un garçon de cabine, fait monter sur le pont... Et...

— Silence ! hurle l'homme aux cheveux bouclés, visiblement de plus en plus nerveux.

On entend encore des coups de feu, quelque part sur l'un des ponts au-dessus d'eux. Tous retiennent leur souffle... Se regardent les uns les autres... Ils savent, ils *sentent* que quelque chose de très grave vient de se passer et que la catastrophe, en suspens depuis des heures et des heures, vient enfin de se produire.

— Où est mon mari ? crie la femme de Léon Klinghoffer.

— Votre mari est à l'infirmerie, dit le terroriste. Par contre, si les Israéliens ne cèdent pas, vous sauterez tous avec le bateau.

Personne n'est dupe, évidemment. Talonnés par la peur, terrassés par la fatigue, les passagers se serrent les uns contre les autres. Ils ne forment plus à présent qu'un seul corps et restent ainsi jusqu'au soir, quand le bateau arrive au large du port de Larnaca, à Chypre.

Nouvelle négociation... Nouvel échec... Deux ou trois heures plus tard, le bateau fait route vers Port-Saïd où il arrive au petit matin. Les négociations reprennent encore. Longues. Pénibles. Confuses aussi, sans doute. Mais plus personne n'écoute. Personne n'y croit vraiment. Quand, vers midi, la voix du commandant de Rosa dit :

— Tout est OK à bord ! Tout le monde se porte bien !

quand les deux terroristes lèvent le doigt en forme de V, quittent le salon Arazzi et laissent les passagers sans surveillance, tout le monde n'a, bien entendu, qu'un nom à l'esprit, celui de Léon Klinghoffer.

Paris, octobre 1987

A l'époque où, comme tout le monde, dans la presse et la télévision, je suivais, scandalisé, la prise d'otages de l'*Achille Lauro,* j'ignorais que Marjory, la veuve de Sidney, et sa fille Marilyn se trouvaient sur le cargo. Je l'ai appris, aussi surprenant que cela paraisse, un an et demi plus tard, quand, venu à New York pour la sortie de *La Mémoire d'Abraham,* je les ai toutes deux rencontrées. En écoutant leur récit, désordonné, entrecoupé d'appréciations personnelles et parfois contradictoires, je me souvins des prédictions de Benjamin Ben Eliezer. Oui, l'aventure de l'*Achille Lauro* illustrait mieux qu'aucune autre la banalisation de la terreur. Car quoi de plus frivole qu'une croisière, ce cadre idéal pour oublier les soucis et les agressions de la vie quotidienne ? Quel chemin parcouru en si peu de temps par ce « terrorisme médiatique », cher à Hidar Assadi ! Et comme on était loin de l'« exploit » de Zarka ! Avec l'*Achille Lauro* le terrorisme rejoignait définitivement le sordide. C'est cette dérive autant que la présence de mes personnages sur le bateau qui me donna l'envie de mener ma propre enquête.

La chance m'a souri : la compagnie maritime propriétaire de l'*Achille Lauro,* apprenant par un entrefilet mon intention de consacrer quelques pages à ce détournement, m'invita sur le cargo et c'est ainsi que je me retrouvai, le 8 octobre 1987, en compagnie du commandant Gerardo de Rosa, sur le pont du fameux bateau amarré dans le port de Naples. Rien n'avait changé, ni le programme des excursions, ni l'équipage, ni le capitaine. Mais, parmi les quelques centaines de passagers avides d'un dernier rayon de soleil ou curieux de nouveaux paysages, j'étais bien le seul à m'intéresser à une histoire pourtant pas si ancienne.

— Le 8 octobre, vers 15 heures, commence le capitaine, je me tenais sur le pont de commandement lorsque retentirent deux coups de feu. C'était tout à fait inattendu. Jusque-là, les terroristes s'étaient contentés de tirer des rafales de mitraillette en l'air, pour nous effrayer. J'allais me précipiter, mais Mahmoud, le terroriste chargé de me surveiller, m'en empêcha. Quelques instants plus tard, Molky, un de ses complices accourait, un passeport ouvert à la main. C'était celui de Klinghoffer.

— Que vous a-t-il dit ?

— Américain, kaputt !

Étrange, me dis-je, de voir comment parmi tant de langues, parmi tant d'expressions et de mots, ce jeune Palestinien né bien après la guerre choisissait ce mot-ci pour annoncer la mort d'un Juif. « Kaputt »... Ce cri, ce glapissement que j'ai entendu pour la première fois vociférer par des nazis dans le ghetto de Varsovie... D'un seul coup, la mort de ce vieux juif paralytique, et la vision d'un enfant les mains en l'air devant des fusils nazis dans le ghetto se superposèrent dans mon esprit, devinrent un seul et même événement.

— A l'arrivée du bateau à Port-Saïd, continue le commandant, Abou Abbas m'avait déclaré, en présence de plusieurs journalistes : « Le commando a été contraint de prendre le contrôle du paquebot, alors que son objectif initial visait l'ennemi israélien. Nous rendrons publiques ultérieurement les raisons qui ont empêché nos camarades de débarquer à Achdod et de prendre le contrôle du navire. » Mensonge, bien entendu. Grossier mensonge. Car il y avait un cinquième homme dans cette sanglante affaire. Quel homme ? Un homme d'une cinquantaine d'années, un peu gras, un peu chauve, l'œil légèrement exophtalmique, une moustache noire fournie, comme en témoigne un cliché pris par hasard par le photographe du bord. Sur son passeport, un nom étrange : Pedros Floros. C'était incontestablement un professionnel. Un de ces spécialistes du terrorisme international à qui l'on a fait appel pour préparer de gros coups. C'est sûrement lui le véritable organisateur du détournement.

Je regarde la photo que me montre le vieux loup de mer et il me semble y reconnaître, d'après le récit de Marjory, l'homme qui l'avait courtisée. Ne s'était-il pas présenté comme péruvien ? sous le nom de Antonio Ramirez ? Brusquement, l'idée me vint qu'il s'agissait peut-être de Jael el-Ardja, l'homme que Sidney avait rencontré dans l'avion à son retour de Beyrouth et qui, selon Benjamin Ben Eliezer, était chargé de l'attentat contre David Ben Gourion. J'interrogeai plus avant. Et, le cœur battant, j'appris que si les quatre terroristes partageaient la même cabine sans hublot, V 82, Pedros Floros, lui, disposait d'une cabine de luxe, située sur l'un des ponts supérieurs. De surcroît et comme le prouva l'enquête, il avait fait le voyage, une première fois, un mois plus tôt, « pour repérer les lieux ». Le soir de la réception traditionnelle lors de laquelle les passagers avaient présenté leurs vœux au capitaine, l'homme, au lieu de se nommer, se contenta de déposer un mince chapelet d'ambre dans la main du capitaine et de murmurer : « Allah ! »

De plus en plus étrange, me dis-je. Car pourquoi ce geste ? Pour prévenir le capitaine d'un danger ? Mais pourquoi, dans ce cas, ne pas l'avoir fait plus clairement ? A-t-il eu peur ? Mais de qui ? C'étaient là les questions du capitaine. Pour ma part, je crois surtout que Jael el-Ardja, alias Pedros Floros ou Antonio Ramirez, ayant échoué déjà dans l'une de ses entreprises, était tout bonnement superstitieux et voulait ainsi conjurer le sort. Que la présence d'un couple de jeunes Israéliens avec lesquels Marilyn s'était liée d'amitié, ait pu le décider à quitter inopinément le navire à

420

Alexandrie est possible, mais, à mon avis, peu probable — car guère professionnel. Possible, en revanche, qu'il y ait eu une sixième personne, le *deus ex-machina* ignoré de la presse.

Mais voici le plus curieux. Au début de ce mois de septembre, quelques jours avant le départ de la croisière, Gerardo de Rosa reçut par la poste un présent : un bijou en or, représentant deux oiseaux superposés. Et, sur une carte, quelques mots en arabe, griffonnés en lettres latines : « *Kaïdar Aleyk Salam.* » *Aleyk Salam*, c'est clair, veut dire : allez en paix. Mais « Kaïdar » ? Ni les Égyptiens au Caire, ni les Israéliens à Tel-Aviv ne purent m'en donner l'explication.

Après six jours de mer, l'*Achille Lauro* accosta enfin à Haïfa. Les haut-parleurs diffusaient l'air fameux de *La Traviata*.

— Comme le jour où les quatre terroristes pénétrèrent dans la salle à manger, les armes à la main, dit le commandant Gerardo de Rosa.

Quand je racontai tout cela à Arié, il sourit d'un air légèrement suffisant qui m'agaça un peu. Il m'emmena ensuite déjeuner dans un petit restaurant, rue Dizengoff, l'un des rares à servir encore, en Israël, le bouillon avec des *kneidlekh* et de la carpe farcie. Il faisait beau et nous nous installâmes dehors. Le seul détail de mon récit qui semblait le surprendre concernait le dernier cadeau reçu par la poste par le commandant de Rosa. Quant au mot « Kaïdar », il avait son interprétation : c'était un prénom et ce prénom était celui de Hidar.

— Ce serait lui le sixième personnage ? demandai-je.

Arié ne répondit pas mais me fit un clin d'œil.

— Il devait aussi y avoir un agent israélien à bord, continuai-je. Quelqu'un que Hidar connaissait.

— Ah ? fit Arié.

— Mais oui, c'est comme un puzzle. Tant que tu n'as pas trouvé l'emplacement de chaque pièce, tu ne reconnais pas l'image. Mais dès que les pièces du puzzle se mettent en place, l'image apparaît nette, évidente.

Contrairement au commandant Gerardo de Rosa, je crois, moi, à l'affirmation d'Abou Abbas. L'objectif des terroristes était, en effet, Achdod et c'est même la raison de la présence sur le bateau de Jael el-Ardja. C'est lui — et là-dessus le commandant a raison — qui devait préparer et superviser l'opération. La présence de Hidar, par contre, s'explique, me semble-t-il, par la volonté des Soviétiques d'empêcher les Palestiniens de commettre l'irréparable. Un massacre de civils à ce moment-là aurait nui à l'image d'Arafat. L'agent israélien était, en quelque sorte, l'allié de Hidar. Leurs buts se rejoignaient. Sauf que ni l'un ni l'autre n'avaient prévu l'imprévu : c'est-à-dire, comme toujours, la folie des hommes. Jael el-Ardja suit le conseil de Hidar et, sans prévenir le commando pour ne pas le « griller », disparaît à Alexandrie. Hidar le suit, lui-même poursuivi par l'agent israélien. Et tous commettent alors une erreur : les quatre terroristes, abandonnés à leur sort et sans plan précis pour leur action à Achdod, n'abandonnent pas la partie et s'inventent même une action de rechange.

Arié sourit tristement :

— L'archer est le modèle pour le sage, disent les Chinois : quand il a manqué le centre de la cible, il ne s'en prend qu'à lui-même.

— Tu veux dire ?

— Tu sais, j'ai toujours aimé la littérature d'action... Hemingway, Von Salomon, Malraux... Je viens de terminer *Pour qui sonne le glas*... Quand tu parles d'un bateau qui fait une croisière en Méditerranée, cela n'intéresse personne. Fais-le visiter par une cousine en quête d'aventures, fais-le détourner par un terroriste, fais-y commettre un crime et intervenir un agent pour empêcher un massacre, fais fuir cet agent devant un autre, et, du coup, ton bateau sautera hors de ton livre, comme le lapin du chapeau d'un prestidigitateur.

En l'écoutant parler, je m'aperçus qu'il avait changé, mûri, qu'il s'était cultivé et avait aiguisé ses réflexions.

Il devina ma pensée :

— Je t'étonne, hein ? C'est que nous ne nous connaissons pas.

422

Après quoi il demanda l'addition et nous remontâmes la rue Dizengoff à pied. La rue était presque vide, fermée en partie à la circulation. C'était Shabbat. Le ciel était bleu, l'air transparent et les promeneurs voués au plaisir de la flânerie.

Je n'aime pas les villes désœuvrées, sans rythme, sans mouvement. Les avenues sont faites pour passer. Les maisons pour vivre ou travailler. La ville n'est pas faite pour la promenade, le pur loisir. Histoire de tromper mon angoisse, je questionnai Arié sur sa mère et sa femme. Judith est à nouveau enceinte. Quant à Richard, il est parti s'installer dans une colonie de peuplement près de Hebron. Et puis, brusquement, comme nous arrivions à la hauteur du théâtre national Habimah, il m'annonça, mine de rien, qu'il avait terminé son rapport sur la mort de Hugo.

J'accusai le coup, feignant de prendre la chose avec autant de flegme que lui. Quand je lui en demandai copie, il refusa en riant. Puis, se ravisant, me dit qu'il pourrait me le faire lire, à son bureau, au Centre.

— Et Hidar? demandai-je. Sais-tu où il en est?

Arié me regarda gravement, passa la main dans sa chevelure bouclée et répéta :

— Où il en est? En danger. J'aurais bien voulu l'aider, mais je ne vois pas comment.

Je sentis qu'il ne m'en dirait pas plus — et me tus.

48

TEL-AVIV

HUGO. LE RAPPORT D'ARIÉ

Objet : Hugo (David) Halter. Né le 27 novembre 1915, à Berlin. Mort le 27 mars 1961, victime d'un attentat sur la route de Tel-Aviv-Jérusalem.

Attentat non revendiqué.

Hugo Halter est né dans une famille d'imprimeurs, dans un milieu orthodoxe. Son enfance se passe sans problèmes majeurs. Il étudie dans une école juive et, très tôt, apprend le métier de son père. L'arrivée de Hitler au pouvoir le rapproche, jeune ouvrier de dix-huit ans, des milieux socialistes. Sa mère meurt en 1935. Lors de la Nuit de Cristal, le 8 novembre 1938, l'imprimerie de son père est saccagée. La police y trouve des tracts antinazis. Son père et son frère sont arrêtés et envoyés à Dachau. Hugo parvient à s'échapper.

En janvier 1939, après de longues péripéties, Hugo arrive à Varsovie. Son grand-oncle, Abraham Halter, l'aide à partir pour l'Amérique. Il s'embarque le 19 février 1939 sur le paquebot *Jan Bothory*. A New York, le Joint Distribution Commitee l'accueille, lui trouve un logement. Un ami d'Abraham, Kastoff, le fait entrer comme metteur en pages à l'imprimerie du quotidien yiddish *Forward*. Dans les couloirs du journal, il se heurte un jour à une réfugiée du nom de Sarah Roth. Elle est hongroise et préposée au courrier. Ils se lient, vivent ensemble par intermittence ; et attendent un enfant.

1939-1940. Pendant cette période, Hugo Halter tente,

par tous les moyens, d'alerter l'opinion publique sur le danger que court le judaïsme européen. Le 18 août 1940, Sarah Roth meurt en couches. L'enfant, Abraham, est prit en charge par les Lubavitch. Il se fera écraser par une voiture, à Brooklyn, quatre ans plus tard alors que Hugo se trouvera engagé dans la guerre, en Europe.

Le 20 septembre 1941, il rencontre le rabbin Stephen Wise, le président du Congrès juif mondial et son second, Nahum Goldman. Il met sur pied un attentat contre Fritz Kuhn, président de l'association pronazie « L'amitié germano-américaine », mais au dernier moment y renonce. Il envoie plusieurs lettres au *New York Times,* qui ne les publie pas.

Le 20 décembre 1941, après la déclaration de guerre, Hugo est l'un des premiers engagés volontaires. Le 8 novembre 1942, il est envoyé au Maroc, à Casablanca, le général Omar Bradley, chef du 11e corps d'armée, débarqué en Tunisie, réclame un interprète. Il arrive à Tunis en février 1943, découvre le monde arabe, se lie d'amitié avec Marwan Assadi, l'un des dirigeants du néo-Destour. Il retrouvera son fils Hidar, quelques années plus tard, à Berlin. Le 10 mai 1943, il participe à la libération de Hammam-Lif.

En juillet 1944, il est envoyé à Palerme, puis à Naples. Le 18 août, il débarque, avec la 36e division du général Dahlouist, à Saint-Raphaël, en France. Il se retrouve officier de liaison du général Montgomery dans les Ardennes. Dépêché, en janvier 1945, auprès des forces françaises du général de Lattre de Tassigny, près de Strasbourg, il est blessé sur le Rhin, le 12 février 1945.

Si sa vie jusqu'à cette date n'est guère mystérieuse, et correspond à peu près aux récits qu'il en a lui-même donnés, tout ce qui suit a été transposé, modelé, aménagé par lui selon l'idée qu'il se faisait du monde et de ses propres devoirs.

Parmi les affaires que la police trouva dans sa chambre de l'hôtel Dan, à Tel-Aviv, et qu'elle transmit à Mordekhaï Halter, mon père, se trouvaient quelques livres dont un rituel de prières en hébreu et en anglais.

Mon père fit tout suivre à Paris. Mais, je ne saurais dire pourquoi, garda les livres par-devers lui. Et c'est ainsi que je découvris, un jour, dans le rituel de prières, parmi les extraits du Traité des Principes, une sentence soulignée d'un trait de crayon bleu. Elle était du rabbin Eliezer, fils d'Azaryah : « Sans la loi, pas de civilisation, sans civilisation pas de loi. Sans sagesse point de piété, sans piété point de sagesse ; sans savoir pas de raisonnement, sans raisonnement pas de savoir ; sans pain point d'études, sans études point de pain. » C'est à dessein que je m'arrête sur cette phrase soulignée de la main de Hugo. Elle me paraît, à bien des égards, éclairer sa vie.

Cela dit, tous les témoignages concordent : au moment de sa blessure, Hugo est sioniste. 1/ Il croit qu'après la guerre, un État juif naîtra en Palestine ; 2/ Il croit à la coexistence entre Juifs et Arabes ; 3/ Il reproche à l'Occident, et surtout aux États-Unis, d'être entrés trop tard en guerre en sacrifiant ainsi le judaïsme européen.

Sa blessure l'aura profondément marqué. D'après le témoignage du docteur Sam Rappoport qui l'a soigné pendant près d'un an à Miami, dans un centre de convalescence pour les officiers américains blessés en Europe, Hugo se sentait coupable de n'avoir pas su préserver la mémoire familiale, en laissant couvrir de son sang le document qu'Abraham lui avait confié. Coupable aussi de n'avoir pas pu, comme il l'avait rêvé, participer en personne à la prise et à la destruction de Berlin.

Au centre de convalescence, il semble s'être fixé quelques objectifs. Il pensait que le devoir d'un survivant était de préserver le souvenir de la Shoah et de reconstituer la mémoire de son peuple. Ces deux tâches l'amenaient, tout naturellement selon lui, à participer à la création d'un État contribuant lui-même au triomphe de la paix dans le monde.

Le docteur Rappoport parle aussi de la reconnaissance, quasi-hystérique, qu'il éprouvait à l'endroit des Furchmuller qui lui avaient sauvé la vie. Ce qui, toujours selon le docteur Rappoport, le rendait exagéré-ment dépendant de Sigrid Furchmuller — laquelle devint, par la suite, sa femme.

La vie de Hugo se complique à partir de sa rencontre avec la jeune Allemande. Cette rencontre ne correspond pas au récit qu'il en a fait. En fuyant l'avant-poste de l'armée allemande près de Strasbourg, Hugo tombe sur Sigrid, mais elle n'est pas seule ; son frère, Hans, l'accompagne. Ils ne soignent pas Hugo sur place, comme il le prétendit par la suite, mais emmènent le blessé à Kiel, où l'armée allemande est en pleine déroute. Les Furchmuller n'ont nullement besoin de Hugo pour blanchir la jeune Sigrid. Par contre, le père de Sigrid, Wolfgang Furchmuller, général de la Wehrmacht, avait besoin d'un témoignage pour échapper aux poursuites. Il devint plus tard un collaborateur du général Gehlen, le tout puissant patron des services secrets de la République fédérale allemande — mais devait, avant cela, être blanchi.

Hugo Halter prétendit avoir, après la guerre, repris sa place à l'imprimerie du quotidien yiddish de New York, *Forward.* Ce n'est pas tout à fait exact. Il n'y demeura qu'un semestre car Sigrid, qui ne se plaisait pas à New York, était repartie à Kiel où il la rejoint dès Noël 1945. Dans les environs, il découvre l'un de ces camps de « personnes déplacées » aménagés par les alliés pour les survivants des camps de la mort. Il y rencontre Moshe Sneh, un émissaire du « Mossad Alya Beth », l'organisation de l'émigration clandestine attachée au Mossad. Moshe Sneh est venu en Allemagne pour superviser le départ clandestin des Juifs pour la Palestine.

Presque trois ans plus tard, le 20 mai 1948, six jours après la proclamation de l'État d'Israël, Hugo se rend avec cet homme à Prague pour négocier un achat d'armes. Les Tchèques, pourtant, tardent à acheminer ces armes vers Israël. Pendant ce temps, la situation en Israël se dégrade. Les armées arabes envahissent le jeune État juif. Et c'est alors, je pense, que Sigrid a pu suggérer à Hugo de s'adresser directement aux Soviétiques. La rencontre, organisée par le frère de la jeune femme, Hans, a lieu à Berlin le 27 mai 1948. J'ai la preuve que Hugo a rencontré, ce jour-là, à 9 heures du matin, pour le petit déjeuner, au café Kranzler, sur Kurfürsterdam, l'envoyé des services secrets soviétiques, Vladimir Volossatov, qui promet de débloquer les armes. Mais en posant des conditions.

Là-dessus, je n'ai pas de preuves, mais je crois comprendre que Hugo, promettant de collaborer avec les Soviétiques, ne savait pas où cela allait le mener. Il s'aperçut d'ailleurs que sa femme et le frère de celle-ci collaboraient déjà. Pour lui l'essentiel, à cette époque, était de sauver les Juifs qui avaient survécu à l'enfer nazi et de préserver l'État d'Israël. Probable aussi que le fait que la transaction ait lieu à Berlin, sa ville natale, joua un rôle important. Vis-à-vis de l'Allemagne, sa position était claire : « pardonner sans jamais oublier ». Pour l'heure, en tout cas, les armes étaient débloquées et Hugo était devenu une taupe soviétique. Une taupe très particulière. Une sorte d'agent double dont le second commanditaire n'était autre que lui-même. Mais enfin, une taupe tout de même. Je m'explique : Hugo croyait que grâce aux moyens mis à sa disposition par les Soviétiques, il pourrait, à sa manière, promouvoir la paix. Mieux : il était persuadé d'être capable de les amener à soutenir une opération qui, à la limite, pourrait leur échapper. Naïveté ? Non. Une réflexion froide, cynique. Il avait un objectif. Peu lui importait le prix à payer pour l'atteindre. C'est ainsi, par exemple, que lors de la première Conférence mondiale pour la paix, en juin 1948, il persuade les responsables du KGB de l'immense intérêt qu'il y aurait pour l'URSS à travailler à un dialogue entre Arabes et Israéliens.

En décembre 1953, exactement le 12 décembre, à 15 h 30, à Francfort, il rencontre pour la première fois Israël Beer, le conseiller personnel de David Ben Gourion, au ministère israélien de la Défense. Et c'est encore Hans Furchmuller qui recommande l'un à l'autre. Hugo Halter et Israël Beer se lient d'amitié. Hugo est persuadé qu'Israël Beer est animé par une volonté identique à la sienne d'assurer l'avenir d'Israël. Beer l'encourage à poursuivre ses contacts. Il lui conseille même d'aller au Caire pour rencontrer Sami Scharaf, un proche de Nasser.

Au mois de février 1955, Hugo, toujours accompagné de sa femme Sigrid, arrive au Caire, fait la connaissance de Sami Scharaf et, grâce à lui, rencontre Nasser. De là, il se rend aussitôt, via Chypre, en Israël, pour rendre compte à Beer de ses conversations avec le Président égyptien. Beer lui promet alors de l'introduire auprès de David Ben Gourion et lui demande de transmettre à Hans Furchmuller un dossier que celui-ci attend. Hugo s'exécute. Le 21 mai 1956, il remet le dossier à Hans. J'ai la preuve, aujourd'hui, que ce dossier contenait le plan de l'attaque tripartite Israéliens-Français-Anglais contre l'Égypte, attaque appelée communément la campagne de Suez.

J'en étais arrivé à ce point du rapport quand Arié interrompit ma lecture.

— J'ai oublié de te raconter une histoire fantastique, fit-il avec toute sa fougue juvénile.

— Oui ?

— Tu te souviens de Zvika Amihay, le Bulgare ? Je t'en ai parlé… Celui qui avait été chargé par Benjamin Ben Eliezer de me communiquer les dossiers de Hugo et de Hidar. Je t'ai parlé aussi de son comportement bizarre… Je l'ai signalé à Benjamin qui, méfiant, a ordonné une enquête. Eh bien voilà : imagine-toi qu'on vient de découvrir que Zvika travaillait pour les Russes ! Tu te rends compte, une taupe à l'Aman !

49

TEL-AVIV

HUGO. LE RAPPORT D'ARIÉ (2)

La campagne de Suez débute le 29 octobre 1956 et ses préparatifs demeurent secrets jusqu'au tout dernier moment. Les services israéliens sont pourtant persuadés que les Soviétiques en étaient informés, même s'ils n'ont pas cru nécessaire d'en prévenir Nasser. Pourquoi ? Parce que les difficultés de l'Égypte les réjouissaient plutôt et ne pouvaient que la rendre plus dépendante encore de leur aide.

Un an plus tard, le 25 septembre 1957, Hugo Halter se trouve à nouveau à Berlin. Puis, lors d'une manifestation contre les violences racistes aux USA, à Little Rock, Arkansas, il rencontre par hasard Hidar, le fils de son vieil ami Marwan Assadi, venu aux États-Unis pour assister à un congrès. D'après les documents en notre possession, cette rencontre n'était pas fortuite. Arabe, proche des organisations palestiniennes, Hidar deviendra rapidement un homme précieux dans la stratégie de paix de Hugo. Celui-ci, quelque peu irrité par la surveillance exercée sur lui par la famille Furchmuller, est heureux d'y échapper grâce à ce nouvel allié. A l'époque il ne sait pas qu'il reste toujours sous contrôle soviétique.

Hugo Halter commence alors à voyager seul. Il rencontre, le 10 décembre 1957 à 18 heures, à Tel-Aviv, David Ben Gourion. Puis, avec Hidar Assadi, il fait plusieurs voyages à Beyrouth et fait la connaissance de Ghassan Kanafani. Chose étrange, tous les agents que j'ai pu rencontrer donnent l'impression d'individus intelligents, beaux parleurs, mais doués d'un amour-propre excessif. Hugo Halter n'a pas échappé à la règle. « L'orgueil précède la ruine et la hauteur précède la chute. »

Toujours est-il qu'il réussit à organiser deux rencontres israélo-arabes. L'une à Florence, le 12-13 juin 1959, grâce à l'aide du maire de la ville, Giorgio La Pira ; l'autre, à Bologne, le 14 avril 1960, sous l'égide du maire communiste Guido Fanti. Je suis persuadé par ailleurs que, parallèlement à son objectif principal, il continue à œuvrer à la reconstitution de l'histoire familiale. C'était une dette qu'il avait contractée, disait-il, à l'égard du grand-oncle Abraham... Ainsi ai-je pu retrouver la trace de son passage à Soncino, dans la province de Crémone, en Italie, à Lublin, en Pologne, à Amsterdam et même à Istanbul. A cette époque, on le voit beaucoup avec le père Roberto Cerutti, un jésuite, directeur général de Radio-Vatican, très influent auprès du Pape. Il complote, organise des séminaires judéo-chrétiens, tente de créer un comité œcuménique pour Jérusalem. Il n'est pas impossible que Hugo ait pu recevoir de l'argent du Vatican. Mais je ne pourrais pas le prouver.

Au milieu du mois de mai 1960, Hugo Halter rejoint Sigrid, qui se trouve en visite chez son père à Mönchengladbach, en RFA. C'est à partir de ce moment que son comportement échappe à la logique. Il quitte en effet l'Allemagne pour Beyrouth où il rencontre Hidar. Nos agents, au Liban, l'ont vu à plusieurs reprises à la Grotte aux Pigeons. Puis, il se rend à Moscou où il rencontre plusieurs hauts fonctionnaires du KGB ainsi que des dirigeants du Comité de solidarité avec les peuples d'Afrique et d'Asie. De Moscou, il gagne Paris, mais n'y rencontre pas son cousin Salomon : il reprend le jour même un avion d'Air-France pour New York. Je pense pouvoir reconstituer aujourd'hui son trajet à partir de sa visite à Mönchengladbach, jusqu'à sa mort sur la route de Tel-Aviv à Jérusalem, en mars 1961.

Le 12 mai 1960, Hugo Halter est donc à Mönchen-gladbach l'invité de son beau-père, Wolfgang Furchmuller qui travaille, il le sait, pour les services de renseignements de la RFA. Ce qu'il ne sait pas, en revanche, c'est qu'il va voir Israël Beer se promenant dans le jardin des Services, en compagnie du patron même de Wolfgang Furchmuller, le général Reinhard Gehlen ! Il en parle certainement à Sigrid qui est étonnée à son tour que son époux, proche d'Israël Beer, ne connaisse pas l'engagement de ce dernier auprès des Soviétiques. Elle demande aussitôt à Hugo de garder tout cela secret. Officiellement, le père de Sigrid ignore tout des activités de sa fille et de son fils et le général Gehlen celles d'Israël Beer. Je peux affirmer aujourd'hui que les services secrets de la RFA connaissent parfaitement les agissements du conseiller de David Ben Gourion, ainsi que ses contacts permanents avec Hans Furchmuller et, à travers lui, avec la HVA, le Haupt Verwaltung Aufklärung, les services secrets de la RDA. Mais cela ne le dérangeait nullement. Au contraire, en suivant la famille Furchmuller à la trace, le général Gehlen obtenait tous les renseignements presque en même temps que les Soviétiques.

Pour Hugo Halter, c'est un choc. Il vient de comprendre que l'action qu'il a engagée et qu'il croyait contrôler lui échappe complètement. Au lieu d'utiliser les Soviétiques, il se fait manœuvrer, depuis des années, par eux. Quel type de sentiments l'anime à ce moment-là ? Ce que je puis dire c'est qu'il commence, dès lors, à voyager beaucoup. Trop. J'ai pu relever un voyage à Moscou. Deux aux États-Unis, où il n'était pas revenu depuis deux ans. Puis un voyage à Tunis et un autre à nouveau aux États-Unis. Cette fébrilité s'explique, selon moi, par sa volonté de se dégager de la toile d'araignée où il s'était emmêlé.

A Moscou, le 22 juin 1960, à 15 heures, il rencontre Vladimir Volossatov, auprès de qui il espère trouver conseil. Celui-ci lui parle des importantes dépenses engagées par ses services et dont les reçus, signés de la main de Hugo, se trouvent en sa possession. Hugo s'affole. Il se dit naïvement, cette fois, que s'il parvient à rembourser les sommes engagées pour les colloques et les voyages qu'ont financés ses encombrants amis, il pourra retrouver sa liberté. Il en parle à Hidar Assadi qu'il retrouve à Tunis, le 3 septembre 1960, à l'hôtel Africa, avenue Bourguiba. Ce que lui conseille Hidar Assadi ? Mystère. Ce que je peux dire c'est que l'homme, piégé par son désir de paix, arrive à New York au début du mois d'octobre. Il rend visite à Shimon Weber, directeur du quotidien yiddish *Forward,* chez lui, à son domicile de Brooklyn. Shimon Weber, que j'ai eu l'occasion d'interroger, le trouve inquiet, désireux de reprendre sa place à l'imprimerie du journal. On le voit souvent, à cette époque, dans la synagogue centrale, au coin de la Lexington Avenue et de la 55e Rue, à New York, sans phylactères et sans châle de prière, en train de méditer.

Le 11 octobre, il se présente à la banque Manufacturers Hanover Trust, à l'agence de 407, Broadway, où il a conservé un compte. Il y demande un prêt de 300 000 dollars ! John MacKinsey, qui était alors en charge de son compte, est mort peu de temps après. Je n'ai donc pas pu l'interroger. Mais je sais que le lendemain de cette visite, le 12 octobre, Hugo Halter rencontre son cousin Sidney pour lui demander de bien vouloir garantir ce prêt.

C'est alors, je pense, qu'il décide de faire éclater toute l'affaire. Il prend un billet pour Tel-Aviv via Paris. Prend contact, au téléphone, avec le général Shmuel Gonen qu'il avait connu il y a des années chez David Ben Gourion et qu'il avait revu début 1960. A Paris, il projette, enfin, de rencontrer ses cousins, Salomon, Perl et leur fils Marek. Quelle n'a pas dû être sa surprise de trouver à l'hôtel Madison, boulevard Saint-Germain à Paris, où il avait réservé une chambre, sa femme Sigrid, probablement, alertée par Vladimir Volossatov. C'est donc avec elle qu'il rend visite à Salomon Halter. Et c'est aussi avec elle qu'il arrive en Israël.

D'après Shmuel Gonen, Hugo Halter a décommandé le rendez-vous à trois reprises. Pour moi, il n'y a qu'une explication à cela : il cherche — et ne parvient pas — à échapper à la vigilance de Sigrid. Pendant ce temps, les Soviétiques cherchent, eux, le moyen de l'empêcher de révéler toute l'affaire au Mossad et de brûler ainsi Israël Beer, l'un de leurs meilleurs agents au Proche-Orient. Visiblement, ils n'ont pas trouvé de meilleure solution que sa liquidation pure et simple. C'est Victor Tchebrikov qui, selon toute vraisemblance, décide l'attentat. Hidar Assadi s'y oppose. Une réunion a même lieu à Moscou, le 27 janvier 1961, au cours de laquelle il tente de défendre sa thèse et la cause de son ami. Rien n'y fait. La sentence est confirmée. Et c'est lui, Hidar, qui, par une diabolique ruse du sort, est chargé de communiquer la décision, ainsi que les détails de sa mise en œuvre, à Waddi Haddad. Le 4 mars 1961, Assadi rencontre le Palestinien à Beyrouth, à la centrale du FPLP. D'après les quelques témoignages que j'ai pu recueillir, il semble qu'il se risque à quelques ultimes tentatives de sabotage ; et, sachant notamment que Hugo Halter a rendez-vous avec le général Gonen et deux agents du Mossad le dimanche 28 mars, à Jérusalem, il persuade Waddi Haddad que ce rendez-vous a lieu non le dimanche, mais le samedi 27. Ce qu'il ne pouvait pourtant prévoir c'est que les relations entre Hugo et sa femme seraient parvenues, entre-temps, à un degré de tension extraordinaire et que, pour décourager Sigrid de l'accompagner le lendemain, il ne trouva pas de meilleure parade que de monter effectivement à Jérusalem, ce samedi 27, par la route où l'attendaient les tueurs de Waddi Haddad. Les jeux de toute façon étaient faits, quoi qu'il arrive, quelques ruses ou scrupules que déploie Assadi, il ne pouvait plus faire échec à ce qui devenait son destin. L'ironie — grimaçante — de l'histoire voulant qu'Israël Beer ait été démasqué par le chef du Mossad, Isser Harel, deux jours auparavant. Gardée secrète, son arrestation fut annoncée officiellement la nuit précédant le Seder de Pâques, le

31 mars 1961, à 2 h 30 du matin. Mais le cousin de mon père était déjà mort. Et il était, à l'évidence, mort pour rien.

Ce sont là toutes les informations que j'ai pu recueillir sur la mort de Hugo Halter.

Rapport rédigé le 7 octobre 1987

Paris, septembre 1988

Le rapport d'Arié sur la mort de Hugo m'avait laissé perplexe. Même s'il répondait à certaines des questions que je m'étais posées je n'y trouvais pourtant de réponse ni à l'énigme du personnage ni à celle de mon étrange, insistant, rapport à lui. J'avais choisi cet homme comme véhicule de la mémoire familiale. Je l'avais transformé en témoin de l'espoir et de l'échec de la génération des survivants. J'en avais fait le symbole même de tous ces hommes qui, parce qu'ils sont les derniers vestiges d'un monde qui n'existe plus, n'ont pas le droit de penser, de sentir ou d'agir comme si cette destruction n'avait pas eu lieu. Avais-je tort ? Ne l'avais-je pas investi d'une exigence, d'un rêve qui m'appartenaient en propre ? Peut-être... Oui, peut-être... Mais ainsi va la vie... Ainsi allaient *nos* vies... Quand un auteur et son personnage vivent les mêmes situations à quelques années de distance, quand il s'établit entre eux, par-delà l'écart du temps et des générations, une si troublante parenté, comment ne pas prendre son parti — et ne pas tirer *tout le parti* — de cette identification ?

A présent, cette histoire est finie. Toutes ces voix d'Abraham, de Mordekhaï, de Sidney, d'Anna-Maria, tous ces fantômes que j'ai tenté, à travers ces pages, de ressusciter et d'incarner, vont se taire à nouveau. En sorte qu'en brûlant le rouleau d'Abraham, puis en tuant

Hugo, bref en détruisant ces deux relais d'une mémoire deux fois millénaire, je me retrouve brusquement seul, confronté au vertige de l'oubli.

Quelques mois après la fin de cette aventure, alors que les visages de tous ces héros et demi-héros commençaient à pâlir dans mon souvenir, je reçus un étrange coup de téléphone :

— *Te racordas de mi ?* me demanda une voix avec un fort accent argentin.

— Non, dis-je. Qui êtes-vous… ?

La voix hésita un instant. Je crus qu'elle allait raccrocher et puis elle lâcha, comme à regret :

— C'est Julio Feldman.

Julio Feldman ! L'énoncé même de ce nom me fit tressaillir. C'était un an à peine après la dénonciation et la mort d'Anna-Maria. Et ce revenant, là, au bout du fil…

— Je suis à Paris, continua-t-il… Un éditeur va publier mes poèmes en français. Je voudrais te voir…

Nous nous rencontrâmes au premier étage du café de Cluny, là même où, quelques années plus tôt, j'avais eu mon ultime rendez-vous avec Vladimir Volossatov. Julio avait changé. Ses cheveux, sa moustache, sa peau même et ses mains avaient blanchi. Tout en lui était pâle, fatigué. Et il avait l'air, vraiment, d'une sorte de spectre…

— Je suis content de te revoir, me dit-il… Oui, réellement content.

Et il se mit à parler — longuement, interminablement, d'une voix étouffée, presque inaudible. J'appris ainsi que sa propre fille avait été torturée et se trouvait dans une clinique à Buenos Aires. Que son fils aîné avait été tué, que le cadet avait disparu. Et que sa femme, choquée par tant de malheur, était soignée dans un hôpital psychiatrique de la banlieue de Rome…

— C'est la faute des fascistes argentins, gronda-t-il en levant sur moi un regard plein de haine. Mais c'est aussi un peu la nôtre… Nous étions devenus des petits chefs…

Sans perspective, sans analyse de la situation réelle...
Capables d'envoyer à la mort toute une génération...
Au lieu de combattre le fascisme, nous l'avons alimenté...

Je ne disais rien. Qu'aurais-je dit ? Et Julio Feldman poursuivit, de la même voix absente :

— J'ai rompu définitivement avec les Montoneros. C'était difficile, je t'assure. Tellement difficile ! Le mouvement était devenu ma famille. En le quittant, je me retrouvais nulle part, dans le néant... Peut-on vivre sans racines ? Sans savoir d'où on vient, où on va, ce qu'on espère. En arrivant à Rome, j'ai écrit à ma mère. Tu te souviens de ma mère, n'est-ce pas ? Elle se trouve à présent dans un hospice juif à Buenos Aires. Eh bien, je lui ai donc écrit. Et dans cette lettre, va donc savoir pourquoi, je lui ai demandé de me raconter son histoire et sa vie... Elle l'a fait, voici sa réponse. Je viens juste de la recevoir...

Julio sortit de sa poche une enveloppe et en retira quelques feuillets bleus remplis d'une écriture irrégulière.

— Je voudrais te la lire, dit-il... Enfin quelques passages... Tu veux bien ?

Dans un espagnol approximatif, la vieille dame racontait son enfance dans un petit village juif de Lituanie. Elle décrivait son grand-père, le rabbin. Elle racontait que chaque fois qu'une guerre ou un pogrom menaçaient la communauté, l'aïeul réunissait toute la famille, sortait d'un vieux coffre un rouleau de parchemin sur lequel avaient été inscrits les noms des chefs de la famille depuis le XVIIᵉ siècle, leurs dates de naissance et de mort. A haute voix, il lisait alors les noms, les dates... Les noms, les dates.. et ainsi de suite, comme une prière. « C'était pour nous plus qu'une prière, écrivait-elle. C'était la preuve de notre survie, de notre indestructibilité. »

Julio lut encore. Mais je ne l'écoutais plus que d'une oreille distraite. Sa lettre venait, sans le savoir, de me fournir la clé que je cherchais en vain — et depuis si longtemps. Que lui, Julio Feldman, ce furieux, cet enragé, cet homme qui du passé avait voulu faire table rase, que lui, le Montonero terroriste, l'un des plus acharnés à effacer sa propre mémoire, pour ne pas dire sa propre conscience, me lise cette lettre-là — n'était-ce pas le plus extravagant des aveux ?

Chez nous aussi il y avait un livre familial. Chez nous aussi, mon grand-père en parlait. C'est ce rouleau qui fut détruit en 1943, dans le ghetto de Varsovie. C'est lui encore dont quelques feuillets ont été préservés par Hugo jusqu'à sa blessure en 1945, près de Strasbourg. Et c'est Hugo, donc, qui était, dans mon esprit, appelé à devenir le porte-étendard de notre mémoire en lambeaux. Hugo ou la mémoire... Hugo figure emblématique, à mes yeux, de l'être et du destin juifs...

Aujourd'hui, Hugo est mort. Il est mort comme presque tous les survivants de sa génération. Il reste Gloria et Martin, mes cousins argentins, qui vieillissent à Buenos Aires. Marjory, la femme de Sidney, qui vieillit à New York. Marilyn s'est mise en ménage avec un avocat célèbre et s'occupe d'une galerie d'art. Richard a épousé la fille du descendant du rabbin de Gour. Il a déjà quatre enfants et enseigne dans une yeshiva, à Kiryat Arba, près de Hebron. Arié, promu colonel, habite avec Judith et ses trois enfants, à Zahala, près de Tel-Aviv. Sa mère, Sarah, est toujours au kibboutz Dafné. Quant à Aron Lerner il n'a pas quitté Jérusalem et il vient de publier un essai, en hébreu, sur *Ptolomé II Philadelphe et la Bible*. Sa femme Rachel est morte voici deux ans. Sacha vit toujours à Moscou et traverse, sans trop de dommages, les révolutions de palais, au Kremlin. Quant à Hidar Assadi, Arié l'avait prévu : il a été tué par deux extrémistes palestiniens dans un hôtel de Lisbonne. Et Olga, après bien des tracasseries et une campagne de presse aux États-Unis et en France, a pu émigrer, avec ses deux enfants, en Israël. Moi, j'ai fêté mon premier demi-siècle. Plus je vais, plus mon univers se réduit à ces piles de cartons remplis de documents, de lettres et de photos que j'ai hérités de mon père.

L'autre jour, c'était juste avant le Kippour de l'année 5749, après la création du monde par l'Éternel, béni soit-Il, je m'étais, comme tous les ans, rendu au cimetière pour honorer le souvenir de mon père et de ma mère. C'était dimanche. Il y avait, par exception, beaucoup de monde. Et j'avançais d'un pas hésitant sur les pavés recouverts d'une épaisse couche de feuilles d'automne quand, au loin, je remarquai un homme en salopette, en train de nettoyer la tombe de mes parents.

— Vous voilà ! s'exclama-t-il quand il me vit. Je suis heureux de vous connaître... Depuis des années que je balaie cette tombe, c'est la première fois que je vous rencontre...

Et comme je l'observais, à la fois étonné de ce ton grondeur et ému de sa sollicitude :

— Je suis un pauvre Juif... Un Juif entre des millions... Mais je nettoie les tombes et vous, vous écrivez des livres... Les livres sont des tombes. Les tombes sont des livres. Et nous faisons au fond, vous et moi, le même métier. Dommage que je revienne chaque année — et que vous ayez laissé, vous, votre *Mémoire d'Abraham* inachevée.

Il ne me donna pas son nom et je n'eus pas la présence d'esprit de le lui demander. Je le regardai pendant un moment s'éloigner dans l'allée et, m'approchant de la tombe, je dis la prière. Comme mon père, comme mon grand-père, comme mon arrière-grand-père et ainsi depuis des générations.

TABLE DES MATIÈRES

Achevé d'imprimer en août 1990
sur les presses de l'Imprimerie Bussière,
à Saint-Amand (Cher)